The 3RD DISTRICT Series

S. J. Garrett

Edited by: Vikki Becker/Enchanted Editing
Cover Art: Stacy J. Garrett

Any resemblance to persons living or deceased is purely coincidental. Unless you're a friend of the author. Nothing is sacred when you are friends with a writer.

ISBN: 978-0-9991070-2-7

Other Titles by S.J. Garrett

CHRONICLE Series

Chronicle of Destiny

Chronicle of Summer

ETERNITY Series

Ghost Eyes

DESCENDANTS Series

Shadow on the Sea

3rd DISTRICT Series

The Shaughnessy File

The Carmichael File

The Dease File

The Lucino File

The Taber File

Singles

Until the Dawn Breaks

To all those who believe in happy ever after: this one is for you.

The SHAUGHNESSY File

PROLOGUE

There was a place known as the 3rd District.

When viewed from a plane, it resembled a small triangle located in the edge of New York City, New York. From space, it could not be seen. It was not a landmark. It was not a place of great historical import. It was, for all intents and purposes, a backwater area in a bustling city of hundreds of thousands of people.

It was also the place where magic lived. If your life crossed the roads of 3rd District, it was said, you would find true love and live happily ever after. You would find a true faerie tale story.

This story is one of them.

Folder One

AENYA

CHAPTER ONE

"I'll be frank, Mr. Michaels. My daughter is the apple of my eye and my pride and joy. The fact that she has been directly disobeying me is very distressing."

From where he was sitting in Sullivan Shaughnessy's office, Hiro Michaels watched the older man pace back and forth across the carpet behind his desk and decided that was a vast understatement.

Sullivan was moving with the manner of a man who had discovered the world was actually flat and his ships had just sailed off the end. Being a wise man, Hiro decided to remain in his seat and not get in the way. "I was only told the conditions of the offer," he finally said. "Why don't you tell me the reasons behind it?"

Sullivan stopped pacing and took his seat once more. Leaning on his desk, his head in his hands, he explained, "My daughter, Aenya, has aspirations of being a dancer. Not that I doubt her skill, but it's not the sort of career I want my child in. I want her to be able to support herself, or at least *be* supported by a decent husband. I have since forbidden her from going out at night and dancing at clubs, hoping it'll curb her desires."

"Her brother mentioned you lock her in at night."

"Yes." He sighed. "And when she looks at me with those big brown eyes . . . it damn near kills me. She's horribly spoiled. Her mother died in childbirth and Aenya is so like her . . . He got up again and went to pour himself a glass of tea that was sitting on the drink bar. "Anyway, I began to notice lately that her shoe bill was incredibly high."

"Her . . . shoe bill?" Hiro lifted a brow. "How so?"

"A new pair of dancing shoes, every day, for the last six weeks!" He offered the bill, and Hiro whistled softly through his teeth as he saw the amount. "Exactly my reaction. And the worst part is that she does not leave her room as far as we know. If she was dancing in the house, Taegan would hear her since his room is on the floor right underneath."

"Taegan Shaughnessy, your eldest son." It wasn't a question. Hiro knew as much about the family as anyone would; the Shaughnessy Corporation was very big in society. He was also friends with Kienan Shaughnessy, the youngest son and Aenya's older brother.

"Yes." Sullivan drummed his fingers on the edge of his desk. "Aenya refuses to tell me anything, so I decided to try to force her hand. I arranged a contract that says that if any man can determine within three days where she goes every night, he can have her hand in marriage."

"Then she's not yet twenty-one," Hiro surmised. "How old is she?"

"Eighteen." he sighed deeply. "The law raising the age of majority to twenty-one was a great idea in theory. I actually voted for the damn thing. Now it's just a pain in the ass." He rubbed his forehead. "I didn't expect my daughter to be so . . ."

Hiro hid a smile. "So much like her father?"

He wanted to take offense but he couldn't. It was hard to take offense at the truth. "At this point, I've been hoping she would confess. She has not only held firm, but all potential suitors have completely failed. You're my last hope, Hiro."

Hiro frowned thoughtfully as he looked at the contract. "This contract also offers shares in the company."

"It's a family company," Sullivan explained. "All family members receive shares. I have tried my best to weed out the ones only interested in the company; I do not want my daughter to be in an unhappy marriage. My deepest hope is to find a man she will eventually love, even if it takes a while. Not all love comes at first sight, of course."

Somehow, Hiro got the feeling Sullivan didn't entirely believe it. There was the slightest of smiles on his lips. "Of course," he responded promptly. Really, what else could he say?

"Are you interested?"

"May I meet her first?" he asked. He smiled. "Hardly seems ideal for me to agree when I'm not certain if I will even like her, let alone wish her for my wife. I know nothing about her other than she is willful, devious, and apparently quite spoiled."

Sullivan laughed at the accurate summation. "Oh, you'll like her. Aenya may be all those things, but she is far more. She's an absolutely wonderful young woman, and more than her doting father think so." He walked over to the intercom and pressed a button. "Shelly, send my daughter in." There was a murmured response, and he walked back around behind his desk. "Don't be startled by her appearance. The family wolf follows her everywhere."

Family . . . wolf? Hiro began to wonder just what the hell he had gotten himself into when the side door opened and he turned his head to see Aenya Shaughnessy walk in, like a princess arriving for court.

He decided that the coffee was spiked. Or maybe he had been in the sun too long. There was no way in hell a mere look at a woman could turn a man's mind into mush and bring every single pulse he had to blinding life. There was no denying Aenya was an exceptionally lovely young woman, mature beyond her years, but a single look at her shouldn't have had his heart pounding so hard it was impossible to breathe.

She was on the shorter side; probably a foot shorter than him, and he was six-one. She had a slender, graceful figure with baby fine sandy blonde hair and large honey brown eyes. She wore a pale pink dress covered in cherry blossoms that should have been a century out of date but looked perfectly at home on such a modern female. It suited her in a way that was more elemental than fashionable.

Her utter femininity and delicate appearance was not marred at all by the slender black and gray wolf sitting by her ankle. The wolf was taller than average and reached just over Aenya's hip. It was also distinctly female, for Aenya had tied a sassy pink bow around the wolf's neck.

The very picture of innocence, she flashed a smile at her father that revealed dimples in her cheeks. "You called for me, Daddy?"

Hiro was instantly on his guard. His calm, analytical brain kicked in and overrode his surprising desire. He wasn't buying the sweetness and light kick. She was intelligent enough to get out of a locked room without being caught, and she was Sullivan Shaughnessy's daughter. She would be a formidable opponent to any who dared test her.

If Sullivan suspected his daughter was up to anything, he didn't show it as she walked over and kissed his cheek. "I did indeed. I'd like you to meet Hiro Michaels. He has come here today to discuss the contract."

Something that was anger and annoyance flashed across her face so quickly that it was nearly gone before it was truly there. Hiro's sharp eyes missed nothing, yet she was all smiles when she turned to him. Her eyes even managed to sparkle merrily. "So," she said after a quick study, "you're another hunter, huh? Well, at least you're young."

"Aenya!" Sullivan scolded gently.

"It's true!" She pouted prettily. "Most of the men who have come through are too old for me. Daddy, can't you rethink this?"

"Tell me where you go," he countered softly, "and the contract is voided."

Hiro found himself holding his breath. On one hand, he wanted her to confess so that she was no longer under this burden. On the other, he wanted her to continue the charade so he had time to get closer to her. This honey-eyed dancer with a modern mind in an old-fashioned dress was *everything* he had ever wanted.

She didn't hesitate. "No."

Sullivan sighed, expecting no less. "Very well. You are excused, little one. And take the wolf. She's chewing on my slippers again."

Aenya giggled, and it was a sound of pure enchantment. "Come on, Stormy." She waved a hand at her pet then shot Hiro a look that was as challenging as it was innocent. For a moment, the guileless brown eyes revealed the wildness inside. "Good luck, Mr. Michaels. If you decide to take this contract, you'll need more than youth on your side." With a dancer's grace, she turned and left the room, Stormy padding along at her heels.

The door hadn't even fully shut behind her before Hiro swiveled on his seat, picked up a pen, and scrawled his name across the bottom of the contract. Something satisfied gleamed in Sullivan's eyes as he watched. "Good luck, son," the older man murmured. "You'll need it."

Since Hiro had come over with a suitcase, just in case, all he had to do was bring his bag up to the door. The Shaughnessy home (mansion, frankly) had servants to help run it. An older butler, who looked more like Michael Gough's version of Alfred from *Batman & Robin,* than Michael Caine's version in *The Dark Knight,* happily absconded with Hiro's suitcase to take it upstairs to the room he would be using.

Bemused, Hiro headed toward the back of the house where he could see patio doors leading to an immense garden. Aenya was sitting on the edge of a pond with her feet dangling in the water. When he was close, she asked without looking up, "Why, Mr. Michaels? Money? Fame?"

He chose his words very carefully. "A . . . vision, I suppose. And call me Hiro, please. I can't quite bring myself to call you 'Miss Shaughnessy' and me using your first name and you not using mine went out of style when your dress was made."

Her smile flickered across her face. "It's a family heirloom. But 'Hiro' it is." She looked up at him. "Nobody seems to understand, Hiro. This isn't a game. It isn't a bit of rebellion because I think I should be an adult and I'm legally not. I don't argue with my father being my guardian. I argue with his trying to stop my dreams. This is my *life*."

Stormy, lying with her head on Aenya's lap, whined softly. He suspected it was in agreement. The wolf's eyes were far more intelligent than he had ever seen in any animal. "Maybe he wants to protect you," he offered.

"Oh, undoubtedly," she agreed. "I know his motives." She nudged Stormy, then got to her feet. She swung around to smile at him. "You're by far the hottest guy to come through here lately. And just because I think so, just because you know so, don't expect me to lower my guard."

A black brow lifted over pine green eyes. It was one thing to be attractive and know it. It was another to have it blatantly pointed out. How the hell Sullivan thought his baby girl was shy was a mystery to him. "Thank you?" He deliberately made it a question and saw her quick grin. With a shrug of one shoulder, and a matching smile, he said, "Don't expect me to be like the others in any way, shape, or form."

"True," she admitted, "you're already different. You're talking to me as if I'm a human and not a prize. I've had to double-check periodically to make sure there isn't a 'for sale' sign around my neck."

Gravely, he said, "And prime real estate is so expensive these days." He studied her face curiously. "You're still in high school?" he asked.

She sighed. "Yes. And yes, I'm eighteen, and yes I'll be nineteen around graduation. My birthday is in June." It was currently November. "I started school late. My father is a smidge overprotective."

"I hadn't noticed," he murmured blandly.

"He's so subtle, isn't he?" She shrugged one shoulder as she let him help her up the slippery incline away from the pond. "The school has allowed my 'suitors' to follow me around to my classes; I presume you will be doing it as well."

He was fascinated. She truly was very small. She wasn't just short; she was also incredibly slender and fine boned. It took considerable strength not to pull her into his arms and see how well she fit. Stormy's presence helped his control. She looked ready to chew on his ankle.

"You presume right," he decided. With honest sympathy, he said, "I take it the school is enjoying this."

"Bad enough I'm a Shaughnessy," she muttered, her brows pulling together into a scowl, "but now this. I could punch them all!"

After a thoughtful moment, he decided, "You are cute as hell."

Her mouth fell open. She warily took a step back, her cheeks turning a pink as becoming as her dress. Without a further word, she whirled and fled into the house, nearly knocking over one of her brothers as he sleepily staggered past with a cup of coffee in hand.

That was interesting, Hiro decided. She confronted him head-on about his being attractive, but turned skittish when he indicated he thought she was cute. He would have to see if he could piece together that puzzle at the same time as the others. If anything, today wouldn't be boring.

Aenya didn't stop running until she was safely in her room. She cursed herself as she swiftly changed out of her dress and switched into her school uniform. She *loathed* her school uniform. She understood it was a requirement for a private school, but she *hated* the way the clothes looked and how oddly vulnerable she felt in the knee-length skirt. The sexism didn't appeal to her either.

She had a secret compromise that no one except her brothers knew about. She wore a pair of dancing shorts under her uniform. That way if some jerk wanted to try to flip her skirt, he wouldn't get a peep show. Even at private schools, teenage males were perverts.

She scowled as she looked in her mirror. It hardly seemed fair that she was eighteen and still in school. Okay, she wasn't officially an adult until she was twenty-one, but she wanted to be out of high school and start working on college. She only had three classes; she was bored out of her mind.

With a sigh, she left the room and headed downstairs to the dining room. Hiro was already there and so were her brothers. The only open spot was next to Hiro, so, reluctantly, she went and sat down. Thankfully, she had a brother on her other side.

Peeking at Hiro from the corner of her eye, she felt again that flutter in her heart and somewhere lower in her belly. Attractive? Yeah, he was. Attracted to him? Yeah, she was. And *attraction* was the understatement of the century. She was in so much trouble.

Over a wide yawn, her brother Kienan said, "At leasht we can trusht Hiro."

"Try it without the yawn," the second eldest brother, Mel, said as he squinted at the textbook in front of him.

"Glasses," both his siblings said.

Muttering, he put them on. "I hate math."

"That's why I cram it down your throat," Taegan noted in amusement. He was the eldest at twenty-eight, followed by Mel at twenty-four, Kienan at twenty, and Aenya at the age of eighteen.

Hiro was mentally acquainted with all of them. Part of his job as a private investigator was to find information; before coming over to the house, he had been sure to get all the information he could. Of course, the fact that he had been friends with Kienan for several years helped.

He looked at Taegan curiously. The older man was a math instructor at the college his brothers attended. As the eldest, he had been the next in line to inherit the company, but obviously he hadn't—that duty was currently on Mel's shoulders. And thinking it, he asked Taegan, "Did your dad blow a gasket when you decided not to follow in his wolf-chewed slippers?"

Kienan almost fell out of his chair laughing. Taegan pulled him upright without looking. He tipped his glasses down to study Hiro then smiled. "A little. You know, I must say I'm impressed. You're better than the rest who have come through. You're actually genuinely interested in us."

"If I'm to marry Aenya," he countered calmly, and felt her bristle, "then I ought to know my brothers-in-law."

Mel peered over the top of his glasses, reluctantly intrigued, and impressed by the new male in their midst. "You're cocky."

"Confident." He smiled. "Your baby brother is cocky."

"I'm self-assured," Kienan muttered.

"You're cocky," his three siblings and Hiro retorted.

Aenya said nothing as a lively discussion ensued. She was *not* happy. She didn't want Hiro to win her brothers' favor. She didn't want him to become a part of the family. She didn't want to like him, or be attracted to him. She didn't want to be so aware of him, conscious of even his leg bumping hers. Unfortunately, her wants didn't seem to be counting for much.

When Sullivan walked into the dining room, she was grateful for the distraction. "Morning, Daddy!" she called cheerfully. Her heart fluttered as she felt Hiro's gaze on her face. Eyes that color in a face that handsome couldn't possibly be healthy for women. Why didn't he have a Surgeon General's warning somewhere?

"Good morning, kids." Sullivan sat down at the table with surprising grace. He was still a lean and attractive man in a black suit even though he was creeping into his sixties. Proving it might be more genetics than healthy living, he groaned when he saw the fresh fruit being put in front of him. "Why do I have fruit and you have bacon?"

"Because your cholesterol was far too high when you went to the doctor last," Taegan explained. He sharply rapped Kienan's wrist with a spoon when he tried to sneak their father a piece of the forbidden pork. "We like you healthy and fit."

"My children are tyrants." With a grumble, Sullivan began to eat the fruit.

"Not that they take after their father," Hiro noted.

The four siblings exchanged a grin with their father. No one could deny it. Sullivan Shaughnessy was known for his steel fist in a velvet glove ways; it was practically a family motto.

"What about you, Hiro?" Mel asked. "Kien said you're a private investigator. I remember you saved his ass a few years ago."

Hiro nodded. "It was in high school. I was a senior and he was a freshman. Some other seniors decided that he needed to learn the 'laws of reality' or some such crap. They decided to try to beat him up."

"Hiro decided they wouldn't," Kienan added dryly. "I was left standing there with my mouth hanging to my knees, not a scratch on me. He got a black eye, though. Someone snuck in a punch."

"I didn't duck fast enough." Hiro smiled. "Anyway, it's not a worry now. I understand someone went into martial arts after the incident. And got a black belt."

"Two." Pride filled Aenya's voice. "And he's won tournaments."

"So you naturally want to solve problems?" Sullivan asked Hiro.

"Oh, very much so. I'm the guy who never played Sudoku because it was too easy." He flicked a glance at Aenya who was pointedly staring at her plate. "I'm tenacious and stubborn. When I set my eyes on a goal, I always get it. And I *never* leave a puzzle undone."

"I have to get ready for class." She got to her feet quickly. "Excuse me."

Mel watched her run out of the dining room. He had seen her run from the conversation at the pond, too. He turned back to study Hiro. "Aenya isn't usually like this," he said thoughtfully. "You've really got her nervous. I've never seen her run from *anything*. She's little, but she's spirited."

"Willful," their father muttered.

Hiro agreed with both, but was too polite to say it. Instead, he said, "Maybe because she senses she's met her match." He glanced at Sullivan. "May I take her to school?"

"Normally the chauffeur takes her." Sullivan eyed him. "What kind of car do you drive?"

"I don't."

Taegan quirked a brow at Mel and Kienan then all three looked at Sullivan. Both Taegan and Kienan owned motorcycles, and Sullivan had expressly forbidden Aenya to ride with either because she was small.

Sullivan hesitated then very slowly said, "I will trust you to keep her safe." He sighed. "I'm well aware that I've been . . . harsh about her safety. If she comes through unscathed, then I'll be willing to let her ride with you sometimes, Kienan."

"Geez, finally. Drives me *nuts* when she gives me that big-eyed look and I have to tell her no."

Hiro got to his feet. "In that case, I need to go make sure she doesn't desert me. Please excuse me."

All four males watched him leave the room, then Sullivan turned to his sons. Taegan studied his father then asked quietly, "Are you sure about this, Father?" He wasn't referring to the motorcycle ride, and they all knew it.

"I'm sure. I saw this morning precisely what Kienan suspected I would. I'm *desperate*, boys. Kien, you had better be right about all of it."

"I am." He wasn't being cocky; he was just confident.

On a sigh, Sullivan took a drink from his coffee mug then promptly sputtered. "What is this? It tastes like some sort of fiber supplement. Where's my coffee?"

"Your blood pressure was high too."

CHAPTER TWO

Aenya was sitting on the steps of her house pulling her shoes on when she heard the purr of a well-kept engine. Warily, she looked up to see Hiro sitting on the back of a gleaming white motorcycle at the edge of the long driveway.

Her romantic heart wobbled in her chest. It wasn't quite the image of a handsome prince on a white horse that she had sometimes fantasized about, but it was pretty close. After all, what prince rode horses down the middle of New York City? Any prince worth his salt would choose modern horses. Try as she might, she couldn't shake the image of him as a prince. Did the bike *have* to be white?

She went down the driveway toward him carefully, trying to get her tongue unstuck from the top of her mouth. If she started babbling incoherently, then she would lose more ground than she could afford. As she got closer, she realized his hair was windblown and his shoulders were strong and powerful under his leather jacket. *Dangerous*. This man was completely dangerous.

She had stopped more than five feet away from him. Sensing she was suddenly wary, he held out his hand to her, as gentle as he would be if trying to coax a scared wild animal. And she was wild. All of her family had a wild spirit.

"Want a ride?" He kept his voice as soothing as he could.

She slowly moved closer and looked at the bike in longing. "Daddy said I couldn't ride one because I was too small. I've always been much smaller than everyone for my whole life. Weaker sometimes too."

That was interesting. He filed it for review and investigation later. "You look quite strong to me." Keeping his movements slow and deliberate, he held out the extra helmet he had borrowed from Kienan. "Your chauffeur was happy for a morning off, and Sullivan had no true issues with my taking you to school. So you either get to ride, or walk."

She put her hand in his and let him draw her closer. She waited patiently while he fastened the helmet on her then her heart flipped up as he lifted her effortlessly onto the bike in front of him. The skirt demanded she ride sidesaddle, but it still rode up as she scooted into place. His hand touched her outer leg warmly and then gently pulled her skirt down and tucked it in where it couldn't be caught in the wind. In that moment, she began to trust him despite the battle they were locked in.

He felt her body relax and let out the breath he had been holding. "Put your arms around my waist and hold on." His eyes danced behind his sunglasses. "I'd hate to lose you. Your father would happily hire hit men."

Her eyes sparkled in return. "We're Irish, not Italian."

"No accents, though," he noted as he walked the bike down toward the street.

"Mmm, no. Not really. Well, we *kind* of do. Mostly it's only noticeable when we lose our tempers. Taegan's is the strongest. I always giggle at him because there are words he says that always have a brogue. Daddy hides his *really* well, but oooh, I used to play games with Kienan under the board table. When he wants to make a point, he goes full Irish."

"I bet you learned some interesting words that way."

Her smile was angelic. "I save them for special occasions."

He was in danger of being absolutely crazy about her, he decided as they made their way down the roads toward the high school. It was the same one all the Shaughnessys and Hiro had attended, and the route was well remembered. He found himself quite impressed with his passenger, too. She held onto his waist with just enough strength to keep her balance but showed no fear. If anything, the delight in her eyes was clear that she was enjoying herself.

She stiffened slightly as they rode into the parking lot, however. A lot of students were standing around, and all were snickering and pointing as they saw her getting off Hiro's bike. She said nothing as she pulled her helmet off. As soon as Hiro removed his helmet, she saw nearly every female present widen their eyes. She really couldn't blame them.

"Wow," one girl said distinctly. She called, "Is he your boyfriend?"

"It's the stupid contract thing again." Aenya concentrated on looking in her backpack for her building pass. The school required all students to carry passes to even get on the grounds.

Hiro's eyes swept over the teenagers in the area. Most were smirking or snickering. He caught more than one snippet of conversation that indicated everyone found Aenya's predicament to be vastly entertaining. Some of the males even watched her with an open lust that objectified rather than admired. He shifted closer to Aenya protectively and narrowed his eyes. The boys were smart enough to sense he was beyond their league. They slunk into the building.

"Savages," he muttered.

Aenya blinked up at him as they headed toward the school office to get him a visitor badge. The office was very amenable to the goings-on. Frankly, they had little choice. The Shaughnessy Corp. had invested much money in the school and kept it afloat when budget crises had threatened.

While Hiro went into the office to get a pass, she stayed in the hall. She just didn't feel like facing the sympathetic secretary. Students passed around her, but they were a blur. To be truthful, her mind was a million miles away. Every minute she spent in Hiro Michaels' company was a minute more that she liked him.

She closed her eyes. It was so stressful! It didn't help that she was madly attracted to him. The entire ride she had been vividly aware of his strong arms around her and his muscular chest right near her face, perfect for leaning against. Whenever his green eyes landed on her, she was tempted to lift up and kiss him.

But she *liked* him, too. He was funny and witty. He didn't object to her personality, and he certainly accepted the wildness inside her that she knew he had seen. Was that why he was so different from the rest? Some others had been handsome, and all had been intelligent in some way. Her dig at his age had been a misnomer. Sullivan allowed no male over thirty to enter the contract.

But when she had seen Hiro . . . her breath had stopped. Her heart had begun racing and she had felt a heat in her blood and body that every female instinct identified. Desire. Lust. *Hunger.* There were dozens of words for it. Just looking at a man shouldn't have been that devastating, but his impact on her was akin to Hurricane Katrina's impact on New Orleans.

She cared about the outcome of this particular contract. She had never cared before. She had felt no guilt for deceiving and destroying the hopes of countless other men. Hiro . . . she hated the idea of deceiving him. She almost wanted to ask him if he would want to date her if there was no contract involved. She was half afraid he would say no, and that alone scared her.

Her heart began to pound harder, and her mouth went dry. Was she falling in love with him? How? She had known him barely three hours! But in those three hours, she had learned he was easy with other people, intelligent, and witty. He was conscious of the difference in their heights and handled her, not as if she was fragile, but with the care that said he knew he could hurt her and didn't want to. He had been a gentleman, not taking advantage of the ride to the school, and he had been open and honest with her.

She was in *deep* trouble. The sooner she got rid of him, the better.

"Hey, Aenya."

The male voice jerked her out of her thoughts, and she looked up quickly. Her shoulders tensed slightly. The young man in front of her was her age, several inches taller, and attractive enough. He was also one of the biggest jerks in the school. "Hey." She kept her voice carefully neutral.

"So when're you going to go out with me?" He flexed one arm at her. "I could always come apply for the contract. Give the new guy competition."

She sniffed slightly. There *was* no competition. Hiro had more muscles in one arm than Leroy did in his entire body. "You can't even pass Pre-Algebra. What makes you think you can figure out what dozens of other *adult* men have failed to?"

"You think you're so much better than the rest of us because you're a Shaughnessy. Far as I'm concerned, you're nothing but a spoiled bitch that is being sold to the highest bidder." He bit the words out, unaware of the dark shadow looming behind him. "I hope you get used up by some guy. Then you'll know you're no better than the rest of us. Grk!"

She had looked away, but at the odd noise he made, her head jerked around and she discovered Hiro had him by the back of the neck and had lifted him off the ground. Her mouth fell open.

"You know," Hiro said calmly, ignoring Leroy's mad wiggling, "I'm only six or seven years older than you. Technically, we're in the same generation. The era I was eighteen in is identical to the one you're in." His voice dropped to a dangerous octave. "I *never* insulted a good woman because I wanted her more than common sense."

He let Leroy go, but the younger male couldn't get his feet under himself and landed on his ass. That, naturally, made everyone in the area start laughing. Hiro looked at Aenya's face then stepped into the office again for a moment. When he came out, he gently took her elbow and began escorting her to the exit. "Let's go, princess."

She stared at the ground, not looking at him even when he pulled her closer and tucked her under his arm in a manner that was both protective and possessive. She felt humiliated down to her very core. Only when she saw that they were leaving the building did her head come up quickly. "Where are we going?"

"Where do you want to go?" he countered. When she tried to get away, he stopped walking and brought her around to face him. He lifted her chin until their eyes met. "Aenya," he said softly, gently, "I know you see me as your enemy."

"Aren't you?" Her eyes met and held his evenly. "These are my dreams that I'm fighting for. Something I've wanted ever since I was three and told I could take ballet. Ever since I had to work harder than other girls because I wasn't tall enough to reach the barre until I was older. When I had to wear higher than average heels for ballroom because I was that much shorter than my partners. I want this, Hiro. Badly. A husband won't fit in."

He gently tucked a stray strand of hair behind her ear. It was not the time to tell her that he was a trained dancer himself and knew intimately how hard it was to be good when you were of average height let alone when you were at a disadvantage. "Well, you're stuck in this contract unless you want to tell Sullivan where you go at night." She shook her head and he smiled. He wasn't surprised. "Alright. Then you're stuck with me as well. Your father has offered me something I want very badly."

Her lips turned down. "Stocks, just like all the others. Sometimes I wish *our* share of the market would dip just like everyone else's."

"Sadly, your father has too many fingers in too many pies."

"And has yet to find a plum."

"His name is actually Jack Horner? That's not very Irish."

She bit her lip, but a giggle escaped anyway. Even when she didn't want to like him, she did. And it took great power to hide the pain cutting inside her. She wanted him to want her. She didn't want him to look at her and see dollar signs. She wanted him to see a woman he desired.

They had reached the bike. He handed her the helmet and watched her fasten it on. "So, where to?" he asked. "I'll take you anywhere you want to go."

She hesitated then made her decision. "Can we swing by the college? I have a friend who attends classes there. Normally we'd meet after school, but I might as well meet her early. She keeps me up-to-date on what's going on with my brothers' college."

He grinned. "Ah-ha! So you're as possessive of them as they are of you."

She gave him a look as if he was mad. "And you only *just* noticed this? Shaughnessys stick together through rain, shine, snow, and chicken pox."

"Chicken pox."

"All at the same time. I was seven, Kienan was nine, Mel was thirteen, and Taegan was a miserable seventeen." She grinned. "Daddy vowed that if we ever all got sick at the same time again, he was going to quarantine us at a hospital and make us be their problem."

He laughed and lifted her up onto the back before swinging up behind her. "Will your friend know to meet you early?"

"I'll send her a text message when I get to the place where we usually meet." As they began to ride out of the lot, she gave in to the urge to follow her heart. She softly laid her head on his shoulder. He felt strong and secure. He even smelled good, like something comforting and welcoming. His heartbeat was sure and steady. Nothing could ever hurt her if she was in his arms.

When they got to the college, he obediently parked on the other side of the lot from where the fountain was located. "Why am I stopping here?" he asked her mildly.

She shook her head as she quickly texted a message over her cell phone. He could only watch in admiration; he wasn't that fast even on a good day. After the message was sent, she put the phone in her pocket. "You're stopping here because I don't want you to scare Madelyne. She has an aversion to handsome men. Now stay here!"

He quirked a brow as she hurried across the lot. Not that he doubted her, but now she really had his interest. He gave her a good minute head start then began to follow her. He had a natural ability to blend in with the background, something he often used in his line of work. It allowed him to remain less than twenty feet behind her without her even noticing.

When they reached the fountain, he crouched down to watch. She sat on the side of the fountain and swung her feet lightly. After a few moments, she looked up with a genuine and welcoming smile. "Madelyne!"

He shifted his gaze to see another young woman approaching. Intrigued, he studied her closer. She was, without a doubt, one of the plainest girls he had ever seen. There was nothing extraordinary about her face or figure or coloring. She had hair an unusual shade of dove gray and spirited violet eyes, but he wouldn't have called either attribute overly compelling. She simply was what she was.

When she sat beside Aenya, he couldn't help but feel that he was looking at a nightingale sitting beside a swan. They were markedly different and yet neither seemed to notice. If Madelyne felt discomfort around a beautiful woman, then it didn't show. And if Aenya felt sorry for her plain friend, it also didn't show. He had the feeling that neither had even noticed they were different at all, and it was wonderful.

As he moved closer, he heard Aenya say, "Madelyne, did you bring it? Please?"

"Yes, of course." Madelyne Winters was rummaging in her bag as she spoke. "I'm sorry it has once more come to this, but I have it. I take it you have another suitor?"

"Yes. I need to get rid of him quickly. He's too intelligent. He's a private investigator and he's friends with Kienan." Aenya didn't mention her unfortunate attraction to him, but she was sure Madelyne suspected. She was sensitive like that.

"All things to make it difficult." Madelyne emerged from her bag with a small canning jar. "Here you go. A few drops in something he drinks will knock him out for a full night. No side effects at all. He'll wake up with a good night's sleep." She laughed. "Well, I admit, there have been a few people I know who have complained of odd dreams, but one in twenty is a small margin."

As Hiro watched Aenya tuck the jar into her backpack, a slow smile began to curve his lips. Devious, intelligent, and spoiled. He could also add cunning and slightly terrifying to the list now. She had been drugging her suitors the entire time so that they slept the night away, none the wiser. Naturally, no man would admit such a thing, so there was no way Sullivan would have suspected.

He would just have to avoid drinking anything she gave him if it ever left his sight. Still smiling, he edged back from the scene and headed for his bike. Much to his surprise, he found Stormy sitting beside it with a lump of material in her mouth. Her tail thumped in greeting when she saw him.

"Hey, put that down," he scolded as he bent to tug the material away. She let go instantly and looked at him expectantly. A little shiver went down his back as he met her eyes. This was *not* a normal wolf. "I'm beginning to wonder where you're from," he murmured.

She pawed at the material and he decided to humor her. He obligingly shook out the material to discover it was a large piece of burlap big enough to cover even a larger man. It resembled a painter's drop cloth but the colored splatters seemed more deliberate than accidental. "Okay, now what? Am I supposed to use it to cover my bike?"

He tossed it over the bike as a joke . . . and discovered the joke was on him when the bike promptly disappeared. "Holy shit," he managed to say, looking around sharply to be sure no one was watching. There was no one close, and he cautiously patted for the bike. It was definitely still there, but it was just as definitely invisible. He pulled the blanket off and the bike reappeared. "Well, well," he murmured. He began to grin. "Whose side are you on, girl?"

Stormy cocked her head, gave the wolf equivalent of a smirk, and loped off gracefully. He decided to completely ignore the fact that no one even seemed to realize there was a wolf running around, even a wolf with a pink bow. Some questions were best left unasked. Instead, he folded the blanket and stuffed it into the bag on the side of his bike. It would be quite handy.

Aenya came running up to him a few moments later with a smile on her face. "Okay, let's go."

She was so relaxed and at ease that he immediately began to like Madelyne. Her plain appearance hid a beautiful heart for her to so completely bring back Aenya's cheer. Unconditional acceptance on both sides of the friendship. He hoped Madelyne wasn't really wary of handsome men. He would love to meet her.

"Where do you want to go now?" he asked.

She hopped up onto the bike. "I want to play hooky. I've never done that before. We can get to know each other. I want to know everything about you."

He plopped her helmet on her head and smiled internally as he sensed her game. "I thought you didn't want to like me."

"I don't," she admitted readily. "A good tactician knows that to defeat an enemy, you need to know an enemy. Isn't that your intent as well? Well, I have the most to lose, so I get to play twenty questions first. Take me out for Chinese, and I'll start asking. I'll even be fair and only ask ten. You get the other half."

He laughed outright and swung up on the bike behind her. "How your father can think you're an angel is beyond me. You're no angel, princess." When she grinned up at him, the wild spirit visible in her eyes, he felt sixteen again and noticing a beautiful girl for the first time. In a way, he felt sorry for Leroy. The impact was devastating at any age.

The place that he chose was a noisy diner several miles away. It served the best Chinese food outside of China but it was nearly hidden between two giant restaurants. Aenya almost didn't see it was there until they were parked and approaching the doors. Once inside, the smell was so heavenly that she took a deep breath in contentment. "Oh yum."

In bemusement, he watched her heap a plate as high as his as they went along the buffet. "Where do you *put* it?" he demanded. "You can't even weigh over one hundred pounds!"

She glowered. "I do too weigh over a hundred pounds!" Not by much, but enough that she felt justified in defending herself.

She blinked when he put down his plate and then gave a startled yelp as he caught her around the waist and lifted her off her feet. He held her for a moment, then put her back down. "One hundred five." He picked up his plate again.

She glared at the people behind her as they snickered and giggled. Bad enough he had checked, but he had been *right*. That burned. "To answer the original question," she said pointedly, "I burn energy very quickly. I can out-eat Kienan, and he's the bottomless pit of the family."

They grabbed a table in a corner where they could squeeze together into a booth. Despite how noisy the place was, the tables were oddly quiet. The diner had been built with custom acoustics that drew sound up from tables rather than dispersing it outward.

"I'm going to come back here with Mel," she decided. "He loves Chinese."

He tilted his head. "Out of curiosity, is Mel a nickname? It doesn't seem to fit in with the rest of your names."

She looked around then lowered her voice. "It's short for Melville. It was our grandfather's name. But Mel *hates* his name, so he only goes by Mel. The only way anyone will ever know is if they look at his birth certificate."

"Gotcha. So, what do you want to know from me?"

She considered things. "Where were you born?"

"Miami. We moved to New York when I was toddler." He stole a shrimp from her plate and nimbly dodged her chopsticks.

Naturally, that meant war. She snitched an eggroll in retaliation. "What's your family like?"

"Small but fun. Mom and Dad co-own a flower shop. It's a family thing, too. They wanted me to take over, but I have absolutely no design aesthetic so it'll probably go to one of my cousins. She's lethal with bouquets." Because he knew she wanted to know, and he didn't want her to waste a question, he offered, "I have no brothers and sisters. And the flower shop is called Belladawn. Not like the poison but dawn as in sunrise." He blocked her from grabbing a meat bun and eyed her chow mien.

Her eyes widened then began to sparkle merrily. "They make beautiful bouquets, yes." When he quirked a brow, she giggled. "Ask me later how I know, when you have your questions."

"Fair enough."

"Where did you go to school and what did you major in?" She smartly rapped his wrist when he made a grab for chow mien. He could have a fair shot at anything except that.

"I went to the same high school as you, obviously, since that's where I met Kienan, but I also went to the college where your brothers are. I majored in Criminal Justice and got a minor in, er, Performing Arts."

She almost asked what art, but he seemed uncomfortable so she didn't bother. It was probably something 'girly,' she decided, like costuming or such. And, because she was a good sport, she gave him some of her chow mien. She was having more fun than she had ever imagined. It was almost like a date. "Have you ever lived anywhere but America?"

"No, but I've traveled overseas. I've been to England, France, China, and New Zealand. The next place I've wanted to go was Ireland. I'll take you with me; you'd love your ancestral homeland."

She decided to ignore that, not wanting to argue over who would win and who would lose. "What are your likes and dislikes?"

"Be more specific."

"Food for now. Asking anything else would use up all my questions."

"Clever girl." He contemplated his answers. "I like fresh fruits and veggies. I hate white meat of any kind. I will, however, carnivorously devour red meat, particularly hamburgers. I'm not a wine snob, but I could probably identify the minute differences in beer. I'm a Coke person versus a Pepsi person, but I like Mountain Dew. Hmm . . . not picky about desserts at all. If it has sugar, I'll probably eat it. Except fried Twinkies. Ew."

She snickered into her glass of tea. "What sort of sports do you like?"

"Basketball is my game of choice." He gave a little salute. "I never played on a team with your brother because I'm not suicidal. Neither high school nor college, I might add. However, it was kind of unspoken knowledge around campus that I could give Mel a run for his money."

"Shh. Don't let him hear you say that. He's still sore when he loses in family matches. We all play." Pleasantly full, she pushed her plate away. She loved Chinese food, and she was discovering a new hunger. She was hungry to learn everything about Hiro that she could. Every answer made her like him more. Oh, they didn't have entirely matching likes and dislikes, but it was *how* he told her things that she loved. "Let's see . . . favorite color?"

His eyes swept over her face slowly. "Brown," he said softly. "Honey brown. That rich and golden color that reminds me of summer tea and the best of candies. Like your eyes."

Breath lodged in her chest, she tore her gaze away. No one had ever looked at her like that before. "What are your plans for the future?"

The minute the words left her mouth, she kicked herself. She didn't want to hear his answer. She was sure she didn't. She didn't want her family connections to ruin this beautiful conversation. No one before had been so open with her. She had been either a piece of property or, worse, a spoiled little kid. Hiro was different. He treated her like the woman she was and showed respect for her as a person.

For a moment, she nearly considered throwing out the sleeping potion. She could chuck it out, let him follow her, and maybe he would understand. If anyone would, it would be him. But she couldn't risk it. She couldn't! There was so little time left . . .

He considered his words very carefully then decided to answer honestly. "I want a settled life. A family. I want the adventure of everyday life. In my line of work, I've been shot at, slept in cramped cars, and seen some pretty bad things. But . . . I'd give it all up for the right home." His eyes met hers. "The right woman. A loving wife."

Silence stretched. They both knew it was a subtle dig. She didn't want to be married, and that meant she would never be a loving wife. But he was becoming much attuned to his honey-eyed, dancing princess. He was almost positive that she wanted him as badly as he wanted her. And if she did, it gave him a leverage that no other suitor had ever or would ever have.

She decided on the coward's route and took her tray over to the trashcan. "You won't find one with me," she said curtly. "Chase your dreams elsewhere, Hiro."

"You don't want to ask your last question?" he asked softly as he dumped his tray as well.

"I'll hold it in reserve for when I think of something important. If I promise not to ask anything you wouldn't want to tell, would you promise to tell me the absolute truth?"

"Without hesitation," he agreed calmly.

She turned around and found that he was right behind her. He was looking at her so intently that she saw herself reflected in his green eyes. That flutter in her body came back with a vengeance and the urge to touch him was nearly uncontrollable. She hastily put her hands in her pockets.

He just smiled and put a hand lightly on the middle of her back to escort her from the diner and back toward the motorcycle. Her innocence was his best ally because she couldn't hide her physical or emotional reactions. He was as ruthless as she was, fully intending to take every advantage he could.

"Exactly who did you meet earlier, anyway?" he asked casually.

The tension left her shoulders. "A friend. Her name is Madelyne Winters. She's my best friend. She's from 3rd District." She glanced up at him as she said it.

He tilted his head thoughtfully. "I'm not sure I know of the 3rd District."

"Few do." She pulled her helmet on. "It's a small part of NYC. Very small; only a few miles big in all directions. If you Google it, it won't even show up. It's mostly businesses but there are a few residences as well. Enforcers operate out of there."

"Now them I know."

"Most do. Anyway, 3rd District looks old-fashioned on the surface. Old-style buildings from most recognizable periods of history. Everything inside is modernized, naturally, but going there is like going back in time. Madelyne runs an inn there, and lives there." She smiled. "There are rumors about 3rd District, you know."

"What sort of rumors?" He quirked a brow.

"Magic. They say that 3rd District is the home of magic. If you believe in the impossible, then you'll find it. Faerie tales, werewolves, and the like."

He opened his mouth to dismiss it out of hand then changed his mind. He had seen impossible things. He believed in magic. Why couldn't it live in a District where it could be protected from those who would tear it apart in the name of science and civilization? "I believe you," he decided.

She blinked. "That's a surprise. You admit to believing in magic?"

"Of course." He said it so simply that she believed him. "I've seen it and felt it. It's everywhere if you know where to look for it."

She was quiet for long moments then looked at him very seriously. "I don't understand you."

"You will." He tucked a stray strand of hair behind her ear. "You will, I promise. And I'll show you a magic that even your District might envy."

CHAPTER THREE

The rest of the day passed in a blur. Aenya lost track of the places that Hiro took her to see. She hadn't even realized her hometown was full of that many interesting places. She found herself oddly grateful for his sensitivity, too; the first place they stopped was a store where she could buy a new set of clothes to wear instead of her school uniform.

She almost got the first pants and shirt to come to hand, but her feminine side rebelled. Instead, she got a pair of snug jeans that flattered her legs and a junior-tee that was her favorite shade of pale pink. When Hiro smiled at her, she felt truly beautiful. Damn it, why couldn't he be interested in her because of *her*?

It was almost dinnertime by the time they were on their way home. Since she was in jeans, this time she got to ride behind Hiro with her arms around his waist. She felt no less safe and secure. She had picked up the rhythm of the bike and was fully comfortable with turns. The only blip on the happy day was that it *was* a happy day.

It had been a daylong date. She knew it. But though it had been an amazing and wonderful experience for her, she felt certain it had been merely a weapon wielded by her 'suitor'. She was fairly sure he was attracted to her, though, and that helped. She was half-tempted to kiss him, just to see what he would do. Her instincts told her it would be like baiting a hungry tiger with green eyes, but it was still tempting.

They parked the bike in its borrowed spot at the Shaughnessy manor and then made their way toward the front door where Sullivan clearly waited for them. Stormy sat beside his ankle, but she looked vastly more amused than her master did. She even woofed in greeting, the sound odd coming from a wolf of her caliber.

Hiro stopped walking and let Aenya go forward. When she was in front of her father, she lowered her gaze. Sullivan regarded her for long moments then asked quietly, "Did you ditch school, Aenya?"

"Yes," she admitted softly. She offered no excuse.

He ruffled her hair gently. "Good." She looked at him in shock, and he grinned at her. "All students need to play hooky at least once in their life. It's a rule. And anyway," he added mildly, "more than one person felt compelled to call me about the scene at school." His eyes met Hiro's. "Something I'm sure neither of you would have told me about."

"Because you worry too much as it is," she reminded him primly.

"Hurry and wash up for dinner." He headed back into the house, refusing to acknowledge that she was right.

"I thought for sure he'd get a shotgun," Hiro said musingly to Aenya as he stepped up beside her.

"It's not our style. If you ever piss off my dad or brothers, you'll know when a fist lands in your face." She grinned up at him. "And, by the way, that also goes for me. Kienan has taught me how to make a good punch."

"That's because he's smart." He sensed the guardedness coming back long before it reached her face. "Don't worry. I won't assume that today means you'll lower your guard."

"Good," she retorted evenly. "Because even though I would call you a friend now, I'm not going to give up." She turned on her heel and disappeared into the house with Stormy following her amiably.

When she got to her room, she wasn't surprised to find one of her brothers. She also wasn't surprised to find him frowning. It was a favored pastime of Mel's. "Now what?" She disappeared into her large closet to find something more comfortable to wear for dinner. "You're going to have some serious wrinkles by the time you're thirty if you keep that up."

He ignored that and ruffled Stormy's fur as she leapt up onto Aenya's bed to listen. He had taken mercy on her earlier and removed the pink ribbon. It just didn't suit her.

"Look," he told his sister, "I know you think you have no choice about things, but you might want to change whatever tactics you've been employing. I got Kienan to talk about Hiro. You've met your match, sis. And to hear his past clients talk, he's borderline psychic."

She pulled on a yellow sundress then walked out of the closet. She sat down on the bed beside her brother and turned to face him. She fully trusted her brothers' instincts. "Mel, what do you think about Hiro? Honestly. Not just on the basis of what other people have said, but on your own experience."

"You won't hit me?"

"Not this time."

He smiled. That was his sister! "I think he's a great guy. He had a serious reputation at school for sticking up for the underdog. He crammed classes and challenged others so that he got his Bachelor's degree within two years instead of four. To put it the easiest way I can, if these were normal circumstances, I'd be completely encouraging him dating my baby sister. We all would be."

"But things aren't normal." She went over to her mirror and began to brush her hair. "He doesn't want me, Mel." She couldn't quite keep the longing out of her voice. "Just the family connection."

Her brother was a wise man. He covered his mouth to hide a grin. She seemed to be the only person who hadn't realized that Hiro wanted her so badly he could taste it. Every male in the house was dead certain that he had signed the contract for the chance to have Aenya and would have signed it even if stocks weren't involved.

It was Hiro's job to tell her, though. There were some things a brother simply did not want to say to his sister. Still smiling, Mel got to his feet. "Well, be that as it may, you better be careful. Hiro will catch you when you're looking the other way." He ruffled her hair with the same affection he had ruffled Stormy's then left the room.

She sighed and headed downstairs as well. Playing by ear wasn't her strong suit, but she was going to have to try. And it was for that reason that she was nonplussed to reach her chair in the dining room to discover a peach rose sitting on the seat. She picked it up warily and looked around. Most everyone else was already present. "Where'd this come from?"

Taegan was grading homework and making notes. "It was there when I got here." Bemused, he made a red checkmark. How could a college level student add two and two and get three? The kid probably had a future in politics.

"Me, too." Kienan looked like he was sitting with his head on the table, but the beeping from his area belied that he was playing a Nintendo DS under the table. "Damn it!" He sat up with his game. "He blew me up!" he said crossly. "Oy!" He made a grab as Mel walked past and took the DS. "I was winning!"

"And you overrode my save file for it." He closed the game and pocketed the device as he sat down. He smiled at Aenya. "Ask Hiro. He got here first."

"Magic," Hiro offered. Aenya frowned at him and he gently caught her hand to bring her knuckles to his lips. "It's a gift. No strings attached, no hidden agendas. I may not have flower aesthetic, but I know roses."

"No kidding." She put the rose by her plate as she sat down. She didn't want to accept the gesture because there was an underlying romance in it. Romance had nothing to do with the current events. Yet she couldn't bear to give it back. "I hate my life," she decided on a sigh.

Sullivan walked into the dining room at that point and scowled. "If you're feeding me more vegetables . . ."

"Artfully disguised vegetables," Taegan promised. He pushed his glasses higher on his nose as he smiled. "Father, we like you healthy even if you're not happy. You'll just have to handle our bossiness."

"And you're soooo good at it." Aenya grinned at Hiro. "Taegan's a den mother in disguise. And he's so much older than me that he's really been more like a second dad than a big brother."

"Someone has to keep you in line." Her brother quirked a brow in amusement. "You're too inclined to run haywire." He turned to Hiro as Kienan reached across him for the potatoes. "You're our last hope, you see."

"Hey!" Aenya was not only indignant but also a little hurt. "What happened to family sticking together?" She let tears well in her eyes. "How can you be that mean?"

"Don't make your sister cry." Sullivan probed at the orange bits in his food. He hoped they weren't carrots. He hated carrots.

"Oh, she's just playing." Taegan reached across the table to lightly pinch Aenya's nose. His eyes were the same honey brown as hers, and both pairs sparkled merrily. "She's just putting on a show, and we all know it. If she was really upset, she'd be shouting at me."

"She's loud when she's angry," Kienan apologized to Hiro.

"And spoiled," Mel added. "Did we mention spoiled?"

"Unfortunately," Sullivan said, seeing his daughter's pout, "I am forced to agree with all three of them." She stuck her tongue out at him, and he just chuckled. It was promptly followed by a frown at his plate. "Are there peas in this?"

"No," all his kids said.

It was a fascinating and beautiful family dynamic that Hiro felt privileged to be a part of. No matter how much money they had, no matter how much power, no matter the servants or grand house . . . this was a family. They hadn't been sheltered from reality as they were often accused. If anything, he thought, glancing to the side where a portrait sat in a place of honor, they knew more than most.

Compelled, he got to his feet to go look at the image. It was a family photo of a lovely blonde woman holding three young boys that had to be the Shaughnessy brothers. Since the woman was very pregnant—humorously wearing a shirt saying

'Baby On Board'—he assumed it was from right before Aenya's birth. Taegan was around ten, Mel around six, and Kienan was two. Such young ages to lose a parent.

"Your late wife?" he asked Sullivan softly.

"Yes." Something eternally sad lingered in the older man's eyes as he looked at the portrait. "The only woman I've ever loved. When I die, I'll join her again." Even after nearly twenty years, the pain was sharp. "Aenya favors her most in appearance, but Kienan and Mel have her eyes. Taegan got her kindness, and Mel . . . well, he seems to have inherited her lack of discipline for studies."

"Mom almost flunked high school," Mel muttered. "I've never been that bad."

"No, but you're dangerously close." Taegan's smile looked almost amused. "Your grades continue to drop like this and you might end up with a tutor for general education."

Mel lost some of the color in his face. There was only one general education tutor at the college, and everyone knew her reputation. "I don't study well. It's in one ear and out the other. And you can stop snickering, Hiro!" he muttered. "I may not have your brain, but I can whip you at basketball, punk."

"Hiro says you can't," Aenya offered with a touch of glee. When he glared at her, she shot him a challenging look. All was fair in love and war.

"Ha." Mel's smile turned confident, self-assured, and dangerously beautiful. It was a smile that marked all Shaughnessy males, and Aenya had often said it was their most lethal weapon. If directed specifically at a female of compatible hormones, she lost all ability to think straight. "You wish, Michaels. You want a match?"

"I'm on Hiro's side!" Kienan decided as he grabbed a dessert from the tray being carried past. "Ooh, vanilla!" He dug into the ice cream happily. "I've seen Hiro play. He's *good*, Mel."

"Fine then." Mel looked at his older brother. "You with me, Taegan?"

"Naturally." Taegan nimbly took the pudding his father had grabbed and traded him for another. "Sorbet, Father. No pudding."

"Me!" When Taegan offered the pudding, Aenya took it happily. "So while you guys are all dudes and stuff, am I supposed to just sit on the sidelines and wave pompoms?" Her eyes slid to Sullivan's and he winked. "Okay, then." She sat back with a smile no less confident than Mel's. "Daddy and I will play the winners."

Hiro choked on his water.

"Which concerns you?" Kienan asked with a grin. "Dad or Aenya?"

"Aenya. Sullivan looks like he gets the iron in his diet by eating nails. Aenya barely reaches your shoulder, Kien, and you're the shortest of all of us. She's also got to be at least eighty pounds lighter than you!"

"At least he didn't automatically assume she doesn't know how to play," Mel told Taegan.

"He's smarter than that."

Sullivan was sulking over his sorbet but was glad to comment, "Oh, Aenya can play, Hiro, I assure you. She was on the girls' team for both her freshman and junior years of high school. No cheerleading for my daughter. She went right onto the courts." He grinned proudly. "That's my girl."

After dinner, everyone went into the family room. Since it was Friday, Aenya had no homework and wouldn't have even if she hadn't skipped school. Mel and Kienan had no weekend assignments. The three of them and Hiro, instead, entered into a lively game of Monopoly. Taegan and Sullivan refereed and kept things legal in between doing their own work.

Aenya was vividly conscious of how easily Hiro had meshed into the family unit. He seemed as if he belonged there. She had to force herself to remember that he wasn't simply her boyfriend. *Damn* that stupid contract, and *damn* the reasons she had been caught dancing at night.

It was getting late by the time Kienan won the game. Everyone split up to go to bed. Aenya found herself escorting Hiro upstairs to where their rooms were located. For convenience, he had the room right beside hers. It was, in fact, connected to hers through an internal door. It had never been more than a nuisance before.

A guard was standing outside Aenya's door. Hiro knew he was there as much to keep Aenya safe from any suitor as he was there to keep her inside. He stopped outside his own door and looked at her. "Well."

"Well." She cleared her throat and prayed she wasn't blushing. "You know the rules. And I'd be lying if I wished you good luck, so, good night." She turned on her heel and went into her room, and she only let out her breath when she heard the door lock behind her. Almost helplessly, her eyes went to the connecting door. She had never before thought that a door could seem so . . . dangerously intimate.

She let out a longer breath and went to where there was a tray with a pot of tea and two cups. She had always asked for tea before bed; it helped her wind down to sleep. It was her own luck that it provided such a convenient way to drug her suitors.

She took her time. She washed off what little makeup she was wearing then changed into the ugliest, dowdiest, most unappealing nightgown she owned. It was practically a flannel tent and entirely concealed anything and everything appealing about her body. She *loathed* that nightgown and only kept it because it was good for body armor she could sleep in.

She went to the tea and poured two cups. She fetched the potion and added a few drops to Hiro's tea before she could change her mind. Then, steeling herself, she picked up the tray and went over to the connecting door. "Hey, Hiro?" she called.

The door opened and she almost bobbled the tray. Her eyes slowly widened until they were pools of honey color. Her mouth went dry. He wasn't wearing a shirt and his pajama pants rode low on his hips. He was as beautiful and sculpted as any statue of a Greek god. Every muscle was defined and alluring. His skin was lightly tanned and the light sprinkling of hair across his spectacular chest seemed to *beg* for her touch. "I . . ." It was all she could manage.

He took the tray from her before she dropped it. Its presence didn't surprise him, but it also held no importance at that moment. He put it to the side then lifted his hands to frame her face and tilt her head back. A flush rode her elegant cheekbones that he knew wasn't entirely embarrassment. Her pulse beat at the same frantic rhythm that his did. "Hi," he said softly.

"Could you put a shirt on?" She closed her eyes to remove temptation from sight.

"Why?"

"Because you're making me very nervous."

The admission made her vulnerable, and he knew it. Out of respect for her, he released her entirely and pulled on his pajama shirt. As he fastened a few buttons, he studied her intently. A grin tugged at his lips. "That is the ugliest nightgown I've ever seen in my life."

She cautiously opened her eyes and relaxed as she saw that the shirt was mostly buttoned. She had never before been flustered by seeing a half-naked male. Hell, she lived with *brothers*. A handsome male form was hardly foreign. But Hiro . . . in every way, he was different. For one thing, he sure as heck wasn't her brother. For another, he just felt unique to her. Something inside him called to something inside her.

She put it aside to the best of her ability. "I wouldn't want to give anyone the wrong idea."

He decided not to tell her that he found her sexy as hell in everything she wore. "Fair enough." He walked over to look at the tray. "What is this, anyway?"

"Tea. I always have tea before bed, and I thought I'd share." She shrugged one shoulder. "You don't have to have some. It's not a peace offering." She picked up one of the cups and took a sip. "I've had tea with all my suitors. It's like fraternizing with the enemy."

Clever girl. By continuing to play on their competition, she ensured the fact that her opponent wouldn't automatically assume foul play. Defending herself and the tea would raise suspicion. He was not only impressed, he was also quite delighted. He would be bored with a woman who couldn't keep him on his toes. "In that case, I'll have some as well." He picked up the cup and started to take a sip when he spotted a perfect distraction. "Is that Stormy pawing under your door?"

She turned and sighed. "Yes. I have to tell them to let her in. Hang on."

The minute she went into the other room, he swiftly dumped his tea in the plant beside him. He poured a fresh cup and was sipping it when she returned. He had banked on her not spiking the entire pot just in case she needed to pour herself another cup. "Good tea," he told her. "Little stronger than I'm used to, but good regardless."

"I like my tea on the stronger side, sorry." She felt her stomach quiver with guilt and nerves. It was too late now. She quickly finished her tea and put the cup down. "Good night, Hiro."

As she went to lift the tray, his hand closed around her wrist gently. She stopped breathing entirely. She was in deep water, well over her head. If he tried to get physical with her, she wasn't sure she had the will to shout for help.

Sensing the rise of her nerves, he feigned a yawn. "Sorry." He shook his head for good measure. "Will you at least tell me if you like me?"

She felt the tension leave her shoulders. She could pull this off for a few minutes. "Well, yes. I do."

"How much?" He used his grip to pull her slowly into his arms, and he savored the feel of her curves pressing against his aching body. To his immense satisfaction, he discovered he had been right. She did fit perfectly in his arms. He lowered his head and began to trail soft kisses over her jaw. "And in what way?"

Warning bells went off in her mind but she found she had no will to listen to them as his soft breath and kisses stole her strength. His fingers, where they were pressed against her lower back, felt hot. The heat slowly spread through every nerve she possessed. "A lot, I guess, but . . ." She lost her words as his lips touched hers. "Hiro, stop it," she whispered.

"No." Giving in to the urge, he buried his hands in her hair and tilted her head back. "I like you, a lot. Guess how." He didn't give her a chance to answer as his mouth settled heavily over hers. His control wavered violently. He had to kiss her, taste her, more than he needed to breathe.

Her eyes opened wide in shock and she tried to jerk backwards out of his grip. He held her firmly and pulled her closer so that she was forced to put her hands on his chest if she wanted to get away. She did so . . . and the heat of his body made her palms tingle. The kiss was soft, and gentle, as if he was wary of frightening her away. As far as first kisses went, it was a doozy. With an innocent trust in his self-control, she hesitantly kissed him back, parting her lips slightly in response to the pressure of his.

The nuclear bomb on Hiroshima had made less of an impact than that kiss as he took immediate advantage and deepened the embrace, his tongue surging past her lips to tangle with hers. Nerves promptly evaporated in hunger. She moved closer, and her hands lifted to curl around his neck.

He taught her how to kiss, and dragged her closer against his body to feed from her mouth. She even tasted like honey, and the touch of her skin was addicting. Aching, desperate, he caught the edge of the nightgown and drew it up until his hand could rest on the heated flesh of her leg.

She panicked and tore her mouth free to gulp in air. "No, no, bad idea, stop now!" Her entire body quivered as hard as his did, but the first stirring of fear had moved inside her heart. For the first time, she knew just how badly out of her league she was with him. If he tried to push the issue, she had no way of fighting him. She wanted him too badly.

He fought for control and won, but barely. He buried his face in her hair and muttered, "Magic. I told you." He let more of his weight sink against her and felt her stagger slightly as she almost lost her balance. "I'm a little sleepy, Aenya. Guess I was punchy. I'm sorry. Don't be afraid."

"Okay. I trust you." She was only a little surprised to find that it was true. Even having been scorched by his kiss, she trusted him to not take advantage of her. She tried to balance him and turn him at the same time. "Maybe if you lay down for a moment, you'll be okay."

He let her guide him toward the bed, and he forced himself to resist the urge to tumble her down onto it with him. He was walking a thin line; his entire body throbbed with stifled desire. "Whatever you can say about me," his voice was slightly rough, "never doubt how badly I want you."

"I'm not *that* naïve," she assured him, her heart skipping happily in her chest. "I had noticed, I assure you." How could she have missed it? The way they had been plastered together had ensured she felt every inch of his body. There was a vast difference between a physical innocence and a mental one.

As he was dumped onto the bed, he looked up at her. Her soft hair tumbled forward over her shoulders and her lips were swollen from his. On a groan, he rolled onto his side and closed his eyes. "Remove thyself, temptation incarnate."

She found herself smiling as she edged back toward the door. "Don't make any assumptions, Hiro. I just decided I wanted my first kiss to be interesting."

Softly he murmured, "Then give me a scale. One to ten for the first kiss."

She hesitated, then sighed. "A twelve, damn you. Now shut up." She grabbed the tray, went into her room, and shut the door. She leaned against it for a few moments and only relaxed when she heard the soft sound of snoring. Even his snoring sounded appealing, she thought in disgruntlement.

Her eyes went to where Stormy was laying on the bed and she suddenly found herself grinning. "Okay, it was a ninety-six, but I refuse to admit that on the grounds that it would be used against me."

A little spring in her step, she went into her closet and happily stripped off the ugly nightgown. She debated her choices then decided to wear a loose, flowing red skirt and a snug white camisole. Both were specially designed for dancers and she would feel perfectly comfortable no matter what type of dancing she decided on.

As she pulled on low-heeled dance shoes, she had to muffle giggles. She had overheard her father and Kienan talking. Kienan had wanted to know why Sullivan was letting her buy new shoes every day. Sullivan's theory was that since so far they couldn't stop her, he would rather see the shoes have the wear and tear than her feet.

She contemplated her feet for a moment. They were lined with more calluses than Kienan's were, and he was a martial artist. She was proud of every single mark.

She hurriedly put on a light touch of makeup and spread glitter across her face. She put on a few select pieces of jewelry before sneaking over to the connecting door to peek inside. Sure enough, there was a lump under the covers, still snoring lightly. Leaving the door open slightly because it would confound him when he woke the next morning, she dashed over to her bed and pushed it out of the way.

The secret passage hidden in the wall wasn't even known to her father. She had found it purely by accident when she was sixteen. She had been moving her furniture around and Stormy had bumped the wall when she was trying to get out of the way. A little digging had uncovered that the passage had been built back in the late 1800s when the house had been built. Aenya still wasn't sure *why,* but she was grateful.

At the end of the very long tunnel, she opened another door to find a young woman waiting for her. She dressed similarly to Aenya and had the same glitter on her face. "You're late!" she scolded.

Aenya smiled. "Sorry!"

Hands linked, they ran giggling to where a car waited for them. The drive was a short one for 3rd District was not far away, and at that time of night, the traffic was light. The club that they were heading toward sat in the center of the District, but the smaller size of the District made the trip barely noticeable.

The 3rd District. You couldn't research it on the internet. It wasn't in Wikipedia's immense database as more than a set of coordinates. Google and MapQuest didn't even know it existed. Even New Yorkers were mostly unaware of its presence. But it was there, it was alive, and it breathed and pulsed with magic and mystery.

And it was there that the hottest club in New York City was located. They called it the Faerie Club, and it was far from mainstream. You only knew about it if someone told you. If you were compelled by something inside urging you to go, then there was something you needed that you could only find there.

The two girls went into the club with laughter and were immediately absorbed by the gathering of people. Music pounded out of the speakers without being deafening, and dancers crowded the floor. Around the edges of the floor, people of all ages sat playing games or talking. Some younger kids were even doing homework, and the occasional toddler could be seen.

There wasn't a single drop of alcohol on the grounds. Anyone who wanted to smoke had to go at least a block away. No drugs of any shape or form were permitted. There would be no missing the rules; they were posted clearly beside the entrance where a very large man served as a physical deterrent to any who wanted to cause trouble.

Hiro was enchanted as he followed Aenya in his invisible cloak. If this was where she went every night, then he understood completely. In his short career, he had seen places that teenagers should have never known of and yet were going to all the same. The Faerie Club was a breath of fresh, peach-scented, air. It was wonderful.

So was Aenya. He leaned on the rail over the dance pit and watched as she moved across the floor, dancing with different men and women alike. He had seen many dancers. He had danced with many partners. He had still never seen anyone like Aenya. She had the rare grace and perfection that came once in a lifetime to one truly spectacular dancer. She was the Faerie Club's reigning princess, uncontested for her crown.

The understanding didn't come with a blaze of blinding recognition. It didn't send off rockets and whistles like their kiss had done. It was just a quiet little click inside his heart. It made sense of everything, confirmed what he had suspected all along.

He was in love with her.

And because he loved her, he knew he would never be able to keep her. If he kept her secret, he would have to leave. If he told her secret, she would hate him forever. She would never believe that he had done all of this for love. A woman who had been burned was always wary of more flames.

Damned if he did and damned if he didn't, but he still had another day and night to think of something. If he could only build some trust in her! Convince her that he was her ally. Maybe he could get her to tell him about this place, convince her that he loved her. He just needed more information about her. He turned to go toward the stairs, but, softly behind him, he heard a woman say, "Come over here for a while."

Startled, he looked to the side to see a woman sitting in the shadows of a table. Her entire face was hidden from sight except for her piercing yellow eyes. They were eyes that saw everything for they had seen directly through his invisibility. He didn't hesitate to shrug off the cloak, and he was vastly amused when no one even batted a lash that he had appeared out of nowhere. He walked over to the table. "And you are?"

"You're in love with Aenya Shaughnessy." It wasn't a question, nor had she answered his.

Try as he might, he couldn't make out her face. It vexed him because there was something familiar about her. "Yes," he finally sighed. "Tell me, how did she find this place?"

"Eventually, if they need to, everyone finds 3rd District. Even you, Hiro Michaels." The woman reached for her glass of water, and he noticed that her short nails were as sharp as claws. "What will you do with your dancing princess?" she asked.

He turned his gaze toward the floor where Aenya was dancing a jive so fast and expertly that it was a wonder smoke didn't emerge from the floor. He couldn't even see her feet!

"Whatever I can to keep her," he decided as he turned back around. He was alone, though, for the woman had disappeared as mysteriously as she had arrived.

Only vaguely intrigued rather than alarmed, he put his cloak back on and walked over to the rail to watch. He found himself not sleepy in the slightest as he watched Aenya dance the night away and wear through her shoes visibly. On one hand, he wasn't surprised. He hadn't thought any feet could ever move that fast. On the other hand, he felt like she needed a better cobbler. You would think she could afford one.

As dawn began to hint at the horizon, patrons began to drift home. Aenya was driven back to where she had been picked up, and she snuck back down into the passage. Stormy was waiting for her, as always. Quickly, her feet aching, she hurried toward her home and her room, wanting to be in bed if anyone came to wake her up. It was a Saturday, though, so she could sleep in as late as she wanted.

The first thing she did when she got to her room was change back into her nightgown. Only then did she creep over to the connecting room and peek inside. Hiro was still asleep, this time sprawled on top of the covers on his stomach. Thankfully, he wasn't snoring anymore. She muffled a giggle as she bit her lip. She tiptoed quietly into the room to pull the blanket over him.

He really was beautiful, she thought as she studied his face with a hunger she didn't want to examine. Giving in to the urge, she softly touched his cheek, needing to feel his warm skin. He stirred, and she snatched her hand back before whirling and darting into her room. She started to throw her ruined shoes into the garbage then stopped.

She smirked a little and set the shoes just inside Hiro's door so that he would see them when he woke up. Giggling softly, she crawled into her bed and pulled the blankets up to her chin. It was akin to throwing down a gauntlet, but she figured that as long as she could hold onto her control for another day, everything would be just fine.

Stormy climbed up beside her and Aenya draped an arm across her back. She always felt safe near her wolf. Contented, tired, she fell asleep easily.

In the other room, Hiro studied the shoes on his floor and felt his lips twitch. The little witch. She was challenging him, and he had to assume she knew it or she wouldn't have done it. She wanted to make this a battle of wills, and he was more than happy to oblige. The prize was well worth it, and though she didn't know it, he had already won.

Now he just needed to make sure that she didn't lose at the same time.

CHAPTER FOUR

The morning sun was strong through the window when Aenya finally began to stir. With a sleepy mumble, she rolled over and pulled her pillow over her head. She had barely been asleep for two hours. Oh, sure, she was used to it, but she had been having such an interesting dream about a half-naked Hiro and those wonderful hands of his.

"Aenya."

Red color climbed her face as she realized that it was his presence that had disturbed her sleep. He was in her room with her, and judging by the sound of his voice, he was right next to her bed. She hastily sat up and pulled the pillow off her head. Half her hair fell in her eyes, and she swiped at it as she tried to bring him into focus.

He had dressed in a casual denim shirt and jeans, and he stood leaning against the wall beside the bed. A pair of familiar, and trashed, dance shoes dangled from his fingers. She held up a hand to forestall anything he might say. "Please, save all commentary until I have caffeine in my system and my brain returns from dreamland."

It was just as well she needed a moment. He needed several. She looked so wonderfully rumpled and flushed that he wanted to slide into the bed with her and remove the horrid nightgown that marred her beauty. He cleared his throat. "At least admit that you're challenging me."

"Well, you failed one night already." She patted away a yawn and took the robe that Stormy brought her. She pulled it on and slid out of bed. "You didn't stop me from dancing." She gave a long stretch that had his pulse spiking like a thermometer in July. "Day after tomorrow, you're gone."

"We'll just see, Aenya. In the meantime, I have another day to get to know you, and I'd like to spend it with you somewhere other than the middle of the city. Will you trust me enough to go on a trip with me?"

She looked at him warily before deciding it didn't matter. She had promised him ten questions and she had the feeling she would rather have some privacy herself. She didn't trust him to stick with the normal 'getting to know you' bit.

"Okay," she finally said. "Can I wear a skirt, or are we going somewhere that jeans are better?"

He couldn't resist. "I'd prefer a skirt. You've got stunning legs, and I wouldn't mind an excuse to get my hands on them."

"You jerk!" She chucked her hairbrush at him, but he was quick and ducked into his room. The door shut just in time, and the brush thumped against it harmlessly. As she heard his chuckle, she gave a little growl and turned to Stormy. "Men are such idiots!"

Stormy's tail thumped on the bed in agreement, and her canine eyes held amusement. Because Aenya refused to give Hiro the satisfaction, she pulled on a yellow t-shirt covered in sunflowers and a pair of white jeans. Feeling defiant, she went out her now unlocked door and headed downstairs toward the dining room where the morning buffet was waiting.

Hiro was already sitting at the table, and when he saw her, he burst into laughter. Kienan, dragging his feet and his eyes at half-mast, staggered into the dining room and mumbled, "What is so funny at the crack of dawn?"

"It's almost ten, Kien." Because of polite company, he refrained from telling Aenya that he had deliberately manipulated her into wearing jeans because they flattered the hell out of her legs.

Kienan, however, was not blind despite being half-awake. "Stop staring at my sister's ass." He grabbed a cup of coffee and headed for the back garden, hoping for fresh air to aid with waking him up. He hated mornings.

There was a loud splash and a lot of male cursing a few moments later. "That bank is slipperier than it looks," Aenya told Hiro.

"And I'm sure Kienan is much more awake now," he countered dryly in return.

As Kienan stomped soaking wet past the dining room, Sullivan walked in. Aenya smiled. "Morning, Daddy." She walked over to kiss his cheek and nimbly took his coffee mug away. "No."

"Aenya, light of my life and my dearest daughter, have some mercy for your poor father?" He sat down at the table and squinted at the glass of juice she put in front of him. "Oranges?"

"Mangos. You hate oranges." She hugged him tightly with her arms around his neck. "I don't want you to get sick, Daddy. Please? Try to be a good sport? For me?" She gave him a look out of big and pleading brown eyes and he visibly crumbled.

"Alright, alright." He reluctantly began to eat his whole-wheat toast. As he did, he glanced at Hiro. "I saw the shoes on the banister. I assume you did not stop her."

"No, sir. I confess I was very tired last night. I was asleep when my head hit the pillow. But I'm such a light sleeper, it amazes me I did not hear her." He saw the little smirk that crossed Aenya's face and couldn't resist getting a little revenge. "Just so you know, sir," he added casually, "I kissed Aenya last night."

Aenya and Sullivan both choked on their drinks. Mel walked into the dining room, stopped, blinked, then turned around and walked away. Taegan walked in a few seconds later. "Mel is laughing so hard that he's literally on the floor. I presume I missed something."

"I just told your father that I kissed Aenya." Hiro's smile was calm.

Taegan nodded sagely as he saw the bright red on his sister's cheeks. "Since we certainly didn't hear her screaming bloody murder, then she must not have minded much." He was moving as he spoke, and the spoon that she threw at him missed him entirely.

Sullivan cleared his throat. "Aenya, something you want to say?"

She shot Hiro a furious look. "It was *nothing*. It was just a kiss. And it wasn't even that good of a kiss," she lied, turning up her nose. She was going to *kill* him! How dare he mention something like that?

Her father just sighed and rubbed his forehead. "I don't think I'm even going to say anything about this. I'm just going to forget you ever mentioned it." He dunked a piece of toast in his juice and discovered it improved the flavor of both. "What are the plans for today?"

"Aenya and I are going out today. I want to get to know her better. After that, I don't know." Hiro glanced at Taegan. "We ought to have that match this evening before dinner. Might as well get the slaughter over with."

"In your dreams, kid." Taegan pulled his glasses off and put them on top of his head. His smile was almost challenging and hinted that the same wild spirit lurked inside him that was inside all the Shaughnessys. "I'm not such a geek that I can't hold my own on a court." He waved a finger at Aenya as she giggled softly. "Stop that. Just because you beat me one-on-one is no reason to gloat."

"Sure it is." She felt better now that the conversation had gone back to normal. She was still blushing though, and seeing Mel still snickering as he entered the dining room didn't help any. Just wait until she got Hiro alone! Oh he was going to get it!

She got her opportunity an hour later as she stood at the edge of the driveway and waited for him to bring his bike around. He stopped next to her and got off and then promptly ducked as she took a swing for him. She missed entirely and spun around, throwing herself off balance as she fell backward.

Laughing, he caught her under the arms and held her steady. "You deserved that, you little brat! For one thing, you lied blatantly. For another, I don't want your family thinking I'm taking advantage of you."

"I can't believe you said that to my *father*!" she wailed. "How am I supposed to face him? This is so humiliating! First that stupid contract and now this! What will he think?"

Once more, he couldn't resist. "That I'm pragmatic enough to want to know if I can handle bedding my wife should I win?" he suggested. She went still with shock, her mouth falling open, then she began to struggle furiously to get out of his grip. He couldn't help but be pleasantly surprised with her strength; she was much stronger than she looked. "Calm down, honey."

"No! Let me go, and I'll kill you! How *dare* you! You son-of-a—!" Her words were stopped sharply as he twisted her in his arms, bent his head, and took her mouth with a wild hunger that brought her own to life with a blaze of fire.

She gave a little jerk of shock before a soft sound of need slipped past her lips and was muffled by his. It wasn't the gentle initiation kiss of the night before. It was more. It was a detonation. She was helpless in her own desire, helpless to his. She found herself returning the kiss as hotly as it was given, her body beginning to throb and ache as she struggled to be closer.

When he lifted his head, his eyes brilliant green and his breath coming quickly, she discovered she was dangling, off her feet, with her arms around his neck and his around her hips. She was breathing just as hard as he was, her body demanding more and more of his touch, pleasure stinging her nerves wherever they touched.

"I hate you," she managed to say, but her voice was too husky with desire to be believable.

"If you did, then we wouldn't have this problem." His voice was no less rough. He kissed her again quickly and then let her go before he couldn't at all. He swung onto the bike and pulled on his helmet. Conversationally, he said, "I got onto a tear when I was twenty-one and stupid. I was legal, so I promptly went drinking. I had this thing called a 'Nuclear Surprise.' I don't know what was in it, but it went right to my head and exploded. I was nice and happy and fuzzy for several hours. Woke up the next morning and wanted to die."

She pulled on her helmet and got onto the bike in front of him. "What's your point?"

"Your impact is twice as devastating, and so far, I don't have a hangover." He grinned when she started to laugh. "That's better. I'd rather have you laughing at me than threatening to kill me."

"Stop being an ass, then."

"And yet my ass is so cute."

She opened her mouth, then closed it. "No comment."

He coaxed teasingly, "Oh come on, Aenya. You can be honest. I'll be honest. I stare at your ass a lot. It's so nice and firm and those jeans do really nice things for your legs."

She tried not to, but he was being so utterly ridiculous that she had to giggle. "I ought to slap you for that." She didn't, though. She just wrapped her arms around his waist instead and held on tightly. Her hands landed on his waist at the back, and she had to bite her lip to keep from giggling again. Sadly, he was right. He did have a cute ass.

She began to drift lightly as they took off down the road. It felt so nice to be in his arms, and she was so tired from the night before. He was strong and confident, his shoulders just right for resting her head on. His heartbeat was still uneven and it thrilled something inside her soul. It was powerful to know that she could deeply affect such a strong man.

That strength was one of the biggest lures to her. He made her feel safe and cherished. She had never really liked being small, but she loved it when she was in his arms. She loved being in his arms, period. The next time he kissed her, there was no telling what might happen. The only reason either of their kisses had ended was because of his control, not hers. Knowing that, oddly, only made her trust him more.

"Aenya," he murmured sometime later. "Wake up, baby."

"Huh?" She lifted her head, surprised to discover that she had fallen asleep. She sat upright and looked around. They were riding slowly through a quiet suburb full of well-manicured lawns and people enjoying their Saturday morning. "Where are we?"

"You'll see." He pulled into a driveway and parked. He got off the bike and removed his helmet, and then he helped her off and removed hers. With her tucked under his arm, he headed for the front door of the house they were approaching.

She began to get a sinking feeling in the pit of her stomach as she saw all the stunning flowers growing in the garden. "Hiro . . ."

The front door opened as they got close and a woman with familiar green eyes happily descended the steps to hug him enthusiastically. "What a wonderful surprise!" She gave him a smacking kiss. "I've missed you like mad! You don't visit enough!"

"Work is busy lately, Mom." He smiled as he hugged her back just as tightly. Still smiling, he turned and held a hand toward Aenya. "Meet Aenya."

Maria Michaels turned and regarded the blushing young woman, and she studied her with a mother's knowing eye. Hiro had never brought a girlfriend over to 'meet his family' before, and that told Maria that her son's feelings were very serious. Aenya's visible embarrassment was evidence that she was as surprised by the visit as Maria. "Hello, Aenya. I'm Maria, Hiro's mother. You're a friend of his?"

Aenya's eyes shot daggers at Hiro's back as he headed into the house. "It remains to be seen." Her manners took over and she smiled at Maria. "I'm sorry for imposing upon you so suddenly. You have a lovely home."

"Stop showing off your etiquette training," Hiro scolded over his shoulder.

"At least I *have* manners, you ass!" The instant the words left her mouth, she went red from ear to ear. She whirled toward Maria in horror with her hands covering her mouth. Maria, however, was laughing too hard to notice. "I am *so* sorry!"

"Oh, no, no! Please don't!" Maria took her hand and brought her into the house. "I think you're delightful! You're welcome in our home anytime, even if you dump Hiro. If he dumps you, I'm disowning him."

She decided it would be too complicated to explain that they weren't dating and that it was more like a betrothal without her consent. Instead, she followed Maria to the family room where Hiro was engaged in a lively argument with a man who had to be his father. They had the same hair color and same build.

"Zeke," Maria said with a smile. "Meet Aenya. She's Hiro's friend."

Zeke Michaels lifted a brow as he looked at Aenya. He looked at his son. "Are you keeping this one? Because you're an idiot if you don't, and I didn't raise an idiot."

"It's a bit complicated." He walked over to Aenya and ran a hand lightly down her hair. "If I get the chance, I'm keeping her, yes. I'll explain later. We're just passing through because I wanted you to meet her."

"Well, it's good to meet you." Zeke studied Aenya curiously. The name was familiar. "Aenya . . . ?"

Very reluctantly, she muttered, "Shaughnessy."

Zeke and Maria's brows lifted almost simultaneously. Anyone who read the news knew about Sullivan Shaughnessy's desperation to find out where his daughter was dancing at night. Reporters were being curiously kind about the situation, writing with more sympathy than one might expect, but they were still telling the tale.

"I see," Zeke said. And he did. If Hiro was involved, then he loved Aenya. It was that simple. "Well, Shaughnessy or not, you're always welcome in our home." He grinned. "Say hi to your dad for me."

She had to grin back. "I will." She stifled a sigh as Hiro began to drag her toward the door. "I can walk, damn it! Stop dragging me or I'll make Stormy chew on your leather jacket! My wolf has sharp teeth!"

"Wolf?" Zeke and Maria both asked as the door shut.

Hiro swung Aenya up into his arms and kept walking, grinning as she kicked her feet in annoyance. "If we'd stayed any longer, they'd have disowned me and kept you." He kept walking and headed past the motorcycle, much to her puzzlement. "Did you like them?"

"Yes, now put me down!" She huffed as he did so, then her heart flipped over in her chest again as he took her hand and linked their fingers together. It felt . . . normal to be walking with him down the sidewalk like that. She gave in to the urge and rested her head on his shoulder. "Where're we going?"

"Just there." He pointed and she saw that they were heading toward a park not far ahead of them in the distance. It was quiet this time of morning and none of the kids had arrived for the day.

It was just a small park with a well-built wooden playground set and sand filling in around it. Flowers bloomed all around the grass patches, and someone had left a sandcastle abandoned in the middle. A lone basketball sat under the tire swing, and the regular swings squeaked lightly as they swung slowly back and forth in the breeze.

"It's so friendly." She walked over to one of the swings and sat down. She pushed it lightly with her foot. "Well," she added with a wry smile, "I guess this is the part where you get a chance at your ten questions." The setting didn't surprise her. It made her feel oddly safe and secure, and she suspected it made him feel the same way.

"Fair's fair." He leaned on the slide to watch her. "What was your mother like?"

Startled, she looked at him. It seemed a question from left field. "I don't know personally, but my brothers have always told me about her so that I don't feel left out." She rocked the swing gently. "She was always a lady in public but she was seriously temperamental. I guess she and Daddy would always get into arguments that ended with cookies and flowers. Bad cookies," she added on a laugh. "The class she almost flunked was Home Ec. She couldn't cook."

"Flowers." He smiled. "From my parent's shop, I bet. No wonder you knew the name of the place, and Dad said to tell your dad hi."

"That'd be why." She turned her gaze toward the sky and decided to tell him the rest without his asking. "I was born prematurely, Hiro. I was supposed to be born in September."

He went very still. Her birthday was in the beginning of June. Even presuming that she had originally been due at the beginning of September, that was still three months early. "Jesus." His heart clenched in his chest. He knew how hard preemie babies struggled to survive. Those that did were miracles. It was no wonder she was so small.

Softly, she continued, "Mom was coming home from picking up Taegan at school and there was a car accident. He got a broken arm and she had internal bleeding. They got it stopped, but she went into labor, and the bleeding started again." Tears slid slowly down her cheeks. "The choice was her life or mine. They could abort me and stop the bleeding, or they could deliver me and risk her life. She chose mine."

"For a while, they thought she might pull through, but she died a week later. I didn't get out of the intensive care unit for almost four months. Daddy and my brothers fought over me, arguing over who would get to hold me, and who would get to feed me, and who would change me. Even Kienan wanted to take care of me." She smiled through her tears. "I love them all so much."

It explained Sullivan's desperate actions. For a man who had lost his wife and was risking losing his child as well, any action, no matter how desperate, was called for. Her brothers were a little more relaxed, but Hiro had noticed Kienan was very possessive of his sister, to the point he had literally hired him to hopefully help her.

When Kienan had shown up at his office, he hadn't been sure what to think. The situation was, to say the least, outrageous. But Kienan had been insistent, saying that he wanted to give Aenya a chance to find someone she could at least learn to love. He was certain, somehow, that Hiro was that person. Hiro hadn't been so sure himself until the day before when he had seen a pair of honey brown eyes and been hit by lightning. It fried his mind better than that stupid Nuclear Surprise.

Wanting to lighten the mood, he sat down on the swing next to her. "What do you like? What do you dislike? And, yes, that counts as two questions."

She blinked then smiled, grateful for the change of subject. "Turnabout's fair play, right? Let's see . . . well, I like most anything. I'm not a picky eater, but I absolutely *hate* beets. Despise them with a passion. And let's see . . . favorite color is pink. I'm a girly girl," she warned him.

He thought of the bedroom decorated in pink and lace and covered a laugh. "I hadn't noticed."

"I dislike stupid things. Not just people, but things. Like . . . letters mailed two days after they were written. Stuff like that." She cocked her head slightly. "Some stupid things amuse me though. Like men."

He applauded her lightly. "Have you ever been traveling?"

"Like out of New York? Sure. We go to Florida for a week every summer and Colorado for a week every winter. It's awesome." She snickered. "I've been forbidden from wearing a bikini until I'm twenty-one though. I almost caused someone to drown."

He thought of the elegant and slender body she possessed and sighed wistfully. "I can imagine why." Sea sirens only wished they were as beautiful as his princess. "How did you meet Madelyne?"

She smiled. "Stormy ran away from home and we were trying to track her down. I ended up wandering into the 3rd District and got lost. Madelyne found me, and when we got to her inn, Stormy was there. Madelyne had found her and was going to call the number on the tag when she found me instead. We became friends." It had been Madelyne who had introduced her to the Faerie Club, she thought wistfully.

"Tell me more about the 3rd District." He watched her face. "When was it built?"

"Well, according to Madelyne, it was built in 333 B.C. I know," she winced wryly when he lifted a brow, "that's well before America was 'civilized.' But there were indigenous tribes here even then. Heck, I think it was when some Norsemen came down to the area that the District was built as some sort of haven. And every nation that ever encountered the District has left it alone. So it's evolved along with society, always one step behind and one step forward.

"I love it there. I feel *normal*. But then again, by their standards, I *am* normal. I've met some . . . amazing people there. The stories are unusual to say the least. And the Enforcers operate out of there, so they have some pretty interesting stories, too. I think that's part of the reason no one has ever tried to change 3rd District. No one wants to take on the Enforcers because no one is really sure how much power they have."

She got up and wandered over to where the basketball was sitting. She took aim at the basket and made her shot. It went in with nothing but net from almost thirty feet away.

"Holy hell," Hiro murmured. "Did you really play basketball?"

She turned to laugh at him. "Yes, really. Everyone so hyped on me to be a cheerleader when tryouts came around that I tried out for the team just to spite everybody. Not only did I end up as captain for two years, but I led our team to both championships those years. And won." She climbed up into the tower of one of the structures. "You're down to three questions," she teased him.

"Okay, so here's a random question like yours about color. What's your favorite song?"

"It's not one you'll hear on a radio." She leaned on the rail. "It's a song Madelyne wrote. It's about magic and faerie tales. And her voice is *amazing*. You wouldn't think a voice like hers would come out of someone so plain. Susan Boyle has *nothing* on Madelyne."

He moved closer and asked very softly, "What are your dreams, Aenya? Why do you dance every night?"

She went very still. Then, finally, she gave a soft sigh and sat on the top of the slide. "I was waiting for that," she admitted. She tilted her head back and closed her eyes. "I want to dance, Hiro. I want it with everything I am. If I couldn't dance, it would destroy me. When I started this year of school, I told Daddy that I wanted to go to a special dance school instead of college. I told him I had been offered an internship with a large company. He refused."

"He worries about losing you," he said quietly. "He just wants you to be provided for."

"If he'd give me a chance, he'd see that I've got what it takes to make my dreams a reality. Our entire family company is built around that very concept, and he doesn't even realize I've got as much potential as his favorite small businesses." She opened her eyes and stared at the sky. "I just want to be free. If I can just hold on till my twenty-first birthday, I can do whatever I want . . ."

What right did he have to destroy her dreams? Heart sinking, he held his hands up to her. "Come down and we'll go back, Aenya."

She said nothing as she let him help her down. She could sense his withdrawal and it hurt her deeper than she had ever imagined. She didn't blame him. Who wanted to be caught in a contract that would force him to marry a woman who would always want something else?

Yet something had changed. She felt it as she walked with him back toward the bike. If, somehow, she lost this battle, then she would never have the will to make his life hell. She would hurt, and she would suffer, but she would take whatever affection she could get from him. She had done the stupidest thing possible. She had fallen in love with a man who would never love her. Unable to help herself, she asked, "Would you have ever asked me out if things were normal?"

He hesitated for long moments. Truthfully, he would have skipped the dating stage and gone straight to her father to ask for her hand. He would have used every weapon at his disposal to convince the woman he loved to give in. Dating? It would have never crossed his mind. "I don't know," he finally hedged.

Pain blossomed inside her heart and stayed there as they retrieved the bike and began to head back toward the city. Any way she looked at it, she was doomed to be miserable. If she let him win, then she would lose her dreams and would have to suffer marrying a man who, at most, felt affection for her. If she won, then she would never see him again.

And what if she did win? Another suitor would come through. Then another. Then another. What if she didn't manage to trick them all? What if someone was immune to the potion? She would really lose then and be forced to marry a man she hated. She wasn't hopeful enough to think it would be a marriage in name only though her stomach churned at the thought of letting any man but Hiro touch her.

And yet . . . her mind began to move quickly. Hiro wanted her. He wanted her as terribly as she wanted him. Maybe that could be turned into love. Maybe if she gave him everything she could, she could make him understand her better. Maybe he would love her. Maybe he would let her have her dreams.

Maybe.

Maybe.

Maybe.

It was all maybes. There were no positives except for one: she absolutely would have no man other than Hiro Michaels for her first lover. She straightened up and moved as close to his ear as she could. "If I asked you to be my first lover, what would you say?"

He almost dumped the bike. He swiftly pulled off the road and stared at her in shock. What in the *hell* was going through that terrifyingly sharp mind? "Alright, please repeat that when I'm not worried that I'm going to crash us."

She couldn't quite meet his eyes as her cheeks turned red. "I wanted to know what you'd say if I asked you to be my first lover."

"I'd say . . . why?" He kept his voice even with effort. She had thrown him for a loop, and it was hard to fight his deepest instincts. He had been resisting the urge to carry her away ever since he had met her. "I thought you didn't want to like me."

"I didn't. But I do. And I don't like how we've been forced into this situation. To be honest, I like you more than I've ever liked anyone else. There's something about you. I'm drawn to it. And . . . it occurred to me rather blindingly that someday I might mess up and be forced to marry someone that I loathe. I don't want to give them the satisfaction." Her eyes lifted to his. "I want to make one decision for myself for once. And I want you to be my first lover. I know you want me, and I know you said you liked me. That's enough." For now, she added mentally.

He ran a thumb over her lips, tempted to remove her helmet so he could get his hands in her hair. "I want you like I've never wanted anything before. But I'm not going to let anything keep me from my goals. You can't seduce me into walking away."

"I'm not trying to. I just . . . I just want my first time to be with someone I desire. If it's the only time I ever feel real desire for a man, then I want to have the memory to cling to." She let out a breath. "We can both go into this with our eyes open. We know it will change neither of our minds."

He fought with himself violently. In the end, he realized he could refuse her nothing. If things ended badly, he too wanted to cling onto this memory. He still hadn't figured out how to give them both what they wanted. She liked him. It was a start. Perhaps the explosive hunger between them could help fan flames even more elemental.

He started the bike up again and turned for another road. She remained silent as long as she could, but when she saw they were heading away from her home rather than toward it, she felt her heart begin beating harder. When they stopped at a light, she asked, "Where are we going?"

"My apartment. I'm not taking you to a hotel. You deserve better than that." He could feel the trembling in her body and it matched the trembling inside his heart. He was terrified of hurting her, or losing her, or ruining the trust she was giving him so generously.

As they pulled into the parking lot of the apartment complex, her eyes went wide. "This is not an apartment," she said decisively. "It's a condo. And it's an upscale condo. In fact, I think Daddy invested in this complex." As he lifted her off the bike and she pulled off her helmet, she asked warily, "You're rather well off, aren't you?"

"I get by." He possessively held her closer as they headed up the stairs toward where his apartment was located. It was the corner one, and on the top floor so he had a lot of privacy, which he much preferred.

She loved it the instant she walked inside. It was light and airy and he hadn't cluttered it with a ton of furniture. There was a giant oversized couch that she couldn't resist going over to and sitting down on. It promptly tried to swallow her up.

"Is this a couch or a bed?" she asked him laughingly.

"Both. Sometimes I'm working too hard and fall asleep where I'm sitting." He hung up his jacket before walking over to kneel in front of her. "You said you trust me. Do you mean it?" She nodded and he let out a little breath. "Good." Watching her eyes, he reached out and unfastened her jacket for her.

She let him remove it and half expected him to go for the edge of her shirt right after. Instead, she made a startled sound as he lifted her into his arms and carried her down the hall toward his bedroom. Her heart was beating so hard that she wondered how he couldn't hear it. "Hiro, if I panic, I'm sorry. I'm just nervous."

"If you panic, we stop." He stopped beside the bed and slowly lowered her to the top of the covers. Her hair tumbled around her shoulders and across the sapphire-colored pillowcase. His breath came in sharply. "No matter how hard it is," he added huskily. "At least I'll try. God, Aenya, do you have any idea how badly I want you?"

"Teach me." Her hands reached for his and their fingers laced together. His head lowered slowly and their lips met, softly at first then with growing passion as nerves gave way to their hearts.

Unspoken between them, their feelings welled up and swept them both away. It was like a dance just for the two of them. His fingers skimmed lightly down her side then slipped under the edge of her shirt. Unlike the night before when his hot hand had touched her bare flesh, this time she didn't panic. Her fingers lifted and framed his face, holding him closer to her as she willingly sank into the promise of his kiss. He tasted like lemonade. As if he had just eaten a piece of lemon candy. It was an addicting flavor and she made a sound of disappointment as he eased her back.

When she realized he was slowly removing her shirt, she blushed. She didn't stop him, though, and her arms came up to shield her breasts as he tossed the top to the side. She was wearing a bra, but she still felt almost horribly exposed.

He forgot how to breathe. "Yeah," he murmured thickly, skimming a knuckle over the top curve of her breast, "I feel for the poor sap who almost drowned. I'd gladly drown for you, too." His hand cupped the back of her head and he dragged her against him again for another hungry kiss. His teeth nipped at her lower lip teasingly.

A soft moan was her only answer and she forgot to shield herself as her hands went to the buttons of his shirt. Her fingers were trembling almost too hard and she finally dropped them into her lap. His free hand lowered and caught her hands, and then lifted them again to hold them against his chest until the trembling eased. "It's alright," he murmured, trailing kisses down the side of her neck. She tasted like honey and summertime. He hadn't known it would be so addicting.

Taking a slow breath, which was all she could manage because it was hard to breathe when his mouth was planting hot kisses along her shoulder, she began to unbutton his shirt again. She got it open and spread her hands across his chest slowly, feeling again that tingling in her palms. "Hiro," she whispered softly, her head falling back.

He shrugged out of the shirt and tossed it aside. He then slowly lowered her to the bed again. His hand ran sensuously over her bare stomach. She trembled, and he smiled as he kissed her again. Against her lips, he asked, "Scared?"

She shook her head. "No." She wasn't, not really. She was a little nervous, but not scared. She did gulp a quick breath of air, however, as his fingers unfastened her jeans. As they slowly slid down her legs, she clutched his shoulders for balance, her head spinning. His fingers trailed over her legs, and the skin was suddenly so sensitive that it seemed as if she felt every line of his fingerprints.

He knew the exact instant her hunger overrode her nerves. Tension shot into her muscles, and she twisted against him as if to follow his hands. Delight made him light-headed. He rolled her underneath him and caught his weight so that he didn't hurt her. Eagerly he ran kisses over the top curves of her breasts, his lips tugging at the lace that covered them.

On a shudder, she caught her fingers in his hair and held him closer. She felt too hot, as if she was going to go up in flames, and she could barely breathe in the thick and heavy air. Her breasts ached and so did between her legs. Everywhere she had a pulse, she could feel it pounding with the drugging rhythm of a drum.

Lifting her slightly, he unfastened her bra and then dropped it over the bed as well. His mouth went dry, and he softly ran the back of his hand down the outside curve of her breast. The nipple tightened and flushed and he couldn't resist the temptation to bend and cover the point with his mouth.

She couldn't stop a soft cry as lightning scored her insides. It was pleasure almost unbearably strong and her dazed mind accepted the fact that she had gotten herself in further than she was going to be able to safely emerge from again. Gripping onto him tightly, her nails digging little crescents into his shoulders, she arched against him in a plea for more.

Her eyes flew wide with sudden shock as she felt his hand on the bare skin of her inner thigh and slowly moving upward. She was naked, she realized, and she buried her flaming face against his shoulder. "Where'd my underwear go?" she managed to ask.

"Magic," he told her, his free hand tilting her head back. He kissed her hard, then his lips curved. "And besides, there were little ribbons on the hip. You looked like a really nice Christmas present. The best ever."

"Don't be a pervert!" The last word was a gasp as his knuckles brushed over her in an intimate caress. Her legs came together protectively and trapped his hand against her heated flesh. She moaned softly as he teased her with his fingers, finding all the sensitive places on her body. Places she hadn't even envisioned owning. "Stop."

"Are you scared?" He held her closer protectively. He was shaking with stifled desire but he wanted to see her go completely wild in his arms. He wanted to pleasure her until she knew beyond a doubt she belonged to him. "Hold onto me. I'll keep you safe."

"Hiro, stop." She squeezed her eyes shut as her body shook with hunger, pleasure making it impossible to breathe. Breathing wasn't important. Nothing was important but Hiro. She would have cried out, but his mouth sealed hers shut, his tongue dueling with hers hungrily. His fingers were insistent, and she twisted against him desperately.

The terrible tension snapped. Ecstasy swept over her entire body, pleasure consuming her until she couldn't think or breathe. All she could do was hold onto him wildly, finding him to be her only anchor. Even when the wave ebbed, she couldn't let go of him. The strength drained from her body and left soft ripples of satisfaction fluttering inside.

The best she could manage to say was, "Wow."

He felt no less shaken. He was suddenly out of his depth, too, never daring dream of finding someone like her. His hunger for her was a living thing inside him, his body tight and desperate for relief.

"Aenya." He tilted her face up so that he could kiss her again. Even as his hands moved over her again, awakening her senses once more, he didn't release her from the kiss. He couldn't get enough of her. He didn't think he ever would. "Let me love you," he said against her lips. "I need you so badly."

"Yes." She reluctantly released him as he slipped out of her arms and she watched him curiously as he stripped off the rest of his clothes. She realized a bit distantly she was no longer embarrassed, no longer nervous. It was as if everything inside her had finally embraced this decision she had made. Why had she ever been nervous to begin with?

With immense curiosity, she rose to her knees on the bed and looked at him eagerly. She wanted to run her hands over him and explore him, especially where he was so obviously aroused, but she didn't quite have the courage for that. Not yet, at least. Her eyes shifted to his stomach and she sucked in a painful breath as she saw something she had been too flustered to see the night before.

There was a scar across his lower stomach; a nasty looking mark that spoke of a painful wound. She knew, somehow, that she was staring at a bullet wound. Stricken, she looked up at him. "Hiro."

"It's okay. I'll explain later." He lowered her to the bed again and forced his hands to be gentle as they skimmed over her curves. He wanted her wild again, so hot for him that any pain was brief. It was hard to restrain himself, and he prayed for an outcome where he would someday be able to see if he would ever be sated with her. He strongly doubted it.

She gave up her innocence without hesitation, winding her arms around his shoulders and gripping her fingers into the sweaty slopes of his back. He watched her face as he slowly took her and saw the way her breath hitched. Instantly he stopped. "It's okay. I'm sorry." His mouth rushed over her face to comfort and he tasted her tears. "Aenya, damn it, don't cry."

"Then don't stop! I want you, Hiro. Just you. Please. It doesn't hurt that badly." It was more a burning than a pain and her body somehow knew there was something behind it. She couldn't control the arch of her hips any more than she could stop her own heart. She *craved* him.

On a low groan, he stopped fighting and surged into her in a single stroke. She gave a strangled little yelp, and he froze, terrified he had hurt her, but her feet hooked behind his thighs and she pressed herself closer against him. It was just a little gesture but it broke his control. "I'm sorry," he said into her hair as he began to drive into her with more power than precision.

She wanted to tell him it was okay, she didn't mind, but she couldn't speak. That terrible pleasure that demanded release from its pressure was climbing again. This time she eagerly embraced it. Her breaths became whimpers and her nails dug into his shoulders. When the release came, it was harder and hotter than before, ripping a cry from her throat that she muffled against his neck.

The ripples of her inner muscles were too much for him to bear. Shuddering, he could only hold onto her fiercely, ecstasy unlike any before consuming him, emptying his heart and soul in her as deeply as it did his body. He had told her he would show her the magic, but she had shown him instead. And he knew, knew beyond a doubt, that this was a magic that they would only find together.

He wrapped her protectively in his arms and rolled onto his side. He stared over the top of her head at the wall across the room as she snuggled close. Even if he had to steal her, she belonged with him, and he would not let her go. There had to be a way for him to win the contract and for her to have her dreams too. There had to be!

CHAPTER FIVE

They slept for a while, tangled together with a sheet haphazardly thrown over them. When Aenya stirred and sat up, it roused Hiro enough to reach for her. "Where're you going?" he murmured drowsily.

"Nowhere."

The soft muted pain in her voice brought him fully awake. He opened his eyes to find her sitting beside him and looking at the scar on his stomach. "Aenya."

She gently reached out to put a hand over the old wound. Her fingertips trembled. "Where did you get this?" she asked softly. "It looks so horrible."

"I was in junior high. I had the unfortunate timing of being at a bus stop when a member of a gang was there. His rivals happened to drive by and open up fire. I, and an old woman, were innocent bystanders. She didn't survive the trip to the hospital. The bullet only went across my stomach, not directly in, so I somehow made it. The cops who got there before the ambulance . . . they saved my life."

Tears welled in her eyes. She could have lost him before ever knowing he existed. Needing to feel his arms around her, she lay down and put her head on his shoulder. He immediately turned and pulled her close. "Is that why you went into criminal justice? You wanted to give something back? Or was your name going to your head?"

"Hush you." He snuggled her closer. "It was probably a combination of both. I never really questioned my path after that." He glanced over her head and sighed as he saw the clock. "It's getting late. We should head back to your house if we want to have our basketball game." He sat up and looked at her lying so naturally and comfortably in his bed. "Regrets?" he asked softly.

"No." She turned her face into his hand as he cupped her cheek. "No matter what happens, I can say that my first time was special."

"You still think that I won't win?"

"I'm positive." Try as she might, it was getting harder and harder to remind herself that she had to play things out. She wanted nothing more than to crawl into his arms and tell him that she loved him and didn't want him to go. She couldn't even tell anymore what she wanted most: him or her dance.

Pushing it aside, she sat up and swung her feet over the side of the bed. She promptly winced. He was at her side in a flash and lifted her into his arms to carry her into the master bathroom. "You need a hot shower," he told her. "I'm not putting you onto the bike if you're sore."

"I'm not *that* sore. Just a little bit." She couldn't resist taking a shower anyway. It was just so intimate to be bathing in her lover's bathroom. But was he actually her lover? It was just a one-night stand, right? Or a one-day stand, as it were.

One *hell* of a one-day stand, she decided as she stood under the shower spray. She felt as if she was glowing, and there was no embarrassment as she washed away the evidence of their lovemaking. It was only as she did so that something finally occurred to her belatedly. She wasn't on birth control, and he hadn't used protection.

She rushed through washing her hair and drying it. She hurried out of the shower and wrapped herself in a towel as she went into the bedroom. A calendar sat on the dresser. She swiftly counted days. She was *very* regular with her periods, so she could be sure on timing. Unless the gods really were pissed off at her, she should start her period in a matter of days. She should be safe.

And yet . . . realizing it, made her immensely sad. Having known Hiro's passion and her own, she couldn't bear the idea of ever being in any other man's arms, let alone having his child. She wanted Hiro. Wanted a family with him. Shaughnessys *needed* family.

She kept the knowledge to herself, knowing that nothing was foolproof and the gods knew she had been enough of a fool over Hiro lately. Instead, she got dressed and headed for the living room. When she got there, she was amused to discover he was reading a romance novel. "I wasn't expecting that."

"There are no laws against men liking romance." He put the book up on a shelf and got to his feet. "Have I sufficiently sacrificed my manly image?"

She giggled as she let him help her with her jacket. "I don't think your image can suffer too badly." She considered that, then added impishly, "At least not until I whip you on the court. When you're crying like a baby, *then* your manly image will be SOL."

He laughed outright as they reached the parking lot. He exuberantly swung her up into his arms and in a wild circle. He was absolutely crazy about her. Knowing she wouldn't believe him, he said only, "You make me very happy, Aenya. I hope you know that."

It wasn't the same as love, but it was the beginnings of hope. She hugged him tightly. If she was wrong and she found she was pregnant, then she would run away from home and force him to go with her. Eventually he would have to love her. She was a loveable type, or so said her brothers.

They found Kienan waiting on the driveway at home with a basketball in his hands. He had a sixth sense for Aenya and had known she was almost home. "There you are!" he called cheerfully. "We're ready to play if you are." He watched Hiro help her off the bike, and his eyes narrowed sharply and dangerously. She looked at him and he was promptly all smiles. "You should put something better on, sis."

"Okay." She kissed his cheek and then jogged into the house.

As soon as the door shut, his fist slammed into Hiro's jaw. Before the older male could recover, he had grabbed him by the shirt and slammed him into the garage wall. "You son-of-a-bitch!" he snarled. "I *trusted* you, Hiro! You think I'm an idiot?! I saw how Aenya looked!"

Hiro didn't bother to try and fight his way loose. Kienan may have been two inches shorter but he was much stronger and vastly better trained. The fact that Hiro's jaw was throbbing but not swelling was evidence of that.

"No," he said evenly. "I don't think you're an idiot. I knew you'd all notice even though Aenya doesn't seem to think so." His eyes narrowed sharply. "And I'm going to tell you something I don't dare tell her."

"And that is?" Kienan challenged.

"I'm in love with her. But she'll never believe me because of this fucking contract."

Kienan stared into his eyes with an oddly piercing gaze and then released him and stepped back. "I had hoped you would. That's why I went to you. When I described you to my brothers and Dad, they were all in agreement with me that you were perfect for Aenya. That's why I hired you."

"As to that . . ." He pulled out his wallet and removed the check inside. He handed it to Kienan. "I'm firing myself. Nothing personal."

Kienan's grin came lightning quick across his face as he tore up the check. "And that's why I trusted you," he said simply. Something dangerous flickered across his eyes. "But I don't want my sister hurt. If you hurt her . . ."

"I'm doing my level best not to. I'm going to make her as happy as I can, Kien." He eyed his friend. "Just don't go hitting me again or I'll hit back and break your pretty nose." He caught movement from the corner of his eyes and turned his head to see Aenya jogging toward them in a pair of jean shorts and a sports bra. His pulse spiked through the roof. "No wonder you forbid the bikini," he murmured.

Kienan snorted. "The dork swam into a pier and knocked himself cold. Even the lifeguard was laughing almost too hard to save him."

"Okay, let's go." Aenya frowned as she saw the slight swelling on Hiro's jaw. "What happened?"

"A bee stung me." He grinned over her head as Kienan flipped him off behind her back. He glanced down at her with a smile. "Are you hoping to distract me with the shorts?"

"Hardly. I'll be moving so fast you won't get a chance to see my legs." She waved at her other two brothers and her father as she saw that they were on the court already. It had been built into the backyard when she had joined the team and the whole family used it whenever they could.

Mel and Taegan were wearing loose tank tops so Kienan and Hiro both stripped their shirts off. Aenya felt a slight blush warm her cheeks. She cleared her throat and sat on one of the benches, her eyes following Hiro helplessly. She had been held by that body, and underneath it. She shouldn't be blushing at seeing it again. But, damn it, he was too sexy! Her fingers itched to run all over him.

His reputation as a player was not exaggerated. He was definitely just as good as Mel, and her brother was lethal. Taegan and Kienan were equally matched in skill, so it really was down to Hiro and Mel and who could outwit the other. The score remained consistently tied and that meant the deciding factor would come down to time.

"Go Mel!" Aenya shouted. When Hiro glared at her, she blew him a kiss impishly.

"Thirty seconds!" Sullivan called.

Kienan had control of the ball. He shot around Taegan and made his way toward the basket. Mel tried to get in his way but Hiro intercepted, forcing Mel to pull up short before they collided. Kienan made the shot and the ball bounced off the rim and into the air. Everyone watched with their breath held as the ball flipped into the air. When it came down, it went through the net.

"Time!" Sullivan called. "Hiro and Kienan are the winners!" Mel said something distinctly unpleasant under his breath, and Sullivan just laughed. "Now boys, let's be good sports."

Kienan flexed the muscles in his arm. "So, Aenya, ready to get your ass whipped? No offense, Dad, but you're getting old."

The way Sullivan went down the short stacked bleachers to the court, no one would have ever guessed his age. "I'll show you old," he said mildly. Oh, it was harder to catch a breath lately, but that didn't mean he couldn't keep up with his kids on a court.

"Kick his ass, Dad," Mel muttered. "Gloating bastards." Despite the cool weather, he was hot from the match. He dumped half his bottle of water over his head rather than drink it. Aenya had better marry Hiro so that Mel had a chance at a rematch. He wasn't going to settle for being punked by a non-team player.

Taegan watched as the match began, the stopwatch swinging lightly from his fingers. The look on Hiro's face was absolutely priceless when he realized how good Aenya was at the game. Her height, which was her greatest disadvantage, was also her greatest weapon.

"Did you notice?" he murmured when Mel sat next to him.

"What, am I blind?" Mel sighed and rubbed the back of his neck. "On one hand, I want to be an outraged big brother and kick his ass for touching my baby sister. On the other hand, I know Aenya. She wouldn't have let him touch her unless she wanted him to. And it was definitely a mutual decision. The way they look at each other . . ."

"And she thinks we won't notice." Taegan shook his head.

"What the hell is she going to do if he fails?" Mel wondered quietly.

"I get the feeling that Hiro hasn't been playing all his cards. He knows something. I'm positive of it. This morning . . . something rang false in what he said. And I've always been sensitive to lies, so . . ." He sat up straighter and added calmly, "I'm willing to trust him with my sister. I will, however, have to hurt him, regardless, for his lack of honesty with her."

"Hit him on my behalf too," Mel offered.

He grinned briefly and then picked up the stopwatch. He had been calculating the points automatically even during the conversation. Numbers were his specialty. "Thirty seconds!" he called. "Aenya's team has a three point lead!"

Hiro said something explicit and rude under his breath. He couldn't get a hand on Aenya because she was so small, and she was so ridiculously agile that she was like a flash across the court. And how in the hell could anyone that short make a basket from that far? "Hold still!" he almost snarled.

She laughed in his face and ducked around him. She whirled and shot the ball at her father. Hiro was blocking the goal and it was time to show her stuff. She wouldn't want him to think he was the only one with tricks. "Daddy, rim it!"

"Hell!" Kienan whirled as his father shot the basketball. "Hiro, grab her! Tackle her! Do *something*!"

Hiro tried, really he did, but she ducked and slid between his legs. Before he could turn, she sprang to her feet and leapt into the air. The ball bounced off the rim and she caught it to dunk it through the net.

"Time!" Taegan called. Beside him, Mel was laughing so hard he couldn't breathe. With a grin, Taegan said, "The Rim Dunk is Aenya's specialty. No one expects her to be able to jump that high. She has all the agility of a gazelle. And she's so small that she can duck through most opponents' legs."

Aenya was holding onto the rim of the basketball net and let go to drop down into Kienan's arms. He hugged her fiercely, then ruffled her hair. "I hate you! I never want to talk to you again!" He gave her a smacking kiss. He was so proud of her that losing didn't really matter.

She got free of his grip and went over to hug Sullivan tightly. They exchanged a high five, and then she turned and gave Hiro a triumphant look. "Your manly image is officially forfeit, Michaels. You just lost a match to a woman half your size."

Everyone, Hiro included, began to laugh. Mel hoisted Aenya up onto his shoulders as they made their way back toward the house. "Make way, make way!" he called, and had the servants laughing as they cleared a path. "Her highness has royally trumped the invading knight."

Dinner was lively that night, as was normal, even though it was later than usual since they had all needed showers. Hiro was still nursing a sulk over dessert and so was Mel. That, naturally, amused everyone else immensely.

"Oh don't be such spoilsports," Aenya scolded them teasingly. "Honestly, you're too much alike in some ways."

"We are not," both males groused.

She just shook her head. It didn't surprise her that she had fallen in love with a man who was that much like her brothers. With a large stretch, she got to her feet. "It's late and I'm tired. I'm turning in early." She walked over to her father and kissed his cheek. "G'night, Daddy. Good match today."

Everyone remained silent as they heard her going upstairs. Only when the door shut did the Shaughnessys turn to look at Hiro. All four, nearly identical, pairs of eyes had varying levels of annoyance and warning.

Hiro held up his hands. "I'm in love with her. She asked me to be her first." The frustration filled his voice for a moment. "How in the name of hell was I supposed to say no?"

"If you do not find where she dances by morning, you must forfeit the contract," Sullivan reminded him quietly. "And if you forfeit the contract, you are not eligible to attempt a second time. Until the terms of the contract are met, it remains active."

Hiro looked at him evenly. "Come hell or high water, Mr. Shaughnessy, Aenya will be mine. I could care less about your company. In fact, you can take your shares and burn them. I have no need for your money. Do I, Taegan?" He shot the question challengingly across the table.

Taegan quirked a brow. "Most don't find me digging in their history."

"You cover your tracks well, particularly since you have a third party assisting you, but I do this sort of thing for a living—and I was expecting it. Why don't you tell your family what you found?"

Taegan removed his glasses and put them on the table. "To put it simply, Hiro's grandfather was a very intelligent man. He ran a fairly sizable investment fund for many years. When he saw the potential downturn in the market, he cashed out and put the money into savings. Upon his death last year, Hiro became the sole heir."

"Which investment fund?" Sullivan asked curiously.

"Archway Financial."

"Well." That was about all Mel could say.

"I see." Sullivan leaned back in his chair and studied Hiro. A man who was the heir to the fortune of what had once been one of the top five biggest investment houses certainly didn't need additional money, even from Shaughnessy Corporation. "The contract is still binding."

"With loopholes so big I could drive a bus through them." Hiro got to his feet. "And I will take advantage of every single one as needed. Now, if you'll excuse me, I'm going to turn in as well." He looked at Taegan. "Feel free to hit me at your leisure. Kienan already did."

"I'm holding it in reserve." Taegan watched Hiro leave the dining room and remarked to no one in particular, "Am I the only one of us with an image in their mind of two bulls yanking different directions on the same rope without realizing they're on the same side?"

"No," his brothers and father decided.

Upstairs, Aenya indulged in a long bath. All the bedrooms in the house had their own bathroom, which was much to their advantage. She would hate to share a bathroom with one of her brothers. They were all meticulous in their organization, and she left stuff all over the counters.

Because there was no need to keep up the farce—she absolutely did *not* want to confront her lover if she was wearing that horrible nightgown—she instead opted to wear the prettiest pair of pajamas she owned. They were pale peach in color and made of soft, silky material. They hugged her body and flattered every curve.

As she picked up the potion to add some to Hiro's tea, her fingers shook. The trembling came from the inside out and could not be controlled. Cursing herself, she grabbed for her courage and added the potion to the tea. Then, bracing her shoulders, she picked up the tray.

He was waiting for her when she knocked lightly on the door. He opened it instantly and smiled when he saw the tray. His lover was nothing if not an incredibly strong woman. "Ah, a midnight snack." As she put the tray down, he realized what she was wearing. His body heated and tightened with greedy hunger. "Well."

"I couldn't bring myself to wear that ugly nightgown for you," she admitted.

"I'm going to tell you something." He tugged her into his arms and ran his hands up under the back of the shirt. "Even in it, I thought you were the sexiest woman alive." He lowered his head and nibbled along the line of her jaw. "Of course, I like you naked even more. Think I could seduce you into staying home tonight?"

Her knees went weak as heat rose swiftly. Shivering in delight, she tilted her head to give him better access. "It would delay the inevitable." She still didn't resist when his lips claimed hers. Her arms wound around his shoulders and she rose onto her toes to improve their fit. She loved how he kissed her. That alone was pure pleasure.

When they slowly drew apart, their eyes met. Unspoken words seemed to flow between them. She took a deep breath and released him to step back. Casually, she handed him his tea. "You're far too good at that."

He smiled at her. "I'll take that as a compliment." He gave a grimace and rubbed his jaw. There was barely any swelling from where Kienan had hit him but it still ached.

"I can grab you an icepack," she offered. "All the bathrooms have first aid kits."

"Thanks." The instant she had gone into the bathroom, he dumped out his tea and poured fresh. When she returned and handed him the pack, it looked as if nothing had changed. He held the pack to his chin with one hand and sipped his tea with the other. "Out of curiosity, what's your dance of preference?"

"That's a hard one." She considered things. "I've tried and trained in several styles but for the last few years I've really concentrated on Latin." She gave him a sheepish grin. "I always feel really sexy but don't you *dare* tell my brothers. They already have problems when they see me in class or performance."

"I'm surprised your father hasn't stopped you entirely." He added a yawn for punctuation.

"He loves me," she said simply. "He wouldn't take away dance from me entirely. He just doesn't want it to be more than a hobby." She covered a smile as she saw him starting to sway a little. "Maybe you should lay down, Hiro. I think you're coming down off the adrenaline of the match. I once saw Mel fall asleep into his dinner plate."

"I'm telling him you're blabbing his secrets." He obligingly lay down on his bed and turned on his side away from her. "I'm not looking at you," he murmured, deliberately slurring his words, "else I might pull you into this bed with me."

Her body clenched with heat and hunger and love. It was a deadly combination that nearly overrode her control. Somehow she held on long enough to hear him beginning to snore softly. Strangely, he hadn't snored when they had slept together. Maybe he was just conscious of bed partners. It was oddly endearing.

She took the tray back into her room and went into her closet. It was Masquerade Night at the Faerie Club. Because she felt defiant and miserable, she pulled out her sexiest dancing dress. It was deep rose with beads and lace, and the silk material clung to every curve of her body. It split to the hip on her right side and the material was very stretchy to accommodate anything she might do. The neckline plunged daringly in the front, and slender but strong straps held it up. The supportive bra that went underneath was nearly invisible, giving the impression she could fall out anytime.

Her mask was an elaborate confection of white and pink, something that covered the entirety of her face except for her lips and eyes. In the light of the Club, even her eyes would seem invisible. She artfully pinned and piled her hair up high, and only wore lipstick since the mask covered everything else.

She pulled on her shoes, fastened them tightly, and decided against jewelry. Even as she was hurrying down the passage toward her ride, she was still miserable. She didn't want to go to the Club alone. She wanted to go with Hiro. She had seen the way he moved and was suspicious he might know how to dance. If so, she *really* wanted to dance with him just once, even if she was better.

Her mood didn't improve when she reached the Club. There was a sign in the front that clearly said 'For Sale by Owner.' On a panicked sound, she rushed into the Club and to where the owner was tending bar. "Please, please, tell me it's not this bad!" she pleaded. "Grandma, please!"

The owner was in her seventies and had no one to inherit. Everyone called her Grandma, no matter who they were. Because she had no family, she had been slowly bowing under the pressure of running the place alone. "I'm sorry, honey," she said softly. "I can't manage the bills anymore. I'm getting too old. I'm praying to find a good buyer else we'll close entirely."

"Can't the Enforcers do anything?" Aenya felt desperate.

"When I spoke with Rhianna Taber, she said she had already tried something and could only wait for the results." Grandma sighed and looked around the room at all the people laughing and enjoying themselves as they attempted to identify each other behind masks. "The Faerie Club was built for people like you who have nowhere else to go. People who need to feel normal. If only I could afford decent advertising to bring in more people and a good manager to keep us running exactly as we are."

"I'll think of something," Aenya vowed. If she had to, she would get together a collection. There had to be *something* that could be done. She swung around to head for the dance floor and walked right into someone. "Oomph!" She looked up quickly to find herself staring at a tall man in a mask that covered his entire face. Something was . . . familiar about him, and it was a little intriguing to see that he wore an outfit that matched hers. "I'm sorry."

Hiro felt his stomach relax when she didn't recognize him. He had been intending to do his invisibility bit, but when he had gotten to the club, Stormy had been sitting outside with the mask and a bag of clothes. He was *seriously* beginning to suspect that wolf.

Because he was fairly sure Aenya would recognize his voice, he deliberately spoke in French. "My apologies as well, miss."

She didn't bat an eyelash. "Mutual apologies are the best," she answered, her accent and speech as fluent as his.

"I'm new here," he said as he took her elbow to escort her to a table. "I don't suppose you can tell me about this place."

She sighed and dropped down onto a bench. "The Faerie Club is a place for people like me who have dreams and want to live them. We come here to dance and talk anonymously, to forget that in real life most of us are for some reason or another pushed out of normal society.

"There are no drugs here. No alcohol. Everything that we eat here is healthy and the drinks are all fruit based. They have a papaya fizzy water that's to die for. It's a family place because kids come here too." She lowered her head and rested her cheek on her arms. "But because it's not mainstream, we can't pull as many people in as we need to stay afloat. Now they have to sell," she whispered. "If someone buys the club who doesn't understand . . . it'll all change."

So that was why. His heart ached for her and for all those present. They knew their dream would end and were driven to enjoy every minute they could. It made sense; Aenya was smart. She could have bided her time until she was twenty-one and then changed her career without her father's refusal. Taegan himself had done it successfully. Aenya had been so blatant, though, that everyone had known, and now she was trapped.

"What if someone you trusted bought the place?" he asked her softly.

Her laugh sounded sad. "Oh, I know someone who could afford it. In fact, it wouldn't even make a dent in his finances. But he doesn't want me to dance, and I don't want him to know about this place."

"It's a pity. I saw you last night and you were amazing. I'm a trained dancer myself, in fact." He stood and offered a hand to her as the music changed to something drugging and slow, an invitation for lovers to move together. "Dance with me."

It wasn't a request, but she found no will to refuse. Her hand slipped into his and she let him draw her down to the dance floor. Her body was already finding the rhythm of the dance, swaying with a seduction that transcended age and gender. Everyone watching was entranced.

As her partner turned her into the dance, she found herself trusting him implicitly and without question. He knew her body, and his touch was familiar. She closed her eyes, trusting him further, feeling as if she was falling into a dream. It was Hiro with her. Her soul and body knew it even when her eyes did not.

"Just dream," he murmured in her ear, and his voice was suddenly Hiro's voice. "And I'll dream with you."

They dominated the floor. Everyone else pulled back to give them plenty of room, not wanting to miss a moment. Aenya's eyes never opened but she never missed a step. Hiro was always there, handling her body with a gentleness that added to the romance and seduction of their dance.

When the music ended, there were no dry eyes in the club. Even the children were spellbound, watching with rapt adoration. They loved Aenya. Everyone knew it was her. No one danced like she did. Her partner was a mystery, and a stranger. Yet there was no question in anyone's mind that he loved the woman he had danced with.

Aenya opened her eyes slowly and turned around. Her partner was gone. Even her mind now insisted it was Hiro, but it made absolutely no sense. And if it wasn't Hiro, what was she supposed to do? She felt seduced by the dance and it felt as if she had betrayed Hiro. Yet, at the same time, it *had* to be Hiro because no one else knew her body so well. It was too confusing!

She pushed it off and away to the best of her ability. She lost herself in the rest of the night by dancing with some of her favorite people. Some were really good dancers. Others were really bad. She had fun with each and every one. She even joined in an energetic circle dance with a bunch of the kids.

As dawn was beginning to creep near, everyone was shocked to hear Grandma give a loud gasp. Everything came to a stop as they all turned to look at her. She was on the phone and talking excitedly, her hands waving in the air. When she hung up the phone, she promptly burst into tears.

One of the young men nearby helped her into a chair. Aenya hurried over and knelt beside the old patron that had given them all a home. "What's wrong?" she asked urgently. "Is something wrong?"

"No, no!" Grandma took a deep breath. "It's wonderful! We're saved! I just got off the phone with a businessman who saw the sign outside. He said he's been watching the Club for a few days now and he would hate to see it go under. He's going to pay off the debts and bring in a new manager to make sure the Club never changes."

A resounding cheer rose throughout the room. Aenya found herself grinning. "That's wonderful! Do you know who it was? We'd all love to thank him!"

"He didn't actually give me his name, but he said he would be coming by tomorrow morning with the check. We'll have the first dance tomorrow night in his honor." Grandma got to her feet. "Now then, all of you scat and go home. We'll never have to worry again."

Aenya floated almost the entire way home, giddy with happiness. She wouldn't have to dance all night anymore. She could go back to being more secretive and go for only a few hours each night. Her father wouldn't have to use the contract anymore because he would assume she had stopped.

Contract.

Hiro.

Pain exploded inside her chest as she stood in her bathroom getting ready for bed. The second night had ended, and Hiro would have to fulfill the terms of the contract in the morning. If he didn't, then he would have to disappear from her life forever.

At least she had the Faerie Club, she thought fiercely. At least she still had her dreams. Maybe her partner would come back and dance with her again. Maybe he could make her forget Hiro.

Even as she thought it, she knew it was hopeless. She would never forget Hiro. Her dreams were cold comfort when she looked at the long and lonely years ahead without the man she loved. Her hands went to her stomach. In that moment, she prayed with everything she was that the timing was wrong.

Trembling, she took her shoes and left them just inside Hiro's room. She then crawled into her bed and curled up. Stormy climbed up next to her, and Aenya hugged her tightly as she buried her face in her fur. And giving in to the pain, she cried herself to sleep. Why was life always so unfair?

CHAPTER SIX

Stormy woke Aenya a few hours later by nudging her insistently. At first, Aenya didn't want to wake, but then she became aware of the utter silence in the room beside hers. She scrambled out of bed and pulled on her robe. When she went into Hiro's room, it was empty. Every sign that he had been there was gone.

Heart pounding in her throat, she changed clothes as fast as she could, yanking on the first jeans and shirt to come to hand. Her door was unlocked once more, and she rushed downstairs toward her father's office. Hiro's suitcase was outside the door. She threw the door open without knocking.

Sullivan looked up and found a smile for her. "We were waiting for you. Have a seat, Aenya."

On rubbery legs, she walked over to the second chair and sat down. Hiro was sitting in the first and he wasn't looking at her. "So," she said as evenly as she could. "This is the third day."

"Yes, it is." Sullivan looked at Hiro. "You know the terms. And I can tell from these shoes that you did not stop her last night, either." It wasn't a question, for the shoes he referred to were sitting on his desk.

"No, I didn't." Hiro's voice was both calm and even.

"Do you know where my daughter dances every night?"

"Yes, I do." He didn't look at Aenya even when she leapt out of her chair in shock. "Twice now I have followed Aenya to a place known as the Faerie Club in the 3rd District."

Sullivan slowly rubbed his chin, not yet looking at his daughter. "I have not heard of it."

"No, I imagine not. It's a good place, sir. It's oriented toward people of all ages and maintains a family atmosphere. While I was there, I did not hear a single objectionable song, unless you have something against polka. The drinks are all fruit based and there is no alcohol on site, nor are there drugs of any kind. I witnessed no fights, no bad language. It was like a dream come true for parents, honestly. I wish I had found it myself and sooner. Aenya dances there and rules the floor. I've never seen anyone better." He did look at her then and saw the soundless fall of tears down her cheeks. "She lives her dream there."

Sullivan studied his daughter. "Is this true, Aenya?"

She closed her eyes and nodded tightly. "It is." She opened her eyes, her lips trembling. "I've been dancing there for almost two years; you just didn't know until recently. The Club was in danger of closing and we were all so desperate to spend every minute there we could. It's a wonderful place, Daddy, I swear. Please . . . please don't make me stop going!"

"It's no longer my business," he said quietly. "Hiro has fulfilled the terms of the contract. You will be his wife."

"No!" She shook her head furiously. "I won't marry a man who does not love me!"

"Aenya, the contract is binding and I am your legal guardian. You like Hiro. You gave yourself to him," he added in a hard tone. When his daughter's eyes flared with shock, he nodded curtly. "Did you think I wouldn't know?"

"I hoped you wouldn't." She straightened her back, her eyes fixed on the wall across from her. "I hope you're happy, Hiro. You've got the rich bride you wanted. And obviously if you wanted to stop me from dancing, you can. I didn't fool you at all."

Hiro got to his feet. "I don't want to stop you from dancing. Do I look like that much of a bastard? I *saw* you. I *saw* how much you love to dance." He took her hand and placed a slip of paper in it. When she looked at it, he said quietly, "The Faerie Club is yours, Aenya. This check will pay off its debts, and you will be its new owner. You will be its new manager, and I know you'll keep it alive. You can dance as much as you want. And . . ." He looked at Sullivan. "As per the stipulations in the contract, having fulfilled its terms, I am free to reject the reward. I am doing so. Aenya may make her own decisions about her life. She can marry whomever she wants and go wherever she wants."

Aenya was staring at the check in such shock that she didn't hear him leave until the door shut behind him. She looked up sharply and took a step toward the door. Her hand tightened around the check. "Why?" she whispered. "You were so sure this was what you wanted."

"He never wanted the shares, Aenya," Sullivan said quietly. "He wanted you. It was only after he saw you that he signed the contract. Last night, he told me and your brothers that we could burn the shares for all he cared. This morning, he told me that he knew you'd never believe him if he told you he loves you. You've been so badly burned by this whole ordeal. But he does love you, baby. I know he does."

"He never told me!" Her breath hitched as she held the check against her heart. "I wanted him to love me so badly . . . I would have believed him."

"Did you tell him that?" He got to his feet. "Unless you go to him, Aenya, you'll never see him again. Kienan told me that Hiro has put his condo up for sale. He's making arrangements to leave the city entirely."

A horn honked outside the window and she looked over in surprise to see Kienan on his motorcycle. "Hey!" he called through the open window. "I know where he's heading! Let's go drop off your check then track him down!" When she hesitated, he snapped, "I'm not letting my hard work go to waste! You need to grow up, Aenya! What good is a dream if you don't fight for it? You fought for your dancing. Now fight for Hiro!"

She whirled and ran from the room. She stopped only long enough to yank on sneakers and rushed outside to where he was waiting. She stuffed the check in her pocket and pulled on her helmet. She climbed onto the bike behind him and grabbed his waist. "Hurry!"

"You got it!" He took off quickly and proceeded to cut through traffic as he headed for the 3rd District. "You know," he called over his shoulder, "I was sure you were going to completely mess everything up."

"What do you mean?" she called back.

"I hired Hiro. I'm the one who told him to come and take a shot at the contract. I was pretty certain that he would fall for you once he met you, and vice versa." He winced as she hit the back of his helmet. "Ow!"

"You jerk!" she shouted. "I wouldn't have worried so much if all of you had been more honest with me!"

"And like you were honest with us!" He winced as she hit him again. "I knew that Hiro was well off. He inherited a serious chunk of change from his grandfather. He doesn't need any part of our company, kid. He only wanted you."

"I have to admit, I'm not entirely surprised." She thought about his condo and motorcycle. Few private investigators could have afforded both. Both were also owned outright and that meant he had paid cash. "I hope it's not too late."

The Faerie Club was quiet at that time of morning. She hurried around to the back where Grandma had a small apartment attached to the club. Most people in 3rd District lived in places attached to their place of work. Grandma cried when she got the check, and Aenya didn't blame her. "I didn't know last night," Aenya admitted. "I didn't know that someone would buy the Club for me. I promise I'm going to make you proud!"

"I have no doubt in you." Grandma waved a hand. "Come in and talk."

"I can't," she apologized. "I have to go find someone."

"Your partner from last night? He's in the Club. He came by a little while ago and asked if he could say goodbye. I guess he's on his way back home."

She frowned. "You speak French?"

"He spoke English with me."

Warning bells went off in her mind. "I think I had better go have a word with him." She turned to go back to the front of the Club, and, no surprise, Kienan was nowhere in sight. Eyes narrowed slightly, she went into the Club. A man in a mask sat studying the dance pit with his back to her. Gee, interestingly, his hair was black.

"So," she asked in French, "you speak English?"

"I speak many languages," he countered in the same without turning. "I hear you're no longer engaged."

"Funny." She walked closer, arms crossed. She switched to English on purpose. "I don't recall anyone here knowing I was engaged. But as it happens, you're right. It's only temporary, though. I'm going to chase my former fiancé down. He's an idiot."

"He seems to think so, too." Hiro got to his feet and turned around. He pulled the mask off and dropped it on a table. There was a darkening bruise on his jaw, and his eyes were haunted, but his stride was deliberate as he walked toward her. She held her ground and he caged her against a table. "Why are you chasing after your idiot fiancé?"

She closed her eyes. "I decided I wanted to ask my last question. We made a promise, you see." When he cursed and paced away, she opened her eyes. "We promised that if I didn't ask anything you wouldn't want to answer, you would answer me truthfully."

"Yes, we did." Impatience gnawed at him. He had laid it all on the line and she wanted to ask him a stupid question. "So ask," he shot at her.

Very quietly, she asked, "Why did you sign the contract, Hiro?"

He went very still and slowly turned around. Understanding had filled her honey eyes. She already knew the answer, and she was giving him the chance to tell her. She would believe him. He slowly walked toward her, longing for her with every fiber of his being. "Because I loved you the moment I laid eyes on you. A dancing princess. I was helpless against you."

Tears slid down her cheeks. "Then don't go away," she whispered. "Stay with me. Screw the contract. I love you, Hiro. So much so it's been destroying me. You gave me my dream and it means nothing without you."

On a low sound of need, he snatched her into his arms and held her fiercely. "Thank god," he muttered over and over again, his lips rushing over her face, memorizing her with painful hunger. "I was doing everything I could to make you trust me. To make you love me. When you asked me to be your first, I was praying it would help bind you to me. But you seemed so practical!"

Her laugh was almost a hiccupping sob. "Practical? I was desperate!" She took a deep breath, her hands running compulsively over his arms, needing to feel him close. "I'm not on birth control."

"I know." His voice had roughened. "Timing?"

"Poor, but I was praying." Her lips trembled. "I realized it last night. I'd run away if I found I was pregnant. Then I'd find you and make you stay with me until you loved me."

"Too late. I'm already mad with loving you." He shot her a dirty look. "You are never allowed to dance like that with any man but me, by the way. I will very happily be your partner for any future dances that involve scraps of silk and lace and highly seductive music."

"Yes, as to that." She eyed him. "How did you follow me? I can assume you knew about the potion and avoided it. But how did you follow me without my seeing you?"

"Like this." He took a step back from her and picked up the material he had dropped near his suitcase. He twirled it like a matador, then said, "Now you see me," and pulled the cloak over his body. "Now you don't!"

She rubbed her eyes, stunned. He had completely disappeared right before her eyes. She warily took a step forward and shrieked as she was unceremoniously caught around the waist and tumbled onto the floor. "Hiro!" The yelp turned to laughter as he tucked her underneath him. "Okay, when'd you learn to dance?"

He pulled off the cloak and tossed it over the railing out of sight. "I've been training most of my life," he confessed. "I didn't tell you because I didn't want you to think I was using dance to get to you."

"It's an absolute waste of your talents," she decided. "You need to give up being a private investigator—or at least the dangerous parts—and help me win lots of competitions that will produce much publicity for my Club so that it never worries for patrons."

"I need a better offer than that. And I recall we aren't engaged anymore."

"Then ask me to marry you. Or I can ask you. I'd get on my knees but I seem to be pinned to a dance floor."

"You look very lovely on a dance floor in any fashion." He lowered his head until their lips were a breath apart. "Will you marry me, Aenya Shaughnessy? Will you be my partner in life and in dance? Help me raise bunches of tiny terrors to drive your father and brothers crazy with?"

"Yes, Hiro Michaels. I will." As he kissed her, she started to frame his face with her hands, but he sucked in a breath and reminded her that he had a bruise on his jaw. "Oh, I'm sorry!" She blinked and squinted at the mark. "What happened? You didn't have that this morning."

"Taegan slugged me for walking out," he muttered. "I should have believed you about the hitting when angry thing. I've been hit or nearly hit by all of you Shaughnessy siblings except Mel."

"When did Kienan . . ." Her voice trailed off and she rolled her eyes with a smile. "A bee sting. Sure. No more fighting with my brothers, got it?"

"Not even at the bachelor party, before the strippers arrive?"

"No! Pervert. No strippers."

"You're going to be a demanding wife, aren't you?"

"Yeah. Scared yet?"

"Shaking in my boots." He smiled and kissed her again lingeringly. Demanding or not, she was absolutely perfect for him in every way. Everything had worked out exactly as it was meant.

Back at the Shaughnessy house, Sullivan was still at his desk staring at the contract in front of him when it suddenly glowed and the word 'Complete' appeared on the top. Grinning, lightheaded with relief, he folded it and handed it to Stormy who was sitting beside his desk. "Return it with my regards."

Like a gleeful cherub, he got to his feet and hurried to the door to call for his housekeeper. He had a wedding to organize! He couldn't wait to see his daughter dancing at her wedding. She had always taken his breath away. He couldn't be any prouder of her.

CHAPTER SEVEN

The red haired woman looked up at the knock on her door and smiled when she saw who was entering. On a chair next to her was a neatly folded swath of burlap. "Ah, there you are," she said. "Got something for me?"

She swiveled around on her chair and took the contract that Stormy held out to her. She opened it and smiled in satisfaction. "Beautiful." She scrawled her notes across the bottom, and then tucked it into the open folder on her desk. As she closed it, it also reflected the word 'Complete' and she slid it into a drawer that said 'Shaughnessy' on it. There were close to one hundred files in there already.

"Only three left, isn't it now?" She reached for a blank contract on her desk. "Let's get to work, shall we? Oh, and remind me to send a nice wedding gift with you. I have some music that they're bound to simply love."

Status: File In Progress

Analysis: To catch a dancing princess, you only need to know the right steps.

Folder Two

KIENAN

CHAPTER EIGHT

The fighting and cursing could be heard from across the house. In fact, it was probably heard from the street even though the house was set back from it by a large driveway and vast front garden.

Hiro was walking past the front door of his future father-in-law's office when he saw his fiancée suddenly rush out the door, slam it, and lean back against it. Her cheeks were flaming red. He coughed. If there was anything he had gotten used to in the week he had resided in the Shaughnessy household, it was that the family did everything loud and large.

"Bad morning?" he offered.

She glowered at him. "*You* go in there and try to be a mediator. Kienan's either going to blow a fuse or Daddy's going to have a heart attack." She blew out a hard breath that stirred her pale bangs. "I need a distraction. Distract me please."

He smiled and swung an arm around her shoulders to escort her away from the door. He wasn't stupid enough to go in there when he could hear both Shaughnessy males shouting. "Gladly."

Inside the office, Kienan leaned across the desk to get in his father's face. He had never been one to back away from a fight. "You're being unreasonable, Dad!"

"Unreasonable!" Sullivan leaned equally across the table so he was eye to eye with his son. "Just because I don't want my children to throw their lives away, I'm unreasonable!"

"You let Taegan do what he wanted!"

"That's because he didn't tell me his plans until he was twenty-one! Damn it!" Sullivan sat back in his chair. First Aenya, now Kienan. Thank *god* Mel was both of legal age and levelheaded.

Kienan's chocolate eyes were tinted slightly red, evidence of his flying temper. Though no red hair marked the Shaughnessy bloodline, their tempers were pure, one hundred percent Irish. "I'm tired of pretending to care about my linguistic studies! I just want a *chance*! You're letting Aenya have a chance!"

"Ha! There was no letting involved on my part! She's Hiro's problem now, and I have every confidence he can catch her if she falls." Sullivan raked his hands through his hair. Why the hell did his kids have to be so much like him? They dreamed big and chased those dreams with all their soul.

As Kienan dropped back down into his chair, Sullivan contemplated the slender wolf sitting beside him. Stormy had been with the family longer than he remembered. In fact, he was fairly sure she had been there before even he was born, and he was climbing into his sixties with every day. Whenever she decided to attach to someone in their family, they rose up and fought harder for their dreams. There was more as well, but he was wary to examine it too closely until he was more certain. It was, to say the least, a very odd situation.

It had been a nice and normal morning until Kienan had walked in and dropped his bombshell. He had plopped down into one of the chairs and announced he was changing his major from Linguistics to Music Composition and Performance.

Sullivan didn't doubt his son's talent. Kienan had an amazing voice and a brilliant talent with most any instrument he chose to pick up. In fact, everyone in the family had some sort of musical skill. Aenya was a dancer, of course. Mel could play on a piano any piece of music after hearing it once. Taegan played several instruments.

However, Sullivan wanted his children to be able to support themselves. God only knew that they refused to accept anything more than an allowance from him, but even Kienan was the only one still receiving that. Taegan had his pay as a teacher. Aenya now received money from the club she owned. Mel drew a paycheck from the Shaughnessy Corp. where he was already working.

Aware that Kienan was watching him, he rubbed his forehead. "Why can't you just get hired at Aenya's club? You could do it as a side job, and then have a regular job to support yourself."

"For one thing, I don't want to work for my sister. I love her, but she's a Shaughnessy, too. She's just as good a businesswoman as you and Mel are businessmen. We'd kill each other. And anyway, I want more. I want to have the world hear my voice."

"It's a hard world to break into," his father warned him. "It's even more stressful than my company. I just want to make sure you're taken care of, and, damn it, I'm still your guardian for almost another full year."

"Was that a general curse or just 'cause you're tired of me?"

"Both, you brat."

They glared at each other, then the younger grinned cheekily. "I'm adorable, and you love me, Dad. You're just a pain in the ass."

"My son takes after me," Sullivan retorted. He found himself thankfully diverted by his phone ringing and Stormy pawing at the drawer beside him. He picked up the phone when he recognized the number on Caller ID. "Shaughnessy." There was a long silence as he listened to whoever was on the other end of the line. He looked down and opened the drawer Stormy was pawing at.

Stormy walked back over to Kienan, and he bent down to scratch her head. Ever since Aenya had gotten engaged to Hiro, Stormy had been hanging around Kienan more. Not that he minded. He had always liked the family wolf. She had always seemed like a big sister or parental unit when he was kid. He even had a vivid memory of her carrying him by the seat of his pants to keep him out of the pond when he was two.

Sullivan was still listening to whoever was on the phone. He was reading over the papers he had pulled out, and he had even put his glasses on. That meant he was serious. Kienan idly leaned back so his chair was on two legs and propped his feet on the edge of the desk. He didn't mind if business interrupted the argument. His dad kicked ass in the corporate world.

"Since everything went so well before," Sullivan finally said, "I will trust your judgment yet again, Ms. Taber. Do I want to know how you arrange all of these things?" He listened, then laughed. "No, I didn't think I did. Good day." He hung up the phone and pulled his glasses off with a sigh. "Alright, Kien. I want to make a deal with you."

"'sup?"

"If you're willing to dedicate a weekend to music and come up with one original song with sale potential, I will help you arrange a chance to sell it."

Kienan fell out of his chair with a thump. "Ouch!" Stormy promptly began licking his face and he sputtered and shoved at her. "Damn dog! Let me up!" She obligingly moved and he flipped gracefully to his feet, his martial arts training long ingrained after many years. "Thanks for the shock, Dad."

"You're welcome." Sullivan slid the contract across the desk as Kienan righted his chair. "Here. If you're worried I'll renege, it's all here in print. Read it for yourself."

Kienan didn't have Mel's vanity; he didn't mind wearing reading glasses. All the men in the family wore them. He pulled them out of his pocket and stuck them on his nose as he sat down. He picked up the contract and began to read.

He was, in his heart, his father's son. It didn't take long for him to skim over the details. The contract was oddly clear of the legalese that was common in the business world. It stated, rather plainly, that he would be given a full weekend to concentrate solely on music. Should he return with a song with sale potential, to be determined by an independent party, then Sullivan's contacts within the Enforcers would arrange said sale. The Enforcers were possibly one of the biggest companies in America. It didn't surprise Kienan that they would have music contacts.

In fact, there was only one thing that puzzled him at all. He dropped the contract to tap a finger on the last line. "Here. 'This contract is considered complete only on the basis of the signee's dreams coming true. If they do not find what they are seeking, this contract is considered null and void.' That's a bit vague, isn't it?"

"It's in all Enforcers' contracts. It was, in fact, in your sister's contract as well." Sullivan tugged the contract back and twirled it around so he could see it. "Lodgings have already been arranged for you since it is very difficult to find a place with the correct atmosphere for an artist of any type. As such, you will be staying at an inn within the 3rd District. The Enforcers know the owner and have booked the entire place for the weekend. It will be just you and the innkeeper."

Kienan frowned and crossed his arms. "I'm getting a really good deal here. Where's the catch? There's always a catch."

"Not this time." Sullivan sighed. "Kienan, I don't want to demolish your dreams. I just want to be certain you are provided for. If that means I go to some very strange extremes, then so be it."

"Strange is the understatement of the year," he muttered.

"It's not as easy as it sounds," his father warned him. "You have to come back with a unique, sellable, song. Otherwise you have to continue with your Linguistics studies." Kienan was fluent in nearly ten languages and had been headed toward a job as a translator with the Shaughnessy Corp. They had worldwide contacts.

As he watched Sullivan sign the contract, Kienan drummed his fingers on his arm. "So, in other words, I put a gamble on this weekend. I risk it all for a chance at my dreams. Hell, it's more of a deal than Aenya got. She never even had a choice. And yet all that went well, so I guess it's not such a raw deal. What the hell. Gimme a pen."

While he scrawled his name across the bottom of the contract, Sullivan spotted a strangely satisfied look on Stormy's face. It made him wonder just what his son would really be finding at the Gentle Brook Inn. That he would find his dreams was a given. It was just a question of whether his dreams would be the same when he left as when he arrived.

Dreams could, after all, change very quickly.

CHAPTER NINE

Taegan stood in the doorway of his baby brother's room and watched with a slightly lifted brow as Kienan packed a suitcase. The facts were slim at the moment. All he knew was that Kienan had come out of the office with a glint in his eye and a determined stride.

He had always known Kienan was a musical time bomb and had, in fact, expected an explosion much sooner. That Kienan had waited this long was the impressive part. Then again, after the events with Aenya, perhaps he felt he had a chance. Taegan propped a shoulder against the door and asked, "What's the story?"

"Dad offered me a deal." Kienan straightened up with a shirt over his shoulder. "He offered me a contract, which is more than he did for Aenya. I accepted the offer, so I'm off for a weekend to concentrate on my music."

Taegan walked over to sit on the bed and Stormy jumped up next to him. He gently ruffled her fur and companionably kept a hand on her back. She was too alone sometimes. She needed family as badly the Shaughnessys did. "Where's the catch, Kien? Father wouldn't just give in like this. You know how stubborn he is. You should have just waited a year."

"I have to take the chance *now*, Taegan." He looked at the guitar case leaning against the wall. "Somehow, I'm absolutely certain that if I don't take a chance now, I'll miss out on something that could define my life and give me everything I ever wanted." On a sigh, he shut the suitcase. "The basic deal is that I go away for a weekend to concentrate. If I come back with a sellable song, I get my chance. If I don't, I continue on as I am."

"That's risky, Kien." Taegan frowned slightly. "Doesn't that mean that even when you're twenty-one, you'll have to continue Linguistics? You wouldn't be able to take another chance just because you're an official adult."

"Yeah. But I'm going to try."

"You've never composed a song in a weekend before," his older brother noted softly.

"I've never tried. If I get the right inspiration, I can do anything. When I come home, I'm going to have one of the greatest songs you've ever heard."

Taegan was silent for long moments, his eyes lingering on Stormy, then he smiled and got to his feet. "I'm looking forward to it. If you make it a love song, we can convince Aenya to let you sing at her wedding."

"Wouldn't take much convincing." He smiled ruefully. "I think I've already been blackmailed into it. And is it weird to be the bride's brother *and* the groom's best man?"

Taegan laughed. "Not around here." He ruffled first Stormy's fur, then Kienan's hair. "Take the sidecar and bring Stormy along. She'll be good company."

"If she wants to go." Kienan smiled at her. "Want to go?" She wagged her tail happily and he laughed. "I figured. C'mon, girl. Let's get going. You'll like riding by motorcycle. It's the kind of thing I think you'll appreciate."

With the wolf at his heels, he headed downstairs and out to the large garage where all the vehicles were kept. He, Taegan, and Hiro owned motorcycles. Sullivan had a sleek little hybrid. Mel had a restored 1970 Mustang that he doted on. Aenya didn't have a car yet, but she was contemplating a motorcycle too. Kienan grinned. He loved his sister.

There was one sidecar that everyone with a bike shared. He attached it and stuck his suitcase in. Stormy jumped in as well and he made sure she was securely fastened in.

As he was looking at the map to Gentle Brook Inn, Aenya suddenly came running into the garage. She skidded to a stop and smiled. "Don't forget to say hi for me."

He blinked, then remembered. "Oh, yeah. One of your friends works at the inn I'm going to. I forgot about that. If she's there, sure, I'll say hi. Her name is Evelyn right?"

"Madelyne!" She poked him in the chest. "She's wary of handsome men, so be nice to her, got it?" She frowned when he leaned over to kiss her forehead. She knew he would never do anything to deliberately hurt anyone, let alone a woman, but she absolutely felt as if the warning was important. "Promise me."

"Of course I promise." He pulled on his helmet. "See you on Sunday afternoon." When she had moved, he fired up his bike and backed down the driveway. Once on the street, he took off for the familiar roads leading to the 3rd District. He had been there several times lately, mostly to visit Aenya's club. He liked it there as much as she did. In many ways, he wasn't surprised that it was where he was being sent for the weekend.

The District was mostly small businesses. The people who worked there also lived there, with very few exceptions. Most businesses were attached to apartments or small houses where the owners lived. There was a very small residential area, but it was mostly run down. Deliberately, he thought, to keep outsiders from hustling in. He was fairly sure a computer teacher from college lived there.

The Gentle Brook Inn was less than four blocks from the Faerie Club. The Inn was a popular resort location due to the fact that it possessed at least three different hot springs, all naturally fed from a brook that ran beside the inn. The brook was from an underground vein; it had never run dry.

Bamboo trees and ferns of all shapes and sizes lined the front of the inn, and the walkway was covered in a riot of flowers blooming in every color. There were flowers that he was certain he had never heard of, let alone seen, before. There was a gentle, relaxing feel to the inn and he felt the tension in his shoulders disappear without his having really known it was there to begin with.

He spotted a small parking lot and rode slowly over to park. As he was pulling his suitcase out of the sidecar, he heard Stormy give a happy bark and take off running toward the inn. There came a startled feminine yelp that almost immediately turned to a laugh, and the woman said, "Easy, girl! Down now!"

His stomach quivered with a sudden and shocking longing. Sheer heat seemed to surge in his veins and every nerve in his body revved at the same time. In bemused understanding, he stood there and realized he was attracted to the owner of the voice. It was a little puzzling. Oh, the voice was powerful and beautiful, but he had never before encountered such a ferocious lust before, and certainly not just because of a *voice*.

More than a little intrigued, he turned around to see who or what Stormy had found. When his eyes fell on the young woman with Stormy, he felt the ground move under his feet even as his heart began to beat harder. It was the last thing he would have expected to happen for the young woman was potentially the plainest girl he had ever seen in his life.

Her hair was dove gray and pinned up on her head in a thick coil of braids. Her eyes were slightly tilted at the corner but not enough to be considered exotic. The color was of violets just starting to open, neither rich nor blushing.

She stood at slightly taller than average height with a slender frame, but there was nothing extremely spectacular about her figure either. Her legs were only a little longer than normal, and her hands were graceful. There was nothing about her that was designed to inspire lust or attraction in the general populace.

And yet, he realized in fascination as he walked toward her slowly, he was enthralled. Attracted. The hard fist of lust had punched in and left him with the most powerful urge to taste her smiling lips and feel her soft-looking skin. More still, his heart ached even harder. Lust was really longing and the longing was as emotional as physical.

The birds hadn't stopped singing and the sun still shined, but he felt cushioned in a pocket that only contained the two of them. He had known beautiful women. He'd had one or two for a lover. He couldn't remember their faces anymore. They had been wiped from his mind for all time by this plain nightingale in an old-fashioned gray dress.

"Welcome to the Gentle Brook Inn." She held out a hand. "I'm Madelyne Winters, the owner and keeper." As he continued to stare at her with a fascinated look on his face, she blinked in bemusement. Most people, men in particular, passed right over her. "Mr. Shaughnessy?"

He shook his head quickly. "Sorry. I was off somewhere." He took her hand and was delighted with her firm handshake. He was also fascinated by her soft skin. It felt like down feathers. "It's nice to meet you, Madelyne. I'm Kienan." The name registered finally. "Oh! *You're* Madelyne! Aenya told me to tell you hi." His eyes sparkled merrily. "Hi."

Aenya was going to burn in hell. Madelyne was going to kill her friend when she saw her next, because she had neglected to mention that Kienan was by far the most beautiful of her brothers. Madelyne had seen Mel in passing at college and she was currently in one of Taegan's classes. Kienan smoked them both.

Men that gorgeous should have had sirens go off when they were near helpless females. He was the shortest Shaughnessy brother, but that didn't make him short. He was barely shy of six feet tall with a strong and muscular body designed to inspire feminine heatstroke. He moved with predatory grace like a large cat, light and agile on his feet. His golden brown hair flopped into his chocolaty brown eyes. They were an artist's eyes, full of dreams and visions.

And she was hopelessly outmatched. She always was when faced with beauty, especially men. She slipped her hand free of his and retreated into professional mode. "The Gentle Brook Inn is yours for the weekend, Mr. Shaughnessy," she told him as she walked inside. "We have four hot springs, two for each gender. Unfortunately, the men's springs are currently broken as the heater decided to fall apart right before winter. You can still go into the spring, but it'll be a smidge cold. Your room is on the first floor, second on the left down this first hall."

She even walked like a lady. He followed her but didn't really listen to her words. All he could hear was the beautiful, melodic sound of her voice and it danced over his skin like invisible fingers. He really didn't need the encouragement. Though the dress muffled her figure, his deft eye suspected she had some very lovely, if subtle, curves under her unflattering clothes. He had never been interested in overly curvy girls anyway.

She started to turn, and he hastily lifted his gaze to smile. "I guess this is a little unusual. Having just one guest. I hope you're being fully reimbursed."

"Oh of course. The Enforcers look after me very closely. And anyway, one or one hundred, I treat all guests the same." She smiled as she handed him his key. "Dinner is at six, but if you're hungry at other times, you can ring the bell. Small my inn may be, but we assuredly have room service."

"Even at midnight?" he teased.

Laughter filled her eyes and took his breath. "Yes, even then. I'm mostly nocturnal." She turned her gaze toward the window where the morning sun was streaming in. "I follow the nightingale's path."

"Nightingale?" He glanced up from signing the register. "What nightingale?"

"It's one of the many legends of the 3rd District." She knelt and ran a hand over Stormy's head. "Do you believe in legends, Mr. Shaughnessy?"

"It's Kienan. My father is Mr. Shaughnessy." He leaned against the counter and cocked his head slightly. "I suppose I do," he finally said. "I don't dismiss them out of hand but I always think they need to be taken with a grain of salt."

"A wise attitude to have, Kienan." She glanced up at him, her violet eyes bottomless with mysteries and secrets. "Especially around this area of town. We all protect our legends."

"Tell me about the nightingale then," he offered. When she tilted her head slightly, he smiled and reached out a hand to help her up. "Your voice is beautiful. I like hearing you talk. So, talk to me. Keep me company while I unpack."

"If you like." She fell into step beside him as they went down the hall, Stormy padding by her ankle companionably. "The nightingale's legend is a sad one, as most are. Once, a long, long time ago, a swan fell in love with a human. In order to become human himself, he needed to sacrifice something great. So he gave up his beauty and was turned human. His love, however, was afraid of him.

"One night as he sat lamenting his sorrow, a small bird hopped into his lap. It was a plain, very ordinary bird. The human was going to turn her away, but she offered to help him win his love if only he would offer her a home. He decided that it couldn't hurt to accept such a deal and agreed. To his amazement, the little bird began to sing.

"The nightingale, you see, is a bird whose only beauty comes from its voice. In the dark of the night, when it sings, you forget how plain it is. Needless to say the man won his ladylove and his beauty was restored. The nightingale asked to be granted her home; none else would have her for she was so plain.

"The man refused. Now that he had his lover and his beauty, he did not want such a plain little bird hanging around. He turned her away, telling her that only when she was beautiful would he ever allow her entry into his home." She fell silent for a moment, aware Kienan was listening avidly. She continued softly, "After a while the man felt guilty and decided to seek the nightingale out. He found her wounded in a forest, pierced by a hunter's arrow which had been aiming for another swan.

"As she died, she told him she did not blame him for his ways. He blamed himself instead, and in his grief, he built a curse upon them both. Only when the nightingale finds herself a home will he be free. They say that at night, the nightingale can be heard singing her songs of sadness, always seeking the home she cannot have. Sometimes, too, you can hear the hunter who has always cursed the little bird that kept him from his prize."

Kienan's breath unraveled. There was a painful hitch inside his chest as if he had experienced every pain the characters in the tale had. "Maddie, have you ever considered a career as a storyteller or bard or something?"

The nickname briefly startled her. She brushed it off with a laugh and decided to accept it. He was obviously an informal type of man. "I'll take that as a compliment." She walked over to the window in the room and opened it to let in sunshine and fresh air. She took a deep breath and turned around. "The nightingale can be heard singing near here every night, you know. Maybe you'll hear her."

"Have you ever looked for her?" He watched her intently, memorizing her face. There was . . . just something about her. Something he couldn't get out of his mind. Every minute in her company made him want her more. Need her more. He was beginning to think he needed her more than he needed air.

"No, she likes her privacy as much as I do." Her mouth went dry as she saw the way he watched her intently. She had never been stared at like that before, as if she was absolutely vital to someone. Unnerved, she took a little step back. Red color climbed her cheeks. "Is something wrong?"

"No, actually." He walked slowly toward her, not wanting to frighten her. Aenya's warning rang in his head. Not to his surprise, Madelyne backed up until she bumped into the wall. He moved even closer and placed a hand on the wall to keep her trapped. Instinctively, he turned so that his body cut off everything around her. "There's nothing wrong. I just have this odd situation."

She had to clear her throat to find her voice. He smelled like wild, wicked danger and the promise of happily ever after. "And that is?" Her voice belied her feelings, sounding huskier and longing. The ferocious desire for him was, to say the least, a problem.

"I'm attracted to you, and I don't even know why." Her eyes widened with shock and her mouth fell open. He grinned. "It struck me that way too, actually. But I've decided to go with the flow. I just figured I ought to warn you since I'm going to spend an inordinate amount of time staring at you."

"Don't joke around!" She pushed him aside and ducked toward the door. Her heart raced furiously in her chest and there was a pain underneath. "Men like you don't want women like me. I don't appreciate the joke, Mr. Shaughnessy!"

"My name is Kienan." He linked his hands behind his head in the picture of casualness, but his body tensed slightly like a tiger ready to pounce. Something wild shifted in his artist eyes. "You better use it instead of my last name."

"Why?"

"Because otherwise I'll do something drastic." His smile turned slow, wicked, and outrageously beautiful. It was the smile that marked all Shaughnessy men, and he used it deliberately as a way to catch the woman he wanted.

Her color rose as her entire body flushed with heat. A smile like that made a woman feel as if she had just been stroked in every sensitive place on her body. "Drastic?" Her voice came out nearly breathless despite her best efforts. "Like what?"

His smile turned into a masculine challenge. "Why don't you call me by my last name and find out?"

She gave in to the coward's urge and fled the room so fast that the door slammed behind her. Her entire world had just flipped inside out and she felt like Alice falling down the rabbit hole. Hearing him clucking his tongue at her softly wasn't enough to make her dare going back into the room.

Her eyes fell on Stormy at the end of the hall. The wolf's eyes seemed guileless, but her tail wagged happily. Madelyne's eyes narrowed. "I absolutely hate you." She turned on her heel and stalked away down the hall, her skirts swishing around her ankles. She wasn't surprised when Stormy followed her with a little smirk on her face. Nothing fazed her.

Kienan gave Madelyne plenty of room; he knew he had made his point well enough. She needed room to breathe and he gave it to her. Instead, he stayed in his room and fiddled with his guitar. There was a melody in the back of his mind. Snippets of words flashed through his thoughts but wouldn't form lyrics. Nothing could seem to make it to his fingers to be captured. In frustration, he launched into a rousing rendition of Yankee Doodle.

Laughter made him look up in surprise to see Madelyne standing in the doorway. Her eyes sparkled merrily. Politely she said, "Dinner is ready, but if you'd rather keep playing, please do. I could make you some macaroni."

"Oh, be quiet!" he groused as he got to his feet. He put the guitar aside and followed her as she headed toward the dining room. As if he wasn't hungry for all knowledge about her that he could have, he asked casually, "How old are you, Maddie? You seem a bit young to be an innkeeper."

"I'm nineteen," she offered. "I go to the same college as you." She gestured him in to the dining room.

As he sat down, he considered her words. "I never noticed you before."

"Most don't." There was no sadness in her voice. Just a simple acceptance of the truth. She put a plate in front of him, and then headed for the door to the kitchen. She felt his curious gaze and smiled over her shoulder. "You're a guest, Kienan. I don't eat with the guests."

He contemplated the door as it shut behind her. Unless he was mistaken—and he highly doubted he was—this was a woman in some serious need of TLC. Her loneliness was practically visible, and his reliable sixth sense told him that she had become so used to rejection that it was automatic to assume more. It appalled him to think that so many would judge on basis of appearance. Her warm and open personality should have drawn droves of people. Even if he hadn't been attracted to her, he would have liked her and wanted to be her friend.

And she really wasn't that plain. Every time he looked at her, she somehow got more and more lovely. Whether it was because her very plainness was appealing or because her personality was shining through, he didn't know. Frankly, if beauty was measured by a person's heart, she would be exquisite.

Decision made, he picked up his plate and went into the kitchen. She was in the process of wiping down a counter and looked at him in surprise. "Is something wrong? Too much garlic in the sauce?"

"It smells *amazing*," he told her sincerely. Then he lied without compunction, "I'm used to eating dinner with lots of people. I figured I'd eat in here with you. Besides, you're good company." He sat down at the counter across from her and scooped up a big bite of pasta. As the flavor exploded on his tongue, his eyes nearly rolled back. "Holy jumping Christ on a motorcycle." He stared at his plate. "Promise you'll marry me and cook for me, please?"

A giggle escaped before she could stop it. "You're so different, Kienan. But it's in a good way." She leaned on the counter and watched him with a smile. "You and your sister have much in common."

"She's an incorrigible brat," he said around a mouthful.

Her eyes danced. "Well . . ."

He nearly choked, then began to laugh. "You're terrible!" Content with her humor, for it was much like his own, he looked around the kitchen. It was a gourmet chef's dream, but there was only one apron hanging from the hooks. There was no sign that anyone other than Madelyne lived or worked there. "May I ask what happened to your parents? I mean, obviously you're alone here."

"They were killed when I was ten. Some psycho was high on something and decided he wanted to rid 3rd District of its witches. Among the casualties were my parents. A few others lost family members that day as well." She ran a hand over the stainless steel countertop. "I thought I'd have to move and be adopted, but the Enforcers bought the inn and said that because they knew I wanted it, they wanted me to have it." She smiled suddenly. "Rhianna Taber is the closest thing to a mother I have. She's my legal guardian, and she and her partner have raised me. If you want to see something amusing, watch a businesswoman slap on an apron over a five hundred dollar suit and start mopping."

Stormy made a sound suspiciously like a snicker. Kienan ignored it. With a smile, he pushed his plate across the counter. "That was wonderful. What's for dessert?"

"You really are a bottomless pit just like your sister." She smiled. "Dessert is a soufflé."

As she started to go past him to retrieve the dish from the oven, he caught her by the wrist. "What," he asked softly, "if I wanted something plainer?" She went very still and he drew her steadily closer as he stood. Pointedly, he caged her between his body and the counter. "You didn't believe me when I said I wanted you."

Her heart was beating fast enough that it was impossible to breathe. His body gave off waves of heat that urged her to simply lean forward and rest her head on his broad shoulder. She could, she thought distantly. She could lean on him, and he would hold her. She hadn't been held in so long . . .

She stiffened her spine and stared at his collar. It was safer than staring into his velvety eyes and sinking into him. "Why should I believe something like that? I own mirrors, Kienan. I know what I look like. And I know what you look like. Men, especially handsome men, do not want a plain woman like me."

"Mirrors only show what's on the surface," he countered with a slight shrug. "They don't reflect my desire for music any more than they reflect your tenderness. And that sort of a thing, Maddie," he caught her chin and tilted her head back, "would appeal to the right man a lot more certainly than any amount of beauty. Besides," his head lowered and his lips skimmed along her jaw, "the longer I look at you, the more beautiful you are to me."

She couldn't breathe and couldn't think, her entire body beginning to tingle as if it had awakened just for the first time. "Don't lie," she whispered.

"I don't lie," he whispered back, his lips teasing hers. He watched her eyes darken to purple, like the most powerful of storms, and his lips curved slightly. "Better get your soufflé."

She gasped and wrenched herself free from his grip. She rushed to the oven, but it was too late. The top had already collapsed entirely, and the edges were beginning to burn. Resigned, she dumped the soufflé into the garbage; she would not serve something that had burned. Instead, she got out the ice cream she had been intending to serve with it and scooped some into a bowl.

As she set it in front of Kienan, he gave her a quick grin. "Vanilla was always my favorite."

Giving in for the second time to her coward's urge, she hurried to the doorway. "Good night, Kienan. Breakfast is whenever you wake up so just ring me so that I know. Oh," she added over her shoulder, "remember to watch out for the nightingale. You would probably scare her. Any sane female would be scared of you."

He watched her go before thoughtfully taking a bite of the ice cream. It was homemade and had little bits of real vanilla in it to give it bite. It was just like its creator. It was unassuming and plain until you got close, then it became irresistible and made everything else seem overdone and over-the-top. As vanilla had been his favorite flavor for his entire life, he thought it entirely fitting that he wanted a woman who was vanilla incarnate.

He just had to convince her that he wouldn't be swayed away by the soufflés of the world.

CHAPTER TEN

As Kienan laid in bed that night and stared at the ceiling, he was unable to fall asleep for the thoughts whirling through his head. He had come here to chase his dreams of music, to take a chance, to have everything he had always wanted. All that had gone flying out the window the instant he had seen Madelyne. How could he even think about music when his thoughts were consumed with her?

There had to be another reason why she was careful to keep people away. It couldn't be because she wasn't lovely. Hell, five minutes in her company and anyone with half a brain would realize what a wonderful person she was inside. Even in a superficial world, people wanted to be near others who made them happy. She brought sunshine and smiles to a very gloomy world.

There had to be something more. And everything inside him, every instinct he owned, tore at him with a fierce vengeance, insisting that he protect her from everything. He had to shelter her from those who would try to hurt her. He was a protector by nature, but this went deeper than that, and he knew it. This urge came from his very soul.

On a wry sigh, he got out of bed and went to the window where the garden beyond was shrouded in shadows and moonlight. Really, he wasn't too surprised. He had been expecting it when he had turned around and felt the world stop as he looked into violet eyes. He, the flighty and irresponsible one, was in love.

Hiro had once said that realizing he loved Aenya had felt like a click in his heart. Kienan hadn't heard a click. He hadn't heard anything. It had all slammed into him like a fist from a gauntlet. It left him reeling and wobbling, his breath gone and his senses dazed. And there was pain, too, thinking of how hard it would be to help heal Madelyne so that she believed he loved her. Thank *god* Aenya had warned him else he might have really ruined things.

With a sigh, he opened the window and closed his eyes. The night was calm and quiet. Then, slowly into the stillness, he began to hear something. He couldn't identify it initially, but as he listened harder, he realized he could hear someone singing. It belonged to a woman, and the lonely haunting melody made goose bumps rise on his skin. He had never heard anything that incredible before. It didn't sound human.

When the purple moon is high in the sky, I walk through the heat of a savannah

His heart began to thud dully in his chest as he straightened and stared out the window intently, trying to see if he could spot anything. There was nothing but the swaying of trees in the night wind and the shimmering of the moon above. No indication that anyone was in the garden, anywhere.

When the pain is too much for my heart, my nightingale's melody soothes my tears

Was it really the nightingale singing? He didn't care. He simply closed his eyes and let the music wrap around him. He felt something nudge his hand and looked down to see Stormy watching him, her canine eyes filled with grief. She walked over to the guitar leaning against the wall and pawed at it lightly.

After a moment's hesitation, he got up and walked over to pick up the guitar. As he sat at the window again, he felt the soft breezes blowing around him. They should have been cool but they were warm as he lifted the guitar. He didn't know if he could possibly soothe a nightingale's pain, but he wanted her to know she wasn't completely alone.

It wasn't hard to pick up the melody. He began to play along after a few beats. There was more there, he thought. So much more that the song could say. But, for that moment, he simply lost himself in the joy of the music, sharing the night with the lonely ghost singing outside his window.

When he heard light knocking on his door a few hours later, he was barely cognizant. He had stayed up the entire night playing with the nightingale. As the first light of dawn had appeared, the voice had disappeared as if afraid of facing the light of day. He had put his guitar away and fallen into bed.

It was now ten o'clock and he had severely overslept. With a distinct curse in Spanish, he rolled over and pulled the blankets up to his chin. Mornings were good for nothing except sleeping. Or snuggling a vanilla flavored nightingale, but despite her knocking on the door, he doubted she would get into bed with him. Damn it.

When there was no answer beyond the curse, Madelyne opened the door slightly and peeked inside. She bit her lip to hide a snicker as she saw the lump under the blankets. She had been expressly ordered by her own role in the contract to make sure that he was awake by ten in the morning so that he had ample writing time. On a sigh, she opened the door and walked in.

He was more sensitive than she had given him credit for. She stood beside the bed and studied his sleeping face with a hunger she didn't want to admit, let alone examine closely. He was wonderfully beautiful, and her fingers itched to touch him. His hair always fell in his face, and this time she couldn't stop herself from gently brushing the strands back.

She had heard him the entire night. He had true talent; not many could pick up a song he had never heard before and play it for hours without sheet music. She sighed and skimmed her fingers down his cheek. What was she going to do with him?

To her surprise, his fingers suddenly closed around her wrist. Before she could catch her breath, he had tumbled her across him onto the bed and turned to pin her beneath his body.

He was half-naked, and the sight of his strong chest made her mouth dry. He was almost unbearably hot, his body giving off waves of heat that sank into her and touched the wounded parts of her that had seemed frozen solid. If she put her arms around him, he would hold her, and she caught herself as her hands were lifting.

He had thought it would be a nice way to teach her not to pet him while he was asleep, but the plan had backfired. Now he knew how she fit in his arms, her soft curves molding perfectly against his body. Her skin felt as soft as down feathers and was smooth and fragrant. Her scent, apples and vanilla, went to his head.

Her hair was already pinned up and he wanted to see it down. He deliberately began to remove every pin he found and tossed them over the side of the bed where they bounced on the wood floor. The sheer number of pins was staggering, and he combed his fingers through her hair to make sure he had not missed one. When he was sure, he leaned back and lifted her so that she wasn't lying on her hair and holding it in place.

Her hair came down eagerly and stole his breath. Unbound, her hair had to be at least as long as she was tall and it spilled across the bed to fall over the side. It was the same fragrant scent as her skin and just as soft. As fine as silk but incredibly thick with no hair products to detract from its presence.

He buried his fingers in it with a sense of wonder. "Why do you hide it?" he asked softly. "It's incredible."

"It's a vanity," she managed to say. She felt exposed and vulnerable with her hair down. He was seeing something that nearly no one else had ever seen. "I keep intending to get it cut."

"Don't you dare!" He drew her closer and buried his face in her hair to seek the gentle curve of her ear. When he found it, he nibbled gently and heard her breath break softly. The little sound sent licks of fire through his entire body.

He lifted his head to see her face and studied her intently. Now used to her features, his eyes began to pick out little details, like the fact that her lips were a little fuller than average and just right for kissing. Her lashes were long and thick and smoky gray; she probably never had to wear any sort of makeup. He knew nothing about her face had changed. It was his eyes that had changed. He saw her with the eyes of a man in love, and because he loved her, he found her completely and utterly . . . "Beautiful," he said softly.

Her startled gaze lifted to his. "Don't be ridiculous," she said curtly. "No matter how badly you might . . . might want to get laid, don't assume I'm going to buy something stupid like that."

His eyes danced. "Well, I definitely want to get laid," he conceded, "but it's not because I woke up horny. I want *you* and only you. Morning, noon, or night. Deal with it." Before she could argue, he lowered his head and kissed her. A shudder rippled through his strong body at her flavor. She was soft everywhere, her lips the perfect shape to mold to his. He would never get enough.

She tried to stiffen her body and keep her lips tightly sealed but she had no more resistance to him than the sun did to the dawn. On a low moan, she lifted her hands and curled them around his neck, holding him closer even as her lips parted to let him in.

The kiss turned wild and carnal as his tongue tangled hotly with hers. His hands lowered and in a single sweep went entirely over her body, leaving her feeling as if he had just branded her completely. Still kissing her, unable to get enough of her, he began to unfasten the front of her dress. He felt desperate for the feel of her skin.

He did stop kissing her as he felt the dress open, and he levered himself up so he could see. Delighted, he skimmed a knuckle over the top curve of her breast gently hidden behind a lace bra. "Who'd have thought?" He lowered his head and trailed his lips over where his fingers had gone.

She flushed both with embarrassment and desire as his lips left a wake of heat behind. "Well," she said, "it's my underwear. Who's likely to see it?" The last word was a gasp as his mouth found the hardened peak of one nipple and tugged lightly. Pleasure spread from her breasts outward, and she realized in a sense of panic that if she didn't stop him, he wouldn't stop at all. "No," she gasped and lifted her hands to cover herself as he deftly opened the front of her bra.

If he had thought it was just nerves, then he would have just loved her past them. He glanced at her eyes to gauge her emotions, and he saw genuine fear. He took a deep breath to get a hold of himself. It wasn't an easy feat when he was so desperate for her that he felt as if he was going to explode, but he would be *damned* if he hurt her.

Because he didn't trust his self-control, he rolled to the side, onto his back and put an arm over his eyes. She scrambled up quickly and his breath hissed in as her hair dragged across his skin like silken fire. He warily opened one eye to see her standing a few feet away with her arms defensively crossed.

He stopped breathing entirely. Curtained in her hair, which did indeed touch the floor, her entire being spoke of unconscious sensuality. No, she wasn't beautiful, but *damn* she was sexy. Even behind her arms he could see the gentle curve of her breasts, and his hands burned to touch her. Roughly he said, "I don't care what you call it, but I want you until I can't think."

She began to button her dress with shaking fingers. "I'm not what you think I am," she said quietly. "I'm not a virgin, Kienan, scared by the unknown."

He thought of her stunned response in his arms and the shock in her eyes as she had felt pleasure for what was clearly the first time. "Why?"

"Why what?" She didn't look at him and cursed her clumsy hands that she couldn't finish fixing her clothes.

He got to his feet and brushed her hands aside to button the dress for her. "Why aren't you a virgin?" he asked calmly. "Because the asshole who was your first, clearly didn't teach you anything about what a woman should feel in a decent man's arms. Mind you, it wouldn't be anything compared to what is between us, but that's because I'm *the* man for you, and that's a big difference."

She flushed. "This is hardly an appropriate conversation to be having."

"I'm the man who is going to be your lover. Therefore, any conversation between us is appropriate." He gently settled his hands on her shoulders and pulled her against him. She gave in after a moment and rested her forehead against his shoulder. "Tell me, Maddie. And give me a name so I can kill him."

She just sighed. "It was two years ago; it's in the past. But . . . well, to make a long story short, he was the most popular guy in the school. He suddenly asked me out and began to date me, and I was flattered. I was stupid," she amended softly. "When he asked, I was stupid enough to agree. It was unimpressive and hurt." She shrugged one shoulder. "I figured it took practice."

"Let me guess." He kept his voice even with effort. "He did it on a dare."

She looked up at him in surprise. "Yes, how did you know?"

"I know my gender, ashamed of it as I am sometimes." He caught her chin in his hand. "There's a big difference between him and me, Maddie. For one, I have a higher respect for any woman than that. For two, I happen to be head over heels in love with you." He gave her a hard kiss on her startled lips, then released her entirely. "So when's breakfast?"

She made a little sound of frustration. "You confuse me. What is it you want from me, Kienan? You could have your choice of women. Why *me*?"

"I don't know. I just looked at you and knew you were mine." He watched her flee toward the door and added softly, "And if you put your hair back up, I will most definitely take it as a challenge, honey. In ten seconds, I will have your hair down and you naked in my arms." He smiled slowly and lethally. "And then I'll teach you what that idiot should have back then."

With a little gulp, she ducked out of the room and fled down the hall to her bedroom. She swiftly brushed her hair, removing the signs of his fingers in it, then reached for her hairpins. She hesitated, however, her fingers hovering over the little jar. She *knew* he wouldn't have said it unless he meant it, and she knew she had an alarming lack of control around him. Compromising, she tied her hair at the base of her neck with a ribbon. At least it would be out of the way.

Now knowing the bottomless pit he could be, she then went into the kitchen and began to make breakfast. Stormy was on her heels and she shot the wolf a fierce glower. "I'm going to murder you, and then I'm going to go explain to Rhianna why her prize 'pet' is gone. I'm sure she'd sympathize!"

Stormy snorted lightly and laid down on the floor under the table. Madelyne sighed faintly and got to work. She had just transferred a huge stack of pancakes onto a platter when Kienan walked in fully dressed. Unfortunately for her heart rate, he wore a sleeveless black shirt that let her see every muscle in his arms. There were a good many to see.

Distracted, she accidentally grabbed the metal part of the skillet and burned her hand. "Ow!"

He moved instantly to her side and ushered her to the sink. As her hand was held under the cold water, she glared up at him. She didn't need to see the little smile at the corner of his mouth to know he had done it on purpose. "Damn you."

"I just wanted to be sure you appreciated what you're getting." He nuzzled his nose into her hair. As long as she didn't confine all that glorious gray silk, she could do anything else with it that she wanted. "I want you to want me, Maddie."

That should have been the least of his worries. She was as subtle as neon, and he knew it! Still, her heart fluttered when he lifted her hand to his lips and kissed the burn mark. He was incredibly gentle with her, always sensing when she felt off balance. It was as if he knew that her vulnerability to his beauty was paired with her fear of it.

He released her and wandered over to sniff at the pancakes. "Is this homemade?"

She dried her hands. The burn barely hurt anymore. "Why use a mix when homemade is better?"

He gave her such a charming and boyish grin that her heart flipped into her throat and stayed lodged there even as her stomach quivered warningly with heat and hunger for something other than pancakes. Trying to ignore it, she walked into the dining room and set down the syrup, butter, and jelly. Aware he was watching her, she carried out the pancakes as well.

She had no sooner gotten back into the kitchen than he was following her with the pancakes again. Exasperated, she put her hands on her hips. "Out, Kienan. You are a guest and should be treated as such."

"Nuh-uh." He sat down at the kitchen counter, a stubborn set to his chin. "I wanna be with you." He pulled his best puppy dog expression and looked so pitiful that it startled a laugh out of her. He grinned and lavishly poured syrup over his pancakes. "You're too alone all the time."

She gave up with a sigh. "Alright, alright." She kept an eye on him as he ate breakfast and she went about cleaning up the kitchen. It was a novel concept to have someone wanting to spend time with her. She still couldn't even figure out why he wanted her. That he did want her, she didn't doubt. As she had said, she wasn't innocent. It was the 'why' that had her all confused inside. What *did* he see when he looked at her?

He suddenly came up behind her, and his arms stole around her waist. He rested his chin on her shoulder and looked out the window they were facing. It looked out into the rest of 3rd District, and children ran everywhere. Despite herself, she felt something inside eagerly soaking up the feel of his arms. "Kienan?"

"Hmm?" He turned his head to brush his lips over her ear. "You needed cuddling, and I felt compelled to give you some. And I won't argue that I'm enjoying it, too." He slowly released her so that she could turn around to face him. "Would you show me around the area? It looks wonderful outside."

Puzzled, she tilted her head. "You're here to write, not play tourist."

"But I need inspiration. Please, Maddie?" He skimmed a finger down her cheek and then across her lips. "You're supposed to be tending to your guest's needs, right?"

Her lips tingled and she tried to press them together to stop it. "Within reason, Kienan. I'm not a harem girl."

He swallowed hard as she licked her lips. Beautiful? No. Attractive? No. Sexy? *Hell* yes. And she had absolutely no idea of her devastating impact. If she had been doing it on purpose, he wouldn't have been able to stop himself from tumbling her down onto her kitchen floor. "So," he had to force his tone to remain light, "then it's reasonable to show me around, right?"

Her sigh was internal this time as she gave in and headed for the door. "Let me go change clothes."

"Put jeans on," he called after her. When she eyed him, he grinned. "What? I want to see your legs. I can't tell you how beautiful they are if I can't see them." He had to snicker as she said something rude under her breath in French, and he whistled lightly as she disappeared out of the kitchen. Try as she might, his elusive nightingale was not a gentle innkeeper.

Nightingale.

The little click in his mind put together many different puzzle pieces. Her voice, even just her regular speaking voice, carried a very potent power. It was tangible power likely able to bend reality. Hey, she was from 3rd District, after all. And the nightingale he had heard singing the night before had sung with the exact same type of power unleashed. Was Madelyne pretending to be the nightingale's ghost?

No, that didn't make sense. She had no reason to playact in such a way. There was something more going on. Something that he felt oddly pulled into. His hand slowly went to his lower right hip and covered a mark he'd had since he was born. He didn't believe in coincidences, and 3rd District was the home to magic. Everything had to be connected.

Upstairs, Madelyne studied her closet, then sighed and pulled out a long skirt and blouse. She simply didn't own any jeans or pants of any kind. At least, none she would wear outside. She had some that she wore solely for cleaning. And as she studied her closet, she was forced to accept that she owned nothing trendy. Her clothes suited a woman thrice her age.

It was why, when she got downstairs and Kienan clucked his tongue at her, she retorted, "Cluck, cluck, yourself. I don't own jeans."

"Pity." He linked his hands behind his head as he followed her out of the inn. "Were you born here?"

She hesitated, then admitted, "Yes. My family has lived here for centuries." She glanced at him to see him smiling. "It doesn't bother you? There are . . . interesting stories about this place."

"I think it's amazing. And to be honest, I love it here. When I'm here, I feel like I belong." He was quiet for a few moments. He had never admitted it out loud, but he wanted her to know. "I'm not exactly normal either. I'm . . . sensitive to some people's energy. My sister is one of them. You would be another. I always know when Aenya is close, and I swear I can sometimes read your emotions, Maddie."

That explained a lot. She looked up at his face. "Your whole family is special, Kienan. I could feel something inside Aenya, too. I don't think it's fully manifested yet. It might be her age. And Professor Shaughnessy is definitely sensitive to emotions too. It's obvious to me at least. What about your other brother?"

"I'm not sure," he admitted. "We're all wild spirits, but his is . . . volatile, I guess. He's very, *very* careful to control it. Whatever his 'gift' is, it might be connected." He smiled suddenly. "Think we have an ancestor from 3rd District?"

"Do you want there to be?"

"If it would make me belong here? Absolutely. I can *breathe* here, Maddie. Those kids waving and smiling at me? They're doing it because they see a stranger they want to meet. They're not doing it because I'm a Shaughnessy. I love it here."

"You're an amazing man, Kienan Shaughnessy." Her heart skipped a beat as he took her hand and laced their fingers together. It felt natural to be walking down the sidewalk with him. Most people from outside the 3rd District looked and felt like outsiders, but he didn't. He looked and felt like a resident.

"Madelyne!" A little girl came running up and grabbed onto her skirt. Her face was streaked with tears. "I promise I was watering it and giving it sunshine!" She hiccupped on a sob. "But it *died*! I really tried, Madelyne! Make it better!"

"Wait here," she told Kienan. "I'll go see if the plant can be saved."

"Sure." He waited only long enough for them to go around the corner before he followed. He moved just close enough to hear what was going on, and by looking in a window across the street, he could see the events clearly.

There were a few other children gathered around what looked like a miserably dying flower of some kind. The bulb was brown and drooping, no signs of color or life. Madelyne knelt and gently cupped her hands around the bulb, and a soft wind began to blow. Her voice rose with haunting cadence to sing a song of morning and rebirth. And when she opened her hand, the bulb bloomed and unfurled into a brilliant sunflower. Flushed with life and health, it seemed to glow in the sunshine.

Heart pounding, Kienan leaned against the building behind him. She had definitely been the singer he had heard the night before. But *how* had she done that? It was one thing to say that he thought her voice could bend reality, but *seeing* it was doubly intriguing. There definitely had to be a good reason for why she sang at night with such pain and grief. It made him wonder where in the legend of the nightingale she belonged.

It also made him wonder where he belonged as well.

CHAPTER ELEVEN

When Madelyne rejoined Kienan, he was watching kids play hopscotch across the street. Absently he said, "When I was seven, Dad gave me and Aenya a box of chalks to draw on the driveway with. Within a few minutes, Mel was drawing too. And shortly thereafter Taegan was involved. We covered the entire driveway in loops and squiggles and flowers and aliens."

She smiled. "What did your dad say?"

"Before or after he stopped laughing?" He turned to smile at her. "Our chauffeur was terrified to drive any vehicle over it. Everyone wanted to keep it intact. So in the middle of the night, us four kids snuck out and washed it away. In the morning we swore it was gremlins. After that we were really careful to keep our chalk drawings to places where they wouldn't be trampled."

"You're all so close. You're so lucky, Kien." Her breath caught as he once more linked their fingers together. This time he brought her hand to his lips. "I always wondered what having siblings must be like."

"Riotous," he decided. "But fun." He tucked her close as he began walking down the sidewalk. Since she wasn't inclined to mention the event he had witnessed, he asked, "Will it live, doctor?"

Gravely, she answered, "It will need much care and love but it should play the piano again."

"Piano playing flowers. Man, 3rd District definitely has some interesting flora. The fauna won't suddenly, you know, break into musical numbers, right? I'm not sure I could handle walking through a Disney movie."

This time she couldn't stop the giggles. "You never liked Bambi?"

His grimace was not entirely joking. "It hit a bit too close to home. Dad rented it without thinking when Aenya was six or so. We got as far as Bambi's mom getting killed. It then took Taegan and Dad a solid hour to get me and Aenya, and Mel, to stop crying."

"Oh, Kienan." Hurting for him, she brought his hand up to her cheek. "I know how much it hurts to lose a parent. And you must have been just a baby."

"Two. But we had Aenya. She helped fill in the holes. If we'd lost her too, the entire family would have fallen apart." He found a smile. "Let's talk about something else. Tell me about the kids."

"Many of them are orphans who didn't fit in at any other shelter. Rhianna keeps a shelter here in 3rd District for kids like them. A friend of mine, Audra Alexandrios, serves as a tutor so that they get the full benefit of schooling without the censure of public schools."

His eyes widened slightly. "She's a professor at college, isn't she?"

She slid a smiling glance at him. "She is."

"She has an . . . interesting reputation."

"That she does. But her heart is good."

"What about that guy?" He indicated a man who was hanging up colorful tapestries for sale in front of a small shop.

"He's a tailor and weaver. A few of the blankets at the inn were made by him. His blankets are very special. They can bond with owners to aid with healing when sick or to do other things." She pointed to a young couple pushing a stroller with twins down the other side of the street. "He made them a blanket to help them have a child when they'd been trying for years."

"And they got twins." He smiled. "I like that."

It was evening by the time they got back to the inn. She had never enjoyed a day so much. He was *hungry* for knowledge. He had asked questions about everyone and everything, showing only fascination for the stories that bordered on fantastical. He had even played a short game of basketball with several kids and showed them how to make proper baskets.

It was such an oddity to her. She had always seen beauty as carrying a certain disregard for intelligence. Most of the beautiful people she had known had never looked past the surface. But Kienan, for all his amazing physical beauty, seemed to be just as beautiful on the inside.

The entire District probably thought he was her boyfriend. He had held her hand the entire time and had stolen more than one quick kiss. When one little girl had exclaimed with delight that he had kissed Madelyne, he had promptly scooped the girl up and given her a smacking kiss on her ice cream streaked cheek 'just to be fair to other pretty girls.'

Unfortunately, for all her enjoyment of the day, Madelyne was exhausted. The mental and physical war she was waging inside had taken their toll. Her days were always long, and she had been under other stresses lately as well. The broken heater was just another in a line of problems lately.

Kienan, showing his sharp sensitivity, followed her into the kitchen. Before she could grab her apron, he lifted her up into his arms and carried her over to a chair. She hastily grabbed his shoulders for balance. "Kien! What are you doing?"

"I'm going to make dinner. Mind you, it won't be fancy, but you're drained, Maddie." He knelt and studied her face intently. "When was the last time someone took care of you?" Her silence was an answer and it broke his heart. He framed her face with one hand, his touch and eyes equally tender. "Just say the word, and I'll take care of you forever."

"No." It was getting harder and harder to say just that one word, as if her resistance was slowly crumbling. She didn't know what he wanted, but she didn't expect it to last. She had reached for the stars twice and both times she had hit the ground so hard she had nearly shattered. She refused to try for three.

"I'll make you change your mind eventually," he said softly as he stood. "But, for now, you stay right there."

It felt odd to be sitting in her own kitchen while someone else cooked, but she knew there was no stopping him. With a little sigh, she folded her arms on the table and rested her head. She was careful not to fall asleep. He wasn't above kissing her awake, and she didn't trust her control. She was fairly sure she didn't have any at all.

What was it about him that called to her? Was it because he might very well be 3rd District descended? Maybe in part, but it was more than that. He was funny and witty, brilliant and sensitive. He *felt* so much. There was a bright light inside him that expanded out and lit up everyone around him. What was wrong with her? It wasn't just the desire for him, though god only knew that was only getting worse.

A plate was suddenly set in front of her and she straightened up in surprise. As she blinked at the plate, she felt her lips quivering. "You made me a peanut butter and jelly sandwich."

He sat across from her with two of the same. "I told you I can't cook. I can make a killer PB&J, though."

He had no way of knowing, she thought, tears beginning to well in her eyes. He had no way of knowing that her parents had always made PB&J sandwiches for Saturday dinner. They had called it their special feast because no one else would eat such a thing on a Saturday night. In her mind, PB&Js had become synonymous with a loving family.

In a blind sort of terror, she realized finally what was wrong with her. She was in love with him. In barely twenty-four hours he had become a vital part of her life and her heart. That stupid sandwich had been the final straw. He had known, subconsciously, what to give her to make her happy and he had done it.

Terrified, she pushed the plate away. "Thank you, but I'm not hungry."

He frowned as she ran out of the kitchen and the door swung wildly behind her. He had been positive she would like a PB&J for dinner. Yet there had been tears in her eyes and fear underneath them as she had looked at him. He wanted to go after her, to cuddle her and promise to make everything better. The only thing that stopped him was the knowledge that she might claw at him like a wildcat if he tried.

Stormy whined softly as she stopped next to his chair. He sighed and rubbed her head gently. "I know, Stormy. But sometimes it's best to give her space. Trust me, I want to comfort her. I think it would just make it worse right now."

He finished his own dinner and dumped the uneaten sandwich in the garbage. He put the plates in the sink and headed down the hall to his room. It was the second night. He was due to go home the next day and have a presentable song for his father. What the hell was he going to do?

He tried to fiddle around with his guitar but the only tune he could bring to mind was the song the nightingale had been singing. He let his mind drift as he thought about songs and love and dancing. The basic beat of the nightingale's song began to throb in his blood, and he grabbed sheet music to write out the rhythm playing in his mind. He grabbed more music and built a harmony with a guitar and piano.

Inspired, he completely forgot the time and began to add more instruments, building a full set to compliment the singer's voice. He wasn't fully conscious of what he was doing until he actually sat back and read the lyrics he had written. He had written a love duet. A song of seduction and love and music. He had written a song for Madelyne to sing with him.

His concentration broke. He sighed and leaned back in his chair as he pushed his glasses up to rub his nose. His chances of getting her on a stage or in a studio were slim to nonexistent. She was a reverse snob. She had been burned so many times that she assumed everyone else would burn her too.

If he burned her with anything, it would be with desire. He burned to have her in his arms again, to taste every inch of her impossibly soft skin. She burned too. He knew it. She just had no more of an idea how to control things than he did, and her reaction was to retreat.

A little stiff from sitting too long, he got to his feet and went to the window to stare across the garden. It was almost midnight and the moonlight complemented the landscape perfectly. It seemed to call to the wildness inside him, and it stirred something inside his soul, so that he wanted to go outside and walk in the midnight garden.

When the purple moon is high in the sky, I walk through the heat of a savannah

When the pain is too much for my heart, my nightingale's melody soothes my tears

He went very still, his mouth going dry as he heard the soft singing. Without giving himself a chance to think, he turned and yanked on his jacket as protection against the cold night air. He started to pick up his guitar, and then changed his mind and left it. He wanted only to confirm what his heart was telling him.

I want to regain the innocence of my youth

But there are no more hopes for me to cling to

Heart pounding, he hurried down the hall and toward the back of the inn. He didn't see Madelyne on the way, nor was there any light under the door that he suspected was her bedroom. He paused a moment, eased the door open, and looked inside. She wasn't there, but it was clearly her room for it smelled of apples and vanilla.

He headed out the back. He tried to be as quiet as possible as he went down the worn pathways of the garden. He could hear the whispering of the hot springs and realized he was drawing close to the women's springs. It had to be the women's side because there was steam lifting in the air to curl like ethereal wisps in lamplight.

His stomach tightened with sudden hunger. If Madelyne was bathing, he had no idea if he could control himself and keep from going to her side.

In the night, the nightingale sings, bringing a change in the wind

He pushed aside an extremely large fern and held his breath as he ducked down. He almost cursed as Stormy ran past him, but he was able to maintain his hidden position. He wasn't breathing. He didn't think he would ever breathe again.

Madelyne was indeed at the spring but not bathing. She was sitting on the side with her feet dangling in the water and her long hair loosely fluttering behind her in the breeze. She sang softly, her voice carrying all the millions of cadences that hundreds of thousands of people struggled to learn one by one.

She had wings.

In the night, the nightingale prays, bringing a change in my dreams

He swallowed hard, but his mouth was dry as a bone. Extending from her back was a pair of brown wings. There were flecks of red within them, and little bits of white. As far as wings went, they weren't extremely beautiful. The color wasn't lustrous, nor was it abundant in variety and shape. They were simply wings of a smaller size that indicated she probably couldn't fly.

It explained a lot. She wasn't a ghost: she was a flesh and blood woman. Yet she *was* the nightingale in the legend. Whether she had existed for all those centuries, or she had been reborn, he couldn't begin to guess. He wanted to change the story. This one would not end in tragedy. If his stubborn nightingale would open her eyes, then she would realize there was a home right in front of her.

Once more he lightly touched the mark on his hip. His suspicions were growing. As quietly as he could, he eased out of the bushes and went back to his room. His mind was going millions of miles per second. He had his song. He definitely knew it was sellable. He just needed Madelyne to be his partner. It wouldn't be as good as a solo, it needed to be sung as a duet. He had deliberately written the woman's part to take advantage of her brilliant voice.

He needed to find a way to finagle more time to convince her to be his partner, not just in music, but in life, as well. He tried to remember the details of the contract. There had to be a loophole in there somewhere. There had to be a way for him to have everything he wanted and give the woman he loved everything she needed.

He awoke the next morning to light knocking on his door. He tried to convince himself she would come in, but he knew she was too smart for that a second time. He muttered under his breath and got out of bed. When he opened the door, all he said was, "Yes, it's morning. Unless you're getting into bed with me, go away."

She cleared her throat. She was more tempted by the offer than she wanted to admit. He was shirtless again, and his pajama pants were low on the hip. He looked like an invitation to break a few commandments. "It's eleven in the morning," she informed him. "You're scheduled for check out at noon."

"Crap. Right." He eyed her intently. She had her hair up again, and he was tempted to pull the pins out. He simply didn't have the time for what he wanted, and she knew it, if the smug look in her eyes was any indication. She had deliberately waited to wake him up. "If you think that my checking out will make me forget about you, think again!"

She blinked as the door shut in her face. He clearly wasn't a morning person. She shook her head and went to the lobby to finish up the paperwork. Despite what he thought, she had no doubt in her mind that once he was away from the District, he would completely forget her. A face like hers didn't linger in anyone's memory.

It was a painful and sobering thought. She sank down to her knees, wrapped her arms around Stormy's neck, and buried her face in her fur. "Why did you bring him here?" she asked in despair. "It's so hopeless for the both of us!"

An hour later, Kienan walked into the lobby and over to the desk. He was wearing his jacket and sunglasses and carrying a suitcase. Putting on her best innkeeper smile, she took the key he was holding out to her. "I hope you'll stay here again, Kienan. I like seeing return visitors."

She stood behind the desk on purpose in an attempt to keep things impersonal. To her shock, he yanked his sunglasses off, dropped them on the counter, and then cleared the top in a single graceful leap. He yanked her into his arms before she could say a word. One hand gripped the back of her head and the other splayed across her lower back. "You will not," he snarled softly, "make this seem so unimportant, nightingale!"

His mouth came down on hers, hard and hungry, and try as she might, she couldn't control her response to him. Even as his head slanted to deepen the kiss, her lips were parting to meet his passion head on. Her fingers lifted and slid into his hair, curled in and held on. She felt hot and wild and breathless with need, craving the drugging delight of his touch.

He turned and trapped her against the wall. Her body pressed to his, and he felt incredible. Small sounds of pleasure slipped through her lips only to be muffled by his. He shuddered, craving her with a force that was painful. He wanted nothing more than to drag her onto the floor and show her how serious he was, but there was no time, damn it!

As suddenly as he had grabbed her, he released her and backed up a step. Her entire body was weak, trembling with desire, and she had to brace a hand against the wall to hold herself up. Her first lover had never gotten even a fraction of a response like that from her, especially not with a single kiss. She swallowed hard as she grabbed for control. "Goodbye, Kienan."

He stared at her for long moments before cursing softly in French. As he went around the counter again and scooped up his glasses, he shot over his shoulder, "This is not the end, nightingale. You better get used to having me around because hell, high water, or curses, you will be mine."

As the inn door shut behind him, she had the sharp sensation that it was less a threat than a promise.

Aenya was waiting for Kienan on the porch when he got home. Dragging his suitcase as he went, he tried to ignore his sister as she fell into step beside him. "Well?" she demanded. "Did you get anywhere? Do you have a song? Did you see Madelyne? Wasn't she awesome?"

He turned his head to snarl at her and then slammed his bedroom door in her face. She could only stare at the door in utter shock. He had *never* lost his temper with her before. Not like that. She heard someone clearing their throat and turned her head to see Hiro trying his best not to smile. "What is wrong with him?" she demanded.

Hiro, having had a similar experience when trying to win her, had a strong feeling he knew precisely what was wrong with the youngest Shaughnessy brother. Trying to find a delicate way of phrasing it, he finally said, "I think he met Madelyne. And I think he liked her a little too much."

She was anything but slow and her mouth formed an 'O' silently. She considered that for a few moments. Carefully, she finally said, "I told you that Madelyne distrusts beautiful men. Kienan's handsome. I can see this is not going to be easy."

"Something tells me the entire weekend was not easy on your brother." He heard the door moving and pulled her back a step so they were out of Kienan's way as he emerged from his room. Since discretion really was the better part of valor, neither Hiro nor Aenya said a word.

Kienan started to walk down the hall, and then paused. He turned around to say to his sister, "I'm in love with Maddie. I also tried to seduce her. Anything you want to say?" His tone made it a challenge.

A bit weakly she offered, "Good luck?" She winced slightly as he stomped down the hall. Now that she was actually looking, she was fairly sure she saw steam coming from the top of his head that had nothing at all to do with temper. "Oh boy," she said on a sigh. "Here we go again." She glared toward where Stormy was following Kienan. "I'm beginning to suspect that wolf."

Hiro was, too, but said nothing as he remembered a woman with yellow eyes at the Faerie Club. Some things he didn't want to understand.

Sullivan was fighting with his computer as Kienan walked into his office. Giving up on the stubborn program for the time being, he swiveled in his chair to smile at his son. "Well, how was it?" The smile began to fade as he saw the determined glint in the corner of Kienan's eyes. "Kien?"

"One," Kienan leaned forward and planted his hands on the desk, "I have a song. But I need the time to polish it and get a partner. A week, tops. By the talent show at the college, okay? I'll perform it there and you can make your judgment then. The contract says that an outside party has to review the song, and it's best if they see me under pressure."

"That sounds fair enough," he conceded. He wasn't surprised Kienan had caught that little detail. He picked up his tea and studied his son curiously. "What's the other thing?"

"I want permission to get married."

He choked on his tea. Gasping, he set the glass down and grabbed a tissue to blot at his eyes. After a few moments he was able to breathe again, and he stared at Kienan in utter shock. "In a weekend, less than forty-eight hours, you come back with a song *and* a future bride?"

"Future bride if I can get her to agree. She's stubborn as hell!" Kienan threw himself down in the company chair and swung his legs over the side. "She's the innkeeper at the Gentle Brook Inn, and Aenya's friend. I just looked at her and knew."

Sullivan drummed his fingers lightly on the top of his desk. Oddly, now that the shock had passed, he found himself unsurprised. His eyes lowered to Stormy briefly, then lifted to Kienan again. "Tell me about her," he finally decided.

"She's an orphan. She's run the inn her whole life, with help from the person in charge of the Enforcers, I guess. She's got an incredible sense of humor and has more than a bit of a temper. She tries to come across as being very reserved and elegant, but she's not at all. Oh, she can definitely be elegant," he added wryly, "but it's more a polish than a real finish. She's got more kindness and gentleness than anyone I can think of, and she needs some serious TLC from the right guy, especially because she's been burned. That guy is going to be me."

Sullivan thought it was very telling that he had yet to mention what Madelyne looked like. Hormones alone were not a strong basis for a relationship. A good helping hand, certainly, but they were useless without something deeper. "And what does she look like?"

"She's about five-seven, slender. Extremely long gray hair and violet eyes. From an objective standpoint, she's very plain, very ordinary. I guess she'd be the kind of girl you'd pass over in a crowd, but five minutes in her company—hell, two—and you can't mistake how beautiful she is inside. Every time I look at her I can't stand to look away. In my eyes, she's perfect." His voice was simple, but completely sincere.

With a soft sigh, Sullivan accepted the inevitable. "Alright. I hereby extend the contract for a week to allow you the time to prepare and perform at the contest. As for your Madelyne, I also give my blessings and my advice as well. Women who have been burned, especially intelligent ones, are very cautious of being burned again."

"I'm aware of that." He hopped to his feet. "I've told her how I feel, but she doesn't want to listen. So, I've decided to go on to plan B and show her that I'm completely serious."

"And how are you going to do that?"

"You still got the number for that flower place you always got bouquets for Mom from? You know, the one run by Hiro's parents. And do you think they'd give me a discount because I'm Hiro's future brother-in-law?"

CHAPTER TWELVE

The college where Madelyne attended school was the same one that all the Shaughnessy males attended. It was an hour's trip from the 3rd District and required multiple bus transfers. It was the best university in the area, though, and she refused to waste a dime of the generous tuition that Rhianna gave her.

It was a delicate balance that she walked. She couldn't always attend classes physically because of her inn. Sometimes she had to stay at home to take care of guests. Rhianna had thankfully worked out an arrangement with the college, and Madelyne was able to do her work online when she couldn't be there physically. So far it had been working.

She was majoring in Business Management with a minor in Music Composition. She was in one of Taegan's math classes—Advanced Calculus—and had been enjoying him as a teacher all semester. After the weekend she had just had, however, she found herself tempted to skip class for reasons that had nothing to do with the inn. How in the world was she supposed to face Professor Shaughnessy when his baby brother had just spent the better part of forty-eight hours trying to seduce her?

She had never considered herself a coward. She told herself to grow up and walked into the classroom as if her life hadn't changed. She waved when others waved at her and smiled at everyone. It actually took her a moment before she realized there was a lot of giggling going on. Her stomach sinking, she slowly turned to look at the desk where she always sat. A cheerful bouquet of sunflowers greeted her.

Her bag fell on the floor with a thump as she lost her grip on the handle. She could only gape at the desk. She was so shocked that she jumped when a girl grabbed her arm enthusiastically. "It's so romantic!" the girl said happily. "Madelyne, it's wonderful! Who is it from?"

She spotted a card in the bouquet and plucked it free. The handwriting was instantly familiar to her, but the message read *'To a nightingale from an adoring swan.'*

"You idiot," she whispered softly. Did he know what she was?

"Madelyne has a secret admirer!" the other girl called happily to the rest of the class.

"No! No! I don't!" She waved her hands quickly. "It's got to be a mistake! No one would give me flowers!"

"Professor Shaughnessy brought them in himself. They were left on his desk with a note that specifically had your name on it." One of the boys grinned as he leaned on the top of his desk. "I don't think there's a mistake, Madelyne, and why would there be? You're so nice that you absolutely should have an admirer."

"My boyfriend was telling me the other day," one of the other girls commented, "that he sometimes wished I was more like Madelyne because she's so open-minded and fun to be around. I couldn't even get mad because he was right," she added on a laugh.

Feeling woefully out of step and wondering what had happened to the world, Madelyne sank down onto her chair and buried her face in her arms. First Kienan and now her classmates. Had everyone suddenly gone blind? Or was she the one who had been blind all along? Oh, it was all too confusing!

When Taegan walked in, she couldn't bring herself to meet his eyes. "Morning," she mumbled.

"Madelyne, I'd like to talk to you after class." His voice was gentle and calming, a hint of a brogue softening the words. "It's nothing serious; don't spend an hour worrying." He got to the front of the class and began to take roll. He was smiling inside. She had always been one of his favorite students anyway. He would like having her for a sister.

When class was done, she waited by the door for him, and then fell into step beside him as they headed toward his office. She carried her flowers to put them in her art locker until she could figure out how to take them home. They were really beautiful. If he had given her roses, she could have easily thrown them away!

As they walked into the office, she asked, "What did you need to see me about, Professor?"

He shut the door with a sigh and walked over to sit behind his desk. He pulled off his glasses and dropped them on the table in front of him. "I'm not speaking to you as a teacher," he admitted ruefully. She went very still, and he gestured to the chair across from him. "Sit down, Maddie." The use of her nickname was deliberate.

She warily sat down and he studied her intently. He had always been saddened to see how much she held herself back from others. Her classmates idolized her, and she had never had a clue until that morning. Kienan's methods, blunt as they were, were at the least helping her see her own worth. If he ever found who had hurt her so badly, Taegan would very happily help him deal with the offender. "Maddie, I think you should transfer to another math class."

She sighed. "I was afraid of that. It'd look bad on both of us if your brother's current interest was in your class. But it's just fleeting, Taegan, really. It'll fade." Taegan had insisted on informality outside of the classroom, wanting to be available for students to talk to if they were having trouble, academic or not. She had never before felt comfortable calling him by his first name but things had definitely changed.

Bemused, he leaned back in his chair. "You haven't heard what Kienan did when he came home yesterday?"

"No . . ."

He cleared his throat. "I believe he went into our father's office and demanded permission to marry."

"He did *what*?!" She leapt to her feet and her bag fell on the floor with a thump. "What is *wrong* with that man? I said no to an affair and now he's talking about marriage?" She made a disgusted sound. "Did someone drop him on his head too much when he was a baby? There's something not firing right in his brain!"

He coughed but couldn't quite disguise the laugh. It had suddenly become quite obvious why Kienan was in love with her. She would be an absolutely perfect addition to their family, and she was strong enough to keep Kienan in line. Their father was going to adore her. "Well, I know he had some interesting escapades, but I think his brain remained intact. That being said, I love Kienan very dearly, and I wanted to make a pitch for him. He doesn't know about this," he added.

She slowly sat down again and folded her hands in her lap. She stared at the front of the desk rather than at him. She felt horribly embarrassed and couldn't help but wonder if he would still be so accepting of her if he knew what she really was.

He considered her for a moment before leaning back in his chair. "Kienan is an unusual young man," he started slowly. "I suppose some boys who grew up without a mother might lean toward being very casual and harsh with women. Whether it was Aenya's presence or something inside Kienan naturally, he's always been very protective of everyone, especially women. He would sooner die than hurt anyone, and he's a fierce defender. It was such a terror helping Father raise him because of that very thing. He's easily hurt."

She looked up quickly. "He never indicated anything like that to me."

"He wouldn't, not if he wanted to protect you, which he most definitely does." He went around the desk and knelt to put a hand on hers. "I love him very dearly, and I can see how much he loves you. All I ask is that you try to open your heart to him. He won't betray you, Maddie. When Kienan is serious, he's serious for life."

Her lower lip trembling slightly, she whispered, "He just doesn't understand. The novelty will wear off and everything will be normal again."

He got to his feet with an odd smile on his lips. "I can see you've got a lot to learn about men in general, and men in love in particular. Speaking as a future big brother, I'd start sewing your wedding dress."

"Thanks a lot!" She got to her feet and snatched up her bag. She slapped the sunflowers down on the desk, her eyes snapping sparks. "Tell your brother to keep his flowers. I don't want them."

As the door swung shut behind her, he grinned slightly to himself. He knew full well what his brother had been up to all morning.

It didn't take long for her to figure it out herself. Her next class had another bouquet of flowers, another note from a swan, and another giggling room full of students. She gave the flowers to one of the other girls and tried to ignore everyone for the next hour.

It was to her folly that it was Monday and all of her classes met on Mondays (with them falling on other days the rest of the week). She found more flowers at her next class, delivered by a teacher so that no one knew who was behind them. Even the teacher wasn't sure since the flowers had arrived anonymously at his office. Rumors were flying and fingers were being pointed. She was sure that Kienan was deliberately having fun with the entire school.

It came to a head while she was sitting at a lunch table in the cafeteria. The other people at the table fell silent suddenly and she looked up to see Kienan approaching with a single yellow carnation. The entire room went quiet as everyone noticed him. Red color slowly climbed her face.

"Special delivery!" he told her cheerfully as he reached her side. "I caught the teacher at the door and decided to save him a trip."

If she hadn't been sure that he was behind it, she would have never suspected him. She warily got to her feet and took the carnation he was holding out. The card was blank and she blinked at it. "It's not signed." What *was* this maddening male up to?

"It's not?" He peered at the card. "How are you supposed to know who it's from then? Ah! Wait. I bet this will help." He reached into his pocket and pulled out a pen. Before she could stop him, he had taken the card and scrawled his distinctive signature across it. "There. That ought to do it."

"Oh my god!" a girl in the back of the room blurted excitedly. "Kienan Shaughnessy is *courting* Madelyne Winters!"

The entire room erupted into an excited buzz. It was the most interesting thing to happen in a long time, and definitely the most romantic thing to happen *ever*.

"No!" Madelyne said hastily, trying to wave her hands in the air for attention. "No, he's not! Kienan," she pleaded, looking at her 'admirer,' "tell them the truth!"

"What truth?" He grinned. "I am courting you, nightingale." He was quick enough to dodge the punch she threw, but he wasn't quick enough to escape her other hand. It came up and threw the contents of her glass of tea in his face. He swiped the liquid out of his eyes in time to see her sweep out of the cafeteria with all the grandeur of a queen.

Everyone else watched her leave as well. The door shut behind her, and all eyes turned toward him expectantly. He shook the tea out of his hair and said musingly, "Plan C it is." He swiftly headed for the exit.

He left behind a clamor in the cafeteria. Everyone was absolutely certain they were going to love every minute of this scenario. Bets were made, and Kienan led the margin by an almost unanimous decision. It wasn't a question of whether he would win; it was merely a matter of *when*.

By the end of her second-to-last class, Madelyne was ready to go home and never emerge again. Kienan was still delivering flowers to her classes by way of the teacher but he had started signing his initials. Now everyone knew. It was enough to drive a sane woman crazy, and she felt the urge to throw a tantrum growing quickly.

At her wit's end, she ditched class for the first time in her life. She left the campus and hurried toward the bus stop down the street. It sat in front of a cheerful salon known for hiring college interns. Even with photos of glamorous models in the windows, she had always felt oddly comfortable there.

As she was passing by, however, she was surprised to hear a young woman shout, "Hey, hang on! Yes, you with the awesome gray hair!"

She had to assume the voice was referring to her since no one else was around. She turned around to see a nearly frighteningly beautiful young woman hurrying toward her. She was shorter than Madelyne, but not as short as Aenya, and had thick black hair that was artfully curled and piled on top of her head. Her eyes were the same smoky black, nearly doe-shaped, and her lashes seemed long and lovely. Her body was graceful and well curved in a way that surely stopped traffic.

As always, Madelyne felt horribly out of her league. "Who, me?" she asked warily.

"Of course!" The woman came to a stop beside her and smiled. "I'm Kalliope, or Kally if you like. I work in the salon here. Please, please, *please* will you let me style your hair?" She clasped her hands together and winked. "I'm working on my degree and I love makeovers! You've got such *amazing* hair. It deserves an amazing cut!"

Madelyne could only gape at her. "I'm sorry?" she finally managed to say. "Surely you're mistaken."

"Me? Mistaken about hair? Not a chance." Kalliope flicked a finger at her own curls. "I know my stuff, hon." She began to circle Madelyne slowly. "I admit, you're not the belle of the ball, but you've got something a lot of people wish for."

"I do?"

"Sure. Here's some advice." Kalliope leaned closer. "The grass is always greener on the other side. Therefore, people who are plain want to be beautiful. And those who are beautiful sometimes wish to be plain." She shrugged one shoulder. "I've wished to be plain sometimes myself. When you're beautiful, people demand things of you. After a while, I learned to use it like a weapon if needed."

Madelyne was fascinated not only by her attitude but her entire manner. "And you stopped me because . . . ?"

"You have major potential. Your face is normal, but we can give you a different kind of appeal with makeup to play up what you have. And your hair is completely your best feature. I can't wait to style it. Also, far as I can see you've got a nice, regular figure. Some flattering clothes would really show it to its best advantage. 'A bird may not change its color, but it can change its feathers.' Right?" She smiled.

Madelyne wanted to laugh. Her new friend had no idea how eerily accurate she was. She didn't give herself time to debate; she just took a breath and said, "Okay. Where do we start?" She got her answer as Kalliope caught her wrist and dragged her into the salon. "Whoa! I'm Madelyne Winters, a freshman at college. You're . . . ?"

"Oh, I'm sorry. Tavoularis. Kalliope Tavoularis." Kalliope urged her toward the washing station. "I'm the heiress to Tavoularis Industries. I guess we could be considered associates, considering what Kienan Shaughnessy is up to." She smiled innocently as Madelyne groaned. "I'm a senior at college. Because of my major, I hang out with Mel Shaughnessy a lot, and I have one of Taegan's classes. I hear things."

Madelyne sat down on a seat with a sigh. "It's a fleeting fancy."

Kalliope looped an arm around her shoulders. "Hmm, don't think so. Let's try it from a different angle." She went around and knelt down to be on eye level with her. "Madelyne, do you love Kienan? Ah!" she added, waving a finger in the air. "No lies or denials. Just yes or no."

"Yes," she whispered.

"Then let me have a chance to make you over, and I'll show you how to use every weapon nature gave us as women in order to make him yours."

It was more for Madelyne's confidence than anything. Mel was one of Kalliope's friends, and he had, rather subtly, indicated some of his suspicions regarding the difficulties of the relationship. Having seen some of the day's events, Kalliope was fully onboard to help Kienan get his lady. They were *perfect* for each other.

"I guess we could try," Madelyne conceded reluctantly. "It hurts to fail though."

"Then don't fail. If I want something, I go after it until I have it. It's just the way I am." She removed all the pins in Madelyne's hair and whistled softly as the length came down. "Okay, I am *so* not cutting this! Maybe some feathering . . ."

It was with some morbid fascination that Madelyne found her hair being fully scrubbed clean before she was escorted to a styling chair. Kalliope turned her away from the mirror so that she couldn't see what she was doing, and she could only bide her time by mentally chewing on her nails. She had never let anyone do anything to her hair before. It had always seemed like putting pretty pillows on an unattractive couch.

"Well, talk to me," Kalliope coaxed. "I've never seen someone your age with gray hair. You spend your time worrying as a career *and* hobby?"

She had to smile. "No, it's genetic. All children of my father's bloodline are fully gray by the time they're preteens. Our hair just doesn't hold onto its color. I *think* I was once a brunette. I really don't remember. I'm so used to having gray hair."

"It totally suits you." Kalliope began to trim more than split ends. "And it's so *soft*. I feel like I'm cutting feathers. People don't have allergic reactions around you, right?" She was rewarded with a laugh, which was exactly what she wanted. Madelyne's voice was wonderful to listen to, and she looked like she was in dire need of a friend. Kalliope knew how it felt; she needed a friend too. Maybe that was another reason Mel had nudged her. He was good at that stuff.

"Hair goop or hair spritz?" she offered as she was getting ready to use the hair dryer.

"Neither if possible. I'd just have to wash it out."

She sighed. "You poor neglected child. Has no one taught you the nuances of hair care and beautification? Style virgins are so vexing sometimes." She worked quickly and expertly, brushing out Madelyne's hair in a way that it didn't need product.

"Are you sure about this, Kally?"

The note of worry in her voice made Kalliope give her a hug with her free arm. "Of course! You're going to look cute and sexy and knock Kienan Shaughnessy on his attractive ass." She twirled the chair around toward the mirror. "Voila! My masterpiece!"

Taking a deep breath, Madelyne opened her eyes and looked in the mirror. Her eyes slowly widened and she looked harder. She was still no raving beauty, but the feathered effect had shortened the hair around her face and made it steadily longer until it reached the back and her ankles. It softened the lines on her face and made her sort of appealing somehow. "How did you *do* that?"

Kalliope blew on her nails. "Magic. It's like decorating a plain couch. You put some pretty pillows on it and suddenly everything looks good." She blinked when Madelyne gaped at her. "Did I say something wrong?"

"Something *very* unnerving, actually." The exact same analogy but with different reactions. That, more than anything, told her that perhaps it was time to change her way of thinking. She took a deep breath. She had money in her savings account. It was supposed to go toward the heater repair, but she could put it off for another month or two. Tourist season hadn't started yet. "Do you have any advice for clothes shopping? I think you can tell I'm hopeless."

"Untutored," Kalliope corrected, "not hopeless. Hey, Ben!" She began to gather up her station. When an older man peered around the corner of the back room, she grinned at him. "I'm going to take off early. I don't have any appointments."

"Can you do that?" Madelyne blinked as she was ushered out of the salon. She felt as if she was being carried along by an unstoppable wave. "I mean, can you just walk out for the afternoon?"

"Sure! Cosmetology is just a minor; my major is Business Management like yours. I want to take my daddy's company." She grinned as they reached her bright blue Camry. It looked as sleek and stylish as its owner. "Mind you, he told me I couldn't have it until either he dies or I give him a grandkid. Considering I've said I won't marry for less than love, I suppose it'll be a while." Madelyne had to laugh at that and she took a quick bow. "So," she asked as she slid into the car, "where to? What's the budget?"

"Reasonable, but a small splurge wouldn't hurt."

"Well of course there has to be a splurge! Where's the fun without it? Besides," she continued blithely, "you're coming to my birthday party and it's going to be amazingly fancy. You need a dress. Something in a blue tone to bring out your eyes. Or red, just to drive Kienan crazy."

Madelyne liked the idea a little too much for her own sanity. "Has anyone told you that you're a bad influence, Kally?" she asked.

"All the time." Kalliope grinned at her and then gunned the engine so that they sailed off down the road. All Madelyne found herself capable of doing was laughing and holding on for dear life. She was enjoying herself so much that she didn't recognize the sound of her cell phone when it began to ring.

Kalliope glanced down at her bag. "That's you, not me. Mine plays Metallica."

She *really* liked Kalliope, Madelyne decided, and pulled out her cell. She didn't know the number and answered warily, "Hello?"

"There you are, nightingale! You ran away from me!"

Pure instinct had her snapping the phone closed almost before Kienan stopped speaking. When Kalliope slowly lifted a brow at her, she said a bit weakly, "I think I just hung up on a short-tempered Irishman."

"Oh, *nice* one." There was more admiration than censure in Kalliope's voice. "Give him ten seconds and he'll call back breathing fire." She snickered as the phone began to ring rather insistently. "He dials faster than I do."

"He doesn't have those nails."

Kalliope admired her well-manicured nails and their rich green color. "We'll have to get yours done too."

Suspecting that arguing wouldn't sway her new friend, Madelyne gave in before there could be a fight. She cautiously answered her phone, "Hello?"

"That was NOT funny!" Kienan wasn't breathing fire, but he was definitely annoyed. "You hang up on me again, and I'll come hunt you down in person." He huffed out a breath and then suddenly sighed. "However, I guess I can't blame you. What will it take to convince you that I'm serious, Maddie?"

"I don't know." She stared out the window but didn't see anything except a blur. "Kienan, I've been down this route before. I just . . . I just don't want to risk everything again. I lost a lot when I did before."

"Give me a chance." His voice was soft and firm. "Just a chance, nightingale. Give me a chance to show you how much I love you. I'll make it as public as possible. I'll tell everyone. Just give me a chance. Please. If you wanted me begging, here I am."

She closed her eyes. "You ask too much," she whispered.

"I want everything. And I'll give you everything in return. Somehow, I'll prove it." He gently hung the phone up.

She let go of the phone and it dropped into her lap where it closed itself. She became aware that Kalliope had stopped the car and was looking at her expectantly. "It hurts," she whispered. "I hate this! I want him, so badly, but I'm so afraid! It destroyed me before! I still haven't recovered!"

"Recovered from what?" Kalliope murmured softly.

"The curse." The words were out before she could stop them and she looked at Kalliope swiftly.

Kalliope examined her nails but she was watching Madelyne under her lashes. "I'm beginning to think you're less afraid of him not loving you, than you are of his loving you and being hurt to protect you. Or should I say that you might die protecting him . . . again?" She smiled when she received a sharp look. "One hears legends in the 3rd District. I go to the Faerie Club a lot."

Madelyne took a deep breath. "I just can't take the risk."

"You know, if it comes down to it, I think Kienan is smart enough to know how to change the past. The cycle can be broken." She got out of the car and gestured to the mall in front of them. "Let's start here. Start with the things you can change. They're like ripples in water. Eventually they spread."

Madelyne got out of the car, hesitated, then said slowly, "Kally . . . thank you. I hope you find that true love you're waiting for."

Kalliope smiled, but there was a touch of sadness in the corner. "Me too. Now, let's shop. Forget the stuff about men. Let's focus on us women, okay?" She caught Madelyne's hand and drew her along toward the mall. "We definitely need to get you stocked up on a combination of casual and professional clothes. I mean, you're an innkeeper. You need to have that old world charm but modern elegance combination."

Madelyne eyed the store she was being dragged into. "I'm leaving myself in your knowledgeable hands for I am completely out of my league here. I don't even own any jeans other than the ones I wear to clean in."

Kalliope looked up from a rack with such a look of horror on her face that Madelyne burst into laughter. All eyes in the store swung toward her and instantly everyone was smiling. Her laughter seemed to demand it. She lit the entire store with it.

"Thank god that I found you," Kalliope said fervently. "You were on a path to complete disaster."

"What's going on?" a saleswoman asked as she approached.

"She doesn't own any jeans. Not a single pair of pants to show off her legs."

A look of horror not dissimilar from Kalliope's crossed the saleswoman's face. "Alright then," she said. She nodded decisively. "You're in good hands, my dear. We're going to make you look like a million dollars."

"I'd settle for a hundred," Madelyne admitted.

"Never settle." Kalliope held a sassy shirt up in front of Madelyne to check her coloring. "Rule One of being a woman. Never settle for less than the best." She winked mischievously. "It's a rule I was sure you knew. You picked Kienan, didn't you?"

Oddly, she found she couldn't argue with that. Bemused, she found herself being shoved into a dressing room while Kalliope and several merry saleswomen helped pick out an entirely new wardrobe. She could have sworn the full moon wasn't for another two weeks. The entire world had gone nuts in three days.

CHAPTER THIRTEEN

Madelyne found herself highly bemused by her new friend. Kalliope had dragged her through ninety percent of the stores in the mall, ruthlessly taking advantage of sales and discounts (and her company's clout) to ensure that Madelyne got a full, complete wardrobe for the lowest cost possible.

She had then driven Madelyne home, dropped her off, and promised cheerfully to drive her to campus the next day. Madelyne had ended up carrying a dozen bags into her room and unpacking them on her bed. Jeans, slacks, skirts, shirts, blouses, tank tops, camisoles, dresses . . . they had gone slightly overboard. She had clothes for all seasons, not just the winter the city was happily diving into.

There was one additional item that was in its own box. She left it to the side as she emptied out all of her old clothes and dumped them into the now empty bags. Kalliope had promised to find a thrift store they could be taken to, so they didn't go to waste.

Once her closet was empty, she began to hang up her new clothes. Meticulous as always, she sorted them into casual, work, and school, then by type. She took delight in all the colors and textures as she did. Apparently her skin tone and hair color had made her perfect for pastels. There were only occasional bright splashes of color; most everything was soft and soothing.

She couldn't help but blush slightly as she also unpacked her new underwear and lingerie. It was another 'grave offense' in Kalliope's book that any woman over sixteen didn't own at least one pretty nightgown or piece of lingerie to hide under her clothes. The important thing, she had said, was to make yourself feel good. It didn't matter if no one else ever saw it. It was so you stopped and looked at yourself in a mirror and felt happy.

She had then blithely helped pick out a scrap of purple and black lace and silk that was designed to do nothing except seduce. It was to be Madelyne's secret weapon against Kienan if she ever felt he was close to walking away. Any man who walked away from a woman in a teddy like that was not worth keeping, or so she said.

Once everything was put away, she turned her attention to the lone box. It had been the single most expensive item, but it hadn't been paid for out of her pocket. Kalliope had discovered that her birthday was only recently past and felt honor bound to get her friend a belated gift. It was also to Kalliope's advantage because it was the perfect thing for Madelyne to wear to Kalliope's upcoming birthday extravaganza.

The ball gown was violet silk in a color that was nearly identical to Madelyne's eyes. It was cut with a princess bodice to best frame her slender bust line. The sleeves were spaghetti straps lined with small glittering beads that traveled down along the edge of the bodice. The silk was covered by sheer, shimmery lavender material that also became a train in the back where it fell all the way to Madelyne's ankles.

The matching shoes were low heels in violet color and covered with more beading. There was a hairpiece for it, and she was under strict orders to see no one, except Kalliope, to have her hair done for the party. As if she would trust anyone else!

After a quick shower to wash away the strange day, she decided to start as she would go on. She dressed in a pair of slim jeans that flattered her legs and a pale yellow camisole with lace straps. And, looking in the mirror, she actually felt as if she might be kind of cute. Oh, she would never look like Kalliope or Aenya, or a lot of the girls at school, but there was definitely something, finally, appealing about her looks.

The front bell rang and she tilted her head. Because of her school schedule, the inn didn't book walk-in travelers unless there was an emergency. Everything was by reservation. There was no one scheduled for check-in for at least a few weeks.

"Coming!" she called as she walked down the hall. To her surprise, she saw a man in a work uniform standing at the front desk. "Hello, I'm the owner. May I help you?"

He turned to smile at her. "Miss Winters?" He glanced down at the clipboard he was carrying. "Broken water heater on the men's springs? I'm here to fix it."

"Oh, I can't afford it right now! I was going to arrange for this next month. I didn't already send in an order without thinking, did I?" She suddenly got a sinking feeling in her stomach. "Wait. Who ordered this?" Her violet eyes began to snap.

He coughed. "I was just asked to fix the heater. It was paid for ahead of time. I was told not to say who had arranged it." Judging by the temper in Madelyne Winters' eyes, he was beginning to understand why. "The springs are out back, right? I'll just go take care of things." He grabbed his toolkit and made a hasty exit toward the back garden.

She said nothing for long moments, then, smiling a little to herself, she grabbed a phone book. She skimmed the pages for the number she wanted and calmly dialed the phone. When the other side was answered, she said sweetly, "Mr. Shaughnessy? Hello, this is Madelyne Winters with the Gentle Brook Inn. I do appreciate the gesture of good will from your youngest son, but I would much prefer a business gesture. Perhaps we can make a deal?"

Ten minutes later, she hung up the phone and felt quite satisfied with herself. The fax machine under the counter began to spit out some documents and she read over them lightly. Content, she signed them, then faxed them back. She began to log the repair and the deal into the computer as she started counting mentally.

The phone rang just as she got to one hundred. He was getting slower. She smiled and picked up the phone. "Gentle Brook Inn."

"You are NOT funny, nightingale!" Kienan was audibly annoyed. "It was a *gift*. How dare you call my father and make it a business arrangement?" Clearly quoting from memory, he bit out, "'In return for the repair of a broken water heater, Aenya Shaughnessy and Hiro Michaels may spend their two-week honeymoon free of charge in one of Gentle Brook Inn's large honeymoon suites.'" His breath huffed out. "Damn it, Maddie, you know why I did it!"

"I know, Kienan," she agreed gently. "And you know in your heart why I can't accept it. Though your heart guided you, and though my heart would like to accept, I have pride as well. And sometimes pride is more important than hearts." She softly hung up the phone.

The repairman walked back into the lobby and cleared his throat. "Everything is taken care of, Miss Winters."

She sighed and smiled at him. "I won't lose my temper with the innocent messenger. Am I correct in assuming that a warranty was included so that if something else happens, I just call and it'll be fixed?" His color rose slightly. "That man," she said in exasperation. "Well, thank you. If you're ever in the area on a weekend, swing by. There are always extra cookies around."

He smiled at her. Gentle Brook Inn's owner was as appealing and calming as the place she operated. "I'll take you up on that." He tipped his hat. "Good evening, Miss Winters."

Once he was gone, she got out a clipboard and began to continue her examination of the inn. It was a project she had been working on for a few weeks. The inn was up-to-date electrically with properly grounded outlets wherever they needed to be, and the plumbing was as modern as possible. Those had been critical needs and they had been taken care of by the Enforcers as a birthday gift for her. The inn had many other things that should be done as well. It was a two-story building with a total of seven regular rooms and three honeymoon suites. Technically, 'inn' was a misnomer since it was more of a bed and breakfast.

The only place with updated décor was in the kitchen, which had almost been a 'have-to' as well. Everything else needed to be updated. She didn't want to change the style of the inn; she just wanted to make it fresh and new. Some rooms needed to be renovated entirely. She wanted to remove the carpet and put in hardwood floors. Some walls needed to be moved to make the rooms more uniform in size. And if it meant sacrificing one of the small rooms, she would love to put in a small elevator, so the inn would be handicap accessible.

Her list was growing by leaps and bounds. By the time she went to bed, she was well aware that the amount of money needed to bring Gentle Brook Inn up-to-date, so that it was true competition with bigger places, was potentially beyond her reach.

She would need an investor. She could think of two companies, three potentially, that might be willing to invest because they knew her personally, but she didn't want that. She wanted to prove she could make things work. Maybe Kalliope could give her some advice. Certainly the older woman had changed everything else about Madelyne's life. She was going to be dangerous when she took her daddy's company.

The next morning was no less daunting than the night before, but she decided to keep her chin high. She pulled on another pair of jeans, a white sweater with a scoop neck, and pretty white sneakers. She left her hair down and used a little bit of gel to keep it styled out of her eyes. And having been tutored quite carefully, she was even able to use her new makeup kit to enhance her eyes and lips. "Why," she complained to her reflection as she felt her heart beating, "is this so nerve-wracking?"

A cheerful honking horn caught her attention and she picked up her backpack. She locked the doors to the inn and then went down to get in Kalliope's car. As always, the black-haired heiress looked as if she had stepped off a runway. Oddly, Madelyne didn't feel that outmatched anymore. "Am I supposed to be nervous?"

Kalliope contemplated that as she navigated traffic. "Yes," she decided. "Because it means you feel you look good and you want verification from other members of the species. Some people will look at you oddly, I'm sure, because you've done a total one-eighty. But most people are going to either accept it without comment or be ecstatic because they will feel like you're approachable now. The ones with snippy things to say are the ones who would have been snippy even if you were being your normal self."

"You taking Psych 101?"

"Cosmetology. Stylists are notorious for reading their clients. It eventually turns into an ability to read people in general." She eyed Madelyne's hair. "Not bad, kid. For a newbie, you did that pretty good. If you comb out the excess next time, it won't feel as tacky to your fingers."

Madelyne stopped fiddling with her hair. She smiled. "You're amazing, Kally."

"Ain't I? Don't forget we're having lunch together. You promised to bring enough for both of us. I've heard rumors about your cooking."

She patted her backpack. "Plenty for both of us. I'll meet you at the fountain." Her confidence felt higher than ever as she walked toward her art locker; she had a watercolors class first on Tuesdays. Kalliope's unquestioning support was doing miracles.

Her friend proved herself to indeed be astute. By the time she got to her locker, she had collected more compliments than she had ever heard in her entire life. Once more she was Alice tumbling down the rabbit hole. Again, wondering if the moon was full and just pretending it wasn't, she slammed her locker and found Kienan on the other side. She leapt backward on a yelp. "Kien! Don't *do* that!"

He could only stare at her, barely breathing. In wonder and delight, he reached out to run his fingers through her hair. It looked even softer and more alluring. Her body was perfect to his eyes, shaped *just* for his hands. Her hips and breasts were rounded just enough to entice his fingers into touching. She had done some strange female thing, and her eyes looked large and sultry. Beautiful? Had he thought she was beautiful? She was *exquisite*. "Nightingale."

The word was little more than a husky rumble of male desire. His brown eyes smoldered as they swept over her. His fingers, when he cupped her cheek, were hot. A soft tremor seemed to be going through his entire body. To think she made such a powerful creature weak enough to tremble . . . Almost helplessly, she found herself swaying toward him, the heat spreading through her as well. If he didn't kiss her, she was going to die.

His breath hitched and his head lowered. Despite the hunger in both their bodies, he kissed her with a tenderness and generosity that was more seductive than a thousand wild embraces. Her hands fell weakly to her sides in sheer bliss.

He sensed the surrender and slowly eased back until there was barely a breath between their lips. He only distantly heard students giggling as they went past. His world had narrowed so that it only included his nightingale. "I love you," he vowed with all the conviction in his soul. "Please, believe me."

"I do." The words slipped past her guard before she could stop them.

When had it happened? When had it finally sunk in that this incredibly beautiful man truly loved her? She couldn't even question herself, not when she saw the brilliant joy slowly lighting his eyes. It blazed from the depths of his heart and soul, illuminating her in his love.

Unfortunately, believing him didn't change one critical fact: she was cursed. She had been cursed for centuries. Curses didn't go away when you died. They just came back more vicious than ever. More than once over her life, she had felt the slimy sensation of being watched. The hunter was out there, lurking in his new life. He would never rest until he killed the one she loved.

The one she loved was a protector. He would sacrifice his life for hers without hesitation. If the hunter learned it, realized that Kienan's weakness was his incredible depth of emotion, then none of the Shaughnessys would be safe. Madelyne wouldn't be safe. And Kienan would die. For his own sake, she had to keep her love inside. No one could know how badly she loved this man.

"What's wrong, Maddie?" He brushed his lips over her forehead to remove the lines forming there. "You're frowning. You feel so sad." The largest hurdle had been cleared. She believed him. Now he just needed to make her fall for him in return. "I can't bear it if you're sad."

"Not sad," she lied. "Embarrassed. You're making quite a scene."

"Yeah." He eased back and grinned. "You're entitled to a few." He stole a quick kiss and snatched her portfolio and books up before she could get to them. "Allow me, my lady." He gave a courtly bow and almost dropped everything. He caught the books quickly and gave her a sheepish grin.

She bit her lip but couldn't quite hide a snicker. "You're an idiot." She fell into step beside him as he headed down the hall. "Thank you, by the way."

He knew to what she was referring. "You're welcome." Softer he added, "I am sorry. It never occurred to me that it might wound your pride. I just wanted to do something for you." He shot her a sour look. "You told on me, to my dad, damn it. I got a lecture!"

She smiled and took her books at the door to her class. "Serves you right, doesn't it?" She firmly shut the door in his face and walked over to her seat. A low wolf whistle made her look over in surprise and one of the boys winked at her. Surprised, she could only blink.

"What?" He grinned. "It was meant sincerely, promise. You look kinda cute today. Wear your hair down more. I'd hit on you, but Kienan would thrash me soundly, and he has a black belt."

"He . . . he does?" Her eyes widened. "I didn't know that." It wasn't entirely unexpected, however. And it certainly explained why his body was spectacularly corded with muscle. Her pulse fluttered just remembering how all that delightful weight had felt against her.

At lunchtime, she met up with Kalliope at the fountain in the quad area. "Hungry?" she asked her friend as she sat down.

"Famished!" Kalliope took the sandwich being held out. "Is this homemade bread?"

"And homegrown veggies. The meat is from a deli near 3rd District. Closest thing to homegrown that you can get in NYC. I made the dressing, too." Madelyne happily bit into her own sandwich. "You said you liked turkey."

"Gobble." Kalliope bit in and rolled her eyes. "Oh man. No wonder Kienan wants to marry you. You cook like a goddess. How much would I have to pay you to get you to cater my birthday party?"

Madelyne laughed. "Thanks."

"No, seriously." She smiled. "I'm asking sincerely. I haven't settled on a caterer yet. And I can afford the best so I absolutely want it. We can make it a business deal if you like so that our friendship doesn't get in the way. It'll be a lot of food, and I know it'll take a lot of your time. And I absolutely want to pay you as you deserve."

"I'll make you a deal." Madelyne finished off her sandwich. "You can hire me to cater the regular food, but your birthday cake will be my gift to you."

"Done!" She pulled out her iPhone and began making notes on one of the applications. "I'll talk with my dad tonight. We'll do some research, find the proper rate, then make the deal official." She glanced up as she heard the quad beginning to buzz. She grinned. "Incoming stud at nine o'clock, and he's carrying a wrapped package."

Madelyne bit her lip to hide a laugh and turned to see Kienan approaching. He was indeed carrying a gaily-wrapped package in his hands. It wasn't very large and he was carrying it with visible gentleness. "Kien," she said warningly when he was close.

He just grinned and put the package in her hands very softly. "Be very careful," he warned. "It's very fragile, and I can't take it back."

She stifled a sigh and began to unwrap the paper. Expecting to find something very expensive and outrageous, she was stunned speechless as she lifted the lid on the top of the box to find herself staring at a bed of material and a sleeping kitten.

It was no bigger than the palm of her hand and it was probably the most mismatched kitten she had ever seen in her life. It was no purebred, that was for certain. Its nose was kind of scrunched, and its fur was on the shaggier side. Its base color was off white and it had stripes and splotches in every shade of brown and orange possible.

"You gave me a kitten," she whispered, reaching into the box and gently lifting the baby out. It fit in her palms and opened its eyes slightly as it gave a pitiful sounding mew. Its eyes were almost peridot in color and its nose was pink. "Kienan, it's a baby."

"A baby girl, in fact." He crouched down so he could see her face. "When I went to the shelter, there were purebreds and beautiful kittens as far as the eye could see. This little lady was hiding in the back of the cage. Apparently she was from an accidental pregnancy, and the owner had thrown her out. The people at the shelter figured she had little appeal and kept her out of sight.

"Thing is," he continued softly, "she reminded me of you. She may not be part of the norm, she may never win any prizes, but to the right person she would be absolutely perfect. She doesn't change. She doesn't *have* to change. The eyes looking at her love her for everything she is. With enough time, maybe she'll see how much value she has."

She lifted the kitten to her cheek and closed her eyes as tears spilled down her face. She had always wanted a pet but she had never been able to find the right one. "She's so tiny," she whispered, gently lowering the kitten to her lap where it curled up to sleep.

"She'll need someone to take care of her." He gently covered her hand and the kitten both, his hand enough larger that both were protectively sheltered. "She'll need you, Maddie."

"No one's ever needed me." Her startled gaze lifted as his free hand softly cupped her cheek. "Kien . . ."

"I need you," he said softly. "But not just in my heart. I need your voice." When she blinked at him, he smiled. "I found my inspiration in you, Maddie. That last night, I stayed up late writing a song for us. I know it's the song that will give me all my dreams. I just need you to sing with me. Together we can show everyone at the talent show that I've got what it takes. Please. Help me."

"I can't." She lifted her hands and framed his face, for the first time touching him of her own will. "Kien, there are so many things complicating this. I want to sing with you, but it's too dangerous. I don't dare sing in public. Please understand." She gave away all her emotions when she sang, and anyone hearing her would know she loved him.

He was silent for long moments and then got to his feet. "I wonder if the swan felt this way," he said quietly.

"Swan?" She looked up from where she had been putting the kitten back in her nest.

"The swan the nightingale gave her life for." He looked at her intently, his eyes darkened to almost black. "I wonder if this was the way he felt, watching the one he loved sacrifice herself for him. No matter what his family or anyone said, he would have wanted just her."

Kalliope watched him walk away. She murmured softly, "Somehow, I think he knows what you are, hon."

"I think so, too." Madelyne smiled sadly. "That reincarnation thing is a real bitch, isn't it?" She got to her feet and picked up the box with her kitten. She was going to have to ditch again, but she really couldn't regret it much.

When Kienan arrived at the inn much later, it was just turning into evening. He wanted to coax Madelyne into going on a date with him and was looking forward to seeing how she and her pet were getting along.

He got his answer for the second question when he walked into the lobby and heard her exclaim, "No, stop wiggling!" Something splashed loudly and she groused, "I will never be a mother."

Trying not to laugh, he left Stormy to guard the door and wandered toward the kitchen where he had heard the sounds coming from. Not to his surprise, he found Madelyne trying to bathe her kitten. He leaned in the doorway and grinned as he watched. "She's just playing."

"I noticed." She caught the kitten in a towel and began to gently dry her. "She got into the plants and was filthy. Scatterbrained little scamp."

"You should name her that." She quirked a brow, and he quirked one back in amusement. "Scatterbrain. If the name fits and all."

"If that was true, you'd be named Troublemaker!" She rubbed her cheek against the kitten's fur before setting her gently down on the floor. "Scatterbrain it is." Leaving the kitten to her own devices, she began to clean up the spill of water on the floor. "What are you here for, Kienan? Don't tell me you're actually going to try and ask me out. That's a little silly at this point."

"Well, a man could hope." It was time to take one of the biggest risks of his life. He glanced down the hall. The kitten was walking toward Stormy fearlessly and the wolf was eyeing the small creature as if it was poisonous. She wasn't especially fond of cats, but when the kitten cuddled up close, she sighed and laid down. She was a protector at heart. Kienan had every confidence that Scatterbrain would be well protected.

Madelyne was wringing out the washcloth in the sink when his hands settled on her hips. Her heart gave a dull thud in her chest even as heat seemed to spread from his fingers outward and made it hard to breathe. "Kienan?" she whispered.

She still wore the low cut sweater, and it was wonderfully easy for him to lower his head and press his lips to the curve of her shoulder where it met her neck. She even tasted like vanilla, but with the crispness of apple. The taste went to his head. "Let me touch you," he whispered, his arms sliding around her waist to pull her more firmly back against him. "Let me love you."

She trembled as he began to trail soft kisses along the line of her neck. She could almost literally feel her strength fading, and her head tilted unconsciously to the side to give him better access. "I'm scared," she whispered. "If I gave myself to you and you walked out while I was asleep . . ."

Fury made his fingers tighten on her hips and his voice was equally tight as he said, "I will kill him if I find him. That's something no decent man does to any woman." He turned her in his arms and used his free hand to tilt her head back. "I would *never* do that to you," he vowed fiercely. "You couldn't make me leave if you tried!"

She closed her eyes for long moments. A small and hurting part of her cynically suggested that this would be a good way to find out if he was really serious. Another part tried to tell her that she might be able to keep him if she gave him what he wanted.

In the end, what made her choose was the memory of his gentleness and the look in his eyes as he watched her. Her heart craved his closeness no matter how long it lasted. If this ended horribly, at least she would know she had belonged to him. She loved him. She could do nothing less than give him everything.

"Okay," she finally whispered in a trembling voice. She lifted her arms to wind them around his neck. "I trust you."

Relief almost made him lightheaded and he caught her closer against him, so tightly she almost couldn't breathe. He swiftly released her only to scoop her up into his arms. "I swear you won't regret this," he promised softly as he carried her out of the kitchen and down the hall.

Astonished at his strength, her heart quivering in her chest, she could only manage to bury her face against his shoulder and hold on tightly. The room spun dizzyingly around her head and she took a quick breath as she felt him lowering her to the top of her bed. "Turn the light off," she pleaded.

"Hell no." His fingers moved with confidence to the edge of her sweater and he quickly pulled it up and over her head. As her hair fluttered and slowly drifted down around her body, he sucked in a sharp breath, desire fisting into his stomach and gleefully holding on. He was literally aching fit to burst, desperate to feel her skin under his hands. "You're beautiful."

"Liar." Her breath caught as his knuckles skimmed over the top of her breast bared by her low cut silk bra. She felt too hot, her skin ready to burst into flame. Her wings ached restlessly. That alone was frightening for she had never before encountered a feeling that consumed her entire body.

"Mm, you'll just have to trust me. I'm the one looking at you." She was soft skin and slender curves, and he wanted to ravish and plunder. Hands shaking slightly, he drew her toward him until her hands lifted and flattened against his chest. "I want to be gentle," he whispered as he brushed soft kisses over her face. "Give me a few moments to find some control before I go after you like a chocoholic on a sundae binge."

A shudder went through her body. She had never wanted anyone like this. She had never *been* wanted like this. Throwing caution to the winds, she took a deep breath and began to unbutton his shirt. She pulled the edges apart and slid her hands inside where she could smooth her palms over the hot skin of his chest. "Dessert's on," she said huskily.

He gave a rough laugh and then dragged her closer, his mouth capturing hers. Her lips parted instantly, and he curled his tongue around hers. A shudder wracked his body at the taste of her. For the life of him he couldn't get enough of her taste, as if it had been centuries since he had last held her.

His hands rushed over her swiftly, learning every curve, and the feel of her was somehow familiar. He knew how her body felt, how she was sensitive on the inner curve of her hip. He knew that a little pressure in the middle of her back made her arch fluidly toward him.

He hungrily caught the edge of her bra in his teeth and dragged it down even as his fingers found the clasp and opened it. She could only moan softly as his mouth captured one nipple and tugged sharply, sending the same tug echoing through her body. Mindless, willingly losing herself in the wildness of his passion and her own, she yanked his shirt down his arms until he shrugged out of it impatiently.

The sight of his golden skin tempted her. She reached for him to run her hands eagerly over his muscles. She had never before known that sort of freedom, and the desire to know him completely was new. She reveled in it, and in understanding for the first time what it meant to be a lover—a true lover. There was power in knowing she made such a strong creature weak.

His lips covered hers again, and she held him closer, where he could not escape. She felt his fingers trying to unfasten her jeans but they were trembling too much to do any good. "What, are you nervous?" she teased. She nipped at his ear and enjoyed the way he shuddered.

"You terrify me. Any sane man would be terrified." His lips raced over her face wildly, hungrily. "I'm so scared I can't run away. You'll have to keep me. I'm housebroken." He kissed her in between every word. "And lots of fun."

She started to laugh but it turned into a gasp as he got her jeans open and ran his knuckles across the skin of her lower stomach. Lightning sparked from his touch. She twisted against him and lifted her hips so he could remove her jeans entirely. Her underwear went with them but she felt no embarrassment.

And for the first time in her life, as she felt his hot gaze raking over her naked body, she felt beautiful. She didn't know what quirk of fate had made him different, that he would see so differently, but he was there. She would fight the devil himself to hold him. "I love you!" she whispered fiercely as she threw her arms around him.

He went still for a moment. On a low sound of need he sank into her arms and kissed her as deeply as he could. "I love you," he whispered against her lips, over and over again, as if the words had been kept inside him too long to be bottled anymore.

His hands skimmed down the outside of her hips then up again, sensitizing her skin almost unbearably. Still breathing his love with every kiss, he shifted down her body, his lips trailing over her breasts, teasing the little birthmarks along the sides that almost looked like the outline of feathers.

Before she could catch a breath, his hand had slipped between her legs and his palm ruffled the gray curls at the apex of her thighs. The feel of his fingers teasing her was maddening, and she clung onto his arms tightly. She was being shaken apart by the pleasure taking her over. It had to stop somehow, eventually, because she couldn't take it anymore . . .

His weight left her suddenly, and her eyes opened in shock. "Kien?" she managed to ask. He had left her so tightly knotted with desire that she could barely breathe. She would kill him with a dull knife if he was leaving.

"I'm not going anywhere," he promised as he quickly shed the rest of his clothes. He pounced, much like a great cat, and caught her in his arms to roll with her over the top of the bed until she was breathless from laughter as well.

The laugh changed to a strangled cry as he tucked her underneath him and his hard flesh began to sink into her body. She grabbed his shoulders desperately and held on tightly, the lash of pleasure sharper than she had thought.

He stopped moving and she dug her nails into his shoulders, "What're you doing?" she managed to ask.

"I thought I hurt you." His entire body trembled with the strength he exerted to stay still. She felt like hot silk and he was wild to bury himself inside her as deeply as he could, until they were completely one and nothing separated them. One thought glaringly burst in his mind and he gulped air. "Tell me you're on birth control."

It had never even occurred to her. She knew the risk that they were taking and knew that if she said 'no' he would somehow find the strength to stop. She didn't want him to stop; she wanted to feel him inside her, to be his entirely in a way she had never been anyone else's. "Yes," she lied, her voice barely a whisper.

He kissed her deeply on a low groan, his tongue tangling with hers even as he thrust into her completely. Her startled gasp was muffled by his mouth, and he broke the kiss to rain kisses over her face softly. "Am I hurting you? You're so tight."

"No." It had never felt like that before. More powerful, more intimate, and far more wonderful. She slowly twisted underneath him to savor every sensation.

"Stop wiggling," he muttered into her hair, clinging to control with his teeth and toes. She fit like a glove, and he could feel ecstasy beckoning, his skin prickling with the electric tension. His breath hissed out as she clenched her muscles around him. "Maddie!"

"Then do something!" She wrapped herself around him as tightly as she could and held onto him with desperate strength as he began to drive quickly in and out of her body. Heat drowned her, and her breath was almost a sob as she tried to endure the pleasure gripping her body. It snapped with a suddenness that took her breath and unbearable ecstasy swept over her senses. She could only hold onto him fiercely as he buried himself one last time inside her and shuddered as his release consumed his entire body.

He was heavy, but she didn't mind. He felt wonderful as a blanket, and his heat sank all the way inside her soul. She felt sated and replete, contented all the way to her soul. He groaned suddenly, and it made her smile with smug satisfaction. She had worn him out as much as he had worn her out. She would have been happy to stay that way, but he rolled off her to the side and onto his back. The look on his face made a chill ripple through her. Try as she might, she couldn't stop her sudden terror.

He didn't even look at her as he threw an arm over his eyes. "You lied, nightingale."

She gulped softly. "No, I didn't."

"The hell you didn't. Why would you be on birth control? You were convinced you'd never catch a lover." He lowered his arm to eye her. "I might have made you pregnant."

She closed her eyes as despair rose inside. "I'm sorry," she whispered. She sat up, intending to leave the bed, but quick as a snake his arm shot out and wrapped around her waist to hold her in place. "Kienan?" she asked hesitantly.

"You're not going anywhere." He firmly drew her down until she was lying beside him. He turned onto his side and anchored her with an arm around her waist. "When was your last period?" he asked softly as he ran a hand slowly over her body. She blushed at the question and he skimmed a knuckle over her stomach. "When, nightingale?"

"It ended only yesterday," she finally admitted. "We should be safe."

"No wonder you were so crabby!" he muttered. He winced as she hit his shoulder. "Well, damn it, you were! I swear the nicest girls can become downright shrews! My sister isn't worth talking to when she's on her period. She'll snap your head off! Not that I begrudge you guys that, but don't take it out on the innocent bystanders!"

She glared at him. "Innocent bystander, my ass!" Her breath caught as his hand slid between her legs. "Cut it out!" She tried to wiggle loose but only trapped his hand more firmly. "Kien, we can't! Once is stupid, twice is asking for trouble."

"I have protection in my jeans; I just forgot it," he admitted. "It was how I convinced myself to take a gamble. But as soon as I had you in my arms, nothing else seemed to matter. I knew, at the back of my mind, that you weren't on birth control. And I wanted that. I didn't want anything between us." He lowered his head to trail his lips over her shoulder.

"Me neither," she admitted a bit breathlessly.

He lifted his head and framed her face gently with a hand. His brown eyes were as soft as velvet. "Tell me now," he urged softly. "Tell me now when your mind is in control. I need more than something given in the heat of the moment."

Her eyes closed helplessly. She couldn't lie about something that important. "I love you," she admitted achingly. "But it changes nothing, Kienan. You don't know what I am."

"Then tell me." His free hand smoothed slowly over her body, the calluses on his fingers scraping deliberately.

"I'm afraid. You'd never understand." Her breath caught as his fingers slid between her legs once more, unerringly finding where she was most sensitive. "Kienan!"

"I understand that you're the woman I love." He began to shift slowly down her body, caressing and worshipping every inch. "That's all that matters, nightingale. The past doesn't matter. Only the future. You're my future. I'm yours." His lips curved against the swell of her hip. "If you have to explain, save it for the honeymoon."

Any protest she wanted to make was lost as his lips and hands incited her senses to riot. She was drowning in him, unable to resist his tenderness any more than she could resist his passion. But, even then, she knew she had to tell him. Not telling him was a lie by omission, and he deserved so much more. He deserved more than a plain innkeeper, but she couldn't let him go yet. That would come in the morning. Right then he was hers, and she held onto him with all the love in her heart.

CHAPTER FOURTEEN

Kienan awoke around midnight and realized he was alone in bed. Scatterbrain was curled up asleep on his chest. He gently lifted her off and put her on the pillow as he sat up. Madelyne was nowhere in the room but her side of the bed was warm so she had only just left.

He knew where she had gone. He got out of bed and pulled on his jeans quickly. Not that he minded walking around naked, but he had a feeling she might be annoyed. She had an adorable prudish streak.

A prickle went down his back and he turned sharply toward the window. He was being watched. His regular sight told him there was nothing outside the window except the garden and moonlight. He didn't need his eyes, though. He felt it through his sixth sense, and the gaze was volatile and deadly.

When the purple moon is high in the sky, I walk through the heat of a savannah

When the pain is too much for my heart, my nightingale's melody soothes my tears

He went very still as he heard the singing. He yanked his shirt on without buttoning it and hurried out of the bedroom and across the empty lobby. Stormy was sitting at the back door, whining to go out, and he opened the door for them both.

I want to regain the innocence of my youth

But there are no more hopes for me to cling to

The hot springs whispered and murmured as if to play the melody of the nightingale's song. He knew he wasn't breathing, but didn't care as he went as quickly down the path as he could. He still felt as if he was being watched and it was stirring every protective instinct he owned. Madelyne was in danger.

In the night, the nightingale sings, bringing a change in the wind

In the night, the nightingale prays, bringing a change in my dreams

As he drew close to the women's hot springs, he slowed his steps to make as little noise as possible. He crouched down and eased aside the ferns to look into the bathing area. His breath came in sharply as he saw Madelyne wading through the hot spring. She wore nothing but her loose hair and her wings.

When my wings are unable to fly anymore, I can still soar the skies on the notes of a song

And when I cannot see the way out of nightmares, my nightingale's melody becomes my light

There was no place on her body that he hadn't touched or caressed, but fresh desire still prowled through his blood as he watched her. Even now, she could be carrying his child. He wanted her to be pregnant. He wanted to watch the life growing in her, knowing that they had created it together. He had never really thought of himself as a future father, but now that the idea had settled in his brain, it was very appealing. Family was as critical to him as breathing, and he wanted to start his own with Madelyne.

He straightened and pushed aside the bushes to walk toward the hot spring. She stopped singing and turned toward him sharply, her arms crossing defensively across her chest. Terror beat hard in her chest as she watched him. He would turn away from her now. She was sure of it!

He smiled at her, and the terror went away. He held out a hand, his eyes soft. "Come to me, nightingale." When she had hesitantly crossed to him, he reached down and lifted her with easy strength out of the hot spring. "You're beautiful," he murmured. "Why didn't you tell me?"

"I was afraid." Her lips turned down. "Most men would think themselves seduced by a . . . a witch or something."

"I," he decided after a moment of thought, "would be a most willing participant if you decided to seduce me. But if you're going to use potions for it, please, refrain from putting an IX on them."

She bit her lip and tried not to giggle. "You're ridiculous! I'm not a witch!" Her breath caught as he skimmed a knuckle down the curve of her breast where the birthmark was located. "I'm her. In the legend. I'm the nightingale. This is my second life."

"I know." He drew one of her hands up to rest over his heart. "I've known for a while. And there's something I haven't told you, Maddie." He shrugged out of his shirt and put it around her shoulders. He then stepped back and waited.

She ran her eyes over him and wondered what she was supposed to be looking to find. She found it quickly and her breath caught in her chest. With his jeans riding low on his hips, the little birthmark on his lower right hip was very visible. It was the mark of feathers, and it was nearly white against his golden skin. Most would think it was a tattoo, but she knew better. She didn't know how she hadn't noticed it before. "It was you," she breathed. "You were the swan I saved."

"It came to me rather blindingly the other night." He began to gently fasten the shirt for her. She had started to shiver. "It had been nagging at me for a while, your legend of the nightingale. You'd never explained what the second swan's role was and why he was there. It seemed a bit odd for him to just somehow be there with the nightingale, in a place where poachers often were."

"I never knew. Not then and not now." She didn't resist when he pulled her over to a bench and sat down with her on his lap. She couldn't bring herself to meet his eyes. "It's fuzzy from back then. It comes as hazy vignettes of emotions and brief words. All I know for sure was that I loved you. Somehow, despite being betrayed by one swan, I loved another. I wanted only to protect you. That's why I . . . I did what I did."

"I started having vignettes of my own yesterday. And I'll tell you what happened." He framed her face with his free hand. "I saw you flying through the trees. You were so sad, so lonely. I was drawn to you. I loved you. I decided to leave my flock and go with you anywhere. It was dangerous, yes, but it didn't matter to me. When you died for me . . . I had nothing left to live for." His voice turned quiet and firm. "I flew into the sun."

She took a sharp breath and shook her head quickly. "No. No!" Tears burned her eyes. "How *could* you?! What did I die for if you didn't live?"

"Do you honestly think any life is worth living without you?" he demanded roughly. "Would you live on without me if I was dead?"

Her eyes closed as the tears spilled down her cheeks. "No," she finally whispered. "I couldn't bear it." Her eyes opened then, intent and fierce. "Knowing all this, you must understand why I can't sing with you. Why I can't let anyone know I love you. We were reborn *and so was he*!"

"He?"

"Oh, god." She stared at him through her hands, stricken. "You didn't realize? I'm *cursed*, Kienan! It's not the swan's curse that keeps him from resting until I have a home. There's something else, something more. When the swan built the curse on us both . . . the poacher was there. And he bound himself into the curse. He will never rest until he destroys any chance I have at finding a home."

He could only stare at her. Didn't she see what was really going on? The answer was right there in front of her. Determination filled his heart. "I think I know how to break both curses, but you're going to have to trust me more than you've ever trusted me before."

Before she could form a response to that, they both heard the rustling of bushes. She scrambled to her feet and ducked behind him as he stood. The shirt covered her decently enough but she had to wear it low on her arms so that it went underneath her wings in the back. She felt very vulnerable.

A man walked out of the bushes with all the casual grace of someone walking into a restaurant. He was dressed regularly enough in slacks and a shirt, but there was a long and wicked knife in his hand. It was held with the competence of someone who knew how to kill. "Good evening," he said pleasantly.

Kienan's shoulders tensed slightly. "Trespassing isn't exactly a good thing around here," he said curtly. "The Enforcers take their District seriously. And I take this inn very seriously. Kindly leave."

"Afraid I can't do that. I believe you're a Shaughnessy, aren't you? Ah, of course you are. Everyone knows the youngest Shaughnessy 'prince' has been smitten with a common peasant." Something dark and malevolent flickered across his face.

Madelyne recognized it even as Kienan did. Despite her best efforts, everyone knew she was in love with Kienan and he with her. It had drawn out the poacher with violent fury and deadly intent. It tore at her as she felt Kienan's body tense. She knew her lover. He would risk himself to protect her. She couldn't bear the idea of his beautiful body covered in blood.

"And what if I am?" Kienan's voice stayed calm. "You have a problem with the Shaughnessy Corp?" He looked closer and realized why the face was familiar. "Ah. I recognize you. Dad and Mel were talking about you, I believe. Let's see . . . I think it had something to do with illegal bookkeeping. You inflated your own stock so that people paid for something with no value. Dad helped the police set you up so you hung yourself with your own rope. I thought you were in jail."

"That's what bail is for." He suddenly sprang forward with almost unnatural speed, something mad in his eyes. The knife was lifted high and curved to hit Kienan directly.

Without thinking, Madelyne knocked Kienan aside and left herself in the path of the knife. She knew only that she couldn't let him die again. He fell over the bench and tried to get his feet underneath himself. "Maddie!" he screamed.

A wild and vicious growl rose on the air with all the force and fury of a guardian wolf enraged. Stormy lunged from the shadows and leapt directly into the path of the knife. It raked across her face, split skin and fur, and sprayed blood. The blade's path continued and struck her in the flank. It remained there and yanked from the attacker's hand as she went through the air. She landed several feet away and did not move. Blood pooled slowly under her body.

"Oh god!" Madelyne flew toward the wolf as fast as she could.

The attacker took a step after her, but Kienan leapt over the top of the bench and lunged forward. Before the would-be killer could block, Kienan's fist slammed into his jaw and sent him flying. He spun around with his heel but the man caught his leg and tried to throw it away. Kienan had trained too long to fall for that. He turned the throw into a flip and his other foot got the man in the chin with bone-shattering force. His opponent was unconscious before he hit the ground.

"Stay with her," Kienan ordered Madelyne. "I'm calling the cops and a vet." He ran down the path quickly, his bare feet slapping against the tile.

Tears streaming down her cheeks, she ran her fingers over Stormy's fur gently. She could feel the rise and fall of her breath, shallow though it was. "You idiot," she whispered. "Damn it, why'd you do it? For him, for me? If you die, you'll never be free. Don't die, please!"

A groan caught her attention and she looked over to see the attacker stirring. Fury rose inside her and she walked over to look down at him. His eyes opened blearily and she knelt down beside him. Quite firmly, she pressed on his broken jaw. His eyes rolled with pain and knocked him out once more. "I ought to kill you here, you bastard," she said fiercely. She folded her wings away as she stood once more. "If she dies, there will be nowhere you can hide. I will be *your* curse!"

Police and medics arrived minutes later. Kienan told them what had happened as Madelyne and a paramedic tried to stop Stormy's bleeding while they waited for the vet. To Madelyne's surprise, the vet arrived with a familiar red-haired woman in tow. "Rhianna!" She leapt to her feet and hugged the shorter woman tightly. "Rhianna . . . she . . ."

"I know." Rhianna Taber held her surrogate daughter tighter and rocked gently. Her gaze when she looked at the vet was fierce. "Take her back to headquarters to treat her. And if anything happens to her, you're looking for a new job."

"Yes'm." The vet had Stormy lifted onto the ambulance and they took off down the street with sirens blaring even as the attacker was loaded onto the other truck and taken the other way.

Kienan warily approached where the two women were standing. He had never met Rhianna Taber before, but he knew of her. He knew she had been the force behind his sister's contract as well as his own. He knew she was connected in some way to Stormy since the wolf served as courier. He knew she was a co-owner of Enforcers and had been for at least three decades. She had to be in her fifties, at the minimum, but she barely looked out of her twenties.

Rhianna looked him over once before holding out a hand. "So you're the youngest Shaughnessy male. Your father is a shark, and I very much enjoy working with him." The Enforcers had alliances with dozens of companies, including the Shaughnessy Corp. Not quite a merger, not quite a partnership. It was more like a mutually beneficial relationship for all.

"Thanks." He shook her hand, still wary. She was Madelyne's adopted mother (legal guardian, his ass), and he was sleeping with Madelyne. "I intend to marry Maddie," he finally said. "I want your permission."

"Kienan!" Mortified, Madelyne released Rhianna and glared at her lover. "This is hardly the time!"

"There won't be any better." He held Rhianna's black eyes intently. "I know what she is, and I don't care. I love her, and I want her to be my wife. My father is in agreement."

Rhianna said nothing for a few moments and tapped a scarlet fingernail against her hip. She was in casual clothes but still every inch the businesswoman. "And if I refuse?" she finally asked calmly.

His face tightened. "I'd take her away. I love her too much to let her go, even when she is fighting me. I won't let anyone hurt her, ever again. So, please." He bowed deeply, stunning Madelyne. "I ask again. Give me permission to marry Maddie."

Rhianna smiled. He was just the same as any other Shaughnessy she had ever met. A wild spirit with a generous heart and a willingness to fight for love. "You're one hell of a kid. Yes, you have my permission, and my blessings." She touched Madelyne's face gently. "The rest is up to her now. Good luck, both of you. I'll call when I find out what Stormy's condition is."

"Thank you," Madelyne whispered. She turned her face into Kienan's shoulder as Rhianna walked away. "Kienan, just because she said . . . it changes nothing. You saw what happened. Stormy might . . ." Her voice broke, unable to bear the very idea.

"Maddie, take a chance." He brought her hand to his lips. "I know you've suffered under your curses, but there's a way out of them both. You said it yourself that they were connected. You'd see the answer if you'd just open your eyes." He let her go slowly. "Saturday is the contest. I'm going to lay it all on the line there. If you don't sing, I won't. I want you more than my music, and if I go big without you, I'll never have you. I'm laying my dreams and my heart at your feet, nightingale."

She felt cold as he walked away toward the inn. "Where are you going?"

"Home." He looked over his shoulder. "I've done everything I can. You have to fly to me of your own will, Madelyne." He smiled suddenly even though it was strained around the edges. "How do you hide those anyway?"

"They push in and out of the skin on my back," she whispered. "It's genetic. They get smaller when they go away, and grow when they come out."

"They're beautiful, you know." He gently shut the inn door and she wrapped her arms around herself. She felt cold all the way to her bones. She simply didn't know if she was strong enough to give him what he wanted and what she so desperately longed for herself.

As soon as everyone was gone, she went into the inn and to her room. Except for the shirt she was wearing, there was no sign that Kienan had been there. Or was there? A sheaf of papers sitting on her dresser called her attention, and she walked over to look at them. Her heart leapt. It was music. It was the song he had written.

She found herself pouring over every note, memorizing every word. It shook her. He had written this for them, for her. She could see where his understanding of her skill had driven him to give her the harder notes, the higher pitches. Her voice would blend with his as naturally as their bodies had come together.

Feeling very cold, she heaped extra blankets on the bed. Scatterbrain snuggled against her, but gave little comfort for the moment. The phone rang two hours later and brought the news that Stormy would be fine, but scarred for life. It nearly broke Madelyne. She was almost crying when she called Kienan's cell phone. She wasn't surprised when he answered immediately.

"She'll be fine," she said without greeting.

He let out a ragged breath. "Thank god." He was silent for long moments then added softly, "A lonely bed is a cold one, Maddie, no matter how many blankets you have. You'll always be warm in my arms, though." Softly, he hung up the phone.

She stared at the blankets and felt fresh tears burning her eyes. How had he known? Holding his shirt tight because it carried his scent, she curled up and closed her eyes, wishing with all she was for the strength to reach for her own dreams. She just didn't know what to do.

By the time Saturday came around, the betting pool was higher than ever. Madelyne was avoiding Kienan, and every time he looked at her, he watched her with a longing that made nearly everyone on campus wildly envious. Even when they began to pester Taegan and Mel, who lived with Kienan, and Kalliope, who was Madelyne's best friend, no one could get a straight answer as to what was going on.

The talent competition had pulled people from all over the city, even Rhianna from the Enforcers, Kalliope's father from Tavoularis Industries, and Sullivan. The Shaughnessy patriarch was clearly waiting for his son's performance; he held the contract they had signed a week prior. Madelyne, watching him from the back of the room, felt her stomach quiver.

Kalliope leaned against the wall next to her suddenly and murmured, "What holds you back?"

"Ever loved someone so much you'd die for them?" she asked starkly.

After a momentary pause, Kalliope said softly, "No."

"When you do, you'll understand." She pressed her hands to her eyes, but pulled them down quickly when she heard Kienan's name announced. Her heart began to beat in her chest. Surely he would reach for his dreams!

His keyboard was already set up and he walked over to it with his lethal and beautiful stride. As he hit the first chord, he opened his eyes and met her gaze across the room. She knew the music intimately, and she was stunned when the verse started and he did not sing. The room began to shift nervously, and Sullivan frowned.

"Speaking as someone who knows what it's like to long for true love," Kalliope said quietly, "it's very foolish to throw it away when you have it. You're not a fool, Madelyne Winters, and stronger than you think. No curse can stand up to love, hon."

On a shuddering breath, Madelyne stopped fighting. Kalliope was right. Kienan was right. And if he could take a risk like this, then so could she. She waited for the music to come around again and began walking toward the stage, her stomach clenching in nerves as she lifted her voice.

Even when I'm alone I can feel the beat inside my heart

An excited buzz raced through the room as everyone began to murmur excitedly. No one had realized her lovely speaking voice was only the tip of the vocal iceberg that was her incredible talent. Kienan's eyes lit with delight. He kept playing and picked up the next line in the song.

So even when you're apart from me we can dance together

The stage was too high to climb onto and the only stairs were backstage. Before she could figure out how to get to him, Taegan stepped forward and caught her around the waist. He lifted her up gently and made it easy for her to climb up onto the stage. She smiled at him as Kienan continued to sing.

The brush of your body against mine, the scent of your perfume

The touch of your hand on my own, the heat of your skin

Her eyes met his and he inclined his head with a smile toward where the microphone stand waited. She ignored it and walked over to sit beside him on the bench. She pulled the mic down where they both could use it. She smiled as well, and he let out a soft breath as she picked up her part in the lyrics.

Come with me into the darkness where the light is hiding

Come with me where seduction itself is another dance

The audience cheered loudly. Kienan's entire family was grinning. Kalliope all but jumped up and down at the back of the auditorium. Rhianna, from where she was watching, couldn't help but grin as well. She needed to go to her office and make a call or two. She got to her feet and walked out of the auditorium silently as she heard the voices behind her meshing into a perfect harmony.

No matter how the music changes around us
The music in our hearts will never change

Even when I'm alone I can feel the beat inside of my heart
So even when you're apart from me we can dance together

Swaying like the falling stars as you fall into my arms
Spinning like the colorful turrets on a merry-go-round

Come with me into the night where the moon sings high
Come with me where the nightingale practices her scales

No matter how the world around us changes the times
The time in this dance will always be one on one

Even when I'm alone I can feel the beat inside of my heart
So even when you're apart from me we can dance together
Even when I'm dreaming, I can feel the memory of this dance
So even when you're sleeping far away, we can dance together

They didn't win. The winner was a sophomore who could fiddle a medley of recognizable rock hits in under two minutes. Even Kienan and Madelyne felt she had earned it. While Madelyne congratulated her backstage, Kienan went looking for his father.

Sullivan was still sitting in the audience and smiled as Kienan sat beside him. "You far exceeded my expectations, son. I'll do whatever I can to make sure you get that sale. You'll have your musical career."

"I don't want it." He had thought long and hard about it. "I want to record this song with Maddie and sell it, yes, but I don't want to go into music as a career. I'm going to keep my major. Being fluent in many languages will help Madelyne with the inn. We could draw in foreign tourists to help turn a nice profit."

Sullivan contemplated that for long moments and then finally asked, "What changed your mind?"

"Maddie. She belongs in the 3rd District and so do I. I realize that now. The inn needs serious renovations, though. Someone needs to invest." A determined look in his eyes proved that he, too, was a Shaughnessy businessman at the core. "I'm going to go over things with Maddie and we'll write a proposal for you to consider. After all, the Shaughnessy Corp. is about investing in dreams and making them come true."

"It is indeed," Sullivan agreed. "And I will give your proposal for the inn the same consideration I'd give any other. I won't let family get in the way. If it isn't sound, I'll tell you so." He, too, understood pride. "If I accept, what will you do?"

"Start the renovations. Maddie and I can live at home until they're completed and move in just before Aenya's wedding. I know she and Hiro are waiting until she's out of high school, but I'm not waiting for Maddie. She needs family, and I need her."

"Your mother would be proud of you," Sullivan said quietly. "As I am. And I will be very pleased to call Madelyne," he paused, then corrected himself deliberately, "call Maddie my daughter."

He smiled. "Thanks, Dad." He got to his feet and headed backstage, following his sixth sense for his lover. It was sharper than ever. He always knew when she was near or far, and even how much distance there was between them. He found her sitting just outside the backstage, perched gracefully on the railing of the stairs like the wild little bird she was inside. He walked up beside her and leaned against the rail. "I turned down the offer for a music career."

She stared at him. "But why? It was what you wanted all along."

"I want you." He smiled up at her. "You're not a jetsetter. You're the kind who likes to nest. So I figure we record and sell just this one song and let it provide supplemental income. And we'll get your inn into working order so it gives some of the bigger chains competition. You'll never have to worry in the middle of the night again. And," he added, "if you do, you can just roll over and punch me, and make me worry with you."

She had to smile. "You're that confident, are you?" She sighed and held her arms out to him. "Alright, I give in. I give up." She went into his arms, and her head rested on his shoulder where it had always belonged. "I'll marry you, and we'll run an inn and raise pets and kids."

"Kids?" He stared at her. "Are you . . . ?"

"No, I don't think so." She smiled up at him. "But I'm hoping."

His breath sighed out softly, the tension and pain fading as he pulled her into his arms. "Come home with me, nightingale," he said softly.

"I'm already there." She knew it was true, felt it as his arms closed around her. The curses, both of them, were gone. "That's all I ever had to do," she said softly. "I just had to trust in you and the home you offered. It was always that simple." She lifted her head to look at him, and her violet eyes were soft and beautiful. "Take me home, Kienan. I've been waiting for you for so long."

Inside the auditorium, Sullivan saw the rest of his family waiting for him and got to his feet to go join them. As he did, the contract fell onto the floor. He picked it up just in time to see the word 'Complete' appear across the top. He smiled.

Stormy carefully limped up beside him; she was bandaged but clearly well on the mend. He knelt and ruffled the fur on her head gently before handing her the contract so that she could carry it in her teeth. "Thank you," he said softly, and sincerely. "But you're part of the family too, so you can't go dying on us. Take that to Ms. Taber, but then take care of yourself for a while."

As he watched her head off and he himself headed toward the door, he regarded his two oldest sons and had to wonder just who would be next.

CHAPTER FIFTEEN

Rhianna studied the contract sitting in front of her. This one had been personal, and she was well pleased with the results. She added her notes to the bottom, smiling as she did, then slipped the contract into the open folder waiting on her desk. The folder glowed as the word 'Complete' appeared and she added it to the end of the Shaughnessy folder.

As she shut the drawer, she glanced across the room. "You took too big a risk," she said quietly but firmly.

The voice that responded was also feminine, but it was huskier and held a note of steel. "I'm risking everything this time. If I don't succeed . . . well, we both know what that means, so let's not go there, shall we? Life or death. Right now they mean the same to me. All I care for is freedom."

"As I see." As she always had, she decided as she pulled out two blank contracts from her desk.

"Two?"

"Mmm. You'll see. Let's get to work, shall we?"

Status: File In Progress

Analysis: The nightingale who has a home always sings a love song.

Folder Three

TAEGAN

CHAPTER SIXTEEN

Among the big businesses in New York City, several names were known to one and all. Like modern day kingdoms, these businesses were handed down through family lines. Unlike more traditional kingdoms, the 'kings' and 'queens' usually put the happiness of their families before anything else. There was never any pressure on an heir to inherit. If they chose not to inherit, then a solution would be reached. It was that easy.

In the world of advertising lived the Viani and Dease families. In the world of investment lived the Shaughnessy and Tavoularis families. Shaughnessy Corp. and Tavoularis Industries were not dissimilar in their operations. Shaughnessy Corp. focused on helping small businesses get up and running. Tavoularis Industries stepped in to keep small businesses from bending under the pressure of large markets without sympathy.

Tavoularis Industries was owned and operated by Jiles Tavoularis. He and his wife had inherited the company from his father and mother, who had in turn inherited from his father's mother and father. It had always been passed down from generation to generation within a short time of the selected heir's marriage. There were extenuating circumstances just in case of deaths and surprise births, but it was generally understood by one and all that an heir could not normally inherit until they were married.

Kalliope hated rules. And she *really* hated rules that dictated she couldn't have one thing without the other. She refused to marry for less than love, and that meant she was still unmarried. Her father refused to let her take control of the company until she was at least engaged. It made for some interesting Saturday mornings.

Some loud ones, in fact.

Even across the mansion, Mara Tavoularis could hear her husband and daughter shouting. She ignored them as she always did. She absolutely refused to take sides in the issue. On one hand, she did agree that Kalliope should be less picky. But on the other hand, she also agreed that she deserved to wait for love. The safest thing for Mara to do was to eat her breakfast and ignore the shouting. So she did.

In Jiles' office, Kalliope paced back and forth in front of her father's desk, her pale legs nothing but a blur under the edge of her short denim skirt. She hadn't had time to do her hair and it tumbled around her back in a wave of black curls. She had been rather unceremoniously ordered to her father's office, and she distinctly resented it.

She planted her hands on the desk and leaned forward. "I am an adult," she snapped. "I am capable of making my own decisions! And I *refuse* to be part of a Cinderella plan! You are not going to ruin my birthday, damn you!"

Jiles rubbed his forehead and bemoaned a fate that had given him a headstrong and stubborn daughter for his heir. This was a fight that had been three years in the making. "Kally," he said as calmly as he could manage, "it's not a Cinderella plan."

"Oh the hell it is!" She straightened and began to pace again. "You're planning to invite all of the eligible bachelors in the vicinity to my birthday party in the hopes that I might pick one. If that's not a Cinderella plan, I don't know what is. If I find a *single* name on that list that I didn't specify, I'm going to make you regret it!"

He grimaced. He knew what she was threatening him with. The simple fact was that he loved his daughter and worshipped the ground she walked on. And as she knew it as well, she knew her most potent weapon was to start crying and make him feel guilty. He couldn't help it. Whenever he saw her tears, he was driven to do whatever he could fix things. It was just vexing that she knew it too. She was a businesswoman to her core. "Kally, let's be reasonable."

"I am being reasonable. You're the one with the issues!" She tossed her hair back as she turned toward the door. "And besides, it would serve you right if I went along with things. You've got this mental hang-up about our position in society. You want me to marry someone of a similar standing. Gee, as I recall, the prince in the story found himself a commoner. It would be your just desserts if I fell for someone who was blue collar." Her black eyes fired with a temper that was nearly regal. "Mark my words, Dad. I. Am. Not. A. Prize!"

The door slammed so hard behind her that a vase sitting on the nearby shelf jumped and fell onto the floor where it shattered and sprayed water and flowers everywhere. On a groan, Jiles lowered his head and began to beat it steadily against the top of his desk. Why couldn't she be happy with a nice business marriage? The Shaughnessy heir, Mel, was only a few months older than she was. It would be a good arrangement. The two companies had flirted with the idea of a merger for a few years. Mel seemed nice and levelheaded. He would be perfect for Kalliope.

Certainly, Mel was levelheaded compared to his little brother and sister, but he was by no means an idiot. Sullivan was on a tear, convinced that since the two youngest of his children had gotten married or engaged, then the oldest two should be as well. Mel was much his father's son. He knew a hostile takeover when it reared its paternal head. He locked himself in his room and announced he was studying. Since his grades bordered on the cusp of no hope, no one went near his door.

Unfortunately, Taegan was another story entirely. He had been enduring Sullivan's not so subtle efforts to get him married off for seven years. He still wasn't sure if it was Sullivan's revenge for his decision to become a teacher instead of inheriting the company.

He sighed and looked at the doorway to his bedroom. Stormy sat there waiting for him. She had been sitting there for ten minutes with all the patience of a saint. He knew he couldn't outwait her and finally put down the pen he had been grading papers with. He was summoned, and he knew it.

He walked over and knelt down to study her. Though he couldn't quite understand the 'how' of the situation, let alone the 'why', he knew very well the 'who.' He had a gift, as most of the Shaughnessys did. His was to recognize energy in and around other living beings. Stormy's had always been familiar.

He gently ran his hands over her side to check on the healing wounds. It had been two weeks since she had been wounded defending Kienan and Madelyne, and she was doing amazingly well. She would always carry the scars, but she would soon be strong and healthy once more.

"You're a strange one," he murmured softly as he studied her face and intelligent yellow eyes. "If I asked you what you really were, would you answer?" Her response was to lick his hand and he smiled. "If you really are who I think you are, that was a very flattering kiss."

She snorted lightly. He got to his feet and dropped his glasses on the desk with a sigh. "C'mon then. You can hang around me all you like." He gave her a wry smile, well aware of what her presence had led to lately. "But I'm afraid I'll be a harder mark than my baby brother and sister."

When he got downstairs, he saw the same brother and sister peering around the corner of the hall and watching Sullivan's study door like one might watch a ticking time bomb. They spotted him, and they both began clapping. Aenya even had a pair of pompoms—god only knew where she had gotten them—and she waved them in encouragement.

On a laugh, he said, "Go away."

"Spoilsport," Kienan groused.

Aenya took his hand in sympathy. "Come on. Let Taegan deal with Daddy. Maddie made breakfast this morning." When her brother perked up, she shook her head. "I still say she spoiled you by marrying you so fast. It went to your head."

"Yeah." Kienan just grinned. "But how else would I have gotten her to cook for us?"

Taegan couldn't argue that the entire family had gotten the benefit of Madelyne's amazing culinary skills. He also couldn't argue that she had spoiled Kienan. He just happened to think that Kienan spoiled her just as much, just as they ought to do.

With a little sigh, he opened the office door and held it long enough to let Stormy in. He then walked in himself and shut the door. "You wanted to see me, Father?"

"Have a seat, Taegan."

Mentally bracing himself, he sat down in one of the chairs. Stormy sat down beside him and firmly aligned herself on his side. He was oddly grateful for the support.

Sullivan took a deep breath. He knew he was in for a fight but he felt compelled to plead his case again. When he had seen Stormy suddenly attach herself to Taegan, he had been ecstatic, sure that his prayers would be answered. The wolf was a good spirit of some kind. He was sure of it. "I'm sure you know why I called you in here."

His son grimaced slightly. "I have a feeling I can give your speech for you." He sighed. "Father . . ." He trailed off as Sullivan held up a hand. Under his breath, he muttered, "Here we go again."

"You're twenty-eight years old, Taegan," Sullivan began. "It's time you considered finding yourself a wife. I was very lenient with your wishes to become a math instructor even though you knew full well I had always expected you to take over the company."

Taegan had to smile at that. "I don't have a head for business. Mel does. He's a much better choice, if he ever gets his grades up. And you really had no chance to argue as you did with Aenya and Kienan. I didn't tell you my plans until I was an adult." Because he loved his father, he willingly admitted, "I would have told you even sooner if the law hadn't changed. I never wanted to get your hopes up, but I knew you would have stopped me."

That law had been a pain in Sullivan's side for several years, though, oddly, he was suddenly looking on it with a kinder eye. It had become almost an aid rather than a hindrance when it came to the happiness of his family. "I can't argue that," he admitted. "And I'm proud of you, Taegan, never doubt that. You got a four-year degree and teaching credentials in a third of the time it takes others. But it's always been tradition . . ."

" . . . Tradition in the family that the eldest marry by thirty and carry on the family name," he finished. He rubbed his forehead. "I have two years left, Father, thank you. I already feel old inside. You don't need to help."

Sullivan knew the feeling, and he knew Taegan had been forced to grow up much faster than normal. He had been only ten when his mother had died, and yet he'd had to step up to help Sullivan raise a newborn Aenya, two-year-old Kienan, and even six-year-old Mel. There was no one who respected Taegan more than Sullivan.

And it was because he loved his son that he said, "Taegan, answer me honestly." He leaned back in his chair. "You haven't dated a single woman since you were twenty-four. If you're gay, I'd appreciate you just saying so."

Taegan could only sigh. "No, I'm not." He rubbed his hands over his face. "There's a reason for it, really. It's just complicated."

Sullivan sighed internally. He had hoped he was right if only because it would be easy to reassure his son that anyone he loved would be welcome, and he could again start looking for the one for him. Shaughnessys needed family. It was part of who and what they were. "Well, what's the reason then?"

Taegan got to his feet and walked over to the window to stare out across the landscape. He had only ever admitted the reason in his mind. It had never come to his lips. "I fear that I am a victim of my own romantic heart." His smile turned sad and wry. "I have the misfortune to be in love with the one woman I can never have. I've loved her for four years. I'll love her until I die. And if I can't have her, I don't want anyone else."

Sullivan looked at him for long moments and then turned his gaze to Stormy. She was watching Taegan too, but when she felt Sullivan's gaze, she turned her head to meet his eyes. She tilted her head a little but it was clear she understood what he was trying to convey. She woofed softly in agreement.

Taegan heard the woof and turned with a smile to kneel and run his hands over her head teasingly, with all the affection he would ruffle his siblings' hair. "She seems to have been a lucky charm lately, so maybe something might change." He looked at his father. "But don't get your hopes up. It's bad for your heart."

Sullivan scowled. "There is nothing wrong with my heart!" He watched the door shut behind his son and the wolf before letting out a sigh. He turned in his chair and looked out the window at the rolling gardens. He didn't know who had captured Taegan's heart. No contract from the Enforcers had mysteriously arrived to help gently nudge things along.

It made him wonder just what this story would be and how it would end.

CHAPTER SEVENTEEN

Taegan taught several different levels of math classes at college, though none that his siblings took. The college frowned sharply on even the slightest hint of impropriety. That didn't stop him from acting as a tutor at home for his younger siblings, of course, but that was under the table.

As most teachers did, he had a few favorite students among all his classes. One was a young man who couldn't do basic math to save his life but could unravel Algebraic equations in his head. Another was Kalliope.

In Latin, she would have been the *decorus procer*. She even looked like a 'beautiful princess' and held one of the best reputations on campus. She was unrivaled for valedictorian, her GPA was a solid 4.0, and she had been voted Homecoming Queen every year she had been at college. She had two courses of study; a major in Business Management and a minor in Cosmetology. She had been tested and retested, and her scores tipped comfortably into the genius range every time.

It was for that reason alone that he realized something was wrong on Monday afternoon. He had always felt particularly attuned to her, and he had known from the moment she arrived that she was out of sorts. Her concentration was absent and she couldn't even add whole numbers, let alone integers.

While everyone was writing down notes from the board, he stopped and knelt next to her desk. "Kalliope," he said softly. "Wait for me after class. I'd like to talk to you."

"Yes, sir." She watched him as he went back to the front of the class. Not that she was the only one. Every female in the class watched Professor Shaughnessy. In fact, the class was mostly female, as were all his classes; it was a phenomena quite well known around the campus. Kalliope could vouch for it personally. She had been in all of his classes.

He was at least a foot taller than she was, and he was strong and muscular. His thick black hair fell into his eyes and clung to the back of his neck. It was never styled and instead left to its own devices, serving a lure to any female with a sense of touch in her fingers. His eyes were honey brown with little flecks of yellow. His face was sheer perfection. He was, without question, the most attractive professor on campus, and one of the three most attractive males over all. The other two were his younger brothers.

He wore glasses to read and was known for sometimes forgetting they were on top of his head. He had the slightest hint of a brogue in his voice, more a flavor of Ireland than an outright accent. Most assumed he had a temper—his brothers certainly did—but he was unfailingly gentle with everyone. He was open and friendly, always ready to lend a hand or an ear, or whatever was needed by anyone.

And she had been in love with him for four years. She acknowledged it inside her heart though she had never spoken of it to anyone, not even Madelyne. She pushed it down where it couldn't be found and acted the same around Taegan as she did anyone else. Never mind that she wanted to run her hands through his hair. Never mind that she longed to feel his hands on her body.

She could even pinpoint the exact moment she had fallen for him. It had been her first day at the school. She had been so nervous that she had found herself bumping into things. One of them had been Taegan. He had smiled at her and told her that he was nervous too because it was his first day as a teacher. She had made sure to take all of his classes ever since. She didn't necessarily love math, but he made it worth it. Even if she hadn't loved him, he would have been her favorite teacher.

After class, she waited by the door for him as he spoke with other students. He wasn't an official campus counselor, but students always went to him first with problems. And he listened. He listened and gave advice. It was for that reason alone that she found herself glad he wanted to talk to her. Maybe he would be open to listening to her, too.

"I'm sorry," he apologized with a smile as he joined her. "Shall we?"

He walked beside her, close enough that he was still with her, but not so close that she felt crowded by his height. She adored that about him. She was short and she knew it, but she hated men who had to point it out. "How tall are you?" she finally asked. She glanced up at him. "I mean, I barely reach your shoulder."

"Six-three." He smiled. "You're not short, Kalliope. You're just . . . compact. Like your car."

She eyed him, but she was smiling. "Let me guess: good things come in small packages? I thought men didn't believe that."

"Only about some things." His smile was as teasing as hers as he held his office door for her. "I like small cars." And the small woman walking beside him, but he didn't say it out loud.

"You'd never fit in one." She dropped her bag on the floor and sat down on the edge of the chair. Her skirt was just short enough that she worried she would stick to the leather seat.

He saw how she was sitting and immediately shrugged out of his jacket. He pulled her up to her feet and put the jacket down on the seat. "Here. Sit comfortably."

"Oh. Thank you." A little flustered, she sat again and settled back in the chair. She tried to keep her gaze as casual as she could while she watched him sit behind his desk. The plain white shirt he wore made his shoulders look even wider. She wanted to cuddle in rather badly. "So what did you want to talk to me about? I know, I was off today."

"Only a little. And as I've never known you to be off about anything, it had me concerned." His eyes darkened as he studied her. "It's obvious something is on your mind, Kalliope. And it clearly has you upset. I thought maybe you might want to talk to someone."

She chewed on her lower lip while she thought about it, unwittingly causing knots of desire to coil inside his body. He had loved her for four years. He had wanted her with a growing obsession to where her laughter alone could turn him on. He had watched her blossom over four years into a woman whose body was his every fantasy and whose mind always kept him guessing and intrigued.

He was patient. As long as she was in his classes—and she had been rather innocently tormenting him by being in them all—he didn't even dare contemplate crossing any lines. Impropriety would ruin them both. But if he could just wait until she graduated, then he might yet have a chance to win her heart.

Of course, graduation wouldn't remove the problem of her father. He was well aware that Jiles Tavoularis wanted his daughter to marry another businessman. Taegan was a Shaughnessy, but he wasn't in line to inherit the company anymore. He didn't want business. In fact, there were only two things he had ever truly wanted. Teaching . . . and Kalliope.

She made up her mind to tell him everything and lifted her gaze to meet his eyes. Her heart instantly skipped a beat. Heat pooled low in her body. She wanted to tell herself she was imagining things, but she was sure, *positive*, that there was desire in his eyes as he looked at her. "Taegan?"

The look was gone as he blinked at her. "My mind was wandering," he apologized. "So, what's troubling you?"

"My father." She propped her chin on her hand. "He's being a pain in the ass. He wants me to get married." Frustrated all over again, she got to her feet and began to pace. Pacing was how she worked out her anger and he wisely stayed seated. "I keep telling him I want to be in love when I marry, but he won't get a clue!"

"What has he done lately to make this rant different than the others?" he shrewdly asked. He was *well* acquainted with the same exact rant from his own father.

She snorted lightly. "Do I look like a prince?" She turned toward him, hands on her hips.

He studied the distinctly female body in front of him, chicly shown in a short black skirt and a partially unbuttoned cream-colored blouse. There was a black scarf around her neck and silver loops dripped from her ears. "Hardly," he said dryly. "A princess perhaps."

"Gee, thanks." She huffed and dropped into the chair again. "My birthday party is coming up in a few days. He wants to change *my* guest list and invite all the bachelors in the nearby vicinity."

He ran his tongue over his teeth. "I see."

"I am NOT a prince in a Cinderella story!" She shook a fist at him. "And stop snickering at me, you brute!" She crossed her arms on a huff as he laughed outright. "I'm going to watch that guest list like a *hawk*. I'm making the invitations personally. Oh, you're invited, too," she added.

"Well, thank you." He leaned back in his chair with a wry smile. "If it's any consolation, my father has been after me for seven years for much the same. It's driving me insane."

She blinked in surprise. "How old are you, Taegan? Only seven years seems a short time. Aren't you in your thirties?"

"Not yet." He smiled. "I'm only twenty-eight. Just turned recently, as a matter of fact."

"Oh!" She suddenly felt less guilty about her feelings. "You're only four years older than me; I turn twenty-four in a few days. I guess I was assuming you were older because you've been teaching for four years."

"I graduated early. I had to," he added ruefully. "My father wasn't entirely happy when I decided not to inherit the company. But the simple fact is that it isn't for me. Mel's much more suited for it than I am. I just don't want to run a company."

"I do." Her gaze was drawn to a photograph of San Francisco that hung on the wall. She didn't need to see the artist signature in the corner to know that he had taken it. It was as beautiful as its creator. "I want to run Tavoularis Industries. I like being in charge, and there's so much we have the potential to do. Daddy doesn't think big enough. I do, and I can make what I think happen."

She sighed and shrugged her shoulders. "It's just a little lonely, I suppose." She smiled wryly. "Maddie's the first real friend I've had in a long time. Usually I get treated with kid gloves by girls, and the boys either want to get into the company, or my pants. None really look at *me*. What I wouldn't give for a normal day, just once!"

The decision, for Taegan, was an easy one. "Do you have any more classes today?"

"No. I usually go to the salon for a few hours."

"Good. I'm also free for the rest of the day." He shut down his computer and smiled. "Why don't we both have a normal day? Let's go have some fun. We both need to pretend for a little while that no one expects anything of us."

She began to smile. "I think I'd enjoy that." She got to her feet and picked up his jacket for him as he came around the desk. As she handed it to him, she rose on her toes to kiss his cheek. "You're a good man, Taegan Shaughnessy."

"I do my best." But it really stung in moments like that when the woman he loved viewed him only as a friend. He would have happily killed to have her look at him as a man, desire in her beautiful black eyes.

"Are we taking your car?" she asked as she followed him out into the afternoon sunshine. It was bright, so she pulled out her sunglasses and slid them on. As she did, she saw him exchanging his regular glasses for sunglasses, and her heart gave a wild thump in her chest.

No math teacher should have looked like that. It was going to be an image stuck in her head whenever she was in class. He was wearing a suit but he had taken off his tie and exchanged his suit jacket for a leather one. He suddenly looked his actual age, and he was attractive enough to stop traffic.

"Hoo boy," she said under her breath. Down girl.

"I don't actually have a car," he was saying. He led the way toward the faculty lot. "I have a bike." His smile turned wry. "I can't afford a good car. Teachers don't make very much, and I refuse to accept anything from my father."

A motorcycle. She managed a weak smile. "As long as you have an extra helmet, I don't mind." Yup, she saw, it was a motorcycle. It was also a *red* motorcycle that gleamed and shined. Her entire view of Taegan had changed very sharply, and she tried to reconcile the two sides of him. "By any chance," she asked, "were you a bad boy in high school?"

He flashed her a grin that was pure wicked danger. It was confident and self-assured and so outrageously beautiful that it made every pulse in her body begin beating all at once. She had heard rumor of the Shaughnessy smile, but rumor had vastly understated its potency. He seemed oblivious of its impact.

"I was a paragon," he assured her, but there was laughter in his voice.

"You were a bad boy. I *knew* it. I knew you weren't that different from your siblings. Kienan and Aenya are obvious about their wild spirit, and Mel does his level best to tame it, but can't wholly hide it. You hide yours the best, but it's definitely there! You're a walking oxymoron." She pulled on the helmet he handed her, and then her heart gave a wild thump again as he swung her up onto the bike in front of him.

He reached around her to turn on the bike and the scent of his skin and cologne curled into her lungs. Really, it should have been her first clue. He smelled wild and untamed, a sharp and romantic scent that made her think of swordsmen and heroes and being carried away for happily ever after.

"So where to?" he asked.

"Well, there's a good movie playing. But it's a chick flick," she warned him.

"Here's a secret that my brothers, and future brother-in-law, will deny unto death. We're all suckers for romance. We all read novels and watch movies. Kienan has been known to cry, but he'd kick my ass if that got out. He has a black belt. It would hurt." He glanced down at her with a smile to see her grinning. "Besides, I hear you're known to watch action flicks."

"Most of them have half-naked men with muscles." She smiled serenely. "I'm a healthy woman, what can I say?" She eyed the masculine arm that was in front of her. He would sell a fortune in movies to women if the arm under the sleeve was even half as built as implied.

She felt oddly safe and secure in his arms as he navigated traffic. His body was angled close to hers as if trying to keep her safe and sheltered. In a way she wasn't surprised. She knew he was as much a protector by nature as Kienan was.

When they parked at the movie theater, she couldn't help asking, "What happened to your mother?" Sadness seemed to move through his eyes and she shook her head quickly. "Never mind. That was personal."

"It's alright, Kally." He used her nickname without thought as he pulled his helmet off. He smoothed a hand through his hair as he considered his words. Then, finally, he said it as simply as he could. "My mother died in childbirth with Aenya. We were in a car accident, and it brought on labor too fast. I ended up with a broken arm and a concussion. When I finally woke, it was to the news that my mother was gone, and my sister was three months premature. We couldn't take her home for months."

"Oh, Taegan." She pulled off her helmet, wanting to hold him and take away the pain in his eyes and voice. Resisting the urge was the hardest thing she had ever done. "What was she like?"

"She hated school." He found a genuine smile. "Her grades were always horrible. But she was kind and friendly, and everyone loved her. She was stubborn to a fault, but you could never hold it against her. I've been told I have her gentleness. I try."

She said nothing as he lifted her off the bike. She looked at where his hands were on her hips firmly but without hurting her. "You are gentle," she said. "You know your strength and can control it. That's gentleness. And you care about everybody so much. That's gentleness, too. I bet you're hurt easily."

He thought about denying it, but knew that she wouldn't believe him. She was too intelligent and far too intuitive. "Yes," he admitted. "I don't make friends easily. I envy Aenya and Kienan for that."

"So . . ." She took his hand as he lifted them quickly, only just realizing how long he had been holding her. "Can I be your friend, and you be mine?" She smiled. "I think we have more in common than most would believe."

"Isn't that like the princess mingling with a commoner?" he asked her.

"You're anything but common, and you know it. So, what do you say, Professor Shaughnessy?" She used the title deliberately with a teasing smile.

"I say you don't call me that unless we're in class, and you have a deal." He couldn't resist lifting his hand and touching her cheek lightly. Her skin was as soft as it looked. He dropped his hand quickly before she could take offense, and he began to walk toward the ticket booth. "My treat," he said over his shoulder.

She touched her cheek lightly before letting out a little breath and following him. If only she wasn't in his class, she thought with a little despair. She would have seduced him in a New York minute. To hell with her father's wishes; she wanted Taegan. But since she was only going to get friendship, she might as well take what she was given and not quibble the details.

Two hours later, however, she was annoyed with him as they walked out of the theater. "She was a moron, I swear! I don't care what your romantic brain thinks, Taegan, she was a moron!"

He glowered at her. "You're being cynical and cynicism means you pay for dinner. Pay up, princess."

"Ass." She went over to a vendor and ordered two giant hot dogs. She slapped one into Taegan's hand. "Doctor it yourself." She slathered hers with everything and took a huge bite. Debates always made her hungry. Around a mouthful she said, "She had a fabulous guy, so why would she run off with a dork like the male lead?"

"Her dork was the prince of her dreams," he reminded her as he ate his own hot dog. "It was supposed to be a romantic star crossed lovers' tale. You said it was supposed to be good, and it was."

She waved a hand at him. "If I had someone, I wouldn't run off just for excitement! I'd stick with him through all the times, even rough ones. If your life is boring, it's because you yourself are boring. Get a makeover, go on a second honeymoon; I don't know. I will never have a midlife crisis."

He grinned at her quickly. The smile then faded and turned gentle as he saw the smear of mustard on her chin. "Hold still." He grabbed a napkin and stepped closer to gently wipe the smear away. Her scent, strawberries and cream, went to his head, and he almost gave in to the urge to kiss her.

Catching himself, he stepped back and tossed the napkin in the garbage. She took a quick breath and listened to her pulse rattling in her body. She had been certain he was about to kiss her. If *Mel* had had this effect on her, she would have leapt at a chance for a business marriage. She would have then dragged him off on a honeymoon to make him forget the business part and made him as mad over her as she was over him.

Unfortunately, the only Shaughnessy she had ever wanted was Taegan, and watching him walk toward his bike, she was forced to accept that he was also the one she would never be able to have.

She let out a little breath and followed him. "Well then," she said. "If you could take me back for my car, I'd be much grateful." She carefully kept her voice light. The evening was suddenly beginning to feel dangerously like a date.

"Of course." His voice was as light as hers for he also sensed the suddenly intimate atmosphere.

Despite it, he couldn't stop himself from keeping her as close as possible on the ride back to campus. The scent of her skin teased his lungs and the heat of her body was a haunting lure. It was self-inflicted torture, and he couldn't stop it.

He took her to where her car was parked rather than drop her at the gate. She gave him back the spare helmet and unlocked her car, aware he was waiting to leave until she was safely inside. She gave him a genuine smile. "Thank you, Taegan. You were right. I needed this afternoon badly. I feel more stable once more. We'll need to do it again."

"I agree."

"G'night, Taegan."

"Good night, princess."

The words were nearly a caress. This time she knew she wasn't mistaken by the desire in his voice. His brogue had softened and thickened, turning such a simple nickname into an intimacy between them. Before she said or did something stupid, she got into her car. She watched him ride out of the lot and slowly rested her head on the steering wheel. If he wanted her in more than just a knee-jerk 'pretty girl with boobs' manner (something she was sadly familiar with) then she was going to have to get rough with him. She *always* got what she wanted.

And she wanted Taegan. It was that easy.

CHAPTER EIGHTEEN

If there was anything the college thrived on, it was rumors. They always started innocently but ended up blowing well out of proportion. A simple rumor about someone with a runny nose could become a Swine Flu outbreak by noon.

Kalliope found herself painfully reminded of the wagging tongues the next day. It started innocently, as it always did, when she found Mel waiting for her outside her English class. "Hey, Mel." She fell companionably into step beside him as they walked down the hall together. "What's up? You're looking a tad blue there, Gibson."

Since he refused to tell where the name Mel had come from, she had taken to associating him with Mel Gibson. He had finally gotten used to it. "Well, my father called yours this morning." When she groaned, he smiled wryly. "That would be my exact reaction. I didn't hear the conversation, but we both know what they're hoping for."

"Yeah." She sighed. "Mel, I love you, but only as a brother. I don't want to date you let alone marry you. It would be immoral in my brain. I mean, I'm Greek but not *that* kind of Greek. That sort of thing went out of style when the Pantheon was built."

"My studies may not be the best, but wasn't the Pantheon in Rome?"

"Good boy! Yes, it was, but they borrowed our gods. Remind me to show you the family crest. It has Zeus on it. It's pretty groovy." She bumped his shoulder with hers. "You know, we could always try pulling a fast one on our parents. We could humor them. Let's pretend to date for a while. Hell, let's get engaged. We'll give it a month then call it off. They can't blame us if we tried, right?"

"That's not a bad idea," he conceded. His sense of humor rivaled his siblings', and he couldn't resist giving her a courtly bow. As sincerely as he could, despite the laughter in his eyes, he asked. "Would you marry me, Kally?"

"Well, okay. Since you asked nicely." She spotted a girl staring at them with her mouth hanging open and felt a sudden wariness. She had almost forgotten the entire college had been expecting the same thing as Jiles and Sullivan. "It's a joke," she stressed. "*Joke.*" She sighed as the girl ran off. "Oh boy, here we go."

"Eh." Mel shrugged one shoulder with a wry smile. "What's the worst that could happen? We were going to trick our dads anyway. When nothing comes of it and we don't act all lovey-dovey then it'll blow over—with everyone. The winds around this school change faster than the industrial average."

With that image in her mind, she was nearly giggling as she walked into her math class. Taegan walked in not long after, and she couldn't stop her smile. Just seeing him made her happy sometimes. "Morning, Professor Shaughnessy." She said it deliberately, hoping for a secret smile.

What she got was a look that froze her to her core. His brown eyes were hard as they flicked over her face and he barely spared her a glance. When he looked at anyone else, he was the same gentle Taegan. When he looked at her, she felt blasted by waves of anger and betrayal.

It *hurt*. She had to curl her nails into her leg under her desk to fight back tears. She couldn't imagine what she had done to make him furious with her. What if he had found out that she was in love with him? Did he hate her now? She could handle anything but that.

Somehow she held onto her control until after class. She gathered her courage and went to his office, needing to know. When she knocked on the door, she could see her hand trembling.

"Come in," he called, and his voice sounded like the normal Taegan.

She opened the door and walked in, and his face shut down as his eyes went cold. It was terrifying. "I don't suppose you could tell me why you're so angry with me," she managed to whisper.

"You neglected to mention yesterday that you and my brother were seeing each other." He felt betrayed in the most horrible way possible. His own brother had stolen her from him, and she hadn't had the courtesy to at least tell him that she was seeing Mel. He lifted a sardonic brow. "You indicated that you were single. That seems to be a lie, doesn't it?"

"I hate you!" The tears welled in her eyes and her outburst startled her as much as it did him. "I'm not seeing Mel!" she shouted, her hands curled into fists. "It was a *joke* we were talking about because of our dads. How *could* you believe something like that? How could you accuse me of lying to you of all people?!" Her voice caught on a sob as she whirled and ran out of the room.

The door slammed behind her violently. He felt worse than slime as he sank down in his chair with his hands pressed to his eyes. He had been jealous, and in that jealousy he had been blind. Because he had been hurt, he had lashed out to make her hurt. So much for him being the mature one in the family. He didn't look up as he heard the door open. "It's a bad time right now."

"I imagine it is," Mel bit out, his voice carrying a brogue clipped with fury. His accent was always fainter than Taegan's, but when he was truly angry, it could be just as thick. He crossed around the desk, grabbed his brother by the collar, and gave him a sharp shake. He was a few inches shorter but he wasn't any smaller overall. "You asshole!" he snarled. "What did you say to Kally? She was crying!"

"I accused her of lying to me." Taegan shoved him back and slumped down in his chair once more. "I let myself believe those stupid rumors. I was cold to her, and when she asked me why, I just accused. I didn't even listen to her." He buried his face in his hands. "*Damn* it!"

Mel fell silent. For long moments he studied his big brother. He eased a hip onto the edge of the desk and crossed his arms. He supposed he should have noticed it sooner. It seemed rather obvious now. "How long have you been in love with Kally?" he asked quietly.

Taegan couldn't deny it, not to his family. "Since I met her."

"Taegan, you idiot." He rubbed a hand over his face. "Kally's like a sister to me. She's my friend and nothing more. This morning, we were talking about our fathers and how they want a business marriage to cement the merger they're considering. We were joking about pretending to be engaged then calling it off to show it wouldn't work, and someone overheard us. They got the wrong idea and the rumors spread."

Feeling even worse, Taegan got to his feet and grabbed his jacket. "I need to go apologize to her."

Mel watched him intently. "You could tell her how you feel."

"No." Taegan's eyes were bleak as he looked at him. "She's my student, Mel. If I crossed any lines then we'd both pay for it. And . . . she deserves someone a lot better than me. Her dad is right about that. Besides, all she wants is friendship from me. So, that's what I'll give."

Friendship didn't make a woman like Kalliope Tavoularis cry as if her heart had been broken, but Mel kept that to himself. "Are you still going to her birthday party? You could steal a dance. No one would think that odd."

"No. My ability to control myself is thin around her, as I'm sure you've just noticed. And anyway," he smiled wryly, "I have papers to grade. I wouldn't want my students to think their grades are as bad as yours."

"Thanks a lot!"

"It is true, though." He shrugged into his jacket. "Keep this up and you'll get a tutor in General Ed."

Mel's skin took a pale cast to it. There was only one general education tutor in the college and there wasn't a single student who wasn't deathly afraid of her. She had to be, beyond a doubt, one of the scariest women anyone had ever known. She rarely left the computer room and even her computer sciences students were in a sort of terrified awe of her. "Don't be evil."

"I'm being honest. Lock the door behind you." Taegan pulled on his sunglasses and made his way as quickly off campus as he could. He knew that the salon where Kalliope worked was only just a block away from the campus. Both his sisters got their hair done there, and, in fact, it was Kalliope who was their stylist. He just hoped she gave him a chance to apologize and didn't come at him with a pair of clippers.

Kalliope knelt behind the counter and organized receipts. She didn't feel like working, but she absolutely needed to get her mind off things. Her manager had been amazingly quiet even though he had seen she was upset. He had simply given her tasks to do and let her be.

She dashed at the tears in her eyes furiously. She hated crying. She hated Taegan for making her cry. She hated that she loved him enough that he could make her cry. She wouldn't have called him an idiot but he had actually *believed* . . . It hurt worse than she had ever imagined. A heart couldn't physically break, but she certainly felt as if there were broken shards inside her chest.

When the bell over the door rang, she was almost pitifully grateful. "Just a second!" she called and swiped at her eyes again. "Can I help you?"

"I don't suppose," Taegan's soft voice asked, "that you have a cure for foot-in-mouth?"

She stood up quickly, the pieces of her heart beating out of rhythm with each other. "It doesn't work on men," she countered waspishly. Her eyes burned with more tears at the sight of him. How dare he look so windblown and gorgeous? Why did he have to look as miserable as she felt? "What do you want? You want to call me a liar again?"

"I need to apologize." He wanted to hug her but knew she would come after him with her nails hooked like claws. "I can't even give you an excuse. I thought I had been lied to, and it hurt. So I hurt you in return. It was childish."

She looked down at the counter. "I thought that I had done something wrong," she whispered. "You were so cold to me. It hurt, a lot."

He studied her long moments before reaching out a hand and lightly cupping her cheek. "I'm not the only one who is easily hurt, am I?" he asked quietly. He softly brushed away the tears that kept welling in her eyes. "I'm so sorry, Kally. Let me be your friend again."

She couldn't stop herself from turning her face into his hand. There was a trembling in his fingers that matched the trembling in her heart. "Always," she said softly. "I forgive you, Taegan. But don't ever assume again. I couldn't marry Mel. He's like a brother to me."

"So he said, too. I thought he was going to hit me when he stormed into the office after you."

She found a smile. "Has he done that before?"

"Once. I was babysitting him and the other two. He wanted to test me, since I was only sixteen and he was twelve—he was obviously far too old to need a babysitter, you know." He found a smile as well. "I tanned his hide, then locked him in his room. Needless to say, he didn't test me like that again."

"He idolizes you, you know." She was sure of it. She was also the tiniest bit envious of the Shaughnessy family. She had always wanted brothers and sisters but she had never gotten them.

"I know." He slowly released her. "What do you want for your birthday present?"

"Pick something out and surprise me. Bring it to the party." When his eyes moved away, she felt her stomach sink. "You're not coming." She had been looking forward to dancing with him, to pretending that he could love her a little.

"I'm sorry, princess." His heart ached as he saw the pain in her eyes. "It's just not a good idea."

"Why not?" She grabbed his arm before he could leave. "Give me one good reason why you shouldn't come. We're friends, aren't we? And what's wrong with a teacher attending a student's party?"

She deserved the truth after the pain he had already caused her. She needed to know why he had to force distance between them. "Because this teacher happens to be attracted to his student."

Her eyes widened, and he felt a bolt of panic as he realized he could not bear to see what lay beyond her surprise. Anger or fear would destroy him. A mutual desire would make it impossible to keep things platonic. Rather than risk hurting her—again—he turned and walked out swiftly.

He found Stormy waiting for him outside. He sighed as she fell into step beside him. She never wore a leash but no one had ever seemed to notice. He had always assumed it was part of her gifts. "You don't need to meddle. I seem to be getting in over my head all on my own." He knelt and ran a hand over her head. "You can't fix everything," he said softly. "No matter how you try. Kalliope's no more a prince than I am Cinderella. Magic doesn't turn pumpkins into coaches and commoners into royalty."

Stormy almost smiled. She wouldn't have bet on that.

The day of Kalliope's birthday party arrived and the entire Shaughnessy household wasn't sure what to do about Taegan. They had been taking turns all day trying to convince him to go, but he had finally stopped listening to them entirely and started locking his door. Not even Aenya could get through to him, and he had *always* listened to her before.

"What is *wrong* with him?" she demanded from Mel as she followed him across the house. The shimmering white skirts of her ball gown swirled around her ankles as she turned and followed him the other way. "I know you know!"

"Alright, alright!" He gave up and stopped trying to escape her. The others came over to join them and he rubbed the back of his neck. "Taegan is in love with Kally." He didn't feel the need to expand on it. It seemed to sum up everything.

"Oh boy," was Kienan's response.

"In other words, he figures he can't have her, so he's not even going to try." Hiro lifted a brow ever so slightly. "I expected better out of him."

"Daddy," Aenya took her father's arm as she saw the musing look on his face, "would Mr. Tavoularis really dislike Taegan? He's not just a teacher. He's still a Shaughnessy. And he's one of the best men around."

"I think," he said slowly, "that Jiles only wants his daughter to be happy. Just as I feel for my children. If Taegan and Kalliope wanted to be together, then Jiles wouldn't stand in the way." He glanced at Stormy who was napping by the doorway. He had a feeling he might finally know where things were going. "It's Taegan and Kalliope's decision about what to do," he finally decided. "They're both adults."

Even when they met up with Madelyne in the 3rd District, Aenya still didn't think Taegan was being smart about things. She shoved it out of her mind, to the best of her ability, as she helped her sister-in-law unload the rental truck they were using to carry the food that Madelyne had made for the party. The catering job hadn't just turned formal, but it had also opened up a whole new set of possibilities for the inn for Madelyne and Kienan.

The party was being held at a place called the Glass Shoe Palace. It was a formal ballroom, converted from an old manor, and could be rented for a few weeks at a time for parties and formal conferences. Kalliope's party was a full-scale formal masquerade ball. All the men wore tuxedos and tails and all the women were in ball gowns. Everyone wore masks.

Everyone except Kalliope. It was as deliberate as the fact that she had requested that everyone wear pastels—it was her birthday, and she deserved to stand out. No pale colors for her; she wore emerald green. The ball gown bodice clung to her body perfectly and the full skirts had emeralds at the point of every tier. She wore emeralds around her neck and dripping from each ear. Her hair was artfully piled high with a delicate coronet of emeralds and silver perched on top.

She didn't make an immediate appearance as people were arriving. She was busy in a dressing room with Madelyne to help her friend get ready. Madelyne's gray hair was exceptionally long but Kalliope took the time to curl all of it so that it hung loosely and vibrantly. That done, she helped her with makeup. "Kienan will fall over."

Madelyne smiled. Somehow Kalliope and Kienan made her forget that she was supposed to be plain. "That would be funny."

"But well deserved." She leaned back. "You, Maddie, are one lovely nightingale."

Madelyne looked in the mirror. She really did look appealing. She *felt* lovely. "And I still say you're a miracle worker."

The door opened and Aenya slipped inside. "We're here," she announced. "The guys are all doing the mingling thing and Kienan told me to come find you." Her eyes met Kalliope's and there was understanding in her gaze. "I'm sorry, Kally. We couldn't convince him to come."

Kalliope looked away. It hurt to look at Aenya sometimes. Her eyes were identical to Taegan's. "Am I so obvious?" she asked achingly. "Is he the only one who doesn't realize I love him?"

Madelyne opened her mouth but closed it when Aenya shook her head. The blonde walked around to look into Kalliope's face. "I think we only noticed," she said carefully, "because Mel told us how badly you were hurt when Taegan was cold to you. You're not a woman who cries easily, but he made you cry." Her smile turned wry. "Been there, done that, as they say."

Kalliope let out a little breath. "That makes me feel a little better. Come on. You can be my ladies-in-waiting and keep the hordes at bay." She walked over to the doors and opened them to sweep into the ballroom with a princess's grace and flair. Madelyne and Aenya followed her, but it was as much to make sure she actually enjoyed herself as it was to keep overly avid suitors off.

It was only their presence that kept Kalliope from slinking away into a corner to hide. It was the party of her dreams, and she was utterly miserable. She danced with everyone who asked, even Kienan and Mel, but it made no difference. She let Aenya teach her a complicated waltz pattern, but the enjoyment was short lived.

Finally at her wits end, she slipped into the gardens for fresh air. With all her heart she wanted the man she loved to be there. She wanted to see him even if only for a little while. If she was to make a birthday wish, it would be simply to have Taegan. He made her entire world so much better by being in it.

A sound made her turn and she was surprised to see a wolf sitting at the edge of the fountain. Since it wore a collar, she wasn't worried it was wild and would attack. She crouched down and held out a hand and then smiled as the wolf rubbed against her fingers. "So you wanted to come to the party, too? Well, it's our secret."

She turned her gaze toward the party in full swing behind the glass doors. "He never even gave me a chance," she murmured softly, "to say how I felt. And now he won't come near me because it could ruin us both. But . . . I don't care. I want to see him. Even for a little while. Silly of me, isn't it? You can't wish someone into being."

She patted the wolf once more then let it be as she got to her feet and braced herself. With a smile that she didn't feel, she swept into the ballroom once more. "So when do I open presents? And if one of them has a spring-loaded pie, there better be enough for everyone."

Taegan didn't unlock his door until the house was quiet. He had finished grading the papers hours ago but he hadn't wanted to give his family ammunition to use against him. He only felt guilty for losing his temper with Aenya. He owed her an apology.

He wasn't hungry, but he forced himself to get something to eat. The servants had been given the weekend off, and he savored the knowledge that he was completely alone. It happened very rarely. Not that he didn't love his family, but right then, he couldn't bear talking to anyone.

It was a stupid fate that made a man fall in love with a woman so beyond his reach that all he could do was suffer. For the first time in his life, he questioned his decision to become a teacher. Would things have been different if he had inherited the company? Really, no, they wouldn't have. If anything, he might never have met Kalliope and gotten to see her smile every week.

His room was on the bottom floor and had doors that opened into the garden. He opened them for fresh air but didn't turn on any lights other than a small lamp as he sat at his desk. In despair, he rested his head on his arms. "Tennyson was an idiot. It isn't better to love and lose than to never love at all."

"Enough with the pity party," a woman's cool voice said suddenly from the patio doors. "It's so unbecoming in a man your age."

He turned sharply, astonished that she had snuck up on him. She stood just outside the doors, leaning against the jamb with a predator's casual stillness. She was cloaked in shadows and he couldn't see her face, but her long black hair fluttered in a light wind.

"You frightened me," he accused. "You should have knocked."

"You'd have told me to go away." She waved a hand in the air. "Well then, Taegan Shaughnessy. How badly do you want your princess? Enough to make a deal with me?"

He said nothing for long moments. He knew who she was. In fact, he had begun to suspect he knew the 'what' as well. He also knew that her word was gold. If she made a promise, then she kept it. She always carried through with anything she said. "What sort of deal?"

"Open your desk."

He did so and discovered a neatly written sheaf of papers. As he skimmed them, he realized it was a contract. It said concisely that she would provide him with the means to disguise himself and attend the party, but he would have to leave by midnight. Bemused, he asked, "Midnight?"

"To be honest, I'm not supposed to be doing things this way. I can only cover my tracks until midnight. Take it or leave it, Taegan. It's your life you're wasting."

"As always, the soul of tact." He looked at the contract again and his lips curved. "I guess this makes me Cinderella and you my faerie godmother."

"Don't *even* go there," she retorted with a bite in her voice that sounded like bared teeth.

"Yes'm." He didn't give himself time to think. He was tired of thinking. For once he just wanted to follow his heart. He grabbed a pen and scrawled his name across the bottom of the contract. As he did, he caught sight of her signature. Seeing it, he asked, "Doesn't your name mean . . . ?"

"Yes." Her tone was dry.

"Whose sense of humor gave you your 'nickname'?"

"Rhianna's. She's twisted like that." She reached into her jacket and pulled out a mask. It looked like a rather plain and ordinary thing, but as light rippled over it, it seemed to glow with magic. "Here's how this works. This is from 3rd District. It's called the Mask of Illusion. When worn, it changes the appearance of the wearer to whatever they wish. It acts as a . . . glamour shield of sorts. Only a very few people would ever know who was behind the mask. So if you wish for blue suede shoes and a new tux, everyone will think you're Elvis."

"My sister is the professional dancer, not I." He got to his feet and walked over to take the mask. He tried to study her face but it was well hidden. "Are you really doing well?" he asked quietly.

"I heal fast. And risks are taken by everyone when love is involved." She flicked a finger at the mask. "Hurry up, handsome. Time's wasting and you only have until midnight. Oh, and Kalliope is wearing emerald green."

He paused as he was about to put the mask on. "You saw her?" The longing couldn't be kept from his voice.

As always, it softened her heart. "Of course. I had to be sure that you two matched. Now, hurry up, the limo is waiting." She turned away, then glanced over her shoulder. He could have sworn she was smiling. "It's a modern pumpkin, if you like. Now, Cinderella, let's go. Your princess awaits. And," she added under her breath as he put the mask on, "don't be an idiot."

The clock was only just ringing eleven o'clock when Kalliope began to have serious thoughts of escaping. She had opened gifts, they'd had Madelyne's outrageously delicious cake, and the party was due to continue for another two hours. She was ready to go home and crawl under the covers until the urge to cry went away.

Quite suddenly, she realized she was being stared at. Her heart began to beat harder as she felt the oddest sensation of déjà vu. She slowly turned around to look at the banister and stairs leading to the entrance of the grand ballroom. Her breath caught in her chest as conversations around her slowly began to die.

A man stood at the top of the stairs, staring at her with a heat in his gaze that burned her from across the room. Though she could not see the color of his eyes, his hair shimmered stark black under the chandeliers. She *knew*. Without a word, she slowly crossed the room toward him. She was only distantly aware that everyone moved out of the way.

He slowly came down the stairs toward her. He wore a tuxedo no different from the other men present, but there was a green waistcoat under his jacket that perfectly matched her dress. Emerald cufflinks kept his sleeves tidy. His mask was elaborate and sculpted, hiding all but his mouth and eyes from view. A bit of a haze of some kind seemed to cover him but she saw through it for she saw with eyes that loved.

All eyes in the room were fixed on them. Mel, at the back of the room, tried to get closer to see what was going on. Because he, too, loved Taegan, his eyes saw through the glamour. He was positive it was his brother descending the stairs. The *how* was what eluded him. The 'why' was obvious.

When Taegan stopped in front of Kalliope, he lifted her hand to his lips and bowed elegantly. "I came to ask for a dance, princess," he said softly.

Only one man had ever called her princess in that tone of voice. Only one man had ever made her pulse flutter with just a touch of his hand. The eyes watching her so unguardedly, so filled with love, were the same honey-colored eyes she had longed for all along.

Her lips trembled as she accepted the gift she was being given. "I would be honored," she whispered, and some inner instinct had her sinking into an elegant curtsey.

Aenya scrambled over to the orchestra. "Waltz!" she hissed at the conductor. "A waltz!" He jumped and turned to the orchestra, and she turned around to look at the dance floor. Her eyes were shining with tears as she clasped her hands together. "It should always be a waltz first." She knew who it was, too.

Everyone had pulled back to give as much room as possible. Kalliope twirled gracefully into Taegan's arms, delighted that her heels made her the perfect height for him. His hand was warm on her waist, and his other hand curled around hers possessively. Even before he stepped her into the dance, the room was spinning around her head.

It was magic. She felt it as they whirled around the floor. Somehow she had known he would know how to waltz. Of course he did. Just as she knew how. Because it was the moment to know, they did. It was that simple.

When the music swelled to an end, they were left in the middle of the floor. Everyone applauded and cheered but she heard nothing except the beat of her heart. When he bowed and moved as if to leave, she grabbed onto his wrist. "No way, Cinderella," she scolded warmly. "You owe me at least until midnight. It's a rule."

He reluctantly let her lead him toward the gardens. Most of the room tried to follow, wanting to know who he was, but they were brought up short as Kienan and Mel got in the way and planted themselves in front of the doors.

"Kally deserves some privacy," Mel warned, his voice soft but very hard. "Don't you think so?" Both brothers' eyes were a challenging shade of chocolate brown, and the crowd backed off hastily.

Kalliope considered her options as she walked in the garden with Taegan. She could play off the charade and pretend like she didn't know who he was. She could tell him she knew and throw caution to the winds. Or she could let him know, and they could pretend as if they didn't. Still contemplating what her preference was, she said sincerely, "Thank you, Cinderella. You showed up at the right time. I was ready to run away from my own party."

She was so beautiful that she took his breath away. She seemed impossibly radiant, too good for a mortal man. His fingers burned to feel her skin, to have her under his hands, to feel her body pressed against his. "I hadn't considered myself Cinderella." He put humor into his voice. "I came in a limo, not a pumpkin."

"A modern carriage is vastly superior to smelling like pumpkin pie for a week. You're not leaving at midnight, are you?"

Her sense of humor was a frightening match to his 'faerie godmother's.' He reached out and skimmed his thumb over her cheek. "I have to," he apologized. "I don't want to get my godmother in trouble." He smiled. "And besides, what kind of Cinderella would I be if I didn't?"

"Would you take your gloves off?" she asked softly. Once he did, she took his hands and lifted them to where she could see them. She knew these hands. They were frequent visitors in her deepest fantasies. "You know," she said carefully, "your hands are familiar."

He went very still. "Are they?"

"Yes, they remind me of my math professor." She released him and walked a few steps away. "I would know, you see, as I've spent the better part of four years fantasizing about his hands. And his eyes. And his lips. Actually, I think there's very little that I haven't had a fantasy about." She turned to look at him and his eyes burned as they watched her. "He said he was attracted to me then walked out before I could answer. I think he's a coward. What about you?"

"Maybe he was," he said softly, longing for her so badly that his hands curled into fists at his side and his entire body trembled. "Maybe he feared your answer."

"Then he's an idiot. Even his own family realized how I felt about him." She moved a step forward. "There's a wall between us. No matter how I love him. No matter how badly I want him. He doesn't think it can be climbed right now." She paused, then added softly, "But it would seem to have chinks in it big enough to allow us a forbidden dance in a magical garden."

Silence fell around them. Even the night creatures were quiet. The music of the ballroom was distant and far away. He very slowly reached out toward her, terrified it was a dream. He was going to wake up and it would have never happened. She made a soft sound of pain and surged forward to press against his chest, her arms stealing around his waist. He closed his arms around her as tightly as he dared, knowing that this, too, was stolen. "Don't cry," he whispered achingly.

"I don't cry!" Yet the tears were sliding down her cheeks and she knew it. She eased back enough to smile up at him. "My mascara is waterproof just in case. I was worried someone might have given me a crank gift."

He gently brushed at the tears clinging to her lashes. His fingers lingered and warmly framed her face. The temptation of her trembling lips lured him in, and he bent his head to softly brush her lips with his. It was nowhere near what he needed, but it was still more than he had dared dream of having. It would have to be enough.

Her lashes fluttered closed and she waited in an agony of need for him to deepen the kiss in the way they both desperately craved. He eased back instead, leaving her with just that faint brush of his lips. He released her entirely, and she opened her eyes to see him watching her longingly. That unfailing gentleness inside him kept him from pushing for more than he thought she wanted to give, and she knew it. The ball was in her court.

She took a deep breath. "How silly of me. The prince is supposed to make all the moves. I had forgotten." She moved forward before he could move back, and she wound her arms around his neck. She rose up onto her toes to kiss him as deeply as she needed. A shudder rippled through her body as she realized he tasted just like he smelled. Danger. Wonderful danger. Her geek was a bad boy at heart, and her bad boy was gentle. "Kiss me, damn you," she muttered against his lips.

His control collapsed in a wave of searing heat. He couldn't resist her any longer. He caught her against his aching body with one arm and used his other hand to tilt her head back, parting her lips for him further. Hungrily he kissed her, tangling his tongue with hers until she made a little sound of pleasure in her throat and her hands fisted into the material of his jacket. Her body arched and strained to press closer, as hungry and aching as his.

Drunk on her taste and scent, he released her lips only to bury his own against the curve of her neck. Breathless, her head spinning, she managed to tease huskily, "Don't leave a mark I can't explain. My daddy owns a shotgun."

It was too damned tempting. He carefully lifted his head and set her back from him about a foot. It removed temptation from reach if not from sight. "You're better than a good wine for going to my head," he said by way of apology.

"They always said my personality was bubbly." She took a deep breath and waved a hand in front of her face lightly. "Have you considered registering your kisses as lethal weapons?" Her eyes closed helplessly as his hand lifted and skimmed over the top curves of her breasts. "That's not fair."

He took a quick breath and put his hands in his pockets. She responded so perfectly to his touch that it drove him mad. He wanted to lower her to the ground, to have her where they were with the moon above and the garden all around. Nothing but them, wild and free. Only this woman had ever called up the wild spirit inside his soul. It was as if years of control meant nothing near her.

Her breath caught as she saw the wicked passion in his eyes. It called to her and reached past all veneers of civilization to the hunger for life inside her soul. She had been waiting for her entire life for someone to look at her and see her for what she was. Now that she had found him, she couldn't even keep him.

She heard the bell tolling midnight and went very still. "You're leaving." It wasn't a question. "Don't. Please." She reached up for his mask, wanting to end the charade, but she heard rustling behind her and instinctively turned. She whirled back on a curse, but it was too late. He had already disappeared.

Lonelier than ever, she started to enter the ballroom again when Aenya and Madelyne descended on her. They firmly escorted her around the crowd and into the bathrooms. Startled, she asked, "Is something wrong?"

Aenya cleared her throat delicately. "You tell us." She pointed at the mirror behind them.

She turned and groaned softly as she saw the distinct mark on her neck. She sank onto the vanity chair and buried her face in her arms. "Damn him," she whispered. "He didn't even leave a glass shoe for me to follow."

"Do you know who it was?" Madelyne made it a question, but she already knew the answer. She had been expecting it. Stormy had been hanging around Taegan, and she, more than any other, knew who and what Stormy was and why she was there.

"Yes." Kalliope took the powder compact Aenya held out to her and began to competently hide the mark on her neck. Her eyes burned with determination. "I'm not letting him get away from me. If he thinks he can kiss me like that and just walk off, he's going to be learning a lesson himself, damn it."

"Good," Aenya muttered.

"Maddie." Kalliope met her friend's eyes in the mirror. "I'm sorry if I was harsh with you about Kienan. But I knew. I knew how much you would continue to hurt. You had a chance I would never get. I wanted you to take it."

"I know. I knew as soon you'd done it, that it was exactly what I had needed." Madelyne hugged her tightly. "You taught me to see value in myself. Now you're just going to have to teach my child the same when you're his or her godmother."

"Well I suppose I . . ." She trailed off and whirled on the seat to stare at Madelyne even as Aenya covered her mouth with her hands. "Does Kienan know?" she demanded.

"Not yet." Madelyne smiled. "I'm saving it for his birthday next month. I only just learned."

Aenya laughed happily and hugged Madelyne tightly. Kalliope got to her feet and hugged her as well, but for the first time she felt an emptiness inside herself as she realized she had lied to Taegan. She didn't want just her daddy's company. She wanted her own family. A husband and a child. She wanted it all. If it would take a fight to get it, then that's just what she would damned well do.

CHAPTER NINETEEN

When they got home, all three Shaughnessy siblings went racing down the hall to Taegan's room. They eased the door open and looked inside, but their big brother was sound asleep in bed. His glasses were on the bedside table next to a book. There was no sign in any shape or fashion that he had gone to the party. Wondering how or what had happened, especially how, they all went to their individual rooms for the night.

Sullivan stayed awake for a while and sat in his study to look out the window at the moon in the sky. It would be full in three weeks. Somehow it felt like a portent of possible devastation. It was a long time before he could shake it off and go to bed.

Taegan awoke the next morning to someone shaking his shoulder and simultaneously waving coffee under his nose. Cursing sleepily in every language he knew, he sat up and pushed the covers aside. He blearily eyed his brother. "I love you," he yawned, "but I'm going to kill you."

Mel didn't bat a lash. "Drink." He put the coffee in his brother's hands and glanced around the room once more, trying desperately to find evidence for what he strongly believed. All he saw was Stormy sleeping at the foot of the bed, the healing wound on her face finally beginning to fade to a normal scar. He owed her so much for saving his baby brother and little sister.

After a few sips, Taegan finally began to feel human again. He raked a hand through his hair. "What do you want? Is this about your grades? Seriously, it could have waited."

"It's not that." Mel frowned. "It's about Kally. How'd you do it, bro?"

"Do what?" He ruffled Stormy's fur gently as she climbed further up the bed to lie beside him with her head on his lap. "I graded papers, read a book, went to sleep." He had also danced with a princess in a magical garden, but that didn't need to be mentioned. Things were complicated enough.

"Pity. You should have seen Kally. Red is really her color."

"She was in green." The words were out of his mouth before he could stop them. As Mel slowly arched a brow and began to smile smugly, Taegan sighed and set his coffee aside. "I knew I should have kicked you out until the caffeine actually circulated in my system."

"Don't suppose you'd be willing to tell me how you managed that. It seems like only our family realized it was you. Seriously. Everyone thought you looked different. Some people thought you were short and others thought you were blond. It was *weird*."

"Umm . . ." His smile and tone were equally rueful. "It's a little complicated."

"Y'think!?" Mel sighed and leaned over to hug him tightly. He hated to see his invincible big brother brokenhearted. "I don't like this. I really don't."

He smiled and ruffled Mel's hair as if he was five again. "There's nothing to worry about. I didn't leave any clues to follow, let alone a glass shoe that only fits my foot, so she can't suddenly come knocking on the door."

"That doesn't mean she won't try." Mel smiled wryly. "She's a very, *very* smart woman."

Kalliope was also a very, *very* pissed woman as she paced back and forth in her room. She was already dressed in jeans and a turtleneck, and she was just waiting for her father to call her down and demand to know what was going on.

Damn, damn, *damn* him. Damn that sneaky, sexy Cinderella! She looked into the mirror and pulled down the edge of her top to see the mark that was visible against her pale skin. She didn't mind its presence as much as the fact that it was all that had been left behind. It wouldn't be enough to track down the man she wanted. She knew where he was but had no ammunition to make him admit it or make her father accept it. Pity he wasn't a vampire. She could use dental records in lieu of a shoe.

There came a light knock on her door and she turned quickly. "Yes?" When she saw her mother peering around the edge, she sighed and sat on the edge of the bed. "Hi, Mom." As Mara sat beside her on the bed, she turned and pressed her face against her mother's shoulder, comforted when her arms went around her. "I wanted to fall in love," she whispered. "I never thought it would be this difficult."

There were no secrets between mother and daughter. Mara knew full well what man had taken her daughter's heart. She whole-heartedly approved. Kalliope was so headstrong that she needed a man as strong as Taegan Shaughnessy. He was old enough to be able to match her where other men her age would fall behind. Jiles would just have to come around. "You looked beautiful together," she offered, rubbing a hand over Kalliope's back.

"Yeah. And he's one hell of a kisser." She smiled wryly and pulled the edge of her top down to show the mark. "Unfortunately, it wouldn't be easy to explain this."

"Hmm, no. I recall a few times I had to hide your father's antics from my own." Mara's eyes danced. "The right man is worth the extra makeup."

"Thanks for that insight." It was more about her parents than she really needed or wanted to know. She sighed and got to her feet to pace again. "If he wasn't my teacher, it would be fine. But if I drop the class, my GPA will suffer. It's too late to drop a class without penalty. And if my GPA drops, I'll lose my place as valedictorian. Dad would be furious."

"Your dad will understand."

"Oh, yeah, I can see me explaining that one. 'Gee Dad, I dropped the class because I wanted to seduce my teacher.' He'd freak!" She raked her hands through her hair and groaned as she heard her father's voice calling her name. "Oh boy, here we go. Will I go to hell for lying to my father's face?"

"Nah. A few white lies for his own peace of mind are sometimes good. As long as he eventually learns the truth, it's fine to fib now. Good luck, honey." Mara watched her daughter leave the room, an ache in her heart. Much as she wanted to, there was nothing she could do to make this easier. Her baby had grown up.

Kalliope smoothed down her hair and braced herself before she went into Jiles' office. "You called?" she asked.

He looked up from where he had been going over the guest list. "Yes, have a seat. Did you have a good time last night?"

"After a while." She smiled at him wryly and decided to play it by ear. "You won, by the way. Your mysterious Cinderella caught my attention."

He coughed and cleared his throat. "Yes, well, I'm afraid that's where I'm confused. I didn't invite anyone else. I asked the guards from the doors and they said that everyone who entered had an invitation. And neither could give me a straight answer as to what he looked like. In fact, I'm still rather puzzled myself."

"So . . ." She made her tone thoughtful. "Whoever he was, he had to be someone I invited. But I could have sworn I knew who everyone there was. I'll have to do some investigating and see if I can find out." She smiled. "I didn't know any of the men I knew were that appealing. He's got my attention, that's for sure."

"Good luck, honey. Let me know who he is, will you?" He was impressed himself, not only with the manner with which the mysterious man had carried himself, but also with his cunning in getting Kalliope's attention.

"Oh I will," she murmured. There were a few things to do first, though, before she considered fighting for her father's agreement. She knew that deep down he just wanted her happiness.

The first step was getting Taegan to even admit he had been there. She had nowhere to move without that, no grounds to use against him. Even though he had refused the company to teach, there was no denying he was still a businessman. She knew she was in for a hostile takeover.

Monday morning brought a new wave of rumors. Everyone was still talking about the party and fingers were pointing. No one could piece together a clear description of the mysterious man. Some thought he was tall, others thought he was short. Some said red hair, others said blond.

Anyone who asked Kalliope couldn't get a straight answer either. She told them all the same thing: she didn't know who he was but she was looking. She wasn't overly fond of lying but felt justified in her reasons. She was biding her time. She needed ammunition and the best way to get information was to talk to an insider.

Mel didn't realize he was about to be kidnapped until he swung around a corner and someone jumped on his back. "Jesus!" Heart pounding, he swung his head around to find Kalliope dangling from his shoulders. "Are you trying to kill me, Kally?"

"March. I need to talk to you. Let's go, Gibson." She held on tight. "I'm not letting go until you spill the beans."

With a sigh, he diverted and stepped into an empty classroom. Once inside, he shut the door. She immediately let him go and hopped off his back. "I can assume you already know the answers," he told her wryly, "but feel free to force them out of me so I don't feel guilty."

"Oh, I can do worse than force." She let her eyes well with tears. "Mel?"

"Gah!" He covered his eyes. "Okay, that's just playing dirty! Ask, you foul creature."

"Was it Taegan at my party? Was he the one who danced with me?"

"Yes. Are you still crying?" He peeked through his fingers and saw the tears were gone. He let out a relieved breath. "How did you know?"

"Well, for one thing," her smile turned a little taunting, "I recognized his hands."

"TMI, thank you."

"Well, that was part of it." She closed her eyes. "I've only ever loved one man, Mel. And when I saw him last night, masked though he was, I knew it was him. I fell in love with a slightly geeky math teacher and was seduced by a bad boy in a mask. Your brother is a walking paradox!"

"Yeah." He had to smile. "He's always been like that. He had to be responsible so early because of Aenya and Kienan that he just sort of bottled up the wild spirit we all have. It's genetic, I'm afraid," he apologized.

"Thanks for the warning," she sighed. She pressed her hands against her eyes tightly. "I love him so much, Mel. It's destroying me. Please, just tell me one thing. Is the only thing that keeps him so distant the impropriety? Does he stay back because he loves me too much, or not enough?"

"It's because it's too much," he admitted quietly. "You could both be ruined if word got out. At this point, whether you stay in his class and risk people knowing, or drop the class to catch him, you could lose your place as valedictorian, and if you do that, your dad will never forgive you or Taegan."

"So it comes down to whether I can wait or not. Either way, I'm going to make my dad mad." She took a deep breath. "I can't wait, Mel. I can't." The tears that lurked in her voice were this time very real. "I've waited so long already, and I can't shake the feeling that if I don't do something now, then nothing will ever be done."

"Then go to him." His voice was simple. "You know the Shaughnessys will stand behind you, no matter what."

"Thank you, Mel." She hugged him tightly before hurrying out of the room to head across campus to the building where the math and computer sciences classes were held. If Taegan wasn't in his office, then she would wait for him until he came back.

As she was passing through the computer wing, she was surprised to see the door to one of the labs open. She knew which one it was. She had heard the rumors too, but she wasn't precisely frightened. She knew how badly things always got exaggerated. More curious than anything, she peered into the darkened room. It was lit only by the light from a computer monitor across the room. The only sound was that of keys clicking as someone typed.

Compelled, somehow, to stop, she asked, "Hello?"

"Hello." The typing stopped as the woman spoke. Her voice sounded cool and calm as if she was never ruffled by anything. There was an oddly welcoming note in her husky voice, though, that made Kalliope relax a little. "Need something?"

"Just curious. The rumors and all." Kalliope walked slowly into the room. As she did, she had the strangest feeling that she had just walked into a room with a predator. She didn't feel threatened, precisely, but the hair on the back of her neck quivered. "You're . . . the computer sciences teacher? Professor Alexandrios?"

"Yes. Audra Alexandrios." Audra leaned back in her chair and regarded the young woman in front of her. Kalliope had a strong mind and will, but she had been using mental compulsions on much stronger people for many years. "You're Kalliope Tavoularis."

"Guess you're not the only one whose reputation carries." Kalliope hesitated then blurted, "Can I ask a question? Hypothetical."

"Hypothetical. Right. Sure, be my guest. Don't expect me to believe you have a friend we're discussing, though. I'm not stupid." Audra began to type again. She was fully able to speak and listen at the same time.

"Well . . . suppose someone is in love with a teacher. Their teacher no less. The teacher loves them as well. Is it worth risking status and reputation to be together?" She realized she was wringing her hands and tucked them into her pockets quickly.

"I've always thought," Audra said calmly without looking up from her computer, "that love was worth risking everything. Take Cinderella, for example. The prince risked his pride entirely by showing the whole world how desperate he was to find the woman he loved. She risked what little safety she had by going to him in the first place."

She half laughed. "You're very intuitive with that, but I get your point." She walked closer, still trying to see Audra's face properly. All she could see were her piercing yellow eyes. The color was unusual, but it might have been a trick of the computer's glow. "What do you think about Professor Shaughnessy?"

"And hypothetical goes out the window." Audra leaned back in her chair and linked her hands behind her head. "He's atypical of his family in some ways since he dreams big, but he refuses to go completely after his dreams. If he would, it wouldn't be difficult, you see."

"You sound like you've known the family a long time."

"Off and on for what feels like a century." She brushed that aside with a wave of her hand. "He's too old to be able to simply follow his gut. The inclination to think too much that comes with age has sunk in. A woman would need to shake him up a little bit, perhaps push him. He's been in charge of his life so long that no one pushes him—not even his father."

Kalliope thought about that for a few moments. She had been starting to suspect those things as well. She hurried toward the door. "Thanks, Professor Alexandrios." She stopped in the doorway and turned back with a quick smile. "You know, you're not as big a beast as everyone thinks."

Audra just smirked slightly to herself. "You have no idea, honey." As the footsteps faded, she opened her mail client and sent a single, one word email across the building.

Taegan heard the beep from his computer and swiveled in his chair to open the email. It was classic Audra. No body to the message; the subject said it all.

Incoming.

He lifted a brow. What on Earth did that mean? She wasn't usually *that* cryptic. He got his answer as his office door opened, and Kalliope stepped into the doorway. Completely unprepared for her presence, he almost couldn't stop himself from leaping up and snatching her into his arms. His mouth went dry, his palms burned, and he grabbed the arms of his chair for support. She wore a peach colored sundress despite the winter air outside and the threat of snow.

Desire for her roughened the edge of his voice without his control as he said, "Good morning."

Her heart fluttered as she heard the edge, and it seemed to caress her everywhere. With a quick breath, she shut the door and walked over to sit down in the visitor's chair. "I thought you might be interested in hearing about the party." Try as she might, she couldn't keep the soft note of memory out of her voice.

Their eyes met. A nearly tangible electric current ran between them. They both knew. They knew they both knew. It was a game where neither knew the rules but the stakes were high. Taegan sent a response to Audra and shut down his computer entirely. He had a feeling that he might need to make a fast exit before he was over his head. "Go ahead," he finally said. "You have my undivided attention."

"It was a really fun party," she started. She got to her feet to walk slowly around the small office. "Everyone was in formal ball clothes and everyone but me was wearing a mask. It was fun seeing who was who. I kept hoping you'd change your mind," she continued, "but when the others showed up without you, I stopped hoping. Aenya told me they tried to convince you, but that you turned stubborn on them."

She ran a finger lightly over the face of a picture showing him as a child holding a wiggling bundle she assumed was Aenya since it wore a pink ribbon. "We had cake. I saved you a piece; I'll bring it by sometime. Oh, and I had presents." She grimaced wryly. "Lots of jewelry and stuff. Not like I didn't have enough. I like Kienan's best though. A weekend stay at the Gentle Brook Inn when it opens again after renovations. Sounds fabulous."

He smiled. "He's good at that sort of thing."

"I noticed. It's why I pushed Maddie at him." She took a quick breath and turned to look at him directly. "We were dancing again when this funny thing happened. I looked up, and I saw this man watching me. He was masked, but I knew him. We danced together, and he kissed me in a moonlit garden. And then he ran off without even leaving a glass slipper behind. I mean, really, what kind of decent Cinderella does that?"

"Kalliope," he said quietly. "No more."

"No." She leaned toward him, her eyes fierce. "We both knew then, and we both know now, that it was you with me in that garden. God, how could I *not* know, Taegan? You haunt my waking hours and make me burn in my dreams." His eyes shot to hers, hot and wild, and she felt an answering emotion well from somewhere deep inside. "Do you dream of me?" she whispered.

He got to his feet, his control threadbare and growing thinner. He moved to go toward the door, but she got firmly into his path and forced him to look at her. "Tell me I'm wrong," she challenged. "Prove me wrong, right here and now."

"How?"

"Kiss me." She lifted her chin slightly when he looked at her in shock. Determination and desperation mingled inside her. "Prove me wrong. That *mysterious stranger* kissed me. I'll know the difference. Worst thing that happens is you get to kiss a hot woman and me a hot man."

"That," he muttered softly, his hand lifting to fist into her loose hair, "is not the worst thing that could happen! Damn you, princess." He dragged her against him, surprising a gasp out of her, then covered her mouth with his in the kiss he had been craving for the last two days and his entire life.

A low moan vibrated in her throat. She threw her arms around him and met his desire equally, recklessly not caring where they were. "I love you!" she whispered fiercely when he lifted his head slightly. "Admit that it was you!"

"It was." He couldn't deny it any longer, not when she was in his arms again. Despite the difference between their heights, her body seemed perfectly formed to mold against him. He had a vision of simply lifting her onto the edge of the desk and finding every inch of her soft skin to imprint her on his memory. A shudder rippled through his body and he caught her even closer. "Kally."

Ready to demand he admit he loved her, for she was sure now that he did, she opened her mouth . . . and the office door suddenly swung open. A student blithely walked in saying, "Hey, Professor Shaughnessy, I have a question about Tuesday's homework." His words came to a startled stop as he saw Kalliope in Taegan's arms. His eyes slowly widened as red color climbed up his neck. "Oh, shit. Umm, sorry!" He backed out hastily and slammed the door.

As if he had been burned, Taegan lifted his hands sharply. "Shit." While Kalliope sank weakly down onto the edge of the chair, he leaned against the edge of the desk. "Well," he sighed, "there go our reputations. Your status as valedictorian will be revoked at the least."

"Do you think that matters to me?!" she snapped at him as she leapt to her feet. "I want you! I don't want anything else! My grades can go to hell. Oh, god." She buried her face in her hands. "You might get fired. I never wanted this, Taegan. I'm so sorry!"

He gently reached out and drew her into his arms. He pressed her face to his shoulder as she sobbed softly. "I know." He softly ran a hand over her back. "I know you didn't. But you understand now why I said this was a bad idea."

She swiped at her eyes. "I guess I'm still a child in some ways."

"No." He pressed his lips to her forehead. "You're just too quick to follow your heart. Sometimes you need to stop and think." He held her closer, uncaring about the passage of time. He had no classes to go to, and she wasn't afraid to skip. Once word spread, they wouldn't be able to see each other on or off campus. It was his last chance to hold her.

It was noon when his phone finally rang. By then, he was sitting with her curled up on his lap. She reluctantly got to her feet as he just as reluctantly let her go. With a bracing sigh, he picked up the phone. "Shaughnessy." He listened for long moments, then said, "I'll be right there." He hung up the phone and turned to where she was standing with her arms crossed protectively. "The school president and council want to see me. You should go home."

"I'll go with you. I'll tell them it wasn't your fault." She turned her face helplessly into his hand as he touched her cheek. "Taegan, please." She couldn't bear the idea of him going into battle alone. And it was a battle. She felt it. Things would have been easy if he had only had a wicked stepmother. He had the school president instead, and that was eons worse. Private campuses abided by different rules than public ones.

"Go home." He leaned down and softly touched her lips with his. It would be the last time he ever tasted her. And because he felt so sure it was, he gave her the truth he had wanted to give her for years. "I love you."

She could only stand there with tears running down her cheeks as he pulled on his jacket and walked out of the office. Helplessly, she sank down onto the chair and buried her face in her hands. "I'm such an idiot!"

A very gentle hand touched her hair so lightly she almost didn't feel it. When she lifted her head sharply, Audra was standing in the room beside her. The sunlight in the room had somehow receded, and shadows hid Audra's face from view once more. It seemed a curious thing, but Kalliope didn't question it.

Audra leaned against the desk and regarded Kalliope. Things were moving forward just as she had thought they would. "Well," she said.

"Well indeed." Her lips trembled. "Do you hate me as much as I'm sure everyone else will?"

"Why would I hate a woman who took a desperate grab for love?" Audra shook her head. "No, Kalliope, I don't hate you. And I don't hate Taegan. It may not make sense, and you may not believe me, but I care about you both."

Oddly, it did make sense somehow, and she did believe her. "Is there any advice you can give me? My attempts at winging it seemed to have backfired."

Audra cocked her head. "I think your best option is to take a few days off. Go stay at a hotel on the other side of town. Let the air clear and everything blow over. When you come back, I think you'll have a better idea of what to do."

"I like that idea." She got to her feet. "Any recommendations for a hotel?" It seemed another compulsion, as if she had to ask.

"Actually, yes." Audra held out a business card. "It's owned by a . . . friend. They won't ask questions or make you uncomfortable. Promise."

Because it was well known that Audra didn't make promises she didn't keep, Kalliope felt her shoulders relax. "I guess I'll go home and see where I stand with my dad, and if it's too bad, I'll go to the hotel. Thank you, Professor Alexandrios."

"Sure." Audra watched Kalliope walk out of the office. She then sat down in the vacated seat and swung her long legs over the arm. With all the patience of a hunter, she waited.

As Taegan headed down the halls, he was able to see firsthand how far and how outrageously word had spread. Students treated him coldly, which wasn't a surprise. Whether Kalliope was willing or not, he had betrayed all of their trust by crossing over a line he should never have gone near. A teacher was supposed to be their role model, and everyone had looked up to him.

It was no surprise to see Kienan in a loud argument with another student and shaking the other kid by his shirt. Kienan was a protector and his temper flared hot. It was, however, a surprise to see Mel almost at blows with another set of students. Mel wasn't known for his fast temper. Who would have thought it?

The entire council was already present when he arrived. "I was expecting this call," he said calmly as he shut the door behind himself. If he felt any discomfort or unease, it was well hidden.

"Have a seat, Taegan." The president leaned forward slightly when he had done so. "To be honest, we're not entirely certain we wish to believe these rumors. Your reputation is sterling and, by this point, the rumors are completely outrageous. Under the circumstances, we're also turning a blind eye to the fights your brothers and sister-in-law got into."

"Madelyne did?" His brows shot up. Madelyne was the least confrontational girl he knew.

One of the members cleared her throat slightly. "I believe that one began when another student referred to Kalliope Tavoularis by a very derogatory name in her presence." She saw the flash of fury in his eyes that was quickly hidden, and she knew that, regardless of the truth, the math teacher was seriously hung up on his student.

"The student who began the rumors is unable to be located right now. I think your brothers have the fear of God in him since they've threatened to murder whoever started this." The president cleared his throat. "Until we can determine his whereabouts and get the truth out of him, we have no choice but to suspend you from classes. You're not fired," he added quickly. "Think of it as a paid vacation."

Taegan took a little breath and asked quietly, "If I may make a request?" When the council nodded, he got to his feet and continued firmly, "Don't punish Kalliope for whatever may have happened. She does not deserve to be suffering for this. Please transfer her from my class to another, and don't let it affect her grade. She deserves to be valedictorian."

As the door shut behind him, one of the women on the council gave a soft sigh. Though he had tried to hide it, his suffering had been clear to anyone looking closely. "David, it's plain he's in love with her. How can we punish something like that? Are we so far entrenched in pomp and propriety that we can't bend the rules a little?"

Taegan wasn't surprised to find Audra in his office, sitting in the visitor's chair with her feet propped on the top of the desk. The afternoon sun slanted across her face and harshly illuminated the healing scar that started at her forehead and crossed down over her nose and to her chin. Whatever beauty she had once possessed had been marred forever by the vicious presence of the scar. It would forever scare and repulse most people.

He wasn't most people. He barely even saw the scar when he looked at her. If anything, looking at the scar brought nothing but respect, admiration, and love. He knew where she had gotten it, and he would forever be grateful for her dedication. He let her be while he packed up his things. But, after a few moments, he realized she was waiting for him to speak first. "Yes?" he asked dryly.

"I take it the council canned you?"

"No, they suspended me with pay. They want to get information from the source before they make a final decision. They don't entirely believe anything they've heard, which is good for me and Kalliope both." He shot her a sour look. "Damn it, you could have warned me a little more clearly! I couldn't control myself."

"Good. Rattling you up is the only way to get you anywhere." She swung her feet down and got to her feet. She flicked her hair back over her shoulder. "You want some advice?"

"From you? Always."

"You need to get away for the weekend," she informed him calmly. "Your family will support you, naturally, but you won't be able to stand seeing their happy relationships. Love that suffers always suffers more when it is around love that doesn't. And anyway, your brothers will nag you."

"You'd know," he murmured. "You've certainly been around us long enough."

She didn't respond to the bait. Instead, she turned and walked out of the office. As the door shut behind her, the oddly frightening and yet protective sense of her presence faded. He was well familiar with it. He could read energy, and hers was one he knew well. He would give things a try at home, but he didn't doubt his friend in the slightest. She knew his family as well as he did.

CHAPTER TWENTY

Kalliope knew the instant she walked in the front door of her house that her father had heard the news because she was immediately summoned to his office. She was hardly surprised. Word traveled fast around her.

Her exit from the campus had felt like a walk through a gauntlet. Half the students had been supportive, but the other half had been brutal and cruel. They had called her names, slung jokes, and made crude propositions. The battering of emotions on top of the highs and lows of the last few days was almost more than she could bear. The hotel looked more and more appealing.

Straightening her back, she walked into her father's office. Pride was all she had left, and she clung onto it with all her strength. She inclined her head slightly when he looked at her. "Yes?"

"What," he asked softly, "was the meaning of the phone call I received? You were found in a compromising position with a teacher? I raised you better than that."

For a moment, she could only stare at him in stunned hurt. "I can't believe you. You'd believe someone else before you even heard what I had to say." Her hands curled into fists at her side. "Yes, I was in Taegan Shaughnessy's office. I'm often in there because he's my friend and listens to me when I need someone to talk to."

"From the sound of things he's slightly more than a friend!" he snapped. He felt furious and betrayed. Taegan had crossed an ethical line that he found appalling. It made him begin to question the entire Shaughnessy family as a whole and rethink the idea of a merger. "I don't want you going near him again."

"You can't stop me." Her eyes glittered fiercely. "I won't bend my life to fit the whims of others."

"You'll damned well do what I say!" He got to his feet. "If you want to inherit this company, then you will do as I say!"

"Then keep your damned company!" The words exploded out of her on a wave of pain and fury. "I'm so *sick* of having to change myself to be good enough for you! It's never been about my skill or my intelligence! I've done everything you ever wanted to make myself be the best possible heir! But now, when I need you on my side, you don't even care! Fuck you, Dad!" She whirled toward the door so he couldn't see the tears trying to fall. "I'm going away somewhere for a few days. I'll come back when you've cooled down. And if you still can't apologize at that time, I'm leaving for good!"

The door slammed violently behind her as she left. Shaking, he slowly lowered his face into his hands and slumped down in his chair. How could she *ever* think that he didn't love and appreciate her? She was his pride and joy.

Mara slipped into the room and walked over to wrap her arms around his shoulders. She had wondered if it might someday come to this. "Neither of you seem to know when to pull back," she murmured softly.

He covered her hands with his. "Or when to leave well enough alone." He let out a breath. "I need to call Sullivan." He reached for the phone, but her hand covered his gently. He sighed and leaned against her. "I guess it can wait. I don't think I want to risk saying something else I'll regret."

Kalliope went upstairs and threw together, in a suitcase, the first clothes to come to hand. Her tears had gone away somewhere. She felt battered and bruised, pushed to the point of breaking. She drove on automatic and followed her car's navigator to get to the hotel Audra had suggested. It was on the other side of the town, big enough to get lost in, and oddly quiet for that time of day. Few cars were in the parking lot, and that suited her just fine. She was able to find a place where her car couldn't be seen in passing.

The manager who ran the place was behind the desk when he heard her walk in. He looked up automatically and was going to call a greeting when he realized her face was familiar. He looked down at the desk in front of him where a small photo sat. It was the same face.

His sharp eyes saw the remnants of grief and tears on her face. She was, indeed, in need of an escape. "Welcome to the Sanctuary Hotel," he told her gently as she came up to the desk. "Are you checking in?"

"Yes, but I don't have a reservation. Do you have a quiet room somewhere that I can hide for a few days?" Her smile was wan. "I'm having a bit of a family fight. I left before I and my father could kill each other."

The key was already sitting next to the photo though he said nothing about it. "Of course. There's a room on the top floor near the back. Only one other room is occupied, across from yours, so you should have plenty of quiet."

She went through the registration process in a sort of haze, signed the paperwork, and then accepted her key. She couldn't even argue when the bellhop insisted on carrying her one suitcase.

The manager watched her go before looking down once more to where there was another photograph and key waiting. He had stopped questioning Rhianna Taber and her odd ways of knowing things before they happened.

She found her room to be tranquil and quiet and just what she needed. She tipped the bellhop before he could try to explain things she already knew and he took that as his cue to leave. As the door shut behind him, she walked over to her bed and curled up into a ball on the top. She couldn't even cry. It hurt too much.

When Taegan got home, it was to a congregation in the kitchen. Mel was sitting on a stool without a shirt. Kienan was holding an icepack over one of his eyes, which was quickly turning black and blue. Madelyne was bandaging his knuckles, and Hiro was taking care of what looked like a couple of nasty abrasions on his upper arm.

The snippets of conversation indicated that he hadn't ducked in time nor had he made a proper fist. Taegan just sighed and kept going down the hall to his room. He dropped his things on the bed and turned to close the door when he realized that Aenya had been following him silently. She stared at him solemnly for long moments before moving closer and wrapping her arms around his waist in a fierce hug.

After all the upheaval of the day, her silent support was nearly his undoing. He lifted her up into his arms and held onto her tightly to take what comfort he could. He pressed his lips to her forehead. "I guess you heard."

"You could say that. It made its way to my high school, Taegan." There was no censure in her eyes or voice. Just steady support. "You want to tell me the truth? I've heard some interesting variations."

He put her down gently and sat on the side of the bed. "I'm in love with Kally, which I'm sure you're already aware of." His sigh was long. "I've been in love with her for years. It was fine when it was unrequited, but she seems to love me as well. Knowing it . . . I find I can't control myself any longer. A student walked into my office and found her in my arms."

"Kissing?" she asked calmly.

"Not at the immediate moment. If he'd been a minute sooner, yes." He smiled wryly. "I don't deny we shared an embrace, but I'm not telling anyone except my family that."

"We would have guessed anyway." She walked over to sit beside him. Her hands covered his wrist softly as she wished with all her soul to make things better. "Where do you stand with the school?"

He studied her hands curiously. "Suspended with pay until they determine what really happened. If my reputation wasn't so solid, I'm sure I'd have been fired." Her hands were burning softly, hotter than usual. Oddly, the pain seemed to have lessened its chokehold. "Aenya . . ."

She lifted her hands with a smile. "I only recently figured out I could do that. I guess it's my gift."

"It suits you." He got to his feet as he heard Sullivan calling for him. "Thanks, Aenya." He brushed another kiss over the top of her head. "Your support means everything."

Sullivan was waiting in his office. When Taegan walked inside, Sullivan studied him intently. "Have a seat."

He shook his head. "I'll stand if it's all the same to you."

"Alright. You want to tell me what really happened?" Sullivan trusted his son to tell him the truth. He had raised Taegan, and he refused to believe any of the rumors he had heard. That there had been some sort of torrid embrace, he had no doubt. The wolf that had just snuck in the door behind him was proof of it.

"To be blunt, sir," Taegan ignored Stormy as she sat beside him in clear alliance, "I am in love with Kalliope and made the foolish mistake of kissing her. I had already released her, but she was still in my arms when the student walked in. Conclusions were drawn. As such, I am on suspension from the college until the council determines their next course of action. I have asked that Kalliope be transferred from my class. She won't suffer for my actions."

"Of course she will." Sullivan lifted a brow. "She loves you, I assume, or she would not have returned your embrace."

"Yes, sir, she does." He smiled sadly. "Her father will hardly approve of me now, not with the smear on my reputation. Pin your hopes for grandchildren on your other children. There will be none from me."

As he left the room, Sullivan got up and walked around the desk to kneel in front of Stormy. "I don't know what you are," he said softly. "I don't know who you are. But I've seen what you're doing for us. So, please, give him a happy ending, too. I can't bear my children to be so miserable."

She rose up to lick his cheek softly in comfort and ran lightly from the room. She caught up with Taegan halfway down the hall and followed him into his room. She sat in the doorway to watch while he packed a suitcase, looking for all the world like a wolf-shaped statue. It was clear she wasn't moving anytime soon.

He smiled wryly. "Alright. What is it you want me to know or do?" Her eyes flickered toward his desk and he walked over to glance at the top. There, printed neatly, were directions to a hotel on the edges of the city. "And if I don't want to go there?" She bared her teeth and he smiled. "I assumed so." He picked up the directions and quickly memorized them. It really wasn't a hard place to reach. "You do plan for everything," he murmured as he picked up his suitcase.

He had no idea how true that was, she thought wryly as she followed him down the hall again.

At the kitchen, he glanced inside to see his siblings. They looked at him expectantly but no one said anything. "No questions," he told them quietly. "I'm just not up to it right now. Kien, I'm borrowing the sidecar. I'm going to stay at a hotel for a few days. I'm hoping things will blow over quickly."

"Sure." Kienan tucked his hands in his pockets and watched as he left the kitchen. His eyes lowered to see Stormy following along in his tracks. He began to smile as he looked at his family. "What's that thing we say in 3rd District, Maddie?"

She smiled in return. "There's no such thing as coincidence."

Oblivious to that little fact, Taegan attached the sidecar to his bike and waited for Stormy to jump in before he put his suitcase in with her. He made sure she was safely secured before pulling on his helmet. A memory teased him of how Kalliope had felt so right riding on the bike with him, and his heart quivered. It would never happen again. He wanted to tell himself that things were better this way, but he couldn't really bring himself to believe it.

The hotel was blessedly large and isolated. He parked out front and saw no familiar cars. Suitcase in hand and Stormy at his side, he walked into the lobby. "Behave yourself," he murmured to her as he saw her eyeing a stray cat wandering outside. "Chicken. You handle Maddie's kitten just fine."

The manager was waiting for him when he came over to the desk. "Welcome to Sanctuary Hotel." His sharp eyes missed none of the strain in his face or the grief darkening his gaze. "Are you checking in?"

"Yes, but I have no reservation. And are pets allowed? I promise she's housebroken. I can get a leash for her as needed."

"Pets are allowed, and as long as she stays at your side while you are in the lobby, you don't need a leash." He would have said a leash wasn't needed at all, but then he would have to explain why the wolf was familiar to him. "We have a quiet room on the top floor. Only one other guest is up there. You'll have plenty of privacy."

"Do I look that bad?" he asked ruefully as he signed the paperwork.

"Worse," the manager admitted. He handed over the key. "If you need anything, just dial 0-4. We have a full room service menu."

"Thanks." He waved off the bellhop and carried his suitcase by himself as he headed for the elevator. Once on the top floor, it wasn't hard to find his room. The one across from him had a 'do not disturb' sign on the handle. He completely sympathized.

He opened his door and smiled with reluctant bemusement when Stormy leapt up onto the bed and laid down to claim a portion for herself. He ruffled her fur gently as he walked over to open the curtains. It was rapidly turning from afternoon into evening, the sun slowly beginning its descent. Sunset was coming quicker these days as winter took hold. If the weathermen were to be believed, it would be snowing in a few days. That suited his mood just fine. He felt cold and bleak himself.

Kalliope awoke to thin moonlight coming in the open curtains. Highly groggy, she staggered over and closed them. She hadn't intended to fall asleep but she wasn't entirely surprised that she had. She looked in a mirror, and she also wasn't surprised that her eyes were a little puffy. Her conscious mind couldn't cry but her subconscious was having no trouble.

There was no reason to repair the damage, and she hadn't brought any makeup anyway. She didn't care who saw her. She didn't feel overly hungry, but she knew she needed to eat. She raked a hand through her tangled hair and opened her door to step into the hall. She had just shut it behind her when she heard clawing at the door across from her.

"Alright!" Taegan exclaimed in exasperation as he opened the door to let Stormy out. "What the hell's wrong with you now?" He broke off in shock as he found himself staring at Kalliope. She stood motionless, staring at him in return.

He looked her over hungrily. He was dreaming. He had to be dreaming. You couldn't conjure someone by wishing for them. Her perfume reached out and curled around him, and he began to breathe again. "Kally," he managed to say.

"Oh my god." She took a quick breath as she saw he was about to go back into his room and shut the door. "No!" She leapt forward and reached for the door to stop it. Her foot caught on the rug in the hall, and she pitched forward without control. She landed safely in his arms as he caught her. On a soft sound, she burrowed closer. She clung on with a wild and desperate strength. "No, please," she whispered against his shoulder. "Don't shut me out."

"Kally." Trembling, he caught her even closer and lifted her off her feet to bury his face against her neck. "What are you doing here?"

"I fought with my father. We both said some pretty horrible things so I left before it got worse." She wrapped her arms around him, afraid she would wake up and find it was another dream. "What about you?"

"My family is behind me one hundred percent, but I couldn't bear seeing Maddie and Kienan, or Hiro and Aenya. It was killing me because I couldn't have you." He eased her back and set her on her feet. "Go back to your room," he told her, his voice strained and aching. "If you stay . . . I don't know if I can stop myself from touching you."

She stepped back, and he closed his eyes tightly, his hands turning into fists at his sides as he heard the door shut. The sound of the lock turning had his eyes opening in shock. She stood just inside the doorway with the closed door at her back. She took a quick breath. "I don't want you to stop."

"I can't protect you." He held her gaze. "I don't carry protection around with me because it's not a game."

"No it's not." She walked toward him slowly. "I'm on the pill," she informed him, her voice calm. "I'm so irregular with my periods that I would get horrendous cramps. I went on the pill to help regulate them. I've only had two lovers, and both are as healthy as am I. Want my records?" It was said with an obvious hint of humor.

"You're making it very hard to tell you to leave." His voice was husky with desire as he lifted his hands to frame her face. It was easy to be gentle when she was finally his to hold as he had wanted for so long. "I love you so much," he murmured. He studied her face and tenderness filled his heart. He brushed at the skin under her eyes. "Were you crying?"

"Yes." She gave him a sour look. "I've cried more the last few days than I ever have in my life, damn you." Her words trailed off as he bent his head and began to brush soft kisses across her eyes and cheek. "We broke the rules already," she whispered. "What's one more?"

"Kally. My beautiful Kalliope." He lifted her into his arms and carried her toward the bed. He lowered her gently to her feet beside it. "I wish . . . if only . . ." He stopped as she reached up and pressed gentle fingers to his lips.

"Change nothing. Not you, not me, not this time. I don't want to ever regret anything." She began to unbutton his shirt slowly, her mouth going dry with every inch of skin she uncovered. He was more muscular than she had thought, more beautiful, and when his shirt was completely removed, she felt a small quiver of feminine fear as she realized how much stronger he was.

He felt the quiver in her fingers and brought them to his lips to kiss each tip softly. He eased closer and ran the kisses down the inside of her arm, up over her slim bicep, and around to the back of her neck. He breathed his love between every kiss. Her arms lifted to wind around him in a reverse hug and his hands settled lightly at her waist as he pressed his lips to her pulse.

Her eyes closed as helpless pleasure washed through her body. "You left a mark last time," she murmured huskily.

"I was too rough." He turned her in his arms and lifted her to her toes, his hands cupping her bottom warmly under her dress. His lips found hers and he sank into the kiss, lazily drawing it out until she softened and swayed against him. Still kissing her, he eased the dress up to her waist and skimmed his knuckles over the hot skin of her stomach.

He released her long enough to remove the dress and then held her hands at her sides as he looked his fill. She wore a pair of matching peach lace panties and bra that seemed only a few shades darker than her skin. The echoes of a tan from the summer were visible in places. He smiled as he realized she wore a bikini often.

She was soft and fragrant curves and long graceful lines. The urge to ravish surged at its chains, but he leashed it tightly. He knew it might be his only time to ever love her. He sank his fingers into her hair and drew her close again for another lingering kiss. The soft moan she gave was the sweetest sound he had heard.

She was floating, unable to breathe or think. She drowned in his caresses, and she couldn't have known his love more surely. When he lifted her in his arms and turned to lower her to the top of the bed, she had to say softly, "Too many novels."

"You disapprove?" He sat beside her on the bed and lightly skimmed his knuckle slowly over her ribcage and steadily higher.

"No, but you," her breath caught as his hand cupped her breast warmly, "are really ruining me for other men. I'll never have another lover. You're going to be," her breath broke again as his head bent and his lips teased her nipple through the lace, "going to be stuck with me."

She moved restlessly beneath him, arching fluidly into his touch as he eased the cups of the bra aside and took a bare nipple into his lips. He suckled softly, savoring the flavor of her skin that was the same no matter where he touched. A flick of his fingers opened her bra so he could drop it over the side of the bed.

She watched him through lowered lashes as she nudged his shoulders. He obligingly rolled onto his back and she rose to her knees beside him. She ran a hand slowly over his chest and thrilled at the knowledge this powerful male was hers. She seemed small and delicate beside him and it was a heady power to be given the freedom of his body.

She softly ran little kisses over his chest. She tasted him thoroughly and the little touches of her tongue made him shudder. Answering wild pleasure shivered through her own body. Her fingers skimmed lightly down the muscles of his arms and up again, and her lips curved against his as she kissed him softly. "Bad boy in disguise."

He turned suddenly and tumbled her onto the bed. He pinned her gently beneath him. "Hardly worthy of a princess." He ran his hand slowly over her legs and up over her hip. He couldn't stop touching her. His heart craved her as deeply as his body did. "But I love you."

She opened her mouth to respond but could only moan softly as his hand slipped under the edge of her underwear and slid downward to caress her slowly. He softly petted her and watched her face with rapt attention as she twisted against his hand, pleasure stealing her breath.

When ecstasy came, it rolled like a wave over her senses. It rocked her to her soul, branded her indelibly as his. Before she could catch a breath, he was kissing her deeply, building her hunger again as his hands stripped her underwear down her legs and away. "Taegan." It was all she could say.

"Kally. You're mine, Kally." He lifted her slightly into the kiss before lowering her once more and surveying her naked body with primitive satisfaction. Even if it was only once, she was his. She would belong to him as she had to no one else. Two lovers or two hundred, they both knew that what was between them was *only* between them. They would never find this anywhere else.

Her hands lowered as he continued to kiss her, and she began to unfasten his pants. He stopped breathing entirely as she slowly slid a hand inside his shorts and cupped him, learning him as completely as he had learned her. "Stop," he said a bit hoarsely. "You'll make me . . ."

"Good." Her voice filled with feminine welcome and delight. Secure in her power, she reveled in touching him.

"I'd rather be inside you." He dragged her hands up his body and kissed the palms with a little nip of his teeth. He released her only long enough to remove his clothes. He was heavy with desire for her, and the sight of her holding her arms out to him made him shudder with need. "I've dreamed of this," he admitted huskily as he sank into her arms. "Of you here, welcoming me. Reality is better than imagination."

She lifted a leg and curled it around his hip to hold him tightly as he braced his weight on his arms over her. Her hands lowered, and their fingers entwined securely as he slid into her in a single stroke. Her breath hitched in her chest and a shudder rippled through her body. It felt like homecoming. Belonging. "Taegan." Her hair tumbled around her shoulders as she twisted slowly beneath him.

If it was wrong, then why was it so very right? He drew their hands up until they were pinned to the pillow beside her head. He held her tightly as he began to slowly slide in and out of her. "Hold onto me," he urged huskily. "Don't let go of me."

Her arms wound around his damp shoulders and she held on tightly as the tension grew. She lifted her head to meet his kiss halfway and sank into the ecstasy of the union. They had to break apart only for air, and she buried her face against his neck, her arms tightening around his shoulder as he poured himself into her. She wished only that tomorrow would never arrive.

Long after she slept beside him, curled protectively into his arms, he remained awake and stared at the clock across the room as it steadily ticked away the seconds and minutes. As it began to grow closer to dawn, he turned and tucked her more firmly under the covers. She reached for him without waking, and he leaned down to kiss her softly and taste her dreams. She settled and curled into the pillow more firmly.

He called himself several kinds of a fool while he dressed. He scrawled a short note on the pad by the phone before ripping the page off and wrapping it around the stem of a rose he removed from the vase in the room. He set it on the pillow where he had slept and then gently brushed her hair from her face. Before he could change his mind, he left the room.

She knew she was alone even before she opened her eyes. She sat up and surveyed the silent room. His suitcase was gone. She noticed the rose belatedly, and she picked up the note to open it. The language looked completely foreign and unknown to her, yet just reading the words made them seem beautiful. She could only imagine how they would sound in Taegan's beautiful voice.

She held the note to her heart and closed her eyes tightly. Even if it was only one night, she couldn't regret it. She traced a finger over the petals of the rose and thought of the story of Cinderella again. It was time she played the tale through to the end. Ideas were forming, tumbling through her mind. Audra had been right. Suddenly she was thinking clearer and more steadily.

There had been a second party in one of the stories, hadn't there?

CHAPTER TWENTY-ONE

Kalliope spent the next few days at the Sanctuary Hotel. She felt secure and grounded once more and ready to take on the world. She was oddly peaceful, too. She refused to believe that she had been given such a wonderful chance at happiness, only to have it slip away. Her fantasies had been trumped by the reality of Taegan's love and desire for her.

The time wasn't spent moping. She made plans and lists and formulated ideas. She was going to have to play both sides. That Taegan had someone on his side was in her favor. She didn't know who it was, but she hoped they really had his best interests in mind.

By the time she was on her way home that Wednesday, she had made her plan of attack. The first step was to find out where she and her father stood. Despite what she had accused him of, she knew he only wanted her to be happy. He was just too entrenched in propriety and status.

She was disinclined to outright lie to him anymore. She was going to have another one of those conversations where they pretended they didn't know what was being said. She was getting rather tired of them. She preferred being blunt.

When she returned to her home, she parked in her spot and headed for the front door. Jiles was sitting on the front steps waiting for her. She warily slowed her steps, not sure what he was doing and thinking. He looked unbearably sad as if he had aged overnight. "Dad?"

He got to his feet, went down the steps, and pulled her into his arms. He rocked her back and forth and buried his face in her hair. "I'm sorry, baby," he murmured achingly. "Please forgive me. I *never* meant to make you feel as if I didn't love you. Of course I love you!" He eased back and gave her a trembling smile. "And I'm proud as hell of you. I couldn't ask for a better daughter."

She let out a little sigh and hugged him tightly, wondering why she was cursed in life to be surrounded by men who were convinced they knew what was best for her. "I know, I know. It's okay, Dad, really. Don't worry about it. Going away made me accept a few things." She walked into the house and set her suitcase down by the door. "Can we go into your office?"

"Of course." He led the way and shut the door behind her as she entered. "What's on your mind, honey?"

She settled herself into one of the chairs and waited while he sat down as well. Carefully, she asked, "Would you say that I'm a . . . fickle woman?"

"Of course not." His answer was swift. "You've always known your heart. It's why it's always been so vexing for me that you wouldn't marry for affection only, hoping for love to grow." He held up a hand. "And, I promise, I'm going to loosen up over that. Just don't wait forever. Retirement has been looking more and more appealing lately. I'm bored."

"Here's the thing." She crossed her arms. "I won't marry for less than love. And all your machinations in the world won't help your cause because I've already found the man I love. He danced with me in a moonlit garden." Her eyes met her father's. "It was a stolen moment, you see. He knew the outside world would never understand."

He opened his mouth, then slowly closed it. Oddly, he found that it made perfect sense of the entire scenario. The only thing he couldn't wrap his mind around was, "I could have sworn he was blond that night," he muttered.

She smiled. "Magic. But here's my question to you." Her eyes darkened, intense and serious. "Do you stand by my decision? I can assure you that he loves me as much as I love him. That he's suffered as much as I have."

"I would stand beside you if you decided to marry a trash collector," he assured her. "You know I love you, but . . ." He sighed. "Things have gotten quite complicated, Kally. The entire city has heard about what happened." He tossed her a newspaper. "See for yourself."

"Hmm." She studied the article. It was devoid of a lot of details, but the author took gleeful delight in Kalliope being caught in a compromising position with a Shaughnessy, particularly one who was her teacher. "And yet they don't even say what really happened. At the *worst* anyone could say was that when that other guy walked in, he saw Taegan hugging me. Seriously."

Her father quirked a brow. "And if he'd walked in a minute earlier?" he asked dryly.

"That's beside the point." Her eyes twinkled for a moment before she grew serious again. "Here's what I want to do. Everyone knows about my birthday party and the mysterious man who caught my attention. I'm going to play this story out.

The Palace is ours for another week. I'm going to have another party on Friday. All the same people from before will be invited. All of them. Invitations can go out tomorrow."

"What of the guards? Unless he shows up with a crowd, they will easily single him out and be able to determine who he is."

"We're not going to have guards this time." Her smile was all business. "The invitations will be keycards to the gate. You have to flash the card to even get inside. A body entering without a card is easily picked up. I wouldn't want to scare him away, you know."

"Are you that sure he'll show up?"

She barely refrained from touching the rose tucked delicately over her ear. "He won't be able to stay away. That I can be sure of."

It took Taegan longer to return home than his lover. He had gone further out of town with the hopes of discouraging her from following him. He couldn't even resent Stormy for deliberately forcing him to confront Kalliope. In many ways, he was deeply grateful. Even if he lived for centuries, he would never forget the woman he loved.

It was Thursday when he finally returned home. He wasn't in the mood to deal with his family just yet so he ducked around into the garden and tried to sneak into his bedroom. He wasn't entirely surprised, however, to discover Aenya waiting for him on the side of the bed. He sighed.

"Hi to you, too." Her eyes searched his face. Whatever she saw seemed to please her, because a little smile played with her lips. "Good thing you got here today." She hugged Stormy as the wolf leapt up beside her. "It would seem that Kalliope is fighting fire with fire. She's having another party tomorrow night. All the same people invited. Same elaborate masquerade."

"I see." His eyes flickered to Stormy who looked both slightly surprised and yet fully pleased. "Well, I can't go, obviously. I'm sure she's just trying to dispel the rumors."

"You could help with that," Aenya noted as she got to her feet.

"You have more confidence in my control than I do," he admitted ruefully. "Now scoot." He nudged her out the door. "Frankly, if I showed my face there, her father would probably kill me."

She contemplated the door as it shut in her face. Hiro's arms slid around her waist, and she leaned back against him. Companionably, she said, "He really had that look. I know that look. I believe it was on your face after we became lovers. And it was definitely on Kienan's after he and Maddie got together. I would bet my club on Kally being at that hotel too."

"Not on purpose," he murmured.

"Well, of course not. Nothing ever happens on purpose around here. At least, not by *our* doing." She blew out a quick breath. "So who is pulling the strings this time? I would have sworn it was Stormy, but she seemed slightly surprised by Kally's actions."

"Then it's no doubt Kally who is pushing things into place. This ought to be interesting."

The speed at which word spread was a double-edged sword. Even though it had made the rumor grow with beanstalk proportions, it also allowed for news of Kalliope's second party to make its rounds with time to spare. By Friday afternoon, she knew that every last person who had accepted an invitation before would be accepting again. Keycards were delivered to those who had given confirmation.

Still, Friday evening, she felt like a nervous wreck. She was taking a *huge* risk and crossing her fingers that not only would Taegan show up, but that he would also leave some sort of clue behind that she could use against him. It had to look as if she had forced Jiles to let her marry whoever she wanted or else he would never believe her.

This time she wore a red silk ball gown with rubies. She selected her jewelry with care to flatter her features, and she used bits of white for accent. Instead of a jeweled circlet, however, she wore a tiny circlet of roses with the one Taegan had given her at the very center. Even after a few days, it hadn't begun to wilt.

Two hours into the party, she was holding court and laughing away all the rumors and assumptions. It didn't take long before there wasn't a person left who honestly believed anything had happened, and all had plans to say so when they were back at school. It was to her advantage that several council members had attended as well. She sought them out deliberately.

"You look lovely, Kalliope," one woman told her.

"Thank you." She sighed. "Tell me honestly. Do you really believe that anything happened between me and Professor Shaughnessy? I mean, the school would say Big Foot was a gym teacher if someone started a rumor."

"True enough," another member admitted. "Are you saying nothing happened?"

"He hugged me." She sighed again as if it was more an annoyance than heartbreak. "I was miserable and upset and you know how he hates to see a friend hurt. And he *is* my friend, thank you."

"That is also true," the woman of before murmured. Her eyes searched Kalliope's but saw nothing underneath the serene surface.

She just didn't know that the serene surface was a cover for a simmering boil of nerves and anticipation. Kalliope was watching the clock and waiting. It was getting later and later. He hadn't shown up with his family, and Mel hadn't known one way or another if he would show up at all. She still knew he would. They were both in over their heads.

It was a very restless and caged Taegan that paced through the Shaughnessy house as the time went by. He wanted to go, to see her just once, but he had given the mask back to Audra. Oh, he could scare up his own mask, but he didn't want to lay a chance on anyone recognizing him. That glamour was more than convenient; it was probably a lifesaver.

Since no one was there to see him, he picked up the invitation and keycard sitting on the kitchen counter. He carried both with him into his room. He hadn't personally accepted the invitation but Sullivan had said in his reply that 'the Shaughnessy family' would attend. Mathematically—and math was Taegan's specialty—that meant he got a keycard too.

The invitation clearly said there were no guards. Entry was via generic—not assigned—keycard. She had made it as easy as possible for him to sneak in. It was clear as day to him. The woman was too smart for her own good. "Damn it," he muttered as he buried his face in his hands, "where the hell are you when I actually need you?"

"Well," came Audra's voice from the balcony. "If you're going to be like that, I'll leave."

He leapt to his feet and turned quickly. She was leaning a shoulder against the balcony door. "Does the contract still stand?" he asked. He didn't bother to hide the desperation in his tone. "Please. I'd take even ten minutes to see her! But I don't want you to get into trouble, either."

"It's moot at this point. Don't worry about me." She held out the mask toward him. "This is the last chance, Cinder-boy. If you fuck this one up, you won't get another. Oh, yeah," she added, "don't forget your watch to keep track of the time."

Kalliope was beginning to think she had failed entirely when she felt the familiar sensation of being watched. Her heart began to pound and she felt her well-loved body throb in recognition of the eyes studying her so hungrily. She turned to see a familiar form standing at the top of the stairs. He had once more dressed to match her.

It took great control not to run across the room and fling herself into his arms. Instead, she walked slowly and met him at the base of the stairs. When he took her hand and brought it to his lips, her lips formed into a trembling smile. "You did come."

"I couldn't stay away. You knew I couldn't. Will you dance with me again, princess?"

Her answer was in her eyes, and he drew her onto the floor as the music began and the others parted to give them room. He twirled her gracefully into his arms, trying to let himself pretend that this was all that mattered, that he didn't crave more with every instant of his being.

From where everyone else watched, there wasn't a single person in that room who doubted that the two staring into each other's eyes were deeply in love. Kalliope glowed with a radiance that made her stunningly beautiful, and the man's hands were both possessive and protective as if he knew she belonged to him. The waltz was an intimacy, almost too intimate to watch. Many felt like they were voyeurs and seeing something never meant for their eyes.

The music came to an end amid applause, and Kalliope quickly escorted Taegan toward the gardens. People once more tried to follow, but they were brought up short by Aenya. She stood in front of the doors with a challenging smile on her lovely face. "Kally gets her privacy," she said pointedly. "Unless you want to deal with her." She pointed down.

Eyes shifted to see the slender gray wolf at her hip, and Stormy's teeth bared in a mockery of a smile. Everyone beat a hasty retreat.

In the garden, Kalliope threw her arms around Taegan's neck and reached up to kiss him. She had missed him more with every day, dying every minute she couldn't see his face or hear his voice. His arms tightened almost painfully around her waist before he loosened his grip and returned her kiss just as desperately.

When they eased apart, she asked, "What time is it? How much time do I have?" She spotted a glint of silver and plucked the pocket watch out of his jacket. She opened it and the clock sneered at her. It was eleven-thirty. "You took too long," she accused on a hitch of breath. "Now I have no time to be with you."

"My faerie godmother got stuck in traffic. Apparently it's hell on broomsticks at this time of night."

"Is she a faerie or witch?" Somehow she managed a smile.

"Sometimes," he said with feeling, "she's both." He framed her face with his hands and searched her features intently. "What did you hope to change, princess? Will this change your father's mind? Even if the rumor is dispelled, even if the council lifts the suspension, I was still your teacher. Your father will never forget that."

"He wants me to be happy. That's all he wants. He wouldn't care what your profession is." She saw the unrelenting expression in her lover's eyes and drew a ragged breath. He was too damn stubborn! "Why did you leave me?" She couldn't keep the pain from her voice. "I know I wasn't *that* experienced, but was I that bad?"

"I left because I couldn't get enough of you," he retorted harshly. "Before my pulse had calmed, I wanted you again." He flicked a finger over the rose in her hair. "The desire I have for you will never go away. And," he added softly as he dragged her against his aching body, "you're one hell of a lover. I've dreamed of you my entire life, damn it."

The sound of Mel clearing his throat caught their attention suddenly. "Mel?" she asked. She felt painfully cold as Taegan released her and stepped back.

"I'm pretending like I don't see anything out here. In fact, I don't because I'm looking at the ballroom." He kept his back turned to give the lie credence. "And because I am looking in the ballroom, I can see your father descending toward this area like Jackson taking Mississippi."

She covered her face with a hand. "Damn it, Mel! You know the Pantheon is in Rome, but you don't remember American history? It was New Orleans, you sieve-minded male!" She turned to speak to Taegan but realized with only a little surprise that he had already disappeared. She looked down at the watch in her hand and closed her fingers around it fiercely. It wasn't a glass shoe, but it would have to do.

She bided her time and brushed off questions until the party ended. She then spent the rest of the night on the internet. She had noticed that the watch was engraved with the same words that had been written on Taegan's note to her. She was desperately trying to find out what they were and what they meant.

She barely noticed the sunrise out her window. She had rejected dozens of languages, even some obscure ones she hadn't known existed. She knew Taegan was multi-lingual and a studier of classic language, but which one was the one so close to his heart that he would leave a note to his lover in it?

A soft scratching at her balcony door was so surprising it nearly sent her tumbling out of her chair. She looked over and saw a familiar wolf patiently sitting outside. She walked over to open the door and knelt down quickly. "What is it?" She realized the wolf was carrying a small bag and took it curiously.

She found three things inside. One was a very familiar mask. Another was a sheaf of papers. The third was a book. Her heart began to beat faster. It was a language book. Pages had been tabbed and she flipped to them quickly. And there, in those pages, she found the translation to the words in the note. "You sappy romantic," she whispered.

She closed the book and looked at the cover. Somehow she wasn't shocked. What else would have been the language of his heart? She turned her attention to the papers and began to read. A smile came slowly and spread across her face. It was a contract. It was a perfect contract and the answer to all her prayers. She now had all the ammunition she needed.

"I don't know who you are," she told the wolf, "but I owe you one!" She kissed the wolf very gently on the scar crossing its face. "Your heart is beautiful." Leaving the visibly bemused wolf on her balcony, she gathered up the things she needed and hurried downstairs to her father's office. It was barely after dawn, but he was always up early.

She walked right in without knocking. Jiles looked up in surprise and his eyes widened as he saw her. He had never seen her look quite so determined or triumphant before. Or exhausted. "Kally?" he asked warily. "Didn't you sleep?"

"I'll sleep when I have the man I love back." She slapped down the watch and the contract. "Here's the deal. He left this watch. It has an engraving in another language. I've since managed to figure out what it is and what it means. It's a very select language, Dad. I'd hazard a guess that of the people invited to the party, only one man would know it."

He began to smile slowly. "I see."

"And so here's the deal. I'm calling together everyone once more. Whichever man can translate, on the spot without help, the inscription on this watch can have my hand in marriage. This contract is a binding document and reads precisely as I have just stated."

Being a businessman, he picked up the contract and read it to be sure. It did, indeed, say precisely what she had. She would bring together all her invited guests for, again, he had entered with an invitation. She would give each *bachelor* a chance to translate, and the one that did would have her hand in marriage. "Are you sure?" he asked her. "Sure this will work?"

"I'm certain." She signed her name across the bottom of the contract and slid it to her father who also signed. She was a legal adult, but his signature ensured that he would not contest the contract, her decision, or her inheritance. "Everyone who was *invited* is invited again. I will personally track down everyone who *received* an invitation to make sure they attend." Her smile was a challenge. "Including my stubborn math professor. After all, shouldn't he be there when I get engaged?"

He leaned back in his chair as he watched her sweep from the room. He began to slowly smile to himself. His daughter was an absolutely brilliant woman, and he was going to greatly enjoy this unveiling. He picked up the phone and dialed. It was finally a good time to call Sullivan.

Monday proved to be a day of surprises, and it started when Kalliope arrived at school. She hadn't entirely been sure whether she would be able to stand going to math class, but as it happened, she didn't need to try. Someone was waiting for her in the parking lot and caught up with her as she reached the path leading toward the math and computer wing. "Hey, Kalliope," the boy called.

She waited for him to catch up and lifted a brow. "What?"

"You need to go to admin." He fell into step beside her as she changed her route. "Hey, I want you to know that the whole school is behind you and Professor Shaughnessy one hundred percent. You'd think this school had its own El Niño the way the wind changes so quickly. Your party was the kicker." He smiled. "And anyway, how can we think you'd be in a compromising position with the professor after we saw the guy you danced with last night?"

She coughed softly. "Oh, indeed. So I guess they found the guy who walked in on us?"

"He's *madly* jealous, Kal." He shook his head. "He's had a crush on you for a while. He started the rumor out of spite. He went to the council this morning and admitted that all he saw was Professor Shaughnessy holding your hand. You were upset, huh?"

"He's a good listener," she said with complete sincerity, though she wondered why the student had suddenly turned the tale even milder than the truth. Still, she wasn't knocking her luck.

She discovered at the administration office that she had been transferred to a new math class. Her grades were not going to be affected and her position as valedictorian was secure.

Not that she had doubted her grassroots efforts, but she was beginning to be a smidge suspicious that someone *else* was pushing things around. She went directly to the computer sciences area and to the computer lab. The door was standing open. As always, the room was dark with only a computer to light it. Audra was definitely present, though, for her typing was audible. "Hey, Professor Alexandrios?" Kalliope called. "Can I talk to you?"

"Sure. Do you want me to listen?"

"Umm, yes?"

"Then wait a second." Audra typed a bit more and then stopped and looked up. "Okay. Now what? I've maxed my quota for good deeds today. In fact I'm going to be doing another one in a few moments so make it quick."

She just smiled. Audra was brash and blunt, but underneath it was a very giving heart. She was sure of it. "I was hoping you could tell me if Taegan is going to be alright as well. My reputation seems to have *mysteriously* cleared this morning. I was hoping his had as well."

Something that had to be a smile flitted across Audra's face though it was barely perceptible in the light. "Interesting timing." She got to her feet and shrugged into the leather jacket draped across the back of her chair. "I'm about to go make sure the council takes the sticks out of their asses and builds a nice bonfire so we can talk about that very subject."

"Professor," she murmured, "you didn't by chance have anything to do with the student's story, or with my grades being kept as is, or any of the other anomalies going on this morning, did you?"

Audra stepped into the doorway, a little smirk playing with her lips. Kalliope studied her face but felt no fear or revulsion. Audra sensed it and rubbed her knuckles over her head as she went past. "Go to class," she shot over her shoulder. "Don't let your grades drop like another Shaughnessy we all know."

"Bite your tongue," she retorted. She smiled, though. She trusted Audra. Leaving things to her, she headed toward her new class.

The thing about Audra was that, no matter where she went, she made her presence felt. So when she walked into the president's meeting room where the council was convening, she didn't bother to start with formalities. "Are you all just going to be asses, or are you going to open your eyes?" she asked bluntly.

The president himself had always been very wary of the tall woman with yellow eyes, and more so since she had been wounded. The scar was like the car wreck you couldn't look away from, unable to feel anything but horror and terror. "Professor Alexandrios," he began, "it's complicated."

"Look at my eyes for once," was her soft suggestion, the words almost a purr, "and try to explain." She walked slowly down the line of chairs. "Taegan Shaughnessy's reputation is gold. The student who saw them has since confessed he told the tale out of jealousy. Kalliope Tavoularis is in another math class, and," she added, leaning on the desk, "they happen to be in love."

"The student and Kalliope?" a woman asked. She shrank back as predatory yellow eyes landed on her face.

"Don't be stupid. It's unflattering." Audra's eyes flicked back to the president's. "To be frank, Taegan and Kalliope have belonged together for years. They withheld announcing an engagement because he really is the best teacher on campus and she needed the best instructor. He has never treated her with special care. Everyone knows that, don't they?"

"Of course." The president loosened his collar as he felt sweat sliding down the back of his neck.

"And since the engagement will be official tonight, you can hardly call things improper, can you?" she challenged.

He swallowed hard. "No, ma'am."

"And you would really hate to see Taegan's reputation ruined just because he can't resist his fiancée, wouldn't you?"

"Yes'm." He glanced along the seats at the rest of the council. No one wanted to cross her, and there was something so compelling about her voice that she had to be instantly believed. "Your opinion is good enough for me, and for all of us. Taegan Shaughnessy can return to teaching as soon as possible. The students will be quite happy."

She straightened and a smirk curved her lips. "Good boy." And turning on her heel, she walked from the room with the graceful and dangerous walk of a true hunter.

CHAPTER TWENTY-TWO

Taegan was crawling on the floor and looking under his bed when he heard his cell phone ring. Exasperated, he got to his feet. He couldn't find his Gaelic dictionary anywhere. He had been using it to write a letter to his grandmother in Ireland. He was only half-fluent at the immediate moment, but the language came so naturally to him that he had been absorbing it for years.

The school president's number glared at him from the screen. His shoulders braced as he answered the call, but the news was such a relief that he sat down hard at his desk. He was lifted from suspension and could return to work the following day. It had been bad enough to lose Kalliope, but losing his job would have been more than he could handle.

After hanging up, he reached for his watch only to belatedly realize he had left it with Kalliope. At the back of his mind stirred a bit of unease. He didn't *think* she could find a way to use it against him, but, really, he didn't put anything past her. She was too brilliant for his peace of mind.

It was quiet in the house. Everyone who had school was there. Sullivan was at work. Hiro was probably elbow deep in the latest case he was handling—he had shifted into primarily missing person's cases, particularly runaways. It made the whole family, especially Aenya, happy that he was less likely to get shot at.

Taegan wandered from window to window, restless and lonely. Until the day he died, he would never forget Kalliope. If he died an old bachelor, so be it. He wanted no one else. He would devote his attention to spoiling whatever nieces and nephews he might be blessed to have. Hopefully sooner rather than later. He kind of missed having kids around.

A muffled sound from the direction of the stairs had his brows pulling together. He quickly went to the second floor and toward Kienan's room. "Kien?" He could have sworn he was at class. He opened the door, and the sound identified itself as retching. Suddenly suspicious, he went to the adjacent bathroom.

Sure enough, Madelyne was bent over the toilet as spasms shook her slender body. He wet a cloth in the sink and knelt to press it to her forehead. Her startled gaze swung to his, guilt in her violet eyes. He just smiled. "When were you going to tell him? And when were you going to tell us?"

She sagged against him weakly, too tired to sit up straight. Morning sickness had hit hard and with a vengeance. "I was sort of hoping to wait until his birthday," she whispered, "but he'll worry now."

"He's good at that. Here, let's get you into bed, little sister." He gently lifted her into his arms and carried her into the bedroom to settle her on the bed. "Just rest, got it? No reason to overwork yourself. The first new generation of Shaughnessy needs to be properly cultivated to weed out Kienan's genes."

She gave a weak laugh. "I'll be fine by evening, promise." She regarded him for long moments and sadness filled her eyes. "Why can't you be happy? It kills me seeing you and Kally so lonely and hurting. You should have kids of your own."

He gently brushed her bangs from her face. "I know, but it's just not possible." He leaned over and kissed her forehead. "When you're feeling better, ring for some soup. It always helped my mother. Especially when she was carrying Kienan."

She groaned. "I hope it's not a sign. I can barely keep up with one of him! I don't need two!"

He laughed and tucked a blanket around her securely. He found himself oddly happy despite his internal grief; he envied his brother a great deal, but he loved him enough to be thrilled for him as well. He would have to talk to Aenya about planning a baby shower at the Faerie Club.

Rather than mope, he put himself into his own studies. Since he couldn't find his dictionary, he concentrated on what he did know, studying with the same intensity he asked of his students. It wasn't until it was close to evening that he realized he had been writing the same phrase over and over again.

"Damn it," he muttered as he put down his pen. He turned slightly and jolted as he saw his brother sitting on his bed. "Mel! For god's sake, don't sneak up on me."

"I didn't. I only just sat down." Something determined glinted in his chocolate eyes. "You need to come with us. Kally has called a meeting for everyone 'who received an invitation to her parties.' She didn't say who attended. She said who received an *invitation*. That includes you, bro."

"I can't go, Mel."

"You *have* to, Taegan. Kally jumped on my back out of nowhere earlier today and told me to tell you that if you didn't show up, then she was going to bring the party here so that you had no choice but to attend. She had that look in her eye. She meant it. And frankly? She terrifies me."

"What is she up to?" he muttered mostly to himself. "I left nothing behind that she would . . ." He broke off. The pocket watch with the engraving in Gaelic. She knew he was old-school Irish. Of anyone at the party, only the Shaughnessys would be likely to know Gaelic. If she had figured out that that was the language . . .

"Let's go." Mel grabbed Taegan's wrist as he saw a brief moment of surrender. He firmly dragged his big brother down the hall and into the kitchen where the others were waiting. "Let's get going before he tries to escape."

Taegan couldn't have escaped if he wanted. Mel was dragging him and Hiro and Aenya were shoving him. Kienan was escorting Madelyne since she was still tired, and the happiness on his face told its own story, as did the way Sullivan hovered like a hen around a chick.

His heart quivered. He wanted a child of his own. A child with Kalliope. A terrifying combination of his stubbornness and her brilliance. She would be an amazing mother and would blend all aspects of her life with ease. With all the flair and style she possessed, she would walk a boardroom with a toddler on her hip. If any woman could have it all, she could.

They were the last to arrive at the Glass Shoe Palace, and everyone had gathered in the ballroom. As they entered, it was clear that Kalliope wasn't taking chances. Several guards took roll and marked off every name. The fact that all names were marked made it obvious that everyone had sensed the seriousness.

There was very little room to stand, but they managed to find places. They even found a chair for Madelyne. Taegan was barely aware of anyone else, his eyes riveted to Kalliope as she stood at the top of the stairs and talked with her father. She was thinner, and there were dark circles under her eyes. He knew she was eating and sleeping no more than he was.

After a few minutes, she waved her hands to get everyone's attention. "Alright," she announced distinctly. "I'm sure everyone is wondering what's going on. Well, I'm going to be as brief and clear as I can. To begin with, as everyone knows that I've been in a Cinderella story lately, I've decided to play it out."

She came down the stairs very slowly. "I'm in love," she said very calmly. "I've been in love for four years. It was an unrequited love that I was sure would never come to be, but at my birthday party, the man I loved showed up incognito to steal a moment with me. And I knew he loved me, too.

"Then, of course, things went to hell. I thought perhaps he would be scared away, but when I threw another party, he came again." She took a deep breath. "He's a bit of a coward, you see. Even if I stood here and pointed to him right now, he would deny it. I could ask all of you, and if you were him, you'd deny it. He seems to think my father will hate him."

She paused briefly to let that sink in. Slowly, she pulled the contract out of her jacket. "You see this? It's a contract. I and my father have entered into it. My Cinderella made a slight mistake that last party. He left me with something that could only belong to him. And how do I know he has to be here? Because both times he entered by invitation." She pulled out the watch and let it dangle from her fingers. "See this? It has some words on it. If you can translate it right here and now, you can have my hand in marriage."

The room fell silent. Taegan barely kept his jaw from dropping, and he barely noticed when Mel and Kienan both elbowed him sharply.

"That being said, I'd like to have all the bachelors line up please." Her eyes looked as cool as obsidian. "And I want no arguments. If you do not get in line willingly, I have several guards happy to put you there."

Needless to say, the line formed quickly. Even Taegan got in line, though at the very end. He knew he didn't dare refuse. Really, how could he? It would give him away instantly. All he could do was brace his shoulders and prepare to lie to the woman he loved. Her father may have entered a contract, but that didn't mean he would be happy. He refused to tear apart her family.

Kalliope made her way down the line, giving each male only enough time to read the words. If he knew it, it would be clear on his face. Confusion reigned more than anything else. Mel had to admit to knowing the language somewhere but not being sure which it was or what it meant. Unknowingly, that very thing pointed the finger at his elder brother.

All eyes were watching as Kalliope stopped in front of Taegan and held up the watch. She knew damned well what he was thinking and what he might do. She would have done it too. "Do you know this?" she asked him, just as she had asked all the others.

"I don't read Gaelic," he lied.

"I see." She turned, walked two steps away, and smiled. She lifted her chin. "When did I say it was Gaelic, Taegan?" She turned around as everyone backed up quickly with lifted brows. "I believe this is what we call a Freudian Slip." She began to walk toward him slowly, and he took a step back. "If you know it's Gaelic, then you must know what it means."

"What makes you so sure?" He began to feel desperate. He could feel Jiles' intense gaze on the back of his head.

"Well, you see . . ." She pulled out a slip of paper from her pocket. "This was left on my pillow a few days ago, wrapped around a rose." The rose was currently over her ear. "And it's the exact same phrase. And, gee, it's in *your* handwriting. What man would go to the effort of leaving his *lover* a note he didn't understand?"

The entire room started to buzz softly. Kalliope wasn't pulling her punches. Jiles cleared his throat distinctly, and Taegan felt panic bubble up. He turned away and looked at no one. "It's just a coincidence."

He only took two steps before Kalliope snapped, "Taegan Shaughnessy!" He slowly turned back, and she held up the Mask of Illusions. She walked over to him and held the mask up in front of his face. The glamour flickered, but could not hold when the truth was out. Everyone recognized him in that moment.

"There's no such thing as coincidence in 3rd District," Madelyne murmured loudly enough that most heard her in the silence.

Kalliope hurled the mask to the side. Her entire body trembled, her eyes dark with longing. "Tell us what the note means, Taegan."

Very slowly, his hand came up to frame her face. He was trembling just as hard. "'To the one I gave my heart, I give a vow of eternal love.'"

"And will you love me eternally?" She turned her face into his hand helplessly.

He closed his eyes and gave in to the inevitable. He loved her too much to pass up a single chance, no matter how risky. He didn't care about his career or his family. He didn't care about anything except having the woman he loved. "Yes." His eyes opened, fierce and intent. "I've loved you for years. I'll love you until the day I die."

"And I love you." Her lips trembled. "I fell in love with a geeky math teacher, but the bad boy seduced me. I won't have any man but you, Taegan. I love you with all my heart." She looked up at her father. "My contract holds, and you signed it yourself. You can't deny me the right to marry Taegan."

When Taegan looked up at him, Jiles began to smile. "Why would I want to? I think he'll make you a fine husband. Perhaps he can keep you out of trouble!" His eyes twinkled merrily, astonishing everyone except Sullivan and Mara. "Welcome to the family, son. And God help you."

The entire room burst into cheers and applause. Everyone surged forward to congratulate Kalliope and Taegan, but the lights suddenly went out and plunged the room into darkness. By the time someone found the switch, the couple in question had disappeared from the dance floor. All eyes went toward the garden, but with every last Shaughnessy standing in front of the doors, no one was really inclined to go looking. Instead, everyone began to chatter excitedly. It was just like that fascinating family to give everyone another romantic story to talk about!

Kalliope and Taegan ducked swiftly around foliage in the garden until they were away from the doors. "Who killed the lights?" he asked.

"I don't know, but they get a medal!" She let out a little breath and glared at the man she loved. "Damn it, you son-of-a-bitch, you lied!" She leapt at him and beat at his shoulder with her fist. "It almost killed me! If you hadn't slipped up, I don't know what I would have done! Don't ever do that again!"

He caught her close in his arms, a shudder going through his body as he realized she was really his to keep. "No, I won't. I swear." He kissed her hard, then looked at her in puzzlement. "What contract were you referring to anyway?"

"This." She pulled it out of her back pocket and handed it to him. Her stomach fluttered lightly as he put on his glasses, and she decided not to mention that the geek side was very hot, too. He was too arrogant already.

No stranger to contracts, he found what he was looking for quickly. He smiled. That little disclaimer was almost a failsafe since it provided loopholes of all shapes and sizes to ensure the contract was completed correctly. "Of course." He tossed it onto the bench near them and looped his arms lightly around her waist. "You know, I don't exactly recall being asked to marry you," he remarked lightly.

She smiled and linked her hands behind his neck. "Am I supposed to do that?"

"You've been doing such a fine job at playing the prince's role, I figured you would take over that as well." He ran his hands slowly over her back and savored the feel of her under his hands. "You wanted to play this story out to the happily ever after part, didn't you?"

As her smile spread across her face, it could have illuminated the entire District. "Will you marry me, Taegan Shaughnessy, and help me run a business and raise children? I want it all. I want to be a businesswoman, I want to be a wife, and I want to be a mother. I want to be your wife and the mother of your children."

"Yes, Kalliope Tavoularis, I'll marry you." He glanced to the side and wasn't surprised to see a familiar small box sitting on the bench. His faerie godmother was quite good at that sort of thing. "I have something for you," he told her as he picked up the box. "It's been in the family for one hundred and fifty years. It has been passed from firstborn to firstborn."

Lips trembling, she opened the box to see a delicate silver ring with a pearl set in the center. "Oh my god," she managed to say. "It's beautiful."

He removed it from the box and slowly slid it over her finger. "You know what? This ring has never belonged to any couple that didn't love each other for as long a time as they were given together. My family has been blessed, you see."

"I think I'm the one who is blessed!" She threw her arms around him happily and laughed as he spun her in a wild circle.

The contract on the bench glowed softly as the word 'Complete' appeared. Stormy picked it up with another contract she was already carrying and ran gracefully across the garden to leap over the fence without effort.

Kalliope stared at the sight. "That wolf . . . I know that wolf."

"That," he said, his voice warm, "was my faerie godmother. She's been pretty busy lately." He snorted very softly. "God help you, Mel. You're the last one standing."

His lover grinned. "He won't be for long."

CHAPTER TWENTY-THREE

Rhianna studied both completed contracts and added her notes before sliding them into the folder in front of her. The Mask of Illusions sat beside her on a chair. As she closed the folder, she looked across the room. "I gave you a lot more leniency than I'm supposed to. You know that, don't you?"

Audra watched as she slid the folder into a drawer labeled with the Shaughnessy name. She could have described every folder in there by heart. They were all engraved in her memory. "I know," she whispered.

"I can't lend you anymore props," Rhianna warned quietly. "You're going to have to do this one on your own, and it will be the hardest one yet. It's the last one, time is running out, and he's the most stubborn and willful Shaughnessy yet." She reached into her desk and pulled out a fresh contract. "Let's get started, shall we? Oh," she added with a smile, "make a note to remind me to have a nice gift picked out for Taegan and Kalliope."

"I'll add it to my To-Do list," was the waspish response. It wasn't like she had anything else important to do.

Status: File In Progress

Analysis: Pumpkins become coaches and commoners become royalty when love is the magic involved.

Folder Four

MEL

CHAPTER TWENTY-FOUR

If the saying that what goes up must come down was true, then it was also true that something continually going down eventually had to hit rock bottom—especially grades.

Mel was brushing his hair the following Saturday morning when his future sister-in-law stepped into the doorway and struck a dramatic pose. He didn't bat a lash. "Now what do you want?" he asked warily.

Kalliope began a pointed examination of her nails. "You're being summoned, Gibson."

"Must you persist in calling me that?" he muttered.

"Tell me your full name and I'll stop associating you with Hollywood."

"You *wish*."

She just smirked a little. "Suit yourself. But the fact remains that you are indeed being summoned. I do believe that *someone* around here has been watching his grades steadily nosedive. I think you're digging to China in fact."

The hairbrush hit the dresser with a thump as he glared at her. "Must you be so damned smug about this?"

She didn't hesitate. "Yes. And I believe that Taegan sent me to fetch you for the very reason that he knew I wanted to rub this in."

"Oh, god." He covered his face with his hands and scrubbed hard. "Taegan's in there with Dad? Now I know I'm doomed. Kally, for the love of God, have mercy," he pleaded. "Find some graciousness. Tell them I ran away. Or that I'm enlisting in the Navy."

"As cute as you'd be in uniform," she grabbed his wrist and began to drag him down the hall to the stairs, "they ain't going to buy it. Let's go, Shaughnessy. Suck it up and quit whining."

Having heard the commotion, Kienan stuck his head out of his room. "'sup?" he asked with a lifted brow. "You running away with Mel this time? You're not trying to make your way through the Shaughnessys, are you? Not that I don't think you're cute, but Maddie would kill you."

"Maddie scares me," she assured him gravely. "You're safe from my wicked wiles. As it happens, I'm not taking Mel away. I'm taking him to the Office." The intonation of the word was more suited to dramatic music than the cheerful radio playing somewhere downstairs. "Papa's going to chew on Mel."

"Does he need dental floss?" He grinned. "And can I watch?"

Mel flipped his middle finger at his brother and gave a startled yelp as Kalliope continued dragging him down the stairs. His stomach was sinking into his feet and his heart was somewhere in his throat. He knew what he was going to hear and it was the stuff of nightmares. "Where's Stormy when I need her?" he muttered.

She had been hanging around him for the last couple days, keeping him company amid a family full of recently, and happily, engaged or married couples. Ever since Taegan and Kalliope had formally announced their engagement, Stormy had attached herself to Mel.

It was a suspicious pattern. Everyone in the household was *positive* she had been behind the events lately, even though they had no way of proving it. She did things that defied all laws of reality and nature. Taegan seemed to know something but he certainly wasn't telling. It left Mel feeling oddly out of sorts, especially because Stormy had disappeared on Friday, and no one had seen her since. Was he that hard to play matchmaker with?

His thoughts stumbled to a halt as he found himself in front of his father's office. Kalliope threw the door open and shoved him in firmly. Despite being nine inches shorter and considerably smaller, she was terrifyingly strong. He found himself in the office before he could blink. Cheerfully, she called, "One boy sacrifice as ordered! Have fun." She winked at Taegan around Mel's shoulder as she left the room and shut the door.

Sullivan had to smile as he looked at his oldest son. "Taegan, the best thing you've ever done was bring her home."

Taegan laughed. "Believe me, I know." He was well aware that only Kalliope with her fierce and wild spirit would suit him. All the Shaughnessys had wild spirits, and whoever they loved needed to be just as wild. It had been more than a bit of a challenge for their 'guardian angel,' of that he was sure.

She would find Mel the hardest of all. Of all the Shaughnessys, his spirit was the wildest. The veneer of civilization was simply that—a veneer. He walked the line between modern man and ancient man, the edge where modern mentality could not completely dominate a primitive instinct to conquer and defend. It was why he was so much more suited to be the heir to the family company. And it was why he would be immensely difficult to match to any woman. Her spirit would have to be just as wild and primitive.

Mel barely withheld a fidget as his brother studied him. He summoned his best 'devil-may-care' smile and walked over to sit down in the visitor's chair. The hair on the back of his neck lifted as he sensed peril of some kind imminent. "So what holiday are we celebrating with a sacrifice? And why do I feel like I've been called to the principal's office?"

"Mel." Sullivan leaned forward and pushed a stack of papers across the desk. As his son picked them up, he said, "I asked Taegan to pull your records at college. You're scheduled for graduation in May. You didn't tell me your grades were this bad."

A bit weakly, he said, "A 'C' is one hundred in Roman numerals, and a 'D' is fifty, right? Does that make it a little better?" He got a narrow eyed look from matching pairs of golden eyes and gulped slightly. "Sorry."

Taegan put his glasses on and picked up the top page of the transcript. "You're going to hate me," he said calmly, "but I'm acting as a teacher, not a brother. I've been discussing things with Father and we are thinking of holding up your graduation for a year."

Mel leapt out of his chair in shock. "What! You can't do that!"

"We can, and we will," Sullivan said firmly. "Mel, you're not an idiot. None of my children are. But you're not putting any effort into learning. If," he continued in a hard tone, "you want to inherit my company, you will have to prove you actually want it. Otherwise, I may just name Kalliope as my heir."

"Oh great. Pick her over me." It was a matter of principle only because he liked Kalliope and knew she was a hell of a businesswoman. She would be taking over her father's company within a few weeks of her own graduation and marriage. "Come on, how about some familial leniency?"

"You've had too much leniency!" Sullivan leaned back in his chair on a sigh. "Mel, I'm sorry. I've made my mind up."

Before Mel could speak, something distinctly scratched at the glass doors leading into the garden behind Sullivan. All three males turned to see Stormy patiently sitting outside with a sheaf of papers in her mouth. Her tail wagged more with pent up energy than with canine happiness for her owners. In fact, no one in the family believed they owned her. She owned *them*.

"Salvation," Mel muttered.

Sullivan opened the doors with a smile and ruffled Stormy's fur gently. "What did you bring me this time?" He took the document from her and wasn't surprised in the slightest to see that it was a contract. He also wasn't surprised to see where it had come from. "Let's see." He put the contract on the desk and put on his glasses to read better. Taegan leaned over his shoulder.

Stormy pointedly walked over to where Mel was and sat beside him. The message was clear: she was on his side. Taegan looked up from the contract and smiled to himself as he began to turn ideas over in his mind. He had a feeling she didn't know what she was getting herself into.

"Alright, Mel," Sullivan finally said as he sat back. "I have a deal to offer you. I will withhold my threat to prevent your graduation if you can show marked improvement within the next week and begin to bring your grades up. You're in Winter Intercession right now. The classes are very short to begin with. Midterms are Friday. If you can score at least a B in two of your five classes, I will not hold up graduation."

Mel carefully asked, "And where's the catch?"

His brother grinned quickly. "You will be assigned a tutor for your five classes. She normally handles General Education, but she's adept in all fields."

The color drained from his face. "No. Oh no. Please no. Why do you hate me?" he pleaded.

"I don't hate you. She's the best we have. Starting Monday morning you will be reporting to Audra Alexandrios and she will be tutoring you. Since you will need a distraction-free environment, she has agreed to allow you to live with her for the next week."

"Can she do that?"

"You think the council would tell her no?"

He winced. "Guess not. But why does she care?"

"That's for her to decide to tell if she's inclined." Taegan held up the contract where Audra's curiously wild signature was visible. "As you can see, she has already agreed and signed. She's even doing this for no extra pay, Mel."

That she would help out of pity, just made him feel worse. He was getting pity from the beast of the campus. Just *great*.

"It comes down to two choices," Sullivan noted as he signed the contract. "You can either accept a tutor and work to pull your grades up, or you can just let things stand and be held back a year from graduation."

He sighed and slumped over in the chair. He really had no choice. Stormy nudged his hand and he glowered at her. "Couldn't you have found a better solution?" She lifted one canine brow and he sighed as he reached for the contract. It was a blur and he squinted at the bottom.

"Glasses," Sullivan and Taegan both said.

With a mutter, he put them on and brought the page into focus. He hated wearing glasses despite the fact that all the males in the family wore them. They felt too much like a handicap. He picked up a pen and scrawled his name across the bottom of the page. Dropping the pen again, he glowered at his family. "If I get eaten, I'm haunting all of you. No one who lives in 3rd District is normal, not even Madelyne. But she's not a beast like I've heard about Professor Alexandrios!"

Taegan glanced at Stormy, saw her faint smirk, and had to cover a smile. His brother had no idea. So who would their dear tutor be pulling onto his brother's path? It would be interesting to say the least.

Before Mel had even walked into the grounds of the college Monday morning, word had already spread. Students were waiting for him when he locked his car, and they tagged onto his heels with nervous chatter. His head began to be filled with all of their legends and rumors. One thing stood out to all of them as it always had: Audra Alexandrios lived in 3rd District.

Of course he knew that Madelyne was from 3rd District, too, but she seemed normal enough. He knew she had some kind of special gift, though not what it was. He didn't mind; so far, she hadn't turned anyone into any frogs or anything, and if she did decide to do it, the person probably deserved it. And, anyway, all the Shaughnessys themselves had special gifts. His lay in physical abilities. The simple fact was that he was ten times faster, stronger, and more agile than normal humans.

It was harder to hide than his siblings' gifts. He had to keep himself under strict control and withhold himself to what the proper limits of his body should be. As he walked slowly down the hall toward the computer sciences wing where his tutor had her office, he had the sinking feeling that he might need all of his extra skills. The school thrived on outrageous rumors, and try as he might, he was listening.

Professor Alexandrios graded fairly, but was intolerant of stupid mistakes.

She always wore black like she was going to a funeral.

She was tall and towered over people, making them feel like she was going to attack.

She was big and brawny, like a female football player.

She blew ice with her every breath. She could freeze computers by glaring at them.

Her eyes were like a demon's eyes, yellow and predatory.

Her nails were sharp like claws and could likely etch steel.

She always sat in the dark, never in the light. When she was in the light, she was horribly disfigured by a terrifying scar across her face.

She was a vampire. She was a demon. The rumors went on and on until his knees were almost knocking together as he walked. His palms were slick with sweat and his mouth dry. His footsteps echoed loudly down the hall of the sciences wing as he slowly approached where the computer room was situated.

There was no light in the room from the overheads, just the odd blue colored light from the computer across the room. The room was silent and he took a hesitant step inside, his heart thudding in his chest so loudly that it seemed to echo in the room. "Hello?" he whispered. Clearing his throat again, he called, "Hello? Professor Alexandrios? Are you here?"

The overheads came on suddenly and flooded the room with light even as a finger touched his shoulder. Strangling a yelp of fright, he leapt forward and whirled around as a sardonic woman's voice said, "Turning on the light usually helps with locating people, kid."

His heart still beating in his throat, he stared in surprise at the woman standing behind him. If this was Audra Alexandrios, then the rumors were grossly exaggerated. She was definitely wearing black, but it was just a black buttoned shirt and slacks, no more or less than any other teacher. She *was* tall, though, maybe two inches shorter than him and he was six-foot even. She was not, however, big and brawny. She was sleek and well curved, her muscles as nicely defined as her hips and bust.

Her eyes were yellow with a ring of amber around the pupil.

They didn't make him think of demons. They made him think of hawks and eagles and wolves. Of predators who were most beautiful on the hunt. They also held a deep and seemingly bottomless intelligence as if she had seen and done it all. Her nails definitely looked sharp. They were unpainted but well kept. Her hands were strong and somehow very feminine anyway. Her age . . . he couldn't guess at. She looked to be in her twenties, but she had been teaching for at least ten years.

The only rumor that held absolutely true was that her face was indeed marked with a scar. It had healed, thankfully, though it was supposedly recent. It was a shade of color that wasn't quite purple but wasn't quite rose either. It started at the scalp on the right side of her face and then traveled down over her nose and to her chin on the left side. It was at least an inch wide where it crossed over her nose.

Though behind the scar there was a strong hint of immense beauty, the scar somehow marred it entirely. It was impossible to look around the scar to what it so effectively hid. It brought a strong sense of menace to her face that was matched by her icy eyes. She truly looked as if she deserved the nickname the students had given her.

They called her a beast.

She examined her nails while she waited for him to get a hold of himself. She hadn't been able to resist the urge to scare him. He had been so obviously believing every rumor he heard that he had been expecting a scare. She would hate to disappoint him. He had also jumped much higher than anyone else, so that added to her amusement.

She watched him from under her lashes. He was quite typical of his family in many ways. For one thing, he was outrageously beautiful. His hair was only a few shades darker than Kienan's golden brown hair, and they shared the same chocolate colored eyes, but Mel's face was softer around the edges like Aenya's. It gave him an almost sultry appeal.

He was two inches taller than Audra, broad in the shoulder, and lean all over. He only occasionally lifted weights, preferring to get his workouts from playing sports—especially basketball. He had been team captain until his grades nosedived. She had always loved to watch him play. There was something about the way he moved, a sense of wildness, that she had always admired and respected.

Matching him was going to be a *bitch*. She had even seen strong-willed women intimidated by his hidden spirit.

"Professor?"

His voice startled her and she lifted a brow. "Yes?"

"I was wondering where the scar came from. It looks like you barely survived."

At the note of empathy, she felt her back stiffen. She flicked her hair over her shoulder as she went past him. Unbound, her hair fell to her hips in a black curtain. "I'm just a hard tutor to work with," she informed him. She dropped into her chair at the computer. "I often pull grades to see who is failing miserably. Congrats. You're the worst I've seen yet."

His back stiffened. She had no warmth in her at all. He had no idea what Taegan seemed to see in her. He had called her a *friend*. Like she knew what a friend was. In a frigid tone, he said, "I don't need your charity or your sarcasm."

"As a matter of fact, you do. If I kowtowed to you like everyone else, you'd think you could run roughshod over me." She glanced at him over the monitor, the blue light giving a frightening cast to the scar. "You're going to have to learn to not be in charge any longer. You'll do what I say, when I say it."

"You're just a tutor," he sniped. "Why should I bow to you?"

"Because I'm your last hope." He hissed through his teeth, and she smirked. "Don't like the truth? Well, get used to it." She began to type on the keyboard. "Your bags are being delivered to my place as we speak. We'll start with your language skills tonight. What language are you studying?"

"Japanese." The word was nearly a snarl, a distinct brogue beginning to color his voice.

"Good. That's easier for you to pick up after the others you're fluent in. Welcome to the real world, handsome," she added, seeing the boiling temper in his eyes. "Sometimes there are people who really do know more than you."

He seethed and snapped his back teeth together to refrain from the retort bubbling inside him. There was nothing appealing about her. He had begun to wonder for a few moments if her appearance was only an aberration, that there was something underneath that was worth knowing, but now he knew the truth: she really was, without a doubt, an utter beast.

Taegan, leaning outside the door, covered his face with a hand. If they didn't find some sort of harmony, Audra would never be able to help Mel with what he *truly* needed help in. She was his only hope of a happy ending—and he might just be hers.

If they didn't kill each other first.

CHAPTER TWENTY-FIVE

The day went downhill from where it had started. Mel found himself dodging sly comments and rude insinuations the entire day. It was clear that the entire college was taking some rather gleeful delight in his fall from grace. Most had known his grades were bad, but they hadn't known *how* bad until now.

His only reprieve came in the form of his family. Kalliope shared a class with him, and no one was smart enough to cross her. She made a point of sitting next to him, too. She was not yet a Shaughnessy, but she was still family. Everyone knew that the Shaughnessys stuck together.

He only had two classes on Mondays, so he bided his time while he waited for Audra. He was going to follow her back to the 3rd District since he didn't know where she lived. She taught three classes on Mondays, and he found himself hanging out in the parking lot near his car.

The snow laid thinly on the ground. It had finally arrived in New York, and since it was the first fall, it was already melting off. More snow was expected for the next few days, potentially enough to allow the kids in the city to build the snowmen they had been waiting for all year.

He sighed and tilted his head back to look at the sky. Even though it was only just starting to turn into evening, he could see the moon. It was nearly full. As always, the sight of it made something stir inside. Sometimes he snuck out of the house when the moon was full and let himself run across the acreage he lived on. He had never told anyone, though he was fairly sure that Sullivan had seen him once or twice.

The sensation of trouble caused the hair on his neck to stir and warned him he was no longer alone long before he heard the sound of boots crunching ice. His eyes slanted to the side to see three other young men swaggering toward him. All wore the familiar jersey of the basketball team.

If the smirks were any indication, they had also heard about what was going on. The one walking in the front was the ringleader. He had become team captain after Mel dropped out, but it was known around campus that he simply wasn't as good. When Mel had dropped out, he had never lost a game. Ever since joining the team, Steve hadn't *won* a game.

Steve sauntered forward with a nasty smirk. "So I heard this interesting rumor." His friends snickered and he grinned at them. It felt good to finally have one up on Mel.

"I'm sure you did." Mel kept his voice even with effort. "Rumors fly around this school faster than they do around the White House. Which ones are you referring to?"

"Oh, just an interesting story about a guy whose grades are so bad that he not only got kicked off the team, but his daddy might hold back his graduation."

Anger began a slow boil inside. "Actually," he countered pleasantly, "I wasn't kicked off the team. I dropped willingly. The coach was willing to overlook my bad grades because he knew the guy who would take my place wasn't half as good as I am." He paused before adding smoothly, "And it looks like he was right. How many games you won, Rutabaga?"

"Rudaveg!" Steve's eyes narrowed. "None of your business, Shaughnessy. You think you're hot shit because your daddy runs a big corporation and you're the little prince set to inherit. I doubt you could survive in the *real* world."

"Which world is that?" He crossed his arms. "Is that the world where I bully and terrorize other people to make myself feel better? Or the world where the only reason I don't have five DUIs on my record is because my daddy is a policeman? Or is it the world where my casual disregard for women has left at least two girls wondering if they're pregnant . . . or worse?"

Steve grabbed him by the collar of his jacket and his face twisted with a snarl. "You don't know shit about shit!"

Mel grabbed his hand and jerked it off his jacket without effort. He gave him a shove that, while appearing casual, sent the other male stumbling back several steps. "It's only fair," he retorted, his body tensed slightly, "as your breath smells like shit."

Steve lunged forward, fist raised, and Mel braced to duck. To his surprise, Steve's arm was suddenly thrown to the side, and his forward momentum had him hurtling onto the ground where he rolled a few feet before stopping. As his friends knelt beside him, Steve sat up holding his hand. "What the hell! Something hit my hand and numbed it!" It was already swelling up. He looked around swiftly and saw an innocuous rock sitting nearby. It hadn't been there before. "That hit me!"

"Be glad it only hit a nerve and not a bone."

The voice was so frigid and cold that the snow seemed to solidify further, defying the sun itself. Mel's eyes widened slightly and he turned to see Audra standing nearby with one hand propped on her hip. The other hand held another rock and she was lightly tossing it up and down. Her eyes looked as cold as her voice sounded.

Steve went several different shades of white before settling on a sickly pallor. "P-professor Alexandrios!" He scrambled to his feet as quickly as he could. "W-we were just talking. Right, Mel?"

"I had no idea you did your talking with your fists," Mel retorted. He linked his hands behind his head. Oddly, against all reason, he felt safe with Audra there.

"You . . . !" He broke off as Audra moved a step closer. He was taller and larger but there was no one in the world who terrified him more. His eyes fixed onto the scar on her face and couldn't tear free. His throat worked, but he couldn't swallow past the sawdust in his mouth. His heart pounded so hard it should have burst.

"I believe team rules indicate that brawling is just as bad as low grades." Her hair fluttered into her face as a wind blew softly. "Consider it part of my generous soul that I don't report you to the coach." Her eyes hardened. "Get lost."

The three males ran off so fast that they slipped and tripped over the snow as they scrambled to get out of the parking lot and to safety.

"Wow." Mel blew out a hard breath. "Hey, professor . . ."

"Save it. I don't need thanks, and I don't care if you thought you had it handled. They're assholes and I have a personal dislike of assholes." She turned and began walking across the lot toward where she had parked her black motorcycle. "Follow me, and don't get lost. I won't go looking for you."

Seething and snapping internally, he got into his car. It wasn't hard to keep her in sight as she was careful not to navigate in a way he couldn't follow. He didn't know if she simply didn't have a preference for splitting lanes of traffic or if she was conscious of him following her. Knowing her, it was probably the former. She had made her contempt quite clear.

Still, he was trying to look on the bright side. He was going to be staying in the 3rd District. There was just something about the place for him. No matter how different he felt from the rest of the world, sometimes, when he was in the District, he felt like he was home. He felt comfortable, normal even. If that was part of the magic, then he was a believer. If a real faerie had come and knocked on his window, he wouldn't have batted a single lash.

They said that no one who was born in 3rd District was normal. Audra lived there, certainly, but that didn't mean she had been born there. He wouldn't have been too surprised though. Like she could be considered normal!

But he *was* surprised when he saw where he was following her. The one residential area of 3rd District was, by most other standards, little more than a slum. The streets looked as if they needed repair and so did the buildings. An odd gloom hovered over the area as if the very air felt the weight of sadness and grief.

Her home was no more than a small two-story building. The driveway was only just big enough for her bike and Mel's car. Long before he had parked and turned off the engine, she had parked her bike and gotten off. And, before his fascinated gaze, he watched as a swarm of elementary school-aged children rushed toward her happily. Slowly, he got out of his car, something moving deep inside his heart.

She was smiling. He couldn't catch her words, but her voice sounded warm and gentle. Her hands were gentle as she ruffled hair. The love she had for the children came across clearly, and the children loved her just as visibly. There was no fear on their faces. No revulsion. Just a strong hero worship and acceptance of her for what she was.

Guilt filled him. He had to have misjudged her. No one who was truly nasty and cold to their core could have ever been so truly kind with children. Hating himself for judging on appearances, he shut his car door. He instantly found himself the recipient of many fascinated stares. "Hi. I'm Mel."

Audra murmured something low, and the kids ran off giggling. When she straightened and looked at Mel, however, her gaze had chilled once more. She turned and went up to the front door without a word.

He followed her and looked around with intense curiosity. It wasn't really a house. It was something that had been turned into one. It didn't look as if it had been renovated in at least one hundred years. All of the structure retained its original construction. As he stepped inside and saw his suitcases, he felt his stomach clench with more guilt. "Professor . . . I want to apologize."

"Ah, the prince speaks." She kicked the door shut and took off her jacket. She tossed it over the edge of a rickety looking banister that led upstairs. "Don't bother apologizing to a peasant, your majesty. I choose to live here willingly. The kids are orphans. I protect them from predators and tutor them so that they do not have to go to school where no one will understand them." As she went into the kitchen, she added, "Call me Audra, will you? We're not at school, and I loathe formality."

Feeling a little like he had missed something, he followed her. "Where are you from anyway?"

Her lips quirked. "Let's call it another time and leave it there." She poured a cup of cold coffee and stuck it in the microwave. "Take your bags upstairs. There's a guest room at the end of the hall. Get yourself comfortable, and we'll get down to business. This isn't a vacation, kid."

He felt his back stiffen slightly. Her kindness was clearly only for children. "Yes'm." The word was as clipped as a cold wind. He turned sharply and grabbed his bags to haul them upstairs. He cursed softly under his breath the entire way. Either he was more spoiled than he thought, or she had a serious personality problem.

Saying the guest room was at the end of the hall upstairs was a bit misleading. There wasn't much of a hall and it only had three doors. One was shut tightly and he assumed it was Audra's room. The second door led into a decent sized bathroom. The third door opened into an unoccupied bedroom.

When he walked inside, he saw it was quite sparse in decor; there was only a queen-sized bed, a dresser, a lamp, and a chair near the window. There was an exceptionally tiny closet as well. It didn't even have a door.

He began the task of unpacking and putting things away and hanging up things that needed to be hung. It was a welcome diversion that helped get his mind off his current situation and the maddening female downstairs that seemed to have a talent for getting under his skin.

When he opened a small drawer, he unexpectedly discovered a small painting. It looked like an old-fashioned family portrait from the mid to late 1800s, but the people in it told him it was probably just a commission.

It was a family portrait of what looked like seven siblings. One of them was Audra and she was distinctly the oldest. He couldn't guess how old she was in the portrait, but she was laughing and smiling. Several kids were climbing over her. A slender boy with eyes that seemed to be the same striking color as hers was caught in the circle of her arms. Mel found himself grinning as he looked at the joy in everyone's faces. It reminded him of his family. This was a family that would yell at each other and then turn around and play cards to decide who was right.

His smile slowly faded as he put down the picture. A little chill touched his skin. Something must have happened. She had given no indication that she had a family, and she lived alone. What had happened to turn such a vibrant woman into such a cold and remote one? He knew he couldn't ask. She would never answer. Still, it shifted his mind, yet again, about her. It seemed to have been shifting all day.

He changed into jeans and a sweatshirt and headed down the stairs slowly, his Japanese language book under his arm. He felt as if nothing was real anymore. In fact, he had a feeling he had left reality behind when he had entered the District.

Audra was waiting in the living room in front of a coffee table. Books and papers spread in front of her. When she sensed his presence, she said fluently, "*Konban'wa.*"

He almost dropped his books. She had no accent. She spoke Japanese as if she had been speaking it from birth. Her English was also without accent, and it was impossible to determine which she had been born speaking. He couldn't even put his finger on her ethnicity to begin with. "You're bilingual?"

"Multi," she corrected. "Like your brother, I speak several languages. I picked up Japanese a few years ago." It had been, precisely, fifty years since she had met a Japanese exchange student after World War II and been fascinated enough to learn the language. That wasn't something she could drop in casual conversation, though. "Have a seat."

He walked over to sit down beside her. When he did, he felt something quiver inside his chest. She seemed . . . smaller when he was up close. Not small, exactly, but he definitely felt bigger. It was a curious feeling. "You surprised me," he admitted. "You're really good with kids. Do you have siblings?"

He watched her face intently and saw the flash of ripe pain that flickered through her eyes. It was like seeing a glimpse of hell before it disappeared. She gave him a cool and steady look. "No." She turned back to the book and flipped it open. "Let's start here. Let's see what you've got down."

He proceeded to show her. His basic grasp of the language was strong, and his accent was as good as it was going to get for the time being. His pronunciation was actually quite strong, and he didn't mangle the trickier aspects. His vocabulary was minimal, but that could only come with practice. His true hang up, as it was with most learning the language, was grammar.

As she began to write out the various tenses and the way verbs used them, she asked, "Out of curiosity, what brought on the urge to learn *Nihon'go*?"

He sighed as he rubbed the back of his neck. "Well, I already know Spanish and French. Kally is trying to teach me Greek. The Shaughnessy Corp. has some strong connections with a company in Japan, and I don't want to always rely on a translator. It's not fair to make them learn my language if I can't learn theirs."

"You really want to take over the kingdom, huh?"

"Yeah." He found a smile. "Growing up, I was a little resentful of Taegan that he was the heir apparent. I knew he didn't want it, but he went along with things. When he became a legal adult and suddenly switched to teaching, I was so happy. For him and for me. I walked right into Dad's office, sat down, and told him that I wanted to take his place."

"You were only seventeen," she noted. "And you were sure?" The question wasn't just for form, though she suspected the answer. She had never been able to read him the way she read the others. He was amazingly resistant to compulsion abilities as well.

"I was definitely sure."

"Hmm." She slid the paper in front of him. "Alright, let's start here. You change verb endings to denote tense . . ."

As she talked, she made notes. It wasn't until she realized that he was too quiet that she knew something was off. She tossed her pencil down in annoyance as she looked at him. He was dead asleep on top of his books, his head on his arms like a child.

"If you keep falling asleep in class, I can see why you're flunking!" More disgruntled than genuinely annoyed, she leaned closer to take his shoulder and give him a shake. He couldn't sleep his way to a good grade.

Her hand stopped in the air as she looked at him. The lamplight slanted through his brown hair and turned it to the color of dark honey. It was soft and vibrant, as wild as its owner. A few locks tumbled into his eyes and more fell over his cheek. His skin was still lightly tanned from summer and his lips were sculpted in a way designed to devastate the feminine pulse rate. He was, without question, the most beautiful male she had seen in her long life.

Without thinking about it, she tenderly brushed his hair back from his face and tucked it behind his ear. Her lips curved as she saw the small earring he wore. It was such a tiny symbol of rebellion, but it spoke volumes about his personality. Even in his sleep, perhaps especially then, there was a hint of danger in him that was deeply seductive. He was a predator, a hunter, and that quality was magnetic to her.

Shock froze her still. She was attracted to him. No, attraction was too mild a word. As she looked at him, she was consumed with a steadily growing hunger to taste his stubborn lips and get her hands in the pelt he called hair. She wanted his hands on her, to savor the little calluses that proved he worked hard and wasn't afraid to get dirty.

She had always cared for the Shaughnessy family, but he was different. Terrified of him and herself, she yanked her hand back and got to her feet quickly. This was *bad*. She couldn't get involved, not like this. It could destroy her. Distance. She needed distance. She scrawled a note on the paper and then rushed to the front door. She ran out into the moonlight . . . and seemed to disappear.

The only reason he woke was because the door slammed. He leapt to his feet with a curse. "I'm so sorry, Audra!" he blurted quickly. He looked around but she was nowhere in sight and the house felt empty. He looked down at the table and saw the note; it was in Japanese, unfortunately. He frowned and crouched to squint at it. It was gibberish at first but as he broke down the structure and words, he realized it said she would be back later. With a sigh, he began to wander slowly through the house. He hoped he hadn't insulted her too badly.

The first floor was no bigger than the second. It had a kitchen, a small dining room currently being used to hold storage, and the living room. Something tugged at him, and he found himself going upstairs. He hesitated outside her door before slowly opening it and walking inside.

Sensitivity to emotions was more Taegan's forte than his, but as soon as he walked into the room, he felt the sadness buried in the walls. He could hear a cry in the back of his mind, a sense of despair and terror that rose in the air like a wail or a scream. It made the hair on his arms stand up.

The room looked barely lived in as if she spent little time there. There was even a bit of dust sitting on the dresser undisturbed. The light from the moon was strong enough to illuminate several details such as the battered wood floors, but it was the walls that truly caught his attention.

He walked closer and ran his fingers lightly over the marks he could see. It felt like a claw had ripped through the wall and someone had tried to plaster and paint over it. As his eyes adjusted to the gloom, he saw marks all over the room. His throat closed with rising pain. It looked . . . it looked like a war had been fought.

Deeply disturbed, he backed out of the room and shut the door. How could she bear to sleep in there? He couldn't bear walking in there.

The house was still empty, and he could feel it. Needing fresh air, he headed back downstairs to pull on shoes and a jacket. He opened the front door and stepped outside, but came to a stop as he saw Stormy sitting on the sidewalk watching him. She had been running hard if the little leaves stuck to her fur were any clue.

He sat down on the front step and held out a hand. She immediately came over and licked his fingers gently. He began to run his hands gently over her fur and removed all the leaves and twigs. "Played hard, huh?" he asked her softly. "I know that feeling. I do that sometimes, too. Just go running wildly." He glanced up at the sky. "When the moon is full, we can go running together."

She rested her head on his lap and he gently stroked her fur. He felt comforted by her presence. He always had been. In some ways he had been jealous of her attention to his siblings. He had always wished she belonged to him alone.

Sighing, he looked at the clouds drifting across the sky. "I royally screwed that one up." His smile filled with self-disrespect. "I let myself believe rumor and then let my first impressions cloud me. I know she was deliberately feeding them, but I really should have known better. Now she's pissed at me." He laughed softly. "She spends a lot of time pissed at people, I think."

He leaned his head back against the door, oddly comfortable to be sitting outside in the night with a wolf at his side. "She's not really all that bad." When Stormy lifted her head in surprise, he rubbed her ears soothingly. "Really, she's not. Oh she's prickly as hell, rude, and pretty darn mean when inclined, but she's *brilliant*. The kids love her, and she loves them so much. I think she's just been alone for too long. When I saw the pain in her eyes when I asked about her family . . . I think that's what clued me in. Maybe she just needs a friend."

He straightened with a wry laugh. "As if she'd let me try! I think I gave her just as bad an impression as she gave me. She thinks I'm a spoiled brat, just like everyone else does. And maybe I am a little spoiled. I grew up without a need for anything, and I've always had servants."

He fell quiet for a moment. "I don't take it for granted. I know how to cook and clean. We all do. If something ever happened and we found ourselves without means, we'd know how to survive. Hell, I could repair cars for a living. I'm good at it. Hiro swears that his bike has never run better." There was pride in his voice for a moment. "I guess it was the one class I really paid attention to."

Stormy cocked her head and there seemed to be a question in her eyes. He tilted his head slightly in response. "I don't hate school. Not really. I just have trouble learning from lecture. I listen and I listen but it never seems to stay in place. If I take notes, it helps a little, but if I lose my notes, I'm screwed. I need hands-on experiences. I kicked ass in Science because it was all about lab work.

"It's like . . . everything gets all crammed in my head and dissolves. It's like because I have so many physical gifts, I didn't get any mental ones. Well, I guess." He frowned. "There are times when I've concentrated hard and made people believe me, but I don't think it's the same thing. I just wish there was someone I could explain this stuff to." She woofed softly and he smiled as he ruffled her fur. "Well, other than you. You're the best listener around, but you can't fix these problems. Maybe you can set me up with a nice bookworm," his voice warmed, "and she can teach me how to study better."

He got to his feet and glanced around, missing the brief flash of jealousy that flickered across her eyes. She was beginning to have deep suspicions about Mel Shaughnessy. All the little quirks that made him difficult to match were beginning to paint a familiar picture. Time would tell if she was right. If she was, it would to be harder than she thought to match him . . . especially when the thought of handing him over to another female seemed distasteful suddenly.

He sighed and drew her attention again. "I guess Audra isn't going to be back for a while. I *really* pissed her off. I hope she lets me apologize. Oh well, since she's not here, she can't argue if I have company over." He opened the door and gave a courtly bow. "After you, my lady."

Agreeably, she walked into the house and followed him as he headed into the living room. She watched as he put away the books and stacked the papers neatly. She wasn't surprised; he and his brothers were terribly meticulous about being organized. Aenya was the messy one in the household.

There was no predicting his actions ahead of time. He changed direction too easily. She followed him curiously as he headed upstairs. She had no idea what bedtime habits he had. She had never followed him into his room before. At first she had been focused on his siblings, and lately she had been trying to get the contract started. And, too, maybe she had been subconsciously wary of the intimacy of sleeping on his bed—in any form.

It was, therefore, with fascinated delight that she sat in the doorway and watched as he stripped down to his shorts. She wasn't going to argue with her current form when it gave her such a delightful free admission to view a body like his. He was strong and muscular from head to heels, sleek and so masculine that he would trip the signals of anyone with compatible hormones. Even in her current body, she felt her mouth go slightly dry, her heart beginning to skip a beat. He reminded her of a male wolf. She hadn't seen a body like that in a long time, but she had never forgotten.

He pulled on pajamas, blissfully unaware of her thoughts, then climbed into bed. He spotted her hesitating in the doorway and smiled suddenly. It was a slow and devastating curve of his lips, self-assured, and confident. It was a smile well designed by nature to serve as a lure to a mate, and he used it without compunction or knowledge of what it truly was meant to do.

She had always called it the Shaughnessy smile because it had been wielded by all men of the bloodline for as far back as she remembered. She just hadn't realized how lethal it could be when it got turned on a woman directly. She was not immune to it herself, not when it came from Mel. She padded across the room and jumped up to lay beside him.

He was holding a book, and she nudged at the glasses laying on the covers. He put them on with a wry smile for his own vanity. She genuinely had no idea why he was vain about them. They did many amazing things to an already stunning appearance.

She remained by his side until he finally fell asleep. He did so sitting up, his glasses sliding down his nose, and the book on his chest. She didn't want to wake him, so she softly slipped from the bed and left the room.

When Audra opened the door an hour later, he hadn't moved. She sighed wryly and walked soundlessly across the room to remove the book from his hands. She carefully removed his glasses as well and placed both items on the dresser. Then, gently, she eased him down so he was sleeping properly. She sat beside him for a moment and studied his face.

A friend. She lifted a hand and ran a finger softly down his cheek. She was afraid to let him try. Afraid to let him even closer. Already she could feel the haunting lure that was his eerie wolf-like persona and traits.

She was afraid she was falling in love with him herself, and that would only lead to tragedy for both of them.

CHAPTER TWENTY-SIX

Mel stumbled downstairs the next morning to the smell of bacon and pancakes. When he peered into the kitchen, it was to find Audra competently assembling two plates of breakfast. He sat down at the counter warily, not sure what to say or think. He had woken up lying down and distinctly remembered falling asleep while reading.

She put a plate in front of him and slid him a cup of coffee. "It's edible," she assured him. "The coffee might be strong, though. I prefer it that way."

He took a cautious sip but found nothing wrong with the taste. "Actually, this is the way I prefer my coffee." He picked up the syrup and poured lavishly over the fluffy cakes. "And this smells incredible."

She sat down at the counter across from him with her own breakfast and was just as generous with the syrup. "I figured that if I had to eat my own cooking, it might as well taste good." She bit into the bacon happily. She ate plenty of vegetables and grains, but she preferred meat to anything else. "Sleep well?"

"Yeah." He didn't bother to ask. She would never answer. Instead, he said carefully, "If I wanted to apologize, would you be willing to listen? I was an idiot. I've seen how stupid rumors get, but I still believed."

She said nothing for many moments. He wanted to be her friend. It couldn't hurt to try. Just as carefully, she said, "Mel, I'm a loner. I have been a long time. I'm not always good with people. Any blame also lies with me. I deliberately let you believe everything you heard. It seemed . . . safer."

"So, then." He offered a hand. "Let's start again. I won't act quite so spoiled, and you won't treat me like I'm a viral disease of some kind." Very slowly, as if it was foreign to her, she put her hand in his. He closed his fingers around hers and smiled. "There. Fresh start. Okay?"

"Okay." She slipped her hand free and picked up her fork. "Eat your breakfast," she ordered.

"Yes'm." Oddly, this time he didn't feel at all offended by her manner. He was starting to look under the surface, and what he was beginning to see slowly grew more and more intriguing.

His upbeat mood lasted until he got to school and parked on campus. From the minute he left his car, he found himself inundated with catcalls and whistles. Leering comments and sly looks were thrown at him the entire way to class. Some were subtle. Others were downright rude.

It didn't help any that when he walked away from his backpack for a second, he came back to a note pinned to it. The note read clearly *Beauty and the Beast* and there was a very disgusting, very lewd picture accompanying it. He threw it away instantly. Pride made his back straight as he walked, but embarrassment made his stomach churn.

Class wasn't even a reprieve. Students took turns kicking his chair or accidentally dropping more notes on his desk. He didn't bother to open any of them. He considered reporting the events, but he wasn't entirely sure the school could or would do anything. And, if he told, then Taegan would find out and he would probably get himself in trouble again.

It was one of the most confusing mornings he had ever experienced. By the time lunch came, he was left at a loss. The culmination of the day occurred when he sat down at a table and everyone else stood up and walked away. What the *hell* was going on this time? Was this just because he needed a tutor?

Kalliope suddenly sat down beside him with her lunch tray. "Assholes," she announced. She took a big bite of her pizza. "I'll explain after I eat. I'm starving."

"Me too." Madelyne sat down across from her with her own lunch, her violet eyes sparkling. "I usually am about this time of day."

"Well, you're eating for two." Kienan sat down beside her and dug into the paper sack he carried. "What'd you make anyway?" His voice was muffled as he stuck his head in the bag. "Smells like pasta."

"Get out of there," Kalliope scolded.

"You're not my mother," he muttered.

"No, I'm your new big sister. It's far worse and scarier." She grinned evilly. "You've never had one of those before. Maddie, better protect him or I'll run him ragged."

Mel felt the tension in his shoulders ease and he smiled as he listened to their bickering. He knew what they were doing. They were firmly aligning themselves on his side and showing the entire school that they would back him without hesitation. If you messed with one, you messed with all of them.

And because it was obvious they knew what was in the air, he leaned on the table and asked quietly, "Would someone tell me what's going on? Is this just because of my grades?"

His siblings exchanged a quick look. Kalliope, being the bluntest, finally cleared her throat delicately. "Well, as we all know, rumors fly around this school at light speed in a way NASA really should harness. And the newest rumor, currently ignored by teachers, FYI, is that you and Professor Alexandrios are lovers."

He choked on the water he had just taken a sip of. "What!" He stared at his sister-in-law as if she had grown another head. "Where did *that* come from?! She's just my tutor! We only met yesterday!"

"I did a little digging," Kienan admitted. "And I think the rumors originated with Steve Rudaveg. He's made no secret of the fact that he's pissed at Professor Alexandrios. Word is spreading that she stopped him from attacking you, and she never once laid a hand on him."

"It's like a puppy barking at a wolf," Madelyne muttered under her breath. "She'll eat him for lunch!"

"No kidding!" Anger filled Mel's eyes. "Guess that explains the comments all morning. I wouldn't repeat them to my brothers, let alone my sisters." He blew out a long breath. "Crap. Well, let him blow hot air. It'll all go away. No one would dare mess with Audra. She'd scare them silly."

Kalliope laughed. "Yes, she would!" She smiled and rested her chin on her hands. "So is Stormy still hanging around you? We haven't seen her lately."

"Actually," he frowned slightly, "I haven't seen her that often lately, either. But she did show up last night and hung around outside with me."

As casually as he could, Kienan asked, "Just you two? No one else showed up?"

"No one." Mel smiled wryly. "I know what you're implying, but she doesn't seem to be doing anything to try and introduce me to someone special. She's just there, keeping me company." His smile turned a little sheepish. "Funny as it is . . . I don't feel neglected. Her company is enough for me, I guess."

Something stirred inside Madelyne's eyes. Something that looked suspiciously like fear. Kienan, sharply attuned to his family let alone to his wife, turned toward her and his eyes darkened. "Maddie?" He put one hand on the back of her neck. His other hand rested protectively over her lower belly where their child slept. "What's wrong?"

"Nothing." She brushed a kiss over his lips and shrugged off his hands as she got to her feet. "I have someone I need to go talk to." She scooped up her backpack and hurried out of the cafeteria, her long hair fluttering behind her. She was terrified, her heart freezing inside her chest as she ran across to the computer sciences area.

"Audra!" She didn't wait for acknowledgement before opening the door to her friend's office and walking in. "What are you waiting for?" she demanded.

Audra looked up from her computer and scowled fiercely. "Do you think I'm enjoying this?" she snapped back. "This is harder than it ever was before?"

"Why?" Madelyne challenged. "Because it's the last? You should be scared! *I'm* scared! I don't want to lose someone else I love!" She took a quick breath and then threw out a hand as the room whirled on its axis. Audra promptly appeared at her side and gently eased her into a chair. "Damn it," she muttered. "Don't tell the family!"

A smile softened Audra's face as she gently touched Madelyne's stomach. "The stronger the will of the child, the more it affects the mother," she offered softly. "That's what we always said in my clan." Her nose flared slightly as she analyzed Madelyne's scent. "And I think you should be on your guard. It's a boy."

"I can't keep up with one of Kienan, let alone two!" The words were more exasperated than despairing. She sobered and covered Audra's hands with hers. "Why, Audra? Why is this one so much harder? You've always been so quick and sure, arranging scenarios so your chosen couple meets." She searched her friend's eyes intently, looking for a sign her suspicions were right.

"Mel is different." Audra got to her feet and walked over to the window. "Normally it's easy. I memorize the scent of my Shaughnessy. I search the city for his or her perfect match. When I find it, I either take advantage of current situations or arrange them to suit my needs." Her eyes closed. "I've been over this city thousands of times. I can't match Mel. He's so unique, so powerful. If his mate existed, then she should be here. It's simply how it is. If his scent is producing the call to a mate—and it is—then his mate is here."

Madelyne watched her for long moments. Then, softly, "And what about you? What about your scent?"

She laughed sadly. "Don't pin hopes on me for cubs to spoil, Maddie." She closed her eyes and pressed her forehead against the cold window glass. "As long as you are alive, I don't mind. When I'm gone, you'll be here with Kienan. To me that is everything. I'd give my life for any of you in an instant. It's the least of what I owe."

"You saved my life!" Madelyne shouted as she leapt to her feet. "You saved Kienan's life! And though we didn't know it then, you saved our unborn child! You almost *died* for us, Audra! I don't want you to die! The answer is there in front of you but you're too stubborn to see it!"

As she whirled and fled from the office, the door shutting wildly behind her, Audra slowly sat down once more. She tried to bring the monitor into focus but she was already thinking of her next course of action. She was well aware of the rumors around campus and she was equally aware of the source. She would be handling the problem without any effort; she had dealt with far more complex and powerful minds than Steve Rudaveg.

Mel had been hurt over the rumors. She had been unobtrusively watching him all day. He had lifted his chin and straightened his back with a warrior's pride, but she knew him well enough to see the pain underneath. It made fury boil in her heart. *No one* EVER hurt her family, especially not Mel.

She scowled at herself at the direction of her thoughts. She was there to take care of the Shaughnessys. She had loved all of them the same. Her feelings for Mel were no different than her feelings for Aenya or Sullivan.

Yet, as she lifted her hand, she was haunted by the memory of his skin and hair and how he had looked in the lamplight. She remembered his wild spirit and nearly wolf-like abilities. And she remembered a body that had stirred her own, raising desires stronger than she had ever before felt in her life. "Damn it," she whispered.

Classes were done. She turned off her computer and got to her feet. She had time before the end of the day. An elementary school sat around the corner, and the kids often came from it to play on the college campus where the snow always took longer to melt off. Even as other parts of the city looked clean, the college was still a winter wonderland.

What she needed was some time with some people who looked at her and saw inside. Both before and after the scar, children had always seen her as she was. They had never been afraid, never hesitated to show her they loved her. It was as if they knew she loved children more than she loved anything else.

As she walked toward the area where she could hear the kids playing, she let herself remember a time when she had always had children around. She had been young and whole, her existence bright. She had been looking at a future where she could hold a child of her own, to hear laughter around every corner.

The laughter had turned to screams. Blood had stained the snow. And her future had changed for all time. There would be no children of her own. No one to stand by her side. No one left to run across the land at midnight under a full moon. She was alone. She closed her eyes and pushed it aside as she went around a corner. It wasn't worth thinking about.

She got an unexpected reprieve from her thoughts in the shape of an immense snowball smacking her directly in the face. It sent her back a step with a curse and she swiped at her eyes, well aware of the giggling of kids. When she could see again, it was to immediately spot Mel standing with a bunch of kids, a look of mingled shock and horror in his eyes. "Mel . . ." she said warningly.

He coughed. "I was . . . well. The kids. Wanted to see if I could shoot a snowball like a basketball. I wasn't expecting you." He coughed again and this time it was clear that he was struggling against laughter. "Sorry."

She shook her hair vigorously to remove the remaining snow. It didn't help. A soccer ball struck the side of the building and sent more snow tumbling off the roof and onto her head. With a resigned sigh, she watched the kids and Mel laugh until they were holding their stomachs.

Her heart clenched as she listened to Mel. His laughter was . . . beautiful. Like his temper, his laughter carried the flavor of his Irish heritage, the brogue velvety on her sensitive ears. Striving for neutral territory, she bent and scooped up a snowball. He wanted friendship. It was worth trying.

He straightened with the intent of trying to apologize again, but a snowball smacked directly into his nose. The kids cheered. Pointedly, he wiped the snow from his face. His smile was as challenging as Audra's. "This means war, you know."

The kids were more than happy to split up between the two adults. Forts were built and lines were drawn. The kids could wildly chuck snowballs with more enthusiasm than aim. Audra and Mel had specialties. Mel could send a snowball airborne and bomb someone. Audra was a big league pitcher, sneaking out shots so fast that no one saw them coming. It wasn't long before they were the only two left standing.

Relying on her natural speed, she began to pummel him mercilessly until he lost his balance and fell into a snow bank. While the children cheered loudly, she gave a quick nod of satisfaction. "You're no angel, but you make a decent impression of one." She winked at the kids and sent them off into fits of the giggles.

A teacher began to wave for attention and the kids ran off happily. Mel managed to get to his feet and shot Audra a wicked grin. "You'd better run, teach, or I'll get you back so fast."

She knew she could outrun him, but the idea of a chase warmed her blood and stirred deep-seated instincts. "Try it," she challenged. She turned and took off running into the trees nearby, so fast and agile that her feet barely touched the snow.

Something also stirred inside him. In a blink he was chasing after her, without hesitation unleashing his natural speed and agility. A snowball was in his hand. He got a glimpse of her as she ducked around a large pine, and he hurled the snowball. She dodged gracefully, her yellow eyes alight. "Too slow," she taunted. As she ducked into the trees again, her laughter rose up and broke free.

The sound curled around him and raked at him with velvet claws. It lured and beckoned, an ancient call that he couldn't recognize consciously, but he felt it vibrate through his subconscious. The snowball fight was forgotten as he went after her again. This time it was something more. The change from playful to predator was instantaneous.

She didn't realize what had happened until she found herself pausing by a tree to determine his location. Quite suddenly, she realized he was behind her. His body barely brushed against hers, and his heat and scent seemed to sear into her nerves. His fingers brushed the nape of her neck so softly she almost didn't feel it. The velvety threat only belatedly registered. She immediately forgot the innocent game. She darted away from him agilely and threw a taunting look over her shoulder. Her body was heating, her heart pounding.

The game continued. She would hide, and he would find her. Their bodies would brush. His fingers might skim her nape, the touch as sensual as it was threatening. She would deliberately leave herself open just long enough for him to get close, and then she would dance out of reach with a ripple of laughter.

It wasn't until she heard a soft rumble from his chest one of the times she got away that she finally realized what had happened. Without thinking about it, they had fallen into the mating hunt of a werewolf. She stopped in shock, her eyes widening as she felt the wild beat of hunger in her blood. Not only had he responded *instantly* to the chase, he was more than keeping up. With all the primitive dominance of an alpha male, he was *letting* her escape his grip just to prolong the chase.

He pounced on her from the shadows almost before she realized he was there. He caught her around the waist and tumbled her down onto the snow. She immediately tried to throw him off, but he flipped her over again and pinned her under his heavier weight. His hands caught her wrists and kept her held submissively beneath him. "Gotcha!" The word was almost a breathless growl.

Their eyes met and locked. She tested his grip and found it unbreakable. Despite the vulnerable position, she felt safer than she ever had in her life. Her heart beat hard, and her pulse throbbed in her neck visibly. The desire in his eyes as he gazed at her had hot fists of lust curling inside her body. She could feel the heated urgency of his arousal pressed against her. For wolves, the chase itself was an act of desire. Both had responded with all the savagery of those with wolf spirits.

But was it *her* that he wanted? She couldn't tell. She searched his eyes for any sign that he knew who it was he held. Would any woman have triggered his deeper instincts? She was torn between hunger for him to want her and for him to let her go. Alpha to alpha, he called to her in every way.

He stared down at her, his eyes raking hotly over her face. Halfway through the chase he had become conscious of what was happening, and he had let it go on. When she had danced away from him one of those times, he had looked into her and seen something he wanted. He still saw it. The scar seemed invisible to his eyes now. He wanted her more than he had ever wanted any woman in his life. His wildness commanded him, and she was just as wild.

As his lips lowered and the tip of his tongue traced the scar, her entire body shuddered with raw pleasure. To lick a wound was the act of a mated wolf. *He wasn't her mate*! Her mind insisted it even as her body and soul responded with eagerness to the tiny touches of his tongue. His mouth came to settle over hers and her mind went away entirely.

She arched her body to press further against his. Her mouth opened under his demandingly to accept the aggressive thrust of his tongue. His powerful shoulders trembled even as her body did, sparks leaping between them with such fury that their hair crackled in the static.

Hotter, harder, wilder. It wasn't enough. It went on and on until a low moan vibrated in her throat. She couldn't get enough of his taste or scent, that wonderfully unique flavor that was his alone and made it impossible to find his mate.

The thought made her stiffen as she realized what was happening. She tore her mouth free and gulped in the cold air. "Mel. Stop. Bad idea." A gasp caught in her throat as he buried his mouth against her shoulder and bit sharply in a warning little nip of possession. "Mel." She put as much command into her voice as she could. "Stop."

His head lifted, and shock exploded inside her soul. His eyes. His eyes carried the wild and feral soul of an alpha male wolf. A thin ring of amber had appeared around the rim of his pupil as a visible manifestation of the physical powers he possessed. If he didn't want to let her go, then she wouldn't get free. The worst part, the very worst part, was that she did not want to get free. Alpha to alpha. Male to female. He called to everything that she had ever been and might ever be.

"Mel." She said it again and exerted her will against his. Her only hope to stop the insanity was that he did not yet know the power of his mind.

He blew out a breath and looked away for long moments. It was a struggle to regain control of himself. He hadn't scared her away with what was inside him. If anything, she had responded back. He could feel the heat of her body and hear the thudding of her pulse matching his. Her scent was sharp and lush, a beckoning temptation. "Hang on," he managed to say roughly.

"Since I would appear to be pinned down," there was a touch of dryness in her voice, "I can't hold on to anything."

He released her quickly and moved away. As she sat up, he looked away in shame. "I'm sorry. I'm not sure what happened."

"Humans are animals, too. Chases spark primitive instincts, and you're a fairly primitive guy, I think." She kept her voice deliberately light. They were walking a thin tightrope. She would never have gotten free if he had been fully aware and cognizant of his own nature. To be honest, she probably wouldn't have tried.

"You may be right." He glanced at her. "But I have to admit that the more I'm around you, the more I want to know." He searched her eyes for any sign that she was still as shaken as he was. He saw nothing. Because he had never before felt anything like what had just happened, he let it lie. Maybe she was right. Maybe she was wrong. It wasn't the time to examine it, not when his body was aching so badly that even the cold snow was no help. "Well, let's pretend that didn't just happen, okay?" His lips curved. "But you're one hell of a kisser, Audra."

Her lips curved to match his. "Back at you, kid." She let him pull her to her feet and fell into step beside him as they began to head back toward the campus parking lot. He exerted a visible effort over himself and kept a foot of distance between them. She was grateful for it. He still smelled too damn tempting.

Deciding to put things back to normal, she said, "You fell asleep in the middle of lessons last night." From the corner of her eye, she saw his cheeks heat. Casually she continued, "I thought we'd try something a little different. Did you know there's a Japanese museum near here?"

Startled, he looked at her. "No."

"It's a very cool place. The entire tour is given in Japanese with a translator for those who speak English. All tourists go there, so you'd probably find yourself plopped down in a roomful of people speaking Japanese. Languages need to be learned by immersion so you'll do better there than my cramming verbs and tenses down your throat."

"I . . . hmm."

"Let's go by the house to drop off the bike, then take your car, okay?"

"Yeah. Sure." He rubbed the back of his neck, wondering at the timing of her decision and his conversation with Stormy the night before. Something tried to prod at his mind but he instinctively shied away. He wasn't ready to understand. "I guess it can't hurt to try." He searched his jacket and came up with his keys. The way they had tumbled over the snow, he had been worried he had lost them.

They parted at the parking lot so Audra could head for her bike. And though she was halfway across the lot and he made no sound, she knew instantly that there was something wrong. It came as a sharp slicing sensation through her heart. She was rushing back to his side before she was even aware of it. As she stopped beside him, she saw why.

Mel's beloved 1970 Mustang, carefully restored by his own hands, had been destroyed. The windows were smashed apart. The tires had been slashed. Gouges from some sort of sharp object had torn apart the paint on every surface. The hood wasn't resting properly, and when she lifted it, she saw that the engine had been covered in something dark and sticky. It smelled like tar.

It wasn't even dark yet; it was only evening. Nearly all the cars were gone except for the ones belonging to faculty. Her sharp eyes spotted Kalliope's car some distance away. She wasn't surprised; the young heiress had evening classes. Where she and Mel stood was isolated a little from any place that the crime could have been witnessed from.

She stepped closer to Mel. He hadn't moved an inch. "Well," she said. "Interesting." She looked at his face and the agony in his eyes made fury swell inside her heart. "You loved your car."

"I worked so hard. Months on end in every spare minute." He touched a cracked side window with trembling fingers. The side mirrors hung from their wires like broken arms. "I saved my allowances from the time I was ten to the time I was twenty. For my twentieth birthday, Dad gave me the last thousand I needed to have enough to buy and fix the car. I know it's old, but . . . I wanted this car."

"Can you afford to have it repaired?"

"If it can be repaired, yeah. I draw a paycheck from the company now since I'm already serving several roles. It's just . . . it's like . . ." He couldn't find the words, hurt and frustration welling inside him.

"It's like you were violated. I know." She would make sure the culprit was taken care of for him. Mel was *hers* regardless of whether or not her heart was involved. No one ever hurt her family. "Call a tow," she told him. "I'll go borrow Taegan's extra helmet." She took two steps away then stopped. She looked back over her shoulder. "I won't let anyone hurt you again, Mel."

He looked up in surprise and watched her as she walked toward the campus. His hurt blessedly diverted into admiration. She had, he decided, an incredibly sexy walk. Probably the sexiest walk he had ever seen on a female. It was like watching a predator or a hunter move, sleek and dangerous in a way that raised his pulse and reminded him just how she had felt under him. Her hips were definitely curved just right.

By the time she returned, a helmet under her arm and a very furious Taegan following her, the tow truck was just arriving to take the car away. Fury flashed in Taegan's gaze when he saw the sadness in his brother's eyes as he sat on a bench to watch. "If you don't handle things," he warned quietly, "I will. And I'm likely to get fired if I do."

"It's handled." She flashed him a smile that showed her teeth. "They can't catch me." She walked over to Mel and knelt to hold the helmet out to him. "There's nothing we can do right now," she told him quietly. "So don't give them the satisfaction of showing how much this hurts."

He nodded and got to his feet as she stood. He pulled the helmet on and looked at his brother. "I'll figure out what to do later. Right now we're going to a Japanese museum." Taegan lifted a brow, and he smiled. "Hands-on learning for language. Maybe I'll do better if it's all I'm hearing."

"Good luck." Taegan's eyes missed nothing as Mel got on the back of Audra's bike. There was something in the way their bodies touched, in the way his arms went around her waist that spoke more than words. A smile curved his lips as the bike sped away. When he felt Kalliope slipping her hand into his, he glanced down at her. "Hands-on lessons indeed."

"Mmm. He definitely had that look." She leaned her head on his shoulder and smiled up at him. "When did you first expect this outcome? I admit I began to wonder when he said he hadn't met anyone else."

"From the beginning," he admitted. He drew her closer and swung her hand up to his lips as they walked back onto campus. "No meddling," he scolded lightly. "They can handle things fine, and," he added when she smiled innocently, "leave Steve Rudaveg to Audra. Trust me, she can handle him."

"Oh, come on. Just a little threat?"

"No."

She huffed. "Ever since we got engaged, you've been so bossy."

He swung her up into his arms. "That's because you get into trouble easily. In fact, you're getting into trouble right now."

She grinned. "I still think you need a couch in your office. That desk just isn't comfy."

At the museum, Mel found himself plunged into another world. As he and Audra walked along with the tour, he was inundated from all sides with the language. There were two tour guides, one for each language, and nearly everyone around them was speaking Japanese. It sounded like gobblygook at first, with only the words making sense and not the meaning.

But, slowly, he began to pick out the different verbs and tenses, using the English translator talking at the same time to get a better idea of the meaning. -Masu meaning present. -Masen meaning negative. -Mashita meaning past.

Audra watched him intently and could almost see the moment it clicked in his brain. She had wanted to see if he was right about his learning ability, and she knew now that he was. He really did learn better with a demonstration.

Tuning out the tour guides, she watched him instead, fascinated with the way he began to immediately speak in Japanese. Once it had unraveled, the syntaxes had connected and he was able to form proper sentences. He spoke almost as good as the natives, a feat that impressed more than one visitor. Several smiling looks were directed at him as he talked to the visitors in their own language.

He was also on a slightly euphoric high. They got outside the building and he caught her in his arms to spontaneously swing her in a quick circle. "You're the best tutor ever!" he announced with a grin.

For the second time that day, she felt extremely outmatched physically. She cleared her throat. "Mel. Put me down."

"Oh, sorry." He put her on her feet with a care that made her heart flutter. Unaware of it, he stretched his hands over his head. "It finally makes sense, you know? I can't wait to get to class. The dragon won't know what hit her!"

She coughed lightly. She really should tell him not to call Professor Nobunaga bad names, but she really couldn't argue with the assessment. Even Audra was preferred as a teacher over Nobunaga, and that said something. "Since Japanese is fine, we can work on your history next."

He grimaced. "How do you have a hands-on lesson about history? A time machine?"

"Hardly. You just need someone who knows the subject well and doesn't mind talking about it." She pulled on her helmet, a slight smirk curving her lips. "Like me. I give a hell of a lecture, and I promise to draw you plenty of pictures and diagrams. I'll also," she added as he got on the bike behind her, "pour tea down your throat to keep you awake."

He felt a dull flush warm his cheeks. "Yes'm," he mumbled. As he slid his arms around her waist more firmly to hold on, he wondered to himself if he would ever fall asleep on her again. There was something about her now that he couldn't get out of his mind. It would fade if it was just the chase, but deep inside, he had the feeling it never would. If it didn't, he was going to have to figure out what the hell to do next.

CHAPTER TWENTY-SEVEN

Mel was still buzzing happily by the time they got back to Audra's place. Bemused at him, Audra went into the kitchen to start a pot of tea. It was a special blend that had no caffeine but the natural components made it even more effective. It also promoted clearer thinking.

While it brewed, she went upstairs and changed clothes. She was more aware of Mel's presence down the hall than she wanted to be. Her body still ached and throbbed. When she looked into the mirror, she could see the mark on her neck from his teeth. The little brand of possession was a stark reminder that for the first time in one hundred and fifty years she had met a male wolf that matched her.

She owned little to no makeup. Luckily, the one thing she did own was powder. She covered the mark to the best of her ability before going downstairs to pour the tea. As she was setting two cups on the coffee table, Mel came down the stairs. She tried to keep her eyes to herself, but she missed nothing of the way he moved fluidly, muscles rippling under jeans and t-shirt. How had she missed the signs for twenty-four years? And where had she been when he had been running under the moon? She would have run at his side.

"What kind of tea is it?" He sat down and picked up one of the cups.

"Drinkable kind."

"Well, I wouldn't want to bathe in it." He sniffed at the liquid but caught nothing familiar except mint. The urge to tease was irresistible. "You didn't put a witch's brew in it or anything, right?"

She rolled her eyes expressively. "Sure, I grow nightshade out back with the azaleas and moonflowers. Shut up and drink your damn tea."

His grin flashed quickly. "Yes'm." He obediently sipped the tea. The flavor instantly spread through his mouth. Mint, certainly, but more as well. Things he couldn't identify but tasted good all the same. "Nice stuff." As if he hadn't discovered a hunger to learn everything about her he could, he asked casually, "Do you prefer coffee or tea?"

"Coffee in the morning, tea any time after noon." She sat beside him. "Both have to be strong. I have sensitive taste buds so I tend to be heavy on flavor. Never eat any spaghetti I might make. Madelyne says I could kill vampires at five miles."

"So you've known Maddie a long time? It wasn't until real recently she mentioned you were a friend. And I know Taegan calls you a friend."

Something warm moved inside her heart. She knew Madelyne knew what she was, and though he had never expressly said so, she was sure Taegan did as well. She cherished their friendship, especially Taegan's. If he ever knew what she had done, even his kindness might change. "I've known Maddie for many years," she said carefully. "I sometimes work with the Enforcers so I've known her through Rhianna Taber."

"Gotcha." He let it lie; he knew when to fight his battles. Little steps at a time, that was how to handle Audra. "So, history."

"Which time period?"

"Early 1900s America." His smile was all innocence. "You know, before women's suffrage and the world went to hell." He wasn't disappointed when she turned a slowly arched brow toward him. Deliberately, he said, "1930 was a bad year."

She leaned over and pinched his ear. "For one, I'm telling your sisters you said that. For two, you know full well it was 1929." She barely kept a smile hidden. The playful teasing was as thrilling in its own way as the more adult teasing of earlier. "Now then. Let's get started."

He scooted closer to watch and listen closely as she began to talk. She was *really* good at lecturing. Her voice fluctuated with dozens of nuances, her tone alone imparting as much information as her words. She used pop culture and modern references to illustrate moods and attitudes, giving his brain something it could easily comprehend. And above all, she talked as if she had been there. The information began to sink into his brain . . . and stay.

As she was flipping pages for information on World War I, he glanced at her face. "How old are you?" Her brows lifted over amused yellow eyes and he coughed. "Sorry. I know it's rude. But you look so young, and you know so much. I would swear you'd been there the way you talk."

"That's the mark of a good lecture," she countered calmly. "If you don't sound knowledgeable, then why should anyone care what you think? I've heard some bad lectures myself. In fact, I wasn't the first to walk out of the room. When I went to the cafe, I saw a stone gargoyle drinking coffee like his life depended on it."

He grinned at that. "Your sense of humor is as warped as mine."

"I'm not sure that's a compliment." After a few moments, she noted, "Fair's fair. My turn for a personal question. Why's a guy like you still single? You're handsome, smart, and rich. You ought to be at least solidly hooked."

"Gee, thanks." He fiddled with his pencil, gazing unseeing at his books. "I guess I never met anyone worth being serious over. And after what's happened with my family . . . well, I suppose I'm waiting now for that special someone to come my way."

"Oh?" She kept her voice casual. "What happened with your siblings?"

"Within a month, they've all either gotten married or engaged." He leaned back on his hands with a whimsical smile. "We have this family wolf. She's become a lucky charm for us, or maybe she's just a good faerie in disguise. She's been helping us all find someone. She hasn't been around me much, though. Maybe there's no one for me."

"There's someone for everyone," she whispered as she put her pencil down. Pain and sadness mingled inside her. It was her indecision that made him feel as if he was meant to be alone. He deserved so much better, and time was getting so much shorter.

"Even you?" She looked at him in surprise, and he smiled. "You're pretty cool when someone gets to know you. Oh, you're still rude and blunt, but it's part of your charm, I think. And, frankly, under that scar is a really hot chick. Rumor says the scar is recent, so why aren't you married with a litter of kids to raise into hellions?" The question hung between them. He knew it was immensely personal and none of his business. It was almost a test of their friendship.

She very nearly found an excuse, but she just couldn't lie to him anymore. She took a deep breath. "I was engaged once. He was murdered. I guess I've never gotten over it." His hand covered hers gently and she looked down in surprise. It was the first time other than the incident in the snow where he had touched her of his own volition. "Mel."

"I'm sorry," he said softly. His heart hurt for her and for how much she must have loved her fiancé to still cling to his memory. Jealousy rose savagely for a moment, but he firmly shoved it down again. It, like the chase, needed to be examined when the event was well past. He smiled instead. "I'll introduce you to Stormy, okay? Maybe she can help. Taegan swears she is his faerie godmother."

She barely refrained from making a face. She was going to kick Taegan. The smartass. "He did pull a convincing Cinderella," she admitted. "The school is still talking about it."

A snicker was his response. "It'll get better. Kalliope is actually having glass shoes made so she can wear them at her wedding."

She bit her lip but a snicker emerged anyway. She adored that girl. Of all the mates she had given to the Shaughnessys, only Kalliope had ever worked harder than Audra. And thinking of her duties reminded her that she had something else to deal with. She closed the history book. "I'm feeling a little tired. It's been a stressful week. Why don't we make it an early night?"

"Sure." He watched her head up the stairs, his eyes lingering on her hips and legs with wistful yearning. He turned his attention to the notes and began to gather them up. He started to close his book but hesitated and opened it again. He squinted at the page.

From up the stairs came, "Glasses."

"How does she do that?" he muttered, but he obligingly put his glasses on so he could read the book. The trick, he remembered her saying, wasn't to think of it as something that had happened, but something that could. Like a novel, or an interesting story. Think of a character, place them there, and build their world.

Taking it from that perspective, he began to read, shortly losing himself in the setting and the scenario. The facts he mentally filed away without notice. The opinions he mentally debated until he understood the value each had. He hit an interesting part that he wanted Audra to clarify and took the book with him upstairs. "Audra?" he called.

There was no response and he eased her door open carefully. There was no one inside and it looked as if she hadn't touched her bed. He frowned, wondering where she had gotten off to, if she was so tired. The woman needed a keeper, seriously. Shrugging slightly, he took the book with him and decided to read in bed. He was tired, too.

Steve Rudaveg was on his way home from a late game when he began to feel as if he was being watched. A chill went down his back and the palms of his hands began to sweat. His heart beat a little faster, his eyes moving restlessly around.

Danger. Danger was close.

Without even truly being aware of it, he began to walk faster. Though the nearly full moon had been bright, a cloud suddenly passed in front and plunged the street into a darkness not even the streetlights could penetrate.

Footsteps echoed eerily behind him. He turned sharply, but no one was there. His breath coming faster, he began to run down the sidewalk, desperately looking for where he had parked his car. When he stopped for a breath, a shadow moved in an alley and feral yellow eyes watched him. His voice emerged as only a strangled yelp. The wolf was nearly as tall as his hip, teeth bared, as low, menacing growls reverberated in the air.

He turned and ran the other way. He stumbled into a kid's playground and tripped over the edge of a sandbox. He landed with a thud on the ground and felt the wolf's breath near his ankle. With wild desperation, he clawed away to his feet and turned around. The wolf was watching him, slowly stalking forward. Taunting laughter seemed to ripple in his mind.

No escape.

The words echoed from the wolf's mind to his. He scrambled back and landed on his ass once more. "Get away from me!" The words were little more than a high-pitched squeal.

You called me here. Jealousy and rumor summon me like a hangman to the gallows. You knew you shouldn't spread rumors. You knew you shouldn't have ruined His car.

"Y-yes!" he stammered hastily. "I knew!"

And you're going to go to the college police and confess, aren't you.

"Yes!" he yelped. In that moment he would have agreed to anything. And when the wolf growled softly and crouched low, he threw his arms over his head in terror. "Don't eat me!" he wailed as the wolf lunged toward him.

Nothing happened. He slowly lowered his arms, his breath coming so hard and fast that it left a cloud of steam in the frigid air. There was nothing around him. No wolf. Nothing. The clouds were passing from in front of the moon. The night was quiet and still, crickets chirping cheerfully.

He ran the entire way home and didn't breathe again until he was in his room and under the covers on his bed.

Audra was still smiling to herself when she returned home. There she had been, all set to 'convince' the punk with her compulsion powers to turn himself in, and instead all she had needed to do was terrify him. Not that that had been hard either. Chasing rabbits took more effort.

The house was silent, and she first went to Mel's room to peek inside. He was sitting up in bed, dead asleep, glasses slipping down his nose. Something warm moved through her as she slipped into the room and went over to his side. The man needed a keeper, seriously.

She gently removed his glasses and helped tuck him into bed. Her lips curved as she saw what he had been reading. If he set his mind to something, he gave it his everything.

He mumbled something and turned onto his side to snuggle into the pillow. Tenderly, she brushed his hair out of his eyes. He was as beautiful inside as he was outside. He was so wild and free, tugging at her in ways she hadn't felt before. She quickly left when he stirred again. The last thing she needed was to be caught there.

She went down the hall to her room and ignored the way chills always flowed over her skin each time she entered. It felt chilly enough that she pulled on an oversized sleep shirt. She usually slept in the nude but it truly was cold, colder than usual.

It was almost always difficult to fall asleep in that room. In many ways, she had always been almost pitifully grateful for the duties that allowed her to spend her time at the Shaughnessy home. There she could sleep. There she could rest. This night, however, she was so tired that she was asleep within minutes of her eyes closing.

And this time she dreamed.

The torches were burning. Children were screaming. The forests were ablaze with hellfire, the sound of guns firing, echoing loudly and bitterly. She ran as fast as her body was able, blood stinging her eyes and staining her skin where it slowly flowed from wounds of all shapes and sizes. She was praying. Praying with her every breath as she ran toward where the children had been hidden. There had to be hope!

There was none. Even before she ran into the shelter, she could smell the death. Claw marks lined the walls and gouged out chunks of wood and stone. Blood covered every surface. Bodies littered the floor. Humans who had attacked and who had defended. Werewolves who had resisted death to the last moment.

Screaming for Kalin, screaming his name again and again, she tore up the floor and rushed down toward the basement. She could hear their screaming, hear their cries, the sounds imbedded in the very walls. And she knew they were already dead for she did not hear the sounds of their hearts beating.

The basement was covered with bodies. No one moved. No one breathed. Even the smallest, a child of barely two, lay like an abandoned doll with bullet holes riddling her body. Two figures struggled before a moonlit window, and she lunged forward to close her hands around the neck of the murderer. It snapped like a twig and he dropped. Kalin fell, and she held him tightly to her breast, knowing he, too, would be dead shortly. Even then, he did not move or breathe, his life bleeding away into her hands.

Her howl of rage and of grief shattered the night air as she vowed for vengeance against the humans who had done this to her people.

"Audra! Audra!"

Her eyes shot open and she saw Mel leaning over her. On a low snarl, she lunged for him with her hands hooked like claws. He caught her wrists and held her away with unthinking power, his grip gentle despite the strength. "Audra!" he said again, eyes dark with worry. "It's me! It's Mel!"

His voice finally penetrated the haze of her mind. The fight drained out of her, and she slumped against him weakly, tired to her very soul. Shaken, he wrapped his arms around her and pressed her head to his shoulder. "Wow. Jesus, you don't dream lightly, do you? Your scream scared the hell out of me. When I got here, you were thrashing like the hounds of hell were after you."

She said nothing as she turned her face into his shoulder. She had never been held after the nightmares before. It was an odd, foreign feeling, but the warmth and security of his arms slowly seeped into her body and melted the cold. His heart, though slightly unsteady, sounded strong and sure under her ear. She pressed closer unthinkingly, needing the feeling of safety that only this man had ever given her.

He felt his heart quiver. She had always seemed so strong, so unbreakable, but she was human, too, with fears and nightmares. His arms tightened, and he slowly ran his hand over her back soothingly. Without thought, he rubbed his cheek against her hair. Had anyone ever held her before? He didn't think so. "Want to talk about it?" he asked softly.

"No." Talk about it? She fought a shudder. She could barely accept that it had even happened. She slowly eased back from his embrace and looked at her hands. Though it had long been washed away, there were times she felt as if the blood was buried in her skin.

His hands suddenly slid under hers. Something quivered inside her soul. His hands were bigger than hers, his skin barely darker. She was only two inches shorter than he was, but he was so strong and powerful that she felt safe and secure. And when his hands slowly closed over hers, the touch was as possessive as it was protective.

"When was the last time you were held?" he asked softly.

"I don't remember," she admitted just as softly. "I never felt comfortable letting anyone close." Her lips twisted with a mockery of a smile. "It didn't matter. No one wanted to be close. I'm not talking about the scars. Something inside me . . . scares people."

"Not me." Her eyes lifted to his and he lowered his forehead to hers. "Not anymore. Yeah, you scared the hell out of me at first. You even admit to doing it on purpose. But . . . I'm not afraid of you. Not anymore. There's nothing you could say or do that would make me decide I didn't want to know you or comfort you. Or be your friend."

Her eyes closed. Though she knew he believed what he said, she knew he was wrong. At best, all she could say was, "Thanks."

"Hey." He eased back and smiled. "I know what you need. Come on." He got to his feet and held out a hand to her. "Come with me. When's the last time someone did something nice for you?"

"I'm not sure. Which century is this again?" Her heart soared when he laughed, his eyes twinkling in his handsome face. And though she knew it was stupid, she reached out and put her hand in his to let him tug her out of the bed. Something was happening. She had the feeling of freefalling without knowing where she would land.

He led her down to the kitchen and began to rummage in the fridge. Curious, she sat at the counter and watched him. He got out milk and then got a pan. "What are you doing?"

"Making some warm chocolate milk." He found the cocoa in a cabinet and added it to the milk in the pan. "It's what Dad always did when we had nightmares. He'd make us some warm chocolate milk and we'd talk until we were ready to sleep again."

"Oh." She rested her cheek on her arms as she watched him. She had forgotten that family tradition, and it felt odd to be part of it in this way. "What are we going to talk about?"

He contemplated how he wanted to ask what he wanted to know. When the milk was ready, he poured a mug and set it in front of her. She seemed oddly fragile as she sat at the counter in nothing but a giant shirt that did nothing to disguise her long and tempting legs. "I know you don't want to talk about the nightmare," he said carefully, "but will you at least tell me if the dream is connected to the walls?" When she went still, he gave a slight shrug. "Even I could hear the pain in this house. Why do you live here?"

"Because I have to. I can't explain." She sipped the milk and found that it was strangely soothing. "But I admit I do have trouble sleeping in that bedroom. Lots of nightmares. Usually I end up sleeping on the couch."

He sat across from her and let the subject lie. "Let's talk about something else." He smiled. "I'll tell you a secret if you tell me a secret. I'll even go first." He made a point of looking around and kept his voice low as if the secret was of grave importance. "My full name is Melville. I was named for my grandfather. But I *hate* my name. You'd only ever see it on my birth certificate."

She found a smile. She felt oddly trusted that he would tell her. Of course, she couldn't tell him that she had always known. "If Kalliope offers me enough money, I'm blabbing."

"Give me a chance to better the offer."

"Will do." Her eyes closed partially as the milk rested warmly in her body and his companionship lulled her toward sleep. "I'm afraid of cats," she finally confessed, her voice drowsy. "Give me the willies something fierce. Whenever I see one, I sometimes can't help chasing them off."

"I could see you running after them with a broom," he decided. He grinned. "Yeah, I could see that. The tough computer sciences teacher that terrifies the campus. The beast of the college is afraid of cats and loves children. Your fan club would have a field day."

Her voice slightly slurred as her eyes closed, she mumbled, "I don't have a fan club. I fired them for holding parties and not inviting me."

He opened his mouth to find a retort when he realized she had fallen asleep at the table. Her lashes rested like dark crescents against her skin. A soft smile curved his lips and he went around the table to gently gather her into his arms. Her head fell against his shoulder, her breath softly feathering over his skin.

He let out a long breath as he carried her up the stairs. With the way everything she did or said seemed to make him want her more, he was growing strongly suspicious that her bullshit about the chase was purely that. Maybe it had shocked his eyes open, but it sure as hell wasn't the only reason. He didn't mind; he was willing to give it more time for her sake. She needed to believe it too.

He didn't take her to her room. He took her to his and settled her on his bed. He tucked her in tenderly and drew the covers up over her shoulders. She promptly rolled over and curled up on her side. "Kalin," she mumbled sleepily.

He hesitated but tucked in the blanket more securely anyway. He couldn't help wondering if Kalin was her dead lover. He also couldn't help his jealousy at the thought. He softly smoothed her hair back from her face and traced his thumb down the scar. With a soft sigh, he left the room to go downstairs. He was going to be the one on the couch that night, but he didn't regret it in the slightest.

She awoke the next morning to his scent surrounding her. She sat up quickly and looked around in shock. She was in his bed and in his room. His presence had permeated everything, blanketing her subconscious with its comforting energy. She felt more rested than she had in a century.

She warily got up and went downstairs, sure she was wrong, but when she went into the living room, she found him sprawled dead asleep on the couch. With that unquestioning generosity of his, he had given her his bed so that she would get true sleep. Once more, inside her soul, she felt something falling and hovering on the precipice of hitting . . . something.

A book dangled from his fingers and his glasses were falling off his face. She gently removed the glasses and picked up the book. It was his math book. She bit her lips and tried not to laugh.

She bent to tuck the blanket around his shoulders better and he gave a sleepy mumble that sounded like a math equation. Smiling, she shook her head and brushed his hair back from his cheek. His head turned and his lips brushed over her fingers. His scent lifted and curled around her, wild and wonderful . . . and that something landed inside her and brought understanding.

It was her.

It was her scent that matched his. *She* was his mate. All she had to do was close her eyes to find him in a room of millions. He could call her name from miles away and she would hear him. She was in love with him, this wild and untamed man who looked into her eyes fearlessly and gave his friendship unconditionally. No other would ever suit him. No other would ever suit her.

Pain and despair welled inside her as she buried her face in her hands. Her only hope for salvation was finding him true love, but if he knew what she had done, he would *never* feel for her as she felt for him. No matter if it destroyed her, she would have to try to find him another mate. Someone who was whole. Someone who deserved him.

Someone who wasn't a murderess.

CHAPTER TWENTY-EIGHT

Mel awoke once more to the smell of breakfast cooking. This time he woke with a start and fell off the couch with a thump. As he sprawled on the floor, he realized there were feet standing in front of him. They were nice feet, attached to slender ankles that flowed into what he knew were exceptionally nice legs even though they were currently covered by black jeans. "Morning," he said.

Audra crouched down. "Morning," she told him gravely. She had decided to ignore her revelations until she could talk to the one person who could possibly help. "Sleep well?"

"I think the better question," he rolled over and got to his feet nimbly, "is whether or not *you* slept well." He searched her face. There was something behind her eyes that he couldn't catch, but there was indeed more rest to her face. "I'm glad," he said softly.

"Food is in the kitchen," she informed him.

"So I smell." He stretched and covered a yawn. "I'll go grab a quick shower and be right there." A thought occurred and he frowned. "How am I getting to school?"

"You can go with me, but I'm just dropping you off. An emergency came up that I have to take care of. I've called a substitute in to my classes today." She headed into the kitchen. "So hurry up. We haven't got all day."

Smiling a little to himself, he went upstairs.

After dropping him off at school, she made a beeline back to the 3rd District and the immense skyscraper that served as the Enforcers' headquarters. It was thirty-six floors high and sleek and elegant in its design. It had undergone many renovations over the centuries to keep up with the times, and currently it was glass and metal. When the sun was rising or setting, it reflected in the windows and made them glow like fire. It was one of the most beautiful sights in New York.

The Enforcers had been formed when the District had, and they maintained the buildings and protected the people. They had alliances with multiple large corporations, and the mutually beneficial relationships ensured that the Enforcers were never without an edge in any market. Some suspected they even had federal backing, but it could not be proven.

Audra was a regular in the building. She had been there so often that she didn't even wear her badge. The guards merely waved her in. However, the top few floors were under strict access, so she had to use her badge on the elevator to go all the way to the very top floor. As she rode upward, she let herself remember a time when she'd had to take the stairs. Thank god for modern conveniences.

Without waiting to knock, she walked right into Rhianna's office and said, "For the love of God, Rhianna, tell me you have five minutes."

Rhianna's elegant brows rose slowly toward her red bangs. She smiled and closed the document she had been reading. She was a shorter woman with a thick mane of red hair and vibrant black eyes. Beautiful by any standards, she also had a regal and commanding air. Her powers were immense though the extent of them was unknown to all, even her partner.

She studied Audra intently, well aware of the clock slowly ticking away in the back of her mind. "If this is about Madelyne, I'm already aware. Imagine." She gave a little laugh of delight. "Me, a grandmother, after all this time. Eric says I need to learn to knit."

Audra didn't bother to sit down. She stood behind the visitor's chair, her fingers wrapped around the back so hard that her knuckles were white. "You're old enough to be someone's *ancestor* but that's neither here nor there." She took a quick breath. "I need an extension. Please. Anything."

Sadness clouded Rhianna's face. "I can't, Audra. It's too close. There's nothing I can do now. I can't amend a contract this late in the process." She began to frown. "Why? What's wrong? I knew he would be difficult, but surely . . ." Her voice trailed off as she saw the agony in Audra's eyes. "Oh. I see." She ran a hand through her hair, not sure what to say. She had hoped this would be much easier. "When did this occur?"

"I realized it this morning." Audra shook her head quickly. "What am I supposed to do, Rhi? He's a Shaughnessy. If he knew what I'd done . . ." Her voice broke as a shudder ripped through her body. "My god, he would hate me! *I* hate me for it!"

Rhianna got up and walked around the desk to help her into the chair. She knelt down beside her friend. "Audra, you know that if you don't find him true love . . ."

"I know." She closed her eyes, tears beginning to slide down her cheeks. "But how can I find him someone else when I know that his scent only matches mine?" She drew a deep breath. "Rhianna . . . he's a wolf. It should be impossible, but somehow the District blood in the Shaughnessy line has manifested wholly inside him. He's a werewolf. He's an alpha male, no less."

"If you are meant to be his mate," Rhianna noted mildly, "he could be nothing less. Has he shifted or compelled?"

"His mind has *tried* to compel; he said he felt as if he had influenced someone. As for shifting, no. But he could. If he needed, he could. The Amber Mark is in his eyes now. If he finds himself with a great need, he could shift." She lowered her head. "I can't even tell him what he is," she added softly. "Not without telling him what I am. And if I do . . . he'll hate me for that, too."

"Then be as open as you can. Give him a side of you that you've never given anyone else. Know that you gave the man you loved everything. Just that alone can ensure you have no regrets." Rhianna tilted her head slightly. "Have you any idea how he feels about you?"

"He wants me." She shrugged one shoulder. "At the least, he seems to. The Amber Mark appeared because he was chasing me. We fell into the mating hunt of werewolves and it got to us both. I played it off as just primitive instinct, and he bought it."

"You don't suppose he might actually want you, do you? To begin with, he wouldn't have fallen into that hunt if there was nothing inside to spark it. For another, I might add, once you get past a cactus' bite, its flesh is sweet."

"Thanks. Thanks a bunch." She gestured at her face. "Trust me, I know my lack of appeal. Even before . . . I scared people." She didn't scare Mel anymore, she remembered then, her heart skipping a beat.

"You're a tad overwhelming, dear." Rhianna got to her feet. "Very few humans know how to deal with a true hunter. Try as you might, you can't hide what you are. Oh, you can pretend for a while, but you're no civilized pet in the slightest. Humans have survived so long because they can feel when a predator is close." She paused before adding smoothly, "Which is partly Mel's problem, I believe. His predatory nature is barely concealed as a wild spirit only."

Audra slowly got to her feet. "I can only play things by ear now. I don't . . . I don't think I'll be able to do it, Rhi." Her smile was sad but accepting. "Wolves mate for life. I can't hand him over to another woman." She let out a long breath and pulled a letter out of her pocket. She dropped it on the chair. "When it's done . . . give that to Mel."

The door shut behind her and Rhianna picked up the glass statuette on her desk. She hurled it furiously at the wall where it shattered into millions of pieces.

Softly, a male voice asked from another doorway, "What do we do?"

His partner looked at the fragmented remains of the statuette. It was like seeing how her heart felt inside. "Whatever we have to." And though soft, her voice was hard as steel.

Mel had braced himself for another day of snide comments and trouble, but it was as if the day before had never happened. Students greeted him cordially. Others waved at him across the quad. Teachers asked with genuine concern about his ruined car.

He went looking for Kalliope at the first available opportunity. He caught her as she was coming out of a class and promptly grabbed her around the waist. He lifted her off her feet and stalked down the hall. "You're coming with me."

"I hadn't noticed." She braced an elbow on his shoulder and ignored her dangling feet. "Are we having some issues, Gibson?"

He put her down when they were out of hearing of other students. "Okay, talk," he ordered. "You have ears like a damn alley cat and you know *everything* happening on campus. So what the hell is going on?"

She lifted her brows. "Oh, you mean the 24-Hour flip-flop. Well, it would seem that Steve Rudaveg went to Administration this morning and confessed to not only spreading the rumors but also vandalizing your car. He was escorted off campus by some very nice policemen just before you got here. You'll probably get a call tonight. And since the student body blows with the wind, everything's fine now."

"What did you do to him?" he accused.

"Me?" She scowled. "Why must you always blame me?"

"Because you're usually at fault."

"Damn it." She hated when he was right. All of the Shaughnessys had her number now. "As a matter of fact," she said with dignity, "I did nothing. In and amongst his ramblings, Rutabaga mentioned an encounter with a wolf. In the middle of NYC at night. If you want answers, look to Stormy. Where's she been lately anyway?"

"I've seen her once or twice lately." He sighed wryly. "I think I'm causing her difficulty." He waved it off with a shrug. To be honest, he wasn't minding it that much anymore. Somehow he couldn't miss Stormy if he had Audra around. "How are things at home?"

"Kind of boring. It's like a deck of cards that's missing an entire suit." She gave his arm a light punch. "Hang in there. Two days to midterms, and everything will be fine. We're pulling for you."

"Thanks." He watched her walk away and then headed for his own class. He decided to go with the flow and pretended like nothing had happened, opting for the high road instead of ignoring his fellow classmates for their two-faced attitudes.

To his surprise, within a few minutes of being seated in class, an attractive young woman dropped down onto the seat beside him. Since she sat down without any books, he lifted a brow. "Can I help you?"

"I'm new on campus, and I'm just here to hit on you," she said with a laugh. She offered a hand. "Kate Willowby. I don't suppose you're free this evening."

He studied her. She was assuredly attractive with short brown hair and lively blue eyes. Shorter than average, around Kalliope's height, and with a lovely, shapely figure. She carried herself well and there was a definite humor inside her. He made his decision easily, wondering if she might finally make sense of everything. "Sure. I have a tutoring session, but it could be ended early. How does dinner sound?"

"It sounds like a date." She scribbled her address on his notepad. "I live a block or two away from 3rd District, so I'm not hard to find. You're staying with Professor Alexandrios, right?" When he nodded, she gave a little shiver. "She's a bit scary." She smiled. "But I guess she isn't so bad."

"Agreed."

She hopped to her feet. "See you later, Mel."

"Later indeed." He waved when she disappeared into the hall and turned his attention to the front as the teacher called for roll. He put his cute date out of his mind and settled in to learn. Much to his immense shock, he was ahead of his class. It was History, and he had always lagged behind. He was now several chapters ahead, and even the teacher noticed.

The same thing happened in both his Math and Japanese classes. By the time lunch came around, he was beginning to seriously think he would be able to fulfill his end of the bargain. He was even whistling lightly as he joined his family for lunch.

"Well, you're cheerful," Kienan remarked. "Where's my brother, and what did you do with him?"

"I'm not that bad," he muttered as he sat down. "I," he announced, "happen to be ahead of my classes, and I have a date. I'm entitled to be cheerful." He watched Kalliope and Madelyne exchange a quick look. "Problem?"

"No. Who's the date with?" Madelyne asked it casually, but her stomach was clenching in a way that had nothing to do with morning sickness.

"Kate. New girl. Really cute."

"Hmm." Kalliope said nothing more than that.

He was the first to finish lunch since the others took their time. As soon as he had left the table, Kienan muttered, "I didn't think new students could start at midterm time."

"They can't." Madelyne frowned.

"Stormy?" Kalliope wondered.

"No." Madelyne pressed her hands to her stomach, her fingers shaking. Not even Kienan's arms wrapping around her could take away her trepidation. "Something else is going on." She couldn't even say whether it was good or bad. Time was running out.

Audra was waiting for Mel outside when his last class ended for the day. As he approached whistling, she lifted a brow. "Are we cheerful for no good reason today?"

"You and my family." He sighed. "Am I always grumpy?"

"Yes."

"At least *pretend* like you don't agree." He stuck his tongue out at her but still smiled. He liked it when she was teasing him. "As it would happen, I have a date tonight. Can we make the tutoring a short session?" While he spoke, he pulled on his helmet and got on the bike behind her.

The knife that drove into her heart was sharp and serrated. It was almost a physical blow, driving the breath from her lungs. Her nails curled into the handlebars of her bike as she fought for control. *Hers*. Everything inside her seemed to snarl at once, feral with possessive rage.

He felt her body quivering slightly but said nothing. When they got home, however, he pulled off his helmet with a frown. "What's wrong?"

"Nothing." The effort of fighting for control made her voice cold and clipped. "Heaven forbid school come in the way of hormones. Have your date. In fact, why don't we skip tonight altogether?" She jerked her helmet off and tucked it under her arm.

He caught her arm as she started to walk away. He felt a little shocked. It had been a long time since she had acted that way. It hurt more than he had imagined. "Audra, what's wrong?"

She turned on him, her eyes nearly as feral as she felt. "Seeing someone gamble with their future pisses me off." The words were almost snarled. "Some people don't even have a future!" She jerked her arm free and disappeared into the house.

He waited a few moments before going into the house as well. Somehow he wasn't surprised when he checked and found no sign of her. There had to be a secret door somewhere that he didn't know about.

The entire time he was getting ready, he bounced back and forth between whether or not he still wanted to go out. Ever since the 'chase,' he had felt more sharply attuned to Audra. He was sure that her lashing out was the result of pain and not anger. He wanted to track her down and find out what was wrong so he could make it better. The only thing that stopped him was knowing she would go for his eyes if he did.

He killed time by reading a book. When it was time to leave, he put on his jacket and left the house. Kate really didn't live far away. It would be easy to walk to her place and then to the restaurant where they wanted to have dinner.

To his surprise, he found Stormy sitting outside on the sidewalk. He instantly brightened. "Hey, there you are." He knelt and ran a hand over her head as she nudged his leg. "Where have you been? I was feeling a little neglected." He rubbed his cheek over her fur, comforted with her presence. "I missed you." He straightened with a smile. "I might be usurping your job, but I might have met someone on my own."

When he started to step forward, she planted herself in his path. Her ears were laid back, and her teeth almost bared. If he tried to step to either side, a low growl vibrated from her throat. He wasn't stupid. He got the point. "Stormy, I can't just stand her up. I know what you're telling me, but I'm not that much of a jerk. Now come on. You can come with me."

Her fur didn't lie flat, but she stopped growling as she fell into step beside him. She would have dragged him back by the seat of his pants if she could have, but he wasn't two anymore. *Really* wasn't two anymore, she thought, glancing over him wistfully.

The silence held for a few moments until he murmured, "I hurt Audra. I didn't mean to, Stormy. Really. I'm not even sure how I did. I guess she just doesn't want me to fail. She's very odd about it, but she cares for me. Last night . . ." He trailed off for a moment. "It was different to have her lean on me. I wanted to protect her. I still do."

She looked up at him in shock and he rubbed the back of his neck. "Yeah, I know. She's the least likely person to need protecting. She's such a strong woman. But she's been hurt too much, I think. I don't want to be another one on the list. If I could, I'd keep her safe from everything."

He stopped walking as he realized he had reached Kate's door. He took a breath and then walked up and knocked. The door opened instantly and Kate smiled at him. In a long sleeved blouse and black skirt, she was even lovelier than he remembered. Her eyes sparkled. "Good evening!" A low growl caught her attention and she looked down. "Umm, Mel? Tell me she's yours."

"Stormy!" He caught his wolf's collar and pulled her back. "Stop that!" He knelt down and caught her face in his hands. He held her eyes intently. There was something oddly familiar about them, but once more his mind shied away. "Be nice or go home."

Stormy stopped growling but didn't fully relax. She sat down obediently, and even let Kate pet her head gently. Her eyes measured her rival intently. She looked like a ball of cotton candy compared to a prime piece of steak. Fluffy and insubstantial and not nearly enough for an alpha male. As she watched them walk away, she laid down with her eyes narrowed. She didn't like her one bit. She didn't even *have* a scent.

Mel and Kate walked to the restaurant they had chosen earlier via text message. It was a sit down place, but it wasn't terribly formal. Once they were seated and had appetizers, they looked over the menu. "I want something with vegetables," she decided. "How about you, Mel?"

"I'm eyeing the rare steak." He smiled wryly. "I've been craving red meat lately."

"You carnivore you." Her voice was teasing.

As dinner progressed, he found her to be a lively companion with a sharp wit and clever mind. He enjoyed himself, and her company, but it didn't take long for him to start wishing it was Audra there with him instead. She could have walked into a fancy restaurant in her black jeans and been treated like a queen.

The longer the evening drew on, the more certain he became that his desire for Audra was not a result of primal instinct. He didn't want Kate, no matter how lovely she was. She didn't have thick black hair like a mane, and she didn't have a hunter's yellow eyes. She was too short for him, and she wasn't that strong. She was too nice, not acerbic enough.

She wasn't Audra, and Audra was the only woman he wanted.

Stormy was still lying on the sidewalk when they returned home, and as Kate turned to unlock her door, she said cheerfully, "That was fun, the three of us."

"Three of us?" Mel blinked.

"Yes. You, me, and the woman you were wishing I was." Dull color filled his cheeks and she gave a sigh. "Oh, well. The good ones are always taken. It was fun anyway. If you want her," she added as she went into her house, "go after her, okay? If I'm going to lose out on a great guy, I want to lose him to a great woman."

"I will." He had to smile. "Thanks, Kate. I really am sorry." The door shut and he let out a long sigh. He walked over to where Stormy was waiting and knelt down to run a hand gently over her head. She looked up at him expectantly, and he sighed again. "Okay, you were right. Just don't gloat." He stood and began to walk down the sidewalk with his wolf walking companionably beside him. "I don't want Kate." He tucked his hands in his pocket. "I want Audra."

She stopped dead in her tracks for long moments. She shook it off quickly and hurried to catch up. Once she had, he said thoughtfully, "It hit me pretty hard the other day. When I kissed her . . . god. There's no way to describe how *right* it felt. It was the hottest kiss I've ever had the luxury of experiencing, and my hunger for her hasn't gone away. It just keeps growing. The scent of her skin is maddening. The curve of her neck . . . I have the almost unbearable urge to bite her there. I want her like hell on fire, and I have no idea what to do about it.

"She doesn't think she's beautiful, but she is inside. There's something about her . . . something different. Once I got past the scar and her surface attitude, I began to look at her as a whole. And there's a whole lot to Audra. She's rude, and brash, and she's definitely mean. But . . . that's Audra. I like the way she is."

The house was dark when they arrived. He could only assume Audra was still out. He held the door open for Stormy and shut and locked it behind them both. As he headed up the stairs, he began unbuttoning his shirt. "I'm not sure what to do," he mused. He dropped his shirt on the chair in his room. "Maybe if I sleep on it, I'll get a clue."

She had stopped listening. Her eyes were riveted to the back of his left shoulder. There, right where the muscles of his back rippled when he moved his arms, was the telltale wolf's head. The black tattoo was a birthmark that differentiated between regular werewolves and alpha ones. A regular wolf had a black claw. Only an alpha had the wolf's head.

If put under enough pressure, he would not be able to resist the urge to transform. The first change was demanded by nature, but he would have perfect control after it. She could only be glad she had left the knowledge behind for him. Even when she was gone, the wolves would continue.

She leapt up onto the bed and laid down to watch as he changed into sweatpants. He was so beautiful to her eyes. He always had been. When he got into bed, she couldn't resist moving closer to rest her head on his lap. His fingers moved softly over her head but couldn't wholly soothe her. Being told that a man wanted you like hell on fire was murder on self-control.

She stayed beside him until he fell asleep. Once he had, she leapt down and ran through the house to her balcony. She leapt over the side and landed gracefully on the grass outside. She was going to run until she was too tired to drop. If she did, perhaps the unbearable urge to change back, strip naked, and climb into his bed would go away. It would be stupid, but it was tempting.

Still, for the time being, it was enough to know he wanted her. It had been a long time since anyone had.

CHAPTER TWENTY-NINE

Mel awoke the next morning to a mind that was crystal clear. If he wanted Audra—and he assuredly did—then he needed to make the first move. It was a move that had to be made when there was no excuse she could use for his behavior. She couldn't have any reason to push him away.

"Primitive instinct, my ass," he muttered as he got out of bed. It was early, barely dawn, but there would be no better time.

He headed down the hall and walked right into her room without knocking. Cheerfully he called, "How can a man apologize if you keep running off and then sleeping the morning away?" He flicked the light on, and she sat up instantly, cursing sleepily in another language he had never heard. At that moment, he wasn't sure he remembered his own name.

She was naked. Wonderfully, gloriously, naked. The blankets had fallen to her waist and he could see every inch of her silky skin. Her strong shoulders flowed down into breasts that were high and shapely and perfectly formed to fill his hands. Her ribcage was elegant, and her stomach was trim. He saw her only as a whole at first, but then his eyes truly focused and he began to see the smallest details.

Her body was riddled with scars. Small ones all over her ribcage as if she had been shot. There was a vicious one across her lower belly in the same color as the one across her face; it too was still fairly new. Pain ripped him apart inside as he wondered how she had survived whatever had happened. "Audra."

Sleep finally lifted. She realized he was staring at her and she hastily grabbed a sheet to cover herself. She tugged it up to her chin and narrowed her eyes warningly. "Your father failed. He seems to have missed one."

"One what?"

"A gentleman!" She threw her pillow at him. "Get out of my room, you bastard. This isn't a peep show, and I want my sleep!" She rolled over and jerked the sheet over her head. It was promptly jerked down again and whisked away entirely. Cursing, she sat up and crossed her arms across her breasts. "Mel!" She glared at him fiercely.

"Well, it was already too late," he said reasonably.

She tried to hit him, but he was faster. He caught her wrist and yanked her off balance. She tried to twist free but by the time the dust settled, she was pinned underneath him entirely with his weight keeping her prisoner. Her hands were once more cuffed over her head. "This is getting to be a bad habit of yours!" she almost snarled.

Softly, he said, "You're beautiful, Audra."

She went very still, her eyes widening. Something that was shock and panic moved in her yellow gaze before anger spiked once more. "The hell I am. Put your glasses on and look again." Her stomach quivered as he continued to gaze at her, his chocolate gaze melting her. "I'm scarred," she reminded him curtly. "There's no way that could possibly turn you on."

He said nothing as he looked her over. The scars went all the way down her legs as well, more small marks where something had ripped through flesh. Thin lines from a blade. The worst was the ragged mark across her stomach. He shifted his grip on her wrists to one hand and slid his freed hand under her. His fingers found a matching scar on her lower back and more small scars all over her upper back. She had been *run though the stomach* at some point in time.

She closed her eyes tightly and turned her head away. She felt exposed and ripped raw. She could fool herself into believing her body was attractive as long as she had clothes on, but if she was naked, every flaw was laid bare. No man in his right mind would ever want her and she knew it. Something hot landed on her shoulder and she looked up quickly to see tears in Mel's eyes. Suffering had turned his eyes black. Her own eyes slowly widened. "Mel . . ."

"God, Audra." His voice was strained. "How did you survive? It destroys me to think of how much pain you must have felt!" He lowered his head for a moment, struggling for control. He wanted to kiss and caress every mark, to remove even the memory of pain. His eyes fell on the little black birthmark on her hip, and it was a welcome distraction. He skimmed a knuckle over it softly. "Nice. A tattoo?"

"Birthmark," she admitted. It was hard to lie to a man who had you naked in his arms. It only added another layer of guilt as she remembered all the other lies she had told. She tugged lightly at her hands, but he had her held firmly. Heat began to slowly roll through her blood as she saw that he was still only in sweatpants. His chest was broad and powerful, and her mouth watered just looking at him. "This is a bad idea," she whispered, her eyes lifting to his. Her toes curled as she saw darkness in his eyes that was no longer pain but pure, raw, hunger.

"So what?" He lowered his head, his lips teasing hers. "I'll show you," he murmured, "how much I want you. I'd never lie to you about that."

But I've lied to you, she thought in despair. A shudder went through her body as his mouth touched hers, and she struggled between acceptance and denial, resistance and surrender. He wanted her. Despite all odds, he wanted her.

A child's scream rent the morning air. His head jerked up in shock. He released her and rolled to his feet. She was only a step behind him as they ran down the stairs, and she yanked on a shirt over her body as she went. She followed him outside and they rushed around the side of the building. She took in the entire scene within moments.

A man had a small girl by the wrist and was dragging her down the street. She resisted fiercely, small wings on her back fluttering madly, she tried to pull out of his grip. "Let go of her!" Mel shouted.

The man looked up and light glinted off the blade in his hand. Something moved inside Mel and awoke with a rush. Audra sensed it and knew that he was about to forcefully change for the first time. She couldn't let him put himself in danger. Her decision was made in a second. She lunged forward with a snarl, and her body glowed and shifted as she changed into the form of the wolf.

She struck the man's chest with all fours and took him flat to the sidewalk. The child was set free, and she rushed over to fly into Mel's arms. He barely noticed. He could only stand still in shock, staring at what he was seeing, disbelief and dim horror filling him. He knew the wolf. How could he not?

Audra was Stormy.

The shock was enough to open his mind to all the little things he had never wanted to understand. Anger began a slow boil and grew into a simmering rage as he realized how badly he had been lied to, how badly he and his whole family had been manipulated. He put the child down. "Call a policeman," he ordered quietly.

"Audra will protect us." The girl popped her thumb in her mouth. "She always protects us. She'll make him go away."

He observed the way 'Stormy' was growling with her teeth inches from the man's throat. He half expected her to eat him, and he couldn't really begrudge her that at the least. Yet she wasn't attacking. Her eyes were locked with the assailant, and Mel could almost feel a conversation happening. After a few moments, she backed up a step and the man got to his feet before turning and walking away with a dazed look in his eyes.

"Audra!" The child lunged forward and wrapped her arms around the wolf's neck. "You saved me!" She held on as Audra changed back and found herself clinging to the woman's neck. She held on tighter and snuggled close. "Thank you."

"Do not," Audra said firmly, steel in her voice, "ever go outside unescorted again, Nell. I will beat you until you can't sit for a month!" She turned her face into the child's hair and knew her entire body was trembling. It wasn't just from fear at nearly losing a child, but with dread for the coming confrontation. Mel was furious.

She put Nell down and watched her run into the orphanage again. Then, hiding as much of her trembling as possible, she turned to Mel and gestured to the house. "After you."

He turned and walked into the house, his body stiff with anger, and she tried to brace herself for when he unleashed it. She wasn't sure she could handle it.

He let it loose the instant the door shut behind her. "My god," he said through his teeth. The words were clipped and came out with the full force of his accent. "You really played me for a fool, didn't you? You've been manipulating my whole family, playing at the family pet . . . you listened to me babble about my dreams and things I've never told anyone else! Faerie godmother, my ass!"

She kept her voice even with effort. "If you had asked me, I'd have told the truth."

"How was I supposed to know?!" he shouted. He turned and began to pace furiously. He raked his hands through his hair. "God," he muttered, "I've been lusting after the family pet. My siblings will have a fit."

The blow was well placed, and she tucked it where it couldn't be seen. "Yes," she said coolly. "I am a family pet. I was once the alpha of a proud werewolf clan that was destroyed. I was their greatest warrior. Now I'm a pet, only here because I am guiding your family on its path."

He snapped, "Don't sound so ill used. You've had it good for a long time now. What? Were you bored and in need of a hobby? Pity for the lowly human family?" His head snapped to the side as her palm cracked across his cheek.

"It's not a hobby!" she shouted. "It's my life! And do you think it was any easier on me?! I've wanted you for so long, and I knew I would never have you if you knew the truth! For a few precious days, you looked at me as if I wasn't what everyone has always known me to be. You knew from the beginning, Mel Shaughnessy! You knew I was a beast! In your own mind, you condemned me and you *were right*! Get out of my house. Don't come near me again!"

She ran up the stairs faster than any human ever could and a door slammed so hard that the building shook. Shaking slightly, he slowly sank down to sit on the side of the couch. He felt like scum and lower than dirt. Like an idiot, he had lashed out to hurt because he was hurting. It was an unfortunate family trait that he had thought he didn't have. His temper began to cool, and he began to see things through her eyes. And as he did, he realized nothing had truly changed.

He still wanted her. Human or werewolf, he wanted her. Where was the difference in his telling her his secrets and dreams while she was a wolf than while she was human? Wasn't that part of getting to know someone? Also, she had her self-imposed job to find them all a true love. If she wanted to match him, then she needed to know him.

He had known he was making things hard for 'Stormy,' but now he finally understood why. How was she going to find him true love when he was all tangled up with her in her human form? The simple answer was . . . she wasn't. He didn't want anyone else. He wanted her. Were his feelings love? He didn't know. But he knew, absolutely knew, that he could not let her go. They had a chance at something special.

He climbed the stairs slowly. He could hear the shower running and somehow he heard her crying though not a sound emerged. He paused outside the door for long moments and then nodded once. Burning his bridges, as they said.

She stood under the pounding water and let it wash away her tears. It couldn't wash away her pain, and it welled endlessly inside her, hurting more than any bullet or sword could. She just wished it was all over with already, that the pain was gone. Freedom didn't matter anymore. She just wanted to be away from the pain.

She didn't blame Mel. She had been expecting his reaction all along. It was just so much worse coming on the heels of the morning's events. For the first time in a time longer than she could remember, she had felt desired. Someone had wanted her despite all odds. Even though it had only happened once and would never happen again, she held the memory close.

His scent unexpectedly seemed to sear into her lungs. The wolf mark throbbed softly. Her head jerked up in shock. She hadn't heard the door open, but strong masculine arms were suddenly wrapping around her waist and drawing her back against an equally strong body. She couldn't breathe, too afraid to hope. "Mel?" She twisted enough to look up at his face.

"I'm sorry." He pressed his lips to the curve of her shoulder and tasted the freshness of her skin. "Forgive me, please. I was an ass. Don't close me out."

A shudder of pleasure rippled through her body. Her neck was the most sensitive place on her body, and she was unable to resist his touch to begin with. Her eyes closed and her head fell back weakly as his hands slid slowly over her body to learn her curves. "This is a mistake," she whispered.

"It doesn't feel like one." He could feel each little pucker under his fingers as his hands glided over her stomach. He wished he could take them all away and erase even the memory of pain. "I want you until I can't breathe." His lips curved. "But I already told you that."

"No, you don't." She gasped as he drew her hips firmly back against him so that she couldn't mistake his arousal pressed against her.

"How old are you again?" he teased softly, catching the rim of her ear in his teeth lightly. "That's not a cell phone in my pocket."

"You," her breath broke as his hands closed over her breasts and rubbed slowly, sending fire flicking through her veins, "you don't have pockets. You're naked."

"So are you. And you're very beautiful naked." He turned her in his arms and his hands sank into her wet hair to tilt her head back. Before she could voice the protest he sensed, he covered her mouth with his. He kissed her as deeply as he could, drinking from her wildly, his tongue tangling with hers.

She fisted her hands into his hair on a low moan and met the kiss with an equal passion. She couldn't fight any longer. She loved him, and he was her perfect mate. If she didn't hold him inside her body soon, she would go mad.

He dragged her closer with one arm and turned off the water with his free hand. Still kissing her, ravenous for her taste, he boosted her in his arms and left the shower and bathroom. She expected to find herself on the bed in her room, but to her surprise he went down the hall into his room instead. "What are you doing?"

He tumbled her down onto the bed and kissed her so deeply that her body arched helplessly toward his. "No ghosts," he muttered as he raced his lips over her face. "No bad memories, no nightmares. Nothing but us." His lips traveled the length of the scar. "Thank you," he whispered. "You gave me my brother and sister, and my baby nephew."

"Madelyne is my friend." She shuddered as the tip of his tongue once more caressed the scar. The little healing touch seemed to reach all the way to her soul. She quivered helplessly in his arms as his lips buried against the curve of her neck, right where he had said he was so interested. His teeth nipped sharply in a wolf's love bite, jerking a ragged moan from her throat.

Ravenous for her flesh, desperate to remove all bad memories, he slowly made his way down her body, his lips and tongue tracing and soothing every scar. She was wild in his arms, wonderfully free and uninhibited. He knew he was out of control, felt nothing restraining him as his teeth nipped at her hip right over the birthmark. She responded as if she had been made for him.

As his teeth nipped again, almost playfully this time, pleasure flooded her body and left her feeling clean. The cold had been banished in fire, and she reached for him eagerly. She wanted to know that wonderful body, to leave her own mark as a warning to any female who dared look at her mate.

He caught her hands and held them at her sides. "Not yet," he murmured, and closed his lips over her nipple and sucked strongly. Her response was a muffled cry, and she arched against him desperately.

He was relentless in his pursuit to drive her out of her mind. Her breath was almost a sob as she struggled to free her hands. "Stop, too much!" His hot breath washed over the sensitive skin of her inner thighs and she stopped breathing entirely. "Let me loose, you fiend!"

His husky laughter was as seductive as his touch, and his lips touched her in a thrilling caress. Her entire body shuddered. He was gentle but ruthless and drove her higher and higher until the tension shattered and left wild ecstasy behind. It wasn't enough. His grip loosened just a fraction, and she broke her hands free with a wild twist of her body that had desire gleefully stabbing through his body.

Rolling quickly, she pinned him beneath her and her hands locked with his. "I want you crazy," she muttered against his shoulder. She bit sharply, unable to control the instinct urging her to mark him as her own. He shuddered, his eyes as feral as hers as he looked up at her. Power flooded her wildly and hotly.

Hers. Even if only for a little while, he was hers.

Hungry to imprint him on her very soul, she petted and caressed him from head to heels, her lips tracing hot designs across his skin. His muscles knotted with desire, and she dazedly felt the rise of her own need. She felt drunk on him as if she couldn't get enough. A little purr of pleasure in her throat, she rose over him, her lips seeking his. Her fingers slid down his body, curled around his erection, and his control broke.

He dragged her hand up to curl around his neck and rolled swiftly to pin her. He caught her hips and dragged her up against him. Before she could catch her breath, he was sinking into her, stretching her completely, desperate to feel her pulsing around him. When he was in her to the hilt, he stopped and buried his lips against her throat to taste her pulse. Seamless, perfect. Audra. She was *his*.

She strangled a cry in her throat as his teeth closed sharply over her neck. He sucked softly on the skin to soothe it and flames licked over her nerves, making her writhe beneath him wildly. "Mel, please!"

He dragged her closer, his mouth sealing hers as he began to drive in and out of her quickly. He was going out of his mind; he would never have enough of her soon enough. The pleasure grew to unbearable heights but wouldn't end; it felt wilder and hotter than anything before. It slammed into him without warning and a low groan ripped from his chest as he surrendered to the wild ecstasy.

It was too much for her to bear, and she clung onto him as wicked waves of pleasure washed over her. His arms locked around her tighter, and she felt inside as the part of her that was the wolf, the part that had never been tamed, calmed and quieted. It brought a sense of completion and peace that she had never thought possible. And when his body shuddered, his weight pressing her deeper to the mattress, she knew he, too, had felt the joy of finally finding his perfect match.

She didn't bother to move for a long time. She simply lay peacefully in his arms and listened to the clock tick softly in the background. He stirred finally and slowly lifted himself onto his arms. His eyes swept over her face possessively. "Hey," he said huskily, his lips feathering over her face. "You going to sleep on me?"

"Under you." Her voice was drowsy with satisfaction. "There's a difference." She found the energy to open her eyes as he shifted to lie beside her. "It wasn't a complaint." His hand moved slowly over her skin, and when it slid down to rest over the scar on her stomach, she closed her eyes. "Mel," she started, but stopped when his hand moved up to touch her lips. His thumb traced their shape and then down along her scar as if it was just another part of her body for him to caress.

"I know. I'm so sorry." He gathered her closer, his eyes closing as he thought about the unfairness in life. Someone as giving as Audra, someone who loved children so deeply, deserved a chance at children of her own.

"I've learned to accept it," she admitted softly, her hands stroking slowly over his shoulders. She turned her head and glanced at the clock. She promptly sighed and turned her face into his shoulder. "You need to get ready for class, and so do I."

"I don't wanna." He smiled down at her. "Wanna play hooky?" He kissed her softly, but the way her lips clung to his made hunger stir anew. The kiss turned carnal quickly. He eased back enough to huskily tease, "I'm not worried about my grades. I have this really good tutor. Mind you, she's kind of bitchy, but she's really hot."

She snorted lightly and twisted to pin him to the bed instead. "Who's bitchy? I'll have you know I'm a paragon of good graces." She sighed and rested against his chest. One day. She already knew how it was going to end. She could steal one day. "Oh, give me the phone," she finally sighed. "I'll call in." She tasted his pulse softly, liked it, and lingered there. "Want a hands-on lesson, kid?"

"Depends on what subject." He skimmed a knuckle down her ribcage, fascinated by her skin. She was utterly beautiful. Scars and all. There was something inside her, some purity that shined through any surface imperfection.

"Mmm. How about a time in history when women walked around half naked?"

"I like my women completely naked. And, hey, convenient, you are." He grinned as she braced herself over him. "As always, I'm glad to learn. Am I going to be graded?"

Her lips curved as they met his. "Maybe you are."

The next time she felt compelled to move, it was only because he rolled onto his back and dragged her over on top of him. He had, once more, managed to get her pinned. She was finding she really liked his dominant side. Then again, it *was* to be expected. He was her perfect match. Alpha to alpha. Male to female. At some point during the day, she was going to have to teach him how an alpha female dominated her male. He would greatly enjoy it.

Thinking about it made her realize that there were still secrets she was keeping. She couldn't tell him all of it. One of the secrets could yet make him hate her. She also could not tell him that she was his perfect mate. If she did, he would never find the will to love again. More than anything, she wanted him happy in the end. She could at the least tell him what he was, though. "Mel?"

"Hmm? Going to give me my grades now?"

Her lips curved against her will. "What's higher than an A+?"

"I'm not sure. We can invent something." He tucked his hands under his head as she slid off his chest and rose to her knees beside him. He could feel the seriousness in her mood. "Is there more you need to tell me?" he asked quietly.

"Yes." She lowered her gaze and let out a little breath. "The Shaughnessy family . . . the first Shaughnessy I aided was a man named Kay Shaughnessy. He was the founder of the Shaughnessy Corporation."

He blinked. "That was one hundred fifty years ago."

"You remember when you asked my age? I think the proper response is roughly around one hundred eighty-nine."

"I can handle that. Older women are sexy. And you look amazing for your age." He skimmed a hand over her hip. "Is that supposed to scare me? Hell, Audra, you're a werewolf. If that doesn't scare me, nothing will."

"How about the fact that you are also a werewolf?" He went very still and she lowered her gaze. "Kay's perfect match was a young woman from 3rd District named Raven. Her blood, though thinned over the years, has given each Shaughnessy child a gift. All of you knew you had a gift. It manifested in small ways as was to be expected of thin blood. But you . . . you are different."

He let out a long breath as things finally began to make sense. "My strength and speed. My agility. The feralness inside me that you so revel in. My dominating personality and the wildness that scares most people. When did you realize?"

"When you were chasing me."

He snorted softly. "Primitive instinct, my ass!"

"It was technically true. It just happened to be primitive *wolf* instinct. You fell so naturally into the mating hunt of a wolf that it shocked me. Then when you pinned me, when you nipped at my neck, I saw your eyes." She lifted her gaze to look into those same eyes. Beautiful chocolate brown with the amber rim. "The Amber Mark. It's in your eyes, too, now. I'm surprised you didn't notice it. Only a wolf has that mark."

As she took a breath, he let his out. "And there's more."

"A little bit." She drew his hand to the birthmark on her hip. "This is the mark of an alpha. I am an alpha female wolf. It means I am the strongest and fastest of all female wolves born. I am the leader of all female wolves should there be any others. There is only ever one alpha per gender per generation for the clan."

His eyes slowly widened. "I don't have a mark."

"Yes, you do. It's on your back shoulder. I saw it the other night. It is the proof that you are an alpha male werewolf. Given enough pressure, you will change into the wolf for the first time. After that, you will be in control."

There were dozens of things he could have said. He could see she was waiting for rejection or fear, but all he felt was a curious sense of understanding. "It makes sense," he finally said, "of everything about me. Everything about you and me. The way we come together." A flustered look suddenly crossed his face. "I bit you."

She lowered her lashes to hide a smile. "Repeatedly. And have you noticed you're a bit, hmm, dominating, shall we say, with me? It's the alpha instinct. You have to be on top. Especially of me, because you *know* instinctively that I could take control."

He reached out and tumbled her onto his chest once more. "Any time you want to return the favor," he tugged her down so that he could feather his lips over her neck, "feel free. I think I can handle letting you take charge. You being so much older and wiser."

As his lips found hers, she let herself sink into him. Tears burned her eyes but never fell. He might never love her, but he accepted her. He wanted her. She could do nothing but give him everything. As Rhianna had said, it meant there would be no regrets.

She wanted to regret nothing about him.

CHAPTER THIRTY

Friday was midterms for Mel's classes. Audra had given her midterms the day before so she stayed home while he went to school. It was one of the hardest things he had ever done to leave her sleeping in his bed. He had grown addicted to the way she felt and tasted, to the way her scent always seemed so *right*. And as a lover . . . as a lover, she was something else.

She was as wild and free as he was, unafraid of the volatile passion that exploded between them. No matter how out of control he got, she matched him. He didn't have to fear hurting her. He didn't have to fear that whatever was inside him would terrify her. He was, however, a little wary to see what reactions he got at school. He felt different. He was different.

It was a visible difference. Males and females alike watched him a little warily when he approached. Once he spoke to them, showed he was the same Mel, they relaxed and the wariness went away. Mostly. The wolf inside him was close under the surface and humans were instinctively attuned to predators.

It made him realize just how long and lonely Audra's life had been. It was little wonder she had spent so much time as a wolf with his family. They loved her unconditionally. She still didn't talk about herself, but he knew he had all the time in the world to get her to open up. He had moved her into his room with him, and she hadn't had another nightmare since.

All his midterms were in the morning. He actually liked it that way because it meant he could go home early. He had a rather cranky alpha female who would be waiting impatiently to hear the results of her hard work. Even being lovers hadn't stopped her from shoving as much information in his head as possible. He kinda suspected it was making her *more* determined. She had a bigger interest in his well-being now.

The first class for the day was Japanese. It was clutch time, do or die. He finished his paper well ahead of the rest of the class and could only sweat out the results. When the teacher walked past his desk and placed his test on it upside down, he almost didn't want to look. He carefully peeked up the edge and a cheerful 'A-' at the top seemed to stare up at him. He looked up in shock and found Nobunaga smiling at him.

An A. Him, Mel Shaughnessy, with an A. It nearly made him giddy. It also drove him to do his best in all his classes. With every A or B, his spirit rose. It couldn't even be diminished when he got a C in Geography. He *hated* Geography, no matter how many cities and states and countries he was forcefully fed.

He had borrowed Audra's motorcycle to get to school, and on the way home, he stopped to buy a bouquet of flowers. A little spring was in his step as he entered the house. "Audra, I'm home! Guess what?"

There was no response. With a frown, he dropped his bag by the door and climbed the stairs. "Audra?" To his surprise, he found her curled in a miserable heap on his bed. She was coughing weakly as if she didn't have the strength for anything else. "Audra. It's okay, baby." He walked over and sat beside her to gently press his hand to her forehead. She was burning up. "Got yourself a bug, did you?"

"Yes. Go away." She jerked the covers over her head, cranky and miserable. They were immediately jerked down again and a shiver roughened her skin. "I'm cold," she complained.

"You've got a really high fever." He scooped her up into his arms and carried her down to the bathroom. He ran lukewarm water in the tub and gently stripped off the borrowed shirt she wore. "Thief," he teased gently. "That's my best shirt."

"It was there. It smelled like you." She let her head drop onto his shoulder.

"It looks better on you than on me." He gently lifted her into the tub and felt his heart ache when she bit back a whimper of pain. "I know, honey." He gently began to wash her, soothing her heated skin with a soft sponge. "Why didn't you say you were sick?"

"I didn't know until I woke up." She leaned weakly against his shoulder. She couldn't tell him, had no way of explaining, what was truly happening. Her body was beginning the process that would end her contract with the Enforcers. It felt so good to be taken care of, so wonderful to have him caring for her. She could only revel in his tenderness.

He gently lifted her out of the tub and held her steady as he dried her. Her skin was already cooler and she wasn't shivering violently anymore. He gently tucked her back into the shirt and carried her back to their bedroom. As he slid her under the covers, he asked, "Do you feel well enough for some good news?"

"Good news is always welcome." Her eyes had fallen half closed but they opened again as she saw the flowers he was holding out. Her heart thumped painfully. Only the children had ever given her flowers before. "For me? What for?"

"You're one badass tutor, Professor Alexandrios." He grinned at her. "Guess who aced his midterms."

She began to smile. "You did? That's wonderful. Now you won't have to worry about your graduation at all." Tears burned her eyes suddenly as she realized she wouldn't be there for it. "I'm . . . really happy." She turned her face into his shoulder and held onto him with a desperate sort of strength. "Sorry."

"You don't feel good. You're entitled." He tucked her in securely. "I get to pamper you for a while now," he informed her gravely. "You're going to have to lie there and take it like a good little wolf." To take the sting out of the words, he leaned over to steal a kiss. "And if I get sick, you can boss me around."

"I don't need an excuse." She didn't argue as she laid there and watched him tidy up the room. His presence was so soft and comforting that she felt herself sliding toward sleep. She would always cherish how safe he had made her feel. How wanted. With a little sigh, she curled up and fell asleep.

He glanced over and a smile softened his face as he walked over to sit beside her. He gently brushed the hair back from her face, his fingers smoothing down her cheek. He didn't like seeing her sick, but he liked being able to take care of her, especially because no one else had. He wouldn't mind doing it for the rest of his life.

His hand froze as he realized where his thoughts had gone. A little breath shuddered out his lips. Well. That was unexpected. He was in love with her.

He began to smile. Truthfully, it wasn't so unexpected. Stormy had attached herself to him with the intent of finding him true love, and she had done exactly that. It just happened to be her personally. But, really, even the logical part of his brain could understand why. Who would suit an alpha male wolf better than an alpha female wolf, and vice versa?

She might not believe him but he was determined to convince her and make her stay with him. When she went home with him, as she damned well would, she would not go home as a pet. She would go as his lover and future wife. Wolves mated for life, and it was time she truly claimed the place in their family that she had always owned.

He started to reach for her shoulder to wake her and tell her, but the phone rang and startled him. He quickly grabbed it before it could wake her. "Alexandrios residence."

"Mel!" It was Taegan, and there was a trace of panic in his voice. "Thank god! We've been trying to call you all morning but your cell was off!" He drew a ragged breath. "You have to come to the hospital. Dad's had a heart attack. He's in surgery right now. We don't know how bad it is."

The color drained from his face. "Oh, shit. Okay, yeah, I'm on my way! I'll be right there." He hung up the phone and turned to look at Audra. She was in no shape to go anywhere, but she would understand. He would just come back on Saturday after he was sure Sullivan would be fine. That he would be fine was not up for debate in his mind.

He wrote her a note and packed his things. He wasn't leaving them there. When he came back tomorrow, he was going to convince her to come home with him where she had always belonged. She needed family, and the Shaughnessys were the only one for her. His siblings and his dad would love her true self even more than they had loved her as a wolf.

That done, he called for the family chauffeur. He needed to get to the hospital and refused to wait for a cab. There was no way he was going to lose his father.

When Audra awoke not long later, she knew she was alone in the house. She carefully got out of bed and walked on rubbery legs to where she could see a note sitting on the dresser. The room, she noticed, carried no sign of Mel except for the shirt she still wore.

The note was short and simple. *'Dad's in the hospital. I'll be back tomorrow afternoon if everything's okay. Get some rest.'*

Tears slowly welled up in her eyes and slid down her cheeks. Gathering all her strength, she went into her bedroom and simply pulled on jeans under his shirt; she couldn't bear to let go of that tiny connection to him. It was all she had left. She picked up the phone and began to make calls. She had been planning for this for so long that everything was done on automatic.

When Mel got to the emergency room, he saw his entire family was already there. Aenya was on Hiro's lap, sobbing in his shoulder, and Taegan was pacing like a caged animal. Kalliope was curled up on her chair, her face streaked with tears, and Kienan was holding Madelyne. Mel's stomach clenched. "Is he okay? Do we know anything?" he asked.

Taegan shook his head. "Not yet. It caught us all off guard. He was arguing with Kienan about something, like always, then he suddenly went gray and collapsed. The paramedics think Kienan doing CPR saved his life, but we don't know that yet for certain."

"Stupid old man," Kienan said roughly. "The doctors told him to watch his heart!" Tears slid slowly down his face. "He can't die. He's too young to die."

It was close to ten o'clock that night before the doctor came to them. He surveyed the drawn faces in the room then looked at Taegan who was clearly the eldest. "He'll make it," he announced.

Taegan sagged against the wall as Kalliope gave a little cry and flew into his arms. Kienan and Madelyne nearly fell out of their shared chair. Aenya just cried harder, this time in relief, as she clung to Hiro. He held her tighter, his face as raggedly relieved as the rest. Mel felt so lightheaded so fast that he had to hastily sit down.

"How is he?" Taegan asked. He held onto Kalliope with all his strength, his entire body shaking.

"We had to do a bypass since one of the arteries was completely clogged. A stent took care of the other one." The doctor checked his notes. "He had a lower than average vitamin count and his iron was borderline. His blood pressure bottomed out at one point but we got him back." He let out a little breath, exhausted to his core. "We're going to keep him in CICU overnight. If he's doing this well tomorrow morning, we can probably move him to a regular room." He found a smile. "Go home and sleep, kids. He's not ready to give up yet."

"He's going to make it," Mel repeated softly as the doctor walked out. "Thank god." He raked his hands through his hair, already thinking of everything that needed doing. The most important thing on his list was calling his lover. "I should tell Audra as soon as I can."

All eyes swung toward him. They had all noticed the difference inside him but there really hadn't been a time to say anything about it. Naturally, it was Kalliope who went right to the point. "You're in love with Professor Alexandrios."

"Yeah." His smile softened. "She matches me in every way. I love her so much, guys. If I've ever made fun of you, you have my utmost apologies right now."

"Accepted," Kienan said promptly. He found a grin. "I never believed she was that bad a person." He felt the trembling in Madelyne's body and frowned as he held her tighter. "What's wrong, nightingale?"

"Did you tell her?" she demanded of Mel.

"No, not yet. I was going to, but she was asleep." She leapt to her feet and rushed into the bathroom, and he rubbed the back of his neck in confusion. Her mood swings lately had been just flat out strange. "Does anyone know what the hell is wrong with her?"

"Impending motherhood?" Kienan offered, but he was frowning at the bathroom door. "Aenya, Kally . . ."

"We're on it." Kalliope was already heading for the bathroom with Aenya on her heels. "You! Maddie! Talk, damn it!" They disappeared into the bathroom and the door swung behind them.

Mel didn't wait to find out whether or not anyone found out what was wrong with Madelyne. They all decided to go home, and he was the only one who didn't need to wait for one of the women, so he left by himself. The chauffeur was more than happy to pick him up, and he was just as relieved to hear that Sullivan would be fine.

It wasn't until Mel was standing in his bedroom that he realized how lonely it seemed without Audra. His bed was big, but he missed having her wrapped around him like a breathing blanket. She had a tendency to wiggle on top of him and sleep draped over him. It was very cold without her warmth. He needed to bring her home, and soon. She had always belonged to him and he to her, but they had never known. Knowing it now, he refused to waste more time.

Sullivan was moved into a regular room Saturday afternoon, and everyone took turns visiting him in the hospital. Mel went last and made sure he brought his midterms with him. He was fairly sure where the conversation was going to go.

He started it by walking in the room and saying, "If you wanted to hit on pretty nurses, there are better ways of going about it, Dad."

Sullivan smiled wryly and moved his bed enough he could sit up slightly. "Well, I hardly intended to do it." He fumbled slightly as Mel hugged him. It had been a long time since his boys had hugged him. "Stop that. The women were bad enough."

Mel pulled over the visitor's chair and sat with a smile. "Kally is going to make you miserable. She's already planning a meal schedule, and Maddie is helping find tasty but healthy alternatives to the things you dislike. God help you now, Dad."

"Maybe they can keep me here longer," he agreed on a grimace. He loved Kalliope but she was hell on wheels just like the rest of his kids.

"You wish," his son retorted dryly.

Silence fell for a few moments as Sullivan gathered his thoughts. He finally sighed softly. "Mel, I'm going to be retiring when you graduate. This has seriously made me realize my mortality, and I'm ready to turn the reins over to you and focus on being a grandfather. And, of course, until I'm out of here, I'm counting on you to handle things at the company."

"Absolutely. If it makes you feel any better, by the way," he dropped his midterms on Sullivan's lap, "take a look. I graduate in the spring, as planned."

Sullivan felt his recently battered heart swell with delight and relief. "Mel, I'm so proud of you." He cleared his throat slightly and tried to find a subtle way to ask. "Is there . . . you know, anything else you'd like to tell me?"

Mel laughed. "Don't be subtle. Yes, there's something else. I've decided to get married."

"Wait, call it a hunch . . . the tutor?"

"Good hunch." He tried to find a way to explain. "Audra is a werewolf, Dad," he finally said. "And she's been . . . rather involved in our lives, if you take my meaning. Stormy won't come home if I bring Audra."

It took Sullivan a second to understand. "I see." He cleared his throat. "Well." A werewolf. Well, Madelyne wasn't human either, so he could take it in stride. It was just a little unnerving to think that a wolf he had called a pet at one point was about to be his daughter-in-law. "How does she feel about things?"

"She's hurt. Badly. Or rather, she's been hurt. I don't know the details, but her entire body is riddled with scars. It's made people turn her away, and made them turn away in revulsion." He lifted his gaze, his eyes stark. "But I love her. No matter how rude and brash she is, I love her. Her heart . . . if you get close enough to her, her heart shines through it all. She's so beautiful inside."

"Then why haven't you brought her to me, boy? Go and find her and bring her to me so I can meet her properly." He watched intently as Mel left the room. His stomach was tight with dread. Just before he'd had the attack, he had been looking at the contract. It had been flashing red, but the word hadn't been 'Complete.' It had been 'Void.' Something was wrong.

Something was very wrong, Mel realized when he arrived at Audra's house. Her motorcycle was gone, and the curtains were drawn in every window. His mouth dry with fear, he ran up the stairs and unlocked the door to rush into the house. "Audra!"

In growing shock, he looked around the room at all the sheets that covered every piece of furniture. He raced up the stairs and found more of the same. There was no sign that she was there or had ever been there. She was gone.

His heart shattering in his chest, he slowly sank down to sit on the steps and wondered what the hell was going on. She had been sick, so how could she have done all this? And why? She knew he was coming back. What the hell was going on around here?!

His cell phone startled him by ringing loudly in the silence, and he slowly pulled it out of his pocket. He didn't know the number but still answered. "Shaughnessy."

"My name is Rhianna Taber. We've never met," a woman's voice said quietly, "but I work with your father, and soon I will be working with you. I need you to come to Enforcers' Headquarters. Immediately. Bring your contract when you do. This is, literally, a matter of life and death."

His heart began to pound dully in his chest. "Whose?" he managed to ask.

"Audra Alexandrios'."

CHAPTER THIRTY-ONE

There was a guard waiting at the doors of the Enforcers when Mel arrived. The guard escorted him to the elevator and rode with him all the way to the top floor. "Second door," he said and then left him alone on the floor.

Mel headed quickly down the hall and opened the second door. "Ms. Taber?" To his utter shock, he found himself looking at Kate Willowby. "Kate?!"

"Not exactly." She reached up and pressed the blue earring she wore. Her image wavered, shifted, and then splintered. It left behind a woman with rich red hair and deep black eyes. She wore a blue visor that she removed and tossed onto a chair. "A modern variation on the Mask of Illusions that your brother borrowed. You needed a push, so I gave it."

He sagged against the door as she went around behind the desk and sat down. "I'm afraid I don't understand."

Rhianna folded her hands on her desk and inclined her head at the free chair. "Sit down. There's not much time left." When he had complied, she studied him with eyes that were haunted. "May I see your contract?" He handed it over and she studied it intently. Her stomach rolled threateningly. "I see." She took a deep breath and reached into a drawer. She pulled out a scroll and passed it across to him. "This is the contract Audra Alexandrios has with Enforcers. It completes tonight, at midnight."

He didn't open the scroll. His fingers were shaking too hard. He simply put it on the desk again. "And?" Try as he might, his voice still shook. Terror choked him. Something inside howled in pain and denial. "What is all this? What is Audra? What happened to her? Why was she with my family? Ms. Taber, please tell me!"

She pressed her fingers to the bridge of her nose. "Little over one hundred and fifty years ago, there was a clan of werewolves living here in 3rd District. Audra was one of them. She was, beyond a doubt, their greatest warrior and most beloved member. She had a full family with six younger siblings. Kalin, the eldest, was her partner on the hunt."

So that was Kalin. "What happened?"

"A raid was raised by humans and they went into the forests that used to be nearby, the place where the clan lived. It was a slaughter. A massacre. Audra led the defenses, but even she can't outrun bullets. By the time she had killed the enemy, her entire clan was decimated.

"The house where she lives? It had been her family's home. She returned there, but it was in shambles. I'm sure you've seen the marks that remain. The blood and death . . . it was horrendous. The children of the village had been hidden there, and she went to find them. Unfortunately, a human had found them first. They were all dead. Kalin died in her arms not long after."

He closed his eyes as he thought of the screams in the walls and Audra's nightmares. Rhianna didn't look up, the story pouring out of her as if she had been holding it too long. "Audra went mad. Vowed vengeance on the humans who had arranged the slaughter. Among those she attacked was a Shaughnessy, one of your ancestors. She killed both husband and wife, and she was going to kill the child as well when soldiers caught her. They were going to kill her then and there but Enforcers stepped in.

"She could have been justified in her actions except that she had acted blindly. The Shaughnessys had been innocent. So, in an effort to stave off her execution, Enforcers offered a contract. She would stay with the family for as long as it took to make one hundred Shaughnessy children find love. A clock started from the day your ancestor came of age. She would have one hundred and fifty years to help his descendants, and if she could, she would be free of her execution. If not . . ."

"She dies." His voice was as stark as his eyes as he leaned forward urgently. "You said her contract completes tonight at midnight. You mean she's failed?"

"You're the hundredth," she said simply.

"But I love *her.* Doesn't that count for anything?" he shouted as he leapt to his feet.

Her composure cracked and she shot to her feet as well. "No!" she shouted back. "Feeling it isn't enough! You have to tell her! The words only have power if you say them! Audra loves you more than you know! She would be furious if she knew I had told you any of this now!"

"I have to find her!" He flattened his hands on the desk. "You have to tell me where she is!"

"I've looked! I can't find her anywhere!" She let out a ragged breath and drew a letter out of her desk. "She told me to give this to you tomorrow. I'm giving it to you now. Please, Mel. For the love of Zeus, help her. I've done all I can. You're the only one who can find her now!"

He took the letter and opened it quickly. He had recognized Audra's handwriting instantly. His hands shaking, he pulled out his glasses so he could read.

Mel,

If you're reading this, I'm gone. I'm sorry. I'm so sorry. I should have told you, but I didn't want you to feel obligated. It would have been so simple if you'd been anything but the wonderful man you are. I fell in love with you. You wondered why Stormy couldn't match you. It's because 'Stormy' let herself get involved.

I'm a werewolf. I was bound to protect your family and took the wolf's form to do it. Don't hate me, please. If I hadn't fallen for you, it would never have mattered. But I did. You're so unique, Mel. You're a human who is truly a werewolf. If you let yourself, you'll be able to access all of the skills that are yours by rights. You'll need to change under pressure the first time to gain control of your wolf form. When you feel it rise inside, just reach for it. It's that easy. I know you'll be fine. You have more strength and courage than any man I have ever known.

Remember me when the moon is full. And remember that I love you.

P.S. Study, damn it. Don't waste my hard work!

Tears slowly slid down his cheeks. Classic Audra. He folded the letter to tuck it safely in his pocket. "What time is it?" he demanded.

"Six."

"Only six hours," he whispered. "You have my cell number," he shouted as he ran toward the door. "Call me if you hear anything! I'm going to find her if it's the last thing I ever do!"

He tore the city apart in his quest to find her, but no matter where he went, who he asked, the response was always the same. No one had seen her. No one knew who she was. It was as if she had never existed. Yet Mel, with his sharpened senses growing slowly sharper, recognized the signs of compulsion. She *had* been through; she was erasing her presence.

Something inside had stirred and was raging. He was a werewolf. Her scent was seared inside him. Alpha to alpha. He reached without hesitation for that something inside and let it take him. It took only a moment to change to the shape of the wolf. It was a welcome and comforting change, familiar and warm.

His nose was thousands of times more acute in that form. He rushed through the city tracking her scent, seeking her with the single-minded determination of a mated male. In the end, he only found himself back at her home. It was where her scent ended and began. He shifted back and went inside, but she still was not there.

It was close to midnight and despair wrenched his heart and soul. He climbed the stairs to her bedroom and sat on the side of the bed as the walls cried their grief. Helplessly, his gaze sought the clock and the time.

11:55.

His eyes closed on a wave of pain, but a sound made him instantly look up. To his shock, he saw a young boy standing in the doorway. He was insubstantial and pale, and Mel realized in disbelief that he had to be staring at a ghost. The boy had Audra's eyes.

"Kalin?" he whispered.

The boy nodded and ran out of the room. Mel raced after him and followed him down to the living room. The boy pointed at the floor, and he began to pull up the torn carpet. "Of course," he muttered. "They hid the children here!"

The carpet came up and revealed a trapdoor. He yanked it up and descended the stairs as quickly as he could. He rushed down the cold hallway toward where he could see a spot of moonlight ahead of him. His mate's scent was rich and strong down there, summoning him to her side. He burst into the underground room and felt the walls scream.

Audra stood by a window that faced the full moon in the sky. She was pale and visibly weak but she was alive. "Audra," he managed to whisper.

Her head swung toward him in shock. "Mel!" Coughing wracked her body and she lost her hold on the window. He caught her before she fell on the floor, and she closed her eyes helplessly. "I didn't want you to see me like this!"

"Why didn't you tell me?" he demanded roughly.

"You deserve more than me. I killed your ancestors." Her eyes closed as tears spilled down her cheeks. "Innocent blood is on my hands. You deserve so much more! A woman who is whole, who is worthy of you!"

He heard in the distance as a clock began to toll the hour and desperately clutched her closer. "No!" he shouted. "No! I don't want anyone else! I love you, Audra Alexandrios! I don't care what you look like or what you've done! *I love you*!"

The bell stopped tolling midnight and she was motionless in his arms. Gut wrenching pain boiled up, and he lowered his head as sobs shook his body. It had never mattered. Nothing else had ever mattered. All he had ever wanted was her all along, and he hadn't known until too late!

A sudden light startled him, and he straightened up quickly as her entire body began to glow. Before his stunned eyes, the scars that marked her body began to glow with light one by one and disappear. He began to count them as they disappeared, and as the last scar, the one across her face, began to glow, he realized that she had been bearing exactly one hundred scars. The same number of Shaughnessys she had helped to find love.

The glow faded and he held his breath as he prayed to every deity he knew. She drew a sudden sharp breath, as if her lungs had been too long without air, and her eyes opened. She stared up at him without comprehension for long moments and then slowly lifted a hand to touch her face. "The scars," she whispered. "They're gone."

"I never saw them." He framed her face with his hand. "I love you, Audra. Werewolf, huntress or," his lips curved, "faerie godmother. I don't care. I love you exactly as you are."

Tears slowly slid down her cheeks as she wrapped her arms around his shoulders. "I love you too," she whispered, and she saw over his shoulder the young boy watching them from the stairs. *Thank you, Kalin*, she thought. *Goodbye*.

The spirit lifted a hand in farewell as he disappeared. And, as he did, the walls slowly stopped screaming as if all those who were gone were finally able to rest.

EPILOGUE

Rhianna sat in her office and stared pensively at the two contracts before her as she heard the clock slowly tolling its merciless melody outside her window. Both contracts flickered . . . and the word 'Complete' appeared across both of them.

The first laugh startled her as it slipped through her lips. It continued as she scrawled notes across the bottom of both contracts and slid them into a folder that glowed softly as the word 'Complete' appeared. She opened her drawer, slid the folder inside, and closed it. It only belatedly dawned on her that she was laughing *and* crying. She leapt to her feet joyously. "Riku!" she called to the office next to hers. "Get out a bottle of champagne!"

"Hot damn!" was the response. "Are we celebrating what I hope we are?"

"Damn right! Hurry up!" She knelt and locked the drawer beside her, her heart swelling happily as the drawer sealed itself and the word 'Finished' appeared across the front in bold red letters. Yes, the Shaughnessy File *was* good and finished.

She caught movement from the corner of her eye and stood to look. Her gaze softened as she saw the ghost standing inside the window. "Thank you," she said softly. "I owe you one, Kalin."

The little boy just smiled and waved a hand before disappearing into the waning moonlight. She watched him go and then turned with her hands on her hips to demand, "Where's my champagne?"

Status: File Complete

Analysis: The beauty wins the beast when the beast shows the beauty inside.

Turn the page for a bonus story about the first Shaughnessy, and for a peek into another world . . .

Bonus Folder

KAY

CHAPTER ONE

A little over one hundred and fifty years ago, America was entering an industrial revolution following the end of a bitter civil war. Inside New York, a second revolution was also occurring. It was a revolution of religion. Sides split and formed their own new units. And, caught in the middle, used as cannon fodder by the insanely fanatic who chose neither side, was the 3rd District in New York City.

The massacre took place in the dead of the night. Humans armed with weapons of all kinds plunged into the woods near the District and laid to waste the entire werewolf clan that had called the trees home. Men, women, and children were thoughtlessly slaughtered. Viewed as unspeakable, horrific, and inhuman, innocent blood was spilled. Only one werewolf survived.

The leaders and protectors of the 3rd District, the Enforcers, were enraged. Rhianna Taber's displeasure was felt when her powers erected an impenetrable barrier around her District. Eric Mason's fury was felt when his elemental powers ripped a river from its bed and sent it tearing through the homes of the murderers.

Rhianna and Eric were co-owners, partners, and best friends. They worked in tandem without thought, often by thought alone, and shared a single-minded determination to protect their people. When they heard that the surviving werewolf had attacked the Shaughnessy family, the Enforcers were quick to act. They argued her case before the governor himself, and then even to the President. Both distinguished gentlemen considered Eric and Rhianna friends. The werewolf's sentence was commuted so long as the Enforcers took her on. They agreed.

A new law was signed shortly thereafter by the governor. If any ever dared to harm a single denizen of 3rd District, they would be immediately arrested and brought before the Supreme Court. An uneasy sort of acceptance began as the 'normal' people came to grips with the unique beings within 3rd District. The people of 3rd District accepted the tentative truce, but they always watched warily when a stranger arrived.

There was one woman in particular who was truly terrified. Some people who were 3rd District born, like her, were finding their marriages annulled for every reason possible so that the person they were wed to didn't find themselves attached to the stigma. This woman held a very, very powerful position and was very well cared for. She was also pregnant.

She feared that if her husband learned she was 3rd District born, he would strip her of her position. And what would he do if he found out his child was therefore also an 'unusual'? Out of fear for her own security, she fled out of the city to the mountains by professing a fear of losing her child.

When the child was born, it was a lovely little girl. Her eyes and hair were pitch black, strong evidence of her paternal bloodline. Her mother despised her, for the child also had a small wave birthmark over her hip that declared her maternal water elf bloodline. If that mark had been gone . . . her mother would have never needed to worry.

The mother stood at the window with her child in her hands and considered hurling her to the ground and killing her. Only a fear of retribution for murder made her hesitate.

"I wish . . . I wish you'd turn into a raven and fly away!" she shouted.

To her shock, the child began to glow. She turned into the shape of a baby raven and flew away out the window on a mournful cry. The mother was fearful at first, afraid the child would die and she would be a murderess, but then she told herself that it was out of her hands. Anything that befell the child now would not be her fault.

Hugging the information close, she returned to her husband and tearfully told him the child had died in childbirth. He believed her, and she felt no fear for her position. Unfortunately, or perhaps fortunately, it turned out that life itself did not look kindly on what had occurred. She discovered very shortly that she would have no other children.

The raven flew and flew, crying the whole time. Rhianna Taber heard the cries and went looking for the child, wondering what was causing it to be so afraid. When she found her, she knew. She took the baby home personally and tried to determine what she should do next. It was her partner's suggestion to form a contract for her to hopefully dispel at least some of the curse. She agreed, and the child became known as Raven Childrose.

Over the next few years, the people of the state learned to be more lenient with the 3rd District. It was still a slightly uneasy truce, but the hostility had dimmed. Most were certain that within a short amount of time no one would even remember the coup at all. Rhianna personally knew that by the time a century was past, no one would even know the 3rd District was more than a rumor.

Indeed, only a handful of people remembered the coup by the time summer rolled around nineteen years later. Even the young survivor of the Shaughnessy family, now twenty-one, had trouble remembering. It was to his advantage in some ways, most thought. What person would want to remember something so terrifying?

Kay Shaughnessy didn't find it to be terrifying. He had no memories of his parents, so he couldn't miss them. And he certainly had no memories of the werewolf that had tried to eat him, so he had no reason to be afraid of wolves. In fact, his dearest friend was a wolf and always by his side. He called her Stormy.

As he tended to the repairs of his small boat, he glanced over to the side where Stormy was lying in the sunlight. She seemed to be asleep, but he knew better. He smiled. "You always look so lazy," he told her. He always talked to her as if she understood. It made him feel less lonely. "If a cat ran by you *might* be stirred to action, but only then."

Her tail thumped on the ground in agreement and she opened one eye to regard him. He turned back to what he was doing and ignored the sweat rolling down his face and back. It was sweltering hot, but if he went home without repairing the crack, then his adopted father would beat him.

It didn't take too much to set him off, as it never had over the course of his life. His 'parents' had taken him in on the premise that they hated the idea of a child being without a family, but within the first two years of his life they had squandered his family's money and begun treating him little better than a slave. By the time he was ten they had progressed to forcing him to work for his keep, beating him whenever he didn't make the 'proper' amount.

Now at twenty-one, he was indebted to them. He couldn't go to school and learn a trade, and he could not make enough money to pay back what they declared was his fair amount. Some nights he wished to simply curl up and die.

He felt a nudge at his elbow and looked down to see Stormy sitting beside him. She had the bucket of water. He gratefully put the tools down to lift the dipper and take a drink. He never asked how she did things like that. He simply believed in the magic.

As he stared at his reflection in the water, he said softly, "There are days when I wish that werewolf had eaten me."

She huffed softly. He smiled and ran his hands through her fur. "I know. Then you'd be alone. I guess if we're going to be alone, at least we're alone together." He hugged her tight for a moment before turning back to his task. A leaky boat was a disaster waiting to happen with his job.

He ferried people up and down the river to take them wherever they needed for a few coins. Some people even gave him tips because they liked his handsome face with its white-blond hair and brown eyes. His soft Irish accent claimed he was of immigrant blood, but he was kind and friendly, and people admired him regardless.

It took him an hour, but the boat was finally repaired, and he was able to get underway again. He wore a hat to shield his eyes from the harsh glare of the river, and his clothes were sturdy even if they weren't in the best of condition. Many a head was shaken over the sad state of the Shaughnessy heir.

It was mid-morning, and he had a full day of sailing ahead. He set out immediately with Stormy riding along as both mascot and protector. Some of the types who got on the boat were questionable, but a single look at her exceptionally sharp teeth made them behave properly.

By the time evening came around, his bag of money felt refreshingly full. He began to sail his way home and watched the moon rising in the distance. It was cool and peaceful, and he felt his shoulders begin to relax a little.

As he approached a bridge, he saw, much to his surprise, a young woman sitting on the rail and staring into the distance. Her hair shined ebony black in the moonlight with silvery highlights. He couldn't guess at the color of the dress she wore, but it looked pale with cherry blossoms scattered across it.

A shiver went down his back. "A ghost?" he whispered, and he heard Stormy snort softly. He glanced at her with a smile. "Well, she might be."

He realized shortly that she wasn't a ghost when a couple of men crossing the bridge began to harass her. He couldn't hear their words, but her body language said she was frightened. He began to frown as he got off on the shore and tied his boat. His motions were automatic, and his eyes were on the scene.

One of the men suddenly made a grab for the girl, and she jerked backwards instinctively. Her feet slipped off the edge of the bridge, and she fell into the river with a little shriek. The men ran off, and Kay swiftly raced to the shore and dove in. It wasn't hard to find her under the water with her pale clothes, but she wasn't strong enough to kick to the surface with all the material weighing her down.

He seized her under the arms and propelled them both to the surface. "Are you okay?" he asked urgently.

She clung to his shoulder with one hand and used her other to sling her wet, and now unbound, hair out of her eyes. "Yes. I'm dreadfully sorry about this. I can't swim," she apologized. "My foster mother said learning to swim would interfere with my destiny."

"I'd like to know how." He was exceptionally strong from his years on the river, and he found it easy to carry them both back to the shore. They staggered out of the water and then collapsed onto the grass.

Both were silent for a moment before she gave a muffled giggle. He tried to hide it, but he snickered. It took only a moment to have them both laughing, and he pushed himself up into a sitting position. "Well, that was certainly the most interesting way I've ever ended a day." He smiled, and it was a swift and devastating curve of his lips that fluttered the pulse of all the females he had ever met. It was all the more lethal because he didn't have a clue about its impact. "Shall I take you home?"

"Oh, no." She shook her head swiftly and stung her cheeks with her wet hair. With a sigh, she caught two handfuls and began to wring out the river water. "I will be fine, I promise." She gave a little grimace. "If I can just get some of this water out first. I look like a wet dog."

He tried not to stare, really he did. He couldn't help it though. Even though it was night, the moon was full and the light was strong. He could see that his 'ghost' was not only almost unbearably lovely in her features, but her dress also molded to her body like a second skin. He could see every curve, and every curve was worth seeing. "I've never seen a wet dog look like you," he admitted honestly, and then felt his cheeks warm. "That is . . ."

She gave a little cough, her cheeks darkening in a way that indicated she, too, was blushing. "Thank you, I think." She got to her feet and blinked as she realized she could feel the grass. She looked down and frowned. "I lost my shoes."

He opened his mouth to offer to go find them when his wolf—his very wet wolf—suddenly sat between them and dropped the shoes on the ground. "Stormy!" He stared for a moment, then, with characteristic humor, said, "This is a wet dog. She is not to be confused with you."

The girl giggled softly as she took her shoes and carefully put them on. Stormy, with a touch of indignity, shook herself enthusiastically and sprayed fresh river water everywhere. Kay laughed as he got to his feet. "Alright, alright! I know when I'm beaten! Ladies always stick together, don't they?"

The girl smiled. "I wouldn't call myself a lady."

He looked at her in surprise. "I would."

"Thank you, I think." She reached out and took one of his hands. She turned it over to place some coins there. "This is for rescuing me." When he started to protest, she shook her head quickly. "No, I want to. You're a good man, Kay Shaughnessy."

He frowned. "How did you know my name?"

She smiled. "Just because everyone does." She hesitated for a moment before rising on her toes and kissing his cheek. "Thank you again." She gave him a graceful curtsey. "You make an incredible hero."

He touched his cheek with his free hand and looked down at his hand to discover he was holding several dollars. Shocked, he jerked his head up. "Wait!" he said quickly, but he was not entirely surprised to realize she had disappeared into the moonlight.

At first, he didn't want to accept such a gift, but then he realized how late it was and that his father would be horribly furious. The money might allow him to escape intact. Holding his breath, he hurried up through the streets and back toward the farm where he lived. Not to his surprise, his adopted father Richard Johnston was standing on the steps in an aggressive stance.

Kay quickly dropped to his knees. "Please! I know I am late, but I was escorting a high-class lady to her home after she had a mishap on the river. She paid me well!"

"Really." Richard's tone could only be called menacing. "Then where is the money?"

Kay tossed the bag to him and it landed at his feet. As he sorted through the funds, Kay held his breath. He was praying, praying with everything he was, that this time he would be okay and would make it through.

Richard gave a little grunt. "This seems to be more than enough. There are scraps in the barn waiting for you." He went back into the house and slammed the door hard enough that the entire structure rattled.

Kay's breath unraveled slowly. Stormy whined and nuzzled him, and he wrapped his arms around her neck tightly. "We're okay," he whispered. "We'll be okay this time. Are you hungry? I am."

He got to his feet and hurried to the barn that he called home. He found the plate of scraps near the lantern, and it had been covered to keep out bugs. For that he was dimly grateful. He could only assume they didn't want him getting sick because it meant he could not work.

He carried the plate with him as he climbed into the loft. Stormy was very agile and followed him up the ladder despite the sharp angle. He always made sure her bed was aired, and he fluffed the straw for her with a smile. "There. Fit for a queen."

He only had two different changes of clothes, so he took off his still wet clothing and put on the dry ones. He could hang the wet ones to dry overnight. He picked through the scraps to find the edible ones and made sure that he and Stormy both had a share. She almost balked, but since he wouldn't eat until she did, she reluctantly gave in.

Finally, exhausted, he curled up on his bed of hay and straw and went to sleep. He had a tattered blanket to cover him but he fell asleep before reaching for it. Instead, a woman with yellow eyes gently tucked it around him and brushed his hair from his eyes. He was hers to protect, by god, and protect him she would.

Now she needed only to figure out how to arrange his happiness as well.

CHAPTER TWO

Kay's days were always the same. He would wake early in the morning and go down to the pump to get cold water to wash his face. Sometimes another plate of scraps would be sitting on the back porch. Whenever it wasn't, he would go into the city early and ferry a food merchant down river as a payment for some breakfast.

After that, his day would really begin. He would work his way up and down the river by ferrying people wherever they needed to go. Stormy was always with him, and it eased the lonely times to talk to her. There were times when he would look longingly at the school where the children of good families attended and wish to go himself. His reading skills were minimal at best.

One afternoon that week, while he was taking a break, he was surprised when a woman sat beside him on the bench overlooking the river. She was almost stunningly beautiful with vivid red hair and piercing black eyes. He knew immediately that he looked upon a woman of very high standing. He felt grubby and outclassed sitting beside her.

Her dark blue dress had a design around the bottom of what looked like patterns he had seen in a book. He thought they had been from a country far beyond even England. She was *tiny* too. Maybe not short, but she was very slender. As he stood slightly taller than average, he felt like a giant. He swiftly stood. "I'm sorry," he apologized. "I'll move."

"Why?" Her eyes smiled at him.

"I smell like the river," he admitted shamefully. "It must be distressing to you."

"Not at all. Sit down, please." When he had done so, and very warily, she turned to take stock of his appearance. She was *not* pleased with what she saw.

It had nothing to do with his looks. He had outrageously beautiful features paired with unusual and stunning coloring. Even among the blonds of the world, his hair stood out. His eyes held a wild spirit barely kept in check, and it gave a mischievous sparkle to the golden color. If there was one thing Rhianna Taber appreciated in anyone, it was a mischievous, wild spirit. She certainly had her own.

No, what displeased her was the state of his clothing, and the fact that he seemed too thin for his size. A young man of his height should not have been so slender that it was a wonder his bones supported his muscles at all. There were shadows under his eyes, and his cheeks were more hollowed than thin.

Little sparks that her partner liked to call her 'temper sparks' appeared in her eyes. "May I make a deal with you?" she asked. When he frowned thoughtfully, she smiled and touched his hand. "You look like you are in need of a good meal. I need a ride upriver. How about a trade?"

He thought of a real meal and his stomach clenched. He always felt hungry because he never got to eat his fill. There were times he wondered if his body ran on sheer stubbornness. "Well . . ." he hedged.

"No arguing," she ordered briskly. She got to her feet and pulled him up as well to tug him along with her as she walked. "I don't take no for an answer from anyone." Sensing his astonishment, she smiled. "My name is Rhianna Taber. I'm co-owner of the Enforcers."

He stopped dead in his tracks which forced her to stop as well. His jaw had fallen open. He knew the Enforcers as well as anyone else did. They were the biggest company in New York and they rivaled the governor for power. They protected a section of the city known as the 3rd District.

The 3rd District was where magic lived. It had been there that the werewolves had lived, and it was there that the bloody massacre had occurred. He did not fear the District or those who lived there. He was fascinated. If Rhianna was the leader of Enforcers, then she was probably really old. It never even occurred to him that a woman shouldn't be in charge of a large company, though it had often been thought by others. Of course, they had shortly changed their minds when they met her.

Without thinking, he blurted, "You look so young!" Indeed, she looked to be barely out of her twenties.

Her smile came quickly. "I do like you. Come along, Kay. I intend to feed you a proper meal for once." Since he seemed to have lost his resistance, she found it very easy to pull him along behind her.

She took him to a restaurant nearby and ordered them both large dinners. With satisfaction, she watched as he began to eat. His manners were impeccable, but he made short work of his meal. She was satisfied to see some of the haunted look fade from his eyes as well. "Talk to me," she offered.

"About what, ma'am? Er, miss." He corrected himself hastily as he remembered the rumor that she was unwed.

"About you." She smiled. "I was there that night some nineteen years ago. I'm curious how you're doing these days. I see being attacked by a werewolf does not give you a fear of wolves." She indicated Stormy lying patiently outside in the sun.

He smiled as he picked up a piece of bread. "I don't fear wolves. Why should I?" he asked curiously. "The werewolf who attacked my family was entitled to her fury, even if we were innocent. It wasn't like she was a murderer."

She considered that. "Then you don't hate the 3rd District?"

"No." His lethal smile flashed quickly. "I envy you who live there."

Hiding a smile of her own, she had to wonder if he had any idea how stunning his smile could be. She hoped it would carry on down through future generations. "Envy?" she repeated. "How so?"

"You belong," he said simply. "It's your home. You belong there. Everyone there supports each other. I envy that. I've never had a home."

"No?" She began to drum her fingers on her leg under the edge of the table. "Then where have you been living?"

"With my adopted family." He opened his mouth to say everything was fine, but something in the ancient black eyes watching him made him change his mind. He couldn't lie, not to her. "I live in the barn," he admitted softly. In a rush he added, "It's truly not so bad. They give me scraps to eat, and I have clothes. There's a roof over my head, and I have a blanket for when it's cold."

The sparks were in her eyes again. "I see. And the money you make?"

"I'm indebted to them for raising me. I have to make enough money to pay them back." He blinked as he saw her eyes. He had never seen a literal manifestation of temper before. "It truly is okay. Mr. Johnston only beats me when I don't make enough. Oh!" He covered his mouth quickly.

She did not normally anger easily, but it took all her considerable willpower to remain seated and not go knock down Richard Johnston's door. "I won't tell," she promised. "Are you full, Kay?"

He looked down in surprise. He had eaten everything on his plate, and he felt very full. "Yes, thank you. I've never gotten to eat my fill before. I'll ferry you wherever you need, Miss Taber."

"Thank you very much." She let him escort her out of the restaurant and back to where the boat was waiting. She smiled as she watched him navigate the river. When Stormy nudged her hand, she ruffled her fur lightly. "Well," she murmured softly for her ears only, "I wouldn't call this interfering. It's more like watching over one of my own. He does have a contract, after all." And it was beginning to look like Richard had heavily violated it.

When Kay assisted her out of the boat, she smiled at him. "I wish you well, Kay." She waved merrily as he sailed back down the river. She felt someone join her, and her smile faded as the sparks in her eyes came back. "If I asked you to shove a lightning bolt up someone's ass, would you do it?"

Her partner looked the direction Kay was sailing, and his eyes were as displeased as hers. "Quite gladly," Eric Mason murmured softly. "Quite gladly, indeed."

The shock of the morning's events lingered with Kay, and he couldn't figure out what exactly had occurred. It made the day pass much quicker than ever, having his stomach full, and he wasn't nearly as tired as he normally was when he tied his boat off that evening. He even had enough time to count the money he had made.

His full stomach lurched, however, as he counted the coins. He hadn't made enough for his weekly share, and he was short by a dollar or so. The day was done, and there was no time for him to find a quick job. His throat tight, he made his way toward home.

Richard stood on the porch, his entire body ready to do battle. Terror made Kay's palms slick but his back was straight as he walked over and put the bag of money in his hand. He backed up a step and waited.

Richard counted the coins and turned a narrow eyed gaze on him. "You're short by two dollars. Were you goofing off on the river today instead of working?"

He had learned over the years that denying and fighting it would only make it worse. He said nothing. Instead, he kept his chin high and his back straight. He refused to cry and show the weakness that Richard always claimed he had.

Richard's face tightened. He had always hated this boy. He had taken him in for the money that came with him, but there was something so innately proud about Kay that he despised. He wanted to break him. "No arguments?"

At that point, Kay figured that things couldn't get worse. "Why waste my words when they fall on deaf ears?"

Fury lit Richard's eyes, and he came down the steps swiftly with his fist lifted. The first hit knocked Kay backward as the punch landed on his jaw. Though he had always taken the beatings without an argument, something inside him snapped and he leapt at Richard with both fists.

Richard was stunned enough that Kay managed to get in several good shots. Then, with a snarl, he grabbed Kay's shirt and hurled him into the side of the house. In a rage, he went after the younger man with fists and feet, mercilessly beating him with all his strength.

Kay curled into himself and bit his lower lip hard to bite back sounds of pain; dying couldn't hurt that bad. Sometimes he wished he *would* die so that it all went away. He couldn't even feel pain anymore. It had all turned white hot and numbing. His breathing was labored, and he suspected that maybe something had been broken. A particularly sharp kick landed in his back and rattled his ribs with a pain he hadn't known existed. He couldn't stop a whimper.

There came a low and vicious snarl on the night air, and Stormy lunged out of the darkness at Richard's throat. He cursed and staggered back away from Kay as Stormy braced herself in front of him, snarling in a way that showed all of her sharp teeth.

Richard backed off, breathing hard. "He brought it on himself."

She didn't move, and he slammed into the house. As soon as the door shut, Kay tried to move. He couldn't, though. Not without pain screaming through his body. He was bleeding too, from his skin splitting under the force of the blows. He dug his nails into the dirt and dragged with all his strength to pull himself onto his knees. His eyes focused blearily on the barn. It could have been a mile away instead of twenty feet. He could do it. He had done it before.

Stormy whimpered, and he thought for a moment she was sympathizing with him. A rustle surprised him, and he was surprised more when he realized someone had knelt beside him. As if moving through mud, he turned his head and saw that the young woman from earlier in the week had joined him. "You . . ."

"Shh." Her lips were thinned with anger, and her eyes filled with concern as she glanced at the quiet house behind them. "Let me help." She wasn't very big, but she knew she could do at least enough to help him walk. She would drag him if needed to get him away from there.

She had never met anyone so unthinkingly kind before. He hadn't known her, and yet he had dived into a river to save her. There was no calculation in him, no fear. He accepted Stormy readily despite what had happened to him. He was as rare as a diamond in the rough, and just as precious.

He tried to get to his feet, but it hurt too badly and he fell to his knees. "Sorry," he managed to say.

She set her chin. "I'm not giving up. Stormy, help me." She took hold of him under the arms, and Stormy grabbed a mouthful of his shirt, and together they struggled and dragged him toward the barn.

It hurt like hell, but he gritted his teeth and tried to help. They staggered into the barn, and he looked at the ladder toward the loft where his bed was located. He knew he would never make it. Instead, he collapsed onto the nearest pile of hay. "Leave me here," he groaned. "I've imposed enough."

He didn't hear anything else for a moment and assumed that she had left. She had repaid his kindness and had no reason to linger. He was so sure of it that he was doubly startled when he felt her kneel beside him on the hay and begin opening his shirt. His eyes popped wide in surprise. "Wha?" She was leaning over him, her hair falling down, and the scent drifted toward him like rain. It was beautiful. "Who are you?"

"My name is Raven Childrose." She took a sharp breath as she saw the marks across his chest. It infuriated her. It was an incredibly beautiful body and a sin to mark it, and the idea of anyone at all being hurt like that made her mad.

Scars of older wounds marked his smooth skin, and the newest ones from that night were open and bloody welts. There were rapidly darkening bruises everywhere, and she could tell from the way he breathed that at least one rib was cracked. Tears welled in her eyes. "How can you stand it?" she whispered.

"I don't have too much of a choice." He watched as she got to her feet and left the barn. When she came back, she was carrying a pail of water that she set down before kneeling beside him again. "You don't have to do this," he told her quietly. "I've gotten through this before."

She shot him a quick look. "I don't like it." She ripped a long strip of material off the end of her petticoat and dipped it in the water. "Even if you hadn't helped me, I'd still do this. I can't stand seeing someone be hurt. I would be a doctor if they would let me learn. I must settle for reading books, I suppose."

He braced himself for the cold water but, to his amazement, it was warm. He frowned. "How did you do that?"

Red color climbed her cheeks. "Do what?"

"Make the water warm. The pump is always cold." His eyes closed tiredly as she continued to clean the wounds. "Are you from 3rd District?"

She hesitated before she resumed gently cleaning the wounds. "Yes," she admitted softly. "I have water elf blood. I can manipulate it to some extent, like changing the temperature." She gingerly touched the bruises dotting his flesh. "I cannot believe someone would be so horribly cruel."

"I suppose I am used to it." He continued to watch her, fascinated with the way she moved and the gentleness in her features. She was unbearably lovely, and he wanted her more than ever. It had been sparked that night by the river, but now it was getting more powerful. He knew her to be incredibly beyond his reach, that it would always be hopeless, and it broke his heart. "You must be a nobleman's daughter."

She flinched slightly and turned to take the bandages Stormy was holding. She didn't ask where she had gotten them, and neither did Kay. "Why do you say that?" She scooted closer and tried to help him sit up.

He pushed himself upright and had to wait for a moment to let the dizziness pass. He carefully shrugged out of his shirt and held his arms up as she began to wrap the bandages around his chest. He tried not to notice, he really did, but his eyes couldn't miss seeing that her bodice was partially unbuttoned. He could see the gentle swell of her breasts underneath.

Raven was not like most women. She had, after all, been raised in the 3rd District by the entire community, including Rhianna Taber. She had been given an understanding of men and women that wouldn't be commonplace in young adults until another century had passed. It was because of that understanding that she noticed within a few moments that he was distinctly attracted to her. In fact, she would have had trouble missing it with how she was leaning over him and all but sitting on his lap. She swiftly sat upright, her eyes wide. "You can't want me," she blurted.

He stared at her as if she was insane. "Why not?"

"Because . . . just because!" She felt flustered, and she knew she sounded it, too. "Men don't . . . I mean . . . they've never . . . I'm not . . ." She gave up and covered her burning cheeks with her hands. "Oh this is going so wrong!"

He tested the bandages, found they were snug, and tried to breathe a little more normally. It still hurt, but not quite as bad. He took the pail and material and began cleaning the wounds on his arms and legs himself. "Try at the top," he suggested with a smile. "Because I know I like you."

Her pulse fluttered wildly in her body at the sight of his smile. She had never seen anything that lethally beautiful before. "Alright." She took a long breath. "I'm not a noblewoman. I was thrown out by my mother. I was raised in 3rd District by everyone. And I . . . well, I just have nothing to offer a man."

He tossed the material aside where it landed with a wet plop on the barn floor. Anger churned inside his heart. How could anyone as kind and beautiful as her not have a hundred suitors? He had no idea who had put such a stupid idea in her head, and he wouldn't have minded giving them a kick of their own. "I think you're incredible," he told her honestly. "If I wasn't just a poor river ferryman, I'd be courting you."

She frowned. "No."

"Yes."

"You don't know me!"

"I want to." He smiled. "But since I can't court you, will you be friends with me instead?" When she eyed him warily, he held up his hands with a sad smile. "I think I could fall in love with you, Raven, but you're so far beyond my reach. I know that I can't ever have you, so will you at least be friends with me?"

Her heart clenched in her chest. He had no idea how wrong he was. It wasn't that he wasn't good enough for her; it was the other way around. She didn't deserve a man as wonderful and handsome as Kay. "I've never had friends," she whispered. "Not real ones."

"Me neither." He couldn't stop himself from reaching out and threading his fingers through her hair. It felt as soft as feathers. If it could have been woven into cloth, it would have been the finest of silks. "Will you visit me?" He smiled. "When neither of us are in life or death situations?"

She had to smile even though she fought a fierce urge to go into his arms. She wanted to be held, just once, by someone who thought she was beautiful. "I have, umm, things to do during the day. I can only visit at night."

"Me, too." He felt battered and tired, but oddly more at peace than he ever had before. With a little sigh, he almost fell over. She caught him and gently eased him down onto the hay. "Guess I'm just tired," he apologized.

"You have reason." She took the blanket Stormy had fetched, and she gently tucked it around him. He was asleep a few moments later, and she watched him for a long time. When she felt dawn was a mere hour away, she got to her feet and walked out of the barn. Stormy tried to stop her but she shook her head. "You have your contract," she said softly, "and I have mine. He deserves more than me."

Stormy highly doubted that, but kept the thought to herself as she went back into the barn and curled up next to Kay. The first few lights of dawn eventually spilled in the window and she watched quietly. A few moments later, a black raven flew across the face of the sun on a mournful cry.

Every Enforcers' contract had a clause or condition to be met. Stormy knew it for a fact. She just had to figure out what Raven's was, and use it.

CHAPTER THREE

Kay awoke a little after dawn to a body that was stiff and sore in every muscle. He painfully got to his feet and forced himself to go to the pump for cold water. He barely spared a glance for the house. He knew there would be no scraps.

He was almost tempted to think it had all been a dream, but his wounds were definitely bound, and he could still smell the scent of Raven's skin and hair if he breathed deeply. It hadn't helped any that he'd had a particularly vivid dream about kissing her. He had never kissed any girl before, but his dream self certainly seemed to know what he was doing.

His feelings puzzled him in a way. They had only met twice, and yet she had become incredibly important to him. Those brief two meetings had taught him everything he needed to know about her. She was sweet and shy, gentle and caring, and she was also strong-willed, smart, proud, and beautiful. She had an independent streak that he found more alluring than alarming.

"It's so odd," he murmured. When Stormy tilted her head, he smiled at her. "Love at first sight. I think I know what it is now. It's Raven." A particularly smug look crossed her face and he laughed even though it hurt. "I thought that would please you. Don't think I don't know what you're up to!"

He got his drink of water and walked carefully back into the barn. He changed his clothes because his current ones were both dirty and muddy, but it was not easy. With an inner pride that nothing could break, he squared his back and began to walk painfully toward the river in the distance.

It hurt. Every step felt like torture, and he couldn't turn without hurting from head to heel. On top of that, his stomach was growling loudly with painful hunger. He carefully climbed onto his boat and began to check all the parts to be sure everything was in working order. He never went out without a onceover.

Stormy began to sniff the deck in a search for something. He let her be and sat down heavily on the floor. He tried to convince himself that it didn't really hurt as bad as he thought, but it didn't work. Then, suddenly, Stormy sat beside him with something in her mouth. He turned his head carefully and found she had a basket.

He was further shocked to find it packed with food. Hot cakes, sausages, bread, and potatoes. It looked as good as it smelled, and his mouth watered. A pink ribbon tied around the handle caught his eye, and the gentle scent of rain drifted to him over the food. It must have been Raven who left it for him. He removed the ribbon and tucked it reverently into his sleeve for safety.

He had enough time to eat, and he made short work of the food. It felt wonderful to eat his fill again. Everything tasted incredible, and he didn't think it was just because his taste buds were underworked. He liked the idea that Raven had made it for him. He just wished he could do something to take care of her in return.

Once he was done, he forced himself to get to work. It was painfully difficult to navigate the river turns, but Stormy stood directly beside him and helped keep him from falling over. She also helped grab the pole and pull it through the water, giving his arms a much-needed rest.

The day seemed to drag on but he focused only on his work. His passengers all noticed the bruise on his chin, and the way he moved carefully, and they suspected they knew what had occurred. There just wasn't anything they could do for him.

During a rough patch in the river, he almost lost control of the boat and one of the passengers hastily stepped over and grabbed the pole before it went flying. "Easy," he told Kay with a smile. He seemed older than Kay, though it was hard to determine by how much, and there were wings of white in his brown hair. He stood not much taller, but he was distinctly bigger, because Kay was not at his full potential.

"Thank you," Kay said shamefully. "I'm just a little clumsy today."

"Little wonder." The man studied him knowingly. "Cracked a rib, did you?"

"I fell out of the barn loft," he lied automatically. He started to reach for the pole again when the ribbon in his sleeve got free and tried to fly off. "Oh! Grab it!"

The man moved as fast as the wind and snagged the ribbon before it could get far. He offered it to Kay with a smile. "A gift from a lady friend?" When the boy's cheeks flushed, Eric Mason felt almost amazingly old. Thinking it, he promptly heard Rhianna's laughter in his mind. He ignored her. "Have you given her something in return?"

"Well, no." Kay frowned. "I don't have any money of my own. Everything I make goes toward my living."

"Ah." Eric took his hand and dropped a few coins in his palm. "Consider this a tip. Buy something nice for your lady. I think she'd be pleasantly surprised."

He wanted to argue, but Eric had already walked away. Even though he knew he ought to save the money for the future in case he ever came up short, he really, really wanted to buy something for Raven. He tied the money into a handkerchief and tucked it safely in his pocket.

As the day wore on, it got harder and harder to steer. Even Stormy's help did not fully help. The pole was clumsy enough under good circumstances. It wobbled too much at the top, and it nearly bobbed out of his hands more than once. One particularly bad dip found him being unexpectedly saved when a raven flew up and landed on the top of the pole. Her weight was just enough counterbalance that his work became instantly easier. He smiled and ran a hand down her soft feathers. "Thank you." A little frown touched his lips as he looked at his fingers. Oddly, the raven's feathers were as soft as, well, Raven's hair.

He put it out of his mind and took advantage of the help from his companions to finish the day with enough money to keep Richard happy. He even finished a little ahead of schedule. As soon as he tied the boat, he hurried quickly into a nearby square where some shops were located.

The raven had flown off at the first sign of sunset so it was just Kay and Stormy browsing the shops. He had no idea what he wanted to get, but when he saw the store selling jewelry, something caught his eye.

It was a matching set of cameo and ring. The cameo was carved from pearl and had the relief of a woman's profile. The ring was also pearl, and little silver threads wrapped around it. He was certain he wouldn't have enough, but when he checked the price it was exactly the right amount. He bought it immediately and tied it safely inside his shirt where it couldn't be found.

It had gotten dark, and he hurried home as quickly as his injured body would let him. Richard again waited on the porch, and Kay handed him the bag of money without a word. That done, he turned and headed toward the barn.

Richard snorted derisively. "Where do you think you are going?"

Kay stopped but didn't look back. "The money is there. And even if it weren't, if you beat me again, I could die this time. You wouldn't want that, right? Then you'd be out your source of funds. I know there are no scraps waiting for me. Right now, I don't care."

Richard snarled, "Do you want me to kill you, you little upstart?!"

Kay looked at him. "Sometimes, yes. Go ahead. I can't stop you." When Richard only slammed into the house, he let out the breath he had been holding. "I'm an idiot," he muttered under his breath. "What was I doing, provoking him like that?"

He made his way to the barn and climbed one step at a time into the loft. He lit the single lantern he had and then just sat there for a few moments to let his muscles stop yelling at him. He eventually pulled out the single book he owned and tried again to go over the passages. It had been a gift from a passenger when he was a child, and it alone had taught him what little he knew how to read.

The scent of vegetables and chicken reached his nose unexpectedly, and he frowned. Maybe the meals lately had made him start to hallucinate. He eased to the edge of the loft and peered downstairs just in case he was wrong. He wasn't. Raven had just set another basket on the ground and steam wafted from it gently. Stormy pranced around her ankles happily and Raven shushed her softly. "He'll hear," she whispered.

Stormy, naturally, chose to bark at that moment and Kay laughed. Raven looked up swiftly and her cheeks turned as pink as the cherry blossoms on her dress. "I didn't mean to disturb you." She bit her lip nervously. "I was just going to leave this and go."

"No." He shook his head. "I was hoping you would come see me. Would you come up here?"

She hesitated visibly but finally picked up the basket and carried it with her as she went up the ladder. He helped her onto the loft. He studied her for a moment before smiling and reaching for the ribbons in her hair. She swatted at his hands, flustered. "No, stop!" She could only sigh as her hair came down. "It's not proper to take your hair down around people."

"I'm not people. I'm your friend. You like it this way more, too. I can see it on your face." He reached eagerly for the basket. "What did you bring?" He happily purveyed the small feast waiting for him. "I saw the breakfast this morning and enjoyed it very much. Thank you."

Her color deepened. "I just . . . wanted to make you something. I know you don't get to eat much." She watched with deep pleasure as he began to eat contentedly. Though Rhianna had told her time and again not to be bound by the rules of society and to strive to be more than 'just a wife,' she knew that she would never be happier than when she was trying to take care of the people she loved.

She supposed it was her own silly fault, falling in love with Kay. It had happened so quickly that she hadn't even seen it was a danger. When she had seen him get beaten . . . she had wanted to unleash a flood on Richard. And then, today, she hadn't been able to help herself from following Kay. She had even helped him steer but when sunset had come she had been forced to leave.

Something would happen that night. Something to change her life. Somehow she knew it. She had tried to sneak in and out to avoid it, but she hadn't truly been surprised that Stormy would thwart her attempts. She also knew what the wolf was doing. She pushed it aside for the time being. "How old are you, Kay?" She wanted to know everything.

"Twenty-one." He set the basket aside. His happy tummy was full yet again. "What about you?"

"Nineteen."

His eyes widened. "And you're not married." He remembered her words of the night before and still could hardly believe it. "I can't believe that some man hasn't swept you off your feet. You're incredible."

"I'm not." She closed her eyes and tears glimmered under her lashes. "My mother tried to kill me when I was born because I was visibly of the 3rd District. It was right after the coup, and people were scared still. Rhianna of the Enforcers saved me, and the whole district helped raise me."

His face tightened with anger. "If I ever met your mother, I'd probably hurt her, and I hate the idea of hurting women." She looked at him in shock, and he reached out to run his hand down her cheek. "I lied to you, Raven," he said softly. He smiled. "I'm already in love with you."

She tried to jerk backwards in shock but Stormy bumped her firmly from behind and sent her flying into Kay's arms. He gave a soft grunt as his ribs protested but his arms instinctively closed around her tightly. He had nothing to base his feelings on, yet something inside told him no other would fit so perfectly in his arms.

Her eyes slowly closed and she pressed closer without thought. Joy seemed to blossom inside her heart at the feel of his arms. She felt . . . safe. Cherished. And yet, there was an odd hunger moving inside her body as well. Her lashes lifted to see his slightly open shirt, and the revealed skin made her tempted to press her lips right there.

The unusual emotions rioting through her heart and body in no way distracted her from whatever was poking her in the shoulder. She tried to pull away and his arms tightened. "Don't move away," he protested. "I like holding you. If I get my courage back, I'm going to kiss you."

She blushed. "I wouldn't protest but there's something digging into my shoulder."

He remembered suddenly and released her. "Oh!" He reached into his shirt and came out with the handkerchief he had wrapped the gift inside. "Here." He held it out with a smile. "I wanted to get you something, and someone gave me a tip, so . . ."

With trembling fingers, she opened the handkerchief to discover the cameo and ring. Her mouth opened soundlessly and then closed several times in sheer disbelief. "I can't accept this!" she protested.

"Yes, you can." He took the cameo and leaned in closer to fasten it to the edge of her bodice. Her scent curled around him, and he gave in to the urge to bury his nose against the curve where her neck met her shoulder. "I love how you smell," he murmured softly. "Like fresh rain." Not even fully conscious of his actions, he moved lower and his fingers unfastened some buttons so his nose could nuzzle into the opening in the bodice.

Her heart began to beat harder, and her breath hitched in her lungs as she felt his hot breath on the sensitive skin between her breasts. "What're you doing?" she managed to ask. "Kay."

He straightened up quickly. "I . . . I don't know. I'm sorry, did I scare you?" He felt both sheepish and embarrassed for having given in to such a shameful urge. It didn't help any that his body ached in an entirely new way as desire gleefully ripped through his blood. He was a healthy young man who had been interested in a pretty girl once or twice. Never like that, though. Never to the point of forgetting himself.

"No." She reached up and touched the cameo with a smile. "It's beautiful." She made a startled sound as he picked up her hand and slid the ring over her finger. "No, don't do that. It looks . . ."

"I know." He smiled almost shyly. "If I could, I would give you a real ring. But I don't deserve you."

"Stop it!" She shook her head swiftly and her hair flew around her shoulders. "It's not you, Kay, it's me! I don't deserve *you*, don't you understand? I'm 3rd District born, and I have no family. I don't even have a place to call home! My parents . . . at least your parents loved you!" Tears ran down her cheeks. "Do you think I don't want a home? A husband and children? If I could, I would marry you the minute you asked!"

He almost stopped breathing. "Are you in love with me, too?"

"Yes." Defeated, her shoulders slumped. "But we both know it's hopeless." When his hands framed her face, she met his golden colored gaze and felt as if she was sinking into the promise it made. "Are you going to kiss me?" she whispered.

"May I?" he whispered back. He drew her closer until she was sitting on his lap. The pain in his body had faded as if it had never been. The only pain he felt was a longing to hold her as close as he could.

"You shouldn't but . . ." Her lashes fluttered closed. "Please."

He wasn't going to ask twice and lowered his head toward hers. Unfortunately, lack of experience for both meant the embrace was a little awkward and their noses banged smartly together. "Ouch!" He pulled back, askance. "Raven, are you okay?"

She wiggled her nose. "Yes, but, ouch." Her eyes met his and she tried not to, honestly, but a giggle escaped anyway. "You missed."

He started snickering too. "I'm sorry. I've never kissed a girl before." The sound of her laughter enchanted him. It just seemed impossibly beautiful. Before he could stop himself, he bent his head and caught her smiling lips with his own.

She even tasted like rainwater. The taste of her spread through him like a wave and made the arousal he had been ignoring since she had arrived all the more painful. His hands lifted to frame her face, and he remembered in his dream how he had kissed her. He glided his tongue over her lips, trying to tempt her into opening her mouth.

She had taken a startled breath when he kissed her, and she couldn't get it back. Heat radiated from his body, and every nerve she possessed was tingling deliciously. Her body felt hot and achy, and she shifted closer without conscious thought to wind her arms around his neck.

She felt his tongue teasing her lips and parted them without hesitation, eager to know his taste. It was rich honey, and it went to her head faster than the wine she had once secretly tried. His tongue touched hers and startled her for a moment before she gave a little sigh and returned the tiny caress. She was more than willing to be seduced by this man.

The kiss lengthened and unraveled in silence until a little whimper escaped her when he lifted his head. Their eyes met and she trembled as she saw the hunger swirling in his eyes. "Again?" he asked softly, his voice rough.

"Please." Her hands slid up into his hair and tugged to urge him closer. When he complied, she trembled with need as the kiss erupted between them. His confidence had grown, and he kissed her with an edge of desire that stole her breath. In the space of a moment, the soft desire inside sharpened into raw lust.

He couldn't get enough. Hunger deepened the kiss until it was nothing but a tangle of tongues and lips. He had to touch her, to know her in every possible way. His hands lifted and plucked at the buttons on her dress until the bodice was unfastened entirely. The edges of the dress opened instantly and slid over her skin like a hungry lover. He could only wish it was him who touched her so intimately.

She couldn't muffle a soft moan as his hands slid under her opened dress and curved around her waist. Even through her thin corset, his heat burned her. She twisted toward his touch, begging silently for more. It was only when she felt his lips leave hers and bury against the pulse racing in her throat that she realized what was going on.

"Oh!" Her voice was nothing more than a breathless sound. "Stop. Kay, stop!"

He stopped, but it took him several moments to find self-control. He had never wanted anything in his life more than he wanted her. He released her slowly and clenched his hands into fists at his side. He didn't look at her as she got off his lap and fixed her clothes. If he did, he would not be able to keep himself from touching her again. "You really have to marry me," he decided with as much humor as he could.

She smoothed her dress with trembling fingers. Her stupid corset already made it impossible to breathe without adding the recent events to things. "Why?" Even as she asked it, she knew it was a stupid question. They were friends, they were in love, and they had almost set the hay on fire. Rhianna had called it one of the perfect combinations for a lasting relationship, and Raven could no longer doubt her. It felt as if the entire world hovered beyond her reach.

"Because." He looked at her with eyes that burned. "I've never felt that before. I know you haven't either. And I'm *sure* we never will again unless it's together. So, we ought to marry."

"Kay . . ." She caught sight of the moon starting to wane and realized it was no longer late and instead very early. "I have to go!" She hurried down the ladder and out of the loft. "Kay, I'm so sorry! Just . . . just forget it, please!"

He could not forget it, nor could he forget the pain in her eyes. He sat watching the night sky and waited for the dawn to come. The sun began to rise with all of its splendor, and he thought he saw the form of a raven flying across the sky. Her sad cries ripped at his heart and soul.

He thought he might be starting to understand, and understanding brought determination. So much in his life had been taken away before he was able to fight for it, but not this. Not Raven. He would fight to the death for her if needed.

First, he needed advice. There was only one person he trusted and that was an old priest who lived very far down the river. He didn't hesitate as he hurried to his boat and set off to go visit. He would be pushing it to have enough time to make his daily quota, but this was more than worth it.

"Father Evans!" he called as he got off the boat and hurried toward the church not far beyond. "Father Evans!"

The old priest was sweeping the steps of the church and smiled as he saw Kay. "Ah, I wondered when you would arrive, young man. Come, sit with me. I will give you a drink to ease the pain of your wounds, and you can tell me of the woman who took your heart."

Kay smiled as he followed Father Evans and shortly found himself sitting on the steps with an odd herbal concoction in his hands. It tasted sort of bitter but he trusted Father Evans' medicines implicitly and drank the entire thing. The pains and aches almost immediately began to fade. "Thank you, Father Evans."

"You are very welcome, son." Evans sat down on the stairs beside him. "Now, tell me of this woman who captivated you."

"Her name is Raven Childrose." He looked in the distance thoughtfully. "I met her by accident, and then she happened to be near my home when I was beaten the other night. We became friends, but I've been in love with her the whole time, I think."

Evans tugged on his long beard. "A coincidence, Kay?" When Kay nodded, he smiled. "There are no coincidences around those of 3rd District. This was meant to be." He crossed his arms inside his sleeves and studied the sun rising in the east. "In some places," he murmured, "it is whispered that there are two beings who watch over the fate of lovers. I've always thought it was so. Perhaps one, or both, is watching over you."

Kay smiled. "I like that." He studied the ground intently. "I think Raven is cursed, Father Evans. She says no man has ever wanted her for a wife. But I do. I want her to belong to me, and I want to belong to her. But . . . if we marry, Richard would have to approve before anyone would ever perform the ceremony."

"I do not answer to Richard Johnston," Evans countered serenely. "I answer to God for my morality, and I answer to the government for my legality. You are an adult, and you are not a slave—no matter what you may think. If your lady agrees, I will perform the ceremony and take care of the paperwork that goes with it."

"Really?" Kay looked at him in surprise.

"I would be honored."

"Then I'll find the courage and ask her," he decided firmly. He leapt to his feet as he heard the birds beginning to sing. "I have to go, but thank you!" With a wave of his hand, he hurried back down toward his boat, hoping only to make it through the day. If he could survive to seeing Raven again, then everything would be alright. He was sure of it.

CHAPTER FOUR

Kay was not entirely surprised when the morning passed without the raven showing up to join him. Somehow he just knew that the raven was *his* Raven. She probably didn't think he would understand. Maybe he didn't, but he did accept it. He would find a way to fix everything.

The morning stretched on and he continued to work. Much to his terror, he realized Richard was in town that day and keeping a close eye on him. Kay tried to ignore him and focus on his sailing but it was very difficult. His passengers noticed everything, and fury rose among them all. They just couldn't do anything!

Evening finally arrived, and he began to think everything might be okay. It all took a nosedive when a sudden fire caught life at one of the shops along the shore. People scrambled to safety, but almost not in time. An explosion from the fire getting into gunpowder sent flaming bits of roof and wall flying everywhere.

Kay could not steer fast enough to get away, and one of the massive chunks struck the small boat with enough force to punch a hole in the wood. Flames swiftly began to eat through everything. Because he knew it was either abandon the boat or possibly go down with it, he dove over the side and swam away with Stormy close behind.

He got to the opposite shore and pulled himself out in time to see the boat beginning to sink. Terror choked him suddenly. He had no way of making his living without the boat. His eyes shot across the shore and he saw Richard walking toward the nearest bridge with a nearly inhuman look of rage on his face.

Kay felt sick. If he stayed there, he was dead. He scrambled up to his feet despite the pains his chest gave him and took off running into the woods nearby. He had youth and agility on his side, and running over grass would make him impossible to track. Even knowing it, he didn't let it lull him into a false sense of security. He kept running and praying for nightfall. He could hide in the darkness.

Dark eventually fell and he huddled behind a tree to catch his breath. A step nearby had him leaping to his feet instinctively. Instead of the raging madman he expected, it was actually Raven that ran out of the bushes. She flung herself into his arms desperately, and it staggered him a step. His arms closed around her fiercely and he buried his face in her hair. "Raven."

"I saw the wreck!" Her entire body shook as she clung onto him tighter. "And I saw Mr. Johnston coming after you! I knew . . . I knew he'd kill you if he found you! Kay, please! You can't go back there!"

"I won't, I promise." His fingers found the ribbons in her hair and plucked them out so that the chignon came down and unraveled. He immediately buried his face in the strands and breathed in the scent of rain. "I'll find somewhere safe, I promise."

"I know somewhere." Her lips trembled as she eased back. "It's horribly improper of me to do so, but I can take you home with me. I live just inside 3rd District, in a home under an oak tree." She tilted her head. "Does that alarm you?"

He shook his head. "I've always believed in magic. If you told me you lived in a palace on top of clouds, it wouldn't surprise me." He took her hand tightly and followed her through the trees toward the 3rd District.

He felt it the instant they entered. His entire body seemed to prickle with awareness of power. He watched curiously as she fit a key into a hole in a tree and then smiled as the tree crawled by its roots to the side to reveal a staircase. "I think I could like this place."

She felt her shoulders relax, and she smiled. "I'm glad." She went down the stairs with him close behind, and the tree moved back into place overhead. Blushing, she lit a lantern and hung it safely out of the way. "It's small," she said in a rush, "but you're welcome to stay as long as you need."

The small house was more like a one-room living space. There was a stove for cooking and strange plants sitting beside it that he assumed were something like firewood. Lanterns hung from the ceiling and she lit one of them for more light. There was a fireplace as well, and a hand carved bed of immense proportions.

Seeing his curious gaze, she went over to the bed and sat on the edge of it. "It was a gift for me from Rhianna. She said that I deserved to have something spectacular for my sixteenth birthday. Even a king wouldn't have something this grand."

He studied the height. "I'd be afraid of falling out of it." The intimacy of the place struck him all at once. They were completely alone, and she was sitting on the side of a bed piled with blankets and pillows. His body tightened on a surge of desire. "Raven . . ."

She swiftly got to her feet, her heart pounding madly inside her chest. She knew she wouldn't have been so nervous if she hadn't been so sure that the next time he touched her she wouldn't be able to stop him. She wanted him so terribly. "Well . . . you could probably use a bath. I know you must be uncomfortable."

He looked down and realized he was covered in river water and mud. He grimaced. It didn't make him want her less, but it made it easier to find control. He would sooner cut his hands off than touch her while he was that dirty. "I don't have clean clothes," he apologized.

"That's okay." She smiled. "Riku, that is, Eric Mason, gave me some clothes for you the other day. I just never got a chance to bring them to you." She got them out of a trunk at the end of the bed and held them out. "Here. I'll wait outside while you bathe."

He would have liked her to stay but knew it would be improper as long as they weren't married. He watched her use her powers to fill a large copper tub with hot water before disappearing up the stairs. He had never seen a tub quite like it before, but it looked plenty big enough for him. He swiftly stripped off his ruined clothes and grabbed the cake of soap nearby. It felt good to scrub off all the dirt from his skin and hair though it also felt quite strange to be that clean. He normally just got a river bath once a week or so. It really wasn't the same thing.

When he was done, he got out and dried off with a thick blanket that had been set out with the clothes. He then turned his attention to the clothes themselves. He felt almost embarrassed with how fine the material was, but he liked the warmth. The coat and slacks he liked even more with their blue-black material and little lightning bolt stitching at the cuffs. He pulled on new socks and sturdy boots, stood up, and his mind was boggled when he looked at the mirror.

He began to smile after a moment. He felt overdressed, and yet he was only dressed properly for once. He quickly climbed the stairs to find Raven and complained as he went, "I feel overdressed."

She muffled a giggle from where she was sitting on a rock watching the stars. "I know the feeling. I very rarely wear a bustle, and I only reluctantly wear a corset if I'm going outside. Every time I do, I feel rather odd."

"I think you're beautiful no matter how you look," he told her honestly as he sat beside her.

She smiled, secretly pleased. "Thank you." She took a quick breath as she saw him, and her eyes widened slightly. Dressed so properly, he looked like the prince of her secret fantasies there to rescue her. "You look handsome," she said softly.

"Good." He turned toward her more fully and lifted a hand to catch her hair and thread his fingers through it. "I want you to find me irresistible." He tugged her closer for a light kiss. "Then maybe you'll agree to marry me."

Her eyes closed as despair welled. "I can't," she whispered. "You know what I am, Kay. I know you do."

"Not entirely. Tell me what happened, please." He pulled her into his arms and held on tightly.

She sighed. She was sure he would change his mind when he knew, but for that moment she savored the feel of his embrace. "When I was born, my mother hated me, so she cursed me. I turned into a raven. Rhianna found me, and Enforcers were able to make a contract for me, changing the curse a little. By day, I have to become a raven. At night, I am a woman." She closed her eyes and waited.

He thought about it for a few moments. "So?"

Her eyes opened in surprise. "So? What do you mean 'so'? Kay, no man in his right mind wants a woman who is cursed and can't run his house during the day! And there's no guarantee I could ever have children either!"

"Well, I don't care!" His brows pulled together in a scowl. "As long as I could hold you at least at night, I would be happy. I can cook and clean during the day if needed. Or . . . or I can become nocturnal. We can sleep during the day and live at night. I don't mind. As for children . . . well, I don't have a legacy to pass on. I just love you, Raven."

She shook her head sharply. "You don't believe me!"

"I do, but I still want to marry you!" His expression grew determined. "I'll prove it. Come on." He pulled her up to her feet and began heading with purpose toward the District proper. He was sure someone would lend them a carriage. "We're going to get married."

She stopped so sharply that he stopped for fear of hurting her arm. Shocked, she stared at him. "B-but . . . if you changed your mind . . ." Her voice dropped to an anguished whisper. "I couldn't bear it!"

He turned and caught her arms to lift her off her feet until their eyes met. "I love you," he repeated firmly. "I'll say it over and over again. From the moment I pulled you out of the river, I loved you." He smiled. "Someone told me there are no coincidences around those from 3rd District. That means this is destiny."

"Well spoken." Father Evans smiled when Kay hastily put Raven down and both turned quickly. He lowered a hand and patted Stormy on the head. "Stormy came and fetched me. I now see why."

Raven felt as if the floor had fallen out from under her feet. "B-but . . . !" She looked up at Kay, and his golden eyes shimmered with an endless well of sheer determination . . . and love. He meant it. Wonder began to fill her heart. He truly wanted her. He truly wanted to marry her. How could she ever deny him? "Alright," she conceded shyly. "I'll marry you, Kay."

His breath released on a rush of air. "I was getting scared," he said under his breath. He held her tightly for a moment as he looked at Evans. "You said you would marry us if we wished. Please, Father Evans."

Evans smiled. "I would be honored, Kay."

And so, they were married. It seemed rather astonishing to Raven; she had always thought it would be very complicated, but it wasn't, not really. Before she knew it, Kay was kissing her, and she was his wife. A little thrill went through her as she threw her arms around him. He was hers, too. Her husband. Now no one could ever take him away.

"Good luck," Father Evans told them both. He wandered off further into the woods, and Stormy followed him. He smiled though he did not look at her. "These eyes are old and have seen a lot," he murmured. "Sometimes they even see things that will come to be. Guard this family well, young wolf. Your destiny is tied to them."

She snorted softly under her breath. No, really? She wouldn't have guessed.

"We're married," Raven told Kay, the astonishment still on her face. "I . . . I can't quite believe it. I never thought it would ever happen . . ."

His grin could have lit the forest. "Me neither, but now you're mine." He drew her closer and rocked her in his arms. Now no one could ever take her away. "We'll make a home somewhere."

"We can stay under the tree for now." She smiled shyly. "It's *our* home now, not just mine." Her heart fluttered a little as he took her hand and began walking back through the trees. She felt a little nervous, but it couldn't stop her heart. Even if, somehow, things ended badly, she wanted to belong to him.

She used the key once more and the tree shifted to the side. Before she could go down the stairs, her husband scooped her up into his arms and started down them personally. She clutched his shoulders, eyes wide. "What're you doing?"

"I thought it was a tradition."

"Well, yes, but . . ." Flustered, she fell silent. It was almost unbearably romantic, and her heart fluttered wildly. A prince, she thought again, but one in disguise. Or perhaps a fallen prince because his kingdom had been taken away.

The romantic moment was thoroughly ruined a few moments later as he stubbed his toe on the tub and tripped. She muffled a shriek as they tumbled, and her breath whooshed out as they hit the floor.

To her astonishment, she realized he had wrapped his arms around her so that her head was protected. He was still sprawled over her, and her pulse began to pound in her body. He was heavy, but something inside wanted to purr with delight. Her fingers itched to touch him and find out what he felt like.

Despite the jostle to his ribs, he was more mortified than injured as he lifted his head. "Are you okay?" The words died as he saw the look in her eyes. It was the same helpless, longing look he knew was often in his own gaze whenever he looked at her. The desire he had been determinedly ignoring roared back hotter than ever before.

She licked her lips at a touch of nerves. "I should bathe," she whispered. "Prepare myself."

"And stall for time?" he whispered back.

"That, too." Her eyes closed helplessly as he freed one hand and cupped her cheek. His fingers were warm, and the heat shivered through her softly. "I love you, Kay."

"I love you too, Raven." His smile spread. "Raven Shaughnessy. It has a nice sound to it."

She turned her face into his hand. "I've never had a family before."

"Me neither. We'll make a new family together." He lowered his head to brush soft kisses over her face and tasted her skin tenderly. "I need to warn you. I have no experience at this. It's all instinct. You'll have to tell me if I'm doing something right."

She softly slid her hands up around to the back of his neck. "So far I like it." She smiled as her nerves seemed to fade away. There just wasn't any room for them. "I'm a terrible hussy, and probably completely improper for suggesting it, but since I don't have any experience either, can I explore you, too?"

His breath hitched at the idea of having her hands all over him. "Please do." He rolled off her and winced vividly as his body finally protested painfully. He saw her frown, and he shook his head. "I'm fine."

"No, you're not." She helped him stand and urged him over to the bed so that he sat on the side. "Take off your jacket and shirt. I want to see the wounds." Fully expecting him to follow orders, she went over to where she kept medicines and began rummaging inside. When she turned around again, her breath came in sharply.

He had indeed removed his jacket and shirt. He also hadn't rewrapped the bandages after his bath, and she could see every wound clearly. There were fist-sized bruises of mottled purple and red, and the places where his skin had been broken open were dull and partially scabbed over.

His body was full of tempting, sculpted lines. All his years of hard work had given him much muscle, and the recent meals had helped fill out the lines of his face and body more. Rather than thin, he seemed sleek. To see such imperfections on his perfect body . . . she entertained a brief idea of pecking out Richard's eyes.

Her hands were steady as she fetched a bowl of water and some cloth. She crossed over to her husband and sat beside him on the bed. Tenderly, she began tending to all the wounds by cleaning them thoroughly and carefully rubbing herbs into the bruises to bring down the swelling. "I could kill him for this," she whispered fiercely.

He watched her under lowered lashes, taking great enjoyment in having her hands running over his chest. He didn't know if she realized it was arousing him to have her tending to him but he thought they might both enjoy it if he returned the favor. "I'm used to it." There was a shrug in his voice as he said, "He used to whip me."

Her head shot up sharply. "What?" Her black eyes were fierce as she tugged at his shoulders, and he obligingly turned around so his back was towards her. Tears welled in her eyes as she saw the old scar marks across his back from where a whip had been laid. She fiercely wrapped her arms around him and pressed her lips to his back. "I hate him for this."

He shuddered at the feel of her lips. Pleasure seemed to radiate from his back outwards as she began to press soft kisses over all the marks. "Raven," he managed to say. "You ought to stop."

"Why?" She nuzzled his shoulder. "You're my husband."

"Yes, but it's not fair." With a grace and speed that surprised her, he suddenly turned around and caught her into his arms. "I want to touch you, too."

The heat of his skin was shocking, and the feel was electrifying as her hands flattened on his chest over his heart. Without giving herself time to be embarrassed, she leaned forward and darted her tongue over his collarbone. He shivered, and delight filled her. "I can't believe I'm here with you."

He buried his hand in her hair and tilted her head back. "I can't either," he admitted softly. Unable to hold himself back any longer, he bent his head and kissed her deeply, his tongue slipping into her mouth to tangle with her own. She tasted like fresh rain. It was addicting.

On a soft sound of need, she slid her hands around the back of his neck and drew him closer. She was beginning to feel feverish, her clothes too hot and confining. By the time his lips released hers, she could hardly breathe for the hunger to feel him touching her. "Kay," she whispered. "Please."

He slowly unbuttoned her bodice and dropped it over the side of the bed. The corset was next to be unlaced. He found nothing beneath the silk material except even silkier soft skin. He gently tugged it away and then lifted her to her feet. They unfastened the skirt together and it fell to the floor. Her petticoats and pantalets went next. In moments she wore nothing but lamplight as she eased once more onto the bed beside him. Shadows partially concealed her from view in a tempting tease.

He had nothing to compare her to, but he felt as if she was somehow perfect. Her trim figure needed no corset, and her curves were gentle and supple. Her skin was pale from lack of sun, and a soft flush made her radiant. He couldn't resist slowly running a finger across her collarbone, and he watched her face intently as he did.

Her eyes closed as she waited in an agony of suspension for him to truly touch her. Her body ached, and her breasts felt hot and heavy. Everywhere his fingers touched there was a wave of fire left behind. His hand suddenly cupped her breast and the lash of pleasure shocked her. She arched toward his touch helplessly on a low moan, the nipple swelling on a rush.

Encouraged, he began to trail kisses over her neck and shoulders, delighted at her taste. He slowly worked his way lower, and his hands trembled with the force of his need. He had dreamed of this, dreamed of touching her. Reality was better than he had dared dream. He closed his lips hungrily around the tip of one breast and thrilled at the whimper she gave as she twisted against him.

Suddenly ravenous, he caressed her with lips and teeth, his hands rushing over her sides and up higher to cup her breasts. He raced his kisses over her chest and tasted every inch of her flesh. She began to tremble, and a fierce throbbing began between her legs. Instinctively, her legs shifted to press together.

He barely noticed as he laid her back on the bed. He simply looked his fill for a moment, feeling his body throbbing lightly with the wild urge to possess her. She was so beautiful! The sight of black curls at the apex of her thighs was tempting, and his fingers skimmed over her stomach and lower.

When his lips covered hers, she went into the kiss eagerly. Her hands skidded over his shoulders and her nails scraped lightly. She felt wild for him, as if she couldn't get enough. She unexpectedly felt his fingers sliding through the curls shielding where she was most vulnerable, and she made a grab for his wrist in embarrassment.

He didn't let her deter him, and his fingers slid lower until he was cupping the heart of her. She was hot and wet, and his fingers slid through her folds to caress her intimately. She gave a little cry that thrilled him, and he used his free hand to drag her closer for another kiss as his fingers explored her softly.

Tension gripped her body and she whimpered thinly as she felt the pleasure getting stronger. Desire drowned her nerves and she released his wrist to clutch his shoulders. One of his fingers slipped inside her again, and she couldn't control a desperate arch of her hips. It wasn't enough. She needed something more. "Kay," she pleaded. "Something's wrong."

Somehow he was certain something was *right.* He continued to caress her and felt a greedy thrill as she surged against him, her body calling to him with a lure he couldn't resist. "Touch me," he urged against her lips. "I want to feel your hands."

She couldn't have stopped herself if she had tried. Her hands eagerly lifted and explored his chest with a sensuality she hadn't been able to release when tending to him. Her fingertips brushed over his nipples, and he shuddered. Encouraged, she did it again, and she was delighted when he moaned softly. She felt drugged on pleasure and her nails bit into his shoulders lightly when his fingers stroked her softly.

With a little surge of strength, she twisted her body and sent him tumbling off her. His eyes almost crossed as she almost pounced on him, and her lips and fingers caressed his skin. It didn't hurt. Nothing could hurt when she touched him.

She had been tipsy once in her life, when she had tried wine for the first time a year or two before. Now, for the first time, she understood what it meant to be drunk. She drowned in her lover, and there was no room for shyness inside, not with how his presence filled her. She helped him remove his pants without hesitation and then simply stared at him.

She had been raised by an open-minded community. She knew full well about sex and babies, and the differences between men and women. It had always seemed so clinical before, but now it was a little unnerving as she beheld the vivid evidence that he wanted her. Her curiosity overrode her nerves and she reached out to touch him with a soft finger.

He hissed softly and bit back a groan; the small touch was like a lightning bolt. He grit his teeth and fought his body, trying to keep from losing control as she explored him. Finally he couldn't take it anymore and rolled her over to pin her beneath him as his mouth devoured hers.

"Your ribs!" she protested breathlessly. She whimpered as he settled between her legs and she felt his hot flesh rubbing against her. Instinctively, her legs wound around his hips. "Kay!"

"Forget my ribs." His mouth rushed over her face, and one hand held her tightly to him. "I can't wait. I need to be inside you." He reached between them with his other hand and caressed her, needing her breathless cries to know she wanted him just as terribly. His erection nestled against her, and as he flexed his hips, he pushed slowly inside. "Raven?"

"If you stop," she warned thickly, "I'll be forced to do something drastic!" Her breath caught as he pushed slowly deeper, and her body slowly stretched to hold him. It hurt a little, but it stirred something deeper inside. She craved having him as close as possible.

On a groan, he buried his face in her hair and surged into her fully. She was hot and wet, and the feeling was electrifying, drawing his body taut with desire. Terrified he might have hurt her, he lifted his head and rained kisses over her face. "Did I hurt you?"

"No." She trembled and returned the kisses almost ravenously. It was what she had wanted, but . . . she needed something more. She didn't understand it but felt it beckoning her. Without conscious thought, her hips arched against him, and it sent off a shockwave through them both. Helplessly, she twisted beneath him. "Kay, do something, please!"

Instinct took over, and his lips sealed hers as he began to slowly slide out of her only to drive deeply back in. Again and again, until he felt as if he might break from the tension, he drove into her, hungry for everything he could have from her.

Her fingers clenched into his hair as the pleasure grew and grew until it suddenly erupted with a force that stunned her. Ecstasy rolled over her without stopping, and she muffled a cry against the side of his neck as she clung onto him. She felt the shudder that ripped through his strong body, and then he was buried in her to the hilt, his head thrown back as he gave in to their pleasure. She had never seen anything more wildly beautiful.

He managed to not collapse on top of her, but he was exhausted. He was also stunned. There was, he realized in vague surprise, a difference between knowing the mechanics of something, and experiencing it firsthand with someone you loved. He turned his head and kissed her deeply. "Are you okay?" he asked softly.

Her eyes opened slightly and a smile curved her lips. "Yes." Her arms slid more fully around him, keeping him close when he would have moved. "I can't think of a word to describe how I feel except 'happy,' but that isn't even close." Her eyes opened wide suddenly. "Oh! Your ribs!"

"They're fine." He felt them twinge in argument but ignored them. He carefully rolled to the side and tugged her closer so that she was protectively tucked against him. "You're my wife now, completely. I'm never letting you go."

Tears burned her eyes as she burrowed closer. "I just hope you feel that way tomorrow morning," she whispered, "when you wake and find that your wife has become a bird."

"Watch me." He held her securely and closed his eyes. He knew that nothing could possibly change his mind.

He awoke hours later to the realization it was after dawn because there was sunlight filtering through the pipe where the stove went above ground. Raven wasn't in his arms. He frowned as he realized he had wanted to wake with her beside him. A soft sound reached his ears, and he looked around swiftly to see a raven sitting on the trunk. She was crying softly.

He immediately got out of bed and lifted her into his arms. He rubbed his cheek over her feathers, and she stopped crying. Her black eyes looked at him in despair. He tightened his hold on her protectively. "I don't care," he said softly. "You're still my wife. You're still my Raven. I'll find a way to free you, I swear it. Just promise never to fly away."

She sighed softly and rubbed her head against his chin in acceptance. He continued to tenderly stroke her feathers and knew that nothing mattered except that they were together. Bird or woman, she was the one he loved more than anything. He would protect her from everything. "I love you, Raven," he vowed quietly.

She closed her eyes and nestled closer. She finally believed that he meant it. Perhaps someday everything would be alright. She wanted to believe in the happily ever after Rhianna had always told her belonged to true lovers. She had found her true lover. They deserved a happy ending.

CHAPTER FIVE

Kay gently set Raven down on the end of the bed and looked for his clothes. Once he was fully dressed, he sat down and frowned thoughtfully. "I suppose the first thing I need to do is to find somewhere I can work." His stomach rumbled loudly, and he cleared his throat. "Sorry."

She flew over to the stove and flapped her wings to get his attention. He walked over with a tilt of his head, and his brows lifted. Breakfast sat waiting on the top of the stove, and it was still steaming warm. She had taken the time to make him something before her change. He tenderly caressed her feathers, love making his eyes soften. "I don't deserve you."

Pleasure filled her heart and she landed on his shoulder so that she could be close to him. It made her very happy to watch him devour his meal, and she really hoped that she could bring him breakfast in bed someday. He was long overdue to be pampered by someone who loved him!

Perhaps a bit amusingly, he was thinking the same thing about her. He deeply liked the idea of completely and thoroughly spoiling his lover as soon as she could be human during the day. Barring that, he would spoil her mercilessly at night instead.

Content in many ways, he put the plate back and smiled. "Let's go into town. I'm not going to be afraid anymore. I know I still owe him money, but he can't force me to be a slave anymore. I can just pay him back in installments."

She frowned mentally but nuzzled his cheek. She didn't think it right that he should have to pay Richard anything, not after how he had been treated his whole life. She could only hope that Stormy was on her way to talk to Rhianna and Eric and tell them what was going on.

It was not yet mid-morning when they got to the city center nearby, and the townspeople greeted Kay with smiles and laughter. Several waved cheerfully. Kay had no idea what had happened, but he got his explanation when one gentleman stopped to greet him, "We all heard from Father Evans that you got married yesterday!" His smile was wide. "We're all happy for you. Where's your bride?"

"Resting." Kay smiled in return. "She's a very delicate woman. Ow!" He rubbed his ear as Raven pecked at it with her beak. He barely hid a laugh; he did not find it surprising that she disliked being labeled as delicate. "Thank you," he said to the man. "Your support means a lot."

"We've always liked you, Kay," the man told him seriously. "If we could have found a way to get Johnston off you, we would have. I know today is a day to rest for you, but tomorrow come see me, and I'll find you a job at my shop." He smiled. "You'll need to support your family."

"Thank you very much!" Surprised, Kay watched him walk away and wondered if the entire city had been on his side without his knowledge. It was an oddly freeing feeling. Deeply curious, he wandered down to the river and sat on a bench to study it. Now that it wasn't his prison, he was able to admire it. "It feels odd to simply stop and relax."

Raven agreed but wished fiercely that she could be sitting there beside him and holding his hand. She gave a startled chirp as he suddenly lifted her off his shoulder and onto his lap, and his nimble fingers smoothed over her feathers. It was akin to when he ran his hands through her hair and very pleasurable. She snuggled under his hand contentedly. How had she been lucky enough to find this particular man?

His hand stopped and she felt tension fill in his fingers. She swiftly looked up and saw Richard Johnston standing less than twenty feet away with an inhuman sort of fury on his face. In that moment, she knew she was looking into the face of evil. She bristled and prepared to do whatever it took to protect her husband.

Kay felt curiously unafraid. He had known the confrontation was inevitable. Because he needed the leverage, he got to his feet. His confidence began to grow more as he realized something he never had before: Richard was the smaller man. He stood at five-seven, at most, and he had more fat than muscle on his frame. Kay stood taller and the steady meals lately had been adding more weight to his already present muscle.

He began to smile. "Good morning, Richard." A soft wind ruffled his hair, and the soothing sensation felt like someone stood behind him in support. Raven's little trill of greeting implied it might not be just his imagination. He gently put her down on the bench. "I assume you're here to congratulate me on my marriage."

Good boy, a familiar woman's voice murmured in his mind. *Keep him talking. Let him hang himself.*

Richard's face twisted with rage. "What woman would want a nobody like you?"

"A wonderful woman," he countered. "One I love very dearly. She is a true lady."

"A whore no doubt." Richard spit at the ground near his feet. "You deserve each other."

Never one to flare with quick temper, Kay found he had to fight for control. He could handle insults to himself, but *never* to Raven. "Actually, we do." His faint accent thickened slightly in warning. "And I really do not care what you have to say." He lowered a hand and rubbed his fingers over Raven's head to comfort her rising distress. "May I assume we have your well wishes?"

"I own you!" the older man roared. "You owe me for raising you all of these years!" He seemed completely unaware of the crowd that had gathered around them. More than one man was armed on the chance that things turned physical. "You owe your life to me!"

Since it seemed he didn't want to keep the truth hidden, Kay didn't feel alarmed at the idea of it all coming out. "Is that why you beat me nearly to death whenever I didn't make what you deemed was the right amount?" His voice was bland and without inflection.

"A boy like you has no idea of his betters! You deserved to be beaten! And who would care if you died?! A homeless, useless child with no family! No money of his own!" Richard took a step closer. "You owe me!"

"For what? Living in the barn my whole life? For working like a slave? For being beaten? For knowing that you were wasting my family's money when there was nothing I could do about it?" Every word made nineteen years of suppressed fury rise hotter and hotter. His hands clenched into fists at his sides. "You're a disgusting, pathetic old man!"

"How dare you?!" Richard lunged forward on a roar, beefy fists raised in warning.

Raven shot into the air on a screech, and her talons raked across his face. Blood flew as he shrieked in fear and pain. He grabbed her out of the air and hurled her violently aside. She landed safely in a familiar man's arms, but she looked distinctly dazed.

Kay saw red. "Don't ever touch her again!" He took a single gliding step forward, and his fist cracked across Richard's jaw so hard that he was sent flying into the river beside them. "I owe you nothing," Kay warned in a dangerously soft voice, "except contempt!"

"Indeed." Eric walked forward, and he had Raven securely held in his arms. His ice blue eyes were dispassionate as he watched the man struggling to stay afloat in the river. "Richard Johnston, did you not sign a contract with Enforcers that stated you would care for Kay Shaughnessy as if he were your own son?"

Rhianna walked up to stand beside her partner and took Raven from Eric to hand her to Kay. "I believe he did, Riku," she countered calmly, "and in light of the evidence, I believe this is a breach of contract. What did the stipulations state?"

"An eye for an eye, Rhi." He reached down to haul Richard out of the river. Eric was not much bigger than Kay but he was immensely stronger. "Let's take him to the sheriff, shall we?" He smiled at Kay. "Consider any debt you *might* have owed to be completely null and void."

Stunned, Kay stood holding Raven and watched Eric head off down the road, all but dragging Richard by the seat of his pants. A little shiver touched his skin for a moment and he held the raven in his arms closer. "He won't make it to the sheriff, will he?" he asked Rhianna softly.

"No," she told him gently. She lowered a hand and scratched Stormy behind the ears as the slender wolf came up and sat beside her. "Richard has been destroyed by his own greed. There is nothing but evil inside him. Part of the Enforcers' role is to destroy evil. Riku will handle things." She smiled. "Now come along with me. We're going to the Enforcers' office to talk."

"Alright." He gave her an odd look as they began walking down the road toward the carriage waiting. "I thought . . . for a moment, I was sure I heard you in my mind. And that wind . . . it felt as if it came from Mr. Mason."

Her smile spread. "Perhaps. We of 3rd District are . . . singularly blessed." She had to laugh softly as he quickly beat her to the carriage and offered a hand to help her up. "Blood will tell. You're a true gentleman at heart." She let him assist her and then took a seat as he joined her. Stormy and Raven sat on the seats beside them.

The Enforcers' building was the largest in the District and in fact the largest in most of the city. It boasted an impressive number of stories and the architecture rivaled the capitol building. Kay loved it on sight, and the entire 3rd District. Where parts of the main city were beginning to be modernized, the styles starting to change, 3rd District was still the same as it had been for centuries.

Rhianna ushered them straight up to the top floor where she and Eric had their offices. Once inside, she took the pins out of her hair and shook out the thick red mass so that it swung around her shoulders. "I do hate those." Rubbing her scalp, she went over to her desk and had a seat behind it. "Sit down, Kay."

He did so, still looking around curiously. Everything in the office had been made from hand carved wood with an eye for detail and design. It was clearly made by the same craftsman who had made Raven's bed. His color climbed as he remembered how comfortable that bed had been when he had been lying in it with Raven snuggled beside him.

Rhianna covered a smile. She truly liked him, this kind boy with dreams in his eyes and a wild spirit in his heart. They were traits she hoped were passed down through the generations along with his beautiful smile. "Well," she started, "to begin with, congratulations on your marriage."

He smiled and smoothed his fingers over Raven's feathers when she landed on his lap. "Thank you." His face grew serious. "Miss Taber, please, tell me. Is there any way to break this curse on Raven?"

"Call me Rhianna." She toyed with a pen. "What would you do if I told you there wasn't?"

His face tightened. "I'd find a way to support us by working during the day, and I'd spend every minute of the night with her. I love Raven," he vowed intensely. "I don't care what she is!"

She smiled suddenly. "I see why your paths crossed. You are truly meant for one another." Perhaps things would be just fine for Stormy after all. Well, if they could all go this smoothly, of course. "There is a way to break the curse," she announced.

His eyes widened. "Really? How? I'll do anything!"

"First . . ." She held up a hand. "Let me explain something, alright? About the 3rd District and its origins." She folded her hands on her desk. "It started many, many centuries ago, before I was born." She tilted her head. "If I told you there were other worlds out there, worlds that cannot be seen by the naked eye, what would you think?"

He thought about it. "I'd think that doesn't sound very wrong," he decided. "I believe in magic, Rhianna."

"Good, good." She settled back in her chair. "There *is* such a world out there; one that lies parallel to this one. It is known as Mirage. Have you ever, on a truly hot day, thought you saw something there but got closer and discovered it was gone?" He nodded and she smiled. "You were seeing a piece of the world known as Mirage, a place of magic. A century or two before I was born, it drifted too close to Earth and became stuck."

"Stuck?" He cocked his head. "How does a world get stuck?"

"Simply because the River Styx runs like a band around the world, right under New York in fact, and Mirage consists entirely of magic. The two got meshed together. The river is now a gateway between worlds." She swirled a finger in the air. "This district is built directly over where the Styx is closest to the surface."

"Magic," Eric added from the doorway, "is literally born here. It affects all of New York, really, but much more thinly. It took a long time for people to evolve as they did. Rhianna's and my generation was the beginning of the truly powerful and visible changes. We chose to build our district on this location so that the magic was always cycling. Now any child born here, even to normal parents, will be gifted."

"So why call it the 3rd District?" Kay wondered. "Why not give it a real name, befitting it?"

Eric's smile spread as he walked over to sit on the edge of Rhianna's desk. "What makes you think we didn't? You see, Kay, when you hear us say '3rd', you are hearing the number three."

"As if it were the third district built," Kay agreed. "It's not?"

"Actually, it was originally named 'thierde,' which is pronounced the same way. It is a word in the language of Mirage that means 'sanctuary of magic.'" Rhianna spread her hands as his eyes widened. "As time went past, people forgot the meaning. We let them. This world is not . . . comfortable with magic. We had thought that most had forgotten, but the slaughter of the werewolves proved us wrong. In a hundred years, I'm sure we'll be nothing but a myth once more."

"Let it happen." His voice was firm. "If it keeps everyone safe, then let it happen." He smiled as Raven nuzzled his hand. "How does this matter to Raven's curse?"

"It's very simple, Kay." Eric crossed his arms. "To break the curse, her feathers must be changed from black to white, and the only way to do that is to immerse her in the River Styx. It is the river that not only connects to Mirage, but sailing along it will also take you to the afterworld where we all go when we die. It is a river of life, death, and rebirth."

Kay leapt to his feet. "I'll do it! I'll take Raven there and break this curse!"

Rhianna smiled. "Good boy. Stormy knows the way, so she will take you there. And, Kay, remember: you cannot touch the river yourself. If you fall within it, you will die."

He nodded firmly. "I won't. I'll come back as soon as I can, and Raven will be walking beside me no matter what time of day it is." Holding an astonished Raven close in his arms, he left the office and followed Stormy as she hurried down the hall.

The door shut behind him, and Rhianna looked at Eric. "Well?"

"He's gone." He didn't elaborate on the details but there was a hardness in his blue eyes for a moment before disappearing. "When I spoke to the governor to tell him how the Shaughnessy heir was doing, he was delighted to hear of his marriage. He wants to meet Kay and Raven once the curse is lifted. The only trouble is that his ex-wife looked . . . a bit alarmed."

"As I imagine she would. If her sin is exposed, she will be labeled as an attempted murderess." She drummed her fingers on her desk. "My only concern now is that *all* the people from 3rd District know how to find the River Styx."

He studied her. "Rhi, have I ever told you that I often think you manipulate people and the only reason there are no coincidences in 3rd District is because of you?"

"Daily."

"Just thought I'd mention it again for good measure."

Raven could not fight a bundle of nerves and huddled against Kay's shoulder for security; was this really going to work? Kay had his own nerves, but he was damned determined that he would make things work out. Nerves turned to puzzlement as he followed Stormy down below the first floor of the building into what looked like a basement. They then went down another set of stairs into a dungeon. "Where are we going?"

Stormy pawed at the wall. He touched it, and a door appeared. Startled, he jerked his hand away and the door disappeared. He touched it again curiously and the door once more appeared. With a quick breath, he pushed on the door and it swung outward into blinding white light.

Stormy nudged him through the door, and he hastily covered his eyes against the brightness. The door silently swung shut behind them, and he slowly lowered his arm as he felt the light fading.

He discovered he was standing on the edge of the world. At the least, that was how it felt. He stood at the top of a sharp cliff, and he could see a series of more cliffs ahead that slowly dropped downward as if they were a giant's stairs. The last one in the distance seemed to drop off into nothing at all.

Wildflowers bloomed everywhere in a riot of colors. He knelt to pick one, and it turned into a butterfly. Another flower was left in its place, and he ran a hand over the top of several blooms. A curtain of butterflies swirled into the air and toward the sky, and it was then that he finally noticed the most spectacular part of that beautiful place.

The sky seemed to be a relatively normal blue, but in the middle, suspended like an illusion, was the appearance of another world. He could see forests and rivers, lakes and towns. It looked like nothing he had ever seen before, and certainly nothing like New York. Castles dotted the landscape and he could almost hear the trumpets. It was grand and beautiful. "Is that Mirage?" he asked softly. "It's amazing."

Stormy took off running down the field, and he hurried after her with Raven flying along beside him. When he had first stood there looking around, it had seemed like such a long distance. By the time evening fell, he knew that they would reach the end the next day. Perhaps time moved at a different rate there.

They were all tired so they stopped where they were to rest for the night. The sun also set in that magical place, and he watched it slowly sink in a fiery blaze of color. Just as it disappeared beyond the horizon, he realized Raven had started to glow softly. The light swirled up and around her, and as it faded away, she was once more a woman. She was also naked, and she blushed profusely as she wrapped her arms around herself.

"Now you know why I always hid," she whispered. "Unfortunately, my clothes never change with me. I turn back and I'm naked." She looked up in surprise as she felt him wrapping his jacket around her shoulders. "Thank you."

He knelt beside her and drew her into his arms as his lips sought hers. He had craved her taste and touch every second of every minute. "Welcome home," he murmured. He slowly lowered her down until she was lying in the flowers. "I missed touching you."

Stormy, being a wise and rather discrete wolf, took off. Neither Raven nor Kay noticed. She tenderly ran her hands over his face and savored the feel of his skin. "It was the hardest thing I've ever done, leaving your arms this morning." She burrowed against him on a soft sound of need. "I've never needed anyone like I need you. I love you so much!"

He caught her close and kissed her deeply, his body shaking with the force of his emotions. He knew how she felt. He knew, precisely, how she felt. If he lost her, he would be willing to jump into the Styx to find her again.

"So that's Mirage," she murmured drowsily hours later as they were snuggled together watching the sky. Her head was tucked on his shoulder and they were using his jacket as a blanket. She had never been more content. "It's beautiful. I always knew it was there, but I'd never seen it."

"I didn't even know it was there." His hand stroked over her back slowly. "It seems so odd to me, in some ways, to think of everything that has happened. But . . . but I like it. Let's make sure that our children always believe in magic."

She straightened up, startled. "You want children with me?" He looked at her oddly and she shook her head. "But we can't be sure I can have them." Blushing furiously, she whispered, "I've never . . . my body hasn't . . . monthly I don't . . ."

He frowned. "I'm still not following."

She bit her lip as her cheeks turned pink. "Women . . . monthly . . . well, they bleed. And that's how they know that they can have children, but aren't pregnant." She shook her head. "I'll teach you to read and then give you a book on it. It's so embarrassing!"

He felt slightly embarrassed himself, and also quite sympathetic for women of the world. "Basically what you are saying is that since you've never . . . you know . . . you can't be sure your body is capable?"

"Yes," she whispered.

His lips firmed. "We'll figure it out. I think if we wish for anything hard enough, we can have it." He rolled over and tucked her protectively underneath him. "Rhianna and Eric are old and wise. They might know something. And if not . . . then maybe we can adopt." He smiled. "We would do much better than the Johnstons."

She smiled and pulled him close. "Yes," she agreed softly. "We would."

As dawn was beginning to rise, she left his arms. He awoke instantly and sat up with a frown to watch as she walked a few steps away. Somehow he heard her tears inside his heart, and he knew this was why the raven cried every morning. He quickly got to his feet and wrapped his arms around her. "Don't cry," he urged.

She trembled and closed her eyes as her head fell back against his shoulder. "I'm alone."

"No, you're not. Not anymore." He held onto her tightly and felt the rise of her power inside. Light consumed her and swirled around them both as the sunrise washed over them. Moments later, he was holding nothing but air, and the raven was sitting on the flowers in front of him.

She took a breath as if to cry but he knelt and lifted her into his arms. "Don't cry," he said again, rubbing his cheek over her feathers. "I'm here with you always." He eased back and smiled. "I love you."

She nuzzled her head against his shoulder and finally let go of the pain she had endured her entire life. No, she wasn't alone. She would never be alone at dawn again, not as long as she had him.

Stormy rejoined them not long after he had gotten dressed again, and they all continued on their way toward the canyon that marked the western edge of the River Styx. When they reached it, Kay carefully got down on his knees and peered over the side. His eyes slowly widened.

The River Styx was nothing like any river he had ever seen before. It wasn't blue at all, and it wasn't even a clear color that reflected blue. It looked visibly, richly, silver and white. It flowed gently and steadily, and he felt his stomach quiver as he saw a small boat sailing down it. A cloaked person was pushing it along and he gave a nervous laugh as he saw the skeletal hands holding the steering pole. "I do not want to know who that is."

He straightened and smiled at Raven as she landed beside him. "Are you ready?" He heard Stormy suddenly growl softly with menace and turned his head sharply to see several soldiers approaching them quickly. He got to his feet and braced his shoulders. "What are you doing here?"

"Orders from the First Lady." One of the men drew a bayonet. "We're here to kill you and the bird."

"No!" He stepped in front of Raven defensively. "You won't touch her!" Even when the soldier aimed the tip of the weapon under his chin, he didn't back down. "Go back to where you came from! You don't belong here!"

The blade was pressed harder, and it drew blood. Raven gave a chilling cry and shot at the soldier's face with her talons extended. His scream of agony echoed everywhere and sent butterflies in mad flight as she clawed at his eyes and ripped flesh. The other soldiers were too horrified to move.

The first soldier managed to grab her and twisted her wing sharply. Bone and cartilage broke loudly in the eerie silence. With a shout, he hurled her over the side of the cliff.

"Raven!" Kay lunged for the edge and dove over the side after her. A broken wing meant she could not fly. She would never survive the fall into the river unless something bigger broke the surface first.

"Well." The solder could barely see as he swiped at his bleeding face. "That's that."

A low, menacing growl rose on the air, and they all turned to see the wolf glowing. Hearts stopped dead as the wolf's body stretched up and became a familiar figure. Everyone knew who she was and what she had done. The scent of their terror filled the air as she slowly walked toward them. They knew their lives were done.

Raven had closed her eyes to prepare for the impact, but they flew wide again as she felt one of Kay's arms close around her. She flapped her good wing and struggled wildly, but he drew her closer with a tender smile. "If we die, we die together." The words came from him with absolute calm.

They plunged into the River Styx. Kay's half-dive managed to break the surface enough to keep them from dying on impact, but it still nearly knocked him out. His arm loosened and freed Raven, and she had suffered no ill effects from the landing. The water surged around her sharply, and he watched dazedly as her feathers turned to white. She would be okay.

The light engulfed her as it always did at sunset though it was only the middle of the day. The transformation had never hurt until that moment when it stitched her broken arm back together and healed it. The light slowly faded, and she found herself staring at her hands. The curse's heavy presence had lifted from her soul. All she had to do was kick her legs and she would float to the surface and be free.

She turned her head and saw Kay suspended in the middle of the river. He would die if he remained there for much longer, and yet there was no way to free him. He was normal. Normal people could not go into the river lest they never leave again.

Without hesitation, she kicked her way over and wrapped her arms around him. He started to struggle then, shaking his head adamantly, but she just smiled and leaned up to kiss him softly. She didn't want to live without him, curse or no curse. If he was doomed, then so was she. "If we die," she mouthed tenderly, "then we die together."

His eyes softened and he moved his arms enough to pull her close. The weight of the river covered them both and dragged them deeper, compressing their lungs until the last bubble of air was forced from their lips.

The bubbles merged together over their heads and began emitting a soft golden light. The light swept down over them, severed the ties the river held on them, and held the waters back. Fresh air that carried a soft scent of peaches surrounded them and both breathed it in deeply. Neither knew what was happening though they were grateful.

The light swirled around them and carried them up toward the surface, and then it carried them even further up to the top edge of the cliff. It set them down gently amid the flowers. Raven pushed herself up to a sitting position and shoved her wet hair out of her eyes. "Why?" she asked softly.

"Because," a man's voice answered just as softly from within the light, "those who are willing to die for love are the ones who truly deserve to live."

The light faded away and the scent of peaches disappeared. Shivering, she wrapped her arms around herself and looked aside to see Kay carefully sitting up. She threw her arms around him on a surge of joy and nearly knocked them both over again.

His arms closed around her fiercely, and he buried his face in her hair. "We did it," he murmured. "We really did it."

"Idiot!" She pressed her face to his shoulder, her shoulders shaking as she began to sob. "You were going to die! How could you think I'd ever want to live without you?!"

He gently framed her face and leaned down to kiss her. "You'd do the same for me." He held her close and looked around, but there was no sign of the soldiers. He spotted Stormy sitting not very far beyond them, though, and there was blood from a gash across her front haunch. She looked relatively intact overall.

He just smiled. He had always suspected he knew who and what she was, but it was her secret to tell if she ever wanted. He felt honored to call her his friend. "Thank you," he told her softly, and saw her surprise. "For everything."

CHAPTER SIX

By the time they got back to the Enforcers' entrance, both Raven and Kay were desperate for clean clothes. He was wearing only his shirt and pants, and she was wearing his jacket. The clothes were stiff from drying in the sun and slightly dirty from being used as blankets at night.

The only bright spot that either had found was the morning they had woken together at sunrise with her still safely curled in his arms. Even as dawn had washed over them, the only glow inside her had been the happiness she felt. She had always hated the dawn, but now she loved it and the way it made Kay's white hair shine brilliantly.

Stormy limped along at their side, and her wound had been dressed by a makeshift bandage torn from the edge of the shirt. She was just as happy to see the exit as they were. Kay opened the door, and she ran in on a loud bark. Her claws skidded on the floor as she ran up the stairs.

Moments later, Eric came down the stairs with her yanking him by his pant leg. "Yes, I'm hurrying," he told her. "Impatient thing." He spotted Kay and Raven and had to smile. "Ah, so the heroes return triumphantly. Well done, children."

Raven felt horribly embarrassed standing there in nothing but Kay's jacket, and she hid partially behind her husband. Never mind that Riku was like an uncle or surrogate father to her. It was still embarrassing! "Thank you, but . . . is there somewhere we can bathe and get clean clothes, Riku?"

Rhianna came down the stairs with two blankets over her arms. "Naturally." She gave one to each of them and then smiled as they wrapped themselves up firmly. "Once you have bathed and rested, come and see me. There's much we have to discuss. And you," she added to Stormy, "come with me to get bandaged up. Troublemaker."

Kay and Raven were shown to a guest room on the second floor and both were more than happy to take advantage of the private bath attached to it. The water was cold, naturally, since no one had known when they would return, but Raven used her powers and had it steaming hot in short order.

She shamelessly admired her husband as he stripped off his dirty clothes. He truly was as beautiful inside as out. The wounds had wholly disappeared after the trip into the River Styx, and even the scars had faded more. Perhaps in a few years they would fade entirely.

He caught her gaze and was warmed. He liked knowing she found him attractive. He smiled and reached over to begin unwrapping her from the blanket and jacket. "You're so beautiful," he told her, "that it seems a shame to cover you up now that I can see you in the daylight."

"It feels so odd," she admitted, holding onto his shoulders as he lifted her and carried her into the tub with him. As he sat down and held her on his lap, she slid her arms around his neck and studied his face intently. "Would you have truly stayed with me if the curse could have never been broken?"

"Yes." He tugged her down for a kiss. "I love you exactly as you are." He eased her back and picked up the cake of soap to begin gently washing her. "And I'm going to warn you now that I'll do everything in my power to spoil you entirely."

"Oh." It was the best she could manage as his hands sent ripples of pleasure through her body and stirred her senses. "I think you're taking advantage of my weakness for you." She shuddered as his fingers slid between her legs.

He smiled. "I just can't keep my hands off you."

"Can we . . . in a bathtub?"

"I know a water elf. She won't let the floor get wet."

When they walked into Rhianna's office an hour or two later, Stormy sniffed at Raven and gave a happy bark as her tail began wagging enthusiastically. Rhianna and Eric both hid smiles as they got to their feet. "Feeling better?" Rhianna asked blandly.

Kay and Raven both blushed profusely. At least there was no evidence. The water had stayed off the floor, but Raven still couldn't figure out how she had been able to concentrate at all. "Yes, thank you." She smoothed a hand over her cherry blossom dress. "Where did you find this? I left it at home."

"I know an elemental master," Rhianna noted dryly. "He has his way with trees."

"Hush, you."

Kay smiled. "You seem like brother and sister."

"Heaven forbid I be related to this shrew." Eric didn't deny the charge though, and neither did Rhianna. They had been best friends for centuries and were very much like family in many ways. Truthfully, they *were* family, in all the ways that counted. "Have a seat. We want to hear what happened."

"Alright." Kay sat down on one of the chairs. Raven took the seat beside him and he automatically laced their fingers together. "Everything went normally until we got to the river. These soldiers came from out of nowhere and told us they were there under the First Lady's orders to kill Raven and me."

"One of them threatened Kay and cut him." Raven lowered her gaze. "I attacked him with my talons. He broke my wing and threw me over the cliff. Kay dove after me and we both went into the river."

Rhianna lifted a brow slightly. "And yet you both sit here alive."

"Well . . ." Kay frowned. "Raven had thought to stay there with me, so that we died together." His hand tightened around hers for a moment. "But there was this light, this golden light. It gave us air and we could smell peaches."

Rhianna went very still and drew Eric's puzzled gaze. "And?" she asked softly.

"It carried us out of the river and to safety. A man's voice told us that only those who are willing to die for love truly deserve to live." Raven frowned as she saw Rhianna's fingers tremble for a moment on her teacup. "Are you alright, Rhianna?"

"Yes." She firmly blocked Eric out of her mind and told herself to get a grip. Still, her heart beat hard within her chest. "Well, clearly, this light was someone with a soft spot for true love." She found a smile and it was natural. "As for the soldiers . . . well, we can explain that."

"Can I make a guess?" Kay asked.

"Certainly."

"Raven is the governor's daughter, isn't she?" He felt her incredulous gaze and looked at her with a smile. "It just seems to add up. The First Lady shouldn't have cared one way or another about you, unless she was afraid that your existence would prove she was a murderess."

"A *very* sharp young man," Eric murmured for Rhianna's ears only. Louder, he said, "You are correct, Kay. When Raven was born, her mother feared for her position if her husband knew she was from the 3rd District. So she cursed her daughter and pretended the child was stillborn."

"She has paid a price," Rhianna murmured. "She can have no more children. More importantly, her husband eventually divorced her to marry a woman he loved far deeper. Rumor says he could not bear to remain with his first wife because of their lost child. I strongly suspect he at least senses something."

"I still don't know why he let her stay on as First Lady after the divorce," Eric muttered.

"Pity," Rhianna told him.

"I . . ." Raven slowly shook her head. "I can't be the governor's daughter!"

"Why not?" Eric asked. "As a matter of fact, this is quite opportune timing. The governor wanted to meet Kay and see how he is faring since the incident nineteen years ago. I think it only fitting that he meet his firstborn child." When he saw the distress on her face, he smiled gently. "Raven, I think you will be surprised. Your father will love you, I'm sure of it."

She wasn't nearly so sure, but she was willing to give it an attempt. She put on a thick and enveloping cloak to hide her features from sight until Eric deemed the right time to reveal her. Kay was the only reason she held any courage, and she clung tightly to his hand as they were shown in to see the governor.

The capitol was grander than she might have ever imagined. Kay was no less stunned, but he was fascinated as well by the architecture. He had always been fascinated by buildings and the ways they could be made. He liked secret passages, too. He had always wanted a home with one or two.

Eric seemed perfectly comfortable as he walked into the governor's office and bowed deeply. "I have brought Kay Shaughnessy and his wife." He heard a slight strangled gasp from where the First Lady stood, and he slid a cold blue gaze toward her. "Is something wrong, my lady?"

"No, no!" She averted her gaze swiftly.

Looking at her, Raven felt nothing but anger. This was the woman who had given birth to her, and this was also the woman who had tried to kill her. Objectively, she could see where she had gotten her looks. Her mother still looked quite beautiful at her later age, but the similarities were purely superficial. Her mother's eyes were narrowed and cruel, and little lines at the corners made her look far older than she was.

In stark contrast, the governor's second wife had soft features that no doubt made her seem deceptively youthful. Kindness edged her face and time would always sit gently on her shoulders because she treated others gently in turn. She stood closest to the governor and had a hand resting on his arm. Hiding just behind the folds of her elaborate dress was a little boy no more than five years old.

Raven's breath hitched as she looked at the governor. There was no denying that this man was her father; they possessed the same black eyes and dark hair. He seemed a bit plain, yet some inner beauty made him larger than life. He had been only a prominent lawyer at the time of her birth, and he had worked his way up the ladder over the years. He was now a well-loved governor that always thought of his people first.

Eric gently placed a hand on Kay's shoulder. "This is Kay," he said to the governor. "He is twenty-one years of age now. He was raised by Richard Johnston."

The governor frowned. "Mr. Johnston has not been seen lately."

"He breached an Enforcers' contract." Eric's voice was almost gentle. "He let himself be eaten away by evil. He abused Kay and treated him worse than a slave. He squandered all of the Shaughnessy wealth and forced Kay to work like a dog to make more. Regardless, Kay has become a man among men."

Kay knew he was blushing but couldn't help it. The governor smiled; the handsome young man's manner was refreshing and endearing. "So I see. Tell me, Kay, is there anything you would ask from me? I feel I owe you a service for not noticing all these years how you were treated. I helped get the approval to you entering that household."

"Hold onto that thought," Eric noted when he saw how speechless Kay was. "You see, I have some advice to ask from you. Let me tell you a tale, and you tell me what should be done."

"Very well. You have my undivided attention, Riku." The governor smiled as his son climbed onto his lap. "Most of it anyway."

"This is the tale: A woman feared for her own safety because she was 3rd District born. Out of that fear, she cursed her newly born child and condemned it to become a raven. This child was given a contract by us, and she was allowed to be a woman by night and a raven by day. She grew up to be a wonderful young woman, well loved by all she met. She eventually fell in love and got married. Her husband loved her in spite of the curse but sought to break it. They looked for a solution together.

"The mother heard of this, and she feared her secret would come out. She sent assassins to kill her child and son-in-law so that the secret could not be revealed. Now, the woman and her husband survived this ordeal and the curse was lifted. Quite a happily ever after, isn't it? My question is about the mother. Thrice attempted murder, lying, child endangerment . . . the list could go on. What ought to be her punishment?"

The governor was thinking, and he did not notice his first wife's agitation, or the nearly deadly look Eric sent her. His second wife did, and she glanced immediately to the cloaked figure standing just behind Kay. It did not take much to guess the tale was a true one, not when the 3rd District was involved. Her heart ached, and she fought an urge to scoop up the lost raven and promise everything would be fine.

"Well," the governor finally said, "I would not want to argue my feelings in court, of course, but if the evidence was heavy enough, I would say the mother had earned herself a life in prison or worse."

The First Lady began to weep softly, and Eric walked over to stand behind Raven. "Well said, sir. Tell me then, do you know this young woman?" And before she could stop him, he whisked her cloak off and revealed her to one and all.

The governor's breath lodged in his chest painfully as he found himself staring into his own eyes, set into a face as beautiful as his first wife's had once been. He *knew*. Fury swelled in his heart, and he turned toward his ex-wife. "Explain yourself," he said menacingly.

"I'm so sorry!" she burst out on a sob. "I was so terrified you would throw me aside! I didn't want to live on the streets or go back to my family! I was certain if you learned I was 3rd District born that you would toss me aside, and I would have to work so hard again! I had no choice!"

"Everyone in 3rd District is under government protection!" he roared as he got to his feet. "I am *honored* to call Riku and Rhianna my friends! How dare you! You tried to kill our daughter! You do not deserve to even associate yourself with the people of that District! Be gone from my sight! I let you keep your duties all these years only because I thought you grieved over our child. You are relieved of every single one, and with much relief, I might add!"

Security guards hurried inside and took the sobbing woman away to await her fate within the local jail. Kay could not bring himself to care one way or another. All he cared about was Raven. He gently pulled her into his arms and buried his face in her hair. "It will be alright," he said softly. "I promise."

The governor straightened and crossed his arms. "Come here, child." When both looked at him, he beetled his brows at them. "Come here, Raven Shaughnessy. I am your father, and I command your obedience!"

Her knees shaking, she slowly crossed the room to stand before him. She would have curtseyed but she was terrified that she would fall on her face. He stepped toward her, and she squeezed her eyes shut. To her shock, she felt his hands gently framing her face, and his fingers were trembling. Her eyes flew open.

His smile trembled too, and tears glimmered in his eyes as he studied his child. "Look at you," he breathed. "You have my eyes, but you have your mother's beauty. My daughter. I thought . . ." His voice broke and he gathered her close against his heart. "I thought you lost to me forever."

She began to cry softly and held onto him tightly. "I thought you didn't want me!" she sobbed.

"No, never that!" He eased her away and wiped at her tears. "I'm honored to call you my daughter." He looked to where his true wife stood. There were tears in her eyes as well. "What say you, madam?"

"Raven," the proper First Lady said softly as she stepped forward. "I can have no more children. My son is the only child I may ever have. I always wished, so hard, for a daughter. I would be honored to be your mother, if you would let me."

Raven's lips trembled. "I have no idea how to handle parents."

"Mostly we will simply be bossy and interfere with your life," her stepmother teased gently. She reached out and hugged Raven close to rock her gently. "I wished for a daughter. It seems I got my wish. Our District miracle."

The governor pulled his son forward from where he had been hiding and nudged him toward Raven. "This is your big sister," he told him gently. "Go and greet her properly."

The little boy walked forward and wrapped his arms around Raven's leg in a happy hug. She buried her face in her hands as she sobbed harder. She whirled around and nearly flew into Kay's arms.

"Why is she crying?" the little boy asked Eric.

"She's happy," Eric promised him. He smiled at the governor. "Now, as to Kay . . ."

"Yes." He retook his seat and studied Kay intently. "Whether you intended to or not, you seem to have married my daughter. Her dowry is quite considerable, and if you wish it, a part of my land is yours."

"I thank you for your generosity," Kay told him, "but all I want is Raven. I would ask simply for the means to get any sort of training I might need in order to support her. I'm afraid I do not read very well as I never attended school."

He tugged on his beard lightly. "You do not wish for land and money?"

Kay smiled. "Not that I do not earn myself."

The First Lady leaned down and whispered in her husband's ear. He listened closely and began to smile. "Then this is how it shall be. You will accept Raven's dowry. Ah!" He held up a hand as Kay tried to protest. "Your father-in-law is speaking, boy. As I said, you will accept Raven's dowry. But you will return it to me as payment for a parcel of land. I will then give to you, as a wedding gift, a fine house. It will be built on your land. And, as my wife's gift to you, you will be sent to the finest master of whatever craft you wish to learn."

Eric covered a smile as Kay and Raven both stared at the governor in shock. "Well, Kay?" Eric asked. "What do you wish to learn?"

"I . . . well, I would be interested in learning accounting." Kay was still highly puzzled. "I always dreamed when I was much younger that I would learn how to make money, and then I would invest in others' dreams so that they could do it, too."

"And are you good at this?" the governor asked curiously.

"I learned many things listening to the passengers of my boat trips. Richard may have hated me, but he always invested in what I suggested. It doubled the profits."

He nodded firmly. "Then you will attend the best of schools, and when that is done, I will give you my own personal funds to invest. And who knows? Perhaps you will even be able to make a fine company out of your dreams." Almost pointedly he added, "One to pass on to your children?"

Eric laughed. "Don't worry. You'll have your grandchildren within a few months." Raven and Kay stared at him, and he winked. "Why do you think Stormy looked so pleased with herself?" Leaving them to have that sink in, he bowed deeply. "Good day, all of you." Without another word, he walked out.

Because the governor insisted on having Raven stay in his manor so he could get to know her better, Kay and Raven found themselves being shown to a grand bedroom where they could stay. High quality clothes were laid out for them, and she fingered the material of one of the dresses. "It seems too fine for me."

He slid his arms around her waist. "I like you in this dress best anyway. We should save it for our daughter or granddaughter."

She turned and wrapped her arms around him with a smile. "What if we only have boys for many generations?"

"I'm sure we'll find ourselves a female descendant somewhere." He lowered his forehead until it touched hers. "I love you, Raven Shaughnessy."

"And I love you." She framed his face with his hands, memorizing his features. "I never dared to dream for someone like you. I was so certain I would always be bound to the night, never able to embrace the dawn. You brought me the day, Kay. You rescued me."

"Does that mean we'll live happily ever after now?" he teased her softly, his heart swelling inside. He loved her more than anything in the world. When she smiled, he felt as if there would never be anything wrong again.

"Yes." Her eyes shimmered with love as she gazed at him. "Yes, I think it does." Her happy ending was right there in his arms. Her emotions welled up inside like a wave, and she rose on her toes to kiss him. Every faerie tale with a happy ending always ended with a kiss powerful enough to build dreams on, and she wasn't about to change the pattern there.

And if their kiss was truly the power for their dreams, then their dreams would never fade. They would never be broken down again.

EPILOGUE

Eric looked into Rhianna's office as he went past. "Everything is taken care of."

"So I see," she murmured as she looked at the two contracts she held. Both of them glowed suddenly, and the word 'Complete' appeared on both. With a smile, she added some notes to the bottom and slipped them into a folder. She then opened an empty drawer to put the folder inside. On the outside of the drawer she carefully wrote 'Shaughnessy File.'

"There." She glanced toward the figure standing on the other side of the room. "One down, ninety-nine to go."

"Good for me," a woman's voice muttered.

"You enjoyed it," she scolded her lightly. "I won't hear otherwise." Well satisfied with the events, she stretched her arms over her head. "I think that someday Kay's company will be one of the biggest in New York. And I see a lovely young woman with blonde hair and the Shaughnessy eyes wearing a cherry blossom dress."

"Are you looking into your crystal ball again?" the woman asked dryly.

She shook her head. "Call it a hunch."

The woman groaned. "I hate your hunches. They always mean more trouble for me."

She thought of the visions she'd had and just smiled.

Status: File Begun

Analysis: A man poor on wealth can be rich on love

The CARMICHAEL File

Folder One

RAYNA

CHAPTER ONE

Seventeen years ago. . .

When the father arrived at Enforcers Headquarters, he was pale and drawn. He was also nearly inconsolable as he desperately tried to explain what was wrong to the lobby receptionist. Finally, at a loss, the young woman simply called up to the top floor. She relayed what she knew and listened to the answer. She hung up and said only, "Mr. Mason will be down in a minute."

Lucas Carmichael found himself unable to sit as he paced back and forth through the lobby. All eyes watched him in concern. Though he was only part of 3rd District by marriage, he was a member nonetheless. Everyone in the District stuck together.

A tall and distinguished man walked into the lobby a minute later. His calm ice-blue eyes missed nothing. The sharp sensation of fear stung his skin, but it came only from the outside and not within. He walked over and firmly got in Lucas' path, forcing the other man to pull up short. "Sit down."

No one had ever refused to listen to an order from Eric Mason, particularly when he spoke in the firm tone of command. Lucas sat down. He gripped his shaking hands together and stared at the floor. "You protect everyone in 3rd District," he finally blurted. "You and Ms. Taber have gifts. You can—you can forcefully interfere with outside forces and powers."

Eric sat down beside him and lifted an ash colored brow. "Yes," he conceded. He offered nothing further. "What happened?"

As before, Lucas could not stop the words from spilling out. "You know my wife and I have two daughters."

"Rayna and Mika." Warmth filled Eric's voice. "They are well loved by those who meet them. Mika should be nine now, and Rayna four?"

"Someone wants them dead."

The words dropped like bombs into the lobby. Everything came to a halt. All eyes shifted. Horror filled some gazes. Fury filled others. The young receptionist immediately left her post and went to fetch a glass of water. When she brought it over, Eric took it without looking away from Lucas. "Drink this," he ordered.

Lucas shook his head. "Why would anyone want my girls dead? They're so beautiful. So giving." The glass was firmly pushed against his mouth and it was drink or choke. He drank. As the water slid down his throat, it brought a cooling sensation that helped to steady his mind and emotions.

The receptionist watched him critically for a moment before going back to her post. Eric set the glass aside and braced his arms on his legs as he leaned forward. "How do you know someone wants them dead?"

"I saw it." He drew a ragged breath. "Neither girl has a lick of modesty. When I told them they could go swimming if they got their suits on, they were pulling off their clothes before they got to their room. And I saw it." His voice dropped so low even Eric almost couldn't hear him. "The Bloody Check."

"Son-of-a-bitch." Eric raked a hand through his ashy hair and stirred the white streaks over his ears. His mind automatically attuned itself to his partner's, and her rage almost shook the building. Almost at the same time, they both calmed and began to think logically. There was only one course. The details would be tricky, though.

Rhianna Taber walked into the lobby a few minutes later. A folder was in her hand. She walked over to the two men and inclined her head. "Let's go into a conference room." She gestured across the hall.

The two men stood. Lucas went first, still almost dazed despite the water of clarity. Eric gestured Rhianna to go before him, like the old-world gentleman he still pretended to be. She arched a red brow and then just shook her head and went into the conference room. He went in behind her and shut the doors firmly.

"Mr. Carmichael," Rhianna began as she sat down, "you know your wife was prophesized to give birth to two exceptionally powerful beings. Two very special children that we of the Enforcers fully intended to recruit eventually."

"What are they?"

"I don't know," she admitted. "My touch on the future is vague at times. Impressions and hunches mostly. All I know definitively is that Rayna and Mika are critical to the peace of the entire world, let alone the peace of our District."

"Is," his voice broke for a moment, "is that why someone would issue a Bloody Contract for them?"

"It's a strong likelihood." Eric leaned back in his chair. "But we're going to have no way of knowing why someone is so afraid of what are clearly powers of good until the girls are at least twenty-one. Their powers should fully manifest at that time. It won't be sooner. They are only half-3rd District. We just need to be sure they make it to that age."

"I'll do anything!" Lucas vowed.

Rhianna and Eric exchanged a long look before he took the folder from her and opened it. He pulled out the stack of papers inside and slid them to Lucas. "Here is what we are offering. It is a two-fold deal. When the person who ordered the Bloody Contract makes an attempt for Rayna, she will emerge miraculously from a mere accident . . . except she will be asleep. She will remain in a coma until her twenty-first birthday, cared for at a strictly controlled Enforcers' hospital. Once she awakens, her powers will combine with ours to nullify the Bloody Contract."

Lucas drew a bracing breath. "And Mika?"

"We can't use the same contract for both." Eric rubbed the bridge of his nose. "It would be too obvious. Hers will have to be slightly different. She will survive however many accidents necessary for her to reach twenty years of age. At that age, one of the accidents will place her within a matching coma. She will remain asleep until Rayna awakens. And the same will happen for her that happens for Rayna."

A little chill went down Lucas' back. "They could sleep for . . . for years! They won't know anything of the world they enter! And what if something happens when they are children? How will they grow and learn?"

"Enforcers have been investigating the possibilities associated with subliminal learning," Rhianna offered. "We have learned, conclusively, that things heard while asleep can remain. It may be a shot in the dark, but we could use these study results to formulate learning tapes for the girls. If their minds can learn, then they will wake with only a few hang-ups to their development. Reading would be a big one, but not insurmountable."

"I'll take care of the details of the tapes if needed," Eric promised quietly.

Lucas took a long, bracing breath. The idea of his babies being stuck in a coma for potentially years was terrifying, but it was more terrifying to think they might die. Without letting himself think, he signed his name across the bottom of the contracts. Eric and Rhianna signed as well, and the girls' safety was officially in Enforcers' hands.

Outside the building, it almost seemed as if something screamed in fury. Rhianna's eyes didn't waver though something came and went in Eric's eyes. Something that sent a chill down Lucas' back and yet simultaneously reassured him. If his girls were to be saved, then only these two could do it.

A few days later, only just arriving back from a trip, his daughters were happily riding with their mother and aunt in a car zooming down a freeway; neither had any idea of the danger and their parents had no intention of telling them unless necessary.

They had gone out of town to visit the girls' uncle and give him support in the family's difficult times. Lucas had nearly lost the family company. At a loss for what to do, he had turned the reigns over to his brother in the hopes that a fresh start would pull them back from the brink. Thankfully, it seemed to be working. The entire family was relieved.

Aunt Yvonne was Lucas' sister-in-law. She had picked up the girls and their mother and was now bringing them home. Rayna and Mika both liked her a lot. She always smelled like cookies, and if there was anything better to smell like, neither girl could envision it.

It was late at night but they still hit a snarl of traffic. As they continued along, bumper to bumper, Rayna pressed her nose to the window to look at New York City. It glowed and sparkled with millions of lights.

Her attention was diverted when she saw shadows moving along the side of the road. Frowning, she tried to see better. She was an exceptionally small girl, and she was still in a toddler's car seat at four years old. Her height in no way detracted from her mental growth. Her mind was much further along than her young age indicated. With precise clarity, she said, "I see people."

"On a freeway?" Yvonne's voice was warm. "At night? I hope they don't get hit."

Mika tried to lean over to see what Rayna was watching. She was in a special seat for older children, but she was also small for her nine years. She was also quite nimble and smart, and she wiggled out of her harness to scoot over to her sister. "Let me see!"

"Mika!" their mother ordered sharply. "Get back in your seat, young lady!"

"You sure she isn't Houdini reincarnated?" her sister-in-law groused.

The two girls peered out the window. The people were doing something. They seemed to be acting weird, too. They weaved back and forth as if dizzy, and they staggered up onto the freeway. A chill went down Rayna's back as the car began to move faster, the traffic finally clearing. "Mommy . . ."

At the note of fear, both adults glanced back at her. Something, no one would ever know what, made Yvonne jerk her gaze back around to the road. With a shriek, she slammed on her brakes as she saw the figure crossing the freeway on foot.

The car went out of control and careened across the lanes, causing horns to blare and brakes to screech. Miraculously, no other cars were hit. Not so miraculously, the uncontrolled car hit the side of the embankment . . . and went into the air over the side.

By the time the ambulance arrived, a crowd had already gathered. Motorists had pulled over to rush to the wreck to provide help. The mother had been killed on impact. Yvonne was only alive because one of those who had stopped knew CPR. The quick thinking motorist relinquished her position to the paramedics and jumped into the on-going search. Yvonne had tried to say something about her nieces before losing consciousness.

The car was a mangled mess, but it was clear where a car seat had been torn free. Flashlights illuminated the area as did floodlights when copters arrived. People called for the girls, but there was no true hope of finding them alive.

When Eric arrived on the scene, he joined in the search as well. He made his way down the steep slope of grass as he headed for the gully at the bottom. It was the line marker between private land and state highway. He didn't cross over as he moved down the gully with confidence. The wind shifted and it led him swiftly to a slightly hidden shallow that most eyes would have passed over.

He found Rayna in that shallow. She had been torn out of her car seat and was lying like a broken doll. Though he knew *she would be fine, his fingers trembled slightly as he checked for a pulse. It was there. Unsteady but strong. A quick look told him that she had only bruises and scratches from the ordeal.*

He shrugged out of his jacket and gently wrapped her up. Almost possessively, he lifted her into his arms and kept her close. She was truly tiny, her Faeriekin blood evident. He softly rubbed his cheek over her white hair. "It's okay, sleeping beauty," he murmured softly. "You'll be fine now. I promise."

He made his way back to where the paramedics were located. He nearly had to force himself to let her go so that she could be examined. There was just something about her that had grabbed onto his heart and not let go. He watched her be taken away to the Enforcers' hospital and then turned his attention to finding Mika. Oddly, he wasn't entirely surprised she could not be found, even as dawn approached. There was no such thing as coincidence.

He went to the hospital as soon as the search party disbanded for sleep before trying again. He said nothing to them of their futile efforts. In truth, it always warmed his heart that so many strangers would pull together to give help where it was most needed.

He found Lucas sitting outside Rayna's room. Grief had aged him within a matter of hours. Eric walked over to kneel in front of him. "I am sorry," he said quietly, "but we are not gods. We can't stop everything. If we could, we wouldn't even have needed the contract that has likely saved her life."

"She'll wake as a four-year-old in an adult body." Lucas looked at him with dull eyes. "How will she ever cope?"

"She will be an adult," he disagreed. "I will arrange for the subliminal tapes to cover everything from regular schooling to modern events to pop culture to as much as she might have learned simply being in school. She will be completely innocent," he warned, "and trusting, though. Some things simply cannot be taught by anything other than experience."

Lucas said nothing. What could he say? He had no control over anything, not even his own life. Not even the precious lives of his babies or his beloved wife. "Will they find Mika?" he asked faintly.

Eric gave him the truth though it was a painful one. "No. But she will live. You will see her again. I swear it." When there was no response, he got to his feet. His eyes drifted to the room where Rayna slept. Heart aching, he went inside and shut the door.

She was pale and still. She breathed on her own but she was not awake. Once the hospital was sure she would not wake, she would be hooked up to other machines to provide nourishment for her growing body. It seemed almost obscene, the thought of a little girl confined to a hospital bed for years.

Something about her felt achingly lonely. Her world had fallen silent. Even when she listened to her tapes, her world would be alone. It broke his heart. He pulled the visitor chair over and sat down beside her. Gently he covered her hand with one of his. "Hey," he said softly. "I know you're scared. But you're not alone. I'm here with you now. I won't let anything happen to you. You like flowers, don't you? Well, when you wake up, I know a garden I can take you to see. It grows against a castle in the mountains, covered by clouds and sheltered from even the harshest snow and rain . . ."

One year ago . . .

Eric walked in the hospital room with a bouquet of flowers in his hand. It was Saturday at two. Every week, at that exact time, he always came to visit Rayna. He had never missed a single day. He came on holidays too. Her birthday and Christmas. Any day that she deserved more than usual to have someone by her side.

As he sat down beside her, he gently covered her hand with his. He talked to her of anything and everything in the world. He told her some of the funny moments of trying to upgrade all the computers in Enforcers, and of the world events that might interest her. For fifteen years, she had grown like a flower in a greenhouse. He told her of that too, describing how her face had matured and her hair had grown. He laughingly told her that she still wasn't tall. At twenty, she might be five-foot even but likely no more.

There were times where he felt as if she was listening to him. He felt as if she truly heard him. His powers of the mind, the abilities that picked up on the signals of the minds of other beings, always seemed to hum louder when he talked to her. And he talked to her of everything he could. It felt as if he could tell her anything, even things he had never told anyone else.

It would be another year until she awoke. Another long, lonely year. He so badly wanted to see her smile, to hear her talking back to him. She seemed to be a light in the darkness to him. He brought her hand to his cheek and closed his eyes. "I wish you could wake up, Rayna," he murmured. "This world needs you. There's so much you have to do and see. You never deserved this future. I just wish . . ." His voice trailed off. Wishes were useless. Her contract bound her.

Her hand moved. Shocked, he stared at her face, sure he had imagined it. Her hand moved again, distinctly more deliberate than a muscle twitch. The machines monitoring her began to record the signals of a waking mind. In his own mind, he could feel the feathery brush of a strong presence reaching out. She was waking up, but it should have been impossible!

He leapt to his feet and rushed out into the hall. "Doctor!" he barked, and the tone of command made everyone leap to do his bidding.

When Rayna opened her eyes a few minutes later, her gaze was blurry at best. Odd images swam above her with faces distorted like a funhouse mirror. One of the faces looked like her father but he seemed much older. Another face was attached to a body in a white coat; a doctor, probably. No other faces looked down at her. "Who . . ." Her voice broke against her will.

"Easy, little one," the doctor soothed. He was already checking her pulse and examining her eyes. "Your voice and eyes haven't been used in a long time. It will take a while for the nerves to come up to speed."

She drew a deep breath and focused. She could see and understand hundreds of dozens of things in her mind. She had no memories to associate to her knowledge. It was just there. She remembered going to preschool and learning about numbers. Suddenly here, in her mind, she knew how to multiply and divide complex equations. She knew what an equation was.

There was more than that, though. Something more important. A garden near a castle in the mountain. It had been described so clearly that she felt she had already been there. She drew a breath and concentrated. "Who?" she asked again, stronger.

The doctor and Lucas exchanged a look. They knew what she was asking. Carefully, Lucas asked, "Who what, Rayna?" Firm orders still rang in his ears.

"With me. Who? Talked." Her lashes fluttered closed. "He called to me . . . So lonely . . ."

"There was no one here, Rayna," he lied softly. "It was just a dream."

She didn't doubt her father but she also didn't entirely believe him. A dream didn't leave her hand tingling with the warmth of being held and it didn't leave her heart aching with the loneliness for another being.

Present . . .

Everyone in New York City knew Rhianna Taber on sight. She was the face on the front of Enforcers that handled day-to-day tasks and oversaw the usual meetings and business problems that came with running one of the biggest companies in America.

The opposite was true of Eric Mason. Only his name was known by many since it was on everything she signed. They were equal partners and co-owners, but he never attended meetings and never handled the casual business. His duties were more detail oriented. If he showed up at a business owned by Enforcers, then it was because someone had screwed up, and everyone knew it.

He and Rhianna had a give and take relationship. They gave each other hell and at the same time took care of each other. They were the same age with only a few months separating them (with Rhianna being older). They denied a familial connection, but anyone who met them knew that they were more like twins than partners. They worked seamlessly together.

It was why, when she tapped a scarlet fingernail on the document in front her, he was already reaching for it before her finger was done moving. Both were sitting at her desk going over some . . . interesting developments. "Look," she offered. "A coincidence."

A wry smile crossed his handsome face. "Rhi, there's no such thing as coincidence around people from the 3rd District."

"Still blame me for that?" she asked idly.

"Yes."

"At least you're reliable in your opinions."

He shook his head slightly and then raked a hand through his hair in agitation. "So let me get this straight. Budgets Inc. has gone on along merrily without a single restructure or reorganization for several years. Now, when they have at their fingertips one of the brightest minds around, they don't want to promote her up through the ranks?"

She regarded him with a smile. "Riku," she used the nickname with the affection of a longtime friend, "you're going to worry the rest of your hair white."

He glowered at her. "The streaks are not because I'm old," he reminded her. "It's genetic."

"Yes, but we *are* old, Riku."

"Shut up, Rhi." He leaned back in his chair and studied the report intently. "Something smells rotten and it's not that perfume you're wearing."

"Audra's idea of a crank gift. I had to wear it at least once." She swiveled to face her computer and began to type quickly despite her long red nails. "I got my hands on the personnel data for Budgets. From the day she started there, mysterious accidents have kept occurring. They're documented, but it's as if no one wants to see a pattern. But that isn't surprising considering the *other* thing."

He glanced up at the note in her voice. "What other thing?"

"I got into the manager's email."

"Do I want to know how?" he asked ruefully.

"No." Her black eyes snapped with the sparks that meant her temper was on the rise. "This manager is the one that works directly over Rayna. In his inbox and trashcan, I've found emails dating back to the beginning of her employment six months ago. Every single email is a litany of the same. Harassment. Her coworkers seem to be taking vicious delight in terrorizing her. She attached any relevant emails and attachments to her emails to her manager, and since the latest was as of this morning, I'd have to say he's done absolutely shit."

That alone told him that it was severe: she never swore. Eyes narrowed, he leaned forward to look over her shoulder. A little electrical hum filled the air around him, evidence of his own growing anger. "And we've received no report. How nice. What kind of harassment?"

"Well, several of the emails are lists of statistics on coma victims. The percentage of who wake up, the amount of mental damage, the erosion of mental and motor skills." Her voice reflected her disgust. "There are photographs of CAT scans of coma victims' minds, showing the places where brain matter deteriorated. It's *disgusting*. And then there are those who make snide comments about her not being a miracle and how it must be a scam because no one could wake from a sixteen-year coma without a lick of damage."

"So she's being harassed," he said quietly, "and there are mysterious accidents occurring. Nearly fatal accidents that everyone is turning a blind eye to. Why does she stay there?"

"No one else would hire her," she admitted simply. "And it was the only one of our companies that had an opening we could get her into without the experience most other places demand. The girl *is* brilliant, Riku. But she's very innocent and that puts her at a big risk. These accidents should *not* be happening. Her contract was solid."

"She woke up too early," he murmured, an unknown note of wistfulness in his voice.

"And whose fault was that?" She lifted a brow.

He sighed and got to his feet. "Mine, yes, I know. It's not like I intended to wake her up," he added defensively. "Hell, Rhi, you know I'd never do anything to hurt that girl! I'd sooner drown myself."

"You can't drown, Riku."

"It was a metaphor, dear." He raked a hand through his hair again and ruffled the aforementioned white streaks. There really was no other option than to go and take a look at the company and find out not only what the hell was going on, but also to find out what was happening around Rayna Carmichael. Her contract was not completed until her birthday arrived, and she was not safe from the death that she had been marked for. It was a week to her birthday. He could take care of things for a week.

"I'm going to head over there tomorrow," Rhianna said suddenly and caught his attention. "It shouldn't be a problem."

"No."

"Pardon?"

He cleared his throat. "Sorry, it slipped out. Sometimes I forget to be tactful and erudite. What I meant to say was, I'll go instead of you. Your face is far too well known. I'll get a feel for the layout, the people and such, and keep an eye on our sleeping princess. If I go in undercover then no one will tense up and put forward their best face. I'll be able to see things as they really are."

She watched him head through the connecting door into his office, and she covered a smile as she turned back to the papers on her desk. She had no doubt that he would indeed see everything clearly. He would be with Truth, and Truth always laid bare everything to the light.

CHAPTER TWO

She was known as the Miracle Girl of the 3rd District, but as Rayna Carmichael hurried down the sidewalk toward the front door of the office where she worked, she didn't feel much like a miracle. It was another of those days where her coordination was sketchy at best and she couldn't quite get a grip on her depth perception.

The physical problems were the least of her worries. She felt lost mentally, slightly adrift in a very weird world. She couldn't even watch the news or read the paper. She didn't understand anything happening, so why try to torture herself? Thankfully, it had also become a good excuse for her ignorance. Sometimes she felt like she was still asleep.

But there really was no denying she was a medical miracle. She had survived a horrendous car crash without a single broken bone, survived a sixteen-year coma, and then within a short time of her awakening as a twenty-year-old, she had been on the same level mentally as her peers. Most who met her couldn't tell she had never gone to school. In fact, it was impossible to tell, especially because she had a gift with computers.

The only thing that gave her away was her lack of an ability to communicate in writing. Her reading skills were minimal; she always carried a dictionary. Her writing skills most closely resembled an elementary school student. She was trying to teach herself, but it was a painfully slow process when she constantly had to look things up.

As always, her shoulders were braced when she reached her desk. The humiliation was to be brief that morning, though, since only one or two nasty notes had been left for her. She tore them up and shredded them without reading them. She immediately straightened up her area to remove any other evidence. She hated her desk to be messy, and others messed it up just to torment her. She had the receptionist desk, and it always looked bad to clients if she had clutter around.

She logged onto her computer after dumping the shred bin. Her desktop appeared, and she discovered it had been changed to a graphic image of the damage done to a coma victim's brain. She promptly changed the wallpaper to the cutest, fluffiest kitten she could find and then began to trace the residue the culprit had left behind. She had quickly learned how to manipulate the internal server the company ran on, and she used it to take a small measure of justice for herself.

She opened her opponent's email, carefully read through a couple, found what she wanted, and forwarded it to the woman's husband. She would be so busy trying to explain to her husband why she was calling a coworker 'love nuggets' that she wouldn't bug Rayna again for a while. It certainly didn't sound like something she ought to be calling an associate.

A financial advisor going past her desk stopped to eye her menacingly. A great number of people in the company disliked her purely because no one else ever did. She was beautiful and kind, and she had an innocent trust that let her see the good in mankind. She took delight in the smallest things. Everyone who met her loved her, and because of it, she brought out the worst in people who embraced crueler emotions.

Rayna looked up at the woman beside her desk and lifted her chin slightly in an almost dare. The woman opened her mouth but shut it as the front door opened. She scuttled away swiftly instead. Rayna clenched her hands together under her desk and found a smile for the old man that had entered. The smile softened her face and made her violet eyes light up the entire room. When she smiled, everything was right with the world. "Good morning!"

"Good morning!" He smiled back. The highlight of his entire week was coming in to Budgets Inc. to go over his retirement stocks. Every visit, rain or shine, Rayna was there to greet him. Her smile was his sunshine. "How are you, my dear?"

"Awake." She smiled as she said it. She got to her feet and made her way carefully around her desk, moving slowly to avoid hitting things. She tried to keep them in the same places, but her coworkers moved them to torment her. "Here, have a seat." She helped him into one of the chairs. "You're always early," she teased. "You need to find someone to budget your time!"

He gave a cackle that turned into a cough. She immediately got him a cup of water, and he smiled at her. "You’re an angel, Rayna."

Her cheeks turned bright pink. "Not me." She got to her feet and went around behind her desk again. Shoulders tensed, she picked up her phone and dialed a number. When the other side was answered, she said, "Mr. Meadows here to see you."

"I told you not to buzz me when people are early!" was the snapped response. "Don't you have any working brain cells, or were they all killed in the coma? Call me when it's actually nine o'clock, you idiot!"

She winced as the phone slammed down on the other side. She slowly hung up her own phone and fought the tears rising to choke her. "It's my job," she whispered softly. She drew several deep breaths and ignored the fact that Mr. Meadows was watching her. She didn't want him to worry, but it was so hard to keep calm when all she wanted was to curl up and cry. Being an adult could be nothing but a frustration.

The bell chimed over the door. Relieved, she turned with a smile. "Good morning," she started to say, only to have the words slowly die and fade away. Her eyes widened and red color swept up her cheeks. The sudden breathlessness was entirely foreign but oddly familiar.

She had never truly been able to understand the concept of attraction. Some of the kinder women had tried to helpfully point out what they felt were attractive men, but she simply hadn't gotten it. She had finally decided that she simply wasn't mature enough to be attracted to anyone yet, or perhaps she might just not be capable of attraction at all.

Apparently, she had been wrong.

The newcomer standing just inside the doorway made her feel flushed as she looked at him. He was tall and broad shouldered with a lean and beautiful strength. It was a strength well displayed in his short-sleeved shirt and blue jeans. His arms were corded with muscles that hypnotized her. She wanted to touch them, just to see if they were as strong as they looked.

She couldn't guess at his age, but he was definitely an adult. A bone-deep calmness in his ice-blue eyes seemed to say he had done, and seen, it all. The youth to his features made her guess he might be in his late twenties, and he was more perfectly beautiful than any TV star. His ashy brown hair *begged* to be touched, and the little white wings of hair over his ears just added to the temptation.

Without looking away from him, her fingers flew over the keys of her keyboard as she sent an email to one of the few coworkers she liked and trusted. *Attractive men? The short word for them?*

Her eyes flickered to her monitor as the response came back quickly. *??? You mean 'hot'? ☺Should I be coming up there, Rayna?*

The man cleared his throat and smiled a little. Rayna blinked and realized he was holding out a clipboard to her. He was also wearing a hip holster that held gardening tools. "Oh!" She leapt to her feet, blushing brightly. "I'm so sorry; I was busy staring at you." Her eyes popped wide. "I mean . . ."

Eric barely hid a second smile. She was so wonderfully sweet! And lovely as well; she was lovelier than he remembered. Her silvery dove hair had been cropped closely around her face and nearly resembled fine feathers. Her eyes were colored the delicate violet hue of morning glories just beginning to wake. Soft and fair skin without blemishes covered her entirely. Not an ounce of makeup touched her skin but she didn't need it. Nature itself had given her an untarnished beauty.

As she took the clipboard from him, his eyes sparkled. Even in her low-heeled shoes, she didn't quite reach his shoulder. More than her height made her small, though. She possessed an overall deceptive fragility thanks to fine bones and supple curves. She could not be mistaken for a teenager, though. It was a curious magic.

His faerie princess. He couldn't stop the delight at seeing her again but kept his voice casual as he said, "Enforcers sent me out. The front area is in some desperate need of maintenance. I thought I'd sign in and get to work. Does everyone come through here?"

"Umm-hmm." She was studying the clipboard. The paperwork had been written as simply and plainly as possible, and it was very easy for her to read. "I'm the receptionist. And, sir, your figures are wrong. You undercharged us." She handed him the clipboard back. "Based on your estimated hours of work and pay per hour, we should actually owe you close to three hundred dollars more at the end of your job. Two hundred ninety-five dollars and twenty-six cents, to be precise."

He stared at her for a moment. He had known she was brilliant, but she had managed to surprise him. She had absorbed her subliminal tapes with a hungry attention, her attention fixated powerfully enough that the machines recording her brainwaves had almost busted. Now she had just done long multiplication and division in her mind faster than a lot of scholars could do it with a calculator. She needed to be tested, and soon, so that she could get at least the high school degree she deserved. "You must have studied a lot in school," he said, putting admiration in his tone as he fixed the clipboard. "Why aren't you a financial advisor?"

"Good question!" Meadows harrumphed. "Rayna is the nicest, sweetest girl in this building!" He thumped his cane on the floor to add emphasis.

"Yes, she's *such* a miracle," one woman concurred snidely as she went past. "Rayna never went to school and yet she's so smart! She doesn't have a high school diploma let alone a college degree. Used to be we'd call people like that either stupid or lazy. Or both. "

Rayna didn't respond. She stared at Eric's collar because she was too humiliated to meet his eyes. Fiercely she clenched her hands into fists at her sides and bit down on her lower lip. The urge to cry faded, and she took a quick breath before looking up at him with a smile that didn't reach her eyes. "She's right. I don't have an education. I never went to school. I was in a coma. They gave me subliminal tapes that taught me everything."

The pain in her eyes tore at him. He fought to maintain his self-control and not fry that self-righteous bitch to a crisp with lightning. He never harmed weaker beings, but the violent urge was strong. *No* one hurt his faerie princess. "I see." He kept his tone deliberately light. "Well, I don't think someone without a degree is an idiot. I don't have one either."

"Oh." She blinked and then smiled genuinely. Her eyes sparkled. "No wonder your math is bad. Oops!" She covered her mouth with a hand. "Sorry. I sort of tend to say what's on my mind. I'm trying to learn not to."

"Don't change," he suggested. He took the clipboard back when she had signed it. "You'd make a lot of people, including me, very sad."

"And me!"

She smiled at Meadows. "Thank you, and you, sir." She heard the phone ring and quickly sat back down to pick it up. "Budgets Inc., this is Rayna. May I help you?" She waved a little as Eric left and then again as Meadows finally headed back to his meeting. The call was a long one, and she tuned out the rest of the office as she walked the caller through one of the company's customer spreadsheets. It wasn't a requirement, but why should she turn him over to someone who didn't care and would be rude? Besides, spreadsheets were numbers and she definitely knew numbers where she might never know words.

It was only when she hung up the phone that she realized a bunch of women had gathered at the window in front of her desk. It faced the front of the building where the sorely neglected front lawn and landscaping were located. She frowned. What on Earth were they all doing there? Since when did they care about the lawn?

She got her answer as one woman purred, "Look at that ass. That is one fine piece of flesh."

"Look at his *arms*." Another woman sighed. "That is one first class body wasted on such a low class job."

"Think he'd ride a woman as competently as a lawnmower?" another asked slyly.

"I don't know, but let's have that mower bronzed if it manages to rip his shirt off."

Rayna's frown deepened as she got to her feet and moved closer to see outside. Sure enough, Eric was outside and he was fighting with the lawnmower. The jeep-like device had decided to resist his control, and his shirt had snagged on the fender. It definitely looked like it was in imminent danger of being torn off.

She studied him for a long moment. He really was beautiful. Something wild and free clung to his presence. If he answered to anyone, it was whatever gods he might believe in. He could not be bound by rules and regulations; if he followed them, it was because he genuinely believed in them. Anger simmered in her heart at the disrespect the other women showed. No one deserved to be treated that way, especially not him.

She knew she would get the sharp edge of someone's fury, but she couldn't stop herself from stepping up in his defense. "You know," she said softly, "if it was a bunch of men standing here saying these things about a woman, you would accuse them of harassment."

There was a collective gasp as all ten women turned to look at her. Outrage rose swiftly. "How dare you accuse us of harassment!" someone snapped.

She linked her hands behind her back and her nails dug into her palms. "I didn't say that. I simply stated a fact. You chose to blame yourself because you knew I spoke the truth."

Knowing she was right—both times!—only made the horde angrier. Most stomped off in furious and indignant huffs. The ringleader, one of the higher-level managers, pinned Rayna with an icy glare. "You know, it doesn't surprise me that you stick up for him." Her voice sounded as bitter as winter. "You're nothing but a nobody. An uncultured little idiot from that backwater 3rd District. Frankly, you're probably not even human. *Less* than human. You should have stayed asleep. No one wants you in our world."

As she turned on an ice pick heel and stalked down the hall, Rayna bit down hard on her lower lip. It was only when she tasted blood that her tears subsided. The pain choked her for long moments. She started to sit down at her desk again when someone going outside opened the front door. A waft of furiously hot air slapped her. Her eyes went to where Eric was digging in the ground. Sweat gleamed visibly across his skin, and a quick look revealed no water cooler nearby. Concerned, she got to her feet.

Outside, Eric swiped an arm across his forehead. It was hot, his back was killing him, and he was in heaven. Gardening was more of an obsession than a hobby. If he couldn't feel the dirt between his fingers, catch the scent of flowers . . . he would stop existing. Hell, Rhianna had put him in charge of the Enforcers Headquarters' gardens just so he would have something to do and stop pestering her. At least there he didn't have to deal with a temperamental mower, he thought crossly. Stupid thing had to be possessed.

His mind could not wholly focus on the job. He had seen the altercation at the window. He didn't know what had been said, but the body language had spoken volumes. He would have ignored the entire scene if he hadn't seen Rayna intervene. If she had been hurt . . .

"Sir?"

He straightened in surprise at the sound of her voice. She stood just a foot away, and she had a frosty bottle of water in her hands.

In a violet sundress with a white vest, she looked as fresh and pure as any of his orchids. Her shoes, he saw then, had been specially made to help her balance and were fastened on with straps. They should have made her look younger, but they only emphasized the graceful lines of her legs—and those were pure, one hundred, glorious, percent adult woman.

He cleared his throat as he realized where his mind seemed determined to wander. "Yes?"

"I thought you might be thirsty. It's so hot out here." She held the bottle out to him with a smile. "My name is Rayna Carmichael. What's yours?"

"Riku." He used his nickname without compunction. He gratefully took the bottle and opened it. "Thank you, Miss Carmichael."

She shook her head. "It's just Rayna. I'm not comfortable with formality, and besides, you're old." She went pink as he lifted a brow. "I meant older than me. I'm sorry. My language skills are very bad at times. I never know how to say what I want." Her eyes flickered back toward the office. "They're always horrible but I never say anything. And whenever I find the courage to say something, they say something worse. I'm not sure why I try."

He removed his glove and reached out a hand to run his thumb lightly over her lower lip. It looked slightly bruised and swollen, and he could see where she had bitten hard enough to draw blood. "Biting your lip?" he asked softly.

"Yes. Trying not to cry." Her eyes searched his face. There was something about his touch that was familiar. His soft, almost velvety, voice seemed to be imprinted in her ears. "Where did I meet you?" she asked softly. "I'm sure I have. I recognize your voice."

The fact that she had no idea her words could be taken as flirting was just another part of her charm. He didn't think she even knew what flirting was, and it made her utterly refreshing in such a superficial world. "I'm sure I'd remember if we'd formally met. You're beautiful."

"Really?" A blush touched her cheeks. "Thank you."

"You sound surprised."

"I guess I never thought about it." She tilted her head. "People are so focused on beauty that I assumed I had none. It's as if . . . beauty is all that can make people special. But it's not right." Something faraway seemed to move in her eyes, something that shifted and flowed like feathery power. "There is always right and wrong in the world. Black and white. You just have to know how to push aside the shadows."

A little chill rippled down his back as he began to understand her slowly growing power. She had the power of Truth. How it would manifest, he didn't know, but she saw with such childlike innocence that she could use her powers without tearing herself apart. Perhaps the coma had been more of a salvation than anyone had known.

It was still a painful power. His heart ached at what she would go through. He wanted to protect her from her own gifts. Carefully, he said, "I think you're right. About being wrong." He grinned sheepishly as he realized how it sounded. "Right?"

She giggled softly. The sound was pure enchantment. "Right!" She glanced at her watch and winced. "I have to go." She reached out to touch his hand with hers. "If you need anything," she told him, "ask for me. I'll help however I can."

As he watched her run back toward the entrance, he slowly lifted his hand to look at it. How could *anyone* treat a creature so open and giving with such cruelty? His fascination and near obsession with her over the years just seemed to be growing. Come hell or high water, he would keep her safe.

When her birthday was past and her contract was complete, he was taking her to Enforcers where her mind and skills could be used properly. A flower would die without room for its roots to grow, and he refused to see her wither. Enforcers was the perfect garden for her, and he fully intended to be there to tend to her and make sure she blossomed.

His obsession, however, was beginning to be a little alarming. He was attracted to her. Well, who wouldn't be? He told himself fiercely, over and over again, that it was simply a natural reaction to the fact that she was beautiful. He had not even *once* considered kissing away the hurt on her lip. Never. Not once. Hadn't been in his mind.

A soft laugh fluttered through that same mind. *Liar*, came Rhianna's voice teasingly.

Shut up, Rhi, he muttered mentally. *Go away, damn it.*

Mental bonds were more hindrance than help when it came to his 'sister', so he ignored her as he always did when she was being a pest. He focused his attention on his work and kept his ears always alert to the people coming and going. People talked frankly as they walked past him, as if he was part of the scenery. His head began to pound under the litany of complaints he heard.

By the time the workday was ending, he was ready for a shower and a strong drink. It wasn't the heat, it was the humanity! Humans could be such bastards. Muttering under his breath, he pulled his gloves off and slapped them against his leg. Dust promptly rose. He coughed and muttered more distinctly. He heard a soft giggle and turned his head to see Rayna standing next to him. A jacket sat around her shoulders and her bag was in her arms. "Hi," she said. Her eyes twinkled.

"Whoops." He grinned. "You didn't hear me, did you?"

"Just a little." Her eyes sparkled all the more as she crouched beside him. "Your day was as long as mine, so it's okay." She pulled a tissue out of her pocket and began to wipe at the smear of dirt on his cheek. "You really like your job, huh?"

He could not move or think properly as she cleaned his cheek. She was so open and giving that it almost drove him mad. He found himself craving those very qualities, but his knees shook with the terror of protecting her. He wanted her hidden behind arbors and garden walls where she couldn't be found by anyone else. "Yes, I do." He found a smile. "Do you like your job, Rayna?"

"It's boring." She shrugged one shoulder. "I always get done with my work quickly and no one else wants to give me anything. I work on my reading in the downtimes by looking at the contracts and agreements and so on."

"You don't read?' he asked softly, hurting for her.

"I do, but not well. Hazards of being in a coma when you're a child," she said with a false sort of cheerfulness. She got to her feet and pushed her hair back as it tried to blow into her face on a warm breeze. "I'll see you tomorrow, Riku." She smiled more naturally. "At least, I'd like to. You're a good person." She bent and kissed his cheek before hurrying away down the walkway.

He reached up and touched his cheek, smiling to himself. Then, gathering his equipment, he began to pack up for the evening. She lived in 3rd District. She was safe there. He wouldn't need to worry about her again until tomorrow. For now, he was going home and getting cleaned up, and pretending that he hadn't wanted to turn his head and meet her lips with his own.

He was in *deep* trouble.

CHAPTER THREE

Eric was never one to give less than his all when he was on a project, and his project was two-fold since he really did feel compelled to do the landscape. So, bright and early the next morning, he was heading for Budgets Inc. He wanted to be there when people first arrived so that he could see how things were at that time.

To his surprise, he wasn't the first one there. Rayna was sitting in the break area under an umbrella, her head tucked on her arms as if she was asleep. Several books lay open around her, and he walked slowly closer, wondering what she was reading.

One of the books was about art. Another was on computers. A third was on grammar and sentence structure, and a dictionary lay just under it. His heart ached for her. He quietly knelt beside her and studied her sleeping face. Seeing her here was so much better than seeing her in the hospital. A flush of life clung to her cheeks, and her beauty looked as soft and ethereal as her Faeriekin blood implied.

The sun had not raised high enough to bring the summer heat, and a chill still infused the air. He didn't want her to get frozen, so he softly touched her shoulder. "Rayna?" He kept his voice gentle. The last thing he ever wanted to do was frighten her.

Despite his care, there was a trace of pure terror and panic when her eyes opened. Her eyes focused on him, and she blinked drowsily as the fear faded. "Riku?" She carefully sat up and a shiver roughened her skin.

He immediately removed his light jacket and put it around her shoulders. He bit back a smile; it was almost three times too big. "What're you doing out here?" He couldn't stop himself from brushing her hair out of her eyes. "I thought the office didn't open for another hour. Why are you sleeping out here?"

"It's quiet." She rubbed at her eyes with a soft yawn like a child. "I don't sleep well so I end up napping in places." She shivered despite the jacket and drew the edges further closed. "I accidentally napped in the break room once. I've been careful not to do it again."

Anger carefully hidden, he eased onto the bench beside her and studied her face. "Why don't you just spend more time at home?"

"I live alone." She picked at the paint peeling on the table. "My father lives in the Bronx."

"That's a fair distance away from here. And, aren't you only twenty?" The law lifting the age of majority to twenty-one had been a large spot of trouble for many people over the last few years, but he had always, and would always, stand by it. Some kids needed those few extra years. Others, like Rayna, were too advanced for their age.

"I am but . . ." She lowered her gaze. "I asked for independence. My father was smothering me. I love him, but I couldn't live that way. I couldn't blink or breathe or do anything without him there. I wanted to go to school," her voice was wistful, "but he refused to even let me out of the house. So I got my legal freedom and moved back to the 3rd District where I was born."

"I would think," he said carefully, "that a man who lost his wife and a daughter would be desperate to hold onto his other daughter, especially if she had been asleep for sixteen years."

Her smile was sad. "I know he loves me. And I love him. But I just didn't fit into his world. I don't have a world of my own. My life is like my apartment. Small and cold. At least out here, I feel a little less out of my depth."

It took every single ounce of two thousand years' worth of self-control not to pull her into his arms. He knew the complex where she lived. She had one of the smallest apartments. The simple fact was that she couldn't afford more on her current salary. She barely made over minimum wage.

Unaware of his thoughts, she offered him a genuine smile. "Anyway, I like being here early. This way I'm at my desk when the office opens."

"Let's get some coffee," he offered. "There's a truck around back. I saw it as I was coming in. Want to come with me?"

"Sure." She swung her feet around and stood up. She nearly bumped her head on the umbrella, but she ducked in the nick of time. Despite the mishap, she moved with a startling grace. Aware he was staring, she blinked at him. "Is something wrong?"

"You must have worked so hard," he murmured. "Physically, to be able to coordinate as well as you do."

"It hurt," she admitted with a child's candid honesty. "My muscles had never been moved. I only stopped using a cane or walker about seven months ago. It was five months of almost constant pain before that. And I still have trouble with my height perception. And my eyes." She rubbed at them again. "If I can get the money, I want to go see an eye doctor. My doctor from the hospital said that because my eyes were not used when I was growing, they never developed as they should."

"You'd be very cute in glasses," he told her gravely. In the back of his mind churned unformed plans for getting her in to the best eye doctor in town. If she didn't want glasses, there were plenty of laser surgery technologies.

She considered the idea of wearing glasses. A lack of vanity meant her only concern was, "I hope I can get them in a color I like." She fell into step beside him as he began walking around the side of the building. She snuggled further into the coat, intrigued by the way it had absorbed his warmth. "How old are you?"

"Old enough I feel it," he said with emphasis. He gestured to the white wings in his hair. "Don't let these fool you. They're genetic. All the men in my family get them. Women get black streaks, unless they have black hair. My aunt had very dark hair, and her streaks appeared with an almost red hue."

"I like it on you," she decided. "It's nice. It makes you look . . ." Frustration crossed her face as she tried to find the word she wanted. "Like . . . a gentleman. No." She rubbed her forehead. "What's that word? The one meaning refined or unique, or something?"

It dawned. "Distinguished?" he murmured, once more feeling his heart ache for her. Truly, it seemed as if the ache never went away. It just changed between sympathy to pain to enchantment to obsession.

"Yes!" She gratefully took the cup of coffee he handed her, and she was completely oblivious to the longing looks from the young man selling the coffee. "I spend hours on Wikipedia," she confessed. "And I read dictionaries. But I never know *what* word I need, so I can't look it up. I've thought about memorizing the entire darn thing."

"You're one hell of a woman, Rayna Carmichael. I don't think I've ever admired anyone more." It was nothing less than the absolute truth.

She blinked at him, then smiled. "Thank you. To be honest, I kind of admire you."

He lifted his brows in surprise. "Me?"

"Sure. You do what you love without caring how others perceive it." She sat down on the edge of a picnic bench and swung her feet lightly.

"What makes you think I love my job?" he asked her curiously.

She frowned at him. "Well, why do it if you don't?" She fell silent for a few moments and studied the ground. "Sorry," she finally said. "Guess I'm childish. I forgot adults don't always get to do what they want."

"What do you want to do?" He eased onto the bench beside her and angled his body so that his knees brushed hers. He noticed her fingertips were slightly whiter than usual and picked up her hands to warm them between his.

"I want to go to school." She stared at their hands but didn't seem to be seeing anything. "I want to learn about computers. I've been teaching myself, and I've learned it quickly. I mean, it's mostly numbers, and I'm really good with numbers." She looked around and saw no one else, but she still lowered her voice. "I can hack into most systems," she confessed. "And I once made Mr. Oppenheim's computer run only in binary."

He burst into laughter. "I'd have paid to see the look on his face!"

Her smile lightened her face and the entire area. "It was funny! He looked like a pink cabbage, all wrinkled and mad! He hopped around for hours until someone came and fixed it." She slipped her hands deeper into his. He was so warm and strong. He was much bigger than she was but she felt nothing except kindness inside him. He made her feel safe in a way she never had before. No matter what he said, she was sure she had met him somewhere. And she was sure she had missed him. "You're a good man." His brows lifted and she tilted her head. "No one's ever said that?"

"Ah, no. I think the nicest thing I've ever been called is intimidating. The worst things . . . well, you're too young to hear them." He paused briefly. "You know, I think *I'm* too young to hear them."

He was rewarded with a giggle. "Then they're all wrong." She slipped her hands free and got to her feet. She removed his jacket and held it out to him. "I have to go now. And Riku . . . thank you. You don't treat me like I'll break, and you don't treat me like I'm some sort of freak. I can just be me." She bent to kiss his cheek softly and hurried away toward the front of the building.

Silence lingered until he heard the coffee seller clearing his throat. Startled, he looked over. "Yes?" He could barely see the man inside the truck so he got to his feet and walked over. "Is something wrong?"

"No." The other male was attractive and probably in his late twenties. He was also slightly uneasy as he mumbled, "You, ah, have a thing for Rayna?" When Eric slowly lifted a brow, he flushed. "Thing is," he said earnestly, "I really like her.

She's sweet and innocent and so pretty. I'd love to ask her out sometime but she has no clue I'm attracted to her, and I don't want to make her stop visiting. I've been trying to get my courage up but . . ."

Something shook inside Eric. It was dark and violent, nearly calling up his powers over the elements. As it was, clouds swept briefly across the sky. Before he could stop himself he said, "Rayna belongs to me. Don't waste your time, kid."

"Lucky bastard," he sighed sadly.

Suddenly realizing what he had said, Eric swiftly left the area and headed for the front where his work was waiting. What the hell was wrong with him? He had no claim to Rayna other than where her safety was related. Even that was sketchy at best. Why had he warned off someone who seemed like a decent guy? He put it out of his mind as he got out his tools. It was time to get his mind off Rayna and focus on the other part of why he was there.

He kept his eye on the people coming and going. After a while, he moved closer to the building and worked right under the front window where Rayna's desk was situated. She opened it after a few moments to let in the morning air, and he was able to perfectly hear everything that went on. It took only a few minutes before he realized how good she truly was at her job.

She handled every customer that came to the desk with the same friendly personality, and it was clear all of them would have preferred to deal with her than anyone else. He counted at least ten people she helped at the desk rather than referring them back; her knowledge of policies and procedures was absolute.

She was the same on the phone, patiently walking people through lengthy documents without ever once losing her composure. She repeated herself as needed, and her voice was always warm and friendly. Her skill was underscored for Eric by the fact that she had probably never *read* the documents; she had learned solely on listening and observing. He could barely imagine what she might be like with better reading comprehension.

Why the *hell* was a woman like that working a front desk? Annoyance gnawed inside him at the utter waste of talent. Damn it, they could just train her up the ranks and take advantage of her natural learning ability!

He got to his feet and yanked his gloves off. He stuffed them in the back pocket of his jeans as he headed down the walkway toward the parking lot. He pulled his cell phone out and punched speed dial. When the other side was picked up, he said without preamble, "I want the monthly employee appraisal reports."

"Okay." Rhianna went through her files and tucked the phone between her ear and her shoulder. "Any reason why in particular?"

"I want Rayna's reports. Rhi, she's even more brilliant than we thought. She handles herself like a queen and has the warm and open manner of a real lady. She's also good with customers and probably knows as much about this place as the accountants themselves. The clients even have a real preference for her." He kept an eye on the building as he spoke, not wanting someone to overhear.

"Then why is she still a secretary," she murmured, and it was mostly to herself. She was reading Rayna's reports, and her brows slowly climbed. "I see nothing at all mentioning that in here. Her reports are just good enough to keep her, but not so good as to have her recommended for promotion. Average, average, average." She snorted rudely. "Needs improvement on her ability to read instructions. What a surprise. They *know* she can't read well. They give her written instructions just to give her a chance to screw up."

"I think it's jealousy," he said flatly, and described what he had seen the day before. He could all but hear the steam coming out her ears from temper, and knew the sparks were in her eyes again. "They don't like that someone without any degree is better than they are. I miss the old days," he muttered in frustration, "when people didn't need those damned pieces of paper."

"Now you really sound old." She drummed her nails lightly on the top of her desk. "With reports like this, we can't hire her from her current position. She'd have to be fired or leave the job first so we can pick her up as a new employee entirely. Find out whatever you can and I'll start a workup for a restructure. Once we have names, we'll go from there."

"Okay." He saw Rayna leaving the building for a break and his attention splintered. "Later, Rhi," he murmured and hung up on her knowing chuckle.

Rayna glanced to where Riku usually was but didn't see him. It was disappointing as she walked slowly down the path that went around the building. She had been completely aware of his presence outside her window. Her skin still tingled and she felt warm from the inside out for once. She had the curious feeling that she was holding her breath until she saw him again.

A familiar hand holding a clutch of wildflowers suddenly lowered in front of her face. Startled, she turned her head to find herself looking into Eric's smiling blue eyes. "You surprised me, Riku." She looked back at the flowers. "They're lovely. Are these the ones you're planting?"

"I think they might be for you," he told her gravely.

"Me?" Her eyes widened. "No one's ever given me flowers." As soon as she said it, she frowned. "No . . . someone did. On my birthdays. I think." She gave him an apologetic frown. "Sometimes I could swear I know things from my coma, but it doesn't make sense. My father swore he was the only one who visited me."

The lost note in her voice broke his heart. His determination to keep his identity secret suddenly seemed to pale compared to her confusion. He couldn't tell her now, though. It was already too late. He had to play things through until she was safe. "Maybe he didn't know," he offered. "But, regardless, these are for you."

She took the flowers and buried her nose in them. They smelled wonderful. "Why?"

"Because they reminded me of you," he told her simply. He had seen the flowers growing in a bed of roses and hadn't liked the idea of just getting rid of them. There was a lot of courage in growing so beautiful in a place where beauty took a different shape, just like Rayna.

"Oh." She regarded him for a few moments before smiling. "Can I spend my break time with you?"

"Of course." He waited until she sat down on the curb, and then sat down beside her and stretched out his legs. He noticed she was doing the same and smiled because the capris she wore revealed a nice length of leg. He wasn't surprised she'd had trouble with her height perception; her legs were beautifully long and shapely. It was hard to fight the urge to run a hand down them.

There was a peaceful quiet for a few moments. A sort of buzzing began to skim across his mind, and he realized it was coming from her. She seemed to be nearly vibrating with frustrated anger and confusion. "If you need to vent," he offered idly, "be my guest. Your coworkers giving you issues again?"

She said nothing for a few moments, somehow unsurprised that he had guessed, then she sighed and drew her legs up to wrap her arms around them. "Well," she hedged, "I don't want to be a tattletale but . . ." The frustration that had been bubbling up finally spilled over. She had never had a friend to talk to about work before. "It's making me crazy!" she finally blurted.

"What is, sweetheart?" The endearment was out before he could stop it, but she either didn't notice or didn't mind.

"Everyone!" She got to her feet to pace back and forth. "The manager is sleeping with one of the advisors." She blinked. "Well, not sleeping I guess but they're, well, you know." Blushing, she waved it aside and ignored his quick grin. "Because of it, he gives her preferential treatment and she's an *idiot*. I don't care how many degrees she has.

"Nobody listens to the clients, and they all end up leaving frustrated and angry. I've had to talk dozens into not changing companies because they were so upset. And the people who do know what they're doing are left underappreciated because they're too new to be mean."

She whirled and looked at him with vivid violet eyes. "Why?" she demanded. "Why do people have to be mean in order to get anywhere? Why can't someone be nice and be able to do just as well? What makes people lie and cheat? I don't understand it!"

He felt the ground tremble under his feet and a strong gust of wind whipped her silver hair around her face. He let out a little breath and curbed his power. She had pulled a very deep, almost instinctual, response from him. "I don't know," he admitted quietly. He got to his feet and gently tucked her hair behind her ear. As he did, he spotted a bruise on her cheek. He frowned darkly and bent to see it better. "What the hell is this? Did someone hit you?"

"No." Her color rose as he stood so close to her. His breath smelled like peppermints, as if he had eaten some candy. His skin smelled like fresh grass and rich dirt. It smelled wonderful, wild, and earthy like summertime. It had always been her favorite season. "I . . ." She tried to catch her scattered thoughts as her pulse thudded in her body. "I'm clumsy," she whispered. "Weird accidents happen."

"Like what?" She smelled sweet and fresh like wildflowers. It was shredding his control to bits, leaving him with a wild urge to carry her down to the grass and see if she tasted as pure as her soul felt. He warily eased back a step, not trusting himself. It didn't help any that he could see the sudden awareness in her eyes, a sort of startled desire as if she didn't even understand her own body. Did she want him as badly as he wanted her? The thought gnawed happily on his aching body and hormones.

She took a quick breath and told herself to get a grip as he stepped back. What on earth was wrong with her? Her entire body ached, and she felt as if she was a magnet helplessly drawn to him. Her hands literally burned to feel his hair and skin. She wanted . . . she had no idea *what* she wanted. "Well, I, uhm." She took another breath. "Well, strange things happen."

"What sort of things?"

"Ladders almost fall on me, books and such. Someone accidentally put rat poison next to the sugar. I almost put it in my cup but one of the nicer men stopped me. I also almost fell down the stairs once when someone bumped into me. Just stupid things." She tried to smile. "If it'll happen, it happens to me."

"Your name isn't Murphy," he murmured, anger in his stomach. She looked frightened and lost as if she had no friends in the world.

"Huh?"

He shook his head. "Sorry. Murphy's Law joke. Look it up on your Wiki. So what happened this morning?" He lightly touched her cheek.

"There was a computer monitor sitting on top of a shelf." She shrugged one shoulder. "I walked under it and it decided to fall. One of the janitors yanked me out of the way in time and the cord whipped around and hit my cheek. Considering it almost flattened my head, I don't mind."

"I see. Well, I'm glad you're okay," he told her softly. "It would upset me if you were hurt." That was an understatement. If he found someone who had deliberately harmed her, he would unleash floods that put Hurricane Katrina to shame.

"Thank you." She looked at her watch and gasped. "Whoops. I'll be late getting back. Can I join you for lunch too?" Her eyes sparkled. "I like being with you."

"I'd be honored." He gave her a courtly bow and enjoyed listening to her giggle. With a smile, he watched as she began to jog lightly back toward the building. He even got a moment to admire the curve of her bottom as she knelt to re-lace her sneakers. Small, yes, but she was one of Mother Nature's most glorious creations.

Wind gusted across his face, and he turned his head sharply as he heard a cracking sound. There was an immense tree branch over Rayna's head, likely as big as she was, and it was beginning to break off the tree. "Rayna!" he shouted as he lunged toward her.

She stood and turned only to muffle a shriek as he slammed into her and sent them rolling several feet away, just as the branch crashed to the ground right where they had been. Shaking from head to heel, she burrowed against his body. Somehow his arms around her made her feel safe and secure. "Oh god," she whispered. "Why me?!"

He didn't answer, and he kept one arm around her waist and the other hand under her head to protect her from striking it. Tension lined his body, and he stared intently at the tree as he sought its spirit. There was no response. It was, as far as could be seen, just a near accident.

Her shaking registered finally. He looked down to see tears seeping under her lashes and falling down her cheeks slowly. His heart broke. "Rayna," he said roughly. "Don't cry. God, don't cry."

"Why, Riku?" She curled her fingers into his shirt and held onto him for dear life. It felt as if she had no anchor anywhere. "Why is this happening to me? I should have stayed asleep! Maybe I should have just died!"

"No!" he countered fiercely. "I'm not going to let *anything* happen to you!" Their eyes met and he couldn't fight the battle any longer. Not when she looked like she had nothing left. She had *him*. She would never be alone again. He lowered his head and hungrily took her lips with his, pure fire burning through his body at the taste and feel of her.

Her eyes went wide, red color climbing her face. He realized, belatedly, she had never been kissed before, let alone kissed by a man who wanted her, and almost lifted his head. But then her hands came up to frame his face with innocent trust. Something slumberous filled her eyes as her body shifted instinctively to be closer. On a tortured groan, he sank into the kiss once more and drew her as close as he could.

Hot. She was burning up. A strange pleasure rushed through her body, every nerve ending alive. Everywhere she felt his skin, felt his weight, her body sent out wild messages of pure delight. Each touch fueled her hunger for more. She didn't know what was happening but she didn't fear it. She trusted him to teach her.

When his head finally lifted, she felt unnervingly cold and lost, wishing only for the feel of his kiss once more. "Riku," she whispered, studying his face. "You kissed me."

"Yeah." His voice was a rough caress. If she didn't stop looking at him with that innocent desire in her eyes, he was going to do it again, and again, until she was kissing him back, needing him as he needed her. His sleeping beauty was waking in more ways than one, with her body now waking as a woman. And he knew, beyond a doubt, that he could not bear the idea of anyone else waking her. "I liked it."

"Oh." A shy smile touched her lips. "I've never been kissed before," she whispered. "But I liked how you kissed me."

He gave a soft groan that turned into a laugh. He had never known honesty could be so dangerous. "Rayna, sweetheart, saying something like that to a man is hell on his hormones." He sat up carefully and pulled her up as well. She was covered in dirt and grass and there were scratches all over her calves. Someone was going to pay deeply for putting marks on her. "If anyone hassles you," he said with steel in his voice, "tell me."

"Why would they . . ." Innocent, yes, but she was quick. Her cheeks slowly turned red. "You mean they might think we . . . that you . . . that I . . . Oh no. But you just kissed me because I was crying!"

"No." He rubbed his thumb gently over the bruise on her cheek. "I kissed you because I want you." He helped her to her feet and caught her hands when she started to brush the dirt off. "Don't. I'll walk you back and explain what happened."

"Okay." She was limping slightly, but when she felt his concern, she tried to hide it. She thought she might have pulled something in her ankle because it didn't quite want to support her weight without pain. "I'm okay."

He pushed the door open and called, "Anyone have an ace bandage? A tree branch tried to crush Rayna." Not to his surprise, no one came running with concern except for the janitor. "Here," Eric said, and helped ease Rayna onto her chair. "I'll leave her to you," he told the janitor when he saw he was armed with a first aid kit. Over the other man's head, he winked slightly at Rayna and smiled when she blushed prettily. "Don't worry about lunch," he told her. "I forgot my, uh, boss wants to see me. I'll be back tomorrow. Lunch then, definitely."

"Okay." She winced as the antiseptic burned her leg. "Ow." Distracted by the process, she didn't even see when he left the building. When the janitor had finished and wrapped her ankle, she used a bottle of water and a tissue to wipe away the dirt. She just ignored her coworkers when they smirked as they went past.

At lunch, she decided to eat at her desk and went onto the internet. You could find anything on the net, including information on men and women, relationships, and sex. She wanted a definition for what she was feeling and figured it was related to all three. She found her answer shortly. *'Passion - a powerful emotion, such as love, joy, hatred, or anger. Ardent love. Strong sexual desire; lust. The object of such love or desire.'*

That was interesting, she decided, and looked up 'lust.' It was even more fascinating. *'An intense or unrestrained sexual craving.'* Remembering the word Eric had used, she looked up 'want' as well. *'To desire greatly, to crave.'* So he wanted her in a sexual manner. He felt desire for her. She thought she might feel the same, and wondered not only how to find out, but if she had the courage to even try.

CHAPTER FOUR

The door blew open on a powerful gust of wind. Being as it was the top floor of the building, and the window was shut, Rhianna didn't bother to look up from the email she was reading from her adopted daughter. "Hello, Riku," she said calmly.

Eric stalked into her office, over to her desk, and leaned over to plant both hands on the top. The resulting thump made her paperweight rattle. "Rhi!" he snapped in annoyance. "Stop it at once!"

She lifted a brow. "What am I being accused of now?"

"The Shaughnessys," he retorted succinctly, "were a bad influence on you!"

The family he referred to was a family that Rhianna had issued contracts on for more than one hundred and fifty years. The final one had been completed about five years prior. A former Enforcer member had also been under contract, and had been assisting the Shaughnessys to fall in love as part of her deal. She, herself, had married the last one and was expecting her second child soon.

Rhianna idly propped her cheek on her hand as she studied her best friend. "I take it," her voice was amused, "that you're having a wee bit of trouble with our young princess." Since it wasn't a question, she didn't really expect an answer.

He answered anyway. "Yes, damn it!" He straightened and stalked away and raked his hands through his hair. "Damn it to hell, Rhi, I want her so badly I can taste it! And it's *worse* because I'm falling over my own feet for her!" Literal flames flicked from the white wings in his hair, evidence of his unrestrained emotion for Rayna and his lingering frustration. "I kissed her."

She began to read her letter again. "Why blame me then? You're the one who followed his hormones and discovered more than he expected. How does Rayna feel about things?"

"I don't think she really knows. Hell, Rhi, she'd never been kissed before." Frustration simmered inside his voice and eyes. "It wouldn't be so bad if I could convince myself that's all the more reason to let her go."

"Instead you want to teach her all about men and the mysteries of being a woman." She quirked a brow slightly. "Well, if you're having this much trouble," she began as she got to her feet, "I'll just call in someone else."

"No!" He saw her raise one elegant brow and cursed softly. He raked his hands through his hair again. "Hell." He glowered at her as she laughed at him. "Stop gloating," he muttered as he stalked into his office. "It's rude!"

She winced good-naturedly as he slammed the door, and then bit her lip to hide a chuckle. Things were progressing nicely. Nicely indeed. It probably wouldn't even hurt to send Rayna an email. Anonymously of course. If the girl was half the hacker she seemed, she might even trace it back to Rhianna. She looked forward to the challenge of stopping her.

The next wave of harassment began the next morning. Rayna got to work to discover that someone had been leaving little notes all over her desk and in all her folders. Some just had words. Others had disgusting and disturbing images. Even though her mind did not understand entirely what she was looking at, she did understand the intent.

She destroyed all the notes that she found and booted her computer. The wallpaper had been changed again. She changed it back quickly, her fingers beginning to tremble. Anger simmering under her pain, she once more traced the route back to the person who had gotten in. She contemplated her options before deciding to use remote access to get into the man's iPhone. She then proceeded to erase everything and reset it to factory default.

That done, she got into her own computer's protocols and erected password protection for everything. If anyone tried to get into her computer without a password, they would lock the system down entirely.

She knew it was futile, but she reported the emails to her manager. She promptly got a response that said she was blowing things out of proportion and would be suspended if she tried to cause trouble again. Rayna, not knowing the legalities or policies of Enforcers, who owned the company, believed him. With nothing else she could do, she began to count the time until break and lunch when she could see Riku again.

An hour later, she was surprised to receive a random email. She hesitated but went ahead and opened it. There was no return address and no subject. The body of the email read, *Ask him about his family*.

Trying to trace the sender only brought a string of useless information. She sat back in her chair with a frown. She would have to try later to see if she could break through. In the meantime, her mind was occupied by the message itself. She could only assume it was referring to Riku.

It made her begin to wonder. She hadn't asked anything about him yet. It felt a little startling as she realized how deeply she wanted to know everything. She had asked Remy, and her older friend had gently cautioned her against confusing lust with love, but she was still somehow sure she was falling in love and not just lust.

When her break arrived, she quickly locked her computer and got to her feet. She rushed out of the building and down the sidewalk. Eric was at the end trying to operate an edging machine. He saw her and stopped the machine as he turned with a smile. "Hey there." To his utter surprise, she leapt into his arms and clung on tightly, her feet dangling as she held onto his neck. "Rayna, what's wrong?"

She just shook her head and pressed her face against his shoulder, feeling safe again. He went with his instincts and wrapped his arms around her to hold her closer. He walked over to where there was shade under an oak tree and sat down on the bench with her held safely on his lap. "It's alright," he murmured, pressing his lips to her hair. "Tell me."

"They were at it again this morning," she whispered. "They had put notes everywhere, and someone had changed my desktop. There were emails too . . ." She shuddered lightly. "I told my manager but he said if I bothered him again I would be suspended. I just . . . I just really wanted to see you. I knew you'd make me feel better."

His arms tightened for a moment against his will. He carefully relaxed them and eased her back to frame her face with his hands. "Listen to me," he urged quietly. "If the manager won't listen, contact Enforcers directly."

She gave him a sad smile. "Why would they listen to me?"

His eyes narrowed slightly for a moment. Enforcers was dedicated solely to protecting those of 3rd District. How could she not know that they would move heaven and hell if she was being tormented? Heads were going to roll when he found out who had deceived her. "Try calling," he suggested softly. "Ask for Rhianna Taber and give your name."

"Why would she know *my* name?" She shrugged one shoulder. "It's okay. I don't mind it so much." She rested her head on his shoulder with a little sigh. "It's okay as long as you're here. I'll miss you when you're done with the landscaping."

"Rayna . . ." He closed his eyes and held her closer. The idea of never seeing her again, never holding her in his arms, was a nightmare.

"I was wondering . . ." She ran a finger over the chain of the necklace he was wearing and wondered what was on it. It was under his shirt somewhere and she wasn't brave enough to go looking, no matter how much she was tempted. "Would you tell me about your family?"

"Ah . . . hmm." He thought about things for a few moments. He hadn't really thought about his family in a very, very long time. "It was," he said slowly, "a difficult family to live in. A difficult time. I'm from 3rd District, too," he added with a smile. "So you know the stigma." He nuzzled his nose into her hair softly. "I fell into the family tradition, learned some special skills. Things happened and I lost my family. My best friend and I both did."

"I'm sorry." She lifted her head and frowned. "It must have hurt so much. I . . ." She looked down at her hands. "The car accident . . . it killed my mother and I lost my big sister. My family is just my aunt and uncle and my father now. I don't see my aunt or uncle much. They're normal."

In other words, not 3rd District. "I'm sorry, Rayna. It must still hurt since it's like yesterday for you."

She looked at him in surprise. "Yes, yes it is. You're the only one who has ever seemed to understand that." She clenched her hands into fists in her lap. "I went to sleep one night and woke up sixteen years later. I was four and woke up almost twenty. Sixteen years . . . it feels like a single night."

"No wonder you have trouble sleeping." He gently covered her hand with his.

"Yeah." She looked up at him and studied his face. "I was looking up things," she blurted suddenly. "I, uhm . . ." She began to blush. "You said," she whispered, "you wanted me. I think I want you, too."

"I see. You only think you do?" He kept his voice teasing with effort. A tremor was starting from his soul outward, the quake rumbling in his body. He could barely keep his hands off her to begin with without having her so honestly admitting her emotions.

"Well, I'm not sure. I've never wanted anyone before. Would . . ."

"What, sweetheart?"

"Would you kiss me again?" she whispered. "I liked it." She looked up at him with a shy smile. "Teach me how to kiss."

The quake gathered fury, straining at its bounds. He forced his hands to be gentle as he smoothed her hair out of her face. Their skin brushed lightly and he nearly felt light headed. His gaze dropped to her lips, his pulse throbbing everywhere at once. "Do you have any idea," he asked roughly, "how badly I want you? I'm terrified of hurting you."

"You would never hurt me." She was sure of it. She lifted her hands to lightly touch his face, and her skin tingled with sheer delight. He was so hot and strong. Her fingers moved unconsciously, caressing his skin. "Please, Riku. I want to know why you're so different for me." She slowly drew her touch away though it was hard. The way he was looking at her stole her breath.

He took a deep breath and cupped her cheek warmly. "Knowing you've only ever wanted me . . ." A shudder rippled through his powerful body. "I'll fight anyone who tries to take you from me." He knew he didn't deserve her, but he craved her more than life. She was like the elements that made him up. Critical. Essential.

"Really?" she whispered in return.

"Really." He lightly touched her lips with his and tasted the curve of her smile. Her lower lip had a slightly metallic taste and he knew that she had been biting it again. "Rayna . . ." His voice was aching as his tongue touched the sore and soothed it. Surprise filled her morning glory eyes and he brushed her lips with his again. "Yes?"

"You . . . I mean . . . tell me what to do," she finally finished simply.

"I can't." His lips curved. "Kissing has a tendency to prevent speaking. That's okay, though, because demonstrating is so much better." Her lips had curved as well and he cupped her chin and tilted her head back slightly. The sunlight filtered across her face and his breath caught. "Rayna."

Her eyes closed as his mouth settled on hers, and everything seemed to fade away into the background. His tongue glided over her lips and the feeling made her breath catch. She wondered what he was doing.

Open your mouth.

It was his voice in her mind, and she didn't question how she had heard it. Hesitantly, she did as he asked, and a searing wave of heat flooded her as he deepened the kiss, his tongue surging into her mouth to tangle with hers. Her skin flushed, and she felt her breasts throb with a pleasure that was almost pain, almost as if they were begging for his touch. Trying to stop it, she pressed against him and unconsciously deepened the kiss further.

A shudder went through his body. His jeans felt too tight and confining, all of his clothes abrading his skin. He wanted nothing between them. He wanted to savor her soft skin against his. And when she tentatively returned the kiss, his control shook violently. He carefully eased back until there was a breath between their lips. "Got it yet?" he asked huskily. "Or should I kiss you again?"

"Yes. Please." She shivered as he did as asked, his mouth moving on hers with a hunger she instinctively recognized. Delight streaked through her, and she clung to him tightly as he deepened the kiss, his hands moving over her back in caressing sweeps that spread the heat through her entire body. His hand slid around her body and softly cupped her breast. Her nerves awoke with a vengeance and she gave a little gasp of fright at the sharp longing that went through her body. The pleasure was intense and shocking. "Riku," she managed to say when he released her lips.

He knew. He gently ran his hand down her ribs and around to her back. Holding her against him, he held his breath and counted to ten. Then he counted to fifty. Even counting to one hundred didn't tame his raging hunger. At that point, he was fairly sure nothing ever would. Some fires were never meant to go out. "Are you sure," he managed to ask, his voice like rough silk, "you haven't done that before?"

A shyly pleased smile lit her face, and she nuzzled against his neck. "Yes." Joy spread through her as she recognized the craving and hunger inside herself. If this was passion, then no wonder it was considered so dangerous. "Riku . . . I want you," she whispered.

A shudder wracked his body. "Don't say that," he muttered into her hair.

Horrified, she jerked back. "It's wrong?" she asked. "Did I say something wrong?"

"It's not wrong, Rayna! It's just hell on my self-control!" She blinked at him, and he said bluntly, "I want to make love to you." Her color rose instantly and he found a smile. She had been *very* busy with Wikipedia's cross-reference system. "Admitting something like that makes it very hard to keep my hands to myself."

"Should I . . . should I not have lunch with you?" She held her breath.

He saw the naked longing in her eyes and ran a hand through his hair to make sure he wasn't giving off flames. Sure as hell he was hot enough to do it! "No," he said. "I want you to have lunch with me." His grin turned wolfish for a moment. "I wouldn't mind having you *for* lunch." He lowered his head to teasingly nibble at her lower lip so she couldn't mistake his meaning.

She got it. Blushing, but smiling, she ran her fingers down his cheek. She couldn't stop herself. "Good." She slid off his lap and regarded him for a few moments. She leaned forward and kissed him lightly and then straightened and ran toward the office building.

He touched his lips and considered the merits of turning the garden hose's cold water on himself full blast. Letting out a long breath, he leaned back against the tree and stared at the blue sky overhead. Rhianna was right, though he hated to admit it. He didn't need her meddling in his affairs. He was falling in love without anyone's help at all.

He didn't see Rayna again until lunchtime, which was to his advantage because it gave him a chance to lurk beneath her window again, and listen to the goings on. His hand tightened around his spade at one point, as he listened to the sly remarks of a few of the women. Rayna would be biting her lip again. It made him furious, furious enough that he decided to take a walk down to the other side and work over there. It removed the temptation to throw thunderbolts.

To his cynical amusement, a woman leaving the building spotted him and started over toward him deliberately. She was, he observed objectively, really quite stunning in appearance but could not hold a candle to Rayna in his eyes. She was also walking with the slight sway to her hips that indicated she was a veteran of sexual affairs.

He wasn't impressed. Even if he hadn't been aware that she was acting out of an attempt to hurt Rayna, he wouldn't have been impressed. Her thoughts were open and un-jumbled, completely without complication to anyone let alone a mental master such as Eric. He gave her a once over and then turned back to his flowers without a word.

"Ahem." She cleared her throat distinctly.

He turned with a slightly lifted brow. Though she couldn't have been that close to thirty, he couldn't resist saying, "Yes ma'am?"

The slight emphasis in his voice made something in her eyes flicker. It disappeared quickly and she bent down to see the flowers better. "I just love flowers," she cooed. She shifted her weight, giving him a clear view of her generous bust. "Don't you just love roses?"

"I love all flowers, but roses aren't my favorite. They're common. I prefer wildflowers that grow against everybody's wishes." His smile was as cool and deliberate as his words. "Wildflowers are much more radiant. There's an honesty in them that makes them irresistible. And they don't have thorns."

Her cheeks flushed an angry shade of red. "I'm not surprised you prefer that little . . . nobody! You're nothing but a gardener and she's uncultured and completely unsophisticated! Sure, she's pretty enough, but she doesn't even know how to dress herself properly!"

"Odd." He turned back to his flowers, a little infuriating smile on his lips. "She looked as if she knew what she was doing when she got dressed." He deliberately sighed wistfully. "I wish she could wear shorts to work."

She gaped at him for a moment. A hiss of fury slipped past her lips and she stalked a few feet away.

Sensitive to Rayna as always, Eric knew when she started to approach. He stood and turned around to see her jogging toward him. When her eyes met his, he gave her a slow and masculine smile. It was a deliberate statement of intent. It said clearly that he had found the woman he wanted and looked forward to having her in his arms again. He wanted the message clear to the roses in the area that he had made his choice.

The message was adorably lost on Rayna, but she still knew his smile was completely for her alone. She glowed softly with happiness as she stopped in front of him. Her arms were wrapped around a large lunchbox. She was slightly flushed as well, and he skimmed a finger down her cheek. "Don't run in this heat."

"I didn't want you to get hungry," she protested.

"I'm always hungry around you." He put a possessive arm around her waist as he began walking. He knew that the 'rose' was shortly going to be spreading more rumors, but that was fine by him. He would make his move soon and remove Rayna from their clutches forever. His wildflower needed a new garden and gardener.

"I, uhm, I hope you don't mind," Rayna mumbled, peeking up at him, "but I sort of *made* lunch."

"You made lunch?" He looked at her in surprise as she set the box down on a table underneath several large trees. Curious, he watched as she removed the lid and let the tempting smell inside waft out. His mouth began to water. "If it tastes even remotely as good as it looks," he said with feeling, "I'll be your slave forever."

She giggled softly and sat down beside him. "I wanted to do something nice for you. I don't know if anyone has ever taken care of you before and I kind of wanted to." She leaned her head on his shoulder. "You make me feel as if I'm needed, even just a little. It's a nice feeling. And . . . I need you a lot too, I guess," she admitted in a soft rush. "You make everything seem like it'll be okay."

He closed his eyes as a wave of emotion rushed through him. There were different levels of need. This was the first time in his life anyone had ever simply needed him to be there. Just him. There with her. She didn't know what he was or where he was from or the power he held, and she needed him anyway.

She had made him lunch. The simple gesture was the final straw. He couldn't even determine when it had begun. When he had found her in the woods after a terrifying car accident? Over the years when he had spent all his free time with her, keeping her company when no one else would? When he had walked into an office and his sleeping beauty had smiled at him with morning glory eyes? It didn't matter when. The truth was there in front of him. He was in love with her. Had always been in love with her.

"Rayna." His voice came out strained. "I want to kiss you again."

"Oh." A shy smile lit her face and she moved closer to him. She tilted her face up invitingly. She had been hoping he would. She had discovered that when she wasn't around him, she felt as though a part of her soul was missing.

The innocent action made his control shudder but his hands were gentle as he framed her face and lowered his head. He kept the kiss tender, lingering over the flavor that was so uniquely her own. She knew what to do now and met the lazy surge of his tongue with her own, tentative but unafraid.

Wind began to blow, swirling around them, and he pulled himself under control with effort. Easing back slightly, he stared down into her face and studied her flushed cheeks and swollen lips. The lower one had been bitten again, and he gave in to the urge to soothe the sting with his tongue. "Don't do that," he murmured.

"But if I cry, they get worse," she whispered.

"Don't cry. You're far better than any of them. Hold your head high, Rayna." He nuzzled his nose into her hair and felt something cool touch his skin. He looked closer and began to slowly smile. "Well, well," he murmured.

She gasped and went furiously red as she lifted a hand to cover her ear. With a laugh, he caught her wrist and pulled it into her lap. He pulled her hair back with his free hand and smiled all over again as he saw her ear. She had triple-pierced ears, the third ring nothing more than a little silver cuff around the top edge of her ear. Her silvery hair hid it almost entirely from view. "What brought on the urge for multiple piercings, love?"

Horribly embarrassed, she mumbled, "I was trying to 'act my age.' I liked it so I kept it. But I was worried someone might think it was weird or something. Does it look okay?"

"It's enchanting." He nibbled on the rim of her ear and listened to her take a quick breath of combined surprise and desire. His. She was going to be his. He would make his move the very next day and then take her away where he could protect her from everybody. And once everything was done, he was going to dedicate all of his attention to capturing her heart and claiming her as his wife. He had a nice castle with a vast garden that his sleeping princess would simply love.

CHAPTER FIVE

Lunch consisted of baked chicken, homemade bread, salad, and a slice of purely decadent peach cobbler. Eric ate his share with gratitude and delight. Contented, he sighed deeply. "Honey, you are one hell of a cook." He wistfully eyed what was left of her slice of cobbler. "You can cook for me anytime. I can't believe you can cook like this when you've only been mobile for seven months!"

She gave him what was left of her cobbler with a smile. It was a smile that turned into a giggle when he didn't even pretend to look guilty. "I like to learn," she said happily. "I can't learn enough to be content. Some of the easiest books to read are cookbooks, so I've read all of them. And I like it. It's fun."

"And you're *good* at it." He helped her pack the containers away. "As if you couldn't tell by me licking the plate."

She glowed softly with happiness as she smiled at him. "I could cook you dinner some time."

Temptation swirled through him but he firmly leashed it. He could wait. There was time. "I'd love that. How about this weekend?" He picked up her hand and kissed her fingers. Her fingers tenderly touched his lips in turn, and he pressed her palm against his cheek, just wanting to savor her touch. "Lunch is almost over. I need to return you to the greenhouse."

"Greenhouse?"

"You remind me of my beautiful flowers," he admitted.

Her eyes softened until they were the color of morning glories in glorious bloom. She didn't want to go anywhere. She wanted to sit with him in the summer sun and simply pass the time. She had always felt as if she had time to make up for, but now she wanted nothing more than to make time stop entirely.

He eased a hand into her thick hair and tugged her closer so that their lips met. He lingered for a moment until he could release her with a tender smile. He deliberately licked his lips. "Cobbler." When she giggled, he skimmed a thumb over her delicate cheekbone. "Let's go. Don't let them bring you down."

"If I have you, it's okay." She got to her feet and her heart thudded powerfully in her chest as he took her hand and entwined their fingers. He was so much bigger that she should have been afraid, but she wasn't. She felt safe and cherished as if she was the most important thing in his world. Her heart reveled in it.

When they were halfway down the sidewalk, he squeezed her hand and let go so she headed toward the building alone. There was a package outside the door and she knelt to scoop it up. The hair on the back of his neck stirred and he looked up sharply to see a large stack of roofing tiles teetering on the edge of the roof.

"Rayna! Move!" He shot forward using his wind magic to propel him faster. His hand closed around her wrist and he jerked her up into his arms. He leapt backward just as the tile crashed to the ground where she had been. The tiles shattered and bits of rock flew everywhere.

She was shaking, he noticed. That was fine; he was too. He buried his face in her hair and held her fiercely. "That scared me to death," he muttered. "I see what you mean about weird things." He looked up at the roof and let his eyes glow with the gold color that marked his powers visibly. The menacing presence faded. Turning back to Rayna, he asked, "Are you okay?"

"Yeah." She gulped air. Tears and panic were held as tightly inside as possible. "You looked really cool," she said, trying for humor. "I could have sworn you were commanding the wind." She frowned suddenly. "You're 3rd District born. Was it you after all?"

That much he could tell her. "Yes. Do you know what you can do?" He knew what her powers were made *of*, but not precisely what they could *do*. If she had a better idea, then it would help him and Rhianna immensely.

"I dunno." She shrugged one shoulder. "My mother was the one from 3rd District, but I don't think she got a chance to tell me or my sister before the accident. I have very few memories at all, really. It's like I have no memories before waking."

His heart aching, he cuddled her for a moment before gently putting her on her feet. "Report the incident," he told her. "Trust me, even if the manager doesn't report it himself, something *will* be done."

She smiled. She trusted him without question. "Okay. I believe you." She stepped around the debris and walked into the building. Eric, his deepest instincts on the prowl, went back to his work under her window. He didn't want her to be far from his sight or hearing.

The roses were looking for blood again. He didn't say anything but he let a soft wind blow in the window—despite it being closed. He heard a soft giggle and smiled, his mission accomplished. He also took a few minutes to call Rhianna but shortly returned to work.

The window opened suddenly "How," came Rayna's voice over his head, "did you do that?"

He looked up to find her leaning on the windowsill. "Do what?" he asked innocently.

"I reported the incident and my manager told me to not worry about it. A few minutes later he's contacting me full of apologies with the promise the building would be checked for safety hazards." She poked him in the nose. "I know you did it."

"Who, me? I'm just a gardener with a little special ability." He caught her hand and nipped at the pad of her finger gently, just for the sheer delight of hearing her breath break and seeing her color rise.

She slipped her hand free, quickly, and went back to her desk before he made her forget her own name. She didn't notice it, but everyone else did shortly, that she was visibly happy. His unwavering support and love gave her a self-confidence that made her radiantly beautiful.

And, for some reason, the women couldn't snipe at her. It was harder and harder to even look at her, as if she was making them uncomfortably aware of their own shortcomings. It had always been that way, as if they had to face the truth around her. Before, it had driven them to be cold and cruel. Now, they couldn't even bear it.

Rayna had to work a little late that day because of a letter she had to finish typing, and she was sure that Eric had already gone home. She felt oddly lonely and disappointed. But maybe it was better, she decided as she headed out of the building. Now she wouldn't go home to a lonely house after having just been in his arms.

To her surprise, he stood at the end of the walkway with his hands tucked in his jacket pockets. He smiled at her, and emotion welled up inside her in a long, vibrant wave that choked her. She rode on it without hesitation and ran down the sidewalk toward him. He expected her this time, and as she leapt into his arms, he caught her close and spun her around.

She laughed and wrapped her arms around his neck tightly. "I wanted to see you," she said happily. "I was worried you'd left already."

"What sort of man would I be if I didn't walk you to your car?" he teased as he set her down gently.

She flushed slightly. "I don't own a car. I ride the bus." Embarrassed, she said, "I don't know how to drive, let alone have the money to take lessons. I can afford to live, but that's it."

"Well, allow me to be your chariot then," he offered with a courteous bow. He straightened and smiled. "I saved for a long time to afford my car." It was a lie, but there was no other way to explain how a gardener could afford the sleek little sports car. Rhianna had laughed at him for months after he had gotten it but, damn it, if she could have a screaming red motorcycle, then he could have his car.

"Okay." She stayed close to him as they walked across the parking lot, and she felt for the first time as if she wasn't alone anymore. The sound of tires squealing made her frown, and she wrinkled her nose as the smell of burning rubber filled the air. "Lead foot."

"Where'd you learn that term? Wiki?"

She grinned suddenly. "My friend Remy. She says she has one."

He laughed. As he swung an arm around her shoulders, he saw a car barreling toward them across the lot far faster than was safe.

It was aimed at Rayna.

Reflex kicked in. He tackled her and sent them both tumbling across the asphalt so that the car shot past where they had been. The car slammed on the brakes and did a donut to swerve around and come back at them.

He wrapped Rayna safely in his arms and quickly rolled them between two parked cars. The driver aiming for them missed entirely, and seemed to sense a third attempt would be too risky. They drove out of the lot as fast as he or she had arrived. Eric tried to get a glimpse of the license, but it was gone before he could focus.

Rayna was shaking so hard her teeth were chattering. Terror flooded him and he sat up quickly. He ran his hands over her to make sure she hadn't broken anything; her bones were too delicate to endure that much trauma! She was scraped and bleeding from nicks, but she was otherwise fine. "God," he said roughly, and pulled her into his arms. "If I hadn't been here . . ."

"All these accidents . . ." she whispered, and there was a soft whimper in her voice that ripped at him.

He framed her face with hands that were still trembling. "It wasn't an accident, sweetheart. That car was deliberately aiming for us. For you. They couldn't care less about me." He got to his feet and lifted her up into his arms. "I'm taking you home where you're safe."

"Please!" she blurted. She grabbed his arms as he put her in his car. "Will you stay with me just a little while? So I'm not alone."

He ran his hand through her hair. "Alright," he murmured. He knew beyond a doubt how the night was likely to end. It was inevitable. She was, as yet, too innocent to understand, but he did. The emotion between them was too powerful to be restrained for much longer, and as there were never any coincidences around those in 3rd District (he *still* blamed Rhianna for that), he knew that what bound him and Rayna could not be stopped. "Where do you live?" he asked. He had to ask. She would wonder how he knew where she lived, otherwise.

She gave him the directions and settled back in her seat. "It looks a little rundown," she warned him, "but it's safer that way. We keep the residential areas looking like they're beyond hope so outsiders don't try to take over."

He smiled at her. "I'm from 3rd District, too, remember? I know what it's really like." Ruefully, he added, "Considering the rumors that fly, I'm glad I'm from there so that I understand the truth."

She knew what he meant. Rumors were all over New York, and even beyond, about the old-fashioned place known as 3rd District. It wasn't like Manhattan or the Bronx. It wasn't even like a small town within a city. It simply was what it was, and it had been that way even long before the time when New York had been New Amsterdam.

In appearance, the District held fast to the historical styles that had built it and grown within it over the periods. The most modern looking building besides Enforcers Headquarters still looked as if it had been built in the mid-1800s. Yet there was more to the District than its historical value. There was magic. Everyone whispered of the people who were different. And everyone knew that if you were drawn to the District, eventually your dreams would come true.

The apartment building she lived in wasn't very big and neither were the apartments. There were bigger places but, as she had said, she couldn't afford them. Eric parked the car outside her place and followed her in as she unlocked the front door.

Apartment was too big a word. It was more like a studio: one giant room and a bathroom. The tiny kitchen was enclosed behind a counter and she had put her bed behind a series of folding screens to give her a semblance of having a bedroom. Her furniture consisted of a table and two chairs, a well-used beanbag chair next to a bookcase, and a couple of lamps. No more.

"It's very small," she apologized. "I'm sorry. It's also really cold at night and hot during the day." She shrugged one shoulder. "I can't afford to turn the heater or air conditioning on. I usually just take a hot shower and get into my pajamas and robe."

He ran a knuckle down her cheek. "It's fine, Rayna." He glanced around the room again and this time his eyes fell on a painting hanging over the kitchen sink. His breath caught as he walked toward it slowly. It was an exquisite representation of the sun setting behind Enforcers Headquarters. "My god," he breathed. "How did you manage to afford this?"

She cleared her throat. "I didn't."

"It was a gift?" He couldn't tear his eyes away.

"No. I," she coughed lightly, "I painted it." When he looked at her in shock, she blushed and looked at the floor. "I painted it. I could only afford one canvas, so I've only done this one." Impulsively, she took it down and held it out to him. "Here."

"Rayna," he said, stunned. He had never known anyone like her. So open and giving. And brilliant. Dear god, she was stunningly brilliant and talented. He would make sure she had it all, he thought fiercely as he took the painting and set it safely on the counter. She would have the time for schooling and the money to buy as many canvases as she wanted. He would love to have her help redecorate his office. Hell, he would set her loose on the entire building.

Silence fell between them as they watched one another. Tension grew stronger and stretched as two bodies, two hearts, and two souls stirred with growing hunger. She drew a quick breath, sensing the odd atmosphere, and it frightened her a little. She had never felt anything like it before. She took a wary step backward and whispered, "I'm just going to take a shower."

He watched her flee into the bathroom and took several long breaths to grab for composure and control. He wanted her so bad that even his teeth hurt. He heard the shower running and went around the counter to get himself a cup of coffee. It was cold, and he nuked it in the microwave before taking a bracing sip. Resigned, he studied his cup. Even a day old, her coffee was delicious.

She stood under the pouring water and tilted her face into the spray. The scratches stung as the water hit them but she ignored the pain. Her mind was buzzing, refusing to settle down. Over and over again, her memory flashed to the moment she had seen the car coming at them. The tires squealed in her ears. The downside of her ability to memorize things she learned was her inability to forget other things, especially things she really wanted to forget.

A new memory flashed across her eyes suddenly. Tires squealing, her mother screaming. The sense of a jarring impact and then flying through the air. Then . . . nothing. She covered her ears on a terrified cry.

Instants later, Eric jerked the shower door open. "Rayna?" he asked in worry. "Are you hurt after all?"

She didn't even heed her nakedness; she threw herself into his arms on a soft sob. "I heard it!" she said into his shoulder. "I could hear the tires from the accident! I remembered what happened when I was four! I thought it was happening again!"

"It's okay, sweetheart. I'm here." He grabbed a towel and wrapped it around her gently, removing temptation from sight even if not from memory. Dear god, she was stunning. Long legs and graceful curves, slim as an orchid and twice as lovely. There wasn't a blemish on her body but for the single mark over her left hip. Just seeing it filled him with anger.

When a contract for death—a Bloody Contract—was made on a member of 3rd District, their body showed the contract as a small red check known as a Bloody Mark. Her Mark would disappear on her twenty-first birthday, providing he could keep her alive that long.

He gathered her up in his arms and carried her out of the bathroom. He moved around the screens and gently set her down on top of her bed. It was a plain twin bed, only just big enough for her. He figured his feet would hang off the end. "No more tears," he soothed. He rubbed another towel over her hair softly. "It'll be alright. You're here, everything's fine."

"Riku." She turned her face into his hand when he cupped her cheek gently. "I'm so much trouble," she whispered. "All those stupid accidents and then that car . . . I should have just stayed asleep forever." Tears slid down her cheeks. "It's better than being so alone."

"You're not alone," he insisted fiercely, his heart breaking. "I'm here." Tears continued to glide down her cheeks, and on a soft groan, he scooped her up onto his lap. His lips rushed over her face to steal the tears. "Don't cry," he whispered. "God, Rayna, how can you think you're alone? I can't make myself leave you no matter how much I know I should!"

A powerful, bone deep sense of conviction filled her, and she wound her arms around his neck. "I don't want you to go. Stay with me. Teach me how to love you." Her lips trembled. "Unless you don't want me anymore."

He caught one of her hands, brought it down his body, and pressed it against his erection straining against his jeans. She blushed brightly and tried to jerk her hand back but he held her gently. "A man can't lie about this," he teased her softly, his breath hitching slightly as the heat of her skin burned him.

Warmth gathered inside and pooled low in her belly, making her ache curiously. She was suddenly vividly aware of the differences in their bodies and felt infinitely feminine and . . . powerful. It was power to know that he wanted her. This man who could have any woman he wanted had chosen *her*. "Riku," she whispered, looking at him with naked longing on her face.

"Are you sure?" He drew her hand up to rest over his heart.

"Very sure. Please, love me."

She leaned up and kissed him softly, briefly startling him, but he caught his balance and deepened the kiss, lazily curling his tongue around hers. When she was truly secure in being his lover, she would be a force to be reckoned with. It made his knees weak with delight.

She trembled softly and he eased back enough to ask, "Frightened?"

"No." She slid her arms around his neck and held on as he slowly lowered her to the top of her bed. She wasn't afraid. Anticipation was filling her. She felt hot and feverish, and a restless sensation of pleasure, that rushed through her blood, made her quiver beneath him.

He sensed it with relief. He had been afraid her nerves would be stronger than her heart and body. He gently skimmed his fingers over the curves of her breast above the towel, savoring her soft skin. Her nipples tightened and passion flushed her skin as her eyes closed in surrender.

"Rayna," he murmured, softly running kisses over her face and down along her neck and shoulder. She trembled softly and her fingers moved convulsively in his hair. Impatience churned, and he held tightly to his control as he began to unwrap the towel slowly. She deserved all the tenderness he could find for her. They could explore desperation later. "Let me see you."

"And you." She slid her hands down to the buttons of his shirt. "I want to know everything." She slowly opened the buttons, fascinated by the golden skin she revealed and the hard muscle beneath. The chain he wore had a pendant at the end, and she reached for it curiously.

It was a flat disc of some strange metal with the symbols for all the elements etched into it. She could feel the age and the power, and it made her skin prickle in recognition. Lying against his chest as it did, it was somehow a stark reminder of how powerful he was, both with the wind and physically. Instead of frightening her, the knowledge comforted her, and she threw her arms around his neck.

He held her a moment and then slowly released her and laid her down again. The towel was open now and revealed her beauty, brilliantly. Her skin was soft peach and her breasts were curved perfectly for his hands. Her hips were delicately shaped, and her stomach trim.

His lips slowly curved as he saw something else. "Well, well," he murmured, and lightly touched the little silver hoop she wore as a belly button ring. "Hiding this, were we?"

She smiled shyly, completely unembarrassed and not bothering to question why. "It would be out of place at work."

"So it would." He didn't bother to resist the temptation. He slid down her body and pressed kisses to her soft stomach before teasing where the hoop rested. Her breath caught and her fingers curled into the material of his shirt. He impatiently shrugged it off and ran his hands slowly over her sides.

She quivered again as his wandering hands sent fire licking right to her core. She wanted more: more of his touch and to touch him more. She started to say so, but his lips closed over the point of one breast and the lash of pleasure was so shocking she couldn't stop a soft cry.

She tasted like fresh river water, pure and clean. He felt ravenous for her taste and could barely keep his hands gentle as they ran over her without stopping. He caressed her breast with lips and gentle teeth and then lavished the same attention on its twin.

She began to shake in his arms like a plucked string and her breath was only a soft pant as he slid his hand slowly down her body, ruffling the soft silver curls shielding her most vulnerable flesh. The scent of her was rich, like wildflowers in full bloom. Trying to soften the shock, his mouth covered hers just as his fingers slipped between her legs.

Her startled gasp was muffled by his mouth and a quiver rippled through her body. He deepened the kiss further until it was almost out of control, and his fingers carefully parted the folds protecting her. A shudder went through his body. She was hot and wet, her desire for him as complete as his for her. "Rayna," he said thickly, burying his lips against her throat and tasting her pulse.

She couldn't answer, caught in a suspension between pleasure and pain, her body demanding something she couldn't recognize let alone name. Desperate, she clutched at him, her head pressing back against the pillows as he slowly slid a finger inside her. "Are you okay?" he murmured huskily, watching her face with rapt attention.

"Yes," she managed to whisper. "Riku, please!" She didn't know what she wanted, but she knew beyond a doubt he would be able to help. She trusted him with her body as completely as she had with her heart.

His thumb shifted, pressed against nerves she had never known were there, and her senses came apart in a blinding rush of light and color. She would have cried out with ecstasy but his mouth was on hers again and he was kissing her deeply.

The waves went on and on until she thought she might faint from the pleasure. It ebbed then, and she gulped air as her body relaxed in his arms. "Riku." It was barely breathed in wonder.

The lazy purr to her voice felt like a physical caress. His eyes raptly memorized her face. He had looked his whole life for her. He had been waiting for her for so long. His other half. The one element he had never been able to truly master. His light.

She felt drowsy and satiated, and dimly flabbergasted at how powerful desire could be. None of her reading had mentioned that. It also hadn't mentioned it wasn't long satisfied. She strangled a gasp as she felt his fingers slowly caressing her. The tension rushed back wildly on a surge of pleasure and she could only manage to say, "What are you doing to me?"

"Did you think that was all?" His mouth rushed over her face hungrily. "There's more. So much more. Let me have you, Rayna. Please. We belong together."

Certainty filled her. "Yes." She returned his kisses eagerly and pressed her body against his. With a hungry sort of pleasure, she ran her hands over his shoulders and chest, learning the feel of his skin. She wanted to taste him, too, to see if he tasted like peppermints everywhere. "Can I . . . can I touch you?" she whispered.

He shuddered. "Later," he promised huskily. "Right now I need you too badly." He gave her another kiss before rolling off the bed to remove the rest of his clothes.

She watched him intently, her color rising as she saw how aroused he was. A shiver of fear rippled through her. She knew the mechanics, knew what was going to happen, but didn't see how it would possibly work. It seemed a little frightening, but this was *Riku*. He would never hurt her. He watched her as well, waiting for her response. If she was afraid, then he would stop and she would never know what it meant to be complete. She wanted him, and she shyly smiled at him in welcome.

He returned to her on a hoarse sound of need that might have been her name, and his weight sank them into the mattress. He buried his hands in her hair and tilted her head up as he kissed her deeply. Her arms wrapped around him, holding him tightly, and a shudder went through his body. "Hold me," he muttered. "Tightly. God, I need you!"

Her breath hitched as his hands slowly drew her legs apart until there was room for him to rest between them. She could feel him, hard and hot, at the entrance of her body, but he didn't move. He just kept kissing her with a desperate sort of hunger that had her passion flaring wildly to life. Helplessly, her hips arched against him as the ache spread.

His control holding by thin threads, he braced his weight on his hands and slowly entered her. Sweat broke out on his skin. She was hot and tight and fit him perfectly. Tears slid under her lashes and he knew he was hurting her, but he couldn't stop. A tortured groan rumbled in his chest as he surged into her fully, burying himself to the hilt.

She gave a startled yelp and clutched at his shoulders. There wasn't really any *pain* as much as a startling sense of being stretched and filled. It was both oddly foreign and yet just as oddly familiar and wonderful. His entire body trembled as he fought to stay still for fear of hurting her. She took a deep breath and savored how it felt. It was beautiful. "I'm okay." She breathed it into his ear as she wound her arms around his neck. "We fit."

His control cracked. Fit? They *belonged* together. "Hold onto me," he urged roughly. "Just hold on and I'll protect you!" He slowly withdrew from her body and then sank in again, his lips seeking hers eagerly. He slowly slid a hand down between them and caressed the bundle of nerves he had found before.

She could only cling onto him desperately as he began to move faster, driving deeper. His knowing fingers added to her pleasure as it churned and surged through her body. It grew hotter and hotter, stronger and stronger, and she couldn't contain a whimper as her desperation began to border pain.

His hands cupped her hips and dragged her against him tighter as he surged into her a final time, and she gave a wild cry as the tension broke and sent her body careening through ecstasy without restraint. His low groan echoed in the air as his own release claimed him, and she held him fiercely, refusing to ever let go.

The silence afterward was soft and welcome as they rested and found their breath again. The apartment no longer seemed cold, but a chill finally touched his sweat dampened body and he knew she would feel it even more acutely with her smaller size. He thought she had fallen asleep—which was adorable as hell—but she tightened her hold when he tried to ease away from her. "No," she mumbled into his shoulder. "I don't care if everyone does it."

He wondered where her mind had gone this time. "I'm not leaving," he reassured her, and he couldn't keep the note of possession out of his voice. She was his completely. He had never wanted any woman like that, and he had never been wanted the way she wanted him. Even then, his pulse barely normal, he wanted her all over again. "Everyone?" he thought to ask.

"I read somewhere," she nuzzled her nose against his shoulder, "men usually leave after."

He thought for a moment to find a suitable way to explain. Slowly, he finally said, "There are different levels of desire. When it's just a superficial feeling, once the 'itch is scratched' it goes away and, yes, the person visiting usually leaves. Men are the stereotype, but it's not gender specific. On the other hand, when the desire is deep and real, when you can't breathe for wanting someone," his voice deepened without his control, "when you're consumed with so much emotion it overwhelms you . . . that's a feeling that doesn't leave. And if it's there, the owners of it don't want to part."

"Oh." She tilted her head back to look up at him, picking out the details of his face in the lamp lit room. "Is that what the true meaning of a lover is? Are we lovers?"

"A lover," he ran a hand through her hair, "is one who loves. So, yes, we are lovers. And not even wild horses are dragging me from this bed."

She hid a smile. "It's too small for you." She wiggled her feet against his leg, well aware his feet were dangling. "We could make a bed on the floor," she suggested. She lowered her gaze. "That is, if you want to spend the entire night."

"I want to," he said with regret, "but my clean clothes are at home. I do need to leave early enough for a shower and such." He studied her face intently and picked out the features with a feeling akin to awe. He had a feeling that he would die without her. "Would you move in with me?" he asked suddenly.

Her eyes widened with surprise. "What?" She clung to his shoulders tightly as he got off the bed and swung her up into his arms. "Move in . . . with you? But why?" She sat on the edge of the beanbag as he pulled blankets and pillows down to the floor to make them a soft nest.

When it was complete, he lifted her into his arms again and settled her gently in the bed he had made. He joined her quickly, rolled them in the blankets, and then settled back with her sprawled over the top of him. She adjusted herself a bit, clearly unused to using a person as a pillow, but shortly snuggled closer. She fit perfectly in his arms as if she had always belonged there. "I want," he told her softly, "to have you with me always. I want to be able to wake in the morning and see your face. And," he added with warm amusement, "my bed is bigger."

She giggled at that and then sobered. "I'd like to live with you," she admitted, "but my father might object. I know I'm not under his guardianship, but I don't want to hurt him."

He smiled internally. Lucas would never object to the safety and happiness of his daughter. "Well, I'll meet him, and then ask you again. I won't let you get away from me now, Rayna."

"Okay." She let out a little sigh and cuddled against him. The pendant he still wore pinched her skin, and she wiggled a little until she could grab the disc and lift it. "Where did you get it?"

"It was made for me when I was born." Impulsively, he slipped the chain off and slid it over her head. "Here. I want you to have it." A deep sense of delight filled him as she sat up slightly and the pendant fell to rest against the top of her stomach. A tempting image filled his mind of her swollen with his child, and his breath caught. It could have already happened. Ah hell. That went onto the list of things he would need to talk to her about if she hadn't already Wiki'ed it. "Rayna . . ."

She inexplicably smiled at him, almost as if she could read his mind. "Would you believe that the one thing that never unnerved me about waking as an adult was the, uhm, *interesting* thing that happens every month?"

He began to smile as well. "I had half expected that to be the thing that unnerved you *most.*"

She shook her head. "I got lucky. I started one before I was released from the hospital. One of the nurses sat me down and told me everything. I had already picked up some of it from my 'birds and the bees' tape. It came up again recently while I was looking up desire and sex." A hint of pink touched her cheeks. "I can count much better than I can read, and I'm regular. We're safe."

"It's not foolproof," he tenderly told her.

"It's not?"

"Nature is a very fickle thing, love." He skimmed a knuckle over her belly. "I wouldn't mind it if we weren't safe."

She thought of being a mother, and while it deeply appealed, she was practical enough to admit, "I don't know anything about babies." She smiled shyly. "I wouldn't mind learning, though. If you were there."

"I'm not going *anywhere.*" He started to draw her toward him, his lips seeking hers, when he caught trace of a familiar scent.

Fire.

He jerked her down against him just as the window shattered and a gas canister already ablaze was hurled inside. "Shit!" He leapt up and jerked on his jeans. She scrambled up after him, and he yanked his shirt on over her head. He scooped her up into his arms and raced for the door.

The thick wood burst into wild flames as someone outside set it on fire as well. It took only seconds to choke them both on the smoke. Fury lined his face and a low snarl emerged from his throat. Flames licked through his hair as he held Rayna with one arm. He lifted his other hand and aimed at the flames. "Open!" he barked.

The flames obeyed the command and pulled back from the door. One hard kick opened it, and he carried her out into the night amid the sounds of people screaming and sirens blaring as fire trucks arrived.

There was enough of a fire break between apartments to keep the flames from spreading, and people flooded the area as they banded together to control the blaze until firemen arrived. Eric carried Rayna away from the crowd and leaned against the hood of his car as he held her fiercely in his arms. His heart thudded in his chest with terror. If he hadn't been there . . . "Are you okay?" he asked her.

She was shaking so hard that her teeth rattled. "Yes. Th-they tried t-to kill us." She burrowed against him on a low sound of fear. "When will it stop?! What did I ever do?!"

He heard the sound of a familiar motorcycle and looked up to see Rhianna arriving. The fact that she wore street clothes and no makeup told him that she had been yanked from a sound sleep—she never went out without her 'armor'. Her face was white as she looked for him. When she spotted him, he gave a slight nod, and she visibly blew out a breath. She immediately turned and began snapping out orders that everyone leapt to obey.

Rhianna would handle everything, so Eric put Rayna into the car and drove to the inn a block away. It was *very* well defended, and only a fool would try to touch her there. When they arrived, he wasn't at all surprised to see a very pregnant woman with black hair standing on the front steps. "Hello, Audra," he said as he got out of the car.

"What the hell is going on?" Audra Shaughnessy demanded. Her eyes fell on Rayna, and a brow slowly lifted as she recognized her and the possession in Eric's touch. Her nose flared softly as she caught the combining of their scents. "Well," was all she said.

Rayna was oblivious to the byplay. She could only stare at Audra with something akin to awe. She felt positively tiny next to the tall woman, and there was a predatory sensation to Audra that was oddly comforting. She was a protector. Rayna was certain.

They all heard a loud explosion and turned sharply to see Rayna's apartment going up in a mushroom cloud. Audra cursed softly in another language and blocked the doorway with her body as a little boy holding a wiggling wolf cub in his arms approached the door. "Go inside," she said quietly, steel in her tone. "Find your father and uncle. Have your mother prepare a room for our guest."

The little boy ran to do her bidding, shouting for his parents, but Rayna didn't hear him. Her eyes were fixed on the blazing building. The explosion sounded over and over in her ears until she was hearing screams as well, echoes of the present and the past overlapping and blurring.

It wasn't just her immediate past. It was a further past. One her mind could not comprehend. Something slimy and evil slithering toward her, rising over her with brutal menace. It wanted her dead. It had approached her with a waver to its steps, as if it was dizzy or drunk.

Before her mind could try to process the ancient memory, other memories intruded. The car accident. The people who had been watching the traffic. The person who had staggered in front of the car as if dizzy or drunk. *It was the same people*!

A choked scream emerged from her throat, and she clamped her hands over her ears. Voices. She could hear so many voices. Physical voices of those going past overlapped with their voices in her mind. Their voices said it was tragedy. Their minds said they were grateful it wasn't them.

She only distantly became aware of Eric shouting her name. Her eyes lifted to his but she couldn't quite focus on him. She couldn't hear the voice of his mind. The pain in his voice was truth. "The accident . . ." Unable to withstand any more, her eyes closed and she slumped against him.

"Rayna!" He pressed his hand against the pendant she wore and used it to connect to her mind. It was alive and wild, nearly reading as static with its fury. Even Eric, as powerful as he was, had to fight to find out what was happening. He had to peel away layers and layers until he finally saw, at last, what it was that she could do.

For all intents and purposes, she had become a human lie detector. She could hear the truth amid myriads of lies. Her powers of Truth were awakening too soon. Her birthday wasn't until Saturday. Two days. She shouldn't have awakened. He painfully buried his face in her hair. She was always waking too soon, pushing past safety. And when she woke, no matter what he said, she would know the truth of him.

Audra studied him intently. "I've known you for over a century," she said mildly. "I've never seen you like this."

"I hadn't found Rayna." He lifted Rayna fully into his arms as he turned to look at his friend. "Audra, I must ask for your help. Please guard her."

"Bring her inside, Riku," Madelyne Shaughnessy said softly from behind her sister-in-law. "She'll be safe here." She smiled at Audra. "You go rest."

"Damned overprotective den mothers!" Audra stalked off with a mutter, her stride still lengthy and graceful despite the eight-month curve of her stomach. "Kalin," she ordered the wolf pup, "stop chewing on your cousin's ankle." Content her son would obey, she went into the guest room she and her husband were using.

Eric smiled and followed Madelyne as she headed toward another room. "I appreciate this, Maddie."

She gave him a teasing smile. "It's just a little odd to think I might have a sort of stepmother who is younger than me." He had played as big a role in raising her as Rhianna had; she had always seen them equally as her adopted parents. Her heart ached a little to see the emotion on his face as he gently placed Rayna on the bed, but it was a good ache.

"Protect her," he said in a quiet voice as he walked to the door. His eyes moved to the tall man standing behind Madelyne, his hand resting possessively on her hip. "Kienan, I'm trusting you as well."

"She'll be safe," Kienan Shaughnessy assured him firmly. He grinned slightly. "We get to go to the wedding, right?"

"Hush," his wife scolded.

Knowing Rayna was in good hands, Eric headed for the door with long and determined strides. He was going to join Rhianna in bashing heads together and then he was going to go home and plan for the next day. It was going to be a bitch. His only salvation lay in Rayna's truth ability allowing her to see why he had deceived her. He could not lose her now.

CHAPTER SIX

When Rayna awoke, it was to the early morning light streaming in through gauzy curtains. She sat up with a jerk and looked around wildly, terrified because she didn't know where she was or how she had gotten there. How much time had passed?!

The door opened and a rather plain looking young woman peered around the edge at her. The first thing out of her mouth was, "It's the morning after the fire."

Rayna's shoulders relaxed and she slumped over. "Thank you," she whispered. A thought made her look up and glance around. "Where am I? And where's Riku?"

Madelyne searched her eyes but saw no understanding for her lover's true identity. Mentally wincing, she walked into the room. This was not going to be easy for Rayna *or* for Eric. "You're at the Gentle Brook Inn, and Riku said he would see you at work if you want, but he would prefer you stay here and rest."

"Oh." She picked at the top of the blanket, a soft blush warming her cheeks as she remembered the events prior to the fire. "He's . . . we're . . ."

"I know." Madelyne smiled as she opened the window to let in the fresh air. "He loves you very much." She walked over and sat on the edge of the bed. "My name is Madelyne Shaughnessy. I run the inn."

"Oh. Of course." She had heard all about the Shaughnessys. Mel Shaughnessy was one of two owners and operators of the Shaughnessy-Tavoularis Conglomeration and had a wonderful reputation as a brilliant CEO and generally decent guy. His wife was a computer sciences teacher at a college. Madelyne would have to be his sister-in-law, married to Kienan, the youngest Shaughnessy male. "It's nice to meet you." She smiled. "My name is Rayna Carmichael."

"It's nice to meet you too, Rayna." Madelyne glanced at the door as it opened and her sister-in-law stepped into the doorway. "Mel better have done that shopping," she scolded as she saw the bag Audra held.

Audra snorted. "Brian's shop is barely down the street. Don't be silly." She walked over and set the bag down before easing herself carefully onto the side of the bed. "So." She studied Rayna. "The princess is awake."

Rayna ducked down slightly and pulled the blanket over herself more tightly. She felt positively outclassed between the calming Madelyne and the brilliantly stunning Audra. "Yes. I . . . I woke a year ago."

Audra's brows shot up and then lowered quickly. "I see. Excuse me, I have a call to make." She got to her feet and walked out of the room.

"Did I . . . did I offend her?" Rayna asked warily.

"No, Audra's always like that." Madelyne snagged the bag with a smile. "Here, she went and got you some clothes."

"Oh. Thank you. I'll pay you back."

"Sure, we can figure that out later." *She doesn't need to worry about it.*

Rayna blinked as she heard Madelyne's voice on top of itself. There was no delay between them yet somehow she could hear both phrases clearly and distinctly. Slowly she said, "You don't want me to repay you." When Madelyne lifted a brow, she rubbed her forehead. "I . . . I can hear the truth over a lie. I remember. My mother told me that once."

"That is not an easy power. Have a shower," Madelyne offered gently. "Get dressed and come have some breakfast." She got to her feet with a smile. "If you insist on going to work, Kienan said he'd give you a ride."

"Oh. Thank you." Rayna waited until she had left the room before opening the bag and looking inside. Underwear, bra, comfortable cotton pants, and a cute sleeveless shirt with cherries all over it. Audra knew how to shop. There were even shoes in the bag.

She took a shower first to wash away the smoke and grime. She also blushed vividly as she washed away the evidence of making love with Riku. If she hadn't done so much reading, she might have been alarmed by the mess. Instead, it just made a warm glow bloom inside her. She belonged to someone, and he to her. It was wonderful.

The clothes felt strangely soothing to wear and helped settle her nerves more. But, then, she knew about the maker's gifts. Just another 3rd District miracle worker. She stepped out into the hall and looked around. A little boy with brown hair already going gray shot past being chased by a little black wolf cub. She saw a man with dark golden brown hair grinning at the sight as well and asked, "His pet?"

"His cousin." Mel Shaughnessy straightened and offered a hand. "My son no less. I'm Mel. You must be Rayna."

"Yes." As she took his hand, she suddenly felt the same predatory sensation from him as she had felt from Audra. It was a sensation that made her feel safe and protected. She spotted an amber rim around his pupils, and it dawned on her at last that Mel and Audra were werewolves. No wonder they felt so safe to be around! "Nice to meet you, Mr. Shaughnessy."

"Mel." He smiled. "Too many Shaughnessys around here. You'll get confused." He led the way toward the kitchen and said over his shoulder, "Kalin, leave your cousin alone." He smiled wryly at Rayna. "He's learning to hunt."

"Oh." Bemused, she went into the kitchen ahead of him and found Audra in a lively argument with another man who bore a striking resemblance to Mel. She could only assume she was looking at Kienan Shaughnessy. "Good morning," she said hesitantly.

"Good morning!" Kienan gave Audra a firm glare. "Sit down, damn it." Assuming she would obey, which she did with a curse, he walked over to smile at Rayna. "Well, you're Rayna. Maddie was right; you are cute."

"Stop embarrassing her!" Madelyne nudged her husband aside and escorted Rayna to a chair. "It could be worse," she consoled her. "Aenya and her husband are off on a trip to England, and Taegan is teaching today while Kally walks a boardroom." She thought about that. "Stalks. She stalks a boardroom, and with a three-year-old on her hip."

Rayna watched them without shame. It was an amazing whirl of life and color. A complete family unit. A little black haired toddler tried to climb onto her lap and she picked him up, recognizing Mel's eyes and assuming he was the wolf child. She *really* wanted a child too. Hers and Riku's. Maybe they would be lucky and Nature would be in a fickle mood.

She was a few minutes late to work and had to brace herself as she walked in the front door. Luckily for her, the first person she saw was Remy Germaine. Her friend eyed her intently and then nodded decisively. "You look good," she said.

"Despite the incident, I feel good," Rayna admitted. She waved Remy closer after a quick look around. When the taller woman leaned down, she whispered, "I have a lover."

Remy grinned. "Well, duh, hon. You're *glowing*. I'm insanely jealous," she added woefully. "My ex-husband never made me glow."

"That's why he was your ex." Rayna sat down at her computer. "How's Nicole?"

"Madly missing you. She wants me to bring her here to see you." Remy leaned on the counter. She loved Rayna as much as she loved her sisters and daughter. She was glad that Riku had come along to bring such joy to her. She deserved the best.

Several women came hurrying over. Remy bristled distinctly, something dangerous flickering in her eyes. The other women paid her no heed as they clustered around Rayna. "Are you okay?" one asked with genuine concern. "Everyone's heard about the fire."

"I'm fine," Rayna told her.

"Well, it's a good thing you weren't hurt!" another female said. *She should have been scarred! Then she wouldn't so beautiful anymore!*

Rayna booted her computer without looking up. "I don't need your false pity. Be quiet or go away."

Remy's brows lifted and she nearly cheered. The other women were more taken aback. "Well!" one said. Snidely she added, "I see the gardener put steel in your spine. You're not better than us now, honey. You're just another woman who spread her legs." *Lucky bitch.*

Rayna smiled. "Jealousy isn't flattering to you. And besides, I can have a fling if I want. I'm an adult. And it's . . ." Her voice stopped. Literally stopped dead, her vocal cords freezing. Startled, she pressed a hand to her throat. She had tried to say it was just casual, but the words wouldn't come out. Because it was a lie?

She tried a second time, but again the words wouldn't come out. What then, she wondered. If it wasn't a fling, wasn't an affair, what was it? The frustration welled and she blurted, "I'm in love with him!"

The other women could think of nothing to say. Silent, they all walked away. Remy coughed and leaned on the counter again. She studied the shocked expression on Rayna's face. "Didn't notice, did we?" she asked gently. "Hell, kid. I noticed it the first day."

"I'm in love," Rayna whispered. Blinding joy rose inside her and she leapt to her feet. "I have to tell him! Is he outside?" She hurried to the window.

"Nuh-uh. Haven't seen him this morning. He might be dealing with paperwork related to the fire. He's the type who would want you protected." Remy ruffled her hair. "You bring him over for dinner, okay? If Nicole has him wrapped around her finger within five minutes, he's worth keeping."

Before she could answer, Mr. Oppenheim rushed into the area. "Everyone!" he barked. "Look sharp and get everything in order! Enforcers is on their way over! Eric Mason himself is coming down to discuss a reorganization of the company as well as to discuss company policy!" He turned and leveled a finger at Rayna. "Your complaints did this! I want you out of sight when he arrives!"

The entire office went into a flurry of panic, especially when they saw that the limo had already arrived outside. Remy rushed to prepare a conference room. A crowd gathered, and Rayna was rudely shoved to the back. As short as she was, she couldn't see a thing, even when the door opened. There came a loud gasp and a few women gave strangled shrieks. Rayna, frustrated, jumped up a little in an effort to see.

Someone planted their elbow sharply in her side and sent her tumbling. "Ow!" She landed with a thump on the floor and rubbed her side. It belatedly dawned on her that a stark silence had fallen and she turned her head to discover that the crowd had parted. There was a man in a suit standing in front of her.

She looked up and all the color drained from her face. Spots swam before her eyes as she stared at Eric's face, certain it was all some big mistake. It couldn't be possible. Riku couldn't be Eric Mason, he couldn't! He was a gardener! "R-riku?" she whispered.

"Riku is a nickname my friends gave me," Eric told her calmly, fighting the violent urge to pull her into his arms and promise it would be alright. She looked lost and adrift, and he felt her pain as if it was his own. "My name is Eric Mason. I believe I'm your boss."

There was an uncomfortable silence, and Oppenheim stepped forward with a false smile. "Mr. Mason, shall we go into the conference room? I'll have a secretary join us. Let's see . . ." He looked over the crowd.

"Bring Rayna." Eric didn't bother to look to see if his order was followed. He started walking down the hall with a stride that made light bounce off his well-tailored suit and broad shoulders. "She'll do a fine job."

Rayna scrambled to her feet to escape, but Oppenheim ushered her down the hall as well. Terrified, in a panic, she instinctively turned her abilities off, too afraid to hear what Eric had to say. The action was pure self-preservation and she had no idea she had done it. She simply couldn't bear to hear whatever his heart might have to say.

The conference room was used for larger meetings but Eric walked in as if he owned it—in fact, he technically did. He set his briefcase on the table before the seat at the head and gestured for Oppenheim and Rayna to also sit. She did so, warily, and well down the table from him. It broke his heart. "Let's get started," he suggested, and sat down.

"Mr. Mason," Oppenheim began, "I don't understand how this meeting is called for."

"Silence." Eric cut across his words with a steely look. "I've been watching the company for days now, posing as a gardener, and I am highly disappointed with what I have seen here. Rhianna Taber and I have decided it's time for changes. Long overdue changes."

He began to remove documents from his briefcase. "I have compiled a list of names and positions. You can see for yourself what changes I intend to make. Recognition for hard work is always to be encouraged, and you are personally aware of this. You wouldn't be a manager at all without our recognition program. This company has fallen to the wolves." Mentally, he sent an apology to Mel and Audra. He would work with wolves like them any day. "Customer service suffers and the manner of the department is disgusting.

"We've pulled all of your past emails. Harassment, Mr. Oppenheim, is not an amusing matter. You had an employee who was being threatened, emotionally and mentally abused, and you did nothing to stop it. You told her she would be suspended for complaining. Clients have continually reported complaints of snobbishness and rudeness." He drummed his fingers lightly on the table. "I experienced the derogatory nature firsthand. If my orders are not met, I will completely erase the company of the dead weight and begin anew."

Oppenheim was turning an interesting shade of red and green like a Christmas tree. Red with shame, and green with fear. Rayna couldn't help but enjoy it. Served him right, the bully. At least what Eric was doing was for the good of the hard workers. He had believed everything she told him. It was a small comfort.

Oppenheim swallowed hard and looked over the organization chart in front of him. Seeing Remy Germaine's name at the top in what was currently his position was sickening. Other obvious changes stood out, but one in particular was distinctly glaring. "I, uh, don't see Rayna Carmichael's name on this chart."

Rayna's head jerked around, and Eric smiled coolly. "Yes, because she's being fired." Her color drained and he once more fought the urge to go to her. As soon as this was done, he was going to take her away and make up for all of it! "Rhianna and I have discussed things and we wish her to be hired on at Enforcers HQ. She's too good a worker to be wasted here. As you're aware," he added in a hard tone. "The false appraisals make that clear. Were you afraid to have her possibly promoted over you? As it stands, we have to fire her here, and hire her on new at Enforcers because of this."

Rayna stared at Oppenheim in shock, and he refused to meet her eyes. "She, well . . . she's . . ." Lacking a defense, he went on the offense. "How do I know you're not doing this because you're screwing her?" he asked bluntly. "Your actions, Mr. Mason, speak of impropriety and favoritism!"

Eric, trusting Rayna's ability to hear the truth, lied, "It was always purely business for me. Why would I want her for a wife?"

Rayna recoiled as if struck. Nausea bubbled up and she shot to her feet. "Excuse me," she whispered thinly, and ran out of the office. She wanted to cry and to scream, to rage against fate. How *could* he?! She had *trusted* him!

"Serves you right," one woman laughed as she saw Rayna. "Got yours, didn't you?"

The fury welled up and Rayna turned on her without warning. "Yes I did! I'm sure it amuses you to no end! You're all nothing but narrow-minded bitches who can't accept their own faults when they're flung into your faces! If you don't like facing your shortcomings, then never look into a mirror again! Until you speak the honest truth to yourself, mirrors will crack when you gaze upon them!"

The women recoiled away from her in fear as they sensed the power in her. She didn't notice. She gathered her bag and bolted from the building. "I quit!" she shouted over her shoulder. "Tell Mr. Mason he no longer has to fire me!"

When she got outside, she saw a familiar car at the curb in front of the limo. Her uncle was just getting out. "Uncle Larry?" On a little hitch of breath, she ran toward him and leapt into his arms. "Take me with you!" she pleaded. "I need to get away!"

Larry Carmichael caught her in surprise and patted her back. "Of course!" He ushered her into the car. "I caught wind of what happened," he explained. "It frightened me, so I came to make sure you were all right. I'll take you home and it'll be fine."

Eric sensed her leave the grounds only when he felt the sudden sharp stretching of the lines of power between his soul and the pendant she wore. "Shit!" He leapt to his feet. Her ability must have turned off, he realized in terror. She wouldn't have left without him otherwise. Dear god, how he must have hurt her! "Oppenheim," he snapped, "get started on these plans! I have to go find Rayna!"

Leaving Oppenheim gaping, he tore down the hall and came to a sharp stop in the lobby as he saw the women staring horrified at a broken mirror. "What the hell?" He went around them and toward the door. "Rayna!" he shouted. "Rayna!!"

Remy walked up and grabbed his arm. Her green eyes were icy. "Come with me." She stalked outside and dragged him with her. Once out the doors, she rounded on him. "You *idiot*!" she shouted. "Do you have any idea what you just did?!"

He felt the warning sensation of her power and knew she was truly pissed. He also knew who she was; he knew everyone in the District. "Rayna can hear the truth over lies," he told her swiftly. "She turned off her ability and heard me tell a lie that hurt her. You have to tell me where she is!"

Her eyes missed nothing. The suffering and fear on his face was real. "Her uncle picked her up," she said curtly. "He lives in Manhattan."

"How would he . . ." The color drained from his face. "What kind of car does he drive?"

"A blue Taurus."

The same kind of car that had almost hit them. A lump of ice settled in his stomach. Had Rayna walked right into a den of snakes, certain she was safe? "I have to find her," he shouted over his shoulder as he ran down the sidewalk. If anything happened to her, he would destroy everything in his path!

As the car headed down the freeway, Rayna closed her eyes and curled up as small as she could. "Thanks," she whispered.

"Any time. What happened, anyway?" Larry demanded.

"Someone's trying to kill me, and I took a lover, but he only did it to find out about the company." She swiped at her eyes. "I just want to curl up and die. My father will have a heart attack if you tell him."

"Ever since he almost lost the company," he said quietly, "it's been hard on him emotionally, especially with your coma and all. I won't tell him about all this, promise."

"Thank you." When they got to the large house, she followed her uncle inside and sent a little wave toward her aunt who was cooking in the kitchen. "I'll just stay a few days," she promised. "Long enough to find a new apartment."

"That's fine, you know we're glad to have you." Yvonne leaned in from the kitchen. "Have some lunch and go take a nap. It'll be better afterward, honey."

"Okay." She didn't feel much like eating, but she worked her way through a bowl of chicken soup, not wanting her aunt or uncle to worry. To her surprise, she began to feel sleepy shortly thereafter. "I guess I am tired," she admitted over a yawn. "It was an eventful night." Her cheeks flushed faintly as she remember how eventful.

"Go upstairs and rest then," her uncle soothed. "We'll wake you for dinner."

"Okay." She got to her feet and headed upstairs to the guestroom, rubbing her eyes sleepily. She didn't know if she would sleep well or not, but she was certainly tired. With a little sigh, she kicked her shoes off and curled up on top of the bed. Maybe just a little nap would help make everything better.

Hours passed. She didn't know what time it was, but she became aware of someone shouting her name in her mind, over and over, demanding she wake up. She forced her way up through the layers of sleep, dimly terrified at how hard it was to wake herself up. She had to literally force her eyes open, and her entire body felt like lead. When she did manage to open her eyes, it was to find her uncle standing over her with a knife in his hand.

Shock reverberated through her soul, and her mind instinctively gave a wild mental cry, shouting Eric's name as she saw the muscles in her uncle's arm tensing. *Riku! Please!* Her mind screamed his name over and over again, reaching for him blindly the way he had reached for her.

The window shattered in a blinding rush of snow and wind. The blizzard swept into the room, slammed into Larry's chest, and flung him violently into the other wall. Eric swung in the window and landed like a large cat on the ground, the black cloak he wore flaring around his body in the wind. Flames licked down along the white locks in his hair and lightning crackled around his left hand. "Stay away from my woman!" he snarled gutturally.

Rayna fought for control of her body. She had no strength and her muscles refused to obey. There was an odd taste in her mouth, mingling with the remnants of the taste of the soup. Her innocent mind didn't want to accept that she might have been drugged, but she was far too smart to truly discount it.

Her eyes fixed on Eric as he straightened and stood in the center of the blizzard. He commanded it as skillfully as he had commanded the meeting. But, here, he was beautiful. "Riku," she managed to whisper.

"Rayna, for god's sake, wake up!" He didn't take his eyes off of Larry. "You turned your abilities off, sweetheart! If you hadn't, you would have known!" He took a ragged breath. "Your uncle has been trying to kill you!"

"No!" Larry shouted. "It was all *his* doing! He forced me to do it! He was using me like he used you! I'm family, Rayna! Listen to me!"

"Rayna." Eric didn't look at her but his mouth was dry with terror. "Please."

She got her feet under herself and staggered forward a step. She felt betrayed and used by everyone, but she knew something with bone deep certainty. She still trusted Eric. She wore his pendant. He had called her his woman. She trusted him more than her uncle! "Riku!" She flung herself at him with her remaining strength, and his arms closed around her, fiercely.

A shudder went through his body as he held her tighter. His mind sought hers, pinpointed the wall she had made, and erased it. She couldn't exist with that wall in her mind, not and survive. It was nearly midnight, and when it was, it would be Saturday. It would be her birthday. She would be twenty-one. She shuddered in his grip, her eyes opening wide, the color turning white. Her power rose wildly as the seconds ticked mercilessly toward midnight.

Larry lunged forward and closed his hands around her wrist. "Rayna!" he pleaded urgently. "Please listen to me!"

A clock began to toll loudly somewhere, and her powers unlocked with a vengeance. It didn't matter whether she heard the lie or touched someone who lied. She would hear the truth. She *was* Truth. Larry's truth poured into her through his hands just before Eric flung him away with a lightning bolt to the chest.

"The truth," she whispered softly, her voice echoing eerily, "will set you free."

The command was the deepest and greatest of her abilities. Larry screamed in terror and horror as his body mutated into a shape echoing his deepest inner soul. Eric held Rayna closer and his stomach churned as Larry melted into the shape of a deadly, venomous, cobra.

The cobra lunged forward, and Eric pushed Rayna one way as he went the other. Fire swirled down his arm and flung the cobra away violently. It began to slither off, realizing it was outmatched, and he started to go after it. "Come back, you bastard!"

Rayna began to sway on her feet and her vision grayed at the edges as her mind rushed into overdrive and then simply shut down. "Riku, I love you," she whispered, and tumbled to the floor in a curtain of silver hair.

"Rayna!" Terrified, he abandoned the cobra and lifted her into his arms. Was this from the drug . . . or also a result of the incomplete contract?

Rhianna found Eric sitting in the lobby of the Enforcers' hospital and staring blindly at the floor. She softly eased onto the seat beside him and wrapped her arms around his shoulders tightly. After a few moments, he asked in a strained voice, "Well? The doctors got the drug flushed of her system, but she won't wake. Tell me, damn it!"

She closed her eyes for a moment and then sighed and released him. "She doesn't want to wake up," she admitted quietly.

His head jerked toward her. "What?"

"She's scared." She raked a hand through her tangled hair. It was wild from her race to the hospital. Her surrogate brother had given her too many scares these last few days. "When I tried to link to her, all I got was wild static, like the kind that stems from fear."

"Do you think the contract has anything to do with this?"

She was silent for long moments. "No," she finally said. "Today's her twenty-first birthday."

He began to curse softly under his breath. Pressing his face into his hands, he whispered, "She turned her ability off. She thought I was telling the truth when I said I was involved with her for business reasons."

She gently rubbed a hand over his back. There was nothing she could do for him that she had not already done. "Talk to her," she suggested softly. "Tell her everything. Tell her the full truth. You have to wake her, Eric, like you did before."

"I don't know how I did!"

"Then kiss her goodbye," she said simply. "I'm sorry, Riku." She pressed her lips to his cheek, got to her feet, and walked out of the lobby.

He stayed there for several minutes before he finally got to his feet and walked slowly down the halls toward the room where Rayna was resting. The guard outside stepped to the side to let him in and shut the door softly behind him.

Rayna was lying as she had for so long, motionless and still in a hospital bed. Machines beeped softly, reading her vital signs as normal. She almost looked as if she was merely taking a nap.

He drew the visitor chair closer to the bed and sat down. He picked up her hand and pressed it to his cheek. His eyes closed as he prayed in a way he had never prayed before. "Hey," he said softly. "I'm so sorry, Rayna. I never meant to hurt you. I was so certain that you would hear the truth, so I lied. I shouldn't have done it, I know. I hurt you and put you into danger. It took all my power to find you again."

He was silent for long moments. She deserved the full truth. "My name is Eric Mason but my birth name was Erikulen. That's where my nickname of Riku came from. I'm co-owner of Enforcers. I have been since the year 333BC when I and Rhianna helped build 3rd District and established Enforcers to protect it.

"I'm an elemental master. I was born to a family of what you would call warlocks who specialized in elements. I got a full dose of them all, and I had them mastered by the time I was your age. The pendant I gave you was made as a symbol of my power. It connects us, you know. I'm surprised it didn't tell you about me.

"Before 3rd District was built, there was nowhere for people like Rhianna and I and our families to go for safety. We lived as nomads, wandering the East Coast. At that time, the East Coast was a large network of united indigenous people. The people were the ancestors of the Native Americans that met English settlers.

"In the year 334BC, I was training to be a warrior with another tribe in another village. Rhianna showed up one day, in a terror, and demanded I return to our village. When we got there it was a sea of fire and blood." He closed his eyes. "We couldn't save anyone. All we could do was flee to the north, gathering as many people of power as we could, bringing them away from those who hated them.

"Rhianna and I knew there needed to be a safe haven for our kind, no matter what form they took. We built 3rd District as our own tribe and formed Enforcers. As the area grew, so did Enforcers. When each new form of government came along, they saw we didn't care if they were in charge, so long as they gave us protection if we needed it. Once they knew that, they were content to let us be. By the 1700s, Enforcers was a power to rival the king overseas. He worried until he saw that we had no care for anything but protecting 3rd District. His support continued. When the country was revolutionized, the congress and new president offered their support. It's stayed ever since.

"Over the years, 3rd District became a legend. We let it, kept cultivating it, making sure that just enough mystery remained to keep the wrong people away. Nowadays, people can accept, fairly easily, our existence as nothing but conjecture and rumor."

He stopped talking again. He closed his eyes for a moment and rubbed his cheek against her hand. It was so cold. "I'm over two thousand years old," he murmured. "People have come and gone, in my life, for centuries. I've made friends and I've made enemies. I've never been in love . . . until you.

"When your father approached the Enforcers, saying you and your sister had been marked for death, and he didn't know why, Rhianna and I were outraged. We agreed on a contract for both of you. For you, instead of dying in an accident, you would be put into a coma until your twenty-first birthday.

"The accident occurred, and I joined the search. I found you under an oak tree." He gave a soft laugh. "You were so tiny! You're still nothing but a little thing, but back then even more so. And beautiful even then. It killed me to think that something like this had to happen to any child, but most especially to you.

"I couldn't stay away. Every weekend, every year, I visited you, just to talk like this. I talked about the weather and things that were happening. I talked about you, described how your face and body were maturing. I kept hoping my voice was reaching you, so you weren't alone. I guess it was, because you woke too early."

Pain filled his eyes. "I'm sorry, Rayna. I never meant to put you in so much danger. If you'd slept until today, none of this would have happened. But because you were awake, we knew we needed to protect you. We made sure you had a job, and place to live, when you left home.

"We realized a week ago just how terrible things were at Budgets. Rhianna decided to go in and check things out and protect you. I volunteered to go in her place. I told her it was because she was too recognizable, but that wasn't the truth, though I didn't know it until later. The truth, Rayna, is that I've loved you in some way or another since I met you.

"I denied it, hid it, and fought it. But I loved you. How could I not? You're the other half of me. For all my mastery of the elements, light always eluded me. You brought the light with you. Until I met you, I never knew what it meant to be complete. Without you, there's nothing but loneliness. You once said you needed me. I need you, too, more than anything else."

He got to his feet and looked down at her peaceful face. He lifted his hand and gently cupped her cheek to skim his thumb over her cheekbone. "I know how scary it is out here. Your powers must terrify you. If," his voice broke, "if you want to stay asleep, then I won't stop you. If you're happier where you are, then stay there. I'll come and visit you, talk to you, and wait until you're ready to come back to me. I'll be waiting." He leaned down and touched her lips lightly with his, and the tears he couldn't stop slid down his cheeks to land on her skin. "I love you," he whispered. Before his control crumpled entirely, he straightened and turned to go to the door.

"Riku?"

He froze with shock. His heart began to pound, and he looked down to find her eyes opening. Shaking, he eased onto the bed beside her. "Rayna?" he managed to ask.

"I heard you," she whispered. "It was you all those years. You brought me back."

His trembling hands lifted and framed her face as she sat up in the bed. "I can't live without you," he whispered, and the words not only rang true, but his deepest emotions poured into her through the contact. "I love you," he added softly and drew her closer until their lips met in a tender kiss.

It was the only truth that had ever mattered.

CHAPTER SEVEN

Rhianna was reading a file when Eric walked in through the connecting door. "What are you still doing here?" she asked. "Don't you have a flight to catch?"

"Not just yet." He sat down on the edge of her desk and waited until she looked up. "I thought you'd like to know what Rayna found by hacking through the computers of her father's old company."

She smiled. "That girl is dangerous. Get her pregnant so she stays busy and out of my databases."

He grinned. "I'm working on it, but it won't stop her." He sobered quickly. "It seems Larry Carmichael was not happy his older brother had inherited the company. He laid a trap and baited it so well that his brother couldn't get out. When the dust settled, Larry stepped in and saved the company, and Lucas turned it all over to him, convinced that it had been his fault."

"Then why the contract for death?" she murmured.

"We won't know until we find Mika Carmichael. Is there any sign of her at all? We both know she survived. She had to. I haven't heard of any other young women entering inexplicable comas, let alone waking when Rayna did, so something must have gone wrong somewhere."

She held up Mika's contract. "Something is happening, that's for sure."

He took the contract and lifted a brow as he saw the words 'In Progress' across it. "Well." He dropped the contract back onto the desk. "Keep us informed."

"You bet. Have a good honeymoon and send me photos. I love that old castle."

"You got it." He walked back into his office and shut the door behind him. A smile instantly lit his face as he saw Rayna sitting on the edge of his desk. He immediately crossed to her and drew her into his arms for a kiss. His wife. It still thrilled him.

She melted against him with a little sound of pleasure and smiled as he eased back. "Keep it up and we'll miss the flight. And Rhi might be irked at us again."

"It's not like that couch is uncomfortable. At least, you weren't complaining at the time. And the doors are soundproof." He skimmed a hand through her hair. "We don't know," he said quietly. "We're looking."

"Okay." She trusted him to do whatever he could. She got to her feet with a steadily growing grace. Her eyes had recently been mended through advanced laser surgery, and it had a dramatic impact on her movement. Thoughtfully, she glanced at the closed door. "She's waiting," she murmured. "Do you know who for?"

"No. I've never really known." He slid an arm around her shoulders.

"I hope she finds him." She closed her eyes. "We all deserve a happy ending."

Listening from the other side of the door, Rhianna could only smile. Rayna was perfect for Eric, just as she had always thought. She walked back over to her desk and picked up Rayna's contract in time to see it sign as 'Complete.' She added a few notes and slipped it into the folder on her desk. She slid it into one of her drawers where she then wrote 'Carmichael' across the front.

What Eric didn't know, she thought impishly, wouldn't hurt him.

Status: File Begun

Analysis: A sleeping princess dreams of love, and only a man who loves her can waken her.

Folder Two

GWYN

CHAPTER EIGHT

When the car accident happened, Mika was flung far from the car because she wasn't wearing her seatbelt and harness. She went sailing clear over a gully and to the other side, where she hit with a painful impact. Something in her arm crunched frighteningly as she found herself tumbling head over heels for several feet.

She skidded to a stop and began to cry with fear and pain as she realized her arm wasn't moving right. She called for her mom and her aunt, and her sister too, but no one could hear her over the sirens.

She tried to get up to go find them, but a rustling in the bushes made her freeze with terror. She turned her head and watched as a pack of snakes slithered out of the bushes and steadily advanced toward her. Terrified, she whirled and ran, scrambling as hard as she could with a broken arm.

She broke through some foliage, and found herself in the air as the ground gave way. She dropped and went rolling down the hill before finally coming to a stop against the side of a cabin. The blow knocked her unconscious, and she couldn't see the snakes as they drew closer.

"Hey!" a young man snapped as he yanked the door open. "Who's out there?" When there was no response, he looked around and saw the snakes closing in on the girl. "Give me my gun!" he barked into the house, and his youngest brother scrambled to give it to him. The man quickly shot at the snakes, and they took off in fear.

"What's going on?" The second eldest peered around the door as his older brother rushed over to the figure on the ground. His eyes widened. "Oh holy hell, there's a kid out there!"

"Whaaat?!" There was a veritable stampede as five other brothers came rushing to the door and tripped over one another.

The eldest ignored them as he knelt beside the little girl. He could tell on a single look that her arm was broken, and she was scraped and bleeding from her multiple falls. He gently eased her into his arms and carried her toward the house. "Get me some hot water!" he ordered. He saw the youngest goggling and glared at him. "Joseff!"

"Oh!" Joseff, at nine, was the baby in the family and quick to follow orders because his brothers loved giving them. He got the hot water and towels, and then hovered nearby as he watched his oldest brother removing the girl's clothes to get to the wounds. "Who is she? Is she okay?" In his hovering, he actually began to hover. His feet lifted off the floor entirely.

The second oldest caught him and put him down. "Joseff, calm down. Heul," he addressed the oldest, "is she alive?"

"Yeah." Heul gently began to clean the wounds. "Poor baby must have fallen down the hill."

"How old is she?" The question came from identical eleven-year-old twins.

"No clue. She's so tiny!" It startled Heul. Even Joseff wasn't that little! The faerie princess who had fallen into their house was no bigger than a minute, looking like a five-year-old in size. At least Joseff looked his age at nine. In fact, he was unusual in his family because he was normal sized. Everyone else was very tall.

"Can we keep her?" This time the question came from the thirteen-year-old sitting on the kitchen table.

"She's not a pet!" the fifteen-year-old felt compelled to jump in. "Right, Arian?"

Arian, the second oldest, was busy rummaging in a clothes trunk so his voice was muffled when he said, "She probably has a family."

"She can't go back." Heul's voice was flat with fury.

"Why not?" Arian walked over with a frown, one of Joseff's shirts over his arm. He saw instantly what Heul had and sucked a sharp breath in. "Shit. Shit shit shit. She's 3rd District."

"What's that got to do with anything? We're from there too," Joseff demanded. "And that's my shirt!"

"Look."

Everyone crowded around the couch to get a better look, and the three oldest all understood what they were looking at. The little girl was marked for death. Right over her left hip was the glaring red checkmark that meant someone had contracted for her death. "A Bloody Check on a kid. Someone wants her dead," the thirteen-year-old muttered. "That's way not cool."

"So we protect her!" The fractionally taller of the twins was usually the spokesperson. "We'll make her our sister! But, how old is she? Owen, can you see?"

Owen was the fifteen-year-old. He lifted a hand and gently touched the girl's cheek to seek her mind with his. He received a wild whirl of static . . . then nothing. Startled, he yanked his hand back. "She's really powerful, whatever she is. Her mind locked me out. But I think she's nine or so."

"My age!" Joseff's face lit with delight.

"Let's get her arm set." Heul gently tucked the girl into the shirt Arian handed him. "Someone bring me a slat of wood." The thirteen-year-old had already been at it and was holding out a small plank. "Thanks, Gavin."

"But . . . what if she doesn't want to stay?" Arian leaned on the edge of the couch. "She has a family, I'm sure."

The little girl began to stir, a little whimper coming from her throat as her arm throbbed painfully. Heul murmured softly to her, his heart hurting. It killed him to see a baby so hurt. He lifted her onto his lap and cuddled her, rocking gently as she began to wake up. His brothers climbed around him, gathering closer, wanting her to know she was safe.

"I hurt." She whimpered and clung onto Heul with her good arm. "I hurt!"

"I know, I know. Shh. It's okay, you're safe." He smoothed her tangled white hair back from her face. "Can you tell us your name?"

She opened her mouth but nothing came out. Tears welled up in her eyes. "No. I don't remember."

"What!" The twins almost fell off the couch.

Owen was levelheaded. He leaned further over the couch so she could see him. "That's okay," he told her softly. "If you don't remember, we'll be your family. All of us will be your big brothers."

She sniffled and rubbed her eyes on Heul's shirt. "Really?"

"Yeah!" Joseff grinned at her. "You can be like my twin, okay, 'cause we're the same age and all." He frowned suddenly and looked at Arian. "Where's she going to sleep?"

"We'll build a bunk bed for your room for now," Arian promised. He leaned on his arms on the back of the couch. "I'm Arian Trahern. That's Heul, the eldest. Then there's Owen, Gavin, Tomos, Seisyll, and Joseff. He's the baby, like you."

"I'm not a baby!"

The little girl smiled but it wobbled at the edges and broke all their hearts. Giving in, she turned her face into Heul's shoulder and began to cry as she held onto him as tightly as she could. He said nothing. He just rocked her gently back and forth, trying to comfort and soothe. After a while, she slipped into an exhausted sleep, simply too worn out from the trauma to remain awake when she knew she was safe.

"Girls cry a lot," Tomos mumbled.

"You cried when you fell off the roof," Seisyll reminded him.

"Did not!"

"So what do we call her?" Arian asked Heul.

Silence fell on the entire room. Eyes and feet shifted. Finally, Joseff said, "She has hair as white as snow, like Grandma did. So . . . Gwyn?"

"That's nice." Heul smiled. "Gavin, you up to some computer B&E?"

"Ooh, with permission? Sweet!"

Present . . .

The words were splashed across every headline. 'Miracle Girl Gets Married.' Gwyn Trahern stared at the newspaper picture of the happy couple as they stood outside the Gentle Brook Inn and exchanged vows. The young woman . . . there was something very familiar about her beyond the eerie fact that they were damn near enough alike in appearance to be mistaken for twins.

"What are you reading?" one of her older brothers asked as he peered over her head.

She set the paper down where he could see. "This." She frowned deeply. "I think I know her." She saw the worry on his face and smiled. "Oh, don't scowl, Gavin, you'll wrinkle."

"Gee thanks." He regarded the paper intently and watched his baby sister's face from the corner of his eye. "Do you think it's from before you came to us?" he finally asked when the silence got to him.

"Don't know." She smiled at him. "It doesn't bother me. I like the family I have. Even if," she added impishly, "they are over-protective."

"You're too little!" he complained good-naturedly as she got up and went to the stove for coffee. "We feel like . . . like giants!"

She muffled a soft giggle. Her brothers, with the exception of her twin, were all over six feet in height. She was five-one. She weighed slightly over one hundred pounds. Her brothers felt like giants; she felt like a faerie! She was completely dwarfed by them. Then again, she was also the youngest. Height seemed to scale downward with age.

Heul was the oldest, at thirty-six, and a height of six-seven. Arian was next oldest, at thirty-four, and the two years had taken away two inches. Owen came after him with another loss of two years but only about half an inch. Gavin followed at thirty, but he was shorter by just a single inch. Identical twins Tomos and Seisyll were two years younger than Gavin, but actually stood at Owen's six-four height.

Joseff, Gwyn's own twin, blamed their elder twin brothers for the fact that he *should* have been six-foot but was instead a mere five-seven. It was a height well used, though, as he was proportionately not that much smaller than their brothers. He and Gwyn weren't blood related, which accounted for her delicate frame, but they were somewhat linked mentally and might as well have been born twins. They even celebrated their birthdays together.

Gwyn had given up being vexed by being the baby in terms of age and size. She was actually bemused by the entire thing. Her brothers looked perfectly at home on a construction site; she could only imagine the hilarity if they were like bakers or something. "Can I go with you to the site?" she asked.

"No!" Gavin glared at her. "Not a chance."

She considered throwing her coffee mug at him. "Oh come on!" she complained. "It wasn't even my fault, and Joseff saved me, and no one got hurt!"

"No." Heul took her mug from her as he went through the kitchen. "And don't drink the coffee, sprite. You'll get hyper."

"Hyper!" She glowered indignantly. "Well, see if I cook dinner for you again! Find a wife and make her do it!" She took endless delight in needling Heul about being single. Well, all of her brothers really, but especially Heul. "I think all of you are spoiled," she announced. She crossed her arms and set her chin in a mutinous line. "You're so used to having me around that you can't take care of yourselves. I think I'll move out."

Heul choked on his coffee and Gavin fell out of his chair. Owen, walking into the kitchen, could only say in a complaining tone of voice, "Great, there goes dinner. Nice, guys. Real nice."

CHAPTER NINE

The phone rang as she was fastening her pearl necklace on. Smiling wryly, Gwyn picked up the phone without looking at the ID. "Rice cooks for an hour, and make sure it's covered with water first or it'll burn."

"You're an angel," Tomos said with feeling. "And if we all get on our knees and beg very prettily, would you please, please, please make us a cake?"

She muffled a giggle and slipped her earrings on. "You guys are horrible! You act like I'm five million miles away, and I'm only just down the street!"

"It's too far," he retorted with feeling.

His sister sighed. She had lived with her brothers for seventeen years. At twenty-six, she had no reason to stay with them any longer, other than her love for them. They had lived on private land for the first three years of her life with them, and then they had all moved into an abandoned building in the 3rd District. They had turned it into a company and a home alike. The company, Driven Snow Architecture, now had one of the best reputations in the country.

While her brothers were the contractors and construction workers equally, she was an interior designer. She was also the voice for the company and took on the tasks of arranging contracts, working with clients, and doing the actual design of the buildings. She had dual majors in Architecture and Design, and Interior Design.

She knew one of the reasons she was in charge of meeting clients was the same reason her brothers were terrified to have her out of their sight: everyone who met her loved her, and she made friends with all she met. She didn't think it was a *bad* thing, but her brothers sure did! They just didn't listen when she told them she was also a good judge of character.

"Caaaaake," Tomos intoned in her ear.

She burst into laughter. "Oh alright! I'll bake a cake for you!" She sighed fondly. "Are you sure you love me because I'm your sister, or do you love me because I can cook?"

"We'd love you even if you burned water," he assured her. "But I won't deny that we *really* love your cooking." The grin was in his voice as he added, "At least you don't have to worry about cleaning up behind us anymore. Unless you want to, of course."

"Ha!" She hung up on him. She was smiling as she did, though. She loved her brothers.

There was a surprising summer storm falling outside so she shrugged into the jacket for her suit. She wasn't sure how she would juggle an umbrella and a briefcase, but she was willing to give it a go. She had an important meeting that she refused to be late for.

The call had come through a week prior. A company that made and produced computer video games was looking to move into a larger building. They wanted to hire Driven Snow. She was on her way to meet with the owner to discuss a contract. Joseff and Gavin, diehard game players, were ecstatic.

She liked Memories' games herself. They were well built and designed, and they always had such beautiful art and stories. She cried her way through a lot of them, which was okay because Tomos did too.

Because she didn't own a car, she caught a taxi and settled back for the ride. Unfortunately, it was morning rush hour and traffic was brutally heavy. The taxi got stuck mere blocks from her destination. "I'm sorry, Miss Trahern," the driver apologized over his shoulder. Since his car covered her area, he often provided her ride. He didn't mind. She was a delight to have around.

"It's not your fault." She smiled. "I don't mind walking. In fact," she rummaged in her purse for the payment, "I'm paying you for the full trip. The extra is a tip. Buy your wife something pretty."

He laughed. "You're an amazing young woman, Miss Trahern."

"Ha. Tell it to my brothers!" She opened the taxi door and then opened her umbrella. Traffic was at a standstill, and she hustled through the cars to the sidewalk. Moving as quickly as she could, she made her way down the sidewalk around busy passersby. Much to her chagrin, her umbrella was stolen in a gust of wind and she stepped right in a puddle. Oooh. She hated it when days acted like that!

Taylor Vincent was not a patient man by nature but he had learned the art of waiting over his thirty-two years. For most of his life, he had wanted to own his own business. Now he did. For most of his life, he had wanted to make the art and stories in his brain something to be enjoyed by all. Now he did.

Owning and operating Memories was no small feat. He worked twice as hard as any of his programmers and developers. He had to write the stories, draw all the concept art, and provide the backgrounds. He then had to review everything and make sure any changes flowed with his original idea. He always listened to suggestions from his employees, too. After a 3D animator had once suggested he change a male lead to a female lead, the game had ended up even better than he had hoped. He now made sure everyone got a copy of the script before it went in for production.

He didn't run things solo, though. So he had more time to focus on his art, he had an administrative assistant. He gave her free reign to make decisions as long as she kept him up to date. Since she knew her way around business, he had never had to worry about anything. Except for his distressing lack of patience.

Tired of pacing his office while he waited for the architect from Driven Snow, he headed down to the lobby of the large building that Memories shared with other companies. Ten minutes might as well have been ten hours. And, anyway, the rain outside was very inspiring so he brought his sketchpad with him.

The security guards in the lobby were used to seeing him with his sketchpad. Much to the bemusement of the guards and his employees, the artist often won out over the businessman in Taylor Vincent.

He tuned everything out around him, only vaguely listening to the doors opening and closing. He had been trying for a week to design a faerie princess for the next game he was working on. He just couldn't picture her in his mind. Kind and beautiful but spirited. Waving a wand, he thought with humor, but not to cast magic. She was horrible at magic. A fireball might turn into an inferno or fail to light even a candle.

A feminine giggle cut across his thoughts and instantly stole his attention. His heart gave a wild clench in his chest and then kicked into overdrive. He looked up, in shock, to see the security guard offering his arm to a young woman trying to put her shoe back on. The guard was smiling widely and said something that had the young woman giggling again. The sound seemed to dance teasingly through Taylor's heart and soul.

As if sensing his gaze, she looked right at him and gave him an impish smile. The entire world went away from around him in a wash of color. There she was. His faerie princess, smiling at him in a rain-splashed suit the color of fresh snow.

Her hair was the same, a wild tumble of white curls that framed a face too beautiful to be real. Her eyes were an unusual shade of purple-gray, like the storm clouds that brought thunder and lightning. She was tiny, only barely over five feet in height, and had a slender frame and gently curved figure. She was stunning. Breathtaking. If she had sprouted faerie wings, he wouldn't have batted a lash.

He moved closer helplessly. He had to know who she was. Where she was going. Where she was from. He needed to know everything.

"I'm Gwyn Trahern," she was saying to the guard. "I'm the architect from Driven Snow Architecture. I'm here for a meeting with Mr. Vincent." When the guard pointed at Taylor, she glanced over and smiled, her eyes crinkling mischievously at the corners. "Oops." In a soft voice, she whispered to the guard, "I thought he was the artist!"

"He's both," he whispered back.

"Oh. Oops."

Hopelessly enchanted, Taylor walked closer. When he got close, he realized in delight that she was truly faerie sized and barely reached his shoulder. He felt immensely bigger despite the leanness of his build. It brought up a sudden urge to defend and protect. He should have kept that sword one of his employees had given him as a prank gift. "I am indeed Taylor Vincent," he told her. "It's a pleasure to meet you, Miss Trahern."

She shook her head and made the pearls she wore at each ear glimmer softly. "Gwyn, please."

"Gwen as in Guinevere?"

"Gwyn as in G-W-Y-N." She smiled. "It means 'snow' in Welsh."

His eyes moved over her soft skin and white hair. "Good call on your parents' behalf." Something pained flickered in her eyes before it disappeared. "Did I say something to hurt you?" he asked softly.

"Just a little, but it's okay. My parents died a long time ago. I never knew them. My eldest brother Heul has raised me and our other six brothers. We own Driven Snow together. It's a family thing."

He tucked his sketchbook under one arm and offered his other. Her hand settled lightly on the crook of his elbow as he escorted her toward the elevator. "Eight siblings," he murmured ruefully. "And you're the only girl?"

"The one and only *and* the baby." She giggled when he winced. "It's not that bad," she reassured him. "Most of the time they don't try to lock me in a tower. Well, they've threatened it, but they know I could get out. I'd cry." She nodded sagely. "My brothers are suckers for tears."

"Most men are."

"If you men cried more yourself, you wouldn't be such babies about it." When they stopped on the second floor, another man got on board. She was quick to move when she saw the stack of boxes he carried was unstable. She caught the top one before it fell. "Whoops! Here, I have it."

"Thanks!" He gave her a grateful smile. "Just stick it back on top."

"It'll just fall again." She smiled. "I don't mind carrying it. Which floor?"

"Fifth." He ran his eyes over her with a masculine appreciation that annoyed Taylor. "Are you new?"

"Me? No." Her eyes sparkled. "I'm the architect from Driven Snow. Mr. Vincent is looking to hire my company. I'm hoping to charm him into signing over a fortune," she added gravely, but the twinkle in her eyes belied her words. "Lacking that, I'm going to wow him with my amazing architectural talents."

As the doors on the fifth floor opened, the man took the box back and got off the elevator. Wistfully, he watched as the doors shut again. Taylor Vincent was one lucky bastard, and he would be an idiot if he didn't hire the lovely faerie with the mesmerizing smile.

By the time they made their way to the twentieth floor and down the winding halls toward his office, Taylor was more enchanted than ever. Gwyn seemed to have absolutely no idea of her impact on people. She had a smile for everyone, a giggle for just the wonder of living, and her eyes sparkled merrily at an inner joke the universe might never get. She was truly as kind as she was beautiful, and he craved the opportunity to sketch her.

"Before we sit down," he offered impulsively, "would you like to see everyone at work?"

Her face brightened. "I'd love to! I've always wondered what went on behind the scenes! The credits are always so long and I know everyone is important!" She giggled. "You even gave a credit to the people who deliver pizza!"

Overhearing her, one worker called, "That pizza guy is a *life saver* when we're on a deadline." He peeked over the top of a cubicle. His blue eyes looked woebegone behind thin-rimmed glasses. "Can I have an office? Please? That way if I work through the night, I can have a couch to sleep on."

"You can have a red stapler," someone else called.

"Ha ha ha. You're such a riot." He slunk back down into his cubicle.

Taylor sighed. "Welcome to Bedlam. Really, we do work here." The affection was clear in his voice. "The smartass is Marie. She does battle scenario programming. The geek with glasses was Blake. He's a text input processor. I.e. he checks for typos."

"BIG typos," came Blake's voice. "'Cause Veronica can't type."

"Bite me, four-eyes!" a woman's voice retorted from across the room.

"And that's Veronica," Taylor offered, trying not to smile. "In case you couldn't tell, she's also a scenario builder."

By that point, Gwyn was giggling without stop and the hand covering her mouth could not hide it. No matter how big the company was, it was clear that everyone worked together as if they were family. She felt perfectly comfortable and natural there, as if she belonged. It made her more determined than ever to win this contract. These people deserved an amazing new building all their own.

Taylor showed her around and let her see the programming and building going on. She was fascinated with the 3D capture and delighted by seeing a landscape built one layer at a time. As she leaned over the modeler's shoulder, she said, "It might be my A&D degree, but I think you've accidentally got a 16th century style on a 12th century building."

"Aw, hell. Bless your degree. You're right." The young woman made a few mouse clicks and fixed the offending roofline. "You want to try? Ever used a CAD program?"

"Yes." She looked at the computer wistfully. "But I'm better with modern design." She smiled. "I'll leave this stuff to the experts. You're much more talented with it than I am."

"Keep her!" someone whispered loudly from across the room.

"We're quitting if you don't!" someone else called.

Taylor laughed. "And on that note, let's go talk business." He once more offered his arm and led her through the maze of cubicles toward the conference room. "And just think, this is just one of our three floors. There's two times this amount of smartass talent running around."

"We don't run," an older man countered as he peered around his cubicle wall. "You said we couldn't be trusted to not be carrying scissors."

"Neither can I," Gwyn admitted in a stage whisper. She smiled up at Taylor as she heard the laughter behind her. "I like your employees. They're wonderful. And you're pretty wonderful too. You know them all by name. I think that's why your games are so wonderful. Everyone loves their job and it shows."

He had nothing to say to that. He felt humbled. When he glanced over his shoulder, he could see all of his employees peering over and around their cubicles, looks of fascination and delight on their faces as they watched Gwyn. He didn't blame them.

And, therefore, he was doubly astonished when they reached the conference room and found his assistant glaring fiercely at Gwyn. "This is our architect?" she snapped. "Taylor, are you an idiot? What does someone like her know about design? All she's good for is using her looks and batting her lashes to get a deal!"

Gwyn recovered from the attack before he did. She offered a hesitant smile. "Maybe you should reserve judgment until you see my work. I'm actually quite good, and it has nothing to do with my appearance." She smiled then, with genuine friendliness. "Thank you, though. My brothers say I'm too pretty, too."

Taylor cleared his throat. "Gwyn, meet Melissa Washburn. She's my assistant." He very rarely reminded Melissa that she had no real position of power. He only did it when he wanted to remind her that his word was law.

Melissa's eyes flashed angrily as she got the point. She gave Gwyn a once over. "I hope you're as good as you say you are, else you'll never get anywhere."

Gwyn kept her smile. "Well, you can join us and find out for yourself." She winced as Melissa whirled and slammed into her office. She frowned at Taylor. "I didn't intend to offend her."

It didn't take a genius to recognize a woman's jealousy. He wasn't entirely surprised by it. Melissa had always been exceptionally proud of being the most attractive female in the company. In every way, Gwyn trumped her. "She's just cranky today," he finally said. He smiled, offering to share the joke. "She got up on the wrong side of the wrong person's bed."

"If she'd gotten up on the right side of the right person's bed, she'd have been smiling." Her eyes twinkled. "I'm glad it's not personal. I don't like offending people." She went into the conference room and set down her briefcase while he shut the door. She was momentarily startled as he held a chair for her, but she sat down with a smile that flashed the dimples at the corner of her eyes. "Thank you."

He sat down across from her. "Before we get started, I have something I need to say." She tilted her head and he smiled. He wanted to capture that expression too. "I absolutely have to sketch you."

"Me?!"

"Yes. If you don't mind."

"Oh." Flustered, she felt her cheeks heat. "No, no, I don't mind. It just surprised me." She smiled suddenly. "I wasn't expecting you to be the artist for the games as well as the producer. No wonder you have such beautiful eyes." She went red and covered her mouth as he lifted a brow. "Oops. I meant you've got an artist's eyes."

She hadn't, however, been wrong with the first statement either. Her new client was deadly gorgeous. His hair had a fascinating shade of smoky gray, almost as if he should have had black hair but it had never darkened all the way. His eyes had the full hue of black, but it reminded her of obsidian with the way it seemed to possess a rainbow of colors inside the darkness. They seemed both dreamy and suave, as if he saw beautiful things that he had the intelligence to grab. He was lean and muscular with a sort of predatory grace that no amount of tailored suits could hide. He should have been a model, not an artist.

He had an earring. The little gold hoop seemed so out of place at first that she wasn't sure she had seen it clearly. She looked again and then smiled to herself as she opened her briefcase. A rebel, she decided, and thought she liked him all the more for it. "Well, Mr. Vincent, shall we get started?"

"Taylor, if you don't mind." He watched her with elemental male hunger in his eyes. She had a way of moving that had every hormone he possessed sitting up at attention and wanting to howl at the moon. Her lack of awareness of her own appeal was just part of her charm.

"Taylor, then." She pulled folders out of her case and spread them out. "Because Memories is growing quickly," she began, "it needs to be a building bigger than your immediate need. Also, it needs to be something new and unique, because otherwise it will get lost in the shuffle. I've provided for a game lobby as well."

"A lobby." He leaned back in his chair. "What for?"

She smiled. "A place on the first floor where people can come in and demo your games and buy merchandise. In the interior design plans, I've arranged to have the lobby decorated with no images but original sketches, ones like the kind that recently sold on eBay for two thousand dollars."

He coughed lightly. His rather sadistic employees had taken great delight in posting the listing everywhere. He had nearly had a heart attack. "It was a giveaway," he explained. "I didn't expect that, I assure you!"

She giggled softly. "Most don't." She flipped open the top folder and slid it across to him. "The basic blueprints are already included care of Owen Trahern. He's the one who takes my sketches and makes them feasible."

He stared in stunned disbelief at the pictures in front of him. She had done a full drawing, showing the building from all possible angles, and every image was as good as a photograph even though it was rendered in blue pencil and black ink. 'Talented' was not the word for her.

The building she depicted was five stories in height. It sat on the corner of a street and took full advantage of the western/northern view in order to catch the sunset in the windows. It was marble and glass with a water fountain surrounded by a brilliant garden in the front. "This is . . . amazing," he managed to say.

"The garden is already plotted as well. Tomos Trahern is our landscaper." She flipped through another folder. "He's already laid out the groundwork, for lack of a better word, and has a list of suppliers for what he needs to make our image a reality. Also," she slid across another folder, "here are the interior design plans. I wanted to avoid the worn effect of so many buildings where they're all the same inside."

He opened the folder eagerly, more and more delighted with everything he saw. "This is stunning. Really, really stunning. I've dreamed and imagined having my own building and company, and you've made the first a reality. You managed to capture exactly what I wanted. You're hired."

She laughed at him. "We at Driven Snow like to give a customer their full money's worth. As time goes, if we discover impracticalities we weren't able to plan for, we'll adjust the designs as needed. You'll likely see me at the site before construction but not often during."

"Why not?" He frowned.

She sighed. "I could give you a line about not being needed but it's actually just stupid family dynamics."

His frown became a grin. "Overprotective brothers?"

"Yes!" She pouted when he laughed at her. "When I was twenty, there was almost an accident. I and my brother Joseff were surveying a site and a piling came loose. It would have knocked me off the second floor but he got me out of the way. Ever since, they've panicked if I go near a site."

"Is it only overprotective brothers, or do you have an overprotective boyfriend as well?" he asked casually. She hadn't mentioned one, but he thought it better to double check.

"Just brothers." Her eyes danced merrily. "They scared all potential candidates away."

"You sound so crushed." He said it dryly, but a mingled relief and delight inside told him that he might be getting too far in over his head already.

"Well, I figure if I find one who can't scare, he's worth keeping. The rest weren't." She began to gather up her folders. "You can keep these copies for yourself. I have the originals. If you decide to make changes, let me know, and we'll sit down and hash them out."

"Give me just a moment to get the contracts you emailed me the other day." He got to his feet to step into his office across the hall, and he wasn't very surprised to find Melissa in there seething. "Yes?" he asked as he got the paperwork from his files.

"Well?" she demanded.

"Yes, I'm hiring her." He turned and gave her a bland look. "Jealousy is unbecoming on you, Melissa. Just because she's more beautiful doesn't mean you have to be snide to her. She treated you with genuine kindness and you snapped at her."

She drummed her fingers on her arm. "You think she's more beautiful than me?"

"To quote another faerie tale, she's the fairest in the land. And, FYI, that's not just applicable to her looks. It applies to her heart, too. She doesn't judge on appearances, unlike someone else around here. She's also damned talented, just as promised." He turned on his heel and walked out without anything more.

Gwyn was still waiting for him in the conference room, but she was peeking at his sketchbook. She jumped guiltily and dropped it on the table. She tried to look innocent, and he grinned. "Help yourself."

She didn't need to be asked twice and scooped up the book to begin actually skimming through the pages. The absolute delight on her face made him feel as if he was Rembrandt, or Michelangelo, or Da Vinci. As if he was the greatest artist known in the world. "You like it?" he asked softly as he sat down.

"It's amazing! Oh!" She giggled. "I love the werewolf! He looks like he'd eat me for lunch, but he's got a kitten on his shoulder! And look at the soldier! He's so handsome!" She looked at him, eyes merry and guileless. "He looks kind of like you."

He winced sheepishly. "Guilty." He would have liked to take it as a flirtation but she seemed blissfully oblivious to how her words sounded. It was refreshing and wonderful at the same time. "You don't think it's a bad thing for a soldier to fall for a faerie princess?"

"Why should I?" She smiled at him as she handed the sketchbook back. "Love is love, no matter what shape it takes." She laughed. "I'm from 3rd District, though, so I guess it's little wonder I'd think that, right?" Her eyes sparkled with merry mysteries. "Magic comes to us with our breakfast."

Delight filled him. Was his faerie princess truly a faerie? He would have been ecstatic if he could find out it was true. "Will you have lunch with me today?" he asked as she signed the contract. He hated the idea of not getting more time to spend with her. "We could discuss the building some more."

"I'd love to, but I have another site I need to visit. Another hopeless dreamer like you." Her mischievous smile took the sting out of the words as she stood and picked up her briefcase. "Driven Snow is very glad to have you hire us. And so am I," she added softly. "You're a good person, Taylor Vincent."

By the close of business, the entire building, and not just Memories, was aware of her beauty and gentleness. The security guards were visibly smitten with her, and any person who had spoken to her was in awe. She truly was the faerie princess of the company, and she had woven spells with a simple smile. Half a dozen people called Taylor and told him personally that he would be an idiot to lose her—professionally or personally.

He wasn't an idiot. He intended to keep her as long as he could. She brought fresh air and a renewed sense of life with her. She also turned out to be a wonderful muse. Within minutes of her departure, he was in his office and sketching madly.

Melissa was in his office, too, and pacing with anger. He only listened with half an ear, but she didn't notice it as she walked around furiously. "They told me I couldn't even hold a candle to her!" she fumed.

"Mm-hmm."

"They dared compare us!" She found it outrageous. "Me, compared to that unsophisticated little nobody from that backwater district! I went to the most prestigious schools in the country and my shoes cost more than her entire suit!" She stopped for a breath and finally realized he wasn't even listening. "Taylor!"

"What!" He looked up, startled.

Annoyed, she reached over and took his sketchpad. "Now what are you on about?" To her dismay and disgust, she found herself looking at a picture of Gwyn Trahern depicted as a faerie princess. She had an adorable look of disgruntlement on her face as she stared up at the bird perched on her head. "Jesus, this is unbelievable."

He took his sketch back with dignity. "Try some graciousness," he suggested to her curtly. "And perhaps you might be able to compete with Gwyn. Now, good night. Lock the door as you leave."

She seethed to herself but left the office and the building. Somehow she refrained from slamming doors as she did so. She was still pissed, and it was worse knowing Gwyn truly was as talented as she was beautiful. Even though Melissa didn't want to, she loved the designs. She wouldn't have minded teaching the little upstart a thing or two, though!

A slithering sound echoed behind her as she was unlocking her car, and she felt a chill. When she turned, there was nothing behind her. Disturbed, she started to get into her car when sharp pain exploded in her leg as if something had just bitten her. She crumpled to the ground unconscious, the venom gliding through her veins even as the cobra glided away from the scene.

CHAPTER TEN

It was midnight before Taylor gave up on trying to sleep. Nerves and excitement coiled so tightly inside him that he felt like a rubber ball let loose in a rubber factory. He hadn't felt that way in six years. Not since he had first formed Memories with a handful of workers—including Blake and Veronica—and set out to grab his dream. Now he stood on the cusp of realizing the next big step of his dreams. His own building.

He had saved and saved until he could afford the land. His employees had helped. Each had willingly taken a five percent pay cut to pour more funds into the land. In return, he had offered each some stock in the company. Now the land was his, outright, and the building was going to be paid for with a loan. As long as he kept his company going strongly for the next twenty years, eventually the building would be his, entirely, too.

Full of restless energy, he got out his sketchpad and began drawing. He normally only did concept art that was turned into full designs by other artists he employed, but the images were so strong in his mind that he found himself drawing more than concepts and sketching full scenes and character depictions.

It wasn't until dawn crept in that he realized he had drawn dozens of sketches of his faerie princess. His white haired, stormy eyed, faerie princess. He softly traced a finger over the line of her face. It was imprinted in his memory. He knew, no matter how long he lived, that he would never forget it. He was definitely smitten.

He wasn't due at the office that day. Unless they were under a short deadline, everyone took Saturdays and Sundays off. Unfortunately for him, that meant he had two whole days to pace and fidget with nothing to do. He cleaned up the apartment, made breakfast, and sketched a comical image of his werewolf being turned into a frog by the magically inept faerie.

He gave up around seven in the morning. There was no law against visiting his own land, and that's what he wanted to do. He wanted to see the site where his building would be going up and pretend it was already done. He had a good imagination.

He drove to the site eagerly, not sure what to expect to see after a day of having Driven Snow on board. When he parked at the site, though, he found himself unsurprised. Supplies and equipment had already been delivered and the foundation was nearly completely dug. A large stack of pilings and steel beams sat facing the foundation, and he headed for it. It would be a perfect perch for studying his kingdom.

As he rounded the edge of the stack, he got a swift surprise as he discovered he wasn't the only one there. Gwyn was perched on the pilings, a morning wind ruffling her hair and pulling out the curls before letting them spring back.

The punch of lust was so staggering that he put a hand out to brace himself. It seemed to rip from his soul outward, a silent detonation of hunger that made his body ache and burn. The longing to touch her, to taste her, was breathtaking and powerful. He wanted nothing more than to know if she tasted as pure as her name implied.

She wore a pair of pale blue jeans, faded from many washes, and a soft, peach-colored camisole. His hands burned to find the softer flesh under the cotton. Smitten? Had he thought he was smitten? He was enthralled. He walked forward slowly, not wanting to startle her. "Good morning."

She still jumped a little, her head swinging around toward him quickly. When she saw him, her eyes lit from within with delight. "Good morning!" Her eyes sparkled. "Come to survey your kingdom, m'lord soldier? I admit, I couldn't stay away, either." She returned her gaze to the empty ground as if already seeing it built.

The déjà vu stunned him. He stared at her, astonished that she would quote his faerie princess in the game without ever once knowing the script or plot. "I thought I might view the land." He leaned against the stack beside her. "I never thought I'd find a faerie here viewing it, too."

"A faerie!" She giggled softly. "Well, I can't confirm or deny it, sadly, but my brothers have nicknamed me 'sprite' because I'm so little and quick to get into trouble."

"You admit it?" He grinned at her.

She grinned back. "To everyone but them." She stretched largely, oblivious to his hungry gaze following the ripple and movement of her curves. "And you better not tell." She spotted movement and held up her hand. To his wonder, a bluebird flew over and landed delicately on her fingers. She brought it down to rub her cheek against its feathers. "Hi there."

He mentally photographed the image; it needed to be drawn as well. "How did you get into this business?" he asked. He couldn't control his hunger to know everything about her. "I know it's family owned, but still."

"They wouldn't let me learn to build, so I had to go into the planning stages." She giggled softly. "Like I said before, I have seven brothers. All bigger, all older. My twin is the only one who isn't super bigger than me. They all do construction, but they also specialize in different fields. Heul, my eldest brother, wanted us to do something together so this was what we settled on."

"A twin?" He smiled. "How much older?" Her gaze lowered, and he began to frown. "What's wrong, Gwyn?"

She took a deep breath. She couldn't lie. She had never been able to lie. And she didn't *want* to lie to Taylor. "I don't know," she admitted softly. She released the bluebird and watched it fly away. "I'm adopted. They found me when I was nine and took me in as their sister. I have amnesia. I have no memories of my life before they found me. Joseff and I share his birthday since we know we're the same age. Owen can 'sense' minds. He was able to pick out that I was nine and my birthday was in May. Joseff's birthday is in May, so we share it. I might even be older than him, but there's no knowing. I hope I'm not. He likes not being the baby anymore."

"Have you ever gone looking for your family?" he asked quietly. His heart ached for her. He had a painful childhood of his own that he had often wished to forget, but it suddenly seemed as if never knowing his origins would be worse.

"I never felt a need to." Her fingers moved unconsciously to her hip and then away, the movement so brief it wasn't noticeable. "I don't even know my real name. Joseff picked Gwyn for my name because of the color of my hair. I looked like their—our—grandmother, who was named Gwyn, too."

The lost note in her voice tugged at him. He gently reached out and ran his fingers through her hair. She looked at him in surprise and was caught by the rainbows in his eyes. Her entire body came alive all at once, a flush of heat spreading across her skin. Her pulse began to throb everywhere. In wonder, she reached out a hand and touched his face, her fingertips reacting with delight at the feel of his skin. Was this why he had never left her mind? The feelings inside her were so right that she knew they were truer than anything she had ever known before.

"I thought it was just me," he murmured huskily, his breath caught at the naked longing in her eyes. "I thought I was the only one."

"I thought there was something wrong with me, that I never felt this way for anyone." Her voice was just as soft and just as husky with desire. "But I see, now, that it was because I'd never met you."

He eased his hand more fully into her hair and cupped the back of her head as he drew her toward him. Her lashes fluttered closed, and his muscles knotted with painful desire. "Gwyn," he murmured, their lips barely touching. His heated breath made her shiver softly with wonderful pleasure.

"Hey!" a sharp male voice snapped. "What are you doing to my sister, you ass?"

He released her as if his hands were on fire. She didn't look surprised, but she certainly looked annoyed as she turned a fierce glare on the one who had spoken. "He was going to kiss me, thank you very much, Seisyll! And, I'll have you know, I wasn't exactly fighting!"

Taylor hastily straightened as the man approached them. When he drew even, Taylor, at six feet tall, felt short for the first time in his life.

Seisyll may have been one of the younger Trahern brothers, but he was still bigger than the average man. His eyes carried equal doses of annoyance and discomfort. His short-cut hair did nothing to disguise the strong lines of his face. Taylor half expected him to put on a horned helmet and go looking for a village to plunder.

Gwyn was distinctly dwarfed by her big brother, but she was also distinctly not intimidated. She glared fiercely at him from her perch, which still didn't have her on eye level with him.

"Who is he?" Seisyll asked her, eyeing Taylor intently. He seemed decent enough, but Seisyll distrusted any man that came near his baby sister with lust in his eyes. It didn't matter if she was willing or not. She knew nothing about men and could too easily get her heart bruised.

"Our client, Seisyll." He gaped at her, and she blushed. "I couldn't help myself," she admitted. "I know it's improper." When he glared at Taylor, she smartly smacked his arm. "Go away! Stop being such an overprotective ninny!" She glared at him until he gave in and walked off.

"Don't touch my sister," he muttered at Taylor as he went past.

She sighed and gave Taylor a sheepish smile. "Sorry. I told you my brothers were overprotective." She lowered her gaze. "But he's right. We probably shouldn't let our hormones get the better of us." A bit helplessly, she said, "I'm not handling this well. I don't know how to flirt or be coy. I just . . . am me. Everyone says I'm naïve."

"I think you're wonderful," Taylor said honestly as he reached up to help her down off the pilings. She went into his arms with a trust that shook him deeply. It was a miracle her brothers were still sane. In fact, he suddenly sympathized with them. Protecting someone so innocent would be terrifying.

"Really?" Her hands rested lightly on his shoulders as he slowly lowered her to her feet. Their bodies brushed and pressed together in places, making their hearts beat a little faster, a little harder.

"Really." The temptation was too strong. Her scent was like fresh snow, sweet and pure. He drew her even closer, and his hands curved around her small waist. "Gwyn," he murmured.

"You shouldn't," she whispered, but her hands were moving of their own will, her arms winding around his neck. His breath tasted like coffee and was so hot that it sent a wonderful shiver through her body. She wanted his kiss. Wanted it with a vengeance.

"May I kiss you?" he whispered, something about her compelling him to ask rather than take. He would be willing to beg; he was losing himself in the storm clouds of her eyes. For the first time, he truly understood his soldier's obsession with his magically inept faerie princess. He was obsessed, too, and hopelessly enthralled.

"Please." She held her breath as his lips brushed across hers. She waited in agony for him to deepen the kiss, but it didn't happen. Disappointment filled her as he eased back. "That's it?"

"For now." He rubbed his thumb over her cheekbone. "It occurs to me that it is very tacky to kiss a lady I haven't taken out to dinner." He stepped back and lifted her hand to his lips with a courtly bow. "Have dinner with me, my faerie princess. I would be honored. I think I can scare up reservations for a suitable restaurant for a princess."

Her color rose. "I'd like to but . . . oh, you'll laugh!"

"Try me."

"I don't have anything to wear." She fumed as he did, indeed, laugh at her. "Jerk!" She blew out a quick breath. "We all draw paychecks from the company. I won't let them coddle me financially no matter how hard they try. I can live well, have a nice place, whatever I want to eat, but I can't afford to get fancy clothes." She glowered. "Do you have any idea what a fancy, stylish cocktail dress costs these days?"

"I can imagine." He smiled. "Suppose you had a dress. Would you go out with me?"

She laughed and shook her head. "Sure. Let me just find my magic wand and conjure a cocktail dress. Thank you for the offer, though. If you wanted to take me to some place casual, I might be willing. I just can't do fancy." No matter how tempting the thought of him in a formal suit was. No matter how badly she wanted to see him in any and every venue. Her craving for his presence was growing and growing. "I'll see you later. I should be going."

He pulled out his cell phone as he watched her walk away. Magic wand, no, he thought in amusement, because his faerie princess couldn't cast to save her life. Thankfully he knew a few elves who owed him a favor or two.

By the time she got home, she couldn't resist the urge to dig in her closet. She knew it was an exercise in futility, but she looked for anything that might pass as a dinner dress. Her fanciest outfit still walked the edge of being casual, unless she counted her suit, which she didn't. Damn it.

When her phone rang, she picked up to say, "Yes, he kissed me. Go away." She promptly hung up again.

Depressed, she sat down on the edge of her couch and stared at the wall across the room. She was beginning to know how the faerie princess felt: wanting someone so badly it hurt, but knowing it was near impossible. She groaned and fell over on her back. "Why," she asked the ceiling, "do I have to suddenly discover lust at my age? I'm already partway toward being an old maid. I could have happily gone along without wanting sex!"

There came a choked sound from the doorway, and she opened one eye to see the shocked look on her twin's face. It was a comedic twist of features, and she rolled onto her side with a shriek of laughter. "Oh my god, Joseff!" she managed to gasp. "Your face!"

He scraped his hands over his face. "Where do you keep the cleaner?" he mumbled. "I need to bleach my brain!" Because she was still laughing, he walked over to the couch to tweak her ear. "Brat!"

"You," she countered, wiping her eyes, "are the one who just blindly walked on in!" She fell over on a fresh peel of laughter. "If I'd known I could get to my brothers like this before, I'd have gone looking for the right guy sooner!"

He pinched his nose between his fingers. "Okay," he said. "Let me get this straight. You have the hots for the client we acquired just yesterday and Seisyll caught him kissing you."

"No, Seisyll stopped him from kissing me. Taylor sort of kissed me after Seisyll walked away." When he eyed her, she explained, "Sort of kiss. Not a real kiss. No tongues or anything. Just lips. It was really annoying because I wanted him to really kiss me."

"I'm not having this conversation," he told himself. "I'm not." She giggled and he caught her in a headlock. "Was that all?"

"Yeah. He asked me out too, but I turned him down."

"Why? Thought you had the hots for him."

"I do. But he wanted to go somewhere really fancy, and," she glared, "I don't own a dress good enough." She kicked him in the bottom as he fell off the couch with laughter. "Stop it, meanie." Her doorbell rang and she got to her feet. "Anyway, I told him that I'd go out only if I had a dress." It was a deliveryman outside her door, and he had two packages. Puzzled, she signed for them.

"Bet he was annoyed," he decided. "You're so beautiful, and everyone loves you."

She smiled. "Thanks. Still," she sighed as she opened the larger of the two boxes, "it makes me wish I *did* own a dress. I could probably fall for him, Joseff." Her words stumbled to a shocked stop as she stared at what was in the box. "Oh," she breathed. "It's stunning."

"What is?" His brows shot up as she pulled out of the box an evening gown in rich golden yellow. It was a color that most women would never be able to wear but would perfectly compliment Gwyn's skin and hair. "Wow," he managed to say. "That must have been a small fortune!"

"It's beautiful!" She gave in to the urge and held it against her body as she turned in a circle to admire the flow of color and light. "Like something for a princess!" It dawned on her, and she put the dress down. She rummaged in the box again and shortly found the card.

My faerie princess:

You promised if you had a dress, you would join me. Here's the dress and I can't wait to see you in it. I'll pick you up just before seven.

Signed*, an adoring soldier*

"Taylor," she murmured. Her face softened as she ran her fingers over the simple white card. He had done this, she thought, holding the card to her heart. How could she say no? She wanted to see him more than anything.

Joseff watched her face and his stomach gave an odd quiver. His sister, he realized painfully, was a woman. An adult woman, and she was falling in love. It hurt a little because she had always belonged to them and no one else. He almost didn't want to give her up. It was only the glow in her cheeks and her eyes that gave him the will to share. "Well," he finally said.

"Well!" She pulled out the shoes that had been sent as well and set them to the side. She didn't question how Taylor had known her sizes. She was just going to accept the magic. "I guess I have a date," she said laughingly. "Maybe I'll finally get my kiss. He's a good man," she murmured softly. "He does his own art and writing. He knows his employees by name." She smoothed her hand over the dress. "He was like a little kid when he saw the designs. I could see the dreams in his eyes. I want to make them all come true."

Joseff was silent. Then, "Are you in love with him?"

Startled, she looked at him with wide eyes. "I . . . I don't know."

"Then weigh it."

She closed her eyes and envisioned scales in her mind. It was her special gift. She could mentally produce a scale in her mind and put evidence on the two sides. Whichever was heavier was the verdict. She had never been wrong, even in situations where the evidence was nearly balanced.

She weighed out all the evidence. Her emotions and reactions compared to her experiences and the way she normally acted. The answer was immediate, and there was no question to the verdict. If the scale had been physical, it would have hit the table with an immense clang.

Wonder filled her, and she began to smile with delight. She was in love. Love at first sight. "I didn't think it was possible," she whispered. "I thought it was supposed to be hard. People work so hard to find love and I walked blindly into it."

"What about him?" he asked softly.

"I don't know." Her smile turned sad. "I know he likes me. And he's definitely attracted to me. It hurts, a little, to think that I'm in love and the man I love might never feel the same. But I can't stop it. Whatever he wants of me, he can have."

He walked over and hugged her tightly. He could barely remember his life before knowing her. In every way that counted, she was his twin sister. Their minds automatically brushed together if they were near. If he couldn't feel her in his mind, it would drive him nuts. "He'd be an idiot not to love you," he said firmly. He released her and cleared his throat. "So, have a good dinner. And, uhm, be careful. You know."

She blushed as the meaning sank in. "Joseff!"

"I had to say something!" he retorted defensively, and hastily ducked when she took a swipe at him with the box. "I'm going, I'm going!" He moved quickly toward the door to get out of range. He looked at her for a moment, sighed, and finally gave up as he left. He might as well go tell the others and get it over with. They would kill him if he didn't.

She didn't even remember her other package until she was trying on her dress that evening. It gathered at the front and fell in slim lines to her ankles. Her back was left mostly bare and she felt like a princess as she turned in front of her mirror. There was no hope for her hair though. She tried pinning, tying . . . none of it looked right.

Frustrated, she went back into the living room and spotted the other package. There was no return label and she opened it curiously. Inside, on a bed of tissue, she found a beautiful comb set with yellow stones that perfectly matched her dress.

Delighted, she pulled it out and wondered if Taylor had sent it as well. Her doorbell rang and she hurried over to open it. He was on the other side, wildly handsome in a black suit, and she didn't fight the happiness bubbling inside. She jumped into his arms. "It's incredible!"

He managed to hold the flowers he was carrying with one hand and caught her close with the other. Dazed, he stared at her. Incredible was not the word for her. It was too pale a word. She was stunning, more beautiful than any dream he had ever had. "Wow," he said, "that's a fine greeting."

"I'm happy." She closed her eyes and rested her head on his shoulder. "I wanted to see you so much." She released him and smiled as he set her on her feet. "Oh!" she suddenly remembered. "My hair."

"I like it," he murmured huskily. A tempting image teased his mind of seeing it tangled across his pillow. "Leave it down."

"I have a comb for it though." She waved the comb at him. "See?" She caught her hair and began to twist it up, but he snatched the comb from her fingers. "Taylor!" Giggling, she tried to reach for it. "Give it back!"

"No." He held it out of her reach, and she pressed up against him trying to grab it. Her breasts rubbed against his chest and he caught a breath as desire slammed into his bloodstream. She went on her toes without thinking, and his arousal suddenly pressed against the notch of her thighs. She froze.

Their eyes locked, and he tossed the flowers onto the side table to free his hand. He curved it around her bottom and drew her more firmly against him, his eyes burning into hers. She gave a little gasp and her fingers gripped his jacket tightly as her skin flushed with desire. Pleasure radiated from the contact and her body began to throb with need. "Taylor," she managed to whisper.

He shuddered and held her closer, his head bending to take her parted lips. The comb slipped from his hand and fell onto the floor with a small clatter. Even before he heard it starting to hum, he felt his hands beginning to burn. The familiar feeling was one he had learned to associate with danger. He instinctively wrapped Gwyn in his arms and moved back sharply. His eyes narrowed on the comb.

The comb hummed and quivered around on the floor. The spines abruptly fired like spikes out of the body, as the body itself shot backwards just as hard. The spikes hit the molding around the floor and imbedded themselves several inches. Gwyn's startled gasp turned into a little shriek as the comb, itself, exploded and sent pieces everywhere in a three-foot radius.

Shaking, she clung onto Taylor tightly and buried her face in his shoulder. Shaking no less, he wrapped both arms around her. "God," he managed to say. "If I hadn't stopped you . . ." Fury bubbled up and he jerked her back. "Where the hell did you get that?!"

Her teeth chattering slightly, she stammered, "I-it came in the mail. A gift. Arrived with the dress. I thought it was from you." She shook her head quickly when he froze. "No, I don't think you did it. You would never hurt me." Her trust was in her eyes as she rested against him and curled her fingers into his jacket.

He let out a ragged breath. "Thank you," he whispered. He held her close for long moments until her shaking began to ease. He only then reluctantly released her to kneel next to where the spikes had hit the wall. It took a great amount of force to finally pry them out. "If this had gone off while you were wearing it," he said grimly, "you'd be dead."

She tried to smile. "And here my brothers said I had a hard head."

Sensing her need to keep the tone light, he didn't argue with her flippant words. He gathered up the debris and put the pieces on the table. "We should call the cops."

"I'll call them later." She set her chin in a stubborn line. "I refuse to let this ruin my evening."

He looked at his watch and sighed. "Unfortunately, we'll never make it to the restaurant in time. I had to promise we'd be there at precisely 7:30 to get a table."

"Then stay here." She took his hand with hers and smiled. "Have dinner with me here. I can cook something or we can order in."

He shook his head. "I can order something. You set up a place to eat. Leave the food details to me."

"Alright." She released his hand and headed out onto her small patio balcony. The sun was setting in the distance as she unfolded her bistro table and two chairs. A tablecloth and two slipcovers turned the patio set from casual to formal. By the time he came looking for her, she had set out candles and wine glasses and was pouring cider for them both.

His breath caught in his chest. The setting sun illuminated her in a beautiful golden glow and haloed her skin and hair. She looked like his faerie princess. His. No one else's. He wanted her to be his alone, to have her at his side where he could always turn and see her smile. He wanted to be surrounded by the utter rightness of being near her and to spend the rest of his life with her.

His breath unraveled slowly. He had written it, drawn it . . . and now he felt it. Love at first sight. From the moment he had looked up in that crowded lobby and seen her smile, he had been lost for all time. "Gwyn," he said softly as he came up behind her.

She turned and smiled as he pulled her into his arms. She softly rested her hands on his chest. "What?" she asked.

"Nothing, I just wanted to touch you." He heard the doorbell and smiled. "Dinner has arrived." He released her and headed for the door, leaving her to light the candles and wonder what he had arranged.

When he returned, she took one look at the pizza box and burst into laughter. He grinned and served them both slices. "I knew you'd appreciate the humor."

"Twenty minutes is pretty quick, I must say."

"Little place down the road. They deliver within fifteen if you live within three blocks. They have a branch near my apartment." He held her chair for her until she sat down. "You're one in a million." He moved his chair closer and sat down beside her.

"A good thing for the world. Two of me would be frightening." She watched him without shame, admiring the lines of his face and the color of his eyes. "Well, you know all about my sordid family history. What about you? Do your parents live in NYC?" He went very still, something painful and cold moving in his eyes, and her smile faded. "I'm sorry," she said quietly. "It's none of my business." She reached for another slice of pizza. "Tell me about your company instead."

His hand closed over her wrist and he drew her fingers to his lips. "No, I can tell you. It's just hard. Painful." He closed his eyes. "I've never told anyone else what I'm about to tell you. I trust you, Gwyn."

"Don't if it hurts you," she countered. She smiled. "You don't have to tell me anything you don't want to."

He searched her face in wonder. She would accept him as he was, never asking for details. Yet, somehow, the clarity in her eyes and the unwavering sense of rightness drew the story out of him like the morning drew the sunrise. He *had* to tell her. She would understand. Any judgment she passed would be the final one. "I *need* to tell you. You're important to me. I don't want there to be secrets between us."

A soft glow filled her. "Alright. Start at the beginning."

He released her and got to his feet to lean on the balcony. It was easier to tell the story if he wasn't looking at her. "I killed my parents." The words came out starkly and unembellished. "In self-defense because they were making a damned hard effort to kill me first." He blew out a hard breath. "I had a best friend once. We were inseparable. When we were fifteen, he got himself into drugs. It began to destroy his life. It was tearing me up. So I went to my parents for help. They asked if my friend had said anything about a supplier. Since I fully expected them to stop him, I told them where the meet was and that I had already called the cops." His voice grew even quieter. "They found his body the next morning. An overdose."

Her hands curled into fists in her lap. In her mind, her scales silently measured every detail. "I see." She kept her voice even with effort.

He laughed sadly. "Yeah. You probably do. Hindsight makes it obvious to me too."

"And?"

"I went to my parents and demanded to know why they hadn't stopped him. They didn't even make excuses. They just looked at me like I was an idiot. Where did I think their money came from? Selling drugs was just a nice, lucrative side business. And they expected me to keep quiet. As if it hadn't just killed my friend. As if *they* hadn't just killed him. I threatened to go to the police."

"And they tried to kill you, too." It wasn't a question. She got to her feet, her arms wrapped tightly around herself.

"My father had a gun. We fought over it. In the struggle, the gun went off and killed my mother. My father went a little ballistic. He came after me again. I got my hands on a statue. Somehow I managed to hit him before he shot me in the head. It wasn't until the cops arrived that I realized I had already been shot." He rubbed a hand over his shoulder. "It was ruled self-defense."

"As it should have been."

The fierceness in her voice had him turning quickly. She was staring at the moon, tears sliding down her cheeks. "Gwyn." It was all he could say.

"Were you supposed to roll over and die? You have nothing to be ashamed of."

"It doesn't feel that way. I suppose I'll be judged when I go to hell." He made a startled sound as she turned and grabbed his arm. She stared up at him with burning gray eyes. Lightning churned in their depths and he felt an inner recognition of the power inside her. He didn't question it.

"There is no heaven and hell," she told him. "Judgment is done your entire life. The scales tip one way or another. Hear me now, Taylor Vincent, this *is not a sin*. It was justice, and you were the weapon wielded for it."

A shiver went down his back. Her inner conviction convinced him when nothing else could. He lifted a hand and cupped her cheek warmly. "I didn't expect that," he murmured. "You're so gentle inside . . . I was sure you would be disgusted."

"I am." Her eyes returned to normal and she seemed unaware of what she had done. "By their actions." She went into his arms and held onto him tightly. "No parent should ever do anything like that."

"I agree." He closed his arms around her and savored how she felt. "I didn't mean to dump all of that on you," he sighed. "Hell of a thing to say on a first date."

She rubbed her cheek against his chest softly. "I was nearly killed, and you have a tragic past. I think we can call ourselves even. Next time we need to do something tame. You know, like bungee jumping or sky diving."

He laughed at that and slowly released her. They took their seats once more, and they deliberately kept the conversation light as they made their way through the pizza. A lively game of Twenty Questions outted him as a fan of ballet and her as having a cast iron stomach—she had drunk the infamous Coke and milk combination and lived to tell the tale.

It was only when a clock chimed in the distance that they realized it was very late. Their eyes met across the table. His entire body knotted with desire as he envisioned simply picking her up and carrying her to the bedroom. The image was so powerful that his hands lifted before he could stop them. He forced himself to put them down again. "Well. I should go. We can try the restaurant next time."

"Okay." Even she could hear the breathless note to her voice. It just disappointed her that the night had to end at all. At least there would be another. That was something to cling to. "Good night," she said softly as they reached the door.

She started to reach for the knob and he caught her wrist. "We've had our date." His voice was nothing more than a rasp of male hunger. Her entire damned family could have walked up and he wouldn't have cared. He *had* to taste her. "Let me kiss you, Gwyn."

She shivered at the sound of his voice and went into his arms eagerly. She couldn't deny him, not when she needed him just as badly. She went up on her toes and met his kiss halfway, and her arms fiercely coiled around his neck. A wonderful shiver went through her entire body as his hands curved around her hips and dragged her tighter against him.

She tasted like a snow cone, fresh and pure but sweet all at the same time. It was addicting. He slanted his head, parting her lips and gliding his tongue into her mouth. The little purring sound of delight that she made went right to his head. The kiss went wild, and he backed her against the wall as his mouth devoured hers. Her hands fisted into his hair, and she twisted against him. A desperate moan coming from her throat as fire burst in her blood and tore through her body like an inferno. She was going to die if he didn't make love to her. Soon. Now. Before she went out of her mind.

When her body arched against his, he realized that things were getting out of hand. If he didn't let her go now, he wouldn't let her go at all. He forced himself to release her and took a healthy step back. Looking at her didn't help any. She was flushed and wild, just as affected by the kiss as he was. Naked desire burned in her eyes. He lifted a shaking hand and traced the line of her swollen lips.

"Stay with me."

The breathless words against his finger tore at his control. He held on fiercely and made himself lift his hand and step back again. "No. But when this is done," he added huskily, "I will take you away somewhere and throw away the key. I won't embarrass you by getting involved with you now while you work for me. I have too much respect for the work you do. I won't see your reputation ruined."

She watched the door shut behind him and slowly lowered herself down to sit on the floor. She was shaking from the inside out, so empty and aching that it hurt. By the time the project was done, it might be too late. Her hand lowered and touched her hip. She was marked for death, and someone was finally making an attempt to kill her. Unless she was careful, she would die before she ever got a chance to know what it truly meant to be complete. She didn't want Taylor to lose someone else he cared for. Never again.

CHAPTER ELEVEN

Because she knew that she didn't dare keep things a secret, she went to her brothers' home the next morning. Everyone was there and hadn't yet headed out to the site for work. She had a key to the front door still, just like they all had keys to her apartment. She walked right in and into the living room where everyone was gathered.

Seven pairs of eyes lifted, studied her, and seven faces winced. She sighed. She knew what she looked like. "I didn't sleep, okay? He was an absolute gentleman."

"Damn him," Owen said, his voice deadpan.

"Tell me about it!" The frustration leaked into her voice. "He doesn't want to risk my reputation on us being involved while I work for him." She raked a hand through her unruly hair. "But that's not why I'm here." She put down the paper bag holding the remains of the nearly deadly comb. "Someone tried to kill me last night. This comb was sent to me anonymously. If Taylor hadn't been there . . ." She shuddered.

Almost as one, her brothers went off in fury. Joseff and Gavin began to curse rather creatively. Tomos went into a near panic while Seisyll tried to get him to calm down and think straight. Arian and Heul began to argue over the next course of action. And, as always, Owen was the calm, the center of it all.

He sidled over to the couch as Gwyn sat down and tucked her legs under herself. He sat down beside her and wrapped a hand around her ankle. He could calm people through a single touch and used it shamelessly when needed. "So," he said quietly, "want to tell me more about our client?"

She felt her color rise. She was assuming he didn't really want to know about the rather interesting dreams she'd had the night before. She cleared her throat. "Be specific."

"Don't be evasive." He studied her. "I know you care for him, but are you sure he's not behind it?"

"I'm sure." She closed her eyes as silence fell in the room. "I'm sure," she said again. "He's capable of killing. I know it. But . . ." She wrapped her arms around herself. "He treats me kindly and with respect. If he was out to seduce and kill me, he wouldn't have walked away last night, even when I asked him to stay."

"Gwyn," Arian began but stopped when Heul held up a hand.

She didn't notice. "All my life there's been something missing inside me," she whispered. "Not just my memories, but something else. Somehow . . . somehow . . . if I had never met Taylor . . . I know I would have died. I don't think he's going to kill me. I think he's the only one who can save me."

Heul walked over and knelt down to study her face. She did not lie and she had an unfailing sense of right and wrong. What she said was always the truth. "Regardless," he told her quietly, "of whether or not he can, I want you to be extremely careful. Do not accept strange gifts from anyone. Don't go out at night alone. You've been marked for death since you were a child. Until that mark is gone, don't let down your guard."

"What is she going to tell Taylor when he sees it?" Tomos finally spoke up.

Heul coughed lightly. Thinking about Taylor Vincent having his baby sister naked was not a favored pastime. "Well, he's not 3rd District. No need to explain unless necessary. Let him think it's a tattoo."

"I can't lie," Gwyn reminded her brothers.

"Well, hell." Gavin shrugged wryly. "Make sure the lights are off when you jump him."

"Gavin!"

"Whaaat?"

She just sighed and got to her feet. "You guys duke it out. I'm going to head to my office onsite." She glared at them. "Since you guys won't actually let me visit, I have to settle for watching through a window."

The men watched her go and shared a long look. How were they supposed to explain that the piling cord had been cut through, and that the construction sites were walking accident zones? It would be all too horribly easy to kill someone there, especially someone as trusting as Gwyn.

Because it was summertime, the streets of the District were lined with vendors who had set their wares outside. Gwyn loved walking through and looking at the different clothing and items. She rarely bought anything because it was rare to find something she liked well enough to splurge on.

Today was an exception. As she rounded a corner, she saw a rack of laced bodices for sale. The bodices were like something out of the Renaissance, and there was one in the same golden yellow of the dress Taylor had bought her. It had white ribbons to tie it in the back, and there was a small lace ruffle around the bottom edge.

Delighted, she took it off the rack and held it in front of her body. She could almost imagine Taylor's face when he saw her in it, and her stomach quivered with anticipation. She wondered if she would actually have the nerve to seduce him. What if she tried that and maybe he really didn't want her and was just stringing her along?

No, not Taylor. It was probably just that he wasn't emotionally involved despite his tenderness and respect. She wasn't so innocent that she could mistake that he truly wanted her, and he also genuinely liked her. She could work with that. Determinedly, she carried the bodice into the store to buy it.

The store, she saw then, also carried lingerie. She debated with herself for long moments before impulsively buying a matching set of underwear and bra to go under the bodice, and a white sundress she picked out to match it. It was an indulgence but, damn it, someone was trying to kill her, so she was entitled to splurge on pretty clothes to entice the man she wanted to be her lover.

By the time she got to the trailer that was her office, she couldn't resist the temptation. She hurried over to her window and shut the blinds so that no one onsite could see her, especially her brothers. She didn't want them to tease her again, and they always teased her when she was 'acting like *such* a girl.'

She shut her office door as well and then pulled out her packages again. She felt horribly decadent and scandalous as she tried on the lace lingerie and pulled the sundress on. She tugged the bodice on over it and liked the look so much she spun in a giddy circle.

The laces in the back were hard to tie but she managed to tighten them just enough that it enhanced her figure without cutting off her air. Looking down, she blushed. Maybe a shirt would have been better because the sundress wasn't covering as much of her cleavage as she would have liked. Good grief, she actually *had* cleavage. She had never really thought of herself as having too much of a bust, but the bodice was making a big show out of what she did have.

An odd smell drifted into the office and she wrinkled her nose as she hurried over to shut the window. The door opened without warning, and she started to turn to see who had walked in unannounced. Whoever had walked in was right behind her, and they grabbed the laces of her bodice and viciously jerked them closed.

The material constricted her lungs and cut off her air as she tried to turn around to get a hold of the person attacking her. Spots swam in front of her eyes and her vision began to gray out. She gasped for air and felt the laces tighten even more as she staggered. Even as darkness swamped her mind, her lungs burning and pained, her mind screamed for Taylor. He could save her. She knew he could!

He walked into the office a second later, saying, "I had a feeling you would be here. I thought I might as well bring you flowers since I forgot the ones last night and . . ." His voice stopped abruptly as he saw her on the floor near the window. The flowers fell from his hand as he rushed across the room. "Gwyn!"

He could see immediately what was wrong and yanked the letter opener off the desk to slice through the laces. The bodice opened and he beat lightly on her back. She sucked in a breath sharply and began to cough as her starved lungs pulled in air. His hands shaking, he drew her closer. Terror choked his throat. "What the hell were you doing?" he demanded roughly. "Lacing yourself in so tightly!"

"I . . ." She began to cough again, her entire body shaking as shock set in. "I didn't do it," she managed to say. "Someone . . . someone attacked me." On a surge of terror, she threw her arms around his neck. "Oh god! Taylor, someone's trying to kill me!"

"What?!" He jerked her back by the shoulders and searched her eyes. "Are you sure it wasn't just a prank gone too far?"

Tears slid down her cheeks. "No." She caught his hand and drew it up to rest on her hip under her skirt. He felt the little raised checkmark and confusion filled in his eyes. "I'm marked for death," she whispered. "Someone contracted for me to die. It's not an accident."

"Jesus." He caught her closer again as horror flooded him. If he hadn't been so certain he heard her calling . . . if his hands hadn't been burning in the way that always meant danger was near . . . he would have lost her. His faerie princess. "You have to go away," he ordered roughly.

"I can't!" She looked at him fiercely. "I won't run away!"

"The hell you won't!" He got to his feet and lifted her into his arms in one single motion. He plunked her down on the edge of her desk and planted his hands on either side of her hips. "I'm not risking you dying!" he barked.

"I'm willing to risk it!"

"I'm not!" He snatched up her phone and began to punch numbers. The operator answered and he ordered, "Connect me to the number for Enforcers." Gwyn looked at him in shock, and he glared at her intently, daring her to argue. When the phone was picked up, he said, "My name is Taylor Vincent. A woman I know is marked for death and she's from 3rd District."

There was a startled pause before Rhianna said slowly, "Her name?"

"Gwyn Trahern of Driven Snow Architecture. She's twenty-six years old. White hair, storm gray eyes. About five feet tall, one hundred pounds."

"Five-one! And I weigh one-ten, thank you!" Gwyn crossed her arms tightly.

"And a stubborn streak a mile wide," he added. "Someone is trying to kill her. Someone sent her a comb yesterday that not only spewed blades at us, but also exploded on impact. Just now someone attacked her in her office and tried to suffocate her by lacing her too tightly into a bodice."

Rhianna began to have a very strong feeling in the pit of her stomach and made a note to call Eric and Rayna as soon as possible. She had been suspicious about Gwyn Trahern from the moment the family had moved back into the District. "This is important," she told him, "so answer carefully. Who are her parents?"

"She doesn't know. She has amnesia. No memories before she was nine." His brows shot up. "You know her."

"Guard her *closely,* Taylor. I'm going to send my partner and his wife out to meet you tomorrow. I can't get them there any sooner. Do NOT let Gwyn Trahern out of your sight!"

"Understood." He hung up the phone and gave Gwyn a pointed look. "You're not to be out of my sight, and Ms. Taber is sending out an Enforcer tomorrow to look into things. In the meantime, you're coming home with me."

"I can't do that!" She muffled a shriek as he scooped her up off the desk and tossed her over his shoulder. "Put me down!" Mortified color climbed her cheeks as they left the office and she saw her brothers gaping at them. "Taylor!" she wailed. "Have pity!"

He spotted Heul and figured he had to be the eldest since he was certainly the biggest. "I'm taking your sister somewhere safe. Someone is trying to kill her, and I'll be damned before I let it happen. Enforcers will be out tomorrow."

Heul cleared his throat and decided not to say anything. He recognized a very furious and very frustrated male. In that moment, he had no doubt that Taylor was as far in over his head as Gwyn. He watched Taylor put Gwyn into his car, kicking the entire way, and covered a laugh.

Joseff swung down to his level by hanging upside down from a support beam by his ankles. "Did he do what I think he did?" he asked in awe.

"Kidnap your twin? Yes, yes he did." Damned if he couldn't like Taylor for it, he thought in bemusement. Gwyn was kind and gentle, yes, but she had a stubborn streak a mile wide. It was impossible to say no to her, just as it was impossible to make her change her mind. Taylor had just done both.

Gwyn sat in mutinous silence as Taylor drove. She was too upset to even look at him. He was no less upset; in fact, he was furious she had not told him what was going on. It was only when the car slowed and pulled into a driveway that she finally began to pay attention. It was an apartment complex in an upscale part of Brooklyn, and she blinked in confusion. "Where are we?" she asked warily.

"My place." He pulled her out of the car and kept an arm around her waist as they went into the building. He didn't quite trust her not to run away from him.

"This is a bad idea," she whispered. She wasn't sure she could trust herself to be alone with him. She loved him too badly. Wanted him more than she wanted air, and she had just learned how precious air really was.

"Tough." He unlocked his apartment and ushered her inside. He locked the door behind them again and then tossed his jacket over the back of a chair. "This is the only place I figure I can successfully keep a faerie princess, with no self-preservation skills, safe!"

"Thanks a lot!" She poked him in the chest. "Look, wise *soldier*, I'm not going to hide away! It's not right!"

"Right! Not right she says!" He caught her chin in his fingers and tilted her face back so she was forced to look at him. "It's not right either," he ground out, "that I had to find out about your death sentence by walking into your office and seeing you on the floor!"

The truth of his words felt like a physical blow, and she closed her eyes helplessly. "I know," she whispered. "But I didn't know how you'd accept it. I was sure you would back off, and I couldn't bear the idea."

"Back off?" He gave a rough laugh and caught her in his arms. "It's way too late for me to back off now. It was too late when I hired you."

"Then why did you leave me?" she demanded, furious tears burning her eyes. "If I'm going to die, I don't want to die a virgin, never knowing what it means to give myself to the man I love! Oops!" She covered her mouth with her hands, shocked she had just blurted it out.

He went very still. In a faint voice, he said, "I left you because I would be damned if I embarrassed you by making you get involved with a client."

"It's stupid!" she snapped at him. She pushed herself out of his arms. "It's not *right!*"

"No, it's not." His hand closed around the nape of her neck and yanked her against his aching body. "You're fired." Before she could protest, his mouth had come down on hers with an almost bruising force that demanded she hold nothing back.

A shudder went through her body and she stopped struggling to get away, instead throwing herself into his embrace with a wild abandon that made his head spin. The kiss deepened, went wilder and wilder, and he finally just lifted her into his arms and began to stride down the hall.

She didn't help his self-control any by racing hungry kisses over his face. She couldn't get enough of his taste. She felt as if she was starved for him. He dropped her onto her feet beside the bed and kissed her again, his hands quickly stripping the ruined bodice aside and hurling it behind him somewhere. She quickly unbuttoned his shirt and yanked it out of his jeans, just as desperate for more as he was. Why did it feel as if she had been waiting for centuries?

He trembled as her hands spread across his chest. The storm in her eyes had been unleashed and it was drowning them both. He dragged her closer and buried his lips against her throat to taste her pulse. She whimpered low in her throat as his arousal pressed against her stomach, and she went on her toes to hold him closer. "Please," she managed to whisper.

"I'll please you. Nothing's going to stop me." He lifted his head long enough to get a handful of her sundress and strip it up over her head. His mouth went dry. Little scraps of golden lace did amazing things to an already, impossibly, perfect body. "Holy hell."

She laughed suddenly, her voice husky with feminine power. "I was hoping you'd approve. I felt so . . . so sneaky when I bought it. It seemed like a trap or something."

"It worked," he managed to say. "Good god." He eagerly drew her into his arms, his lips seeking hers again. She arched her body against his and it took all of his control to not tumble her onto the floor and take her where they stood.

The room whirled around her head. She gasped as she landed on the bed and his weight sank her into the mattress. His hot hand cupped her breast, and she moaned softly as pleasure streaked from the contact all through her body. Before she could catch a breath, he opened the front clasp on the bra and his palm softly caressed her bare flesh.

She felt like silk and fire. He ran wild kisses over her neck and shoulders and moved steadily lower. He couldn't get enough of her taste and closed his lips over one nipple to suckle sharply. Her back arched on a wild cry and he caught her there, holding her as tightly as he could. Ravenous, he devoured her flesh and raked his lips down across her stomach.

"Taylor," she pleaded, terrified of how high he was pushing her senses. Her voice became a strangled gasp as his fingers slid between her legs and found her softest flesh. He caressed her until she couldn't breathe for the tension consuming her.

"Go higher," he muttered against her throat. He shuddered as he felt how hot and wet she was even through her underwear. He wanted to dive into her, to take her so completely they were one. He stripped the scrap of lace down her legs and lifted his head to survey her naked body with savage satisfaction. "You're mine," he vowed softly.

She opened her mouth to answer but his fingers moved on her bare flesh and she couldn't think, let alone speak. She clung desperately to him and twisted her body against his touch, begging for an end to the ceaseless pleasure. "Taylor!"

His lips closed over the point of one breast just as his thumb pressed against the bundle of nerves at the apex of her thighs. Her entire body jerked in shock and then came apart, wild pleasure washing over her. When the spasms finally ended, she opened her eyes to see him watching her with rapt attention.

His mouth covered hers and she went into the kiss eagerly, a shiver rippling through her body as that alone awoke desire once more. With a rough sound, he forced himself to release her, and stood long enough to quickly shed his clothes. She reached for him as he joined her again, and there was no hesitation in her touch, no shyness, as if she knew this was right. Somehow, he did too.

"I want to touch you," she whispered against his lips when he lifted his head slightly. "I want to know everything."

"Later," he promised, his hands sliding over her flesh.

"Now." She twisted her body and caught him off guard, allowing her to tumble him onto his back. She had him pinned before he could move, and her lips made hot forays across his skin. He shuddered. She smiled, delighted with the knowledge that she could overpower him. She watched her hand gliding over his muscled stomach and trembled with emotion. "I love you," she whispered as she pressed her lips to his shoulder.

She was wild as fire, her hands and lips caressing him hotly. There was only the slightest hesitation in her touch as she curled her hand around his erection to learn the feel of him. He bit back a hoarse groan, and she closed her lips over one flat, male nipple.

His control snapped with a nearly audible sound. One hand fisted into her hair, and he dragged her higher up so he could kiss her greedily. A little sound of pleasure issued from her throat. He rolled and tucked her underneath him desperately. The feel of bare skin against bare skin brought a brief moment of sanity. He caught her face in his hands. "Do you need me to protect you?" he asked roughly.

She shook her head quickly. He didn't know if that meant she was on birth control or simply trusted him, but he didn't care. He knew she had understood the question and all of its potential outcomes. He dragged her legs up and over his arms, opening her to him. "Let me have you," he pleaded, lifting his lips slightly.

"Yes." Her instinctive fear at being so vulnerable was drowned in a searing wave of fire. "Please!" Her breath caught as his hard flesh began to stretch her, and her body tried to adjust to the movement. It ached rather than hurt, but she couldn't bear the idea of him stopping. Her hips arched wildly in an effort to take him, and he shuddered and drove into her completely.

He went still and gulped air as he tried to let her adjust. He would be damned if he hurt her now. His lips raced over her face and caught the trace of tears. He nearly started to pull away but her grip tightened, and her lips found his. She clung on desperately and twisted her body against his to prove she was fine. It was all he needed to know. He began to drive into her again and again, and her breathless cries branded his heart.

The only ache she could feel was the one built from relentless pleasure demanding release. His fingers found some sensitive place along her spine, and it lit up every nerve in her body. Only his hungry kiss kept her cry of ecstasy from escaping out the open window, and her lips equally stole his hoarse groan as he, too, surrendered to the pleasure. Her arms tightened around him fiercely as if afraid he would be torn away from her now that she had claimed him.

He had enough presence of mind to catch his weight on his arms, but that was all he could manage as he kept her locked securely in his arms beneath him. He felt stunned and shaken all the way to his core. He had, in his life, experienced both sex and making love. This didn't seem to be either of those two things. It went far, far beyond the physical and into something damn near spiritual. Magical. It could only grow stronger with time.

He lifted his head and stared at her as he memorized her features. "Gwyn." Her eyes opened and she looked up at him with a questioning look on her face. He gently cupped her cheek and touched her lips with his. "I love you." Her eyes widened, and he eased back with a smile. "I knew it yesterday. How could I not? The faerie princess of my dreams landed in my arms."

Tears burned her eyes and she closed them as her lips trembled. "You fired me, you bully."

"Yes, well, I was desperate." His lips glided over her face and stole her tears. "At that point I'd have done anything to have you. There was no way I'd be able to keep my hands off you, not after your confession." He smiled at her. "How about telling me now? Really telling me, instead of blurting it out in anger."

"It's your fault." She flushed slightly. "You kidnapped me!" On a groan, she covered her face with a hand. "I'll never be able to face my brothers again." He laughed at her and she glowered. She resembled a disgruntled faerie so much that he had to kiss her. When he lifted his head again, she searched his face with an inner hunger she could not fight. "I love you," she whispered.

He trembled slightly and held her closer. "Let me keep you safe," he said into her hair.

"I will not stay cooped up." Her chin set into a stubborn line.

"Then come with me to the office tomorrow." He grinned slightly. "I'll get you to actually model for me." When she blinked, he freed himself from her arms and left the bed to go to his desk.

She admired him without shame, thrilling to the idea of being able to touch him as she pleased. She was startled out of her admiration when he dropped a folder on her stomach. "Oof." She sat up and curiously dumped the folder open. Images spilled across the sheets, and her breath caught.

It was her. He had drawn her as the faerie princess for his game. Her heart swelled with emotion. "I'm not this beautiful," she whispered. "And I don't have wings. And I can't cast magic."

He laughed softly. "Neither can she." He skimmed his fingers through her hair. "I knew, when I saw you, that you were my faerie princess. And like my soldier, I'll do whatever it takes to keep you safe." He drew her into his arms and closed his eyes, his heart tightening with a rush of emotion as she curled trustingly against him. Come hell or high water, he would keep her safe if it was the last thing he ever did.

CHAPTER TWELVE

The day passed in a blur. What little time they didn't spend in bed, they spent either eating together or watching movies on the giant flat screen television that Taylor called his guilty pleasure. Gwyn cooked dinner for them, and after one bite, he informed her that he would be her willing slave if she cooked for him like that all the time.

Through it all, there was a growing suspicion in her mind. He would answer questions before she asked them. If she was thinking his name, he would answer as if she had spoken out loud. He somehow knew when a vase was about to fall on her and moved her out of the way well before it toppled.

If the man wasn't psychic, she was going to eat her hat. Power recognized power and having spent a significant amount of time as physically close to him as a woman could get, she was definitely recognizing the presence of power.

It wasn't until the next morning when she finally decided it was time to bring it up. They were lying together and listening to the sound and scent of a summer rain. She was sprawled over his chest, limp with contented pleasure. With her ear pressed against his chest, she could hear his heartbeat slowly steadying. She really didn't want to go to the office.

"Me neither," he murmured drowsily, his voice as lazy with satisfaction as her body felt.

She contemplated her words for a moment. "I didn't say anything."

"Yes, you did."

"Did not." It wasn't the first time they'd had the exact same conversation. She propped herself up on an elbow and studied her lover's face. "Taylor," she said calmly, "have you ever considered the idea that you might be, shall we say, psychic?"

That got his eyes open quick. He eyed her intently. "Pardon me?"

"You hear me when I don't speak. Your hands burn when there's danger. I *know* you subconsciously heard me when I called your name yesterday. I hate to tell you, but normal people don't do that." She smiled. "Am I missing anything on the list?" He hesitated and she tugged on a lock of his chest hair. "Talk, Taylor."

"Ouch. Brat." He snuggled her closer. "I guess strange things have always happened. Ever since my parents died, I've noticed odd things. Sometimes catching snippets of conversations from other rooms. Picking up on wayward thoughts. The burning hands thing is the big one. When it's directed at someone I know, it's nearly unbearable."

She hesitated. Slowly she asked, "Have you ever sweated blood?"

"Yes," he said warily. "Under extreme pressure. Why?"

She winced. "There's an ability. It's called a Plasma Sense. It's one of the more unnerving abilities to possess. It, uhm, is essentially an early warning system built directly into your blood. That burning in your hands, it's your blood burning. If you ever fully tap your power your hands might be covered with blood as your body tries to send you the warning."

"How useful is that?" he asked on a grimace.

"I'm not sure," she admitted. "The only person I know who had it said that when she looked at her hands, she just *knew* who it was in danger and where they were."

"Pleasant." He blew out a breath. He knew full well that she couldn't tell a lie. Whatever she said, she believed to be true. "What about the telepathy?" It was easier to say than he had thought it would be.

"Most people with power have some sort of mental strength. Since yours is strongest with me, it'll probably never, actually, interfere with your life." She nuzzled his shoulder softly, her simple delight in touching him squeezing his heart. "I don't really know what my own abilities are," she admitted. "But I'm not scared of them now. You'll protect me."

Her honest and innocent trust made him break out in a sweat. "Why are your brothers sane?" he muttered.

"Hey."

"Damn it, woman, you trust too easily!"

"If I waste my time distrusting everyone, then I waste the opportunity to know new people and learn new things." She shrugged one shoulder. "And I'm a good judge of character. The problem with most adults is that they learn to be cynical."

"It's safer."

"It's stupid." She cuddled closer. "If I'd been distrusting of you, we wouldn't be here, you know."

"I'd argue that." He skimmed his hands over her back. "We might not be here right now, but we'd eventually have been here. I wanted you the minute I saw you. I still want you." His fingers slid slowly between her legs and her breath caught. "You respond like you were made for me," he murmured huskily. "Are you too sore to take me again?"

"Yes," she whispered. "Damn it." She made a startled sound and held on as he lifted her into his arms and got to his feet. She almost asked where they were going, but she saw he was heading for the bathroom so assumed it was the shower. She blushed. She was never looking at a shower the same again, not after his idea of washing her.

He gently put her on her feet and ran water in the tub. He smiled. "You take a bath and soak some of the soreness out. I'll make some breakfast."

She eyed him balefully. "Can you cook?"

"Yes, princess." He tweaked her nose lightly. "Not like your gourmet self, but I can cook." He was beginning to understand why her brothers had fought to keep her from moving out. Dear god, the woman could put professionals to shame with her cooking.

"Okay." She sank into the tub on a little wince as he left the room, and then closed her eyes and tilted her head back. She felt just a little sore, but it was understandable, she thought impishly. As demanding as his passion was, hers more than matched it. "So that's why waiting makes it worth it," she murmured to herself

She lingered for a long while until she noticed her fingers wrinkling. Contented, and less sore, she got out of the tub. She could smell bacon and eggs even from the bathroom. She wrapped herself in Taylor's robe and just sighed as the sleeves flopped well past her hands. She cuffed them several times to find her hands again, and she had to hold the bottom, like the train of a skirt, in order to walk safely.

He took one look at her and burst into laughter. She wrinkled her nose. "So I'm tiny. It's not a crime."

"No, but it's cute as hell." He helped her to her seat and bowed deeply. "My lady." She swatted at him and he grinned as he went to get their food. "I like spoiling you," he decided as he sat beside her. "I keep trying to give you flowers, too."

She smiled shyly. "I don't need to be spoiled. I just need you. That's enough to make me happy." She took a bite of her food. A smile tugged at her lips. "You burned the toast."

"Then you make breakfast from now on," he answered casually.

Her heart gave a wild leap of joy that she didn't bother to temper. Riding with it, she threw her arms around him and almost knocked them both over. "Does that mean I can stay with you longer? Sort of . . . live with you?"

"No." He framed her face with his hand. "Gwyn, I don't want you to just move in. I want . . ." He broke off as the phone rang. "Well, hell. Wait here."

She watched him go to the phone, giddy delight in her heart. Was he going to ask her to marry him? She hoped so! She would ask her brothers to give her away, and Joseff could be her maid of honor. Or something like that. Male of honor? Was there a proper term? The best man was for the groom. Brother of honor, maybe.

He hung up the phone and looked at her, his face set. "That was the office. They just got a call that an Enforcer has contacted them and will be there within the hour. We should be there to meet them."

"Okay." She got to her feet and started to clear the table when he touched her cheek and drew her gaze. "Yes?"

"When this is over, we'll talk again," he murmured softly. "Promise."

A warm glow filled her. "Okay." The glow stayed with her the entire way to the office, and it was visible to everyone who looked at her. There wasn't a single person there who doubted she and Taylor were lovers. There also wasn't a single person who doubted that that was the way it should be. Something just always seemed to be right about Gwyn. She didn't judge anyone, so why judge her?

Melissa seemed to have come to a similar feeling because she was waiting outside Taylor's office for them. "Miss Trahern," she said hesitantly, "may I talk to you? I want to apologize. Maybe we could go to the cafeteria or something?"

Gwyn could never carry a grudge. She smiled. "Of course." Taylor smiled at her, and she knew he was fine with it as long as she didn't leave the building. She fell into step beside Melissa. "You don't need to explain or anything," she told her. "It's just nice that you don't hate me anymore."

"It was jealousy!" Melissa lightly waved a ringed hand as they sat down in the cafeteria. There was no one else there but the cleaning men and they were sharing a cup of coffee. "I was horribly jealous of you," she admitted.

"Me?!" Gwyn stared at her in shock. "But,why?"

"I'd been working on getting Taylor to notice me for years, and he was oblivious. You came in and he was worse than a tomcat who caught the scent of a female in heat." She leaned back with a smile as Gwyn coughed and blushed. "Sorry."

"It's okay." Gwyn smiled. "I'm just glad everything's okay now."

"Me, too. Hey, you hungry? I interrupted your breakfast this morning, didn't I?" When Gwyn waved a hand as if to say it didn't matter, she smiled. "Well, I want a snack. Sure you don't want an apple or something?"

Feeling it would be rude to decline, Gwyn nodded with a smile. "Sure." She watched Melissa go to the counter and get two apples and felt a sense of relief that she was going to be able to get along with Taylor's assistant. "I was worried," she admitted as she took the apple and bit in. "I mean, Taylor and I seem to be getting pretty serious. I wanted to be your friend first."

Melissa nibbled at her own apple. "You're such a good person."

A sudden dizziness hit Gwyn. Her head began to spin and the room tilted like a funhouse. She tried to lift a hand to her forehead, but her muscles were growing heavy. Her entire body was starting to feel like dead weight. She tried to get to her feet, but it was almost impossible to move. She fell to her knees, the scales in her mind tilting wildly. "You," she managed to say. "You drugged me."

Melissa caught her by her hair and dragged her head back. "You're such a good person," she repeated with a sneer in her voice. "Too good. Friends? What a laugh. We'll never be friends, little girl, and once you're dead everything will go back to normal. I'll be the most beautiful woman in the company and Taylor will come to be mine."

Gwyn managed to look up into her eyes and pity filled her heart. "I'm sorry," she whispered.

"What for?"

"That you're so empty inside."

She slumped over and Melissa released her in fury. The two cleaners approached quickly and she snapped at them, "Take her somewhere she won't be found! Preferably somewhere I can be sure she won't wake up!"

His hands were burning. Taylor lifted them and stared at them. They had been at it for the last five minutes, and it was steadily growing in force. His skin felt as if it was on fire. Someone knocked on the door, and he looked up quickly. "Yes?"

The door opened and he got to his feet as a tall man with ash brown hair winged with white and a slender young woman with silvery hair entered. The woman bore such a powerful resemblance to Gwyn that he sucked in a sharp breath. They could have been twins; they looked that much alike. "My god," he managed to say. "Who the hell are you?"

"My name is Eric Mason." Eric gently placed a hand on Rayna's shoulder. "This is my wife, Rayna. We're from Enforcers. We're here about Gwyn Trahern." Taylor was still staring at Rayna in shock, and he felt his heart clench. "I take it Rayna resembles your Gwyn."

"Yes." Taylor sat down quickly. "My god," he said again. "You've got to be related to her." His eyes shot to Rayna's. "Were you ever marked for death too?"

"Yes." She lowered her gaze. "My sister and I both were. There was a car accident when I was four and she was nine. She was flung from the car just as I was, but no one ever found her. I didn't wake from my coma until a year ago."

"And you're safe now?" he demanded.

"Yes, because of her contract with Enforcers." Eric dropped a stack of paper on his desk. "Mika Carmichael's contract is still open. The event that was supposed to occur to save her life never happened. Until this contract is fulfilled, she will be at risk. Where is Gwyn now?"

"She went to lunch with my assistant."

Rayna stared at Taylor's hands. "Your hands are burning."

"Yes." He stared at her. "How did you know?"

"We can explain later," Eric said urgently. "Where is Gwyn?"

Taylor was beginning to feel more than a little panicked. When he heard a noise in the office beside his, his stomach clenched. "Melissa!" he barked. He went over to the office door connecting his area to hers and flung it open. She looked at him in alarm and he demanded, "Where is Gwyn?"

"I don't know!" She seemed taken aback by the sight of Rayna, almost as much as he had been. "What is going on?"

"Taylor," Eric urged as he grabbed the younger man's shoulder. "Think! If Gwyn is in immediate danger, you can know if you just open yourself up! You have a very powerful gift for being not of the District!" He narrowed an icy blue gaze on Melissa. "When did you leave Gwyn?"

"We had lunch and then she decided to go out for a bit. I haven't seen her for a while now. Geez, back off! I don't know what happened to her."

Rayna's head jerked toward Melissa. Horror filled her eyes. "Riku!"

Eric didn't hesitate. He lifted a hand and cast wind magic that flung Melissa into her chair and bound her. He didn't need to know what truth Rayna had heard to understand it had to be terrible.

Taylor was barely aware of what they were doing. He was concentrating fiercely on his burning blood. He didn't care what kind of power it was. He needed it. He needed it to save Gwyn. It was the only thing important to him. He could not lose her now!

"What did you do to Gwyn Trahern?" Eric demanded of Melissa.

"Nothing!"

"Lie." Rayna's voice sounded amazingly cold coming from a face so delicate and eyes so naturally giving. "She's trying to kill Gwyn." Her head tilted slightly. "Has *been* trying to kill Gwyn. Thrice attempted."

Melissa stared at her in growing horror as she realized the other woman could see through lies. She looked at Taylor for help and went pale as she saw blood beginning to cover his hands. "What is that?" she managed to whisper.

Taylor stared at the blood. It seemed almost like a projection screen. He could see glimpses of Gwyn's pale face in the red color. She was lying at the bottom of a hole with rain beating down on her. The view seemed to shift and he saw steel and concrete. His head jerked up as the blood disappeared. "I know where she is!"

"Go!" Eric snapped. "We'll stay here. For god's sake, Taylor, hurry!"

He wasted no time as he raced through the building, taking the stairs because the elevator would be too long. He drove faster than was legal but somehow didn't get stopped. Lights changed miraculously for him so that he made the trip in a quarter of the time. Even before the car was fully parked, he leapt out and ran for the site.

No one was there because of the rain. He ran toward the foundation and slid on the mud when he didn't step right. "Gwyn!" he shouted. "Gwyn! Answer me, Gwyn!"

Nothing came back but the sound of his own voice. He slid down into the foundation itself and headed for the four holes where the first structural beams would be placed. Cement spouts were poised over the holes and tarps thrown over the entire thing to keep out water and debris.

Terror choked him as he went to the first hole to yank up the tarp. Nothing. He found her lying at the bottom of the hole under the third one. She almost looked as if she was taking a nap. "Gwyn! Wake up!" There was no response and he looked around sharply. He found a ladder and used it to swiftly climb down into the hole.

His heart only started beating again when he heard her breathing, but it was shallow and she was pale. Cold. She was so cold to the touch. He dug out his cell phone and dialed 911, praying that he wasn't too late. Why wouldn't she wake up?

He discovered the extent of the Enforcers' power quickly. As soon as he mentioned Eric's name, the paramedics prepared to transport her to the Enforcers-owned hospital in the 3rd District. He rode along with them in the ambulance, his fingers desperately entwined with Gwyn's.

At the hospital, he was forced to remain behind as she was rushed into Emergency. He was only dimly aware of when Eric and Rayna arrived. He felt numbed and battered from the inside out. He couldn't say anything as Rayna took him to the waiting room and made him sit down. All he could do was stare blindly at the floor, not even conscious of her gently tucking a warm blanket around his shoulders.

When the Trahern brothers arrived, they rushed into the waiting room and came to sharp stops as they saw Rayna. "Holy hell," Seisyll managed to say. "There're two of them."

She glanced between him and his identical twin but didn't comment on the irony. "I'm Rayna Mason," she told them softly. "Sit down. Gwyn is in Emergency. Riku, that is, my husband, Eric, is with her. I'll tell you what I know, okay?"

Eric remained in Emergency with the doctors and oversaw everything. It came as no surprise to him that Gwyn had been drugged with the same insidious venom that had tried to take Rayna just a month before. It also came as no shock that Gwyn did not wake even after the venom was gone.

When she was moved to a regular room, he gently tried to reach out to her mind. Her brain waves were vastly different from the rest of the world, even among psychics. Like Rayna, she had a built-in defensive system designed to protect an exceptionally powerful mind from outside interference.

He couldn't get a lock on her. The only thing that he could be sure of was that her power was rising rampantly as it tried to find the power Rhianna and Eric emitted. Her contract was trying to fulfill itself, but with Rayna awake, the clause in Gwyn's contract that dictated the length of her coma was completely nulled.

It was the hardest thing he had ever done to walk into the lobby where Taylor and the Trahern brothers waited. All looked as if they had been devastated.

Taylor spotted him first. "Well?" he demanded roughly. "Why won't she wake up?"

Eric wrapped his arms around Rayna when she curled against his side comfortingly. "Seventeen years ago," he began, "Lucas Carmichael came to Enforcers to tell us that his daughters had Bloody Contracts issued against them for their deaths. Contracts were formed to try to negate the effects until the girls came of age. For Rayna, she entered a coma that was to last until her twenty-first birthday. Mika was to enter a coma during her twentieth year and awaken when Rayna did. Once awakened, their power would merge with the powers of the Enforcers and nullify the Bloody Contracts."

Eyes shifted to Rayna in sudden understanding. She nodded slowly. "Gwyn is my sister, Mika Carmichael." She bit her lower lip. "Things got out of control. I accidentally awakened too soon." She covered Eric's hands when he held her closer. "It took Riku a lot of effort to keep me alive until I was twenty-one. Once I was, my contract fulfilled. My Bloody Check disappeared."

Taylor took a quick breath. "So because your contract is completed and Gwyn's isn't, there are loose threads."

Eric looked at Joseff. "No matter how much you wanted to protect her, the minute you saved her from that accident six years ago, you threw everything off balance. She has gone along largely unawakened in power and that means there's nothing to merge with the Enforcers."

"So . . ." Heul swallowed hard. "So there's no telling when she might wake up. She *might* wake up in six years, because that's how long she should have slept, and yet she might not because the contract is partially voided."

"It could be six years, sixty years . . . or six hundred years." Eric lowered his gaze. "We're not gods. There are limits to what Rhianna and I can do. All I can say with certainty is that when she finally awakes, her contract will complete. Her power will join with Enforcers and her Bloody Contract will be nullified."

"Why were they targeted?!" Arian shouted as he leapt to his feet. "Why?! Why would anyone put a mark of death on two girls like Gwyn and Rayna?"

"That," Eric admitted, "is something only they can tell us. And unless Gwyn awakens, we may never know." He released his wife and walked over to where Taylor stared blindly at the wall across the room. "Taylor." When his gaze lifted, Eric said quietly, "I've been here. I know what you're going through. Wake Gwyn. You're the only one who can. She will answer if you call her. She has to. Your mind can tune itself to hers where no other can. Help her find her way back."

Taylor didn't know what he could possibly do, but he knew that he could not bear the idea of living without Gwyn. He painfully got to his feet and went down the hall toward the room where she was being held. The guards let him in, and he felt a punch of pain as he saw the stillness of her body. She looked like she was asleep, but it was worse. It was so much worse.

He drew the visitor's chair closer and reached out to take her hand in his and link their fingers together. He remembered the blood on his hands, and knew he would never fight his abilities again if it meant keeping her safe. He should never have ignored that burning sensation. "Gwyn." He watched her face for a sign of response. "If you can hear me, I'm so sorry." He closed his eyes. "I didn't do a good job of protecting you, faerie. You must hate me so much now."

There was no answer and he moved closer. He pressed her hand to his cheek. "You were right, you know. I am psychic. Scared the hell out of me when my hands were covered in blood, if only because I could see your face and what had been done to you. I went a little mad, I think, when I saw where you were.

"You have to come back to me, you know. How else will I propose to you? I was going to do that this morning but we were interrupted." He looked at the clock and laughed softly. "Okay, it was yesterday morning. It's after midnight now. But it's true. I want you to marry me, Gwyn. In three days you have become more important to me than anything."

He closed his eyes and pressed his lips to her hand. "Please, come back to me," he whispered. "I swear I'll do a better job of protecting you this time, Gwyn. Just trust me again, the way you did before." He stood and looked down at her, his free hand lifting to cup her cheek. "I love you. I'll love you until the end of time. Even if you never wake, I'll never love another. I'll wait for you, forever." He leaned down and touched her lips softly with his, pain almost choking him. He couldn't bear it! Three days before, he hadn't known her. Now, facing a future without her, it was like his worst hell. He couldn't live without her.

She drew a deep breath suddenly. He straightened in shock, hope rushing through him. "Gwyn?" he whispered.

Her eyes opened and she looked up at him with a shy smile on her face. "Good morning," she whispered back. "I heard you calling me. I felt you, in my mind. I couldn't stay away." Her arms lifted to curl around his neck as he gathered her close in his arms, and their lips met with almost desperate longing. The painful burn that had always lingered in her hip where the Bloody Check was located seemed to fade away. As if sensing it, his fingers slid down to her hip. "It's gone," she told him softly. "My contract is complete."

He straightened in shock. "How did you know?" He searched her eyes. "Is your memory back?"

"And then some." A soft note of steel echoed in her voice, that he had never heard before. "My memory is very, *very* old, Taylor." Her eyes met his. "Millennia old." She pressed her lips softly to his and then let him go. "Hold my hand and you will see. I'm going to link with my sister."

He gripped her hand tightly, though he was rightfully puzzled. He could see the rise in her power, and it was power that was fully under control. He could literally *see* her reaching for her sister's mind. And because he was linked to Gwyn, and Eric to Rayna, he could even see Eric's presence as a shadow in Rayna's mind.

Rayna, Gwyn called mentally, *link with me, little sister.*

Rayna's head jerked up and her eyes went unfocused. The violet color seemed to overtake her pupils until they disappeared. Power rose inside her so strongly that it crackled in the air. Eric held tightly to her hand, his mind's eye observing what was happening. The two erratic wavelengths of the sisters merged seamlessly . . . and fused.

At the same time, their heads fell back as a pair of tiny wings emerged from under their hair right behind their ears. Taylor didn't fully understand what he was seeing. Eric did. All the pieces fell into place as he finally understood the critical importance of Rayna and Gwyn's existence to the District and the world. He was already calling Rhianna mentally as he followed Rayna down the hall toward Gwyn's room.

"Gwyn!" Rayna burst into the room, rushed over to her sister's side, and threw her arms around her on a sob. "You scared me!"

Gwyn held her sister fiercely close. "I know." She began to sniffle too, her breath hitching on a sob. "Oh, Rayna, I missed you!" The pain bubbled out of nowhere on the heels of her memories. Her mother was dead. "Oh god," she whimpered. "She didn't deserve to die!"

Taylor felt helpless as he watched the two sisters grieve, and he looked at Eric as the older man tapped his shoulder. Eric inclined his head, and Taylor reluctantly followed him into the hall and closed the door.

The two women clung together as they shared their grief. After a few moments, Rayna finally eased back and looked up at her sister's face to search her eyes intently. "Why didn't you come looking for us? Didn't you want to be with us?"

"I didn't remember." Gwyn wiped her eyes with her hand. "I lost all of my memories in my fall down the hill, and the amnesia stayed until I awoke just now. Those men you saw in the lobby are my brothers. They took me in and raised me. They're some of the finest men I've ever known."

"I like them." Rayna rested her head on her sister's shoulder. "And I like your Taylor. He's kind of like Riku in some ways."

"Yeah." Gwyn found a smile for the first time. "How did you manage to catch a two thousand year old elemental master anyway?" She had sensed him even from her sleep, but she just hadn't cared enough to respond. Only Taylor had reached her heart.

Rayna giggled a little. "I was in a coma," she explained, "for sixteen years after the accident. Riku woke me too soon and my contract was affected. To protect me until my birthday, he came to spend time with me. We fell in love. I ended up in another coma, after Uncle Larry attacked me. Riku called me back, like Taylor called you."

"Does Riku know what we are?" Gwyn asked softly.

She nodded. "I think he does now." She smiled. "Riku knows almost everything. I'm actually holding one secret from him, and I'm really, really proud of it."

She leaned up and whispered in Gwyn's ear, and her sister giggled softly. "Can I watch you tell him?"

"No!" Rayna giggled too.

Out in the hall, Taylor turned to Eric and asked, "Can you explain that, Mr. Mason?"

"Eric or Riku. We're going to be in-laws." Eric leaned against the wall. "Congratulations, by the way. Not many men can claim to have taken goddesses for lovers like we have." He watched Taylor choke on the bottle of water he had pulled from a vending machine. "This surprises you."

"No shit!" Taylor stared at him. "I'm going to assume you were speaking in a metaphorical sense."

"It was literal. Rayna and Mika Carmichael are the Goddesses of Truth and Justice, reborn." Eric looked at him intently. "That's why they were marked for death. There is something evil on the loose, and it is attached to their aunt and uncle. As soon as they awakened, they would track and destroy the evil. That's why Rhianna felt they were critical to Enforcers. We, too, exist to destroy evil."

"How?" Taylor asked. "I noticed Rayna has an ear for hearing lies, and Gwyn has always been firm on right and wrong, but . . ."

"Rayna is Truth. She literally hears the truth over someone's words when they tell a lie. And, if she's touching them, she hears the truth without a word. She can tap the truth of someone's soul and expose it. Sometimes it transforms the body into a shape befitting the soul.

"Gwyn is Justice. When she looks at someone, she can see the balance of their life thus far. One side is the good, one is the bad. What they've done, and what has been done to them. She treats everyone fairly, judging only on the basis of her scales. If one side is tipped too far to either side, she can balance the scales by administering justice. She has to work in conjunction with her sister because some crimes are so heinous they must be exposed as truth before justice can be properly served."

Taylor blew out a hard breath. "Not an easy existence. Explain about this 'evil' thing."

"Do you know what evil is?" Eric asked quietly.

"Yeah." He thought of his childhood. "I grew up with it. I was forced to destroy it."

Eric wasn't surprised. "That's what needs to be done, Taylor. True evil can only be destroyed. And that's what Larry and Yvonne Carmichael contracted with to put the Bloody Check on their nieces. It was prophesized before the girls were born that their mother—a Faeriekin princess, by the way—would give birth to two exceptionally powerful beings. No one knew what the girls could do, precisely, but you can be sure the evil attached to Larry did. It influenced him to arrange for their deaths. The people Rayna saw during the accident were its minions."

"Then you stepped in," he summed up. "Well, fine. That explains the why. But, and I really hate to point this out, the aforementioned uncle and aunt are still out there somewhere, and I don't see them giving up if they know our goddesses are capable of destroying them."

"That's why," came Gwyn's voice from the doorway, "we're going to go gunning for them for once." She stood side by side with her little sister, their hands tightly laced together. "We'll expose them for the murderers they are, and then justice will be served. For now, we'll start with Melissa. She does not deserve to get off without being judged."

"It's going to be hell living with you, isn't it?" Taylor complained. She stuck her tongue out at him, and he felt his heart ease as he saw that nothing had really changed. Goddess or not, she was still the same impish, faerie princess who had stolen his heart. "While all of you talk to Melissa, I'm going to go back to the office and see if I can't find a paper trail for us to use. Normal mortals wouldn't understand this whole situation."

"He's starting to sound like one of us," Eric noted dryly, and made his wife giggle softly. "Let's get to work."

CHAPTER THIRTEEN

When Gwyn walked into the lobby, her brothers were staring at the floor. She propped her hands on her hips. "Man, you'd think someone had died."

Seven heads jerked up. "Gwyn," Heul breathed.

With a whoop, Joseff shot across the room to scoop her up in his arms and swing her around exuberantly. "I missed you!" he said into her hair. "Man, you scared us!" His mind automatically searched for hers, felt her touch, and his shoulders relaxed. But, curiously, he felt something more. He looked at Rayna. "You're mentally linked?"

She smiled. "Seems so."

He considered that. "I can handle that," he decided. "That is, if you don't mind that Gwyn and I are like twins too."

"I think it's wonderful." She rose up on her toes to kiss his cheek. "I envy her a little." She smiled a little sadly. "My father and I are still not comfortable with each other. Riku and Rhianna are my only family other than Gwyn."

"Ah, wrong answer." Gavin scooped her up and hugged her. "Now you have seven brothers." He gave Gwyn a pained look. "Geez, I wish I'd been warned that there was more than one of you."

She stuck her tongue out at him. Arian glanced around but didn't see Taylor. "Where's your boyfriend?" he asked.

"He went back to his office to try to find a paper route to help explain what happened," she said dryly.

Something dangerous moved in Eric's eyes. "In the meantime, the girls and I need to go talk to Melissa Washburn."

"Don't worry." Gwyn hugged Heul tightly. "We'll come over later and tell you everything. I'm not suddenly going to stop being your sister just because I no longer have amnesia. Really, I'm not Mika Carmichael anymore. I'm Gwyn Trahern." She smiled impishly. "Until I and Taylor marry anyway."

"Oh alright," Seisyll groused. "We'll go blow up concrete and pound on steel until we feel better."

As the seven trooped out, Gwyn realized Rayna was staring at her with wide eyes. With her truth sense, she knew Seisyll hadn't been lying. Giggling, she hugged her sister. "They're construction workers. I'm an interior designer." She contemplated that. "Actually, not anymore." She looked at Eric. "I think I've been recruited."

"Hopefully," he admitted. "Enforcers needs you, Gwyn. You and Rayna both." He deliberately sighed. "And Taylor too, I guess. He has some use. But he can be a part-timer. Hate to waste all his creative talent."

"How gracious of you," she murmured drolly.

Rayna giggled as she cuddled against Eric's side. "Don't mind him. You'll get used to him." She rubbed her cheek against his chest softly. "He's not nearly as terrifying as he wants to pretend to be."

"Only for you," he promised softly. "Now let's get going."

Melissa was being held in the dungeons of the Enforcers' headquarters. Rayna, upon learning that, frowned at Eric and asked, "You have a dungeon?"

Gwyn giggled. He just sighed. "Kindly recall that I am old, and this company was founded before what is now considered civilization." He ran a hand through Rayna's hair, and skimmed his fingers over the little silver wings almost hidden within her thick locks. Most would never notice them. "Don't tease."

She shared a smile with Gwyn. "We're honor bound to tease you," she giggled. "Gwyn especially. I have dibs on Taylor."

"With my complete permission," Gwyn added impishly. "My brothers are going to have fun with you, Riku. They've adopted Rayna, so now *she* has seven big brothers."

"Gavin was right. You two should definitely have warning labels," he grumbled. He held the door in the dungeon cell for them so they could enter ahead of him.

Melissa heard the door and turned from the barred window to demand her release only to realize who was in the doorway. The color drained from her face, and she slowly sank down to the ground with her back pressed against the wall in shock and terror. "No," she managed to say. "You're dead!"

Gwyn leaned a shoulder against the doorframe. "No, very much alive. I can't die before I get married, you know. It wouldn't be fair."

"Fair! Fair! What do you know about fairness?" Melissa screamed at her.

Eric couldn't resist the humor. "Gwyn is the fairest woman in the land. Only her sister is her equal."

"Sister!" She saw the pint sized silver haired woman walking toward her and shrank back. There was something terrifying about her, as if she saw straight into her soul and exposed every truth.

"Rayna," Eric warned, "watch your thumb."

"What on Earth does THAT mean?" Melissa got her answer as Rayna's small fist suddenly landed on her jaw and snapped her head around. She hit damned hard for such a tiny thing. Melissa stared at her in shock. "The hell!"

"That was for Taylor, since he said he can't hit a woman." She rubbed her knuckles and walked over to Eric with a frown. "That hurt."

"I'll take you to Kienan to learn to make a proper fist." He kissed her fingers and watched over the top of her head as Melissa got to her feet. The other woman was visibly shaking. "We have a few questions. Truth will determine the value of your answers, and Justice will administer punishment." When she said nothing, he asked, "Did you help contract for Rayna and Mika Carmichael's deaths?"

"What?! No!"

"Truth." Rayna looked at her sister. "She wasn't involved that far."

"Yeah, I can see it." Gwyn frowned. "Why did you try to kill me then?" The scale was heavily unbalanced to the point of needing punishment administered, but it seemed a bit odd when Melissa's worst trait was jealousy. There had to be more.

"I didn't try to kill you!"

"Lie." Rayna's hair rippled lightly with power. "The truth shall set you free." Her quiet voice sounded as firm as steel. Her violet eyes flickered with bits of lightning. "You will tell us the truth, starting from the beginning when you tipped the scales."

An odd sheen settled over Melissa's eyes as the power took hold. "I hate beautiful women who get more attention than me." Her voice was without inflection, her eyes staring straight ahead. "In college, I arranged for a girl to be attacked because I wanted her boyfriend. I got an employee at another company fired when she won an in-company beauty contest instead of me. I hate Veronica too. I was planning to arrange an accident. Gwyn was more important. Taylor wanted her. I wanted to ruin her name and make her look like trash."

Sometimes the evil wasn't far under the surface. Sometimes it could be in human flesh. Eric felt exceptionally violent and crossed his arms. Softly, Rayna asked, "When did your plans change to murder?"

"When the snake bit me. I woke up in the morning and felt very clear. If Gwyn was dead, then Taylor would look at me. I used to build bombs for fun when I was a kid, so I disguised one as a comb and sent it to Gwyn. It didn't work. I loitered at the construction site, hoping that I could drop something on her. I saw her trying on that stupid outfit and tried to suffocate her. Finally, I just decided to drug her." She held up her hand where she wore a ring.

Eric walked over and took the ring away. When he twisted the face, a little needle extended. A quick sniff told him that it was the same venomous drug used on both sisters. "She must have used this to drug the apple." He studied the ring. "This has the Carmichael family crest." He looked at her. "Where did you get this?"

"The snake dropped it."

"Snake." It finally registered, and Rayna looked at Eric in horror. "Uncle Larry?"

"Uncle Larry?" Gwyn echoed.

"I exposed his true self when he tried to attack me," she explained. "It turned him into a cobra. Whatever evil we are facing must take the form of a snake. It latches onto those easily converted to true evil." She took a sharp breath as a memory from the distant past filled her mind. She grabbed Gwyn's hand. "Sis . . ."

"Yeah." Gwyn put an arm around her shoulders. "Nahga." She looked at Eric. He didn't seem surprised. "Did you suspect it was the Snake God?"

"I had a suspicion," he admitted. "It's his style, and snakes seem to be cropping up everywhere." He studied both their faces and saw fear mixed with determination. "Are you sure you can face him again? You're stronger now, but what happened back then is sharp enough in your minds that I can see it from Rayna." It made him feel slightly ill.

"We can do it," Rayna said softly. Almost achingly, she asked, "Do you think he corrupted Uncle Larry and Aunt Yvonne?" She couldn't bear the thought of the beloved aunt and uncle of her childhood being so horrible.

He crossed to her and pulled her into his arms. "I'm sorry, sweetheart," he said into her hair. "I'm sorry. He couldn't have latched onto them without something to latch on to. Larry Carmichael formulated the plan to destroy Lucas long before Nahga entered the scene." He offered his hand to Gwyn and pulled her close as well. Their belief in the goodness of mankind was their greatest weakness as well as their greatest strength.

Gwyn eased back after a moment. "What do we do with her?" She pointed at Melissa. "Even without being poisoned, she's done some terrible things. What she told us wasn't everything. I can see the evidence in my mind." Because she was unfailingly fair, she didn't say what she had learned. The disgust in her eyes made it unnecessary, though. "The scales need balancing."

"Let's get the poison out of her first since, I presume, death is not what is needed." Eric held up a hand and water magic surrounded Melissa. He began to increase the heat until she started sweating and then used her opened pores to allow his magic into her skin. The poison from the snake's bite was forced out through the same wound on her ankle it had entered through, and it took the form of a snake as well.

It slithered toward Gwyn but was repelled violently by an invisible barrier around her. Her contract was complete. Evil could not kill her while she was under Enforcers' protection. With a vicious hiss, the snake slithered out the door.

Melissa collapsed onto the floor. Gwyn walked over to kneel beside her. "For one who acted out of jealousy and vanity," she murmured, "I take from you the one thing you covetously horde." Power rippled through her eyes. "Let justice be done."

Even Eric flinched when her beauty melted away to leave nothing but a horribly grotesque appearance behind. He doubted anyone would ever look at her and mistake her features for anything except a reflection of the cruelty inside her heart.

The scales balanced once more, Gwyn walked over to her family. "Where is the snake going?"

"It has to know it has lost," Eric muttered.

"It does." Rayna's eyes slowly widened. "It will want to strike back at us. It will want to hurt Gwyn." She took a sharp breath as Gwyn paled. "It'll go after Taylor!"

Taylor logged onto Melissa's computer and began to go through the files and programs, his ire rising as he saw that she had been documenting her actions. It was annoying to think anyone would be so stupid as to keep an electronic diary on their work computer detailing her plans to kill someone. It was more annoying to think she worked for him. She hadn't even used passwords to close access to the files. Was she *trying* to get caught?

His hands began to burn.

He lifted his hands and stared at them. "What the hell? Gwyn is safe now." He heard knocking on his office door and left Melissa's to cross into his own. "Come in," he said curtly. "But I'm afraid I'm a bit busy right now."

The man and woman that walked in just smiled at him. "You have time for us, I'm sure," the woman said, and she lifted the gun in her hand to aim it at his chest. "We're going for a ride, Mr. Vincent."

He felt himself oddly unsurprised. He lifted his hands and studied the blood that quickly covered them. The answers were there, and the blood faded as he lowered his hands once more. The woman was staring at him, and he shrugged. "Sorry. Strange psychic ability that I can't yet control. It's supposed to warn me when I'm in danger, but it seems to delay in doing so until said danger has already arrived."

She couldn't help but wince. "Pleasant."

"Meh." He came around the desk calmly. "You can put the gun away. I'm not an idiot. You don't want someone to be suspicious." He willingly walked with them from the office as if there was nothing at all odd going on. He would *not* risk his employees' lives. Blake kept a sword at his desk, and he would probably try to use it. "Mind introducing yourselves?"

"Larry and Yvonne Carmichael." Yvonne was doing all the talking, which didn't surprise Taylor since he had to assume it took a lot of concentration for Larry to maintain a human appearance. When he breathed out, the tip of his tongue could be seen, and it was distinctly forked. "You ruined things," she hissed softly. "The girls are gunning for us, and so we're going to hit them where it hurts."

Taylor got into the car that waited at the curb and linked his hands behind his head as he leaned back. "Are you going to just kill me, or are you going to make them watch?" he asked conversationally.

"Oh we want them to watch." She smiled at him. "But we're not stupid enough to have them be there in person. We're going to let a few friends of ours have their way with you and then we'll bleed you out slowly. We'll film the whole thing."

"Ah. Gotcha." He closed his eyes as if he didn't care, but his mind sought Gwyn's. Even across miles, their minds were meant to touch. The bloody vision had shown him what to do, and it was wonderfully easy to let his mind merge with hers.

Between his danger sense and her ability to track evil, their mind link provided a trail more accurate than the best GPS device. "Live feed or recorded? I'd hate to have your bandwidth cut out in the middle."

"Very cute." She watched his face and felt a flicker of frustration that he didn't seem to care. Either he was an idiot or he was stupidly expecting to be rescued. She couldn't wait to see his smug and cocky attitude wiped away.

The place they went to was a normal looking house in the suburbs. No one seemed to pay any attention, and a few neighbors even waved cheerfully. Taylor mentally applauded the wisdom of hiding in plain sight.

The house felt almost unbearably hot. Yvonne fiddled with the thermostat while Larry opened a window. An obedient breeze blew in the room and Taylor wondered if anyone had noticed there was no wind in the front of the house. "When do the games begin?" he asked. "This whole hostage thing is really not frightening me."

Larry abruptly turned into a large cobra and lashed at him on a hiss. Yvonne hurriedly stepped between them. "Don't kill him yet!" she ordered. "If he dies now, it defeats the whole purpose." She shivered as the wind turned biting cold. "What is this?"

"Got to watch out for those unexpected blizzards." Taylor closed his hand around a vase. "They come from out of nowhere!"

He hurled the water into her face and the wind froze it solid, preventing her from seeing or breathing. She struggled wildly and dropped to her knees as she clawed at the ice. Her struggles became weaker until she blacked out entirely. The ice melted as her body hit the floor with a thump.

Taylor ducked as the cobra tried to hit him. "What took so long?" he demanded.

Eric swung in the window. "Traffic."

"Gee thanks!" He ducked again and dodged around the edge of the hall. "Not that I'm complaining, but, damn it, were you waiting for them to shoot me?"

"I didn't have an open shot! You could be more grateful, kid!" Eric fired a stream of fire at the cobra that had it recoiling in pain. "You're still alive!"

He ducked as the cobra's tail slammed into the wall where his head had been and sent plaster flying everywhere. "That's looking debatable!"

"Stop arguing!" Gwyn and Rayna had come in through the back door of the kitchen and were at the edge of the living room.

"Release Yvonne!" Eric ordered Rayna. "Hurry! Unless they're both exposed, neither can be destroyed! Nahga split himself into two pieces, and we have to destroy them both together! Don't hesitate, no matter what!"

Rayna nodded once and looked at her aunt intently. "And the truth shall set you free!"

"Rayna!" Gwyn grabbed her sister and they dropped to the ground as Yvonne transformed into a cobra the same size as her husband, and both snakes lashed at them. They stayed low to the ground as the two cobras merged into a single being so tall it nearly burst through the roof. Venom dripped from its fangs and burned through the carpet. Its tail lashed around and hit both Eric and Taylor, sending them flying into opposite walls as they tried to get to their lovers.

"Nahga," Gwyn whispered. She remembered him. A memory of a far distant past where evil had overcome the light of truth and justice, and plunged the world into darkness and despair. No hope. There had been no hope.

"Gwyn." Rayna's voice shook. "Kill it, quickly!" She remembered as well, and it ripped her in two. She couldn't bear the memories.

Gwyn took a breath to release her power but the cobra was prepared and blew a scalding blast of hot breath at her and Rayna. They both went flying into the kitchen and crashed into the sink. They painfully tried to get to their feet as the cobra advanced.

"Hey!" Taylor had gotten his hands on the gun and fired without hesitation to draw the cobra's attention. Eric started firing bullets of ice, and Nahga tried to snap at them with its jaws. Too late, it realized it had turned its back on the real threat.

"And justice be done!" Gwyn shouted, the wings on her head opening fully and radiating her power in a searing wave that washed across the room like a tidal wave and slammed into Nahga.

There was no ceremony with its death. It was obliterated so fast that there was a popping sound as air rushed in to fill the space left behind. Silence fell on the house as Taylor dropped the gun on the floor and Eric lowered his hands.

Gwyn took a deep breath. For the first time, she felt as if she could truly breathe. The weight of the past was gone. She could live, truly live, and without fear. No one wanted her dead. She gave a glad little cry and raced across the floor to leap into Taylor's arms.

He caught her close and buried his face in her hair, needing her soft scent and warmth to banish the terror of the last few days. It was over. Finally, it was over. Into her hair, he asked, "Is this the part where someone says 'they lived happily ever after'?"

"You're the writer," she said into his shoulder. "How does your game end?"

"The faerie princess gets a hundred lifetimes with her soldier for every year she spent in fear." His lips curved. "So, presumably, she would be stuck with him forever. For them it's a happily ever after."

Her eyes closed as she smiled. "It sounds like one to me, too."

CHAPTER FOURTEEN

Rhianna heard the giggling long before she heard the footsteps. She didn't look up from the file in front of her as she smiled to herself. "Come in," she called. The door eased open, and two of her favorite people peeked around the door at her. She smiled. "What are you up to?"

Gwyn and Rayna crossed the room quickly, the latter not hampered by her sixth-month pregnancy in the slightest. The former was carrying a gaily-wrapped package that she held out with a smile. "A little bird told us," she said cheerfully. "Happy birthday!"

Rhianna glanced at the door that joined her office to Eric's and snorted as she heard him whistling like a bird. "I can imagine." She took the package and unwrapped it curiously, only to start laughing as she saw the game within. "This faerie looks familiar."

Gwyn's color rose slightly. "I tried to convince Taylor to change it, but he's very stubborn."

"A good quality in the right man. And it's entirely accurate. You are both Faeriekin princesses." She opened her CD drive and popped the disc in to let it load. She loved the games from Memories; this one wasn't even supposed to be released for another month.

"Now that you have your gift, we have a favor to ask," Gwyn announced.

"Oh?" She arched a brow.

"Yes." The sisters exchanged a smile. "We want to 'help' our brothers." Rayna's voice was solemn.

Rhianna began to smile. "What's good for the goose is good for the gander?"

"What goes around comes around. Turnabout is fair play. Pick your metaphor." Gwyn linked her hands behind her back. "We have plans, you see, and we're going to need you and Riku to help. We were thinking a contract. You know. Just to make sure things go the way we want them."

"Have you got someone in mind?" Eric asked from the doorway. He had been wondering what they were up to. He had seen them talking and giggling together for a week.

"Oh definitely." Rayna's eyes twinkled. "We've been learning by watching you," she added innocently. "Everything should be in place by Gwyn and Taylor's wedding next week."

"You two *definitely* should have warning labels." Eric went back into his office with a shake of his head.

"I must agree," Rhianna noted dryly. "But I will be quite happy to help however I can. The happiness of those in 3rd District comes first. Let me see what I can come up with."

"You're the best!" Rayna said happily as she went around the desk to hug her tightly. When she eased back and let go, she met Rhianna's eyes very seriously. "Is *he* trapped too?"

Her leader, and surrogate sister-in-law, went very still. "I'm sorry?" she asked softly.

"The one you're waiting for. Is he trapped, too?"

She was silent for long moments before she sighed softly and rested her arms on her desk. "I don't know," she admitted with simple honesty.

"I hope you find him." Rayna gave her a kiss on the cheek and then headed for Eric's door.

Gwyn likewise started toward the main one. She stopped there and looked back over her shoulder. "You're not a bad person, no matter what you think you've done so far. The scales are balanced. You'll find him."

Rhianna watched both doors shut and leaned back in her chair with a little smile. Having Truth and Justice around was often unnerving, but it was very comforting as well. Gwyn had just given her a sense of peace she hadn't had in a long time.

She studied the contract on her desk, wrote some notes on the bottom, and closed the folder. It promptly flashed the word 'Complete.' She swiveled and slid it into the drawer with its twin. She smiled as the drawer started to flash the word 'Finished' but changed its mind and remained blank instead. Things weren't done *quite* yet.

Status: File ~~Complete~~ In Progress

Analysis: To balance the scales of love, you just need to be the fairest in the land.

Folder Three

TRAHERN

CHAPTER FIFTEEN

Of all the people in the wedding party, and all the people attending the reception, only the bride and groom were calm. Their friends and family ran a gauntlet of emotions that swung between excited and nervous. On the groom's side of the immense garden, Taylor was greatly amused to see his friends and employees acting like they were the ones getting married. On the bride's side of the garden, Gwyn was fascinated at watching her normally levelheaded brothers act like they were readying themselves for a noose. "Guys? You do remember I'm the one getting married, right?"

Her sister giggled softly. "Stop moving, Gwyn! I'll smear your eyeshadow."

"Sorry, Rayna." Gwyn obligingly turned back to her little sister so that she could continue applying makeup.

Rayna smiled and deftly swiped shadow over Gwyn's eyes. Neither sister normally wore makeup, but the fantastical setting had demanded more than lip-gloss. It had taken Rayna two weeks to perfect her technique, and another two for Gwyn to decide on the look she wanted.

The shimmering glitter across Rayna's cheeks matched the shimmering threads in her violet dress. She figured it was probably her husband influencing Taylor that had resulted in her costume making her look like a living flower. She liked it. It seemed fitting that a faerie bride have a flower spirit for a matron-of-honor. "You're not mad at me, are you, Joseff?" she called across the room.

He stopped yanking on his collar and turned immediately to smile. "Of course not! Gwyn's enough of a sadist to have tried to put *me* in that dress, and it looks much better on you."

Gavin snorted softly. "Gwyn wouldn't do that," he said solemnly. "Would you?"

"Mmm. Maybe." Though her eyes were closed, it was a sure bet her eyes sparkled. Rayna's certainly were, and the passing time had only made them act more and more like twins. Gwyn felt quite blessed to be able to say she had two twins.

Rayna studied her new brothers from the corner of her eye. Though mostly Welsh in blood, they looked much like Vikings that had been dropped in the middle of New York. Half had pale blond hair, the other had yellow blond. All eyes were different shades of blue. All were almost lethally handsome. They were giving, loving, and brilliant on top of it.

And every last one of them was single. It had been the bane of Gwyn's life and was now Rayna's puzzle. How did seven such spectacular men manage to escape matrimony for so long? Ah, well. The sisters shared a smiling look. They wouldn't escape much longer.

The door opened and Rhianna peered around the side. "Ah," she said in satisfaction. "Good. Looking like that, Taylor would have to be an idiot to try and escape."

Gwyn grinned. "I'd just chase him down."

"That's my girl."

As the door shut, Rayna looked at her brothers and giggled as she saw all were standing at attention with something akin to terrified fascination on their faces. "She doesn't bite! Rhianna is *really* nice. She's like my sister-in-law, so you have to like her, okay?"

"She runs one of the largest companies in the entire country," Tomos noted in awe. "She and Eric are almost *always* in the newspapers. It's like meeting a celebrity!"

"She's just Rhianna," Gwyn said simply. She got to her feet and smoothed out her voluminous skirts. The wedding gown was a pure romantic indulgence. Designed to flatter her graceful figure and snowy white hair, its creation had been nearly slaved over by her soon-to-be-husband. He was *such* an artist sometimes; it wasn't perfect until he couldn't find anything left to pick apart.

The garden in front of the newly opened Memories building had been transformed into a fantasy garden for a fantasy wedding. All guests wore elaborate costumes, and many wore masks. Since all seven brothers were giving Gwyn away, they were all wearing specially designed, formal uniforms that made them resemble princes. Tall and slightly intimidating princes, but princes regardless.

"Riku's feeling guilty," Rayna informed Gwyn, almost impishly. When Gwyn tilted her head, Rayna giggled. "He married me so quickly that we didn't have a real wedding. Now he feels like he cheated me or something."

"You want one?" Gavin wrapped his arms around her to hug her snugly. "We could step in to give you away. Or would your father want to do that?"

She shook her head. "He doesn't leave his house anymore." She smiled, genuinely. "He did what he needed to do. He couldn't live without our mom unless I and Gwyn needed him. Now that we've found our places, he can let go." She sighed softly. "He's normal, but he loved a Faeriekin. That 'mating for life' thing is pretty cross species when power is involved."

Matching looks of wariness crossed seven faces. The sisters hid a shared smile. "Now then." Gwyn picked up her bouquet of sunflowers. "I feel like getting married. Let's get this over with so I can kidnap my husband for our honeymoon."

When they got to the end of the aisle that she would walk down, they could see Taylor waiting near the arbor with the priest. Even the priest had gotten into the spirit of things and was dressed like a wizard out of medieval times. Taylor wore what looked like an elaborate dress uniform for a soldier. Eric, dressed like a rather intimidating warlock, was beside him as his best man.

In age order, the Trahern brothers moved down the aisle to take a spot. Joseff remained with Gwyn and Rayna. A small body in a tiny pink dress appeared out of nowhere and squeezed up between the three adults. She tugged firmly on Rayna's skirt. "Rayna!" Nicole Germaine asked plaintively. "Can I go throw flowers?"

Rayna knelt down and firmly fixed her skirt and wings. The flower girl looked like the perfect little faerie. At five, she was almost frighteningly intelligent for her age, thinking and acting on a much higher level, but she was still very much a little girl. The idea of being the faerie flower girl had tickled her pink. "There," Rayna said, "now you can go."

Nicole brightened happily, her vivid green eyes filled with delight. The crop of rusty red curls on her head bounced merrily as she turned and began to skip down the aisle, throwing flower petals with great abandon. Sadly, few made it onto the aisle itself. Most ended up on the Traherns.

By the time she reached the end where Heul waited, her basket was empty. She looked up at him and her lower lip quivered. "I ran out."

He brushed the ones off his jacket into her basket. She waved at him and he knelt down as close to her height as possible. She planted a big kiss on his cheek and then scampered over to the arbor to enthusiastically throw her last handful. Every last person in the audience was either snickering or grinning by that point, including Rhianna.

The priest blew a petal off his nose and tried desperately not to smile as he looked at the young woman on the piano. Since both Gwyn and Taylor hated organ music, they had compromised on a piano. The pianist was, in fact, an aunt to the audacious little flower girl and had the same rusty red hair. Her eyes were turquoise green instead.

Rayna waited for her cue before walking down the aisle serenely. She did her best to not giggle at the sight of her big brothers covered in flowers, but it was hard. Gavin winked at her as he bowed, and she bit her lip. She managed to make it to the arbor without mishap—she had been terrified she would trip—and she took her spot. As she looked at Eric, his smile warmed her from the inside out. She didn't need a ceremony. She had him.

Joseff escorted Gwyn to Seisyll, who took her to Tomos, who took her to Gavin, who took her to Owen, who took her to Arian, who finally took her to Heul. They were a marked contrast, the eldest and youngest, but there was enough of a resemblance in their coloring and features that no one had ever questioned whether she was a Trahern.

He escorted her toward the arbor, and Taylor walked forward to meet them. "I will care for her," the groom said calmly. His eyes never left Gwyn's face.

"Will you love her?" Heul was proud of himself for not forgetting his lines.

"I can do no other."

"Then I give her to you." He offered Gwyn's hand to Taylor. He bent to kiss his sister's cheek and then moved back to his place, hoping like hell his eyes weren't as damp with tears as they felt. Damn it, she wasn't supposed to grow up that soon.

Taylor escorted Gwyn to the waiting priest, and they were finally wed. When the priest said Taylor could kiss the bride, he was more than happy to swing her up into his arms enthusiastically. The cheering became whistles and clapping as it became quickly obvious the couple wasn't in a hurry to stop. Eric kicked Taylor's ankle. "Young eyes," he warned softly.

Taylor let go of Gwyn to see Nicole watching with wide eyes. He burst into laughter and scooped her up in his arms. "You did great," he told her. As he escorted Gwyn down the aisle, he passed the small child off to another woman with dark red hair. "Thanks, Remy," he murmured.

Remy smiled. "Anytime. Rayna and Gwyn are both dear friends."

The reception was held inside the lobby of the building. It, too, had been turned into a vast storybook scene. Many smiling glances were sent toward some of the artwork on the wall. It was no secret that Taylor had used Gwyn as a muse for his recent game.

Joseff liked parties as much as the next person, and the people in attendance were nice, but he didn't know how to dance and was really bad at mingling. He sidled his way toward the side exit, slowly but surely seeking escape. No one was looking, and he ducked into the hall. Letting out a little breath, he sent a mental apology to his sister. She just snorted at him in response.

The hall led to a side exit where another garden resided. Hands in pockets, he headed toward the doors. He needed to be outside where it was open. The evening closed around him peacefully, and he took a deep breath.

A sound caught his attention, and he slowly made his way toward the side of a large gazebo designed to offer relief from the sun in the summer. He cautiously peered around the side . . . and found himself face to face with the most shockingly beautiful young woman he had ever seen.

Her rusty red hair was pulled up so that ringlets cascaded around her fair features. Her eyes were a deep, turquoise green and framed by almost ridiculously long lashes. She wore the costume of an old-fashioned bard, and the laced corset flattered a distinctly curvaceous body. They both straightened up, and he discovered, to his everlasting delight, that she was clearly shorter. If she was taller than Gwyn, it was only by a thin margin. "Hi." He recognized her suddenly. "You played the piano."

"Hi." She smiled. "Yes I did."

Freckles. She had freckles. He was enchanted. "I'm Joseff Trahern." He offered a hand.

"Lexie Germaine." She shook his hand solemnly and felt her heart flutter wildly as he then brought her hand to his lips and bowed deeply. She had been staring at him since she had seen him the first time. He was so gorgeous! She had actually been afraid to speak to him; she tended to trip over her tongue when she was nervous. He looked like every girl's secret prince charming, and the way he smiled at her had her pulse going faster than an Irish fiddler's bow.

"Lexie." He liked it. "Is it short for anything?"

She took a breath. "Brace yourself. It's Alexandriana Genevieve."

He shook his head slightly and rubbed his ear. "I'm not sure I heard that properly, let alone could attempt to repeat it. Lexie, it is." He kept hold of her hand, unable to make himself let go. "I want you to know now," he informed her, "that if I do not ask you to dance, it's because I can't dance and I'd embarrass you."

"Well, if you did ask, I'd have to decline because *I* can't dance, and I wouldn't want to embarrass you, either."

They shared a conspiratorial grin. "How about a walk?" he offered.

"See, that I can do. I've even been doing it for twenty-one years. I'm an expert." She let him tuck her hand into the curve of his elbow. "So you built this building with your brothers? It's beautiful."

"I do mostly windows," he said with a smile. "We're all adept builders, but we also specialize. Like, I work with glass, and Tomos does landscapes. What about you?"

"I work with my sisters. We own an interior design company. We all specialize in different styles and have other special talents. Mine is Traditional, and I'm a stained glass artist."

"Sisters? How many?"

"Uhm, six."

"Six!" The name finally registered. "Wait, Germaine. You're Remy's little sister, right? Kingdom Design?"

"Yup!" She smiled. "I'm the baby. We're *this* close to getting Remy to join us. She's wasted on working with numbers at that budget company." The music from inside drifted out suddenly and curled around her. "I love this song." It was a slow song designed to entice couples to sway together. "The singers are from 3rd District like me."

"Me, too."

Their eyes met and both fell silent. Two hearts beat far faster than normal. When he brushed a stray curl out of her face, her hands lifted to rest over his chest. He was so strong that she felt deliciously small and delicate. Something stirred along her mind like a soft voice. The voice of his heart. It was a voice she had been waiting to hear.

They moved together without words, her head tucking onto his shoulder as he wrapped his arms around her. You didn't need steps to slow dance. Just a willing heart. There were two between them. Two hearts beating as one.

When the song ended, they didn't move. After a moment, she asked, "Joseff?"

"Mmm?"

"Is it supposed to be that easy?"

He didn't need to ask for clarification. He knew. "I never thought so, but I saw it happen to Gwyn." He looked down at her. "Let's test if we're right. There are supposed to be fireworks if I kiss you, correct?"

Breathless, she stared up at him. "Please. Test. I'm always happy to experiment." His head lowered and his lips brushed hers. Sparks seemed to leap. Her blood heated wildly. Brushed again. Her entire body began to ache. She looked into his eyes, and they were as dark and hungry as she felt. She wound her arms around his neck and rose onto her toes to kiss him with all the unleashed emotion in her soul.

When they finally parted for air, her careful hairdo had been completely demolished by his fingers. Feeling them buried in her hair, however, was worth every lost pin. "Fireworks?" she whispered.

"Is it the Fourth of July already? I'd swear the celebration was right over us."

Her lips curved even as his did. A bit guilty as she remembered something, she sighed and reluctantly released him. "Joseff . . . I need to tell you something. A locket in my family had a gift for us seven sisters. We were each given a wish. All of us, except Remy, wished for true love." She looked up at him in worry. "Maybe what we have is because of that wish."

"Is that supposed to be bad?" he wondered. "I mean, you didn't ask for *my* love, specifically. Maybe the wish's power just helped us find each other." His brain belatedly began to connect the dots. "Wait. This is a little coincidental."

"There is no such thing as coincidence in 3rd District," his love reminded him.

"That's my point. Seven sisters. Seven brothers. Six sisters who wished for love. One just *happens* to find that love with one of the brothers. Youngest to youngest." Her eyes had slowly widened and he was beginning to grin. "What did Remy wish for?"

"She didn't. It was right after she got divorced. Then Chase died a year later. She still cared for him, so it was hard. I think she's afraid to upset Nicole's life more. Poor thing doesn't even remember Chase."

"Heul needs family. Sounds like Remy does too. And Heul *loves* kids." He grinned. "Let's go find Rayna and Gwyn. We're going to need help."

She held tight to his hand as he hurried toward the door. "Help with what?"

"Nudging those wishes along. Remy and Heul might be harder because she didn't wish, but I'm sure it'll be perfect! C'mon, Lex."

"My legs are shorter than yours. Yikes!" She grabbed his shoulders as he swept her up into his arms. "Wow." She stared at his profile. "That was . . . that was really romantic. Do it again any time you like."

"Man, you're perfect for me." He put her down on her feet when they reached the other door and both slipped into the reception. Muffling giggles, they made their way across the room to where Rayna and Eric were sitting with Gwyn and Taylor. Both sisters had taken off their shoes briefly and had their feet on their husbands' laps.

When Joseff and Lexie reached them, four pairs of eyes went to where their hands were clasped. "Well," Taylor said.

"Ha! Told you so!" Rayna told Eric almost gleefully.

Gwyn's eyes twinkled. "Hi, Lexie."

"Hi, Gwyn." Lexie's eyes were twinkling too. "Can I keep Joseff?"

"Sure. Feel free."

"And there's something else." Joseff pulled over two more chairs and sat down with Lexie beside him. "We want to set up her six sisters with our six brothers. There's this thing about seven wishes, and a locket, and coincidences."

"There are none in 3rd District." Eric glanced across the room at Rhianna, and she just smiled. He wasn't surprised.

"Wish I'd known that," Taylor groused.

"Wouldn't have done you any good," Gwyn apologized. "Now then." She leaned in and so did the other five. "To be honest, Rayna and I had already thought of it," she admitted softly. "And we've got things in place to begin making the dominoes fall. We're not taking chances. And since Taylor and I won't be here, I'm going to have to rely on you and Lexie to take our place. Rayna and Eric and Rhianna will help out, definitely."

"What's the plan?" Joseff asked.

"Arranging situations," Rayna offered. "We're just going to set up the right circumstances and see what happens."

"Details please?" Lexie asked.

By the time Rayna and Gwyn were done explaining, Joseff and Lexie were both grinning. "That's . . . that's diabolical," Joseff finally said. "But it's so simple. So perfect. If anything will happen, that's the scenario to set it up in." He glanced around the room. "And we've got the right start."

The others followed his gaze. It was fairly easy to pick out the Trahern brothers because all were tall and blond. Likewise, the Germaine sisters were easy to see for they were also on the tall side, except they were red haired. The red hair ran from dark to rust and all eyes were different shades of green.

Without fail, someone was staring at someone else. If a Trahern wasn't staring at a Germaine, a Germaine was staring at a Trahern. The very distinct, pointed, difference lay with Remy and Heul. They seemed quite determined not to look at each other at all.

"Hey, Eric?" Taylor asked absently. "How good is your control of that wind?

"Absolute."

"You're just horrible," Gwyn decided solemnly. She gave her husband a contented kiss. "And I absolutely love you."

The reception continued. Gwyn danced with all of her brothers. The cake was cut and served. And, finally, it was time for the bouquet and garter. While Gwyn was trying to find her precarious footing on a chair, Lexie and her older sister Jennifer descended on Remy. "You!" Lexie scolded. "Come on."

"Oh come on!" Remy sighed as she found herself dragged toward the cluster of single women. "I'm a mother!"

"And you're single. Ergo, you're eligible. There is no law that says previously married women can't catch a bouquet. Half the men here have been ogling you." Jen shoved Remy forward. "Give one of them a thrill, geez."

Gwyn hid a smile and chucked her bouquet over her shoulder. As if carried on the wind, it sailed through the air over outstretched hands and landed in Remy's arms. "That's great!" another Germaine sister, Samantha, said as she hugged Remy. "I'm not even upset I didn't catch it because you did!"

Remy had nothing she could say to that. And her daughter was watching with rapt adoration and delight, so she couldn't really argue either. She just sighed and moved out of the way. It was just a myth. No one really believed the people who got the garter and the bouquet would marry. She genuinely didn't even think that lace and flowers could predict future weddings anyway. That was pushing it, even for the District.

As the bachelors lined up to catch the garter, a plaintive voice said, "Tall people in the back! That's not fair."

Obligingly, the Trahern brothers minus Joseff moved to the back. Really, they didn't need to be in the front. They already had an advantage. Gavin, being Gavin, couldn't help but shout, "Taylor, stop flirting with my sister and just get her garter!"

Amid the laughter, Taylor retorted, "Her skirt is attacking me."

"You wanted it poofy!" Gwyn giggled like crazy. "And stop tickling me!"

"I'm about to try to catch my sister's garter," Arian said warily. "Isn't that blasphemous?"

"Shush!" Taylor straightened and smoothed Gwyn's skirt back into place. Without looking away from her face, he chucked the garter over his shoulder

Magically, mysteriously, it flew across the top of the crowd and landed in Heul's hands. The most interesting thing was that he hadn't even been reaching for it. He had lifted his hands to avoid bumping into someone. As he stared at the scrap of lace and silk in his hand, it dawned on him. His eyes narrowed toward his sister, who merely smiled angelically.

"You have to dance with Remy!" Lexie grabbed his hand and began to draw him toward the floor. "Come on! It's tradition!"

Joseff and Tomos were pointedly escorting Remy onto the floor at the same time. When Heul and Remy found themselves face to face, neither found a word to say. Heart pounding, she struggled against an urge to run. Why did this man get under her skin? One look at him and she was sixteen again, discovering the joys of the male of the species. He was so strong. Masculine. Everything she could ever want. "Uhm."

"They won't leave us alone unless we comply," he murmured softly. He handed off the garter and then took the bouquet and handed it away as well. He tugged her closer and stepped forward. She automatically stepped back and the dance started before she was even conscious of it.

For him, it was an exercise in self-torture. He had wanted Remy Germaine since he had laid eyes on her. She was so strong emotionally, holding together her family in a way he had held his own. He respected and admired her, and the way she looked in a slim, black. sorceress dress made his body hunger and ache in entirely new ways. Just looking at a woman had never made him burn before.

"Oh man," Jen whispered to another sister. "Look at how he's looking at her!"

Henrietta, Rie to her friends and family, sighed gustily. "Yeah." Her eyes drifted across the room to where the Trahern twins were standing. One of them, she wasn't sure which, just seemed to be more handsome to her than his brother. It was curious because they were quite identical except for hair length. Her eyes met the blue eyes of the one with short hair, and her toes curled in her shoes at the way he slowly smiled. "I think it's genetic."

By the end of the dance, the entire room was at least ninety percent sure that the myth might be more than just that. When the music ended, Remy and Heul hastily parted and went to opposite sides of the room. They didn't look at each other at all for the rest of the reception. In fact, their determination to ignore each other was quite clear.

"Let the games begin," Josef murmured to Lexie.

She just grinned.

CHAPTER SIXTEEN

When Joseff walked into the living room one morning a few days later, he discovered Heul deep in thought as he stared at a letter. "Problem?" the younger brother asked.

"Your sister."

"Which one?"

"Your twin!"

"Ah." He sat down on an armchair and threw his legs over the side. "What did she do? Oh," he added. "I have a date tonight. I won't be home until late."

Heul eyed him intently. "Correct me if I'm wrong, but haven't you gone on a date with Lexie Germaine every single night for the last five days?"

Politely, he asked, "Is that a problem?"

"No," Heul muttered as he went back to the letter. He liked Lexie, but her oldest sister haunted his waking days and sleepless nights. Then, too, there was Joseff. Heul had always felt more like a father than a brother. He knew that he had lost Joseff to Lexie. His family was slowly drifting into their own ways.

"So what did Gwyn do now?"

Heul sighed and handed over the letter. "See for yourself. If you read between the lines, you can all but hear her giggling when she wrote it. It's a very nice, very polite letter of resignation. Enforcers has offered her a full time position as a consultant. She and Rayna are going to work as a team."

"Yikes. If they walked into a boardroom together, I'd panic." Joseff could indeed hear his twin's giggles in the letter, and he didn't need to read it to know the contents. He handed it back over. "I guess that means we're without an interior designer for Driven Snow." Casually, he added, "You know, Lexie's sisters own an interior design company, Kingdom Designs. She mentioned they were thinking of finding a construction firm to partner with, to share the burden of the economy."

Heul slowly narrowed his eyes on his baby brother. "You and Gwyn are doing that creepy mental thing again. She mentions the exact same thing in here."

"Probably because she and I talked about it first." He shrugged one shoulder. "She felt guilty about abandoning us. I think we ought to give it a trial run. See what happens. I mean, do *you* want Gwyn to come back all happy from her honeymoon only to be filled with guilt?"

"Not at all." Heul stared at the letter for a moment. Abruptly he asked, "Does Remy work there now? I know you said Lexie and her sisters were trying to convince her."

"She does indeed. She got fed up with stifling her artistic side. And she wants Nicole to grow up thinking you can chase your dreams, so she decided to chase her own. She joined Kingdom Design and the other six put her in charge." Blithely, he continued, "She's pretty much the same level as you. When Gwyn and I were talking, we were thinking, for the trial run, that we'd see if we can work together on any type of project. We'll just match up brother to sister on the basis of what they do individually, rather than shared."

Heul grunted softly as he sat back on the couch. "And you just happen to specialize in glass blowing, and Lexie is a stained glass artist."

"That's what gave us the idea," he admitted readily. "The fact that I'm in love with her is moot. We'd have worked well together despite it. If two people, two *specialists*, can work together, then builders can work with designers. We aim for the hardest scenario so that the easiest is, well, easy."

His big brother stared at him for long moments and then stared out the window. Finally, with a distinct sense of impending doom, Heul said, "Fine. Call Lexie. If she can convince her sisters, then we can convince our brothers." Sourly, he added, "Unless you two have already planned all of it out."

"Not *all* of it," Joseff denied. He smiled. "But we definitely have a good start. Let's go find the other guys."

Kingdom Design was run from a smaller building in 3rd District. The seven co-owners were all born of the District and had lived there for their entire lives. After their parents died, when Remy was twenty-two, she took on the task of raising all six of her siblings, even eleven-year-old Lexie. She had forced herself to take a desk job so that her sisters were provided for. Then, years later, she'd had Nicole to care for as well.

Now, at thirty-two, she found herself a divorcee and a single mother to a five-year-old. She and Chase hadn't loved each other enough to stay married, but he had been a good man and one of her dearest friends. He had wanted to help raise their daughter. Now he was gone. She had stopped grieving, but the effects lingered.

She had finally settled into her life. Perhaps that was why it was so frustrating to stand at the window in her office and find her thoughts consumed with Heul Trahern. "Men are not supposed to take over a woman's mind," she muttered.

Behind her, Lexie said cheerfully, "The right men are!" She tossed herself down in a chair with a suitably dramatic flair. Her upswept curls bounced merrily. "Joseff is on my mind *constantly*. I'm going to marry him."

Remy had to smile as she turned around. "Really? Hadn't guessed." She sat on the side of the desk, one ear open toward the hallway where Nicole was chasing a remote control car all over the place. "He's a good man."

"Indeed." Lexie linked her hands behind her head. "Anyway, I want to talk to you. You know how we were talking about combining with a construction company? Well, Joseff says that Driven Snow just lost their interior designer. Gwyn got stolen by Enforcers."

One side of Remy knew it was a brilliant match. The other side had been seduced by a pair of blue eyes and a smoldering dance in a storybook room. "Lex . . ."

"You're such a chicken!" She sighed dramatically. "Remy, I'm not asking you to sleep with Heul. Though it'd do you both good, I'm sure. I'm just asking you to work with him. Joseff and I were thinking of a trial run. Y'know, matching artist to artist. If we can do small projects together that focus on us and our specialties, then we can work together as a collective group."

"And naturally, you and Joseff would work well together."

"I ain't denying that that is definitely what made us think of it, but we'd work well together even if we weren't nuts over each other. We were comparing his brothers to my sisters and we found lots of ways this could work. Yeah, unfortunately, you'd have to work with Heul, but you guys are the oldest. Actually," she laughed, "it was pretty funny how it broke down in birth order. Someone had a field day when they planned our families."

Remy let out a long breath. "Let's ask the others. If they're up for it, we can try it. We've got nothing to lose."

"Awesome!" Lexie hopped to her feet. "I'll go round them up!" Whistling softly, she headed out of the room.

Ten minutes later, all seven sisters were crowded into their conference room. Remy, as was her way, sat as far from the front of the table as she could. Next to her was Lexie. On Lexie's other side was Jennifer, the next oldest to Remy. She was thirty and five-eight with rust red hair and peridot green eyes. She tended to be the quickest to temper but could also be the quietest when she was thinking.

Across from Jen was Samantha, the next oldest. She was five-eight as well, twenty-eight, her hair was dark red, and her eyes were lime green. She wore thick glasses, much to her annoyance as no one else wore them. They suited her quite well, however, and enhanced her eyes.

Next to Sam was Tabitha. Tabby was twenty-six, five foot nine, rusty haired, and her eyes were pine green. She was the quietest of her family. She rarely touched anyone and had to be coaxed into opening up and laughing. Her powers were not comfortable for her, or anyone.

Next to Tabby were Belle and Rie. Identical twins with dark red hair and teal green eyes. They were twenty-three years old and five-seven, and Belle was the fractionally older. Rie wore her hair to her hips. Belle's hair was shorter and riotous with curls. Rie could be the more outgoing, Belle was the not-so-closet romantic. All seven sisters shared a similar beauty, and they had more than once caused a double take if they went out in public at the same time.

"So." Jen leaned on the table. "What's up?"

"I have a proposal for you." Lexie hopped up to sit on the side of the table. "Driven Snow Architecture is in need of an interior designer or two. We were thinking of joining with a construction company. Joseff and I think we ought to try a trial run." She outlined the plan briefly and followed up with, "We all have to be willing to do this, so if one person doesn't want to, then we won't."

"I'm for it," Jen decided. "They're decent guys. And," she grinned, "like it'd be a hardship to work with guys who are that hot."

Lexie looked around the table and saw all her sisters in agreement, even Remy, though hers was more reluctant. She gleefully bounced to her feet. "Great! I'll call Joseff!"

The Germaine sisters arrived a few hours later at the Driven Snow Architecture building. Like their own building, it was in two parts. The front was the actual business, and the back was where the Traherns lived. Almost everyone who worked in 3rd District lived in homes attached to their place of business.

The fact that they were all District-born, and therefore subject to the mystical laws of their home, was in the back of everyone's mind as they all marched into a large conference room. The males sat on one side of the table, the females on the other. Amusingly, perhaps unintentionally, they sat in order of birth. For Remy and Heul, it was a study in frustration. They carefully avoided looking into each other's eyes.

"Well," Joseff said cheerfully. "This ought to be fun!"

"I bet." Gavin tried his level best not to stare at the quiet redhead across the table from him. There was something in her large green eyes that tugged at everything inside him. And she was tall. He liked tall females. She appealed emotionally and physically, and he couldn't have been more delighted at the chance to get to know her. His sharp eyes hadn't missed, however, that she didn't shake hands or even touch her sisters. He longed to know why. "How is this working?"

Lexie hopped up and began to hand out contracts. "Rayna gave these to me. Since our businesses are overseen by Enforcers, they will be keeping an eye on our potential merger. So here's how it'll work. Joseff and I went over everyone's skills and came up with a game plan."

"First up is Remy and Heul." Joseff looked at his notes. "Since her specific talent is in designing buildings, and Heul builds 'em, we figured they could work on a small building. A dollhouse for Nicole's birthday or something."

Remy had to smile. "She'd love that."

"Then next are Arian and Jen." Lexie paused beside her sister. "Since you both work with wood as a carpenter and woodworker, respectively, we found a client who wants a hand-crafted bed made. Here's his information." She handed over a card to Jen.

"Then Owen and Sam." Joseff found a set of drawings in his folder and gave them to Lexie to pass down the line. "Owen specializes in turning drawings into blueprints, and Sam is a 3D modeler. They can work on turning those drawings into a full set of blueprints and 3D models."

Sam looked down, trying not to show that she was as happy as she was. Owen was by far her favorite of the Trahern males. There was just something about him. If he turned out to be half as attracted to her as she was to him, she would have him. It was that simple.

"And next," Lexie continued, "we have Gavin and Tabby. Gavin specializes in electrical work and Tabby is awesome with mapping and diagramming things that need fixing. We'll have you guys work on this project." She handed a card to Gavin. "An old building that needs rewiring. It hasn't been touched in fifty years."

He grimaced. "Good god, who knows what will be in those walls."

Tabby smiled at him almost shyly. "Don't worry. If it's in there, we'll find it."

Joseff covered a smile. "Annnnd next are Tomos and Belle. Both of you are landscapers."

"Gee, are we landscaping something?" Tomos asked dryly. He grinned at Belle and she grinned back. Inside his chest, he felt his heart clench. Though Belle and Rie were identical, he found only Belle to be attractive. She took his breath away. Working with her, getting to know her, was something he had wanted since he had seen her at the wedding.

"Good guess!" Lexie handed Belle some documents. "The guy who wants the hand carved bed wants his mansion garden redone. Hey, he's got the money, we got the talent. It works for me."

"And lastly, Seisyll and Rie. You both work with metal. Seisyll is a welder and Rie is a metal sculptor. We couldn't find any special projects for you together, but we thought you could give each other's job a try. Mutual respect would be just as effective." Joseff was sitting next to Seisyll so he handed him the papers he needed. "A building needs some work and a chick from the Bronx wants a statue. Pick the order you want to do them."

"Does everyone feel okay with things?" Lexie asked.

"And what will you two be doing?" Owen countered dryly.

"We have a project, too." Joseff smiled. "We got a special order for a detailed stained glass piece. It'll take both of us to do it. We figure if we haven't killed each other by the end, we'll pick a wedding date."

There was a moment of silence before Sam decided, "I'm in." She signed the contract in front of her and slid it across the table to Owen. He paused for a moment and then signed as well. In a matter of moments, everyone had signed their contracts, even Remy and Heul, although they showed much more reluctance.

As Lexie collected the contracts, her eyes met Joseff's across the table. They both began to smile.

CHAPTER SEVENTEEN

By mutual agreement, the teams met the following morning at one or the other's preferred place of work. For Arian and Jen, that meant meeting at Jen's woodshop. It was a small room converted from a garage attached to Kingdom Design's building.

Arian wasn't in the best of moods as he headed for the shop early in the morning. He hadn't slept a minute the night before, haunted by a pair of peridot-colored eyes. Jennifer Germaine was long-legged, willowy, and beautiful. He would have expected her to be a model instead of a woodworker, but he had seen her hands. They were elegant and shapely, but marked with the little scars and calluses that showed she had paid the price for her work.

His own hands showed the wear and tear of almost twenty years of hard work. He could build, construct, and arrange steel beams with the best of them, but his first love was lumber. When Driven Snow built a building, no matter the size, once the steel frame was done, he took over with internal woodwork. If they worked on a house, he was in charge almost from the start.

The sweet and fresh scent of recently shaved pinewood filled his nose as he headed toward the open door to the shop. He could hear the very busy sound of a saw of some kind. Wisely, he didn't say anything as he stepped into the doorway; he didn't want to startle anyone with a saw. He cautiously looked in the room and quickly forgot everything he might have said.

Jen stood at a workbench, her unruly red hair tied on top of her head. She wore goggles to protect her eyes, and they were the only spot on her body not covered in sawdust and woodchips. She was bent over the table and delicately cutting out a curved line in the piece of wood she held. Her long legs were wrapped with well-worn blue jeans and a snug tank top flattered her upper body.

She was breathtaking. He could only stand there staring at her. It felt as if he had been punched in the gut. There wasn't supposed to be such a thing as the perfect woman. Yet, in his book, Jen was perfection personified. Was there any man alive who could resist a redheaded artist who could make sawdust look sexy?

She turned off the saw and straightened up. When she saw him, she smiled and put her goggles on top of her head. "Good morning," she said cheerfully. As he continued to stare, her heart began to beat faster. Self-consciously, she brushed at the sawdust on her face. "What?"

"I think you're sexy," he finally said. "I want that stated now."

"Oh." She cleared her throat. What was she supposed to say to that? Was she supposed to admit that she thought he was God's gift to female woodworkers? In blue jeans and plain t-shirt, he was over six feet of mouthwatering muscle and breathtaking beauty. She had been hoping they wouldn't be paired together. How was she supposed to concentrate? She had been ogling him since the wedding!

"So." He walked into the shop and took a deep breath. "I love that smell."

She grinned. "I'll give you five bucks if you can name each one."

He lifted a brow and then grinned as well. "Pine, maple, oak and . . ." He sniffed the air. "Cedar."

"Ooh." She pulled out her wallet and handed over five dollars. "You have a nose like a bloodhound." She removed the slat of wood she was working on and carried it over to another table. "I saw from our instructions that the bed was supposed to be in a more traditional style, so I've been working on some details."

He walked over and leaned over her shoulder to look. The wood was beginning to shape into something that might have been a curved part to a headboard. The true detail would be her hand carving. "So if I need help, I know you know your way around a jig saw."

She sniffed. "And a circular one, thank you." She could only hope a bit desperately that he hadn't noticed how fast her pulse was racing. He smelled like cherry wood. It was her absolute favorite. And he was so big and hot. For one of the few times in her life, she felt small as he moved closer.

Belatedly, he realized he was crowding her. He started to step back when his eyes lowered to the delicate line of her throat. Her pulse tripped as hard as his did. Relief made him lightheaded. He wasn't the only one feeling the madness. He moved closer and lifted one hand to lightly rest on her hip. "Question."

"Sure." The word was almost a squeak, and she cleared her throat. "I mean, sure."

"Are you afraid of me, or attracted to me?"

She considered lying. Then she considered being evasive. She even considered losing her temper. Finally, she just sighed. "I think it might be a rather intimidating combination of both." She looked up at him with a frown. "I'm not the type to just look at a man and start lusting after him. I'm out of my depth. I saw you at the wedding and was terrified you'd talk to me, and I'd act like an idiot."

"So far you're not acting like an idiot." He wiped a smudge of sawdust off her face and his hand lingered warmly. "In fact, I like how frank you are." He eased back.

Her quick smile was rueful. "So he says now. Wait until I *really* get comfortable with you. Remy blames every single swear word that Lexie knows on me. The sad part is that Lexie only knows half my vocabulary. I have a tendency to be, uhm, vocal with my temper."

"Me too." He grinned. "And I yell."

"Loudly?"

"'fraid so."

"Good. So do I." She grinned, too. "And I think this may work out after all. I think I'm starting to really like you."

"It's mutual." He looked at the clock. "Wasn't our client supposed to come by this morning to go over the details?"

"He was indeed." She looked down at her clothes. "Hopefully he won't take offense that I've already gotten started." She brushed at the wood chips and sawdust but it didn't help. "I must look like I was rolling in the bin."

He refrained from mentioning that that was part of why she seemed so sexy to him. Instead, he began to move around the shop, examining the equipment and supplies. She was as fully outfitted as he was. He felt as at home here as he did back at his shop.

A man cleared his throat and drew their attention toward the door. There they found a rather portly man in a suit staring at them. He seemed pleasant enough in appearance, but there was something in the corner of his eye that Jen didn't like. The feeling compounded when his eyes slid over her, very slowly, and lingered on her breasts and hips.

Before she was even fully conscious of her discomfort, Arian suddenly stepped slightly in front of her and shielded her with his body. "May I help you?" he asked pleasantly.

The man had to tilt back slightly to meet his eyes. A lip curled in slight disdain. "My name is Davis Harkin."

"Assemblyman Harkin?" He lifted a brow slightly.

"None other." Harkin swept his gaze over the shop. "I was told I could find Jennifer Germaine and Arian Trahern here. I presume you are they?"

"Good presumption." Jen kept her hands in her pockets. She didn't like the way Harkin looked at her. In fact, she didn't like the way he looked at her shop. He felt slimy and disgusting, and she refused to even shake his hand. "I'm Jennifer, this is Arian."

He offered a hand to her but Arian took it instead. Pointedly, Arian applied subtle force. "Nice to meet you, Assemblyman Harkin," he said pleasantly, but his blue eyes were cold. "I will assume you are our client?"

Harkin wasn't stupid enough to try to get into a pissing contest with Arian Trahern. He looked like he ate nails for breakfast and had steel girders for lunch. "Yes, yes I am." He flicked a glance over Jen again, something covetous in his eyes. "I felt it was time to upgrade my furniture, and I wanted to start with a new bed. Something fancy and handmade. I assure you, I can pay for it."

"Traditional, I believe I heard mentioned." Jen stayed slightly behind Arian; he felt like a protective shield. Chills ran down her back and she felt sick to her stomach. "Four posters, full headboard and footboard?"

"Indeed." Harkin got his hand back from Arian but all his fingers were numb. It was vaguely alarming, because he didn't recall Arian applying force. He tried to step to the side to see Jen better, but Arian shifted his weight and continued to block his full view. "I need it within two days. Tomorrow afternoon if possible."

Jen looked up at Arian as he glanced over his shoulder. He nodded slightly in agreement and turned back to Harkin. "Done," he said. "King size?"

"Yes. Room for two."

The way he said it nearly made Jen gag. Her fingers curled unconsciously into the back of Arian's shirt. He shifted back only the slightest bit, but it made her feel enveloped in his strength and heat. Safe. Protected. "We'll get started right away." She was proud of her even tone, though her stomach rolled worse than a marble on a ship deck.

Harkin paused, looked at her, and sensed, more than saw, Arian's alertness. "Very well. I will return tomorrow." He took his leave quickly, backing out of the shop without taking his eyes off Arian. He somehow felt that turning his back could be lethal.

As soon as he was gone, Jen bolted for the garbage can and proceeded to throw up all of her breakfast. While the spasms wracked her body, she was only vaguely aware of Arian gently holding her and giving her whatever support he could. When the attack ended, she had no strength to stop him as he lifted her into his arms and carried her over to the couch against the wall. He put her down as delicately as glass and went to grab a bottle of water from the cooler.

He knelt in front of her to offer it, and she found a wan smile. "I suppose this would be the ideal time to mention my gift. I'm a...barometer, I guess is how we've classified it. The higher the reading of one of the 'seven deadly sins,' the more sick I get." She took a sip of the water and then saluted lightly with the bottle. "Greed and sloth seemed high on his list."

"I do not want you to meet him alone. Ever." His voice was hard, even though the hand resting on her knee was gentle. "Do you hear me, Jennifer? Do *not* ever see him alone. I don't trust the bastard, and I'd hate to have to kill him. Killing a politician would be bad publicity."

"Depends on which paper ran the notice." She lifted a brow slowly. "And I will agree on the grounds that I am a fully grown and intelligent woman, not on the grounds that you have just ordered me to do something. You have no authority over me."

He leaned in suddenly, and they were nose to nose. Her pulse and heart kicked into overdrive. Breathless, she stared at him. There were little flecks of darker blue in his eyes, like chips of the sky. It took considerable effort not to lean forward and press her lips to his.

"How's that barometer of yours around me?" His voice was little more than a rumble of male desire.

"Silent," she managed to say.

"Then it's not as accurate as you think. Right now, your 'lust' sensor should be on full alert." He nipped at her full lower lip before backing up and straightening. "I'm going to start cutting out the frame. Once your stomach settles, you can help me or start the detailing."

Her stomach didn't need settling anymore. It was her libido that needed help. She let out a long breath. She had the very sneaky feeling that she had fallen in love. Sure as hell, there couldn't be any other reason for why he jerked at her heart and soul as strongly as her body. She watched him almost helplessly. She had once wished for true love. Did wishes really come true?

Steadier, she got to her feet, and walked over to her detailing table where smaller tools were laid out. She grabbed a sketchpad and began to draw quickly, outlining what she thought the bed should look like. It was to her credit that she didn't jump when Arian's arm suddenly slid around her shoulders and he tugged her against him so he could see over her head. "Well?" she asked.

"I like it." He ran a finger over the line of a poster. It was inlaid with beautiful details. "Which is easier? To carve a poster, or to carve a casing for a poster? I can make a poster to scale and you can carve into it, or I can make a smaller one and we can attach details."

"For stability sake, we should carve into the poster. But, frankly, I don't see his bed getting that much usage, no matter what he infers."

He decided he was absolutely crazy for his red haired partner. If he wasn't looking at her, he was thinking about her. And when he was looking at her, all he could think of was pulling her into his arms and tasting her lips. It was more than that, though. She was acerbic and strong willed in ways that he loved. When she smiled, he felt like he was looking into paradise. He would go crazy if he couldn't have her at his side, always. "Let's go with simple. I'll make the posters smaller."

They settled into an easy rhythm. She put on the radio in the background after a while, so they had something to listen to other than the whine and whir of power tools. She narrowed in and focused on her detailing. Under her skillful hands, the little accents started to bloom. As he worked, the entire bed frame began to come to life. At first there were planks of wood. Then there was the rough outline of a bed. He only gave it a temporary assembly, because it needed to be taken apart for more detailing later.

As the sun was setting, he was beginning to sand and smooth in preparation for stain. She still worked on details. The pain in her lower back finally got to her, and she put down her tools to stretch largely. The clock cheerfully said it was nearly one in the morning. "I think we need some sleep."

He watched her hungrily. The way the light rippled over her when she stretched had done dangerous things to his already aching body. "Don't suppose you'd mind if I fell asleep on the couch."

"Not at all." She got to her feet carefully. "I'll probably only sleep a few hours then come back to do more work. Is that okay?"

"Sure." He busied himself with cleaning up anything they wouldn't use the next day while she closed and locked all the doors. Finally he just couldn't take it anymore.

When she turned from locking the door, he was right behind her. Breath lodged in her chest, she backed into the wall as he loomed in dangerously, seductively close. This time her barometer seemed to be going off the chart, but it didn't make her stomach sick. There was a deep difference between selfish lust and a lust born of deeper emotions. She just couldn't tell if it was his or hers that had her sensors spiking.

His head slowly bent until his breath was hot on her lips. He stayed there, his eyes keeping hers captive. He waited with the stillness of a predator, and his body seemed to vibrate with desperate hunger. She knew, was certain, that he would back off and not press the issue if she told him no. She couldn't do it, not when she wanted him just as terribly. She slid her arms up around his neck, rose on her toes, and met his kiss with aching desire.

The kiss turned into the most devastating experience of her life. He didn't just kiss her; he *consumed* her. Despite the blatant carnal nature of his tongue tangling with hers, he kissed her with a famished need, long, and deep, and drugging. It seemed as if he was imprinting her taste inside him. Her entire body went hot and weak, only his arm around her waist keeping her on her feet.

He lifted his head, and his eyes burned. She couldn't even find her voice or her mind. In fact, she wasn't sure she entirely remembered who she was or where she was. The best she could get her jumbled thoughts and riotous hormones around was, "Wow."

His teeth nipped at her lips and her knees shook. He shifted, and pressed closer so she couldn't mistake his body's desire for her. The languid, slumberous darkening to her eyes made a shudder rip through his body. If merely kissing her was hotter than foreplay with other women, how the hell would he survive if she was in his bed? Or hers. The couch was also looking appealing. "Are you going to stay with me? Or invite me in?" His voice was a purr against her ear as his teeth nibbled enticingly.

She wanted to. God, she wanted to with every fiber of her being, but she hadn't gotten to thirty without learning who she was and what she wanted and needed. She had decided on an 'all or none' commitment, knowing only that would make her happy. "Not yet," she managed to say. Not until she knew she could keep him.

He slowly released her, his hands sliding over her body with a possessive touch. "Okay." His lips quirked. "But know that I only have the strength to release you because you said 'yet' and not 'never.'"

"What, am I stupid?" She shoved her hair out of her eyes. "Are all of you Traherns alike?"

"To our knowledge."

"Then no wonder Lexie lost her mind." She pressed against his body for a moment to find his ready strength. His arms curled around her, and she let herself soak in his comforting embrace. As she did, she acknowledged what was inside. She loved him. Her wish had come true. But did he love her? Well, if not, then she would change it. "Good night, Arian."

He released her and watched her go into the building through an attached door. He let out a long breath and eyed the couch. He would never fit, but perhaps the cramped corners would help distract him from his body's cranky messages.

When Jen walked into the house, she saw Lexie looking at her gravely. "Not a word," she muttered as she stomped past. "I need a cold shower." Ignoring her baby sister's distinct giggles, she went upstairs.

She only managed to get a few hours of sleep, and what few hours she got were not very restful. She had never realized before how cold and lonely it could be to sleep by herself. She should have offered to share her bed, she thought, as she stared at the ceiling. Arian had the bedrock decency to sleep with her but not seduce her unless she wanted it.

A little guilty that he was sleeping on the couch, she got out of bed and got dressed. When she walked into the shop and saw him sprawled on the couch, his legs hanging over the arm, she had to bite her lip to hide a smile. She walked over and leaned down to brush his lips with hers. "Wake up, sleeping beauty," she murmured.

Drowsily, he said, "That's my baby sister."

"Snow White?"

"T'other sister."

She shook her head affectionately. "You have the most fascinating family, Arian."

One eye cracked open and then closed on a groan. "It's not morning."

"Afraid so. It happens every day in fact. Usually around the same time of day." She moved back hastily as his hands lifted. "Don't you dare." He swung his legs around and sat up, and she held out the coffee she was holding. "Careful. Rie made it, and I could use it to clean my saw."

He gratefully accepted the cup. The coffee was hot, strong, and could have etched steel. He drank half the cup in a single gulp. His sleep hadn't been any more restful than hers; the small couch had done nothing to distract his mind or body. "How much work do we have left?"

"If you'll take over using the jig saw to cut out shapes, not much at all. A few hours." She rolled her shoulders and neck. "The nearly all-nighter helped. Oh god." The last was added as his hands settled on her neck and began to rub. She relaxed under his hands as his fingers found and firmly removed every knot. With a soft whimper of pleasure, she braced a hand on the table.

The little sound went through him like lightning. He bent his head to brush his lips over her ear. "When we're done," he breathed softly, "want me to get rid of all of them? All over your body?"

"Yeah." She leaned back against him, her head finding the perfect spot on his shoulder. "But I won't promise to sleep with you."

"I wouldn't expect you to." He feathered a kiss over her cheek and slowly released her. "It was an offer made without strings, Jen." He contemplated her. "Why Jen instead of Jenny?"

She lifted a brow. "Do I look like a Jenny?"

"No. It's too . . . perky."

She opened her mouth but closed it without protest. She laughed. "Damn, it's hard to be offended at the truth." She turned to lean up and brush his lips with her own. "Let's get this thing finished."

With him focusing on cutting, she was able to focus on the detailed carving. Sure, there were machines to do that kind of work, but it really wasn't the same as doing it by hand. While she finished the last piece, he attached everything together.

When the bed was finally done, they both stepped back to survey their work. "Damn," he said.

"I'll see your 'Damn' and raise you a 'Holy Hell.'" She ran a hand over the footboard. "This is definitely the best thing I've ever made. I *hate* the idea of giving it to that slimy worm. He doesn't deserve something this nice."

"We'll make another one," he decided. "Even better than this one."

"Deal."

He tossed his goggles onto the table. "I don't know about you, but breakfast didn't stay long. There's a restaurant a few blocks away that does dine-out. I'll pick something up. What do you want?"

She thought about it. "Anything edible. I'm not picky." She smiled as he dropped a casual kiss across her lips before heading out the side door. Arian, she had learned, was a very physical man. He showed affection with touch. A hand on the shoulder, a skim of his fingers through her hair, a kiss on the lips or cheek. A woman would never question his feelings for her, and she was beginning to think her handsome Viking was the tiniest bit infatuated with her as well.

She busied herself with starting to put away tools. All the doors were shut and the radio was playing, so she danced her way around the tables. A knock on the side door had her brows lifting, and she walked over to open it. Her stomach instantly rolled and she was on her guard. "Assemblyman Harkin, hello."

Harkin glanced over her shoulder, saw no sign of Arian, and couldn't have been more delighted. He had already had a bad morning and didn't want to deal with this Trahern brother, too. "Hello, Miss Germaine. I came to see progress."

She reluctantly stepped back and mentally prayed for Arian to come back quickly. If needed, she thought Lexie and Joseff might be in Lexie's shop on the other side of the building, but she wasn't sure she could call them in time if Harkin pulled something. "We're done, in fact."

He spotted the bed and his mouth fell open. "Well." Astonished, he walked closer to see it better. He had never seen finer craftsmanship. "This is impressive work by both of you. Every penny is well spent."

She sat down at the workbench. Her hand rested on the top, ready to reach for a sharp tool if needed. Her stomach rocked and rolled. "Arian and I haven't discussed price," she said, though she was filled with disgust at watching him touch the bed. "He just stepped out, so why don't we wait for him to come back?"

"Nonsense. Name your price." He moved closer to her. "I assure you, I can meet it." His eyes slid over her. "Any price."

Temper began a slow boil and alleviated the sickness. "I am not for sale," she warned, her voice clipped. "And I do not appreciate the way you look at me or address me. Harassment is a strong word, Mr. Harkin, but I'm not afraid to use it."

"Don't be silly. Who would believe you?" He put a hand on her leg and slid it up her thigh. "It's your word against mine. Now, name your price."

Just as her hand curled around a carving tool, a dark shadow filled the doorway and blocked the sunlight. Arian was on Harkin in a blink, his hand closing around the other man's and prying it off Jen with little effort. "You don't touch a woman without permission," he snarled. "Especially not mine!"

"I'll have you arrested for assault!" Harkin squeaked. He couldn't feel his arm, and his fingers were a blaze of agony.

"Before or after I send security tapes to the press?" He applied force and drove Harkin slowly back toward the door. His entire body vibrated with rage. "There are cameras in this shop, Assemblyman. And even your money couldn't buy your way out."

"Wh-what about your job?" Harkin was nearly doubled in pain, the words a gasp. If his fingers weren't broken, they were assuredly going to be dislocated.

"We're firing ourselves. We don't want your money, and you certainly don't deserve our work!" Arian shoved him out the door so hard that he landed on his ass on the cement, his useless arm hanging at his side. "Good day." He slammed the door hard enough that the walls shook, and then turned his gaze on Jen. Something volatile and deadly churned in his eyes. "You let him in."

"Was I supposed to let him rot outside?" she snapped. She dropped the tool she had grabbed. "I was trying to stall for you to get back!" She fiercely rubbed a hand over her leg. "He *touched* me!" Despite her anger, her voice hitched. "His hand felt slimy!"

He crossed the room swiftly, and his hand brushed hers aside. As his hot palm swept over her leg, even the lingering remnants of Harkin's horrible touch faded. When he snatched her up off her seat, she threw her arms around his neck and kissed him with all the pent up fury in her heart.

Just as fast, his anger turned to hunger, and he tumbled her down onto the floor of the shop. "He touched you!" he said against her lips. His fingers rushed over her work shirt, unbuttoning it as fast as he could. He had to have her naked. Had to touch her. Love her. "Damn you, Jennifer!"

It only barely crossed her mind to stop him. Barely. For a split second. It was, after all, the middle of the afternoon and they were on the sawdust and wood chip covered floor of her workshop. The pungent scent of wood combined with his own ripe, wonderful scent and any protest died. She needed him. Wanted him. And, damn it, she was going to have him.

The next time she found any energy or will to think or speak, she was lying sprawled underneath him. Her body was still quivering and shaking in the aftermath of ecstasy. Her legs were locked around his hips and her arms around his shoulders. Against her chest, she could feel his heart still hammering as hard as hers. "Wow," she managed to say.

His lips curved against her neck. "I'll see your 'Wow' and raise you a 'Holy Hell.'" He carefully lifted his head. "Am I too heavy?"

"Not really. But the wood chips are digging into my back." She held on with a laugh as he rolled and pulled her on top of him. She sat up, straddling his hips, and shook her hair back. Their bodies were still joined, and she felt the sudden leap of his arousal slowly stretching her again. It sent off streamers of pleasure, and her lashes dropped. "It's a good thing there aren't really cameras in here," she said huskily.

"Yeah." His voice was just as rough as he stared up at her. She was rumpled and flushed and covered in sawdust and wood chips. She was the most stunning thing he had ever seen. "Jen, I think we're just going to have to get married. I can't seem to stand the idea of you rolling over wood chips with any other man."

"I suppose that's fair." She flexed her hips for the sheer torture of seeing his eyes darken. "I'd hate to find you rolling on sawdust with any other woman. What do you suppose we keep the bed for our honeymoon? We can reinforce the posters. I'm sure we'll give it a *lot* of use." Her breath caught as his hands slid slowly up her body. "I don't suppose I could get a vow of everlasting love, could I?"

His fingers tangled in her hair, and he drew her down until their lips met softly and sweetly. "Yes to all of it," he breathed. He kissed her again, deeper and sweeter. "Hell yes I love you, Jen. I think I have all along."

Tears burned her eyes. "I love you, too," she whispered. "I wished for true love once. I never expected the powers-that-be to give me someone like you." She slowly straightened and stretched, knowing it did wicked things to him when she did. "Now make love to me."

"I thought that's what I had already done."

"Do it again."

"As my lady wishes." His lips curved. "After all, when you wish for something, you apparently have to have it."

Her eyes smoldered with love, and laughter, and desire. "Of course."

Listening on the other side of the door, Lexie and Joseff shared a grin and a high five. One down, five to go.

CHAPTER EIGHTEEN

Owen and Sam decided to meet at Kingdom Design as well, since Sam's computer lab hiding on the second floor of the building was better outfitted. First thing in the morning on the day after the meeting, Owen knocked on the front door. It was opened by a rather harried looking Belle. Or Rie. He wasn't sure which was which yet. "Morning . . .?"

"Belle. Sam's on the second floor. Gotta go, bye!"

He moved aside as she zipped out the door. He smiled wryly to himself. Tomos had better watch himself. He knew full well that his little brother was smitten with Belle, and if she was half as charming as she seemed, Tomos was a doomed man.

As he climbed the stairs, he contemplated his own future. From the moment he had laid eyes on Samantha Germaine, he had been fascinated by her. She was by far the most outgoing of the Germaine sisters, but there was a hint of vulnerability inside her large green eyes that tugged at his nurturing heart. She wore extremely thick glasses, and he had the feeling they weren't the run-of-the-mill kind. They added to the hint of vulnerability and seemed oddly appealing.

Was he attracted to her? With every fiber of his being. She was lush, and sultry, and the kind of tempting siren who would, very easily, lure happy sailors to their doom. He was practical and levelheaded. He understood the lack of coincidence in 3rd District, and he understood symmetry. His startling hunger for Sam Germaine would, no doubt, turn into affection and then to love. He was prepared for it. Even fascinated by it.

He was not prepared to walk into her computer room and have the floor drop out from under his feet so fast and sharp that he was falling before he knew he had stepped off a cliff. She was curled up on a window seat next to a bay window and reading a thick book. The morning sun turned her dark red hair to the rich, lush color of red wine, the kind that lingered on his tongue and was the embodiment of flavor.

Her skin was flawless like porcelain, and freckles scattered across the top of her nose and her high cheekbones. Her lips were tempting red, carnal and inviting. Her body was shapely and made as if from his fantasies. She sensed his gaze and looked at him. And she smiled.

Owen hit the ground. Hard.

The gut punch nearly knocked him back a step. Reeling, he could only stare. Every thought of being calm and practical dissolved. *It wasn't supposed to be that easy!* But it was. Between the slam of desire at seeing her to the heart wrenching beauty of her smile, he had fallen in love.

He very carefully hid it inside until he was more ready to deal with it. Even as his practical mind said it had to be mutual eventually, his heart was going ninety miles an hour with agitated ponderings. How was he supposed to handle Sam now? He knew she was hell on wheels; he could sense she was like Gavin, and god only knew that Gavin was a terror. If she knew she could have anything she wanted just by smiling, he would be doomed.

"Owen?" Sam tilted her head as she got to her feet. "Something wrong? You're just standing there." And making her pulse dance like a drunken frat boy at Mardi Gras. The way his cerulean eyes had darkened as they swept over her face had stolen her breath. She hoped it was a sign he wanted her as badly as she had wanted him since she had first seen him.

Unfortunately, his eyes cleared, and he smiled in a way that seemed only friendly. "Not at all. I was just surprised, because I didn't realize you were as big a book geek as I am."

Her back teeth clicked together. "I am not a geek."

"I didn't mean it to be offensive," he protested. "I see it's a sore spot, so I'll let it be." He walked further into the room and smiled. Though the computer desk and set up was totally high-tech and modern, the rest of the room was as feminine as it could get. "I feel much like Gallagher must have felt encountering the Lilliputs."

She smirked. "Suck it up, and be a man about it." She walked over to the drafting table and easily adjusted it. "There. Now you'll fit. Should I find a chair more suitable to your frame, Mr. Gallagher?"

This time it was his back teeth that clicked together. It took considerable effort not to let his temper flare. It seemed surprisingly quick, for once. "I think I can make do." He put the case he was carrying down on the top of the table. "I have the drawings here. Let's work on the first blueprint for the outside and then move inward. As I work on them, you can do the modeling."

"Fair enough." She pulled another chair over and sat down beside him. Deliberately, she leaned in, so he was sure to notice her presence. He didn't even bat a lash. "How does this work for you?"

"I have to calculate the rough dimensions of the drawn buildings and translate them to a blueprint." He wished like hell she would back up. Her perfume made his mouth water. And, damn it, he wished she would button her shirt all the way. The tempting swell of her breasts made his fingers itch.

"Oh so you're not all brawn. Sometimes it's hard to tell." Her eyes widened innocently. "I mean, you know all the stereotypes."

"Like the one about redheads having a temper?"

"It's not a stereotype if it's true. All us Germaines have a temper. Bad ones. And did I mention that most of us tend to yell?"

"No wonder you aren't married."

That stung. She straightened up and crossed her arms. "I'll have you know," she retorted stiffly, "that we all set our standards very high and no men have ever held up to them. I haven't met a single one yet."

Equally stung, he nodded sagely as if he didn't want to give her a good shake. "I know how that feels. We Traherns set our standards pretty high as well. I don't think I've ever met a woman who could compare. I always leaned toward short brunettes, personally." It was a lie, but he couldn't resist the dig.

She got to her feet with a sharp motion and went over to her computer to start booting it up. It was as much to keep from getting mad as it was to hide how much that had hurt. So she wasn't the perfect woman. There was no such thing as perfection. So what if she was tall and red haired? So what if she wasn't some kind of meek little mouse that he could boss around? He would be bored. Quiet and practical as he was, he was still too strong a man to be happy with a woman he could run roughshod over.

Things were quiet for the next two hours. Neither spoke except to make preliminary decisions about building materials, room dimensions, and other details for her to plug into her modeling program. It was homegrown and specially made to suit her needs. She didn't even want to know how Tabby had fused so many different program elements into her 'Modelmaker 2000.'

When the silence finally got to her, she asked, "How did you lose your parents?"

"Car accident. You?"

She had to smile. "Our ever-so-practical parents decided to go mountain climbing. When Dad fell off a cliff, he was hooked to Mom for safety. They both fell all the way down the mountain. We've always thought that it was just like them to go out together and so spectacularly."

"You were only eighteen," he murmured.

"Small 'only' margin. I was halfway through my degree. Remy held us all together. Jen and I helped however we could." She looked at him to see him watching her, his eyes dark with shared empathy. Her heart lurched and stopped for long moments. When it started again, it was no longer her own.

A little shaken, she turned back to her computer. She hadn't been expecting that. She hadn't expected to fall in love. Was he the one she had wished for all along? When she had made her wish for true love, she had never truly expected to get it, let alone with a man like Owen Trahern.

Silence fell once more. He handed over the first set of blueprints, and she got to work. His handwriting was very precise and his calculations were fabulous. She didn't have to question anything. She could simply lose herself in the construction of the delicate flower shop. She loved modeling. Seeing a building spring up with a few mouse clicks was her favorite thing.

However, as the day became evening and then turned into night, her eyes became strained. It was only when his hands settled on her shoulders and pulled her back from the monitor that she realized how close she had gotten. "Oops." She rubbed at her eyes. "Sorry."

"Don't be sorry. I didn't notice either. I think my neck is permanently stuck sideways." He rolled his shoulders. "Let's close up shop and start again in the morning." He peered at a clock. "Hmm. Amended. Let's start again later."

She squinted at the clock. "It's not midnight."

"Afraid it is."

"Ugh." She pulled off her glasses to better rub at her eyes. "See you later then."

"Good night, Sam." He hesitated, brushed a hand over her hair, and then left the room. He headed down to the first floor and unexpectedly found Lexie sitting on the stairs. He quirked a brow. "And here I thought you'd be with Joseff."

She smiled at up at him. "He went to get a bag. Remy told him to just stop being wishy-washy and spend the entire night. We'll be trading back and forth until we get our own place." She eyed him shrewdly. "You like Sam, huh?" Before he could speak, she continued on blithely, "In case it wasn't mentioned, I can read people. I hear the voice of people's hearts. And yours? Yeah. LOUD."

He smiled. "No wonder you've got Joseff hooked."

"He says it's because I'm a good kisser." She nodded sagely. "He said he was addicted."

He bent and gave her a quick kiss like he would give either of his sisters. "Nah, not that impressive."

"Hey," Joseff complained as he came in the front door. "Lips off my girl. Get your own." He studied Owen's face but said nothing about what he saw. "How's the project?"

"Moving along." He hesitated, then asked Lexie, "Why does Sam wear glasses?"

Her gaze lowered. "It's her decision to tell if she wants to."

Sensing the sadness, Owen let it be and left for the night. He went home and went to bed, but he wasn't entirely surprised when he couldn't go to sleep. He was fairly sure that he and the others were being set up, and he didn't know whether he wanted to yell at his meddling Enforcer family members or thank them.

He headed back over to Kingdom Design the next morning. When he got there, Sam was leaning on the open sill of her window. She looked as lovely and fresh as a storybook princess. Owen, a closet romantic, couldn't help but be charmed. "Good morning," he called up to her. "Sleep well?"

She looked down to answer, and her glasses slipped off her nose. He tried to jump forward, but he wasn't quite fast enough. The glasses hit a large rock in the garden and promptly shattered. "Shit!" he cursed. He quickly gathered up the pieces and looked up. She hadn't moved, and there was horror in her eyes.

He took the stairs two at a time and went into her room. She hadn't budged from the window. "It's okay, Sam," he urged. "We can make this work." He looked closer and realized her shoulders were shaking. "Come over here," he added gently. "It's not the end of the world."

"I can't," she whispered.

"Why not?" He began to frown. "If you're near-sighted, then . . ."

"I'm not." She turned around very carefully, her hands gripping the wall. Tears slid down her cheeks. "I'm legally blind, Owen. All I see right now is a blurred wash of color. No details. Nothing." More tears slid free. "I can't even see where you're standing. I could be in front of a cliff and wouldn't know."

He moved toward her carefully but her eyes didn't blink. He waved a hand gently in front of her eyes and she didn't flinch. Her gaze was completely unfocused, unable to grab onto anything. "Do you have spare glasses?" he asked as calmly as he could.

"No. Th-they're so expensive. Experimental glass. They're fragile but they allow me to see. I'm better with 3D than 2D, so computers are okay for me, but I have trouble reading on paper. I make myself do it anyway because I love books." Her lips trembled and she reached out a hand blindly. "Where are you?" Her voice quivered.

He caught her hand and drew it to his heart. "Here," he said softly. He eased her away from the window and took her over to the couch. "Sit." When she had, he sat beside her. He never once released her. His heart was breaking. His sassy, confident, and rather aggravating partner seemed more fragile than her glasses. "What happened?" he asked softly. He stroked his thumb over her cheekbone. "Was it from birth?"

She shook her head and desperately held onto his hand. Her other hand covered the one on her cheek. Even with him right beside her, she saw nothing but a blur. The blur was so extreme that not even movement penetrated it. Sometimes she thought she saw something shift, but she could never be sure it wasn't just her imagination. Only color could move across her sight but it never had form. She wanted to crawl into Owen's arms and make everything go away, but she was terrified of moving.

As if sensing it, he pulled her into his arms and pressed her head to his shoulder. "Close your eyes," he said softly. "Then you won't see anything because you want it to be that way."

She closed her eyes and everything steadied. Her body relaxed against him. "You would think I ought to have great eyesight, considering my gift," she murmured. "I'm a pentachromat. I have five cones in my eyes for receiving color, unlike normal humans who have three. There's so much color in the world, Owen. I can't even describe it."

He rubbed his cheek against her hair. "No wonder you're an artist. How did you lose your sight?"

"When I was five, my kindergarten class was attacked by a psychotic woman. I don't remember the exact details of what set her off. She planted a bomb in my classroom and kept us all hostage while she screamed at the police. The others were eventually released. I wasn't."

He went very still. "I remember that event. I remember watching it on the news. I was nine." He took a sharp breath. "God. I do remember that. She detonated the bomb while you were both inside the room."

"It was faulty. It wasn't as big as she thought it would be. It killed her." Her lower lip trembled. "All I remember was seeing this immense fireball of heat. The next thing I know, I'm waking in the hospital and I can't see anything except a permanent blur of color. The explosion damaged my eyes in ways that even surgery could not fix."

He flinched harshly. With a soothing murmur, he pulled her closer and sought to use his power to keep her calm. "And the glasses?"

"Pure experimentation, but they work for me. It'll take me a few months to save for a new pair." She tried to smile but it wobbled. "Maybe I can call on my distant family relation through Lexie to Gwyn or Rayna, and Enforcers can help me out."

"You're not alone, honey. We'd all help chip in."

"But what do we do *now*?" She wiped her eyes on his shirt. "I can't uphold the end of my bargain. I can't see, so how can I use a computer?"

He took a long breath. "If you are willing to trust me, there is a way. My primary abilities are of the mind. I can sense and read things about people. I have, on occasion, merged my mind with one of my brothers so we could share data. When we did, we could see out each other's eyes as needed."

She didn't lift her head but she was suddenly alert. "Would that work for me?"

"It can't hurt to try. But here's the thing." He framed her face with his hands. "Doing this means that there will be no secrets between us. You're going to see everything inside me and I'll see everything inside you. And if you don't trust me, it'll never work at all. Your mind will reject me."

He would see everything. That meant he would see all her desperate love and desire. She lowered her head. He would have known anyway. Eventually he wouldn't have been able to mistake it. "Okay," she said softly.

She didn't really know what to expect. There were all sorts of stories and legends about mind merges and what they were like. Much to her surprise, she at first didn't feel anything at all when he merged his mind to hers. Then, without warning, it hit her. Like a shot of straight whiskey to her blood, the rush flooded her head. The tidal wave of memories and thoughts and feelings dragged her under so fast that she nearly panicked and pulled out. But then she saw something. Something beautiful and wondrous. It was his most cherished memory, most cherished emotion.

Her.

She saw herself reflected in his eyes. She saw his acceptance of what might happen and his shock for what did. His vulnerability. And his hunger. Her breath shortened as his hunger whipped up her own. And there, surging at careful chains, was his love. He loved her.

Owen, reeling from the onslaught of her emotions and thoughts, hadn't realized she had clamped onto his most carefully hidden secret, until he noticed she was swinging her hand blindly. "What are you doing?"

"Trying to find you so I can hit you!" she shouted. "You gave me no clue that you were attracted to me! Or that you were in love with me! I was going nuts trying to get you to notice me, and you were pretending like it was nothing! Hold still so I can hit you!"

An absurd urge to laugh rose inside him. Her emotions were laid bare before him. It was fairly obvious, now, that they were both idiots. "I knew at the start that this was bound to happen, and yet I stupidly kept it inside, never thinking that your sharp tongue might be because you were feeling rejected. So much for my being the levelheaded one."

"Steady as a rock," she retorted waspishly, "but about as dense! Oooh! Damn you, Owen Trahern! I ought to kick you!"

"You can't even see to hit me," he pointed out practically. "So kicking is out."

She lowered a hand, patted forward, and found his chest. She pinched sharply and was rewarded by his yelp. "Yeah, but I fight like a girl!" She opened her eyes reflexively and the room spun eerily on its axis. Everything abruptly settled, and it was in crystal clear, sharp detail. An explosion of color surrounded her like the inside of a prism. She took a sharp breath in shock. "That's not possible."

"I told you that you could use my eyes." His face was impossibly tender as he looked down at her. His blue eyes seemed to be made of a million flecks of other colors. "That doesn't just mean you see what I see. It means you can literally borrow my *ability* to see." He framed her face with his hands. "You have the most amazingly complex and beautiful mind I have ever seen or touched. It's going to tear out a piece of me when we let go."

"Then don't." She smiled up at him. "I'm in love with you, and you're in love with me. That seems to be a good reason to keep this mind merge. I mean, you don't have to. People in love don't *have* to be together, so you could walk out the door." She paused, then added deliberately, "Of course, I'd have to chase you down. I may be blind, but I'm sneaky."

He rubbed a hand over where she had pinched him. "I'd noticed." He cupped the back of her head and drew her up so that her lips met his. The kiss was soft, and sweet, and wonderful. His feelings and hers; they were a jumbled mass that fueled both. Hunger rose sharply and burst into a firestorm. Ravenous for him, she threw her arms around his neck and kissed him wildly as her body arched against his to relieve the pressure.

He twisted and tumbled her down onto the couch. As his mouth devoured hers, his hands slid under her shirt and began to memorize every inch of her soft flesh. Old scars marked her body from the explosions and he lingered over each to erase the memory. "You better stop me," he muttered against her lips, "or I'll take you right here!"

An out-of-control Owen was the sexiest thing she had ever experienced. "Don't you dare stop!" He rose over her, his eyes burning, and she lifted her hands to frame his face. Very seriously, she asked, "Owen, will you marry me? If I waited for you to ask, your practical mind would wait *forever* for 'the right moment.' This is it, and I'm not waiting. I love you, I want to marry you, and eventually, I want to have your children."

He slowly began to smile. "You are the most incredible person I have ever met." He kissed her again, slowly, with a famished heat, until she seemed to melt underneath him with a purr of pleasure in her throat. "Yes," he said softly. "I'll marry you, Sam Germaine. I'll share my eyes with you if you share your heart."

"I just want *your* heart."

"It's yours." He feathered kisses over her face softly and began to slowly make his way down her body as he tugged her shirt up and out of his way. "How's that wishes coming true thing working for you? Am I a suitable choice for a girl who wished for true love?" Her answering emotion nearly took all the strength from his arms. On a groan, he gathered her fiercely close. "Out loud," he rasped. "Say it out loud."

"The girl who wished for true love," she whispered, "could never have dared imagine you. The woman who wished for true love could ask for nothing more." She muffled a giggle suddenly. "Owen, aren't we supposed to be working?"

"Later." He buried his face between her breasts. "Much later. Maybe this afternoon."

They didn't get much work done that afternoon, either. Eventually they gave up and snuck down to her bedroom. As they cuddled together, she rested her head on his shoulder and listened to his heart. She had stopped using his eyes but was no longer so afraid of being blind. She wasn't alone inside her rainbow world anymore. "When do we tell the others?" she asked idly.

He linked his hands under his head. "We'll tell them as we see them, and they no doubt guess, but I think we won't be the only ones with news. Coincidentally, we both have five other siblings paired up. And this makes us two for two of matched couples."

Her lips curved. "But, Owen, there's no such thing as coincidence in 3rd District."

"Exactly."

CHAPTER NINETEEN

When Gavin got outside the meeting room, he saw Tabby walking down the hall ahead of him. He hurried down to catch up with her. "Hey," he said as he fell into step beside her. As he did, he didn't miss the way she edged away. He also didn't miss that she wore long sleeves and jeans despite the heat outside, and her hands were in her pockets. The only bit of skin showing was her face.

It was a beautiful bit of skin, tempting and alluring. His eyes ran over her face eagerly. She seemed so delicate compared to her sisters. She was, by far, the most slender and had the most fragile feeling to her. She would glance at him out the corner of her eye, and the wary flashes of pine green were stirring up every urge possible to go out and slay dragons for her.

She really wished he wouldn't stare at her. It was making her entire body heat and long for things it could not have.

Her hands were in her pockets as much for his safety as her own. They wanted nothing more than to get into the thick mop he called hair and to trace the strong line of his jaw, to feel the scrape of the neat goatee on his chin.

Dear god, her partner was *hot*. HOT. Capital letters, bold, underlined, italics. His voice fluttered along everything feminine inside her whenever he spoke. When they got outside, she finally asked softly, "Can you not stare at me?"

He shot her a lethal grin. "Well, I *can* but I don't want to. You're really pretty, Tabby." He stopped walking and turned to face her. Deliberately, he held out a hand. "Let's be formally introduced. I'm Gavin Trahern, computer hacker extraordinaire and electrical wiring genius."

She looked at his hand but didn't take it. "Tabitha Germaine, or Tabby to most everyone. I'm a computer programmer and programing specialist. I design diagnostic programs on the fly, tailored to situations."

He started to lift his hand to her cheek and she flinched back sharply. He dropped his hand. "Okay," he said quietly. "This could be difficult. I'm from a very physical family. We show affection with touch, and I like you, so I'm inclined to want to touch you in passing." *There* was an understatement. The way he wanted to touch her had nothing to do with family, and nothing to do with casual. "You want to tell me why you're afraid of me?"

She looked up swiftly. "No, it's not you. I'm not afraid of you." Miserably, she said, "My 'gift' for being 3rd District born can be painful to other people and to me. It's transmitted via physical contact. So please don't touch me."

There was a long silence. Then, "When was the last time you were hugged, Tabby Cat?"

Her eyes widened slightly at the nickname. "Tabby Cat?" she echoed. He just smiled and she frowned, choosing instead to focus on the question. "I don't remember," she admitted. "Probably when I was a kid. The problem kicked in when I was five."

"What would happen if I touched you?" Because he had to. Needed to. Craved to. The ache in his body paled when compared to the ache in his heart. His kitten desperately needed someone to hold and cuddle her. Belatedly, something dawned on him and his eyes slowly widened. "Tabby . . . you've *never* been able to touch *anyone*?"

She looked at him miserably, knowing well what he was really asking. "No, I haven't." She let out a long breath. "You don't have to be delicate around me, Gavin. If you tell bawdy jokes, you're not going to offend a fragile virgin. Just because I've never been kissed doesn't mean my mind isn't an adult's."

The sheer fact that she blushed slightly seemed to argue with her words, but he didn't push it. He was still reeling that she had been entirely isolated from any physical contact for that many years. The injustice of it churned inside him. She was so beautiful, and sexy, and sweet. She had known idiots in her life. He would have happily risked anything to have her for his own.

Would risk anything.

The thud inside his heart was not entirely unexpected. He had landed in love. Falling? He had been doing that since he had looked across a conference table and seen a pair of haunted green eyes watching him. Being Gavin, he didn't bother to hide or evade the situation. "Okay, Tabby cat," he said. "We need to talk. Follow me."

Puzzled, she followed him around the side of the building to where there was a small garden. He sat down on a bench, and she sat down as far from him as she could. "What's wrong?" she asked. "Are you . . . offended?"

"Hell, no." He turned to face her. "Here's the thing, Tabby Cat. I'm in love with you. I just realized it about thirty seconds ago." As her eyes widened, he continued on, "It's not really surprising, actually. I've wanted you since I saw you, and you were pulling on my heartstrings with more skill than a concert violinist.

"That being said, what would happen if I touched you? Would it kill me?" When she shook her head, he scooted closer. "Just be exceptionally painful?" Sparks seemed to almost literally leap between them as he leaned in. His entire body was heavy with desire to touch her. He bent his head, intent on claiming the soft pink lips luring him to his doom.

She hastily shot off the bench and moved out of reach. "You are *dangerous!*" she blurted. Her pulse was scrambling and her lips were tingling, and he hadn't even touched her! He stood and began to stalk toward her, and she backed up quickly. "No!" she said sharply. "Gavin, please! I don't want to hurt you! If-if we're going to work together, you're going to have to get over this."

He grinned. "How does one get over being in love, Tabby Cat?"

"Stop calling me that!" she demanded in exasperation.

"No. It suits you. You're sleek, and feminine, and you could really do with a good dose of petting from the right man." His blue eyes smoldered. "Like me."

"My abilities won't magically turn off," she whispered. "Don't you think I've *tried*?"

"What are they? Tell me and maybe I can find a way around them." She shook her head, and he shook his head in return. "I get the feeling you're a little bit afraid, Tabby Cat. Not just of me, but of yourself. What idiot blamed you when you accidentally hurt him with your powers?" She was silent. "Clearly there was one."

"I didn't say that."

"You didn't have to." He hooked his thumbs through his belt loops. "Okay. I'll try to be patient. I can't promise to succeed. I have a tendency to grab what I want, when I want it. And I want you. Let's meet at the project tomorrow, and we can get to know each other. And if you decide to trust me, then you can tell me what your gift is."

She took a deep breath. She wanted to run away as fast as possible, but she couldn't do it. She wanted to be with Gavin. She wanted to see his quick smile, to see his midnight blue eyes lighten when he was amused. And dear god she wanted to kiss him. Her entire body throbbed with heat. Her breasts ached, and she crossed her arms quickly. His eyes lowered and his lips curved as if he knew. She decided on the coward's route. "See you tomorrow." She turned and hurried away as fast as she could.

He sank down to sit on the bench and put his head in his hands. When he sensed Joseff sit beside him, he said ruefully, "You have my sincerest apologies for the hell I gave you the last few days over Lexie."

Joseff cleared his throat. "Apology accepted. I take it you like Tabby?" He got a sideways look from wry, and warning blue eyes. He grinned. "Ah."

"Great understatement there." Gavin straightened up with a sigh. "There must be some mystical compatibility between our two bloodlines. And our children are going to confuse the hell out of everyone." He scrubbed his hands over his face. "Boy, aren't I the optimistic one? I haven't even kissed her."

"You know," Joseff said, "Lexie told me that Tabby and Sam were the two with the biggest handicaps but they had responded in polar opposite ways. Sam is outgoing and blunt. Tabby is shy and soft-spoken. And no," he added, "I don't know what their handicaps are. But Lexie said that Tabby's one, and only, attempt at having a boyfriend ended up with him hospitalized. She was fourteen at the time."

He winced. "Yeah. I can see why she's been a bit traumatized." He got to his feet. "I'm not without my own skills," he mused. "If the world wants to be so 'coincidental' as to match seven brothers with seven sisters, then there *has* to be a way. And I'm damned well going to find it."

His confidence lasted only as long as it took to get to the project site. He got out of his car, took one look at the dilapidated house, and began to curse rather creatively.

To say the house was falling apart would be putting it politely. It was decades old and hadn't been upgraded once. The last owner had moved out years before and had left it alone. When she had died, her granddaughter had sold it to a real estate company to be refurbished and resold.

"Are you kidding me?" Tabby complained behind him. "There's got to be rats in there. And bugs. Did I mention I dislike rats and bugs?"

"They won't bite, I'm sure," he promised her. He turned with a smile, but the smile slowly faded as he looked at her. Hunger rose and rattled at the bars of its cage. He hadn't slept all night, aching and frustrated in body and heart. And now she stood there looking so beautiful that it was pure torture. His hands started to lift, and she took a slight step back. He forced himself to put his hands down. "Good morning."

As his rough voice swept over her, she felt like the cat he had called her. Every pulse point began to throb, heat surging in her blood. Aching, empty, her body made its demands known. It was doubly frustrating because she had always been able to ignore her body before. There was no ignoring her desire for Gavin. "Morning."

The slight rasp to her voice didn't make it any easier for him to keep his hands to himself. She wanted him as badly as he wanted her. It was *deeply* tempting for him, especially because he knew she didn't have any real idea of what kind of pleasure they could share. He really wanted to replace her loneliness with joy. "Tabby Cat."

She held her laptop in front of her like a shield. "Let's go inside and see what it's like in there."

He took a deep breath. "Good idea." He gestured her ahead and fell into step behind her. His lips curved slightly as he watched her hips. She was slender but she was shapely in all his favorite places.

"Are you staring at my butt?" she asked with a slight dryness to her voice.

"Your hips," he admitted candidly. "But now that you mention it, your butt is quite nice, too."

"How kind." She felt the heat in her cheeks and wished it wasn't so telling. She simply wasn't used to men, or teasing them and being teased. It had always seemed so much easier to just stay away from them entirely than to accidentally tempt someone with something they couldn't have. She had the feeling that she could sneeze and it would tempt Gavin.

The house had been gutted. All plaster and drywall had been torn down. All that was left standing were the wooden beams, and they were showing signs of rot. The wiring and plumbing also remained, and he eyed some of the cords. "That is not code."

She smiled wryly. "Sure it is. It's 1958 code."

"Mmkay. It ain't 1958, babe." He looked at her suddenly, askance. "Er, sorry. I didn't mean to offend."

"Calling me 'babe'?" She shook her head. "I'm hard to offend. It's just a nickname and you don't mean it in a derogatory manner. It's no different than 'dude.'"

"Dude."

"Dude." She nodded sagely. "One of my college friends was from California. Her lingo rubbed off on me. For an entire year, I couldn't seem to get that word out of my dialogue. And it's androgynous. It works for men and women."

"Dudette."

"Nope!" Her eyes began to sparkle. "Hasn't been 'in' since the 1980s."

Enchanted by her all over again, he offered, "Make you a deal. You take no offense if I call you babe, and I take none if you call me dude."

"Deal." She looked around at the floor and found a spot she wasn't afraid to sit on. She settled down and unpacked her laptop. While it was booting, she pulled out a sensor and tossed it to him. "Attach that to your meter. It'll hook you to my laptop."

"Cool." He studied the sensor, and then opened his meter's back and attached the cords. He put the cover back on and knelt to begin inspecting an outlet. "It's not grounded." He began to take readings. "Ugh. It's spiking somewhere."

She typed on her keyboard swiftly. "Start checking all the outlets. We can create a diagram of the house, and I can track down the short." She watched her computer as he moved from outlet to outlet. "Based on the image I'm getting, there is only one outlet per room."

"Seems like it. Make a note that we need to add more outlets. Ideally, we'd want one per wall per room. Grounded, of course."

"No hairdryers killing lights?"

"Not unless the owner wants to go to work with an afro."

She bit her lip as she made notes. "So what got you into wiring?"

His lips curved as he began to check light switches. "Well, I was always into trouble. All I ever heard was 'you're grounded.' I finally took it as a sign and specialized in electrics and electronics. That way if I was told I was grounded, it was a compliment." He enjoyed the sound of her soft giggles. "What about you, Tabby Cat?"

"Hmm." She studied her laptop screen. "Hard to say. It was one of the few things I could do safely. And it's fun for me. Being able to build and design security protocols helps with our company. A lot of people like to have homegrown security systems that dig right into the wiring."

"Damn. Wish I had thought of that." He began to check the wiring itself. In more than one place, the wires were corroded or worn. "I want a closer look." He made his way through the beams to where the breaker box was located. He double-checked that everything was off before heading back to the wires. Using pliers, he began to pull them apart. "Yick."

She found herself deeply amused as the day progressed. His choice in words was steadily getting more creative as they found the extent of the damage. "You know," she finally said, "at this point, we ought to just tear it all out and start over.

We've got a list of faults, breaks, frays, and corrosion. The time and cost it would take to repair and play patchwork isn't worth much when it'd have to be done again later."

"I think you're right." He straightened from where he was stripping the end of the wires in an outlet to see their current state. A scuttling nose had him looking down, and he saw an immense rat running between his feet. He hastily stepped back. "Company."

She looked up and blinked as she saw the rat. So long as it didn't come near her, she had no issue. She looked at Gavin's face, and a smile began to blossom. "Gavin?"

He backed up as the rat came closer. "What?"

"Are you afraid of rats?"

"No!" He hastily back-stepped again. "Damn thing is taunting me!"

She put her laptop aside and got to her feet. She couldn't help the smile on her face or keep it out of her voice. "Gavin, you do remember you're over six feet tall, right? And it's only a rat."

"It's a mangy football with feet!"

He shot her a look of such helpless horror that she felt her smile reaching all the way into her heart. The warm glow seemed to melt all the cold loneliness inside. With a breathless sort of wonder, she could only memorize his face with her eyes.

She was in love with him. This impossible, stubborn man who could rewire a house in his sleep but was afraid of rats. This over six foot tall linebacker of a construction worker who was so gentle with her that she wanted to cling onto him in a way she could not dare do.

Pushing it where it couldn't be found, for she knew he would take ruthless advantage, she walked over and used her shoe to nudge the rat. It scampered off, and she shuddered. "Yuck." Still smiling, she looked up at Gavin. "Chicken. Your 'Tabby Cat' had to scare off the big, terrible rat."

He looked at her for long moments, then grinned. "My hero," he said gravely. Without thinking, he lifted his hand to touch her cheek.

She backed up so sharply that she tripped over the meter on the floor. She backed into the wall and her hand connected with the wires. An immense electrical flare went up, the light sharp and blinding, and every wire in the house shorted and blew apart. When the light faded, the smell of burned plastic and copper filled the air. Smoke drifted up from the wiring, and anywhere the wooden beams were near the wires, the wood was charred and blackened. She looked completely unharmed, but her eyes were filled with misery, and her rusty red hair had frazzled at the ends.

Gavin was silent for long moments. "Okay," he finally said after a minute. "Let's talk, honey."

Shoulders slumped, she moved away from the wall and kept almost two feet of distance between them. She walked over to a window and stared outside. It was easier than looking at him. "I have a very powerful electric field around me. You know how you can build up a static charge with your body? Mine's about the five million watt version. I experimented once. I sat in a chair for *hours* without moving. I discharged the field beforehand. At the end of the time, I touched some wire. It blew apart. I guess I absorb it from the air and not the ground."

"How did it start?"

"It was dormant until I electrocuted myself." She sighed. "By the way, when parents tell you not to stick a penny in an outlet, *listen to them*." She caught sight of her reflection in the glass and scowled as she tried to smooth down her hair. "After that, no one could touch me without getting nasty shocks. We thought it was the length of time between shocks, but the jolt never seemed to get better between discharges. But it definitely got worse the longer between them."

"And the accident that made you give up?"

Her lower lip quivered. "Jackson Sanchez. Cutest guy in ninth grade. Nicest guy in the school. He asked me out. I wanted to believe that my curse wouldn't ruin my life. He was okay with me not touching anyone. Everyone knew I was different. But he really wanted to kiss me." A tear slid down her cheek. "All he did was take my hand. And I electrocuted him. He ended up in the hospital for a month. He didn't blame me, Gavin. I blamed me. Other kids blamed me. I went into home study. It was easier."

"So for twelve years, you've had no other physical contact. No wonder you blew out the wiring here."

She braced her shoulders. He sounded more musing than mad, but she was still braced. She slowly turned and found, in surprise, that he was right behind her. She backed up, but the window was right behind her, and she couldn't move. "No!" she said sharply. "Don't touch me!" His hands lifted toward her, and she flinched, her eyes squeezing shut. "I don't want to hurt you!" she nearly wailed.

His fingers softly skimmed her cheek and threaded into her thick hair. Nothing happened. Her eyes flew open as his other hand closed around her wrist. It slowly slid up her sleeve so that his warm hand could caress her flesh. Shaken to her core, she stared at him. "How?"

"You didn't notice?" he asked softly. He smoothed down her hair, erasing the static clinging to her rusty-colored locks, so that they fell back into place. He then curled that hand around the back of her neck. Tenderly he stroked her skin. "Hadn't you wondered why I wasn't wearing gloves to work with the wires? Even with the breaker off, it's not a good idea."

"I . . . I hadn't noticed." Her eyes closed with helpless pleasure as his hot hands softly stroked over her skin. She could feel the line of his fingerprints. Just those little touches on her arm and neck were wildly arousing. Her entire body was heating and aching until she almost couldn't breathe.

"Damn, you're sensitive." There was wonder in his voice. "I wonder what'll happen if I kiss you, Tabby Cat." He eased closer, his body pressing to hers. The feel of her curves molding to his body was wildly erotic, especially when she nearly purred at the sensation. She seemed to go entirely weak, only his weight and his hand on her neck holding her up. "God, Tabby Cat," he said roughly. "We were made for each other."

"What are you?" she managed to whisper. She couldn't think, couldn't speak. He was so hard and hot. And safe. Dear god, the feel of him was safety, and security, and the seductive promise of comfort. Someone to hold. Someone to hold her. She felt starved for the feel of his arms. Her lips trembled. "Is it prosaic to ask for a hug at this moment?"

He yanked her into his grip as his arms fiercely banded around her. "Never!" he vowed hoarsely. "Jesus, when were you last hugged, Tabby Cat?" He buried his face against her neck as he lifted her off her feet. "I'm never letting you go!"

She carefully wrapped her arms around him. It felt . . . odd. But it was a wonderful odd. A beautiful odd. His strength seemed to sink into her and suddenly she was holding onto him just as tightly, wishing she could absorb herself into him. Her body arched to press closer.

He dragged her head back and took her mouth with his. There was no first kiss hesitation. He kissed her as if he had the right, his lips almost bruising as he eagerly devoured her, his tongue tangling with hers hotly, daring her to meet him halfway. And when she followed his lead, brazenly but hesitatingly stealing the kiss, he felt as if he would go up in flames.

He tore free and gulped in air. "We have three options," he rasped. "We can try to sneak into your house. We can try to sneak into my house. Or we can find a hotel."

"Where's the 'try to ignore this and get back to work' option?" she asked breathlessly. She clung onto his shoulders for support, because her legs felt too weak to hold her up. Only his arms kept her upright.

"You think we can?" he demanded incredulously. "Damn it, woman, are you mad?" He gave her a little shake. "I'm in love with you. And if you tell me you're not in love with me, I'm calling you a liar."

"What makes you so sure?"

He lifted her higher. "Wrap your legs around my hips." When she had, he turned and began walking for the door. He kept one arm around her waist and bent to pick up the laptop. That in hand, he went out the door. "I know you love me," he finally said, "because you have to. I won't accept anything else. It might not happen right now. But I'm going to make it happen. I want your love, Tabby Cat, so I'm going to have it."

She took a deep breath. "Hotel."

He didn't waste a second in putting her in his car and getting into the driver side. In minutes they were on the freeway. "I should feel guilty," he decided, "but I don't. I want you to myself. We can deal with our giggling siblings later. Much later. Like next week."

"Gavin." She smiled at him. "We still have a job." She poked his arm, a little thrill inside her that she could touch him. "Now explain yourself."

"I have a dampening field. It's the easiest way to explain it. I could grab a live wire and it wouldn't do shit. I could get hit by lightning and *possibly* singe my hair. I'm a friggin block of rubber for all intents and purposes." He shot her a grin. "Insults bounce off too, just a warning. So anything you might be putting out, I'm absorbing. We're a perfect match, Tabby Cat. And no matter how long it takes, I'm going to make you see it, too."

She thought about it for long moments. Her eyes closed as she settled back in her seat. "Gavin, will you marry me?"

"In a heartbeat," he responded instantly. "God knows I'll be miserable without you."

"And you'll be my lover?"

"Every chance I get."

"I might not be able to have kids," she warned him. "I mean, we can't know how my power will affect a baby."

"So we spoil our future nieces and nephews."

She took a deep breath. "Will you love me forever?"

"Haven't you been listening?" he demanded. "I'll love you until I die. Hell, I'll love you after that. We'll have to be buried together, and some day three hundred years from now, they'll unearth us to find two happily fused skeletons. Or we'll be cranky old ghosts and haunt badly wired houses while chasing each other around the attic."

She began to laugh almost helplessly. "Oh, Gavin! That's so horrible!" She leaned over and pressed her lips softly to the corner of his mouth. "I love you," she breathed softly.

"You'd better," he said, his voice strained. "And keep your lips off me, Tabby Cat, or we'll never make it to the hotel."

She settled back in her seat once more. "You just want me around to scare off rats."

The smile he gave her was tender and teasing all at the same time. "I was always a cat person."

CHAPTER TWENTY

The morning after the meeting, Rie went to wake her sister before she left to meet Seisyll. Not to her surprise, Belle was a lump under the blankets. She walked over, turned on the timer of the clock, and walked out.

The alarm went off ten seconds later with all the bells, whistles, and banging of a fire truck running through a Fourth of July parade. Belle jolted awake so hard and fast that she almost tumbled out of bed. Blearily, she peered at the clock. Her eyes popped wide open as she saw what time it read. "Crap!"

She hastily scrambled out of bed in a flurry of dark red hair and silk nightgown. She rushed down the hall to the bathroom, rushed through a shower, and then also rushed through her room to get dressed. Her hair was still damp as she skidded down the stairs. A plate with toast and scrambled eggs was on the counter. Grateful to her twin, she gulped down breakfast.

The doorbell rang and she hurried over to open the door. She found Owen Trahern on the other side, and he blinked at her. "Morning . . .?" His voice trailed off.

"Belle. Sam's on the second floor. Gotta go, bye!" She ducked around him and ran down the sidewalk toward the car she shared with Jen. Her sister didn't need it that day, so she was in charge. She could have kicked herself. She hated being late! She also really hated keeping a hot guy waiting.

She wasn't sure what it was, but there was something about Tomos Trahern that had instantly gotten her attention. Staring across the table at identical faces, she had found her eyes fixed to Tomos. His ponytail seemed to beg to have a woman's fingers in it, and there was something soft and dreamy in his pale blue eyes. Her heart fluttered when he smiled. Oooh. The man was dangerous to any woman's sanity, let alone a romantic woman's sanity. He looked like a man quite happy to find a white horse and rescue a damsel in distress.

When she pulled into the driveway of the old manor, she saw fairly quickly why the place needed work. The front area alone was in desperate need of help. There were more weeds than flowers. Barren dirt patches seemed like missing teeth in the garden's lopsided smile.

She got out of the car with a grimace. Bemused, she studied the beat-up pickup truck she had parked beside. It took character to own something like that. She wondered who it belonged to; she doubted it was a man. Few men would admit to owning a white truck with a series of faerie bumper stickers.

The front door was standing open. The entire manor was over eight thousand square feet, and there was a centralized atrium that also needed work. She blew out a quick breath when she found it. It wasn't as bad as the rest, but it needed help. It definitely seemed that the owner of the mansion didn't know anything about plants. The rest of the place was well designed and excessively luxurious.

Curious, she made her way through the rest of the house toward the back. There was no backdoor on the first floor so she headed up. A little turned around, she finally went through a bedroom toward a balcony. She could just shimmy over the side. Her sisters teasingly called her Trinity since she could jump off buildings a la *The Matrix*. Their best guess was that she could lower the force of gravity around her body.

She stepped onto the balcony and got a perfect bird's eye view of the vast back garden. It was *huge*. A large hedge maze took up the majority, but there were other areas, as well. Something that had likely once been a pond, and dilapidated flower rows. It was a bit depressing to say the least. She mentally began to catalogue what needed to be done. She and Tomos would need to call in backup. Thankfully, she knew a few workers she could call on. He probably did too.

Something rustled. She looked down quickly to find Tomos standing under the balcony and looking up at her. In the morning sun, he seemed like a golden god. A Viking prince there to carry her away. There was something in his eyes, something hot and soft all at the same time. Something that made her heart flutter and her pulse spike. "Hi," she managed to say.

He felt gleeful talons of desire rake his body at the breathless sound of her voice. When he had seen her on the balcony, he had been irresistibly drawn toward her. He had wanted her since the first time he had seen her. She smiled almost shyly at him, and he found himself falling helplessly in love. This stunning, red-haired princess was the woman of his dreams. He was sure of it. "Hi." Prosaic as it was, it was all that came to mind.

Silence fell for long moments. Finally, she said, "I can't figure out what to say. I feel like I ought to say something from *Romeo and Juliet*, but I hated that story."

"You and me both," he agreed with feeling. "Give me happy endings or give me nothing at all. It should've stayed a comedy." He moved closer, hands tucked in pockets. "How about this? Rapunzel, Rapunzel, let down your hair."

She grabbed a handful of her hair and studied it. It was wild with curls and only hung to just past her shoulders. "No, I don't think that'll work either." She leaned on the balcony rail. "I can't think of any other balcony scenes though. At least, not with a meeting sort of theme. I've seen plenty of princes scale balconies, but *that* is definitely a faerie tale quirk. I've never met a man strong enough to scale a balcony."

He lifted one blond brow. "Really now." Feeling slightly challenged, he looked around.

Warily, she asked, "Tomos . . . what are you doing?"

"Proving you wrong." He studied the wall next to the balcony. It was brick and mortar and just uneven enough to make climbing it plausible.

"If you fall on your ass, I reserve the right to laugh at you before helping."

"I'd expect nothing less." He got a grip on the brick and began to climb. It wasn't a question of strength. It was the actual amount of surface he had to grab. Luckily for him, there were plenty of bricks protruding just enough to allow him to climb fairly easily.

Eyes wide, breathless, she stared at him as he pulled himself over the side of the balcony. "Well." It was the only thing she could say.

He grinned at her mischievously. "Thank you, milady." He gave a courtly, sweeping bow.

She could only look at him in bemusement. Princes weren't supposed to be wearing torn blue jeans and a scruffy t-shirt saying '*I'm the GOOD twin. Really.*' They weren't supposed be wearing mud caked boots and a faded bandana. And they sure as hell weren't supposed to be so lethally male and overwhelming.

Yet when she had once wished for true love, she had wished for her perfect match. Not *the* perfect man, but the perfect man for *her*. And here he was. Her secret prince, her romantic fantasy lover, who could climb balconies and go muck around a garden with her.

She was in love.

She realized belatedly that he had stepped closer, and his pale blue eyes carried all the answers to her secret dreams. Striving for even ground, she held out a hand. "Let's get this back on track. I'm Belle Germaine and I am a hopeless romantic who likes playing with flowers."

He took her hand with a matching smile. "I'm Tomos Trahern and I am also a hopeless romantic who likes to play with flowers." He brought her hand to his lips softly, simply because a handshake didn't feel right on a balcony with a woman he would happily climb any tower to find. "Does Rie kill plants like Seisyll does?"

She nodded sagely. "Sadly, yes. She says I hogged the genes related to growth. It's just as well. She hogged the genes related to time and direction."

"Uh oh. Let me guess. You'll get us lost *and* we'll be late."

"In a nutshell? 'Fraid so." She tugged lightly at her hand. "Can I have that back now?"

"If you insist." He released her slowly, his fingers caressing the soft skin of her palm. Watching her as intently as he was, he saw the soft flush that rose high on her cheeks and the telltale beating of her pulse in her neck. Elation filled him. He could work with attraction. He could make her love him the way he so desperately needed.

He stepped forward and she forced herself to hold her ground even though he was looming deliciously over her. At five-seven, she had never felt particularly small before. Caught in the shadow of his body, his heat curling around her seductively, she felt positively tiny. Of course, the way he was looking at her didn't help. She felt as if he was a hungry wolf eyeing a particularly tasty bunny.

"I think we need to clear the air." His voice deepened without his control. "One, we need to work together. Two, we're both hopeless romantics. Three, I've wanted you since I saw you. We're going to have some serious tension at times. We're going to have to try to be practical."

"I agree with all of the above." She took a deep breath but it wasn't the smartest thing she had ever done. He smelled like rich, wild nature and the promise of earthy sensuality. "And I want you, too. When we're done with this job, we need to look at where we stand."

The irony of the romantics of their families being practical wasn't lost on him, but he also understood that they, more than anyone else, needed to be sure they weren't deluding themselves. At least, she needed to be sure. He already was. He had waited twenty-eight years to give his heart and he had recognized the event when it happened.

He eased back a step. "So. Let's go examine this sorely neglected garden. Our client is supposed to come by after stopping to see Jen and Arian."

"Okay." Unable to resist, she ran at the side of the balcony and leapt over. She landed as gracefully as a tiger on the grass and turned to look up at him. His jaw was hanging open. She promptly burst into laughter. "Your face!"

Deciding to show off as well, he sniffed slightly. "Why jump when you can fly?"

Before her fascinated gaze, his body began to twist and contort, feathers blooming over his skin as his face lengthened and his overall shape began to shrink. In seconds, there was a large falcon in his place. He flew into the air and over the side of the balcony and then zoomed for her head.

She ducked with a shriek of laughter. When he came at her again, she took off running. She looked over her shoulder to see where he was, but saw no sight of him. She ran right into his warm body a second later. His arms snapped around her waist to keep her from falling. "Gotcha!" he said.

She grabbed his arms for balance, still laughing. "So you can shift?"

"Nothing smaller than a large bird," he confirmed. "I can't quite compact myself enough to become a mouse." He released her and stretched. "As it is, I always get a little cramped in smaller bodies."

"I can't imagine why," she murmured dryly. She grabbed his hand. "C'mon. Let's start looking around." She pulled out her iPhone and stuck a stylus over her ear. "You talk, I'll take notes. My memory is selective."

"What does it select to remember?"

"I can quote every great romance novel, movie, or play known to mankind dating back to the 1600s. I cannot, however, name any presidents other than the current one, and if you ask me where China is, I *might* find it on a map with some clues."

"Isn't that the big country near France?"

He asked it innocently enough that she blinked for a moment before grinning. "You flunked Geography too, huh?" When he grinned back and winked, she realized that she truly liked him just as much as she loved him. "Did you swap with Seisyll to cheat in class?"

"Never!"

He denied it so vehemently that she knew he was lying. The twinkle in his eye was a giveaway as well. "And I never swapped with Rie," she said staunchly. "Now, let's get to work."

Hip to hip, they made their way through the sorely neglected garden while she took notes. More than once, one or both of them muttered the phrase 'low maintenance.' They didn't even bother to tackle the hedge maze. It just needed a decent pruning.

A sudden chill went down her back. Before she was even fully conscious of it, Tomos was at her side. His broad shoulders sheltered her protectively. "What is it?" he asked in a low voice.

"Someone's staring at me." She moved closer to him without thought.

He wrapped an arm around her waist and looked around. His eyes fell on an affluent looking man walking toward them. There was something in his eyes as he looked at Belle that made Tomos' hackles rise. "Play along," he murmured so softly only she heard. She gave a nearly imperceptible nod. Lifting his voice, he said, "Hello. I'm Tomos Trahern. This is my fiancée, Belle Germaine. I presume you're our client." He offered a hand.

The man looked at his hand as if it was a snake before very carefully accepting the handshake. His eyes never entirely strayed from Belle. "I am Assemblyman Davis Harkin. I just came from meeting your brother and your sister."

Tomos hid a grin. If Harkin had looked at Jen the way he was looking at Belle, he had a good idea why he had been so wary of shaking hands. Arian wasn't very subtle with his abilities sometimes. "I'm sure they will do a good job for you," he said pleasantly. Unable to resist, he applied subtle force to the hand he held until Harkin's eyes swung toward him warily. "She's beautiful, isn't she? I can't take my eyes off her either."

Belle had never considered herself the type to need rescuing, but there was definitely something thrilling about having someone stand up for her. She watched their hands in fascination. If Tomos was exerting effort, it didn't show. On the other hand, Harkin's knuckles were white.

"Yes, she is." When he got his hand back, Harkin stepped back quickly. Thank *god* he didn't have to deal with more than two of the Trahern brothers. If it hadn't been for the fear of retribution from Enforcers, he would have destroyed their reputations. How *dare* they treat him like this? "So, I apologize for the state of the garden. It went to hell long before I moved in, and I lack any sort of gardening skills. I intend to hire a gardener, however, so don't worry about making sure I can't kill it. The grander the better."

His eyes had strayed back to Belle again. She pointedly leaned against Tomos' arm and smoothed a hand over his wrist in a tender gesture. "We can make it very grand. Do you have any preferences? Cottage style? Tropical?"

"Whatever will best suit the house." He looked at her hand, slightly offended. What did this Viking have that he didn't have? These women had no taste at all. "I leave it in your hands."

"Why don't we take our leave now," Tomos offered, "and we'll start designing something for your land. Do you have all the notes, *mon belle amour*?"

She almost lifted a brow. She should have known he would speak French. "I do."

"Then we'll see you later, Assemblyman." He kept her safely tucked under his arm as they walked away, but he was well aware that Harkin was staring at Belle very intently. If it had been a look of simple desire or attraction, he wouldn't have minded it much. The look in Harkin's eyes, however, was greedy and cold and disgusting. When they were out of earshot, he murmured, "Did we have an escape clause in the contract?"

"Not that I remember," she said regretfully. "Let's go back to your HQ and get to work. The sooner we're done, the better. I'm willing to pull an all-nighter if you are."

"Done." He released her as they reached their cars. "Meet you on the backside of Driven Snow's building." He hesitated for a moment and then leaned down to lightly brush her lips with his. "He won't touch you," he breathed softly. He released her and went to his truck.

She lightly touched her lips as she watched him get into his truck. The whimsy made her smile. Her prince wore mud-caked boots and drove a white truck decorated with faeries. Only she would have such an unlikely hero.

She followed him back to the building. It was quiet inside since everyone else was out working on their own projects. Curiously, she followed him upstairs. "Where is your lair?" she quipped.

He sent her a smile. "In my room. I hope you don't fear I have dastardly purposes."

She gave a gusty sigh. "And here I was hoping for some sort of romantic ravishment. You disappoint me, Tomos."

"Don't tempt me."

The low mutter was nearly a growl. It reverberated through her nerves until her entire body heated and softened. Despite his light attitude, he wanted her as badly as she wanted him. She let out a soft breath. Damn it, she was sure. Why couldn't he be sure? She didn't think she could wait until the project was done.

She followed him into his room and promptly smiled. To call it a disaster would be polite. Clothes were strewn everywhere, and bookcases filled with books on landscape and plants were crammed together with romantic movies and novels. The bed was nearly a lake and took up a good portion of the room. Taking up the rest was an armchair for reading and a desk with a high tech computer set-up. "Maid's year off?" she asked politely.

Dull red climbed his cheeks. "Er, yeah."

"We must have the same maid."

Their eyes met, and he smiled. "Dust bunnies under the bed?"

She snorted softly. "I have colonies. Jen swears they're going to come to life and invade the city." He unearthed a corner of the bed for her, and she sat down comfortably. She kicked off her shoes and crossed her legs. "Okay. Let's do this."

With him manning his landscaping program and her manually looking through books for ideas, they fell into an easy rhythm. Ideas were punctuated with movie quotes, and Latin plant names were deliberately mangled until both were laughing.

They had so much fun that it was after midnight before he looked at a clock. "Damn. Is it that late?"

She rubbed at her eyes. "My internal clock says it is." She covered a massive yawn. "Sorry."

"No don't be." He rolled his shoulders. "I'd say we've got a solid plan. We can present this to Harkin tomorrow and arrange for him to buy the plants needed. Normally we'd pay for the purchase and invoice the cost, but I do *not* trust that man."

"Me neither." She rubbed at her eyes again. "Give me some coffee and I'll be good to drive."

He smiled. "Sure."

As he walked out of the room, she got to her feet to stretch. She peered at the computer, adjusted a retaining wall in their design, and sat down on the bed again. It felt soft and comfortable, and she couldn't resist lying down on her side. She would just close her eyes and get her second wind.

When he walked back into the room with two cups of coffee, he found her dead asleep and curled up on his bed. It was a toss-up whether his body or his heart ached harder. He put the coffee aside and walked over to look down at her. Almost reverently, he ran a finger down the freckles on her cheek.

She snuggled into the pillow with a sleepy mumble. He knew he should wake her, but he just couldn't bring himself to do it. Instead, he saved their design, closed the program, and shut down the computer. He cleared off the rest of the bed, closed the door, and turned out the light.

He got onto the bed as carefully as he could. He tugged Belle back against him and cuddled her against his chest. She snuggled closer but did not wake. He draped an arm lightly over her waist and savored having her in his arms and his bed. If he could do nothing but hold her like that forever, he would be a very happy man.

She awoke the next morning when the sun got into her face. She rolled over to get away from it and found herself snuggling into a hard male body. Startled, her eyes opened wide. She was curled against Tomos' chest and his arm was draped over her waist. He was still fully dressed and just as asleep as she had been.

Her heart quivered. She must have fallen asleep while he was getting coffee. And instead of waking her, he had just snuggled up beside her and gone to sleep as well. She lifted a hand to softly touch his face. His chin was just a little rough, stubble scraping deliciously over her palm. His eyes opened and she felt suddenly shy. "Hi," she whispered.

"Hi." He memorized her face and the soft flush to her cheeks and glow in her eyes. Dear god, she was beautiful! "You know," he said softly, "I know you have an identical twin, but I just don't find her as beautiful as I find you. From the moment I saw you, I couldn't tear my eyes away. I must be attracted to your heart and soul. God knows I'm attracted to your body, but there has to be more."

Her breath hitched as he turned his lips into her hand and softly kissed her palm. "I have the same problem," she admitted softly. "I just don't find Seisyll as attractive as I find you. You take my breath away, Tomos."

His hand slid slowly up her back to cup the back of her neck. He drew her toward him slowly, giving her plenty of time to get away, but that was the last thing she wanted. She sighed softly and lifted her chin to meet his kiss halfway, craving the feel of his lips on hers.

The kiss was soft and tender, drugging and consuming. Her lips parted on a second sigh and he deepened the kiss to let his tongue softly tangle with hers. Heat rose without hurry, the pleasure long and luxurious. Even the hunger of their bodies had softened to give way to the hunger of two hearts and one shared soul.

He shifted and tumbled her onto her back. He braced himself over her, still drinking from her in those consuming kisses that stole her thoughts and her breath. One hand cupped the back of her head. The other smoothed slowly over her body to memorize her curves and leave an indelible imprint.

Both were breathing hard when their lips finally parted. Quivering with need, she couldn't find any strength to move. She was going to die if she didn't feel his weight on her, feel his hot skin. Her hands pressed against his chest and her fingers kneaded sensually. "Tomos."

"I should stop." The words were breathed against her lips as he began to softly trail kisses over her face. "Imagine the embarrassment if one of my brothers walked in." He teased her ear by nibbling lightly. "Stop me, *mon belle amour*."

She cast around in her mind for something, anything, that might stop him. And finally only one thing came to mind. "I'm a virgin."

His head came up quickly. "What?"

She cleared her throat. She knew she was blushing. "You heard me." She gave him a helpless look. "I'm a romantic, remember? I never felt compelled to experiment just for the sake of my body. And, frankly? Until I met you, my body was always easy to ignore. I wanted to wait until I met someone I couldn't ignore." She sighed. "You'd never get it."

"Yes," he said quietly, "I would."

Her eyes met his and everything inside seemed to melt as she saw the steadiness in his gaze. "Oh." The word was almost nothing but a breath. "Really?"

"Really." He lightly kissed her again. "There was never any ignoring you, Belle." He pressed his forehead to hers. "Let's go over to the manor and get the meeting done with. Then we can chase each other through the flower aisles at the nursery." He took another kiss, unable to resist her softly swollen lips. "And then, when we're done with the project, we'll see where we stand."

"Or lie."

His lips curved. "That, too." He released her and rolled to his feet. His jeans felt far too tight but he ignored his clamoring body to the best of his ability. "You want to go home for fresh clothes?"

She pointedly kept her gaze on his face as she sat up. "And listen to my sisters harass me? Mm no thanks." An idea occurred to her. "Let me borrow a shirt."

"A shirt."

"Yes, the article of clothing that goes on the top of the body, often worn over a bra if you're a woman." She grinned a little when he sighed. "Well, I don't mind wearing the same jeans again, but a different shirt is a subliminal message that I probably changed clothes. People notice tops before they notice bottoms. And if I'm wearing *your* shirt, it looks more like I spent the night with you." She added smoothly, "Actually, it would appear I did."

"Body armor against a pervert. Sounds good to me." He rummaged in his closet. "It'll be too big."

"So?" When he handed her the dark blue shirt, she contemplated it. "I like your taste in color." She stripped off her t-shirt without embarrassment. She pulled on the loaner shirt and was amused because she didn't even need to unbutton it. Listening to his breath break was wildly arousing. She wanted him to want her. She needed it.

Of course, she was left to stare at his bare chest when he pulled his shirt off. Mouth dry, she watched helplessly as the muscles of his chest rippled in the morning light. Even after he pulled on a fresh shirt, the memory had burned in her brain. Gravely, she said, "You do realize I will forever look at you and remember your bare chest, right?"

With equal gravity he said, "It seems fair. I'll forever remember that bit of lace and silk that you call a bra. Is that even legal?"

"Assuredly." She paused, then offered, "Wait until you see what's hiding in the back of my dresser."

"You're an evil woman," he groaned. Putting it forcefully out of his head, he booted the computer and got the designs printing. "We can grab breakfast on the way out."

They were arriving back at the manor within the hour. They were both riding in his truck this time since there was no need to waste gas on two vehicles. She found it hard not to snuggle into her borrowed shirt. It smelled wonderful, as if it had absorbed the essence of his skin.

They knocked on the door but there was no answer. Together, they headed around to the back. Still no sign of Harkin, but the patio doors were open. "I'll go inside," Tomos said. "I'll be right back." He disappeared into the manor as he called Harkin's name.

Belle wandered a few steps into the maze. It was just high enough that she couldn't see over the top. A familiar chill went down her back and she turned to see Harkin staring at her. He had come up from the side of the building. Without conscious thought, she fled into the maze. All she knew was that she couldn't bear to be near him without Tomos.

Ironically, her ability to get lost served her well in mazes. She found the center within a matter of moments and ducked down behind the gazebo, her heart pounding. Mentally she called for Tomos over and over, unsure if he could hear her. He had never said whether he was mentally strong like most District people were, but she was hoping her own power might be enough.

Harkin walked into the center and clicked his tongue. "Now why did you run? Don't you know that just makes it better?"

The ugly anticipation in his voice made her stomach roll. He was only feet away. She said nothing, wishing she could make herself invisible. His hand suddenly closed around her arm, and she swung her free hand with all her strength. He jerked back and the blow missed, but it also freed her. She darted away. "Don't touch me!"

"Do you really want to cause trouble?" he asked her. "I can make your boyfriend's life very uncomfortable."

Fury filled her eyes. Before she could say anything, there came a low and menacing growl. Her eyes slowly widened and she stopped breathing. At the look on her face, Harkin slowly turned around. Behind him was an immense lion, crouched low and ready to spring. Sharp teeth were bared as it snarled softly. Its tail lashed furiously, and its mane bristled and lifted warningly.

Harkin screamed like a girl and ran out of the center just as the lion tried to pounce on him. He didn't stop running until he was out of the maze. It had to have been an illusion, though he was damned if he knew how it had happened. Those people from 3rd District were *weird.*

Belle stared at the lion. "Tomos?"

It shifted and changed and reformed into the man she loved. His eyes were no less furious. "Are you okay?" He framed her face in his hands. "Did he touch you?"

She shook her head. "I'm fine, thanks to you."

"Scared me half to death." He scooped her up into his arms. "Okay, Belle. I think it's time for some honesty." He headed deliberately for the exit of the maze. "I think we both know we're in love. We're the victims of love at first sight and we're too hopeless of romantics not to know it. We've both been acting like it was just lust."

"I concur," she admitted. She rested her head on his shoulder. "At the risk of raising the romance factor, I made a wish on a lucky locket once that I would find true love with the perfect man for me."

"You're right. That definitely raises the romance factor. Did you ask for a happily ever after too?"

"Of course. I hate sad endings." She snuggled closer. "Let's go home, Tomos. We'll worry about finding a contractual loophole to get out of the job later."

"Much later," he concurred. "Right now, I just want to be with you. We've both waited long enough to find each other."

She looped her arms around his neck with a happy sigh. And they said there was no such thing as perfection.

CHAPTER TWENTY-ONE

After the initial meeting, Rie was on her way down the street toward a café when she heard her name being called. Surprised, she stopped and turned to see Seisyll hurrying toward her. She could be sure of his identity for two very simple facts: he kept his hair much shorter, and she was attracted to him.

It was a curious situation, being attracted to a man with an identical twin, but she simply didn't feel anything for Tomos. She found him to be good looking but without feeling any sort of interest. On the other hand, when she looked at Seisyll, she had the unnerving sensation that all her hormones were standing at attention and saluting the wonder that was testosterone-induced male physique.

She wasn't quite sure what to do about it. When their eyes had met across the dance floor at the wedding, she had half expected to find slag on the floor from the flying sparks. All the Trahern brothers shared this 'look.' It was a way of looking at a woman that made her feel as if she was the *only* woman in his universe.

Seisyll stopped in front of her, and she felt something low in her belly heat and clench. He was definitely looking at her as if every other woman in the world had disappeared. The little curve to his lips and the smoldering heat in his eyes seemed to invoke images of tangled sheets and heated skin and long, lazy desire.

"Where are you going?" he asked her.

"Uhm, café. Felt like some coffee."

"May I join you?"

"Sure." She tucked her hands into her pockets as he fell into step beside her. "So you're the younger twin too, huh?"

He smiled wryly. "Yeah. Ten minutes."

"Thirty." She grinned. "Your twin doesn't let you forget it either?"

"Ha. He's counted the seconds." He tilted his head curiously. "Thirty minutes? That's a long time."

"I wasn't in the right position." She shook her head. "They ended up doing a C-section." She walked into the café and took a contented sniff of the coffee-laden air. She would happily breathe coffee if possible. "But everything turned out okay. Mom was fine and so were Belle and I."

He contemplated her as they ordered their coffee. From the moment he had laid eyes on her at the wedding, something inside her had drawn him. His eyes had wandered to her repeatedly, nearly devoured her appearance in her fire elemental's dress. He had deliberately tried to focus on Belle, but he simply hadn't been attracted. Then, when he had looked at Rie again, it was as if he could see no one else. A curious phenomena, to be sure, but one for which he was grateful. Tomos had a serious thing for Belle.

But what was it about Rie that was different? She was beautiful and shapely, sure, and she possessed the same porcelain skin as her sisters mixed with the same scattering of freckles over her nose. He had looked carefully at the meeting, but there had been no difference in freckle pattern over Belle and Rie's faces. Now *that* was fascinating. Her hair was dark wine red like half of her sisters, and her eyes were an interesting shade of teal green. She was taller than average, which he definitely appreciated, and she was lively and witty.

So what was it that tugged at him? Hell, he could practically see the ropes yanking him toward her. It wasn't just physical, though God only knew that he felt slightly ravenous for her. If he didn't get his hands on her at some point over the next few days, he would go stark raving mad. He *burned* hotter than the welder he used at work. There was something more here. Something less clear. Something that ached when she smiled. Something that was just as hungry, just as longing.

She grabbed a seat at a table out of the way and smiled as he sat across from her. "Is this the 'getting to know your partner' thing?"

"Definitely." He grinned a little. "You have to know my first question."

She sighed. "Yeah. It's usually the first question. 'Rie' is R-I-E. It's short for Henrietta." Even saying it, she winced. "My options for a nickname were Etta, Henri, Hen, or Rie. Rie won."

"And you were named this because . . ."

"Belle is named for our mother's grandmother. I was named for our father's grandmother. Those nice, old-fashioned, colloquial names that torment modern children." She grinned at him. "Not that you'd know about that."

"No kidding!" He leaned back in his seat and studied her. "Rie is a good choice. You absolutely don't look like a Henrietta. Are you the only one with a nickname that she uses because her full name scares her?"

She stuck her tongue out a little for the teasing. "Sam and Jen use their nicknames by choice because they can. If you call them Samantha and Jennifer, they don't mind at all. No Sammy or Jenny though. My companion in name-dom would be Lexie."

"Alexis?"

"Nope."

"Alexandra or 'dria'?"

"Nope." She grinned. "Alexandriana Genevieve."

He choked on his coffee.

She grinned and propped her chin on her hand. "Named for our grandmothers' mothers. Both of them. But she was Lexie from the day she was born. Mom 'n Dad were always good about understanding that they gave us the name and thus gave tribute. It was up to us how we handled it."

"If I have a kid," he decided, "he or she will go without a name until they talk. At that time they can pick their own name."

She kicked him under the table. "You will not! You'll just spend a lot more time thinking about it." As it fell naturally on the ends of the statement, she asked casually, "What does your girlfriend think?"

"I don't have one." He gave her a slow smile. "Until a few days ago, I really hadn't been attracted to anyone enough to contemplate pursuing a serious relationship."

"What happened a few days ago?"

"I saw you at my sister's wedding."

The words fell between them. She almost stopped breathing. He was giving her that look again, the look that said he had tunnel vision and she was the light at the end. His hand slid across the table to cover hers, and before she could blink, he shifted his chair closer so that he was looming close. "Uhm."

"Are you single?" he asked softly, his breath brushing against the skin of her ear and cheek.

"Uhm, yes." She took a deep breath but all she got was the alluring scent of male combined with the aromatic scent of coffee. It was a potent combination.

"Are you attracted to me?"

"Are you nuts?" Her voice was as shaky as she felt. "I'm going out of my mind here. You're *lethal*. Get away from me before I do something really stupid." She turned her head and they were nose-to-nose, almost lip to lip. Her gaze dropped helplessly. He had one hell of a kissable mouth. She had never been happy with kissing before. She had a feeling that he would make her *very* happy. "People are watching."

Without looking away, he drew a veil down around them. "No they're not. As far as anyone can see, we're just sitting here having coffee." He curled one hand around the back of her neck. The other hand rested hotly on her thigh. He couldn't stop himself. With a soft rasp in his voice, he said, "I'm going to kiss you, Rie."

Shivering from just those two little touches, she knew she was doomed. When his head tilted and his lips glided across hers, she was trapped. And when his lips settled, when the heat and power of the kiss poured into her, his taste as wild as the coffee they had been drinking, she knew she was lost.

Her lips parted under his, and a soft sound of desire slipped free as he deepened the kiss and curled his tongue around hers. Her entire body was beginning to ache and yearn. She lifted a hand and splayed it over his chest. Her fingers kneaded sensually. He was so wonderfully big. Hot and hard and masculine.

He carefully lifted his head. Little shudders ripped through his body. Her taste was so unique that he knew he was addicted. He slowly slid his hand up her leg and savored her supple flesh. "Do you have any idea how badly I want you?" The words were little more than a rumble. His breath hissed out as her hand slid down into his lap to rest as light as a butterfly over his straining erection. "Rie, I think you're a tease."

"I think I might be." Her fingers tingled as she lightly tormented him. "You started it. Your hand is almost in the danger zone." His hand was so close to where she ached most that she felt the heat of his skin, even through her clothes. "I don't think I've ever been groped outside a date before."

He forced himself to pull his hands away. Her hands lifted, and he wisely put a few feet between them. "Okay." He drew a long, bracing breath. "Okay. We have a job to be done together. We both know that we're probably a few kisses away from falling in bed together."

"Or on the floor."

He had to smile at that. "Or on the floor. So . . . let's call the job a date. It's a long date to get to know each other. We can evaluate where we stand after that. Why don't we give your metal craft a try first? I have no artistic sense though," he warned.

"That's okay." She smiled. "We'll find some." She got to her feet and looked around. The corner felt cushioned where they were. "What did you do?"

"I can cloak and shield," he admitted. "I blocked our presence from other people. They see what they expect to see." He looked up at her. "What can you do?"

Her smile was sultry and enticing. "You'll have to find out on our date." With a toss of her long hair, she broke past the veil and headed for the exit.

He watched her leave and felt a smile tugging at his lips. He had finally realized what it was about her that pulled at him. It was very simple, actually. He wasn't entirely surprised, based on the evidence. In fact, he was quite content.

Loving Rie was possibly the easiest thing he had ever done.

The next morning, Rie made the effort to ensure that Belle would wake up on time and then went downstairs and left out a plate of breakfast. Honestly, she found it highly amusing that the 'younger' twin was the only one with practical brain cells.

Her practicality seemed to have taken a hike, though. She hadn't slept well thanks to a mind in a state of fluctuation and a body in a distinct state of frustration. She was more than happy to go to her shop and lose herself in the crafting and shaping of metal.

She was so lost in her work that she didn't realize she was no longer alone until she straightened and lifted her safety visor. She promptly saw Seisyll leaning against a table nearby. Her pulse kicked into overdrive. "How long were you standing there?"

"Only a little while." He smiled. "You looked so intent that I didn't want to distract you."

"And you didn't want to be hit by flying slag." She walked closer with a matching smile. "You want to give it a try?"

"First thing's first." He reached out a hand and curled it around the back of her neck to draw her closer. She melted against him happily. Her body aligned perfectly to his as her hands splayed across his chest. He bent his head to kiss her without hurry, contentedly lingering over her taste. When he finally eased back again, he murmured, "Good morning."

Feeling much like every muscle had melted in pleasure, she could only lay against him. "Good morning," she said dreamily.

"You know," he looped his arms around her, "I have to apologize to my brother-in-law."

"Which one?"

"Taylor. I gave him hell when I caught him almost kissing Gwyn."

She nodded sagely. "It would probably be wise, as you seem to be determined to kiss me at every opportunity."

He stole another kiss. "I'm not a hypocrite." He slowly, and very reluctantly, let her go. "Show me how this works. I know the mechanics, but I warn you, again, that I am not very artistic."

She was a patient teacher. She took him through the process of trying to find inspiration and how to make what was in his mind get to his hands and then to the welder. It didn't take long, though, before she realized he was right. He was *really* bad at art.

Biting her lip, she studied the pile of metal he was glaring at. "It's, uhm. Unique."

He shifted his glare to her. "Sure." He scowled and crossed his arms. "It's like the time Joseff tried to show me glasswork. I didn't do bad with blowing glass. When it came to shaping it? Yeah. I made the Picasso of unicorns."

He looked and sounded so sulky that she bit harder on her lip. He shot her a warning look that was a combination of embarrassment and annoyance. Giving in, she covered her mouth as she began to laugh, her eyes dancing as he made a rude noise. "You look like the little boy who can't build anything but a lopsided kite!"

"I never made a lopsided kite." Grudgingly he muttered, "That couldn't fly anyway."

Something shifted and settled inside her as she studied his face. Contentment rose and spread. Love. Finally. She had wished for true love, prayed for it, and had hoped that the magic of her grandmother's name and locket would bring it to her. And it had.

She framed his face and rose up to kiss him softly. His arms curled around her, and his pale blue eyes darkened with hunger and something more. Something that made her heart ache as badly as her body did. "I can't make kites either," she said against his lips.

He snorted softly. "It's an art, according to Gavin." He studied the misshapen piece of metal he had been trying to work with. "Why don't I let you handle this, and you can come help me with the building. It's basic welding work from what I saw this morning."

"You went by before coming over?"

"I had a feeling we'd be going there soon," he muttered. "I told you I had no artistic sense."

She smiled. "Okay. Let's get going. You get to drive. I share a car with Lexie and I promised she could use it today just in case she had to go somewhere."

"Sure."

They cleaned up the shop together and then made their way to the building that was in need of their work. Somehow, she wasn't surprised to see it was an old industrial building. It was all steel beams and little else. Nothing was very appealing about it. "And we're doing what again?" she asked as she got out of the car.

"The building was just bought by a couple of people who want to convert it into an artist workshop. Several of the ceiling beams need repairs and we also are to install some pieces of art."

"Install?"

"Weld 'em to the ceiling."

"Now *that* will be cool." She nodded decisively. "Let's get to it. You point me at something and tell me to weld it shut."

"Would that work on my brothers' mouths?" he asked wistfully.

"No more than it works on my sisters."

They shared a conspiratorial grin. He was much more in his element here, and not needing to worry about aesthetics helped lift his mood. She just laughed at him. They started at the base level and sealed anything that was easy to reach and repair. Once all that was left was the ceiling, he went to get the ladder. When he came back in, he got the shock of his life to see Rie hovering near a beam, welding competently. *Hovering*. "Rie!"

She yelped and lost her concentration. She also promptly started to fall. He was thankfully fast enough to catch her before she could hit the ground. Heart racing, he clutched her close. "You scared the hell out of me!"

She shoved back her visor with a glare. "*I* scared *you*?! You're the one who distracted me! I have to concentrate to stay in the air! It's not easy, thank you!" She crossed her arms in annoyance. "Now put me down and I'll get back to work."

He forced himself to put her down. He set up the ladder and she gracefully floated up to the ceiling again. Side by side, they worked together easily to first repair all the mishaps and tears caused by poorly done deconstruction. Once that was finished, they got to work with hanging the art pieces. That part of the job started with having to decipher the layout drawings they had been given. It was only her eye for art that at last clarified the rather jumbled instructions.

They started welding the work to the beams. He used the ladder to hold the pieces in place while she hovered and secured them. After hanging the first piece, he went to check the drawings. She finished welding the last part and moved back to make sure it was level. Unfortunately, she burned her hand on the beam and lost her concentration. He hastily caught her again. He could only sigh and put her on her feet again.

An hour later, after the fourth mishap, he had had enough. When he caught her, he didn't put her down. He instead headed for the doors. "Alright," he said. "That's it. We're going back to your shop."

"But we're not done!" she protested.

"I've had enough scares, thank you. If you're so determined to give me gray hair, I'm going to give you some by making you teach me to be artistic."

She snorted. "It'll take you fifty years to be artistic."

Easily, he countered, "Fair enough. I'm willing to hang around that long."

Her heart began to beat harder. "Are you now? Well, I suppose Lexie and Joseff will be married for a nice long time, so we'll have plenty of good reasons to see each other."

He put her down slowly and let her body slide along his. Firmly he trapped her against the car. His fingers pulled down her ponytail so that they could get lost in her hair. "That was not what I meant," he said softly.

"Then what did you mean?" She met his eyes evenly.

His free hand smoothed over her cheek before framing her face warmly. "I know it's tacky to propose on a first date, but I can't seem to stop myself. Marry me, Rie. I fell in love with you when I looked at you. Give me a chance to make you fall for me."

She framed his beloved face with her hands. "You can't make me fall for you, Seisyll. I already did that by myself." She leaned up to kiss him softly. "I'll marry you." She smiled. "Did I tell you there was an enchanted locket from my grandmother that gave us sisters each a wish? Seven wishes for seven sisters."

"The grandma you were named for?"

"Mmmhmm. And all of us except for Remy wished for true love. I wished for my perfect match . . . but I could never have imagined you. I wouldn't have dared wish this big."

He had to kiss her for that. When he released her, he asked softly, "What did Remy wish for?"

"She didn't." Sadness moved in her eyes. "I think she's afraid. But Heul . . . he's so perfect for her, Seisyll."

"There's no such thing as coincidence," he murmured.

She eyed him warily. "What are you thinking?"

His smile came slowly and wickedly. "I'm thinking we were set up." He scooped her up and carried her around to put her in the car. "I'm taking you home." He leaned in to kiss her, but she tasted so wonderful that he lingered longer than he intended. He finally broke free and muttered thickly, "Taking you home, *fast*."

She took a deep, trembling breath. "Good idea. I don't think I'll be able to concentrate unless you do, and we both know what happens when I lose my concentration."

He grinned and stole another kiss. "That's okay. I'll just keep catching you." He got to his feet and went around to get in the driver's side. As they were heading back toward where he lived, he asked, "What do you think about all of us, sans Remy and Heul, getting together for a meeting? Working together won't be enough for them. They're going to need another push. We're going to have to waylay them at every turn. We need to get Remy's weaknesses to Heul, and vice-versa."

"Well, Lexie and Joseff set all of us up, so I don't see why we can't get them to help again. But you know who we *really* need? We need Nicole. If she doesn't approve of Heul, our opinions won't matter." She tilted her head. "Let's let things stand for a few days. Finish our projects. On Friday, we'll call everyone together and see where we are."

He shook his head. "I'm never letting you near my sisters. You'd take over the world."

She grinned. "I'll take that as a compliment."

CHAPTER TWENTY-TWO

The morning that Remy was supposed to start work with Heul didn't get off on the right foot. She and Nicole had the entire fifth floor of the building to themselves, and it was on its own air conditioning and heating; she refused to let her sisters pay even part of her own living. Sadly, that meant that some mornings the air went out. It was eighty degrees and climbing when she woke.

She hastily adjusted the thermostat and made a note to call for someone to come fix it. Again. She then went to get coffee, but the timer hadn't gone off, and there was none waiting for her. With a sigh, she went down three flights of stairs to beg coffee off of Lexie. That in hand, she went back upstairs. *Elevator.* They desperately needed an elevator on this side of the building.

She kept an eye on the clock. When it was closer to seven, she went down the hall to Nicole's room. "Rise and shine, baby," she said as she went into the room. She automatically looked at the small bed, but Nicole wasn't there.

Before panic could set in, she heard her say, "Mommy?"

She looked around quickly and saw Nicole sitting in the rocking chair. Her red braid was coming undone and she looked hot and miserable. She was holding a raggedy stuffed dog that she'd had since she was born. "What're you doing up?" Remy walked over and knelt down. "Too hot?"

"I dun' feel good."

Remy gently pressed a hand to her forehead. Alarms went off mentally. She was very warm and it wasn't a sweaty heat from the air. It was a dry feverish heat. "Uh-oh. Stay here, Nic." She went down the hall quickly and came back with the thermometer.

Nicole sat still while it was pressed to her ear, but it was a stillness born of exhaustion and not behavior. She was never still unless she was sick. While Remy waited for the thermometer, her sharp eyes spotted Nicole scratching surreptitiously at her stomach and arms. "Has anyone been sick at school?"

Nicole rubbed at her eyes and scratched her arm again. "Benji Greeber has been out. Ms. Woodrow said he's got . . . uhm . . ." She wrinkled her nose. "Turkey spots."

Remy closed her eyes. "Chicken pox?"

"Yeah, that."

Remy studied the thermometer as it beeped, but she was already resigned to what she knew. "One hundred degrees. C'mere you." She scooped up her daughter and stood her on the bed. Gently she tugged off her sweaty nightgown. On a sigh, she studied the little spots forming across Nicole's stomach and arms. They would be full-fledged pox within a day or two. "You and Benji play together before he got sick?"

Nicole nodded. "We feed the class hamsters together. He pulls on my braid, so I kick him."

"Well, it looks like you got chicken pox too."

"Nooo! Luis from fourth grade sez that if you get chicken pox, you turn into a *chicken*!" The last word was a wail as she burst into tears and grabbed onto Remy's neck. "I dun wanna be a chicken, Mommy!"

"You won't be a chicken! You're going to be hot, and itchy, and miserable for a while, but you won't be a chicken." Remy carried her down the hall into the bathroom. "You get to have a nice cool bath, and then you're going back to bed."

It was a testament to how bad Nicole really felt that she didn't argue with her mother. She didn't splash or make a peep as Remy bathed her gently. She was still quiet when Remy dressed her in a fresh nightgown and tucked her in bed. As Remy re-braided her hair, she asked in a quivering voice, "No chicken?"

"No chicken." Remy handed her the flop-eared dog she loved. "I'll bring my TV in here, okay? You can watch movies and sleep lots. And I'll make you lots of nummy things to make you better in no time."

Her lower lip quivered. "Pudding?"

"I could be persuaded." Remy gently kissed her forehead, her heart aching as always. She loved her daughter more than anything. "Now rest, baby."

She wasted no time in moving her small TV into Nicole's room and hooking it up with the DVD player. She put on Nicole's favorite Disney movie, then headed down the hall to their living room. She could only sigh as she grabbed the phone and dialed the school.

"Golden River Kindergarten."

She braced a shoulder on the wall. "Hello, Ms. Woodrow. This is Remy Germaine, Nicole's mother."

"Good morning, Ms. Germaine!" Ms. Woodrow's voice had her smile in it. "What can I do for you?"

"Warn your parents there's an outbreak of chicken pox. I have a very miserable little chicklette in bed right now."

"Oh dear." Ms. Woodrow sighed. "I was hoping Benji hadn't infected everyone. He's already been out a week. I'll notify the other parents immediately. Once is an occurrence. Twice is an epidemic. Especially among five-year-olds. You tell Nicole that we'll be looking forward to seeing her get better. I'll have someone drop off her lessons for the next two weeks, just in case."

"Thanks, Ms. Woodrow." Remy sighed again and hung up the phone. Her reflection in an antique mirror seemed to smirk at her across the room. She looked flushed and tired and frazzled. In faded sweatpants and a camisole, she looked like a particularly unappealing housewife. "How the mighty have fallen," she groused.

There was a light knock on the wall, and she looked over quickly to see Heul standing at the top of the stairs with a lifted brow. She stared at him for a moment until her memory kicked in. "Oh!" She groaned. "Oh." She covered her face with her hands. "Oh damn."

"Good morning to you as well," he said gravely. "Bad time?"

"I have a five-year-old with chicken pox, and a broken air conditioner that may give out any minute," she retorted crossly. "What do you think?"

He thought she would hit him if he told her that she looked like an invitation to sin. He had never seen her without her self-defensive styled hair and well selected clothing. Seeing the woman underneath her protective shield was highly alluring. The flush to her cheeks made him want to kiss her and make her more flushed. Her hair was haphazardly pinned up with curls sticking out everywhere, all but begging for his hands. Her camisole and sweats did nothing to disguise that her body was all woman.

Carefully hiding it, he said, "I think we should work from here today so you can be on call for Nicole." He grimaced. "I had to get Joseff and Gwyn through a double dose of chicken pox. They were ten. I threatened to have Arian tie them in bed."

Oddly, it made her feel better. Impulsively, she asked, "You want to see Nic? She likes you a lot."

"I'd love to." He kept his hands in his pockets as they headed down the hall. He mentally told himself that he would just peek in, say hello, and step out. Professional. Calm. Distant. He needed to keep himself from being tangled up by these two dangerous Germaine women.

Every thought of being distant left his head when he looked into the small room decorated with yellow and cream. Two miserable green eyes looked at him, capped by a mop of rusty red hair, and he lost his heart. "Hey, baby," he said softly as he walked across the room. He knelt next to her bed. "Gonna be a chicken for a while, huh?"

Nicole's lip quivered. "Will I grow feathers?" She held out her arms.

He gently lifted her up and cuddled her in his arms. She felt small, and delicate, and tugged on every heartstring. He loved all kids but this one got to him the most. "Only a few," he told her solemnly. "But you'll never even see them. They'll just make you itch for a while, and then they'll go away." He rubbed his cheek over her hair softly. "In the meantime, you get to take time off from school and watch movies."

Her lashes drooped. He felt so nice and safe. Like a daddy. She had always wanted a daddy. Someone to make her mommy smile and to make her feel safe. He could beat up that mean Luis from fourth grade. "Mmkay." She looped her arms around his neck and hid her face. She was asleep in seconds.

Remy felt something in her heart twist as she watched them. Nicole never trusted strangers, but she clearly trusted Heul. It made her heart begin to crack open. She didn't want to love Heul, but with every passing minute, she was more afraid that she would. "Want me to take her?" she asked softly.

"No, it's okay." He gently tucked Nicole back into bed and smoothed the covers over her. He waited until they were in the hall again before saying, "We can work from here, Remy. I don't have a problem. The first part is simply planning anyway."

"I suppose so." She tugged on a lock of hair nervously. "If you'll give me a chance to change clothes, I . . ."

He pulled her hand away from her hair. "You look fine," he told her. "Stop worrying so much."

"Ha." She turned and headed down the hall to the living room. "Have a seat. I'm going to go grab my sketchpad. If you want something to drink, there's soda and juice in the fridge." She had taken two steps when she heard the thump that was the thermostat failing. She groaned. "Not now."

"Go get your sketchpad." He nudged her down the hall. "I'll deal with the thermostat." He stepped over to peer at the temperamental device. The cover popped off easily when he took his pocketknife to it. The problem was apparent: one of the wires wasn't staying in place where it belonged. He jimmied it into place again and closed the panel. "Hey, Remy? It's no big deal. I'll ask Gavin to come fix it. He'll have it taken care of in minutes."

"Really?" She stepped over with her sketchpad under her arm. "Last time I had someone out, they said it would need to be replaced entirely."

"Well, eventually, I'm sure it will. But it's just a short in the system. Gavin can handle it." He sat down on the couch and offered a smile. "I don't bite, Remy. Let's sit down and work together. We're both adults. We can stop being such idiots just because we're attracted to each other."

She opened her mouth to deny it but could only sigh. "Yeah." She walked over to sit down across from him. "It's awkward for me," she said carefully. "The last man I was attracted to was Chase, and it didn't work out."

"Want to talk about it?"

Oddly, she did. She had never really talked about things with anyone other than her sisters. "Okay." She began to lightly sketch out the basic shape of the dollhouse. "I met Chase in my last year of college. He was funny, and smart, and we had good times hanging out. We were attracted, thought we were in love. We got married. Yet almost from the honeymoon, we realized the attraction wasn't strong enough. We gave it a year, but it just didn't work. We decided to get a divorce before we ruined our friendship. But then ...I discovered I was pregnant."

"Did you try to make it work?"

She shook her head. "We refused to chance becoming the sort of parents we hated. We went through with the divorce, but we stayed friends. Chase was *ecstatic* about being a father, as much as I was about being a mother. When Nicole was born . . . oh, he loved her so much. We had it all worked out. Visitations and how he'd spend time with her. He'd come over just to watch her sleep. I loved him," she added softly. "I wasn't *in* love, but I loved him."

He wanted to reach out, but knew better. Any jealousy he might have felt was drowned in pain for Remy, and for Chase. "What happened?"

"He loved to go water skiing in the summer. He was really good at it, but there was another skier out there with a less skilled driver. The two boats nearly collided and jerked apart. It jerked Chase and the other skier together. The collision," her voice broke briefly, "the collision was so strong that their heads cracked together. Both fell unconscious. And tangled together, they couldn't be pulled from the water in time. Both drowned. A freak accident."

"Does Nicole remember him?"

"No, thankfully. It's horrible of me, but I'd rather her not remember, than remember and grieve." She took a deep breath. "And you're the only person outside of my family that knows the whole story."

"I'm practically family," he reminded her.

"I suppose so." She contemplated the drawing that was emerging. "How detailed can you get?"

"How big will it be?"

"Probably about four feet high."

"As detailed as you want me to be. I might delegate the tiny carving to Arian or Jen though." He grinned swiftly. "The key to being in charge is to delegate."

"No kidding!" She grinned back at him, in that moment understanding him completely. She added a few more details. "So, turnabout is fair play. Why haven't you taken the fateful plunge?"

"I've never been in love, or thought I was in love." He scooted over so he could see what she was drawing. He was fascinated by the way she could draw and talk at the same time. It was as if two different parts of her brain functioned simultaneously. "And . . ." He hesitated for a moment. "And I've always been . . . lucky to know whether or not something will work. To know exactly what I want."

"Your gift?"

"Mm. You?"

It was her turn to hesitate. "I'm . . . a medium, of sorts."

His brows went up. "Ghosts."

"Ghosts."

"As in Casper and Slimer."

"As in the old guy who used to sell bagels still stands on the corner of the District and wonders why no one can see him."

"He doesn't know he's dead?" He eyed her. "I thought that was just bullshit from *The Sixth Sense.*"

"Not hardly." She shook her head. "Sudden death can be as disorienting to the dead person as to the people left behind." She bit her lower lip, hard, but decided not to tell him the rest. Aiming for humor instead, she said, "I've figured out how to crack up my sisters. I just do an impersonation of Haley Joel Osment."

"Reasonable?"

"Darn reasonable."

"You'll have to show me sometime." He plucked the sketchpad from her hands. The dollhouse looked like a miniature version of an old-fashioned Southern manor. It didn't look like it was backless, however. "Hinged sides so it can open and close?"

"I think so. Gives her double the space but can be stored easily." She took the pad back and began to lightly draw the inside on a fresh sheet of paper. "Do you have moral or religious objections to pink and yellow?"

"I raised a baby sister," he said dryly. "And she's as girly as they get."

The mental image of him trying to take his baby sister shopping made her cover a grin. The Viking in a girl's department store. It might as well be a bull in a china shop. "Good. Nicole loves them."

"Mommy?"

Both looked up instantly to see Nicole standing at the entrance of the room. She was rubbing at her eyes. "Can I have breakfast?" She itched at her arms in agitation. "The feathers are *itchy*."

"I'll take her," Heul murmured. "If you want to handle the food."

It was foreign to lean on someone other than her sisters, but she trusted him implicitly. "Done." She walked over to Nicole and lifted her up. "You want pancakes?" she asked. "I could be persuaded to make some."

"'Kay." Nicole was happy to be passed over to Heul. She snuggled in close, content to be held by him. "Whatcha doing?"

He held up the sketchpad. "We're building a dollhouse for a cute little girl."

"Oh. Will you build me one, too?"

"We might be able to do that. You like this one?"

"Uh-huh." She scratched at her arm again and then at her stomach. "Will it have flowers?" Almost on the heels of the question, she complained, "Being a chicken *itches*! I don't wanna be a chicken anymore!"

"Got a damp cloth?" he asked Remy. She tossed him one over the breakfast bar, and he gently began smoothing it over Nicole's skin. "Here we go," he said softly. "This will help some. Your mommy will get some lotion that will help. But now you know."

"Know what?"

"Why chickens are always running around clucking." His grave voice barely covered the humor in his eyes. "They itch too. And they don't have fingers to scratch with."

Remy bit down on her lower lip to keep from laughing at the wide-eyed look Nicole was giving Heul. She carefully concentrated on flipping the pancakes lest she give him away. Itchy chickens. He was *incorrigible*.

"Do they havta use lotion, too?" Nicole asked. In her fascination, she had forgotten her itchy skin.

"Yep. Farmers will catch and pluck them and dump on lotion. The ones that keep complaining end up getting sold to supermarkets where they're put out of their misery." He nodded sagely. "But little girls who get chicken pox are special. They get to complain all they need to. And your feathers won't grow back once they're gone. Right, Remy?"

"Leave me out of this!" The laughter was in her voice. "It's your story." She carried the plate of pancakes over to the table. "Bring our chick over here and let her eat her mush. I mean breakfast."

Nicole giggled as Heul carried her over to the table. "What's your name?" she asked him.

"Well, where are my manners?" He shook her hand solemnly. "Heul Trahern. I'm Joseff's big brother."

"Ohhhh." She dug into her pancakes happily. "'Kay."

Letting her be, Remy and Heul went back over to the couch. She elbowed him as they sat down. "I can't believe you," she said softly. Laughter made her eyes merry. "That was so bad of you."

"She stopped thinking about the itching, didn't she?" He grinned. "I'll pick up some calamine lotion for you before I come over again tomorrow morning." When she opened her mouth, he narrowed his eyes. "No arguing. Just say 'Thank you, Heul' and we'll move on."

She closed her mouth to smile in bemusement. "Thank you, Heul."

When Nicole had finished her breakfast, she was tired again. This time it was Heul who took her back down the hall to her room. As he was tucking her into bed, she asked, "Why don't you have kids?"

"Hmm." He knelt beside the bed to study her face. "I haven't met a woman I wanted to have kids with."

"What about Mommy?"

Warning bells went off in his head. "What about her?"

"You watch her lots." Her eyes were drooping closed. "An' she watches you."

Out of the mouths of babes. He gently smoothed her hair out of her eyes. "Would you be happy if I was interested in your mom?" It was, to him, one of the most critical aspects of any relationship he and Remy might have.

"Uh-huh. You'd be an awesome daddy." She rolled over and snuggled into her pillow. "Will you come over again tomorrow?"

"Mmm."

"'Kay."

He waited until he was sure she was asleep before he left the room. As he shut the door quietly, he thought of his 'gift' and the things it could and could not tell him. When Joseff had asked him if he was interested in the merger, he had seen the potential outcomes of going ahead or holding back. It had come down to his brothers' happiness weighed against his. Going forward meant that his brothers would find true love . . . and that he wouldn't.

Nothing was set in stone, he reminded himself as he went downstairs. If he wanted, he could fight against what he was shown and change things. He had changed things before, but at a great cost to himself. He wasn't sure yet if he wanted to change things, though. If what he and Remy had was just attraction, then there wouldn't be any problems.

The problem would only be if he was falling in love. And as he looked at Remy across the room, saw the concentration on her face as she sketched, he had a strong feeling that he was.

CHAPTER TWENTY-THREE

Over the next few days, Remy and Heul alternated between working at her home and working at his. Nicole was taken with them to both locations and snuggled into either her bed or a couch where she could be pampered by her six aunts and six future uncles.

The status of her new uncles also came to light over the next few days while Remy and Heul worked on the dollhouse. Every last one of the other partnerships finished their project and came out a couple. In many ways, neither Remy nor Heul was surprised. In many other ways, it just added to the stress of their own relationship. They *knew* their siblings were waiting for signs of orange blossoms.

If anything was flying, it was sparks. Remy was going out of her *mind*. She had stopped being able to sleep at night; her dreams were feverish and plagued by the masculinity that was her partner. He hadn't even kissed her and she burned for his touch. She had never considered herself overly sexual before, but now she was being forced to re-evaluate.

While she was trying to fasten on a pair of earrings Friday morning, she scowled at her reflection. "What the hell is wrong with me?"

"It's called passion, Rem."

She very slowly straightened. There was nothing in the mirror, but when she turned around, there was a very familiar young man sitting on the side of the bed. His tousled black hair was as unruly as she remembered. His face was as handsome, and his eyes as blue. "Well," she finally said.

"Hey."

She rubbed the bridge of her nose. "Sane women do not have conversations with their dead ex-husbands."

Chase Crowley just grinned. "Women who are mediums do." He got to his feet and looked as fit and healthy as he had before he had died. He walked over to take the earring from her and competently fasten it to her ear. "Talk to me, Rem. We were friends. We sucked at being married, but we were awesome at being friends."

"I am not talking about my sex life with you!" she muttered.

"Why not? I'm dead. Who am I going to tell?"

She opened her mouth, then closed it. Bemused, she said, "You still make the absurd sound so . . . reasonable. Tell me, is there an afterlife? No one else has ever said."

He contemplated that. "Well, I haven't played chess with the Grim Reaper, and I sure haven't seen any pearly gates or barbeque pits of doom, so I can't be sure. Mostly it's just a fuzzy gray area. I don't see color now. And you look hot with gray hair, by the way."

She gave a long sigh as she sat down on the side of the bed. When he sat beside her, she gave in. "I'm so confused, Chase. What we had was . . . nice."

"And nice just isn't enough. What have you got with Heul Trahern?"

"Intensity." She pressed a hand to her heart. "He has this way of looking at me that makes me feel like he just stripped me naked and enjoyed every minute. With you, I never . . . I mean . . . it didn't . . ."

He nodded. "Which is as much my blame as yours. You can't blame yourself if I didn't turn you on, Rem. We were *friends*."

"But that's why I'm so confused." She pressed her fingers to her eyes. "Heul is a friend, too. And I want him more than I want air. How can my body crave something it hasn't ever experienced?"

"Nature," he intoned gravely. "Animals wouldn't reproduce if both males and females didn't enjoy sex. Humans just happen to be programmed to have sex for reasons other than reproduction."

"You sound like an anthropologist, Dr. Crowley," his ex-wife muttered.

"Perish the thought!" He crossed his arms. "Let me see if I can reason this out. You have felt inadequate because I couldn't turn you on enough. A combination of bad chemistry and not enough effort, to be sure, so we're equally at blame. And, also, you're wary of giving your heart because you don't want to be hurt again, and you don't want Nicole hurt. On the other hand, you have Heul. You're so attracted to him that, given five minutes and a bottle of syrup, you'd strip him naked and dive in like a secret chocoholic. This is an oddity to you because you've never before had that urge, more's the pity for *me*. At the same time, you're confused because you consider Heul a friend and you're convinced that friends can't be lovers." He paused. "How am I doing?"

"Stay out of my dreams."

"Ah. I'm doing well. I'll continue. Now then. I'm going to point out one simple fact for you: the couples who have lasted longest together are the ones that are friends as well as lovers. It's not the intimacy of making love, Remy, it's the intimacy of sharing your thoughts and your feelings. Not just your body. If you're not comfortable enough with someone to share your every thought, then why be comfortable enough to share your body? Or vice-versa."

"I was comfortable enough with you for both, and it didn't work."

"Mm. That's where we pull in the phenomena of nature known as 'mating for life.' Some animals, like wolves, mate for life. They are chemically programmed by Mother Nature to have one perfect match. Wolves will leave their family pack to find a mate and have their own pack. Many other species are the same way, and humans can be counted among them. Some men and women simply don't respond chemically to any but their perfect mate. There's nothing wrong with them any more than there is anything wrong with someone who does respond chemically to others beyond their natural mate."

"And how do emotions play into this, Dr. Crowley?"

"Oh, those things? They make a mess of *everything*."

She ran both hands through her hair. "For God's sake!" She blinked. "Is there a god?"

"You think I'm telling if there is? Ha. I'm dead, not stupid." He took her hands and held them tightly. "Remy. You can't live your life in the past. You're not living. The ghosts in our bedroom were as much my making as they were yours. You couldn't banish them, and I couldn't make you want to. But your Heul is different. Follow your heart. And be happy."

She took a deep breath and asked the question she had wondered about for years. "Chase . . . do you hate me?"

He shook his head with a smile. "No. If I was meant to know her, I'd have lived longer. I'm her birth father, but I'm not her dad. I don't regret helping create her. I'm proud to have given such an amazing little girl to an amazing woman."

"Now you're sounding a little oogie-boogie for my tastes. You'd think you believed in destiny."

"Who me? I'm just a dead anthropologist who thinks his ex-wife needs a good kick in the rump. Or to get a good tumble in a bed. Sadly, I can't provide the second, but I can give the first." His eyes flickered to the door and back. He smiled. "Bye, Remy."

When Jen opened the door, all she found was Remy glaring at the bed. "Problem?"

"No," Remy muttered as she got to her feet. "Not at all."

"Well," Jen said casually, "we decided to do you a favor. We're taking the midget over to Driven Snow so that you and Heul can relax. I'm letting Heul have command of my shop, so there shouldn't be any trouble. It'll be just you two and you can finish your project quicker. Taking care of Nicole has been taxing you."

"I . . . hmm."

"No secret motives," Jen assured her. "We need this project done so we can hammer out the details. I think we all know the merger is sound. Orange blossoms aside. So you and Heul don't get together. Big deal. There is such a thing as irony."

"Well . . . okay," she reluctantly said. "I know Nicole loves her new uncles. She'll like being over there."

"Yup!" Jen's eyes were completely without guile. "So you have a good day." She pulled the door shut again and looked down the hall to where Arian was standing with Nicole in his arms. She gave them a thumbs-up and both, even Nicole, returned the gesture.

An hour later, Remy found herself in the shop with Heul. They were working on the details of the dollhouse. She was also a painter and color specialist, and she was handling that aspect. While he cut, and carved, and constructed, she added color to small pieces.

When he happened to glance over at one point, he had to hide a smile. "Remy, do you want a headband?"

"Huh?" She blinked at him.

"You're pushing your hair out of your eyes."

"So?" She looked at the mirror across the room and saw instantly what he had. "For crying out loud." She scowled at the smears of yellow and pink on her cheek. "I haven't done that since I was ten. Jeans are fair game, but not my face."

He got a wet cloth and walked over. "Here we go." He stepped close and bent to begin removing the smears. It was self-inflicted torture. He couldn't breathe for wanting to taste her. He couldn't think for thoughts of her. He had stopped sleeping. He was barely eating. His body was in a state of desire that was agony if their skin so much as brushed. Standing this close, she was a tempting offering. Her scent was pungent, and her body seemed wildly seductive in paint stained clothes.

Their eyes met, and he saw the darkening of her hunger for him. She was trembling softly, nearly vibrating with frustration. He could hear the soft struggle she made to keep her breathing even. "How much longer can we ignore this?" he asked softly, his voice a rasp. He tossed the cloth aside without looking. His hands sank into her thick hair and he bent his head to close his teeth lightly over the line of her jaw. "Let me kiss you. For god's sake, Remy, let me kiss you before we both lose our minds."

On a desperate groan, she turned her head and found his mouth with hers. She wound her arms around his neck and dragged him as close as she could. His hands tightened, and he pulled her up into him so that she was nearly bent backwards while he devoured her. Lips clung and burned, teeth scraped. It was madness. Insanity.

She had never been kissed with such famished intensity, and she felt herself sinking into a heated pool of surrender. It was her teeth that nipped at his lip when he moved as if to release her. He groaned and sank into her again, his fingers moving convulsively in her hair as his tongue wildly dueled with hers to gulp in her taste and scent.

Then, suddenly, the embrace went from wild to tender. His fingers softened and so did his kiss. She opened her eyes slightly to find him watching her, his blue eyes as soft and dark as velvet. Something churned inside, something stronger and hotter than desire. He watched her as if she was his entire world.

The thud was painful and hard inside her heart. It seemed to wrench her entire soul. Terrified, she broke free of the kiss and tried to push him away. She was in love with him. Had been in love with him but too terrified to admit it. She could pinpoint the exact moment it had happened. She had walked in to find him rocking Nicole to sleep in the rocking chair. She had looked at him and seen everything she could ever want in a mate.

He loved children and was brilliant with them. He was strong enough to take charge when needed, but not afraid to step down when someone knew more. He gave of himself to his family without thought or consequence. And he watched her as if she was the only woman in his world. This man who was blessed to know what he wanted . . . wanted her.

She tore herself out of his arms and fled out of the shop toward the house. He paused only a moment before following her swiftly. Things were about to come to a very critical point. There were two outcomes before him, and the next five minutes would decide which he chose.

Blocks away, at the Driven Snow building, Nicole was cuddled onto a couch, and watching Sam and Seisyll beat the heck out of Tomos and Jen at a video game. She was happy. She liked her new uncles. She liked to see her aunts be happy, especially Tabby, because Tabby smiled lots now that she was with Gavin. And if she was touching Gavin, she could even hug Nicole. That was Nicole's favorite part. She never got to hug Tabby 'cause Tabby had electric veins, or something.

But there was a blip on her happiness. Thinking it made her frown to herself. She was absolutely, positively certain that she wanted Heul to be her daddy. She loved him *lots*, more than her uncles. As much as she loved her mommy. And he loved her mommy. She was sure of it 'cause he watched her mommy like her uncles watched her aunts. And since her mommy watched him the way her aunts watched her uncles, then her mommy had to love him, too.

"Uh oh," Belle murmured. "She's thinking."

"This is bad?" Owen asked curiously.

Rie jerked a thumb at her niece. "Machiavelli's reincarnation."

"What's up, kidlet?" Gavin sat down next to Nicole on the couch. He had to smile as he looked at her. Her face was lightly colored with spots that made her resemble a pink Dalmatian. She had stopped scratching, though; Arian had wrapped her hands in soft mittens. Keeping her distracted helped too. She was starting up the slope toward being healthy, and that meant she was getting fidgety.

"I want Heul to be my dad." She nodded decisively. "I want him to marry Mommy."

The adults exchanged looks. Then, carefully, Lexie asked, "What if they don't feel that way?"

She rolled her eyes as if adults were too dense to get it. "'Cause they watch each other like you and Unca Joseff look at each other. Or like Unca Gavin and Aunt Tabby. An' 'cause you love each other, that means they gotta love each other, right?"

"Nothing gets past her," Tabby apologized to the men.

"Yikes."

"Well," Joseff said, "we're working on it, Nic. We want them to be happy, too. It might take a while though."

She nodded. "'Kay. I can wait." She contemplated that. "Until Christmas. 'Cause there's a party and I wanna go with my new daddy. He can beat up mean old Luis!"

Seisyll suddenly went pale. "Dear god. What do we do when she's a teenager? Gwyn was bad enough."

The Germaine sisters exchanged a grin as the Trahern brothers all began to look horrified. "Welcome to the family," Sam said drolly.

Remy took the stairs two at a time until she was in the attic. Once surrounded by the familiar scent of dust and time, she was able to release some of the panic. She walked on trembling legs across the room to the large wooden trunk under the window. Heart pounding, she opened the lid and looked inside. There, resting on top, was the gold locket.

She carefully picked it up and turned it over. Tiny little engravings of initials were clear on the back. Seven sets of initials, and six of them darker than the surrounding gold. She lightly touched where she had engraved her own initials but never made a wish.

"Well!" an old woman said suddenly. "A fine kettle of fish you're in now, Remy Germaine!"

She slowly turned her head to see a familiar old woman sitting in what had been, only minutes before, a broken rocking chair. The old woman was knitting competently, her needles clicking and flashing. Her short white hair framed a wrinkled face that still retained its freckles. Her eyes were meadow green and sharp as ever.

All Remy could say was, "You couldn't knit."

"I've been dead for fifteen years. I've had time to learn." Grandma Henrietta watched her oldest chick intently. "I was quite content to chase your grandfather around fluffy clouds. I'm not entirely happy I have to come down here and smack you."

"Then there is a heaven?"

"For me," she said easily. "For others there may be something different. There's a . . . cycle, Remy. We're all a part of it. What we do after death is entirely dependent on our beliefs and our desires and our sins." She waved a hand and almost lost her knitting. She scowled. "I dropped a stitch."

Remy sank down and looked at the locket in her hands. "What do I do?" she whispered softly.

"You could wish for his love. You would have it."

She shook her head quickly. "No. I will not wish for something that I might never get naturally." Her lower lip trembled. "I'd live with the knowledge for my entire life. If he loves me, I want it to be because of me."

"Well of course you do."

Remy eyed her grandmother. "Of course?"

"Naturally. Everyone in 3rd District has the internal workings to mate for life. Some call it chance. Others call it magic. Me? I call it damned lucky and leave it there." She resumed her knitting. "Chase came along in your life when you needed him. He gave you Nicole, and we both know he couldn't be happier for it. If you hadn't had Nicole when you did, you might never have had a child at all."

"And how do I tell Heul that?" she asked achingly. "Tell a man who loves children so badly that if he wanted to be with me, he might never have a child of his own blood?" She got to her feet. "An aberration, they called it. Just a fluke. Some women stop ovulating but don't stop menstruating."

"Frankly, if nature was going to turn off one, she ought to turn off the other." Grandma put down her knitting. "You could wish for that, Remy. That locket has the power to grant anything you wish."

Remy thought of love. She thought of having more children. She loved children as much as Heul did. She thought of a life full of laughter and joy and passion. And she thought of Nicole. Softly, she said, "I wish only for Nicole to be happy. Whatever is needed for her to be happy in her life."

The locket glowed and the initials on the back darkened. Grandma nodded sagely. "A worthy wish. I see Nicole as having a nice, long life. But never forget your own happiness, Remy. She'd be miserable if her mother was sad."

"I'll do my best."

Outside the door, Heul leaned against the wall. His heart ached for Remy. Life was cruel to give her only one child when she had enough love for many. And it hurt him as well for he knew she would never get over what she felt were her own shortcomings. He loved her. He finally knew it for what it was, and only one outcome lay before him.

When Remy stepped onto her floor, she found him waiting for her. "Sorry," she said. "I just . . . I've never felt desire before," she admitted. "Not like that."

"I want to make you an offer." He got to his feet and walked over to her. "It's an offer I don't make lightly."

Her heart began to beat harder. "What kind of offer?"

"We have a one-night stand. We're alone today. Let's be lovers once and see what happens. Afterward, we'll see where we stand, if we want to continue the affair. It's not just new territory for you, Remy. This is way out of my league. I'm in over my head, too."

"You won't want to stay with me," she whispered miserably. "When we step into that bedroom, you won't want to stay."

"Try me."

Before she could blink, he had reached out with that shocking speed of his and literally swept her off her feet. His mouth came down on hers with desperate hunger holding something wild and feral but tender. A helpless moan echoed in her throat as she surrendered. She loved him. Wanted him. If only once, she wanted to live.

He walked into her bedroom and came to a sharp stop. His head lifted. A chill went over her skin as she heard the soft feminine whispers flowing through the room. Shaking, she looked around to see the wispy forms of several women standing at the edges of the room. All very different, but all lovely in some way. Different ages, different ethnicities. All they had in common . . . was Heul.

Touching Remy as he was, he saw them too. "What is this?" he asked her softly.

She braced her shoulders. "The downside of my gift," she said flatly. "Welcome to the ghosts of lovers past. And welcome to one of the big problems Chase and I had. There were only two ghosts to stand around and stare at us, but they were enough. Add in that I just couldn't want him that way . . ."

"Did you even try to banish them?"

"How can I?"

"Easily." He set her down on her feet and began to strip off her clothes. His hands were hot and deliberate as they caressed her slightly chilled skin. "You make me forget they ever existed. Replace their presence with yours. And I'll make you forget they ever existed, too." He lifted her off her feet and pressed his lips to her throat where her pulse was rapid.

"I can't," she started, but the words strangled off into a gasp as one of his hands closed over her breast and sent sensation streaking through her body.

"Yes, you can." He tumbled her down onto the bed and began to slowly kiss and caress his way across her body, leaving no inch untouched, no secret unfound. "God," he said roughly. "I don't know how you found them. How could they ever compare to you? I didn't even remember their faces!"

She opened her eyes slightly to see all but one ghost was gone. The one that remained was smirking at her. Something wild and fierce rose inside her, as hot as her desire and potent with feminine power. Heul was *hers*. She wasn't going to turn him over to anyone, especially not ghosts of the past!

He almost staggered when she suddenly threw herself into his arms and her mouth sought his. She seemed to simply pour herself into the kiss. Her body moved erotically against his, and her hands fluttered over his skin, sensitizing it to a fever pitch. Aching, throbbing, he fell onto his back as her sensual assault continued. "Remy." It was all he could say.

The rough rasp of his words was a physical caress. She knelt across his hips and rushed to open his shirt. She was naked and he wasn't. It wasn't fair at all. With a murmur of wordless delight, she rubbed her hands over his chest and bent to nuzzle her nose through the soft blond curls.

He wasn't a passive participant. His hands swept over her, kneading her breasts and lightly scraping her nipples. He skimmed his hands down her stomach, teased the small stretch marks that were evidence of her child, and then slowly his hands slipped between her legs. He shuddered. She was hot and wet, and as he stroked her softly, he watched her face intently.

She shuddered. A whimper left her lips as the need built. Those rough fingertips were making her entire body throb for more. Helplessly, her hips began to follow his touch. Her head fell back as the heat rose inside until she felt as if she were burning alive. "Heul!" His name was nothing more than a choked cry of desperation.

She found herself on her back a second later. She pushed and shoved at his jeans, almost sobbing with every breath as her body dangled, enticing, on the edge of something . . . on the edge of *something*, and she needed that something more than air.

When he was finally as naked as she was, he dragged her legs over his arms. "Look at me," he managed to say. Her eyes met his and he plunged into her deeply. Fire raced up through his entire body. She was tight and wet and hot; they fit so perfectly, her muscles eagerly clamping down on his aching flesh. Her groan of agonized pleasure seemed to sear him. Brand him. "Do you see any ghosts?" he demanded harshly.

She forced her eyes open. There was no one in the room but them. "No," she managed to whisper.

"That's because there's only you inside me. Only me inside you." He pulled back and thrust forward again. "You never tried to banish them, Remy! Never wanted to. You had to want me enough to make them go away."

"Stop talking," she begged, grabbing at his shoulders for balance.

After that, there were no words for either of them. There was nothing but the driving hunger for each other's body until they couldn't take any more and fell together into a shocking ecstasy that neither would have ever imagined. No ghosts. No inadequacy. There was nothing but them, burning together in a velvet paradise.

Some indeterminable time later, he muttered into her hair, "Your bed is too small."

She smiled against his shoulder. "You're too tall." He lifted his head and she framed his face gently. "Thank you," she said softly.

"You're welcome." He rolled off her only to tug her up against his side. "In case it escaped your notice, I was going absolutely *mad*. I haven't been eating or sleeping." He gave her a fierce glower. "I had never even kissed you, and I wanted you until I was close to insanity. I'm shocked that I lasted as long as I did once I got my hands on you."

She lifted her head to look at the clock. "An hour is an aberration?"

"I prefer three."

"Three!" Her eyes went wide. "Can a body *survive* three hours?"

His smile was slow and lethal as he leaned over her, his hands suddenly gliding over her skin with an intent other than comfort. "You're going to find out."

She awoke much later in the afternoon to find herself alone in bed. He had made good on his promise and she felt like an overcooked noodle. She ached in some muscles, but the others were melted down to puddles of satiated flesh. She had never felt so loved. She had just needed the right man. She had needed Heul. She really hated when Chase was right.

She carefully sat up and looked around. She knew without asking that Heul was not there in the building or anywhere close. A note sat on the nightstand and she picked it up with trembling fingers.

Dear Remy,

Thank you. Thank you for giving me something so precious. Your trust and your body, but something more as well.

I know you're probably mad to wake alone. I'm sorry. But if I stayed, I'd ask for more than you can give. My gift is to see future outcomes. The one I saw . . . it gave you happiness, but it would take you from me. I choose your happiness. I knew all along that in the end I would never have you, no matter how I wanted otherwise.

The dollhouse is done. Nicole ought to love it. If you wish, the merger will go forward. Don't worry about me. I won't demand more of you. But never ever *doubt that you are a warm and sensual woman, and that you'll make the right man very happy.*

Heul

She crushed the note in her hand as her temper flared. He was walking out for *her* own good? Bullshit. Furious, she got out of bed and got dressed. He thought he could make love to her and leave? Over her dead body. Did he think she didn't love him? Well, he was a damned blind idiot! If his note was any indication, he loved her too, and if he did, what the *hell* was he doing walking out? He saw the future, saw her walking away? They would see about that!

At Driven Snow, Heul was sitting in his office with twelve males and females glaring at him. "What?" he demanded. "I'm not in the best of moods, so kindly take yourselves out of my office."

"You *walked out*?!" Belle planted her hands on the desk. "You idiot! Why didn't you tell her you loved her?!"

"She'd never believe me!" he shouted.

Silence fell. No one was sure of what to say. As it happened, no one had to try. The door suddenly slammed open to reveal a tall redhead who was so mad that her eyes were like green flames. "Heul Trahern!" Remy shouted. "What the hell do you think by leaving me alone in bed?"

The others stepped back quickly en masse. "Holy shit," Lexie managed to whisper, eyes wide. She had never seen Remy that mad before.

Heul grabbed onto the edge of the desk before he grabbed Remy. She stalked over and planted her hands on the desk and leaned across to get in his face. "You are an idiot!" she told him. "A big one! In fact, I've never met another idiot who was bigger! You want to tell me what the meaning of this note is?" She leaned back and threw it at him so that it bounced off his head. "What kind of crap is this? You saw me walking away so you walked away first?"

"You think I don't see that you're afraid to love me?" he countered harshly. "That you're afraid to make another mistake?"

"And it didn't stop me from falling in love, did it?" she shouted. "We're both idiots! *You* thought I was so fragile that I wouldn't believe you, and *I* was sure I'd screw things up! Well I'm not fragile and *you* were the one who screwed up!" She gestured sharply at the door. "Tell me you want me to walk out, and I will. If you want me to stay, then I'm staying! If you can handle a woman who sees ghosts—including her dead ex-husband—then I can handle a hardheaded precognitive who doesn't know destiny when it bites him on the ass!"

"Stay." The word came from the deepest part of his soul. "You have to know I love you, Remy. I can't seem to function without you."

"Then you'll have to marry me." She crossed her arms. "If you can handle the fact that I might never have any more children."

"Then share Nicole with me," he said simply. "You know I'll love her as if she was mine. If we want more, we can always adopt." He carefully got to his feet. "Now tell me you love me without shouting at me."

"I love you." She smiled as she said it. The words were easier than she had thought they would be. Oddly, she wasn't worried anymore. How could she make a mistake when everything was fitting together perfectly? Yes, he was her friend, but he was her lover as well. She didn't think she could ever envision having one with him and not having the other. "It's not a mistake this time."

"Well." Gavin cleared his throat. "Does this mean we're going ahead with the merger?"

Remy and Heul glanced at their grinning siblings. To be honest, they had forgotten they were there. Heul coughed. Remy cleared her throat. "Yes," she finally said. "I believe we are." She held out a hand to Heul. "What do you say we call it Seven Wishes Design?"

He took her hand. "I think that sounds perfect." And with easy strength, he yanked her across the top of the desk into his arms and kissed her with all the love in his heart while their brothers and sisters clapped and whistled.

Out in the hall, Nicole carefully closed the door and grinned cheekily. She absolutely *had* to be flower girl for her mommy and daddy. A little skip in her step, she climbed down the stairs to where Rayna and Eric were standing near the door. "Here, Auntie Rayna." She held up the seven contracts she was carrying.

Eric took the contracts while Rayna snuggled Nicole. Satisfied, he watched all seven contracts glow and the word 'Complete' appear. "Perfect," he said softly. "I think Gwyn will be quite happy when she gets home."

Rayna smiled up at him. "Seven wishes for seven sisters and seven happy endings. You can't ask for more."

"Can I ask for a baby brother or sister?" Nicole asked. "'Cause I want one."

Eric and Rayna exchanged a grin. Remy and Heul were in for a quite a shock. Remy had wished for Nicole's happiness, and if Nicole needed a baby sibling to be happy, then that's what she would get.

After all, a locket made from a golden apple of Aphrodite *always* kept its word.

EPILOGUE

When Rhianna was handed the seven contracts, she read them closely. She smiled. "I'd say young Joseff and Lexie did a fine job, wouldn't you?"

"They're naturals," Eric concurred. "Now can we get out of the matchmaking business?"

She slowly lifted a brow. "What are you talking about? We're not in the matchmaking business. We're in a business to ensure the happiness of the people of 3rd District. We've issued thousands of contracts over the years but only half of them deliberately had anything to do with finding someone love."

He stared at her. She stared back, her black eyes guileless. On a mutter, he stalked to his office. They both knew he couldn't prove that she was doing anything on purpose. All he had were hunches and suspicions because, despite her words, anyone associated with a contract from Enforcers—of any type—somehow ended up finding true love.

He stopped at his door and looked at her. "Rhi . . . where did you get the golden apple you made the locket from for Henrietta Germaine? The elder one, I mean."

She arched a brow in the maddening way of hers. "I found it lying around."

He looked at Rayna inside his office, and she made a helpless gesture. Rhianna was telling the truth. "*Damn* it," he groused and stalked into his office. The door shut firmly.

Covering a smile, Rhianna made some notes on the contracts and put them into their proper folders. She slid the folders into the drawer labeled 'Carmichael.' When she locked the drawer, the word 'Finished' appeared. This time she knew it was for real.

She settled back in her chair contentedly. She had indeed told Eric the truth. She really wouldn't call herself a matchmaker. Mostly she just liked to meddle. Was it her fault if happiness and love tended to be synonymous? Of course not. It just happened to fall that way, and she just took advantage of things.

She couldn't help but look forward to what was next. She loved her job.

Status: File Complete

Analysis: Whether you wish for love or happiness, for yourself or others, your wish will only come true when you believe in yourself.

Keep going for a bonus story from Mirage where another pair of lovers are 'coincidentally' brought together, but the one Enforcing their contract is someone entirely new . . .

Bonus Folder

JERAN

CHAPTER ONE

People often see wavering images of things on hot days. As they draw closer, the images disappear and prove they never existed. But they did exist. They existed in another world that lies parallel to Earth. That world was known as Mirage.

When it drifted too close to Earth many centuries ago, it got stuck to the River Styx and thusly stayed connected. Unlike Earth, which drew its magic only from the River Styx, Mirage consisted entirely of magic. To Earthlings, it would be a world of faerie tales. To those of Mirage, Earth was the world of tall tales.

Although only the people of the place known as 3rd District within New York City knew about Mirage's existence, Mirage knew completely about Earth. Many citizens had crossed to Earth to stay, and some had come home with mates. It was always kept a secret if they did.

Some of the 'lower class' people of Mirage thought of Earth as only a faerie tale. Some, like Jeran Windwalker, figured it was just a story parents used to make sure their children didn't go wandering at night. 'Be careful,' his father had often said, 'or an Earthling might kidnap you.'

Jeran was a good boy and often seen as simple-minded. He obeyed his father without question. It was why he still lived at home even though he was nineteen years of age and more than old enough to have gone seeking his fortune in the world.

He was a handsome young man with lavender hair and purple eyes, although he was of slightly shorter height than most males his age. Regardless of his height, farm girls for miles around were smitten with his good looks and the honest and kind heart he had. He was a young man who, almost literally, had his choice of women.

His elder brothers, Jared and Jonah, despised him for it. They were of ages twenty-two and twenty-four, and they were equally handsome, with similar coloring to their youngest brother. They were taller than their brother by five inches, and they had gone out into the world to make their fortunes, only to fail and return home to wait for their father to name his heir and die.

Their father, Julian, loved his boys, but it was Jeran he loved the most. As he lay in his sickbed and watched through a window as Jeran patiently filled a bucket with cool water, he thought again how much he wished that his two eldest were as kind as their brother, or that Jeran was as smart as his older brothers. None were currently suitable to inherit.

Jeran saw his father grimacing as he returned and rushed to his side. "No, don't overdo yourself, Father." He smiled and brought a cup of the cool water he had fetched. "The more you stress yourself out, the sooner you'll die."

Julian regarded his son. "You don't want me to die?"

"Not at all." He busied himself straightening the bed and fluffing the pillows. "You're my only father, so of course I'm loathe to lose you." He smiled, little sparkles appearing in his eyes; the sparkles were just one of the many things the girls loved. "If I had two fathers, then maybe it wouldn't be so bad."

Julian sighed fondly. "You're a brat." He held out a hand that Jeran took tightly. "Tell me, what have your brothers been doing lately?" He had no reservations about taking advantage of Jeran's open nature and quick-to-speak-before-thinking tendency.

"Jonah spent today visiting all of the neighbors, seeing if any of them were looking to sell any time soon. Jared spent his time trying to go courting amongst the girls. He came home quite furious since he couldn't find them." Jeran's voice was puzzled. "I can't understand how he missed them. They were visiting with me while I tended to the horses."

Julian hid a smile. "Ah, well. He is not nearly as open-minded as you. How did Jonah's time go? It's quite a fine idea, actually, seeking to merge our lands."

"Not well, either. None of the other farmers want to deal with him." Again, Jeran was confused. "They're always so open with me and always happy to talk and haggle prices."

Not for the first time, Julian wished with all his heart that Jeran had just a slightly harder personality. If Julian could be surer that he could defend himself on all fronts, he would have named him his heir in a heartbeat and gone to make funeral arrangements.

He was at a loss. All of his sons had flaws. He had no way to decide amongst them. With a sigh, he settled back against his pillows. "I want to rest for a little while, Jeran. I'll call when I wake."

"Alright." Jeran smiled and leaned down to kiss his father's cheek. "No dying in your sleep."

"Yes, yes," he said gruffly. Jeran's open and honest love was humbling. He cherished his son more than anything. "Off with you."

Jeran left the room and shut the door behind him. His smile immediately turned into a frown. Sometimes he wished he had the courage of his brothers. If he did, then he would have been able to tell his father that it had not been Jonah's idea for the merger but his. It was just the most recent in a series of similar events throughout his life.

To be truthful, he was not as simple-minded as most thought. He was simply too nice, and too shy, to speak up for himself. For his entire life, his brothers had been taking his ideas and promoting them as their own. At this time and date, he highly doubted anyone would believe him anyway.

It was evening when the front door slammed open and Jonah and Jared staggered in, both so drunk that Jeran could smell the alcohol from where he stood on the stairs. His nose wrinkled. "Keep quiet. Father is resting."

"Oh suuuure," Jonah slurred, "we'll be quiet. Real quiet. Right, Jared?" He gave his brother a sloppy punch in the arm that sent the already-off-balance male staggering across the room where he crashed into a table. "Shhh!" he said with an exaggerated gesture. "We gotta be quiet. Wouldn't want to scare the geezer to death."

Jared lurched up to his feet and narrowly missed cracking his head open on the closest door. "Right you are. No need to make noise." He walked woozily toward Jeran. "Still baby-sitting, kid? I'd say you ought to get a wife but what woman'd have you?"

Jeran nimbly stepped to the side and watched his brother smack into the wall. He told himself he didn't care. Then he sighed. "I'll make something to get rid of your headaches." It would also sober them up, but he was smart enough not to mention that at least. The first and most important ingredient in the cure was apples. He got out the apple basket and headed out into the back orchards to start gathering.

The apple orchard was an acre in size and the apples the trees produced were the best in the country. They came in every color under the sun from red to white to yellow to green. The ones he wanted were the green apples, and they grew on the trees toward the back. He looked over the orchard as he walked. He didn't need a kingdom. Just this little farm.

There was a loud and indignant squawk from up ahead followed by a feminine shriek. Startled, he dropped the basket and hurried toward the sound. "Hey! What's going on?" As he rounded the corner, he got his answer; the moonlight was bright enough that he could see clearly as the day.

There was a young woman crouched on the ground with her arms thrown over her head to protect herself as a large golden bird tried to peck at her. She wore the plain and simple clothing of a farm girl, so he had to assume she lived nearby. "Cut it out!" he shouted as he ran forward. He scooped up a rock and chucked it at the bird.

His aim was true and he struck the bird in the side. With an outraged cry, it flapped its wings and took off into the sky, shedding golden feathers as it went. He ignored the feathers and knelt beside the girl quickly. "Are you okay, miss? Oh, you're bleeding!" he exclaimed, noticing her arms had been pecked at viciously.

She lowered her arms to look at them and then looked up at him. He took a sharp breath, his eyes widening. He had never before seen such a beautiful girl in his life; her features were too impossibly perfect to be real. Her hair was thick and black, and her eyes were the same, but there were little golden flecks caught in the blackness of them that he likened to stars in the sky.

A long silence descended. Abruptly, he realized he was staring. He flushed. "I'm terribly sorry." He sat down beside her and reached for her arm. He tugged it closer gently so that he could see the marks. There were three of them, all of them deep enough that blood welled up slightly. "They must hurt."

"Very much so." She lowered her lashes and watched him from under them. "I can tend to them myself. I was trespassing, so I'm hardly worth your time."

He gave her a shocked look. "Trespassing or not, I'm not going to walk away." Because injuries were par for the course on a farm, he always carried one or two first aid supplies in the satchel around his waist. He pulled out a strip of bandage and began to gently wind it around her arm. "Besides," he told her, smiling, "I don't worry about trespassers. You were chasing that bird, right, so it was an accident."

"What if I told you I was here to steal some apples, and the bird got in the way?" she asked softly.

"Well, then I'd pretend I hadn't heard. There are *plenty* of apples in this orchard." He finished wrapping the bandage and tied a jaunty bow on the top. "There you go." He smiled at her, his eyes sparkling. "My name is Jeran. I live here. What's your name?"

"Michaela." She searched his face intently, feeling her heart beat harder inside her chest. She had never before seen such a handsome man, and he wasn't a giant like so many others. She was very small herself, and she always hated males who towered over her. And, more importantly, he was honestly kind. Was he the one she needed? "I'm from far away. I was visiting."

"That's okay." He pulled her up to her feet easily and his eyes widened. "You're so small!" he blurted happily. She was only slightly over five feet in height, and therefore he was several inches taller. Since the average height of a female on Mirage was anywhere from five-six to six feet, he was delighted.

She was no less surprised to find her head fit just under his chin. Warmth filled her heart. "Maybe we're destined to be," she laughed as she looked up at him.

"Destined to be what?" he asked curiously.

He really was sweet, she thought. Kind of naïve, but she really liked it. "Never mind. If we are, then you'll find out." She reached up to frame his face and then went on her toes to kiss him quickly.

His eyes widened as she released him. He touched his lips and felt them tingle. He wasn't *that* naïve, and he recognized that there were some potentially potent sparks between him and his starlight beauty. "Promise I'll see you again," he told her.

"Oh I'm sure I can promise that. Thank you, Jeran," she added softer, "for giving me hope." Without another word, she hurried off out of sight. She didn't go very far, though. She ducked down and hid behind a tree so that she could watch him. If he was the one . . . well, she would soon know for certain. She hoped so, with everything she was. She could easily fall in love with a man like Jeran.

Jeran was puzzled but knew he distinctly looked forward to seeing Michaela again. He had never considered courting any girl before because he had never met one that he honestly took a fancy to. Michaela was perfect for him.

With a sigh, he started to pick some apples for the cure for his brothers. As he was carrying them back to the basket, he noticed some of the golden feathers had fallen in as well. Curious, he picked one up. Much to his shock, he realized it was real gold and not just golden colored.

Delighted, he said, "I'll give it to my father. He'll love it. Perhaps it will help him live longer!" He held the basket close and hurried back toward the house. He would share his gift bright and early in the morning. He needed to make the cure for his brothers right then. Gold could wait.

Michaela watched him hurry off and felt tears begin to slide down her cheeks as she slowly sank down to her knees. He was, she thought in dim shock and relief. He truly was the one destined for her. She had thought she would never find him, and realizing she was soon to fall in love was a little terrifying. With a little sigh, she rested her forehead against the tree beside her. "Oh, who am I kidding?" she asked on a wry smile. "I already fell."

Jeran could barely keep the feathers a secret, almost bursting at the seams to tell someone. But because he had already promised, he got to work with the apples and other ingredients needed and made the hangover cure for his brothers. It was no easy feat to make them drink it, but they were so drunk that he finally just poured the concoction down their throats.

He awoke the next morning with the dawn. He quickly hurried into his clothes and went to get the chores done. Once they were completed, he made breakfast. By the time that was done, his brothers were awake and staggering into the dining room. They were sober and not hungover, but both were clearly exhausted.

Jared gave an earsplitting yawn. "Once I'm more awake, I intend to go wife-hunting again. I have no idea where all the women were yesterday, but maybe I scared them off with my dashing good looks."

Jonah snorted over his cup of coffee. "More like they were hiding in abject terror."

Jared opened his mouth to retort and Jeran didn't hesitate to rap him smartly in the back of the head with the spatula. "Ow!" Jared glowered and rubbed his head but couldn't argue with his baby brother; if he did, he wouldn't get fed. Jeran might have been stupid, but he was stubborn.

When breakfast had been cleared, Jeran hurried to his father's room with a tray. "Good morning!" he called cheerfully.

Julian looked over with a smile as he came in. "Good morning, son. As you can see, I decided to live another day."

"Good." He set the tray down and smiled. "Because I brought a gift. They fell off a bird in our orchard." He held out the feathers. "Gold, father. Real gold! Aren't they beautiful?"

Julian stared at the feathers in his hands in shock. Greed churned inside him. "A bird you say? Which direction did it fly?"

"North."

"Jared! Jonah!" he called. When the two other young men had joined him and Jeran, he held out the feathers. "I want you to travel to the north. Find me the bird that shed these feathers! I must have the whole bird!"

Jared stared at the feathers. "Real gold," he breathed.

Jonah was no less stunned. "Well." He snorted. "So what? I don't want to go on some weird journey, thanks. I'll stay here."

Jeran frowned and said softly, "But Jonah, Father seems very insistent. Perhaps having this bird will cure him."

"All the more reason not to go, I think," his brother muttered back.

Julian beetled his brows together. "I will give my farm to whichever of my sons brings back that golden bird."

"Sold!" Jared took off for the barn as fast as he could.

"Hey, you asshole!" Jonah was hot on his heels. "I won't give up that easy!"

Jeran eased down until he was sitting on the side of the bed and took the feathers away from his father. "Don't stress yourself out, Father, please." He studied the feathers and wondered to himself if perhaps there was a spell of some sort over them. He had never before seen his father act like this. Perhaps it would be best if his brothers never found the bird.

Time passed, and days became months. Spring faded into summer, and two months went by. Julian's health stayed steady, and Jeran continued to run the farm as he always had. Still, he would watch the north every evening, waiting for his brothers. Finally, he knew they likely would not return.

"I'm sorry, Father," he said softly.

Julian frowned intently. "I refuse to believe such a thing! I must have that bird, Jeran, understand? I feel as if I will die if I do not."

"Then I will go," he said. "I will find this bird for you." Even as Julian shook his head, Jeran took his hand. "Please, Father! I will have the neighbors watch over things while I am gone, and I will find my brothers and the golden bird, I promise!"

"No, Jeran." Julian felt his heart quiver. Losing Jonah and Jared was not as frightening as losing Jeran. "You're my dearest son, I would never risk you." That and he was worried Jeran was not smart enough to find the bird, but he kept the thought to himself.

The longer he argued, the more he realized Jeran's stubbornness was rearing its head. His mind and heart were set. With a heavy heart, Julian finally gave his blessings and watched out the window the following morning as Jeran set off toward the north with a big backpack full of supplies.

He sadly picked up the feathers sitting on the table beside him and studied them. But, to his utter astonishment, they turned black in his hands like the feathers of a raven. If they were enchanted, he had no idea what the enchantment was, but he did have to wonder just why they had chosen that moment to change. Was it Jeran? What gift did his son have that he did not know about?

CHAPTER TWO

The road was long and dusty, but the sun was bright and warm. As he walked down the trail that led into the woods, Jeran realized he was happier than he had thought he would be. He had never been far from home before, and it was like an adventure to consider seeing so many new things.

He began to whistle as he walked, and there was an added spring in his step. The only thing that marred the niceness of the day was the knowledge that he still didn't know where to find Michaela. He had been scouring the town since the night he met her, but no one had seen or heard of her. A part of him wondered if he had conjured her up.

"Hello."

He stopped in surprise and looked down to see that there was a little golden fox sitting next to him. With a smile, he knelt and patted the small animal gently. "Hi, yourself." Talking animals were as common on Mirage as skyscrapers were on Earth. He didn't find it odd at all to have the fox speaking to him. "Need some help?"

"Actually, I am here to help you." The fox circled him slowly and studied him. Yes, this one would do just fine. Sitting in front of Jeran again, he said, "I understand you are looking for the golden bird."

"I am!" Jeran smiled. "Can you help me?"

"I certainly can." He pointed with one paw down the road. "Down this road, two days hence, you will find a small resting place. It has two inns. One of them will be bright and lively. The other will be dark and gloomy. Whatever you do, stay at the gloomy one."

Jeran thought about that. "I suppose that makes sense. I mean, you can't sleep well at a lively inn."

"Exactly. Now, beyond the rest stop, another couple days away, you will find a kingdom. This is where the golden bird lives. I will tell you how to catch him, but you had better pay close attention!" he scolded. "The bird is kept in its own pen at the back of the palace. Sneak into it and put the bird into the *plain* cage. It will remain quiet and you can escape with it."

Jeran committed the information to memory. He wanted to be sure he did this right. He wanted to prove to his father that he was not simple-minded, and that he could be trusted to run the farm. "Okay," he promised. "Is there any way I can repay you?"

"We can talk about repayment when you are done with your journey," the fox promised.

He straightened. "I understand." He smiled and dug into his bag. He came out with a cookie and offered it to the fox. "As thanks for now." With a renewed spring in his step, he turned and hurried down the road once more.

The fox sniffed the cookie and then nibbled on the edge. It was really quite tasty. He supposed it was a good thing Jeran knew how to cook. Michaela could burn water.

It was indeed two days before Jeran reached the two inns, and it was close to sundown as well. He was exhausted. His feet were sore, and he was dusty and grimy from the road. The idea of being able to sleep in a bed, a real bed, was a haunting lure as he stared at the brightly glowing inn.

He abruptly remembered the fox's advice and realized that resting at a lively inn was not going to allow him to sleep. He turned away from the sight and headed to the slightly gloomy looking inn. Much to his surprise, the interior was not gloomy at all. It was warm and welcoming, and it felt as if all his troubles faded away.

The desk clerk smiled as she saw him. "Good evening! Will you stay for the night?"

"Yes, please." He laid a few coins on the counter and sniffed the air. "Is that food I smell?"

"Naturally. If you'd like to go up to your room, I'll send someone along with a complimentary tray."

"Thank you." He gathered his backpack again and trudged up the stairs slowly. He was hoping very much for a bath before bed. He was used to being dirty because of farm work, but he didn't like wearing dirt overnight.

With much delight, he discovered there was a copper tub filled with hot water waiting for him. Hooray for modern convenience! He eagerly dropped his backpack on the ground and rummaged in it for a change of clothes. There was soap and a towel near the tub so he wasted no time in stripping off his tunic and vest.

He had just reached for his belt when the door opened. In shock, he and Michaela stared at one another. The latter was carrying a tray of food. The moment was broken when they realized what had happened, and he ducked behind a bookcase even as she whipped back out into the hall and out of sight.

There was silence. Then, "Er, hi, Michaela."

"Hi, Jeran." Oh my god, she thought over and over again. He was short but he was *gorgeous*. Though Nature had not given him much in height, it had taken full advantage of what inches were present. Clothes had hidden very nicely that his arms and chest were corded with sleek muscles. Her fingers itched to touch.

"What're you doing here?" He was embarrassed, but only because he had panicked. She was the prettiest girl he had ever known. He wanted to be at his best when he saw her, not sweaty and dirty from days on the road.

"I brought food. I'll just leave it out here."

"Okay but . . ." He grabbed his courage. "Come back later, okay? Like in thirty minutes?"

"But you need sleep."

"I want to see you more."

Her color rose even as her heart fluttered in her chest. "Oh. Well . . . okay." She bent and put the tray on the floor and pushed it around the edge of the door without looking. Quickly she pulled the door shut and hurried down the hall. She needed to do her hair or something. She wanted to be her best when she saw him again.

He wasted no time in stripping and jumping into the tub. He wanted to get as clean as possible and look his best when she got back. He wanted to know where she lived, and why she was working here. His hunger to know everything was matched only by the hunger he felt to hold her in his arms.

Thirty minutes later, he was dressed in clean clothes and finishing his meal when there came a knock on the door. He smiled and went to unlock it. "Hi, Michaela," he said as he opened the door. His voice stuttered to a stop, and he stared at her. She had put her hair up and done something to her face. Some strange female thing that made her already impossibly beautiful features even more unforgettable.

Self-consciously, she patted her hair. "Is something wrong?"

He was bemused. He had never realized that seeing her hair up would make the urge to get his hands into it worse. He had to fight to keep from taking it down for her. "I was just surprised." He stepped back to let her in and shut the door behind her. "Do you work here?" he asked as he walked over to the table and pulled out a chair for her.

"No." She smiled as she sat down. "I befriended the clerk recently. I offered to bring the tray up so she could rest herself." She folded her arms on the table as she studied him curiously. "You're so far from home." She had begun to think he would never start down the path leading to her.

He sighed. "Well, remember the golden bird?" He gave her a quick rundown and summed up by adding, "I just want to prove I'm not stupid."

She straightened, the golden flecks in her eyes snapping like sparks. "That's ridiculous! You're just too nice, that's all." She contentedly studied the lines of his face and his purple colored eyes. "So you're the baby in the family?" she asked.

"Yeah." He was no less content in admiring her black eyes with their golden flecks. "I turned nineteen a few months ago. How about you?"

She smiled. "I'm the spoiled brat since I'm an only child. I turned twenty a little while ago."

His eyes widened. "You're older than me!"

She frowned. "Is . . . is that bad?"

"No, but why aren't you waiting for a prince, or something? I mean . . . you're just the kind of girl they'd want!"

Her lashes lowered slightly. "Am I?"

"Well . . . sure." He gave her a puzzled look. "You're beautiful and funny, kind and gentle. You're also intelligent and strong. What prince wouldn't be smitten with you? I mean, I know I am, and I'm no prince." It belatedly dawned on him what he had said as he saw her wide eyes. "Oops."

"You're . . . smitten with me?" she asked softly.

"Yeah." He smiled. "I was really disappointed, you know. I went looking for you the next day but no one had seen you or heard of you." He reached out and took her hand. "I want to court you, if you'll let me."

"Court me?" She was nearly breathless. "For . . . for marriage?"

"If you'll let me." His eyes crinkled at the corners as he smiled. "I'm falling in love with you."

Michaela, in her twenty years of life, had seen dozens of princes. She had been romanced by some of the best. She had heard every flowery word, every pretty compliment, and been given every rose. As Jeran pulled a wildflower out of a vase and tucked it over her ear, she realized that his honest and simple nature was exactly everything she had ever wanted. "I'm glad," she said softly, her eyes glowing. "Because I'm falling for you, too."

His smile faded. "But . . .?"

She closed her eyes sadly. "There are . . . complications."

"Another suitor?" he asked in dismay.

"No, not at all." She got to her feet to pace away a few steps, her arms tightly crossed. "Jeran, I'm not what you think I am. I'm . . ." Her voice stopped sharply and she felt an impotent frustration. She could never talk of it. She was free to walk at night, but her curse stopped her voice if she tried to speak of it.

"You're what?" He walked over to her. "If there's something wrong, I want to fix it if I can." He took her hands with his and held them tightly. "Michaela, please. Tell me what's wrong."

"I can't!" On a sound of despair, she pressed against his chest and pulled her arms free to wrap them around his waist. "I want to, but I can't! Promise me! Promise me you'll keep looking for the golden bird."

He felt his heart flutter suddenly. "Michaela, are you cursed?" Fear and anger mixed inside him. His gentle Michaela . . . the idea of anyone cursing her, in any way, made him furious. If he found the person, he would probably hurt them.

"I can't talk about it!" She held him tighter. "Just hold me for a moment!"

His arms went around her, and he lowered his head toward hers. "Okay. I'll hold you as long as you need."

She drew a deep breath and got a grip on herself. Reluctantly she pulled out of his arms. "You should rest. I'm so sorry."

He just as reluctantly released her and watched her go to the door. "Michaela?" When she looked back, he smiled. "When I see you next time, I'm going to kiss you, okay? I wanted to this time, but you're scared."

Her lips trembled as her broken heart mended a little. She loved him so much. She would have loved him even if he wasn't her destiny. "I'm going to hold you to that, Jeran Windwalker. And I'm never scared when I'm with you."

He quietly locked the door behind her. Determination filled his heart. He would find the golden bird to save his father, and then he would find a way to save his Michaela as well. Protecting them was more important than anything.

A few days later, he found himself staring at the high brick wall of a castle courtyard. He was stumped. He could not figure out a single way to get himself up and over the wall without attracting the attention of everyone in the courtyard.

He took off his backpack and began to pace restlessly. He wished that he could have his brothers' intelligence just once or that he could think in complicated ways. The only idea he had at all was walking up to the gate and asking to look around.

He blinked and looked at his backpack. He knelt and dug inside it and came out with a book. It was half-full of sketches he had done of things he had seen. They weren't great sketches, but he wanted to remember everything clearly.

Wondering if it would work, he went over to the gate and up to the guards. "Hi. Can I come inside to draw the castle?"

The guards shrugged. "Sure," one said, and moved his axe out of the way so he could enter.

He scuttled past them, wondering why people called *him* stupid. It was a nice castle, he saw, and wished he really had the time to draw it like he wanted. Maybe later. He was in too much of a hurry to get the golden bird and give it to his father. More than that, he didn't know how, but he was sure the bird would somehow lead him to Michaela.

The pen was on the backside of the courtyard, and he snuck inside quickly. He immediately spotted the bird. It was sleeping on a perch at the back of the room. He quietly crept toward it. A look around revealed the plain wooden cage. As he was reaching for it, he realized that a bird this spectacular deserved something better. There was a golden cage nearby so he scooped it up instead.

The bird was silent as he picked it up, but the instant he tried to put it in the cage, it woke up and began to complain very loudly. He dropped the cage and grabbed the plain one. The bird silenced but it was too late. Guards were already bursting into the room with weapons drawn. "You! Boy! Drop the bird!" one barked

He opened his hands but the bird seemed to have taken a fancy to him and began climbing all over his shoulders and head. "I can't," he said. "I tried, sorry." It was kind of a cute bird. It was plump like a chicken but it was plump with feathers and not fat. It had a rounded beak and the tips were sharp for pecking. It had a long sweeping tail and its wings were sturdy. Since it wasn't much bigger than a housecat, it was really extra adorable.

"Bring them both." The guard grabbed Jeran's arm and dragged him along as he went into the palace proper. The bird obediently followed in their wake.

Jeran was mortified as he found himself shoved to the floor in front of the king's throne. The king was an older man with a long graying beard and beady black eyes. Jeran had no idea what kind of ruler he was, but he was terrified regardless.

The king studied him. "Name?"

"Jeran Windwalker, majesty." He took a quick breath and blurted, "Please, please, let me go! My father is sick and dying and I have to bring the golden bird to him or he might die anyway! I'm the only one left to run the farm, and my father needs me very badly, and there's a girl that I'm in love with who is cursed, and this bird might help her, so please!"

The king studied him for a few moments. "You seem like an honest lad. More importantly, the bird seems to have taken a fancy to you, and lord knows it hated all of us."

Since the bird was on Jeran's shoulder and cooing happily, he could hardly argue the point.

"Here is what I shall do," the king decided. "You will go to the neighboring kingdom and fetch me their golden horse. I have wanted it for a long time. When you return with it, I will give you the bird to save your father and your love. How is that?"

Jeran leapt to his feet. "Oh thank you! You won't regret it!" He plucked the bird off his shoulder and handed it to the nearest guard despite the bird's annoyed squawk. "I promise! I'll return as soon as I have the horse!" He whirled and ran out quickly, determined not to mess up again.

As he went, everyone in the throne room looked at the floor where golden feathers had fallen from the bird's wings. It was obvious the minute Jeran was gone. The feathers turned to black.

Outside, Jeran hurried to pick up his backpack. The neighboring kingdom was close enough that he could see it from there, so it was easy to get onto the road and start walking. He felt like the idiot that his brothers called him. He had been given specific orders and he had messed them up. He just couldn't help it. He hated seeing anyone, animal or human, not being given what they truly deserved. Still . . . he supposed he was lucky the bird liked him. It would make going home much easier.

"Did you mess things up?"

He looked down swiftly to see the fox walking beside him. His color rose. "I know, I know! Don't berate me, please," he said miserably. "I'm already feeling like enough of an idiot. I just . . . I just thought it deserved better."

"Do you think that gold is so important?" the fox asked.

He frowned. "Well, no. I don't really think money means that much to me. But it was a royal pet. It's much more than common. And it deserved better. Anyone deserves better. I mean, if I'm going to make it live on a farm, it ought to have something special for itself."

"I am going to tell you something important, so listen close." The fox glanced up at him. "You think you are common and have nothing to offer, but you have something inside that is more special than anything. I am not telling you what. I *will* tell you that because of what is inside, that golden bird will see any cage it is ever put in as being beautiful as gold . . . as long as you are the one who chose it."

He frowned thoughtfully. "It didn't want the golden cage because the king chose it."

"Exactly! Now, as to your new problem . . ."

Jeran looked down. "I know I have no right to ask, but if you can help, please do. If only for the people counting on me."

The fox smiled. So typically Jeran. He had no idea of his own worth. "Alright then. Here is what you do. It is the same situation, really. The golden horse has refused any owner. All those who have possessed him have wanted him only because his mane sheds golden threads. But as long as the heart is greedy, the threads are useless."

"That poor horse." Jeran frowned. "I almost don't want to give him to that greedy old king. He figures if the bird is gone, he needs more money."

"The bird is useless to him for the same reason, actually. Anyway, what you need to do is find the horse and put the plain bridle on him. You have to ride him out of the stable and the guards will not notice. Once you are outside the walls, you will be safe."

He nodded. "Right. I'll try not to mess this one up." He smiled as the fox snorted softly and wandered off. He supposed good faeries and helpful spirits came in all shapes and sizes.

When the sun finally set, he was not very far from the next kingdom. He stopped to set up camp and sat down with his back against a tree. He wasn't very tired. He was hopeful. He had no idea what Michaela's curse was, but he was fairly sure she was only able to roam at night. He hoped she would come to him again. He wanted to see her more than anything.

An hour passed, then two. It was dark, and he was hungry. Regretfully, he began to make something to eat. He guessed Michaela wasn't able to find him now, just like she hadn't on those other nights on the road. He finished his dinner and got to his feet to go put the scraps out for the animals. As he was straightening, he heard a sound.

He turned quickly but only just in time to have someone plow into him and take them both down to the ground. When the dust settled, he found himself on his back in the dirt with a familiar female sprawled over him. Despite the moment, he smiled. "Hi, Michaela."

She cleared her throat. "Hi, Jeran." She carefully pushed herself up into a sitting position and then realized she was pinning him down. She blushed and scrambled off him. "I'm so sorry! I was hurrying to see you and tripped over some pesky little animal."

He propped himself up on his elbow, content now that she was back with him. "I didn't mind. I was wishing to see you, and I guess I got my wish." He sat up fully and looked at her sadly as she sat beside him. "I messed up, Michaela. I'm so sorry."

"Messed up?" She frowned. "How?" She listened as he told her about the bird and wished she could reassure him that what he had done was actually a good thing. "You're still working hard, though. And you befriended the bird. That's the first important thing."

"What else do I have to do?" he asked simply. He reached out and framed her face gently. "I want to take you home with me, Michaela. We could run my father's farm together. In the morning, the orchards are always so beautiful. You could help me work the fields, or work in the house, or whatever you wanted. We could have a family ourselves, to pass the farm to when we're old."

Tears slid down her cheeks, and her lips trembled. It was a dream. A wonderful dream. He was offering her the most basic and simple of lives, something she wanted more than anything. "I can't cook," she whispered.

He smiled and brushed her tears away, not noticing how dark they were against her skin. "That's okay. I can." He moved closer and his hands framed her face. "May I kiss you now?"

In an answer, she slid her arms around his neck and drew him closer. She rose up slightly to press her lips to his. He tasted like dreams. Like a dream she had waited so long to find. "I love you," she whispered softly.

He trembled slightly and caught her closer as he bent his head and deepened the kiss. In this he knew exactly what he was doing. The knowledge was inside his mind and stamped in his heart. Because it was Michaela, he knew everything. Her taste, like golden strawberries, went through him powerfully. Desire tightened his body in a rush.

She shuddered as the kiss went even deeper and her body awakened with wild passion. She eagerly met the kiss headlong, her tongue tangling with his as he darted it into her mouth. She was too hot, her skin feeling too sensitive. More. She needed more of him. She couldn't get enough. She had been waiting so long for him.

She made a startled sound as he suddenly scooped her up onto his lap. The sound turned to a soft whimper as he pressed his lips to her shoulder and nudged aside the edge of her bodice strap. She almost couldn't breathe; her laces felt too tight. Her breasts ached for his touch and she wanted to beg him to touch her.

"I think I should stop." Even as he said it, he was rushing his hungry mouth over the upper curves of her breasts. He had been right from the beginning. What was there between them was more than powerful; it was downright *explosive*. It took a considerable amount of willpower to not tumble her onto the grass and drive her as crazy as he felt.

"Don't, please." She caught him closer, her fingers digging into his shoulders. She felt the light edge of his teeth scrape over her sensitive skin, and her nipples tightened in a rush, sending ricochets of pleasure through her body. "Jeran."

He lifted his head carefully and drew her closer, holding her tightly until he could get a grip on himself. "Not here," he told her, a slight rasp in his voice that thrilled her. "It's not safe, and you deserve better."

"Do not," she said against his shoulder.

"You do, too. And, besides, it'd probably be uncomfortable with rocks and sticks poking us, and we'd both get filthy."

She sighed. "Do you have to be so practical?" She lifted her head, wryly resigned to discovering she wanted him to the point of frustration but unable to help that same frustration. "If I took off my clothes and wrapped myself around you like a coat, would you be able to stop?"

His purple eyes turned almost black and raw hunger for her moved in his gaze. "No," he told her softly. "But I'd hope you would be willing to wait until we're married."

She made a soft sound of frustration and got off his lap. "What if it doesn't happen? What if you can't save me, Jeran?"

"I will." There was no hesitation in his voice. "You know how important gold is to other people?" When she nodded, he cupped her cheek. "Well, that's what you are worth to me. You're worth *more* than gold. You're everything. I love you, you know that."

She found a smile even though it trembled. His ironic use of words was not lost on her. "I know." She wrapped her arms around him and held on tight for a moment. "I trust you, Jeran. I know you'll save me. And when this is all over, we'll go back to your farm and give your daddy grandchildren to dote on so he has a reason to live a long time."

He smiled and held her closer. "It's a deal."

CHAPTER THREE

Jeran awoke the following morning to a dead campfire and the dawn sliding over his face. He carefully sat up and looked around, a bit puzzled as to where he was and what he was doing there. Memory returned with the sound of a bird calling, and he scrubbed his hands over his eyes swiftly.

Michaela had left him around midnight over his protests. He knew she couldn't stay but he had at least wanted her to know that he wanted her to be with him. He had wanted to kiss her again but he hadn't trusted himself to stop.

All he could do was keep on going. With a little sigh, he got to his feet and cleaned up his campfire. It took only a short amount of time until the area looked as if it had never been disturbed. He got something to eat out of his bag and munched on it as he began to walk down the road toward the next kingdom.

A shiver went down his back suddenly as he hit the main road and left the forest. It was possible to see for quite a distance, and when he glanced to the north, he could see the outline of a dark and forbidding castle.

It was black and gray, and the sky was dark above it. It was clearly a cursed place, and malevolent energy seethed around every tower. He felt a chill just looking at it. It was scary to think that somewhere, someone had done something to be cursed, whether it was earned or not. Worse still was the tiny smidgen of fear in his heart that he might have to go there himself.

He stopped dead in his tracks and stared at the castle. Maybe Michaela was a member of the castle. Maybe she was one of the servants and she was cursed by proxy. If the entire place was cursed, then she was an innocent bystander. His heart firmed. If that was the case, he would storm the walls until he found her. She belonged to him, damn it.

"You know," the fox said conversationally as he materialized at his side, "your simple-mindedness is a good thing sometimes."

Jeran looked down. "How so?"

"It makes you more possessive." He smiled. "And when you know something is yours, you will fight for it." There was, for a moment, sadness in his eyes. "Many a man with a complicated mind or personality would envy you. They have to learn the hard way to fight for love."

"Like you?" Jeran asked softly.

"Ah, there is that surprising astuteness!" He shook his head. "Never mind about me. This is about you." He pulled a rolled up piece of paper from out of thin air and placed it at Jeran's feet. "This is a contract. It is a binding document. When you free Michaela, you both need to sign it."

Jeran picked up the paper and studied it. He couldn't read a single word as it was in a language he did not know. "What is it for?"

The fox smiled. "When you and Michaela are together, you will be able to read it. I will pick it up once it is signed. Good luck, Jeran."

Jeran frowned and watched the fox wander off. More curious than alarmed, he tucked the contract away safely in his bag and continued down the road toward the kingdom where the golden horse was located. Plain bridle, he told himself over and over again. Don't be stupid!

It was evening by the time he found himself outside the castle. This time he didn't think the guards would be stupid enough to let him in on the premise of drawing. He put down his backpack and began to pace back and forth as he thought.

Something tickled his leg. He glanced down absently and realized that some of the feathers from the golden bird had gotten stuck to his bag. He picked them up and studied them intently. Crossing his fingers, he blew hard and sent them flying through the air at the guards.

"Hey, are those golden feathers?" one asked his partner as he watched the items in question flutter past.

"Quick, grab 'em!" The other made a grab, but the feathers were fast enough to get beyond his reach.

While the two guards chased after the feathers, Jeran quickly shot forward and snuck around the gate and into the courtyard. His heart pounded in his chest, and his palms were slick with sweat from nerves. As quietly and stealthily as he could, he made his way to the stables where he was sure the golden horse was held.

The stables were warm and dry as he entered, and he spotted the horse immediately. It had a stall all of its own. It was an average sized beast with a white coat and a mane and tail of pure golden strands. He hesitantly approached as the horse watched him warily.

When he was a foot away, the horse stepped forward and sniffed at him. It liked whatever it smelled, since it snorted and butted against his chest. He let out the breath he was holding and rubbed a hand between the horse's ears. "Good boy," he said softly.

He swiftly looked around and spotted the plain bridle. His nose wrinkled. It was plain material, but it was covered in gaudy accessories. Annoyed, he took off the excess decoration. "You don't need diamonds on a bridle," he muttered. "It would hurt the horse's skin!" He dropped the valuable gems on the floor where they bounced uselessly.

The golden horse nodded its head as if in agreement, and he swiftly slipped the bridle on and adjusted the bit expertly. Not worrying about a saddle, he went to swing onto the horse's back when he saw the bandage wrapped around its ankle. He stopped and knelt to look. The golden horse had hurt itself somehow, and the wound was only just mending.

He *knew* he was breaking the rules he was under, but riding a horse when it was wounded was one of the cruelest things he could think of. He had medicines in his backpack. Maybe he could sneak out and back in as easily as he had the first time.

Before he could move, the stable doors flew open and guards surged in with weapons drawn. He ducked as the guards lunged forward, but to his surprise, the golden horse gave a furious whinny and planted itself in front of him, stopping the guards cold. "Wow," he said softly, shocked. "Thank you."

"Let's take him to the king," one guard muttered. "If we harm him, the horse will attack us."

And so, much to his dismay, Jeran once more found himself escorted to the king. The entire castle was nonplussed, however, for the golden horse followed him the entire way and right into the throne room. "Get that horse out!" the prime minister ordered.

"We can't," the guard said apologetically.

The horse, happily nibbling on Jeran's hair, snorted softly. Jeran felt his cheeks heat slightly. "I'm sorry," he said apologetically. "Your neighbor told me to get the horse in exchange for a bird I need."

"Damn it!" The king was more resigned than annoyed. "Not again! He's always after this horse!" He studied Jeran intently. He could not doubt that the young man was good at heart and a decent person. Not when the golden horse was so visibly smitten with him. The horse had hated all of them and had turned to black the instant any touched it. Jeran had a hand on the horse's neck and it remained gold.

He made his decision. "Here is what I shall do. I will give you the horse if you will fetch me the princess from the neighboring kingdom. Her father gave her to me in marriage, but I have yet to retrieve her. The kingdom is cursed, and I cannot enter. You, however, could."

Jeran's stomach flipped. "Can't I opt for the community service option?"

"No. Fetch me my bride, and I will give you the horse."

He sighed. "Okay." Reluctantly, he turned and left the throne room.

The horse was forced to stay behind. As it watched him go, its coat and mane turned to black as it laid down sadly in despair. It would not sleep nor eat until its true master returned.

Jeran retrieved his backpack, and morosely headed into the forest to find a place to camp since it was dark. It took an hour before he found a hidden pathway between some bushes. He curiously followed it as it wound around scenery until he heard the sound of water. It sounded like a waterfall.

As he rounded the edge of thick trees, he beheld what he sought. It came out of a tall cliff and fell into a pond that drained via a small stream. Judging by the steam, it was a hot spring of sorts. He thought of a bath and was delighted as he put down his bag. Belatedly, he heard soft singing, and his eyes went to the waterfall. His eyes widened even as the singing stopped abruptly.

Michaela. Michaela was bathing under the waterfall, and she was gloriously naked. His entire body heated, and desire knotted his muscles. Her eyes were wide as she stared at him, and he couldn't stop himself from hungrily devouring her with his eyes. It suddenly dawned on him what he was doing, and he quickly ducked around a tree. "Uh, hi, Michaela."

"Hi, Jeran." She ducked behind the waterfall, arms around herself. Her entire body was flushed and not from the hot spring. The single encompassing look he had given her out of his beautiful, purple eyes had been more potent than a thousand compliments from other men. It took considerable willpower to not go wrap herself around him and bring him into the spring with her.

"Sorry for peeking. I didn't realize." He kept his back turned, even though his hands were fists at his side to keep from going to her and snatching her up in his arms. If what he felt for her was even marginally like what people felt for money, then he was beginning to understand what the greedy people of the world went through.

"It's okay." She dried herself swiftly and yanked on her clothes. "I guess since you're here, you didn't get the horse."

"I couldn't ride it, not when it was wounded." He sighed. "And now this king wants me to fetch his bride from the cursed kingdom."

Temper sparked in her eyes. Like hell she was any man's bride but Jeran's! She had never been engaged to that greedy bastard. Her father had sold her in exchange for land, but before she could be taken away, the kingdom had been cursed! "I see." She kept her voice neutral as she walked over to where Jeran waited.

"You sound angry." He guessed it was safe and turned around as she reached him. He couldn't stop himself from reaching out and gently cupping her cheek in his hand. Her skin was so wonderfully soft. If the rest of her was as soft as she looked, he was going to be addicted. Heck, he already was. "What's wrong?" he asked softly.

"The princess doesn't want the king." She crossed her arms in agitation. "She was sold by her father for land. All she wanted was to fall in love, and then that happened. I guess either someone took pity on her, or was mad at her father, but the kingdom ended up cursed until she could find a man to love. A man whose heart was as pure as gold."

He studied her face. "You're from the kingdom."

"Yes," she whispered, her eyes closing. "And you're a man whose heart is as pure as gold."

"Then the curse has to stay." He framed her face as her head came up in shock. "I love you, Michaela, not some princess. We'll find another way to break the curse. I don't care if I'm the only man she can love. I only want *your* love."

Tears slid down her cheeks as she turned her face helplessly into his hand. She couldn't tell him. She couldn't tell him what she was without the curse binding her voice. "I love you!" she whispered fiercely. She threw her arms around him. "Remember that! I loved you the minute I saw you!"

"Good. Because I loved you too." He eased her back and bent his head to take her lips with his. He kept the kiss tender at first, but the taste of her seared his nerves with delight, and he caught her closer.

She trembled as the kiss deepened, and she buried her fingers in his hair. She wanted him so terribly! A low moan echoed from her throat as his hands slid down to cup her breast and rub sensuously. Pleasure radiated through her entire body. "Jeran," she whimpered softly as he released her lips to taste the skin of her throat. She prayed to every god she knew that he wouldn't stop this time.

He drew her closer, wanting to feel all of her curves pressed to his body. A shudder went through him, and he eased back to study her face with a hunger he couldn't fight. She was so perfect that he couldn't believe she was his. "Michaela."

"Don't you dare stop," she whispered huskily. "Or I'll do something drastic."

"We have to." It took considerable willpower to release her and let his hands rest on her hips. "I want us to be married first."

She dropped her head onto his shoulder. "Fine, let's go find a preacher and get married. Like *now*. Curse or no curse, I'm going to be your wife if it's the last thing I ever do!" She shot him a fierce look. "I've never known a man who was so perfect for me. I've been offered kingdoms and fortunes, but it means *nothing* compared to that simple life you offer. I've dreamed of such a thing my entire life!"

He caught her closer again and buried his face in her hair. "The minute the curse is lifted, we're getting married," he promised. "I want to return home with you as my bride." He eased back again and smiled. "Then we can go on a honeymoon and lock the doors behind us."

She leaned up to kiss him hard. "Good!" She released him with a sigh and walked a step away. "Do you know how to break the curse?"

"Not yet. Do you?"

"Yes." She looked at him. "You must go to the princess' room and call her by name. She will wake only for a man with a heart of gold. Once she wakes, you must take her from the palace. Once she is away, the curse will break."

He frowned. "I'll go right back in for you, Michaela. I promise. I won't leave without you."

"I know." She smiled. "But I'm sure everything will be fine. I believe in you." She leaned up to kiss him again, lingering over his taste and the way it felt to have his arms around her. He made her feel safe and cherished. She was doted on by her kingdom, but she had never felt loved until she had looked into Jeran's purple eyes and seen his love for *who* she was, not *what* she was. "If you hadn't met me," she asked, "would you have wanted the princess?"

"I don't know." He smiled. "If she's like you, sure."

"And what if I was a princess and not some simple farm girl?" She held her breath. It was as close to telling him the truth as she could without being silenced.

He rolled his eyes. "Michaela, I love *you*. Your wit and your kindness, your humor and your strength. I love all the funny little quirks that make you up, including the way you chew on your nails when you're nervous."

"I do not!" She belatedly realized she was indeed nibbling on her nails and swiftly put her hands behind her back. "So, even if I was a rich girl, you would want me?"

He pulled her snuggly against him for the sheer torture of feeling her curves. "Michaela," his voice was tender with amusement, "I want you right now. You could be ugly, and I'd want you. I don't care what you're wearing, or how much you own. Let's look at it this way. If you *were* a princess, would you stop loving me? I'm just a farm boy."

"Of course not!" She was indignant. "Any woman worth her salt, let alone a princess, would be willing to be your bride simply because of who you are." He poked her nose gently and she had to sigh with a smile. "Okay. You made your point." She leaned up to kiss him again, but his taste was so tempting that she lingered longer than she intended.

His hands tightened for a moment before he set her away firmly. "Be good."

"But you make it so tempting to be bad," she complained. Obligingly, and feeling wonderfully desired, she moved back a few steps. "I should be going anyway. You need rest." She hesitated, wanting to kiss him good night, but knowing that they were both at the edges of their control. "Good night," she whispered, then turned and fled into the trees.

He let out a long breath and looked longingly at the hot spring. He was beginning to wish it was icy cold. He had been observing all kinds of animals in mating season his entire life, and for the first time he was beginning to understand why it was always such a frantic time. If he didn't get his hands on Michaela soon, he was going to go crazy.

A thought occurred to him and he realized he had no ring for her. He went swiftly hunting through the trees until he had found the perfect piece of wood. He took it back with him and got out his knife from his backpack. He would just make her a ring. One that was completely and uniquely hers.

It was mid-morning the next day before he was heading back onto the road. He had stayed up late to finish the ring and so had slept late as well. Now, as he stood facing the gloomy kingdom in the distance, he felt the beginnings of nerves all over again. There was so much riding on this!

Firming his heart, he started walking. It was evening before he entered the domain of the kingdom, and he knew the instant he had. The land went from lush and green to dead and brown. The sky went from blue to malevolent gray. Dangerous power seethed like shadows around the towers and around the base of the walls.

All the farmlands had been cursed as well. Everyone in the kingdom had been cursed. He saw the extent of the curse as he walked. People were unconscious wherever they had been working last. Even the animals had been affected.

Letting out a careful breath, he continued toward the castle even though it was steadily growing darker. There was no way he was going to camp out in this place. He was going to break the curse, find Michaela, and get the hell away. The princess would just have to go with them and deal with the king herself.

The castle gates hung partially open. He carefully pushed them apart and walked inside. It was even gloomier and more dangerous inside the courtyard. He had no idea where to look for the princess, but as he studied the surrounding turrets and towers, he noticed that the energy was the worst around one particularly high tower.

He took a deep breath and entered the castle proper to head toward the tower. He was nervous again. If he was the one who could wake the princess, then she might wake and fall for him or something. He didn't want to hurt her feelings, but he was in love with Michaela. Maybe whoever had cursed the kingdom had accounted for that. He hoped so.

The guards outside the tower had fallen in front of the door, and he gingerly stepped over them to enter. He slowly climbed the stairs, listening to his steps echo hollowly off the brick walls. When he reached the closed door, he took another deep breath and braced himself. Slowly and carefully he pushed the door open.

The tower was a bedroom. It was decorated the way he imagined any princess' bedroom would be, with elaborate furniture and little charms and baubles. The bed was a big four poster with gauzy curtains. Through them he could just make out the form of the princess. Something was familiar about her, and he went still in shock.

Dropping his backpack, he rushed to the side of the bed and pulled back the curtains. His eyes widened and his throat closed. He could not speak. *Michaela*. It was Michaela that lay before him, her face as serene as a tranquil pool. Unlike the times he had seen her before, her hair was not black. It was gold. It was the pure rich color of gold. She wore a white dress edged in gold trim and there was a golden pendant around her throat. His Michaela was the princess. Her words of the night before made much more sense now, and the reasons why she had never been able to speak of the curse short of how to break it.

His eyes ran over her face eagerly. She looked precisely the same to him. Only her hair color had changed, and he thought that this was as beautiful as her black hair. She deserved so much more than a simple farm boy, he thought, gently reaching out a hand to touch her cheek, but in her own words she had said she loved him and wanted the life he offered. He was going to hold her to it.

He leaned down until their lips were a breath apart. "Michaela," he said softly. "Wake up. I'm here now."

Her lashes fluttered and slowly lifted. Delight filled him as he saw that her eyes were the same black pools as always, still scattered with golden flecks. His golden princess. He had always seen her as such even before knowing it was literally true. Her lips slowly curved, and she lifted her hands to frame his face. "Hi, Jeran," she said huskily.

"Hi, Michaela." He kissed her softly and then simply gathered her close in his arms. "I don't deserve a princess," he said softly.

"That's okay," she said just as softly, holding him tight. "I'm a farm girl at heart." She reluctantly released him and let him pull her to her feet. With a touch of defiance, she removed her pendant and chucked it out the window. "I refuse to wear that again!"

He thought of the golden bird and its golden cage, and the golden horse and its golden bridle. He could only smile, thinking of the ring he had made her. "Let's get out of here." He took her hand and laced their fingers together tightly.

They raced down the tower stairs together and back through the palace. As soon as they broke through the gates and into the surrounding city, there was a crack of thunder across the sky. He swiftly ducked down and pulled her with him around a corner to safety. Both watched the castle pensively as the clouds writhed and seethed.

Then, suddenly, the clouds were gone. The energy lifted and the storm went away. The malevolence in the land went away as well, and all around where they stood, they could see the people beginning to stir. The curse was gone. On a laugh of joy, she leapt into his arms and held onto him fiercely. "I knew you'd save me!"

He swung her in a wild circle and caught her as close as he could. "Of course. You promised to marry me, remember? I'm holding you to that." He lifted her hand and reached into his pocket to draw out the ring he had carved. "It's not gold," he told her as he slid it over her finger.

Her eyes filled with tears. "It looks like gold to me," she whispered, treasuring this small thing he had made more than she had ever treasured anything else. He had made it for her alone, and it fit perfectly. Nothing could be more valuable in her eyes.

CHAPTER FOUR

Because the city was waking, neither Jeran nor Michaela wanted to stay there for long. They wanted to get somewhere beyond the kingdom to where they would be free. The minute it was discovered that she was gone and the curse was lifted, there would be a massive search party sent out.

As they attempted to sneak through the back of the city, he remarked, "I don't think your father will be happy."

"No, really?" she muttered. "He sold me!"

"I wouldn't mind giving him a piece of my mind about that," he muttered in return. He caught movement out the corner of his eye and turned quickly. He put her behind him protectively. She was so vividly obvious with her white dress and golden hair that anyone who saw her would recognize her.

To their surprise, they found themselves looking at an old man standing in the doorway of a brightly lit inn. He was looking at them curiously, his iridescent blue eyes oddly youthful and ancient all at the same time. He began to smile. "Come on in, children."

Jeran and Michaela exchanged a quick look. "Sir," Michaela said very slowly, "you know who I am, right?"

He chuckled softly. "You are this young man's bride, are you not?" He winked at her.

She immediately brightened. "Of course!" She held onto Jeran's hand tightly as he followed the old man into the inn. It felt so odd to her to be awake and walking freely. She had been allowed to roam at night, but she had always felt as if there was a ball and chain attached to her ankle.

The old man escorted them to a large room on the third floor and offered the key to Jeran. "Here you are, my boy. If you want a bite to eat, just ring the bell, and I will have someone send something on up."

"Thank you for your generosity," Jeran said as he put the key in his pocket. The old man walked away, and he ushered Michaela into the room and shut the door behind her. His shoulders relaxed and he let out a long breath. "We lucked out, didn't we? Umph!"

He staggered and lost his balance, falling onto the ground with a thump as Michaela literally launched herself into his arms. Desire roared through him in a cheerful wave as he stared at her caging him to the carpet. Her golden hair tumbled around her shoulders and spilled forward to brush against his skin. "I understand now," he murmured.

"Understand what?" She hadn't been intending to knock him flat, but she wasn't arguing. She felt like the most cherished being in the world if his arms were around her. Her pulse pounded eagerly, and her lips tingled with the hunger to feel his again. She was *not* taking no for an answer tonight. Not when he was hers at last.

"Greedy people." He lifted a hand and threaded his fingers through her hair. "I see now why they covet their gold so deeply. I'd kill anyone who took you from me." His other hand curved around her waist and tested the resilience of her soft flesh. The fabric of her dress was silk, and he found himself thinking it wasn't as soft as her skin. "It doesn't suit you."

She lowered her lashes, knowing precisely how his mind had wandered. "Then take it off me," she offered, her voice husky with invitation. "I want to be your wife, Jeran."

"But you aren't, not yet." He stared longingly at the curve of her breasts where they were gently revealed by the low cut of her bodice. He wanted to press his lips there and taste her heartbeat. He wanted to know every secret she possessed, but he would be *damned* if he broke his promise. "You deserve to be wed first."

She made a sound of frustration and got to her feet. "Because I'm a princess?" she asked scathingly.

He shot to his feet and caught her wrist to yank her into his arms. "Because I love you!" he shouted. "Because you're special simply by being you! You deserve to have the wedding of your dreams and everything you've ever wanted!"

"All I want is you!" She pressed against him and lifted her hands to bury her fingers in his hair. She rose on her toes and eagerly covered his mouth with hers, kissing him with all the frustration and pent up desire she felt. His taste alone sent a shudder through her body. She *craved* him.

His control snapped and he jerked her even tighter against him as he returned the kiss ravenously. He couldn't get enough of her flavor, and he curled his tongue around hers demandingly. It didn't seem to matter anymore. Nothing mattered but making her his. He tumbled her down onto the floor, not even realizing the bed was right beside them. "Michaela," he said roughly, pressing his lips to her throat.

"I will *kill* you if you stop!" She dug her fingers into his shirt and thrilled at how it felt to have his weight pressing her to the floor. "I'll go out of my mind if you don't touch me."

"Nothing could stop me." He shifted his weight so that he was beside her and began to unlace her dress with trembling fingers. It fell open with a soft rustle of sound, and his breath wedged in his chest as he stared at her. Her breasts were impossibly perfect to him, and the sight of them hidden behind a gold lace bra was more tempting than water after thirst. "You're so beautiful."

"You're noticing now?" She shivered as his finger curved down the outside of her breast and sent ripples of pleasure through her nerves. "You saw me naked."

"Just a glimpse." He drew her up to a sitting position and took a swift breath as her hair spilled down over her shoulders and nearly hid her figure from sight. "But this is much, much better. Now I can touch you."

Her only response was a soft moan as he bent his head and nuzzled between her hair, seeking the curve of her breast. When he found it, his lips trailed soft kisses over every curve as if memorizing her. His free hand lifted and curved around her other breast, his palm rubbing the nipple and making her voice splinter with a soft cry. "Jeran . . ."

"How am I doing?" he asked huskily. He felt addicted to the flavor of her skin and greedily closed his lips around the hardened nipple that begged for his touch. She tasted like strawberries everywhere and the lace in his way frustrated him. "I'm still learning," he said against her skin. His teeth scraped lightly.

She shuddered and reached behind herself for something, anything, to anchor herself. "If there's a test," she managed to whimper as his lips suckled at her strongly, "then you'll pass it!" She couldn't breathe, could barely think. Her entire body seemed to be throbbing with need. "Take your time later!" Her back arched helplessly as he tugged her bra aside and his lips were suddenly on her bare skin.

Her hand found his backpack and she curled her hand into it to ground herself. Something inside was sharp, however, and sliced her finger. The pain was shocking enough to break her out of the sensual haze clouding her brain. "Ouch!"

His head came up swiftly. "What? What's wrong?" He saw the little line of blood on her finger and swiftly brought her hand to his lips and kissed the wound. "What did you hit?"

"I don't know." She forgot the pain as she felt his tongue touching the cut and soothing it. Her breath hitched. "It was in your backpack."

He kept a firm hold on her finger with his to stop the bleeding and used his free hand to drag the bag closer. It was hard to concentrate on anything other than the half-naked woman beside him. His body was hard and hot with desire for her. Nothing short of her injury would have stopped him. "There shouldn't be anything sharp in here. The knife is closed."

The scroll the fox had given him was sticking out of the top and the edge of the paper glinted in the lamplight. He immediately realized what had happened. "You cut yourself on the paper."

"Oh." She curled her free hand around the back of his neck. "Well, if that's all . . ." She groaned in frustration as he pulled out the scroll and began to open it. "Read later! Ooh, damn you, Jeran Windwalker!" She blinked as he held the scroll in front of her face. "What?"

"This." His voice was warm with love. "It was given to me by a, er, friend. I couldn't read it before, but he assured me that when you were with me, I would be able to. He was right. Read what it says, Michaela."

She muttered under her breath and took the scroll from him. "Alright!" With a sigh she began to read, "'This contract is a binding and legal document that can and will be Enforced to the highest degree. This document is to certify that the signees below, Michaela Sandstorm and Jeran Windwalker, are hereby lawfully married and as such are entitled . . .'" Her voice broke off, and she stared at the scroll. "What!"

He took it from her with a smile. "That's the important part, but it also goes on to verify that I rescued you, and what I did to be with you. So, by signing it, we're married." He waved it in front of her face. "Willing to wait long enough to sign this? Provided you still want this farm boy."

"Give me a damn pen." She grabbed the backpack and dug in it until she found a pen he used for inking his art. "I want my farm boy!" she said, aggrieved. "My whole problem is that I want my farm boy until I'm insane, and I'm madly in love with him, and he keeps stalling!"

His grin felt like it could split his face. "That's odd. Because he seems to be equally insane for his princess and just as madly in love with her." He watched her sign the contract and then took it from her to sign as well. "You're my wife now, Michaela Windwalker. No one can dispute that."

"Good!" She took the contract and chucked it over her shoulder before throwing herself against him and leaning up to kiss him with a hunger that had not dimmed once. "Mine now," she muttered as she began to unlace his tunic as swiftly as her trembling fingers would let her. "My husband."

"Always." He scooped her up into his arms and rolled to his feet. His fingers were trembling just as much as he carried her to the bed. Desire. Need. Hunger. Love. There was no word big enough for the emotions churning inside him as he laid her down on the soft white sheets. "I love you."

She smiled up at him. "Promise?" She held up her pinky to him.

He linked their pinkies together. "Promise." His heart so full it might burst, he shrugged out of his tunic and tossed it to the side. With as much care as he could, he went to work on the rest of her dress so he could remove it entirely.

She trembled as his fingers brushed against her skin and sent little sparks along her nerves. "You could always just rip it. I never cared for it anyway."

"But then you'll have nothing to wear." He lowered his head to begin trailing hungry kisses over her breasts. He dropped the dress to the side, then removed her bra and dropped it as well. "I'm the only one who can see you naked."

"Good point." She lifted her hands and ran them slowly over his chest, thrilling at how his skin felt and delighted by every muscle. "Little Jeran. I bet the girls back home were always around when you were hard at work and shirtless."

He lifted his head, surprised. "Yes, they were. How did you know?"

She wound her arms around him on a happy laugh. "Promise me you'll never change." She pressed her lips to his shoulder to taste his skin. Her farm boy worked for a living and it showed. She remembered her sight of him when she had accidentally walked in on him about to bathe, and she realized that it was far more thrilling now that he was close at hand. "You're so beautiful."

"I am not." He curved a hand around her hip and tugged her closer as he bent his head to taste her silken skin. She was wonderfully soft! "My brothers are more handsome."

"I don't believe you." Her eyes met his, and she smiled. "And even if I did, I'd still prefer you."

There was a long silence as tension grew between them. Then, even as he was reaching for her, she was reaching for him, and their mouths met and fused in a wild kiss. With a hunger he no longer needed to fight, he began to run his hands over every inch of her he could. His hands were shaking, but he couldn't stop it. He needed her more than air.

She could only grab onto his shoulders for an anchor as his hands set fires wherever they went. Her body was hot and restless, craving more and more from him. Her skin was so sensitive that just the brush of his hair was enough to drive her wild. "Jeran, hurry!" she pleaded as his mouth moved voraciously over her breasts.

He barely heard her. He swiftly stripped her panties off and leaned back to stare at her naked body. His breath came in and stayed there as he stared at her. "There's supposed to be no such thing as perfection," he whispered huskily. "Apparently they never met you."

She couldn't form a response to that before he was kissing her again, his mouth as hungry as his hands and nearly as rough. It sent her senses spinning dizzily with delight, and she curled her fingers into his hair to keep him close.

She nearly stopped breathing entirely as she felt his hand curving over the sensitive skin of her inner thigh. She felt as if she was waiting forever before his fingers finally slid upward and cupped the heart of her. The touch was electrifying, and pleasure ricocheted through her entire system. It still wasn't enough.

He shuddered as he felt the slick heat of her against his fingers. He petted her, watching her face with rapt attention as her body twisted in his arms. Her eyes opened to meet his, and the golden flecks were more dominant than the black, as if they had gone liquid gold with her emotions.

He couldn't stand it anymore and released her long enough to strip off the rest of his clothes. If he waited any longer to claim her as his, he was sure he would go out of his mind. He returned quickly to her side and kissed her deeply, unable to resist the lure of her swollen lips. "I won't hurt you, I promise!"

She closed her eyes in sheer delight as his weight settled over her. "It never crossed my mind," she said huskily. She curled her long legs around his hips instinctively, wanting to bind him to her in every way possible. Her fingers slid up to clench in his hair and she held him close as their mouths met again.

The feel of his hard arousal pressing against her made her hold her breath. As she felt him slowly sinking into her, stretching her thoroughly, her breath unraveled on a soft moan that was pleasure and pain combined. She wanted him deeper but she felt too stretched. Her nails bit into his shoulders. "Jeran," she whimpered.

"I'm sorry." He shuddered as he raced his lips over her face. She was like hot silk beneath him, and she fit him like a glove. His breath hissed out as she clenched her muscles around him. "Don't do that," he managed to say. "I don't want to hurt you!"

"Then do something!" She clenched her nails into his shoulders and twisted beneath him. The pain was nothing. She needed him inside her to ease the unbearable pressure that made her feel as if she would be broken in two. "Please!"

A tortured sound rumbled in his chest as he gathered her close and surged into her in a single stroke. Electricity seemed to race through his body and some inner pain he hadn't been able to define seemed to ease at last. "Michaela." He caught her tears with his lips and kissed her hungrily. "I'm sorry."

"It doesn't hurt." Her words became a soft gasp as his hips flexed, and he began to slowly stroke in and out of her. The terrible tension rushed back in wildly until she was clinging onto him with all her strength, her breaths nothing but soft sobs against his shoulder as she tried to cope with the ceaseless pleasure.

Something inside seemed to shatter, and ecstasy rushed over her like a wave. She would have cried out but he was kissing her again, and he took her cry into himself. Her muscles caressed him with every pulse of her pleasure, and he shuddered as he buried himself to the hilt and let the ecstasy consume him as it had her.

His lips met hers again with a touch of desperation, needing to know her taste again. For the first time in his life, he finally felt as if he had found where he belonged. He gathered her close and held her with all his strength as he buried his face in her hair. She was his wife in every sense of the word. He would be damned if he let someone take her away.

She let out a soft sigh and burrowed closer against her husband's warmth. "Jeran?" she murmured.

"Hmm?"

"You were right, damn it." She smiled and rubbed her cheek against his shoulder. "It was worth waiting for."

He smiled. "It was very worth waiting for." He snuggled her closer, and the feel of her soft and fragrant skin was enough to make his body tighten with fresh desire. He softly tasted the curve of her ear and listened to her breath hitch. "Guess what?"

"What?" Her eyes closed slightly as she felt her body heat with a suddenness that took her breath.

"I want you again."

On a contented sigh, she drew him closer. "Good. I want you again, too."

They were awakened the following morning by a loud knock on the door. "Open in the name of the king!" a man bellowed.

"Can I refuse in the name of the princess?" Jeran shouted back in annoyance.

Michaela dissolved into giggles as she tumbled off his chest and watched him look for his pants. She fell over onto her back on a happy sigh and stretched largely. She felt incredible. Her body felt as if it was singing, and she ached in some places. The ache was just as delightful, and it was a constant reminder that she had claimed her husband as thoroughly as he had claimed her.

He pulled his tunic on and looked at where she was lying on the bed with the sunlight flowing over her soft skin. His heart swelled in his chest as he crossed to her and leaned down to kiss her softly. "Good morning, by the way," he said huskily.

"Good morning." She threaded her fingers through his thick, lavender hair happily. Another pounding on the door made her groan. "Damn it! I'll kill them all!" She scrambled out of the bed and scooped up her clothes to begin getting dressed. As soon as her laces were firmly tied, she raked her hands through her hair. "Do I look like I was just tumbling in a bed?"

He studied her and the way she looked wonderfully rumpled and flushed as if she had indeed just been tumbling over a bed with him. "Yes," he said, his voice slightly rough. "Makes me want to tumble you more."

"Good." She stalked over to open the door. "My husband and I," she said with a slight edge to her voice, "were sleeping."

The handful of guards standing outside the door in full armor and weaponry could only stare at her in shock. Then, with a slight scramble, every single one dropped to their knees quickly. "P-princess Michaela!" the leader stammered. "My lady, we did not realize you were in there as well!"

She rolled her eyes. "Well, where *else* would I be? You knew Jeran was the one who saved everyone, so obviously I had to be with him!"

The guards fidgeted nervously, clearly uncomfortable with envisioning their princess in any man's bed. "Your father presumed you had run away," the leader said. "He demanded we find you, and we thought to start with the one who broke the curse."

She looked at Jeran. "Let's go see the old man and get it over with. If he thinks I'm marrying that bastard next door, he has another think coming."

Jeran had to grin. His princess had the mouth of any farm girl. He loved her all the more for it. "As my lady commands," he said, loving amusement in his voice. He took her hand and their fingers laced together tightly as they left the room and edged carefully around the guards. "Do they always do that?" he asked her in a whisper.

"Yes," she whispered back. "It's annoying! Do you have the scroll?"

"It's in my pocket." He wasn't letting it out of his sight and didn't trust himself to not lose his backpack, which was itself over his shoulder.

The entire place seemed vastly different without the curse hovering over it, but there was something about it that he still didn't like. After a moment of thought, he realized that he didn't like it because he was viewing it through Michaela's eyes and was able to see it for the golden cage it was.

The king was clearly displeased as he stared at his daughter. "Where is your royal pendant?" he demanded.

"I threw it away." She smiled. "I have no need of it." She held up her hand where her wooden wedding ring rested. "I'm married, Father. And as such, I will be traveling with my husband to his home."

The king stared at Jeran. "And where is your kingdom?"

He straightened his back. "I have none. I can offer Michaela nothing but my love and a simple farm life."

"Which is more than enough for her," his wife pointed out to her father. She leveled a finger in the astonished ruler's face. "I want Jeran. Nothing more, nothing less. You sold me like I was a piece of property! Even before Jeran knew I was a princess, he loved me!" She smiled with feminine smugness. "And believe me, we're *completely* married now so there's nothing you can do."

A couple of ladies-in-waiting began to giggle softly. Some of the guards had to turn away to hide grins. The king could only stare in horror. Finally, on a sigh, he sat back on his throne. "Alright. I know when I'm defeated. You are married?"

Jeran pulled out the scroll and walked forward to offer it. "It is a binding contract," he said. "And I'll fight anyone who tries to take her away from me."

The king studied the scroll and looked at the bottom. "I am to sign this as well?" When Jeran tilted his head, he indicated the blank line below the couple's names. "My name is here. It is to indicate I verify this document and the events mentioned within."

"I suppose so, then." Jeran took the scroll back once it had been signed and went back over to Michaela. "We have your blessings?" he asked the king.

The king studied the two of them, and the way Michaela seemed to glow softly with happiness as she leaned against Jeran's shoulder. He couldn't find it in his heart to be upset or angered, not when they were so obviously in love. "Yes," he finally said. "You have my blessings, provided you come back to visit with grandbabies for me to spoil."

"It's a deal!" Michaela said, then leapt into Jeran's arms happily and kissed him in front of the entire castle. All who were observing began to cheer. Jeran could only smile and hold her closer. Living with Michaela was going to be a terror, but incredibly fun. His father would adore her.

CHAPTER FIVE

The following morning found Michaela and Jeran waking up in the woods not far beyond the castle of the neighboring kingdom. They were taking their time on their way back and enjoying every minute they could together. That, and they were trying to find a way for Jeran to keep Michaela at his side, get his horse, and his bird, and get home without trouble.

"Well," she said as she washed her face in the stream they were sitting beside, "disguising me is easy once we're past this kingdom. I'll get some normal clothes and braid my hair, and no one will be any wiser *despite* my coloring."

He admired the way the sunlight filtered over her face. "Only if you let me unbraid it for you at night. I like your hair the way it is."

"So I shouldn't get it cut?" she teased.

"You better not." He leaned over to kiss her. It still sent a thrill through him, and he knew it would likely never go away. "It might make me lose my temper, and I've never done that before."

Her brows lifted. "You've never lost your temper." She winced. "I hope I'm not the target when you do. You'll probably be really scary." She thought about things. "But really, *really*, sexy."

He flushed. "Stop it." He tugged her close and rested his chin on the top of her head. "I don't even want to let that greedy king see you." He smiled. "Well, I guess that makes me greedy too."

"This is a good kind of greedy." She rested a hand over his heart and sighed softly. "So who was this friend who gave you advice before? Perhaps he can give you advice now."

"You called?" the fox asked suddenly from beside them, making her stifle a yelp, and Jeran nearly sent them both tumbling into the stream. The fox hid a smile. He adored both of them very dearly. "My apologies."

"Your friend is a talking fox?" Michaela asked her husband.

"Yes, he is." Jeran smiled and offered a cookie to the fox. "I don't suppose you can help me get home, can you? I got the last task right, didn't I?" He nuzzled his nose into Michaela's hair. "I claimed my golden princess."

"And how," she murmured.

The fox snickered and nibbled on the cookie. "Mmm. I can tell Michaela did not make these. She would have set the kitchen on fire again." He dodged when she tried to swat him. "He would have found out eventually."

She glowered. The fact that he knew her biggest mishap didn't bother her as much as that he had blabbed. "Tattletale."

Jeran just smiled. "I don't mind. I can cook for the both of us. I can do the mending too as needed."

She stuck her tongue out at him. "I can sew, thank you, and quite nicely. I can manage to take care of any mending that is needed." She ran her eyes over him. "Especially if I cause it personally." She flicked a finger at the slightly torn edge of his collar. "Sorry about that, by the way."

He grinned. "I didn't mind." If there was anything sexier than his wife pinning him to the ground and stripping him, he had yet to hear of it. He loved the bold and sassy side of her more than anything.

The fox chuckled at them both. "I can see that you are indeed well suited. I knew that you would be." Before they could call him on his near admission, he continued, "Because I like both of you, I will tell you how to get home. That contract of yours will end up being the most important part."

"You mean the extra lines for signatures?" Michaela asked.

"Precisely. You see, this contract will only show the signer their role within it. In other words, you two will see the whole thing. This king who owns the horse will see only that Jeran retrieved the golden princess. Jeran, you will need to insist the king sign the contract and give you the horse before you give him Michaela. Ask to test it out first and then pull Michaela up with you."

"I see." Jeran smiled. "Once he has signed the contract, he cannot back out. He'll think he's making a trade when he's actually just confirming my work. Are we invisible when riding the horse?" he asked curiously.

"You may as well be." The fox smiled. "Only those who are pure at heart will see you until you wish otherwise."

"That will make getting away easier," Michaela agreed. She smiled. "And I think I see what we do at the first kingdom. It's nearly the same thing. You can ask for the king to sign before you'll give him the horse, then ask for your bird, and once we have it, we can take off!"

"It almost feels like stealing," Jeran remarked.

"Well, you *do* own them, you know." The fox playfully butted against Jeran and Michaela both. "It is not stealing. It is taking back what is rightfully yours." As he was starting to walk away, he added, "Oh, and when you get to the inn to rest for the night, make sure not to buy any dead carcasses."

"Ew!" Michaela exclaimed. "Why would we?"

"Just do not do it, trust me."

Jeran's nose was as wrinkled as Michaela's. "I should hope I wouldn't buy a dead carcass." He got to his feet and reached down to draw her up as well. He frowned as he suddenly noticed the little scrapes and nicks on her hands. "Where did these come from?"

She blushed. "Well . . . It's really bad but . . ." She reached into her pocket and pulled out a slightly misshapen ring made of the same wood as her own. "I tried to make this last night after you fell asleep. It's not nearly as beautiful as the one you made."

He took the ring from her and held it up to the sunlight to see it better. It was probably one of the worst carvings he had ever seen. He loved it immediately. "It's perfect," he told her. He held it out to her. "Here. Put it on me properly."

Her face lightened with a radiant smile. "You really are something special." She took his hand and slid the ring over his ring finger slowly, delighted to discover it fit. "I was worried it would be too small."

"Looks just right to me." He threaded his fingers through her hair and leaned down to kiss her softly. "Let's go," he said softly. "And if your feet get tired, tell me. I'll carry you."

"You will not." She let out a contented sigh and leaned against his arm as they began to walk down the road. "When will you let me peek into that sketchbook of yours?"

He smiled. "Anytime you want. But you're in there too."

"What!" Her brows shot up. "Me?"

"Lots of you. They don't do you justice though."

"I'll decide that, thank you." She was secretly pleased. Her husband was probably the most incredible man in the world, she decided happily. In light of her happiness, she couldn't even really resent that darn fox for possibly having a hand in her curse.

Her happiness began to turn into trepidation as they drew closer to the castle. Jeran squeezed her hand tightly and she drew strength from him as always. Because she knew it was crucial that no one realize she wanted to be with him, she searched her memory for an idea of how a spoiled princess should act. "Quick, carry me," she told him.

"Are you hurt?" He frowned swiftly.

"No, but I want to pretend like I'm spoiled."

"Good luck with that." He tied his backpack on his hip and smiled as she climbed onto his back. He got a firm grip on her legs around her skirts so that he didn't worry she would fall and realized he enjoyed it because he could feel every one of her curves. "You're light."

"You're a smart man," she mumbled. "Never tell a woman she's heavy."

"I wouldn't mind even if you were." His stride never changed as he walked toward the castle gates, and he knew the instant the guards recognized him. They boggled at the sight of Michaela on his back and then they turned and raced into the castle.

He put Michaela down on her feet but kept her firmly behind his body as the guards fetched the king. In a whine, she demanded, "You dropped me!"

"You wouldn't stop complaining," he retorted, but it took all his willpower to resist snickering. He felt like an utter fool. As he saw the king approaching, he felt Michaela tense. "Your majesty, I retrieved the golden princess."

"So there you are, Michaela." The king glared at her. "All this trouble you caused!" She said nothing and he turned to Jeran. "Give her to me and you shall have your horse."

"Please forgive me," Jeran apologized, "but I have found myself going through quite an ordeal. I would prefer if you signed this contract verifying what I did, and gave me my horse to test, before I give the princess to you."

The king nodded. "Naturally, my boy. Let's see this contract." He took the document that was offered and read it swiftly. It stated very plainly that Jeran Windwalker had stormed a kingdom, broken a curse, and retrieved a princess. Since it was quite nicely to the point, he had no objections to signing. "Bring the horse!" he ordered the stable master standing near.

The man obeyed and led the golden horse out of the barn. Its leg was healed now, and it was wearing the plain bridle Jeran had picked. Its ears perked up as it saw Jeran, and it eagerly trotted over to butt against him. The black coat and mane turned back to gold, and it happily began to chew on his hair.

Michaela had to muffle a giggle. She couldn't help but wonder if it was just some odd quirk amongst her and her 'brethren', but they all seemed to love Jeran's hair. Perhaps because it was as soft and strong as his heart.

Her stomach fluttered lightly with desire as she watched him swing up onto the horse's back. There was something very seductive about the sight of him on horseback. It made him seem stronger and more giving and more wonderful. So much more of everything he already was. With a sense of wonder, she realized that here, truly, was the man of her dreams riding in to rescue her.

"Are you satisfied now?" the king asked, eyeing her covetously.

Jeran smiled. "I am." He walked the horse around the courtyard briefly. He kicked it lightly in the sides and it shot forward. He leaned down out of the saddle and scooped Michaela up into his arms and onto the horse before him, removing her from the king's reach.

The instant she was on the horse it was as if all three of them suddenly disappeared into thin air. Only a few of the servants could see them still, but every last person heard Michaela's delighted laughter amid the sound of thundering hooves as they took off out through the gates.

Jeran let the golden horse run at its own speed as they raced across fields and through trees. He couldn't help but grin down at Michaela as he felt her wrap her arms around his waist. "I wouldn't let you fall."

"I know." She gave a little nervous laugh. "But I'm not the best rider in the world either."

He burst into laughter. "You have no ladylike graces, do you?"

"No." She sulked. "I was feeling rebellious when the lessons were insisted on." She smiled and cuddled closer. "But that's okay. I'm sure I can learn everything I need to. I'd much rather be out playing in an orchard than sitting and sewing any day." She rubbed her cheek against him. "Your neighboring farm girls will be so disappointed, I'm sure."

"You'll win them over." He was sure of it. He looked around and began to measure the distance of the sun in the sky and the distance they still had to go to get to the last kingdom. "We should camp for the night."

"It's only the afternoon," she protested, then saw the heated look in his eyes. "Oh." It was the best she could manage. Well, who was she to argue with her husband when he had that look in his eyes?

It wasn't until much later after the sun had set and the moon was rising that she thought to ask, "Will you tell me about your brothers?" She curled more snugly against his side, content to use his cloak as a blanket. "I get the feeling that you don't like them even as you love them."

He tucked his hands under his head. "Yes," he finally said on a sigh. "You put it correctly. I love them because they're my brothers, but there are times I almost wish I could hate them. All my life they've been taking my ideas and using them as their own. I don't mind that too much, really. I suppose it's just the idea that they are willing to do such a thing."

She slowly smoothed a hand over his chest. "You said your father was ill?"

"Yes." Worry darkened his face. "I don't want him to die, Michaela. I love him more than anything except you. Even if I go home and he gives the farm to Jared or Jonah, I don't mind as long as he lives."

"You deserve the farm. You've worked so hard, Jeran." She set her chin. "He's your father, so he's not a fool. But if he does give the farm to them, then we'll go make our own and *prove* him wrong."

He smiled. "You just want to be in charge of something. It's the princess in you."

"I do not!" She tried to hold her indignation but couldn't. She smiled and held him tighter. "I think it's just that I want to be in charge of my own life and know that something belongs to me and only me."

"You have me." He rolled and tucked her protectively underneath him. "I will always be yours alone."

She smiled. "I can settle for that."

The next morning as they were getting dressed, she thought to ask, "Where will I get some normal clothes?" She fingered the silk of her dress, not wanting to put it back on. "I'd sooner go naked than wear this again."

He opened his mouth to respond when he spotted an unfamiliar bag sitting on the ground next to his backpack. He curiously knelt and opened it only to discover a set of clean clothes that looked like they might fit his slender wife. "How about these?"

She was delighted as he pulled the clothes out. There was a nice and sturdy pair of leggings with a tunic-dress and a thick cloak, all of which looked like they would be incredibly comfortable. "Oh! They're wonderful!" She held them up in front of herself. "I bet your friend did this."

He smiled. "I think so." He watched her as she changed, and his eyes lingered on the curves of her body as she did so. No matter what she wore, she was always beautiful to him. The tunic-dress reached her knees, but when she belted it around her waist, it fit precisely like it was supposed to.

"It's not a dress." She couldn't have been happier. "I always wanted to be able to wear leggings but they're a *commoner's* piece of clothing." She twirled in a delighted circle. "But now I'm a commoner too. How do I look?"

"Like a princess," he said softly, his voice tender. "You'll always be one to me."

Her eyes stung with tears for a moment. "Well, you've always looked like a prince to me, so I suppose we're going to live happily ever after." She caught her hair and began to braid it swiftly down her back. She tied the end with a piece of string and then took the hat he offered her. She pulled it onto her head at a jaunty angle. "Will I pass?"

"With flying colors." He pulled her close for a kiss before releasing her to whistle for their horse. It trotted over and stood patiently as he lifted her up before climbing up behind her. "We ought to name him," he remarked.

"Hmm." She rested against him while she thought about it. She was glad to concentrate on something. Her stomach felt a little funny now that she was in motion. She seemed slightly queasy and it was annoying. "Let's see . . . How about Coal?"

The horse snorted even as Jeran did, both with humor. "Because he isn't, or because it's an undervalued item?" he asked shrewdly.

"Both." She smiled. "Coal is the cold man's gold just as water is to someone who is thirsty, or food to a starving man or . . ."

"You to me." He kissed her softly when she looked at him in astonishment. "Don't look so surprised." He snuggled her closer against him. "Take a nap if you like. I can see you don't feel well."

"I'm not sick," she grumbled. "I never get sick." Much to her surprise, however, she was asleep within moments, lulled by Coal's steady trot and by Jeran's easy strength and warmth.

She woke to Jeran's tender kiss. With a sigh, she curled closer. "Are we home?" she asked.

"No, we're outside the kingdom." He was loathe to wake her. He had never felt as contented as he had riding across the land with her sleeping so peacefully in his arms. He was a little worried though. When they reached the crossover town, where the inns were located, he was making her go to a doctor to be sure she was fine.

"Oh." She rubbed her eyes. "I'm awake now. What should I do?"

"Make sure I don't do something stupid."

"Sounds easy enough." She straightened as they rode into the courtyard so that she wasn't reclining against him. He would need his hands free. As she looked around at the people, all she could think was that every kingdom she had ever seen was precisely the same. It was no wonder it held no appeal to her.

The guards had gone to fetch the king the instant they had recognized Jeran. The king came out into the courtyard, and the expression on his face was heavily put upon. He had reason. The golden bird, now black in color, was sitting on his head. "Windwalker!" he barked. "Take this damned bird!"

Jeran bit his lip to hide a laugh. "Yes, your majesty, as soon as we take care of things. Would you sign this?" He leaned down to offer the contract. "It's to verify what I've done. I want to make sure everything is nice and finished."

He took the contract and studied Michaela. "Your love?" he asked.

"She is." Jeran smiled.

"Ah. Well done, lad." He looked at the contract, and it read as exactly what Jeran had said it would. It stated quite plainly that he had retrieved a golden horse from the neighboring kingdom and was thusly entitled to the golden bird. "This looks perfectly fine." He signed his name on the line and handed the contract back. "Now get this bird off my head!"

Jeran laughed. "Yes, your majesty." He leaned down and plucked the bird off the king. It gave a happy squawk and turned back to gold as it began to climb all over Jeran and Michaela both. It settled down on Michaela's lap and began to make a sound that was half a purr and half a twitter.

Before anyone could say a word, Jeran, Michaela, and Coal seemed to simply vanish before everyone's eyes. The king gaped for a moment and then had to brace himself when wind was kicked up around him as the horse and its riders took off. He suddenly burst into laughter. "Well, I suppose I earned that." They did say, after all, that the greedy men in the world were the ones who always ended up the poorest.

Jeran and Michaela waited to camp that night until they were sure they were well away from the kingdom. Not that they didn't trust the king, but they both wouldn't rest peacefully until they were home where they belonged. In fact, they didn't rest very peacefully that night anyway, because the golden bird seemed to like Michaela's hair and spent the entire night chewing on her braid.

By the time they were riding into the small town a few days later, Michaela was resigned to the bird that was attached to the end of her braid. "Maybe I'll make a new fashion style," she muttered.

Jeran, as had become habit over the last few days, plucked the bird off her braid and put it in his backpack. Eventually it would get free and zero in on her braid again, but he hardly blamed it. His fingers often got stuck to her hair too. "How are you feeling?" he asked her, hugging her lightly. She had gotten sick a few hours after setting out that morning and his worry was increased for it.

"Better now." She sighed as he stopped in front of the inn and dismounted. "Tomorrow morning before we leave, I'll go see the doctor in town and see if he has any herbs that will help. I think it's just the stress. It's been a very trying time, you know."

"I know. But when we get home we can relax all we want to." He smiled at her. "Once we know my father is fine, we can go on a trip somewhere to be alone, just the two of us. Where do you want to go?" He lifted her down easily and held her while she found her balance.

"The ocean," she decided. "I've never been there before. It's not far is it?"

"No, not far at all." He gave a coin to the stable boy standing near. and he led Coal off to the stables for the night. With an arm around Michaela's waist, Jeran headed into the inn. As ever, it was quiet and peaceful and he knew they would both be able to rest peacefully despite the golden bird—now named Lead because she was so heavy—potentially chewing on their hair.

In fact, they did sleep peacefully. They were woken rather abruptly, however, by the sounds of shouting outside. Jeran sleepily got out of bed and walked over to look out the window. There was a group of people gathered around the hanging tree. "Just a hanging," he said on a yawn.

"Ugh." Michaela raked a hand through her hair. "It's too early for that."

"Apparently not." He frowned, wondering why something seemed odd. He looked closer at the crowd and suddenly went pale. He recognized the two standing under the tree with nooses around their necks. "Oh my god! It's my brothers!"

"What?" She scrambled over to him. "Oh dear!" She could tell they were his brothers; they were just as handsome as her husband. But, as she had thought, she much preferred Jeran's shorter height and softer smile. His brothers looked hard around the edges. "What are we going to do?"

"I have to find out what they did." He gave her a swift kiss and grabbed his clothes to get dressed. "Go to the doctor and get checked over. I'll see if I can save their carcasses. It wouldn't be the first time."

She felt a sudden chill as she watched him hurry out of the room. The fox's words danced in her ears, and she couldn't shake the feeling that something terrible was about to occur. She took a deep breath and got dressed. She was going to the doctor and then she was getting her husband and they were leaving.

He hurried down to the square and over to the hanging tree. "Hey what's going on?" he asked the owner of the other inn. "What's the commotion about?"

The owner was happy to explain, "These two idiots racked up an immense bill at my inn with all their drinking and partying. In an effort to pay for it, they tried to steal from some other patrons. Then they got into a fight over it. They *deserve* to hang."

He sighed. It figured, didn't it? "What if I paid their bill and for the damages from the fight? They're my brothers," he said apologetically. "I have to help them even when I'm ashamed of them."

The owner studied him briefly. "Sure." He smiled. "You seem like a good young man. If you can cover the bill, I'll consider it a done deal."

Jonah and Jared, overhearing this, were so relieved that they nearly collapsed and hung themselves regardless. When they were cut loose and freed, they immediately hugged Jeran enthusiastically. "Jeran!" Jonah exclaimed. "We knew we could count on you!"

Jeran pushed them both away with a sigh. "Of course. I can't believe you!" he scolded. "Partying for *months* while Father and I worried about you!" He sat down on a bench near the well while his brothers got themselves drinks. "I had to go looking for the golden bird myself!"

Jared snorted. "I still say it was nothing but a joke."

Jeran smiled. "No, it wasn't." He opened his backpack and Lead instantly stuck her head out with an indignant squawk. "I found the bird. And I also got a golden horse." He pointed to where Coal was waiting near the inn. His smile brightened as he saw Michaela hurrying toward him, and he completely missed the sudden looks of greed that crossed his brothers' faces. "And I found a golden princess."

Michaela was nearly giddy with delight. She wasn't sick. She was pregnant. She was going to have Jeran's child. She couldn't wait to tell him. "Jeran!" She threw herself into his arms with a happy laugh. "I have wonderful news!"

"Tell me later, Michaela." He smiled at her. "As long as you're not sick, that's all that matters."

"Not at all." She smiled. "You sure I can't tell you now?" When he shook his head, she sighed. "Oh alright." She turned to Jonah and Jared, and her smile dimmed. She was well acquainted with the greed in mankind. She recognized it instantly inside them. "Hello. I'm Jeran's wife, Michaela."

The two brothers looked at her, their eyes lingering on her hair and figure with a greed that churned her stomach. It also made Jeran's eyes narrow sharply. He would tolerate a lot from his brothers, but never this. If they didn't treat Michaela respectfully, he would kick them both. "Brothers," he said warningly.

"Aw, it's no big deal!" Jonah took his shoulders with a big smile. "We're family."

Before he could say anything in response, Jonah had suddenly given him a shove. "Jeran!" Michaela shouted, lunging forward as her husband staggered backwards and began to fall into the well. "*Jeran*!" She fell to her knees beside the well but could see nothing. All she could hear was a resounding splash. There was no other sound.

Tearing pain welled up inside her and she leapt to her feet as black tears streamed down her cheeks. "You bastards!" she shouted. She came up short as Jared suddenly aimed a dagger at her. Ice hardened her heart and her hands moved protectively to touch her stomach.

"Here's the deal," Jared said. "You don't tell anyone the truth, and we'll let you pick which one of us you marry. Open your pretty mouth and we'll kill you."

Her eyes narrowed. A part of her didn't want to live without Jeran. She wouldn't have cared about her fate if she hadn't been carrying their child. If it was the last thing she ever did, she would have her child and let his or her appearance prove who her true husband was. "I won't say anything at all," she said, her tone almost emotionless. "I will remain silent until the day I die."

"Good. No one likes a talkative woman anyway." Jonah caught her wrist and dragged her along behind him toward the golden horse. His smile swiftly turned to a frown as he realized the horse had inexplicably turned to black. "What the hell?" He looked at Michaela. "What is that?"

She said nothing. Jared could only shrug; he had his arms around Lead to keep her from flying away. She was still a golden bird, but the feathers she shed were turning to black as they fell to the ground. Neither brother knew what to make of it. Still, they didn't care. They had all the evidence they needed to prove to their father that they had done the deed and not Jeran.

As they rode away, Michaela looked back toward the well where Jeran had fallen. Grief nearly tore her in two. Why should someone so kind be the one who suffered? She had found him only to lose him. Turning her gaze toward the sun in the distance, she closed her eyes. Her hair almost immediately turned from gold to black and startled both Jared and Jonah. It made no sense to them in the slightest. Oh well. A princess was a princess.

CHAPTER SIX

The well in the town was not shallow. It was quite deep and never ran dry. As such, when Jeran landed at the bottom, he landed purely in water. He did not strike the bottom and die as his brothers had intended. Instead, he was able to swim to the surface and tread water. His first emotion was grief. He had never imagined his brothers would betray him like that.

Then, finally, he began to become mad. For the first time in his life, he became truly enraged. He'd had enough. For his whole life, his brothers had been taking away anything that was his that they wanted. He would be *damned* if they took Michaela.

The end of a rope fell down into the water beside him. He looked up toward the top of the well to see the fox perched on the edge and staring down at him. "Get out of there," the fox ordered. "Damn it, boy! I told you not to buy dead carcasses!"

"Be more specific next time!" he retorted as he began to climb out. "Next time say 'don't rescue your brothers even though you love them, because they're assholes and will try to kill you!'"

The fox's brows shot up. "Well." It was the best he could think to say. "So, little Jeran finally loses his temper."

He began to wring water out of his clothes with short and jerky motions. "Yes, he does. I'm through with being nice." His eyes swept over the area quickly. It was easy to tell that his brothers had taken off with Michaela, as well as Coal and Lead. "Michaela is *my* wife." The idea of how much pain she must be in was just more fuel on the fire of his anger. "Any more good advice?"

The fox thought about it. "Do not tuck your thumb under your fingers."

It made little sense but he committed it to memory. "Done." With a controlled sort of energy, he picked up his backpack and slung it over his shoulder. He was going home, and he was claiming what was rightfully his: Michaela and the farm. Michaela most of all.

Julian was still alive when Jonah and Jared returned home. He was vastly puzzled by their sudden appearance and the young woman they brought with them, but he was alive. He was also deeply saddened. He was sure now that Jeran would never come home. A part of him wanted to die right there but he resisted the feeling. Charon couldn't ferry him down the Styx just yet. "Well, who is she?" he asked Jonah.

"We rescued her from a dragon." Jonah was thinking as fast as he could. "She's a princess. We haven't decided who she's going to marry. And, uh, the horse is the fastest in the land. Oh, and we got the bird too. So you need to give us the farm now."

Julian studied Michaela and the sadness that seemed to be etched into her face. The girl was grieving, of that he was sure. "What is your name, my dear?" When there was no response, his frown deepened. "Are you well?"

"She's a mute," Jared blurted. "All the trauma, you know. Go into the kitchen and make dinner, Michaela. We'll take care of the horse and bird."

She shot him a scathing look before stalking into the kitchen. She was actually glad now that she couldn't cook. She hoped they both got sick and died!

Julian wasn't an idiot. He knew as he looked at his plate of dinner that she had no domestic talent. He didn't doubt that she was a princess, but he highly doubted that she would have been destined to marry any man that was as domestically inept as she was. And there was no denying that his eldest two sons were indeed inept.

He bided his time for a day, watching her intently while Jonah and Jared argued over who was more worthy to inherit. The more he watched her, the more sure he was that she was far better suited to his missing son. He was also more and more sure that she was pregnant. She was sick every morning, and she often touched her stomach when no one was watching. He remembered his wife vividly even after many years, and how she, too, had acted.

Finally, one morning two days later, he made his way to the living room where Michaela sat at the window and stared across the land. She spent nearly all her time there, the very sad looking golden bird beside her. The bird shed only black feathers. The horse would not eat. Michaela had the look of a woman grieving for someone she loved. Julian was beginning to suspect there was more here than met the eye.

"It's a pity you're mute," he said as he sat beside her. "I'd love to hear about your family." When she said nothing, he leaned back in his chair with a sigh. "Well, I'll tell you about mine if you'd like." He watched her face intently. "I actually have a third son, you know. He was my greatest pride. So kind you had to love him."

She closed her eyes helplessly as tears welled up inside. She cried every night and yet it seemed there were more tears still to cry. On a broken sound, she buried her face in her hands. She couldn't bear to hear about Jeran, not when her soul seemed to be dying without him.

Julian sighed softly and reached out to take her hands. He lifted her left and looked at the ring resting there. He knew the workmanship instantly. "Michaela," he said gently, "I know you are Jeran's wife." He smiled when her head swung toward him. "I'm old, daughter. My eyes have seen a lot. It was Jeran who rescued you, wasn't it?"

She said nothing. She couldn't. She feared for the life of her child, and for Julian. She did not doubt Jonah or Jared's ruthlessness. They would kill their father if they thought it would assist their own greed.

Julian didn't need her to say a word. He could see it in her eyes. "Where is Jeran, Michaela? What did Jonah and Julian do?" That they were at fault, he did not doubt. How else would they have come to be with Michaela and not Jeran? "How many lies have they told?"

"Lies? What lies?" Jared laughed but the sound was strained as he and Jonah stood in the doorway. They were terrified. Ever since they had woken that morning they had felt as if their world, which had seemed so perfect, was about to fall apart. "What are you telling him, Michaela?"

"You said she was mute," Julian noted as he got to his feet.

"She can write," Jonah defended their lies. He walked over to put a hand on her shoulder in what looked like a friendly gesture but his fingers bit in cruelly and she flinched at the pain. "Are you smearing our good names, princess? For shame."

As Julian stared at his two sons, he wondered how he could have been so blind for so long. How had he fooled himself into thinking they were good at heart? How long had Jeran been covering for them, protecting them at the cost of his own happiness? "Where is your brother?" he asked, his voice very quiet.

"What? Jeran?" Jared laughed, but his palms were sweating. "We never saw him at all."

"I see." Julian's hands curled into fists. "And how did you come to find Michaela again?"

"We, er, stormed a tower and fought a wizard, right, Jared?" Jonah was beginning to sweat as well, and he carefully took a step away from Michaela.

"You said it was a dragon." Fury tightened Julian's face. "Where is Jeran? I am not the senile fool you believe me to be! Michaela wears a ring that Jeran made, and when I mentioned him to her, it drove her to tears! What did you do to your brother? Have I raised murderers?"

"Shut up, old man!" Jonah gave him a shove and sent him sprawling on the floor. "Do you have any idea how tired we are of Jeran? It's always Jeran this, Jeran that! We proved we were better than him, didn't we? He's a simple, stupid boy!"

"Yeah," came Jeran's voice behind them, "but he was smart enough to learn to swim."

Everyone turned sharply to see him standing in the open doorway. Michaela couldn't breathe. Almost afraid to believe, she took a slow step toward him. He held out his hands to her, and on a sob, she rushed forward and leapt into his arms. "Jeran! You're alive!" She clung onto him desperately, shaking with her emotions. "I thought you were dead!" she sobbed into his shoulder.

"I'm alive." He held her fiercely for a moment, his face buried in her hair, and then he lifted his head and looked his brothers dead in the eye. They both swallowed hard and went white as they looked at Michaela and saw that her hair was turning to gold from black like the night sky taken over by the light of the sun.

"Th-that's impossible!" Jared managed to say.

Jeran held Michaela with one arm and used his other hand to pull the scroll out of his pocket. He held it out to his father without taking his eyes from his brothers. "This contract is a verification of what has occurred. It states Michaela is my wife, and it details the deeds I have done to win her and to claim the golden bird. It is signed by three kings, one of which is Michaela's own father. The horse in the corral is also mine; I'm sure it will be just as glad to see me as my wife is."

Julian put the scroll down without looking at it. He did not doubt Jeran in the slightest. His son did not lie. He was stunned at the transformation in him, however. He had never seen Jeran sounding so forceful. He had never thought he would see it, but he was seeing it then: his little boy was a grown man. "What happened to delay your return?"

"Jonah and Jared were set to be hung for thievery and for causing immense damages in a fight. Both of these events were caused, by the way, by their racking up immense bills at an inn over the course of these last few months." Jeran spotted the bruises on Michaela's shoulder and his fury grew. "I paid their debts and freed them. In return, they shoved me into a well. A friend helped me get out."

Jonah gave a shaky laugh. He had never before been afraid of Jeran, but right then he was positively terrified of him. Jeran in a fury was something he hoped to hell he never saw again. "Father, how can you believe him?"

"Because he has never lied to me." Julian got to his feet painfully and braced himself against the table. "And because he has brought the evidence of it to me." He looked at Michaela. "What say you?"

"Everything Jeran says is true." She lifted her chin. "I am Princess Michaela of the Sandstorm Kingdom. Jeran is my husband. These two," she gestured at Jared and Jonah, "threatened to kill me if I told the truth."

"I see." He was unsurprised by the news.

Jeran set Michaela gently aside and walked toward his brothers. "You know," he said, "all my life you two have taken what was mine and claimed it for your own. It didn't bother me because I loved you. If you had never taken Michaela from me, I would have never bothered to tell the truth. I would have let you lie about why you were delayed and never have corrected you. I'm through, now, with being nice to you."

Jared snorted even though his knees wanted to knock. "What? Are you going to hurt us? You can't even hit properly."

Jeran lifted his hands and curled them into fists. Then he smiled and untucked his thumb from under his fingers. He tightened his fists and suddenly struck. The first punch knocked Jared on his ass. The second sent Jonah onto the floor beside him. "Try me," he challenged. "Get up and I'll hit you again."

Holding his bleeding nose, Jonah said, "That's okay. We'll stay down here."

Jeran turned and gave a laugh as Michaela leapt into his arms. This time he caught her and they didn't go tumbling to the floor as usual. Holding her tightly, he looked at his father. "What do you have to say, Father? I went out into the world. I found the golden bird. I found the woman of my dreams. She's pregnant with my child."

Michaela gave a gasp. "Darn it, Jeran! I was going to tell you! How'd you know?"

He smiled at her. "I'm not completely stupid. I asked the doctor before I left. He was happy to tell me." His hands slid down to rest possessively over her stomach. She was carrying his child. Now that the anger was gone, he was able to savor the joy he felt inside. He couldn't wait to take her away somewhere private so he could study her body. He knew it wouldn't be any different, but he wanted to be able to memorize every change.

Julian eased down onto a chair with a sigh and a smile. "So I see," he murmured. "Even if you had not found all of that, what you showed me when you walked in here would have convinced me. The farm is yours, Jeran. You are the only one I would trust with it. I can die peacefully now."

"Don't you dare," Michaela scolded him. "You have a grandchild to meet and spoil." She turned her head as the other two Windwalker males got to their feet and walked silently out of the house. "I suppose there is no helping some people."

Jeran smiled as Lead flew over to land on his shoulder. "I'm not going to think about them anymore. I've got what I want."

"The farm?" Julian asked.

"Nope." He scooped Michaela up into his arms and spun her in a quick and giddy circle. "My golden princess."

Julian smiled. He supposed it would be worth living long enough to meet his grandchild, particularly if he or she turned out to be just like Jeran. Mirage needed more Jerans to help balance out the greed of mankind.

Jeran and Michaela left on their honeymoon trip the following morning. Julian assured them both that he would still be alive when they returned, and they were able to set out with light hearts. Coal seemed to be sensitive to Michaela's rebellious stomach, and the ride was far smoother than ever.

Content, Michaela snuggled against Jeran. "You were so incredible yesterday," she murmured.

"I was angry," he said. "I'm so sorry, Michaela, for being so stupid."

"That's okay." She suddenly straightened in surprise as she saw a familiar figure in the road ahead. "Isn't that the fox who has been helping us?"

Jeran looked and smiled. "It is." He stopped Coal and then dismounted and helped Michaela down as well. Together they walked down the road to kneel in front of the little fox. Jeran pulled a cookie out of his bag to offer it, as was his way. "Hello again."

"Ooh. Oatmeal." The fox nibbled happily on his treat. "Hello indeed. I am very proud, Jeran. You have learned a very important lesson."

"Don't buy dead carcasses?" Michaela asked innocently.

"Don't put golden birds in golden cages?" Jeran asked.

"Or, when rescuing a princess, make sure to get her completely out of the kingdom before her daddy sends the army to knock on the door?" his wife offered.

"It was more like a pounding than a knocking."

The fox began to laugh. "You know the real lesson."

Jeran smiled. "I do. And I promise I'll try to work harder at knowing when to be nice and when to let someone take the punishment they deserve."

"Something tells me I'm still going to be the one disciplining our child," Michaela countered dryly.

He grinned at her. "Probably." He turned back to the chuckling fox. "I owe you," he said seriously. "Name it, and it is yours."

The fox thought about it. "I ask only that you take the contract that has been signed and give it to a Good Faerie to be delivered to Earth. She will know where to take it precisely. As I cannot take it myself, I must ask this of you."

"Consider it done." Jeran was silent for a moment, and then he said softly, "I hope you find her again, someday." At the startled look shot toward him, he smiled. "The woman that you loved that you learned, too late, to fight for."

The fox was equally silent and then smiled as well. "Thank you, Jeran." With a little bow, he turned and began walking down the road away from them. Within twenty feet he seemed to simply disappear into the sunshine as if dissolving into the light.

"Who do you think he is, or was?" Michaela asked softly.

"I don't know." Jeran stood and pulled her up to her feet as well. "But I think he'll find what we did. What everyone is looking for."

"What's that?"

"Happily ever after."

EPILOGUE

On Earth, there was a place known as 3rd District. Running directly under the district was the River Styx. It was through this mystical river that the world, Mirage, was connected. Resting over the entrance to the Styx was a building in 3rd District known as the Enforcers Headquarters. It was where the company known as the Enforcers was stationed from. They protected and defended the people of the District and also guarded the entrance to the Styx.

Rhianna Taber was one of the two co-owners and founders of Enforcers. She took care of the daily running of the place and the day-to-day business. Her partner took care of the larger processes and business deals they got into. His wife was their resident hacker.

It was for this reason that Rhianna studied the humorous image of herself depicted as a cherub, which was now her wallpaper, and turned to call at the adjoining office, "Riku! Keep Rayna out of my computer, damn it! And tell Taylor to stop being a smartass!"

Her response was a chuckle from her partner and a giggle from his wife. Taylor was another Enforcer, the husband of Rayna's sister, and he was also a game artist and writer. Only he would have drawn such a spectacular image. He and his wife had only just returned from their honeymoon, and they were already jumping into things. Taylor was only a part-timer, since he had his own business, but Gwyn and Rayna worked as a team to uncover truth. They also worked as a team to pester Rhianna.

She just sighed. She was surrounded by smartasses, but she hardly minded. She could be just as bad, if not worse. Why did like always call to like?

She turned to pick up her cup of tea when there was a shimmer, and a scroll appeared on her desk with a flicker of golden light. The scent of peaches seemed to drift gently up from the scroll, and her heart stilled inside her chest.

"Rhi?" Her partner was standing in the doorway watching her. "Is something wrong?"

"No, not at all." She picked up the scroll and carefully blocked Eric from her mind. She covered her emotions with a smile, but even she knew it was strained at the corners. "It's just a contract from Mirage. See?" She held it up. "There's a note on it. 'One for the records.'"

"Ah." Eric shut the door and looked down at the slender woman beside him. Her face was pensive. As she was Truth, he knew, then, that Rhianna had lied blatantly to his face. He just wished he knew why; she had never directly lied to him before, and the knowledge was painful.

In her office, Rhianna traced a finger lightly over the handwritten notes on the scroll. She had never forgotten that handwriting. Forcing it out of her mind, she turned and slid the completed contract into its own folder in her desk drawer. There was no use dwelling on the past, especially at her age.

There was far too much past to dwell on.

Status: File Complete

Analysis: A heart of gold can turn even the simplest of gifts into a treasure fit for a princess.

Folder One

CAMERON

CHAPTER ONE

There were two agencies in New York that companies fought over to have as their designer for ads and campaigns. One company, owned by the Lucino family, was known as Just In Time, Inc. The other company, owned by the Dease family, was known as Two More Minutes, Corp.

Two More Minutes had been formed by Viktor Dease and built from the ground up. When he had married, his wife, Lorcana, had become a partial shareholder. When they had been blessed with two sons, one two years older than the other, Viktor had been wise enough to leave the future of the company in their hands.

Though not very old, Viktor knew not to tempt fate. He wrote up a will and a trust for the company. When each of his sons turned twenty-one, they would each inherit fifty percent of the company, thereby making them the sole proprietors. Kenneth and Cameron, though children, loved their father's company and looked forward to being in charge.

Viktor acted not a moment too soon. Five years later, when Kenneth was twelve and Cameron was ten, Viktor was diagnosed with lung cancer. He passed away within another two years. Lorcana stepped in to take over the company, and though she led well enough, the employees found her to be an unpleasant woman to work with, and for, in equal doses. There wasn't a single person who didn't look forward to the day the two boys would grow up and take over . . .

(One year ago . . .)

The boardroom had filled to the brim with executives. It was a power meeting to let one of the larger conglomerates in New York look for a new and unique style to promote their product. They had considered going to Just In Time, but something had swayed them toward Two More Minutes.

Part of the reason might have been because the company was owned half by Lorcana Dease and the other half by her son Kenneth Dease. He had inherited his share of the company on his twenty-first birthday weeks before and had already made sweeping changes that seemed to be nearly revolutionizing the company.

His younger brother, Cameron, was only nineteen. He would not inherit his share until he turned twenty-one as well. The not-yet-partner put in partial time at the company and the rest into college where he swiftly blazed through Business and Advertising degrees. Same as his brother before, he would complete his Bachelor's degrees within the coming year, marking a scant three years to completion; both brothers had graduated high school early as well. Though neither liked hearing 'prodigy' applied to them, they certainly ticked off the right boxes to earn the moniker.

The power meeting had both brothers present and sitting in to observe and participate. The executives of the other company, be they male or female, couldn't have been happier with that arrangement. The brothers looked as alike as two peas in a pod, nearly resembling twins. Both had shimmering platinum hair and oddly piercing gray-green eyes, and a terribly devastating beauty.

Lorcana disdained sharing the spotlight with anyone, even her own sons, and dictated everything they did—up to and including the way they dressed. Or rather, she only now dictated to Cameron. She had lost control over Kenneth weeks before.

The elder brother had taken swift advantage of the newfound freedom. While Cameron still had to wear his hair short and dress in a suit that did not do a bit of justice to his form, Kenneth had already started letting his hair grow and had immediately taken advantage of the family tailor to get a properly fitted suit for himself. He finally looked, and felt, like he belonged in the room.

Anger and upset churned in Lorcana. As soon as Cameron turned twenty-one, the company would be completely out of her control. It was *her* company. She had married for it. She had given birth to two sons for it when she had hardly been able to stand her husband's touch. Now she would lose it all.

Still, her smile stayed calm and competent as she explained the campaign that she had displayed on the room's large computer screen. "As you can see, we went with a family theme."

One of the executives drummed his fingers lightly on the top of the table. "It's an old campaign."

Kenneth and Cameron exchanged a quick look. They had tried telling their mother that the company wanted a fresh and modern look, but she was so set in her ways she could be the poster woman for cement retail. Their idea, or rather,

Cameron's idea, had been to get away from the family theme and move toward the young couple one. Their generation would start buying now, and continue buying through the future—if they could be hooked.

Cameron cleared his throat. "If I may, we do also have a second idea for you to view."

"Cameron, don't speak until spoken to," Lorcana told him gently, but with an edge to the tone.

He seethed and swallowed his anger. Kenneth just narrowed his eyes fractionally and slid the portfolio holding Cameron's concepts across the table. One of the company's graphic designers had mocked them up on the down low to keep Lorcana from knowing. "Then allow me to speak for him. He and I have both discussed this idea. I find it to be a fresh new look that I believe you'll like." He ignored the warning look his mother shot his direction.

The executives gathered in closer to look at the offer, and they all began to smile. "This is just what we wanted," one female said. "Something new and young. Something to bring in all those 'just legal' youths that want to have a romantic dinner."

Lorcana stopped behind her sons' chairs as the conversation lifted in an excited buzz. "We'll discuss this later," she warned quietly, her tone icy, and she continued down the line.

Cameron and Kenneth exchanged another look. "For the love of god," Kenneth muttered, "hurry and grow up, Cameron, before one or both of us commits murder."

(Present)

The 3rd District. On the surface, it was a place where the sights and sounds of old America could be seen. Only the insides of the buildings had been modernized. All the exteriors stood the same as they had for over two thousand years. The only modern building in the District was the Enforcers' Headquarters, the company owned by Rhianna Taber and Eric Mason.

Enforcers protected the people of the 3rd District and had for centuries. Some people felt fairly sure Rhianna and Eric had run it for centuries too, but there were few who worried over it. The 3rd District was a place where magic gathered. No child born there was born without a special gift.

It did not, however, make the people less 'human'—though some assuredly had less than human blood. They loved and they hated. They cried and they laughed. Eric Mason stood on the doorstep of a small home in the middle of the District and knew that the news he bore would only bring tears. He took a quiet breath and lifted a hand to knock.

The door shortly opened by a slender young woman with surprisingly bright hair. It looked not quite orange and not quite red, and was instead an interesting combination of both that resembled rust. Her eyes glowed dark brown and filled with lively humor as she smiled at Eric. The smile turned a normally cute face into a nearly beautiful one. "Mr. Mason!" Like all residents, she knew Enforcers on sight. "Can I help you?"

He cleared his throat. "May I come in, Sarah?"

Sarah Davidson stepped back easily to let him enter. "Of course. I hope it is quick. I need to go to the airport and pick up my mother and father."

He closed his eyes and cursed mentally. "Sarah, please sit down." He opened his eyes and saw the smile on her face fade. She was young, only twenty, but she held a razor sharp intelligence paired to a nearly psychic-level of astuteness. The look on her face implied she may already know what he needed to say, so he got straight to the point. "There was an accident."

She slowly sank down to sit on the side of the couch. Her dark eyes seemed far too large for her face. "I see."

He knelt in front of her and covered her hand gently with his. "Sarah," he said quietly, "I am sorry. The entire plane went down, and there were no survivors. There was a failure in the engines that could not be avoided. Rayna and I checked and double-checked and there is no mistaking the truth. Neither of your parents survived."

She turned her gaze toward the window and then straightened her back. "At least they were together," she murmured. "They were such lovebirds. They'd have suffered without one another." She turned back to him. "The family company will fall to the shareholders, won't it?"

The Davidsons had owned a small but very profitable ad company that had worked exclusively with small businesses. It had been primarily owned by her parents, but shares had been split amongst investors. Among them was the Shaughnessy-Tavoularis Conglomerate, a company Eric knew very well indeed. "Yes," he admitted. "But there is an alternative."

"What is that?"

"Before coming here, I spoke with Mel Shaughnessy and Kalliope Tavoularis. You are the sole heir to the portion of the company owned by your parents. If you are willing to sell all of that to Mel and Kalliope, they will ensure the company is not dissolved entirely. It will continue to operate as it is, but it will be co-owned by Shaughnessy-Tavoularis."

She let out a long breath. "So, in other words, I give up the keys to the castle that is rightfully mine in order to avoid being the princess devoured by the wolves of the wilds?"

He had to smile. "I suspect Mel and his wife would resent that."

"I suspect you're right." She got to her feet and walked over to the window to stare almost blindly across the landscape. The grief would come later. She would deal with it when she could. Right then her only choice was to accept the deal being offered so generously. Enforcers, and Mel and Kalliope, had gone out of their way to try to help her. The money would support her until she got a job, and she would not endure the guilt of seeing a few dozen people lose *their* jobs. "Alright," she finally said. "What do I need to do?"

It was mostly a lot of paperwork, she discovered. Lots, and lots, and lots of paperwork. She met with Mel and Kalliope multiple times and was able to reassure herself that they would do a good job of maintaining the integrity of her parents' company.

Thankfully, the other complications of her age had been handled by Enforcers as well. At twenty, she was not yet a legal adult. The law raising the age of majority had been in place for many years, and it had eliminated the gap between eighteen and twenty-one. Enforcers had very persuasive lawyers on hand, though. Sarah, so close to being legal, was given her independence and would not need a guardian for her last year as a minor. Effective immediately, she was an adult.

But because she would not own the company, she would not receive funds from it. She also wouldn't have a guardian to help support her until she got up and running. She would need a job to help pay for her living expenses as well as any further college courses she might want to take. The sale price of the company had been *beyond* generous, but that money would not last forever, and she had too large a practical streak to waste time.

Eric helped yet again. He sent job offers her direction that he thought she might be interested in. Finally, she decided to apply for one. It was with the Dease ad company known as Two More Minutes. The position would be as receptionist and secretary to the owners. She would be doing clerical work, but at least she would be surrounded by something she loved.

The night before she was due to start working there, she found herself looking around her new apartment and realizing that she was lonely. She could no longer turn and have her parents there to share her laughter and her odd sense of humor. And, finally, she let herself grieve.

CHAPTER TWO

As Sarah got ready the morning she was due to report in to work for the first time, she stood in front of her closet and fidgeted. She had been told that she needed to be 'casually professional' but that term had such a broad interpretation. She also had the soul of an artist, so she balked at wearing anything resembling a neutral.

Aware the clock was ticking, she grabbed a soft yellow sweater and a pair of black slacks. She paired them with a pair of yellow heels, a black scarf for her hair, and some sassy silver hoop earrings. "Body armor," she decided.

Because it was getting late, she beat a hasty retreat to the kitchen, gulped down coffee, then just as quickly left the apartment and went to get her motorcycle. It was a guilty pleasure, and she knew it, but she couldn't bring herself to sell it. The gas still, barely, cost less than public transit.

She reported in twenty minutes later to the high-rise building that the Deases owned and operated from. The company only took up the highest floors of twenty through thirty; all other floors had been subleased to other companies. No other ad companies, of course.

She studied the directory and felt her amusement well. Executive Services for Two More Minutes sat all the way up on the thirtieth floor. She snorted. "So hot air *does* rise. I always wondered about that."

The other people in the elevator lobby began to laugh. Since that bank of elevators only went to the top ten floors, one man felt safe saying, "You must be the new girl. Welcome aboard. And good luck with the piranha."

"Piranha." She contemplated that as they got on the elevator. "I assume we are discussing my esteemed new boss Lorcana Dease?"

"Bingo! Give the girl a prize."

She shot him a sassy grin as they got off the elevator. "I'd rather have a cookie." She waited in bemusement for him to open the large glass doors that signaled the entrance to Executive Services. She had never understood the need that men had to leap to open doors for her. Was it the hair? She hoped it wasn't the hair; she had never really seen herself as a ginger so much as a paprika. She had a soul (artistic though it was).

As she walked around the corner, she saw a vast open space heralded by a tiny reception desk. Behind the desk sat a series of short cubicles. None reached over three feet tall. If someone sat up, they would likely resemble a gopher emerging from a golf hole. "Wow," she said. "Groundhog Day must be fabulous. If the pit sees its shadow, there's another month of piranha bites."

That made everyone start laughing. One woman with a riotous mane of curly auburn hair walked over with her hand held out. A genuinely warm and welcoming smile lit her face. "I hope you're Sarah!"

"I am indeed," Sarah agreed sagely. "Have been for twenty years, though my mother used to swear they tried to name me Penelope. Apparently I balked."

The other woman grinned. "I'm Louise Pram. We could use someone with your sense of humor around here."

Sarah took her hand and very expertly hid a subtle flinch. Her skin was so sensitive that even the nearly non-existent rasp of her associate's fingerprints felt painful. She had been dealing with it for all of her life, so she had learned to suck it up and ignore the discomfort where needed. "Nice to meet you, Louise. And I promise I packed plenty of piranha food. Hopefully the biting won't be so pronounced."

Louise smiled. "Lorcana, I presume. If we were discussing Kenneth and Cameron . . . well, if they didn't feel like my brothers, they could bite me any time and any way they want."

"And *how*," came a chorus from several voices in the pit.

Muffling a giggle, Sarah followed Louise over to the receptionist desk. It turned out to be bigger than she had initially thought. The small stature was an illusion created by the preponderance of office supplies and surplus items that had been placed everywhere. "Is this the supply office?"

Louise coughed. "No, we have a supply room."

Sarah began to test the quantities of pens on a pad of paper. Half of them didn't work despite having ink inside, and the other half were empty of ink entirely. "Mmhmm. I'd rather have pens that no one else has chewed on. At least I know where my teeth have been." She tossed out or chunked in the recycle bin what was beyond repair or out of date—one pad of paper still listed Viktor Dease as in charge—and then grabbed the nearby cart and loaded it down with the rest.

Louise watched in utter fascination. Sarah had wasted no time in wading in and taking charge. Cameron and Kenneth would absolutely *love* her. This was one person who might just have the backbone to look Lorcana in the eye and tell her 'no.' "The supply room is a closet around the corner," she offered.

"Make sure there's coffee left," someone called. "The Deases ought to be in soon."

"Will do!" Sarah gave a sassy salute and looked at Louise. "I've heard that the two males are very handsome. And your comment of earlier . . ."

"They're *gorgeous*. Almost identical, actually. Most think they're twins on first look."

She grinned. "Resident eye candy is always a welcome thing when working a desk. Do promise me that they come through often."

"Not often enough," Louise said wistfully, and then she and Sarah exchanged a look and began laughing.

"I hate my life," Cameron muttered at his brother as they walked into the building. "Scratch that. I hate my age."

"Six months," Kenneth sympathized. "In six months you'll be twenty-one. The hell will then be over."

"Hell is right!" Cameron crossed his arms and glared at the elevator panel as the cab rose steadily. "Any ideas I have need to come from you so I don't get chewed on! I can't even pick out my own clothes, talk at meetings . . . Shit, I wouldn't even be wearing a decent suit if you hadn't told Mother to jump off."

His big brother pulled an innocent face. "Well, it looks bad on the company, you see, that we all don't dress for success. She would hate to have someone think our work was as sloppy as the way she forced you to dress."

Cameron muttered something uncomplimentary under his breath toward their mother. He could not argue that he owed Kenneth a *lot*. Kenneth had taken a lot of the brunt of their mother's wrath for most of their lives, and especially over the last two years since he had taken over his rightful share. The only reason he hadn't moved out of the family home was because he *refused* to let Cameron face Lorcana alone, or be lonely.

Truthfully, Cameron and Kenneth alike had had relatively lonely lives because they had never really been able to make and keep friends. The only real friend they had made in their lives had been Louise, who had effectively adopted them as her baby brothers from the moment she had been hired. They just kept it quiet lest Lorcana decide to fire her.

And if friends had been scarce, girlfriends had been far more so. Which would have been fine if Cameron had not felt a need for a romantic or physical relationship, but he did. Thinking it, he demanded of Kenneth, "Can you get her to allow me to have a girlfriend while you're busy convincing her to not be a bitch about my clothes?"

"You've had a girlfriend."

"Sneaking around with a girl and making out in the backseat of a car is not the same as having a girlfriend," he muttered. "Call me a stupid romantic, but I want to be with a girl I can actually *date* and, you know, maybe fall in love with and marry."

Kenneth cocked his head. He, too, had felt a similar lack of companionship as his brother, but he'd had more patience to wait. Once Lorcana had been fully removed from the picture, he would start looking around as well. "So, in that vein, what kind of girl do you want?" He had his own ideas about what his brother needed. Cameron had carried heavy chains for a long time, and Kenneth thought he needed someone with serious spunk who could bring humor into his life. If he found the right girl for his brother, he would encourage it however he could.

"Hmm." Cameron contemplated things and finally grinned. "You know, I don't think I have an actual preference. I think I'll just know a girl I want when I meet her. I think I lean toward cute girls, though. Never really been interested in cover models, y'know?" He pushed open the doors to Executive Services and then came to a quick stop. "Whoa."

Kenneth stepped around him and lifted a brow. The reception desk looked unexpectedly immaculate, and a dish of candy sat at the front. "Ooh. M&Ms." He grabbed a few. "Either we're being bribed or the new girl started today. Or both."

"Okay, she's good. Did you meet her?"

"Nope. Mother did not bother with an interview; just hired her based on her resume." Kenneth glanced around and spotted the brunette in question. Technically, she was one of the graphic designers, but she served as office manager as well. Lorcana wouldn't actually hire a *real* office manager, or an actual Executive Secretary, so Louise pulled double duty without double pay—for now. "Hey, Lou! Where's the new girl? We want to introduce ourselves."

"She went to the supply room. After clearing out the mess, she discovered she had nothing but chewed up pens." Louise grinned. "She said that if the pens were to be chewed on, she'd rather it be her own teeth. She knows where they've been."

The brothers exchanged a grin. That alone promised they would like their new secretary. Cameron opened his mouth to say so when he spotted Lorcana standing in the boardroom doorway and tapping her foot impatiently. She was looking at the clock and her lips were drawn into a thin line. "I hate Mondays," he muttered. "She stores up all that ire over the weekend."

Kenneth patted his shoulder sympathetically without a word. Cameron took a quick breath to brace himself and then heard an unfamiliar female voice softly exclaim, "Wow! That's a good gene cookie dough!"

"Cookie dough? Don't you mean gene pool?" one of the other employees asked curiously.

The first voice giggled. "Cookie dough. You know. Cookie cutter cuties."

Cameron forgot his mother. He instantly turned and headed toward the direction of the voice. He could feel himself grinning, and that alone was a first because he almost never grinned on Mondays. He swung around the corner near the supply room and saw one of the graphic designers standing with a young woman he didn't recognize.

He knew, however, that he would never be able to mistake her for anyone else. Her hair was *amazing*. It was straight as a pin and fell to her waist in a fascinating shade of rusty orange. She looked average in height, probably only five or six inches shorter than his five-ten, and her figure seemed subtle rather than curvy. No one would call her pretty, necessarily, but she was cute as hell. He adored her on sight. "We have munchkins in the office!" he proclaimed.

Sarah turned with a grin. "I do not represent the Lollipop Kids, Mr. Lion. And I traded Toto in for a less frilly bike. That basket was just too 1940s."

The other nearly added in his own wise comment when he looked closer at Cameron. There was something in the younger man's eyes and corner of his smile that served as a red flag. Covering a grin, the man edged back until he could sneak away without notice. Had their new princess caught the eye of one of their favorite princes? It was too fabulous for words.

Cameron didn't notice the exit as he held out a hand. "Cameron Dease."

"Sarah Davidson." She took his hand and braced herself, but to her surprise, he didn't hold her hand too tightly. His fingers were strong and warm, and the little rough edges didn't hurt. If anything, it felt quite enjoyable. Her shoulders relaxed. "I'm your new slave labor. I mean receptionist. Shoot. I always do that."

"You mean we didn't make the fine print small enough?" He lifted her hand to his lips and bowed with all the courtly grace of a prince from hundreds of years before. He simply couldn't resist. Something about her just seemed to demand old-world manners. "Welcome to the company, Sarah." He grinned. "A baking company, so to speak."

She smiled impishly. "Well, I could have called you bad boy bookends." The words came out of their own will, which was just as well because she had mostly forgotten how to speak. Her heart had gone into such overdrive, it seemed a miracle she could string any words together. Louise, damn her hide, had lied. Gorgeous? Cameron Dease was sin incarnate.

"Let's go back to cookies." He eased closer without conscious thought and flattened a hand on the wall behind her head to effectively cut off the rest of the office. "And speaking of cookies, have lunch with me."

"I probably shouldn't. You're my boss."

"Not for six months, I'm not. I'm someone who *might* ask you to do something, but I'm not your boss. And even if I was, you can be friends with your boss around here. It's a family company. Informality is cool." His eyes searched her face. She had the most impossibly kissable mouth he had ever seen. He would start with friendship and then see if she wanted more as badly as he was beginning to think he did. "Just lunch," he coaxed.

"Might as well give in," Kenneth offered dryly from their side. "He won't give up until you do."

She blinked and then looked back and forth between them. "I thought cloning humans was illegal."

He laughed. "Okay, we're keeping you." He reached over and caught Cameron's collar. "Leave her alone."

"I'll cry," Cameron warned as he was dragged away. "Please?"

She sighed as if she had been asked to climb Mt. Everest with a toothpick, but she grinned to take the sting out of it. "Oh all right." She couldn't help but like him. He looked like someone in need of some serious laughter. She would just have to ignore her hormones. Seriously, where had they been since puberty? She had been sure they would sleep until she was eighty.

When she returned to her desk, several other coworkers pounced on her. "You go girl!" Louise said. She started to clap Sarah on the shoulder but caught her faint wince and arrested the movement. Poor thing probably had a sunburn. "You didn't mention you had a fishing pole with you."

"I didn't catch him," Sarah protested on a laugh. "We're just having lunch. He's just being friendly. He looks in some serious need of a friend."

"We wouldn't argue that," a man admitted. "Lorcana works Cameron like a slave. Until he's twenty-one or married, he's firmly under her control. It's the worst thing ever, especially because Cameron and Kenneth are incredible at what they do and Lorcana is only so-so."

Sarah tilted her head. "We have permission to call them by their names?"

Louise grinned. "Kenneth made the decision. He said that there were too many Deases running around. If we're going to curse at them, he would rather know precisely who we're cursing at."

"I'm going to like it here," Sarah decided mischievously.

Inside the meeting room, Lorcana glared at Cameron as he and Kenneth walked in. "You kept me waiting." She hated to be kept waiting by anyone, even her own child. Perhaps especially by her own child. Her sons looked far too much like her dead husband for her own tastes.

Cameron felt himself bristle slightly. All the relaxation and fun he had gotten out of his meeting with Sarah seemed to fade away. "I was introducing myself to the new secretary," he told Lorcana politely but with a bite to the words. "I thought it was the proper thing to do since she'll be answering the phones and needs to know who to give messages to."

She walked over to the door and looked across the room to where Sarah had begun to get the computer up and running. Her familiarity with the machine was visible. Lorcana gave a quick nod. "She came highly recommended from Enforcers. Eric Mason himself vouched for her work integrity and skill, and Rhianna Taber had nothing but high praise for her personality. Her other professional references came from Mel Shaughnessy and Kalliope Tavoularis-Shaughnessy. It seemed a waste not to hire her."

And thank god for it, Cameron thought, but he felt more curious than ever about Sarah's history. She could claim two of the biggest companies in America as professional references? It was fascinating, especially since he knew that Enforcers usually only worked with people in 3rd District, and if she was from 3rd District then she was probably not human. He couldn't wait to ask.

"So what is this all about?" Kenneth asked his mother as he sat down beside his brother. "You indicated that this was an urgent meeting. You've come to an important decision of some sort?"

Lorcana linked her hands behind her back as she began to walk around the table. She had been thinking, and thinking, and she knew that she faced losing the company in six months. That Cameron would claim his share was inevitable. Her only hope in holding any control over him was to ensure he married a woman of her choice and blackmail him into signing a pre-nuptial agreement giving his shares to his wife. She could then have the wife sign them over to her. "I've been thinking about things," she said, "and I have decided that Cameron needs to get married."

Cameron choked on his coffee and Kenneth did likewise. "What?!" they both demanded, and loudly enough that several people outside the meeting room looked toward the doors in surprise.

"You're out of your mind!" Cameron shot to his feet. "Why should I get married? You won't even let me date!"

"You're my precious baby boy," she cooed. "I only want your happiness. To that end, I will simply have to select your bride myself. You're still under my guardianship for six months, Cameron. I just want you to be happy."

He felt slightly ill as he sat down. There was no doubt in his mind that any woman *she* picked would make him utterly miserable. She only associated with people who were just like her.

"Here's my idea," she said decisively. "I'm going to invite properly eligible women in for an interview. If they pass the first round, they will come back for a second. Once we've narrowed it down, then we'll have the perfect candidate."

Slightly green at the edges, Kenneth shifted in his seat as she continued on outlining her plans. He leaned over to his brother and murmured, "We need to find a way to stall for time. Six months. We can manage that, right?" Louder, he said, "And when will these . . . interviews, as you put it, begin?" Interviewing for a bride. The idea alone was disgusting.

She beamed. "Why, I thought I might start things up this week. There's no reason to wait. I'm sending out the notices this afternoon!"

Cameron groaned and dropped his head onto the table. "I'm so screwed," he said under his breath. "My life is over." His eyes shifted to the clock. Three hours until lunch. He could endure. Seeing Sarah again would make it better. He just felt sure of it.

As lunchtime drew closer, Sarah had become very comfortable with her new job. She always learned very quickly, and she had been a receptionist for her parents' company whenever their regular had called in sick or gone on vacation.

She was also vividly aware that the meeting that morning had not gone well. For one thing, she and everyone else had heard the shouting. For a second thing, Cameron had left the room looking as if the world was falling down around his head. He had disappeared down the hall to his office, and even from the front she had heard the door shut hard.

She'd had enough. She got to her feet and went over to the coffeepot to pour two cups. With both in hand, she headed for the hall. "Last on the left," Louise said helpfully as Sarah went past. She hid a smile to herself. The entire office would encourage this budding romance if they could. They adored the Dease brothers, and Sarah seemed *perfect* for Cameron.

Sarah moved down the hall and her brows drew together as she realized that Cameron's office was actually a glorified closet next to the supply room. She peeked around the now open door, saw him sitting with his head on his desk, and resolved to remove his clear anxiety. Injecting surprise in her voice, she stepped into the doorway and said, "Hey! They told me that this was the strip club, darn it."

He lifted his head and smiled. He couldn't help it. She came like a breath of fresh air into his windowless little closet. "I could always take my shirt off."

"Let's not, Harry Potter. It might make the others jealous." She walked over and sat on the edge of his desk to offer one of the cups of coffee. "Is this your broom closet under the stairs, Mr. Wizard?"

"Less broom and more dustpan." He looked around with a sigh. "I'd settle for a single window."

She also glanced around. "You need some paintings. Maybe a painting that *looks* like a window. You could hook a little fan to it and make a fake breeze." She propped her chin on her hand. "And add a plant or two."

He tilted his head as he considered her ideas. "I always thought it was a waste of time since I would be leaving."

She laughed. "And you want to be miserable in the time you remain here? Just take the stuff with you." She swung one foot lightly, and he was tickled when he realized that she had an anklet with small ladybugs on it around her ankle. "What happened this morning?" she asked. "I see tooth marks. You got nommed pretty hard methinks."

He leaned back in his chair on a sigh. "My mother wants me to get married."

A pause, then, "Are we talking Cinderella or . . .?"

"I wish! No, she's going to be interviewing potential brides as if hiring someone for a job." He put his head on the desk again. "I can't guess at her reasoning, but it sure as hell can't be good."

"Well, why not look for your own bride?" she offered.

"I'm not legal. She'd have to approve."

"There are *always* loopholes," she pointed out. "Maybe you could find a bride you like and ask her to pretend to be someone your mom might like." She shook her head slightly. "I can't fathom it. A parent doing something like this to their child."

He smiled at her. She really was just what he had needed to feel better. "Your parents must be good ones."

She lowered her gaze and again felt the pain well up without stop. It still hurt to even think of them. "They were," she whispered. "You know the plane crash three months ago? They were in it." She clenched her hands into fists at her sides. "I'm sorry. I need a moment. It hurts so much."

He got to his feet and pulled her into his arms without thinking, wanting only to bring back her smile. "It's okay," he said softly. "I know how you feel. When my father died . . . it was horrible. It was years ago and the pain still sneaks out and slaps me." His heart tightened fiercely as he felt her burrow against him and tuck her head on his shoulder. She felt so . . . right in his arms.

She gave a soft sigh and closed her eyes. She had never been held by anyone other than her parents because it always hurt too much to feel physical contact. For some odd reason, Cameron seemed incapable of hurting her. Even the feel of his shirt wasn't abrasive to her skin. She could still feel each individual thread, but it seemed as oddly soothing as the alluring scent of his skin and cologne.

The mood had shifted to something oddly intimate, and it alarmed her more than a little. To regroup, she sought refuge in humor and sniffed at his collar. "Lavender."

He coughed and released her. "So what?" he asked. "I like it."

"But it's a *girl* scent," she said, putting a whine on the word 'girl.' She was rewarded by a swift grin. "But that's okay," she told him. "I have a preference for fruit, so we shouldn't clash and create The War of the Smells."

He leaned over and sniffed at her hair. It smelled like blueberries. He figured it was just his own bad luck that he adored blueberries. "You're right. Do bakers chase you down on the streets?"

"Only the random ones who sell cookie cutters to parents-to-be," was the teasing retort.

Laughing, he held up his hands. "Okay, I know when I'm defeated." He leaned down and softly touched her cheek with his lips. "Sarah, thank you. You showed up right when I needed you most. I guess it was a lucky coincidence."

Listening outside the door, Kenneth had to smile to himself. He had taken a peek at Sarah's personnel file and recognized her home address. She did indeed live in the 3rd District, and there was a fairly common belief that, when it came to 3rd District, there was no such thing as coincidence. If anything happened, it happened at the whim of destiny.

He lightly rubbed his hands together. There was no law against helping destiny, and he fully intended to help his brother and Sarah. They just . . . belonged together somehow.

CHAPTER THREE

By the time lunch arrived, Sarah was at home with her new job and her new coworkers. By that time as well, her coworkers were absolutely in love with her. Her sense of humor could only be called contagious, and she was quick to respond if someone needed help. She won their eternal devotion by walking around and refilling coffee cups; they were working on a rush order and hadn't had time for a break.

Sarah also resolved to do more office work than strictly assigned to her, to allow Louise to do her *real* job. So, after negotiations and outright emotional blackmail, she got Louise to hand over the tedious task of typing up letters to some of the company's clients to give them status updates. She was so involved in her work that she didn't realize she was no longer alone at her desk until she heard giggling. Without looking up, she asked, "Is that Jason or Freddie behind me?"

Louise tucked her tongue in her cheek. "Well, certainly not Freddie. And if Jason looks that good without his hockey mask, his victims died happy."

Cameron snorted. "Gee, thanks, Lou!" He leaned down to look over Sarah's shoulder. "You type like a demon." He grinned. "And you misspelled 'gratitude.'"

"You distracted me," she accused. "And if you're going to type, type fast." She fixed the typo and tried to ignore the tempting scent of lavender and male skin that teased her nose. She saved the file, locked her computer, and swiveled on her chair. With a smile, she asked, "Ready for lunch?"

"I was ready before I started work." He tugged her gently to her feet and kept a firm grip on her hand as he hauled her behind him out of the office.

"I need my purse!" she protested on a laugh.

"My treat. Stop fighting. Don't make me carry you out."

"Be still my heart, you charmer you." She gave a sigh as she was hauled toward the elevator. "Why don't you just throw me over your shoulder? Good grief, Cam, you couldn't get more caveman-ish if you were swinging a club and wearing a loincloth." Her mind promptly diverted by the mental image and she dragged it back. She was *not* going there.

"I'm desperate," he admitted. "Mondays always suck, but after you left me, my mother started sending me emails of pictures of 'possible candidates.'" He ushered her into the elevator as the doors opened. He didn't admit out loud that he had mentally compared the pictures to Sarah and found them lacking. He was well aware that he was already getting in over his head. He just didn't care.

She leaned against the wall and watched curiously as he used his keycard to access an unlisted floor. "Wow," she said solemnly. "And here I thought the company would have policies against sending dirty pictures."

"Ha. I wish they were dirty pictures. At least then I'd have a *reason* to feel so offended. The photos were of very nice businesswomen. Some posed, like for portraits, and others were more candid, as if caught at work. Mother wanted me to see what my 'choices' were. Choices, my ass! I won't have any say in it."

She linked her hands behind her back. "What about going along with things?" When he lifted a brow, she explained, "A marriage of convenience. Don't sleep with her unless you and she mutually want to. When you're twenty-one, divorce her."

"It crossed my mind," he admitted as the elevator stopped and the doors opened. "But the damage would be done. I have this sinking feeling that Mother is doing this to get her hands on my share of the company."

"Yeah, that wouldn't be a surprise. Company rumor mill works better than the Starbucks coffee grinder." She stepped out of the elevator and followed him up a single flight of stairs. When she pushed open the door at the top and stepped outside, she was surprised to find herself standing on the roof of the building. Further surprising was the realization that the roof was, in fact, a giant greenhouse and atrium. "Wow," she breathed.

"Follow me." He took her hand and drew her into the open doors of the atrium where trees and plants of all shapes and types instantly surrounded them. If it hadn't been for the glass ceiling, someone would forget they stood on a roof in New York City. He studied her face and knew bringing her there had been the right idea. "Like it?" he asked softly.

"It's amazing!" She turned in a slow circle. Impulsively, she took off her shoes to feel the grass under her feet. "This is my idea of a break room!"

"Dad built it way back when he had the building built." He led her through the pathways until the sound of running water grew loud. "But he never gave Mother access to it. The only two keycards are in Kenneth's and my possession. She knows that, but she doesn't really care. She hates most forms of nature, though, I guess to be fair, it's probably as much because she has a lot of allergies as much as anything else."

"So nature hates her as much as she hates it?"

"I plead the Fifth on that one."

She grinned as they rounded a large bush and found a large pool with a waterfall tumbling into the center from some artfully stacked rocks. A picnic lunch sat only a few feet away. She walked over and sat on the edge of the stones lining the pool. "So if the roof leaks, I know who to blame, right? Can you swim in this? It looks pretty big."

"Yup. Twenty feet diameter, seven foot deep at the lowest point." He moved closer and sat down beside her, far closer than was strictly polite. He also leaned in so that she couldn't mistake that he was close. It came as more of an instinct than a conscious decision. He *had* to ensure that he had her attention. He knew he would lose her if he didn't. "Ken and I come here to escape. We know when the other is here, so there won't be interruptions." His breath swept across her nape. "If you look straight ahead, you can see the skyline."

Her heart began to beat harder than a snare drum in a school band. He felt hot and secure, tempting and sinful. If she leaned back, she would be leaning against him. Would he hold her? The depth of her longing to know was a little frightening, so she again sought refuge in humor. She squinted out the windows. "I can see my house from here."

He laughed and eased back. He moved over to the picnic blanket and began to unpack the basket. When she had joined him, he offered her a soda. "I saw that you live in 3rd District."

Her lashes lowered slightly, her eyes watchful and waiting for judgment. "Yes, I do. I was born there."

He visibly brightened. "Then you're not human?"

She blinked at him. "Wow, executives are getting more tactless these days." Her gaze turned wary. "Where's the other shoe, and why do I feel like it will hit my head?"

He scooted closer. "Not from me," he assured her. "I think it's fascinating and amazing. I've met Mel Shaughnessy and his wife. They *totally* can't be human. They hit a chord between terrifying and protective. It was wild."

"Hee." She muffled a full giggle. "Audra and Mel do that." She hesitated and then went with her instincts. "They're werewolves. I've known Audra my whole life, so I knew Mel even before he, uhm, became a professional reference for me. So, yeah, they aren't human. And I'm . . ." She searched for the words. "I wouldn't say I'm not human. But I'm . . . different. Here." She held out a hand.

He curiously took her hand. Goosebumps rose on his skin as he felt a tingle of *something* going through his fingers. Power. It was the only word he could bring to mind. If asked to describe it, he would have never been able to. It simply was. And watching her eyes slowly darken to black from brown seemed oddly erotic. He wanted to make her eyes darken with desire instead of power.

Her fingertips moved over his hand as light as a feather, as if reading him. Then she blinked, her eyes cleared, and she smiled. "You fell off your bike when you were six, and you scraped up this hand." As his eyes widened, she grinned. "There are tiny scars on your hand. I read them." She released his hand. "My skin is so sensitive that I can feel the individual threads in cloth. My clothes are specially made because of it."

"How can you handle touching people then?" he wondered.

She looked at him, startled. "I didn't think you'd pick up on that." She looked away. "It *is* painful, to be honest. Especially because I can read things people have done if I am touching them. Mostly it is in relation to injuries and such." Inner honesty made her admit, "But you don't hurt me. I'm not sure why."

He eased even closer to her and framed her face with his hands. He leaned down and softly brushed his lips over hers, careful to make sure it was just friendly. He had the feeling his Sarah might be a little skittish when it came to romance—and just as inexperienced as himself. "Good," he said softly. "Because I'm a very touchy-feely sort of person and you seem like someone in need of serious hugging."

"I could handle that." She smiled. "Friends who can't hug aren't worth having." She gave him a quick one. She released him with hidden reluctance and reached for something to eat. She would be double damned if she admitted that she wanted more than friendship. She was going to throw toilet paper on Eric Mason's prized sports car if she found out he had known she would click with Cameron. "How goes the shark work?"

He munched on a carrot stick. "It sucks, for me at least." He considered her. "As a consumer, would you pay any attention to the same ad you'd seen a million times before?"

She snorted. "No. I completely tune out." She nibbled on a sandwich. "I take it your mother is stuck in a rut."

"Stuck? Hell, she put a door over the top so she can't get out." He fell over onto his back and linked his hands behind his head. "There's a company that wants to promote shoes. My mother wants to go the old-fashioned route of using models. I keep trying to say we need to jazz it up. Maybe use dancers. Appeal to the younger generation like you and me." He opened one eye. "How old are you?"

"Twenty."

"When's your birthday?"

"Next month." She grinned. "I'm older than you are."

"I like older girls." He went on without missing a beat, "But my point is that we're the new generation of shopper. You need to appeal to us too. We'll be here a lot longer than the older generation. Catch us now with flashy or entertaining ads and keep us with the quality of your product. We'll keep going back."

His style wasn't that vastly different from her parents' so it felt comfortable to her. "Why not go ahead and have Kenneth force your mother to take the idea?"

"Because she said she won't go along with it without support from some big name dancer to be in the ads." He sighed. "And without her support, how can we hope to get any dancers involved? I don't even *know* any dancers!"

"Have you ever been to the Faerie Club in 3rd District?" she asked curiously.

"Sure. Who hasn't? That place is awesome! I'm a decent dancer, but I danced with Aenya Michaels once. Friggin' world champion dancer. She left me in her dust." He sat up with a grin. "Maybe we could go together some time. Relax after work."

"Sure." She wasn't entirely listening, though, as her mind worked very quickly. She had gotten to know all of the Shaughnessy family members during the dealings with Mel and Kalliope. She had met Aenya Michaels, formerly Shaughnessy, as well. She had a strong feeling that if she asked the older woman, she would be glad to assist. Aenya's dancing skills were well known; they had single-handedly turned the Faerie Club into the hottest spot for young adults. She had also won a world dance competition with her husband two years prior.

She startled out of her thoughts as Cameron eased closer to her yet again. He was sitting right beside her now, but slightly behind her. The difference had her suddenly feeling enveloped in his presence. Her pulse kicked into overdrive and she strangled an urge to turn her head and kiss him. She really wished he would stop looming over her like that. It had to be bad for her blood pressure.

The soft hitch in her breath couldn't be disguised by the sound of running water. He slowly ran a finger down her arm and watched as goosebumps followed his touch. A giddy sense of delight and triumph seemed to meld with the steadily growing hunger he had for her smile and her outrageously lovely body. She wanted him as badly as he wanted her. And he felt no guilt whatsoever for being willing to take advantage of her apparent sensitivity to him. "Know something?" he murmured into her ear.

She fought a shiver as his breath teased her. She knew her skin was sensitive everywhere, but her *ear* was an erogenous zone? Whatever genetic gods had put her together had to have been smoking something. "What?" She tried to ease away before she did something stupid.

He just slid even closer. "I think I'm falling in love with you." Her head jerked around and he fought the urge to lean in and take the kiss he craved. They were nose-to-nose, and their lips almost touched. "It's just a warning," he said, his voice slightly huskier than normal. "Because if I do fall in love with you, I will be having you come hell, high water, or my mother."

"Whoa." It was the best she could manage. She had never before heard such a blatant declaration of intent. In fact, she had never known any man with the confidence or courage to consider making one. It terrified her on more than one level, and she sought for balance. "Well, fine then. Since I might be falling for you too, we'll have to see who gets there first, if at all. Kind of like trying to get to a sale at Sak's on Black Friday."

He grinned and eased back. He was beginning to understand her, and in his understanding, he was beginning to form a plan. "Well, we need to go back to work before you're late. Much as neither of us probably wants to go back."

It was to her credit that her knees weren't still weak and she looked perfectly calm as she got back to her desk a few minutes later. The calm gave way to laughter as she saw the post-its that had been stuck all over her monitor. They all said different things, but the general theme was the same: if she wanted Cameron, she had the full support of her coworkers. "I'm not replacing those from supply," she scolded, but with a smile.

The others just grinned and went about their business. After cleaning up the mess, she did likewise. She was, however, still thinking swiftly. As she observed Kenneth and Cameron going into another meeting with Lorcana, she made up her mind. "Someone have a home phone book?" she called. Sometimes, things called for old-fashioned methods. The number she needed could not be found online.

Louise brought one over to her. "What are you up to?"

She flipped pages swiftly. "I'm doing my good deed for the month." She dialed the phone and waited for a few moments. When it was answered, she smiled. "Hey there, Ruthie. Is your mommy there? It's Sarah." Louise opened her mouth and Sarah shook her head. "Aenya? Good afternoon! How are you? Listen," she continued, "I have an idea to run past you."

Ten minutes later, Louise's eyes looked huge as she watched Sarah hang up. "You did not just call Aenya Michaels and ask her to support Cameron's idea."

"Actually, yes I did." Sarah smiled. "It's too complicated to explain, but I know the Shaughnessy family and all its extended branches. Aenya is only four years older than I am. She's one of the nicest people I know. She also knows the complications of bad business owners. She was glad to help."

Twenty minutes later, in the meeting, Cameron felt as if he was hitting his head against a brick wall. His mother wouldn't give way for anything. "Can't you see?" he exploded as he leapt to his feet. "You're going to destroy the company like this! You want it so badly and yet you keep choking it!"

"Don't you dare take that tone with me!" Lorcana snapped back.

"Cameron's right." Kenneth's voice was clipped. "Our business has dropped twenty percent over the last few years. It was only when I took control of my rightful share," he used the phrase deliberately, "that the business started growing again!"

Lorcana opened her mouth to retort sharply when the door opened behind her. She whirled around and shouted, "You are to *never* interrupt a meeting! Get out, now!"

Sarah didn't bat a lash and looked past Lorcana to Cameron. "Your guest is here." Her eyes twinkled and asked him to play along.

He blinked. "Well, uhm, show them in."

She stepped to the side and gestured gracefully. The slender young woman who had been standing behind her walked into the room and swept her honey colored gaze over it swiftly. She had grown up under boardroom tables playing cards with her youngest older brother, and yet she had never heard anything as ridiculous then as what she had heard now. "My name is Aenya Michaels. Which of you two handsome males is Cameron?"

Kenneth's jaw fell open. Lorcana could only stare in shock. Cameron felt a bit off kilter himself, but he recovered and got to his feet. "That would be me." He took her offered hand and wondered when he had entered the looking glass without noticing. "Thank you for joining us."

Her eyes sparkled. "I was glad to hear from you." With a casual sort of confidence, she sat down beside Cameron. She knew it would piss Lorcana off and didn't care one way or another. "When you contacted me with the request that I dance in an ad, I was quite honored. I know what it's like to fight for a dream."

Lorcana whirled on Sarah. "You are not to take any more requests from Cameron!" she ordered sharply. The *nerve* of the girl!

Sarah met her gaze head-on. "Does Cameron draw a paycheck?"

"Well, yes, but . . ."

"And is he a Dease family member?"

"I don't see what . . ."

"Then I will continue to do as he asks me." She lifted her brows. "My job description was that I would be secretary and support to *all* members of the Dease family who work for the company." She gave a graceful and yet subtly mocking curtsy. "Now excuse me please. Kenneth is horrible at filing his papers."

Kenneth grinned swiftly. "Job security." He wanted to laugh out loud. He also wanted to hug Sarah. She had not only done the impossible, but she had stood up to Lorcana at the same time. If it was the last thing he ever did, he would see her get together with Cameron. His baby brother would finally have someone to fight at his side.

Boxed in by her own words, Lorcana had no choice but to go along with Cameron's idea. She would die before admitting that it was a good one, and she sure as hell wouldn't admit to being impressed by Aenya. Aenya was a Shaughnessy by birth and it showed; she was a shark to her core and held her own during the negotiations as well as her elder brother might have.

It was the end of the day by the time the meeting ended. Kenneth had a dinner date and had to hurry out. Lorcana was still in a snit so she took off for home. Cameron got out into the office area and looked around swiftly but Sarah had already left for the day. Disappointed, he wondered how it was possible to know someone for just one day and know they were vital to your existence.

Aenya stepped up beside him. "Walk with me, Cam. I'd like to talk to you, if you don't mind."

"Not at all." He fell into step beside her and glanced at her curiously. "Did Sarah call you?"

"She did." She smiled. "Sarah . . . well, it's her choice to tell how and why, but she got to be very dear to the Shaughnessy family. We've taken her under our wing, so to speak. We told her that if she ever needed help, she could call on any of us. When she told me what was going on here, it annoyed me."

He lifted a brow. "Why?"

"Two reasons. One, because it was stupid." She grinned impishly. "I'm Sullivan Shaughnessy's daughter, and I own my own club. I know stupid business when I see it. And the other reason is because of you." She sighed. "You probably wouldn't remember since I doubt you read the paper when you were fourteen, but, I was forced into a contract with my father. Any man who found out where I danced at night could marry me."

"Yikes." He winced in sympathy.

"My father did it because he loved me and worried, but it still made me mad. It worked out though." She smiled. "I met Hiro. Sneaky bastard found out where I danced *and* stole my heart." She grinned when he laughed. "But the thing is . . . it wasn't coincidence." She turned to face him as they waited for the elevator. "3rd District was involved. And it was involved with my brothers as well."

"Magic."

"It's more than that." She shook her head. "It's a joke, but it's true. There is no such thing as a coincidence around 3rd District. The fact that Sarah is here, that you've met, that you're falling for her . . . it's not a coincidence."

He tilted his head slightly. "Destiny?"

"You know, I'm not sure." She smiled as she got onto the elevator. "But I can say that I'm sure that someday you'll have everything you want. Dreams come true in our District, Cameron." She waved her hand. "See you in a few days to get the rest of the details taken care of."

He smiled but he was thinking hard as the doors closed. He had always believed in magic and in destiny. He had always thought that perhaps there was some being out there, some deity that watched over lovers. The idea that the entire 3rd District might be protected by such a person was an incredible one.

He thought about things critically as he returned home and went to his favorite place in the garden. He had known Sarah for only a single day but he already craved her presence. He wanted to see her again, to talk with her. He wanted to hold her and remove the lingering traces of grief. He wanted to make love to her, to sleep with her all tangled in his arms.

He was so deep in his thoughts that he didn't know Kenneth had joined him until his brother spoke up, "I know they say 'ask and ye shall receive' but I've never known a guy who asked for a girlfriend and found love."

He glanced up at Kenneth with a wry smile as his brother sat beside him. There were two years difference in their ages, yet they had always been as close as the twins they resembled. "Short date?"

"Eh, she canceled. No worries. Tell me about Sarah."

"I want her so badly it hurts," he admitted. "I'm looking forward to work, Ken. I *want* to go to work so I can see her." Awe and pride entered his voice. "Did you see her stand up to Mother?"

"I don't think a princess could have done better. Her parents named her well." Kenneth linked his hands behind his head. "So what do we do? Mother won't change her plans, especially not over someone like Sarah. But *I'm* on your side, you know that."

"Yeah." He let out a long breath. "The first thing is to convince Sarah that we can be more than friends."

"Is she at least attracted to you?"

His grin turned dangerous for a moment with masculine satisfaction. "Most definitely. I plan to take full and complete advantage of that. In the meantime, if you can think of a way to get her on Mother's radar as a potential bride without getting all of us in trouble, please let me know."

"Gladly."

Cameron was the first one at work the following morning, an inner instinct telling him that Sarah was the type to arrive early and leave late. Much to his delight, he found that he was right, and she was already at her desk a full thirty minutes before she was due to start. The entire office wouldn't be arriving for a while yet either, and the area remained nice and quiet.

She didn't know he had joined her. She had her email open but didn't see it. She was still thinking about the same things that had kept her up all night. She had never expected to meet a man that she couldn't bear to be away from for more than a few hours at a time.

She was a virgin by choice (and practicality because of her abilities) but every time she looked at Cameron, all she could think of was throwing on sexy lingerie, climbing onto his lap, and settling in like a dieter on an illegal binge. Why she'd had to fall in love with a person she could never have, she didn't know.

Her skin tingled suddenly and she knew he stood behind her. Ignoring her fluttering heart, she said, "And here I thought the office wasn't haunted. Are you the ghost of hot men past?"

He laughed and leaned down to wrap his arms around her shoulders. "I'm more like the ghost of piranha food past."

She snickered and turned as he released her. More than happy, she returned the hug he had given her. "You're here early, Cam. You trying to be prepared for the auction?"

"Auction?"

She quirked a brow. "Your mother had me contact five of the first brides. They'll be here today bidding on a certain cookie dough cutie."

He groaned. "I wish you were talking about Ken, I really do." He rested his chin on her head and held her closer. She definitely wasn't very curvy, but that just meant she fit perfectly in his arms. "Promise to have lunch with me. I'm going to need you."

Her eyes softened as her heart swelled. There was nothing like being needed by the man you loved. She wanted to take away the sadness in his eyes. "Cam . . ."

"Whoops!" Louise covered her eyes as she entered. "I see nothing. I hear nothing. Just let me get my coffee."

Cameron laughed and released Sarah. "I was just stealing a hug. I need her to keep me sane."

Louise grinned at Sarah. "Not fishing, huh?"

She stuck her tongue out. "I'm just lucky that way." Good luck, she mouthed to Cameron as he headed down the hall. After a moment of thought, she turned and began to type up a document. When Louise joined her, she said, "If Lorcana wants this to be an interview, the candidates ought to have a duty statement."

Her supervisor's brows slowly lifted as she saw what Sarah was typing. "You're an evil woman. Damn, we should have found you sooner."

The five candidates had arrived by ten o'clock. Sarah checked them in but intensely disliked all of them. They were beautiful, cultured, intelligent . . . and radiated an aura of pure ruthless manipulation not dissimilar from Lorcana. Talk about like recognizing like.

Still, she remained friendly and polite and had all of them smiling once they were seated. She simply didn't have the heart to be rude or mean. Casually, she handed out the duty statement. "These are some of the duties you will be undertaking once you marry Cameron Dease. You'll also find a fact sheet about your potential groom."

One female said, "He's only twenty?! I'm not going to marry a man seven years younger than me, I'm sorry." She got to her feet and held out the statement to Sarah. "My apologies, but I didn't know he was that young."

Sarah just smiled. "That's understandable." She snorted mentally in derision. Cameron was more mature than half the males she knew who were older. He had been forced to grow up early just to survive. "Are there any more questions?"

"There aren't any executive parties?" another asked warily.

"No. Lorcana prefers to keep thing strictly professional. She does not encourage fraternizing with other employees in any fashion."

The woman made a disgusted sound and got to her feet. "Sorry. I have a high profile name. I have to be seen. Please give my apologies." She swept out with all the drama of a Hollywood star, and Sarah almost rolled her eyes.

The other three were clearly ambivalent but they remained for the interview. Sarah played her role and showed them into the meeting room and then escorted them out when they were done. Her anger grew with every passing minute. Every time she caught sight of Cameron's face, it looked more and more haggard. It seemed as if the strain was aging him rapidly.

Kenneth left the meeting first and he looked no less stressed. He stopped on his way out to give Sarah his key card. "Cam wants you to meet him for lunch. He worries that Mother might sense something between you and get rid of you."

"But we're just friends," she protested.

He just smiled and walked away. She really was cute as hell. If he hadn't felt so much like a big brother to her, he would have fought Cameron over her. Maybe she had a sister, or a best friend like a sister. It was doubtful though. Perfection was rarely recreated, much to his regret.

With a sigh, she locked her computer and grabbed the lunchbox she had packed. She pointedly ignored the cheers and waves she got but inside she smiled. She worked with smartasses. It made her feel good.

By the time Cameron got to the roof, he was in desperate need of her presence. Her sense of humor and her calming manner. Her soft and fragrant skin and hair, so vastly different from the perfume other women wore. Most of all, he needed her touch to remind him that there was someone who needed *him*.

When he saw her standing at the edge of the pool, a soft wind fluttering her hair, emotion welled up inside him. He was in love. This beautiful creature was the only one meant for him. Riding with it, he moved forward and wrapped his arm around her fiercely. He buried his face in her hair. He couldn't imagine his life without her now.

She wasn't sure what to do for a moment. There was something inside him, some wild and driving emotion that seemed to echo what was inside her own heart. Could he really, possibly, love her as much as she loved him? She shied away from examining it. Things were complicated enough. Instead, she turned in his arms and hugged him tight. "It's okay, Cam. You're safe now."

After a few moments, he reluctantly released her. "I'm sorry. I just . . . needed to be near you."

Warmth unfurled inside her. "Just call me your lode stone. I steal all the yicky stuff and make you feel warm and squishy."

He laughed and drew her over to the picnic blanket. Much to his surprise, he saw the lunch set out. "Wow, where'd you score this?"

"I made it." She felt pleased with his startled look. "Spoiled little rich boy with a piranha for a mother and servants to do everything, I figured you might like something other than fancy gourmet food."

He couldn't have been happier. "Good call!" He dug eagerly into his share. The first bite made his taste buds happily dance. Her cooking skills rivaled her sense of humor for being her best feature. If he ever managed to get a ring on her finger, he would beg for her to make lunch every day. He would even be willing to share her lunch skills with his brother. "I bet none of those 'potential brides' could cook like this."

"Well, maybe, but I doubt they have time." She worked her way through her own share. "They're your stereotypical high-power executives who believe they don't need time for family." She shook her head. "I can think of three large corporations, three of the largest in New York and/or America, and they're all about family. Shoot, I can think of four if you include Enforcers. Sorry, but it's a lie to say you can't have it all. It's all about delegation and killing stereotypes."

"Didn't one of the leaders of Enforcers get married a while back?" he asked curiously.

"About ten months ago, yes." She smiled. "He's so in love with her. She's another of 3rd District's . . . um, miracles."

"Oh yeah!" He snapped his fingers. "I remember her! She was in a coma for like sixteen years and came out of it okay."

"That's Rayna. She's really nice, but not a pushover." She tucked her hair behind her ear. "How bad was it, Cam? Did you even like any of the women? If you like one, there's always the chance you could fall for her and turn something bad into something good." It took a lot of effort to keep her voice from quivering. She wanted him for her own, but she wanted more for him to be happy.

"Ha. Not hardly." He looked at her directly, his eyes more green than gray. "I'd rather have you for my wife."

She took a small, sharp breath. What was she supposed to say to *that*? Her muscles tensed as she prepared to scoot back away from him. "Well, that's certainly the best proposal I've ever had, better than the one in third grade from Oliver Persnickle. He gave me a toad."

His hand shot out and wrapped around the back of her neck, stopping her before she could get away. His other hand closed over her wrist, and he jerked her onto his lap and up against his chest. Her shocked brown eyes slowly widened even as his narrowed slightly. "Don't, Sarah," he warned softly, intently. "Don't hide from me. I see right through you."

She swallowed hard. His body was hot and hard and she wanted nothing more than to merge everything she was to him so they would never be apart. She couldn't breathe, couldn't feel, couldn't *live* without him. "Cameron," she strove to sound patient, "we're friends. That's all. Friends can't get married."

"We're more than that," he told her, "and I'll prove it." He swiftly turned and tumbled her down onto the blanket. Before she could blink, he had covered her body with his own to keep her pinned. He cuffed her hands over her head. "I'm in love with you," he said quietly, and so intensely that she had to believe him. "And I warned you what would happen if I fell."

His hot mouth cut off any response she might have wanted to give. He didn't just kiss her; he consumed her as if he was devouring her. She could only manage a strangled moan as hunger pounded through her body. Everywhere their skin touched brought a dizzying pleasure that was both physical and mental. Information poured into her mind as fire seemed to pour into her blood. Both fed her craving for more.

She arched toward him wildly, ravenously returning the kiss. Her teeth scraped over his lower lip, where he often bit down when he was thinking hard. A low rumble came from his chest and he returned the rough caress. When she gasped, he slicked his tongue into her mouth. She countered and the kiss grew ever hotter until both were shaking.

He broke free on a curse. "Damn," he muttered, pressing a hot and wet kiss to her throat. He resisted the urge to sink in his teeth and mark her as his. "I've never been that turned on by a kiss before." He slowly pressed against her, his aching erection rubbing against her stomach. Her eyes darkened and lust happily clawed at his body. "If you doubt me," his voice sounded rough, "then feel free to check."

"I didn't bring gloves to handle dynamite." Her breath hitched and her body arched helplessly as he released her hands so he could open her blouse. For the life of her, she couldn't move or escape, and she really had no care to even try. Her entire body felt drugged on him, quivering helplessly for more of the wicked pleasure he could give.

He stopped to lavish kisses over every inch of skin he uncovered. By the time he had the blouse halfway open, she was writhing beneath him desperately. She had never imagined her sensitive skin might react like that. "You're evil!" she managed to say, but the words came out as almost a sob.

He muttered something wordless and unclipped the front clasp of her bra. Her hands shot down to cover herself but he caught her wrists and pinned them again, baring her to his gaze. "You know," he said huskily. "I've seen women with better figures."

"But . . .?" she asked breathlessly.

"But I can't seem to remember them. The only thing in my mind is you." He nuzzled the gentle curve of her inner breast and nudged her bra cup aside. Hungrily he closed his mouth over the hardened point of her breast and sucked strongly.

Her back arched and a thin cry came from her throat. She began to shake in his arms and tried to fight free. Her body didn't seem to be her own anymore. She was drowning in pleasure and wanted more, but she was terrified of the strength of her desire. She felt wound so tight that she thought she might break in two. Why wouldn't it *stop*? "Cam," she managed to plead. "Stop."

"You'd hate me if I did." Still ravishing her breasts with his lips and teeth, he began to unfasten her slacks. When they were open far enough, he slid his hand inside them and her panties, seeking the heart of her. Savage satisfaction filled him as he felt the evidence of her arousal, slick and burning against his fingers. "If we were just friends," he said fiercely, "then we wouldn't feel like this."

She couldn't respond. She desperately grabbed for his arms, needing him as an anchor as his softly stroking fingers made the wicked delight worse. One long finger slid inside her body, and her senses came apart in a blinding shockwave of ecstasy. The waves washed over her, each stronger than the last, until she arched wildly underneath him.

Her cry muffled by his hungry kiss. He held her there, his other hand keeping her pressed close. When the tension seemed to flood out of her and she went limp, he gentled the kiss. He slowly lowered her back to the blanket and began to softly smooth his hands over her skin. It was self-inflicted torture. He wanted nothing more than to take her where they were, knowing her desire as intimately as he could, but they had no time.

"Okay," she finally managed to say huskily, "you made your point. I concede defeat." Pleasantly satiated, she slid her arms up around his neck. "But how am I supposed to go back to work and not have every single person there know exactly what I was doing? Or rather, *who*."

He had to laugh at that. She wouldn't be his Sarah without her sense of humor. "The same way I'm not sure how to hide what I *wasn't* doing, and wish like I hell I had been." He kissed her again and lingered over her taste. "Invite me over for dinner tonight." His green eyes burned like gems, and there was no doubt in either of their minds what would occur.

She had never believed in fighting the inevitable. "Come over for dinner," she whispered, "and stay for breakfast."

"Deal!" He kissed her again just for the sheer torture of it and then forced himself to let go. Still, he watched her hungrily as she put her clothes back into order. Except for the flush to her skin, her slightly swollen lips, and the glow in her eyes, it was hard to tell that she had been tumbling over a picnic blanket. Her hair seemed miraculously tidy, and he wanted to muss it up. "Do you believe that I love you?"

She looked at him for a solemn moment before leaning over and framing his face as she kissed him tenderly, giving him all the generosity of her love. "Yes," she said softly against his lips. "And I love you too, Cam. I'm sure you know." She curled closer as he hugged her tightly. "I'll think of something," she decided. "If I have to, I'll get Audra to come beat up your mom."

"Audra?" It took a moment for the name to click. "Audra Shaughnessy?" His eyes widened. "You wouldn't."

"I would. She's a protector of kids. And she's known me since I was a kid." She grinned mischievously. "If I tell her I want you, she'll find a way to make sure I get you. By the fastest means possible."

"You're evil. I knew I loved you." He kissed her again, and then released her entirely. His eyes seemed to glow with happiness despite his obvious frustration. "Let's pretend nothing happened. And then tomorrow we can say that nothing happened the day before, but most definitely did the night following."

She just giggled.

CHAPTER FOUR

Sarah was an intelligent young woman. She stopped in the women's restroom to see how bad the damage was to her appearance. Her hair pleased her with its lack of tangles, but there was no mistaking the effects on her face. Some cold water thankfully brought the flush to her cheeks down to normal and brought down the swelling of her lips.

Her eyes, well, she couldn't do a thing for them. Anyone with half a brain would look at the expression in her eyes and know she had just been well loved. Her humor couldn't help but find it fascinating. She wondered if anyone would have the absolute nerve to say a single thing.

She was back at her desk just as lunch ended, and she knew immediately that Cameron had to have already passed through. Everyone immediately looked at her intently as if to confirm a theory. Based on the smug looks, she could only assume they had guessed right. Then again, it wouldn't be hard to miss the contrast between him looking so frustrated and her looking so relaxed.

Louise wandered over and leaned on the counter. Casually, she examined her nails. "Have a good lunch?" she asked blandly, but a hidden note of laughter gave her away.

Sarah considered her words. "It was certainly an interesting lunch. I've never had cookie dough quite like that before."

Louise was hard-pressed to keep from laughing or grinning. Good for Cameron! She had been hoping he would get more ruthless with Sarah. Considering her 'just ravished' expression, it was fairly obvious what had occurred on the roof. "Going to be having more?"

Sarah smiled wryly. "I think it's my dessert tonight." The entire conversation was absurd but she enjoyed it too much to care.

"You go, girl." Pleased, Louise headed back to her desk.

Down the hall, Cameron was scrolling through Google to find a florist when his brother walked in unannounced. Kenneth studied his younger brother and a smile began to play around the edges of his mouth. "Good lunch?"

Cameron looked over and smiled wryly. "I'm a masochist, but I got my point across to her."

Kenneth shut the door behind him so that no one could walk in. He sat on the edge of Cameron's desk and contemplated the search results on the computer screen. "Then that means we only need to deal with Mother. You know there's no way she'll approve of Sarah, not after she so beautifully stood up to her."

"I'll think of something." Cameron's eyes burned intently as he leaned back. "I'm not willing to even pretend. I'll have Sarah as my wife or no one else." He raked his hands through his hair. "I hate to consider it, but, if it comes down to it, I'll either get a lawyer to have Mother's guardianship revoked, or give up the company entirely. I want to be *happy*, and I guess it's time to decide what that means to me. At the least, I know it includes Sarah."

Kenneth nodded slightly. "I stand by you for either choice. I'll be proud to have Sarah for a little sister." He grinned. "But I might suggest a cold shower in the gym downstairs unless you want Mother to get suspicious. You look a bit, uhm, *distracted*."

Cameron took the advice to heart, but he got the strong feeling that Lorcana already sensed something. Whenever he saw her passing through the office, she would always take a moment to study Sarah intently. It probably wasn't helping, he thought wryly, that he couldn't help but look at Sarah himself. Every time he did, he thought of lunch and the night ahead.

When the bouquet of flowers arrived for Sarah, she found herself all the more amused as she signed for them. There was no card to indicate who they were from, but she (and her coworkers) all knew. Kenneth also knew because he winked one of the times he walked past her desk. Impulsively, she put one of the flowers over her ear, just to enjoy seeing Cameron's eyes light when he looked at her. Lorcana glared at her, but she just looked at her blandly. She had combed the official employee handbook, and Cameron had been right: no rules existed against fraternization. As long as all parties were willing, their private lives were their own.

She rushed home as soon as the day ended. She wanted to get her apartment cleaned up and herself prepared. Damn it, it was going to be her first time, and she wanted to make sure it was special for them both. She was in love and she was going to give herself to the man she loved. That seemed worth some candles and silk.

Once the apartment was clean, she set up electric candles around the living room and bedroom and then contemplated her closet. She didn't want to wear anything that was *too* hard to get back off, and yet she didn't want to be obvious. Finally she settled on a sheath dress in stark black. It was plain and elegant, but it also flattered her hair and skin. She sassily wore nothing underneath it.

Her heart jumped when her doorbell rang. She quickly hurried over and peeked out the spy hole. Her mouth went dry. Men who looked that hot should have been illegal. Or strippers. Cameron still wore his work clothes, but the shirt was partially unbuttoned and his tie hung around his neck. She wanted to muss him up even more, and she opened the door to say, "Alright, the stripper is here. Now for the real fun."

He grinned. "I even brought pizza." He waved the box under her nose temptingly.

"What, no fancy fish or French food we can't even pronounce?" She clucked her tongue as she shut the door behind him. "I feel so cheated."

He ran his eyes over her slowly and felt his hands almost literally itch to touch her. She had never seemed exceptionally beautiful before, more cute than anything, but right then she was the most beautiful woman he had ever seen. He studied the snug form of the dress and how there didn't seem to be any lines marring the flow of the silk. "Are you wearing anything under that?" he asked huskily.

She lowered her lashes with a smile as old and feminine as time. "Perfume."

"Per . . ." He swallowed hard as desire ripped through his body faster than the speed of light. "*Just* perfume?" He put down the pizza on the kitchen counter before he dropped it. If she didn't stop smiling at him, he was going to pounce on her. The candlelit atmosphere just made it more difficult to keep his hands to himself.

"Maybe." She stepped forward and slid her hands up to link around his neck. Her body molded to his perfectly as if they had been meant to go together. "Dinner first, or dessert?" Her lashes fluttered closed as he bent his head and began to trail soft kisses over her ear. Shivers rippled through her body with lazy waves of pleasure. "Cam?" she whispered.

"Hmm?" She even tasted like blueberries, as if she had deliberately worn his favorite flavor and scent just for him. He wanted to taste every inch of her from head to toe, and he ran his hands slowly down her back and over the curve of her bottom. Just as he had thought, there was nothing beneath the dress but her.

"I've never done this before, just so you know." She buried her fingers in his hair, delighted with how it felt.

"I know." He smiled as he lifted his head. "I had guessed that might be the case. Know what?"

"What?"

"I think I've done this before."

She arched a brow, bemused. "You only think?"

"Well, I can't seem to remember anyone else. Just you." He softly took her lips, drawing the kiss out until both their heads were spinning and their pulses beat hard in unison. There was something about her that made him want to take his time, to shower her with all the love they both had missed out on.

Drowning in him, swept away on the drugging pleasure of his touch, she could only catch a startled breath as she found herself lifted into his arms. "Despite my name, I'm not some . . . princess. Put me down."

"I thought girls like romance." He took his best guess and headed down the hall toward where he could see more candlelight.

"Well I'm sure most do, and I do for sure, but . . . it's unnerving." She held on tighter to his shoulders as he lowered her slowly to her feet inside the bedroom. "I didn't imagine this would happen," she whispered. "How can you know someone only two days and know that you had been waiting for them your whole life?"

"Magic." He pulled her closer and kissed her again, shuddering as the taste of her spread through his body and soul. He eagerly ran his hands down over her back and savored the resilience of her skin. It felt ridiculously soft.

She could only manage a faint moan as his touch sent off wild streamers of pleasure through her body. It was as if her skin had become hundreds of times more sensitive to him now, and the barest brush of his skin against hers made her hunger for him grow. "Cameron," she whimpered into his kiss.

He lifted his lips long enough to catch her dress in his hands and slowly peel it upward. He tossed it to the side and for a moment just studied her naked figure with possessive delight. She was still no centerfold, but she was the most incredible thing he had ever seen. "You're beautiful, Sarah," he whispered.

"So are you." Curiously unafraid or shy, she began to unbutton his shirt the rest of the way. When it was finally open, she watched hungrily as he shrugged out of it. He was smooth skin and hard muscle, and put every fireman calendar she could remember to shame. And he was hers. Delight filling her, she skimmed a finger along the line of his chest. "So do you work out, or was this literally God's gift to women like me?"

He grinned, a little flustered but a lot pleased. "Both. I was lucky enough to be born attractive. And I'm not lazy enough to waste that. Ken and I both work out."

"Wow. Bet that alone gets the pulse rate of the other gym-goers up."

He gave in and laughed outright. On a burst of happy energy, he scooped her up into his arms and tumbled her down across the bed. He kissed her wildly, deepening it until her body arched helplessly toward him and her fingers clutched at his shoulders for an anchor.

Hungry for everything, he began to trail hot kisses down her body, lavishing the inner curves of her breasts with caresses. His hands stroked slowly over her sides again and again until he thought he could feel the sensitivity himself.

She took a breath to tell him to stop teasing her when his mouth closed over the point of one breast. She twisted against him on a strangled cry, her desire sharpening to a razor point until she was at the edge of release in moments. Her body began to shake, her legs moving restlessly, as he switched his attention to her other breast.

Sensing her desperation, he slowly slid one hand down to ruffle the rust colored curls at the apex of her thighs. His touch slid lower and he shuddered as he felt the slick heat waiting for him. He wanted to be inside her so badly it hurt, but he also didn't want to hurt her. He wanted her wild in his arms.

She struggled to breathe as his knowing fingers teased and tormented. Somehow he knew exactly how to touch her to drive her insane but not give her the satisfaction her body craved. As his teeth scraped lightly over her stomach, she gave a thin cry. "Sadist!"

He released her on a low curse and stripped the rest of his clothes off. He swiftly returned to her, and his playful pounce sank them both deeper into the soft feather bed. With a touch of desperation, he kissed her again, his tongue surging into her mouth to tease and torment. She returned the kiss just as ravenously, and her fingers raced over every inch of skin she could reach. Her fingers skidded over a few odd scars on his back and the knowledge ripped through her mind. Tears filled her eyes and she clutched him closer. "I love you!"

He dragged her closer and braced her legs over his arms, opening her completely to him. His erection pressed against her opening, sought entry, and slowly he flexed his hips to push inside. Electricity rippled down his back with raw delight and he fought the urge to drive deep. He wanted to always remember that first moment.

Her breath caught and she dug her nails into his shoulders. Her skin was so sensitive that all she could feel was sheer pleasure. It had to be some sort of biological chemistry that made him so very different, but it seemed such a paltry term for what existed between them.

He kissed her again as his arms shifted to hold her as tightly against him as he could. She wrapped herself around him like a vine, some deep instinct urging her to bind him fast to her so that he could never get away. He began to drive in and out of her swiftly, every thrust sending her excitement higher and higher until she thought she would break apart and her thin cry was muffled by his lips.

Something broke. The snapping tension seemed to ricochet through her entire body and soul all at once, the rapture as all-consuming as it was dimly terrifying. She could only clutch onto him desperately as she felt herself drown in ecstasy. And when he shuddered, caught just as she was, her arms tightened and she held him closer as it took them both.

It was a few breathless minutes before he found the energy to lift himself enough to look at her. She looked content, sleepy, and sated. It was a face he wanted to see more often. There were dozens of faces he wanted see on her. He wanted to wake with her in his arms and fall asleep with her at night. Forget having a girlfriend. He wanted her for his wife. There was no law against skipping certain stages when you knew what you wanted. "Are you happy?" he asked softly.

For an answer, she wound her arms tighter around his shoulders. "Ask me when I'm not glowing. On the bright side, we won't need a night light."

He laughed and kissed her lightly. Even with just that, he felt the stirring inside of hunger for her again. Still, honesty, and bedrock integrity, made him say, "Sarah . . ."

"It's highly unlikely." She opened her eyes to smile at him. "I'm due to start my period in a few days, but I'll go to the doctor and get some birth control." Her lashes lowered. "That is, if we're going to be doing this again."

"You bet your ass we will. In the meantime, I'll take care of things for us." He smoothed a hand down to rest over her stomach. "If the timing was wrong, and you are pregnant . . ."

"Yes?"

"Whatever you decision you make, I'll stand beside you completely. And if you decide to keep it . . . I'd be more than willing to be a dad." He rolled over onto his back and took her with him so that she was sprawled over the top of his chest. "And even if we're in the clear, I'll do whatever it takes for you, Sarah. My mother has stopped me from having everything else I wanted. She won't stop me from having you."

She curled closer and rested her head over his heart. "I felt them," she whispered. "The scars on your back. She beat you?"

"Only once. My father caught her and threatened to divorce her if she ever laid a hand on me or Ken again." He ran his hands lightly over her back. "But enough about that. Want to know something funny?"

"Sure." She propped her chin on her hands to study his face in the candlelight. "I'm always interested in a laugh."

"This was the first time I ever made love in a bed." He grinned when her brows lifted in disbelief. "I told you. My mother never let me have a girlfriend. My previous experience consists of sneaking around with girls and testing the shocks of cars. Fords have some good ones, by the way."

She giggled softly. "Makes me wish I didn't own a motorcycle."

He should have known! "You own a motorcycle? That seems slightly out of place for my princess."

"Ha. You're just jealous. Men can't stand when a woman has a better vehicle than they do."

"Sad but true." He linked his hands behind his head. "My car is so old that the original owner was named Flintstone."

"Must be bad in heavy rain."

"Tell me about it. The breaking is hell on my shoes." When she laughed, he held her even closer against him for a moment, savoring how it felt to be there. "I wish I could spend the whole night and wake with you, but my mother might notice I was gone all night." He nuzzled her ear softly. "When I turn twenty-one, I'll move in with you long enough to give my mother time to move out of the house. Then you're coming home with me. As my wife."

It wasn't the most romantic proposal she had ever heard, yet it felt utterly perfect. She smiled and closed her eyes as she cuddled closer. "It's a date."

He left close to one in the morning, and only because he had forced himself. She found it exceptionally hard to sleep without him there to snuggle against. She loved the way he felt against her skin. Her cheerful mood was so strong that when she dressed for work, she took the time to put some curls in her hair and some makeup on. She also wore a skirt that was *slightly* shorter than 'professional' but only an adept eye would notice without a ruler in hand.

She was the first one to the office, as was becoming habit, and she got coffee going. While she contemplated some tea for herself, strong arms suddenly went around her waist. Delighted, she snuggled back against her lover. "I thought you were the perpetually late one."

He smiled and hugged her tighter. He had missed her insanely and had never before noticed how cold and lonely his room could be. When he had seen her standing at the coffee machine, he hadn't been able to keep his hands off her. "Yes but if I get here early, I have enough time to steal a kiss or two."

She turned around to wind her arms around him. "Steal away, my prince. But I might steal them back."

"Promise?" He lowered his head to kiss her when he saw down the collar of her shirt a few shadows on her breasts that weren't from the light. Shocked, he unbuttoned the first two fastenings to see better. Sure enough, there were bruises on her fair flesh. "Oh god. Sarah . . . I . . ."

She laughed and covered his mouth with a hand. "No! It's not your fault. Well okay, *technically* it's your fault. But it's not that you hurt me. Remember, I told you my skin is sensitive. Well, that also means that I bruise faster than a grape. I fell down the stairs once and looked like I had gone ten rounds with the champ. I think I won, but I can't promise it."

He let out a breath. "Okay. I just don't want to hurt you." He gently re-buttoned her shirt and then skimmed a finger over her curls. "Did you make yourself prettier for me? And how short *is* that skirt? I'd swear it wasn't proper, but maybe it's just my wishful thinking."

"I just wanted you to have a fair comparison of me against the potential brides." She fluttered her lashes for emphasis.

"You win. Hands down, you win."

Kenneth stood around the corner and listened to the conversation. He had known instantly when he had seen his brother that morning that Cameron had been rolling around a bed with Sarah and enjoying himself immensely. On one hand, he could not have been happier. On the other, he was worried. He did not want to see Sarah get hurt and he had no doubts about his mother's ruthlessness. Bruises would be the least of the problem.

Her unique gift was certainly interesting though. He filed it away for later review. Something told him it might be usable in ensuring his little brother's happiness. Deciding he had eavesdropped long enough, he came around the corner and headed for the coffee. "You sure you don't want to run away with me instead?"

"I'll fight you over her," Cameron warned, but with a smile.

Sarah clasped a hand to heart. "Why, lucky me. I have the two most eligible males in the building vying for my hand. I don't know how I'll ever choose."

Cameron glanced around, and Kenneth grinned. "It's clear."

"Good." That said, he grabbed Sarah and kissed her so hard that her toes curled inside her shoes. When he released her, he asked, "Now who wins?"

She could only dangle in his arms, her head spinning wildly around her shoulders. "I think I do. Whoo boy." Her sharp ears detected footsteps and she quickly stepped away and smoothed her hair and clothes.

Cameron's good mood was visible to everyone, and more than one smiling glance went Sarah's way. She looked completely unruffled, but there was an added sparkle in her eyes. Even Lorcana noticed and her ire steadily grew, as did her suspicions.

She felt fairly sure Cameron was screwing the girl, and under other circumstances she might not have minded. In fact, if Sarah had been the type she could easily control, she would have wholeheartedly approved of the relationship, especially since it seemed clear that Cameron wasn't thinking with his brain in relation to her.

But the girl had had the absolute nerve to stand up to Lorcana and she despised that. Who did she think she was? She was a nobody from the backwater 3rd District, and she had no fortune to call her own. She came recommended by Shaughnessy-Tavoularis but that meant nothing in the grander scheme of things.

Still, she decided to play it by ear. "Well," she said to Cameron as she entered the meeting room. "You look extra cheerful this morning. Finally decided that I'm right about this whole situation?"

"No, but I've decided to make the best of it." He shrugged and propped his feet on the table. He knew she hated it and therefore did it on purpose as much as he could. "I long ago came to the conclusion that you hate me and want to do everything you can to make us miserable because you are."

Her jaw dropped. Kenneth's did too but then his shock faded to be replaced by sheer delight. Sarah had put some serious steel in Cameron's spine. He couldn't have been happier. And, while Lorcana paced away, he swiftly wrote Sarah's name in on the list of candidates. He knew full well that his mother wouldn't recognize her name; why would she bother herself with such a trivial thing? She barely remembered Louise's name half the time. Something needed to be done, and he could nearly feel a presence urging him to act.

In the front area, Sarah was already beginning to check in the potential brides. A part of her wanted to tell them all to keep their hands off her man, but she covered it with a friendly smile. Really, what could she say that wouldn't get her and Cameron into trouble? She would have to play along until they found a solution.

Two potential brides walked out when they saw the duty statement. The others remained and she did her part to make sure they felt welcome. Observing her, Cameron thought to himself about how she truly seemed to be a real princess in disguise. He fought the urge to rush out there and make it plain that he wanted her only.

Lorcana, going down the list of names, didn't even know who she was calling for as she walked out of the room and said, "Davidson!"

Sarah's eyes widened and she looked around. There were no other brides left, and she was the only one who had the last name of Davidson. She warily got to her feet and walked into the meeting room. "Er, yes?"

Shocked, Lorcana stared at her. "What are you doing in here?"

She blinked. "You called my name."

Lorcana looked down at her list swiftly, and this time looked closer. "Kenneth!" she snapped at her eldest son. "This is your handwriting! Why is she on the list of brides?"

He linked his hands behind his head. "I figured Cam ought to marry the woman he's in love with. Where do you think he was last night?"

With the doors standing open, there was no one who hadn't heard him. Everyone fell silent. Cameron and Sarah mutually stared at him in wide-eyed shock. Lorcana couldn't find her voice at first and then her fury rose wildly. Her face turned red as she whirled on Sarah. "You're fired!" she screamed. "If you think you can sleep your way to the top, you're sadly mistaken, you little bitch!"

"You mean like you did?" Sarah lifted her chin slightly. "You knew Cam had been with me last night when you saw me this morning." Her voice remained perfectly calm. "The only reason you're so mad now is because you *know* that your son stands on the cusp of a happiness you will never have." She turned to the door but briefly stopped and looked back. "You are a pitiful woman, Lorcana Dease."

She held onto her composure until she reached her desk. The pain welled up sharply and she grabbed her purse as she fled out the doors. She knew Kenneth had been trying to help, but it had backfired in the worst way possible. She would never see Cameron again; he would be under twenty-four hour surveillance. How was it fair that she fall in love and have her heart broken all within a twenty-four period?

Cameron's temper blew. He leapt to his feet and slammed his hands on the top of the table. "I've had it!" he shouted. "I've had it! You've done nothing but ruin my life! And for what? A company you don't even know how to fucking run! Well, you know what? I want Sarah more than I want this damn company! Unlike you, I know how to love. I know that it's more precious than any shares, no matter their value! Keep your greed! I hope it keeps you warm. I'll have Sarah as my wife or none other! I'm retaining a lawyer in the morning and having myself relieved of your guardianship! If it means giving up the company, then *so be it*!" He ran out of the office swiftly but Sarah had already left. Cursing, he headed for the stairs.

This time the silence was absolute. Kenneth said nothing. Pride filled him over his brother's actions, and he could not regret what he had done. It had spurred Cameron to do something long overdue. Still, Kenneth could not shake that feeling that he had somehow been manipulated into causing the events. His eyes drifted across the room to a potted plant that, curiously, had begun to bloom with white roses. Where had those come from? They had not been there before the idea had struck him to write down Sarah's name. More magic?

Shaking, Lorcana braced her hands on the table. She had never seen Cameron like that. A part of her was shocked because he had never looked more like his father. She had loathed Viktor, but a part of her had respected him as well.

Someone knocked lightly on the door and the two Deases looked to see Louise standing in the doorway. Politely, she asked Lorcana, "Did we hear you fire Sarah, and Cameron vow to give you the company in order to have her?"

"That about sums it up," Kenneth confirmed.

"I see. Well, in that case we quit. And by we, I mean the entire graphic department." She removed her badge and dropped it on the floor. "We're not going to work for you, Lorcana. We only stayed this long because of Kenneth and Cameron. Bring back Sarah and Cameron, and we'll return. Until then . . . I guess the company is temporarily shut down. Goodbye."

Kenneth and Lorcana both walked over to the door and watched in surprise as every single employee shut down their computers, gathered their bags, and left. Lorcana felt sickened as she watched all of her carefully laid plans fall apart. If only that little bitch had never arrived. "What coincidence is this that I decided to hire *her*?" she asked scathingly.

Kenneth glanced at her as she walked off and decided not to mention the lack of coincidence around 3rd District. She would never understand. Still wondering what in the hell they were supposed to do next, he headed out of the office. He would find where Sarah lived and have a talk with her and Cameron. Maybe the three of them could find a way to win it all.

CHAPTER FIVE

When Sarah got back to 3rd District, she stopped to visit a friend on her way home. They had been friends since kindergarten when they had discovered that they had nearly identical names. It had started as just something to giggle over and then had evolved into their own inside joke. They enjoyed seeing people do double takes.

Things had happened so fast over the last few days that Sarah hadn't had time to tell Sera about the changes in her life. Now she desperately needed her friend's levelheaded, pragmatic, personality, and her quick thinking.

Sera Thomason was watering the flowers in front of her home when she sensed her friend. She looked over at Sarah and snorted. "Well. Someone got laid."

She had to smile. "Is it that obvious?"

Sera tossed short black hair streaked with hot pink out of her gold colored eyes. "Well, to someone who knows you. You have that nicely relaxed look about you. Now you want to tell me why there's so much sadness in your eyes as well, and who I have to kill?"

Sarah took a deep breath. "You know I went to work for the Deases, right?" When Sera lifted a brow, she sat down on a tree stump. "To make a long story short, I fell in love with Cameron Dease."

Sera's gold eyes began to resemble flames as her ire grew. "And he took advantage."

"No." She put her head in her hands. "It would be easier if he had. No, he loves me too. We became lovers. And now his mother has fired me because she's a cold-hearted bitch who wants to make Cameron suffer. She'll have him under lock and key until either she marries him off or he turns twenty-one. Probably the former before the latter."

Sera drummed her fingers on her arm and contemplated the merits of turning into a wild boar and goring Lorcana Dease to death. "All executives are pricks," she noted. "You're better off without any of them."

"You may think that," Sarah said softly, "but you don't know Cameron and his brother. They're different, Sera."

Sera wasn't an empath, but she didn't need to be in order to feel her friend's misery. With a sigh, she relented and sat beside her. "So, what do we do?" Sarah glanced at her, and she smiled and nudged her shoulder. "Hey, we're friends. That's what friends do." Abruptly, a frown marred her brow. "You *were* careful right?"

Sarah coughed. "Well . . ."

She groaned. "Sarah!"

"He made me forget my own name!" she defended herself. "And he was lucky to remember to take his socks off! I was going to go on the pill or something, but I guess it's moot now."

"You know what?" Sera hugged her. "If you do end up pregnant, I'll hire some big thugs to kidnap your Cameron and get him away from his mother. Then you two can 'live in sin' until he's legal."

Sarah hugged her back. "Thanks, Sera." She sighed and got to her feet. "I'm going home. I just can't make my brain work right now."

Sera watched her go and then crossed her arms, a scowl darkening her lovely face. Sarah had been her best friend since they were children. Just as Sarah had stayed by Sera's side through the death of her father and her mother's ailing health, Sera had stayed by Sarah's side during the loss of her parents. Thinking that her friend was suffering and she couldn't do anything pissed her off.

"Excuse me?"

She looked over at the male voice and her brows rose sharply. The young man on the other side of her fence was downright gorgeous with platinum hair and eyes more gray than green. Her eyes narrowed suddenly as she saw that he wore a suit. She got to her feet slowly and walked over to him. Her delicate nose instantly caught a whiff of Sarah's perfume. "You must be Cameron."

Cameron watched the slender female like one would watch a wild animal. She looked quite furious, and he was fairly sure she knew Sarah because of it. A sixth sense told him that Sarah had been through the area lately. He had tried her house first, but she hadn't been there. "I am," he said. "Do you know where Sarah Davidson is?"

"Yes." She bared her teeth. "Now ask me if I'm going to tell you."

He narrowed his eyes. "Are you her friend or not?"

"Oh I'm her friend." She narrowed her own eyes in return. "And as such I'm not going to watch her be torn to pieces by some little boy who can't cut his mother's apron strings."

Temper flared in his eyes and she wondered if he would let it loose. Then, to her everlasting shock, he suddenly dropped onto his knees. "Please," he said, his voice low. "I'm begging you. Where is Sarah?"

"Get up," she begged. "You're really freaking me out here!" She hated seeing men grovel, and his sincerity was so strong that she felt as if she had been kicked by it. He suffered as much as Sarah did. There was one severely lovesick man in front of her right then. She sighed. "Look, I don't want her hurt again."

"I'm going to do my best." His gaze hardened. "I've disowned my mother. It means disowning my company, but I want Sarah more."

She lowered her gaze slightly. "Sarah should be at home by now. She was in no condition to go anywhere else."

He leapt to his feet and gave her an enthusiastic hug. "Thank you!" He swiftly ran off down the road, leaving one very bemused shapeshifter behind him.

"Yeah," she murmured, "you're definitely the one for Sarah."

Back at the company building, Kenneth paced rapidly in the lobby. He didn't know what to do. All he knew was that he had to do *something*. He couldn't stand to see his brother and Sarah suffering, and he was doubly sure that he didn't want to see the company fall into Lorcana's hands, even in part. Cameron had shed blood for his share—literally.

As he swung around again, he came to sharp stop in surprise. Standing just behind him was a short young woman with snowy white hair. Her purple-gray eyes seemed to laugh at a joke only the universe might understand. And she was *tiny*. At only five-eleven, he still felt like a giant. "Er, can I help you?"

"Actually, I can help you." She walked over and held out a sheaf of papers. "I'm from Enforcers."

"Because of Sarah?" he asked shrewdly.

"Mmm."

It wasn't quite an agreement, but something told him not to ask more. He took the papers and unrolled them. His experienced eye instantly recognized that he held a contract. He read it over quickly and then had to go back and read it again. He began to grin slowly. "This is great." He looked up but the young woman had disappeared, leaving behind the scent of roses. "Thanks," he murmured.

He wasted no time in heading for home. The servants at the manor were quick to clear his path. He rarely got that kind of a look on his face, and when he did, you got out of his way.

He didn't bother to knock on the study door. He just walked right in. "Look," he said curtly, "let's call a spade a spade. You want Sarah gone. I want peace in the house."

Lorcana slowly looked at him, her eyes narrowed. She knew he wasn't helping because he was on her side. "Your brother's *happiness* doesn't matter?" she sneered.

Icily, he retorted, "I'd rather find a way to bring him back than to deal with you by myself." He slapped the contract down on the desk. "This is a surefire method. You play nice for one night and we get everything taken care of by morning. This contract says that if Sarah can feel a *pea* through a mattress, then she can marry Cameron. If not, she's out."

"Oh please!" she scoffed. Even she recognized the scenario. "A faerie tale!"

"Fitting for someone from 3rd District, no? I'm not telling them what they're signing. They won't even know. But with their signatures on here, they're trapped into the outcome."

She tapped a scarlet fingernail on the top of the desk, but she couldn't find any way that she *wouldn't* win. Even if the little twit was 'different' in some way like rumor stated, there was no way she could possibly feel a pea under a mattress. "Won't it be squashed?" she asked reluctantly. "I always wondered about that."

"Eh. I'll freeze it beforehand." He met her eyes. "One night. You can pretend to be less than a bitch goddess for one night."

Her face tightened. "You're pretty bold, Kenneth Dease. How dare you talk to your mother like this?"

"Please. Let's be honest here. You married Dad because you wanted the company. You gave birth to me and Cameron under duress because he wanted kids and would have divorced you otherwise." Something cold moved in his eyes. "Dad loved us; he told us all along what you were really like. If he had known he would die and leave us in your *tender* care, he probably would have quit smoking."

She muttered something vile under her breath. With vicious strokes, she signed the contract. "Now get out of my sight," she ordered sharply.

"Gladly." He tucked the contract in his pocket and walked out of the study. It took considerable effort not to slam the door behind him. Now all he had to do was find Sarah and Cameron and get their signatures on the contract without telling them what was going on. He could only hope they still trusted him.

Sarah was curled up on her couch crying into a pillow when she heard the doorbell ring. Unwilling to deal with anyone, she didn't move. She felt miserable and alone. If it was Sera, she would apologize later. If it was a salesman, he could get lost. And if it was Eric . . . ooh. He would *so* get it.

A fist pounded on the door and she nearly jumped out of her skin. Her heart froze in her chest as she heard Cameron calling, "I know you're home, Sarah! Open the damned door. Please. Let me in."

She carefully walked over to the door but didn't open it. "Why are you here?" she asked achingly. "You're just going to make it worse."

"Open the door." His voice softened. "Sarah. Please. Let me in." He held his breath as the silence stretched, then his heart began to beat again as the lock turned and she opened the door. His beating heart promptly broke as he saw the puffiness under her eyes and traces of tears on her face. "Sarah."

Before she could blink, he had moved to catch her in his arms and lift her off her feet. It felt so good to be held by him that all she could do was wrap her arms around his shoulders and cling on.

He walked into the apartment and kicked the door shut. Still holding tight to her, he walked over to the couch and sat down with her on his lap.

"Why did you come here?" she whispered again. "It just hurts more."

"Because I love you." He eased her back and gave her a little shake so that she looked at him. "I'm not losing you, Sarah. Do you think I want any life without you around? Who would I go to when I needed a laugh? Who would I share horror stories of bad coffee with? Who would I make love to just for the sheer joy of sharing my body and heart with?"

Her lips trembled. "You're going to make me cry again!"

He wiped away her tears softly. Quietly, seriously, he said, "I told Mother that I'm getting a lawyer in the morning." He held her when she tried to jerk away. "I'm relieving myself of her guardianship. Yeah, I lose my shares. Big deal. I want you more."

"You can't *do* that!" she cried. "Cam, you *can't*! Men don't give up multi-million dollar companies for women!"

"This man does." He turned sharply and pressed her down onto the couch. His eyes darkened to more green than gray as he pinned her. "Read my lips, Sarah Davidson: I am *not* giving you up!"

When Kenneth suddenly cleared his throat, both lovers looked at him in surprise. "Sorry," he said, "the door was unlocked." He shut the door behind him. "I guess I'm interrupting."

Cameron very reluctantly helped Sarah sit back up. He didn't let her slide off his lap, however. "A little," he conceded. "But I assume you're here for a good reason. And hopefully it's a better idea than what you tried this morning."

"Yeah." He walked over and sat down on one of the chairs facing the couch. "I am *really* sorry, guys. But something needed to happen. We would have been stuck in status quo forever." His smile turned wry. "And, Cam, there isn't much of a company to give up."

"Wha?"

"When Sarah was fired and you vowed to give up the company in order to have her, everyone in Graphics quit." They stared at him, and he raked a hand through his hair. "Seriously. Louise came to the door and told us very politely that she and the others had stayed for me and you, and they would not work for Mother. They then walked out. They won't come back unless you do."

"I would say that's impossible," Sarah said softly, "but I never really believed that word even exists."

Cameron jerked a thumb at the window and the District that lay beyond it. "Par for the course around here, isn't it?" He raked a hand through his hair in a manner not dissimilar from his brother. "So now what do we do? I mean . . . I hate to see the company go under, but I'm not giving up Sarah."

"I would hope not!" Kenneth said. "Look, here's the thing. I had words with Mother. And I may have gotten to an agreement with her."

"Did you sell your soul?" Sarah muttered.

"No, no. It's okay. I got her to agree to letting you come over for dinner and to spend the night. To give you and Cam a chance. I even got her to sign a contract." He pulled the papers out of his jacket. "I just need you two to sign as well so she can't welsh."

"Can I read that?" Cameron asked warily.

Kenneth met his eyes. "Do you trust me, Cam? If you do, then sign without reading this. I promise that tomorrow morning everything will work out."

Cameron and Sarah exchanged a long look and then both nodded slightly. What did they have to lose anyway? Without reading the contract, without bothering to even skim the surface, they both signed at the bottom next to Lorcana's name. "Man, I hope this works," Cameron sighed. "I'm not looking forward to facing my mother."

Sarah wasn't feeling entirely sure herself, but she couldn't let either Cameron or Kenneth down. Cameron was willing to give up a multi-million dollar company for her. Kenneth had put his neck on the line. That was worth finding some courage. "I'll go pack a bag, I guess." She rose to her feet and headed to her bedroom.

The minute she got out of earshot, Cameron demanded, "Tell me straight, Ken: are you getting yourself in trouble over this?"

Kenneth shook his head. "No. And, besides, what can she do to me? I'm an adult. The sooner she's out of our house, the better. You and Sarah can redo the master for yourselves."

Speculatively, Cameron said, "You know, you sound entirely confident that somehow this is going to work out. What do you know that we don't? Should I have been reading between the lines on that contract after all?"

His brother smiled. "Let's just say that simply by being exactly who and what she is, Sarah is going to ensure you both have a happy ending."

Puzzled and yet amiable, he went to help Sarah. Really, at this point he was playing it all by ear. He had always believed in magic, and Aenya's words seemed to, rather appropriately, dance constantly in his mind. He really wanted everything to work out perfectly.

"How do you guys handle dinner?" Sarah asked as she sensed him in the room. "I mean, when I'd have dinner with the extended Shaughnessy family, they were super casual, but your mother is, uhm, a little straight-laced."

"How tactful." He grinned a little. "Why don't we plan on making it fancy? That way you can prove that you're not some poor secretary and I can happily admire you all night. Can you wear that black dress?"

"Maybe." Her eyes began to sparkle merrily as her humor returned. "But I'm not going to tell you what I'll have on under it." She paused, and then murmured, "Or what I don't."

"I foresee myself sneaking into your bed sometime tonight."

"The man's a prophet! And I thought I was the one with the wooky mojo in her bloodline."

The mutual good mood lasted until they got to the Dease family home. Despite her best efforts to keep her smile, Sarah found herself highly wary as the two brothers escorted her into the large manor. The wariness faded, however, as soon as she met the housekeeper. In fact, she began grinning.

The older woman was as plump as a large bird, had snowy white hair, and sported a cherubic-like face. She seemed to descend out of nowhere and grabbed Cameron by the ear. "Cameron Dease!" she scolded, her voice far more youthful than her appearance lent itself to. "What's this I hear about you falling in love?"

"Ouch! C'mon, Tia! Let go!" He wiggled free and rubbed his ear. With a wry smile, he gestured at Sarah. "Meet the woman of my dreams."

"Hi." Sarah smiled angelically. "I'm the woman of his dreams. I'm usually called Sarah."

Tia studied her intently and began to smile. She had a feeling she was going to like this young lady very much. "I'm quite happy to meet you, Sarah. I am Tia. I run the household. I've also raised both these terrors since they were but toddlers."

"Oh so you're the one I need to bribe to get all Cameron's secrets." She nodded sagely. "We'll have to talk price later. I can offer homemade cookies."

With a rich laugh, Tia clapped a rather alarmed-looking Cameron on the shoulder. "I believe I might just be buyable for that price." She took the suitcase Sarah carried and winked saucily. "Should I put this in Cameron's room to save everyone some trouble?" Cameron's cheeks turned pink, and she just clucked her tongue at him. "As if your Tia didn't know!" She tweaked his nose. "I want grandbabies to spoil."

As she disappeared down the hall, Sarah started giggling. "I'm going to like her!"

"Tia is awesome," Kenneth agreed with a grin.

Cameron sighed fondly. "In case you hadn't guessed, she's Ken's and my *real* mother in all the ways that really count. C'mon. We'll give you a tour of the place. You'll like it here."

She didn't just like it. She *loved* it. Despite the size and grandeur and the occasional servants wandering around, it felt like a home. Since she knew full well that Lorcana didn't even know what a home was supposed to be, she could only guess it was Tia that had made sure her two 'sons' felt comfortable. At least she could understand better now how Kenneth and Cameron had become such amazing men despite their birth mother's influence. Love could make all the difference in the world for any child.

Cameron's bedroom was on the third floor. It was also almost as big as her entire apartment, and her eyes widened in wonder at the giant bed taking up a chunk of the floor space. "Holy cow. Was that designed by NASA or something? I swear it defies all laws of spatial relations. Who divided by zero?"

"Hey, I like lots of room."

They exchanged a look. Then, as one, they both ran forward and jumped on the bed. She would have gone skidding off the other side as her silk skirt found no traction on the equally silky covers, but he hastily grabbed her and yanked her back. Sprawled in the middle of the bed, they both started laughing. "That was fun!" she managed to say.

"I'm just glad I caught you! I took a noser into my dresser once. Dad swore the only reason I didn't have a concussion was because my head was so hard!"

"Like father like son?"

He grinned. "So he claimed." He sat up and felt his heart twist as he looked down at her. Her rusty hair had tangled around her shoulders, and glowed more brilliantly orange than ever against the blue comforter. She looked so perfect there in his bed, as if she had always belonged. Unable to resist, he leaned down to kiss her. She sighed softly into his lips as the kiss deepened, and a shiver rippled through her body as he skimmed his fingers down her sensitive skin.

"Ahem."

Against her lips, he muttered, "Go away, Tia."

Tia gave a ladylike snort. "You can work on my grandbabies later. Mrs. Lorcana has said that she wants dinner to be formal, and that you're to be dressed and downstairs in fifteen minutes."

She disappeared from the doorway and he reluctantly released Sarah. "I need to start locking the door."

"That would be more effective if she didn't probably have keys to every door." She scooped up her suitcase and spotted the door leading into the bathroom. "No peeking!" she scolded him as she went in and shut the door.

"Spoilsport! It's not like I haven't seen you naked."

"Yes, but I'm shy."

"And the sun rises in the west, I'm sure."

"See, I knew that stuff about it rising in the east was just a governmental conspiracy."

Grinning, he went into his closet to find clean clothes. As he changed into black slacks and a blue dress shirt, he couldn't help but think again about how much he owed his big brother. Kenneth had done a lot over the last nearly two years to act as a deflector for him, helping him win battles he might not have been able to fight alone. Even the minor scraps, such as the clothing he wore. Kenneth deserved happiness too.

"Shoes or no shoes?" Sarah suddenly asked from the bedroom.

"Shoes. When Mother says formal," he said wryly as he walked out of the closet, "she means . . ." His words trailed off as he saw her. She had done that strange female thing to her hair and face where it didn't *look* like she had done anything, but suddenly her features were more pronounced and her hair was pinned in a way that begged for his fingers to take it down.

The black dress clung to every curve of her body without being too revealing. Having become intimately acquainted with every inch under the dress, he approved wholeheartedly of anything that showed it off. "You're not cute," he told her.

She arched a brow. "I'm not?"

"No. Right now you're gorgeous. And sexy. I thought I preferred cute girls, but I'm becoming a big fan of sexy ones."

On a sigh, she rose on her toes to kiss him happily. "I love you, Cameron Dease. Never change."

"In general or specifically?" He linked his hands around her waist.

"I meant in personality. I would take it as a favor if you at least changed your socks once a day." Her eyes twinkled. "Some change is good for you."

He lowered his forehead to hers with a smile. "The changes you've brought sure are." He held her for a moment and then let go. "Let's go eat dinner with the devil. No food fights, though."

"And the long spoon I brought would be such a good weapon, darn it."

CHAPTER SIX

Kenneth and Lorcana were already in the dining room when Cameron and Sarah arrived. Kenneth got to his feet with a smile when he saw them enter. "You sure you won't run away with me instead, Sarah?"

"You don't like the color blue as much," she told him innocently, "and it goes with my hair so well."

Despite herself, Lorcana found herself asking, "Blue and orange?" Looking at them, she could certainly *see* that the colors blended nicely together, but she hadn't the faintest idea why. She knew advertising when it was good, but she couldn't grasp the art behind it.

"Complimentary colors," Sarah offered kindly. "Like red and green, or yellow and purple." She let Cameron hold her chair and sat down gracefully. "Most people don't know why they work, but they know that they do. I only know because I spent a lot of time with the artists who worked for my parents' company."

"Oh, did they own a business?" Lorcana smiled coolly. "I thought most of those in 3rd District were middle or low class."

Cameron's hands curled into fists under the table, and Sarah covered them gently with one hand. Sweetly, she said, "As a matter of fact, there are few people in the 3rd District who don't own whatever business they work at. We can lay claim to the hottest club in NYC, and one of the most affluent bed and breakfasts as well. The president has even stayed at the Gentle Brook Inn; did you know?" Blithely she continued, "Anyway, my parents owned a small ad company that worked with small businesses."

"What was it called?" Kenneth asked curiously.

"Analogous Ad Company." She smiled. "More color puns." Aware that all three Deases were now staring at her in shock, she blinked. "Did I say something odd?"

"Your parents owned AAC?" Cameron sat back in his chair. "Wow. We tried to buy stock in the company but we couldn't bid high enough. I didn't even make the connection that the reason the company had been bought by the largest shareholders was because the owners had died."

"I couldn't run it by myself," she said softly. "I had to let Mel and Kalliope take over. It was better than seeing it be destroyed. I couldn't have endured that."

"Then you're an orphan?" Lorcana asked.

"Yes, but I'm a legal adult. The Enforcers themselves got me the lawyer that gave me my independence. And I turn twenty-one next month." She smiled angelically. "I've been acting like an adult since I was eighteen though; my parents trusted me to think for myself."

Even Cameron couldn't guess at whether or not she had deliberately insulted Lorcana. His mother was fairly certain she had, but she couldn't prove it. Frustration simmered under the surface in Lorcana. It seemed as if everything she did to make the girl realize she wouldn't fit in just seemed to backfire. "You know," she said, a little bite in her words, "there are a lot of rumors about 3rd District. People say that those who were born there aren't even human."

Sarah sighed gustily. "I told my parents that too, but they *insisted* that they hadn't stolen me from aliens. And my childhood tutor often threatened to eat one of us kids for misbehaving, but I think she might have been a vegetarian, so I doubt she meant it." She propped her chin on her hand. Something powerful flickered across her brown eyes. "If I was able to cast spells, you wouldn't even know I'd done it until too late."

A chill went down Lorcana's back and she rubbed her hands over her arms. She just felt sure she had seen . . . something in Sarah's eyes. It was with much relief that dinner was served at that moment and she didn't have to try to find a retort. She wasn't even sure she had one.

"So you don't have any artistic talent?" Kenneth asked Sarah curiously.

"Define talent." She smiled. "I've always said I had the soul of an artist but lacked the skill to express it. I can draw stick people, but that's only because my best friend *is* an artist and was patient enough to teach me. I've seen her sketch portraits of people on the fly. She's amazing."

Cameron thought about the cocky young woman he had met when he had been looking for Sarah. The slender female had definitely had style and flair, but she had been a lot more . . . forceful than he had come to expect out of freelance artists. She wouldn't take any crap from her clients, that was for sure!

"What made you decide not to go to college?" Lorcana asked politely. "Couldn't you make up your mind on a major?"

Sarah's eyes widened innocently. "What makes you think I didn't go to college? As a matter of fact, I'm currently trying to earn a dual major. I've been studying Advertising and Computer Information Sciences. I've had to take a brief sabbatical since I need to save money for my next semester; my parents were helping to support me. However, I recently entered a scholarship contest and made it to the finals, so I might be set within the next month or so."

"What was the contest?" Cameron kept the grin off his face with effort. The way she seemed to deflect or counter Lorcana's every comment was fabulous.

"Interested students had to write a five-thousand word essay to explain and promote a personal, home grown computer program. In the finals, we actually had to build the program. I decided to take my 'art for dummies' knowledge and built a program that, with only a little input from the user, can accurately and efficiently match colors for everything from interior design to clothing trends."

Kenneth whistled between his teeth. "That's a lot of programming!"

"Tell me about it! I was awake until two a.m. more nights than I can count. Anyway, if I win, I'll be able to have my degrees within the next year. I only have a handful of classes left." She tilted her head and her curls bounced lightly. "Of course, you wouldn't have known that, Lorcana, since I didn't feel the need to put down a 'pending' degree on my application unrelated to secretarial skills. I didn't want you all to think I was using my degree to get my foot in the door."

Lorcana's back teeth clicked together. "Dessert!" she nearly barked at the servants.

While they were all eating, Kenneth took a brief hiatus from the table for a few minutes. When he returned, Lorcana just stared at him. He inclined his head ever so slightly and retook his seat. Mollified, she clenched her hands together and told herself it would all be over soon. She hated Sarah. She hated more the way Cameron looked at her. And she absolutely loathed the fact that there was the smallest seed of respect inside her for the younger woman. She had style, grace, and class.

Clearly thinking the same thing, Kenneth said wryly, "You know, it's so funny. Cam and I are always teasingly called princes because we're set to inherit a modern castle. You're completely the equivalent of a princess whose kingdom was lost."

"Yes, but I'd never do well in exile," Sarah countered woefully. "I'd have no one to talk to. I'm a people person. By the time I returned to civilization, I'd be talking more than the local politicians."

Lorcana threw down her napkin and got to her feet. "I'm going to retire for the evening. Good night."

Everyone was silent while she left the room. Finally, Cameron smiled and said, "That was like a round of tennis! Back and forth, back and forth."

"It's probably the only love your mother will ever know."

"Ouch!" He gave her a smacking kiss. "That was petty, and awful, and I love you all the more for it!"

"You should hear what I've been biting back!" She blew out a breath. "I don't think I've won any points, guys. She still hates me. She still doesn't want me anywhere near Cameron because I make him happy, and if he marries me, she loses all control of the company. It's your guess which she hates more."

"Well, no use thinking about it right now," Kenneth said softly. "Let's just go to bed and deal with things in the morning." He winked. "Try to actually sleep, okay, guys?"

"Tia wants grandkids," Cameron argued, grinning. "We should try to oblige."

"I must be insane to be anywhere near you two!" Sarah got to her feet with a smile. "Your time will come, Kenneth Dease! And I'm going to enjoy watching it."

"It would only be fair," he agreed.

Cameron slipped his arm around Sarah's waist and escorted her out of the dining room. "Damn," he said softly, "that was unreal! She really tried to put you through the wringer." His arm tightened possessively. "You really held your own, though. I was really proud of you."

She rested her head on his shoulder with a sigh. "Thanks, but I'm not overly optimistic about the future. Unless she's swapped with a pod person in the middle of the night, there's no way she'll ever give her blessing tomorrow morning."

He shut the bedroom door behind them and leaned against it. His green eyes were dark and intense as he watched her kick off her shoes. "So what if she doesn't change her mind? I don't care, Sarah. For once in my life, I'm going to make my own decisions. I'm going to fight my own battles. If she still digs in her heels, you and I are going back to your apartment *together*. We can both get new jobs. We can make it work."

"Enforcers has good lawyers." Her smile was slight but real. "I could call Eric Mason or Rhianna Taber and ask for help. They'd give it without hesitation." She took a long breath and then began pulling the pins out of her hair. "What's done is done."

"Stop." He had moved closer without her knowledge and his voice had gone husky with desire. "Let me." He buried his fingers in her hair and sent the remaining pins flying. The few curls in her hair were already stretching out, and he wrapped one around his finger. "Your hair just doesn't like to bend to anything. Just like you."

Her lashes fluttered closed as his hot mouth began to trail kisses over her jaw. That wonderful, now familiar, heat was spreading inside her body. Of their own will, her hands lifted and spread across his chest. He was so hot. Hard and secure, a seductive promise of comfort and pleasure all at the same time. How was it that even his clothes couldn't hurt her skin? They weren't like her clothes; they weren't specially made. It seemed as if everything he was permeated everything he wore. "Cam."

He slowly caught handfuls of her dress and stripped it up over her head. His mouth went dry as he saw what had been hiding underneath. The dark blue silk barely covered her breasts and rode high on her long legs. Sexy garters held up smoky stockings. "I'm glad I didn't know this was under your dress," he managed to say. "I'd have gone crazy."

Her lips curved slowly. "It was an eighteenth birthday gift from my friend. I never thought I'd have a reason to wear it." She wound her arms around his neck and pressed teasingly against his body. "Think you can get it off me without ripping it?"

"Watch me." He bore her down onto the rug, his mouth eagerly rushing across every inch of fragrant skin he could reach. He sensed as much as felt her flinch slightly and immediately rolled over so she was on top. "I didn't even think." His hands stroked slowly up her legs and played with the garters as he went. "No rug burns on your body. No marks at all this time."

By the time they climbed into bed, she wouldn't have cared either way if she had rug burns or not. Seriously, what he could do to her body had to be illegal somewhere. As he pulled the covers over them, she drowsily curled closer against his side. The silk sheets felt deliciously decadent against her skin, which was even more sensitive than usual thanks to him. Thank goodness for his rich-boy preference for the really high thread count sheets. She could sleep on these safely.

"Comfy?" he asked sleepily. He tugged her even closer possessively.

"Mmph." She tucked her nose against his shoulder.

"Good."

Her comfort didn't last long. He shifted position and she naturally adjusted herself to follow. Problem was, as she settled down again, something pressed painfully into her back. It felt as if she had laid down on a rock! Agitated, she tried to find a place to lay that didn't dig into her tender flesh, but the more she moved, the worse it got.

Her restless movements finally got to her lover. "Jesus, what's wrong with you?" He rose onto one elbow to eye her intently.

"There's a lump in the bed!"

He sighed as he understood. "It's probably just a spring. I don't feel anything." He laid down again and dragged her on top of his chest. "Here. Now go to sleep!"

That was easier said than done since feeling him pressed along every inch of her body was highly distracting. But, finally, she was able to drift off to sleep. Once she let herself relax, she realized how comfortable she really felt. He made a nice bed.

She awoke in the early morning to the feel of his hands moving over her body slowly. She surrendered to his touch with a sigh into his kiss. If this was how she was destined to wake every morning, then she was going to be a very happy woman.

As real sunlight began to come in the window some time later, she reluctantly rolled off his chest. The lump in the bed instantly stabbed into her back again. "Ouch!"

"Alright, that's it!" He rolled out of bed and dragged her up as well. "I'm finding this mysterious lump of yours." He began to strip off the covers.

She walked over to the mirror and turned to see her back. She winced. The black and blue bruises were spreading with a vengeance. "May I recommend that we keep my bed?" She rolled her shoulders carefully. "I'm going to be stiff all day. And it hurts. Do you have aspirin around?"

"Yeah, in the medicine cabinet." He sighed. "I can't find anything wrong with the bed, sweetheart. The springs seem to be fine. I guess it's a good thing we'll be using your bed; at least we know it won't make you look like you went three rounds."

"Tell me about it! Now help me get my bra on. It hurts to move my back muscles right now."

"I'd rather help you take it off." He fastened the clasp in the back and then tenderly skimmed his fingers over the bruises. "I'm sorry, Sarah." He gently pressed a kiss to the worst of the marks.

"How were you supposed to know?" She smiled over her shoulder. "Next time I feel something wrong, I'll say something rather than just toss around. I don't think either of us got the sleep we wanted. But let's let Kenneth think we were working on Tia's grandbabies and make him jealous."

He laughed and helped her pull on a sweater. He then got dressed while she packed up her things once more. After a moment of thought, he pulled out a suitcase of his own and began to throw items into it. "I'm an optimistic guy, but I'm not an idiot," he told her. "I'm sure we'll be leaving together."

"I know." She let her fingers entwine with his as they left the room and headed downstairs toward the dining room to get some breakfast and have the final showdown. When they walked in, she was surprised to see both Kenneth and Lorcana staring at her intently. "What?" She automatically looked down. "Is my sweater on backwards?"

"No, not at all." A smug smile began to curse Lorcana's lips. "How did you sleep last night, my dear?"

Instantly wary, she said, "Well enough, thank you, despite the fact that my tossing and turning kept us both awake."

"Tossing and turning?" Kenneth asked.

"Yeah." Cameron sighed. "There was a lump in the bed that she could feel and it bruised her something fierce. I didn't feel anything myself, so I finally made her sleep on top of me."

"Which was vastly more comfortable than a pillow top bed anyway," his lover said impishly. To her shock, Lorcana suddenly walked over to her and grabbed her arm. "Ow! Hey, let go!"

Lorcana tugged Sarah's sweater away from her back and stared in horror at the sight of the bruises covering her fair flesh. "That . . . that's impossible!" She backed up sharply, her face white. "It's impossible!"

"What did you do?" Cameron demanded of Kenneth when his brother started laughing. "Damn it, Ken, I knew you were up to something!"

"Here's that contract you signed." Kenneth pulled it out of his back pocket and handed it over.

It didn't take Cameron long to figure it out. "'Should Party 2 be able to feel to feel a single pea through a high quality mattress, Party 3 will be given full permission and authority by Party 1 to marry said Party 2. This contract will be Enforced to the highest . . .'" He trailed off in shock. "*This* is what we signed?"

"That was a *pea* that I felt?" Sarah yelped.

"I stuck it under the mattress last night." Kenneth grinned. "And there's no denying the evidence that you felt it; you've sure got the bruises to prove it. And that means that you've both fulfilled the terms of the contract, little sister." He glanced at his mother coolly. "And because she signed as well, she can't deny the terms. Cameron has full permission to marry you even though he's not yet legal."

There was nothing Lorcana could say to that. Before her eyes, every one of her plans had crumbled and fallen apart. *The girl had felt a pea through a mattress*! It should have been impossible, but not even she could find a way that this could have been a set up. The bruises on Sarah's back were very real, and they looked very much like what one would expect of someone rolling over a small object.

With a violent oath, she stalked out of the room. Her office door slammed so hard that it shook the entire manor. Kenneth said nothing. Cameron and Sarah said nothing. Then, suddenly, Cameron grinned. "I'm not knocking my luck!" He grabbed Sarah's wrist. "We're getting married *right now* before she finds a way to renege!"

"Ow, my wrist! Yikes!" She grabbed his shoulders for balance as he instead scooped her up and headed with purpose toward the door. Her head spun around on her shoulders. The emotional rollercoaster of the last three days was beginning to take its toll on her thoughts and emotions. It seemed too good to be true. But that contract . . . she had recognized the language. They *had* been set up all along, and she couldn't even be mad over it. She was getting everything she had ever wanted.

An hour later, they were signing the legal paperwork that would make them husband and wife. They had been expecting a long wait, but as soon as they arrived, they had been shown right in to a judge rather just see the clerk. He even took the time to walk them through all the other paperwork they would have to do to make the federal government happy.

"Are you keeping your maiden name?" he asked Sarah.

"Hmm." She thought about it and then smiled. "No, I want Cameron's name. His last name, anyway. I'd look silly answering to his first name."

"Here's the documents you'll need." He slid them to her with a smile. "Just fill them out and bring them by when you can. I'll take care of the rest."

"Not that we're not grateful," Cameron said, "but you're definitely going above and beyond the call of duty. It's not election year, is it?"

The judge laughed. "Not at all, son. As a matter of fact, Rayna Mason from Enforcers called me and told me that the two of you were on your way. I owe the Enforcers a great deal, and this was the least I could do to repay the debt."

Cameron was still pondering that when they finally left the courthouse. "Rayna Mason?"

"She's a specialist with Enforcers," Sarah offered. "She's Eric's wife. You know, the girl who was in a coma for sixteen years."

"How did she . . .?"

She sighed. "Cam, we were set up. From the beginning, probably. That line in the contract about it being Enforced is standard language in all Enforcer contracts. I'd bet money that Kenneth got it from Rayna or Gwyn, or even Eric."

"So the outcome was never in doubt."

She smiled up at him. "Seems so."

"Wow. I guess I didn't need that suitcase after all." When she laughed, he swung her up into his arms and around in a quick circle. "I'm going to love you forever, Sarah Dease." His grin widened. "I like how that sounds. And it'll look great on a name plate for a desk."

"I was fired, remember?"

"I'm in charge now, so you're rehired. You'll be my personal secretary this time. I'm not sharing you with my brother."

She giggled. "That's not fair to him, Cam. I can be both your secretary."

"Okay, fine. But I'll only share you there."

"That's fair. I mean, he's practically your twin, but he's just not my type."

"We'll have to find his type."

"Right now?"

He headed for his car. "Later. Much later. Maybe tomorrow. There's no law against having a honeymoon before a ceremony."

Content, she held onto him tighter. She had changed her mind. She wasn't going to throw toilet paper on Eric's car. She was going to send him and Rayna a *big* bouquet of flowers to thank them. She owed them both so much.

Kenneth was watching the guesthouse be cleaned out when his cell phone rang. He walked away to answer it, but no one was there. Puzzled, he went back to the bench he had left the contract on only to discover it had disappeared. In its place sat a single white rose. Oddly unsurprised, he just smiled. Everything had worked out perfectly. Now he wouldn't need to worry about Cameron's happiness anymore.

It was just a shame that Sarah didn't have a sister.

CHAPTER SEVEN

Rhianna Taber was the face on the front of Enforcers. Eric, as her partner, was normally the one in the shadows. He only went to a meeting when someone had screwed up. Rayna was in charge of Enforcers' information technology section and had the ability to hack into any system in existence. Her sister, Gwyn, worked in the legal department as a consultant. Gwyn's husband, Taylor, was a part-time consultant; he owned his own video game company.

Having all five of them together in one place usually meant that there was something big in the works. So when Rhianna walked into the conference room, she said idly, "We're scaring the natives."

Rayna giggled softly. "Well, naturally." In her arms, contentedly sleeping, rested a baby girl with a cap of silvery hair. "You want to hold her?" she asked.

"Gimme." Rhianna happily took baby Glory to cuddle her. "She's the closest thing to a niece that I have." She sat on the edge of the desk and smiled at the white-haired woman next to Rayna. The two sisters were as nearly identical, if not more so, than the Dease brothers. "Well?"

Gwyn Vincent pulled out the contract and put it on the table. As they all watched, the word 'Complete' appeared across the front. "Done and done well, I might add. Trade you." She took her niece while Rhianna picked up the contract.

The older woman wrote down some notes and then slipped it into a folder that also reflected as being complete. "I have a drawer prepared," she noted. "Room for at least three files. I presume, of course, that there will be at least three."

"Naturally," Taylor agreed absently without looking up from his sketchpad. It went everywhere with him. "I mean, we can't just leave it there."

"One down and two to go, so to speak," Eric offered.

"And just what have we got in mind for part two?" Rhianna arched a brow.

Taylor put down the sketchpad where the others could see. He had just finished drawing an old-fashioned genie lamp. Even as they all watched, smoke began to lift from the spout on the page. With a flash, the lamp disappeared from the page and appeared in the middle of the table. "Fun," he decided.

Rhianna began to smile. "I always knew you had untapped abilities that would be useful."

"I know." Gwyn shot her husband the impish grin that he had always loved. "Isn't he great?"

Status: File Begun

Analysis: The most important things in life are more than skin deep. Beauty, love, and humor. A true princess has all three.

Folder Two
KENNETH

CHAPTER EIGHT

As Cameron's twenty-first birthday drew ever closer, things began to get busy. Lorcana had moved into the guesthouse because she adamantly refused to live under the same roof as Sarah. Since her sons, and daughter-in-law, weren't inclined to share space with her either, it worked for them as well.

Everyone who worked for Two More Minutes came back to work happily when they received word of the outcome. Louise was distinctly the most pleased since Sarah's new position as Executive Secretary meant that *she* was the office manager. That gave Louise plenty of time to focus on her graphics work. Now if they could only find a lead graphic designer! She hated being in charge.

It was two weeks before Cameron's birthday and Lorcana was facing the end of her career. The only reason she even remained in the company at all was because Kenneth and Cameron were transitioning her out. Transitioning her! As if she was an old retiree of no use anymore. She had *earned* this company and now it wouldn't even be hers anymore.

If she wanted to keep a hold of her business, then she needed to find a way to control Kenneth. She didn't fool herself into thinking it would be easy. He was an adult, and he was one of the more intelligent men she had ever met. He was also ridiculously stubborn and unfailingly honest. No, getting him under her control would be damned near impossible.

But not completely.

It stung her that she was even thinking of going this particular route, but she was desperate. She had nothing to lose by grasping at straws. She had already learned that there were indeed some things beyond mortal comprehension. A lowly secretary who could feel a pea through a mattress was one of them. An ancient lamp that might grant wishes was another.

The rumor of the lamp had come to her from one of her cronies as another of those silly 3rd District legends. Supposedly this lamp had a genie inside that could grant wishes. The difficulty lay in that it had been lost into a well somewhere, and there wasn't anyone who could get it out.

She wasn't ready to give up yet, though. There had to be a way!

Kenneth had spent most of the previous six months working elbow-to-elbow with his brother to make sure that Lorcana's departure would be as seamless as possible. While Cameron took on more and more of the internal work, Kenneth found himself working externally to find clients, work with the ones they already had, and oversee their publicity department.

It didn't help any that they didn't have a lead graphic designer anymore. The last one had finally retired the year before; he had been around since the company had been formed by Viktor Dease. With that spot empty, Kenneth had to start reviewing applications with Cameron and prepare to conduct interviews. And worse still, they were in the middle of a big job for an auto company.

When Sarah walked into his office with a cup of coffee, she smiled wryly as she saw him leaning back in his chair with a cloth over his eyes. "I have caffeine, Ken." She brought the cup over and put it down in front of him. "You need a break."

"I need the next two weeks to be over." He straightened and pulled the cloth off his eyes. "Mother is making things as hard as she can for us, and you know it. I can't shake this chill I get whenever I see her." Grimly, he added, "I get the feeling she's up to something."

"You need to get your mind off things," his sister-in-law scolded. "You need to get out of here for a while. Take a day off, Ken, c'mon."

"I have way too much work to do. But," he added as he got to his feet, "I *will* be outside to do it, promise." He smiled suddenly. "You boss Cam around like this too?"

She grinned. "I'd hate for him to be bored."

There were many mysteries in the world, and most of them hid in the 3rd District. Some of them were more of ironic destinies than mysteries, though, Sera Thomason decided to herself as she headed home from her part-time job. Her *former* part-time job since the owner had decided to cut back, and she was the cut he had decided to make. Friggin' stuck-up business owners in Brooklyn. She would have rather dealt with the small businesses in her District any day, but no one needed a budding graphic designer.

"Mom, I'm home," she called as she walked into her house.

"Welcome home, honey." Cecily Thomason looked up with a smile as she saw her daughter walk into the living room. "Did you have a good day?"

"Got canned." Sera plopped down on the tattered chair that her Golden Retriever loved to chew on. "So I guess I'm job hunting. Again. Hey, Milly." She ruffled her dog's fur as she ran up with her favorite rope in her teeth. While they played a light game of tug-of-war, Sera tried to surreptitiously eye her mother. "How do you feel?"

Cecily sighed. "As well as can be expected. Doctor Matthews said he would come by later to check on me. Really, he fusses worse than you do."

"Hey, he has the degree that tells him when fussing is required. I'm just a worrywart." She glanced at the clock and then went into the kitchen with Milly on her heels. "I'll get your medicine."

For the last few years, Cecily's health had been rapidly declining. It seemed as if everything was happening all at the same time. She had been diagnosed with so many things that Sera wasn't even sure she remembered all of them. Every single one required medication to keep it in line. Both mother and daughter had insurance through Enforcers, but that didn't make the payments any easier. Sera worked every odd job she could and sold her art on the corners to make ends meet.

If it hadn't been for the fact that Doctor Lewis Matthews was a childhood friend of Cecily's, Sera doubted that they would even be able to afford to go to a doctor at all. Lewis was more than willing to make house calls and let Sera pay off any bills by mowing his lawn or babysitting his two twin daughters; the widower claimed she kept him sane by entertaining the two five-year-olds. She loved both kids, so couldn't argue the deal worked for everyone.

Her stomach churned as she saw that the medications were running very low. She knew she could ask Sarah for a loan to cover it, but she hated the idea of owing anything to anyone, even her surrogate sister. And she really didn't want Sarah to start worrying again; she was finally happy with her new husband.

There weren't many options left for Sera. She didn't have her degree, and she couldn't get into her chosen field yet. A lot of people were cutting back on part-time workers, and she couldn't go full-time until her mother was strong enough to be home all day by herself. She was going to be stuck in fast food, if she could even find one of *them* hiring. On a sad sigh, she knelt and hugged Milly. "Oh well. We'll make it work, right? Maybe I can train you to do some tricks and we can join the circus."

"Woof!" Milly licked her face enthusiastically.

"Yeah. I can see it now. Sera and her amazing Slobber Dog." She swiped a hand over her face. "Man, your breath smells. Let's go for a walk and you can eat some flowers or something. But not Madelyne's this time! She'd kill us."

CHAPTER NINE

Kenneth was a big believer in understanding his clients. If they wanted to promote to a certain type of people or a certain area, then he needed to visit them and find out what they needed and what they were like. He had a personal pet peeve about seeing billboards in rural areas, or ads for things that people in the area might never need.

Having briefly seen the 3rd District, and having talked to Sarah about it, he knew that it was an untapped area for advertisers. AAC had been their only company because no bigger places would work with such small businesses. Kenneth and Cameron wanted to change their company's standing on that, so Kenneth knew he needed to find out what the District needed.

It was to his advantage that he wasn't known there in the way he was known other places. He deliberately dressed down, opting for the most casual jeans and shirt he could find. In fact, he found himself enjoying the efforts. He so rarely relaxed anymore.

He opted to take the bus as well. Really, his pretty Volvo would have been totally out of place. In fact, if they had allowed it, he would have completely gotten a real horse. The 3rd District was the perfect place for it.

The closest bus stop to the District still had him walking a few blocks. Not that he minded the exercise. He hadn't been able to get to the gym for weeks either. As he walked across the street that marked the entrance to the District, he took a deep breath. The air was somehow . . . cleaner there. It had to be part of the magic.

When he rounded a corner, he was brought up short by several males not much older or younger than himself. He hated to profile people, but he couldn't stop his shoulders from tensing when he saw that they didn't look at all as if they belonged in the District.

"So what's a guy like you doing out here?" one asked slyly. "This isn't a safe part of town, you know." He slipped his hands into his pockets. "What do you say you hand over your wallet and we'll let you go?" A very low and vicious snarl from behind the males had them going white. "Sera."

"Yeah," came her mocking voice, "but I ain't the one snarling at you. That would be Milly. She thinks she's a Rottweiler right now."

Kenneth glanced over the male's shoulder to see a shockingly beautiful young woman holding the leash of a distinctly unhappy Golden Retriever. The dog had her ears back and every single tooth bared as she growled low. "Rottweiler, huh?"

"You should see her German Sheppard impersonation." Sera bared her own teeth in a mockery of a smile. "Should I demonstrate it?"

The thugs weren't that stupid. They ran off as quickly as was possible. As soon as they were out of sight, Milly stopped growling. She sat down and began to wag her tail happily. With the canine equivalent of a grin, she woofed at Kenneth. He found himself grinning. "Thanks for the save, Milly."

He shifted his gaze to his rescue dog's owner. It was with much male appreciation that he studied her long legs and generous figure. They were more emphasized than disguised by her tattered jeans and peasant shirt, and both articles had been liberally streaked with paint. His eyes met her wryly-amused golden ones, and he grinned. "Hi."

She decided she had to like him. She grinned. "Hi. A bit out of your way, aren't you? You're not from the District."

"I felt like visiting." He offered a hand. "Kenneth."

"Sera."

"S-A?"

"S-E. And thanks for asking." She snorted. "Most people never guess right." She laughed when Milly barked. "And this is Milly. She's supposed to be a Golden Retriever."

"She makes a great Rottweiler." He knelt to pet Milly and she wagged her tail harder. "All bark and no bite, aren't you? Hey there, beautiful." He laughed when she licked his face. "Best action I've had in months. Thanks."

He was gorgeous and he loved dogs. Sera automatically gave him points for both. He also looked eerily familiar but she couldn't quite put her finger on it. She hadn't seen *him*, precisely, but she felt sure she had seen someone *like* him.

He got to his feet and his grin widened as he realized how tall she was. She stood only one or two inches shorter than his five-eleven height, and that suited him *just* fine. He liked tall girls. In fact, she was the best of his favorite two female worlds: tall and curvy. The twain didn't usually meet, but here they were rolled into a black haired, sardonic package.

"I'd like it to be stated," he said, "that I am very much attracted to you, and therefore I will be doing my best to get you to go out with me. Tell me you're legal," he begged.

She *really* liked him. "I'm legal," she assured him. "But you're going to have to work hard to get a date. I'm not really a date-type girl. I've never seen the point. I'd as soon stay home and get my sketch on."

"You're an artist?"

"Budding." She tied Milly's leash to her belt loop and tucked her hands in her pockets. "You want to see the District? I can show you around. I live here. Born and bred, in fact."

He fell into step beside her. "So you're gifted?"

"Ooh, how tactful you are! Most ask if I'm not human."

"Are you?" He smiled. "I don't mind either way. Well, as long as, you know, you're not going to have an alien come out of your chest."

"Nah, that's not our shtick around here. We lean toward the more traditional types. Faeries, werewolves, and so on. I'm human, but I'm gifted." She had never been embarrassed by her gift, and she could feel genuine interest and acceptance from him. "Actually, we're not really that secretive about it. We don't flaunt it, but we don't lie about it either."

"Well, what do you do?"

"Shift."

He considered that. "Are we talking about morphing objects?"

"No, myself. I'm a shapeshifter."

"Hmm. I have two reactions to that. The first is 'holy cow!' The second is 'that's so cool!' You can pick your favorite." He smiled when she laughed at him. Her laughter seemed to make her eyes glow like coins. He was even fond of her bright pink hairstreaks, and he had never really been into that before.

"I like them both. Wah!" She threw out her arms for balance as Milly darted to the right and nearly pulled her off her feet. She landed safely in Kenneth's arms when he shot forward, and Milly, deciding this was a new game, ran around them happily, tying them both up in the leash.

"Idiot dog," Sera muttered. She held onto Kenneth's arms for balance as she glared at her pet. Her legs were firmly tied to his and moving might knock them both rather painfully over. "Sorry about that."

She turned her head to meet his eyes and realized that they had come almost nose-to-nose. Because they stood so close in height, they were effectively on eye level. His ridiculously sexy mouth was so close that she could have kissed him without moving at all. Her breath lodged in her chest and her pulse began to hammer as she saw his darkened gray-green eyes watching her with hunger. "Uhm."

His hands tightened on her hips as he pulled her closer. "I'm going to kiss you," he murmured huskily.

"No, you're not!" She flattened her hands on his chest and leaned back as much as she dared. "I just met you!"

"Then you had better find a way to get us untangled. And I'll kiss you later when we've known each other a few more hours."

"Grab the leash," she muttered. Her eyes flew wide as his hand slid hotly over her hip and pointedly grabbed the leash where it pressed against her bottom. With more haste than grace, she grabbed her power and let it take her.

His brows shot up as she suddenly disappeared and a bluebird appeared in midair in her place. "Wow." He held tighter to the leash as Milly realized it was loose and tried to run off. Firmly, he yanked back. "Sit."

Milly sat. Sera flew back a step and turned back to normal. Very warily, she reached out to take the leash from him. "Okay, Kenneth. I have ground rules for you. Hands and lips to yourself unless I say otherwise, got it?

"It wouldn't bother you if you weren't attracted to me just as badly."

"I won't deny that." She wrapped the leash around her wrist. "And you definitely get points for not freaking out that I turned into a bird."

"It was fascinating." He fell into step beside her once more as she headed down the sidewalk. "What can you turn into?"

"Most anything, but there are caveats to it. I have to have a rudimentary understanding of the physiology of whatever I'm becoming else I retain some human features. When I was a kid, I accidentally turned into a bird-human hybrid. I was molting for weeks after."

"Did you get your power from your parents?"

"Yeah. My mom is a shifter. My dad was a conjuror type."

"Was?"

She lowered her gaze. "He died six years ago."

"I lost my dad ten years ago," he said softly. He curled his hands around hers and laced their fingers together. "I know how much it never stops hurting." He brought her hand to his lips briefly. He had a feeling he was in danger of losing his heart to his lovely shapeshifter. It wasn't just desire. It couldn't be, not when he ached to hold her and take away her sadness. "So what do you do, Sera? Do you sell your art?" He knew 3rd District had a strong handcrafted market.

"Sometimes. Mostly I have a bunch of part-time jobs. Well, I did." She scowled. "I just got fired. I *hate* executives and big business. It's all about the bottom line. What pricks."

He groaned mentally. If that wasn't the worst-case scenario, then he didn't know what was. "You hate all executives, or just those that don't care about the lesser man, or woman?"

"All of 'em. Ain't met one yet that I liked. Well . . . okay, I guess there's one I like. My best friend married one a few months ago. He's cool." She tried to tug her hand free, but his grip stayed firm. Reluctantly, she let it be. It was sort of nice to walk holding hands. It almost felt like having a boyfriend, and she hadn't had one of those in two years. It just hadn't been worth the time.

Kenneth was worth every minute, and she liked him more and more every moment. Maybe she would let him kiss her. Oh, she didn't doubt she would enjoy it. Just his presence alone was enough to give her heatstroke. She could only be glad she didn't have any sort of elemental power. She would be starting fires for sure.

"So." He changed the subject pointedly. He needed time to find a way to tell her who he really was without her killing him, *or* running off. "Tell me about the District. I read about how it doesn't have a lot of flashy advertisements and it intrigued me. Seeing it now, I realize what they meant. There aren't a lot of posters or billboards, are there?"

"We're a historical landmark," she retorted dryly. "You think they had billboards back in the 1800s? Please. We like our advertising to be external. Internally, we pass out flyers and stick notices in mailboxes. People have tried to pay Enforcers to put up big signs and stuff, but Rhianna and Eric adamantly refused. If *we* want to advertise, we mostly go the poster route or word of mouth."

"Television?"

"Who can afford it, Ken? It's so expensive!"

Bingo! He couldn't have been happier. Offering cheaper means of television advertising to businesses like those in 3rd District would probably be the perfect place to start. They didn't need much else, although he was pretty sure some discount poster services might be appreciated as well. "Digital or hand-drawn?"

She blinked in bemusement. "I actually understood what you're asking. Go me. Mostly hand-drawn around here. It's that 'old-school' thing. I help out with a lot of that around here when I can. I'm a pro with both acrylics *and* Photoshop/Illustrator. I'm trying to get my degree in Graphic Design."

"Okay, we have to talk. Seriously." He glanced around and saw a quiet bench sitting under some shady trees. "Come over here."

"As if I had a choice," she said dryly as he dragged her along. "What's the deal?" She sat down and tethered Milly to the bench so she couldn't get away. "Something up?"

He sat beside her and took her hands. "Okay. Here's the deal. I . . ." He trailed off as he watched the sun filter across her face. It caressed her skin and made her eyes shimmer with power and mystery. Her short hair seemed to simply beg to be mussed up more by his fingers.

He cupped her cheek with his hand and leaned forward to kiss her. She tasted like sunshine and magic, her lips soft and perfectly made for his. His free hand curled into the back of the bench as he fought to keep the embrace light. The little purring sound she made did nothing for his control, however. He eased back a breath and asked huskily, "Going to hit me?"

"Not if you kiss me again." She slid her hands into his hair as he pulled her closer again. The shivers were starting from the inside out, spreading in heated waves of delight. Dear god, the man knew how to *kiss*. It was stupid, it was probably tacky, and she didn't give a damn. As the kiss deepened, something low in her body clenched with sharp longing. Every nerve ending came alive all at once.

When he slowly broke the kiss, she had to force herself to release him. She looked into his darkened eyes and saw the same swirl of volatile emotions inside him as churned inside her. "Uhm." It was the best she could say.

"Still not going to date me?" He nipped at her lower lip teasingly. His hands slid down her body and then up again, savoring every inch. "I'm not feeling very casual, Sera."

She shuddered as his mouth found a sensitive nerve in her neck and teased it with his teeth. She was going to go crazy if she didn't get his hands on her soon. "Neither am I," she managed to say. When he lifted his head and looked at her, she accepted the inevitable. She had been doomed from the moment she met him. "Oh, the hell with it. Kiss me again."

His lips curved and he slowly slid into the kiss, his lips teasing hers into opening for him. She found herself going under for the third time before she had realized she was in deep water. Slowly, reluctantly, she eased back until there was a breath between them. "Where have you been for the last five years of my life?" she asked huskily.

He ran his thumb over her lower lip. "Only five?" His voice sounded just as thick with desire as hers.

"I didn't realize how nice the male of the species was until I was sixteen." Her lips began to curve. "Of course, at sixteen, you don't have real standards yet, so I thought the paperboy was hot." She took a long, steadying breath. "Five years later, I think have figured out what I like. Even saying that, I don't think I ever set the bar so high as for a man like you."

His eyes lit. "Compliments aren't going to help me find self-control, Sera." His hands again skimmed up her sides and then down. "But I must confess I had a similar thought when I saw you. I've always liked tall women. And I like curvy women. I never thought I'd get both in such a spectacular combination."

"You're so bad for my pulse." She eased back entirely and untied Milly. "I need to be heading for home."

"I'll walk you there." He stood and took her free hand with his. "I want to spend more time with you. And if I know where you live, I can come back tomorrow and pester you mercilessly until you go out with me."

"Gee, I've always wanted a stalker." She smiled as she bumped her shoulder against his to be sure he knew she only joked. "I seriously like you, Kenneth. I'm not normally quick to like people, but I can't seem to help myself with you."

He mentally crossed his fingers and prayed that he could build enough of that like to ensure she didn't hate him when she found out his identity. He just couldn't bear to tell her yet. It was too wonderful to spend time with someone he knew liked him for himself. "So are you on your own or do you live with your mother?"

"I live with my mother." Her gaze lowered. "She can't live alone. She's been so sick lately. It's like everything at once has hit. Among the many other things eating at her, she's diabetic, has Crohn's disease, and just got diagnosed with kidney stones." Her voice broke and then steadied. "Worse, the doctor is now worried about her heart and her liver. She can't eat much; the medications make her sick. She's lost twenty pounds in a *month*." She swiped furiously at her eyes. She *refused* to cry.

"I'm so sorry, baby." He brought her hand to his lips for a long moment, hurting for her. "Is that why you work so hard?"

"Someone has to. I had to put school on hold. I was *so close* to my degree, Ken. I only had general education left. But all my school money had to go to pay for the hospital and the doctors and the meds. I've tried applying for grants and scholarships, but so far no luck." She shook it off. "What about you?"

"I finished my major in three years. Business mostly. I want to run my own company." He shot her a teasing grin. "Will you still like me when I'm high on the food chain?"

"Will you promise to be honest and have goodwill for us lower peons?" Her voice was just as teasing. "Don't worry, Ken. I like you as you are, so unless you completely changed your attitude, I'd still like you. I'm usually a good judge of character." Milly woofed and she laughed. "And so's she."

It was something at the least. "Hey, you want to get lunch?" he asked. "My treat." He grinned when she eyed him. "It's not a date, promise. When I have you on a date, you'll know it." His fingers skimmed down her arm slowly. "Trust me."

"Hoo boy," she said under her breath. Impulsively, she asked, "Do you want to have lunch with me and my mom? I bet she would like the company."

"I'd be honored. And I promise to behave myself. She doesn't have to know I'm trying to seduce her baby girl."

"You're so bad." She just shook her head as she led him toward her home. "Don't be alarmed by the appearance," she warned him. "We keep the area looking ramshackle so that people won't try to bulldoze in."

Even with the warning, he was still slightly nonplussed by the residential area. Anywhere else, he would have called it a slum. But here . . . it seemed oddly inviting. It had to be the people. Residents of all ages wandered around, working in yards, setting out laundry, or simply lounging on porches. Everyone knew everyone else. "Just like you're your own town," he murmured.

"Bingo." Sera unlocked the door and took Milly's leash off so that she could bound inside happily. "Mom!" she called. "I found a stray. I'm going to feed him."

"Sera," Cecily scolded as she stepped into the doorway. When she spotted Kenneth, her exasperated look turned to a smile. "Oh. That sort of stray." She studied him with a mother's speculative eye. "And you are?"

"Kenneth." He smiled. "Sera saved me and I bummed my way into a meal. Please pardon the intrusion, Mrs. . . .?"

"Thomason. But Cecily is just fine. It's nice to meet you, Kenneth." She sighed as Sera darted forward and helped her sit down. "How do you do that? I don't even know I'm tired before you do."

"You shouldn't be up yet." Sera frowned deeply. "You just got over the flu."

"I have to do something," her mother said gently. "I can't let you take all the weight." She smiled when Sera hugged her tightly. "I love you too, honey."

A little pain clenched Kenneth's heart. He'd had Tia growing up, but it had never been the same as this. He had never known what it was like to have a mother that loved unconditionally. He envied Sera a little, and he certainly understood why she was so determined to help Cecily.

"What's wrong?" Sera asked. "You look sad."

Candidly, he admitted, "I was just envying you a little. My mother hates me and my brother. She always has."

"Her loss." Cecily's lips firmed in a way that indicated Sera might be a chip off her mother's block. "Mothers like that don't deserve the name."

"I can't agree more."

"Sit." Sera shoved him into a chair.

"Woof."

She grinned. "Milly's cuter, sorry." She competently began to assemble the ingredients for two sandwiches and a vat of soup. Over her shoulder, she asked, "What was with the interest in advertisement in the District?"

"Morbid curiosity. I've never seen a street without a billboard. That, and I want to find a niche for myself, and I'm interested in all kinds of things." He watched her unashamedly, not noticing Cecily watching him in turn. "You're a graphic artist, right? Can I see some of your work? Or anything you've done?"

"Over the door," Cecily offered.

He turned his head and was struck silent by the brilliant poster. It was an advertisement for the Faerie Club, both hand-drawn and digital all at the same time. The top left started out sketched and then slowly evolved into full digital color by the bottom right corner. In the middle, in the middle of a dance, was a couple. They looked normal in the drawn portion but wore fantastical costumes in the digital. Across the bottom, it read '*Where magic happens.*'

"Wow. Damn, you're good." He tried to remember their advertisement for a lead designer. Had they insisted on a degree? He sure as hell hoped not! Sera would be *perfect*. She had the skills and the personality alike to get the job done.

Cheeks pink, Sera said, "Thanks." She put down a sandwich in front of him and gave her mother a bowl of soup. Content, she sat down with her own sandwich. "Don't feed Milly scraps, no matter how pitiful she looks."

He laughed. "I'll do my best."

They played cards after lunch while Cecily kept things legal. Kenneth was having so much fun that he had no idea how late it had gotten until he saw the clock. "Oops." He grimaced. "I need to go." He had two meetings, and he would be running to one of them. He reluctantly got to his feet. "I'm sorry to run out."

"No, it's okay." Sera walked him to the door with a smile. "Come back anytime." When his hand gently framed her face, she leaned in with a soft sigh to meet his kiss. Her fingers curled possessively for a moment into his shirt. "Come back soon," she said softly.

"Will you miss me?" he asked just as softly. It took considerable willpower to not kiss her again.

"Probably." Her lips curved. "Kiss me again to be sure."

He did so with a smile, lingering over her flavor until he knew he was in danger of not leaving at all. He slowly released her and stepped back. "See you tomorrow." As the door shut quietly, he took a deep breath. He needed a cold shower. In fact, he needed five. He was also suddenly beginning to understand what had happened to Cameron when he had met Sarah. This love at first sight thing was volatile and scary all at the same time.

Sera walked back into the living room and found her mother lifting a brow. She winced. "Well."

Blandly, Cecily said, "I admit, I'm old-fashioned enough to think that at least one date should occur before kissing commences, but I'm also still healthy enough to not blame you in the slightest. I didn't think men were grown that gorgeous in New York."

Sera sat down on the couch with a laugh. "You and me both! He's also witty, personable, and has such a giving heart." She sighed deeply. "I think I'm in love with him. I know we're all wired for true love, but *really*? At first sight?"

"It happens for some." Cecily smiled. "And for others, you need to test the waters before you find the real thing. What's important is to treasure each moment and fight for it. If you're one of the lucky ones to find the real thing from the beginning, then you need to do whatever you can to keep it."

Sera rested her head on her mother's shoulder. "He's a good kisser too."

"The best ones are, honey."

CHAPTER TEN

Kenneth made a point of getting to the office early the next morning so that he could rearrange his schedule. He wanted to spend as much time as possible with Sera. He knew it was absolutely critical to build up her trust before he told her the truth.

As he scowled at his calendar, Louise walked into his office. She studied him for several moments before a smile teased her lips. "Kenneth, how long have I known you?"

"Huh?" He blinked at her. "Five years. You started as an intern when I was starting college." He had always greatly respected her for that simple fact; she was only four years older than he, but she had moved up the ranks quickly.

"Based on that long history, and the lack of formality around here, I'm going to be blunt." She sat on the edge of his desk. "You look like a guy in serious need of getting laid. There's steam coming off your head, boss. Who's the lucky girl?"

"Her name is Sera."

"Well, there's irony."

"Tell me about it." He sighed. "She's also, still ironically, from the 3rd District as well. Unfortunately, she hates executives, and I happened to meet her incognito. So she likes me, but she's temperamental enough to possibly kick my ass when she finds out the truth."

"Okay, are we talking about a mutual case of the hots or . . ."

He raised his hand. "Hi, I'm Kenneth Dease and I'm a victim of love at first sight."

She winced good-naturedly. "And another good man bites the dust. What about her?"

"I *think* it might also be mutual, but I don't think she'd admit it if it was. If anything, there's definitely mutual attraction. I couldn't keep my hands off her."

"Or your lips?"

"Them neither. She wears a rather addicting cinnamon lip-gloss." He raked both hands through his hair this time. "I'm trying to rearrange my schedule so I can free up some time this afternoon to go see her again."

Tongue in cheek, she said, "I hadn't seen those wings before."

"Wings?"

"You know what they say about moths and flames, right?"

"If they looked like Sera, the moths went happily to their doom." He found a smile suddenly. "Why are you still single, Lou? If you weren't so much like our sister, Cam and I would have been fighting over you."

"I'm picky," she retorted dryly. She got to her feet. "Let me know if I can help, okay? Cam's happy. You need to be happy too."

Through some creative finagling, and strategic excuses, he managed to clear his afternoon. The instant his last morning meeting ended, he rushed home to change clothes and then made a beeline for the 3rd District. He felt bemused at himself as he headed for Sera's front door. His heart beat faster than a snare drum, and he was fairly sure he was holding his breath. He had always thought people grew out of those reactions once puberty ended.

Sera was washing dishes when she heard the doorbell. She dried her hands quickly and hurried to answer, her breath held with anticipation. She had been hoping all day to find Kenneth on the other side. Thus far she had been disappointed twice. Once by a kid selling cookies and the other by Dr. Matthews.

This time, when she opened the door, she was rewarded by the sight of Kenneth on her porch. He looked windblown, sexy, and slightly flushed as if he had run the entire way to see her. "Hi." It was the best she could manage, and it came out as breathless as she felt.

"Hi." He curled his hand around the back of her neck and drew her in for a hungry kiss. The taste of her was rich and wild and as potent as the power inside her. "Missed you," he said against her lips as he eased back. He rested his forehead against hers. "Did you miss me?"

"Are you nuts?" Her laugh came out shaky. "I was going out of my mind." She curled against his chest and rested her cheek on his shoulder. His arms closed around her tightly and she felt something inside eagerly soak up the feeling. It wouldn't have been so bad if it had been just her body—though it hadn't helped her sleepless night any. Her heart and her soul seemed starved for him.

"I cleared my afternoon for you." He smiled. "I'm all yours for the rest of the day." When she lifted her head, he leaned in and nibbled at her ear. She had triple pierced ears, and he found it sexy for some reason. "I'm at your command."

The man was temptation incarnate. She knew she could invite him to stay the night and he would be more than willing. She even knew that she wouldn't regret it. He had been right the day before. Whatever there was between them was not casual. It never would be. But it was certainly volatile, and well out of her experience. She needed a little more time. She wasn't nearly as impulsive as most people thought.

"What's going through your mind?" he murmured, his hand cupping her cheek. His eyes searched hers. "I can see so many things flickering across your eyes. Secrets and mysteries." His lips brushed hers. "Tell me everything."

From the living room, Cecily called dryly, "Hi, Kenneth."

He lifted his head with a grin. "Hi, Cecily," he called back. He dropped a kiss on Sera's nose. "I guess the good moms always know everything."

"Boy do they! Get some rest!" she called to her mother. "I'm taking Kenneth with me to pick up the terrible two and drop them at Brian's shop!"

"Have fun!"

"Terrible two?" Kenneth asked curiously. A stab of jealousy made his eyes greener than usual. "Who is Brian?"

"The closest thing to a big brother I have," she assured him with a grin. "Why, Ken, are you jealous?" She got her answer when he dragged her against him and kissed her so hotly that her toes curled in her shoes. "Oh." It was the only thing that came to what remained of her mind.

"Who are the terrible two?" He looped his arm lightly around her waist.

"They're my mother's doctor's daughters." She laughed when he blinked. "Tammy and Tawny. Identical twins. Super cute but super scary smart for their age. They're about five or so. I babysit them in exchange for free doctor's visits for my mother. I also pick them up from school and deliver them to Brian's place. He's Doc Matthew's nephew."

"Biggest little town in New York," he murmured.

"That's one way of putting it."

The elementary school that the two girls attended sat right outside the District. Kenneth carefully kept an eye on the area just in case anyone spotted him. Thankfully, he didn't see anyone who would have reason to recognize him.

It wasn't hard to tell who the girls were. Not only were they most assuredly identical, but they also spotted Sera and gave happy shrieks as they ran down the sidewalk and jumped into her arms. They talked over each other and at the same time, each trying to be the first to tell their favorite person about what they had done that day. He couldn't help but grin as he watched.

"Okay, okay!" Sera put them both down. "Calm down! You can talk my ear off on the way to Cousin Brian. First, meet Kenneth." She turned them around so that they could see him. "Ken, meet Tawny and Tammy. Tam is the one with the short hair."

He knelt down to their height and smiled. "Hi. Nice to meet you." He offered his hand and smiled when they both shook it.

"Are you Sera's boyfriend?" Tawny asked shrewdly.

"No," Sera said.

"Yes," he said at the same time.

The twins giggled as the two adults eyed each other. "Don't encourage him," Sera scolded them with a smile. She took Tammy's hand. "C'mon, troublemakers. And that means all three of you."

As they walked, the girls chattered five miles a minute. It was to Kenneth's credit that he not only managed to keep up, but he was also able to ask questions and listen with obvious attention to the answers. His love for kids seemed very clear, and Sera's heart sighed happily. He was hot, liked dogs, *and* he loved kids. She was going to have to date him after all. Only an idiot would lose a guy like that, and she wasn't an idiot.

Kenneth hadn't known what to expect from 'Brian's shop,' but he knew he would have never guessed right even if he had tried. The small building had large glass windows that displayed brilliant bolts of cloth and handcrafted clothing. Racks of more clothing as well as blankets, curtains, and anything else that could be made of cloth stood in the middle of a slightly overzealous garden.

The bell over the door chimed merrily as they walked in the front door. Inside the tiny room were rows and shelves upon shelves of more beautiful work. A counter wedged into a corner with an old-fashioned cash register on top. Beside it sat a jar that said 'tag trade.' "What's that?" Kenneth asked Sera as the girls ran for a door leading further into the building.

"Tag trade? It's what we do around here. Say I wanted a blanket but didn't have the money. I would take the tag from the blanket and write my name on the back. I'd then drop the tag into the jar. Brian could bring that tag to me and trade it for one of my art pieces of equal value."

"And who said that the barter system couldn't work in America."

"The same people who think the moon landing was a hoax."

They exchanged a grin as a man walked out of the backroom with a twin attached to each ankle. "Did you lose something, Sera?" he asked her dryly, his blue eyes twinkling merrily behind his glasses. He glanced at Kenneth and lifted a brow curiously. Sera had never brought a male over to the shop before. "Well. Hello. I'm Brian Matthews. I own this shop."

"You're one hell of a weaver," Kenneth said sincerely. "And my name is Kenneth."

"Nice to meet you." Brian put the two girls down gently. "I bet you might find some snacks in the fridge," he told them softly. He smiled as they darted into the back happily. "I get them buzzed on sugar and then give them back to their father," he explained to Kenneth. "My grandmother says that it's his just desserts for waiting so long to give her grandkids."

"What are you working on right now?" Sera rummaged through the racks as she spoke. "Anything fancy other than 'that' project?"

"No." He shook his head slightly. "No more special projects for me." She looked at him with fear, and he gently skimmed his hand down her hair. "I'm under contract," he told her. "All I can do is hope and pray."

Kenneth withheld his questions, sensing that there was something very serious being discussed that he didn't understand. Instead, he watched with amusement as Sera and Brian haggled price over a dress she liked. By the time they left the shop, she had the dress in a bag, and Brian had a tag to be used in exchange for a poster.

As they walked down the sidewalk, Kenneth asked softly, "Under contract?"

Her gaze lowered. "Around here that means that he's been signed into Enforcers' direct protection. It always finds a way to ensure that whatever is wrong is made right, but it's never easy." Her hands clenched together. "He's cursed, Ken. And that's all I'm going to say."

"He seems like a nice guy," he offered softly. "He'll get his happy ending."

"Yeah." She shook it off visibly. "Let's find something else to talk about."

"Like what?"

"I don't know." She smiled. "I'm just happy to be with you."

Abruptly, he couldn't keep up the farce anymore. He couldn't bear lying to her, and he was definitely lying by omission. "Can we talk?" he asked softly. He skimmed his fingers through her hair.

"Of course." She glanced around and saw a more secluded spot under some trees. She headed over and leaned against the trunk. Her stomach churned with nerves. He looked very serious, and a little grim. He couldn't technically break up with her if they weren't seeing each other, but if he had decided he didn't want to see her again, she didn't know what she would do. "This isn't going to be some sappy break up, is it?"

"No!" He framed her face with hands. "Get that out of your head right now. I'm not intending on leaving you. I just . . . have something to tell you. And I know you're going to be mad at me, so I'm not sure where to start."

"You're married."

"No."

"You joined the army?"

"No."

"Pity, you'd be hot in uniform." She let out a long breath. "Okay, what's this great secret, Ken?"

"I . . . hell." He lifted her chin slightly and kissed her with all the desperate longing in his heart. As she sensed it, her hands gently rested over his heart. Just that touch seemed to soothe him, and he gentled the kiss. When her lips parted on a soft sigh, he contentedly deepened the embrace. Desire surged at its chains when she teasingly curled her tongue around his, but he held tight to control.

He lifted his head slightly, and her eyes opened. The golden color looked dark and drowsy, and her lips were swollen and sensual. "If that's what you do to me with a kiss," she said huskily, her fingers trembling where they pressed to his chest, "I'm almost afraid to have you for a lover." She took a ragged breath. "You're really scaring me, Ken."

He took a breath just as ragged. "Sera, I am . . ."

"Kenneth Dease!" a woman's voice exclaimed. "What a wonderful surprise!"

He hastily stepped back as the woman hurried over with a wide grin. Sera eyed the older woman intently, recognizing her as a TV news anchor from Manhattan. The cameraman following her looked just as amused as the reporter did. The name belatedly sank in, and she finally realized why Kenneth had been familiar. "Oh my god," she blurted. "You're Cameron's brother! You're Sarah's brother-in-law!"

He blinked. "The friend you said married an executive was Sarah?" He should have known!

"Yeah." Her eyes narrowed slightly. "And that means you're an executive too."

"Kenneth," the reporter quickly broke in, "can I have a minute of your time? I really want to ask you about your company's new campaign using Aenya Michaels. I came here to see her, and finding you was a lucky break."

He cursed softly under his breath. "Later, okay? I was *trying* to fit in."

"Oh." The reporter looked at Sera, saw the temper in her eyes, and winced. "Oh my."

"No worries." Sera took several steps to the side, carefully concealing the fact that her heart felt as if it was shattering inside her chest. She had never known a pain that sharp before. "We were done here, I think." She added softly, "I'm not mad at you, Ken. Okay? Trust me. Around here, we know what it's like to want to find a place where we don't stand out. And . . . Sarah was right about you. You're different than others I've known."

"Sera!" He reached for her arm but she evaded his grip. Before he could stop her, she ran off down the street. "Dammit!"

Miserable, the reporter said, "Kenneth, I'm so sorry. I didn't have any idea."

"No, how could you?" His eyes narrowed on her and the cameraman alike. "I trust I won't be seeing this on the six o'clock news."

"No, of course not! I'm not that kind of reporter." Genuinely unhappy, she added, "Did I mess everything up?"

"No . . . I think the fault lies with me." He took a long breath. "Call me for a comment later." He turned and walked away without waiting for consent. He would call a cab and get back to the office as soon as he could. He needed to talk to Sarah and find out everything he didn't know about his Sera. The woman of his dreams had entered his life, finally, and he would be damned if he let her get away now.

CHAPTER ELEVEN

Sarah was sitting on the side of Cameron's desk and watching him sign something when Kenneth walked in without knocking. "Help," he said without preamble.

His siblings looked at him and two sets of brows winged upward. He looked a little more frazzled than either was used to seeing, and Cameron was fairly sure that he recognized the frustration in the line of his brother's face and body. "Would you like to be more specific?" he asked politely.

Kenneth sighed and sank down in one of the visitor chairs. "Sarah, you have a friend named Sera?"

"Yeah, Sera Thomason." She smiled. "We always called it our personal joke that we had nearly identical names. But we're almost totally opposite in personality. I'm kind of like a peppermint and she's like a red hot."

"More like a cinnamon gumdrop," he muttered.

She pursed her lips as she tried not to laugh. There was only one way he would have known that. "Well, that explains where you've been the last two days. I take it she was wearing that cinnamon lip gloss she likes so much?"

He sighed deeply. "Yeah, she was."

"Okay, this I have to hear." Cameron grinned. "How did you find out what her lip gloss tastes like?"

"Yesterday, I went to the 3rd District to see what they might need in way of advertising. You know we were talking about taking on small businesses, and I figured that since Sarah was from there, we ought to start there. It's an amazing place. Well, I met Sera, with an E, when I almost got into trouble. Milly was doing an impersonation of a Rottweiler."

"You should see her German Sheppard impersonation," Sarah noted gravely.

"So I heard. Well, she, Sera I mean, agreed to show me around and answer my questions. Somewhere between Carroll Lane and Tolkien Avenue, I think I fell in love." He raked his hands through his hair. "And she hates executives. So there I was, stuck between a rock and a hard place. I was *going* to tell her, but I ended up kissing her instead."

"Actions speak louder than words?" Cameron struggled not to laugh.

"Boy do they! I couldn't tell her yet. I was so afraid she'd hate me. I had lunch with her and her mother. Then I went over there again this afternoon. I met more people, fell in love with her a little more. I wanted to make her fall for me before I told her. I think I was close to succeeding when disaster struck."

"Someone recognized you," Sarah guessed.

"Yeah. That stupid reporter from Channel 2 spotted me and gave me away before I could explain. Sera said she understood why I'd hid my identity, but she ran off before I could stop her! Damn it, Sarah, help me out here! What don't I know? Why does she hate executive types so much?"

Sarah tapped a finger against her cheek while she thought about it. "Okay, how much did she tell you about her dad?"

"Just that he died six years ago."

"Okay, so she didn't mention *how* he died?" When he shook his head, she sighed. "He was in a car accident with a drunken driver. The driver who hit him was an executive from one of the big hotel chains. He pretty much bought his way out of a manslaughter charge. Sera and her mother have been struggling hard since then. She won't even let *me* help her, Ken. All she has left is pride. You could go knocking on her door, but she wouldn't let you in anymore. If she climbs out of being lower class, it'll be because she did it herself."

Cameron propped his chin on his hands. "How long would it take her?" he asked.

"I can't guess. It would probably help if she could get a job in her field and make a steady paycheck. She's working part-time."

"Not anymore. She said she was fired," Kenneth muttered.

"Well . . . hell."

"I need a distraction." He got to his feet. "I'm going to start going over applications." Thinking of Sera, he asked wistfully, "Did we really insist on a Bachelor's degree for our lead designer?"

Thinking the same thing, Sarah said, "Afraid so." She handed over the stack. As the door shut behind him, she sighed. "Well, now what do we do? We wanted him to find love, right?"

"Yeah." Cameron sat back in his chair. "We'll figure something out."

Lorcana was getting her nails done when her cell phone rang. She glanced down at the number and recognized it. She carefully pressed the answer button; she always wore an earpiece for her phone in case of just such a situation. "Hello, Patricia. What can I do for you?"

"It's more what I can do for you," her friend said. "You know that lamp thing you were interested in? I just heard about a kid in 3rd District who can *shapeshift*. My son had a college class with her and said she was pretty open about the skill. He even saw her shift once. She might be able to get that lamp for you."

"What's her name?"

"Sera Thomason. I have her address and everything. Actually, the name is familiar. I think my husband had dealings with her family once. I'm not sure. I don't really remember, frankly. She's so deep in the lower class that I'm surprised she even went to college."

"Email me the address," Lorcana said decisively. "If she can get me what I want, I'll be glad to pay her a nice sum. Money talks, even among those weirdoes in that District." She hung up the phone, her lips pursed. Really, she had nothing to lose at that point.

As soon as her nails were done, she called for her chauffeur and gave him the address Patricia had emailed her. She formulated her plan of attack on the way. She was well aware that lower class people clung stubbornly to their petty pride. She couldn't just throw money at the girl; she would probably refuse out of spite. No, she would have to figure out what she really wanted or needed and use that for leverage.

She hated the 3rd District. She always felt out of place there, and she was sure she hadn't mistaken the hostile looks fixed on her. She rang the doorbell on the ramshackle house and resisted an urge to wipe her finger on her skirt. This part of the District looked like it belonged in a slum; a historical slum, but one nonetheless.

When the door cautiously opened, she strove for a friendly smile. "Hello. Are you Sera Thomason?"

Warily, Sera asked, "Why? Who are you? You lost, or something? You're not from the District, that's obvious."

"No, of course not. My name is Lorcana Dease."

Sera knew immediately that she had to be looking at Kenneth and Cameron's mother. It only made her more wary. She knew what Sarah and Cameron had gone through, and the events had put Lorcana very far down in Sera's estimation. What the hell was the old broad doing at *her* house? Did she know about Kenneth? "What can I do for you, Mrs. Dease?"

"May I come in?"

"No, my mother is asleep." She stepped outside and firmly pushed Milly back into the house. The retriever was growling very low in her throat in a way that meant she liked Lorcana no more than Sera did. "Sorry, she's protective." She shut the door. "My mother is ill right now, and I don't want her to wake."

"Understandable. Now, I have a proposition for you, my dear. I understand you're a shapeshifter. There's an item at the bottom of a well that I need you to get for me. I'd be willing to pay you for your time." Lorcana smiled casually. "I own a large company. I assure you, my money is good."

Sera bit her tongue before she asked if that was all that was good about her. "What well, what item, and how much are we talking?"

"The Frisk Well, it's an old lamp, and name your price."

"The Frisk Well? No wonder you need a shifter. Only frogs could get down there safely! Those bricks are slippery as hell." She crossed her arms. "Look, I appreciate the offer, but I'm not interested."

"Not even to buy medicine for your mother?" Lorcana made her voice sympathetic. "It must be very difficult, having a sick mother. Things are so expensive nowadays, after all. Do you have insurance? Does it cover everything?"

"Yes, we do, and no it doesn't." Her eyes narrowed slightly. She really wanted to kick Lorcana to the street. She was everything that Sera had always hated in bigwig, high power executives. She had also tried to make Sarah miserable. Sera was more of a 'two strikes' woman than a three strikes.

And yet . . . she couldn't deny that the money would be well used. It was a job, and god only knew that she had done some she hated for people she intensely disliked. "How much?" she asked again warily.

"Ten thousand?" Lorcana offered. "Would that work for you?"

Ten thousand would cover the medical bills, medicine, *and* groceries for at least a few months. She wouldn't have to rush into a new part-time job. Maybe she would even have a breather to find something she liked. "Okay," she decided.

"Deal." She reluctantly shook Lorcana's hand. It seemed slightly stunning to think such a cold female had given life to two such amazing men. "You know where the well is?"

"Unfortunately, no. Do you?"

"Sure. It's not far from here. Follow me." She tucked her hands in her pockets and headed down the sidewalk, leaving Lorcana to follow at her own pace. Unable to resist, she asked innocently, "Didn't I read somewhere that your son got married?"

"Yes." The word was bitten out. "I just couldn't bear to be in the way of true love."

"You're such a good mother. You must love your sons a lot." She hid a grin as she heard Lorcana make a strangled agreement. Served her right!

The Frisk Well sat near the brooks that fed the Gentle Brook Inn less than a mile away. It was old gray stone covered in mossy vines, and the wooden roof had darkened with age. It was considered a wishing well around the District, and few ever asked for a wish that didn't come true. As such, when someone wished, they made sure it was something they really needed and wanted. Sera had never bothered to wish for her life to be better; it was way too much work for one poor wishing well.

As they stopped next to the well, she lightly put her hands on it. She stayed silent for several moments and Lorcana asked warily, "What are you doing?"

"Thanking the well for letting me jump down inside. Scoff if you like, but we take things seriously around here." A breeze tugged at the streaks in her hair teasingly and the sunlight glinted across her eyes.

Lorcana rubbed her hands over her arms. "Just hurry up."

"Sure thing."

Before her shocked gaze, Sera promptly turned into a small green frog. The older woman took a step back sharply, her heart pounding like mad. First the thing with the pea and the mattress, and now this. She had been pulled into some stupid faerie tale and she *loathed* it. "Get the lamp and get out. This is madness."

Sera hopped into the well and nimbly hopped down the slippery walls toward the water at the bottom. She turned into a fish just before landing and checked the depth of the water. It was only three feet or so, and she went back to normal to stand on her own feet. "Let's see if I can find that lamp."

It was dark as hell down that far since the sun couldn't reach all the way, but she finally found the small lamp wedged into a crevice in the wall. She pried it loose and studied it as best she could. It felt surprisingly heavy for its size. "Now how to get this out."

"Did you find it?" Lorcana called.

"Yeah," Sera called back, "but I'm not sure how to get it out. It's heavy. Seriously. The only bird I could turn into big enough to carry it wouldn't even fit in here! And I can't hop out like a frog."

On a little screech of frustration, Lorcana slammed the lid down on the well. "Rot for all I care! What a useless excursion this was!"

Sera could only stare up at where there had been, moments before, a circle of blue sky. "Hey!" she shouted. "No freaking way she just locked me in here!" She dropped the lamp and turned into a small bird to fly up to the roof. Try as she might, however, she couldn't push the heavy wood out of the way. Furious, frightened, she went back down to the water and changed back once more. "That bitch!"

Psst.

The faint feminine voice had her going very still. "Pardon?" she asked carefully.

The lamp! Rub the lamp, silly!

She scooped up the lamp, poured out the water that had gotten inside, and warily rubbed the side. She had seen stranger things in her life, including faeries who lived inside computers, so she wasn't going to be surprised to find a wishing well spirit living in a lamp.

She *was* surprised, however, when a tiny pink streak shot out the spout and bounced erratically off the sides of the well. On a shriek, she ducked and covered her head protectively before she got hit by flying sparks.

A warm light began to illuminate the area and she cautiously lowered her arms. Her eyes slowly widened as she straightened and stared at the small creature hovering in front of her. "No way," she breathed. "Are you . . . a dragon? Wait, I thought *genies* lived in lamps."

The small dragon snorted and ruffled the fins on her head. "And who said genies had to be human-like, huh? That smoky, wispy thing is *so* out of date." She landed on Sera's shoulder. "I'm Dazzle, and I'm a genie-in-training! You got my lamp, you summoned me, and so you get to use my power! As long as you wish for non-selfish things, I can grant you wishes forever. Selfish wishes deplete my power, and eventually I won't have any more."

"What happens then?"

"I lose the ability to grant wishes. Eventually, if I can't regain any power, I'll disappear."

Sera frowned. "Then would wishing myself out of here be selfish?"

"Nope! That would be a wish of self-preservation, so it's totally cool." Dazzle's face wrinkled up as she concentrated. She began to glow hot pink as she called on her power. "I'm new at teleporting, so hang on tight."

"Oh god." Sera squeezed her eyes closed as she felt the spell hit. When she carefully opened her eyes a moment later, she found herself at the top of a large tree. "Gah!" She grabbed the branch she was on and held tight. "Damn it, aim *lower* next time!"

"Er, sorry about that."

She just sighed and turned into a monkey to climb her way down. She turned back at the bottom and brushed at the muck on her jeans. "Yuck. Man, what a disaster that almost was! I knew she was a bitch, but I didn't know she was *that* nasty. She could have killed me!" She crossed her arms and tried to ignore the fact that Dazzle flew alongside her with the lamp. "No wonder she wanted your lamp. She must've heard it granted wishes."

"Yup yup. That's right. But now I belong to you. You're my master, okay?"

"Just call me Sera." She opened her front door and went inside as quietly as possible. Milly slept near the door but woke up to follow Sera to her bedroom. If she was at all unnerved by Dazzle, it certainly didn't show.

Once the bedroom door shut, Sera stripped off her wet clothes. "I cannot believe this. I don't even know *what* to wish for. And I don't want to wish for selfish things. Can you tell me if something is selfish so I can decide if I really want it?"

"Sure, there are no rules against it."

"Is there anything you can't do?"

"Interfere with free will," was the prompt response. "I can't do something to someone that they wouldn't do by themselves on their own. Like . . . I couldn't make Lorcana a decent person even if every person in the world wished for it. She's bad to the core, seriously. But I could give her horns." She brightened, the fin on the tip of her tail twitching happily. "Wish for that!"

"*No*!" Sera had to grin though. "Tempting as it is." She pulled on fresh clothes and sat down on her bed. "Okay. If I was going to wish for anything, I'd wish for my mom to be healthy again. Can you do that?"

"Absolutely! I can't do it all at once, but I can start making all the problems get better." Dazzle flew over to land on the footboard. "I'll turn her medicine into vitamins." She nodded firmly. "She'll be just fine within a week, just another of the District's miracles."

Sera let out a long breath. "That's fine with me. I just . . . can't lose her too."

"So . . . what do you want for yourself?" Dazzle climbed up the poster on the footboard and perched at the top. "You made a big unselfish wish, and now you can have a selfish one. What do you want?"

"Hmm." She looked at the battered computer sitting on her desk. It barely ran its operating system let alone the programs she needed. "How about a new computer and the non-bootleg versions of the programs I need to do my art?" She laughed. "Well, technically, they'd still be bootleg, huh?"

"I dare anyone to prove that they aren't legal." Dazzle flew over to the computer and around it so fast that her glow blinded Sera briefly. When the glow faded, the old desktop had been replaced with a shiny new model and a stack of discs sat beside it. "You'll have to install them," she apologized. "I'm still learning. Last time I tried to auto-install something, I made the whole machine start speaking in tongues."

"I'll enjoy every minute of it, no worries. How'd you know what kind of comp to give me?" She ran a hand over the top reverently. She also had not one but *two* huge monitors.

"Hey, I might be only just learning my powers, but I know my way around computers. My last master taught me a lot. She was really good with them."

"That's really cool."

"So . . . now what?" Dazzle landed on her shoulder. "There's got to be more. I mean, if you had everything you needed to be happy, then you wouldn't have even woken me up. So there's got to be more."

"I want a job I can love," she said softly. "But I don't think that's something you can give me, Dazzle."

"Hmm." Dazzle thought about that. "What would you need to get your job?"

"A degree, for one thing." A rolled up paper appeared and dropped into her hands. "No way. You did *not* do what I think you just did."

"Sure did." The fins on her head cocked at different angles as she grinned. "It's just a piece of paper. You've got the stuff you need in here." She patted Sera on the head. "And it's all official and stuff. Anyone who checks will see that you graduated this semester."

"Do I have a good GPA?" Sera asked dryly.

"I left it where it was. You can't knock a B+ average, y'know. Now what? I'm having fun! I like granting you wishes. They aren't selfish at all. There's too much good in your heart for that. You're like my last master. She was good too. So I'm gonna do my best, okay, Sera?"

"I feel . . . dazed." She sank down and sat on the floor against her bed. When Milly moved closer, she scratched her ears lightly. "I can't believe this is happening. I mean, sure, I believe in the impossible, but this is surreal even by District standards."

"Well . . . what else do you want?"

Unbidden, an image of Kenneth popped in her mind. "Something you can't give me," she murmured

Speculatively, Dazzle asked, "A man?"

"Bingo."

The dragon-genie tapped her claw on her jaw as she thought about it. "Kenneth Dease, right?"

"I'm not even asking how you knew that."

"Good idea. Well . . . I can't get you *him* per se, but I can get you close to him. Did you know his company is looking for a lead graphic designer?"

Her head jerked up sharply. "What?"

"Yeah, they're doing interviews tomorrow. I could get you an interview. You'd have to get the job yourself, but you'd be close to him." She wiggled her butt in a manner not dissimilar from a cat about to pounce, and a folder appeared on Sera's lap. "That's their qualifications and what you need to bring."

"Let's see." Sera flipped the folder open and ran a finger down the list of knowledge requirements. "I have all these. And I've got the portfolio to prove it." She groaned suddenly. "Wait, I can't do this. Lorcana's going to know who I am."

"She's not doing the hiring." Dazzle's voice sounded smug. "She's being transitioned. You'll be interviewing with Kenneth and Cameron. And they're businessmen enough to hire you only if you're good. They wouldn't hire you *just* because they like you. It'll help though. Ooh! You'll need a nice suit!" She glowed and a stylish black suit appeared on the bed.

"I didn't wish for that," Sera noted warily.

"Pre-emptive wish. You would've wished for it eventually."

"I . . . hmm." She studied her genie. "So just where did you come from again?"

"The lamp." The dragon smiled angelically.

Somehow she got the feeling that that wasn't the whole truth, but she didn't push the issue. She'd had enough to deal with for one day!

CHAPTER TWELVE

Kenneth didn't sleep that night. He couldn't. There were simply too many thoughts tumbling in his mind for him to shut everything down and rest. He wanted to go to Sera. He had to go to her. But what was he supposed to say? She was too conscious of the difference between their classes.

The sleepless night turned out to be more visible than he thought. When he arrived at work the following morning, Louise handed him her cup of coffee as he walked past her desk. "Do I look that bad?" he asked wryly.

"Worse."

"Great." He took the coffee with him as he headed for his office. He had gone over the applications before passing them to Cameron to review. They had five designers they were interested in, and all were available for interviews that day.

To his surprise, there was another application sitting on his desk. "Where'd this come from?" As he picked it up, he went very still. It couldn't be a coincidence. There were no coincidences.

The applicant was Sera.

"That was on my desk when I got here," Cameron offered from the doorway. "I had Sarah call her to come in. She's way more qualified than anyone else we're seeing today. If her portfolio is as good as I'm hoping, our decision will be easy."

Kenneth ran a finger over where she had written 'Bachelor's in Graphic Design, 2016.' "I thought she said that she didn't have her degree."

"I called the college and checked. They confirmed it. Something weird is definitely going on, Ken." He grinned. "But I'm not knocking our luck. If she's coming to you, all the better. You look a little . . . sleepless."

"Get out of my office, Cam."

With a snicker, his brother backed out. "Try not to hit on her during the interview."

"Smartass," he muttered. He tossed the application down on his desk and crossed his arms. Something was definitely up, and as soon as he had a chance, he would pin Sera down and find out what had happened.

He was forced to bide his time. Sera ended up as the last scheduled interview and that meant he had to sit through five other applicants. Not that they weren't talented or genuinely likeable. They just weren't the person he had waited his entire life to find.

Sarah was in the middle of checking out one applicant when she saw Sera walk in. "Sit," she ordered. Her friend smiled wryly and sat down, and she grinned at the young man she was currently helping. "I've known her for years. I can get away with things like that."

He grinned. "I have a friend like that." He winked at Sera. "Good luck."

"Thanks." She waited until he headed out and then walked over to her friend's desk. "Well. Nice digs. That your husband's office behind you?"

"Sure is. He used to have a closet but upgraded recently." Sarah studied her. "Degree, huh?"

"It's a really long story. I promise I'll explain everything later. Let's just say that yesterday hit a whole new level of unreal, even for the District." She blew out a hard breath. "How do I look? I've never worn a suit before."

"You look amazing." Her eyes twinkled. "Sort of sexy, so I do hope Ken can concentrate on your art portfolio and not your physical one." She got to her feet. "I'll show you to the conference room."

"Yeah, sure." Sera's hands tightened around her portfolio as she tried to ignore the way her stomach dipped and rolled like a particularly unhappy ocean. The lamp was tucked safely in her purse but it wouldn't be much use. She was on her own and she knew it.

Kenneth looked up when the door opened and his jaw dropped as he saw her. He was on his feet before he even being conscious of moving. A tailored black suit did amazing things to an already amazing body, but he missed her paint-streaked jeans. She was an artist, not an executive. "Sera."

She held her portfolio like a shield. "I'm interviewing," she warned him. "Keep your hands off!" When Cameron cleared his throat, she found a smile for him. "Hi again. You sure you two aren't twins?"

"Positive," he said dryly. "Nice to see you again, Sera. Now hand over that portfolio." He took it when she held it out and then dropped it on the table to spread out the pieces inside. "While we look at this, tell us what you can do."

She sat down and took a deep breath. She could do this. "Well, I've been self-taught for a long time, but I just completed my degree as well. I know the Adobe Creative Suite . . ."

The brothers listened intently, most of their attention on the work she had brought. Without bias, she had by far the best portfolio of anyone who had interviewed. Kenneth had been expecting it after seeing the piece she had done for the club, but the work in her portfolio was even better. "How are you at work on the fly?" he asked.

She blinked. "Good. Why?"

He slid a sketchpad across to her. "I'm going to describe a concept, and I want you to draw it." He slid across a box of pencils as well.

"Go for it." She held one pencil in her hand and stuck different ones over each ear so they were in easy reach. The gum eraser was brand new; she had to stretch and squish it around until she felt surer it would pick up pencil cleanly.

Unbeknownst to her, all of her actions got added like points to her already high score. "Okay, here's the idea. It's a poster. Flashy, modern, and edgy," he began. "It's an ad for sunglasses. The background is sharp angles so the round edges of the glasses pop. The glasses are red, so give a green background."

"Blue," she argued. "If you want it to pop, then clash your colors. Red against blue will be much more dramatic." She twirled her sketch around. "See? And anyway, people are conditioned to see red and green and think Christmas. You have to be careful with them."

The brothers exchanged a long look. "Okay," Cameron said finally. "You're hired."

The pencil hit the table with a clatter. "I'm *what*?"

Kenneth grinned at her. "Don't sound so shocked. You've got the best qualifications, you've got the best portfolio, and you were willing to argue with your future bosses when they were wrong about an art concept. You're absolutely hired."

"I think I'm going to pass out." She pushed back from the table, her head spinning. "Or I'm going to be sick. I got the job?" She shook her head hard when he came around the table. "Don't touch me. I'm freaking out here. Do you know how badly I wanted this?" she demanded. "It's my *dream*."

"And now you have it." He tugged her up to her feet and kept her possessively tucked under his arm. "And now that business is done, we have some personal things to talk about." He held tighter when she tried to get free. "You might be almost as tall as I am, but I'm certainly stronger. I'm kidnapping Sera," he added as he dragged her past Sarah's desk.

She grinned. "Good."

"Traitor!" her friend muttered. She glanced up and saw Lorcana and felt her stomach clench with fear. "Oh crap."

He spotted his mother and held her tighter. "Problems other than the obvious?"

"Part of the explanation I owe you," she whispered.

Lorcana walked closer and stared intently at Sera. She knew she wasn't imagining things. Really, how could there be two tall females with pink streaks in their hair? The little twit must have found a way out of the well after all. "And you are?"

"Our new lead designer," Kenneth informed her coolly. "And if I play my cards right, she might even agree, finally, to go out with me. She might be your next daughter-in-law, so I wouldn't be burning your bridges yet, Mother."

She hissed something unpleasant under her breath. Suspicious, she eyed them as they walked away. Something smelled rotten around here. What was that little nobody up to?

"Precisely where are you taking me?" Sera demanded.

"My office." He ushered her inside and shut the door firmly. "I don't want interruptions."

"I guess you really want that explanation."

"That's not all I want." He framed her face with his hand and kissed her hungrily. His other hand dropped to her waist and dragged her tighter against his aching body. Desire? It had gone beyond that. This was obsession. Craving. "So you won't date me," he muttered against her lips. "Can we skip to the part where you'll put me out of my misery and let me be your lover?"

"Ken." It was little more than a moan as his hands opened her jacket and got to work on her blouse. She desperately grabbed for control and caught his hands before he could make her forget her name. Her entire body vibrated like a piano string with too much tension in it. "I will not have my first time on top of a desk."

His head lifted quickly. "Pardon?"

She scowled. "Weren't you listening when I said I wasn't casual?"

"You're twenty-one," he said with a matching scowl. "I'm entitled to have believed you'd had to have had at least one serious relationship."

"Not *that* serious. You're the first guy I've ever wanted to be serious about in that way, okay?" She let go of his hands and carefully refastened her blouse, her fingers trembling as she did. He wasn't the only one going out of his mind. How the hell did a body crave something it hadn't had before? No wonder it was called frustration!

He took a long breath. "I used to have self-control. Then I met you." He took a healthy step backward and put his hands in his pockets. It was either that or tumble her down onto the floor. She had worn that damned lip-gloss again and it only enhanced her natural flavor. She looked rumpled and flushed and *damn it* he wanted her so bad it hurt. "Talk. Quick."

She drew a shuddering breath and pressed her fingers to her lips. "So I had a surprise visitor yesterday morning . . ."

By the time she finished explaining, he was staring at her in disbelief. That his mother had tried to kill her was little surprise; he knew her ruthlessness knew no bounds. And that there was a genie-dragon hybrid in a lamp didn't seem so hard to swallow either. It was having all of it together that blew his mind. He slowly sat down in one of the chairs. "Well."

"Please don't be mad," she said softly. "I just . . ."

"Why on Earth would I be mad?" he asked wryly. "We didn't hire you because of your wishes, and I sure as hell wanted you well before you had them. It's just a lot to take it." He pressed his hands together and tapped them against his chin while he thought. As far as he was concerned, nothing had changed. Nothing except that a few more barriers had been knocked down between him and the woman he loved.

"Alright." He got to his feet. "I'm simply going to count my blessings now I have you close enough at hand that I can chip away at your stubbornness." When she warily backed up, he moved closer and trapped her against the desk. His lips skimmed tenderly over her cheek. "Let me be yours," he breathed softly. "I need you, Sera."

Her lashes fluttered closed as his lips claimed hers in a kiss so tender that it stole all the strength from her body. It felt, almost, like he loved her. Could he? Of their own will, her arms wound around his waist to hold on tight. She loved him so much.

They eased apart and his trembling fingers skimmed through her hair. "Let me come over for dinner. You don't have to date me," he coaxed, "but let me be part of your family."

She was so doomed. "Alright," she finally conceded. "Come over for dinner tonight. Mom was feeling so well this morning that she's going to be bored real soon. She'd love company. She likes you a lot."

"Good. Now that we have that settled, let's talk business." He smiled. "You need to meet the people you're going to be working with, and over."

As she heard them approaching the door, Lorcana beat a hasty retreat. Her heart pounded hard with a combination of fury and desperation. Sera had used the lamp. She should have known that was what was going on! At least it was true that the lamp gave wishes. Now she just had to get her hands on it!

When Kenneth and Sera walked into the area where the other designers were located, Louise had to work to cover a smile. "Nice to meet you," she told Sera solemnly. "I'm Louise, but most call me Lou. Since you're not officially my supervisor yet, I feel free to tell you this: please put Kenneth out of our misery. He's been hell to live with these last few days."

"Hush!" Kenneth scolded her. "I'm working on her all by myself, thank you. She's letting me have dinner with her and her mother."

Torn between horror and amusement, Sera had nothing to say to that. She was greatly enjoying herself regardless. It seemed a little . . . daunting that she would not only be working in her field, but that she would be overseeing the work of this many other talented people. She was equally flabbergasted when he showed her into the office she would use. "It's huge!"

"Yeah, our last lead had been here forever. He picked the spot when the place was made. You get to reap the rewards." He leaned against the door and smiled. "Do you still think you're walking through a dream?"

"I should be waking up any minute now," she admitted. She held up her hands warily when he stepped closer. "Don't you dare touch me, Ken!" She darted out of his reach. "Don't you have any self-control?"

"Where you're concerned? No." He snagged her wrist and tugged her close. "Let's get some lunch. Not a date," he assured her. "Just lunch. You've got to be hungry. I know I am. There's a cute bistro not far from here."

"Oh just go out with him!" a male scolded as he went past the open door. "We saw your work; we know you didn't seduce your way into your position."

"Pity for me," Kenneth murmured.

Sera groaned and covered her face with her free hand. "Fine. Alright. Let's get lunch. I didn't eat breakfast, so I am kind of hungry." She freed her hands and stuck them in her pockets. "No more holding my hand, got it?"

"Fair enough." Instead, he lightly rested his hand on the small of her back. The gesture was very possessive and as subtle as neon. Not touch her at all? Over his dead body. This was practically a war that he fought, and he would be damned if he lost.

The bistro was small but lively, and he was a frequent enough visitor that the waiter happily found them a small table out of the way of the crowd. As they settled in with sandwiches and coffee, Sera felt some of the tension fading from her shoulders. She let out a long breath.

"Decompressing?"

She smiled wryly. "Finally. I think it finally sank in. The weights just lifted from my shoulders. I mean, I know my mom is going to get better, but now I can support us until she's on her feet again. I can't depend on Dazzle for everything. That would definitely be selfish."

"You know," he said softly, "my dad would have adored you. He was hell on wheels, but he loved Cam and I. When we were little, and old enough to realize our mother hated us, he told us that he stayed with her because of us. He knew the courts might side with a mother over a father, and he didn't want that chance. If he'd known he would die from lung cancer, he'd have quit smoking."

She gently covered his hand with hers. "I almost envy you," she said just as softly. "You had some warning it might happen. I had none. Dad went out to get ice cream, and a few hours later, a member of Enforcers was at our door to tell us what had happened. A drunk driver."

"Enforcers told you?"

"Yeah. If something affects a member of 3rd District, the Enforcers are notified first. They personally tell the people involved."

"I knew they had clout, but, damn." He turned his hand over and laced their fingers together. "I liked it there," he admitted softly. "When Cam told me it felt like being home, I didn't really understand until I was there myself."

"I can't envision living anywhere else."

He softly rubbed his thumb over her palm. "But could you? Would you be happy in a big place with plenty of room for artistic expression?"

Her heart began to beat harder. "If I knew I was somewhere I would be loved, yes. I can put down roots anywhere as long as I know I will be happy." Barely breathing, she searched his face. "Why do you ask?"

He brought her hand to his lips and kissed her wrist tenderly. "I'll tell you tomorrow morning," he said huskily. "I want to talk to your mother first." He reluctantly released her hand, his fingers caressing her skin as he did. "How do you feel about starting work this afternoon? We have a meeting with a company, and we definitely need your on-the-fly art skills."

"As long as my pay starts this afternoon," she smiled, "I don't mind at all."

He laughed. "A woman after my own heart."

He had no idea, she thought morosely, how bad she really wanted his heart. And his smile. And his body. And damned near everything about him. Men like him could easily make a woman completely lose her sanity.

"By the way," he added an hour later as they walked back into the office, "feel free to dress more casually when you're not going to be at a meeting. If you look around, you can get an idea for the style around here. But if we've got a meeting, then you'll need to break out this lovely suit." Wistfully, he said, "I never thought I'd look forward to meetings."

She glanced down at the suit, half-expecting to find it had suddenly become skintight and made of leather. "It's just a normal skirt."

"On your legs, it's an invitation to ogle." He brought her hand briefly to his lips. "See you at 3:00."

She blew out a breath as he walked away and then firmly walked into her new office. She sat down behind the desk and dropped her head on the top. "What have I gotten into?"

"Ahem."

She glanced up and found Louise in the doorway. "Sorry. Did you need something?"

"Your first official duty." She walked over and put down her timesheet. "Sign please." She eased a hip onto the side of the desk, a smile teasing her lips. "So. Do tell what's going on with you and Kenneth. Obviously you two knew each other before you interviewed."

"By three days. Or maybe two and half?" Sera signed the timesheet and slid it back across the desk, marveling at the concept. *She* approved time now? "It's complicated. I didn't even know he was a Dease until some reporter gave away his identity." She rubbed her forehead. "And there I was, falling real fast for some guy, and he turned out to be in charge of a huge company. I was, until today, seriously low class, Lou."

"A classy low class," Louise told her. "All that bull about position is just that. Around here, it doesn't matter where you're from so much as what you do with your life. Kenneth fell for *you*, hon. He didn't fall for what you might become. Did he even know you were interviewing here?"

"No. Heck, I didn't even know until last minute." She frowned thoughtfully. "You think he might love me?"

Louise sighed affectionately. "You're so cute." She hopped to her feet. "I always wanted a little sister; now I have two between you and Sarah. I just find it ironic that you both supervise me now."

"You're not offended?"

"Heck no! I'd rather focus on my work than keeping this loony bin in line *any* day." She winked. "Just let me know if you need someone to talk to, okay?"

Sera found herself smiling. She would definitely like Louise. Having a big sister sounded pretty wonderful. "You got it. Now get to work." Her smile became a grin. "I always wanted to say that."

"Fun, huh?" With a grin, Louise headed back to her desk. She would have to talk to Michael and Becky and they could start planning a secret bridal shower for Sera. There was no question in her mind how this would end.

Cameron had entered the lobby of the building after running out for a sandwich when he was surprised to see a stranger studying the elevator listing. She was *tiny*. Not only short but overall delicate and slender. Her silvery hair seemed more like feathers than human hair. When she turned and smiled at him, her violet eyes sparkled merrily. "Hello," she said.

"Well, hi." He smiled as he stopped next to her. He had to smile. There was something that felt genuinely likeable about her. "Are you looking for someone?'

"I was looking for you." She held out a folder. "This is important, Cameron, okay? You need to make sure Kenneth and Sera sign this contract."

"Contract?" His eyes widened. "Wait, are you from Enforcers?"

She giggled and ran off through the lobby. "Bye!" she called over her shoulder. She narrowly missed bumping into both the security desk and a person entering, but everyone who watched her had a smile.

Wondering what she had given him, he flipped open the folder and started reading. A slow grin began to cross his face as he saw what was being set up. Not that he had doubted a happy ending, but this would just be insurance. Still, he could only shake his head in bemusement as he hit the call button for the elevator. Enforcers employed some really interesting people. He would have sworn he had just met a wingless faerie.

Sera had settled into her new office by the time the meeting drew close. She had found the supply closet, been cheerfully helped by a graphic geek named Michael, and now had most of what she needed. The other items, such as her preferred choice in sketchpad and drawing utensils, she would bring from home. Electronic drawing tools came courtesy of the job, and she was a very happy camper.

After a glance at the clock, she gathered up her things and headed for the conference room. As she left her office, a cheerful woman with pale blonde hair walked up. "Hi. I'm the tech geek around here."

Sera grinned. "I'm the new art geek. Normally I'm called Sera."

"Emily." She saluted with a CAT cable. "I'm here to hook up your email and stuff. It'll be done by the time you're back from your meeting."

"Great. Thanks." Still marveling at the day, Sera headed for the meeting. She was doing what she loved, and she got to work near the man she loved. Could it get any better?

Cameron waited for her outside the meeting room. "Hey, there you are," he said with a smile. He held out a document. "Your signature, ma'am. Some of the last paperwork for your position. We're informal on most things except procedure."

"Sure." She signed at the bottom without looking twice. "Any hidden language about servitude?"

"It's standard language. Ken didn't write it." He grinned when she stuck her tongue out at him. He had always wanted a big sister. Sure, she wasn't *that* much older, but it still counted. Whistling softly, he waited for Kenneth. When he spotted him, he said, "Last formality and Sera is officially ours. Yours. Well, something to that effect."

Kenneth grinned and scrawled his signature next to Sera's. "Anything about servitude in there?"

"You two think far too much alike." He folded the contract and tucked it safely into a pocket inside his jacket. He refused to let it out of his sight until he was positive it was no longer needed. Like after the honeymoon.

As he walked into the conference room, Lorcana edged around the corner she had been standing near. She checked twice, made sure no one was paying attention, and hurried to Sera's office. The tech was finishing up, and she hid where she wouldn't be seen. Internally, she bemoaned her current state. She had gone from being in charge to being forced to hide so she could steal a lamp from a stupid peon.

Emily left the office and Lorcana darted inside, heart pounding. She spotted Sera's purse and opened it quickly. The lamp sat inside. She snatched it up, zipped the purse closed, and scuttled out of the office. She didn't breathe until she entered the tiny office she had to use until she left for good.

Hands trembling, she rubbed the lamp quickly. A bright pink glow lit the area and she held her breath. When the glow cleared, a small dragon hovered in front of her. "A dragon?" she demanded. "Shouldn't there be a genie?"

"Uh-oh." Dazzle stared at Lorcana. "You're not Sera."

"No." She smiled tightly. "I'm your new master, and you need to grant my wishes. I want the company." She paused as she thought about it. "You know, I want more than that. I want revenge on that stupid shifter and my idiot son. Give me a contract that says Kenneth is willing to marry the woman of my choice and will turn over his shares upon marriage."

Dazzle reluctantly produced the document. "I can't forge his signature," she warned. "It would be interfering with free will; he'd have never signed this willingly, and I can't make it look like he did."

Lorcana scoffed. She picked up a pen and signed Kenneth's name at the bottom of the document; the signature looked nearly identical to his real one. "I've forged my boys' signatures for years. If no one gives me what I want, then I take it. I used to forge their father's signature as well." She studied the contract in satisfaction. "I'll call that nice woman who was willing to marry Cameron and see if she wants Kenneth instead. Everything is going to be just the way I want it." She frowned as Dazzle lost lift and plopped onto the side of the desk. The dragon didn't look . . . healthy. "What's wrong with you?"

"I'm tired. Can I rest, master?"

"Oh. Sure. I'll call you if I need you again." As Dazzle disappeared into the lamp, she picked up the phone and began to punch numbers. Finally. Finally she was going to get what she deserved. And once she had Kenneth's share, it wouldn't be long before she got rid of Cameron as well. Her wish granting dragon would see to it.

CHAPTER THIRTEEN

The meeting went smoothly, and better than expected. While ideas fired from all around the table, Sera kept up with the demand. She produced sketch after sketch, made dozens of changes, and was fast enough to ink anything that became set in stone so she could change around it safely. Though Cameron and Kenneth had come up with the original concept, the company receiving it was very particular about their promotions.

Still, when they left at the end, they looked very happy with the result. They had two print ad concepts that Sera would turn digital, and the ideas from those print ads would be given to the 3D animation unit to be made into a gimmicky television commercial.

The door shut behind them, and Sera held up her carbon covered fingers. "I look like a coal miner," she said ruefully. "I didn't start pushing my hair out of my face, did I?"

"No, you're clean," the lead animator, a woman named Becky, assured her. She grinned suddenly. "And now you know why I work with computer pencils and not physical ones. I never walked out of an art class looking like a zebra." She pondered that. "Okay, I did once, when they made me take fundamentals of art. I vowed off charcoals ever again."

Sera grinned back. "I could tell some horror stories too." She rolled her shoulders and gratefully accepted the napkin Kenneth offered. "Thanks, Ken." She wiped at her fingers. "I've never made so many changes so fast before. It was fun."

"Thank god," Cameron said sincerely. "I was afraid you'd run screaming. You artists are so temperamental."

"We grow artists tough in the District."

Kenneth glanced at the clock. "That's it for the day, guys. Let's break and meet tomorrow morning at eleven. Will that give you enough time to get a rough digital outline?" he asked Sera.

"Since I'm starting at eight, sure." She looked at Becky. "I can send you the digital frame to use to make the character models. You'll have it by ten-ish, okay?"

"That's perfect."

Kenneth smiled as he fell into step beside Sera as they left the office. "You're fitting in like you always belonged here." His hand lightly rested at the small of her back. "I definitely don't care how you got here. I'm just glad you did." He followed her into her office and shut the door behind him.

She eyed him warily. Since the office only had windows to the outside, no one in the main area would see them. Then again, she doubted it would stop him. She edged back as he stalked toward her slowly. There was something not quite civilized in his eyes as he approached. Something dangerous and predatory in the small smile on his lips. She bumped into her desk and leaned back when he leaned in. Her pulse began to beat harder as her entire body heated to flashpoint.

"It was torture," he said raggedly, his voice rough, "to sit there and watch you across the table. I'm shocked I didn't say something stupid. I'm more shocked I didn't simply pounce on you. Are we still strangers?" His hot hands closed around her arms and he gave her a little shake. "Are we strangers, Sera? I don't think we are."

"You terrify me. It's just all too much." She shuddered as he pressed a hot kiss to the side of her neck. Her entire body ached for his. She could actually feel her breasts throbbing with the need to feel his hands. Everywhere she had a pulse, it beat out a crazy rhythm that demanded his caress. Colors whirled at the edge of her vision, hot and bright.

"Sera."

On a moan, she turned her head and found his mouth with hers. His tongue thrust hungrily into her mouth and her knees nearly gave out. Only his hands held her up. The kiss devoured her, dragging her into the erotic spell he could weave so easily over her. She surrendered on a shudder. It hurt too much to fight. She loved him. Needed him. She would never stop. "Your place or mine?" she asked huskily.

His head lifted sharply and his darkened green eyes searched hers. All he saw was a melted pool of hot and welcoming gold. Something mysterious, something feminine, lurked in the depth of her gaze, and a small, ancient smile touched her kiss-swollen lips. "Are you sure?" he demanded.

"I never say anything I don't mean." She wound her arms around his neck and rested her forehead against his. "So, which is it?"

"Mine." His lips slowly curved. "I still want to have dinner with you and Cecily. Then I'll kidnap you back to my place and sneak you into my room."

"Will you have your wicked way with me?"

"I'm going to have you any way I can." His teeth nipped at her lip in a sensual threat. "Consider yourself warned." He slowly released her and his hands slid slowly over her skin as he did. His fingers laced with hers. "Let's go."

She was nearly in a daze as she followed him. To those who observed their exit, there wasn't a single doubt that the couple was on the verge of self-combustion. In fact it seemed quite obvious that they wanted to be alone together, and as quickly as possible. Into the silence of their exit, finally someone said, "At least Ken will be easier to live with tomorrow."

"How did you get here?" Kenneth asked as he escorted Sera out of the building.

"Bus. I don't own a car, and I sure as hell can't ride a bicycle this far."

"That'll change," he said determinedly. "Until you can get a car you want, I'll carpool with you." His lips curved ever so slightly. "Then again, you'll be at my place most nights, so it won't be hard."

How permanent was he thinking? She couldn't guess and she was too afraid to try. He hadn't said he loved her. Did he? He liked her, she knew that. And he definitely wanted her. Was that enough for her to get her happy ending?

Her thoughts halted when she saw the vehicle they approached. Her lips twitched. Her tough, high-level executive boss drove a Volvo. And not just any Volvo, but one that looked like it had been popular before he was born. It was clean, well-taken care of, and certainly dent and scratch free, but it was no flashy sports car. "I was totally not expecting this."

"Hey, I never claimed to go for the high life in everything." He looked at her evenly. "I work in advertising, Sera. I know how to look beyond the surface and see if what's inside is quality. And I don't hesitate to choose the best . . . even when it might not be considered top of the line."

She had the feeling they weren't talking about cars anymore but said nothing about it. She just got in without a word. She felt . . . odd. Suspended in a bubble. It was as reality no longer existed. The world had gone away. There was only her and Kenneth.

She was half-afraid she wouldn't be able to carry on a conversation with her mother, but when she let them into the house, she was surprised to find it empty. "Mom?" She went into the kitchen and saw a note on the fridge. Bemused, she read it twice to be sure.

"Where is she?" Kenneth asked from the doorway.

"On a date."

"A date?" His brows shot up.

"With Doc Matthews." She laughed suddenly. "I *knew* he seemed to have a personal interest. I'm really glad, for them both. They need each other. Seriously, the way he watched Mom was totally not how a normal doctor looks at a patient." She turned with a smile that slowly faded as she saw the look on Kenneth's face. Her breath caught.

"Exactly how did he look at her?" he asked softly.

"Offhand," she managed to whisper, "I'd say it would be roughly like how you're looking at me right now."

The tension stretched as they watched each other. They were alone. They would be alone for hours. She found herself walking toward him slowly, drawn by a force she could not fight. He moved forward equally, and his hand lifted to brush his knuckles over her cheek.

The mood broke rather abruptly when Milly ran into the kitchen with a happy bark. She knocked into Sera, threw Kenneth off balance, and then proceeded to smother both with happy kisses when they landed in a heap on the floor.

"Damn it, Milly!" Sera started laughing as she tried to shove her dog away and get herself untangled from Kenneth at the same time. "What a way to spoil the moment!"

Kenneth propped himself up on his elbows with a grin. "But it's not a bad thing. I was two seconds away from tearing that suit off you and taking you on the kitchen counter." He rolled lithely to his feet before kneeling and lifting her into his arms.

"Gah!" She grabbed his shoulders desperately. "Okay, I know I'm not that heavy but I'm not *that* much smaller than you."

"I just happen to be that much stronger." He nuzzled his nose into her hair so that he could tease the hoop on the top of her ear with the tip of his tongue. Her breath broke and desire clawed at his body. "Direction?" he asked huskily.

"Hall. Left door." The ability to use words of more than one syllable had taken a hike along with her blood pressure.

Milly followed them but stopped when Kenneth shut the door in her face. Content, she curled up outside and her tail wagged happily. She liked her Sera to be happy. And she liked Kenneth. He was a keeper. She would have to teach him to play fetch.

Kenneth slowly let Sera's legs go so that she could stand on her own feet. He glanced around the room curiously and began to smile. It was obvious an artist lived there. It looked a whirl of color and pattern, somehow oddly chaotic and yet entirely harmonious. He couldn't wait to set her loose on his house.

He glanced at her to find her watching him, and the smile slowly left his face. He softly cupped her cheek and drew her in to could kiss her softly. The explosive force of the passion between them had suddenly tamed. Time. They had time. He deepened the kiss one breath at a time until her hands dropped to her sides in surrender.

He slowly eased back and began to unfasten her jacket. Her hands lifted and he brushed them aside. "Let me," he urged huskily. "I've wanted to do this all day." He slid the jacket down her arms and it fell onto the floor softly.

She couldn't find her breath or her will. There was so much more to this than she had ever imagined. She couldn't even tell whether it was her heart or her body that ached more. Couldn't be sure where she ended and he began. When his fingers slid inside her open blouse and skimmed across the top of her breasts, fire licked through her body. What was it in his touch that felt so good to her? "Only you," she said softly, her lashes lowering. "I was waiting."

His hands trembled for a moment. "Sera." Wonder filled his gaze as he let the blouse fall. She seemed impossibly perfect to his eyes with her curves barely held in check by the scrap of white silk hiding her from his gaze. "Look at you," he breathed.

Her lips slowly curved. "I'd rather look at you." She tugged on his tie until he leaned in closer for a kiss. Her nerves had evaporated. She didn't even remember them. Teasingly, she nibbled on his lower lip the way he always did to her. "I used to like my males to be much taller. But your height is so convenient, Kenneth." She eased up only slightly on her toes and blew lightly on his ear. "See?"

Any blood that had still been in his head seemed to gather much lower, fisting into a hard ache that demanded relief. Her fingers teasingly walked down his chest, and his stomach tightened in anticipation. "You're a tease." It was barely more than a rumble.

"Maybe." She nudged at his jacket and watched with hungry eyes as he shrugged out of it impatiently. The white-collar shirt he wore just emphasized the strength in his shoulders and made them seem wide and powerful, perfect for a weary shifter to rest her head on. She unfastened the buttons and laughed as she encountered his undershirt. "And men say women wear too many clothes."

"You do." He shrugged off the shirt and then tugged off his undershirt. Gloriously bare, he rested his hands lightly on her hips as his fingers played with the zipper of her skirt. "How's that?"

She traced a finger down the sculpted line of the muscles on his chest, loving how the pale hair covering them teased her touch. "I wouldn't have expected this from a guy who panders posters."

"He also lifts weights."

"Lucky me." Her lashes lowered slightly as she felt her skirt sliding down her legs. And slowly her lips curved as she heard his breath catch. "I'm not a pantyhose girl," she said solemnly, sensual laughter lurking in the tone.

"Now I'm the lucky one." He reverently skimmed his hand down her leg and tugged at the top of her thigh high stockings. He couldn't even say what was so sexy about them, but the way they emphasized her almost outrageously long legs was beyond belief. He caught her around the waist and lifted her onto the side of the bed. Slowly, like a man unwrapping a particularly anticipated present, he peeled the stockings down her legs and then off entirely.

She fell over onto her back and closed her eyes as she savored the feel of his hands on her body. The bed moved as he sat beside her and she looked up to see him leaning over her. Something beautiful filled his eyes. Something that might very well have been love. Emotion welled and stole her voice. All she could do was reach for him desperately.

He sank into her arms on a groan and kissed her deeply, his tongue dueling hotly with hers. One hand tangled in her wild black hair. The other swept up and down her body without course, almost as if he was memorizing her. Every touch fed the fire and spread the pleasure until her whole body quivered with desperate need.

He grasped the front of her bra and tugged hard. The back broke open and he pulled the offending piece of clothing away and tossed it aside. He bent his head and greedily captured one tight nipple in his mouth. She was cinnamon everywhere; hot and spicy but sweet underneath.

Her back arched wildly and she grabbed his shoulders for balance. Every tug of his mouth tugged at something deeper and made a hot fist begin to gather inside. The ache seemed to center between her legs and spread outward. His name was little more than a cry of desire as he began to trail hot kisses down her stomach. "I'm going nuts," she managed to say.

"I've been nuts for days," he countered thickly. "Jesus, Sera. Where have you been all this time? I didn't even know I needed you." He stripped away her silk panties and eased back enough to sweep a possessive gaze over her naked body. His. Only his.

His fingers slid between her legs and softly slid through the silky black curls hiding her from his touch. Her mouth opened to say something but all that emerged was a soft moan when his fingers found where she ached most.

She was wet and hot, nearly burning him alive. He grasped wildly at control. He hurt with the need to be inside her. And she was ready for him. Dear god, she was ready. Her desire for him was as powerful as his for her. He watched her face raptly as he slowly slid a finger inside her body. His thumb teasingly brushed over the sensitive nerves at the apex of her legs.

Her hips arched wildly and her hands grabbed the covers for support. When he slid a second finger slowly, teasingly, into her, she suddenly jackknifed up and grabbed for him. He fell over onto his back with a rich masculine laugh. "Problem?"

"Two can play that game." She tossed her hair out of her eyes, and their golden color glowed with power and promise. "And you're not naked."

His grin turned dangerous. "That can be fixed."

They unfastened his belt and pants together, and she fiercely stripped them and his shorts down and off his body. When he was as naked as she was, she sat back to look at him. That something deep inside heated and fluttered wildly as she saw how aroused he was. He wanted her. It seemed a glorious thing that he wouldn't care where she was from or that she might not be normal.

His breath hissed in as she lightly ran a fingertip down the length of his throbbing erection. His fingers dug into the blanket beneath him as he fought the urge to drag her over the top of him. The look in her eyes, the nearly wondrous discovery, was worth every agonizing second of torturous pleasure.

Her lips teasingly traced across his chest before nuzzling one flat nipple. Her tongue flicked lightly, as if to just taste, and his body jerked. Thrilling to having him at her mercy, she caressed and petted him softly, tasting anywhere she liked. His shoulder. His stomach. He was impossibly beautiful, impossibly perfect.

Her hot breath teased the tip of his arousal and he cursed under his breath. He caught her around the waist and rolled to pin her again. The soft skin of her legs caressed him as she naturally wrapped them around his hips as if they had been lovers forever. Her hands softly framed his face, her eyes darkening nearly to black as he slowly took her, and the sight was wildly erotic.

When he was as deep as he could go, he buried his face against her neck, his body trembling fiercely. "Sera." It was all he could say. She fit him so perfectly, her body made to align to his. The sensation was pleasure that bordered on pain.

She had no words for him. She could only kiss him, pouring everything she was into that simple thing. It was enough. He took her again and again, each time a little deeper, a little harder, until that something broke inside. It broke with the force of a hurricane, ecstasy rushing over her so hard and fast that there was no resisting it. No words to describe it. And when it took him as well, she could only hold onto him as tight as possible, never wanting to let go.

He caught most of his weight on his elbows as he collapsed against her, but that was the limit of his ability. After a few moments, when he felt surer his voice would work, he asked huskily, "Are you comfortable?"

"Don't mind me." Her eyes didn't open and her voice sounded drowsy with satisfaction. "I'll just stay here a while."

His lips curved. "I guess there's no need to ask if you enjoyed it."

"Never ask questions with obvious answers." She made a disgruntled sound as he gently disentangled their bodies. "I liked you where you were." She felt him leave the bed and opened her eyes curiously. "I thought post-coital glow was supposed to be one of the best parts."

"It is." He opened the door just enough for Milly to dart in. "But someone was being neglected."

Her heart happily melted. When he got back into bed and tugged the covers over them, she cuddled in as close as she could. A thrill filled her at how his arms went around her just right. She watched Milly curl up on the end of the bed with her favorite squeaky toy in her mouth, and she wondered why she didn't simply implode with joy. "I'm so glad my bed is big," she said with wry humor. "It can actually hold two people skirting dangerously close to the six foot mark and a Golden Retriever that doesn't realize she's almost as heavy as her owner."

He smiled and combed his fingers through her hair to tease out the pink streaks. "I always wanted a dog, but we couldn't have pets. They would make a mess. Or they might break something."

"Or they might make you happy," his lover muttered.

"Probably," he admitted. "Sure as hell the house has been happier since Mother went into the guesthouse. Cam's birthday is in barely a week. At that time, she's out for good from both the company and our lives. I can't even call it burning our bridges. There were never any bridges to burn."

"You going to stay all night?"

"I wish I could." He trailed a finger down her arm slowly. "Your mom might be miffed at me."

"Nah, she thinks you're hot. She wouldn't blame me at all."

He snorted softly. "Be that as it may, I still want to talk to her. Then you and I are going to talk about us."

She sighed happily. "I can handle that."

Since there was no knowing when Cecily would be home, he reluctantly left around ten. Sera walked him to the door, wearing nothing but a robe covered in splotches of bright color. She was as vibrant as the art she made and glowed beautifully like a diamond in the rough. He loved her more than anything.

His good mood lasted only until he got home. When he walked into the house, he found Lorcana waiting for him. His smile faded as he hung up his jacket. "What?" he asked her curtly. "I'm tired and you're not welcome in *our* house."

Her smile more closely resembled a sneer. "We'll see about that, Kenneth. I have something you might want to look at. Be glad you got your lust for that little nobody taken care of. You won't be seeing her again."

A chill went slowly down his back. "Now what have you done?"

"Let's go into the office and talk about that, shall we?"

CHAPTER FOURTEEN

Sera woke the following morning feeling as if her entire world was finally right. She had her dream job. The man she loved might just love her as well. Nothing could possibly ever pull her down again.

She had no meetings that day. She opted for a pair of casual pants and a bright shirt that she knew Kenneth would love; he had the soul of an artist, too. She went to collect her purse, and she was startled to realize it wasn't anywhere in the house. In fact, she didn't remember grabbing it out of her office when she left. She wouldn't have normally worried, but Dazzle's lamp had been in there.

She waited for ten minutes, but Kenneth didn't arrive to pick her up. A feeling of trepidation began to fill her heart as she ran through the District to Brian's place. He was always awake early, and though puzzled, he was amiable to driving her to work. He didn't ask anything on the way; he could sense something going on.

She ran into the building, shoved through a surprising crowd of people in the lobby, and impatiently waited for the elevator. She couldn't shake the feeling that there was something terribly wrong. When the elevator dinged, she didn't get a chance to step inside because Louise stepped off. "Thank god," she said. She took Sera's arm and pulled her down the hall. "Sera, there's a big problem."

"What's going on?" She grabbed Louise's arm in turn. "Lou, what's going on? I can feel it. I can feel something wrong."

Louise took a deep breath. She hated what she had to say. "Ken arrived at work this morning looking as if his world had ended. I was so sure he'd be all smiles. We all knew he and you were going to take the logical step in your relationship. He was supposed to be happy!" Her hands curled into fists. "But he wasn't. Apparently he's getting married."

"Wait. What?" Sera leaned against the wall before her legs could give out. Bile rose and she firmly pushed it down. "He's getting married? To who?"

"Janice Benton." Her blue eyes snapped with angry lights. "Let's just say that she and Lorcana get along *fabulously*. I tried to get Ken to tell me what the hell was going on, but he just shut down. All he would say was that sometimes you couldn't win."

Sera shoved past her and scrambled into the elevator. Her new friend stayed right behind her. "I can't accept this. I can't."

"There isn't much time, Sera. The wedding is in less than an hour."

The doors were barely open before Sera ran down the hall into the executive suite. No one in the office smiled. No one laughed. People watched her with sadness and with grief. She barely noticed. She went right into Kenneth's office without knocking. "Ken?" Her heart sank as she saw him sitting with his head in his hands.

He looked up slowly. The woman of his dreams. He had found her and he couldn't even keep her after all. One memory of one beautiful night was going to have to sustain him for a very long time. But her . . . she could have happiness. He just had to make her hate him first. He slowly got to his feet. "Hello."

Her hand curled tightly into the frame of the door. "So. I hear you're getting married in an hour."

"Yeah. Surprised me too. But I'd asked her a long time ago and she'd put me off." He jerked one shoulder up in a mockery of a casual shrug. "Guess our fun is over. Since we're going to have to work together, try not to make any scenes, okay?"

Not Kenneth. The voice seemed to whisper in her mind, but she didn't need to hear it. She knew she was not hearing the truth. For a man supposedly marrying the woman he wanted, he looked amazingly miserable. "Is that what you want, Ken?"

He averted his eyes. "Yeah."

She turned and walked away without another word. It almost seemed to him that he could literally feel her tearing out the biggest part of his heart and soul. On a violent oath, he doubled over and slammed a fist on the top of his desk.

"What the fuck is going on?" Cameron demanded sharply from the doorway. He walked in and violently kicked the door shut. "Ken, what's going on? You left before I could see you this morning, and Sarah and I hurried here expecting you to be walking on air. Instead we're hearing that you're marrying *Janice*. Damn it, bro, you want to explain?"

Kenneth slowly sat down. "You know all that paperwork that we had to sign to transition Mother out? Apparently she snuck something in when we weren't looking. A contract relating to that company we intend to absorb. Among the terms and conditions is a clause saying that, to cement the entire deal, I have to marry Janice because she's the niece of the owner. I can't back out, Cam. Do you realize how many people in that company will lose their job if we don't absorb it?"

"That's impossible." Cameron lightly touched his jacket pocket. Inside it was the contract he had made Sera and Kenneth sign. Suddenly it made all the sense in the world why he had been given it. "She had to have forged it. It has to be fake, Ken."

"And how are we supposed to prove it?" his brother demanded. "And it doesn't matter now anyway." He buried his face in his hands. "I sent Sera away. She must hate me now . . ."

Sera made it halfway through the office before sudden fury made her change her direction. She couldn't work there anymore. She couldn't bear to see Kenneth and know he would never be hers again. But if she was going out, she would go out with a big bang. Someone needed to tell Lorcana Dease off, and she was more than happy to do so.

Lorcana wasn't in her office. Disappointed, she started to leave when she spotted something sticking out of the desk. She moved closer to look and horror filled her. The lamp. It was the lamp. She pulled it out of the desk drawer and stared at the tarnish on the side. Lorcana had stolen the lamp. Had she done something to Kenneth?

No. No, she couldn't have. Dazzle couldn't impact free will. Whatever had happened, he had to be willing. She took a deep breath and rubbed the side of the lamp. Dazzle slowly appeared, but with none of her usual flare preceding her. The small dragon looked tired and sick, but when she saw Sera, she found a smile. "Sera. My real master."

"Oh Dazzle." Sera hugged her close. "I'm so sorry. If I hadn't left your lamp at work, this wouldn't have happened." She rubbed her cheek over her head. "Are you okay?"

"Lorcana's selfish wish used up nearly all my power." Her eyes closed for a moment but opened again. "I can grant you only one more wish, Sera. Then I won't have any more power. But I want to do this. I want you give you something." Her eyes closed again. "You made me so happy with all your unselfish wishes. I wanted to be with you forever . . ."

Sera bit back a sob as she hurried out of the office. She snuck back into her own and put the lamp back in her purse. She knew no one could see Dazzle. She wrote out a letter of resignation and left it on the top of the desk. Then, still keeping Dazzle close, she left the entire area and caught an elevator going down.

The lobby had packed with even more people. The wedding was being held in the auditorium, and even for such short notice, plenty of people had turned out. Other business owners were there, and people from the company Janice represented. Media had arrived, too, from several stations and at least one newspaper.

She made her way through the crowd and edged into the back of the auditorium. The wedding had only just started. Kenneth still didn't look like a happy groom, but Janice certainly glowed happily. Sera had to wonder if anyone had noticed her bouquet was already dying. The red roses had wilted almost entirely.

As the minister began to talk, Dazzle asked softly, "What's your final wish, Sera?"

There was no question in her mind what she wanted. If all Dazzle could grant was one wish, then there was only one thing to be done. She deserved to grant one last unselfish wish to make up for what Lorcana had done. "I want Ken to be happy." The weight of the lamp disappeared from her purse and Dazzle slowly dissolved from sight. Arms empty, heart breaking, she walked out of the auditorium. There was nothing else she could do.

Cameron was sitting in the front row, arms crossed and eyes narrowed, when Sarah suddenly grabbed his arm. He followed her gaze and his eyes widened as he saw the soft pink glow around the corner. He looked around quickly but saw no one looking at him. He promptly snuck from his seat and into the hall. To his surprise, the glow was a dragon. "Who are you?"

"I'm here to grant one last wish for my master." Dazzle glowed softly and a cassette tape appeared in Cameron's hand. "Lorcana Dease forged Kenneth Dease's signature. The evidence is on that tape from her phone. He is not bound by a false contract, but he *is* bound by a true Enforcers one."

He looked down at the tape and then up again but Dazzle had disappeared. A grim set to his chin, he snuck around to where the audio system was situated. He put the cassette in, thanking the gods that the system hadn't been upgraded, and then flipped the switch that transferred the speakers from the microphones to the internal audio.

Seconds later, Lorcana's voice came over the speakers. *Janice, you want to marry Kenneth?*

Janice's voice answered, *Like he wants to marry me. He's onto your games.*

Yeah, well, it doesn't matter. I've got his signature on a contract that says he'll marry you to cement that merger, and once married, he has to give his shares to you.

How'd you get that?

Ha. How do you think? I forged it. It's not the first time I've done it. You think I ran all decisions past those two idiots I gave birth to? Please.

The entire auditorium began to buzz. Horror filled Lorcana's face as angry expressions slowly turned toward her. Reporters leapt forward and shoved microphones into her face. Janice began to look just as terrified as many eyes turned toward her as well.

Cameron darted around the system and jumped up onto the small podium beside his brother. "I've got more proof!" he announced firmly. He pulled out the contract. "This is a different contract entirely. Kenneth signed it willingly not even a few days ago. It states that he will marry the person he loves and no other. It was also signed by Sera Thomason. Sera is from the 3rd District, and this contract is overseen by Enforcers." He grinned at his brother. "And Kenneth remembers signing this one, doesn't he?"

"You sneaky . . ." Kenneth said softly as he understood. "Paperwork, my ass."

"Hey, it was true." He punched his big brother lightly in the shoulder. "Turnabout is fair play. You did it to me."

Before Kenneth could react, Dazzle suddenly appeared before both males. "Don't worry," she told them, "no one else sees me. Ken, you need to hurry! I'm the genie Sera told you about. She used her last wish—my last wish—to wish for you to be happy. So whatever it takes to make you happy, then that's what I am bound to do."

"Take me to Sera," he said instantly. "I need her to be happy. I only need her. Please, take me to her!"

"Okay!"

The bright flash momentarily blinded Cameron. When he could see again, Kenneth had disappeared. As people looked around in confusion, he covered his face with his hands. "Wonderful. How am I going to explain that one?"

Sera hated riding the bus, but there was no way she could walk home. She simply curled up in the back and stared sightlessly out the window as streetlights and signs rolled by. She felt dead inside as if everything had stopped all at once.

When her stop arrived, she barely acknowledged the driver's farewell as she disembarked. She just didn't care about anything. With a deep breath, she turned to go home . . . and felt her broken heart freeze inside her chest.

Kenneth stood behind her.

Her purse hit the ground with a thump. "Ken?" It was little more than a whisper. "I thought you were getting married."

"Someone wished for my happiness." He slowly walked toward her, his eyes dark and intense. "I'm here to take that happiness."

Her hands slowly curled into fists at her side. Tears welled in her eyes but she refused to let them fall. "And what do you need to be happy?"

His hands tenderly framed her face. "You." He rubbed his thumb over her cheek. "You're my happiness, Sera. I love you more than anything. I have from the day I met you. I want you to be my wife. I want you to turn my house into a place of color and laughter. I want you to boss me around at work even though I'm supposed to be in charge."

Her lips trembled into a smile. "I tried to quit."

"It's not official. You have to yell at me and storm out dramatically. It's a rule."

She gave a hiccupping laugh. "You know me. I love rules." His lips found hers and her hands curled around his wrists to keep him close. The tears welled up from somewhere inside that she hadn't known could cry.

"Stop. Sera, please. Stop." His lips rushed over her face to steal her tears.

"I was so scared," she whispered shakily. "I wanted to die, Ken. I knew you weren't happy, even when you were trying to lie to me." She hit his shoulder hard enough to make him wince and then curled her fingers into his shirt to hold on. "I was going to go yell at Lorcana when I found the lamp." Her voice broke on a sob. "Dazzle. She lost her power. Lorcana killed her!"

A bright pink glow startled them both and they looked up in shock as the dragon-genie appeared with a shower of sparks. She looked vibrant and healthy as if she had never been so frighteningly weak. "I'm right here!" she said happily. She flew in loop-de-loops around the lovers. "I told you, didn't I, that good wishes negate selfish ones. So I'm okay now." She landed on Sera's head and peered down into her face. "I can't grant wishes anymore though."

"I don't need anything else." She wound her arms around Kenneth's neck and smiled. "I've got everything I want right here."

It took nearly an hour to get rid of everyone in the lobby. Cameron let Sarah take care of the media while he took care of the guests. Janice and Lorcana were 'taken care of' by two policemen who had just happened to conveniently show up. Louise categorically denied calling them, but no one believed her. One of them was her cousin.

As Cameron waited for the elevator, he felt a presence and turned to see the silvery-haired woman standing behind him. She smiled, her eyes twinkling. "Hi again."

"Hi." He pulled out the contract and handed it to her. "Here you go." Softer, he added, "And thanks."

"You're welcome!"

As she ran off, Sarah stepped up beside him and slipped her hand into his. She softly rested her head on his shoulder. "Bet we see her again."

"Oh?"

"Ever hear the saying about things coming in threes?" Her eyes slid to where Louise stood bickering with a security guard.

He followed her gaze and began to smile. "The best things do, right?"

CHAPTER FIFTEEN

Rhianna was in her office when Rayna walked in with the contract. It read as 'Complete' very clearly across the front. "Tada!" she said as she put it on Rhianna's desk. "Here you go, Rhi."

Rhianna read over the document, added some notes, and slipped it into a folder. It also reflected complete, and she swiveled in her chair to add the folder to a drawer clearly labeled 'Dease.' She closed the drawer, and it remained entirely blank.

"One more, right?" Rayna asked.

"Naturally. In fact, I've been waiting for this one for a long time. It's well overdue for an ending." Her lips curved. "A happy one, of course."

Violet eyes sparkled merrily at her. "Of course."

Status: File In Progress

Analysis: A diamond in the rough always shows its true colors when held by someone who can see the value inside.

Folder Three
LOUISE

CHAPTER SIXTEEN

(Six months ago . . .)

It was warm and sunny in the 3rd District, but it made no difference to those who worked and lived there. Warm or cold, bright or cloudy, those who ran businesses kept their doors open for anyone to walk in. When it was winter, customers might find themselves receiving hot tea or cocoa to combat the chill outside. When it was summer, iced tea or lemonade might be on hand.

Ever since the Faerie Club and the Gentle Brook Inn had taken off in society, the District had had a renewed interest from people on the outside. Rather than rebuff those who came wandering in curiously, the District had opened their doors and their wares and offered a rare glimpse into the magic of their homes.

Among the favorite small shops to visit was the tiny building where Brian Matthews sold his beautiful clothworks. The gentle shopkeeper had a way of making a loom sing, and if it was sewn, it was sewn by hand. He owned only a single old-fashioned sewing machine, but it got little use. The more tedious the detail, the more pride he took.

The irony was, of course, that at least half of New York had seen or owned his work and simply didn't realize. The pieces he sold through big name stores were sold under the pseudonym B. R. Matthews. Brian liked his quiet. He liked his life to be peaceful. And as his twenty-eighth birthday crept dangerously close, his only solace came from his work.

When he turned twenty-eight, he would die.

Marked across his upper chest for all of his life had been twenty-eight small birthmarks shaped like needles. Every year, one more disappeared. His uncle, the doctor in the family, had finally made the connection as to what was occurring when he had seen Brian suffer a minor heart attack on his sixteenth birthday at the very moment one mark faded. The weaver was cursed, and no one knew why.

Brian went on with what was left of his life to the best of his ability. Really, what else could he do? He opened his shop, made his art, and enjoyed the company of his nieces and nephews.

The bell chimed merrily over the door, and he left the back room to see who had entered. To his surprise, he found a familiar red-haired woman waiting for him. "Well." He tucked his hands into his pockets. "Hello, Ms. Taber. I wasn't expecting to see you." He had never met her, but everyone knew the Enforcers' head honcho on sight.

Rhianna smiled at him. "Most aren't. How are you, Brian?"

"Well enough." He held a stunning green dress in front of her. The nearly Grecian style suited her in some elemental fashion. "This was made for you." He offered it with a smile. "My work chooses who it belongs to."

She draped the dress over her arm, and her fingers moved over the soft material gently. "I'll wear it quite proudly." She searched his cerulean blue eyes intently and suddenly smiled. "You would never tell me, would you? You're not the type to burden others."

"Why tell what everyone knows?" he said simply. "Talking of it will not change it." He went behind the small counter. "Tea?"

"Yes, thank you." She put the dress down and accepted the cup he offered. "Brian . . . yours is a gift that we do not want to lose. You are an important part of this District. Everyone who lives here is. The way you can heal with your craft is too needed to be lost."

"But what can you do? We don't even know why I am this way." He rubbed his hand over where the last mark rested on his chest.

She studied him for long moments before murmuring, "Even without Truth here, I can see you are lying, Brian. You know why this is happening."

He looked away. "And it cannot be changed."

"Why can't it?" She reached into her jacket pocket and pulled out a sheaf of papers. "This is a contract, Brian. Enforcers wants to do whatever it can to aid you." She put the contract down in front of him. "We will provide you with ancient thread that will serve as a lure to the right person. With this thread, you must weave a scarf that will have a strand of your hair. Sell it under your pseudonym. It will find its way to the person who can break the curse. At that point . . . you will have to do the rest."

He stared blindly at the contract. "I couldn't survive seeing her again," he said softly, achingly.

Even softer, she said, "And you won't survive if you don't. Time changes people. Souls learn more with every rebirth. You can end things right this time."

"I don't even know how it ended before . . ."

"Then that, too, you must find."

He closed his eyes for a moment before straightening his back. He grabbed a pen and signed the bottom of the contract before he could change his mind. Beside him, a roll of softly glowing multicolored thread appeared on the counter. When he touched it, he could feel the age and the power. The ancient spool had Latin carved into the side, and though he was rusty at the language, he could still read it. "'From the loom of Hestia.'" He glanced at Rhianna. "Where did you find this?"

A little smile touched her lips. "I found it lying around." She tapped a finger lightly on the contract. "It's up to you, Brian."

He smiled wryly. "Wasn't it always?"

(Present day)

Louise was the black sheep in her family, but one that was well loved. She had two older sisters, two older brothers and two younger ones, six aunts, six uncles, fifteen cousins, one or two second cousins, and five nieces and nephews. Of that massive family, of those old enough to have a job, she was the only one who was an artist.

She could lay claim to lawyers, police, businesspeople, a fireman, two ranchers, and assorted other desk job type people that she was related to, and not a single one of them knew a paintbrush could be used for more than painting a wall. She preferred her paint to be electronic these days, but she knew her way well enough around a canvas.

She lived alone in a small apartment in Manhattan. It was the most centralized location to all her family in the city (some were scattered across the country), and it was also close enough to work that her commute didn't become a nightmare. She felt happy enough where she was, but she was also discontent with her life. At twenty-six, she knew her whole life lay ahead of her, but she simply didn't feel truly happy yet.

As she brushed her thick auburn hair and desperately tried to convince her curls to behave, her phone began to ring. She hit the speaker button. "Hi, Mom."

Evelyn Pram sighed deeply. "Lou, you know I love you."

"Oh lord."

"Could you *please* make a flyer for your cousin's wedding?"

She just smiled wryly. Her family accepted her artistic side mostly because they loved to take advantage of it. "Which cousin this time?"

"Elly. She's marrying that nice attorney I told you about."

"Great, more lawyers in the family." She gave up on her hair and tied a bright blue ribbon around it to keep it back from her face. "Shoot me an email with all the details. And, no, I will not be a bridesmaid. That last time I was a bridesmaid for one of my relatives, I ended up looking like the Great Pumpkin in heels."

Her mother snorted softly. "Get married yourself and you can have revenge."

"Ha. I actually have aesthetics, remember?" She hung up the phone over her mother's sputter, but she was smiling as she did. Her parents were very careful not to pressure her into getting married or 'settling down' even though she knew they both worried over how alone she felt.

With a shake of her head, she pulled on her favorite sundress. Summer had hit NYC with a vengeance, and the sun was bright and hot in double doses. The air, smoggy as it could be, seemed fresher and cleaner. Going to work was now a great feeling, and she looked forward to every minute. Her job hadn't changed. The entire company had changed. It had been months since Cameron had claimed his shares, and he and his brother had done a clean sweep to remove all traces of their mother (their not-so-happily-jailed for fraud mother) from the place.

Louise was a happy camper. Her bosses, both of which were more like her brothers, were happy. The women they had married, both of which were like little sisters to her, were happy. She loved working for Sera. She was able to be both supervisor and friend, and she didn't take crap. Especially not from Kenneth, and Louise had snickered more than once to hear them shouting at each other. It was a match made in heaven as far as she was concerned.

The message light on her answering machine blinked as she entered the living room, and she pushed the play button. One message was political junk; some assemblyman wanted to be re-elected. She couldn't have cared less for him or his policies. Another message was to tell her that the DVD she had ordered was at the store for pick-up.

The last message was from her favorite older brother. *Lou, go on a damn vacation and stop stressing everyone out. You're like a paint can that's been shaken too hard. You're going to spew everywhere.*

"Love you too," she muttered. Still, she had to think about it. Maybe she *should* take a day off and play hooky. She could con Sera and Sarah into going with her; they had a dual wedding ceremony coming up and were still hunting for dresses. They had promised Louise that she could pick her own bridesmaid dress, so she had reluctantly agreed to be a shared maid-of-honor.

Her phone began to ring again, and she sighed as she answered. "Hi, Dad."

"My favorite daughter!" Craig Pram had a big booming voice that could keep rowdy teenagers in line as effectively as it did unruly defendants in court. "Would you do your loving father a *big* favor?"

"Now what do you want?" It was more affectionate than exasperated.

"Well, Harry is retiring soon . . ."

"More flyers? Seriously, Dad, you could just open any Office program and fake it yourself."

"But then they wouldn't be professional."

"Professionals get paid. I get emotionally blackmailed!"

"Love you."

She sighed. "No wonder you indulged my desire for art school! Alright, alright. Send me the info and his photos and whatever else you need."

"That's my girl!" He paused and then added, "You know, Lou, we were thinking you really ought to take a vacation. Those Dease boys can spare you a few days."

"Oh don't you start too!" She hung up the phone and glowered at it for long moments. And only the pigeons outside the open window heard her mutter, "I don't need a vacation from work. I need one from my family!"

CHAPTER SEVENTEEN

The first thing Louise did when she got to work was get a cup of coffee. On one sip, she knew Sarah had gotten there first; she made the best brew in the company. Louise had watched her once, and she still had no idea why hers always tasted better. Coffee in hand, she sat down at her desk and booted up her computer.

She had only just started to troll through the half dozen emails when Sera suddenly walked up and leaned on the side of the cubicle. "You," Sera said.

"Me. What's up?"

"Wanna play hooky?"

Louise slowly looked at her. "You're doing that creepy thing again. Stop reading my mind! I was just thinking how nice it might be to take a day off."

Sera grinned. "And even better, it's not being AWOL because your supervisor is making you go. Sarah and I found this sweet shop that we want to look for dresses at. And you've got to come along because you need a dress too."

Sarah suddenly popped up on the other side of the cubicle. "And, seriously, we still need to fill our closets at home. I mean, what's the point of making our husbands complain about losing their closets when we don't even take up a quarter of the space?"

Louise laughed. "Hey, far be it from me to argue!" She closed her mail and began to shut down the computer again. "I still think it's going to be *amazing* to have the double ceremony. I'm not even stressing over being maid-of-honor."

"Why would you be?" Sera asked curiously.

"Haven't you heard about that old superstition that a woman who is too many times a bridesmaid will never be a bride?" She held up her hand. "This will mark my sixth walk down the aisle without being the one in a veil."

Sarah pursed her lips slightly. "I admit that I've never seen you date in the months I've known you. So what gives? You don't want to be married? It's perfectly fine if you don't, you know."

"Hmm." Louise slung her purse over her shoulder as she stood. "I do," she decided at last. "I just haven't met a guy lately that I wanted to date, let alone think about marrying. And I *was* engaged once," she offered, "but it didn't last long. He became convinced that I was seeing someone else, and I wasn't. Kind of put a damper on things."

The two sisters-in-law fell into step beside her and they headed for the exit. Kenneth and Cameron already knew they were sneaking out, so neither worried that they might be missed.

"What exactly are you doing about your dress?" Louise asked Sarah. "I mean . . . you have to have everything specially made for you, so . . ."

"That's the curious thing, Lou." A light summer breeze teased her rusty hair as they walked outside. "Ever since I married Cam . . . my sensitivity has gone down to a much more manageable level. I still bruise like a grape. I still feel *much* more acutely than a normal person. But some of the harder issues are gone. I can feel the threads in cloth, but only if I'm thinking about it."

"It served its purpose," Louise murmured.

Sarah grinned at her. "You're starting to sound like one of us, Lou. You sure you're normal?"

"Normal as I can be considering my family. Hey!" The last was a yelp as a particularly strong wind snagged the ribbon in her hair and whisked it away. It sailed out of sight before any of the women could think about grabbing it. Now freed, Louise's curls danced wildly around her face. She blew a lock out of her eyes. "I need a perm."

"But your hair is curly already," Sera said in confusion.

"Believe it or not, it helps tame the beast. Ah well. At least the wind feels nice." She pulled out her keys and twirled them around a finger. "I'll drive."

The shop that Sera and Sarah had found was located in a nearby mall. The crowds didn't look too bad at that time of morning, and they found a parking spot miraculously close to the entrance they wanted. The shop itself was actually a boutique, and Louise recognized it as they walked in the door. "I've been here," she said decisively. "With all five of the prior brides I've been in a ceremony with. Good choice, gals. They have some sweet dresses here." She winked. "And though pricey, you can afford it now."

A handsome gentleman in a suit and turban came up with a wide grin on his face. "Louise, are you here again? Tell me you're getting married this time."

"Nope. That would be these two." She put a hand on each of her friends' shoulder. "Sera, with an E, is the tall one. Sarah, with an A and an H, is the redhead. They're having a double ceremony since they're marrying brothers."

His brows winged up as the names and the scenario clicked for him. "Ah, the two women who married the Dease brothers, correct? Welcome to Bridal Dreams." He smiled. "I'm Rashid, and I'll be helping you out today. Louise knows I know my dresses."

"He can't get rid of me," she agreed cheerfully. "He keeps hoping I'm going to get married so he can prove his skill by finding me, the pickiest female in the world, the perfect dress."

Sera snickered. "Well, we're picky but not that picky. I'm all about being streamlined and simple. Sarah is totally a romantic and needs a princess' dress. And we need a hot and sexy bridesmaid dress for Lou. She can choose whatever she wants as long as it is blue or green since those are our colors. Any shade of either, too."

Rashid stepped back for a moment and studied all three females intently. Sera looked tall and shapely, as striking as a model. Sarah looked cute and spunky, but somehow innately regal. Louise looked, as always, vibrant and wild-spirited. "I might just know what you need. Let's find a fitting room to get your sizes."

Sera and Sarah got rooms right across from each other. Louise opted to wait to look for her dress until they had what they wanted. That they would find it, she had no doubt. She had seen Rashid in action. He had an amazing ability to read people perfectly.

He returned shortly with two dresses. He gave one to each female and sat down beside Louise on the padded bench in the hall. "So." He looked at her pointedly. "Elly is getting married. She's younger than you are, kid. When Evelyn called to tell me and Jess, she was bemoaning the fact that all her children except you are paired off. Even Deke just got married, and he's your baby brother."

"Twenty-two," she murmured. "Not so much a baby, 'shid."

"We're family, Lou." He bumped her shoulder. "I think I know you well enough. What's going on, hon? It can't be just that you're picky. You're not still hung up on that idiot from three years ago, right?"

"Yes and no." She frowned. "He accused me of cheating. The thing is . . . I *felt* like I was cheating. But not on him. I felt like I was cheating on someone else *with* him."

He sat back. "Huh."

"The few dates I've gone on since have made me feel the same way." She sighed. "I figure if I ever find a guy that I don't get that feeling from, he was probably the person I was cosmically cheating on." She dropped her face into her hands. "I used to think oogie-boogie stuff was crap. Then I met the two dingdongs trying on dresses. Let's just say . . . they changed my mind."

"Who're you calling a dingdong?" Sera demanded.

Louise looked up with a smile but her words got stuck. "Wow," she finally said. "Wow, Sera. You look amazing!"

The gown was pure white silk. No lace or frills adorned it. It clung to Sera's entire body until mid-thigh where it began to flare into a train. The very faintest of shimmery patterns wove into the material and reflected light as she moved. The bodice dipped enough to tease without being overly sexy.

A little giddy, Sera turned in front of the mirrors lining the hall. "I can't believe how beautiful it is! Kenneth's eyes are going to pop out of his head if he sees this." She swung around, eyes sparkling. "I want it. It's perfect!"

"Rashid, one. Picky brides, zero." Louise crossed her arms on a grin.

"Make that Rashid, two." Sarah stepped out of her dressing room with her skirt held in her hands so she could walk. "It's so perfect."

The dress had a full ball gown skirt made of layers of silk, satin, and lace. The top had a corset that laced down the front with fat white ribbons to her waist where the streamers fell into the folds of the skirt. It had no straps or sleeves which suited her smaller frame perfectly. The skirt dragged on the floor behind her for at least two feet. Everything was shimmering white but very faint cream touches brought vivid emphasis to her bright hair.

"I think we might have to hold the men up at the altar," Sera told her sister. "Ken's definitely going to pass out, and Cam's probably going to stutter through everything."

Rashid rubbed his hands together. "Now let's find some accessories. We can then get you in with our seamstress for any alterations needed, though I think there may be few. You are lucky enough to wear off-the-shelf sizes!" He turned his gaze on Louise. "And as for you, I have a few things that ought to be perfect."

Sarah lifted a brow as he headed down the hall. "I get the feeling he knows you other than when he helped your other brides."

"He married my cousin," Louise admitted dryly. "So I'm sort of related to him."

Veils were decided on, along with hairpieces. As soon as Sera and Sarah got back in their street clothes after seeing the lady who would make the alterations, Louise found herself shoved into a dressing room. "No orange!" she said over the door fiercely. "I still haven't forgiven you for that!"

Rashid just laughed and headed for the racks. When he returned, he had a dress draped over his arm in a blue identical to her eyes. He passed it into the dressing room and then winked at the other two women. In a soft voice so his cousin didn't hear, he told them, "If she ever gets to an altar, I already have her dress picked out."

"Nice." Sarah sighed happily as she saw Louise walk out of the dressing room. "Done. Sold. Pack it up, it's going home."

It was a simple dress in silk and satin, but it both clung and swirled around Louise's body in a way that made her look as if she walked through water. Beads scattered across the dress glimmered and rippled in the light. The skirt went to just past her knees and the top stayed up by thin beaded straps. The faintest of green color could be seen if the light hit the dress just right.

"Rashid, three?" he asked hopefully.

Louise could only sigh as she ran a hand down the dress. "Okay, I forgive you for the Great Pumpkin incident."

The gown was added to the other two, and they headed up front to be rung up. As Louise reached for her wallet, Sera caught her wrist. "Add hers to our total," she told Rashid. "We're the ones making her be in the wedding, and that means we pay for it." She arched a brow at Louise when her friend stared at her. "No arguing. I'm your boss and I said so."

Sarah giggled softly. Rashid grinned. "Just for that, I'll give you the employee discount I was going to give Lou." As he handed over the receipt, he added innocently, "There's a lingerie store just down the way that most of our brides go to as well. Tell them to give you the Dream Honeymoon discount."

"Thanks!"

After a giggling tour of the lingerie store, they emerged with several bags among them. Even Louise hadn't been able to resist some of the fancier pieces. Just because she had no one to show them off to didn't mean she wouldn't enjoy wearing them anyway.

That stop set the course for the whole day. They went in and out of nearly every store, and they always came out with more than what they had gone in with. Realizing that it wouldn't all fit in Louise's car, Sarah called for the chauffeur to pick her and Sera up in a few hours.

It was nearing late afternoon by the time they found the last accessory shop on their list. It was a specialty place that sold unique and one-of-a-kind items. The windows had been filled with everything from shoes to purses to hats to scarves. Books and trinkets lined the walls, and revolving stands with jewelry dotted the aisles.

The three women split up to peruse the wares, and Louise found herself wandering a little aimlessly. Many things intrigued her, but nothing really jumped out at her . . . until she reached the back of the shop. Amid the rows of assorted neck and head accessories, there was a satin cushion sitting by itself on a small table. Folded on the middle of the cushion sat a scarf of such brilliance and color that she took a sharp breath.

"Ah." The owner had come up beside her without her knowledge. As old and wrinkled as he was, he looked as if he would be quite at home on a porch yelling at kids to keep off his damn lawn. His faded brown eyes still held wizened intelligence as he studied her and the scarf in turn. "You like this, yes?"

"It's beautiful." She reverently touched the scarf and was sure she felt it tingling all the way from her fingers to her shoulder. "Can I pick it up?"

"I don't know. Can you?"

She scooped it up and unfolded it so that its beauty was unconfined. It felt as soft as silk, as thin as air, but as warm as fleece. She could nearly see through it, and as light passed through, it cast multicolored rainbows on the carpet. It reached roughly four feet in length and six inches wide. The way it slid over her fingers felt nearly sensual. "It's so beautiful." She brushed it against her cheek and marveled at the craftsmanship. She knew it had to be handmade. "Where's it from?"

"It was made by B. R. Matthews."

"Really?" She looked at him in surprise. "I've admired his work for years but could never afford it." Very reluctantly, she forced herself to put the scarf down. "It's probably too expensive for me." She rubbed her fingers over the scarf softly. She just couldn't stand to let go.

The owner picked up the scarf and wrapped it around her neck before she could stop him. "Sometimes the art picks the owner," he told her softly. "This is yours, my dear. I am sure Mr. Matthews would be very pleased."

"Really?" She looked in a mirror and was enchanted with how the scarf seemed to fit perfectly. It wrapped just once around her neck, and the ends fell to her waist in the front and back. It was also light enough it didn't get in the way. In fact, she almost couldn't tell she wore it at all. "Are you sure? It must be worth a fortune."

"I am sure."

Sera came around the corner of a rack and her brows shot skyward as she saw Louise. "There you are. Whoa!" She moved closer and leaned in to see the scarf better. She recognized the work instantly. "B. R. Matthews. Niiice. He makes amazing stuff." She straightened and found a smile though her stomach had begun to quiver with a dangerous combination of nerves and hope. Why hadn't she suspected this sooner? It made sense of *everything*. "It suits you."

"Thanks." Louise knew she shouldn't accept such an expensive gift, but she simply had no willpower to say no. "Thank you, sir," she told the owner softly.

"You are most welcome."

It was evening by the time she helped unload at the Dease manor the bags that had been stuffed in her car. With only her own indulgences left, she headed for home. She felt curiously lighter and more content. Taking a day off had definitely helped.

Her answering machine was blinking faster than a nearsighted blonde with new contacts. She hit the play button and listened with half an ear as she unpacked her purchases. It seemed as if every family member she could lay claim to had called to tell her something or another. Her family intimidated people like Sera and Sarah who had had exceptionally small families while growing up. She couldn't imagine *not* having a big family.

As the apartment fell into blessed silence, she found herself looking into a mirror. She had changed into a nightgown and robe for the evening, but she had left the scarf on. Bemused at herself, she removed it and placed it gently on her dresser. She started to walk away, and it snagged on her sleeve. She freed it and used it to tie her hair back instead, and she let the ends flutter behind her sassily. Someday she wanted to meet B. R. Matthews and tell him how much she loved his work. It seemed to speak to her very soul.

"B. R. Matthews" had a vastly different day. Brian awoke in the morning to the sound of banging on the roof, and he recognized it as the sound of the neighbor's cat hunting birds. Since it was as good an alarm as any, he went ahead and got out of bed.

As always, his day started by putting on a pot of coffee before unlocking the shop. He set out what would be displayed outside and then cleaned up the inside. While he drank his first cup of coffee, he went through the tags in his jar. There weren't many. He would swing by their places later and make the trade final.

Tags sorted, he got his computer running to check his email. There were several new messages. One from his uncle; he had just come back from his honeymoon and wanted a belated wedding gift for his bride. Brian just shook his head. It still amused him that the woman who had always been like his sister was now his step-cousin. He also just glad that Lewis and Cecily had found each other; sometimes true love just took a little longer to go from simmer to boil.

Another message had the weekly newsletter from the Faerie Club. Aenya was expecting her second child and she wanted to hold a party. A second personal message for Brian alone accompanied it. She wanted a baby blanket; she felt sure she would be having a boy this time, but she didn't want to go with the traditional blues that regular stores hyped on, just in case she might be wrong.

By the time he finished the emails, people were already starting to wander in and look around. Friday mornings were always the busiest in the District, followed closely by Sunday afternoons. It was a fascinating phenomenon that he had always found amusing. He sold two blankets and six banners and then helped a very pregnant mother find a dress for her niece's graduation party.

When a lull arrived, he closed for lunch and went into his workroom. An immense loom took up most of the space, but it was all that he needed in there. This was where he worked on his most special projects. He was working on his biggest project at that very moment, and he knew very well that it might be his last. He had been under contract for six months. His birthday stood only days away.

A gust of wind blew the front door open around mid-afternoon, and two identical little girls came running into the shop shrieking, "Cousin Brian!" at the top of their lungs.

He ducked behind the counter. He had played the game with them since they had been old enough to walk. He smiled as he heard their footsteps pattering around the hardwood floors. Then, suddenly, two matching faces popped around the side of the counter. "Found you!" Tawny shouted.

"I just can't hide from you well enough!" He scooped up both and hugged them tight. "How are my favorite girls?"

"We get summer break." Tammy looped her arms around his neck and eyed him owlishly. "How come adults don't get summer break? It's not fair. We want Sera to play with us."

"Sera has a busy job. Unfortunately, adults don't get to play like little kids." He carried them into the kitchen and put each down on a different chair. He got two cups of milk and two cookies and handed one of each to each girl. He sat down at the table with them, an ear cocked toward the front in case anyone came in. "Are you happy with your new sister and mommy?"

Both nodded enthusiastically. "Mama is really nice, and she only scolds if we're really bad," Tawny said. "And she and Daddy are always cuddling, but they let us cuddle too. We get to go spend the weekend with Sera and Ken! They got a puppy to play with Milly, and we get to play with him too!"

"How come there are two Seras?" Tammy demanded.

"They spell their names differently." Brian poured himself some tea. "And it's just one of those little things that life likes to throw at us to make us giggle. Like brothers marrying women with mostly the same name. That sort of thing."

"Oh." The twins nodded, eyes wide, as if they understood entirely.

He covered a smile and let them be while he headed up front to help another customer. When he returned, both girls had started drawing with the paper and crayons he always kept on the table for them. Tammy had no real aesthetics. You had to guess to be sure what she had drawn. Tawny was very much Sera's sister; the girl had a talent beyond her years.

"Brian?" Tammy had stopped drawing.

"What is it, Tam?" He knelt next to her chair.

"Daddy says you're going away soon." Her lower lip quivered. "I don't want you to go away."

"I'm sorry, honey." He gently smoothed back her hair. "I wouldn't go if I had a choice. But this is something beyond my control."

"Where are you going?" Tawny asked. She climbed off her chair and walked over to hug him tightly. "Can we visit you there?"

"No. Someday, when you're a little older, your daddy and mommy will tell you everything. You're not old enough to understand yet. I'm sorry." It broke his heart as both girls clung onto him tightly with tears in their eyes.

"Adults are silly." Tawny wiped her eyes on his shirt. "How come you have to have secrets?"

"Well, when you grow up, you can have your own." It disheartened him to think he wouldn't be there to see them turn into young women. He knew they would be troublemakers, and with Sera for a role model, they would be ass kickers as well. A lethal combination, to be sure. "I tell you what," he said softly. "You want early birthday gifts?"

"Yeah!" Both brightened. Their birthday was in a month, and they had been sad that he wouldn't go to their party. He had always been the most fun to play games with, and he had never once been mad if cake got thrown.

They followed him to the main room of the shop where they found a younger couple exploring things. As Brian rummaged in the racks, the twins went over to the woman and smiled up at her. "Hi."

"Well, hi." She knelt to their height and smiled. "Do you live here?"

"Nuh-uh. Brian's our cousin! We know where everything is." Tammy nodded firmly. "You want help?"

"We were just exploring." The man smiled as well. The twins were too cute to not be smiled at. "But I guess I could use a new tie."

"Okay!" Tawny scampered off and returned momentarily with an armful of ties. "Here! You can find one. Brian makes lots of nice ones." While the man went through them, she asked, "How come boys wear ties?"

"To make up for women wearing pantyhose," the woman explained dryly.

Brian covered a smile. "Tawny. Tammy. Come over here."

"Kay!" The girls skidded around the racks and stopped quickly as they saw him holding up two small dresses. One in blue, Tammy's favorite color, and the other in green, Tawny's favorite. Both looked like something a princess would wear.

"Oh my," the woman murmured as she looked over the top of a rack to watch. "How lovely!"

"Are . . . are these ours?" Tammy gingerly touched one of the dresses.

"I think they might be." He handed the blue one to her and the green one to her sister. "Happy birthday. I figured you might want to wear them to your party, so you get them early."

Tawny hugged her dress tight. She liked the clothes he made. She always felt as if he was hugging her, and he was the best hugger ever. Her lower lip wobbled. "I'd rather you stayed here."

He knelt and hugged them both tightly. "I know," he said softly. "I know."

The twins went home with their father an hour later. Brian helped some more customers and made a brief detour to take care of the tag trades he had pending. He lucked out too; the traded items would make good last gifts for his family. Then, with all that done, he began to work on something else. He had put it off long enough.

As the sun began to set, he finally brought in everything from outside and shut the front door. He turned over the Closed sign, turned the radio on low, and went to get some dinner. He had to admit he loved working from home. The convenience couldn't be beat. He would have said he would miss it, but he had no idea precisely how the afterlife worked. It would be interesting to find out.

His phone began to ring while he was washing the dishes. Since it was the line that connected to his fake name, he answered, "Matthews."

"Hello, Brian."

The familiar old voice made him smile. "Hello, Mr. E. Don't tell me you're out of stock already."

The old man laughed. "Nearly, my boy. Anything of yours seems to simply fly out of here at lightning pace. After all, I carry the elite B. R. Matthews at discount prices. You can't get these sales anywhere else."

Brian laughed and leaned against the counter. "It still amuses me that people don't even realize I'm just a lowly weaver from the District. I don't hide who I am. No one chooses to see." He took a long breath. "Just so you know, I finished my will today. I'm leaving whatever is left in stock to you. I know you'll take care of selling it and getting the money to my family."

"Don't be so quick to have that witnessed, Brian. Something interesting happened today."

The weaver nearly stopped breathing. He slowly sank down onto the chair beside him. "The scarf?" he managed to ask.

"Her eyes were blue."

"Blue eyes." His own cerulean ones closed. "Naturally."

"When she walked in, I knew she would be the one. She had no purpose. No reason to be there. And without asking, without being guided, she found her way to the scarf. She could not put it down. I sent it home with her, Brian. I think if I hadn't, she might have died herself. There is hope, my boy."

He slowly hung up the phone and got to his feet to go look at the tapestry he had been working on. It was more than three-quarters done with only the end left to be completed. Starting from the top, it told a story in memories and vignettes. In the center, surrounded by the story, rested a man and woman.

She had blue eyes.

Very softly, tenderly, he traced a finger over her nearly imperceptible features. "Come back to me," he murmured huskily. "I never stopped waiting for you, just as I promised so long ago."

CHAPTER EIGHTEEN

It took less than two days for everyone to realize Louise was attached to her scarf. Almost literally in some aspects for she never took it off. If it wasn't around her neck, it was tied around her hair. Sometimes she looped it around her waist. It didn't matter where she wore it; no one saw her without it.

Kenneth didn't think too much of it until he saw his wife watching her nearly constantly. He caught Sera's arm and pulled her into the office. He shut the door and asked quietly, "You want to tell me what's wrong? And don't tell me it's nothing. I know you better than that."

Her hands curled together. He pulled her into his arms and she pressed her face to his shoulder. "I'll tell you later when . . . when things end. However they end. I'm just scared and hopeful and feeling useless."

He softly ran his hand down her back. "Okay," he said softly. "When you're ready, tell me. But tell me sooner if I can help."

"No, I need to take the next step. Maybe I'm not supposed to, but I'm damned well not sitting around." She tugged free of his grip and left the office. "Hey, Lou," she said as she crossed to her friend's desk.

"I've almost got the ad for the billboard done," Louise said without glancing up. "Ten minutes or so. I'm currently wrestling with layout. I'm just not happy."

"That's great, but that wasn't what I wanted to ask about." Sera flicked a finger at the ends of the scarf. It was currently tied as a headband around Louise's hair, and it somehow seemed to miraculously be able to keep the riotous curls in line. "You don't take this thing off, Lou. If you told me you slept in it, I wouldn't be surprised." Louise's cheeks warmed, and she gripped her hands together tightly. "I know him," she finally said.

"What?" Louise's head swung around. "B. R. Matthews? You know him?"

"It's a fake name. He's actually my step-cousin. His uncle is my stepfather. The B stands for Brian. The R for Robert. He lives in 3rd District and runs a small shop there. He sells his normal work in big stores and keeps the specialty stuff at home." Somehow she found a smile. "We always laugh at how people buy some poor weaver's wares and never realize they have what is technically a designer label."

"Can I meet him?" Louise snatched up a pen and paper. "Address, please. I've always wanted to meet him and tell him how much admire his work. It's a silly dream, I know. I'll go this weekend."

Sera wrote down the address and wondered how her fingers could be steady. "Actually," she said casually, "he won't be open this weekend. If you want to go, you better go today. It's only mid-morning. If you wanted to take off, I wouldn't stop you. Hey, trust me, I know all about silly dreams and reaching for them, so it would be perfectly fine with me."

"You're the best! I'll finish this then take off." Louise went back to her work, a giddy feeling in her heart and stomach. She would finally get to meet someone she had admired for years. No one knew what he was like, but she felt prepared to like him since Sera so clearly did.

Once she finished the layout and sent it to Sera for review, she shut down her computer and gathered her bags. She knew how to get to the District, and she didn't worry about losing her way. And since it wasn't *that* big, she knew she could find parking and just walk however far she needed.

It was a good plan, except for the fact that she had no real sense of direction to begin with. She was sure she followed Sera's directions precisely, but it didn't take very long before she was rather hopelessly lost. She couldn't even be sure which way went back to her car. She could see the Enforcers immense building in the distance to her left, but it had almost always seemed to be there, no matter how many turns she made.

With a deep sigh, she sat down on one of the benches along the street. A crack of thunder had her morosely looking up at the sky. It had been cloudy all morning, but the weathermen had sworn it wouldn't rain.

A few fat drops of rain landed on her hand and head. It was her only warning. In less than a minute, the clouds opened and it began to pour. She didn't bother to dive for cover. Really, the damage had already been done. She knocked a soggy lock out of her eyes. At least her hair would stay in place for a while.

An umbrella suddenly moved over her head and the rain was kept at bay. Startled, she looked up and found herself staring into a pair of cerulean blue eyes so beautiful that they took her breath. They were set into a face just as shockingly handsome. A trim goatee hugged the line of a strong jaw that she really wouldn't have minded running her fingers down. His black hair had been tied into a small ponytail at the back of his neck.

"Thanks," she managed to say as she felt her entire body flush with heat. Something needy gathered deep inside. Holy hell, what did they put in the water in this District? People, almost as a whole, were utterly gorgeous!

Brian offered her a hand. "Come on. My shop isn't far. You can take shelter there. I had just brought everything inside when I saw you." As her fingers slipped into his, he fought the urge to draw her into his arms. The violent and ferocious desire was the least of his problems, though it did not help. Finally. Finally she had come back to him.

She let him draw her to her feet, and her heart raced wildly as he tucked her under his arm protectively to keep her out of the rain as they hurried down the sidewalk. She hadn't felt a desire like that before, and she didn't even know the guy! She knew he was shorter than average since he didn't tower over her, but boy had Mother Nature used those lesser inches well.

He ushered her into his shop and shut the door as another thunderclap echoed loudly across the sky. He shook the umbrella out and set it aside before pulling off his glasses and wiping them dry. "You must be freezing in those wet clothes."

"Only a little." She wrapped her arms around herself and looked around the shop curiously. It didn't take her long to realize that the wares for sale appeared to be very, very familiar. Her fingers curled into the ends of her curiously dry scarf. "Wait. Don't tell me you're Brian Matthews."

He smiled and handed her a cup of hot tea. "The one and the same."

"What a lucky coincidence." She smiled at him. "I was coming to see your shop. I was given this scarf the other day, and I've always admired your work. I just wanted to tell you how amazing I think it is." She offered her free hand. "I'm Louise Pram. Everyone calls me Lou. I work for Sera."

He should have known. "It's nice to meet you, Lou, and thank you very much for the compliment." He eyed her critically. "You can't go out in this weather, and you certainly can't stand around like that. Why don't you borrow something to wear and wait out the storm?"

"You wouldn't mind?"

"Not at all. I'd rather talk to you than to myself." He went through the racks, studied items, and finally picked a colorful skirt and matching top. "Here." He offered them to her. "These were made for you. You can go through that door," he pointed, "and change. Toss your wet clothes in the dryer."

She ran her fingers over the silky material of the clothes. "I really shouldn't."

His eyes twinkled. "But you will anyway."

She laughed. "I can't help it. I'd never turn down a chance to wear something this beautiful." She hurried into the back and shut the door. She didn't bother to lock it. There was no rational reason why, but she absolutely trusted him. She felt safe with him. She couldn't shake the feeling that it wasn't their first meeting. Everything about him . . . his eyes, his smile, his voice . . . even her attraction to him felt familiar.

The skirt hung to her ankles and felt so light and airy that she decided it had been made of clouds. The top was her favorite kind since it had built-in breast support. That meant she could toss her bra in the dryer too. Thankfully, her underwear had stayed dry. She added her socks to the dryer and set her shoes aside to air dry.

Her sopping wet hair couldn't be helped, but when she walked back into the front, Brian offered her a towel. "Thanks." She rubbed at her hair briskly and studied him curiously. "You've been on the market for ten years, but I'd swear you couldn't be much older than me."

"I turn twenty-eight in a few days." He leaned on the counter to watch her. She glowed brilliantly inside his small space as if it simply couldn't contain the wildness of her soul. "What about you?"

"Twenty-seven in five months." She saluted lightly as she pulled the towel off her head, and she knew, without looking, that her hair had to be a mess. A little smile played at her host's ridiculously kissable mouth. "That bad?" She tugged at a curl.

"Come here."

She didn't think to question why. She simply walked over to where he stood. She didn't find a single protest to voice as his fingers combed through her hair and easily coaxed the curls into taming. He truly wasn't much taller, though she herself stood on the shorter side, and he seemed strong and warm. Secure. The scent of his skin made her feel as if she had come home.

His fingers were still tangled in her hair as if he couldn't quite let go. She couldn't catch her breath as she looked up at him. She had never thought of glasses as sexy, but on him they looked outrageously hot.

Another clap of thunder broke the tension. She stepped back and he picked up his coffee. By tacit agreement, neither said a word about what had almost happened. Instead, she sat down on one of the seats at the counter. "Thanks again for the rescue. I have no sense of direction."

"None at all?"

"Afraid not." She winced wryly. "I'm the only artist in the family. I think that anything related to practicality was used up before my parents got to me. Then again, I have younger siblings that turned out okay, so maybe there was a temporary shortage on genes." She propped her chin on her hand with a smile.

"How many siblings?" He sat down across from her and picked up a bundle of material to begin stitching a hem.

"Six total. I'm fifth in the line-up." She watched his hands in fascination. She had always considered sewing to be slightly feminine, but his nimble hands bespoke pure masculinity. The delicate way they handled the cloth made her wonder what it would be like to feel his touch on her body. "What about you?"

"Only child," he admitted. He glanced up to find her watching him and his fingers tightened on the needle and thread as his body throbbed with hunger. His scarf had curled around her neck and the end lightly danced over her breasts. He wanted to be the cloth covering her, to tie her up in him so she could not escape again. He just did not dare. "I have a couple aunts and uncles," he said, his voice huskier, "one of which is Sera's stepfather."

She very carefully sat up straight, her pulse beating quickly. She knew she had not mistaken the desire in his eyes. It called to the passion inside her so swiftly, so fiercely, that it took her breath. She waited, looked, but that strange feeling of cosmic cheating did not come. Was he the one she had been looking for?

She cast quickly for a neutral subject. She had just met the man! She couldn't jump over the counter and pin him to the floor, no matter how tempting it sounded. Never mind that she didn't feel like she talked to a stranger. "Do you make your own cloth? I'd swear I've never seen anything like it before."

"I do. If I don't weave it by hand, there's a place I can send my designs to and have them make it. I use them only for large projects. Most of the time, it's all by hand." He saw her fingers lightly moving over the scarf and his body tightened with need. He wanted to be the one she touched in that way. "Your scarf was woven by me."

"I never take it off," she admitted. "I just can't bear to let it go." She took a deep breath. "What are you working on there?"

"A shirt." He held it up so that she could see it. "I'm not sure who it will belong to. My work always picks its owner."

"Is that your gift?" When he lifted a brow at her, she smiled. "C'mon. You were born here. Was I not supposed to know? Have you *heard* what's been going on at my office over the last few months? I work for Aladdin!"

"It is my gift. I can deliberately imbue certain items with the ability to heal or give someone protection or help. When I make an item for someone in particular, it becomes attuned to them. No one else will see it in the same way the owner does."

Her heart skipped a beat. Had he . . . made the scarf for her? That was impossible. He had never met her until now! "I think it's amazing," she said honestly. "When Cameron and Kenneth said that the District was like homecoming, I didn't fully understand until I was here. Even when I was lost and wandering the streets, I didn't feel out of place. I could have been happy to wander for hours."

"We often say that those drawn to the District have inside them something that they need that only can be found here. What do you want, Lou? More than anything."

"To be loved." Her color rose as she heard her words. "I know it sounds cheesy," she stammered quickly, "and don't think I don't have a great family, because I do, but I just don't have anywhere to fit in, and my family sometimes looks at me weird and . . ."

He gently pressed his fingers to her lips. A soft smile curved his lips and made his eyes warm. In the lamp lit room, he looked mysterious and welcoming at the same time. A gentleness inside him simply effused the air. It called to her like a lodestone.

"Don't explain yourself," he told her softly. "When you said 'you don't fit in anywhere' it made perfect sense why you were drawn here. We don't belong anywhere else except here." He rubbed his thumb over her cheek and softly brushed at the curls tumbling in her eyes. Was there hope this time? She was very different from the woman he had known before.

Her lips began to tingle with the desperation to feel his on them. "Brian."

His hand lifted as he got to his feet. "Let me show you something."

She took a moment to press her hands to her heart and take a breath. She was quivering, literally trembling, from head to toe with desire. Every tiny brush of his skin against hers brought dizzying pleasure. And it wasn't a *new* feeling. It seemed as if her body already knew his touch, already knew what he could do to her. "Jesus," she muttered.

"Lou?"

She got to her feet and hurried to where he stood near another door. As she walked, the skirt fluttered around her legs. The silky material caressed her suddenly sensitive skin. She would have *sworn* it felt like his hands touching her instead. "Sorry. I was wool gathering."

She watched rather helplessly as a slow smile curved his lips. "I don't work with wool," he told her, "but I could make an exception if you supply some." He put his hand on the small of her back and nudged her into the room. "In here."

The practical part of her brain told her it was stupid to be alone with a man she barely knew because he might have dastardly intentions. The rest of her prayed that he did. She ignored both and stepped into the room. He turned on a lamp and she blinked in the glare. When she saw the loom in the center of the room, her breath caught. "Oh. Oh wow."

She slowly touched the tapestry and felt it pulsing with power. "It's beautiful, Brian," she said softly. She ran her eyes over it, sensing it might be more than just decoration. "What is it? Does it tell a story?"

"It does." He didn't need to see the images to know how it went. It had been engraved inside his soul. "Have you ever heard the tale of the Weaver's Wife?"

"No."

"Do you want to?"

She lightly ran her fingers over the faces within colored thread. "Yes." It came out as little more than a whisper. Somehow . . . she could feel the importance.

"The story starts a long time ago."

She found a smile. "Doesn't it always?"

His knuckles brushed down her arm softly. "There was a poor weaver who lived by himself along the sea. He had no fortune, no claim to fame. His was a simple life. One day, as he was walking to town for thread, he came upon a young woman on the road. She was a wild spirit in a conservative family life, and she did not look upon him poorly. They walked together. They talked together. And they were in love before they reached the town.

"Her family was reluctant to allow her to wed the weaver, but he offered woven silks, the finest ever seen, and her family relented. The two were married and she wore a gown made by her groom's hand, tailored perfectly to fit only her. They were happy together for many years, living by the sea while the waves came in."

He took a step away, seeing only the past. "The weaver could feel a restlessness in his wife. Her spirit could not be tamed. And so he said to her 'go into the world. I cannot go with you.' She went into the world, traveled to a foreign place, and then came home. Her restlessness grew worse, and he told her again 'go into the world. I cannot go with you.' Again, she went to see a far off land. She came home, and she was so restless that the weaver knew she could not be kept. He told her 'go into the world. I cannot go with you." Very softly he said, "And she went."

She found herself gripping the edge of her scarf like a lifeline. Her throat had tightened with pain for the weaver in the tale. How he must have loved his wife to let her go! "And what happened?" she whispered.

"I don't know." He let out a long breath. "I've never known. I don't think anyone knows what happened. I keep hoping I will figure it out so I can finish my tapestry." He finally turned to look at her, and his heart broke at the sight of tears on her cheeks. He rubbed his thumb under her eyes to steal them away. "I did not tell you to make you sad."

"It's not that." She turned her face into his hand almost helplessly. "It's just . . . I could swear I had been there. I felt it so deeply." She drew a ragged breath. "Well, I hope you find that ending, Brian. I'd like to know too."

He led her back into the front shop, and they could both see that it had stopped raining at last. "I suppose I should keep my things indoors tomorrow, just in case," he said wryly. "Whenever they say something on the news, I always assume the opposite."

"That's because you're smart." She sighed. "Guess I better put my clothes back on and get out of your hair."

"You can keep what you're wearing," he told her softly.

"Really?" She looked down in surprise at the clothes. "But . . ."

"Tell you what." He smiled as he leaned against the counter. "You visit me again, and we'll call it a fair trade." He snagged a bag from a hook and held it out. "Put your things in here and I'll walk you to your car." His eyes twinkled. "And I'll be sure to point out the right way to get here."

She had to grin at that. "I don't get embarrassed by the truth." She hurried to the dryer and pulled out her warm clothes. She tucked them into the bag and slung it over her shoulder. "I really am grateful to you."

"Then come back very soon."

She tilted her head slightly and her curls danced around her face. He kept his hands in his pockets before he got his fingers in the auburn locks once more. "Why?" she asked. "You sound like you're in a hurry."

"I won't be here much longer," he said simply.

"Oh." Sadness wrenched her heart. Not that she blamed him if he had decided to move; he really needed more space with the way he was busting at the seams, so to speak. His tone just seemed to indicate that he would be going very far. The thought of not seeing him again terrified her. "I'll come back tomorrow then." She glanced away shyly. "I like spending time with you."

He held out a hand and she took it hesitantly. He laced their fingers together and tugged her closer. She held her breath, praying for a kiss, but all he did was give her a gentle hug with his free arm. Fed up with both of them, she freed her hand and wrapped her arms around his neck firmly. "Hold me. Just once, I want to be held."

The hitch in her voice shattered his control. His arms banded fiercely around her waist as he lifted her off her feet. He buried his face in her hair, savoring the fragrant scent and silken texture. She still smelled like summer and sunshine. He had never forgotten. "Lou."

"It's stupid," she said shakily against his shoulder. "It's ridiculous. But I can't let go of you. I'm scared, Brian. I don't even know why. I feel like something terrible will happen to you if I do. I want to say I just met you, but I didn't. I know I didn't. What's wrong with me?"

"I don't know. But you're not alone. I knew you when I saw you. I think I knew you subconsciously all along." He eased her back and caught a handful of the scarf. "I made this for you." He spoke so softly, so intensely, that she believed him. "It could belong to no other." He brushed a tender kiss across her forehead. "I'll take you to your car."

If it hadn't been for him holding her hand, she knew she would never have had the strength to leave. They stepped outside and she shivered in the still chilled air. Summer storm it may be, the air still felt cool on her skin after being indoors. He released her hand to go back inside, and when he came out again, he wrapped a soft shawl around her shoulders. "I shouldn't accept this," she scolded him.

He smiled. "But you will." He combed his fingers through her hair just for the enjoyment of seeing the curls cling to his fingers. "After all, no smart woman turns down free designer clothes. You seem pretty savvy to me."

She laughed. "I can't argue with any of that." She leaned against his shoulder as they walked down the sidewalk. She saw people smiling at them and couldn't help but smile back. When someone waved, she blew them a kiss. "I bet they think I'm your secret girlfriend."

"They've been bored lately. The giggling will do them good." He tucked her under his arm securely.

"I have to ask. How tall are you? I mean . . . I'm five-three and I'm not very shorter than you."

"Five-six."

She sighed happily. "I could grow fond of shorter men." They had reached her car and she reluctantly stepped free of his arm. She unlocked the door and turned to say goodbye when she realized how close he stood. The urge rose so fast that she couldn't resist. She tossed her bags into the car and then went on her toes to kiss him. She let him go almost as quickly as she had grabbed him and ducked into the car. The taste of him was as wildly tempting and achingly familiar as the rest of him.

He bent to look in the car at her, and his blue eyes burned with passion barely kept in check. "I'll let you go with that," he warned huskily, "but now I owe you one." He shut the door and walked away before she could say a word.

On a shaky breath, she dropped her forehead onto the steering wheel. She had the panicky feeling of going under for the third time and couldn't even remember deciding to get into deep water. She knew she should stay away, let him go, and move on. But she couldn't.

She just couldn't.

CHAPTER NINETEEN

After a sleepless night being haunted by too familiar cerulean eyes, Louise woke very early. She ignored her answering machine, didn't bother to check her mail, and got dressed in clothes to combat the still threatening storms. Another had come overnight, and most assumed another would hit that day.

She hoped to play hooky again, so when she got to work, she didn't bother to start her computer. She instead lurked outside Sera's office. She had a lot of questions for her friend. And as soon as she saw her, she demanded, "I want to know about Brian."

"Yikes!" Sera pressed a hand to her heart. "You came out of nowhere, Lou! I'm too young for a heart attack." She unlocked the door and nudged her older friend inside. She shut the door where no one could overhear and put her bags down behind her desk. "Okay, what do you want to know?"

"Where is he going?"

"Can't tell. That's his choice."

Louise sat down in one of the chairs and gripped her hands together tightly. The scarf tied around her hair seemed oddly less colorful as if responding to her emotions. "What *can* you tell me?" she asked softly. "Please, Sera. I'm begging. I'm in over my head. You've been there."

"Yeah." Sera propped her chin on her hand as she leaned on the desk. "It's damned scary, that's for sure. Why don't you tell me what happened yesterday, and I'll decide what I can tell you. Brian is . . . secretive. There are things only he should tell you."

"I went to see him yesterday and got lost in the storm. He took me to his place and gave me dry clothes. We talked. He told me a story of a tapestry he's making." She took a deep breath. "And we struggled with one ridiculously powerful attraction. We both . . . we both recognized each other somehow. He said he made this scarf for me."

Sera took a long breath. "There's not much else I can tell you other than the fact that he's one of the most amazing people I've known. He loves so much. Gives so much. He would sooner be the one unhappy than see anyone else suffer. I've never heard him raise his voice. Never heard him use anything stronger than 'hell' and that was only when the loom nearly fell over on one of my little stepsisters."

"What am I supposed to do?"

"I don't know," her friend said simply. "I wish I did. But you're of no use to us like this, so take another day off, okay? Go see him. I think any answers that the two of you need can only be found with each other."

"Thanks, Sera." She got to her feet and hurried out of the office.

As Sera buried her face in her hands, Kenneth walked into the office. He went to her side without a word and pulled her into his arms. He had a strong feeling he knew now what was happening. It was scary for everyone involved. There was a lot more at stake here than he had ever imagined.

The neighbor's cats awoke him again, but Brian didn't immediately get out of bed. Truth be told, he hadn't really been sleeping. He hadn't slept much the entire night. He had been tormented by dreams of the past and memories of the present. How was it possible to crave another person so badly? He couldn't remember if it had been like this in the past, but he wouldn't have been surprised.

When he finally dragged himself out of bed, he put on coffee and got to work boxing up items he knew wouldn't sell in the next two days. There was no fear in him. No real sadness. He'd had a long time to get used to his fate. He didn't even want to think that he might be freed of his curse; it was too painful to think of trying and losing.

His regular phone rang and he picked it up. "Hello?"

"Brian, I hear you were seen with a lovely lady yesterday."

He smiled wryly. "You heard right, Uncle Lewis. Her name is Louise Pram. She's a friend of Sera's, and also one of her employees. She got lost out here and I gave her shelter from the storm."

Lewis was silent for long moments. Then, "And?"

"And I don't know," he said simply. "I'm not going to trap her, Uncle. I could not bear it. Am I supposed to sacrifice her happiness just so I can live? I don't think so. I'm sorry. Enforcers tried their best, but I don't think it's going to work." He hung up the phone and considered the merits of locking the front door. He just didn't feel like seeing anyone. She wouldn't come back to him.

"Brian?"

His head jerked up in shock at the sound of her voice. She hovered just inside the front door, something hesitant in her eyes as if she wasn't sure he would welcome her. "Lou." He breathed her name softly, unable to believe she really stood there. "You came back."

"I promised, didn't I? Am . . . am I interrupting anything? I can leave."

"No!" He crossed the room and caught her in his arms. "Don't you dare walk out that door." He buried his face in her hair and savored how it felt to hold her. Even if it was only one more time, at least he could see her. Could touch her. "I didn't really expect you to come back again."

"I had to." She curled her arms around his shoulders and held on tightly. Everything was alright again. Now that she was in his arms, everything was alright. "I needed to see you again."

He let her go with visible reluctance. "Well, you can help me then. I'm working on packing. I know you'll enjoy seeing all the different things I've made." He smiled suddenly. "Say, you want to help me out? I have several things I need to finish and my dressmaker dummy fell apart on me. They should fit you well enough for me to make sure I'm putting them together right."

She cocked her head and smiled. "Sure. That sounds like fun." She laughed. "Gee, I always wanted to be a model but they said I was too short."

"Pity." Something hot filled his eyes as he looked her over slowly. "You certainly have the body for it." He let his fingers linger on her cheek and then dropped his hand and went to the front door. He turned over the Closed sign to give them privacy before leading the way into the back room where he kept works-in-progress.

"How many rooms are there?" she asked curiously. She was ignoring, to the best of her ability, the way he seemed to be looking at her. It wasn't good for her pulse or her control. "I've seen two others than the front now."

"Four, not including the bathroom. The other two rooms are a small kitchen and my bedroom." He hung a sheet from the ceiling to make an impromptu changing area for her. "Here you go. Now you won't worry about modesty." He turned around and lost nearly every thought in his head as he realized she had stripped off her jacket and shirt. The plain black bra gently hugging her beautiful breasts was all about practicality, and he wanted very badly to remove it so that she wore nothing except the light.

Her stomach quivered with nerves but she managed to keep her tone light. "I've never been very modest. And . . ." Much softer she continued, "And I just don't feel uncomfortable with you. I know you somehow. I trust you."

"Don't trust me too much, love." He focused on pulling clothing out of drawers. "I want you very badly."

She had known it, but hearing it sent a thrill through her body. What would it be like to make him lose his control? To have her gentle weaver go wild? She somehow knew that he was the still waters whose depths became dark and volatile. Perhaps that was the very water she had been pulled under. "I trust you," she said again with absolute conviction. "You would not hurt me."

"No," he agreed quietly. "I wouldn't." He handed her a handful of cloth and added casually, "And if you are wondering, I'm comfortable enough with half or completely naked women as well."

"At almost twenty-eight," she murmured drolly, "I would certainly assume so." She shook out the material she had been handed and discovered it was a dress of some kind. Curious, she shed her jeans as well and pulled the dress on over her head.

He closed his eyes as he watched her shimmy into the outfit. This hadn't been such a good idea after all. It would be one serious test of his self-control. She was perfectly formed, her body designed to be held by his. When he opened his eyes again, he found himself grinning despite his desire. "Hmm."

Her lips twitched. "I think this belongs to someone taller than me." The collar of the dress tried to dip toward her waist, and the waist tried to go to her knees. "I think Sera needs this more than I do."

He grabbed a tape measure but briefly paused before lifting it. "Do you mind?"

"Not at all." She held up her arms to allow him to get her measurements. As he checked her bust size, she added in amusement, "The only man in the world who could probably guess my measurements without being offensive is also the only man who would think of double checking."

"I'd have been wrong." He wrote down the numbers on a pad of paper. "You're a bit more curvaceous than I was admiring."

"As opposed to assuming, you were admiring?"

He glanced up from measuring her hips. "I'm not blind." He straightened and smiled. "Strip."

"Yet another thing you can say without being offensive." She tugged off the dress.

"It's a gift." He put the dress in a box with a note for it to be given to Sera and then grabbed another article. "This ought to be much closer."

Much to her relief, it was. Rather than being distinctly too big, it was only a little bit off. She could even see where he hadn't finished piecing it together; among other things, it only had one sleeve. The material felt so soft and silky that she knew he had woven it.

Truthfully, she suspected she would always know the difference. It just seemed that anything he had woven by hand caressed her skin intimately. She was only glad he didn't make lingerie. There was no telling what it would do to her.

She stood patiently while he pinned the missing sleeve in place and held the tape measure so that he could check the length. "I think it's a funny length." She looked down. "The edge hits that no man's land between calf length and ankle length."

"I agree. Let's see if I have something to fix that." He went through three drawers before he found a roll of lace. "Here we are." He knelt at her feet and pinned some in place. "I think that's much better."

"Definitely." She turned in a circle to help him pin all the lace, then gingerly removed the dress with his help so that she didn't get stuck by anything. Even with his care, one of the needles scraped over her shoulder. "Ouch!"

"I'm sorry, Lou." He lightly touched the scratch where it looked angry and red against her fair skin. "It's not bleeding, thankfully." He skimmed his thumb down her shoulder where he could see only a faint tan line. "Sunbathing or tanning salon?"

"Hey, if I'm going to tan, I do it in real sun, not artificial." She couldn't fight a shiver of delight as he trailed his fingers over her skin. His fingers were as soft as the silk they handled, and just as delicate in their touch. "Brian."

His hands curled around her waist hotly as he pressed a tender kiss to the scratch. "I just needed to touch you."

The quivering started from inside and moved outward as his lips softly trailed across her shoulder. Barely breathing, she leaned her head back against his shoulder helplessly. Heat rose with shocking swiftness, her body eagerly craving more of the wicked pleasure. *He wasn't even really touching her*. Just those tiny kisses over her shoulder and his hands around her waist. She was so sharply attuned to him that it began to alarm her. "Brian," she said again.

This time he let her go. "I'm sorry." He averted his gaze. "Get dressed."

She slowly pulled on her clothes again and found them oddly distasteful after having worn his work. Striving for a neutral subject, she asked, "When Sarah had so much trouble with her skin, did you make her clothes? Sarah Davidson, I mean."

"I knew who you meant." He made himself busy by sealing boxes. It was either that or tumbling her down onto the hand woven rug and getting reacquainted with everything new and everything familiar. He wanted her so badly that even his teeth hurt. His jeans felt far too tight on his aching arousal, and he knew full well that there was no hiding it. "And yes, I did. I had always hoped to make her wedding dress someday, but, well, things have happened to both of us."

"That's one way of putting it." Fully dressed again, she bent to help him pick up some pieces of clothing when there came a very loud clap of thunder right over the shop. It was followed closely by the sound of heavy rain. "Seriously," she said dryly, "why have meteorologists when they can't even predict the weather correctly?"

"I have a second cousin in Sacramento, Cali." He shook his head. "She says that if you wait five minutes, the weather changes. More mood swings than the local government."

"Which local government?"

"Any."

They shared a grin. She handed him the items she held and turned to get more. Her toes promptly caught on the rug and it slid across the hardwood floor. It threw her entirely off balance and would have sent her onto the floor if he hadn't moved swiftly and caught her in his arms.

Sadly, he slid on the rug too. They went down hard but landed on a pile of material that cushioned them. She shook her head to clear it and looked up to see him smiling wryly. "Sorry about that," she said sheepishly. "Did I mention that the directional genes weren't the only ones that went on strike when I was born?"

"I've seen the world's greatest dancer slide on this thing. It's not you, trust me."

His smile slowly faded as he looked down at her. She had ended up beneath him in the fall. Her body pressed along every inch of his. Her wild hair reflected more red than brown as it caught the warm hues of the material she laid on. Her perfect mouth curved into a smile, and her blue eyes shimmered in the light.

Her smile disappeared as she stared up at him and saw the look in his eyes. Instead, her lips began to tingle and throb, as if knowing precisely how his mouth would feel and craving the sensation. With trembling fingers, she ran her thumb over his lips and then over his face before burying her hands in his hair.

He bent his head and took the kiss they both needed so badly. His lips were soft and firm all at once; hot and hungry but gentle and tender. The conflicting emotions tugged at everything inside her until the trembling had spread through her whole body. Her lips parted under the pressure of his and a soft whimper caught in her throat as his tongue immediately thrust into her mouth aggressively.

Something broke inside her. She could hear it, let alone feel it. With a low cry, she arched up to deepen the kiss, her fingers curling into his hair to keep him close to her hungry mouth. She couldn't get enough of his taste. She was starved for it.

His hands fisted into her curls and held her head still as he took the kiss even deeper. The taste of her was engraved inside him, so familiar and so welcome that his throat tightened with a swell of emotion he could not fight. He broke free of the kiss and raced wild kisses over her face. Her soft breaths seared him. "Lou. I love you."

She went very still. "What?"

He lifted his head and met her eyes evenly. "I love you. Stay with me."

Terrified, she broke out of his grip and scrambled to her feet. "This is too much. Too fast. I'm not like this. I can't get involved with you." She backed toward the door, breathing too hard and too fast. "I don't know what's wrong with me."

She fled the room and he closed his eyes as he heard the front door open and slam closed. Pain welled up endlessly. He had reached for her again only to encounter the one thing he could not fight: her desperate longing to be free. He fell onto his back and covered his face with his hands. It was over.

She had run two blocks before the tears caught up and forced her to stop. With a low sob, she sank down to the ground against a wall. Just what was she running from? Was she running from his feelings or her own? Why had she panicked? "I'm a coward," she whispered, her face buried in her knees.

She had finally found the person she was cosmically tied to, and she had run away when he told her he loved her. It was fast, outrageous, and it shouldn't be happening. Yet it *was* happening . . . and she could not find the will to change it.

She was in love with him. She had been all along.

A soft throbbing warmth had her lifting her head. Her scarf was pulsing. The gentle touch of the material over her skin had the same sensation as Brian's touch. She gently rubbed the cloth between her fingers. From the day she had picked it up, this moment had been inevitable.

So what if he was leaving? Providing he wasn't going to the moon, she could go with him. If it wasn't far, they could commute. If it was far, she could find another job near him. The only thing she could not give up was Brian himself.

She scrambled to her feet and called herself every name she could think of as she ran back through the pouring rain. Though she had always before gotten easily lost, she found her way to the shop as if something pulled her there. And something did. The man she had loved since before her birth.

The door was still unlocked. She threw it open. "Brian!"

He looked up sharply and felt a wild sense of déjà vu as he saw her in the doorway. She was soaked and shivering, her hair longer than usual because the curls had pulled out. Her eyes weren't quite tamed, were certainly a little wild, and a lot terrified. "Louise." He stayed where he was in the middle of the shop. He could not go to her again.

"It's not you," she said fiercely. "It's me. I'm a coward. I ran from my feelings, not yours." She took two trembling steps toward him. "I love you. I have all along."

Heart pounding, he held his arms out. She cleared the floor in nearly a single leap, her arms going fiercely around his neck even as her legs hooked around his hips. She clung onto him as if he were life itself. "Lou. Dear god, Lou." He held her as tightly as he could, shaking from the inside out.

"Don't let me go," she whispered as she trailed desperate kisses over his neck and face. "Not even for my sake."

He would have to. He knew he would have to. But this was a reprieve from hell, a chance at heaven. He buried his fingers in her hair and dragged her head up for a wild kiss. Unable to release her, he whirled and carried her down the hall to his room without once releasing her lips. She was wild in his arms, her body twisting and pressing against his, her tongue not only accepting the mating thrust of his but returning the gesture readily.

When he swung her around, she broke free of the kiss with a breathless laugh. "Wait! Don't get the bed wet! I'm soaked to the skin!"

He dropped her onto her feet and nearly tore the shirt she wore off over her head. It landed with a wet plop somewhere in the room. "I wanted to do this all day," he admitted roughly. His hands ran up and down her sides just a little harder than usual. "You shouldn't wear anything." His mouth ran hotly down her neck and his teeth tugged at the strap of her bra. "And if you wear anything," he added more fiercely, "it should mine. I'm the only one who can touch you."

"I knew it." Her head fell back as his teeth scraped deliciously. It was only his arms holding her on her shaking legs. "I knew it felt as if . . . as if anything you had woven was touching me like a lover." She laughed huskily. "Don't make me lingerie. I'll lose all ability to think."

"How you tempt a man." He unfastened her jeans and slowly peeled the wet denim down her long legs. She still wore her sandals and he tossed them across the room without care.

Her head was still spinning when he stood and dragged her up for another kiss. The feeling of his clothes against her sensitized skin was erotic, but not nearly close enough to what she wanted. With more desperation than finesse, she rushed to open the buttons on his shirt. One popped off. "Sorry."

His laugh sounded low and seductive. "You know a good tailor."

"Boy, do I." Her sigh came long and happy as he shrugged out of his shirt. He wasn't necessarily built like some men she had known, but his body was defined with just enough muscle to entice. Everything looked gentle about him, and she craved that tenderness even in the middle of the storm surging through her body. "You're beautiful."

"Am I?"

She looked up in surprise. "You sound surprised."

His fingers curled into her thick hair. "Everything is different when you're in love." He tugged her up again and kissed her with a slowly famished heat. The shudder that ripped through her body clawed at him with desire.

He released her and swiftly divested her of her bra. Her underwear went next. As he straightened and stared at her hotly, she realized what he meant. It was one thing to know you were attractive. It was another thing entirely to see yourself in the eyes of the one who loved you.

She reached out a finger and lightly touched the needle shaped mark on his shoulder. "Tattoo?"

"Birthmark."

"How appropriate." She eased in and lightly tasted the mark, and her tongue teased it gently. His strong body jerked and the rush of power filled her. "Just how much can you take?" She nuzzled her way across the dark curls on his chest. "You've been seducing me for days. It's my turn now."

"I've barely touched you." His voice broke as her lips closed over a nipple and tugged. "Lou."

"With your hands, you've barely touched me." She scooped up the fallen scarf and slowly trailed the ends across her skin. "This has touched me all along. You touched me all along."

He looped the scarf around her neck and jerked her against his aching body. "I never stopped touching you." He lifted her and tumbled her down onto the bed. When he saw her lying there, the scarf dancing over her beautiful body, his control broke. He stripped off the rest of his clothes and slid onto the bed beside her. "I need you," he said roughly as he buried his face between her breasts. "Please, Lou."

His mouth captured her nipple and sucked so strongly that her back arched. The ache that had never gone away erupted into a wildfire. She could feel the throbbing need between her legs and she curled a leg over his hip enticingly. "Hurry."

The breathless plea was more than he could bear. They could tease each other later. They had been teasing each other for centuries. On a tortured groan, he caught her mouth with his as he fumbled blindly for the nightstand. "Damn it," he said against her lips when he couldn't open the drawer.

A wild thrill went through her entire body. She nipped sharply at his ear and savored the way he quivered in her grip. "I wonder if I could make you get really creative." Her tongue teased the line of his jaw.

A bit desperately, he got the drawer open and grabbed protection. When she saw the foil packet in his hand, her heart fluttered with emotion. That he would remember something like that even as hungry as they both were . . . it was simply the way he was. Everything about him was so perfect for her. She grabbed his wrist before he could tear it open. "No," she said softly. "Not this time."

It was risky and irresponsible. He had never been either of those things, but he didn't want anything between them either. She was his in a way she would never be anyone else's just as he was hers. He threw the packet to the side and dragged her closer. Slowly, his eyes burning into hers, he began to take her, savoring the sensation of her tight flesh welcoming his possession.

When he was as deep as he could go, he simply stayed there for a long moment. Homecoming. It wasn't a new feeling. He still remembered how it felt to make love to her. How every moment felt perfect. He framed her face with his hands and kissed her ravenously. "I love you."

Her hips arched helplessly, trying to urge him into moving. No cosmic cheating here. *This* was what she had been seeking. She dug her nails into his shoulders demandingly. "I love you. Please!"

He shuddered and gave them both what they needed, thrusting into her again and again until her breaths were sobs and she clung onto him wildly. The tension gathered and coiled, the ceaseless pleasure driving him to take her as hard and deep as he could. He fought it, needing her to be there with him.

It wasn't a long wait. Ecstasy could not be resisted by either. It grabbed them sharply and wouldn't let go, waves of pure delight tearing through their bodies. It went to a level beyond their flesh, into their hearts and souls, even into their minds as the joy of reunion, not discovery, claimed them both.

In the silence after, she lay curled against his chest, listening to him breathe, and realized that she wanted to be nowhere else. She needed nothing else. Finally she had found where she belonged.

CHAPTER TWENTY

The sound of the storm finally clearing woke Louise later that evening. She had lost track of the passage of time entirely. There had been nothing but her and Brian inside her world. Her body ached and tingled after the last few hours, and she savored every sensation. She would have called her lover insatiable, but, really, she was just as bad. She couldn't shake the feeling that they had been making up for lost time.

She turned to cuddle against him and discovered his side of the bed was empty. Startled, she sat up. "Brian?"

"Down here," came his voice from somewhere in the house.

She slipped out of bed and spotted a gorgeous silk robe lying on the end of the mattress. It was a blushing rose pink with a paler cream pattern across it. Enchanted, she lifted it and rubbed her cheek over the soft material. It teased and caressed her like the touch of its maker's fingers, and she knew he had made it for her.

When she slipped it on, it fit perfectly. She used her scarf as a belt and headed down the hall toward Brian's voice. She found him standing at the loom, studying the story of the Weaver's Wife. She slid her arms around his waist and pressed against his back. "What's wrong?" she asked softly.

"I can't see the end." He kept his voice even with effort. He couldn't see the end and the mark had not faded. She loved him, but he could not keep her. Nothing had changed except that he would die knowing what it was like to truly live.

"Is it important?"

"Yes."

She rubbed her cheek against his back. "Why?"

"I can't explain it." He turned and pulled her into his arms. "I knew this robe would be perfect on you." His fingers danced down the sleeve of the robe, caressing the skin beneath as if the silk wasn't even there. "I suspect that if I go through the shop, I'm going to find a lot that I made with you in mind."

"I wouldn't mind wearing a wardrobe entirely created by you." Her lips curved. "Of course, considering my sensitivity to your work, there's no telling what it'll do to me. I might have to take long lunches just to find you and seduce you."

Sadness filled his heart. There would be no long lunches together. He buried his face in her hair for a moment and held on with all his strength.

She paused as she sensed his desperation and then held him in return. She wanted to tell him that whatever was wrong would be made right, but she could not find the words. "What's wrong?" She framed his face with her hands as he lifted his head. "Tell me," she urged softly. "I can't stand to see you so sad, Brian."

"I was just thinking of a cousin of mine. He was diagnosed with cancer and told he only had months to live. He asked me what I would do if I only had a day left to live, and I had no answer for him." He searched her eyes. "What would you do?"

She didn't have to think about it. "I would do everything I had never gotten to do. Then, when I felt that my last moment had arrived, I would choose how I left this world." She softly kissed him, hurting for him. "I'm so sorry, Brian. It must hurt to lose someone you love. And your family is small to begin with."

"I've accepted it." He released her and looked at the tapestry. "I need to ask you a favor," he said softly. "If a time comes that something happens to me before I finish this, I want you to burn it."

"Burn it?!" She took a step back in horror. "You want me to burn something so beautiful?"

"Please, Lou."

Very reluctantly, she finally said, "Alright. But you'll finish it. I know you will." As he turned toward her, she slid her arms up around his neck. "I didn't like waking without you," she told him softly. "I don't even want to be away from you for a minute."

His lips curved. "I think my cousin's leniency with your time off might go only so far, my love." He softly trailed kisses over her face and savored her taste. It had been burned inside him for all time. It would remain there always.

"Oh, I dunno. I bet she wouldn't mind. I have plenty of vacation time owed to me. I hadn't taken a day off in a year or two." She slid her hands slowly over his chest, and her fingers danced across the little needle mark that intrigued her. "And I think she and Sarah and the boys think this is my just desserts. They wanted me to find someone."

He lifted her into his arms and headed back down the hall toward the bedroom. "I'm not wasting a minute," he muttered fiercely. "I've waited too long for you as it is." He lowered her down onto the bed and untied the robe. "I love you, Louise."

The desperation was in his touch again. She didn't question it. She simply gave herself to his embrace with all the love she had. She tried to give him everything, somehow sensing he needed to hold onto her. The wordless fear had come back again, but she absolutely refused to lose him.

The next time she awoke, it was morning. She also awoke to her lover's hands softly moving over her body. The sunlight poured in the window but it did not feel nearly as hot as his skin. She opened her eyes and found herself looking into his cerulean gaze as he watched her tenderly. With a sigh, she tugged him down for a lingering kiss. Now *this* was her idea of starting the day right.

Clanging and banging on the roof broke the mood. "What is that?" she asked warily.

"Neighbor's cat chasing pigeons." He skimmed his hands over her before reluctantly getting out of bed. "Shower?"

She admired the line of his back and decidedly delicious ass and then hopped out of bed as well. "My hair must be a mess." She looked in a mirror and winced. Her curls had officially gone out of control. "I tried to grow my hair out once, hoping it would stretch the curls. It didn't work. I just looked like I had hair that went out of style in the 80s."

"They're not that bad." He caught a handful and tugged lightly. "I love your hair." He turned on the shower full blast and waited for the water to heat. "In you go. There's room enough for two."

Only barely, she found out a moment later, but she wasn't complaining with any excuse to be in close quarters with his amazing beauty. She even let him wash her hair for her, though she had never imagined she would ever want to share that kind of an intimacy.

After the shower, she dried her hair while he shaved. The domesticity of the scene staggered her. Her few lovers had never felt that . . . right to her. Even disregarding the 'cosmic cheating' issue, she had just never felt like having anyone that deeply in her life. Things had been casual. The curious thing now was that this *was* casual. Casual intimacy. Brian fit so perfectly in her life it was as if he had always been there.

She commandeered the small kitchen to cook breakfast while he made coffee. He disappeared to put on clothes and shortly returned to catch her in his arms. He rested his chin on her shoulder contentedly. "I threw your dirty clothes in the washer."

"I can't go naked all day," she noted dryly.

"More's the pity. Actually, I picked something out for you."

"Now you really *are* spoiling me, B. R. Matthews."

His lips curved into an innocent smile that still looked slightly wicked. "Can I help it if I made that many pieces of clothing with you in my mind? I never know something was made for someone until they come and claim it. There's much here for you to claim."

"Well, if you want to put it that way . . ." She dished up the scrambled eggs she had made and grabbed the toast. "Simple and yet protein filled. We need our energy after last night. And yesterday. I can't believe either of us is walking."

He just smiled and picked up his fork.

While he did the dishes, she went and found the clothes he had laid out. To her amusement, in addition to a lovely pale blue skirt and pink camisole, she also had a matching pair of panties and bra, both in the same pale pink. She was further amused to find they fit perfectly. The only downside was that the material had a way of gliding over her skin that most assuredly would be distracting all day. "When'd you start dabbling in women's unmentionables?" she called down the hall.

"I always did," he called back. "It's just not the biggest part of my trade. I literally make just about anything."

Bemused, she picked up the phone and called her office. Sera cheerfully let her take another day of vacation, but this time Louise was sure she heard a note of strain in her friend's voice. As she slowly hung up the phone, she looked to where Brian stood in the doorway. "She's worried about something. She tried to hide it, but I could hear it. I better take only today and go in tomorrow. Something must be falling apart and she's trying to be nice."

"That might be best." He tugged her to her feet and admired how she looked in the clothes he had made. While she had been on the phone, he had boxed up items he wanted to be given to her some time after he was gone. There had been many, just as he had thought all along. "You know what I want to do today?"

"What?"

"Go out."

"I could be persuaded." She tied the scarf around her hair to keep it out of her face and teasingly fluttered the end under his chin. "Where do you want to go?"

"There's a carnival a few blocks away. I've never been to one."

"Really? In that case, we absolutely have to go." She laced her fingers with his as they headed through the house. The front area had been nearly entirely packed. She wanted to ask where he was going, but something kept her from speaking about it. She really wanted him to ask her to go with him, but she wasn't sure if he would. Maybe he needed to move away for a little while and miss her a lot. Then she could call and nag him into letting her go wherever he was. She didn't doubt he loved her, but she suspected he intended to let her go for what he thought was her own good. Over her dead body, he would!

The carnival was lively and fun. He proved to be adept at several of the midway games, and she found herself the reluctant carrier of several strange toys. She didn't mind. She had fun just watching him explore everything. He resembled a big kid who had been let loose on the grounds, and the sudden mental image of a little boy with cerulean eyes and her curly hair nearly took her breath. She really wanted a future with Brian. One that included marriage and kids. Rashid could finally pick her out a dress.

They tried out some of the rides, and all the coaxing in the world wouldn't let Brian convince Louise to get on the most hair-raising one. "No thank you," she said firmly. "My feet stay on terra firma, mmkay?

"What're you afraid of?" he teased. "It's perfectly safe."

"Not a chance in hell." She crossed her arms and set her chin. "You go ahead. I'm staying right here."

"Spoilsport." He brushed a kiss over her lips and hurried to get into line.

She just smiled and sat on a bench to wait for him. She *hated* large roller coasters. She would sooner find a nice, plain one that didn't do loops and turn her upside down or drop her fifty feet in two seconds.

The ride was only a few minutes, and he returned shortly. When he reached her side, he scooped her up into his arms, bags and all, and swung her around in a happy circle. "I saw you from the top," he told her. "And you were so beautiful that it took my breath."

She kissed him with a happy sigh. "Just for that, I might someday go on a larger coaster with you." She felt as much as saw him flinch slightly and her smile faded. "What aren't you telling me?"

"Nothing important." He put her down but kept her close in a way that acted more protective than possessive. It was almost as if he feared she would be torn away. "You want to go for a drive with me? It's only early afternoon. I've always wanted to go into the mountains. Ever since I found you, I've felt like I can do everything I always wanted to."

"I'd go anywhere with you." She smiled. "You drive. You know me and my sense of direction."

The drive was two hours long, but they enjoyed every minute. They took turns switching radio stations and made fun of cars that were either an ugly color or simply looked weird. His car had a convertible top, and they left it down. It ruffled his hair and made her curls dance wildly.

"Just what was it like growing up with six siblings?" he asked her curiously.

"Interesting. By the time I was born, Mom and Dad had things down to a science. Unfortunately, I threw them for a loop. Here they were with four kids who liked science and law and numbers and suddenly their newest one wanted paint and pencils. That sustained me until I discovered the joys of computers and digital art."

"Seduced by the dark side."

"They had good cookies." She shot him a grin as he laughed. "One time, when I was about ten, I really, really wanted to paint a mural. I don't know why. But I really wanted to. No one would let me. So I painted the side of the house."

He tried not to smile. "I'm sure your parents greatly appreciated your talent."

"The fact that mural is still there did not stop them from grounding me at that time." She contentedly leaned back. "What about you? Did you get into trouble as a kid?"

"Who didn't? Let's see . . . my most memorable moment had to be when I got mad at a cousin and sewed him into his blankets. Since I used special thread, he couldn't break out. I was about thirteen at the time. He got revenge by filling my room with frogs. I still hate those things to this day. They give me the creeps."

"I guess I shouldn't wear my cute froggie earrings, huh?"

"Not unless you want to see a grown man cry." He turned off the freeway down a beaten road that wound around some rather sharp bends. From the corner of his eye, he saw she had her eyes tightly closed. "You don't like mountain roads?"

"Not in a car going fifty."

"We're going twenty."

"It feels like fifty!" She opened her eyes only when the car stopped and delight filled her at seeing that they had arrived at a scenic outlook. "Oh how beautiful!"

"I hear it's even better up the bike path." He came around the car and took her hand with his to lace their fingers together. "Come with me."

"Always," she promised softly.

By the time the sun set, they were sitting together on a bench that looked out over the rest of the mountain. From that perch, they could see the skyline of their city beginning to glow in the twilight. His hand softly covered hers, and she knew she had never been happier. She had never spent so much time with someone and loved every second.

"I guess you have to work tomorrow," he murmured softly. He rubbed his thumb over her knuckles tenderly.

"Unfortunately. I need to see what Sera is so worried over. Will you miss me?" she teased.

"Every second."

That something was in his voice again and she straightened up. "What's wrong?" She grabbed his shoulders when he would have turned away. "Damn it, Brian. I know there's something wrong. I can feel it. If you're ready to get rid of me, just say so!"

"No, never that! I'm just thinking of my journey." He rubbed his thumb softly across her cheek. "I thought I was ready, but maybe I'm not."

"I'll come visit you," she promised fiercely. "You can't get rid of me."

Somehow, he managed a genuine smile. "I would never want to get rid of you." He got to his feet and tugged her up as well. "Let's go home. It's getting late, and you need sleep if you're going to fix whatever your coworkers broke."

"I'm just glad I'm not in charge anymore. I mean, I was good at it, but it's just not my thing. I like the peacefulness of letting someone else lead."

He drove her back to where her car was parked in the District and stood patiently beside her as she unlocked it. When she looked up at him, he couldn't bear it any longer. He pulled her into his arms and kissed her as if it would be the last time. "I love you," he said against her lips.

"Brian?" She frowned when he released her. "You're scaring me."

"It's okay. I'm just not sure how to handle my emotions." He stepped back. "Better leave before I don't let you go at all."

"That's more tempting than you want it to be, I'm sure." She slid into the car and looked up at him. "Good night, Brian."

"Goodbye, love."

It wasn't until she got into bed later that she realized what he had said. He had said goodbye, and it hadn't been in a casual 'see you tomorrow' sort of way. Terror stabbed into her heart. *What was wrong*?

She didn't sleep all night. Bright and early the next morning, she made her way to work. She had tucked her fear away to the best of her ability. As soon as she was done with work for the day, she would go by Brian's place and hopefully catch him before he left entirely. He couldn't get all of it done in just eight hours.

She was at her desk when Sera walked in. The taller female went utterly white as she saw her. "Why are you here?" Sera demanded as she rushed to Louise's side. "Why aren't you with Brian?"

Louise leapt to her feet and slammed her hands on the edge of the cubicle wall, drawing startled eyes from everyone there. "What the hell is going on?" she nearly shouted. "What aren't you two telling me? Damn it, Sera! If you know, tell me! Brian wouldn't tell me what was going on, and I *know* he was afraid of something!"

Sera grabbed her arms sharply. "Go to him! Hurry, Lou! You have to go to him before it's too late! He should be at his shop. Make him tell you what's going on! I *can't*. Don't you think I would have if I could? The terms of his contract—" She shut up quickly.

"Contract. He's under contract with Enforcers. There *is* something wrong." Without waiting for consent, she snatched up her purse and rushed out of the office. Tears burned her eyes and closed her throat, and terror clawed at her heart. Even the soft material sliding over her skin could not soothe her. He would not be under contract unless there was a danger of something terrible happening. She needed to save him from whatever was wrong!

It wasn't long before she parked and rushed toward the shop, but it felt like a century. A For Sale sign sat in the front yard, and the blinds were drawn in all the windows. The door was miraculously unlocked and she rushed inside only to stop sharply. Everything was boxed and labeled clearly. The labels didn't have a forwarding address. They had names and instructions. She grabbed some at random.

'Give to Brie.'

'For Aenya; tell her that I made sure it would aid with restless nights teething'

'Sera; she can have it altered by anyone if needed.'

"What is this?" she whispered. She dropped the tags and went into the kitchen. Empty. The bathroom was empty. The bedroom was empty. There was no sign of Brian. Everything was neatly packed and labeled, ready to be distributed to different people. Nothing indicated it would be sent to his new location.

She went into the room with the loom and stopped still. The tapestry was still there, and it was as yet still unfinished. Boxes with her name stood against the walls, and there was a letter pinned to the bottom of the weaving. With trembling hands, she picked it up and recognized her lover's handwriting.

My Louise,

If you're reading this, then you obviously came looking for me. I'm so sorry I couldn't tell you this in person. I just didn't want to ruin what little time we had together. It was precious to me, and much more than I had ever dreamed of.

I'm cursed. The mark on my chest will disappear at the hour of my birth on my birthday. That day is today. When that mark fades, I will die. I've lived with this knowledge most of my life. I was resigned to my fate . . . until you walked in the door.

Three hundred years ago, I was a poor weaver. You were the daughter of an affluent family. You wanted to be free. I let you go. To this very minute, I don't know what happened after that. The tale of the Weaver's Wife is the tale of my life. Of my wife. Of you.

I'm taking your advice to heart. I did things I had never done before. Now I will choose how I go. My last gift to you is in those boxes. The greatest thing I can do for you is to set you free. You would never be happy caged.

I'll love you forever.

Brian

Tears running down her cheeks, she tore open the first box. It was clothing. Every box held more. She could feel the love he had poured into his weaving and knew that he had given her a piece of his soul.

She turned and looked at the tapestry. He had wanted her to burn it if he was unable to finish it. Yet as she stood there and stared at it, she slowly began to realize something. It flowed into her mind as flashes and snippets and images.

She knew how the story ended.

She rushed from the shop and back to her car. The entire time she drove on the freeway, she prayed she wouldn't be too late. She never once worried that she would be lost. She could feel the threads tying her to Brian, and they led her true. Her scarf pulsed hotly around her neck and seemed to be urging her on. Those turns on the mountain that normally terrified her were barely even noticed.

Dirt flew as she parked quickly at the scenic overlook. Desperately, she made her way up the path. "Brian!" she shouted. "Brian, answer me!" No answer returned, but as she rounded a bend, she saw him standing at the edge of the cliff where they had watched the sunset together. His open black shirt rippled in the wind, and the mark on his chest was stark and terrifying.

He sensed her presence for it was engraved inside him. His head lifted sharply and he turned toward her. His eyes flared wide with shock. "Lou. What are you doing here?"

"You idiot!" she shouted at him. Her hands curled into fists at her sides. "You're an idiot! What do you think you're doing?!"

"I'm giving you what you need most," he said simply.

"That was always your problem!" she countered furiously. She swiped at the tears in her eyes. "You were so convinced that I wanted freedom that I believed it too! *I want you*. That's all I've ever wanted! You know how that story ends? I do. I know how it ends!"

He very nearly stepped toward her but forced himself to stay put. "And how does it end?"

"She went to the last foreign land and realized that she wanted her husband to be at her side. She had no care for travel without him. That was why she'd been so restless. She thought he didn't want her!"

His mouth opened and closed. There were no words he could find to that. "What are you saying?"

"I'm saying you cursed yourself, you idiot!" She hurled her shoe at him but he ducked. "So stupidly blind, thinking you knew what I wanted! *I* would have cursed you too!" She kicked the other shoe off and moved closer a step. "You want me to be free? You want to let me go? I'll never be free of you, Brian Matthews. If you think you've got the guts, take away the scarf you gave me. It's a piece of you, isn't it?"

"It is." He carefully walked toward her, every step weighted in lead.

When he reached only a foot in front of her, she grabbed the scarf and flipped it around his neck. She dragged him down and kissed him wildly, pouring everything she was into it. Her heart, her soul, and her tears. She eased back a breath and whispered, "When she got home, she railed at her foolish husband for thinking he knew what she wanted. And what did the weaver say?"

His trembling hands framed her face. "Stay with me. Never leave again."

The mark on his chest glowed brightly for an endless instant and then softly dissolved away until there was nothing left. Her hands, spread on his chest, could feel the steady and powerful beat of his heart.

"I'm alive," he murmured.

"For now!" Her hand curled into a fist and beat against his shoulder. "I'm going to kill you for putting me through this! Damn you, Brian. I would have died without you here."

He tugged the scarf off and curled it tenderly around her neck once more. His hands moved over her without stopping, as he couldn't help himself. He could barely believe that she was there, that he was there, and that they were together as they had always wanted to be. He tugged her up for another kiss that lingered achingly. "Marry me," he whispered against her lips.

She laughed and wrapped her arms around his neck. "I think I did that once. But I'd be willing to do it again. My cousin Rashid will be ecstatic. I think he's had my wedding dress picked out for years."

"Rashid." A smile began to curve his lips. "Does he work at Bridal Dreams?"

"He does." Her brows shot up. "Don't tell me . . ."

"I told you I made a little of everything. If he's been holding the dress that I think he has, then he was right. It was assuredly made for you." He lifted her and began carrying her back toward the car. "We're going to need to go on a long honeymoon somewhere. Where do you want to go?"

"Anywhere," she answered simply, "as long as I have you. That's all I ever wanted. Just you by my side. Never let me go again."

Sitting on a shelf in the quiet shop, the contract from Enforcers had been overlooked for months. As it registered that the conditions in the agreement had been fulfilled, it began to glow softly. The word 'Complete' appeared across the front, and the document folded itself up tightly. Its work was done.

EPILOGUE

Rhianna was in her office reading her email when the front desk paged her to let her know she had a package. With a smile, she went downstairs to the lobby. "What have you got for me, D.J.?"

The receptionist smiled and held out a bubble wrapped package. Across the top, it read *Fragile!* Rhianna opened it very carefully and found two items. One was a contract that glowed brightly. The other was a folded tapestry. When she unfolded it, everyone who watched caught their breath. It was, without question, the most beautiful thing anyone had seen.

She turned and handed it gingerly to D.J. "Have it hung down here so everyone sees it," she told him. "Put it next to Taylor's paintings of the other . . . jobs we've done."

"Yes'm." He gingerly took the tapestry and carried it over to the wall that she had indicated. There was enough room in the center to hang the tapestry, and he waited patiently for a ladder to do so.

Spreading outward from the center where the newest story would hang were brilliant depictions of other tales. One showed a tattered pair of dance shoes sitting on the edge of a banister. Another was of a swan and a nightingale curled together. A third showed a glass slipper and golden pocket watch. The next showed two wolves running under a full moon.

On the other side of the tapestry were more paintings. One showed a princess sleeping in a field of morning glories with a prince kneeling beside her. Beside it hung a picture of a faerie holding a red apple and a soldier keeping a wand out of her reach. The third in the set showed an image of a golden locket with seven sets of stars surrounding it.

As the tapestry was being hung, another worker brought over two new paintings to go with the weaving. One was of a princess lying on a stack of mattresses, smiling down at the man watching her. In his hand rested a pea. The other painting was of a golden genie lamp whose smoke seemed to form the image of a couple embracing.

On the wall across the room could be found two additional paintings. One showed a raven carrying a pink ribbon. The other was of a fat golden bird carrying a set of wooden rings in its beak.

It was quite a collection. Rhianna loved every single one. Still smiling, she went back upstairs to her office. She added notes to the newest contract and slipped it into a folder. As it also glowed in completion, she tucked it securely into the drawer labeled 'Dease.' She shut the drawer and locked it, and the word 'Finished' appeared in red.

Content, she sat back in her chair and stretched her hands high over her head. She had known all along how the story would end.

It had been worth the wait.

Status: File Complete

Analysis: Where there is love, there is always freedom. Sometimes it just takes a while to recognize it for what it is.

Come back with me to the world on the other side of the River Styx. Their stories might just be as critical to safety of the 3rd District as the work Rhianna does is . . .

Bonus Folder
TERRA

CHAPTER ONE

It was hot. It was hot and humid. It seemed as if the very sky was sweating, the oppressive heat clogging the air so that when someone breathed, it felt as if they were breathing molasses.

It was days like those on Mirage that often offered glimpses of the Earth. It hovered there in the distance, just beyond the sight of most. Was it real, or was it a myth? Most knew it was real. Others laughed it off. Yet more wondered what it must be like.

Terra Evermore didn't have the time to wonder, though she had seen the blue planet from the corner of her eye as she drew water from the well. Her day had started early and it would end late. Even in the middle of the day, even under the hottest part of the sun, she had work to do. Her muscles ached and threatened to cramp, and sweat slid down her back under her threadbare tunic and leggings. Her bare feet, callused though they were, still wanted to blister as they crossed over stone and dirt that was hard baked and so hot that water evaporated when it dripped.

When the bucket of water was full, she lugged it precariously toward the manor that she lived in. She could not call it home. It had never been home. Truthfully, she did not really live in the manor at all. She slept out back under a leaky tool shed roof. She was only allowed to sleep inside if snow came; after all, she was no use if she was dead.

Her mistress stood on the steps leading into the kitchen. "What took so long?" she demanded.

"I didn't want to waste water." Terra knew better than to ask for a drink though her throat felt dryer than the dirt under her feet. She simply lugged the bucket up the steps and handed it over. "What do you need me to do next, Mrs. Arcwood?"

Mrs. Arcwood put the bucket of water on the counter in the kitchen with a little grunt. She still couldn't fathom how such a small female could carry the water bucket with little effort. Terra was of slightly shorter than usual height for Mirage since she stood only around five-six or so, and she looked as slender and lithe as a willow. Yet, she was still somehow as strong as a tree that bent in the wind rather than break.

Mrs. Arcwood reluctantly cared for the girl. She had ever since the child had been bought from a servant merchant. Even at ten, Terra had been lovely and smart, and in the eight years since, she had blossomed into a young woman that more than one passing male farmer had admired wistfully.

However, Terra was neither for sale nor was she free. She was an indebted servant sold to pay off her family's debts. She would serve the Arcwoods until she died. Mrs. Arcwood kept her affection for the girl a secret. She knew her husband cared little to nothing about her, and she knew her son did not act the kindest toward females of equal station let alone lesser.

As she poured water into the pot on the stove, she said casually to Terra, "Has Vin been bothering you, Terra? His father and I have told him that he is not to give you orders, and he took it with great resentment."

Terra's stomach rolled. She did not like Vin. She never had. He was five years older than she was, and ever since she had come to the Arcwood household, he had delighted in terrorizing her. He looked at her in a way that made her absolutely terrified to be alone near him. She couldn't be sure what he would do to her, but she knew it would be bad. "I do not be alone near him," she admitted softly. "He . . . alarms me."

Mrs. Arcwood looked at her sharply. "Has he touched you?"

"No!" She shook her head vehemently. "That is why I am always so careful. I get sick when I see him."

"Make sure it stays that way." Mrs. Arcwood handed her a basket. "Chickens."

"Yes ma'am." She headed back out into the heat and over to the chicken coop. Among her chores, this was her favorite. It meant she could get, even briefly, out of the sun.

She was halfway through with the task when a shadow filled the doorway. She looked up quickly and saw Vin standing there. She edged back, her free hand closing around the pitchfork behind her.

A sneer curled his lips. He was handsome, fair and beautiful enough to be a prince, but something cruel always clung to the corner of his eye. "Look what I found," he said slyly. "All alone, little Terra?"

Her pale green eyes narrowed sharply. The color appeared nearly iridescent in the light, and it shimmered in the dark. It was offset by long, and thick, silvery-brown hair. She wore it braided nearly constantly, but it still offered an enticing sight to most men, as much as her slim and lovely body did. "I'm working, Vin. Please leave me be."

He clucked his tongue. "That's *Master* Vin to you."

Her chin lifted slightly. "Mrs. Arcwood has told me that she and Mr. Arcwood have refused you the right to order me around. Therefore you are no master to me. You never will be."

The smile faded from his face as his eyes went cold. "My parents won't be around forever. You won't always avoid being alone near me." He began to stalk closer. "You can be willing or not. I don't care. You're just a slave."

As he moved closer, she swung the pitchfork around and jabbed it lightly into his stomach. He barked out a laugh. "You wouldn't dare!"

"Try me." Her hands tightened. "I'll die before I let you touch me." She pushed harder when he tried to step forward.

He saw something in her eyes, some steady determination, and backed up. "You'll be whipped for this," he snapped. "When I tell my parents that you assaulted me!" He turned and stalked out, and it seemed as if the very air cleared with his exit.

The pitchfork fell on the ground with a clatter as she lost her grip. Shaking, she sat down against the wall. She probably would be whipped, but it would be a better fate than finding herself in his hands.

"Terra!" The roar came from the house, and it was recognizably Mr. Arcwood's voice.

She finished gathering the eggs and left the coop on shaking legs. Her hands tightened around the basket handle as she saw Mr. Arcwood standing at the kitchen door. The same cruelty in Vin's face existed in his father's face. In one hand, Mr. Arcwood carried a familiar cart whip normally used on horses. "What's this I hear about you attacking Vin?" he asked in a viciously soft voice.

Protests were useless, but she tried anyway. "I didn't! He tried to grab me in the coop and I fought him off! All I did was aim the pitchfork at him; he walked into it himself, and not even very hard!"

He grabbed her arm and swung her around to shove her toward the shed where she slept. "If Vin is grabbing you, then let him," he snapped. "What, you think it matters to anyone if you're 'pure'? You'll never be any man's wife, Terra. Don't you dare raise a weapon against anyone in this family again!"

She said nothing. She had never lied before, and she would never lie in the future. If Vin grabbed her, she would fight to her last breath. When they got to the shed and she was released, she turned her back and bowed her head.

He raised the whip . . . then slowly lowered it again. There was something inside her in that moment, some goodness, that stayed his hand and his heart. He dropped the whip to his side. "Next time," he snarled, "I won't be so gracious!"

She turned sharply, shocked, and watched as he stalked into the house. Trembling, she slowly sat down in what little shade the broken roof provided. Her only consolation was that they would all go on a long journey starting the next day; Vin would not have any chance to get her alone.

Even before dawn the next day, she helped to load the wagon. They were going to the kingdom several days' journey away to celebrate the upcoming festival. The king had been gone on a long sabbatical, and he was expected to return in a week. The festival promised parties and celebrations and exotic wares from across the land. Though she would not get to buy anything, Terra looked forward to at least seeing the city.

When the wagon had been fully loaded with supplies and provisions, they set out. Mr. and Mrs. Arcwood rode at the front of the wagon to drive the horses, and an umbrella mounted over their heads shaded them. Vin rode inside the covered wagon where it was cool. Terra rode on the very back, precariously perched on the step. There was no shade, and it was certainly bouncy, but at least she did not have to walk.

"Don't we have to go through those nasty woods?" Vin suddenly asked his parents. "I hear it's cursed."

"So people say," Mr. Arcwood agreed. "But I've never heard of anyone getting eaten in there. Mostly, they say that the Oak Woods is full of trees that are living."

"Aren't all trees living?" Terra asked and then hastily covered her mouth.

Thankfully, Mr. Arcwood didn't take offense at the question. "Perhaps I should have said sentient. It is said that the trees in the Oak Woods are full of will and thought. There's a story about it. Something about an oak tree that lost a love, or whatever. You know how Mirage is." He stopped the wagon so that a crowd of Brownies could scuttle across the street. "Everything is never what it seems."

It was mid-afternoon by the time they entered the woods. Terra loved them instantly. The trees stood immense and towering, stretching thick branches up toward the sky which could barely be seen between the leaves. Roots crisscrossed the land, brown where the sun hit and mossy where they rested in shade. The horrible heat dissipated there, and it was even on the cooler side. The air smelled crisp and clean.

"This place gives me the creeps," Mrs. Arcwood muttered suddenly.

Startled, Terra looked over her shoulder toward the front of the wagon. "It certainly is depressing," Mr. Arcwood agreed.

Terra had no idea what they were thinking; the woods were beautiful! Peaceful and serene. She would have happily stayed there forever. The only downside was that the sudden shift from the hot sun to the cool shade had her shivering after several moments.

Vin leaned out of the wagon and put a blanket around her shoulders. Into her ear, he purred, "Wouldn't want you to get frozen. I like my women to be soft."

She jerked away from him and nearly jerked off the step. "Don't touch me!"

"Vin!" Mrs. Arcwood snapped sharply.

He started to answer when the wagon came to an abrupt halt and sent him tumbling to the ground inside. A pot banged against his head sharply. "Ow! What's going on?" He stuck his head out the front and got his answer. Bandits. Half a dozen bandits had surrounded the wagon.

"Get the goods," one said to the others. His voice cut the air like a whiplash. "Take everything we can carry."

As the bandits walked closer, Terra scrambled down off the wagon and darted around the side. She ran right into Mrs. Arcwood who tugged her closer protectively. Vin and Mr. Arcwood joined them, all of them too terrified to say a word. They could only stand there and watch as the wagon was torn apart and anything of value got stuffed into bags and sacks. When the wagon was only a shell, one of the other bandits lit it on fire.

"What do we do with them?" yet another asked. He ambled closer to Terra and caught her braid in his hand before she could jerk free. "She's a beauty, isn't she? Is she your daughter?" he asked the older couple.

"Yes," Mrs. Arcwood blurted.

"No!" Mr. Arcwood countered. "She's just a servant! You can take her if you let us go."

"Why don't we make this easy?" the lead bandit said casually. "Someone grab the girl. Kill the rest. Then it won't matter, will it?"

Swords and daggers were drawn. Sneers filled faces that crossed everything from boring to handsome. As one grabbed Mrs. Arcwood's arm, she gave Terra a powerful shove and sent her stumbling. "Run!" she shouted. "Run, Terra!"

One of the bandits lunged for Terra, and she whirled and dashed into the trees. Behind her, she could hear Vin starting to scream. It raised the hair on her arms and she clamped her hands over her ears. Equally chilling was when the screams cut off sharply. Desperately trying to shut out the raucous, nearly maniacal laughter, she ran ever deeper into the woods. She didn't know if they were chasing her. She didn't want to stop to find out.

It was only when she realized that she couldn't hear them anymore that she stopped running. She had no idea where she was. She could see nothing but trees and roots everywhere. There was no sign of an exit. The woods were supposed to be days wide and days long. She wouldn't be leaving anytime soon.

Tears rose and choked her as she sank down under an unusually small oak tree. She buried her face in her knees as she sobbed, her whole body shaking violently. Even if she managed to find her way to an exit, what was she supposed to do? She had no money. No food, no water. She had no skills or abilities that she could use to make money. If she didn't die before she found people, she would no doubt find herself as another servant.

By the time the tears spent themselves, it was turning into evening. The woods were growing darker. She had seen no sign of animal life, but it didn't worry her. She had always gotten along with animals of all kinds. Even known predators did not offer her harm. She had even heard Mr. Arcwood once tell a neighbor that their fields were never tormented by wolves or coyotes because she was there. He had seen them sleeping near her shed peacefully, and they had never attacked another animal again. Terra didn't doubt him, though she had never seen the beasts that supposedly liked her.

As twilight began to turn into night, exhaustion caught up. She leaned back against the tree, intending to simply close her eyes and rest. She was cold, tired, and hungry. It would be impossible to sleep. And yet, it was only moments before she was out, her body simply unable to keep up with her emotions.

The calm of night descended and the oak tree stirred. Slowly, tenderly, two branches folded down to curl around her protectively.

Finally. Finally she had come home.

CHAPTER TWO

It was hunger that woke Terra a few hours later. Something smelled so delicious that it had crept into her sleep and called to her. It made her stomach clench hard; she hadn't eaten all day, let alone eaten well for longer. She didn't want to open her eyes to see what was being cooked. She felt warm and secure for once, and the feelings were just as foreign as the thought of being full.

When her brain actually clicked awake a few moments later, she went very still with fear. Memory had rushed back in. That warmth and security actually came from a pair of arms wrapped around her. She was on someone's lap, held against someone's chest. A man's chest; that much she knew for sure without looking.

Her eyes flew wide and she found herself staring up into a shockingly handsome man's face. He looked rough and powerful, his dark brown hair shaggy and uncontrolled. And he was *huge*. Even on his lap, she was shorter and smaller.

Terrified, she began to struggle wildly. "Let me go!" she shouted. She beat at his shoulders and tried to pull out of his arms, but he was vastly stronger than even she was. He continued to hold her firmly and oddly gently. "Let go! Let go!"

In her panic, it took a long time to realize he was saying something. His words slowly permeated the haze in her mind, their soft cadence finally catching her attention. "Calm down, you're safe," he said over and over again. "I'm not going to hurt you. Please, calm down."

Out of breath from the fight, she slumped against him. Tears slid down her cheeks. "Don't hurt me."

The plea in her voice broke his heart. He released her carefully, slowly, wanting to be sure she knew what he was doing. The instant she was free, she shot off his lap and backed away across the entire room. She ducked into a corner and all but curled into herself, her skin white and her green eyes too large in her face.

As slowly as he could, he got to his feet and walked toward her. He kept his hands held out so that she could see he was unarmed. "My name is Nikolas Rivers," he said softly. "What's your name?" There came no response and he knelt down. He knew that his size alone had to be intimidating her; he was much taller than average and very powerful in his build. She looked as if a strong wind might whisk her away. "Please," he coaxed. "Tell me your name."

"Terra," she whispered, her eyes locked on his hands. "Terra Evermore." Her eyes slammed shut as he lifted a hand toward her. When his fingers simply brushed away a smudge of dirt on her face, she looked at him swiftly. Her eyes searched his dark green ones. There appeared to be no sign of malice or cruelty in him. Only gentleness. "You're . . . you're not going to hurt me?" Her voice broke on the words and then came out with a rush. "Please, let me go. If I was trespassing, I didn't mean to!"

"Terra." He took her icy hands in his and softly blew on them to warm them. "I will not harm you. You are safe with me. I saw what happened with the bandits. I am only trying to help you. I would not hurt you."

"Why would you care?" she asked quietly. Her hands laid passively in his grip as if she thought fighting to be futile. "I'm just a servant."

"You looked like a frightened willow tree," he countered. "When I saw you running in the woods, you were so lovely. I treasure trees, and I will treasure you." He tugged lightly on her hands and pulled her to her feet. "You were very brave."

"I was terrified!" she disagreed shakily. She swayed on her feet suddenly, the dizziness sweeping through every inch of her body. She found herself instantly lifted into his arms once more. The fear did not return this time. She hadn't been held in a long time, if ever, but there was something in his touch that felt so kind, so nearly reverent, that she trusted she was safe.

He put her down on a chair next to a table. "You must be starving. When did you last eat?"

"Yesterday." Honesty made her admit, "But it wasn't very much. I didn't often get a lot of food. Just enough to make sure I wouldn't get sick." She took a wistful sniff of the air. Whatever was cooking on the small stove certainly smelled heavenly.

He waited, but when she did not ask for anything, he tucked his anger away carefully and walked over to the stove. "Do you like stew?" he asked her.

"I've never had any."

"Here's your chance."

"I can't repay you," she said miserably.

"Did I ask you to?" He brought a bowl over and put it in front of her. He added a chunk of bread and a glass of water so clean that it looked more blue than clear. "Eat," he urged as he sat down across from her. "There's plenty. I eat a lot, therefore I make a lot." When she still hesitated, he reached over to lift her chin so that she met his eyes. "If you want to repay me for saving you," he said pointedly, "you'll eat. Seeing you fade away would be a complete waste of my time and effort, wouldn't it?"

A sudden smile lit her face and turned her lovely face into an unbearably beautiful one. "I suppose it would." She picked up her spoon and began to eat. The stew tasted as delicious as it smelled, and she forced herself to eat it slowly. She didn't want to get sick, and she didn't want to rush through what might be her only good meal for a long time. "Where are you from?" she asked him. A hesitant smile touched her lips. "I mean, if you don't mind telling me."

"I'm from here," he said simply. "I live in these woods."

"Oh, a woodsman." Well, that certainly explained his build. She looked around the room curiously. There were no windows, and the walls looked more like dirt than wood, though it was rather hard to tell in the light from the single lamp. The room claimed a large bed, a stove, and the table and chairs she sat at. "Where are we?"

"Underground." He smiled when she looked at him in surprise. "There are many mysteries in these woods, Terra."

Something fluttered low in her body at the way he said her name, and it had nothing to do with being hungry. Breathless, she could only stare at him. He was truly the most handsome man she had ever seen, though she wouldn't have called him necessarily beautiful. A sudden heat rushed through her body, shocking and unexpected. She averted her gaze quickly as her cheeks flushed pink.

He curled his hands into fists under the table. He had wanted her from the moment he had laid eyes on her. Her shimmering hair begged for his hands to be lost in it, and her iridescent eyes reflected her every emotion. Though malnourished for too long, her body didn't seem to be thin. She was willowy and slim instead, her figure lithe and seductive without effort.

Holding her as he had for those hours had been self-inflicted torture, but he had done it to combat the terrible chill she had gained from being in the woods too long. More than once he had wanted to kiss her awake. He had never dared hope she would want him, especially not after her initial reaction to him. But now . . . for a moment, there had been something in her eyes. A startled desire followed quickly by shame.

He reached out and covered her hand with his. Her blush deepened. Tenderly, he said, "Terra, look at me." Her eyes reluctantly lifted, and he brought her hand slowly to his lips. Without hurry, keeping his gaze on hers, he softly kissed each slender finger before kissing her palm. His lips pressed to her wrist and he could feel the rapid race of her pulse. "Don't be afraid," he said huskily. "I could not hurt you."

"I'm a servant," she said miserably.

"Your masters are dead." She flinched, and he pressed her hand to his cheek. "You are free, Terra. There is nothing to be ashamed of if you desire me." He slowly smiled. "I'm glad that you do. I wanted you when I saw you in my woods."

Her breath hitched as that something inside stirred. The lethal smile touching her rescuer's lips seemed to simply beg to be kissed. Certainly, she had never kissed anyone before, but he made it very tempting. But he was a woodsman, and she was a former servant. A more unlikely pairing didn't exist.

She dropped her hands into her lap when he released her. "What am I supposed to do, Nikolas?" she asked softly. "I have nowhere to go. I have no skills at anything. I don't even know how to get out of these woods."

"You can stay here tonight," he countered softly. "I must leave soon, but you are welcome to stay. The sleep will do you good."

She looked at the bed longingly. It seemed far too fine for her to touch. "Just give me a blanket and I'll curl up in a corner. I can sleep anywhere."

He didn't push the issue though he had no intention of letting her sleep on the floor. "Since I have a little time left, tell me about yourself," he offered softly. "I'd like to know about the willow I saved."

"I'm a servant, as I said. I was bought eight years ago by the Arcwoods, when I was ten. My parents got into debt very badly." Her gaze lowered. "My mother was ill. My father sold everything to pay for medicine, but it did no good. When she died, he simply . . . gave up. He was gone soon after. The debt fell on my shoulders. The holder of the debt said if I would be a servant, he would call it even. I didn't have a choice."

"So you've been a slave for eight years to a couple who, obviously, cared little about your health." He fought to keep his voice even. "Do you live in the kingdom?"

"No. We're part of the land owned by the king and under his jurisdiction, but we were not in the actual kingdom. When we were attacked, we were heading for the festival."

"It disgusts me that the kingdom would have no idea that children are being sold to pay a debt they had no control over." He ran his hand down her hair softly, the calluses on his fingers snagging on silken strands. The tendrils seemed to lift and follow his touch. "What was it like on the farm where you lived?"

"It was okay, I suppose." His fingers skimmed down her cheek and she rubbed against them unconsciously. His touch was so loving, so tender. It was an alien sensation, but one that she couldn't help but soak up eagerly. That anyone might care about her . . . "I slept outside most of the time, but when it snowed I slept in the kitchen. I always slept with a knife in case Vin found me."

"Vin?"

"The Arcwoods' son." She shuddered. "He always tried to touch me."

"Touch you how?" His voice sounded as grim as he felt.

"He wanted . . ." She made a helpless gesture, embarrassed. "You know what he wanted. You said you did too."

"Wrong." She looked at him in surprise and he drew her hands up to rest over his heart. "He wanted to hurt you in a way no man ever should hurt a woman. I want to love you. I will not, *could never*, hurt you."

She searched his face intently, and slowly, a little flower of happiness began to unfurl inside her heart. It seemed miraculous, but she could see in his eyes, and hear in his voice, his sincerity. Whatever he wanted of her, it was nothing like what Vin wanted. "I trust you, Nikolas," she said with conviction.

Relief nearly made him lightheaded. "Hey, at least call me 'Nik.' You don't need to be formal with me." He hesitated for only a moment before lifting her off her seat and settling her on his lap. She went very stiff for a long moment and then her body slowly relaxed against him. Her head fit perfectly on his shoulder. "There," he said softly into her hair. "Someone around here is long overdue for some cuddling."

Suddenly drowsy, she found herself smiling. "You're a bit big to cuddle but I can try." He laughed out loud and it sounded wonderful on her ears. She rubbed her cheek over his chest softly. He smelled like the woods did. Pure and clean and free. "How tall are you?"

"Six-seven."

He reached an entire foot taller than she did, but it no longer seemed so scary. Somewhere between the way he had treated her after she had attacked him to the way he now held her so safely, her fear had evaporated entirely. She felt . . . happy. Safe. Maybe she was in love with him. She didn't know. She had never loved anyone before. Maybe it was just gratitude. Maybe it was just desire, though 'just' seemed a misnomer the way her pulse clamored at his every touch and every smile. "Nik?" she asked softly.

"Sleep," he countered just as softly. Her soft breath feathered across his skin as she relaxed, and he continued to hold her until he knew for sure that she truly slept. Her skin was nearly translucent even though it carried a soft gold tint from the sun. Dark circles showed starkly under her eyes.

He got to his feet and carried her as if she was the most precious thing in the world. He placed her very softly on the bed and tugged a blanket over her. She snuggled deeper into the pillows with a wordless murmur, and he brushed at the hair falling in her face. He had waited a long time to find her. He had nearly begun to give up hope.

"I won't let you go again, my willow," he promised softly.

He stayed by her side until he sensed the dawn approaching. As he felt the first rays calling him, he softly brushed a kiss across her lips. She stirred, her hand moving as if to reach for him, and he straightened swiftly. With a last longing look, he walked away. It would be a long time until sundown arrived and he could hold her again. He did not worry for her safety. There was nothing in the woods that could harm her. Neither plant nor animal would ever be a danger.

The willow had returned to where she belonged.

CHAPTER THREE

Terra awoke to the sound of birds chirping and a morning breeze caressing her skin. Startled, she sat upright and found she had been sleeping in a soft bed of grass beneath the branches of a tree. She looked around but there was no sign of any shelter nearby, even one that might be underground.

A soft cooing sound caught her attention, and she looked up to see a small dove sitting on a branch over her head. She smiled as she got to her feet. "Hello," she said softly. "Am I hogging your tree?"

The dove cocked his head slightly. "I would not say so," he said after a moment. "I own nothing in these woods. I simply fly where I am needed."

She blinked once, then twice. "You talk?"

"Certainly. Do you?"

She suddenly smiled. "Sometimes my talking got me into trouble. I suppose I do not mind that a dove can converse with me. Do you have a name?"

"I do not. It does not matter though," he added gently. "I would always know when you spoke to me though you spoke not my name." He flew down and landed delicately on her shoulder. "What will you do today, Terra?"

"I do not know." She crossed her arms around herself as she began to walk aimlessly. "I feel a little . . . surreal right now. Did I dream everything? Am I still dreaming? Was Nik even real, little dove?"

"He was as real as you are," he promised. "And you shall as yet see him again. Today is yours. Tonight is his. The time in between is waiting time. So I ask again, what will you do today?"

"I suppose I can only start walking and see where I end up." She tilted her face up toward the sunshine coming through the leaves. "It is so peaceful here. I don't know why people call these woods cursed. Are the trees really sentient?"

"Everything that lives has a spirit. It just so happens that these woods are slightly more willful than most other places." He hopped around to sit on her other shoulder. With his beak, he tugged on a lock of her hair where it had escaped her braid. "Why do you plait your hair?"

The colloquial term sounded fascinating from a dove, but she accepted it at face value. She knew her companion was not normal. Perhaps he was a good spirit in disguise. "I braid my hair to keep it out of my face when I am working. And it is so hot on the farm!" More reluctantly, she added, "And it hides how dirty it is. I only bathe when I can be sure I will not be found. I haven't had a hot bath in years."

"I suspect you have not had clean clothes in years either."

She looked down at her tunic and leggings. Both were caked with dirt, worn all the way through in places, and practically falling to pieces in others. The only thing she wore that remained in any decent condition were her underwear and bra; those were necessities in her book, and she treated them far more carefully than her outerwear. If she could only wash one thing, it was that.

"Well," she said, "I haven't worn these all my life, you know. I only finished growing a short while ago. But they are all I own now." She frowned deeply. "I do not know how I will make money to buy anything should I get out of these woods."

A secretive smile crossed the dove's face. "By the time you get out, you will not have any worry for it any longer."

"If I get out." She sighed and sat down under a tree. "I am so tired. My feet hurt so badly. Yet I know I shouldn't complain; I'm alive." She leaned against the tree trunk and closed her eyes. "I almost wish Nik had not saved me."

The dove flew down to land on her lap. "Would you wish away meeting him?"

"No." She softly stroked the small bird's head and was rewarded by a trilling coo. "That is why I said 'almost.' Last night . . . for the first time, I felt like someone cared about me. I want to see him again," she admitted even softer. "I don't know what I feel. But I want to be with him. He may never love me, but that's okay. I just want to be with someone who cares about me."

The dove watched her for long moments and then flew off into the sky. She let him go and closed her eyes to rest. It was a curious situation to find herself in, to be sure. This sort of thing was supposed to happen to other people, not to people like her.

Sadness suddenly filled her heart. Mrs. Arcwood had tried to save her. She had always found the older woman to be more gentle than her husband or son. She had liked her. Now she was no doubt dead along with Vin and Mr. Arcwood. Try as she might, she couldn't regret that the two males were gone. They had been horrid people. She would carry the scars from Mr. Arcwood's whip forever.

After a brief rest, she got back on her feet and started walking again. She couldn't even tell where the sun sat in the sky, and she had no idea if she was going forward or backward. Nothing looked familiar, but she could not be sure if she would remember what she had already seen. There was no way of knowing how far from the incident that Nikolas had taken her.

Her feet began to hurt. She tried to balance herself on a tree to see if she had cut herself but she was tired enough that she missed the trunk. She instead stumbled past it, and her shirt snagged on a bush that tore out a chunk of material.

The sudden urge to cry welled and she fought it. Crying changed nothing. She simply squared her shoulders and freed her shirt from the bush. If she had to walk naked in the woods, then that's what she would do. There wasn't anyone to see her anyway. Maybe she could make clothes out of leaves.

She rested under a different tree hours later when twilight crept in. As she looked around for a place to sleep, the dove suddenly returned. He flew down to land on her shoulder and dropped a small gold key into her hand. "What is this?" she asked.

"A key."

Exasperated, she said, "I see that!"

He smiled. He had known there lurked a spirited heart under her quiet exterior. There had to be. She would not have endured that long without it. "It is a key to another home under a tree. Follow me; I will take you there. You may take shelter there tonight."

She curiously followed the dove as he flew through the trees. It wasn't very long before he stopped before a mighty pine tree with a trunk wider than Terra. She ran her hands lightly over the bark, and her fingers brushed across a small hole. When she looked closer, she discovered it was a keyhole. She put the key in and turned it, and the entire trunk opened like a door to reveal a staircase.

More fascinated than alarmed, she went down the dark stairs carefully. At the bottom, she found a small room just like the one she had woken in before. A fire burned welcomingly in the stove, and when she went closer, she discovered that technically nothing burned at all. It simply gave light and heat. "Magic," she whispered, enchanted. She had always wanted to see magic.

The dove flew down and landed on a trunk sitting against the wall. "Terra. Come here."

She walked over and opened the trunk. Inside, she saw clothes of silk and satin, the colors rich and the fabrics luxurious. "Oh," she breathed. "They're lovely."

"Wear something," he urged.

"They are too fine for me." She shut the lid regretfully. "And I am filthy in any case." She spotted a basin of water and a washcloth and went over to at least scrub her face and hands clean. Just that simple thing felt delightful. She glanced at the bed wistfully but instead went to sit in front of the stove. It was quiet and calm, and she was tired. Maybe she could take a nap before the owner came home.

When Nikolas came down the stairs less than an hour later, he came to a sharp stop as he saw her curled up in front of the stove. Why wasn't she in the bed, or wearing the clothes he had provided? He walked over to her and knelt down. The dark circles had begun to fade from under her eyes, and her skin seemed healthier. The woods as much as the rest were beginning to take their effect.

He softly smoothed his fingers down her cheek, savoring how it felt to have her close once more. He eased her into his arms and stood, his heart tightening fiercely as she instinctively cuddled against him. One delicate hand curled over his chest as if to grab onto the heart inside.

He placed her softly on the bed and brushed her hair out of her face. Unable to resist, he gently kissed her, needing nothing as much as he needed her taste again. She stirred, a soft sigh captured by his lips, and her lashes lifted slightly. A warm welcome filled her eyes, and she curled her arms around his neck. Her lips parted to invite a deeper embrace.

He groaned softly and took the gift she had given so freely. It was near impossible to keep his touch tender, but he would be damned before he frightened her. Even as he deepened the kiss, his tongue teasing hers and enticing her to return the gesture, his hands ever so lightly skimmed down the side of her body.

A shiver rippled down her nerves of pure delight. Shy but unafraid, she hesitantly began to return the kiss, following his lead without question. He tasted as wonderful as he smelled, his flavor as instantly addicting as the pleasure beginning to steal through her body. She couldn't breathe anymore, but she really didn't care. Breathing wasn't important anyway.

He slowly broke the kiss and searched her eyes. They glowed more iridescent than ever, and looked very sultry with an unconscious sensuality. Not a single trace of fear could be found in her gaze. As her fingers softly traced his lips, he asked huskily, "Did I frighten you?"

"No. It was beautiful. I'd never been kissed before."

Warily, he asked, "Kissed the way I kissed you, or at all?"

She smiled. "At all. I never met anyone I wanted to kiss, and certainly no one wanted a servant girl enough to kiss her without consent."

"I really should apologize."

Her eyes deepened with warm laughter. "But you won't."

His lips curved. "No, I won't." Fascinated, enchanted, he framed her face in his hands. She was warm and vibrant, giving and brave. And smart. He was sure she would disagree, but she seemed to accept and absorb so much so swiftly. A servant? She should be a princess or queen. "You're not going to hit me?" he asked solemnly.

"That would be silly when I kissed you too." When he released her, she sat up gingerly and tried not to touch the bed too much. She didn't even remember getting into the bed, and she felt rather embarrassed at getting the covers dirty. She could see the smudges from her clothes. "I thought I was in front of the stove."

"I moved you." He frowned. "Why didn't you change clothes, Terra? Or get in bed if you were tired?" He fingered the great tear in her tunic. "This is falling apart."

She shook her head. "I couldn't take those things. They were too fine for me."

Temper lit his eyes and he shot to his feet to pace away. "Too fine, she says!"

Wary but not entirely afraid, she watched him carefully. "They were silk, Nik. At best I might someday be a farm girl, but I will never be in a position that deserves to wear something that lovely." She got out of the bed before she made it dirtier.

He swung around and stepped closer so that he towered over her. "I may not be very old," he told her fiercely, "but I have seen my share of ladies, noblewomen, and princesses. Only half of them deserved to wear the silks you claim are too fine for you. It has nothing to do with your birth, willow, and everything to do with what is inside." He blew out a hard breath. "And stop looking at me like that. I'm not mad at you. I'm mad at the idiots who made you think you were without worth."

"I'm sorry." She made a helpless gesture. "I've always had to be very careful of Mr. Arcwood's temper and I couldn't help but be wary of yours. I know you won't hurt me."

There was a significant silence before he asked very softly, "Why were you careful of his temper?" No answer. "Did he hit you?" Again, silence. Nausea churned in his stomach. "Whip you?" Her lashes flinched, and he cursed softly.

Before she quite knew what he would do, he crossed to her and spun her around. Red color flooded her cheeks as he knelt and lifted her tunic away from her back. "Don't look! It's horrible!"

His fingers, though shaking, remained tender as they traced the thin scars on her back. Most were faded and would no doubt disappear entirely someday. Others were much newer, much starker, and would be there for much longer. One particularly vicious mark reached nearly an inch wide. He softly traced the length of it. "He must have been particularly furious."

"I was so tired coming back from the coop that I dropped the basket of eggs and broke everything." A little tremor ran through her body. "Please. Stop looking, Nik."

He smoothed her tunic down and curled his arms around her waist as he pressed his face to her back. "I would never hurt you, let alone like this," he vowed softly, "no matter how angry I might be." He reluctantly released her and got to his feet.

She took a deep breath as she turned to look at him. She could believe him. The horror in his voice, and the pain in his eyes, at seeing how she was marked felt true. This was a man who had no cruelty inside him. "Okay." She started to say something else when her stomach rumbled loudly. Her cheeks went bright pink as he smiled at her. "Uhm."

"I suppose I had better feed you again." He caught her hand and brought her wrist to his lips for a moment. "Come sit down. I'll make something. Or do you want to?"

"I don't cook very well," she admitted shamefully. "Mrs. Arcwood tried very hard to teach me, but I lack some sort of skill at it. At least, when it comes to a stove. I can bake with a stone oven well enough, but those are such luxury items."

"And it seems like only yesterday that running water was a luxury." He competently began to assemble the ingredients for his stew. "Ah, well. I like to cook. Until I was on my own out here, I never really had a chance."

"How old are you?" she asked curiously. "You said 'you may not be very old' and yet you seem much older than me . . ."

He smiled over his shoulder. "How old do you think I am?"

"Thirty-five?"

"Ouch. Twenty-five."

She winced good-naturedly. "Sorry." She propped her chin on her hands and watched him. How such a strong and masculine male could be that gentle amazed her. "Where are you really from, Nik? You talk like a city boy, and yet you are very much a woodsman."

"I am from the city," he admitted after a moment. Letting the stew simmer, he sat at the table and handed her a small loaf of bread to nibble on. "Coming out here wasn't an intent, exactly. I simply found myself unable to leave."

"It is beautiful," she agreed softly. "A dove was telling me that the trees are living creatures. Are they? Can they talk and think? Do they feel?"

"Of course." His voice sounded simple. "They feel and love. They are no different from you and I other than the form they reside within. Those of pure hearts, such as you, find the woods to be beautiful and peaceful. Those who carry malice find the woods to be frightening and uncertain. It is how the trees protect themselves from those who would chop them down carelessly without a single thought for how they feel."

Something painful lodged in her chest. "I don't know why," she said softly, "but it hurts to hear you say that."

She was more sensitive to what happened around them than he had thought. Carefully, he said, "You are a very giving person. I would imagine it would hurt you to think of someone being cruel." He went over to the stove and dished up two servings. As he placed a bowl in front of her, he said teasingly, "My lady."

She smiled shyly. "I am no lady."

"Of birth." He shrugged one shoulder carelessly. "At heart, certainly you are. I'm older and I say so, so you'll just have to trust me."

Her smile spread. "Well, I guess I cannot argue with that." She contentedly began to eat her stew. It was still a marvelous feeling to think that not only was she having a real meal, but that there was someone who wanted her around. If it meant being with Nikolas, she would have been happy to never leave the woods again.

"Terra?"

She looked up quickly. "Yes?"

His breath caught at the glow in her eyes. "Don't look at me like that, willow," he said faintly. "I am having enough trouble keeping my hands off you." He reached out with trembling fingers to caress her cheek. "From the moment you fell into my arms," he murmured softly, "I have never wanted anything more than to have you for my own. I love you very much, willow."

Her mouth opened and then closed. Wonder slowly filled her face and her eyes. She reached out to touch him, her fingers tracing over his beloved face. The warmth unfurled inside her, and finally she understood what it was. It wasn't gratitude. It wasn't just desire.

It was love.

"Nik," she breathed softly.

He reached out and pulled her onto his lap so swiftly that the empty bowls bounced off the table onto the floor. She didn't care. She threw her arms around his neck and met his kiss with all the pent up emotion inside. But this time . . . she realized something distantly. His touch was not unfamiliar. The hunger that stirred inside her blood was not unfamiliar. Even before his arms went around her to hold her close, she knew exactly how it would feel.

Aching, fit to burst, he broke free of the kiss and buried his face against her neck. She quivered in his arms, her breaths coming as quickly as his. Her fingers seemed to be convulsively moving against his scalp as if she couldn't stop herself from caressing him.

"Ask me to stay with you," he pleaded roughly. The faintest of trembles of fear went through her body, and he lifted his head instantly. Confusion had filled her eyes. "It's alright, Terra," he promised gently. "There's time yet."

"I don't understand," she said softly. "Why am I suddenly afraid?"

"You've been through a lot the last few days. Your life has changed completely beyond your control. Now I threaten to change it again." He brought her hand to his lips and tenderly kissed her palm. "You will make this choice, willow. It is entirely your choice if we become lovers. I will wait as patiently as I am able to."

"I'm so sorry, Nik." She pressed her face against his shoulder. Her body felt achy and restless, desperately craving the feeling of his hands, but it couldn't entirely override her nerves. She *wanted* to be his. Why couldn't she ask him to stay?

When she suddenly yawned, he found a real smile. "I suppose it is just as well. I wouldn't want you to fall asleep while I was making love to you. After, perhaps, because then I could have you in my arms."

Only the lightest of blushes on her cheek, she countered, "I'm already in your arms."

"But frustratingly clothed."

She sat upright, eyes wide. "You would want me to sleep *naked* in your arms?"

He arched a brow. "You expected to be wearing boots?"

"Or a nightgown at the least!"

He leaned in and teasingly nibbled at the line of her jaw. "You won't need one. And when you eventually are there, you won't even think of it." The little stinging kisses made their way down her neck to her shoulder. "You shouldn't wear anything except your beauty. Or me."

Flushed with an entirely different heat, she had no words to say to that. She felt silly and naïve, but she had always assumed that couples wore pajamas to bed. But then, really, what did she have to base her assumptions on? The Arcwoods hadn't been an affectionate couple, and Nikolas was proving to be *very* affectionate. She soaked up his attention like a tree would soak up the sun.

Another yawn caught her by surprise. He softly tugged her closer. "Go to sleep," he urged softly, his voice nothing but a rumble in his chest. "I will hold you until I have to leave."

"I wish you did not have to leave," she said sleepily. She curled her hand over his heart. "You seem so tired when I see you, Nik. I can feel it." She sighed softly and closed her eyes. "I want to take care of you too. If I could be with you, I would never want to leave this place."

He closed his eyes as he struggled for control. Even after she slept, he continued to hold her. Every time he left her, it took another piece of his soul. Through the whole long day, even when he could not feel anything else, he felt hunger for her smile and her laugh. For her kiss and her touch. How much longer would he have to wait?

CHAPTER FOUR

Terra woke the following morning to once more find herself outside. This time she did not feel quite so startled by it. The magic in the woods was something to simply be accepted. And she did accept it. She could accept anything.

The sound of a brook caught her attention, and she made her way toward it carefully. Her feet still ached, but not nearly as bad as they had the day before. She was more than happy to sit on the bank of the brook and let her feet dangle inside. The cool water felt wonderful. If she could have found some soap, she would have even bathed. The next time she saw Nikolas, she really wanted to look as good as she could.

"A woman who loves is a vain woman." The dove flew down to land beside her.

She smiled. "I never imagined I would be in love, so I had no real care for my appearance. I suppose that since Nik has seen me at my worst, I ought to be unconcerned, but I don't want him to regret picking me."

"It is natural instinct," he countered gently. "Love is a survival mechanic. It triggers the desire to mate and produce offspring. It, therefore, produces the urge to look your best for your mate. Feeding the beast, if you will."

"You sound like quite the expert."

He ruffled his feathers. "I suppose you could say that."

"Well, perhaps you'll then explain why love is said to be blind."

For a moment, something old and sad crossed the avian face beside her. "When you love," he said softly, "you are supposed to be blind to flaws. You will find your love to be perfect to you. Though others may see them as plain, beastly, or perhaps even a little cold, you will see beyond it to the inside. Blind to the outside, perhaps is the best way to say it. Blind to the outside, accepting of the inside. Loving regardless of both."

She watched him for long moments and then asked softly, "So who was blind to your inner flaws?"

His wry laugh sounded a little sad. "I was blind to my own." He shook it off visibly. "Ah well, we were discussing you, were we not? You love Nikolas as he is. You would love him no matter how he appeared, yes?"

"Yes." There was no question in her mind or heart.

"Good." He hopped closer to the water to look in. He nearly slipped down the bank, but she caught him. "Thank you," he told her. "I am not quite used to this form just yet." His head tilted when she smiled. He smiled as well. "You do not seem surprised."

"Little surprises me anymore." She opened her hands and let him fly up into the air. Feeling refreshed once more, she got to her feet and stretched largely. "I don't know where I will go today," she decided softly, "but I'm not in any hurry or desire to find the exit anymore. If I looked for Nikolas, would I find him?"

"Possibly, but you may not recognize him as he is right now. You are not ready to."

She considered that as she began to walk. Why wouldn't she recognize Nikolas? He was distinctive in many ways. She felt sure she could never pass over him in a crowd, and she felt even surer that there was no way he could disguise himself that she could not see through. She felt attuned to him, as if something at the core of him called to something at the core of her.

She took her time walking through the woods. To her delight, the woodland creatures finally came out of hiding. Birds of all kinds nested in the trees, trilling to one another and to her alike. A long-eared jackrabbit hopped along at her side for a ways before scampering off to play.

Two wolves, a mated pair, welcomed her when she approached where they rested in the shade of some boulders. Tiny cubs curled against the female's side, and Terra cuddled each in turn, giggling when they licked her face. The male wolf rubbed against her softly, and she combed her fingers through his fur to pick out twigs and briars. "There you go." She kissed his forehead softly, marveling at how a beast that wild, that free, could be so welcoming to her.

Deeper in the woods she found a small herd of deer. A large stag with a mighty rack oversaw the many doe that walked at his side. Two tiny fawns teetered on legs that were too long for their bodies. With tiny bleats, they wobbled over to Terra and contentedly bumped against her.

The stag was a little intimidating when he got close for he was much bigger than Terra, and certainly carrying more muscle, but he acted as gentle as the fawns as he bumped his nose against her. She scratched his head around his antlers and smiled at the soft and fuzzy fur that covered them. She wouldn't have guessed his antlers would feel like that.

As twilight drew close, she was sitting under a thick fruit tree with a wildcat purring on her lap. Well, with its head on her lap. The beast was much bigger than an average housecat. The dove flew down from out of nowhere and landed without fear on the beast's back. The cat opened one eye, sighed, and closed it again. Terra just smiled. "Hello."

The dove dropped into her hand the golden key he carried. "There is a place waiting for you."

She gently nudged the wildcat and it reluctantly wandered off. With a large yawn, she got to her feet to follow the dove. "These are called the Oak Woods, but more than oak grows here."

"It used to be all oak trees," the dove explained, "but seeds were carried in by birds and a few other species have sprouted. In the beginning, when the woods were first formed, there were only two trees, and only one was an oak."

"Hmm." Interested but sensing he wouldn't tell more, she instead asked, "I don't suppose I can keep one of these little homes? I love the woods, but a place to actually live would be wonderful."

"They have a purpose, and when they serve it, they will be gone."

"Oh." A little disappointed, but not entirely surprised, she used the key on a lock in a large fir tree. She went down the stairs revealed and found another small room. This one, much to her delight, had one feature that the other two hadn't: it had a bathtub behind an elaborate screen. And not just any bathtub, but one full of steaming hot water. On a chair beside it sat a dish with a bar of soap, a couple fluffy-looking towels, a brush, and a bucket to rinse her hair with. "Is . . . can I use that?" she asked in a hushed voice.

"It is there solely for you."

She didn't need to be told twice. She stripped off all of her clothes and draped them over a chair. She unbraided her hair so that it fell to her hips in a curtain of silvery-brown color. It didn't quite sway with her steps for it was quite dirty, but she had every intention of fixing that as well.

She gingerly got into the tub and found it to be the perfect temperature and depth. She sank in to her chin with a sigh of near bliss. The hot water felt wonderful on her sore muscles and aching feet.

She only lingered a little while. She didn't want the water to go cold, and she didn't know when Nikolas would arrive. She grabbed up the soap and fiercely scrubbed herself clean. It felt as if she removed several layers of dirt. She treated her hair to the same thing, scrubbing it with soap twice before it actually felt clean again. She used the bucket to rinse off the soap and then wrapped herself in the towels to get out.

To her immense chagrin, when she went to grab her clothes to wash them, she discovered they had disappeared. The dove was also nowhere in sight. "You *sneak*," she muttered under her breath.

She reluctantly eyed the trunk sitting to one side. Unless she wanted to go naked for the rest of time, she had no choice but to dig into the fine materials. She hastily dried her hair enough that it didn't drip and then opened the trunk.

She really had no idea if she had any taste since everything looked beautiful to her. She finally settled on a shimmering pale green dress that was so soft and delicate that she felt clumsy just handling it. There was a matching bra and panties to go with it, for which she was grateful since that fink dove had taken *all* of her clothes, but everything was *silk*.

She felt beyond decadent as she pulled the clothes on, but the dress fit so perfectly that she just couldn't bring herself to take it back off and look for something plainer. It fit snug to her chest and waist, and flared out to a fuller skirt as it went to brush the floor. It laced up the front, thankfully, and she got into it easily enough. The sleeves went to her wrists where they flared into a bell shape. Around the edge of the sleeves and the skirt went dark green embroidery of leaves.

There were slippers to match, but she left them off. Her feet felt too happy to confine right then. Instead, she sat down in front of the fire in the stove and began to brush her hair. The concept seemed completely foreign to her, and she had to struggle with several tangles before they let go. She had almost never brushed her hair before; the few times she had been able to wash it, she had braided it immediately after. Perhaps that was why her hair had so many waves; she couldn't recall having wavy hair as a child.

She heard a step on the stairs and looked up with a smile as Nikolas walked in. He stopped sharply as he saw her, and his eyes widened. Nervously, she twisted a lock of hair around her finger. "Do I . . . Do I look okay? I wasn't going to . . . but the dove . . . I mean, he said I could . . ."

"Stop." He took a deep breath for control and came the rest of the way down the stairs. "I just didn't believe my eyes at first." He knelt beside her and caught a handful of her hair. It was as soft as the silk of her dress, resilient, and thick. "You're beautiful, Terra," he said huskily. "You look like a princess."

"Really?" She looked down shyly. "I was hoping you'd like it. I don't know anything about clothes, but I thought that you might like green because you love the woods." And his eyes were green as an oak's leaves, but she kept that to herself, not sure if the observation would embarrass him. Truly, green was becoming her favorite color too. She loved his eyes.

"I like green," he said agreeably, "but I like it when it is the same color as your eyes. Eyes as green as a willow's leaves." He used his grip on her hair to tug her up for a tender kiss. "I missed you," he murmured against her lips.

"I missed you." She buried her face against his shoulder as he held her.

"Would you . . ." He took a deep breath. "Would you be happy here, Terra? Would you be happy with me even if I was a simple woodsman who could not be with you during the day?"

"I could be happy anywhere if I was with you. I just wish I could keep one of these houses! I want so much to have a home to live in. I've never had one. And I could try to learn to cook, so I can take care of you the way you took care of me." She searched his eyes, her breath held. "Why?"

"Will you . . . Can you . . ." He blew out a breath. "Damn it. I've used some of the smoothest lines in the world and I can't even ask the woman I love if she would be my wife."

Her smile lit not just her face but also the entire room. "Yes."

His lips slowly curved. "I didn't actually ask."

"The answer is still yes." She laughed as he shot to his feet with her in his arms, but the laughter died shortly as he kissed her wildly, as if the dam on his emotions had broken free. He didn't kiss her; he *consumed* her. A kiss such as that would have frightened her even the day before. All it did now was bring her desire for him wildly to life. When he finally released her, all she could say breathlessly was, "Nik."

"If I make love to you," he warned huskily, "then it is our wedding night. Ceremony or no, you will be mine and I will be yours. Do you want that, Terra?"

Her lips trembled. "I've never belonged to anyone. No one belonged to me." She wrapped her arms around his neck. "I love you, Nik. I want nothing more than to be with you. Don't let me go."

With a shuddering breath, he carried her over to the bed and gently put her down on the side. He knelt in front of her and searched her eyes for any sign of nerves. All he saw was a shimmering, welcoming glow. Her hands softly framed his face before skimming back into his hair.

He eased onto the bed beside her and began to slowly unlace the dress. His hands looked large and powerful against her delicate build, but there was such a lack of fear inside her that his own nerves faded. He was so afraid of hurting her! But she was strong. Much stronger than even he had guessed. She bent. She did not break. And she came back more resilient than before.

As he tugged the dress slowly up her body, she began to unlace the ties at the collar of his tunic. She released him so that the dress could be tugged off and promptly went back to working on his tunic when it was gone. With his help, the tunic got removed as well.

In wonder, she spread her hands slowly across his chest. He was beautiful. As powerful as an oak, but as gentle as a spring breeze. The muscles of his body looked starkly defined, a reminder of his strength, but the sight of them only made heat gather low in her body. Such a magnificent creature wanted her. She would not question her luck.

"Look at you," he breathed softly. His hands brushed down the outside of her breasts and she caught a breath. "So lovely." He tugged the straps of the bra down until her breasts came free of the cups. The nipples were tight and flushed, begging for his touch. Unable to resist, he bent his head and took one in his mouth gently. Her body jerked in shock and a soft moan rippled from her lips as he sucked softly. She tasted like nothing he had ever known. He couldn't get enough.

Every tug of his mouth tugged deeper. She caught his hair and held him closer, her body arching instinctively in a plea for more. The depth of the pleasure his touch wrought was faintly astonishing. Yet, at the same time, each caress made her want more. She teetered back and forth between hunger and delight until she couldn't breathe or think. "Nik." It was almost a sob.

Her bra disappeared over the side of the bed. He lifted her onto his lap for a ravenous kiss, his hands buried in her hair to keep her possessively close. Her fingers dug into shoulders desperately as she countered his kiss, just as hungry, just as needy. When he didn't deepen the kiss fast enough to suit her, she nipped at his lip warningly. A low masculine laugh rumbled in his chest as he gave her what she wanted, his mouth plundering every secret from hers.

When he released her, she gulped in air that was hot and humid in a way that in no way resembled the farm. It burned her deep inside, and his scent seemed seared into her lungs. She found herself flat on her back with him looming over her, and there was still no fear. Her fingers trembled with need as she ran them over every inch of his body that she could reach. She couldn't feel enough fast enough.

He stripped away her panties and raked his gaze over her swiftly. She was long and graceful with all her height carried in her legs. Her waist was trim, her breasts delicate rather than lush. The silvery-brown curls between her legs served as a delicious lure that sent his fingers trailing slowly down her body.

As his fingers scraped across her stomach, her muscles quivered and tightened. He began to make his way across her skin with his lips and dropped hot little kisses over every inch. The deceptively fragile line of her ribcage, the intriguing little dip near her bellybutton. There was nothing he didn't savor.

Her legs shifted restlessly as he nuzzled the curls that had intrigued him. Then, before he could ask, her legs parted to let him closer. A shudder ripped through his body as every muscle tightened to the point of pain. He skimmed a finger across her most sensitive flesh and listened to her breath break. He kissed her, tasted her, and savored her cries. She was hot and wet, more than ready for him, but she was small enough that he couldn't stop his fear that he would hurt her.

"Nik." The desperate plea in her voice cracked his control. "Please." She didn't know what she asked for, but knew only he could give it to her. Her entire body was aching and tight, straining wildly for an end to the ceaseless pleasure. It was so sharp that it nearly became pain. "Nik!" It was a cry as he kissed her again.

He slowly made his way back up her body until he could take her mouth again. The kiss went wild and carnal, her taste branding them both. She fiercely wrapped her arms around his neck when he started to release her. "No!"

"I'm not leaving you." He stripped off the rest of his clothes as fast as he could. Her green eyes looked dazed with desire, her lips red and swollen. A fine tremor ran through her entire body, and her lovely breasts lifted with her every breath. He sank into her arms again with a tortured sound of need. "I love you." He caught her arms and drew them up around his neck. "Hold me, Terra."

Her arms tightened fiercely. Without asking, as if somehow knowing, she curled her legs around his hips. She held onto him tightly with all her strength. She would never let him go!

Her lips parted on a swift breath as she felt his hard flesh slowly pushing into her body. There was only a brief moment of panic. Just as her body started to tense, she looked into his eyes and saw the wellspring of his emotions. It stole all her fears as surely as it had stolen her heart. She turned her face up for his kiss, telling him without words that she wanted him.

He surged into her completely, and her startled cry was muffled by his lips. He stayed fiercely still, his body shaking. "Are you alright?" Her hips twisted against him and it was enough. He began to thrust in and out slowly at first, giving her time to adjust, but as she began to arch into every motion, his control collapsed entirely. He took her again and again, each time a little deeper, a little harder.

She buried her face against his neck to stifle her cries as the tension broke free and wild ecstasy went cascading through her body. It felt as if she had somehow imploded into a million pieces, never to be whole again without him. He buried his face in her hair as he drove into her one last time and his release claimed him as surely as he had claimed her. It was nothing he had ever experienced before. Nothing he had imagined might exist.

He let himself fall to the bed beside her, and he found a smile when she automatically tightened her leg over his hip to keep them joined. He didn't want to leave her either. He sighed long and deep as he tugged her even closer. "Still want that nightgown?"

The rough quality to his voice seemed to stroke over her body. "S'okay. I think I'll just stay here a while." She smoothed her hand softly across his chest. Neither his heartbeat nor hers had steadied yet, but she loved it. The lingering aches in her body were of a kind that she had no desire to soak out in a tub. "Are you going to touch me again?"

His lips curved. "Let me catch my breath first. You wore me out." He trailed his fingers down her arm slowly. He caught her hand and brought her fingers to his lips. The calluses on her fingers marked of her hard life, and they created pure magic on his body. When she eventually discovered her own power as a lover and tried to have him at her mercy, he would be in trouble. He couldn't wait.

Softly, she asked, "What do you do during the day, Nik?"

He hesitated. "Watch over the woods."

She tilted her head back and looked up at him. "The dove told me that there were once only two trees in these woods. Do you know the story?"

"Mm. Do you want to hear it?" When she nodded, he tugged her closer. "Many centuries ago, most of Mirage was flat and without trees. Seeds fell from the Earth, or so they say, and found themselves to be in exceptionally fertile land. Soon trees grew everywhere. In this area, only two seeds fell. One was a willow seed, the other an oak.

"In this rich land, the two seeds grew with minds and wills. The willow was delicate, tossed about in every wind. The oak grew closer and closer, wishing to protect his beautiful companion. Under the protective shade of the oak's branches, the willow stayed safe from the wind and grew tall and beautiful. As the two trees continued to age, they grew closer and closer until they entwined. When you looked into the branches, you could not tell which was which save for the shape and leaf.

"Other oak trees began to grow around the two, drawn to protect their lord and lady. Soon everyone knew of the mysterious entwined trees, and people came from all over to look and wonder. One who came was a huntsman. He looked upon the trees with disgust. Grown as they were, they overtook the land where he wished to build a home. And so he took an axe and cut them down."

She made a sound of pain, and his arms tightened protectively. "The spirits of the two trees were released, and the sound of the willow's weeping melted the huntsman's cold heart. He could only look with horror at what he had done. But it was too late. The deed had been done. Some say he still lives somewhere in these woods, lamenting what he had so carelessly destroyed."

Her breath hitched on a little sob. Somehow she couldn't believe it was nothing but a story. It cut her far too deep inside. *It was as if she had been there.* "What happened to the willow and oak?"

"No one knows. They say their spirits wander the world, always seeking one another, never able to share the sun again as long as the curse lives." He framed her face with his hands and began to tenderly kiss away her tears. "Shh. I did not tell you to make you cry." When it seemed the tears would not fade, he turned and tucked her underneath him once more. "I'll make you forget," he said huskily.

But even in his loving embrace, she could not entirely forget the tale. It felt important somehow. She was no fool. Her lover called her a willow. She could not see him during the day. She often associated him with oaks. If there was a curse on them, then she was going to break it. He had saved her, and now she needed to save him.

It was that simple.

CHAPTER FIVE

Terra awoke sharply the next morning as she realized she was alone and outside. She sat up quickly and clutched tighter the blanket that had been wrapped around her. Folded on a fallen log close by sat her discarded clothing of the night before, and the slippers had been placed lightly on top.

It belatedly dawned on her that the tree she slept under had its branches curved quite deliberately to form a shelter around her. She looked up swiftly and recognized it as the smaller oak tree she had seen that very first day when she had been running for her life. It stood only a foot or so taller than she did, but its presence just bespoke regality.

Tears welled in her eyes and slid soundlessly down her cheeks as she got to her feet. She wrapped her arms around as much of the trunk as she could and pressed her face to the surprisingly soft bark. "I still love you," she whispered fiercely. "I will never stop loving you, my oaken lover."

The dove suddenly flew down and landed delicately on a branch. "Terra?"

With a yelp, she clutched her blanket tighter. "I'm naked!"

Politely, yet chuckling, he turned his back to let her scramble into her clothing. "Are you decent?" he asked after a few moments.

"Yes, thank you."

He turned around and flew down to land beside where she sat on the log. She was looking at the slippers a bit helplessly, but as much as he wanted to help, he couldn't. He didn't have hands. He pointed a wing at one shoe and then at the proper foot. "Left."

She blushed. "Thank you." She pulled them on gingerly but found them to be surprisingly comfortable. It would be much nicer walking in them than barefooted. She straightened up and ran a hand through her tangled hair. Unbound, it showed the effects of her husband's hands having been in it. "What do I do?" she asked achingly. "He is the oak, and I am the willow. Am I right?"

"You are right," he agreed simply. "The huntsman did not just curse himself; he cursed the entire woods. The minute Nikolas entered the woods, he was forced to retake the oak form during the day. If he leaves the woods before the curse is lifted, the following dawn will find him becoming an oak forever. But you . . . you could break the curse. Only you could for only you have the gentleness inside to forgive even the worst of beasts. That is why all creatures are drawn to you. Near you, there is always peace."

Her eyes lingering on the form of her oak lover longingly. Even like this, he seemed beautiful to her. "What must I do?"

"Sign this." The dove glowed, and a scroll and quill appeared. "We good spirits do things formally around here," he apologized. "And this will give me the authority to tell you *exactly* what needs to be done. You have to do precisely what I tell you!"

A little smile touched her lips as she signed the bottom of the scroll. "I spent my life doing what people told me. I doubt three days has made me forget. If I ever found myself in a position of telling someone *else* what to do, I wouldn't know how to handle it."

He picked up the scroll with his beak and it disappeared. "You would be better at it than most for you are kind. Now then." He hopped onto her lap and ruffled his feathers. "I will lead you to where the huntsman still lives. You must go into his home and walk past him without a word. Do not listen to him! In the room beyond him, you must light only a single candle. With that candle, search for two rings. One will be made of oak wood, the other of willow."

Her brows shot up. "He . . . he made rings from the trees he cut down?"

"He made *wedding* rings," the dove confirmed softly, "for he had seen too late the beauty of the union he had destroyed. The oak ring will fit you; put it on. The willow ring needs to be tied to a ribbon on your bodice. Once you have done those things, go back to the huntsman. You must forgive him, Terra, even though he has cursed the one you love. Even though he may seem to be a cold and cruel creature."

She took a deep breath. "I will do it. I have to. I can't let Nik down. I have to save him as he saved me."

"Good girl." He flew up into the air. "Follow me."

She got to her feet and followed quickly. With her new slippers, she found it much easier to cross the land of the woods. The only downside was that the skirt made it a little more difficult to navigate over and under assorted obstacles. Yet, she was not alone in her journey. When she reached a tall boulder she needed to climb over, a great bear came forward and let her climb onto his back to reach high enough to pull herself up.

When she hit a river that looked too deep to cross safely, beavers swam down the waters pushing a raft made of twigs and logs. They ferried her to the other side without mishap. When she found her sleeve caught by a sticky briar, an eagle flew down and used its sharp beak to free her without tearing away her gown.

It seemed to be hours that she followed the dove. She didn't argue once. He clearly knew where he led her. And soon enough she found her answer as to their destination. He stopped flying and landed on a tree. "There," he said softly.

She stepped around the tree and found herself looking into a small clearing. Trees had been cut away, their stumps left to rot and blacken in the sun. In the place where the willow and oak had stood, there was nothing but broken ground that had never grown back. A hut stood only feet away, beaten and weathered and grayed from age. Some of the panels of wood had rotted and sagged. A pallor hung over the entire place. No smoke curled from the chimney. No light shined from within the filthy windows.

Her hands curled into fists. She braced her shoulders and walked determinedly toward the hut, her heart beating madly inside her chest. She could barely breathe. Her mouth was dry and her throat was tight.

Only the lightest of pushes caused the door to fall open. She stepped into the opening and barely kept back a flinch. The interior looked just as bad as the exterior. Holes in the floor caused the wood to sag. Cobwebs hung in every corner. Dust coated all surfaces. Molded food sat abandoned on a table.

And there, sitting in a rickety chair before a dead hearth, was an old man. He looked shriveled and worn, as battered as his home. His eyes had sunk far into his head, and wrinkles within his wrinkles pulled down his entire face. He was gaunt and pale, his hands gnarled where they gripped the arms of his chair. His clothes resembled something a huntsman might have worn, but they were dirty and torn. The dust on the floor around the chair seemed to say he had not moved from that spot in years.

As she stepped into the home, the floor creaked. Eyes that were a little mad, a lot miserable, and greatly furious fell upon her. "Get out." The voice rasped like dry leaves.

She didn't say a word as she edged across the floor and tried to avoid the rotted places. The thump of his foot on the ground made her flinch but she did not falter.

"Worthless!" the voice spat. "Useless! Unwanted little cow! Who would care to have you around? *Slave*. You are nothing but a servant without a master! No one would want you!"

The words grew ever viler the closer she got to the broken door at the back of the room. She flinched at every syllable, but she did not stop. She did not say a word. Years of cruelty at the hands of Mr. Arcwood and Vin had taught her that silence was the only weapon that worked. She had no need to defend herself.

Her hands shook but she managed to open the door and slip into the room. It was pitch black as she fumbled for a table. Something fell over and broke but she ignored it. At long last, her fingers closed around a candle and a match. She lit the candle and a small area became illuminated. She put the candle in a holder on the table and looked around. The room appeared to be barely more than a closet, and the shelves held boxes upon boxes of junk. Objects of all kinds sat on the floor and crowded a tiny table.

After a few moments of blind fumbling where the candle's light did not reach, she finally found a handcrafted box. She slowly opened the lid. There, resting on a bed of dried leaves, were two wooden rings. One ring was made of wood the same dark brown as Nikolas' hair. The other was a wood of silvery-brown, just like hers.

She picked up the oak ring and slid it over her finger. It fit perfectly. The lighter ring was also bigger, and she knew it would fit Nikolas. She tied it to the ribbon on her dress and then blew out the candle. Shoulders squared, she walked out of the room.

The old man had fallen silent. He neither looked at nor spoke to her as she walked softly toward him. She knelt beside him and looked up into his face. She could not hate him. Sadness welled inside her as she gently covered his hand with hers. "It's okay," she said softly. "I forgive you. How could you know? You've paid, huntsman. You've paid a thousand times over. Only you cannot forgive yourself."

Tears slowly gathered in the old man's faded eyes. They rolled down his wrinkled face as it slowly crumpled. "Willow." His voice broke as he began to sob softly. "How can you forgive me?"

"I never hated you, huntsman. *We* never hated you. You hated yourself. I forgive you. Please. Let go. You do not have to stay here any longer."

A long sigh unraveled from the huntsman's lips. "Thank you, willow." He began to dissolve into shimmers of light. "At last I can rest . . ."

Even as he disappeared, the hut disappeared as well. In moments, she found herself alone, kneeling in the middle of the clearing. Grass already began to grow in where only an hour before it couldn't. Softly, she asked, "Did I . . .?"

"You did," the dove confirmed just as softly as he flew down near her. "The curse is broken."

She immediately turned and ran back the way she had come. She wanted to find Nikolas. She had to find him! If the curse was broken, then surely he would be a man again. She would be able to see him in the sun, to wake in his arms in the morning.

Search as she might, she could not find him. She could not even find the oak tree he had become. Disheartened, she took shelter under another tree entirely. The dove had not arrived. She knew there would be no more little houses under trees. They had, as the dove had said, served their purpose.

Somehow she managed to fall asleep. It was not an entirely restful sleep. Her dreams were tormented by haunting images of oak trees dancing just beyond her reach. She wanted Nikolas. She wanted to be with him so terribly. Had they come that far only to still never be together?

The sunlight on her face woke her in the morning. Sore and stiff from sleeping on the ground, she carefully sat up. Her beautiful clothes were very dirty now, and so was she. Thankfully, when she looked around, she discovered the unexpected yet familiar shape of the trunk that had held her clothes. She instinctively checked for the willow ring and found it had disappeared from her ribbons. "What?"

The dove flew down and landed on the top of the trunk. "Good morning, Terra."

"Good morning," she said softly. Her gaze lowered. "I did not find him, dove. I looked for him, but could not find him."

"Naturally not. He is waiting for you elsewhere. I can lead you to him." He smiled when she looked up swiftly in surprise. "But first, you cannot go back to him looking like this! Come with me. There is a place to bathe not far from here."

She followed him eagerly, caring not so much for the bath as for the hope that soon she would be with her husband. Her *husband*. It was a marvelous thought that someone would belong to her in such a way, and she would belong to him.

The place she was led to turned out to be a small hot spring that looked barely bigger than a tub itself. Soap and towels waited. The dove flew off to give her privacy, and she wasted no time in taking off her dirty clothes and getting into the water. She scrubbed herself clean, thoroughly washed her hair, and dried off as much as she could. Her hair was so thick that it would take an hour, at least, to fully dry without help from a fireplace.

By the time she finished, her dirty clothes had disappeared. In their place came a new gown of pale silver with the same leaf pattern around the sleeves and skirt. It much resembled her last dress, but it had a much fuller skirt, nearly a full bell, like a ball gown. As she tightened all the laces, she startled herself to see her own reflection. She looked like a princess!

Slippers also waited, and she pulled them on her feet. She got them backwards and quickly had to switch them. Maybe wherever she and Nikolas made their home would be the kind of place she could mostly go barefoot. She had a feeling she and shoes might never fully get along.

"Decent?" the dove called.

"Yes, thank you."

He flew down and dropped the cloak he carried. As it landed in her arms, he offered, "Put it on. It will keep you warm and clean."

She almost didn't want to accept the gift. The cloak was real velvet! But, since the dove didn't seem inclined to leave until she did as told, she pulled the cloak on and fastened it securely. It felt very warm, and very comfortable. "Lead the way."

He did so unwaveringly. As the first few hours passed, she began to realize the trees were growing thinner. The sounds of a city had started to grow louder. "Are we leaving the woods?" she asked.

"We are. Nikolas waits in the city."

"Oh." Well, that made some sense. He had said that he had not intended to live in the woods. Perhaps only the curse had kept him there. If he wasn't an actual woodsman, then what was he?

The woods stopped where a road began. The city started not even a hundred yards away. Trumpets blared and the people cheered and laughed loudly. Flowers and banners hung from every rooftop and decorated every corner that she could see. Belatedly, it dawned on her. "That's right, the king was returning after a hiatus." She frowned at the dove. "Are you sure we should go into the city? It must be packed!"

"You will find him." He landed on a fencepost.

"You're leaving me?"

"You do not need me any longer. Goodbye, Terra."

"Goodbye," she said softly as he flew off. With nothing else she could do, she pulled the hood of her cloak over her hair and made her way down the road toward the city. It was amazingly bright and cheerful, a whirl of light and color to a girl who had lived her entire life on farms. She was enchanted with the shops and fascinated by the people who milled the streets. She missed the quiet of the woods, but the city seemed amazingly beautiful in its own way. It was, in fact, liberally covered in trees itself.

"The procession is coming!" someone shouted from a rooftop.

She shortly got crushed in the crowd as people gathered on the sidewalks to wave and cheer. She was both warmed and bemused by the people's obvious love for their king. She had been listening to conversations, and apparently he was a fairly new king. He had inherited the throne only a few years before when his father had died. His sabbatical had been one to mature himself into a better leader.

As the procession began to approach, she couldn't see anything. The crowds had gotten really thick, and most people were taller than she was. She pushed her way through to the front, but someone unintentionally shoved her rather hard and sent her stumbling into the street. The entire procession came to a halt before they ran her over.

Terrified, she covered her face with her hands as she heard someone dismount their horse and approach. She would get into so much trouble! She squeezed her eyes shut as her hood got tugged off her hair. "I'm so sorry!" she blurted.

A tender hand tangled into her hair with an achingly familiar touch. Her head jerked up and around, and she stopped breathing entirely as she beheld the man that knelt beside her in the clothing of a king.

It was Nikolas. *He* was the king.

The morning sun shone down on his hair and made his eyes glow softly with joy as he looked at her. She forgot entirely that there was a crowd watching. She carefully reached up to frame his face with her hands. He turned his head to press a kiss to her palm and then tugged her left hand to his lips. He softly kissed the ring she wore. "My willow."

Lips trembling, she whispered, "The willow ring."

He held up his hand, and the silvery ring resided where it belonged on his finger. It fit perfectly. "When I left to find myself," he murmured huskily, framing her face in his hands, "I never expected to find you as well." He slowly stood and pulled her to her feet as well. Belatedly remembering the crowd, he looked at all the faces of his people. The expressions ranged from surprise to confusion. "The woman before you," he said clearly, "is my wife. She is your new queen. Without her love, without her bravery, I would never have returned home."

The crowd began to cheer loudly, and Terra blushed brightly. "I can't be a queen!" she whispered strongly to him.

His lips curved slowly. "Of course you can. You married a king." He snatched her off her feet into his arms and kissed her with all the love in his heart. To see her in the sunlight, to feel her touch even in the middle of the day . . . He could ask for nothing else. "I love you!" he said fiercely against her lips.

Joy rose and blinded her. "Nik! I love you so much!" She gave a hiccupping little sob, threw her arms around his neck, and kissed him just as wildly as he had kissed her. She would never let him go again!

The cheers became whoops and catcalls as the people realized their king and new queen did not seem intent on ending the embrace anytime soon. "Get a room!" someone shouted over the laughter of the crowd.

Nikolas laughed as well and scooped Terra up off her feet. "If you insist!" He put her on the back of his horse and swung up behind her. He held the reigns with one hand and kept his other arm firmly around her waist. He didn't think he would ever be able to let go of her without fear for at least a few more years. Perhaps centuries. "Are you happy at last, my willow?"

"Very happy." She looked up at him. "But who was that dove, Nik? He was always there for me. He told me everything I needed to do. He claimed to be a good spirit but I don't . . . I don't think he was."

"That was the messenger of love," he told her softly. "The one who helps ensure that we all have a happy ending."

She sighed contentedly and snuggled closer. "Then I guess that's what we had better do."

EPILOGUE

Rhianna Taber was in her office studying a list of names when she felt as much as saw a soft glow coming from her desk. She slowly lowered the document in time to see a scroll tied with a golden ribbon appearing before her. The scent of peaches seemed to dance along her nose and dig velvet claws into her heart and soul.

She carefully unwound the scroll to read it. In classic Enforcers' fashion, the word 'Complete' was boldly marked across the front in red. Yet it was not a contract that had been issued from Enforcers. There was only one other being that could do something like that.

Her trembling fingers were well controlled as she wrote some notes at the bottom of the scroll. She slipped it into a folder and slowly closed it. It was too painful to think about. It was too painful to hope.

Eric Mason had been watching her the entire time, and he quietly shut the connecting office door before turning to look at the other three people behind him. Taylor Vincent stood staring at his hands in a way that did not bode well. "Burning?" Eric asked quietly.

Taylor took a long breath. "I haven't felt this in a long time. There's something dangerous out there, Riku. And it's coming directly for Rhi."

A little shiver roughened Gwyn Vincent's skin, and she turned into his arms. "It's somehow familiar," she said softly, "the dark cloud hovering around her. The scales are *balanced*. I can't understand it."

Even Eric had never known everything about his oldest friend and partner. He tugged his wife, Rayna, into his arms and drew what little comfort he could from her. Whatever was coming for Rhianna would have to go through the four of them first. She was not alone.

The Enforcers protected their own.

Status: File Complete

Analysis: Even the hardest of hearts will soften when faced with an oak's dedication and willow's tears.

Folder One

ISABELLE & GABRIELLE

CHAPTER ONE

(Two years ago)

"Why do we have to have bodyguards?" Isabelle Lucino muttered at her elder brother as they walked down the hall to their father's office. At nineteen, she was four years younger than her brother's age of twenty-three. She was also a whole foot shorter. She blamed their mother's genes; she had been short too.

Rafael sighed deeply. "I am not happy about it either, Bella," he admitted, "but Papa was insistent that it is needed. Do you remember the embezzlement sting that he and I helped the police set up? It worked, but the man we caught is certifiably nuts. He made some rather serious threats against us."

"Have the cops caught him?" She fought a chill.

"He got away before they could." He opened the door to their father's office and walked inside. "We have our wardens, do we?"

Antonio Lucino smiled wryly. "Rafe, I would not do this if it was not necessary. You should have heard your grandfather when I told him. I think he wanted to hire hitmen. I managed to talk him out of it, but if you see any mushroom shaped clouds in the general direction of Italy, hide under the table."

"Have I mentioned that I am glad we are in NYC and not Rome?" Isabelle sat down on the edge of her father's desk. "When do we meet the poor saps who have to follow us everywhere?"

He lifted a brow. "Right now."

Rafael glanced at the door and winced good-naturedly as he saw the two males standing there. One was a young man who couldn't be much older than himself, and the other looked to be in his late twenties. "My apologies."

The younger male grinned. He had an interestingly androgynous face, lively baby blue eyes, and unruly short blond hair. He appeared tall and slender but stood with a casual confidence that Rafael most often saw in exceptionally talented street fighters and martial artists. "I would resent things too, if I was in your shoes," the bodyguard said dryly.

Even his voice seemed an interesting blend of male and female, as if nature simply hadn't been able to decide which to give him. Rafael liked him instantly. "My shoes would not fit you."

"And it's a good thing. My feet complain when inside anything other than sneakers or boots." He gave a slightly cocky salute but his smile looked genuine. "Tori Li."

"Rafael Lucino." He gestured to his sister. "Isabelle."

Isabelle eyed the taller male beside Tori warily. He stood the same height as Rafael, and was roughly the same size, so he would easily tower over her. He was also uncomfortably handsome with dark red hair and chocolate colored eyes. Morosely, she sighed mentally. She could all but see her hormones jumping up and singing hosannas in Italian. They would make things so much more troublesome. "Hello." It was all she offered.

"Hi." His voice sounded calm and amused, and very masculine. The way he stood beside Tori made them into a study in opposites. "My name is Alexander LaGuardia. Everyone calls me Alex."

"Your friends do at least," Tori murmured. "Have you heard what your enemies call you?"

"It's no worse than what *you* call me."

Antonio just smiled. "Alex, you will be in charge of Isabelle's safety. Tori, you will be in charge of Rafael's."

"What on Earth made you decide *that*?" Isabelle demanded. She pointed at Tori. "He is shorter than Rafe!"

Rafael stepped closer to Tori and held a hand out from the top of his head to over the top of the shorter male's. "It is by only half a foot or so. Besides, it is not your size but how you use it. He looks as if he knows what he is doing, and an easily underestimated bodyguard works for me." He eyed Alex. "Yours looks like he eats nails for lunch."

"As a matter of fact," Antonio offered, trying not to smile, "part of the application process included a personality quiz. Not only were Alex and Tori the ones with the highest qualifications, they also had the best matches to your personalities."

"A personality quiz?" Rafael asked warily. "They are our bodyguards, not our dates."

"Very true, but if I want peace in my household, I want to be sure you will get along with each other." Antonio lifted his brows. "Is that understood?"

Isabelle sighed. "*Sì*, Papa."

"Yes, sir." Rafael offered a hand to Tori. "I will try not to make your life too hard."

"That's okay." He shook his hand with a smile. "I need to earn my pay."

Alex walked closer to Isabelle and held out his hand. When she reluctantly took it, he bowed gracefully. "Don't worry," he said sympathetically. "It shouldn't be too long to endure. As soon as the threat is gone, I'll be out of your hair."

"Are you sure we cannot let *Nonno* hire hitmen?" Isabelle muttered at her father. He just laughed, and she withheld another sigh. Dealing with a bodyguard would be bad enough. Dealing with one she was attracted to would be worse. Their personalities matched? What a joke. The sooner things ended, the better.

(Present)

"I was just talking to your *nonno* on the phone," Antonio said wryly from the head of the table. "He wants great-grandbabies."

As one, Isabelle and Rafael groaned and dropped their heads onto the dining room table. Antonio didn't blame them in the slightest.

It was a beautiful Saturday morning in October. The Lucino household was in full swing as usual. Though a weekend, there were fifty million things to be done. Isabelle had a fitting for her wedding dress. Rafael had a luncheon with clients. Antonio had to go in to the office to put out the fires that had cropped up over his day off. Both he and his son were in charge of the family advertising business, Just In Time, Inc., and though they had tried to coax Isabelle into coming on board as well, she had declined. She had no head for art of any kind.

"Who was he aiming his ire at this time?" Rafael asked dryly.

"Well, certainly not Bella since she is engaged, so presumably he meant you, my boy." Antonio grinned when his son groaned anew. "He married your grandmother when he was nineteen. He assumes things are still the same these days. I tried to explain, but you know he never listens to me."

"Does *Nonno* know that Isabelle probably will not be giving him grandbabies either?" Rafael asked dryly. "It is just a business marriage." One that he hoped would eventually be a marriage of love as well, but he kept his thoughts to himself. His sister acted a bit touchy on the subject of her pending nuptials.

"Do I look mad?" his father asked politely. "He does not even believe in business marriages." He cleared his throat and then said passionately, "It is about love, 'Tonio! Love is what is great in this world! Passion drives people and gives your poor father his *bambini* to hold and cherish! I married your mother for love, and we have stayed together more than fifty years!"

Isabelle dissolved into giggles. "You sound just like him!"

He laughed. "After fifty years, I would hope I could make my impressions credible." He glanced over as the door opened, and he smiled instantly. "Ah, there you are. We were waiting to eat until you got here."

"Hey, Tori." Rafael grinned as he saw his friend walking over to sit beside him. Tori had been his bodyguard for two years now. They were the same age, and Tori was slightly smaller, but Rafael had seen him in action. He knew he could be no safer with anyone else. "Did you oversleep again?"

Tori snorted softly. "That would be Alex's shtick. I was just sneaking in an early workout." He took his seat beside Rafael. "Alex is the over sleeper."

Alex just lifted a brow as he sat beside Isabelle. He was ten years her elder, thirty-one to her twenty-one, and after two years, there was nothing he didn't know about her. Because of it, he said dryly, "I was just testing to see if Isabelle's temper would flare, and she'd come track me down. You keep swearing she has a temper and I've yet to see it."

Her elbow landed sharply in his side. "Be glad," she countered haughtily. "My temper is a force to be reckoned with."

"You're Italian," Tori noted. "It's a force of *nature*."

Servants came in with breakfast and began to serve dishes. All wore smiles. The Lucinos did everything loud and passionately. It was one of the reasons it could be so much fun to work for them. The other was the fact that *Signor* Antonio always gave them holidays off with generous bonuses. Even just working for the Lucinos made you part of the family.

After breakfast, Isabelle escaped the table as fast as humanly possible. She hurried upstairs to her room, threw herself onto her bed, and screamed as loud as she could into her pillow. If people didn't stop talking about her marriage, she would *kill* someone! She liked Roberto, but he was as much a brother to her as Rafael. She didn't want to marry either of them!

When Alex stepped into the doorway, he felt entirely unsurprised with the scene. He walked with surprising silence over to the bed and sat on the side. Her ashy brown hair was coming out of its braid, and he resisted an urge to help it be even freer. "Would you like to talk?" he asked her. "I think we're friends too, aren't we?"

She lifted her head, her piercing blue eyes both resigned and reluctant all at once. She was, in his opinion, one of the most beautiful women in the city. It wasn't a passive pretty or a normal lovely. She had a fierce and striking beauty, a nearly sultry one in fact, that turned heads wherever she went. It was mark of her Lucino bloodline being enhanced by her mother's genes; the gene pool had been covetously guarded for centuries until Antonio had married a Caucasian woman and finally brought in some diversity.

"We are friends," she told him, "but you work for Papa. I know you spy on me for him!"

"To some extent," he admitted readily. "Your safety is, first and foremost, my primary duty. But if you told me something in private that had nothing to do with your safety, it would go nowhere else, Bella." He offered a hand to help her sit up. "Now, talk to me."

She sighed deeply as she sat beside him. To be honest, she liked talking to him. In fact, she liked far too much about her bodyguard for her own sanity. His height, his strength, his heart, and his handsome face that just could not be ignored. Two years had done nothing to make her attraction ebb for him; in fact, it had only gotten worse.

The curious thing was that he didn't even technically look that handsome. She had never been able to put her finger on it. He had red hair and chocolate brown eyes—he blamed the combination on a combustible Irish/Italian combined bloodline—and his features went together nicely, but he wasn't classically handsome like Roberto or strikingly beautiful like Rafael. He was just . . . Alex.

He was also as immovable as a mountain, stubborn as a mule, and gentle as a kitten. She had been beating her head against the brick wall of his over-protectiveness for two years. She would be doing it for many more at their current rate. The idiot who had caused all the trouble by making threats against the family still had yet to be caught.

"Is it Roberto?" Alex asked her.

"Yes and no. I mean, I like him. I would not hesitate to say that I love him. He has been Rafe's friend since they were five. But . . . I am not *in* love with him. I know that it is just a business marriage, and that he would not pressure me to become his—his lover, but . . ."

"You're not happy at not marrying for love," he noted shrewdly. "I think you have more of your grandfather in you than you thought."

"Is it too much to ask?" she muttered.

"No," he decided after a moment of thought. "Have you tried telling anyone?"

"Ha. You imply they would listen. They are too happy at making the merger between our companies. 'We have to keep up with that Dease family, Bella. Ever since those boys took over, they have taken some of our clients!' Feh!" She fell onto her back and covered her face with her hands. "I could scream!"

"You did. But I won't tell anyone I noticed."

"*Grazie.*" She groaned when she heard the doorbell ring. "Roberto."

"It's bad form for a bride to be so underwhelmed by her groom's presence."

"Do you have sisters?" she shot at him.

"Two."

"Contemplate marrying one of them and tell me how you would feel!" She reluctantly let him pull her to her feet and crossed her arms tightly as she followed him downstairs. Somehow she found a smile as she saw the dark-haired man waiting for her at the bottom of the steps. "*Ciao,* Roberto."

Roberto Viani smiled and leaned in to kiss her cheek. "*Ciao*, Bella." He tweaked her nose lightly. "Do not look so happy to see me. It is not good for my heart."

She smiled suddenly. "You are going to be miserable married to me. You know you are. You always hated me nagging you, and now I will have a *legal* reason to do it."

"Yes, but I will have a legal reason to tell you to shush." He hugged her with one arm and smiled at Alex. "Hello, Alex. How are you today?"

"Despite Tori poking fun at me and Isabelle accusing me of treason, quite well." He smiled as he said it. He liked Roberto despite the fact that he had an urge to rearrange his too handsome face. Ever since the marriage had been decided months before, Alex had been struggling to keep his jealousy hidden.

"When do we leave for the bridal shop?" Isabelle asked Roberto. "The fitting is in an hour, correct?"

He raked a hand through his black hair. "Isabelle . . . Hell. I told Rafe I did not want to be the one to tell you."

"Tell me what?" she demanded. "Now what are you going on about?"

"Isabelle." Antonio stepped into the doorway to his study. "I am sorry, *cara*, but you are being put on house arrest for an indefinite time." When her mouth fell open, he held up his hands. "I am afraid I do not have a choice. There was a very specific threat that arrived only minutes ago. I have called the police, but there is not much they can do right now."

"What threat?" Alex asked very softly. His hands lightly settled on Isabelle's shoulders protectively.

"'Don't let her out of your sight, old man,'" Rafael quoted from where he leaned in the doorway to the parlor. "'You never know what might happen to such a pretty girl.' The detective that we talked to said that we need to take it very seriously. It could be a prank, but it might not. We would rather find out later it was a prank and have overreacted than see something happen to you because we assumed wrong."

"Your dress is being delivered here for your fitting," Antonio said firmly. "And you do not step foot out of this house unless we are sure the immediate danger is past."

Isabelle's hands slowly curled into fists at her side but she withheld her temper as carefully as she could. Calling the men names and throwing things would be entirely undignified.

Satisfying, but undignified.

Less than ten miles from the Lucino villa, there was a small area of New York City known as the 3rd District.

You couldn't find it on a map. It didn't show up on Google. Even most of NYC was unsure if it really existed. Those who knew of it spoke of it in hushed whispers. The 3rd District, it was said, was the place of magic. No one who lived there was normal. No one who was born there was entirely human.

It was overseen by an immensely large corporation known as the Enforcers. The company had existed since before the Revolutionary War, and some suspicious historians felt sure it had been there in some form even before Columbus had landed on North America's shores. To be sure, Enforcers had a very great amount of power, both corporate and political. People suspected they might even have federal backing, but no one was gutsy enough to ask.

Among the many other things they did, Enforcers' main duty was to watch over the District. Every business in the District was either overseen or owned by Enforcers. In fact, quite a few immediately outside the District were as well, but not as many people knew about those.

The District was mostly commercial, and the people who worked there lived in homes attached to their place of work. The entire place looked like a slice of history; none of the exteriors had been modernized except for Enforcers Headquarters. The purely residential area always looked rundown, but it was deliberately done. No one wanted outsiders coming in. If you wanted to stay, you had always belonged.

It was that simple.

Gabrielle Wisteria was one of the ones who had been born there, but she would have belonged regardless. She was half water elf, and as such had some rather . . . interesting powers over water, and an interesting physical trait she strove to hide by deliberately keeping her ashy brown hair long in the front so that it covered her ears. They were *just* pointed enough to cause lifted brows if seen. She also wore headbands made by a weaver in the District if she was unsure her hair would stay where it belonged.

At twenty-one, she was a legal adult, which was to her advantage because she was also an orphan. She had lost her parents years before in the 9/11 attack on the World Trade Center. She would have become a ward of the state, but Rhianna Taber and Eric Mason from Enforcers had smoothly stepped in and made sure she stayed in the District.

Brie had paid them back in as many ways as she could. She had worked part-time as front desk support, and she still went in willingly if they needed an extra pair of hands for anything. Normally, however, she worked as a waitress at a small restaurant that catered to the tourists who came through the Gentle Brook Inn, the District's primary hub.

"Brie!"

She looked up from collecting empty plates and smiled as she saw her manager. As always, he looked far too rushed and far too preoccupied. "Yes?"

"Kitchen, now." He took the plates from her. "Please!"

She just shook her head and headed for the kitchen. She knew, even before walking in, what she would see. And sure enough, the sink was on strike again. Water spewed in the air and pooled on the floor. The cooks were trying desperately to protect their food by using umbrellas to block the spraying water.

"Oh geez." She walked over to the sink and put her hand over the fountain. "Grab that tub." When it was brought over, she held her hand over it. The water flowed obediently up one arm and then down the other into the tub. In moments, the spray had stopped. "When is he going to replace this thing?"

"When you quit," another waiter said with a grin. He was mopping up the mess on the floor. "If he doesn't have to worry about it, he won't."

"He should pay me extra. Sheesh." She fixed the broken spout on the faucet and turned the water back on. Everything worked fine. "I should have been a plumber. But nooo. I had to be an artist."

The sink incident set the tone for the entire morning. It was a very busy morning, and she found herself practically running to clear dishes from one table before serving people at another. It wouldn't have been so bad if she hadn't been doing the job for two years. She felt so *bored* with it. Nothing ever changed.

"Brie, help!" It was the manager again.

She sighed. Nothing *ever* changed.

Isabelle was in the parlor reading a book when Rafael walked in with a cheerful seamstress from Bridal Dreams, the wedding boutique, following him. "Here you go," he told her with a smile. "And ignore her if she snaps at you."

"I do not take out my anger on the innocent messenger," Isabelle muttered as her brother walked out whistling. She found a smile for the other woman. "I am sorry that you were called out here on such short notice."

"I get paid either way," she assured her. The tag on her blouse said her name was Demi. "Now let's get this gown on you and see if the last alterations are exactly what they need to be. You're so lucky," she added on a sigh. "I'd kill to wear a B. R. Matthews dress down the aisle."

"It just seemed made for me," Isabelle admitted as she locked the parlor door. She didn't trust her brother, or her fiancé, to not pull a prank on her. They could be fifteen, twenty-five, or fifty-five, and they would still be tormenting her.

The alterations were perfect. The dress gathered just right at the bust and fell in shimmering waves past her ankles. As much as she didn't want to marry Roberto, she couldn't help but love her wedding dress. She would have been happier to wear it to marry a man she was in love with, but she would take her enjoyment where she could find it. "The sleeve is a little snug," she noted.

"Let's see . . . ah." Demi used a pin to mark the spot. "The seam was taken in just a bit too far. We can get that fixed just fine. And since it'll be your last fitting, as long as you don't decide to go on a sundae binge, you shouldn't have any more problems."

Isabelle had to laugh at that. "I am allergic to chocolate, so there are no worries about sundaes for me." She got back out of the dress gingerly to avoid the pins and then pulled her regular clothes on once more. Once she had, she unlocked the parlor door. "I do not trust my brother," she explained.

Demi smiled. "I have one too. I know how you feel." She sighed as she gathered up her things. "Your fiancé is so handsome."

"Yes. He is." Isabelle crossed her arms as she followed Demi out into the foyer. Alex and Rafael were waiting for her, and she narrowed her eyes on them both. "What? Is some mysterious person going to attack me in the parlor?" She shot a look at Tori as he approached. "What, are you here to babysit me too?"

Tori backed up carefully, hands in the air. "Easy. I'm unarmed. I only just got here." He bumped into Roberto as the other male came up behind him. "Careful. She's out for blood."

Roberto walked over to Isabelle and caught her shoulders. "It will be over soon, Bella," he said soothingly.

Her blue eyes began to simmer with temper. "The threat or the wedding?"

"Both," he responded calmly. "You are just starting to get nervous."

"I am getting pissed off!" She knocked his hands off her shoulders fiercely. "I do not want to marry you!" she shouted. "I am tired of being told what to do! Did I have a say in any of this? No!" She backed up when he stepped toward her. "Just leave me alone!"

She darted around him and ran up the stairs two at a time. The men remained silent for several moments before, wryly, Tori said to Rafael, "I owe you ten bucks. You're right; she *does* have a temper worse than yours."

A sinking feeling suddenly filled Alex. He got to his feet and swiftly ran up the stairs toward Isabelle's room. The door was locked. "Bella, open the door!" he ordered. There was no response and he cursed softly.

"Let her be," Rafael suggested from the bottom of the stairs. "If she has not come out by dinner, I will get the key from Marco. He has the master key to all the rooms."

Alex sighed and headed back downstairs. There was no way to explain the feeling he had. It was just a feeling that told him Isabelle was getting herself into trouble somehow. He had become acquainted with the feeling; he just didn't understand how or why he had it. "I need a drink," he muttered.

Roberto laughed at him. "I think we all do. Isabelle certainly keeps things entertaining."

By the time Brie had her lunch break, she was at the point of tearing out her hair. "Ooh." She stalked down the street away from the restaurant before she gave in to the urge to kick her boss. "What I wouldn't give to just get a single day away from here!"

She swung around the corner blindly and walked head-on into someone coming toward her. Both of them fell onto the sidewalk. "I'm so sorry," she started to say, but the words disappeared as she stared in shock at the young woman she had run into. The other female stared at her with just as much astonishment.

From the length of their ashy brown hair to the tilt of their clear blue eyes, the two women were perfectly identical. "*Dio,*" Isabelle breathed, her eyes slowly widening further.

"Whatever you just said," Brie managed to say, "I probably concur. Holy shit." She got to her feet carefully and offered a hand to Isabelle. As the other woman stood, she felt her head spin. They were the same height, the same build . . . Anyone looking at them would easily think that they were identical twins.

"I think we might need to talk," Isabelle said. She gave a shaky laugh. "This is surreal!"

"Tell me! C'mon. My apartment is near here." She studied Isabelle, noted the quality of her clothes and the way she walked, and smiled wryly. "You're so not from around here." She pulled off her hat and plopped it on her companion's head. "Here. So people don't stare at us until we get there. I'm less noticeable than you are."

"Talk about a coincidence," Isabelle said softly.

Brie laughed out loud. "You're *definitely* not from around here. Let's go. I think this is going to be one heck of a tale, and I've absolutely got to hear it."

CHAPTER TWO

Brie lived in an apartment in a complex only blocks from where she worked. Isabelle had heard rumors of the rundown state of this portion of the District, but she was a little puzzled to see that it didn't look nearly as bad as it had been made out to be. Something felt oddly welcoming about the area.

The apartment itself was on the smaller side, and it had been filled with all manner of furniture and art. The warm tones in the color and wood both reminded Isabelle of her home with its distinctly Tuscan flavor. "This is wonderful," she told Brie.

"Thanks." Brie shrugged out of her jacket and tossed it casually over the back of a chair. "Grab a seat. Want a soda?"

"*Sì.* I mean, yes, thank you."

"Okay, what the heck is that you're speaking? Spanish?"

"Italian." Isabelle sat at the kitchen counter with a smile. "My name is Isabelle Lucino. I am usually called Bella."

"Gabrielle Wisteria, but Brie for short or I'll smack you." She smiled as she said it. She passed the soda to her companion and had to laugh. "This is so weird. It's like looking into a mirror! We even *sound* alike, except for your accent. But we're definitely not long lost twins or some such junk."

"Can you be sure?" Isabelle asked curiously. "I mean other than the obvious that my parents never divorced; my mother died a few years ago from pneumonia. And there was no reason for her or Papa to give up a child. We like big families."

"Well, that would be one reason. The other is your ears."

"My *ears*?"

Brie pulled off her headband and tugged her hair up and away. "Now don't go freaking out on me."

Isabelle stared in disbelief at the obviously pointed ears on her double. "*Dio*. You are not human?!"

"You make it sound like a bad thing." Brie grinned. "I'm half, thank you, and very proud of my water elf half." She took a sip of her soda. "My mom was the human. My dad was the elf. And my mom was Italian too, by the way. You're a halfsie with something else?"

"It certainly is not elf, I assure you. I know they say everyone has a double somewhere; there is no such thing as perfect genetic uniqueness, but this is truly crazy." She laughed suddenly. "But it is too amazing not to enjoy! It is like finding a sister. I always wanted one. I am surrounded by men all the time!"

Brie offered a hand. "I could use one too. I've never had a lot of friends. I get along with everyone, but I'm not really close to anyone, you know?" When Isabelle took her hand, she smiled. "So what's your life like, Bella? You've got that 'private school' thing imbedded in you, so I know you grew up on the 'right side of the tracks' as it were. How old are you?"

"Twenty-one. Recently, actually. My birthday is in July."

"Heh. April here. I'm older than you by four months." Brie hopped up and sat on the edge of the counter. "Thank god for it, too. It would be too much if we had like the same birthday or whatever."

"Agreed. And, yes, I did grow up in a good family. Have you heard of Just In Time, Inc.?" At the nod, she smiled. "My father is the owner and CEO. My brother is slowly stepping in, though. They pretty well co-run the place now. They tried to get me onboard, but I have no artistic skills." She looked around the apartment wistfully. "Clearly, you do."

"More's the pity. I traded all my practical genes for it." She grabbed a cookie from a jar and offered it. "Chocolate chip?"

"I am allergic to chocolate."

Brie looked at her in horror. "How do you *live*?"

Isabelle laughed. "Quite well as long as I avoid it. It will not kill me, actually. It just makes me very sick. And I get a rash. It is hard to determine which is worse."

"I eat the cookie on your behalf then." She took a big bite and thoughtfully chewed. "So rich girl comes wandering into the District, huh? What gives with that?"

"I lost my temper with my family." Isabelle dropped her head onto her arms with a sigh. "I am getting married to someone who might as well be my brother. It is a business marriage so our companies can merge. I have known Roberto my entire life. I do not want to marry him. And on top of that, there is some sort of death threat against the family. It became personally aimed at me, and I was confined to the house."

Brie winced in sympathy. "Making you a time bomb with an Italian temperament. You go out your bedroom window?"

"Yes." She propped her chin on her hands. "I should be able to get home before they get the master key from our housekeeper. I just needed to *breathe*, Brie. I had heard that the 3rd District was where people went to escape."

"The irony being that when I ran into you, I was trying to escape my life too." Brie grimaced. "I like my boss well enough, but I feel so . . . underwhelmed there. I'm a waitress," she offered. "And since I can fix most problems in the kitchen, I'm pretty vital. But I'm so bored. It's that artsy side you envied. I want challenge and creativity."

"No college?" Isabelle asked curiously.

"No funds and no desire to be indebted to the federal government. Enforcers offered me a scholarship, but it just didn't seem worth it. I told them to give it to someone who needed it more." She sighed. "I'd give anything to be someone else for a day."

Isabelle slowly began to grin. "I think I might know how to solve both our problems. Let us switch!"

"Let us *what*?!" Brie stared at her. "Are you nuts? We'd SO get caught, and we'd get in so much trouble!"

"No, no. I think we can do it! Would your boss mind?"

"No," she said slowly. "He'd probably be amused by it. You wouldn't have to pretend with him. But me . . . your family'd go nuts!" She winced. "And I don't want to kiss your fiancé."

"Do not worry," Isabelle assured her. "It is only a business marriage. I have never kissed Roberto. Come on, Gabrielle. It would be fun!"

"Don't call me Gabrielle," she muttered. She blew out a breath. "I somehow know we're going to regret this, but I can't help but be tickled by the idea. Okay. Hit me with the facts. Tell me what I need to know to pull this off."

"How good is your memory?"

"Good enough, I hope!"

Isabelle started at the top with all the servants and made sure to describe them as best she could. If Brie messed up even once, then they would both be in a lot of trouble. Isabelle had absolute faith in Brie's ability to pull this off, though. "And do not forget," she added, "that I do not talk quite like you do."

"I'll try not to sound like a peasant," Brie retorted dryly. "I'm fairly decent at mimicking most accents, too—remind me to show off my Irish accent I learned from one of the co-owners of the Gentle Brook Inn. Now describe your family."

"Papa is named Antonio. He is on the taller side, over six-foot, and his hair is half-gray and half-dark brown. Brown eyes. My older brother, Rafael, Rafe for short, looks like Papa twenty-five years younger except his eyes are blue like mine. My fiancé is Roberto Viani. He is only slightly shorter than Rafe, and his hair is black. His eyes are a rather interesting shade that is not quite blue. Almost lavender, really."

"Is that it?"

"No, there are two more people. One is Tori Li. He is Rafe's bodyguard. About five-ten, blond and blue-eyed. You cannot miss him. He is this fascinating blend of male and female in just about everything, except perhaps strength. He was amazing when saw him in a delightful co-ed mixed martial arts tournament. He took down almost everyone! The other person is my bodyguard." Her voice softened unconsciously. "Alex LaGuardia."

Brie slowly lifted a brow. "Alex, huh?"

"Same height as my brother, but more powerful. Red hair and brown eyes. Not your normal handsome, but he is . . . breathtaking." Belatedly, she saw how Brie was looking at her. Her cheeks slowly turned pink. "Uhm."

"Bella . . . do we have a bit of a crush on our bodyguard?"

"No!" She waved her hands in the air. "Of course not!"

"I get the feeling I definitely won't be bored," Brie decided dryly. "Your family sounds nuts."

"*Grazie.*"

"You're welcome. I think."

Isabella laughed. "I will have to teach you some words eventually. Well, what do you say? Can we switch?"

"Well . . . we need to tell Enforcers first," Brie said reluctantly. "I wouldn't want them to call you thinking you were me and then getting mad because they didn't know. I owe them a lot, Bella. And besides, it never hurts to have someone watching out for you, right?"

"You mean ask them for permission?"

"Let's put it this way: I might be able to fool your family, but there's no way you'll fool anyone here. Better that we tell Enforcers than have them find out accidentally." Her doorbell rang suddenly and she blinked rapidly. She cautiously went over, peeked out the spyhole, and then sighed as she opened the door. "Don't do that, Gwyn!" she complained. "It's creepy!"

The white haired young woman on the other side of the door just grinned, her gray-purple eyes twinkling merrily. "You can't be surprised. A lot of people saw you two meet, and word came to us." She shot a cheerful smile at Isabelle. "Hi, I'm Gwyn Vincent. I'm from Enforcers."

Isabelle found herself smiling. There was something so likeable about Gwyn that she put everyone around her at ease. "I am Isabelle Lucino."

"Of course you are." Gwyn walked in and put down a tote. From within, she pulled out a stack of papers. "Rhianna says it's perfectly fine to switch, but she wants it formal so that if anyone tries anything with Isabelle, then we, Enforcers, can claim she's under our protection as well. People might mess with most anyone, but no one is dumb enough to mess with us."

Isabelle hesitated only briefly before smiling and signing the bottom of the contract. Brie signed next to her. Gwyn curiously studied their handwriting. "You guys even write similar. That's pretty nifty. I mean, I have two twins and we're not even that much alike."

"You mean triplets," Isabelle said, confused.

"No, she has two twins," Brie corrected dryly. "It's a long story. Thanks, Gwyn!"

"Don't mention it." With a wink, Gwyn collected the contract, stuffed it in her tote, and left the apartment.

"She is *tiny*," Isabelle observed the instant the door shut. "I mean, we are only five-three and I felt *huge* next to her. What is she?"

"Different."

Accepting that, she laughed. "Let us switch clothes and then go talk to your manager! This is going to be so much fun!"

Mr. Prost was understandably puzzled when the two women showed up, but he had as good a sense of humor as anyone born in the District did, as well as a good understanding of how the universe worked. He also liked Isabelle a great deal, finding her to be lovely, personable, and quick to learn. "It's hard work," he warned her.

"I look forward to it. I have never had to work for anything. I think it is time I tried. Brie will get her pay for what I do, right?"

"Naturally." Mr. Prost winked at Brie when she stared at him. "It's not like you're leaving me in the lurch. I think we can get Bella to do a fine job." He sighed heavily. "I suppose I better get that sink fixed though."

And thusly, Brie found herself catching a taxi to the Lucino villa. Following Isabelle's specific directions, she snuck around to the back, climbed up to the balcony, and crept inside the bedroom. Fascinated, she studied the design and décor and found it to be very similar to her own choices at home. It was tidier, though. She wouldn't mind the house arrest if it meant being in a place like this. It was gorgeous! And she had Isabelle's computer logon and password, and Isabelle had hers, so they could exchange emails at night just in case.

They always ate dinner together, she remembered, and they dressed for it. No pajamas allowed. After a quick perusal of Isabelle's closet, she decided on a slim black skirt and a pretty blue blouse. Didn't her partner own any *jeans*? Not a single t-shirt hung anywhere either. It wasn't that her clothes weren't lovely, but Brie knew she would miss her comfy clothes before very long.

They even wore the same size shoes, and she pulled on low-heeled black slippers. She had never worn heels in her life and could only pray she wouldn't break her neck going down the stairs.

A loud knock sounded on the door and made her heart leap. "Bella," a man called through the door. "Open the door this minute. You have sulked all day and Papa is getting worried."

He had to be Rafael. Bracing her shoulders, she hurried to open the door. Sure enough, the male on the other side could have been *her* brother. He looked exactly as he had been described. "I was not sulking," she informed him, mimicking the family accent with surprising ease. "I was resisting an urge to throw something at your hard head."

His brows shot up, then he grinned. "It would do you good. You simmer so long that I am always worried you will blow entirely like you did this morning." He leaned down and kissed her cheek. "Dinner is ready, Bella. And try not to kick Roberto under the table. Last time he tried to retaliate, he kicked *me*."

Having been without a family for years, the obvious love and affection from him acted as a balm to her soul. She followed him downstairs and tried to not be obvious about the way she was trying to take in everything. She wasn't entirely successful since he cocked his head at her and said, "You look like you have never seen the place before."

Carefully, she said, "I suppose I was just realizing how lucky we are."

"I cannot argue with that." He hugged her lightly and grinned when he saw Alex approaching. "Look what I found, Alex. I lured her out with promises of *Nonna*'s fettuccini recipe."

Alex came to a sharp stop as he stared at the young woman before him. She had Isabelle's face. She had Isabelle's eyes. She even had her smile. But she was *not* Isabelle. He had been so used to feeling a gut kick of desire if he so much as caught a glimpse of her that it was shocking when he didn't feel it this time.

Brie searched his eyes and her heart began to race madly. He knew. She could see he knew. She moved forward quickly and caught his arm. "Alex, can we talk? I owe you an apology as much as I owe one to Roberto. Please?"

"Of course." He led her into the parlor. "We'll be right there, Rafael," he called as he shut the door. As he heard the other male's footsteps fade, he turned toward Brie and narrowed his eyes slightly. "So. Who are you?"

"Gabrielle Wisteria, Brie for short." She took a deep breath. "Isabelle and I met a few hours ago. We thought it would be fun to trade places. She's doing my job as a waitress in the 3rd District. I'm here to spend some time with her family. Please don't tell anyone!" she pleaded. "We were both bored, and we thought it might be fun! It knocked both of us for a loop when we met!" She frowned suddenly. "How did you know I wasn't Isabelle, anyway?"

"I would know my Isabelle anywhere," he said simply. "You are as beautiful as she is, but I'm not attracted to you as I am to her. I suppose it is her soul that I want most."

She studied him intently and a smile began to tug at her lips. "You been in love with her all this time?" Geez, and Isabelle had a crush on him in return. They were both idiots in her book. If she'd had a hot guy like this who loved her, she would have been ecstatic.

"I have." He suddenly smiled. "Isabelle uses little to no slang, so you had better watch your speech. You say she is in the District?" At the nod, he sighed deeply. "I had better find an excuse to take a weekend off to go find her. It is my duty to protect her."

"And your honor. And your desire. And . . ."

"Yes, yes. You've made your point." He shook his head in bemusement. "You are identical in the face, but not the personality. Perhaps you can learn from each other. She could use your relaxed air."

"And I could use some polish." She grinned. "Don't be embarrassed to say it. I don't deny the truth." She blew out a breath as she heard someone calling 'her' name. "Don't abandon me yet. Help me get through dinner, I'm begging you."

"Certainly." Wryly amused at the entire situation, he escorted her from the parlor and led the way to the dining room. In a voice so low only she heard, he said, "Go to your papa and kiss his cheek. Then take the seat to his left, beside Roberto."

She took a deep breath and hurried to the older gentleman sitting at the head of the table. She bent to kiss his cheek and smiled. "I am sorry, Papa. I did not mean to worry you. I was having a snit." She shot as lofty a look as she could at Rafael who was sitting to Antonio's right. "It's certainly different from a sulk."

Antonio laughed and kissed her forehead. "*Sì*, Bella, and you are entitled. You have been too well behaved your whole life. Papa is convinced you are a changeling. '*Miei bambini* need more passion, 'Tonio!' Or so he claims."

She bit back a giggle as she turned to take her seat. To her surprise, a dark-haired hunk with seductive lavender eyes was holding her chair. Her breath wedged in her lungs even as her blood heated happily. The sudden fist of desire started somewhere deep and spread outward sharply. She swiftly averted her eyes, feeling the heat in her cheeks. Holy crap, she was lusting after her friend's fiancé. She would burn in hell. "Thank you," she said softly as she sat down.

Roberto stared at her intently as he sat down beside her. She sounded like Isabelle. She looked like Isabelle. She even mimicked most of her mannerisms. Yet he was absolutely positive that she was *not* his fiancée. When he had looked up to see her in the doorway, he had nearly been felled by a sharp hunger to taste her smiling lips and feel her silken skin under his hands.

He watched her intently as she sat beside him. There was a slight hesitation in her hands as if she wasn't entirely sure of which utensil was for what. Her speech, though formal enough, just didn't have the same polish as Isabelle. And with every passing second, his hunger for her grew. Who was this mysterious changeling that seemed to be made of magic in her soul?

If the others noticed anything, it was simply that Isabelle acted suddenly a little more open. Her smile came much quicker, and she laughingly exchanged quips with Tori and Rafael, much to their delight as she had never really verbally sparred with them before. "I think your seclusion did you good, Bella," Rafael told her laughingly. "You are a little different now. A good different."

"Am I? I hadn't noticed a difference." Brie told herself to shut up before she got in deeper. It was just so easy to relax with these people! It was like finding a long lost family. Maybe she and Isabelle could switch again sometime. At least, before she got married. Brie didn't like the way her pulse scrambled at Roberto's every steady look, and he was watching her a *lot.*

His knuckles grazed ever so lightly down her leg and she jolted. "Is something wrong, Isabelle?" Antonio asked curiously.

"Roberto kicked me." She turned up her nose, trying to hide her rapid heartbeat. "I would kick him back, but my legs aren't long enough."

Somehow, she made it through dinner. Making it through the weekend would be *hell* at this pace. As they were adjourning from the table, Alex suddenly said, "Antonio, may I have a word with you and Isabelle? We'll need Tori as well."

Puzzled but amiable, Antonio said, "Certainly, Alex. Rafael, Roberto, please excuse us?"

"Of course." Rafael smiled at Tori. "I will wait for you in the billiards room. I want to win another ten dollars."

"In your dreams."

Roberto studied Brie intently. "I would like to speak with you as well, Bella. I will wait in the parlor."

She absolutely did not want to be alone with him, but she knew she couldn't get out of it. "Of course." As soon as she got upstairs, she would call Isabelle and demand they call this off. There was way too much going on in this weird family!

In Antonio's study, Brie gratefully sat down in one of the chairs. Antonio went around behind his desk and sat down with a wry smile. "Do not tell me you want to quit, Alex. Isabelle cannot have finally made you reach your limits of patience."

"Of course not." Alex lightly rested a hand on Brie's shoulder. "Unfortunately, I have had a family emergency come up. I would ask for the weekend off to make sure everyone is all right. I will come back on Monday morning. Since Isabelle is under house arrest, it should be simple enough for Tori to watch over her as well."

"Absolutely," Antonio agreed. "I do hope everything is well."

"So do I, which is why I'm leaving as soon as I pack a bag." He smiled down at Brie. "Don't cause too much trouble for Tori."

Lacking a more appropriate response, she simply sniffed disdainfully. It was the right response since it made Tori laugh. "Don't worry, Isabelle," he said cheerfully. "I won't be dogging your every step inside the house. Just don't go near the doors or windows else I have an urge to pull you away like we're in some sort of spy movie."

She barely kept from grinning. She really liked Tori. He was so easygoing! She just felt comfortable with him in a way she didn't usually with other people. He felt very real, and very natural. No wonder he and Rafael had become such good friends.

With that meeting done, she very reluctantly went to the parlor for another. She nearly asked Tori to go with her but knew that she had no way of explaining why. She opened the door and peeked inside, and there was no sign of Roberto. Glad he hadn't gotten there yet, she walked over to the fireplace to warm her chilled hands. Hazards of her power: when she became nervous, her hands got as cold as ice.

The door suddenly shut behind her and a lock clicked. She whirled sharply and caught a breath as she saw Roberto leaning against the door. "You startled me," she managed to say.

"Fair enough, *cara*." He crossed his arms as he watched her. "You certainly startled me when you walked into the dining room."

What the hell was *cara*? Isabelle hadn't given her a crash course in Italian terms! She resisted an urge to edge backward. There was really nowhere to go, and he wasn't even that close to her. "You would think you hadn't seen me before."

One side of his mouth kicked up in a lethal smile. "I do not believe I had." He straightened and slowly began to walk toward her. "I do not think we have been introduced, *cara*."

"You're being silly." She found herself backing up to escape his approach. "We've known each other for years." He couldn't have guessed like Alex did. Not unless he was in love with Isabelle too. God, this was just getting more and more complicated!

"No. We have not." He leaned in and caged her against the wall with his hands on either side of her head where she could not escape. As he bent his head, the scent of her curled up and dug into his lungs. She smelled like pure water and magic, and it was a scent that most assuredly did not belong to Isabelle. He would know this mysterious beauty anywhere. "You are not Isabelle," he said very softly near her ear.

A shiver rippled through her body at the heat of his breath, felt even through her headband. He had seemed such a gentleman during dinner, but she realized then that it only acted as a façade. He was no more tamed than she; he just hid it far better. "Of-of course I am."

Just how far would she take the farce? He lifted her chin until she was forced to look at him. "Then you will not mind kissing your fiancé, will you?"

Isabelle had sworn she wouldn't find herself in this predicament! She tried to turn her head away. "You've never wanted to kiss me before." At least, dear god, she hoped he hadn't! Maybe Isabelle hadn't realized her fiancé wanted more than business. "Let me go!"

"That, *cara*," he murmured huskily, "I find I cannot do. You walked into the dining room and took my breath. It is only fair that I take yours." His lips brushed across hers lightly, temptingly, and he savored the sound of her breath hitching. Whoever she was, she wanted him as badly as he wanted her. Mutual madness. "It should not be so alarming," he murmured as he pressed soft kisses along her jaw, "to want your fiancé."

She pushed at his shoulders. "Stop. Please, stop." She wanted to sound forceful, but the breathless tone gave her away. It seemed as if she was going weak all at once, every muscle turning pliant as his incredible mouth traced her face.

His lips settled over hers gently, and his tongue softly teased her lips to open. She gave a shivering little moan and it raked across his body like velvet claws. When her lips parted, he took what she offered, deepening the kiss with a hunger that had simmered for hours. He pressed closer, let her feel how badly he wanted her, and was rewarded with another delicious shiver.

They slowly parted and he stared into her clouded blue eyes. They seethed like the restless surf on an ocean shore. She slowly pressed her trembling fingers to her lips, something like fear moving to replace the desire in her gaze. "You are not Isabelle," he told her roughly. "I never wanted her the way I want you. Who are you?"

"I knew this wouldn't work," she whispered. Her head dropped onto his chest as her shoulders slumped. "I just knew it."

"Easy." He ran his hands softly over her arms to soothe. "Let us sit down and talk." He eased back and drew her over to the settee. He made sure to sit close beside her and left one hand on her knee while his other arm rested across her shoulders. She would run before he got his answers if he didn't hold onto her. "Now then. Will you tell me who I just kissed?"

"Gabrielle Wisteria." She didn't look up at him and kept her gaze on her hands in her lap. "Brie for short. I'm from the 3rd District." She did peek at him then, but he looked more speculative than alarmed. "Isabelle was running away when we met. We thought it might be fun to switch places."

"No wonder Alex took off," he murmured. "He always knew her best. He knew instantly that you were not Bella. I wonder what clued him in."

She kept her mouth shut. Things were awkward enough without telling the man that his fiancé and her bodyguard had the hots for each other.

He studied for several moments, his gaze lingering on the headband she wore. It might as well have been another clue. He had never seen Isabelle wear one before, and it seemed more like a disguise than a fashion statement on Brie. "Gabrielle." He said the name slowly, savoring it. "I like it." He skimmed his knuckles across her cheek. "Would you let me get to know you, Gabrielle?"

"Brie," she muttered.

"Why? Gabrielle is a lovely name."

"Only those close to me can call me that."

"Then I will call you Gabrielle, as I very much wish to be close." He leaned in and tugged lightly at the headband. She went very still, her eyes widening. "What are you hiding, *cara*?" He lifted her chin. "I will kiss you again," he said softly, decisively.

"You're engaged." She broke out of his grip and scrambled to her feet. "I don't *care* if it's 'just a business marriage.' You're still engaged. I'm not a cheater. And if you are, then you're a jerk. Isabelle deserves better than you." Temper lit her eyes when he lifted a brow. "You gonna tell me that you wouldn't take me to bed if I offered? That makes you a jerk."

"I have no intentions of seducing you while I am engaged, *cara*. But I do wish to get to know you. You are here this weekend, yes?" When she nodded, he got to his feet. "Then I will 'court' you. If any ask, we can simply say that we are trying to see what being a couple is like. When Isabelle returns, we will see what we will see then." A little smile crooked his lips. "Tell me, did Alex tell you why he knew you were not Bella?"

"The opposite of you," she muttered. "He *didn't* want me." She studied his face. "You're not surprised."

"Oddly, I am not." He stepped closer but stopped when she retreated. "I am not going to kiss you, Gabrielle. Give me your hand, please." She very cautiously offered her hand, and he drew it to his lips. "My name is Roberto Viani," he said softly. "I am delighted to meet you."

The man was *dangerous*. She freed her hand and rushed out of the parlor as fast as she could unlock the door. If only he hadn't been engaged to Isabelle! Business marriage, nothing. An engagement was a promise, and she refused to be made to feel like she had helped break one.

As Roberto walked out of the parlor, Rafael was coming down the stairs. His brows lifted through his bangs. "Well," he said. "You are looking a little . . . stressed, friend."

Roberto sighed. Though it would have been simple enough to tell Rafael everything, doing so would mean that Brie left. He most assuredly did not want to let her out of his sight until he had no choice. "Something seems to have happened to Bella and I."

Rafael grinned. "That is one way of putting it. Thank *Dio*, that is what I say. I was hoping you two would be happy."

"Well, that remains to be seen. I have decided that I have been a bit lax in the fiancé department, Rafe. I will see if I can court your sister this weekend. She certainly cannot run from me, can she?"

"Not right now, no." He shook his head. "No wonder she seemed so different at dinner. She must be floundering right now since this is so sudden."

Roberto hid a smile. "That is one way of putting it, yes."

CHAPTER THREE

As the oldest of three, with his younger siblings both being sisters, Alex was well used to the fascinating way many women could be as different as night and day between their internal and external personas. He appreciated it, even admired it. Certainly he had been admiring Isabelle for the last two years as much mentally as physically. She came across as being a little distant, a little aloof, but there was a smoldering passion inside her that he had always been helplessly drawn toward.

While he wanted any threat removed from her life, he couldn't help but hope it took longer so that he could build up memories. As soon as she married Roberto, she would be forever beyond his reach. He had once hoped that as soon as he was freed of his duties, he could court her. Now he knew it would never happen.

Finding her in the 3rd District wasn't hard. It seemed that everyone there knew what was going on. He very shortly walked into the restaurant where she was working, though he took great care that she not notice him. It was easy enough to blend into the crowd since it was the dinner rush.

He started smiling within a few moments. Isabelle was having the time of her life. She laughed and smiled as she waited on tables or cleared away dishes. She helped out with the register, learning patiently how to work the machine from another waiter. She obviously worked hard, but she was also clearly enjoying every minute.

He caught another waiter's eye, and when the man walked over, Alex said softly, "I don't suppose I could request the blue-eyed waitress."

The man grinned. "You and nearly every other male here. Sure. Her table list isn't too big. I'll switch with her." With a whistle, he headed over to where Isabelle was stacking receipts. "Hey, Bella. Table Two asked for you specifically. Betcha get a good tip if you flutter your lashes."

She laughed. "You mean Brie would get a good tip. I am making money for her, remember?"

"She'll make you keep the tips, trust me."

"You are probably right." Amused, she grabbed her order pad and headed for Table Two. It was tucked into a quiet, shadowy corner. The man was reading a newspaper, so she couldn't tell his identity yet. "I am Brie," she said cheerfully as she reached the table. "Can I get you some water or coffee?"

Alex put down the paper and grinned when her eyes widened. "And you look surprised, Isabelle. Did you think I wouldn't notice the switch?"

"I do not have time to talk to you right now. I am on the clock, and it is Brie's paycheck." She looked at him pointedly. "Water or *caffè*?"

"Water." He offered the menu from the table. "Just the house soup special, please, and a small side. I already ate dinner."

"Side potato, mashed." She had written it down before realizing she should have made it a question. The simple fact was that she knew him almost as well as she knew herself. All his likes and dislikes. "Uhm, butter?"

"You know I prefer sour cream," he said softly.

"*Sì*." She sighed and took the menu. "Just . . . stay there and do not cause me trouble, Alex!"

"When have I ever?"

"If you only knew," she muttered as she walked away. The man caused her trouble every time he looked at her. Every time he smiled. His casual way of touching her shoulder or tugging on her hair. Her whole family was physically affectionate, but Alex was assuredly *not* like her brother or father, or fiancé.

Thankfully, he seemed to be aware that it was actually Brie's job on the line and he didn't make a scene. He thanked her when she brought over his meal, declined an offer to refill his water, and spent a humorous two minutes trying to decide on dessert. "Cheesecake or pie. Hmm."

She shook her head at him. "You have been spoiled on Peggy's cooking!" she scolded lightly. "It is a wonder that you have not gained fifty pounds over the last two years with the way you inhale her tiramisu!"

He grinned. "I work out with Tori. The kid is a slave driver. He frightens me, really. He's half my size and he drops me on the mat regularly." He put down the dessert listing. "Cheesecake," he decided. "But don't put chocolate on it."

"Why not?" she asked curiously.

"I can share it with you if you don't."

Feeling her cheeks heat, grateful for the low light, she hurried toward the kitchen. As she was coming back out with the dessert, Mr. Prost caught up with her. She smiled as she saw him. He was such a funny man; he seemed to be the rooster whose feathers were always ruffled. "Hello."

"Ah, Bella. Brie will be very happy with how hard you worked." He clapped her on the shoulder lightly. "It's quitting time for you, my girl. You go on home and get some rest. You have the morning shift tomorrow, alright?"

"Very well." She held up the dessert. "Let me just deliver this and then I will clock out. Actually," she put down the plate to take off her apron, "I know this man, so consider me off the clock now, alright?"

"Of course."

She picked up the plate again and carried it over to Alex's table. She put it down in front of him and slid onto the seat across from him. "I am off duty now," she explained when he arched a brow. "And thank *dio*. My feet are killing me." She picked up a fork and broke off a piece of the cake. "What are you doing here, Alex? Did not anyone wonder why you were running off while I was in grave danger?"

"I told them I had a family emergency and since you were supposed to be indoors, Tori could watch over you for me." He crossed his arms and sat back. A dark frown filled his face. "Isabelle, what were you thinking? Running off as you did, you're lucky it was Brie you met. We can't know if anyone is watching the villa."

"I am tired of being a Lucino," she retorted fiercely. "Just once I wanted to make a decision for myself."

He glanced around, saw that the place was preparing to close, and got to his feet. "Let me pay for my meal and then you can take me where you're staying so that we can talk."

"Fine."

Minutes later, they were walking through the lamp lit streets of the District. Even at night, the place felt welcoming to Isabelle, and to Alex as well. People were only just shutting down for the evening. Someone who sold woodworks was carting all manner of items into her home. At another house, a pregnant woman helped her husband carry in beautiful articles of clothing. When she spotted Isabelle and Alex, she waved cheerfully.

Isabelle waved back with a smile. "It is so lovely here. I envy Brie a little." She led the way to the apartment complex and into the small home itself. "This is Brie's place, but she said I could stay here. I guess you can as well."

"How gracious you are." He shrugged off his jacket and hung it up on a hook near the door. He glanced around the apartment and had to smile as he realized that Brie and Isabelle shared more than matching faces. They had similar tastes as well, although Brie's living space seemed to shout that someone with creative talent lived there. Sadly, Isabelle had none.

She sat down on the couch and kicked off her shoes. "Ooh. My feet. I have never stood for so long before! I have an entirely new respect for servers of all kinds."

He sat down beside her and resisted an urge to offer to rub her feet. He wasn't sure he could keep his touch impersonal right then. She looked rumpled and flushed, and much softer and more approachable than she ever had before. The soft golden light in the room just made her beauty more seductive, more alluring.

Unaware of his scrutiny, she asked, "How did you know, Alex? Did Brie get caught?"

"No," he said softly. "I simply knew she was not you. I asked her about it and she told me you two had decided to walk in each other's shoes for the weekend."

"Yes, we did. Now go home." She aimed a glare at him. "You are going to ruin everything if you keep following me!"

"My duty," he reminded her quietly and firmly, "is to see to your safety. I'm not going home until you do."

"I do not want you here!" she shouted at him. "I am so sick of being a Lucino and being so in need of protection! Consider yourself fired, Alexander! I want nothing to do with you!"

Something volatile lit his eyes. "You think I care this much because you're a Lucino. Ha!" His hands closed around her shoulders and he jerked her closer so that she sprawled across his lap. "I don't care what you are, Isabelle. I never have. But thank you for firing me. Now I can do something I've wanted to for two damned years!"

She took a breath to curse at him, but the words were lost when his hungry mouth covered hers. Her eyes went wide with shock for an instant before a searing wave of desire swept through her body. It was so sharp, so compelling, that she found no will to resist it. On a low moan of need, she curled her hands into his shirt and pressed up to deepen the embrace. She had wanted him so badly for so long . . .

His hands released her only to bury his fingers in her hair and pull her ever closer. His mouth was hard and wild, not merely asking for her response but demanding it. When her lips parted, he immediately thrust his tongue inside to taste her. She reminded him of the sweetest of grapes, like the kind made into the best of wines. Addicting. Arousing. She was everything.

He released her as sharply as he had grabbed her. Roughly, he said, "That, Bella, had nothing to do with my being your bodyguard or your being a Lucino. In fact, it was probably the stupidest thing I've ever done in my life." And if she didn't stop staring at him with her slumberous blue eyes, he was going to do it again.

She shook her head sharply and pushed at his shoulders. "Let me go, Alex."

He did so reluctantly though his fingers glided across every inch of skin they could. He was entirely unsurprised when she scooted away from him down the couch. "You can't make me go away," he said quietly, "any more than you can change who you are. And I wouldn't want you to try." A little smile suddenly tugged at his lips. "And since your father hired me, you technically can't fire me either, Bella."

"I am also engaged," she shot at him. "Let us not forget that either!" She raked her hands through her hair. It seemed as if she was shaking from the inside outward. 'Want' was too mild a word for what she felt. 'Lust' was much closer, but even that fell short. She *needed* his touch in a way that was dimly terrifying. If only he hadn't kissed her! Now she knew exactly how wonderful his mouth felt, how delicious his taste was. "*Dio*!" she said fiercely. "How complicated this is! I hope Brie is not having this sort of trouble." She got to her feet with all the dignity she could muster. "You can sleep on the couch. I am going to bed. *Buono notte*."

"Good night," he murmured, watching the sway of her hips as she went down the hall. He wasn't entirely sure he would even manage to sleep with the way his body ached, but at least the couch looked uncomfortable enough to take his mind off things.

Brie awoke the following morning with a bit of a start. The room was unfamiliar, and so was the bed. Memory returned as she listened to the birds chirping outside the window and didn't recognize their voices. She sighed and got out of bed. She was half-tempted to think she had dreamed everything, but a look in the mirror told her that she *still* looked as if she had been kissed senseless. Any man who could leave a visible impact even hours later was one to keep away from sane women.

After a bracing shower in the adjoined bathroom, she felt a little more human again. Well, as human as she could be, she thought impishly as she got dressed. Steeling herself for whatever assault she might come under from Roberto, she made her way downstairs for breakfast. When she reached the foyer, she was surprised by a man in a uniform walking up with a bouquet of water lilies. "For you, *signorina*," he said with a smile.

"Me?" She took the flowers in confusion. "Who sent me flowers?"

"I believe *Signor* Viani did."

"Oh." She hastily handed them back over. "Please put them in water, Marco." At least, she hoped he was Marco! He sure looked like he knew the place and was in charge of it as well.

"Of course." He winked as he took the flowers toward the kitchen.

Water lilies! She furrowed her brow as she headed for the dining room. Either Roberto somehow knew what she was, or he had made an eerily accurate guess. Both made equally unnerving thoughts.

The dining room was empty except for Tori. "Where are Papa and Rafael?" Brie asked.

"In the boardroom upstairs. They're working on a rush order. They stole a client from the Deases, and they're trying to hash out the best possible campaign." He shook his head in amusement. "I keep telling them they need to be in a business other than advertisement. They've got the mentality of pirates!"

She tried not to laugh as she served herself from the buffet that was set out. She definitely liked Tori. "I'm sorry Alex abandoned you," she offered as she sat down across from the bodyguard.

"It's alright. I just hope everything is okay. You know how he loves his sisters."

"Mmm."

They were halfway done with breakfast when Roberto walked into the dining room. He smiled slowly when he saw Brie. "*Ciao, cara*." He walked over and bent to kiss her cheek softly. His lips curved further when he saw the blush climbing her delicate neck. Her pulse beat rapidly, an enticement to press his lips there. Instead, he looked at a very bemused Tori. "*Ciao,* Tori."

"Hi." He propped his chin on his hand and grinned. "I'm not used to seeing you two act all lovey-dovey. It's a nice change of pace, for sure." First chance, he would corner Rafael and find out what had happened to change the direction of the winds blowing. It seemed as if everything had done a complete switch ever since Isabelle had lost her temper.

Roberto leaned over and murmured softly in Brie's ear, "*Grazie* means thank you, if you want to thank me for the flowers."

"*Grazie,*" she said very softly, and it again came out surprisingly fluent. She had never used an accent as comfortably as she did Italian. Must have been her half-blood. "For the flowers." She would have said that she loved water lilies, but she had no idea if Isabelle did. This was so much more complicated than she had been thinking it would be!

Tori excused himself a few moments later, and she very nearly called him back. She absolutely didn't want to be alone with Roberto. "Do you always eat over here?" she asked him softly. "What about your family?"

"It is just me. My parents took off on a world tour a year ago when Papa retired." He smiled. "I have postcards from five different countries and counting. He and Mama are having a grand time. But since that means I am alone at home, I get lonely. Rafe and I have been friends for two decades. I am as at home here as he is at my home." He tugged her to her feet as he stood. "Let us go into the parlor." His smile came slow when she blushed. "Do not worry. I will not have my wicked way with you, *cara*."

"You had better not!" She reluctantly let him tuck her hand into the crook of his arm as they left the dining room. Her fingers flexed softly, automatically testing the resilience of the male flesh under her touch. He was much, *much* stronger than he seemed. Heated lavender eyes flicked a glance at her, and she knew he had felt her curious examination.

Inside the parlor, she escaped his grip and pointedly sat on a chair so that he couldn't sit beside her. He just smiled and sat across from her on the settee where he lounged with the grace of a large feline. "Did you sleep well, Gabrielle?"

"Brie!" She didn't like the way he turned her name into a caress in his velvet voice. "And I did, thank you."

"I did not." A corner of his mouth kicked up.

Her belly tightened with a flutter of raw heat. Her hands curled together in her lap as she fought for control. "You said we were going to get to know one another." She kept her voice steady with effort. "What do you want to know about me?"

"Well, you surely know the first question, *cara*. You said you were from 3rd District."

Her lashes lowered. "I am half water elf."

"A real elf?" He sat up, intrigued. "Are we meaning Santa or Legolas?"

She shot him a dirty look. "Neither, thank you. What, you also think all faeries are the sugar puffs that Disney makes them out be?"

He grinned and held up his hands. "Easy. It was a fair enough question. What does being a water elf mean?"

"It means a certain control over and creation of water." She hesitated and then pulled off her headband. She lifted her hair away from her ears and revealed their delicate points.

Enchanted, he moved closer. He softly reached out and traced the line of her ear, following the gentle lines to her cheek and back to the tip. There was something sexy about her ears, but he couldn't quite determine what it was. Delight filled him as he saw the tiny holes around the tip. "You pierced your ears?"

"Who hasn't these days?"

"I would like to see you wear earrings. I think your ears are lovely." He trailed his fingers over her ear once last time, wistfully. Someday, hopefully soon, he intended to kiss every inch and work his way down.

As soon as he leaned back, she hastily put her headband back on. Her ears were actually tingling from his touch, and the tingles spread deep and wide. She had never guessed her ears would be that sensitive.

"Tell me about your family," he offered. "I assume you must be half Italian to be identical to Isabelle."

"Yes, my mother was. My father was the elf."

He paused. "Was?" He kept his voice as gentle as he could.

"Trade Center." It was all she said.

"*Cara*." Hurting for her, he moved to be kneeling in front of her chair. "I am so sorry. No wonder you were so interested in switching with Bella. You wanted a family again, even for a little while." When she looked at him in surprise, he brought her hand to his lips. "I think I know you quite well even in such a short time, *cara mia.*"

"Alright," she said in exasperation. "Just what are you calling me?"

"Beloved," he said softly.

She snatched her hand back quickly. "I'm not."

"I must disagree." He retook his seat. "What do you wish to know about me?" She said nothing and he sat back comfortably. "I am twenty-five," he offered. "I am the CEO of Inkwell, a small but lucrative advertising company. My father and Antonio have toyed with the idea of a merge since Rafe and I were ten. It seemed very convenient to do so now, with me and Isabelle marrying to cement the deal. There is some strong competition in the market now that Two More Minutes has come under new management." She remained stubbornly silent and he just smiled. "I have two degrees, one in Business Management and the other in Advertising. What about you?"

"I don't have a degree. I didn't see a need for college. Anything I want to learn, I learn on my own. I take free classes when they come up, but I'm mostly self-taught." Reluctantly, she admitted, "I'm an artist. I work best in pencils and charcoals. My day job, what Isabelle is hopefully enjoying, is being a waitress."

It was an utter waste of talent in his book. Artists needed to be *creative*. His native land had been built on art for centuries. It was in his blood even though he lacked the ability to create with any sort of medium. He had always greatly respected those who could, and frequently turned to his artist employees for advice. "I would like to see your art," he murmured.

"Maybe someday."

The doors suddenly opened, and Rafael walked in with a sigh. "*Scusi*, Bella, Roberto. I do not mean to interrupt, but I could use you, Roberto. Papa and I are absolutely stumped at this point. We need some fresh input."

"Naturally." Roberto offered a hand to Brie. "Come with us, *cara*. See what your family does."

"If you can make her interested," Rafael noted dryly, "I will give you twenty dollars, Roberto."

Brie took Roberto's hand and stood. "Just for that," she said loftily, "I will go along."

Rafael stared at her and then started laughing. "Me and my big mouth." He hugged her tight when she was closer. "I should have known you would do that." He wiggled his brows teasingly. "I was half hoping I would walk in on a kiss."

She elbowed him sharply. "Behave yourself."

Chuckling, Rafael walked into the boardroom. "I brought Roberto, and by opening my big mouth, I seem to have gotten Bella as well. It is just as well. Would you mind taking notes, *cara*?"

The affectionate term sounded entirely different coming from Rafael than it did coming from Roberto. She found a smile and picked up the pad of paper sitting on the table. "I can do my best." She took a seat and tried to ignore Roberto sitting next to her. She had the scary feeling that she might be falling in love, and that was even worse than falling in lust. He was *engaged.*

The men began firing ideas back and forth across the table, talking loudly and over the top of each other. She listened, writing down ideas as they were thrown out, but after a few moments, she started to sketch out the scene they were trying to decide. It was an advertising poster for a large food chain, but they couldn't decide on any one particular theme.

She didn't even realize what she was doing until she noticed it had gotten quiet. She looked up quickly to find Antonio and Rafael looking at her curiously. "I'm sorry," she apologized. "Did I miss something?"

"You looked a little distracted, Bella. What are you up to over there?" Antonio asked affectionately. It was just nice to have his daughter interested in the company for once.

"I was . . . uhm." She tried to hide the sketch but Roberto snatched it out of her hand. "Give that back!"

He dropped the paper on the table where the other two males could see it, and both took quick breaths. The sketched outline was not only precisely rendered, it was also very skilled.

"What the . . .?" Rafael looked at Brie sharply. "You are not Isabelle," he breathed. "You cannot be. My sister cannot draw to save her life. No wonder you seemed so . . . different somehow." And no wonder Roberto and Alex had reacted so strangely to her presence! "Who are you?" He made his voice gentle. "You know us, so obviously you and Isabelle met."

She leapt to her feet and fled from the room as fast as possible. "Go after her, boy," Antonio told Roberto quietly. As he also ran out of the room swiftly, Antonio took a deep breath. "I think I know who she is, Rafe." His son looked at him sharply, and he got to his feet. "I need to make a few phone calls. I want to confirm my suspicions."

CHAPTER FOUR

Isabelle awoke in the morning to the smell of coffee and bacon. With a large yawn, she pulled on a robe and padded into the kitchen to see what was going on. She had kind of been looking forward to cooking for herself for once. She had never really gotten a chance to try it before. "Alex?" she asked as she walked over to the counter.

"Good morning," he told her gravely. "I couldn't sleep, and you're on the morning shift, so I thought I'd cook something for us. There wasn't much to choose from, but I thought bacon and eggs would work fine."

"Oh. *Grazie*."

He tightened his grip on the spatula as he stared at her. She was flushed and rumpled, her eyes still sleepy and her cheeks still flushed. It took every ounce of his willpower to resist lifting her into his arms and carrying her down the hall to bed once more. "Bella."

At the rasp in his voice, she took a wary step back, her hand lifting to her throat. "I will just go catch a quick shower," she whispered, and she fled down the hall once more. The entire way, she kicked herself. Why was she so afraid of her own feelings?

Because she was engaged, that's why. Yet . . . she wasn't being *forced* to marry Roberto. She had agreed because she had, foolishly, thought that she would never have Alex. He was the only one she had ever loved, ever wanted. And he wanted her too, which was more than she had dared dream of having.

She thought critically about the situation while she dried her hair. The business marriage didn't *have* to occur to support the merger. It was just a formality to make the paperwork less messy. If she told Roberto that she was in love with Alex, he would certainly agree to let her go. After all, he loved her too; he just wasn't *in* love with her.

Her father and Rafael would be more than happy with the situation. They also wanted her happiness. Besides, they were Italian. They were supposed to do things big and passionately. She felt long overdue for some serious drama. Maybe switching with Brie would have a much bigger, longer reaching effect than alleviating their boredom.

The instant the switch was done, she would talk to Roberto, cancel the engagement, and turn her eye toward Alex. He would be hers come hell or high water. She couldn't be sure of the depth of his feelings, but she absolutely would not settle for just lust. Oh, she would enjoy it, of that she was sure, but she wanted much more. He was still in her father's employ, and that made it stickier, but if she told Antonio she wanted Alex fired so that she could seduce him, her father would probably be willing. Slightly flabbergasted, but willing.

Feeling in control of her life once more, she got dressed in the black slacks and white shirt that made up 'her' work uniform. She would have to get some pants for herself. They were amazingly comfortable. Perhaps Brie would lend her a pair of jeans or two until she could get her own.

She headed back to the kitchen and sat at the counter. The size of the apartment did not lend to a dining room table, and Brie had turned the counter into the eating space. It was cozy and delightful. Isabelle was also pleasantly surprised when Alex handed her a plate with food. "I did not know you could cook."

He smiled. "Well, it's not part of casual conversation usually, and it isn't like I had a need to, living with your family as I have."

"You know," she said thoughtfully, "I do not think I really know as much about you as I thought I did. At least, I do not know the unimportant things. I know *you* but not the extra little details about your life. You are ten years older than I. You have got to have some interesting things to tell me."

He slowly lifted a brow. "This sounds rather like a date, Bella."

She arched a brow in return. "I suppose it does. But that is silly, is it not? After all, I am an engaged woman." She sipped her coffee calmly. "For now."

His hands curled into the edge of the counter. Roughly, he said, "Isabelle, if this is a game you're playing because you feel you need revenge, I don't appreciate it." She looked up at him, her blue eyes clear as the sky, and he felt his muscles knot with ferocious need. "Don't look at me like that."

"How am I looking at you, Alex?" she asked softly.

"Like you want me to touch you."

"That would be silly, no? I am as yet an engaged woman." She delicately finished her breakfast. He was truly quite good in a kitchen, even with something that simple. "Alex, do you remember the day we met?" He nodded slowly and she handed him her plate to put it in the sink. "Until that day, I had been fairly sure that I had skipped the hormonal phase of puberty. Then you walked in." She shook her head. "I had no more worries on that front."

He closed his eyes and counted to ten. "I wanted you the minute I laid eyes on you. But it was so hard to even be your friend that I knew I didn't dare tell you."

She smiled. "Alex, when I am feeling threatened or insecure, how do I react?"

"You get aloof and haughty," he responded promptly. The minute the words left his mouth, he found himself smiling. "You'd think I'd have realized sooner." He went around the counter and cupped her cheek tenderly. She might not love him yet, but she wanted him. She wanted a relationship. He could build from that. "It's good for Roberto that you're dumping him."

"Oh?"

"I've been close to breaking his nose for months," he admitted. "I'm afraid I'm a jealous man."

She suddenly grinned. "You are Irish and Italian. You are the type who would break his nose and *then* yell at him. I still cannot believe how even-tempered you are! The minute I heard about your heritage, I was all set for some good shouting fights in the house, but nothing seems to bother you at all. Such a disappointment, Alexander."

He tugged her up into his arms and enjoyed feeling her body along his. She fit perfectly, as if they had been made to be one. She smelled as wonderful as the rich wine of her taste. "There's only so much room in the house for bad tempers now that yours has been proven."

She went on her toes and linked her hands behind his neck. "So, tell me again. How *did* you know that Brie was not me? Was it her ears?"

He paused, wondering why her ears would have anything to do with it, then pushed it aside. He would ask later. "Actually, it was because I was not attracted to her," he admitted candidly. "She looked like you, sounded like you . . . but I knew she was not you. And she didn't smell right."

"Smell?" She blinked.

"I can't describe it, Bella. I just didn't think she smelled right. But you . . ." He nuzzled her neck softly and breathed in deeply. "You are perfection. Like red wine on a summer evening. Like grapes ripening in the sun."

Her knees went weak. "Alex."

The husky sound of her voice flicked along his nerves. "I would kiss you," he said roughly, "but I fear I might not stop. I will not shame you, Bella. You are still engaged." He slowly released her and his hands slid warmly over her body. "You have work. I will come with you and see if I can be of any use."

"You will distract me," she grumbled, but inside she was delighted. She didn't want to be away from him. She wanted to savor how he wanted her. It would only be better if he loved her as well. Ah, well. She had time to work on that later.

When they arrived at the restaurant, Mr. Prost was more than happy to see them. "Good morning, Isabelle! And who is your friend?"

She smiled. "Alex. He does not have anywhere to go today since he is visiting with me. Could he help in any way?"

"Certainly!" Mr. Prost smiled at Alex, liking the calm man's demeanor. "How do you feel about working a cash register?"

"I haven't done it in fifteen years, but I think I can manage."

"When you were sixteen, I was six," Isabelle murmured.

"Does that bother you?"

"Not at all. It mostly fascinates me." She started to walk away and then glanced over her shoulder with a smile that could only be called sultry. "Try not to distract the patrons."

Mr. Prost chuckled at the look on Alex's face. "I think I ought to worry she will distract you. And I thought Brie had a devastating impact on the male clientele. Like the moon and sun, aren't they?"

"Or water and fire," Alex murmured, unknowingly apt.

Perhaps a bit ironically, noticed by all, was the fact that he wasn't the one who had trouble keeping his mind on his work. It was Isabelle. She didn't miss her tables, didn't drop anything, but she was clearly distracted by the cashier. When she would take him receipts, and he would smile at her, her thoughts would clearly scatter. She very nearly started to serve the wrong things to the wrong tables, catching herself just in time if someone else didn't catch her.

The patrons were highly amused. Mr. Prost was, too. After the third near mishap, he finally shook his head and pulled her aside. "Isabelle, why don't you take the day and visit with your 'friend'? I won't hold it against you or Brie, I promise. You're no good to me like this."

She winced wryly. "I am truly sorry." With a sigh, she took off her apron. "I knew better than to tease him. I was just setting myself up." She walked over to where Alex stood and waited patiently until he finished ringing up the last tab in front of him. "We are being kicked out," she said in amusement.

He just grinned. "Somehow I thought that might happen." With much relief, he turned the last receipts over to another waiter. "And not a moment too soon. I was reminded just how much I hated working in fast food." He held the door for her and followed her out into the morning sunshine.

"Was that your first job?" she asked curiously.

"It was, but I bailed ship as soon as possible."

"Exactly how did you get into the bodyguard business? I saw your resume. It is very impressive."

"It was an accident, actually. I had always been interested in learning self-defense, and I took to it quite well. When I was twenty-four, a friend of my father's was going to be traveling somewhere a bit more hostile and asked if I would go along as a deterrent to would-be assailants."

"Would-be turned into attempted, I presume."

"Correct. I did such a good job that someone else asked to hire me." He shook his head wryly. "I enjoyed it enough that I decided to actually do it as a career. I met Tori about three years ago on another job. He scared the shit out of me. This guy, half my size, had me on the floor in seconds. I still don't know how he does it."

She laughed richly. "He is so unassuming! I suppose that is why he is so effective at his work." She unlocked the apartment door and headed inside. "Oh well," she sighed. "I suppose I ought to get in touch with Brie and see if she wants to call things off early."

She went to the fridge and pulled out the jar of tea she had spotted before. She had barely poured one glass when the front door opened and Brie rushed in. "Brie!" She started to smile but it faded as she saw the look on her friend's face. "Brie?"

"Your fiancé is driving me nuts!" Brie nearly shouted. "And he *kissed* me!"

Alex, somehow, found that entirely unsurprising. Being a wise man, he said nothing and sat down on the couch. It was both fascinating and slightly disturbing to see the two identical women beside each other. Curiously, even at a distance, he knew he would always know which was which. Now seeing them together, he could spot nearly elemental differences in the way they moved.

Isabelle cleared her throat, a bit bemused and lot curious. "Would you like to explain how that happened?"

"He knew I wasn't you. He said it was because he was attracted to me and he'd never been attracted to you." Brie took a deep breath. "And he kissed me." She groaned and covered her face with her hands. "And Vesuvius was just a little volcano seepage."

Isabelle bit her lower lip to hide the smile that wanted to spread. Were things really going to work out that wonderfully well? If Roberto and Brie got together, then it solved so many troubles all at the same time! "Why are you here? Was he that, hmm, intimidating?"

"I goofed." She sighed. "Your dumb brother bet Roberto twenty bucks that *you* wouldn't sit in a meeting. I went just to make him lose. They were talking about a poster, and I just sort of started sketching."

Alex winced. "Isabelle can't draw to save her life."

"Unfortunate, but true." Isabelle lifted a brow. "They caught you." At the nod, she sighed. "Well, that does it. We are going to be in a great deal of trouble. Oh well. It was fun while it lasted, no?"

Brie didn't get a chance to answer. The door opened behind her, and Roberto walked in as if he had a homing signal for her. "*Scusi*," he said to Isabelle and Alex. He caught Brie around the waist and tossed her over his shoulder casually. "Bella, *cara*, I hope you understand when I say I want to cancel our engagement."

She did her best to hide a smile. "Yes. Yes I do."

Brie managed to untangle her tongue and nearly yelped, "Put me down, you bastard! Ooh! What's Italian for bastard? I don't think he's listening to English!"

"*Bastardo*," Isabelle murmured, desperately trying not to laugh.

"Well, *that's* easy to remember. Bastardo! Put me down, Roberto!"

"Eventually."

The door shut behind them and left a thoughtful silence. Isabelle looked at Alex, and he at her. "Well," she finally said. "I would appear to have been 'dumped,' as they say. Oddly, I am not that crushed over it. I suppose I should throw a tantrum and wail and curse his family, but I do not feel quite that dramatic. Do you mind?"

"Not at all." His brows lifted as she walked over and sat down on his lap. Desire tore through his body with the force of a storm as wild as his lover's blood. "Isabelle."

"I am single now," she said softly, linking her hands behind his neck. She teasingly brushed her lips across his. "But I do not want to be, Alex. I know you are still in my papa's employ, but I just don't care anymore."

His hands tangled into her hair and his eyes searched hers. There was something there, something he was terrified of naming for the chance he might be wrong. "Why, Isabelle?" he asked softly, huskily. "What do you want from me?"

"Passion and romance." Her soft hands framed his face. "And love." Her voice trembled softly. "I want that most of all." Softer, against his lips, she said, "*Ti amo,* Alexander." When his hands tightened, her lips curved. "I presume it does not need a translation. You do not need to love me yet," she added simply. "I can wait. But be warned now that I will do whatever it takes to have your heart for mine."

He brought one of her hands down to rest over his heart. It beat as wildly as hers. "It's yours," he said simply. "It always has been. I love you, Bella." He stood with her in his arms and turned determinedly toward the bedroom. "Your papa won't hire hitmen if I seduce his baby girl, will he?"

"Only if you abandon me," she warned gravely. "And in that scenario, you should be more worried about what *I* might do."

His lips curved. "I'll live in fear of your temper for the rest of my days."

She laughed. "As you should."

Roberto didn't put Brie down until they reached where he had parked his car. Unfortunately for her, that location happened to be a block away. Even dangling upside down over his shoulder, she could see the many people they passed. Every single one of them started grinning. "Mercy!" she wailed. "Put me down!"

"Not until I am certain you will not escape again, *cara*." He did put her down to open the passenger door, but only so that he could nudge her inside.

She knew better than to jump out again. She simply crossed her arms and stared out the windshield as he got in the driver's side. "I can't believe you dumped Isabelle!"

"You know she will not be hurt. And she has Alex in any case. I have often wondered over the last two years if there were true sparks between them. I am glad to see it confirmed. I love her a great deal, but only as a brother would. I wish her to be happy."

"And if you don't marry her, what happens to your precious merger?"

"We will have to see, will we not? It should not fall apart simply because I am no longer marrying Antonio's daughter." He glanced at her from the corner of his eye. She looked wild and untamed, as if he had somehow caught a creature of magic and confined it. She also looked frightened and miserable, two emotions he never wanted to see on her face again. "*Cara*," he said tenderly, "do not look so scared of me. You will break my heart."

"I'm more worried about you breaking *my* heart!" she fiercely retorted. "I don't want to fall in love with you, Roberto, because it would only destroy me when I couldn't stay with you!" She blinked as she realized he was parking the car in the driveway to a villa no less impressive than the Lucino one. "Where are we?"

"My home."

She scrambled out of the car and tried to run away down the driveway. He caught her in two long strides and once more flipped her over his shoulder. She began to beat on his back. "Don't you dare!" He walked into the villa, and she felt her cheeks heat as an older housekeeper came hurrying forward. "Oh god," she moaned, covering her face with her hands.

"*Signor* Viani." The woman put her hands on her hips. "What are you doing, young man? Is that . . . *Signorina* Lucino?"

"Actually, no. Bella and I canceled our engagement. This is Gabrielle. It is quite a long story, and I am not entirely in the mood to tell it right now. I will explain later, Maria." He went purposefully up the stairs without truly stopping once.

Maria gave a happy sigh as she hurried toward the kitchen. "Get out a bottle of wine!" she ordered. "We are celebrating."

Roberto walked into his suite and shut and locked the door before putting Brie down once more. She immediately backed away from him with her cheeks brilliantly pink. "Now then," he said softly. "Why are you so certain that you cannot stay with me, Gabrielle?"

"Are you nuts?" she shouted. "I don't know anything about your world! I don't belong in it, Roberto! Friggin' hell, don't you think I've been paying attention this weekend? You and the Lucinos come from the same background; you keep the chlorine in the gene pool and put lifeguards at every turn. I don't think my gene pool even *has* a lifeguard!"

"Clearly, *cara*, you were not paying enough attention." He began to unbutton his shirt as he stalked slowly toward her. "I am not dallying with you." His hands closed around her arms and he jerked her up against his hot body. "I am in love with you!"

"You don't even know me!"

Temper and frustration flared in his twilight colored eyes. "I see words are not doing any good. Let us see if actions can break through your stubbornness, Gabrielle."

Any protest she might have made was stolen by his hungry mouth taking hers. As the heat blasted into her body like a drug, a low whimper tangled in her throat. She wanted him so badly. Loved him so stupidly. Her legs lost their strength, and his hands curled into her hips to keep her standing. He drew her tight against his aching body.

He stole more than her breath. He stole her soul. There was an edge to his hunger, a desperation, as if he was fighting to hold onto her before she escaped. She tried to draw back, but his hand tangled in her hair and pulled her in again.

Her last resistance crumbled. She went on her toes against him, and her hands fisted into his open shirt to keep him closer. Her mouth went wild under his, her tongue tangling with his hotly as she strained to deepen the embrace.

He jerked back and stared down at her. "Mine." It was little more than a rasp. He jerked her shirt free of her skirt and rushed open the buttons, popping several in the process. He neither noticed nor cared. "I will know everything about you, *cara*," he vowed roughly. "And you will know me."

Dazed, she had no will left to resist as her shirt landed on the floor. Her skirt went next. His hands swept slowly, caressingly, over her skin until she shuddered with pleasure. "Touch me." He dropped stinging kisses along the slender line of her neck. "Know me."

The temptation could not be resisted. She pushed the shirt off his shoulders and hungrily took in the sight of his half-naked beauty. He was much more powerful than she had been guessing, every line corded with strong muscle. His golden skin seemed nearly bronzed, and the dark hair that lightly covered it was as soft as a pelt. She spread her hands slowly across his chest, savored his heat and strength, and watched his eyes darken to a violent, stormy color.

He caught her hands in his and brought her palms to his lips. He held her there for a moment, struggling for control before he took her on the floor.

As she sensed it, any lingering doubt swept away. Whether she could keep him or not, she believed that he loved her. She could see it churning in his eyes and feel it in the wild race of his heart. For all his hunger, he was trying not to rush her. He wanted to give her the chance to meet him halfway. How had she *ever* been unsure of him before? He was everything she needed.

She tugged her hands free and pointedly unfastened her bra. She dropped it on the floor and then hooked a finger in his belt loop to tug him closer. "You think you can catch someone like me?" Her voice was husky as she rose on her toes to tease his pulse with the tip of her tongue. "I'm not even human."

A shudder ripped through his body. "I do not care." His arms banded around her waist to lift her off her feet. He tumbled her down onto the top of his bed and savored how it felt to have her pressed against his aching flesh. His hands framed her face, his eyes memorizing her. "Do I need to protect you, Gabrielle?" It was little more than a rasp.

Her name sounded exotic. Foreign. In his voice, it became a caress. "Preferably—for now." Her fingers kneaded at his chest. "Touch me." It was little more than a breathless plea.

Nothing could have stopped him. He tore off the headband she wore and found the edge of her delicate ear with his teeth. She even tasted like magic, wild and unstoppable. He had a vision of a tiny dark haired girl with pointed ears sleeping in her arms, and his hands shook. "*Cara. Ti amo.*"

Some things needed no translation. As his mouth slid hotly across her skin, she buried her fingers in his hair possessively. Hers. Even if only a little while, this beautiful creature was hers.

He nuzzled between her breasts, his hands cupping her soft flesh as gently as he could. The nipples tightened and flushed, begging for his mouth, and his low laugh rippled over her skin as he studied her. "You know," he said thickly, "I think you are slightly better built than Isabelle."

She gave a laugh that turned into a moan as his lips closed over her nipple and tugged. "Don't tell her that!" The moan became a soft cry as he tugged again, his fingers kneading her flesh compulsively. Each tug pulled at something deeper and spread the pleasure into a demanding ache until she twisted under him wildly in a bid for relief.

He slid further down her body, teased her navel and the intriguing little hole near her bellybutton that might mean another sexy piercing. He then moved even lower, to the brown curls, damp with her desire.

Her hips arched desperately at the first teasing touch of his tongue on her most sensitive flesh. His fingers danced over the hot flesh of her thigh and somehow found nerves she hadn't imagined existing. He drove her up ruthlessly and savored her cries as she twisted beneath him.

The ache grew and coiled and tightened until every muscle quivered. She reached for him desperately and tugged at his hair in a bid to make him stop. His mouth closed over a secret bundle of nerves and everything seemed to shatter at once, shocking ecstasy ripping through her body without course. She would have cried out, but she had no voice any longer. He had taken it along with everything else.

With a near violent curse, he rolled to his feet and tore off the rest of his clothes before grabbing protection from the nightstand. As he slid onto the bed beside her once more, he saw steam curling up from her damp flesh. The sight of it clawed at his insides. He had never seen anything that outrageously erotic before. He took her mouth with his for a ravenous kiss as his hands stroked over her body fiercely.

She caught her breath as desire roared to life once more and gave her no room to recover, no room to breathe. Her body throbbed wildly for release in mere moments as if he hadn't just thoroughly satisfied her already. "I'm going to get you for this!" It was almost a sob.

His laugh sounded rich and sultry. "I look forward to it, *cara*." He slid over her, caught her legs over his arms, and slowly began to ease his throbbing arousal inside her. She was wet, more than ready for him, but petite enough that he struggled for control before he hurt her. "*Cara*?"

"If you stop," she gasped, "I'll kill you!" Her arms curled around his shoulders, and her fingers dug into his back demandingly. How could anything ever hurt when he touched her? Maddened by his slow pace, she arched beneath him and drove him deep into her body. Her eyes flew wide with shock and then darkened with hunger.

It was more than he could take. He kissed her wildly as he began to thrust, his tongue mimicking the motion of his hips. He stole her soft cries with his mouth and savored the feel of her silken body. His teeth grit together as he fought for control. Only when she arched and cried out against his mouth did he let go and give in to the need riding him so hard. He buried himself to the hilt and stayed there as ecstasy shuddered through his body. He would *never* let her go.

As he collapsed against her, she buried her face against his neck. He smelled wonderfully sweaty and untamed, and he felt even better. Her whole body seemed to pulse softly as it acknowledged his claim over her. It felt a bit primitive and uncivilized, but so were they. "You Italians," she murmured huskily, "definitely embrace passion, don't you?"

He laughed softly as he slowly rose onto his elbows. "You are Italian as well, *cara*. It is a wonder we did not set the house on fire." He trailed his finger down her arm, thrilled by the tendrils of steam. "I did not expect that."

She opened one eye and closed it again. "And yet, I'm not shocked by it."

"Did I hurt you?"

Her eyes opened quickly. "How could you even think that?"

"I just wanted to be sure." He kissed her softly and lingered over her magic and pure water taste. "*Ti amo*, Gabrielle. I do not think I can live without you. The merger can go to hell as far as I am concerned." He searched her eyes. "Tell me," he urged softly.

Her lips curved into a trembling smile. "I love you."

"Then it will be fine. In the morning, we will call Alex and Isabelle and have them meet us at the Lucino home."

"In the morning?"

He smiled slowly. "I am not done with you yet, *cara*. I may never be."

"Oh." It was little more than a contented sigh. "I suppose I can handle that."

CHAPTER FIVE

As the morning sun began to creep in, Brie was curled in Roberto's arms and sleeping contentedly. He stayed awake and softly smoothed his fingers through her hair and down her arm. He had given up on the hope of ever finding true love, and then she had walked into his life and turned it upside down.

He had never really resented the thought of marrying Isabelle. He loved her, after all, and had thought that perhaps being married might make them erase their brother-sister relationship and allow them to possibly fall in love. And, even if not, he had known they could at least be happy. He had been uncertain of whether or not they would ever be lovers, or have children, but he had accepted that as well in exchange for the merger both companies needed so badly.

But Brie . . . she was so different from Isabelle! They were alike only in appearance, and he was still fascinated at how he could want Brie so badly but only have passing admiration for Isabelle. His Gabrielle was wild, passionate, and sultry in not just her face and body, but in her heart and soul. His lips curved. She was more Italian than she thought.

From the moment he had seen her in the dining room of the Lucino home, he had known in his heart that this moment would be inevitable. He had never been the kind to deny his heart, and he was certainly unafraid to claim what he wanted—especially when she had wanted it just as badly. It had not been easy, but the rewards had been worth every agonizing moment.

She fit into his arms perfectly. Her soft breaths comforted him on a nearly cellular level. To imagine her not in his life was to imagine hell. Yet, he knew she would run away again if she thought that she had destroyed the merger. He did not worry about it himself. He felt confident in himself and in the Lucinos, Rafael in particular. They would make this work. Mergers happened all the time without business marriages. He admitted to some old-fashioned ideals, but that one he could happily abandon.

She stirred sleepily and tucked her face more firmly against his shoulder. "Are you awake?" she asked drowsily. "It's dawn. Go to sleep."

"It is a bit after dawn, Gabrielle." He bent his head to kiss her softly and tenderly coax her awake. "You look quite at home in my bed, *cara*. You will have to stay here more often."

"That's one heck of a commute to my job," she retorted dryly. She trailed her fingers over his face and traced his beloved features. "3rd District isn't exactly around the corner from this part of Brooklyn."

"Mmm. We will figure something out." He had every intention of marrying her, but he knew better than to speak of it just yet. He had her soft and warm in his arms, sleepy and content, and he wasn't about to stir up her temper. "Do you want a hot shower?" he asked. "We can take one before we get breakfast."

"Well, yes, but . . ." A smile began to curve her lips. "Roberto, I have nothing to wear. You tore the buttons off my shirt. And it wasn't even my shirt!"

He just smiled. "I will have Maria get you one of my mother's shirts. They should fit you well enough. She is only a little bigger than you are." He tossed aside the covers and openly admired her naked body. "If I could have you always naked, I would be a happy man." He trailed his fingers over her bellybutton. "Pierced?"

"Yup."

"I would like to see it sometime."

"You have a fetish for jewelry." Her lashes fluttered closed as his lips teasingly nibbled at her ear. She had never known she was sensitive there.

"I have a fetish for you, *cara*. Up with you before I have my wicked way with you again."

She scooted out of bed quickly to go into the adjoined bath. Much to her bemusement, his inclination to not have his wicked way with her only applied to the bed. He took full and deliberate advantage of the close confines of the shower. By the time she stepped out again, she was clean, but her legs barely held her up. "Don't touch me, you fiend," she warned when he stepped closer. "I can barely walk!"

He just laughed and dropped a towel over her head. "I cannot resist you, Gabrielle." When no immediate retort came back, he lifted a brow. "You have stopped objecting to me calling you by your full name?"

"I sort of like it how you say it," she admitted. "And after last night, I don't really imagine you could get closer!"

The sound of the bedroom door opening was clearly heard in the bathroom. "Good morning, *Signor* Viani," Maria called cheerfully. "Good morning, *Signorina* Wisteria. I have brought some clothes from *Signora* Viani's closet for you, *signorina*. I will take yours to be, er, mended. There is a tray of food out here for you two. Please enjoy!"

Roberto chuckled as Brie's cheeks turned red. "She is happy that I have been thoroughly caught by a woman she likes," he offered. "She has known me many years. She chooses to retain the formality of titles, but that does not mean she ever hesitated to box my ears!"

"Did she do it often?" she asked dryly.

"I was an angel, *cara*."

"What's 'malarkey' in Italian?"

He laughed and tugged her into his arms for a fierce hug. "You suit me so well, Gabrielle. No other would do." He lifted her chin for a lingering kiss and then slowly released her. "We will eat breakfast and then I will call Alex. There are many things to do today."

In the 3rd District, Isabelle was the first to wake. She woke slightly disoriented as well for there was a heavy weight across her stomach and she couldn't move. When she turned her head and saw her lover, she began to smile. He was sprawled on his stomach with his arm thrown haphazardly across her waist as if to keep her from escaping. She had no intentions of anything like it.

Content, she admired him as he slept. There was a certain satisfaction in knowing she had worn him out. He had certainly worn her out as well. Her well-loved body still ached in places and reminded her of his thorough possession. If she had realized how wonderful claiming him would be, she wouldn't have wasted the last two years. The only unease she felt was only the very slightest of feelings in regards to her father's reaction. Still, Antonio was much his father's son; he would be thrilled at seeing her throw aside everything for love.

"Alex." She trailed her fingers down his arm and savored his strong muscles. He was incredibly strong and beautiful to her eyes. She had seen him shirtless before; it was hard to avoid when he liked to go swimming in the pool at the villa. She had also seen him working out with Tori, and unlike his partner, Alex stripped to the waist to do so. Even knowing all that, it was still entirely thrilling to have all that mouth-watering male landscape under her hands.

"Five minutes," he muttered into the pillow.

Enchanted with him all over again, she scooted closer until she was next to his ear. "Alexander," she said softly, nibbling at his ear, "it is morning and your lover is famished."

One brown eye opened and peered at her. "She ought to be after yesterday. There I was, all intent on being considerate because it was your first time, and every time I turned around, you were seducing me." He sighed deeply and tugged her ever closer. "I am a happy man."

With a laugh, she nipped at his ear. "Freedom, Alexander. Give it to me or I will have my wicked way with you again."

"Is that supposed to make me let go?" He lifted his arm and rolled onto his side with a smile. He propped himself up on his elbow and studied her contentedly. She was unbelievably beautiful. Giving and generous. And passionate. He had known she was capable of great depth, but she had still surprised him. She wanted him as thoroughly as he wanted her and reveled in their mutual emotions. "I am such a fool," he murmured. "To have wasted two years."

"I was thinking the same of myself." She slid out of bed and stretched languidly, sending sunshine rippling over her golden skin. "I believe I want a shower before food," she decided. She smiled over her shoulder, her blue eyes shielded by her thick lashes. "Do you suppose there is room for two in there?"

"I think we can try." He got out of bed and crossed the room to lift her into his arms. "Should we toss the sheets in the washing machine for Brie?" He carried her into the bathroom and set her delicately on her feet.

"Certainly, but I do not think she will be spending much time here." She laughed as she turned on the shower. "Roberto will not let her go, Alex. You can be sure of that. And I am glad for it," she added softly. "I want them both to be very happy. Meeting Brie was like finding a sister. And she needs *famiglia*."

The shower proved to be only barely big enough to hold them both. There wasn't room for fooling around, though much laughing was done as elbows bumped and hands slipped. As she briskly toweled her hair dry, she said warmly, "My shower is *much* bigger. You will have to sneak in sometime."

He reached out and combed his fingers through her hair. "I don't know how long this threat against you will last," he murmured, "but even if it should end tomorrow, I won't be going anywhere."

"You had better not." She gave him a lofty look. "I would hire kidnappers."

He laughed. "Or send Tori."

"True. He would get the job done quite efficiently."

They had only just finished breakfast when his cell phone began to ring. He snagged it from the counter and smiled wryly when he saw the number. He answered it with, "Are you sane this morning, Roberto, or should we be wary of your hot blooded temper?" He winked when Isabelle grinned at him.

"My temper is just fine." Roberto smiled as he said it. He was watching Brie get dressed, and the look on her face as she fought with the clasp on the back of the dress was adorable. "In fact, I do not think I have ever felt better. How about you?"

"Better than I've been in two years." He tugged Isabelle's hand to his lips and nibbled at the tips of her fingers. "I take it we're going to go back to the Lucino household to explain the goings-on."

"Naturally. I will bring Gabrielle if you bring Isabelle. I am sure Antonio and Rafael are very puzzled, and there is much we all need to discuss, in particular the merger." He tugged Brie closer and fastened the clasp for her. The slim gray silk suited her perfectly, though he rather thought she would prefer jeans. She was simply that type of person, and he loved her for it. "We will see you there."

She crossed her arms as he hung up the phone. "Are you sure?" she asked fretfully. "Not that I *want* you to marry Bella, but I don't want to see the companies struggle because of this."

"The merger will go through," he said confidently. He tipped up her chin and kissed her lingeringly. "Do not worry, *cara mia*. It will all work out." He tucked her under his arm protectively as they left the bedroom to go downstairs. "Do you drive?" he asked curiously as he helped her into the car.

"I have a license, but no vehicle. I usually ride my bike or a bus. Like I said, the commute will suck."

"I will drive you."

The tone was firm enough that she knew he wouldn't take no for an answer, and she had no desire to disagree anyway. With a wry sigh, she settled back in her seat. She wasn't entirely sure what the future held yet. They were in love, and they were lovers. Logic said that someone really ought to mention cohabitation, but she hadn't been thinking logical all weekend. She was playing it by ear at that point.

She would have balked at walking into the Lucino villa, but his hand rested on the small of her back to prevent escape. It was with much relief that she saw Alex and Isabelle arriving in Alex's car. "Bella!" She ran to her friend and they clasped hands. "I'm sorry," she said dryly. "Maria is mending your shirt. Roberto ripped off the buttons!"

Isabelle laughed. "*Sì*, and you both look much happier for it!" She hugged her tightly. "I am so glad," she admitted softly, "that he found you, and you found him. *Sorella mia*." She kissed Brie's cheek softly. At the puzzled look, she smiled. "My sister. I see I must teach you the language of your birth."

"The language of my birth is American. But I might want to learn some things. Mostly so I can yell at Roberto." Brie grinned.

"Those are the easiest words to learn." Hands linked with her friend, Isabelle walked with Brie back over to where their men waited. "Shall we?"

Roberto gestured for them to go first, and they walked into the house before him and Alex. In the foyer, Rafael was leaning against a wall and waiting rather impatiently. Tori stood next to him. As the blond saw the girls enter, his brows went up. "Holy stigmatism, Batman. I'm seeing double."

Rafael walked over and bent slightly to peer into both faces. Curiously, now that they were next to each other, he could see easily which was which. It was something rather elemental, though he couldn't put his finger on it. There were minute differences as well, like Brie's hair being an inch shorter, and Isabelle's eyes being fractionally more olive shaped. "*Dio*," he said wryly as he straightened. "Bad enough there was one beauty, but now two. Your poor brother will never sleep."

"I'm not your sister," Brie pointed out.

"You are now, *cara*." He gestured toward Antonio's office. "Papa is waiting for us." He let the women go on ahead and lingered until they had entered the office. Then, as the males passed him, he murmured, "I suppose I need not ask what occurred over the last day. I will be happy for both of you, and my little sisters, once this mess is straightened out."

Inside the office, Antonio was staring a little blindly at the information before him. The grief staggered him. He had hoped, prayed, and wished with all his might, but he was far too late. All he had left was the beautiful daughter that Sophia had given the world. When he heard the door, he looked up. And despite his grief, he smiled. "Well, this will take much getting used to."

"Are you mad, Papa?" Isabelle asked hesitantly.

"No, Bella. I suppose I am relieved in some ways. You were long overdue for a good tantrum, and in doing so, you have brought home someone I have spent many long years looking for." Every pair of eyebrows lifted, and he sighed. "Please, sit down everyone." His experienced eye didn't miss the way Alex gently helped Isabelle into her seat or the way Roberto stood behind Brie's chair in a way more possessive than polite. He wholeheartedly approved of the entire thing.

"What do you mean you have been searching?" Roberto asked.

"First things first." He smiled at Brie. "Your name, *cara*?"

These people were sure casual with endearments, but she still preferred Roberto's way of saying it. "Gabrielle Wisteria. Most everyone calls me Brie."

"*Cara*, what was your mother's name?"

"Sophia."

"Maiden name?"

"I don't know. She never talked about her family." Her heart began to beat faster and her hands clenched together in her lap. "Why do you ask?" she managed to whisper.

"Twenty-two years ago," he said softly, "my little sister was disowned by our father for choosing to marry a man of 'questionable' lineage. He was from the 3rd District, and back then the stigma was much worse than it is today. Her name was Sophia Lucino. I kept watch on her from a distance for many years, but she somehow slipped out from under my radar. I have been looking for her, or you, ever since."

"Well." It was all Tori could think to say.

"So then Brie is our cousin?" Rafael asked softly. "No wonder she and Isabelle are identical! It is just another mystery that life likes to trip people with." He smiled at Brie. "You have got family in us now."

There was nothing she could say to that. She felt more than a little shell-shocked. She even jumped slightly when Roberto put a hand lightly on her shoulder. "Antonio," he said calmly, "Isabelle and I have called off our engagement. Our affections have turned elsewhere. I would ask that the merger continue solely on the basis of our companies' needs."

"Well, you know," Tori had to point out, "isn't Brie technically a Lucino as well? Marrying her would be the same as marrying Isabelle, right?"

"Hang on!" Brie said quickly. "I didn't agree to any of this!"

"Tori has a good point," Antonio told Roberto, ignoring her outburst. "Would you marry Gabrielle instead, Roberto, to cement the deal?"

"Of course."

Brie leapt to her feet sharply. "That's enough!" she shouted. "You can't just decide who I will and won't marry just because I might be part of this lunatic family!" She pointed at Antonio. "I'm not your sister! Don't think you'll dictate my life just because you're feeling guilty!" She whirled and smacked Roberto's hand aside when he would reach for her. "And you! *If* I marry you, it will be because you're on your knees asking, you got that?"

She whirled on her heel and stalked out of the office with enough force that the door slammed behind her. Isabelle hastily leapt to her feet and followed. All Rafael could say dryly was, "*Sì*, Papa. She is a Lucino."

Brie was partway down the driveway when Isabelle caught up with her. "Don't talk to me," she warned.

Isabelle caught her arm and pulled her to a stop. "Brie." She was smiling as she turned her cousin to face her. "That was brilliant, *cara*!" She hugged her tightly. "I was so proud of you! It took me years to find my temper, and you found yours in minutes! You are a true Lucino after all."

The absurdity of the entire weekend caught up and Brie started laughing. She dropped her head on Isabelle's shoulder. "Oh god. I did not just say all that to your father and Roberto, did I?"

"You did, and it was *wonderful*." She sighed wistfully. "I wish I had done that when I was told they wanted me to marry Roberto. But then, perhaps we might not have met you." She laced their fingers together as they reached the sidewalk. "And I am very happy to have met you, Brie."

"I guess I'm happy I met you too, Bella." The sound of tires screeching reached her ears, and she looked down the street curiously. "I thought this was private property."

"It is." Isabelle began to get a bad feeling in her stomach. "We should go back in."

A long black limo skidded to a stop in front of them before they could get away. And though they backed up quickly, they were forced to stop as two men holding guns got out of the car. "Which one do we want?" one asked someone inside the car.

"Get them both." The voice sounded as careless as it did icy, and both cousins felt a chill run down their backs.

In the office, Alex walked over to Antonio's desk and held out a hand. "I want my contract back," he said calmly. "I'm quitting."

Antonio idly handed it over. "Yet, I presume, you will still defend Bella, no?"

"With my life." He tucked the contract into his back pocket. "But I can't have her for my wife as long as I work for her father. I should have quit before being her lover, but how was I to resist her after two years?"

"Around here," Tori said dryly, "I think they totally understand about passion, Alex." A piercing scream ripped through the air, and he leapt to his feet. "Son of a bitch! Alex!"

Alex was already rushing out of the office. Tori stayed right on his heels, and so did Roberto and Rafael. As one, they ran out of the villa and down the driveway. Brie and Isabelle were struggling with two men trying to shove them into the car. Two other men stood watching the tableau, and both held guns fitted with silencers.

"Let go of my sisters!" Rafael shouted as he lunged down the driveway.

One of the men turned and lifted his gun. Without hesitation, Tori threw himself in front of Rafael and knocked him to the ground. The bullet slammed into Tori's unprotected chest, and blood flew as he staggered back a step. His knees buckled and he fell to the asphalt. Blood began to pool under him.

"Tori!" Isabelle screamed, but there was nothing she could do. She and Brie were both shoved into the limo so hard that they sprawled across the seats painfully. The men got in behind them, and the one who had shot Tori put away his gun as if nothing had happened.

Rafael scrambled to where his bodyguard had fallen. "Tori! *Dio*!" He turned him over and blanched as he saw the gaping hole in his chest. But he was breathing still. It was faint and labored, but he was breathing. "Tori!"

Tori's lashes fluttered slightly. "You . . . okay?" His voice broke on a sharp lance of pain.

Alex ripped off his jacket and folded it up. "Press this to the wound," he told Rafael urgently. He looked at the villa where the servants and Antonio had gathered. "Call 911!" he ordered Marco. "Hurry!" He looked at Roberto and knew his face had to be just as pale, just as stricken. "Isabelle's necklace has a homing signal in it. We can find them."

"I'll drive."

As the two males rushed to where Roberto had parked, Rafael pressed the jacket harder against the wound, praying for it to stop bleeding. Tears welled in his blue eyes as he lowered his head. "Damn you, Tori. You can*not* die on me."

It was only minutes until the ambulance arrived, but it felt like hours. Paramedics rushed to take Rafael's place, and he was pushed back enough that he could not see what they did. "Is he going to live?" he demanded.

One paused, glanced at her colleagues, and then looked at him. "We will do our best. Does, er, he have family?"

"He is part of my family! I will go with you to the hospital." He moved closer once Tori had been put on a stretcher, and took Tori's hand in his. To lose Bella and Brie was bad enough, but to lose Tori as well would devastate him. Closing his eyes, he prayed in a way he had never prayed before.

CHAPTER SIX

"Well, ladies." The voice was both cold and almost mocking. "How kind of you to join us. Please, have a seat."

Brie scrambled up to her knees and helped Isabelle up as well. They both edged back to sit on the nearest bench seat, hands tightly clasped as they tried to avoid being anywhere near the men with guns. It was all Isabelle could do to keep from lunging at the man who had shot Tori.

"I admit," the leader said, looking between them, "I was not expecting this. Which of you is Isabelle Lucino? The other may go free."

Brie squeezed Isabelle's hand tightly. Like *hell* she would abandon her cousin. Isabelle wanted to set Brie free, but she was more terrified to be alone. She clung to Brie's hand as a lifeline. They were in this together.

When it became clear that neither would answer, he settled back in his seat. His handsome face seemed to be carved in stone, and his black eyes looked unnervingly quiet. "The boss can decide what to do with you, then. Whichever of you isn't a Lucino is going to regret she kept her mouth shut." He reached over and cupped Isabelle's chin. "Maybe I will get to enjoy the imposter. You're both very beautiful."

The glass of water sitting on a sideboard suddenly seemed to explode and the water spewed into the air all over him. He jerked back hastily. "Very subtle of you, whichever of you did that."

"Where are we going?" Brie asked softly.

He looked up from wiping the water off his jacket. "It matters little to you. No one will be able to find you."

Isabelle softly touched the necklace she wore. It had been a gift from Alex for her twentieth birthday. She knew full well that it had been chipped just in case anything happened. It had been an amusement before. Now it was a salvation. Careful to mimic Brie's way of speaking, she asked, "Then why can't you tell us where we're going? If we're not going to be rescued . . ."

"Just shut up or we'll gag you both."

They shut up. The windows were tinted enough that looking out was just as hard as looking in. Two of the men sat against each door, completely eliminating the chance of jumping out when the limo stopped. It also didn't seem to stop often. Either they were on a freeway, or they were hitting every green light.

Eventually the limo rolled to a stop and the men got out. They dragged Brie and Isabelle out with them, and both blinked in the harsh sunlight after having been in the dim car for too long. They were nowhere that looked familiar. It was a nice villa of some kind sitting in the middle of its own acreage. It seemed vaguely reminiscent of the Lucino home, but a menace clung to this building.

There was no one around. Neither cousin said a word as they were escorted into the villa. Since neither resisted, the men let them walk under their own power. In the foyer, the leader said to the men, "Take them to a room upstairs and lock them in. I'll go talk to the boss."

The men did as they were told without question. They took the two women upstairs, shoved them into a ridiculously decadent bedroom, and then shut the door. The sound of the lock turning echoed loudly and eerily.

Brie ran over to the window, but it was shut and sealed as well. The window in the attached bathroom was far too small to climb out, especially from the second story. "This is just great," she muttered. "Just great!"

Isabelle sat on the side of the bed and crossed her arms around herself. She couldn't stop shivering. "What are we going to do, Brie?" Her voice broke and she buried her face in her hands. "They shot Tori. *Dio*, what if he dies? I could not bear it! He is part of the family."

Brie sat down next to her. "What the heck is going on, Bella? Why's there a death threat against you? What's up with the bodyguards and house arrest?"

"Two years ago, Papa and Rafael helped catch someone who was involved in a great deal of embezzlement. The man lost out on millions of dollars because of it. He found out that the Lucinos were involved and made some serious threats against us. The cops were not able to catch him, so he has been loose all this time. It was simply safer to hire bodyguards than to wait and hope the police caught the criminal. And he is nuts, Brie. They could give him an insanity defense and it would stick."

"What sort of insane are we talking?" Brie looked around the room as she spoke.

"Well, other than the part where he is trying to kill us, and the part where he set up a pyramid scheme that even Ponzi would shake his head at, he has been heard many times talking to himself. And I do not mean in a normal way. He would hold actual conversations with absolutely no one, and never pleasant ones."

"Great. So we've been kidnapped by a nutso. We have got to get out of here."

"How?"

"I say we knock a guard out and make a break for the door. We're dead either way, right? We can't expect them to simply put us here with three full meals and amenities while this guy nicely asks your dad for an apology." Brie looked at the door sharply as she heard footsteps and then glanced around. She spotted a heavy statuette and hefted it. She was completely playing by ear and praying that it worked. She swiftly darted over to the side of the door where she wouldn't be seen by anyone entering.

The door opened and one of the guards walked in. With much savage satisfaction, she recognized the bastard who had shot Tori. She cracked the statuette over his head with all her strength. He dropped like a stone to the floor and did not move.

"I hope you killed him!" Isabelle said fiercely as she hurried to Brie's side. "We need to get out of here before the others come running!"

A peek into the hall showed it was clear. The foyer downstairs looked empty. Isabelle led the way toward the stairs and hurried down them, listening intently for any sign that someone had heard them and was coming after them. As Brie reached her side, she spotted movement. Instinctively, she shoved her friend into the hall beside them and removed her from sight.

"Well, well, well." The older gentleman who had spoken looked like an executive on his day off. He was cleaned up, well-shaven, and wore an air of authority. Casual khakis and a polo shirt seemed to indicate he might as well be heading to a golf game, but something not quite sane glimmered across his pale eyes. He crossed from the office doorway slowly toward Isabelle. "So you're Antonio's little bitch of a daughter."

"I do not think we have been introduced." She lifted her chin.

"How rude of me, dear. I am Martin Johns." He bowed mockingly. "I believe your father ruined my life."

"Interesting. I heard he helped to catch a thief and a liar. I would say he saved other lives, no?"

His face tightened with fury. "You're going to regret your sassy mouth, Miss Lucino. I intend to break you down until you're begging for your life." Something moved across his eyes. "It told me that you would escape, but I do not think so. My men would never betray me."

On pure gut hunch, Brie stepped forward from the hall to be directly beside Isabelle. As Martin paled, she asked, "How can you be sure you have the right girl? Do you know what Isabelle looks like? She does not have a twin, yet here I stand."

"No . . . no I told them specifically to go after Isabelle! They wouldn't have failed me!"

Isabelle smiled serenely as she laced her hand with Brie's. "And yet here there stand two of us. Which is which, Mr. Johns? Can you tell? Perhaps one of us is an illusion."

"How can you be sure you haven't been drugged, Mr. Johns?" Brie made her voice as gentle as she could. "Maybe we aren't even real. But then, I feel real. Do you feel real?" she asked Isabelle.

"Certainly I feel real. Maybe we are imagining *him*."

"What a silly thought! I would not imagine some like him."

"Oh, so true. What was I thinking?"

Their voices began to take on an identical cadence as they bantered back and forth. And though they wore different clothing, Martin began to lose the ability to distinguish between them. One of them was real. The other was illusion. But what if they were both real? That meant he had the wrong woman, and someone *else* would be after him.

"No, no!" He shook his head sharply as he backed up a step. "I'm just tired," he said fiercely, and it was hard to tell whom he tried to convince. "There's only one of you. You're trying to trick me."

"What trick?" both asked at the same time. The echoing voices sounded unearthly. "We are both real."

The other men suddenly rushed into the area with weapons drawn. "Mr. Johns! What's going on?" one demanded. "Why are they out of their room?"

"You see them? You see both of them?" Martin demanded.

"Well . . . yes sir." The man looked to where the women stood, and he was startled when he realized only one remained there. "Er. Uhm." He looked around quickly but there was no sign of the other female. "Wait."

The other men were just as puzzled for they only saw one woman as well. And yet, when Martin stared, he was sure he still saw two. One was smiling. The other waved. With a screech like nails on a chalkboard, he whirled on his men. "You!" he snapped out. "You did this to me! I knew you would betray me!"

The men, as one, began to edge back. All three faces began to reflect wariness as they saw just how far off the deep end their boss had started to dive. When Martin lunged for one of them, the man was forced to dodge quickly.

Isabelle and Brie carefully edged to the front door. It was locked. Brie, currently holding a watery mirror over herself to keep all but Martin from seeing her, glanced over to see him still attacking his men. Either they didn't want to hurt him or they weren't sure what to do, since all they did was try to stay out of his reach.

"How do we open the door?" Isabelle whispered.

"Do you trust me?"

"Of course!"

Brie wrapped her arms around her and concentrated fiercely. She had never attempted this before, but desperate times called for desperate measures. As her power rose, both began to dissolve. In moments they were nothing but a tendril of water. They flowed out through the open window over the door and then splashed onto the porch where they promptly turned back.

"Ouch!" Isabelle rubbed her sore hip. "The landing lacks something to be desired, Gabrielle."

"I'd never done it before, okay?" She scrambled to her feet and caught Isabelle's hand to tug her up. "Let's get out of Dodge!" Hands clasped, they ran down the sidewalk toward the curving driveway to the street.

Just as they reached the bottom, a familiar green car skidded to a stop. Even before it fully parked, Alex and Roberto leapt out. Isabelle forgot all thoughts of dignity and leapt into Alex's arms. "Alex!" she sobbed against his neck.

Roberto could barely breathe as Brie sprang into his arms. She wrapped her arms and legs around him like a vine, shaking so violently that it was a wonder her delicate bones weren't rattled. "Gabrielle. *Cara.*" He buried his face in her hair. "You scared ten years off my life, *cara.*"

"I've lost twenty!" Alex said shakily as he held Isabelle. He wanted to yell at her for even leaving the house, but she had merely gone after Brie. And naturally Brie wouldn't have known the danger. The thought of what might have happened if Brie had been alone was as terrifying as what had nearly happened to her and Isabelle both.

"Tori." It was a broken sob against his neck. "Is Tori alive?"

"We don't know." He smoothed her hair back with trembling fingers. Fear made his stomach churn violently. "We came right after you two." He gently touched the necklace she wore. "You gave me hell, but you never took it off."

"I knew you would save me if it was ever needed."

Roberto somehow found a laugh. It was easier now that he had Brie warm and safe in his arms again. "Bella, the two of you saved yourselves. We are simply driving the getaway car. The cops are right behind us, so we can leave." He slowly put Brie on her feet and kissed her hard. "We will go to the hospital to see Tori. He is strong. He will be just fine."

Rafael and Antonio were sitting in the emergency waiting room when they arrived. Antonio looked like he had aged ten years in a matter of hours. Rafael was pale and terrified. When he saw his sisters running into the room, he leapt to his feet. "*Dio!*" He rushed forward and caught them both in his arms. "Bella. Brie. *Grazie a Dio*." He kissed Isabelle's forehead and then Brie's. He could have loved his cousin no more if she had actually been his sister.

"Tori." Brie's voice shook as she clung onto him. "What about Tori?"

"He is in surgery." His voice broke but steadied again. "The paramedics think we were in time." He looked up sharply as he saw movement, and he held his sisters tighter as he saw the familiar form of a doctor in the doorway. He held his breath.

"You are the family of Tori Li?" At the nods, the doctor let out a soft breath. "Tori will be fine. He lost a lot of blood, and the bullet tore up his shoulder, but it missed his lungs. It missed everything vital. He'll need to stay in the hospital for at least two weeks, and he will need extensive care at home. He will also need physical therapy." He smiled suddenly. "But, knowing him, he'll be working out within months as if nothing had happened."

"You sound like you know him," Alex observed.

"I've known Tori for years. Now go home and rest. He will be in intensive care for a few hours, and he is sleeping. You may see him tomorrow."

"I will see him now." Rafael's tone booked no argument. "He took that bullet to save my life. He is my closest friend. Please."

The doctor stared at him for several moments before a tiny smile touched his lips. "Very well. Come with me, Mr. Lucino."

They left the room and Antonio got to his feet carefully. He felt every one of his fifty years in that moment. He made his way to his daughter and niece and pulled them both into his arms. "Never scare your poor papa like that again!" he said into Isabelle's hair. He kissed Brie's forehead. "And you, *cara*, are going to be kept under wraps with Bella until the threat has passed." He looked at Alex and Roberto. "The detectives called me while you were on your way here."

Roberto's stomach clenched. "They did not catch the man."

"They arrived moments after you left, but he had gone out the back. They want statements from the girls, but I told them they would have to wait until their family had been reassured." He looked at both Roberto and Alex evenly. "I believe you have things to discuss with my daughters."

"You have been adopted," Isabelle whispered to Brie. "You might as well accept it."

"Gabrielle," Roberto said softly, "I would like to talk to you."

She sniffed at him. With the danger past, her anger with him had returned. Never mind the fact that she really wouldn't have minded jumping on him again. Never mind the fact that when he had seen her, there had been so much emotion in his eyes that it had broken her heart. "I have nothing to say to you."

He sighed. "One day, *cara*, you will learn not to push me." He caught her around the waist and tossed her over his shoulder to carry her out.

"A match made in heaven," Isabelle murmured. She smiled at Alex. "Well, I suppose you have reason to stay on as my bodyguard now."

"I quit, Bella."

"You . . ." Her eyes widened. "You *what*?" She was so astonished that she did not notice her smiling father sneak away to give them privacy. "You quit? *Dio*, Alex! But why?" Her lower lip trembled. "Was this . . . was this incident too much?"

"No." He pulled her into his arms and kissed her tenderly, letting his emotions well in the embrace until she went limp in his arms. Only then did he lift his head. "I love you, Bella. I quit so that I could ask you to be my wife. I can't marry my boss' daughter, after all." He cupped her cheek. "Say yes."

Tears welled in her eyes as she wound her arms around his neck. "*Sì*. Yes. Any way you say it, my answer is yes. *Ti amo*, Alex. Always." Happier than she had ever been in her life, she pressed her face to his shoulder. She should have run away and met Brie sooner. Everything had worked out in the end.

Brie was not nearly in such a good mood. She crossed her arms sullenly, eyes narrowed, as she was carried out over Roberto's shoulder past many giggling nurses and several startled, yet amused, people in the emergency room. "Roberto, I think Mr. Johns wasn't the only who had lost his mind. You need help. You're certifiable. You can't keep running off with me like this!"

"As a matter of fact, Gabrielle, I can. I am much stronger than you are. And do not dare to turn into water to get away. I will find a sponge and absorb you up again."

"I wasn't thinking of it," she muttered. When she was finally put on her feet in the parking lot, she edged away from him a step. "I'm not going anywhere with you. Hear me? I'm not even going to talk to you!"

"You do not have to talk. But you will get in the car or I will put you there."

She made a little sound of frustration and got into the car. He just smiled and went around to the driver's side. He could see many long, happy years fighting with her in his future, and he could not wait. He would have been bored with Isabelle; he knew that now. Fiery as she had revealed herself to be, she was tame compared to her cousin.

Brie remained stubbornly quiet and watched the roads curiously. She had no idea where he was taking her, yet she found herself unsurprised when she recognized that they returned to his home. As the car stopped, she said fiercely, "If you think I'll let you touch me when I'm this pissed off, you have another think coming!"

"You are not talking to me, Gabrielle. Remember? Just come with me. You may be mad at me later if you so wish. For now, I have something I wish to show you." He opened her car door and held out a hand. Triumph flared as she slowly put her hand in his. He should have done this that morning when he had awakened to find her warm and beautiful and perfect in his arms.

To her surprise, he did not take her into the house. He instead led her around the side and to the backgrounds where an extensive garden resided. Statuaries lined stone walkways, and trellises dripped with brilliant flowers. A particularly stunning fountain made her fingers itch for pencil and paper. She knew she could spend hours in these amazing gardens and never be bored. "Wow."

"My grandfather's father built this," he admitted, "when he was younger than I. He met his wife while he was in the middle of building the house." He drew her into a gazebo made of warm toned stone that reflected across her ashy hair and golden skin and made her beauty magically deepen. "He brought her here and turned her to look at the shell of the home he was making. And he told her 'if you will be mine, I will share this with you.'"

"Very sweet," she managed to say, her heart tripping madly. "May I leave now?"

"Every generation since," he went on without pause, "the one who would inherit has brought the one they love to this very spot to make that same promise." He brought her chilled fingers to his lips and then went down on one knee. "*Ti amo*, Gabrielle. Be mine. Be my wife."

"I'm not human," she whispered.

"I do not care. I do not care about the merger either." When her eyes widened, he brought her fingers to his lips and breathed softly on them to warm them. "If Antonio had said that he would not accept a merger without my marriage to Isabelle, I would have walked out. Your Lucino blood is irrelevant. You are my choice, *cara*. You were my choice from the moment I saw you. Be mine."

She looked at him and then at the garden around them. It seemed to speak of promises. Of wishes she had never dared speak aloud. A home. A family. Someone to love her. She looked down into his lavender eyes and saw everything she had ever wanted. "Yes," she said softly. "A million times yes."

"Promise?"

She rolled her eyes. "No, I'm lying."

"Too late." His grin spread. "I have witnesses."

She looked over his head at the villa where many faces were pressed against the windows. She wanted to be embarrassed, she really did, but she found herself laughing instead. She tugged him up to his feet and wound her arms around his neck. "What did your great-grandfather do when his lover said yes?"

"He kissed her."

"Well?" She arched a brow. "I'm waiting."

His rich laugh was still echoing in the garden as he kissed her with all the love in his heart.

CHAPTER SEVEN

"Both Isabelle Lucino and Gabrielle Wisteria are reported to be fine and well. Tori Li, who was shot in the defense of Rafael Lucino, is listed in stable condition and expected to make a full recovery. Anyone with knowledge of the whereabouts of Martin Johns is encouraged to contact the police. A reward has been posted for tips leading to a successful arrest."

Rhianna Taber lifted the remote control and turned off the rest of the news report. She knew everything that had been said and would be said. As co-owner of Enforcers, she had contacts in all places, including the news and police. If it affected a member of 3rd District, she was notified first.

Her partner was sitting on the side of her desk. They had been watching the news together, and Eric Mason's handsome face now looked very grim. "How much control do we have this time, Rhi?"

"Not as much as I want," she admitted. "Tori should never have been wounded, but we can as yet turn it to our advantage and get a happy ending for the entire Lucino family." She picked up the contract the two cousins had signed and watched the word 'Complete' appear. She added her notes to the bottom and then slipped the contract into a folder. It also signed as being completed, and she slipped it into a drawer labeled 'Lucino.'

"You moved very quickly to have Gwyn get them under contract," he noted softly. "Did you know this would happen?"

"No. And that's the entire reason I was worried. When I can't see the outcome," her hands clenched together for a moment, "then I know that evil is on the move." And whenever she felt it, her guilt knew no bounds.

Her partner said nothing for several moments. Then, softly, he asked, "So what do we do next?"

"What else?" She smiled wryly. "We play it by ear."

♀ ♀ ♀

Status: File Begun

Analysis: Be she princess or pauper, every woman is richer when she is loved.

Folder Two

RAFAEL

CHAPTER EIGHT

The hospital room was quiet. Machines beeped steadily. Rafael had been sitting by Tori's side for the last hour or two. It had been almost a week since the incident. In that time, Rafael had spent more time at the hospital than at home. He simply couldn't bear to leave his friend's side. Tori had been nearly *killed*.

The door opened, and the doctor walked in. "Rafael," he said kindly, "go get some coffee. You look like you haven't been sleeping."

"Seeing someone be shot in my defense will do that to someone," Rafael shot back softly. He still got to his feet. "I can take a hint. I will come back shortly."

When the door shut had behind him, the doctor walked over to look down at Tori. "You, young lady," he said quietly, "are damned lucky that someone didn't try to remove your shirt to get to your wound at the scene."

Tori opened her eyes and stared up at the ceiling. It was about all she had the strength for, though she grew stronger with every day. She would be going home tomorrow. Her blood levels had been brought back to normal, and she could actually get out of bed for short bursts. "I know," she sighed quietly.

He sat down beside her and began to check her pulse. "When I first saw you, I was rather surprised," he admitted. "But I went along with things. I've never corrected anyone's assumptions, as you asked. Do you suppose you ought to tell me precisely why you've chosen this sort of life?"

A tiny, self-mocking, smile tugged at her lips. "No one wanted me around when I was a girl."

(Nine years ago)

The girls were whispering again. Tori kept her chin up as she walked down the hall. Her books were clutched to her chest, and she kept her eyes fixed straight ahead. At sixteen, she was too tall, too gangly, and too late for puberty. She stood eight inches over five feet tall, her legs and arms were thin, and she had absolutely no figure. In a school full of teenage girls becoming young women, she had a triple whammy.

As she tried to open her locker, her fingers slid off the lock. She looked in disgust at the greasy hair gel that had been smeared over her locker and now her fingers. Didn't they ever think of anything new?

"Having trouble there, Victoria?" one girl asked snidely as she walked past. "Since you never do anything with that mop you call hair, maybe the gel will be useful!"

Tori ignored the sound of the entire hall laughing. She wiped her fingers on her jeans and opened her locker to switch her books. Her reflection in the built-in mirror on her door sneered at her. Her hair was shorter than half the boys in the school, and her face hovered in a strange middle ground between feminine and masculine. Androgyny wouldn't be that bad if she *felt* androgynous. She just felt too much like a girl to be comfortable with what nature had chosen for her.

"Don't you have gym with her?" a girl said in a loud whisper as she went past.

Her companion laughed rudely. "Yeah, but she should be in the boys' locker room. She has no boobs at all. She doesn't even wear a bra to phys ed!"

People in the hall started laughing again. Tori slammed her locker door and slung her backpack over her shoulder. "If wearing a bra means cutting off the circulation to my brain and making me as stupid as you, then I'll be glad to go without one," she retorted.

"You want to say that again?" The girl went on her toes in an effort to get into Tori's face. "You think you're so tough?"

"Dude." The other girl with her tugged on her arm. "Dude, that's a really bad idea."

"Oh yeah? What's she going to do? She's nothing but a flat-chested beanpole whose mother dumped her in the garbage."

Tori's fist cracked across her jaw so hard that she was knocked flat on her ass. She began to sob with more drama than sincerity, and people rushed to her side with coos of sympathy. Not one spared Tori a single look even though she had been the one provoked. Arms crossed, she went directly to the main office. "I hit Paula Crothers. You might want to suspend me."

Astonished, the secretary stared at her. "Pardon?"

"Suspend me." She sat down in a chair. "I'd welcome it."

By the time her foster parents arrived to pick her up, the principal had decided to not only suspend her, but also recommend that she switch schools entirely. This event was the latest in a long line of them, and the principal didn't feel right punishing her when she was the one being tormented. He just couldn't seem to make anything change at the school for her; the bullies' parents were honestly no better in many ways.

Tori said nothing as the car rolled down the freeway. Her foster parents weren't really quite sure what to say. She was a very giving, very loving person. She had an infectious sense of humor, a sharp wit, and a brilliant mind. She was also an exceptionally talented martial artist with two black belts and several trophies to her record. At sixteen, she was only just starting to shine.

But for her two high school years and prior two junior high years, she had never once come home from school smiling. She talked little about the things that happened, but teachers were more than happy to fill in the details. Today was just another day for Tori.

"I just don't understand," her mother said softly. "How can the entire school dislike you? In our years of fostering, you're by far the most amazing girl we've ever known."

"It's not the entire school." Tori rested her elbow against the car door, her eyes watching billboards rush past. "Just the girls. I get along with the boys just fine. I'm not feminine enough for the girls to want to be seen with me. On the other hand, the boys feel comfortable with me because they don't have to worry about their hormones. I'm just one of the guys. And that's another reason the girls hate me. The hot guys hang out with me."

"You're a late bloomer, Victoria," her father promised softly. "You'll be beautiful one day soon. In the meantime, we should consider home study. Take off the peer pressure a little. Your mind is too good to be wasted."

"Yeah. Whatever. As long as I don't go back to that hellhole, I don't really care."

(Present)

Doctor Singh studied Tori for long moments. "When did you decide to start disguising yourself as a boy?"

"When I graduated high school. I moved to NYC to go to college and decided to forestall any issues with my peers. I decided to let them figure out what they thought I was, and since everyone assumed I was male, I let them. It stung, but at least I could survive, and I could make friends. I never lie about it, and I tell the truth if someone thinks to ask, but for all intents and purposes, Tori Li is a man as far as the world is concerned." She took a long breath. She felt weak and tired again. Just talking wore her out quickly, and it was becoming more and more vexing. "It solved all my problems. Girls aren't offended by me and guys still feel comfortable."

"Yet, somewhere inside, *Victoria* is hiding and wishing she could be free," Doctor Singh murmured.

"I keep her as quiet as I can. Saves my sanity."

The door opened suddenly, and Rafael walked in. A smile lit his face as he saw that she was awake. "Tori." He walked to her side and leaned over the rail to take her hand in his. "You are awake. How do you feel?"

"Tired. Bored."

Doctor Singh chuckled. "The second is a good sign." He got to his feet. "I will leave you two. Do not stay too long, Rafael. Tori needs his sleep."

Rafael kept a firm grip on Tori's hand while he tugged the chair closer. As the door shut, he said teasingly, "As if he thinks that I do not spend time here even when you are sleeping." He searched Tori's face, hating the pallor to his skin and the still dull color of his eyes. "Tell me honestly, Tori. How are you feeling?"

She found a smile for him. "I'm fine, Rafe. I will be fine. I just learned the hard way that I'm not bulletproof. I mean, I always knew I might someday have to make that decision to step in front of someone, so I'm not resenting my job, if that's what you're thinking. I really didn't even think about what I was doing, to be honest. It was pure instinct. I saw the gun aimed at you and . . ."

"And scared me to death," he finished in a low voice. "*Dio*, Tori. If you had died, it would have destroyed me. You may have come into my life as my bodyguard, but you know you are my best friend. Should all the trouble end tomorrow, I would still insist on you being in my life. No one knows me as well as you do."

Something painful that had nothing to do with her injury ripped at her heart. She had become a victim of her own circumstances. For two years, she had been desperately, maddeningly, trying to keep her emotions for her friend under wraps. From the moment she had walked into Antonio's office, she had been ridiculously attracted to Rafael. Over two years those flames had been fanned into something much more elemental and much more dangerous.

The real reason she had thrown herself over him had nothing to do with her contract. She could have been Isabelle's bodyguard and would have done the same thing. She had been in love with Rafael for almost these entire last two years. She would never stop loving him, but he not only thought her a male, but he loved her only as a friend. She genuinely did not think revealing her gender would make any difference in that.

Oh, she knew he wouldn't be mad over it. He and his family were humorously easy-going in some ways. They would realize they had made the mistake by not asking—and, in fact, Antonio *did* know—and they would accept her reasons and all would move on. She just feared losing her closeness with Rafael if he knew, so she kept quiet still. It would be her secret to her grave, whenever that happened. "It's funny," she said softly. "I never really had a close friend."

Rafael looked up in surprise. Tori very rarely ever talked about himself. He had briefly mentioned being in foster homes, and that he had been home schooled, but he had never said more than that. For all his outgoing, personable charm, he was frustratingly secretive. "You have *never* had one? I find that hard to believe, Tori."

"Believe it." She sighed deeply, her lashes drooping. "Sorry."

"No, it is fine." He smiled. "Sleep, Tori. I will be here to protect you."

A little smile touched her lips. "And who is the bodyguard, huh?"

That was his Tori. Rafael kept Tori's hand in his as he watched him slip asleep again. Only when he was sure that Tori was asleep did he bring his hand to his lips and press a kiss to his palm. He had a *big* problem. He had fallen in love with someone he suspected he might never be able to have. How did a supposedly heterosexual man tell his male best friend that he wanted him more than air?

He had honestly wanted Tori from the beginning, and his instant response to him had made him doubt his eyes saying Tori was male. Yet Tori had not corrected anyone, so Rafael had been left to assume Tori's fascinating blend of feminine to masculine had been enough to interest him anyway. After they had begun spending great deals of time together, Rafael had stopped caring entirely what gender his bodyguard may or may not be. Whenever Tori shot him one of those laughing, teasing grins, Rafael was forced to choke a desire to kiss those smiling lips.

He *burned*. Every day made his desire for Tori grow worse. And now . . . now, with Tori wounded, he had been forced to confront his deepest feelings. He was in love with his bodyguard. But, how could he *not* love Tori? His soul burned so brightly that it lit the area around him. In some light, he looked like a particularly attractive man. In other light, he looked like a particularly attractive woman. It was an enchanting sort of magic that Rafael had watched for two years and still didn't understand.

It was unrequited. He accepted that. Tori might never love him the way he loved Tori. But he would be Tori's friend. He would give Tori the family he had always seemed so hungry for. In a way, he almost hoped the man threatening the family would not be caught for a while yet. He wanted Tori close. The question remained, however, how long he would be able to resist the urge to kiss those ridiculously sexy lips that his bodyguard had. That, more than anything, would drive Tori away, and he could not bear even the idea of it happening.

Tori was released from the hospital the following afternoon. She was more than happy to see the last of her room. She was tired of being in bed, tired of constantly being poked and prodded by nurses, and tired of really crappy meals.

Getting dressed proved to be an interesting exercise, but she adamantly refused to wear that stupid hospital gown any longer. Since she could not use her left arm at the moment because it was excruciatingly painful *and* in a sling to put a straightjacket to shame, she was forced to yank on her jeans one handed. Her shirt proved even trickier, and she was scowling at it when a nurse came around the curtain.

"Oh for god's sake, Tori!" The nurse was more exasperated than surprised. "Let me help before you ruin all our hard work!"

She sighed and stopped wrestling with the shirt. She let her arm be limp so that the shirt could be worked over it. Even still, her wound throbbed in annoyance as her arm was put back in its sling. She grimaced and ignored it. She wasn't taking pain pills anymore. She absolutely wanted to get herself back into fighting form as soon as she could. Rafael was still in danger.

"You know," the nurse said casually, "you say you're not beautiful as a woman, but we were all talking about how lovely we think you are."

"You're kind, but you're also lying." She plucked at her shirt with her good hand. "I'm not wearing a bra, and you can't even tell that I'm a woman. I *might* be an AAA cup size, but really, why bother counting that?"

"Being a woman isn't all about your breasts, you know. It's something inside. Something deeper. Something you feel that comes into the air around you. You've probably been driving several men nuts because they're attracted to you but their eyes say you're a male." She smiled when she got a distinctly skeptical look. "Have you tried to be a woman on purpose, Tori? You might be surprised."

"Ha."

"Let's try this." She knelt to help Tori wiggle into her sneakers. "What would it take to change your mind?"

"Hmm. A bust size that can't be hidden by decent cotton and a guy who wants me regardless."

She arched a brow slowly and then hid a smile. She and every other nurse and doctor in the hospital felt nearly entirely certain that Rafael Lucino had a *very* personal emotional investment in his bodyguard. His reaction to Tori's injury and subsequent weakness had crossed the line from a good friend into the realm normally reserved for lovers. "You're just a late bloomer," she contented herself with saying.

"I'm twenty-five!" Tori snorted rudely. "If I haven't bloomed by now, I never will."

Another nurse called, "Are you ready to go?"

"Yes! Get me out of here before I climb the walls one-handed like Spiderman!"

Laughing, the nurse pulled back the curtain to reveal she had brought a wheelchair. She and the first nurse very carefully helped Tori sit down in the chair and firmly covered her with a blanket to combat the chill outside. "Stop pouting," she ordered. "You know the deal was that you could get out of jail early, but only if you were wheeled and not walking."

"Hrmph."

Tori's sour mood lasted until she was wheeled out of the hospital. The sight of Rafael standing next to his car waiting for her lifted her spirits as nothing else could. Just seeing him alive and healthy made every pain, every weakness, worth it.

He slowly smiled when he saw her, and it sent her heart into riotous pounding. He had the most lethal smile she had ever countered, and it constantly served to remind her that as much as puberty had skipped her physically, it had *not* skipped her hormonally. "Get me out of here," she told him dryly to cover her reaction. "They're threatening to tie me to the bed!"

"Well, do not think you will be doing anything except resting at home, either." He walked over and lifted Tori with casual ease out of the wheelchair. When Tori clutched his shoulders, he belatedly realized what he had just done. For a moment, he had entirely forgotten Tori was a male, and a strong one with it. "I am sorry. I did not think."

Knowing damned well she would be breathless if she tried to talk, she managed to simply smile and roll her eyes. It worked. He grinned and put her gingerly into the car. As soon as the door shut, she blew out a hard breath. She was only five inches shorter than he, and she weighed much more than she looked. He had still handled her as if she was Isabelle or Brie's size.

He got into the driver's side and shook his head. "If I offended you, I am sorry, Tori. I did not think for some reason. I did not want you to tire yourself out." He grinned quickly. "If you wish to get back at me when you are strong again, you may hit me if you are inclined."

She slid a glance at him. "It's my left arm injured. I could hit you with my right hand. But since I guess you saved me some strength, I can let you get by."

He laughed. "It has been so lonely without you at home! I have no one to talk to. Brie is living with Roberto, and Isabelle and Alex spend their time together. Even when we all have dinner together, it feels as if there is something missing. You are not there to tease me, or to talk with after dinner. I have not slept this week, Tori. I did not have you to talk with until I was tired."

His problems with insomnia were known only to her, and she only knew because she had caught him awake one night. Most nights since, they had stayed up together, talking or playing billiards, until they both felt tired enough to sleep.

She frowned. "You need to rest, Rafe. I can't protect you well enough if you are sick. Not right now." She put a hand on his arm. "I nearly gave my life for yours. You can't be wasting that, got it? Else I really will hit you!"

He smiled and covered her hand with his for a moment. "With you home, I will be fine. I will simply have to take care of you."

She laughed. "There you go again! Just who is being paid anyway?" She scowled suddenly. "And Antonio had better not still be talking about giving me that bonus!"

His brows lifted. "You heard that? I thought you were asleep."

"I was half in, half out. You Lucinos are loud." She rolled her eyes.

"*Sì*, but we are fun and we look after *famiglia*. You are family."

She couldn't argue that point. Just glad to be out of the hospital, she closed her eyes and settled in for a light nap. It was easy to let down her guard around Rafael. He made her feel loved, even if just a little.

Rafael glanced at Tori from the corner of his eye and then gently brushed the back of his knuckles down Tori's cheek. Tori muttered something wordless and grumpy, and it made his heart ache with tenderness. He loved him so.

A few minutes later, they pulled into the driveway of the Lucino villa. He smiled as he saw the crowd on the porch. "Tori."

She opened her eyes and yawned. "Are we there?" Her words stopped as she saw what waited for her. Her eyes slowly widened. "Wha?"

Every last member of the Lucino household, including the servants, stood on the porch of the villa. Alex and Roberto were helping Antonio hold up a giant sign that said 'Welcome home!'. Isabelle and Brie held flowers. The servants all had balloons or streamers.

Rafael parked the car with a smile. "You were missed."

"I see that!" She waited for him to come help her and let him support her weight as she carefully walked toward the entrance. She could walk on her own, but it would take all her strength. She felt no shame in letting Rafael support her as long as he didn't carry her again. It really was not her style, and it was sexier than she could handle.

"Tori!" The identical cousins rushed down the walkway toward her. "You're home!"

"Hey, no grabbing!" She grinned. "Unless you want to see me cry. My shoulder is killing me." With her free hand, she tugged on Isabelle's braid and then ruffled Brie's hair. The half-elf had cropped her hair to a point just below her shoulders to help tell her and her cousin apart more. "Nice look, Brie. How much fuss did Roberto give you?"

"Just a little, but he warmed up quickly." Brie smiled. "It's not the same without you here."

"Geez." It was all she could say.

When they reached Antonio, the older man let out a long breath. "*Grazie*, Tori. You do not know how much what you did means to me. That being said, do not ever scare us like that again. You are *famiglia*."

Under her breath, she muttered at Alex, "As if I wouldn't do it again. Is he nuts?"

Alex smiled wryly, understanding perfectly. "Can you manage the stairs?" he asked. "Or do you need someone to carry you?" When he was shot a scathing look, he held up his hands with a grin. "You can't kick my ass yet, so you'll just have to suffer if we decide to carry you against your wishes. You don't weigh that much, kid."

She just sighed and then laughed. No matter how much they teased her, no matter how embarrassing it was to be dependent on others, it was still good to be home.

CHAPTER NINE

In slightly less than a month, Tori started using her left arm again. If it hurt, she grit her back teeth and ignored it. The mark had faded into a pink scar that felt tender, but it was not in danger of being reopened. As far as she was concerned, that meant she could start working on getting strength back. She started small and began to move her way upward. Alex, unable to stop her, finally sighed, threw his hands in the air, and agreed to help.

Going on two months after the incident, however, Tori had an entirely different problem on her hands. Because of the shock to her system, she had missed two periods in a row. She didn't complain over that, frankly, because it had always annoyed her to endure the annoyance of having a uterus without having any real need for it to be there. Two months in, her body went back to normal . . . and then some.

She didn't even notice at first until she went to get dressed one morning. She pulled on her shirt, tried to button it, and discovered that it didn't fit. Puzzled, she tugged at the edges of the shirt, but they wouldn't come together. She walked over to look in the mirror, turned to see her profile . . . and got the shock of her life.

She had breasts. They weren't *Playboy* material by any imagination, but her bust had to have increased at least two sizes. *She looked like a woman.*

She jerked on a t-shirt hastily and let out a quick breath as she saw that the folds still hid her chest. She would need to buy a sports bra or two, just to flatten the slight curves so she could skate by without awkward questions. What the hell was going on?

After locking the door so no one could walk in, she grabbed her cell phone and called the hospital. Doctor Singh had given her his direct line in case there was a problem because he knew full well she would not follow his orders. So, when he answered, she said bluntly, "My breasts grew. What did you do to me during surgery?"

There was a startled silence. Finally he said, laughter in his voice, "You have to be the only woman I can think of who would complain. Tori, we did nothing to you."

"Then what's going on? You told me that missing my period was perfectly normal after the severe shock to my system, but you didn't mention that this might happen! I'd swear I've grown two sizes or so. I'm probably an A or something. I'm too afraid to get a tape measure to find out."

"Hmm." He fell silent for several moments as he thought about things. "We had said you were a late bloomer," he said slowly after a minute, "but it could be possible that it was more literal than we thought. Physical and emotional trauma has been proven to be *extremely* hard on a mind and body alike. The shock of being shot might have, well, kick-started a process you were, for whatever reason, stunted from starting earlier. Remember, many women enter their final growth spurt roughly around your age."

She said nothing. Then, softly, she asked, "Would a physical and emotional shock from when I was newly born have been enough to 'stunt my growth' as you put it?"

"That is very likely," he agreed. "In fact, it is probably precisely what could have done it. As a newborn, you are developing and growing every second. It would not have taken much. Did you suffer a trauma, Tori?"

"Yeah." Her eyes closed. "My birth mother threw me in a garbage can."

The silence on the other end of the line was shocked and appalled. "Dear god, Tori," he finally managed to say. "Dear god, I am so sorry. How did you survive?"

"The garbage pickup came by within minutes, I guess. My foster mother told me that the guy who found me saved my life because he wrapped me up in his jacket and rushed me to a hospital." She found a smile suddenly. "I actually got to meet him when I was ten. He cried when he saw me, when I thanked him for saving me."

"I see." And, indeed, he did. It seemed to explain a lot about her personality and hard choices. "Well, I suggest, at this point, that you keep track of changes you notice to your body. If anything happens that is not normal, call me immediately."

"And going through puberty at twenty-five is *normal* to begin with?"

He laughed. "For you, Tori? It would seem so."

She hung up the phone with a huff of annoyance. On one hand, she was sort of tickled at the idea of finally having a figure. On the other hand, she was ready to beat her head against a wall. Why *now*? If she got too much of a figure, then she would have to get really creative to hide it. Her excuse for being allergic to chlorine so she could avoid going swimming only covered so much ground. Things couldn't possibly get worse.

Downstairs, Rafael sat in Antonio's office. He had been arbitrarily summoned by his father almost as soon as breakfast had been over. He was also fairly sure he knew what he was about to hear. The nudges and prods had been going on for five, almost six, years. Over the last two years, they had gotten less subtle, particularly when Antonio had noticed he had stopped dating.

He had no idea how he was supposed to explain things to his father. What was he supposed to say? That the person he loved and wished to marry could not have his children? That the family bloodline would continue only through Isabelle and Brie, but not with the Lucino name?

He didn't question that his father wanted him to be happy. Antonio would stand behind him completely. The rest of the family beyond this branch, including the head of the family in Italy, might not be nearly so accepting or understanding, however.

"Rafael," Antonio suddenly spoke up, "you are causing your papa a great deal of worry. I have not seen you go out with anyone since the trouble started two years ago. Are you so worried of bringing danger to a girlfriend or lover?"

Unsure whether or not he was glad Antonio hadn't guessed the real issue, he hedged, "You must admit, Papa, that in light of recent events, it would certainly be a better idea for me to be discreet."

"You can be discreet without being unhappy." Rafael stared at him, and he arched a brow. "You think I do not know my *bambini*? You are unhappy, Rafe. I do not like it. It has been especially bad since Tori was shot. You are guilty needlessly, and Tori would be the first to say so. His job is to protect you, and it was understood to be a risky task. He has survived and is nearly as good as new. Your guilt will only upset him."

Rafael just sighed. "*Sì*, Papa."

"Now, just so I can tell your *nonno* that you are looking to provide me with an heir, would you please go on a date with one of those nice young women you are always ignoring at work? Any one of them might be true love in disguise, Rafe."

"I suppose I will never hear the end of it if I do not."

"We have the gala opening for a client tomorrow night," Antonio urged. "Ask Theresa to go with you. She is lovely, and friendly. The entire family likes her a great deal, and she would fit in so beautifully with us. You may just not have noticed it yourself."

Rafael had in fact noticed such a thing, but not in a romantic sense. Meeting Theresa had been like meeting a lost sister. Certainly she was very lovely, and possessed a delightful humor, but he had never once been attracted to her. She would make someone very happy as their partner, just not him. Still, he wanted to keep peace in the house. And . . . who knew? Maybe going out with an eligible female might cure him of his obsession with Tori.

And pigs would fly.

"Very well, Papa," he sighed. "I will call Theresa. If you will excuse me?" When Antonio waved him off, he left the office as quickly as he could. Before he could convince himself not to, he went to the nearest phone and flipped through the contacts in the book beside it. Theresa was in charge of the publications desk at the main office, and her phone number was one of the first listed in their contact book. If they needed to pull an old job for reference, she was the one they called. It was Monday; she would be there.

The phone rang once before it picked up. "Just In Time, Publications Desk. This is Theresa."

"*Ciao*, Theresa." He found himself grinning. She always sounded so prim on the phone that he couldn't believe she was his age. "It is Rafael. How are you?"

"Busy." A smile filled her voice. "My bosses are always throwing things at me."

"That is because you are a fine catcher. I, in fact, have another thing to throw at you. I would appear to need a date." At the silence, he could all but imagine her staring at her phone as if it had grown legs. "There is no pressure, Theresa," he said gently. "It is mostly business, a little pleasure. I enjoy spending time with you."

"I'm sorry, you must have dialed the wrong number. You have me mistaken for the busty blonde in the legal department."

He laughed. "You know I do not. Please?"

"I can't believe I'm agreeing to this, but sure. It's not a date, right?"

"We will have to see, won't we? I will pick you up at six." He hung up on her sputter, still smiling. As he stood there contemplating what he had done, his smile began to fade. It felt, a little, as if he was cheating on Tori, but that was ridiculous. Tori, above any, would want him to be happy and find someone special. Never mind that *Tori* was his someone special.

Needing to see him, and to vent, he quickly headed for the gym located in the basement. He knew damned well that Tori would be there pushing himself much harder than he should be for someone who had been shot two months prior.

Tori was lifting weights cautiously with her left arm when she heard steps on the stairs. She hastily put down the dumbbell and dropped on the ground as if doing sit-ups. She hated to get scolded, and everyone seemed inclined to do it if they saw her overworking her arm. She saw Rafael in the doorway, and she sat up again with a smile. "Well, what did Antonio want? He went very 'Don Lucino' on you."

"What else would he want?" he asked ruefully as he offered a hand to help her to her feet. "He is lamenting my being a bachelor at such an old age of twenty-five."

She picked up her towel to hide a grin. "Uh oh. Did you get the 'heir to carry on the family' talk?"

"*Sì*, it was something to that effect." He sighed and sat on the side of a bench to watch as Tori began to put up equipment. There was something about the way he moved that was just so . . . unthinkingly sexy. It had been baffling him for years. "He convinced me to go on a date tomorrow night."

"Well, don't sound so thrilled about it. You'll scare someone." She told her jealous heart to shut up and walked over to sit beside him. She lightly bumped her shoulder against his. "You know that you guys are the modern equivalent of a kingdom. You're the heir apparent, so you need to produce another heir to pass along the throne to. Geez, and I thought this was the 21st century."

"One of these days," he noted ruefully, "you will have to meet *Nonno*. It will all make sense."

"So who's the lucky chick?"

"Theresa Adams."

She pursed her lips thoughtfully. "About five-five, thick and *ridiculously* long brown hair, brown eyes, and roughly one hundred sixty pounds. Works the Publications desk. Wears glasses and could be a model for your classic nerdy bookworm. Pretty and smart. Shy until she warms up."

He had to laugh. "You have an encyclopedia for a brain, Tori!"

"Hey, it's what I do. Where are you taking her?"

"To the gala tomorrow night. I told her it was mostly business and we'd see if it turned into a date. I am hoping that if sparks do not fly, which I doubt they will, at the least I will buy some time with Papa."

"Well, why don't you date anymore anyway? You were quite the playboy before I and Alex got hired. You were always going out. Then . . . nothing. I've heard of people quitting addictions cold turkey, but I didn't think you could do that to dating as well."

His lips twitched. Lacking the freedom to tell the truth, he said only, "It seemed safer for all involved. Ah, well." He got to his feet. "Thank you for listening to me, Tori."

"Anytime," she murmured. She watched him walk out and then raked her hands through her hair. She liked Theresa. That didn't mean she liked seeing her go out with Rafael. She had never considered herself a jealous woman, but she honestly loathed this scenario entirely.

She knew she really should go with Rafael and Theresa to the gala just as a deterrent to any would-be kidnappers, but she couldn't bear the idea of seeing them together. She would have to ask Alex to go in her place. She could just use the excuse that she was worried she wouldn't be up to dealing with trouble if it happened.

And what would she do if Rafael *did* find someone to love? She wasn't sure she could convincingly hide her emotions if that occurred. She wanted him happy, but she didn't want him to be with anyone else. "Friggin' hell," she muttered, dropping her face into her hands. "Now what am I going to do?"

Alex was fine with serving as a one-time guard for Rafael. On the other hand, Rafael felt very disappointed that he wouldn't get to have Tori there. He knew Theresa was his date, but he had been hoping to at least enjoy Tori's company as well.

Upon seeing Rafael's distinct unhappiness, Isabelle followed Alex into their room when he went to get changed. "Do you know what is wrong with Rafe?" she asked her fiancé. "I have never seen him as he has been since the incident."

He hesitated for a moment before sighing and buttoning his dress shirt. "I only have suspicions," he said carefully. "The one who would know best would be Tori, but I suspect Tori is at the heart of the problem." He sought for a way to say what he thought. "If it had been me shot in your defense," he finally said, "how would you have reacted?"

"I suppose I would have acted much as Rafe did. But I am in love with you." When he arched a brow, she grew thoughtful. "Hmm. Indeed, that would make sense of quite a lot. But I did not think Rafael liked men. Perhaps it is just Tori."

He kept the rest of his suspicions to himself and just smiled wryly. "Perhaps so." He lifted her chin and kissed her softly. "Will you wait up for me tonight?" he asked huskily.

Her lips curved. "Perhaps so."

When Alex got to the garage to meet up with Rafael, he was entirely unsurprised to find the younger man quietly staring out across the landscape. Tori was walking with Brie through one of the gardens, and they could be easily seen from the garage. "Rafe?"

Rafael sighed. "*Sì,* Alex."

"I didn't ask anything."

"You were intending to. The answer is still yes. Get in. I will drive tonight. You do not mind riding in the back?" He opened his car door and forced himself to tear his eyes away from the sight of Tori laughing with Brie.

"Of course not. I'm just decoration; you can't make your date ride in the back." Alex got in as well, turning over the possible things he could say to his friend and future brother-in-law. The situation was complicated, frustrating, and potentially futile. "We don't pick who we love," he finally said. "Sometimes it gets picked for us. Brie told me that recently. I blamed her 3rd District upbringing, but I admit, she does seem to be right."

Rafael was still thinking about that when they reached Theresa's house. It was a small place in Brooklyn and not very far from the company headquarters. It looked curiously depressing somehow, even though it was kept in good condition and the garden bloomed happily despite some weeds. In truth, there was nothing at all displeasing about its appearance, but he *felt* depressed looking at it. He couldn't even be sure why.

He rang the doorbell, and Theresa opened the door moments later. She was a curvy and lovely woman with hair so long that it actually brushed the floor when she took it down. It was up now, and she had somehow braided and pinned it into an elegant chignon. The old-fashioned style suited her as much as the demure black dress she wore. "Hello, Rafe," she said with a smile. "All day I kept expecting this to be a joke."

"I would never do that to you." He offered his arm. "You look lovely, Theresa." He spotted movement and glanced up to see an old woman watching them from further in the house. Distrust and disgust mingled in her eyes. "I will bring her home before midnight," he promised.

"See that you do." The door slammed behind them.

Theresa's fingers bit into his arm for a moment, her brown eyes darkening behind her glasses. "My grandmother," she said softly. "She is . . . possessive. She does not like men."

"I will do my best not to give her reason to hate me." He escorted her to the car and opened the passenger door for her. "I believe you know Alex. He is chaperoning me tonight because Tori is still recovering."

Theresa shyly smiled toward Alex. "Hi."

"Hello. Don't mind me. I'm part of the furniture."

Determined to enjoy himself, Rafael forced away thoughts of Tori and the trouble in their lives and focused instead on his date and the gala. It was a big, elaborate party for the company's newest product, and since Just In Time had launched the advertising that promoted it, they were VIP guests. Antonio was not much of a partygoer anymore, blaming his 'advanced' years, and that meant Rafael was in the spotlight to attend. He was more inclined to think his father just wanted an excuse to have a quiet night at home.

With Alex shadowing them discreetly, Rafael and Theresa made their way around the lobby where the product and others in its line were on display. "Technology eludes me," Theresa admitted to Rafael. "I can use a computer well enough, but I am much happier when you give me books. I still carry a CD player," she laughed. "I can't figure out how to work an MP3 one."

"Is that why you applied for our library?"

"That and it was the best paying job I was qualified for. I haven't gone to college. Grandmother doesn't believe in it."

Sensing a touchy subject, he diverted the conversation. "How many books do you read a week?"

"For fun or for work?" She smiled. "More than you probably can contemplate. I read through the archives just for kicks. If I could go to school, I would study English. I love words. I love seeing how words evolve. For example, I saw an ad from the sixties in the archives for the same product we did an ad for last year. They were *completely* different. Not just in style, but in language."

It didn't take long for him to realize there would simply be no sparks with Theresa. She was lovely and fun, but she was simply too even-tempered to suit him as a lover. He had hot blood. He liked to shout and argue and laugh and love. She needed someone with a bit of calm intensity who would protect her gentle nature. They just did not match as more than siblings. If *anything* got confirmed that night, it was that Rafael felt surer than ever that he and Theresa could probably have been twins in another life. He loved her quite intensely, but in the way he loved Isabelle and Brie.

Proving a surprising astuteness as he walked her to her door a few hours later, she said softly, "Don't kick yourself that we didn't click, Rafe. Come on. Did you really think we might? We've been working together for a year. If there were going to be sparks, we'd have seen it by now. You are like . . . like a brother to me, and I think you already knew that."

He smiled wryly. "Was I so obvious?"

"I think it was just instinct." She smiled suddenly. "Love is love, Rafael. It can't be labeled. It can't be made comfortable. It can only be accepted."

He contemplated that as he went back to the car. He knew he had not mistaken her meaning. As he was driving home, he asked Alex, "Tell me something. Am I so transparent to everyone?"

"I only noticed recently," Alex admitted amiably. He wasn't going to pretend to misunderstand the conversation he had heard. "You did an admirable job of pretending, but you went to pieces when Tori was shot. Your reaction was a bit . . . strong."

"Do you have any advice for me? Please, Alexander. I just do not know what to do." He parked the car in the garage at the darkened villa and got out. Only two windows shone with light. One was waiting for Alex in Isabelle's room. The other was in Tori's room.

Alex got out of the car and draped his jacket over his shoulder. "You just need to decide if you want to fight for the one you love. Do you want to live with regret, Rafe, or move forward toward true happiness? It's your call."

Rafael watched him walk toward the villa before turning his gaze toward the second lamp lit window. A night wind ruffled his hair as he took off his jacket and walked with purpose toward the villa. No Lucino worth their salt would ever not fight for love. It was time he fought as well.

Tori's evening did not go much better than his. She played cards with Isabelle and Brie and beat Roberto at billiards. Dinner was lively as always, even with two empty chairs. It was all she could do to keep her eyes from straying to the seat where Rafael always sat. Thinking of some nameless woman someday sitting beside him instead of her was enough to bring her mood down over and over.

Claiming exhaustion, she retreated to her room almost right after dinner. Truly, she was not that tired. She was so acclimated to staying up talking with Rafael that it had become hard to sleep without having seen him.

As she shrugged into her pajama top, she discovered to her chagrin that it too would no longer button. The bottoms could be pulled up to her hips but went no further. Frustrated, she grabbed the tape measure she had reluctantly obtained. Naked but for her underwear, she walked over to her mirror and stared at her reflection—something she very rarely ever did. She was *definitely* getting a figure.

Her hips had grown three inches. Her bust had grown by five. She was staring in consternation at the tape measure when her door suddenly opened and Rafael stepped in. Shocked, she stared at him. She hadn't even realized she had left the door unlocked in the universal Lucino 'come on in' gesture.

He stopped dead in his tracks as he stared at her and slowly ran his eyes down her body. Though slim and slender, there was absolutely no doubt that he stared at a woman. Her hips curved just enough to entice, and her breasts seemed to be the right size to fill his hands.

As his gaze slid back up her body, he saw the vivid scar on her chest near her left breast. His breath wedged in his lungs. The mark was still more red than pink, but it healed rapidly. It was a stark reminder of what she had done and what had been done to save her life.

He raked his gaze over her face. Now that he knew, he felt foolish for not trusting his first instincts. Why hadn't she corrected them? He would have to find out, and find out what *she* wanted to be. For the first time, however, her deceptive androgyny seemed to have evaporated. She appeared to be all woman right then, not even a hint of masculinity in her stricken face and tousled blonde hair. She was, in fact, the sexiest thing he had ever seen, and he had honestly already thought she tipped pretty high on the sexy chart anyway.

He stepped back without a word and shut the door. Heart pounding, she dropped the tape measure and grabbed her t-shirt. She jerked it on and ran to open the door. "Rafe," she said as loudly as she dared in the sleeping house. "Are you . . . are you mad?"

He stopped in front of his door and looked at her. "No, Tori," he said gently. "I am, in fact, unsurprised. I will speak with you tomorrow. *Buono notte, cara.*"

His door shut softly behind him and she went back into her room. She felt confused and a little wary. Why was he suddenly calling her *cara*? Was it just because he now knew she was a woman? On a sigh, she sank down onto the side of her bed. How much more complicated would this get, anyway?

CHAPTER TEN

Rafael didn't sleep at all that night. Even if he hadn't been struggling with insomnia for years, he would have still been awake. Both his body and his mind had tangled up in knots. Frustrated hunger burned in his body, stirred violently by the sight of Tori's beauty. Dozens of questions and guessed answers churned in his head.

Why the hell did she let everyone think she was a man? He could guess that one easily enough; the simple fact that so many people automatically made assumptions about her being male was a strong indicator that she hadn't been (or felt she was) feminine enough as a woman. He called bullshit. He had wanted her for two years. Clearly, whatever signal she put out was strong enough to reach his body and soul even though his eyes had been deceived. He wanted to kick himself for not being polite enough to just *ask* in the first place.

The tape measure was a curious thing. He would definitely ask about that. In fact, there were a ton of things he intended to ask, and he was damned well going to get every single answer. The most important thing he wanted to ask, however, required some . . . parental assistance.

A tiny smile touched his lips. He would try to get some revenge on his father for pulling the 'Don Lucino' act and then he would go find Tori and clear the air. If she wasn't in love with him yet, then he would make sure she was eventually. There was no other he wanted. No other he had ever wanted.

Once full sunshine came in the window, he got out of bed and caught a shower. Breakfast was in an hour, and he wanted his conversation with his father done before then. He felt fairly sure Tori would avoid breakfast with everyone, and that was perfectly fine. He didn't want any observers for their discussion either.

Refreshed and alert, he got dressed and headed downstairs to his father's office. Antonio was a naturally early riser, especially since he and Rafe worked mostly from home. The light was already on and clearly seen under the door. Rafael knocked lightly. "Papa?"

"Come in, Rafe."

A little smile playing with his lips, he went into the office and shut the door. Casually, he walked over and sat down in one of the chairs. "The gala went well," he began. "Theresa was a lovely companion to have along, but I am afraid that she and I will never be more than friends. Perhaps we should consider just adopting her into the *famiglia* instead." He thought about her grandmother. "Something tells me she could use some family love."

"That was my feeling, too. And you at least tried," Antonio commiserated. "That is all I wanted, Rafael."

"Yes, well, seeing her allowed me to open my eyes to something else entirely. Papa, I need you to fire Tori."

Antonio paused as he was lifting his coffee. He slowly put the mug down, a combination of confusion and suspicion in his eyes. "Why would you want Tori fired, Rafael? Are you truly that worried for his safety? He is your bodyguard. It is his duty to put his life on the line. I do not like it either for I care for him a great deal as well, but it must be accepted."

"As a matter of fact, that has little to do with it. I wish to marry Tori."

Antonio looked at his son a bit more critically. "I do not judge, Rafael, but I did not think you were interested in other men."

"I had wondered if I was," he admitted. "But it would seem I am not." He looked at his father a second time and then sighed. So much for his hoped for revenge. "You already knew that Tori is a woman."

"*Sì.*" Antonio smiled. "I ran a full background check on both Tori and Alex when I hired them, and I knew when she came for an interview that she was a woman—only to be surprised when I met her. She told me she would be whatever you and Bella assumed her to be, as that was how she had always done it, so I respected her wishes." He lifted a brow. "How did you come to know?"

Rafael smiled. "When I came home last night, I went to her intending to confess my feelings for her, even thinking she was a man. I walked into her room without knocking, since she had left the door unlocked. She was naked."

"I imagine that was quite awkward."

"I am surprised she did not hit me. Do I have your blessings, Papa? Will you fire her so I may ask her to be my wife?" He smiled a little wryly, a little wistfully. "I have loved her for two years, nearly since she was hired. When she was shot, it shocked me into realizing it. I would have had her for my own even if she had not been a woman. I had accepted that last night. Things are simply less complicated now where the extended *famiglia* is concerned."

"*Sì*," Antonio agreed dryly, "as I will not have to deal with *mio papa*—though I would have for you if it had been needed." He took a long breath and dug in his desk. He pulled out Tori's contract and handed it to Rafael. It felt a little bittersweet to have his eldest finally be in love, no matter how much he had wished for such a thing. "She is no longer under my employ as of this moment. I admit that I am glad for it. I was trying to find a way to keep her with us even when the danger passed. She has become an important part of our family, just as Alex has." He suddenly laughed. "*Dio*, those personality quizzes! I should have known she was setting me up."

"She?" Rafael's brows lifted.

"Rhianna Taber of Enforcers. We have worked with them before, and when I mentioned offhand what I was going to do, she gave me the quizzes to be certain all went well. I should have known what might happen."

"All is well that ends well." Rafael got to his feet. "I am going to go have it out with Tori. I do not think she will be happy, nor will she believe me. But I will win." He looked as confident as he sounded. "Lucinos fight for love, no?"

The first thing he did was go to the kitchen to speak with the cook. "Peggy?" he asked as he walked into the bright kitchen. He stopped to take an appreciative sniff of the air. Everything smelled like cinnamon and pastry. "You are making cinnamon rolls."

"Of course." She shot him a smiling look over her shoulder. She had been with the family since he was ten, and he still loved her cinnamon rolls best. "If you are hungry, breakfast will be ready soon, Rafael."

"That is good, but I was going to ask if Tori had come by."

"He did indeed. Poor thing looked exhausted as if he hadn't slept. He let me know he would not be joining the family for breakfast, so I was preparing a tray for him." Up to her elbows in dough, she inclined her head to where a covered tray sat on the island counter. "Marco was going to take it up in a few minutes."

"I will do so." He peeked under the tray lid. "Is there enough for two?"

"Naturally." She fluttered her lashes at him as if she was as young on the outside as she was on the inside. "I know my kids. I knew you would want to keep him company." Her eyes twinkled merrily. One of the maids had overheard the parental conversation and quickly spread word. "Or, should I say, keep *her* company."

He stared at her. "How did you know?"

"Well, Betsy ratted you out on your conversation with *Signor* Lucino, but we staff have actually known all along. She had to tell us since we would not let her do her own laundry, and we do shopping for her like we do for everyone else. There are things that many women need that many men do not." She began to shape the dough into loaves for the oven. "We have enjoyed watching you fall in love, Rafael, particularly when you did not know the truth of who you loved. You merely *loved*, as you should." She nodded firmly. "She will make a fine *Signora* Lucino."

Rafael just smiled as he shook his head. "'You staff,' you say, but you are all family. I am not that surprised that you knew." He lifted the tray and then put it down again. "Peggy . . ."

She didn't look up, but she smiled. "Marco cut some flowers this morning. They are in the vase in the fridge."

"*Dio*, you frighten me sometimes." He opened the fridge and retrieved the vase of flowers. They were a mix of buds and blooms, caught in the transition between growth and full beauty. They were perfect for his Tori.

Vase on the tray, he carted the entire thing upstairs toward her room. He could not open the door with his hands full, so he called, "Tori? Open the door, please."

"Open it yourself," came the retort. "You're good at that."

He grinned briefly. "*Sì*, but my hands are full, *cara*."

The door jerked open. "Don't call me that!" Her words halted as she saw what he carried. "What is that?"

"Breakfast. Now let me in and I will share it with you. Peggy made cinnamon rolls." He stepped forward, forcing her to fall back or run right into him. She backed up and he carried the tray over to the table near the fireplace. All suites in the villa had their own bathrooms and small sitting area beside either a fireplace or a balcony.

He put the tray down and turned to study her. She wore sweatpants and a very baggy t-shirt, both of which concealed any sign of femininity of her body. Her hair, which had not been cut in three months, skimmed the back of her neck. It had not been brushed yet, and it was mussed and unruly from being slept on.

The morning light tried desperately to emphasize the fascinating hints of masculinity that she had often shown, but it did not seem to be as successful this time. He did not think it was just his eyes that had changed. *She* was changing, and she was blossoming like the buds in the vase. "You are beautiful," he said softly.

"Oh please!" She covered her face with a hand. "You find out I'm a woman and suddenly you're calling me '*cara*' and telling me I am beautiful. What is wrong with you, Rafe? Did you hit your head yesterday?"

"I suppose you could say I was hit," he agreed amiably, "but it was not in the head." He lifted the lid off the tray of food. "You need your strength. Come eat, *cara*."

The intimacy of the way he addressed her had her watching him very warily. When Brie had laughingly said how it was so funny that the same word could sound entirely different from Roberto, Tori had been amused but not entirely understanding of what she meant. She definitely understood now. Rafael turned the endearment into nearly a physical caress when he used it toward her.

She sighed and sat down at the table to take her plate. She was too hungry to argue. "I guess you want to talk."

"Indeed." He sat down across from her and took his plate from the tray. "I have many questions. We will begin with something I should have asked much sooner: do you want to be addressed as male or female, neither, or both? I apologize for not doing this the first day."

"Very few people ever ask me that," she consoled him. She sighed. "Female is my preference. I am cisgender, as far as that goes. I was assigned female at birth, and I identify female, but Mother Nature is a bitch and decided not to give me three for three with my looks and body. I've always made an ugly girl but a passable boy, so it became easier to just let people think I was male instead of constantly being reminded by other people that I was a subpar woman. High school was hell, Rafe. I was tall and I skipped most of puberty. When I went to college, I effectively built a new life from the ground up. It wasn't hard. I didn't have a family to distance myself from."

"And people are so quick to judge that they have never assumed anything other than what you present," he murmured. "And those who know the truth because of legal reasons, such as Papa, keep quiet because you ask them to."

She shrugged. "Being a male allowed people to get to know me. I've never had trouble making friends since. People are more comfortable with a less masculine man than a less feminine woman. As much as it hurts to deny myself, at least I'm not *alone*. Also, Tori is a nickname, so you know. So, depending on what I'm signing, I use either version of my name, both of which are also legal. I tried to make things simple for myself."

"Yet they have grown complicated. You were measuring your breasts last night," he noted calmly. "Is there something wrong?"

A hint of pink touched her cheekbones. "According to the doctor," she muttered, "the physical trauma of being shot kick-started the parts of puberty I missed. My entire body is changing. I'm actually developing a figure, but it's happening so quickly that I can't keep up. None of my clothes fit anymore." She sighed deeply and pushed away her empty plate. "I had intended to tell you," she admitted softly. "I knew my days were limited until it became obvious. I didn't intend you to find out as you did."

"I am not complaining." His blue eyes seemed to smolder as he looked at her. "The view was amazing. You are lovely, Tori. But," he continued even softer, "I have thought so for two years. Be you man or woman, I wanted you. When I came to you last night, I had decided to tell you how I felt."

She stared at him in shock. "You're not funny, Rafael."

"I am not saying it to be amusing. Now, when I went to my father this morning, I admit I intended to have some amusement at his expense."

Humor lit her eyes. "You wanted to use me to get revenge for his 'Don Lucino' act, didn't you?" When he grinned, she just shook her head. "I can't even be offended. It would have been hilarious if he had not already known. Sorry about denying you that." She lifted a brow. "I imagine nothing is going to change, right, now that everything is out in the open? I mean, my identity has not affected my work over the last two years. You all know I am capable."

"Indeed you are." He pulled out the contract and held it up. Deliberately, he tore it in two. "But you have been fired regardless."

"What!" She leapt to her feet, her baby blue eyes firing up with sheer fury. "Because I'm a woman? For god's sake, Rafael, I thought we were friends!"

"We are." He stood and began to stalk around the table toward her. "I just happen to want more than friendship, Tori. And as long as you were employed by my father, you could not be mine." His hands closed around her arms to jerk her soft body against his. Subtle though her curves were, they molded to his frame perfectly, tormenting him with thoughts of how she would feel under his hands. "I cannot marry my bodyguard. But you are no longer that, are you?"

"Are you out of your mind?" she shouted. She slapped her hands on his shoulders and pushed as hard as she could. He stumbled back but still managed to keep his grip on her. He swung around and pinned her against the poster of her bed. Shocked, her eyes flew wide as she felt him from head to toe and assuredly every inch in between.

His lips curved into a devastatingly sensual smile. "You look surprised, *cara*." He pressed closer so that she could not mistake his desire for her. He *ached* for her. "Were you not listening?" He skimmed his lips along the strong line of her jaw.

He loved her height. It put everything within such delightful reach. "For two years I have wanted you. In fact, I do not think I have ever *stopped* wanting you. It just seems to vary in intensity between desperation and obsession."

Head spinning, she grabbed his arms for balance. She shook her head hard, trying to compute what he was telling her. "That's impossible."

"*Sì,* but it is true." He gave her a small shake. "Tell me you do not want me, Tori, and I will let you go."

Her lips trembled. She could not tell him that. She could not bring herself to lie to him over something so important.

"Kiss me, Tori." His lips hovered over hers, his breath flavored with cinnamon and rich coffee. "You gave me my life. I will show you how to live." Something stirred in her eyes that was longing and desperate and afraid, and it ripped at his heart. He needed her so terribly to save his soul.

When his lips took hers, the shocking delight of it sent a shiver through her entire body. That simmering need inside that she had fought so hard to control seemed to boil over wildly. Her arms were pinned and all she could do was feel. He devoured her hungrily, stealing her breath and her will and making her body ache fiercely. Her breasts, sensitive in their growth, throbbed where they pressed against his strong chest.

A low moan vibrated in her throat. His feelings or hers. She couldn't separate them, couldn't find the will to try. She pressed upward to deepen the kiss and shuddered with pleasure as his tongue eagerly curled around hers. He tasted of secret dreams, untamed passion, and of all the things she had thought she would never have.

His hands lifted from her arms and buried in her hair to drag her closer. Quivering with violent hunger, he broke the kiss and buried his mouth hotly against her neck. There was a birthmark there that had always tempted him, and he nipped at it teasingly before soothing the sting with his tongue. "I have wanted this for two years," he said again roughly, his accent thickening. The sound of it made her entire body tremble. "You cannot tell me that I do not want you."

He lifted his head when there was no retort and his stomach knotted hard. Her blue eyes looked dazed and her cheeks flushed. She pressed her lips together for a moment as if she didn't entirely understand why they were swollen. She was the most beautiful creature he had ever seen. "You are beautiful, *cara*." He skimmed his lips over her ear. "*Ti amo*," he breathed. "*Dio*, Tori. I have loved you for years."

She didn't get a chance to answer. Her unlocked bedroom door opened, and Isabelle and Brie walked in. "Tori," Isabelle was saying, "please come have breakfast with us! It is boring without you." She broke off in surprise at the sight of Tori in Rafael's arms. "*Dio*!"

"Ha!" Brie elbowed her cousin. "I told you Rafe wanted Tori!" She eyed Rafael intently. "I still say he should have just admitted he liked guys, too."

Rafael reluctantly released Tori, but he was smiling. "In fact, Tori is a woman," he told his sisters. "There is nothing for me to admit except that I do not care one way or another."

"*Sì,* and that makes sense of everything." Isabelle shook her head in bemusement. "I had always wondered what was different about you, Tori! It is no wonder that I and Brie were always comfortable with you in a way we were not with other men." She frowned suddenly. "Why did you never correct our assumptions? Your choice of industry?"

Tori pushed Rafael firmly and forced him to release her. Her strength was nearly completely back and that meant she was as strong as he, something for which she felt grateful. "I'm not attractive as a woman," she said crossly. "It just seemed simpler. Magically, by being a boy, people stopped calling me ugly. It was nice to be accepted. You wouldn't have even given me the time of day if you'd met me when I was a girl."

"Bzzt," Brie said, "wrong answer! We like *you*, Tori. We don't care what you look like. And anyway, we've all said at least once that you were the kind of man who could rock being a hot guy *or* a hot chick, so, obviously, you're not as unfeminine or ugly as you think. Whatcha think, Bella? I bet we could take Tori out for new clothes and even make *her* think that she was sexy and gorgeous."

Isabelle's eyes twinkled. "*Sì*, Brie. It would be fun."

"Your entire family is nuts!" Tori told Rafael. "I'm glad I was fired; I can get out of here before I'm nuts too!"

"Fired!" Brie's brows shot up.

"Rafael wants to marry her," Isabelle decided. "Like Alex quit so that he could ask me to marry him. As long as Tori worked for Papa, she was off limits to Rafe."

"Quite." Rafael caught Tori around the waist and tugged her closer. "And I will not take no for an answer, *cara*."

Alex knocked on the doorframe over Isabelle's head, and his other hand lightly curled around her waist possessively. "You chose a bad time to fire her, Rafe," he said quietly. "You will need her more than ever to protect you. Another threat has arrived, but it was directed at you."

Isabelle clutched his shirt, her eyes darkening. "Alex, what threat?"

"It was a list of the places he has been to lately. Next to each, it was clearly noted when he had been either alone or away from Tori or I. At the bottom, it said 'I missed the last time, but I won't the next.' We have sent it to the police. They are going to check for fingerprints and do all those things that they do even though we know who sent it."

Tori's eyes darkened with dangerous fury. "Bastard." She glared at Rafael. "Un-fire me, damn it. Do you think I will stand by like some helpless heroine? I was *trained* to protect others, and I have protected you for two years. I was ready to die for you, Rafe. Like *hell* I am going to see all that wasted just because your hormones are out of control!"

"I have an idea!" Brie clapped her hands together. "Let's rehire Tori, but undercover! She can pose as Rafe's fiancée. Since his bodyguard is supposed to be a guy, then no one will look twice at Tori, especially if we call her something else. Is Tori a nickname for anything?"

"Victoria," she muttered.

Rafael loved it instantly. He had liked 'Tori' but somehow he liked her full name more. Perhaps because it represented the side of her that she wanted so badly but felt she could not have. "Let us go talk to Papa," he said. He grabbed Tori's wrist and pulled her along behind him firmly. "You are coming as well."

"Ouch!"

At the yelp, he released her quickly. "*Dio*! Was that your bad arm?"

"No." She smirked in his face. "Sucker." She crossed her arms and went past him firmly. "I can walk by myself. I've done it for a quarter of a century."

Alex wisely hid a grin as he ushered Isabelle and Brie down the hall after Tori. Rafael just smiled and followed them. He loved Tori for everything she was, and he was very happy to know that it was only her gender she had hidden. It was clear that her personality was the same one he had known and loved all along. She would never hesitate to backtalk to him, or to get in his face if she felt he was out of line. She would still kick him under the dinner table or laugh at the way he could be as bossy as his father. She would still stay up at night with him, listening to anything he wanted to talk about. He had never realized it was possible to love one being that much.

Antonio looked up when they all walked in and then hastily sipped his coffee to cover a smile. Roberto, sitting in one of the chairs, arched a brow at Tori before looking at Brie. She nodded sagely. "We walked in on a serious embrace. I'd give it an eight for sheer heat factor. I was pretty impressed. Traumatized—we're talking about my brother here—but impressed.

Tori caught her in a headlock. "You be quiet, troublemaker." She looked at Antonio a bit shamefully. "Antonio, I am truly sorry that it all came out like this. I should have said something sooner to the others, but . . ."

"Say no more." He held up his hands with a smile. "No one is at all upset, for you are still our Tori. You are still a part of this family, and I will still always be grateful to you for saving Rafael's life. I will be glad to call you my daughter-in-law."

"I'm not marrying Rafael!" She released Brie and backed up. "I *might* be willing to go along with Brie's ridiculous charade because it will allow me to protect him, but I will not actually marry him! He's out of his mind."

"*Sì*, as I have been for two years. Put me out of my misery, Victoria."

She glared at him. "I don't like how you say my name. Cut it out."

"Good luck with that," Brie groused dryly. She looked at Antonio. "I had an idea on how to make sure Rafael is safe without being obvious about it. We can't just sit around twiddling our thumbs forever. Isabelle and I are both having to postpone our marriages and honeymoons because of this, and now Rafe will be limited in what he can do for the company. So what if we set a trap?"

"What sort of trap?" Antonio asked with a thoughtful frown.

"We have Tori pose as Rafe's fiancée. He won't be without a bodyguard, but no one else will know that. If we can get Mr. Johns or one of his dumb thugs to lower their guard, maybe they can get caught. He grabbed me and Bella right from in front of this place, and you know he probably hates Rafe more than us. It won't be long until he tries to grab him too. Tori can handle things. We all know she can."

"I hear Detective Franklin in my head," Alex muttered, "and he's saying 'leave it to the cops.'"

"And what have they done so far?" Isabelle demanded. "Nothing! We have done all they told us to do so that we were safe, and Brie and I were still grabbed. Rafael was still nearly killed, and Tori still nearly died. I am tired of sitting and doing nothing! If not this, then I say we call *Nonno* and tell him to find those hitmen he keeps promising!"

Antonio looked at Tori. "It is your decision, Tori," he said quietly. "But know that I, too, have full confidence in you. There is no one else I would trust with Rafael's life. It will be risky, though."

"Please." She shook her head. "If I didn't want risk, I wouldn't even be in this business! But . . . this is not just business." She looked at Rafael. "It's personal, too. It's been personal all along." She blew out a breath. "I'm out of my mind. Fine, I will pose as his fiancée. But it's *just a cover*."

Antonio opened his desk to find a blank employment contract and instead discovered a neatly typed document. He pulled it out in confusion and read over it swiftly. A little smile began to tug at his lips. Entirely unsurprised, much as he had been unsurprised that morning, he placed the contract on the top of the desk and slid it across to Tori and Rafael. "There is no telling how long this may take," he warned Tori. "You could find yourself engaged to Rafael for a year or more."

"A long-term and then broken engagement won't ruin me," she said dryly. "Besides, no one wants me anyway." She signed the bottom of the contract before she could tell herself not to. Truly, there was no other option if she wanted to keep the man she loved safe.

Rafael signed as well and began to smile slowly. "I hope you realize that I will make this engagement very real, *cara mia*. After all, to be believable, people must believe I am madly in love with you. You have heard of method acting, *sì*? To act the part, you must become the part. I look forward to teaching you."

She backed up cautiously, her eyes widening as the sensual threat registered. "Don't you dare!"

"You cannot run from me, Victoria," he warned softly. "You are quite stuck now."

"*Sì*," Isabelle said happily as she grabbed Tori's right arm, "and Brie and I will take you out shopping! You cannot wear your old clothes if you are to be Rafael's wife. You are a woman of high class, and you should dress as such."

"I will begin plans for the engagement party," Antonio decided. "Rafael is my heir. We must have a grand party. Within a week, I believe. I will call Papa tonight and tell him of the good news. He and Mama will want to come out to attend. Let us say we will have it next Saturday. That will give Marco and Peggy plenty of time to prepare everything. It will be here at the villa."

A sort of panicked terror began to fill Tori's eyes as she realized just how deeply she was getting tangled into things. Brie leapt up from her seat and took her left arm firmly, ensuring she was caught and could not run. "Let's go, Tori! We're going to find you a dress that will make Rafe's eyes pop out of his head!"

"Oh god." It was little more than a despairing moan as she was dragged out of the office by her identical captors.

As the door shut behind them, Roberto said idly, "I did not know that Don Lucino would come out to America for a farce engagement."

"Farce? What farce?" Antonio held out the contract.

The other three men moved in closer to read it, and all three began grinning, Rafael most of all. He hadn't even really read what he was signing, trusting his father knew what he was doing.

Clearly written were the words '*This contract is a binding document that can and will be Enforced to the highest degree. Victoria Li, hereafter Party One, and Rafael Lucino, hereafter Party Two, will commence a marital engagement to end in matrimony. During the term of engagement, Party One will serve as a secret bodyguard for Party Two until the threat of danger passes. When said danger has passed, the engagement will become formal and considered true and binding.*'

Rafael quirked a brow in amusement. "Is this contract from Enforcers? I recognize that standard language at the beginning. It is in all their contracts."

"*Sì*. It must have gotten mixed in with other paperwork that Ms. Tabor gave me recently for something else entirely." Antonio sighed fondly. "I will have to be certain to invite Ms. Tabor to the party, no? It seems she has a vested interest in the outcome."

CHAPTER ELEVEN

Isabelle and Brie dragged Tori all the way to her room and shoved her inside. "Find something to wear for now," Brie ordered cheerfully. "We're going to go finish breakfast and then we'll meet you in the garage."

"I will make Alex go with us," Isabelle assured her, "so that we are twice as safe. It will also lend credence to your new persona!"

The door shut behind them, and Tori raked her hands through her hair. It seemed like every time she turned around, things just kept getting more out of hand. Frustrated mentally because she couldn't seem to keep up, and certainly frustrated physically thanks to Rafael, she all but stalked into the bathroom for a shower.

He hadn't just come out of left field; he hadn't even been in the park to begin with! Not once over the last two years had she so much as guessed that he was attracted to her. But then, she willingly admitted, she wouldn't have known what to look for. She had never had anyone of *any* orientation be attracted to her before. She didn't doubt that Rafael wanted her, but she couldn't quite determine what he saw when he looked at her. What did he see that she didn't?

She unexpectedly got her answer when she stepped out of the shower. She briskly toweled her hair dry and tossed it out of her eyes to see her reflection. As she saw her appearance, she was brought up short in sheer surprise. She was . . . kind of pretty. She had gotten so used to seeing herself as she had been years before that she hadn't noticed any changes, and her aversion to mirrors had not helped her case.

She wasn't gangly anymore. Her height had caught up to her arms and legs. Even with them being more muscular than the average woman, they still looked sort of appealing. Her breasts and hips, now more clearly curved, emphasized how naturally slender she was. With her hair a little longer, her face seemed . . . softer.

Curiously subdued, she wrapped herself in a towel and walked into her bedroom. What else wasn't she seeing clearly?

"There you are."

She stifled a yelp and whirled as she clutched her towel tighter. Rafael was sitting at the small table and waiting for her with a tiny smile teasing his lips. "Do you mind?" she demanded. "I've already had a near death experience; I don't need another!"

He got to his feet and walked toward her slowly. She looked damp and flushed and so desirable that he was highly tempted to pounce on her right there. She seemed to sense it because her body shifted fluidly, gracefully, into a slightly more defensive stance. He held up his hands. "I am not going to grab you, Victoria."

"Then what do you want?"

"That is a loaded question, *cara*." He leaned in before she could dodge and softly kissed her. He kept his hands in the air the entire time, even when her lashes lowered and a soft sound of desire slipped past her lips. The little longing whimper raked through his already tortured body. He stepped back and put his hands in his pockets as she looked at him in dazed bemusement. "You are beautiful, Victoria."

She shook her head quickly. "That was sneaky, Rafe!"

He grinned. "There is a saying about love and war."

"Just say whatever you're here to say, you fink." She crossed her arms firmly and then blinked. An odd look crossed her face. He lifted a brow at her, and she sighed. "Getting used to having boobs is not easy after almost twenty-six years of having none. They get in the way."

"But they are lovely," he said wistfully. "I envied your tape measure."

Her color rose slightly. "Why are we discussing my breasts?"

"You brought them up. I am quite a fan of art, so I was compelled to speak on the subject. I was never fond of busty women."

She burst into laughter. "Now you're outright lying! The last chick you dated before all the trouble started looked like she had come off the set of *Baywatch*! She bounced so much when she walked that it's a wonder she didn't give herself a black eye!"

He started laughing. "What an image!" Content, he skimmed his fingers across her cheek. "I am so glad we can still laugh like this," he admitted softly. He brushed his thumb over her cheekbone. "I like knowing that I can tell you anything and that you can say anything to me." His lips curved. "I get the best of all worlds in you, Victoria. A friend and a lover."

"I never said I'd be your lover!"

"It is inevitable," he said simply. "I will not settle for less than everything. I will take your heart for my own." Because guardedness was creeping back into her eyes, he eased back a step. He had time. "You are going shopping for clothes, correct?" When she nodded, he firmed his lips. "I will buy what you need."

"I'm not without money," she said in exasperation. "I've been paid well for keeping your ass out of trouble. I rarely buy anything anyway, so I am entitled to an indulgence or two."

"*Sì*, but since you are, technically, buying these things for your 'job', it only makes sense that I pay for them." He arched a brow, daring her to argue with him. "And I very much want to see you in the best because you by far deserve it. I have told Bella and Brie that you are not to pay for a thing."

She groaned and covered her face with her hands. "Next you will tell me that you told them to buy me lingerie!" She looked up sharply when there was no retort. "You did *not* tell them that."

"I merely said for them to outfit you from the skin out. How they interpret that is entirely their decision. But, *cara*, you *do* need lingerie. You may not be able to go without a bra for much longer unless you wish to give Jill a run for her bouncing money."

He said it so straight-faced that she couldn't help but laugh. "Get out of my room! I need to scare up something that I can wear in public. None of my shirts button anymore," she confessed dryly.

A little smile touched his lips. Holding her gaze with his, he slowly unbuttoned the shirt he wore. He shrugged out of it with a casual ripple of muscle and then wrapped it around her shoulders. He stepped closer and bent his head to skim his lips across her ear. "It will look better on you than me. It should only be just a bit too big." His hand skimmed down her side, heated even through the towel. "I love how tall you are. I do not have to reach to enjoy your beauty."

She wasn't breathing as he walked out of her room shirtless, as casual as if he had been fully dressed. When he had shrugged out of the soft silk, she'd had to fight an urge to run her hands over his powerful chest. She had seen him without a shirt before; he loved to swim and had always coaxed her into going along even if she didn't get in the pool as well. Things had changed now. It seemed as if she could no longer control her emotions or her hormones, and both were steadily going out of control. He had barely touched her and she felt restless and needy.

Unable to resist, she rubbed her cheek over the soft material of the shirt. It had absorbed the heat and scent of his body, and both were a seductive lure.

She dropped the shirt on the bed. She was *not* going to wear it. Unfortunately, she realized quickly that she had no choice. She had managed to find a pair of jeans that had once been too baggy in the hip and waist, but her shirts were out of commission. She could wear one of her t-shirts, but they all looked either like sleepwear or something she would work out in.

Resigned, she pulled on Rafael's shirt and buttoned it. She tied the ends at her waist since it was still long on her and then cuffed the sleeves twice to use her hands. There were a lot of technicalities in life. One technicality was that she stood only five inches shorter than Rafael, and it was definitely a technicality because he was distinctly broader in the shoulder and overall bigger. She should have been able to forget being the stronger of them, but it did not work that way for her. Strangely enough, the bigger her client, the more protective she got. She had never been able to figure that one out.

Knowing that there was no escape, she headed downstairs. Marco was in the foyer sorting what looked like invitations. When he saw her, his smile came bright and delighted. "I am happy for you, *signorina*! *Signor* Rafael could not have chosen a better bride. We are all very happy that you will marry him. You do not need to worry about a thing! Peggy and I will handle the engagement party details!" He winked. "There is time enough for you to learn how to throw a gala."

Lacking anything better, she mumbled a thanks and hurried out the door toward the garage. To her reluctant amusement, Isabelle, Brie, and Alex stood next to the limo that rarely got used. The chauffeur was waiting as well, talking cheerfully with all three. As Tori got closer, he turned and beamed at her. "Congratulations! *Signor* Rafael was so happy when I saw him earlier."

"Isn't that the shirt Rafe was wearing?" Alex asked dryly.

"Mine didn't fit," Tori muttered.

The chauffeur was a wise man. He hid a chuckle as he opened the door for her. As soon as all four passengers had gotten inside, he whistled contentedly to himself as he went to the front of the car. He had won the betting pool that had been going for two years, ever since the staff had learned that Rafael was falling in love. All had known this was inevitable, but they had taken turns guessing how long it would take.

"What's up with the limo anyway?" Tori asked as she settled back in her seat.

"We're planning a slaughter of many stores." Brie pulled out her iPhone and began flipping through her notes. "We're completely going to need the room for bags. Isabelle called ahead to a couple places, and they are going to open early for us when we get there so that we can avoid some of the crowds. I've got a complete list of what we need to get for you. I've seen your closet; it's huge. It can hold everything."

"And so can the closet in the master suite," Isabelle added casually. "It is worth noting since Rafael will take charge of it upon his marriage to you. Papa was already rather gleefully beginning to box up his things. He wanted to turn it over to Rafael after Mama died, but there was tradition to uphold."

"I am *not* marrying Rafe," Tori repeated firmly. "This is just a cover, remember?"

"Why not?" Alex asked bluntly. "You want to tell us that you're not in love with him? I think we all know that already. In fact, Rafe may be the only one who does not know. You didn't take a bullet for him because of your job, Tori, and we both damned well know it."

"Will you give me some room to breathe?" she demanded. "None of you would know how this feels! You all have loving families. You've never doubted that someone wanted you there. You've never looked in a mirror and wondered why God hated you. You never questioned your own blood, afraid that there was something horrible in it!"

"There is nothing but good in you, Victoria," Isabelle said softly, covering her hands gently. "You are the ugly duckling, and we are the swans who welcome you home. We will help you see how beautiful you are inside and out. You were always meant to be part of our *famiglia*. You did not belong with those horrible ducks, ever."

After a long silence, she said softly, "It's hard, Bella. I can't change how I look at myself overnight. I already had a shock this morning after my shower. I looked in the mirror . . . and felt a little attractive. It was like having blinders taken off." She laughed wryly. "I think Rafael was shock therapy."

"It was a shock for us too," Brie agreed dryly. "If he'd been any closer to you, he'd have been on the other side!"

Tori glanced at Alex. "Cover your ears." When he did so with a wry smile, she lowered her voice and said, "You do *not* dare tell Rafe this, but that was my first kiss."

"*Dio*." Isabelle's eyes went wide. "You are joking."

"'Fraid not. Told you no one else wanted me."

"No, that's not how you say it," Brie argued with a grin. "You say that you were too picky to bother with lesser quality. You were holding out for the best." She lightly kicked Alex's ankle. "It's safe now. The icky girl conversation is done."

He just grinned. "I guess we're *all* lucky to have Tori. We men can talk to her as frankly as you women do."

"You are definitely the best of both worlds, Victoria," Isabelle agreed with a smile.

Tori just sighed wryly. She wasn't sure if she would enjoy this outing or not, but she knew she wouldn't be bored. "Just remember I know nothing about dressing like a girl," she warned. "I'm going to have to completely trust you."

"I'm an artist," Brie assured her. "I can add the trendy, stylish kick and Isabelle can make sure that you've got the classy look going on as well."

And thusly, Tori found herself escorted into one of the bigger and more expensive stores in the entire mall. The mall itself was fairly upscale, but this particular store catered to people like the Lucinos. She peeked at one price tag as they went by and then told herself never to look again else she chicken out. In a way, she was glad Rafael was paying; this would have wiped out even her savings.

Alex was a good sport, even when the first stop they went to was the women's lingerie section. He only paid half attention to the conversations and arguments; most of his focus remained on the area around them. They were the only ones in the store other than the clerks, for now, but that didn't mean he would let down his guard.

Tori felt grateful for his presence; Brie and Isabelle were hitting her with so much information that she had no way of being on alert herself. Come to find out, she was just shy of being a B cup, so that was the size bra they got just in case she grew any more. It was one of the stranger feelings she had ever experienced as she tried the first one on. It hit an interesting level between comfortable and uncomfortable, and when she pulled her shirt on over it, she could only gape at the mirror.

"How's it going?" Brie called over the dressing room door.

"I have cleavage. T'hell did that come from?"

"It's going good," she said to Isabelle. To Tori she added, "The manager says that you can go ahead and wear that one if you like; we've got the tag for it to be rung up when we're done. After all, you can't try on much anything else without it."

"Here you go, Victoria." Isabelle handed a hanger with a new article over the top of the door.

Tori took one look at what she was being offered and said quickly, "Initiate! I'm an initiate! I'm not ready for the mystery of the teddy yet!"

"Try it on." Isabelle's tone booked no argument.

"Jesus." She studied the strange blue silk contraption for a minute before figuring out how it was supposed to be put on. It wasn't made to go over a bra, so she had to take her new one off again. Her shoulder twinged in the process, reminding her again that she was still not one hundred percent better. "Ouch. Shit."

"What's wrong?"

"I can't unfasten this damn thing because of my shoulder."

"Pull your arms out of the straps and turn it around so the clasp is in front."

She blinked. She would never have thought of that, and much to her surprise, it worked perfectly. Freed from the device, she donned the teddy. As she looked in the mirror, she could feel the blush climbing from her neck to her forehead. There was a lot less to the garment than she had thought. It left little to nothing to the imagination.

The door cracked open, and Brie peeked in. "Wow!" she said. "Wow, you look great!" Rafael would go bonkers, and that was half the fun, but she kept that thought to herself. Tori was, as she had said, an initiate into the fun of having a lover. "You're pretty sexy, Victoria. Seeing you like this, I totally can't believe we were all fooled."

"Alright, I'll get it too." She shoved Brie back out and shut the door again.

Ten minutes later, the teddy was in a cart along with a few other bras, matching panties, and an outrageously beautiful silk nightgown that Tori was reluctantly in love with. It was also blue, and it was close enough to the color of her eyes that it became extra flattering. Their next stop was the regular women's clothes area.

"Tell me something," Isabelle said suddenly. "Why do you keep your hair so short? Your face could handle longer hair very well."

"It doesn't grow very fast. It's taken three months to even get it to this point, and it's still only an inch or two longer than it used to be. I don't think I'd like long hair. I'd never know what to do with it." Tori eyed her warily. "Why?"

"I was simply thinking that you could get it styled. Something that is easy to manage, but something more flattering than simply chopping all of it off. You have such beautiful hair. I know many women who pay money to get that shade of golden hair, but you have it by nature. When Brie and I get our hair done for the party, you will come with us."

"Yes'm." Tori tucked her hands in her pocket. She knew better than to argue with Isabelle when she got bossy. And, anyway, she was at the reluctantly resigned stage. She was almost enjoying the excursion.

They left the store with two bags of items. Or rather, they obtained two bags. A cheerful clerk would actually take them to the limo so that they could hurry on to their next stop.

The tone for the entire day was set. With an amused Alex following and offering occasional commentary, Tori was taken through at least half the stores in the mall until her cheerful captors decided they had done enough damage. Sensing she was getting overloaded, they decided to make the shoe store their final stop. It was almost evening already.

Tori was not only overloaded but also overwhelmed. She hadn't recognized herself in the mirror once all day. Brie and Isabelle were ruthless in making sure that everything flattered her. Jeans clung to her hips and thighs. Skirts were long to emphasize her height. If a shirt buttoned, it was tailored to tuck in at the sides so it enhanced her bust. If a shirt pulled on, it was either in a baby-doll style, or simply snug. Slacks were tailored in a way not dissimilar from the buttoned shirts. Dresses had either no obvious waist or one cut slightly higher than average.

Tori was fairly sure she would remember nothing of what she had been told. Her consolation in that fact was that she knew everything she now owned could go together. If she pulled it out of her closet, it would work. Brie had stuck to cool tones, primarily blues and greens, and matched them with neutrals.

"Oh what about jewelry?" Isabelle suddenly remembered. "She will need some of that as well. She will wear some of Mama's jewelry to the party since she is Rafael's future wife, but she will need casual pieces."

Tori blinked. "Jewelry? What for?"

Brie pursed her lips as she sought an explanation. "Okay, it's like this. Say you have a room with really nice furniture. You put in accessories to emphasize certain colors and lines to really make the room look completed and awesome. Jewelry is like that for women."

Tori looked at Alex. "My life was so much less complicated as a man."

"I have been thinking the same thing all day," he countered wryly.

"Do you have pierced ears?" Isabelle asked her.

"No, why would I?" Her eyes widened. "Oh hell no. No one is sticking needles in me. I got enough of that in the hospital."

"It doesn't hurt," Brie said in exasperation. "Just a little pinch and a sort of dull punch. No pain. We'll do that after we get shoes. Your ears should be just healed enough for you to wear some fancy earrings at the party. You heal fast."

"Alex, save me," Tori pleaded.

"Sorry, you're on your own." He nudged her into the shoe store. "Stop being a chicken. I've seen you face down men three times your size and wipe the floor with them. You can handle a little body art."

"What size shoe do you wear?" Isabelle asked.

"Men's size seven. I don't know what I wear in women's."

She got her answer after she stuck her foot on a sizing device. She was a size nine and a half, borderline ten. She found herself parked on a padded bench while Brie, Isabelle, and an overly perky salesgirl ravaged the aisles for selections. "I don't know how to wear high heels," Tori muttered. "I'll break my neck!"

"They're not that high," Brie assured her as she brought over several boxes. "You're super tall, Victoria. You don't need high heels like Isabelle and I do. A subtle heel will work the same way on you that higher ones work on us. It's about making your legs look hot."

They settled on nothing higher than two inches. Luckily, Tori wore a pair of her new jeans, and they were able to see how effective the shoes worked at flattering her legs. After the first wobbly steps where she distinctly felt like an overgrown newborn colt, she got the rhythm and was able to walk more comfortably.

"You have incredible balance," Isabelle said happily. "I was certain you would be fine once you got used to it. And because we love you . . ." She held out a pair of chic sneakers. "These will go with any of your jeans."

"Sneakers!" Tori grabbed them and held them against her chest possessively. "My feet will take back some of the nasty things they've been saying about you."

Sandals in black, white, and tan were obtained along with a variety of casual and formal heels in primarily neutral colors so they would match anything. She opted to wear the sneakers out; they were as comfortable as they looked, and she couldn't help but like how they managed to be casual and chic at the same time.

She was so busy admiring them that she didn't realize they had reached the jewelry store until Brie suddenly intoned, "Dun dun *dun*."

She looked up and nearly did a double take. "This is real jewelry."

"You were expecting fake?" Isabelle arched a brow.

"I was expecting something that doesn't scream 'rob me.'"

"They have simple items here as well. We want elegance, not overdone." Isabelle smiled as the man behind the counter came around to greet her. "*Ciao,* Francis. It is good to see you again."

"And you as well." Francis smiled at Alex. "Hello again, Mr. LaGuardia."

"You've been here before?" Tori asked curiously.

"Alex got my engagement ring here." Isabelle held up her left hand where the fiery ruby winked merrily. "He said that he would not give me diamonds because I am too temperamental. I would turn them red. It was best to give me something red to begin with." She smiled at Alex in a way that had others in the store looking over enviously. "He knows me well."

Alex kissed her for that and then tucked her under his arm contentedly. "We're here for Victoria." He gestured to Tori. "She is marrying Isabelle's brother, Rafael. The notices will be out shortly."

"How delightful!" Francis beamed at Tori. "Congratulations! How did you manage to tie him down?"

"Duct tape."

"I think I am going to like you. Well, what exactly can I help you ladies find?"

With his help, they picked out a few discreet necklaces and matching bracelets, none of which got in Tori's way. She even liked the way the bracelets glittered around her wrist. Either her girly side had been asleep with the rest of her hormones, or she had just never felt safe to indulge in it. It could go either way.

Several pairs of earrings were chosen, and she found herself reluctantly sitting on a stool at the counter while Francis used a small pen to mark where the holes in her lobes would go. She looked in a mirror to be sure they were even and then squeezed her eyes shut. She didn't want to watch.

The first one was the shocking one. It definitely felt like a quick punch, but it wasn't entirely painless. It was more like a quick hit before turning into a faint throbbing. By the time she even recognized that it had hurt a little, her other ear had been pierced as well. Surprised, she opened her eyes.

"There," Francis said. "That wasn't so bad."

She looked in the mirror and turned her head to see the tiny silver studs. She actually liked them more than she had thought she would, so she smiled as she said, "I've experienced one of the worst pains known to mankind. I guess this definitely wasn't so bad."

"You have given birth?" he asked curiously as he began to ring up the purchases.

She could have bitten her tongue. "Uhm, no. I had to have shoulder surgery after an accident. I was happy to be drugged, I assure you."

"Nice save," Alex murmured.

By the time Tori dragged herself into her room, it was dark out. She was *exhausted*. They had dropped Brie off with Roberto and gotten burgers to eat since they had missed dinner. Once home, Alex and the chauffeur had grabbed Marco and the gardener to help haul in all of the spoils of the war on the economy.

The bags were all over Tori's room to the point there was really nowhere to walk. She didn't care. She fell face first onto her bed and contemplated not moving for a week. She heeled off her sneakers but that was all she had the energy left to do.

She couldn't even lift her head when she heard her door open. Into her pillow, she muttered, "Shoot me again, please. I'm already dead."

"I see that." Rafael's voice sounded warm with tender amusement. He picked his way gingerly across the room and sat beside her on the bed. Even though he only saw the back, he approved of the efforts. The jeans she wore made a spectacular showing of her lovely bottom. He barely kept from running a hand over it and down her leg. He thought she might be too tired to hit him, but he wasn't going to take the chance. "Tell me you at least had fun."

She propped herself up on her elbows with a wry smile. "I question my sanity, but I think I did. I think the fashion lessons are leaking out my newly pierced ears, but I did enjoy myself most of the time. Your sisters are shopping guerillas. Seriously."

"And that is why I do not go out with Isabelle," he admitted dryly. "I had suspicion that Brie might be just as bad, if not worse for her creative bend." He tugged on a belt loop lightly. "I approve. I am not certain my heart will withstand the sight of you in a dress, *cara*, but I look forward to that as well."

"I'm wearing a bra," she confessed in a mock whisper. "I feel like a grown-up now." When he laughed as she had hoped, she rolled over and sat up. "Are you plotting, Rafael? When I questioned if I needed to get something fancy for our 'engagement' party, I was informed by Isabelle that you were going to 'handle everything' once you knew what sizes I wore."

"That is because I have a surprise for you. You will see it soon enough." He leaned in to peer at her ears in the low light from the single lamp. "You got them pierced. I am glad. As the heir, my mother's jewelry came to me to be given to my future wife." She opened her mouth, and he continued calmly, "It is a Lucino tradition that the fiancée of the heir to the family wear the jewels at the engagement party. It would be questioned by many if you did not."

"Damn it." Sudden amusement made her grin. "Tell me, if Isabelle had been older and therefore the heir, how would that have worked? I don't think Alex would look good in diamonds."

"I am sure he could have managed. The earrings would quite flatter him, but he might resent giving up his beloved Apple Watch for a bracelet." He said it with a straight face, but when she started laughing, he had to laugh as well. "I could not resist. Do not dare tell him I said that, Victoria."

"It's our secret. Now answer seriously."

"Seriously, Isabelle would have worn them herself. Old-fashioned *mia famiglia* may be, but both son and daughter have inherited in the past. Did you know that the Lucino family has been in America for over a hundred years, and has an even longer history in Italy?" When her brows lifted in surprise, he brought her hand to his lips. "I will take you to our land near Rome. We have a *castello*."

"I already get lost in this place," she complained. "You'll never see me again if you take me to a castle. Besides, I'm not the castle type. I don't go in for wine and cheese. I'm more like beer and pizza."

"There is a fifty-two inch television in the *castello* game room."

She blinked. "Wow."

"*Nonno* sneaks in beer when *Nonna* is not looking." He winked. "He claims it is his guilty pleasure."

"I still can't wrap my brain around the fact that eventually you will inherit a castle."

"It will be ours, *cara mia*." He pressed her hand to his heart and curled his free hand around the back of her neck to tug her closer. "I will chase you through the halls when no one is there and enjoy finding you when you are lost. I will show you my homeland. Italy will love you, Victoria, in a way that America never could. I will love you in a way no one else ever has, or ever will."

She could find no will to resist when his lips tenderly claimed hers. Her entire body went weak with a pleasure that was velvety and consuming. This was not the violent hunger of the morning. This was deeper. It seemed as if he kissed her from his very soul, and she couldn't help but surrender. Her heart demanded no less.

He slowly lowered her to the bed and eased back to look down at her. The light was doing its magic over her face again, making her features soft and sultry all at the same time. "It is a curious beauty," he said huskily, framing her face with one hand, "that can have so many facets. You are magic, Victoria. I look at you and see something new. I will spend a lifetime looking at you, and you will never look the same twice. I will lose my breath every time."

"You make me sound like a diamond," she somehow managed to tease. She felt breathless and needy, craving his closeness but equally afraid of it. He said he loved her, and he seemed to truly do so, but everything had changed so swiftly that she was terrified to trust her heart, or his. What if it was merely gratitude and friendship in disguise?

"I believe you are," he said after a moment. "Carbon is placed under extreme pressure and from it comes something beautiful. So, too, were you formed, *cara.* What you have endured has made you beautiful." He brushed her lips with his and slowly released her. "If I stay longer," he murmured huskily, "I may not leave at all."

She sat up and put her hand on his arm with a frown. "Will you sleep?"

"I will now that I have seen you. When I am with you . . . I feel safe. You will protect me. Knowing that, I do not fear my sleep so greatly. Someday soon, I will sleep with you in my arms, and I will rest better than I ever have before." He kissed her one last time. "*Ti amo*," he murmured against her lips. "Come to me, *cara*, anytime. I will love you for all the times no one else would."

She wasn't breathing as she watched him leave her room. A part of her wanted to go chasing after him. The rest of her was too afraid to take that jump. Something would happen soon, though. It had to. What was between them was too volatile to be contained much longer. She just didn't know if she had the courage. Fighting for her life was nothing. Getting shot had been minor. Nearly dying had been an inconvenience. Trusting her heart scared the hell out of her.

CHAPTER TWELVE

The few days until the party proved a flurry of activity. Word spread like wildfire through the media, and Tori was highly unnerved to open a newspaper and see a picture of her and Rafael together. She was more unnerved if she walked past a mirror. Even if she just grabbed the first thing to come to hand out of her closet, she looked . . . good. Pretty. Feminine. It was surreal.

She had gotten smart and stopped thinking about it. She was rolling with the punches, so to speak, and just taking each day at a time. Rafael was either consciously trying to help or subconsciously aware of her unbalance. He didn't push her. He didn't act heavy-handed. He was simply . . . there. He held her hand. He would casually kiss her in passing. If they were together, he was always touching her. A hand on her shoulder or back. An arm around her waist. She had known the family was tactile, but having it focused toward her was both sweet and scary.

They still stayed up talking until they were tired. They still played billiards together. Once they were ready for bed, he would kiss her good night and offer her a place to sleep if she wanted. When she declined, he would simply smile and let it be. She had the unnerving feeling that his patience was the water dripping on the stone of her fear. It kept crumbling away.

The morning of the party, she was in her room, reluctantly flipping through a magazine of hairstyles that Brie had pointedly given her when she heard a large commotion from downstairs. Her brows lifted, and she headed down the hall to look into the foyer.

The commotion was the arrival of an older gentleman who looked like Antonio in twenty years or Rafael in fifty. He wore a pitch-black suit with the confidence of a man half his age, and he still stood tall and proud. He carried a cane, but it seemed more a prop than a necessity. Even at seventy, Vincent Lucino was attractive enough to turn heads. His hair was entirely white, and his sharp blue eyes looked nearly wicked with amusement.

Tori had a strong feeling that Rafael might be a chip off his *nonno's* block. Wary of going downstairs into the happy reunion, she hovered just out of sight. She sensed Brie come up beside her and murmured, "You too?"

"He disowned my mother," she countered just as softly. "He owns a *castle*, Tori. He has more zeroes in his bank account than the U.S. government."

"And where are *miei bambini*?" Vincent suddenly demanded in a booming voice that carried. "Why do they not come to greet their *nonno*, 'Tonio? Have you not been teaching them to respect a great man?"

Antonio laughed. "*Sì*, Papa, I have. That is why they do not come running."

His father laughed and gave him a hard hug. "You are growing old, 'Tonio. I will forgive you for being so rude."

Isabelle came running in from the kitchen, a brilliant smile on her face as she threw herself into her grandfather's arms. "*Nonno*! I am so happy to see you!"

"Ah, Bella!" He lifted her off her feet for a fierce hug. "You are more beautiful than ever! You will give me great-grandbabies, *sì*?"

"*Sì*. You will meet Alex shortly. He has stepped out to run an errand for Rafael." She kissed Vincent's cheeks. "You will love him. He is perfect for me. You will not be able to intimidate him at all."

"That is good."

"Where is Mama?" Antonio asked Vincent curiously. "She is not with you?"

"She could not come this time. She is recovering from pneumonia." At the alarmed looks, he held up his hands. "She is fit and complaining, so I know she will be well. She has demanded that the wedding take place in *il castello*, as is tradition." In an aside, he added, "She is being lazy, 'Tonio, and she does not think I know. Pah! After fifty years of marriage, I know her mind better than she does."

"I wonder what it'll be like to be married for fifty years," Brie murmured to Tori. "You think I'll have gotten used to Roberto by then?"

Tori snorted softly. "You'll have learned all of the cuss words you need, that's for sure."

Rafael suddenly walked up behind them. "You are being cowards. He does not bite." He caught each by the shoulder and began urging them forward toward the stairs. "If you do not show yourselves now, then he will come find you. He has a nose like a bloodhound." As they reached the top of the stairs, he added, "*Nonno*, smile. You are scaring Gabrielle and Victoria."

Vincent's brows lifted. "I am not a scary man, Rafael. You must be mistaken. Your *nonna* is scary." His expression grew thoughtful as he looked at Brie. It was a little surprising to see that she appeared so perfectly identical to Isabelle, but he had seen many amazing things in his long life. "So you are Sophia's child."

It was Rafael's hand in the middle of her back that kept Brie from fleeing. "Yeah."

"'Yeah'? What is this 'yeah' that you Americans use? Why do you not use proper language?" He sighed heavily. "Roberto will bring you to Italy and you will learn culture. Now come greet your grandfather. I am old, and I am foolish, but I learn. If Sophia were alive, she and her husband would be welcomed home."

She hesitantly walked over to him and went on her toes to kiss his cheek. He hugged her tightly, and she carefully hugged him back, her breath unraveling. She had been half-afraid he would kick her out of the house!

"There." He kissed her cheeks and then lightly tweaked her nose. "You are very American, but we can fix that. Do you speak Italian?" She shook her head, and he sighed. "*Sì*, and such a pity. You will learn."

"I am working on it," Roberto said calmly as he walked into the foyer from outside. "*Ciao, Don Lucino. Come sta*?"

"*Benissimo*, Roberto." Vincent smiled. "I suppose I shall have to like you now that you are marrying one of my *bambini*."

"I suppose you shall." Roberto tugged Brie into the circle of his arms with a smile.

"Now, Rafael!" Vincent beetled his brows at his heir. "Where is this woman that has stolen your heart?"

Rafael firmly pulled Tori the rest of the way down the stairs and gave her no option of escape. "This is Victoria Li. She saved my life, *Nonno*. I have since convinced her to live it with me." He brought Tori's hand to his lips and smiled as he looked into her wary eyes. "Do not overwhelm her too greatly. She has never had *famiglia* before."

"Li." Vincent arched a brow. "You are Chinese?" She shook her head. "Japanese?" At the next shake, he pursed his lips. "*Sì*, you do not look Asian. Where does your family come from, Victoria?"

"I don't know. I was raised in a foster home. My name was given to me by a doctor when I was taken to the hospital as a baby. I could be any ethnicity, sorry. I'm pretty sure it's mostly Caucasian since I'm naturally blonde and blue eyed, but I could be any number of European types too."

He studied her critically and nodded firmly. "Then you will do well for the mother of my great-grandbabies. It is good that the family has more new blood introduced. You and Rafael will have beautiful babies for me to spoil."

She could feel the blush climbing her face. "Thanks."

"*Scusi, Nonno*." Isabelle smiled. "I must steal Gabrielle and Victoria so we may go get our hair done. Alex will be meeting us there," she added when three sets of male eyes narrowed in concern. "You must get settled in." She kissed her grandfather's cheek. "We will make ourselves more beautiful so you may show us off."

"If you insist." Vincent smiled as the three women hurried out—Brie and Isabelle mostly dragging Tori—and then turned to Rafael. His smile faded. "Tell me what you know of Victoria. I do not like that she does not know her own heritage. She does not hide well that it bothers her, this not knowing. We will fix it."

Tori was indeed dragging her heels, but only a little bit. Thankfully, they weren't taking the limo again. The chauffeur instead stood next to the regular Cadillac that the family used. It wasn't precisely as subtle as she might have preferred, but it was better than the limo. The windows were tinted in the back, and that helped her feel a little better as well.

As they headed to the salon, Brie asked, "Did you decide anything?"

"No." Tori tugged on a lock of her hair. "I really don't care, Brie, okay? Just as long as I don't have to fuss with it, I'm fine. And no extensions!" she added hastily. "That completely enters the realm of high maintenance. If you want to see me with long hair, you'll simply have to wait a year or two for my hair to grow naturally."

"Nothing curly," Isabelle told Brie. "She is not the curly type." Tori winced at the very idea, and she laughed. "Do not worry, Victoria. You are in good hands."

Alex was waiting for them at the salon, as promised, and looked much like a bull in a china shop. The salon was delicate and elegant, and he was too tall and too masculine to not stand out. He took it in good humor, though, and settled in the waiting room with a magazine where he could keep his eye on all three chairs the women would be in.

Tori found herself introduced to a stylist named Jon and then whisked into the washing station to have her hair fully scrubbed. While he was doing that, he talked cheerfully with Isabelle and Brie about what to do to her. She closed her eyes and tuned them out. They might as well have been speaking in Italian; nothing they said made any sense to her. What the hell was 'feathering'?

After wrapping her hair with a towel, he showed her to the cutting station. "Now," he said, "what I'm going to do is fancy up your hair specifically for tonight. After the party, you can wash out all of the product without any problems. Just blow dry your hair and it'll fall into its natural style." He winked. "Its new natural style. If you want to play with it, a little gel will do wonders. Just leave it to me."

"Do I have any other choice?" she muttered.

"You could go bald and wear a wig."

"Don't tempt me!"

He just grinned as he got to work on her hair. She didn't bother to look in the mirror at herself; she used the reflection to watch everyone and everything else instead. It felt as if someone was watching her, but she couldn't pinpoint anything overt. There were many people who would glance over at her curiously, but none of them seemed dangerous. And yet, she couldn't shake the feeling. When she glanced toward Alex, she could see him tapping a foot lightly on the floor. It was a telling gesture that meant he felt something too.

The hair dryer started whirring and she closed her eyes. The snipping had stopped and Jon was doing something with a strange round brush. "Did you bring the hairpieces?" he asked someone curiously.

"What hairpieces?" she asked warily.

"Keep your eyes closed," Isabelle ordered from somewhere to the side. There was a smile in her voice.

Tori muttered but kept her eyes closed, even when she felt Jon clipping something into her hair on either side of her head. Hair clips? Were they nuts? She was twenty-five, not fifteen.

"Now you can look." Satisfaction filled Jon's voice. "You're going to knock your fiancé on his butt."

Her eyes popped open and she stared at her reflection. He had cut her hair in a way that made it fall more toward her face and soften the lines and angles. It had been fluffed and tousled for more body, and looked . . . elegantly sexy. It was the only way she could think of describing it. She then saw what had been clipped into her hair and her breath caught.

The clips were slender diamond swans opening their wings. Set into her golden hair, they sparkled and shimmered with even the littlest light hitting them. They pulled her hair back away from her ears, and the final effect was so feminine that she could only gape. She very cautiously reached up to touch one of the clips. "Bella," she pleaded, "tell me they're not . . ."

"Oh, they are. They were made just for you."

She would kick Rafael's ass for this. How was she supposed to forget she had *real* diamonds in her hair? She would be terrified of turning her head too fast and accidentally losing one.

Brie's hair ended up being curled and pinned up in ringlets. Isabelle's hair was upswept into an elaborate coil of braids that looked like something out of a princess' guide to fashion. Brie had a sapphire circlet wrapped around her hair. Rubies on a delicate silver net covered Isabelle's coil.

With their hair finished, all three were free to have their nails done. Tori stared in fascinated horror at the little bottles of polish and the assorted nail tips. Brie blessedly came to her rescue. "Don't make her nails long," she told the lady cleaning Tori's nails. "She has a very physical job, and she would break them." She winked at Tori.

The stylist took the advice to heart and only extended Tori's nails enough that they went past her fingertips. "What color polish?" she asked Tori. "What does your dress look like?"

"Good question," Tori muttered.

Isabelle smiled. "She will be in white."

"I'll be in *what*?" Tori gaped at her. "I'll spill something on myself! That's like *asking* for karmic revenge!"

"*Taci*, Victoria." She admired her nails and the rich ruby color they were being painted. "It will all be revealed at home. Tonight you will be a swan."

Tori's nails ended up painted a soft gray color that she would never have imagined could look so pretty. The better part was that she could still make a decent fist without worrying about cutting her palm. The tips were nice and blunt, and not long enough to get in the way. "Thanks, Brie," she murmured as they headed on their way home.

"Don't thank me yet." Her grin turned wicked. "You've still got to put on makeup." Tori groaned, and she laughed. "Bella will hold your hand the entire time."

They snuck in the back through the kitchen with Alex serving as a decoy by entering the front door. Brie wouldn't have minded being seen by Roberto, but neither she nor Isabelle wanted Tori seen until they were completely done.

They ushered her into her room swiftly, and Isabelle instructed, "Put on the dress and we will return as soon as we have also changed. If you cannot fasten the dress, then you may wait for us."

Tori scowled as the door was shut behind her. She had once found Isabelle's bossiness amusing. It had become vexing now that she was the recipient of it. Muttering under her breath, she walked over to the bed where a garment bag had been laid out with two boxes beside it. One looked like a shoebox, and the other could have been anything.

She opened the strange box first and felt her cheeks heat. Neatly folded inside a bed of tissue were a strapless white bra, lace underwear, and sheer flesh-toned stockings. A note on the top from Brie read, *I convinced Isabelle that you weren't a garter type woman. They're normal silk stockings.*

"Thank you, Brie," she muttered.

The shoebox indeed held shoes, she discovered. They were a frothy confection of straps and beads that looked too ridiculously fragile to be worn on feet. A little more wary than before, she carefully opened the garment bag. As she saw what was inside, she stopped breathing.

The dress was definitely white, but the top portion to roughly her hip area was liberally covered with intricate beadwork that seemed to subtly hint at a pattern she couldn't quite decipher. From the hip to probably mid-thigh, the dress was made of white feathers. When she carefully ran her hand over them, she wasn't entirely surprised to discover they were real. Apparently Isabelle had been literal when she had said Tori would be a swan.

With a quick breath for courage, she pulled on her lingerie and then made an attempt to get into the dress. The zipper went up the back from her waist to that elusive place partway up her back that she would have to be a contortionist to reach. Designers were nuts, or they thought women had reverse bending elbows. It was debatable.

The entire thing was snug, even the feathered portion, but not so snug that she felt impaired in her movement. The end of the dress stopped an inch below her knees, more than long enough to go past her thigh-high stockings. The top of the dress had a straight line that just sort of teasingly hinted at the shadow of her cleavage. The straps were wide enough that they covered the tail end of her scar, something she had entirely forgotten about but was glad someone else had remembered. She was proud of the mark, but it would give her identity away.

The door opened and Isabelle peeked in. She sighed happily. "Oh, Victoria! You are lovely!"

"Wow!" Brie peeked around her shoulder. "You're hot, Tori. Totally." She hurried in, looking sleek and sultry in a long skirted dark blue silk dress covered in elaborate beading. She zipped up the back of Tori's dress for her before stepping back to study her critically. She nodded firmly. "Rafe definitely knew what he was doing."

Isabelle put down the case of makeup that she carried "Put on your robe," she told Tori, "so we do not risk your gown." In her red ball gown, she was as sultry as her twin, but she seemed to be more like the flame that smoldered than the flame that burned.

Once Tori was bundled in her robe, Brie got to work on her makeup. "Light," she assured her, "because your face doesn't need a lot. You've got perfect cheekbones."

"I do?"

Her lips thinned. "I'd like to kick all those people who made you feel ugly. You just didn't belong in their world. Different doesn't mean ugly. You absolutely need to look up all of those snotty little snits from high school and send them postcards from the *castello* after you and Rafe get married. Like a 'too bad you're not here' sort of thing. Make them green with envy."

"I'm not marrying Rafe."

Isabelle and Brie shared a smile but said nothing. Tori's protests had been steadily growing weaker, and it was clear that her resistance crumbled. She would tumble right into Rafael's arms if he pushed just a little bit harder. The two of them *belonged* together. It was a crime against love itself if they weren't.

Brie added a pale rose-colored lipstick for a finishing touch and leaned back. "Okay. Lose the robe and look in the mirror."

Tori took off the robe and cautiously walked over to her full-length mirror. The woman that stared back at her was a stranger. She was beautiful and sexy, strong, and yet feminine. She deserved to walk into a ballroom on the arm of a man like Rafael Lucino.

A light knock sounded on the door. "May I come in?" Rafael called.

Brie hurried over to open the door. Rafael walked in, a box in his hand, and stopped sharply as he saw Tori. His eyes slowly widened. He didn't even notice when his sister and cousin slipped out with smiles. His gaze was filled with the sight of the woman he loved.

She was . . . stunning. She looked a little shocked by her reflection and a lot vulnerable as she looked at him. Her hair begged to be mussed by his fingers. Her lips were soft and asking to be kissed. The dress he'd had made for her seemed to flatter everything he loved about her from her long legs to her gentle figure.

"*Dio*, Victoria," he whispered. "You are beautiful." He stepped closer and carefully touched her cheek with his fingers. "I cannot believe you are real."

She couldn't catch her breath. He looked exotic and gorgeous in his black tuxedo, and too handsome for her sanity. A white sash crossed his powerful chest, drawing emphasis to his strong shoulders. She somehow smiled as she tugged on it lightly. "Uh-oh. Have you been marked as the future keeper to the keys of the kingdom?"

"*Sì.*" He put the box on the bed and opened it. "And now you will be marked as my future queen."

Her mouth fell open as he lifted a silver and diamond necklace. "I'm not wearing that."

"Yes, you are. Turn around, *cara mia*." She reluctantly did and he slipped the necklace around her neck and fastened it into place. The nape of her neck was slender and delicate, and he could not resist the urge to press his lips there. She shivered softly and he ran his hands down her arms. "I cannot resist you."

Matching teardrop earrings were fastened to her ears, and he was deft enough to put them on her without bothering her still sensitive lobes. It did nothing good for her pulse, however, to have him standing that close. He smelled wonderful, felt hot and tempting.

"Now then." He picked up a smaller box that had been in the bigger. "It would not do for you to walk in without an engagement ring. And as I want you to keep it for your own, I had best do this properly." He went down on one knee as her eyes widened. "Marry me, Victoria. Marry me for real. Forget everything else. Love me. Be my salvation, my defender. Keep me safe in your arms."

Her stomach dipped with sheer terror, but as she looked into his eyes, she saw something she had never seen before. A trace of nerves, of pain and longing. He had always seemed confident before. So cocky and assured. Yet here . . . he was vulnerable. Wonder began to fill her softly. "You're in love with me."

"Have I not said it enough? I think I have loved you since I met you. Man, woman, neither, or both. It is *you* that I love. I have wanted you all along. You *belong* with me, Victoria. With my family. Please. Marry me."

She took a deep breath. It was real. It was scary and it was real. "I guess since I saved your life," she said huskily, "the least I can do is make sure it stays safe for the next seventy years or so. It was personal this time, Rafe. It should have been a job, but from the beginning it was personal. I didn't take a bullet for you just because it was my job. I wasn't even thinking in that moment. I just . . . loved you."

His breath came out hard and quick. "You scared me, *cara mia*." He stood and pulled her into his arms fiercely. "I would kiss you, but I would muss you up and Brie would yell at me. I will kiss you later when I am free to muss you up as much as I desire."

Someone banged on the door. "Let's go, you two," Alex called. "You're the guests of honor. You can't be late to your own party, and the natives are getting restless."

"We are on our way," Rafael called back. He opened the ring box and pulled out what was within. The delicate silver setting held a diamond just big enough to catch the light, but not big enough to be overwhelming. On the inside of the band, the words '*Ti amo*' had been engraved. "So you always remember you are loved," he said softly as he slid it over her finger.

"Don't make me cry," she pleaded. "I don't cry. I've never cried. I'm not going to be *that* much a girl. I like some of my boy self!"

He laughed and kissed her knuckle over her ring. "As do I. I shall endeavor to make sure you are always smiling, *cara*." He brushed a kiss across her forehead. "Let us go before Alex comes in and fetches us. Are you ready to face a room of wildly jealous people?"

"Jealous of me or you?"

"Me. I fear I might be in grave danger from many gentlemen, Victoria."

She shook her head in amusement, not entirely believing it herself. "I will protect you."

"*Sì, cara*. I have never doubted that for a moment."

CHAPTER THIRTEEN

The layout of the Lucino villa allowed for an immense dining room and an equally immense ballroom. Tori had been in the dining room often enough and was always amused by the way the whole family gathered at one end of the large table. She had peeked into the ballroom once or twice out of curiosity, but she had never actually gone inside.

It was for that reason that she felt suitably impressed when she walked into the room and found it filled with people. The staff had gone overboard with decorations, and the entire place felt like it belonged in the infamous *castello*. She had to force herself to remember she was still in New York and had not been secretly teleported to Italy. It was overwhelming, especially when people began to clap and cheer as they saw her and Rafael. His arm tightened around her waist in support and made it easier to resist an urge to run away.

"Remember, *cara*," he murmured softly, "you are the queen here. There is no one who can compare, no one who would dare try." He skimmed his lips across her temple. He felt humbled by her bravery. He knew that this was exceptionally hard for her because she had never stood in the spotlight before.

"Don't leave my side," she pleaded softly, "or I really will run away."

"I am not going anywhere. Just think of this as your prom night."

"I never went to prom," was her mutter. "The boys didn't want me."

"Then you knew only fools. I would have claimed you for my own without a second thought." He walked further into the room, and his arm around her waist forced her to go with him. "I will introduce you to people, and you will be yourself. Everyone will love you."

She wasn't quite that confident but she was committed. There were a lot of big names in this crowd of people. Several politicians, other corporate owners, businesspeople that the Lucinos had worked with, and other high-class elite made up the majority of the crowd. The rest were the employees of Just In Time, Inc. To her immense relief, the crowd wasn't as big as it had initially appeared; only fifty or so people were in attendance.

She began to relax after the first hour of mingling. People were being genuinely friendly and welcoming. Even the politicians seemed to be truly happy for Rafael, but she took that with a grain of salt. She trusted no one who had to be elected for anything.

It didn't take long for those in the crowd to realize that Rafael was madly in love with his fiancée. He never once left her side and either kept his arm around her waist or held her hand with his. If he looked at her, there was something powerful in his blue eyes. His voice, when he would speak to her, always seemed more intimate.

And Tori? There was no question as to her feelings as well, though there was an obvious shyness or sense of wonder if she looked at her fiancé. Truly, that did not come as a surprise to anyone. Nearly no one in the crowd had ever heard of her before, so she obviously came from a different background entirely. To suddenly jump to the top of the totem pole would be disorienting for anyone. Reactions were a bit tepid to her at first, but she was so friendly, so personable, that even some of the snootier guests found themselves liking her a great deal.

There was, however, one person in the crowd who knew Tori and knew where she had come from. Tori herself did not realize she was there until Rafael escorted her over to meet one of the politicians. "Victoria, *cara*," he said with a smile, "meet Assemblyman Davis Harkin and his new wife, Paula."

Shocked, Tori stared at an equally startled Paula Harkin. The former Paula Crothers, the girl Tori had knocked on her ass so that she could be suspended to escape school.

At twenty-five, Paula was as beautiful as ever, but there were tiny lines already beginning to appear at the corner of her eyes and mouth, as if too much unhappiness had started dragging her down. Still busty and yet petite, she wore an emerald green dress that showed off nearly every one of her assets. It also showed that her formerly trim body looked much skinnier than might be healthy for her size. Her desperation to fit in had only done all the more damage to her internally and externally.

For the first time in her life, Tori realized she did not feel outclassed. Her entire body relaxed. She had always wondered how she would feel if she met someone from her past again, and now she knew. She felt . . . nothing. If she was a swan as her family said, then Paula had to be a duck. They just belonged in two different worlds, neither better nor worse than the other. "As a matter of fact," she said calmly, "Paula and I knew each other years ago. We went to high school together."

Rafael's arm tightened possessively and protectively though he kept his smile. "It is a small world, no?"

Harkin inclined his head with one of those polished 'good guy' smiles that Tori had always hated. "It's a pleasure to meet you, Victoria." He looked her over slowly in a way that made her hackles rise. "Rafael, you have spectacular taste as always. It's good to see a young man marrying for love. I had to wait for my chance." He smiled at Paula affectionately.

Somehow, Tori didn't think love had anything to do with their marriage. Harkin looked old enough to be Paula's father, and the look in his eyes felt more . . . covetous than loving. He may have been pleasant enough in appearance, perhaps, but there was simply something about him that felt disturbing.

Paula forced herself to smile at Tori though it did not reach her eyes. "I didn't expect to see that you were the Victoria Li I once knew."

"I imagine you didn't. Congratulations on your marriage. I'm sure you're very happy together." Tori unconsciously rubbed her cheek lightly against Rafael's shoulder. "I'm sure you're happy for me too."

Paula's back teeth audibly clicked together. Her eyes narrowed with visible jealousy as she stared at Tori. It wasn't fair! The tomboyish caterpillar had somehow turned into a beautiful butterfly, and she had also bagged one of the hottest and most eligible bachelors in the state. The *way* that Rafael looked at her . . . Paula had married Harkin for his power and money, and she hated every minute of her life. Tori was getting more position, far more money, and a gorgeous husband who doted on her to go with it.

Snidely, she said, "It's so odd, Victoria. You disappeared for years. You dropped out of high school and that was all we knew of you."

"Actually," Tori's voice cooled, "I went into home study. I graduated perfectly on time. I chose to come out here for college. I've been working a rather confidential job for the last few years. I met Rafe on the last one."

"Well, at least you've stopped being so ugly."

A startled hush fell on the room as people heard Paula. Her color rose, and her husband began to look uncomfortable. Tori knew that proper etiquette probably called for her to ignore the insult and move on. It was a big party, there were dozens of bigwigs in the crowd, and taking the bait would probably embarrass the Lucinos.

Proper etiquette could go to hell. She'd had enough. "You're right," she told Paula. "I did stop being ugly. Unfortunately for you, your ugliness is still to come. You're going to get old, Princess Paulie, and I'd bet you're not going to do it very graciously."

"Don't call me that!" Paula hissed.

Tori leaned in until they were eye-to-eye. "I still don't know why you hated me or why you went out of your way to make my life hell. In the end I'm the one who is marrying the man of my dreams. I'm the one who will never doubt that my husband will want me even if I get old and wrinkly. The minute your boobs start to sag, you're going to be tossed over for the latest model. You and I both know it. I'd start saving money for some high class plastic surgery if you want to keep your cushy home."

"You can't talk to me like that!"

"Actually, I can. And it feels damn good. Almost as good as the time I knocked you on your ass. Push me, Paulie, and I'll do it again. I'm nine years older, nine years stronger, and nine years meaner." She straightened and turned away. "Fill your flapping jaw with some appetizers. I'd stay away from the bread though; I hear it's bad for ducks."

Several people started laughing as they got the reference. Harkin grabbed Paula's elbow and hustled her away from the scene much faster than would be expected of a man his size. In a voice that carried, Vincent called, "*Sì*, Rafael! You have chosen well! She will give me fierce and fiery *bambini* to spoil!"

Tori's cheeks turned red. "Oh god," she said under her breath. "I did not just make a scene."

"*Sì, cara*, you did." Rafael swung her into his arms with a wide grin. "But Lucinos enjoy making scenes. You will make a fine Lucino. Perhaps you are Italian as well."

She wound her arms around his neck with a sudden smile. "I'm probably a mutt, Rafe, with a little of everything."

"But the Italian is the important part." When she laughed, he ushered her into the middle of the room. "We will dance now. I wish to have you in my arms."

"I don't dance," she blurted in horror. "Rafael, I'll humiliate us both."

"I will teach you." He pulled her into his arms and bent his head to brush her ear with his lips. "There are many things I will teach you. Do not drink too much wine, Victoria. If you are tipsy, then you will not enjoy my lessons nearly as much."

An entirely different sort of heat flushed her body and made her cheeks pink. Her legs went weak but she somehow stayed on her feet by clinging onto his arms. It was nearly impossible to quell an urge to turn her head and kiss his sinfully tempting lips. "Teach me to dance," she invited softly, her voice huskier. "Then teach me everything else later."

A thrilling mix of hunger, laughter, and love filled his eyes. "How you tempt me, *cara*."

On the other side of the room, Antonio was smiling at the sight of his son and future daughter-in-law dancing when a stunning redhead in a green dress walked up to him. The Grecian style to the piece suited her in a way that seemed purely elemental. "You look pleased," Rhianna told him.

"I am well pleased. Did you know all along that this would happen?" He lifted a brow at her.

"Now how would I know that, Antonio?" Her black eyes widened innocently. "It was a coincidence." Her gaze turned faraway as she glanced to where Theresa was looking very unnerved and flustered by the cluster of males standing near her. "There are more as yet to come," she murmured.

"*Scusi*?"

"Nothing." She smiled. "I must excuse myself, Antonio. It was lovely to see you." She offered a hand.

He smiled and bowed gracefully. "A delight as always, Rhianna. Do not be a stranger. You will attend the wedding in Italy, yes?"

"I will do my best to make some free time."

More than one pair of wistful eyes followed her as she walked away. Practicality said she had to be in her fifties, or more, considering how long she had been in charge at Enforcers, but she looked to be barely in her mid-twenties. She was as beautiful and vibrant as any woman half her age.

Antonio had always admired her, and he felt it a great shame that so fine a woman would have been single her whole life. She deserved to have someone to hold her when her work grew too hard. But then, it would take a singularly exceptional person to handle such a powerful female. He hoped he saw it happen in his lifetime.

Tori was ready to escape by the time midnight arrived. With a sympathetic Alex covering for her, she snuck out the back and took off her shoes. Her very happy-to-be-freed feet were silent as she tiptoed through the quiet villa toward her room. Maneuvering on tile in stockings was not easy, though. Thank goodness that her balance was above average.

She spotted a light under her door and her brows drew together. When she peeked the door open, her sigh came long and contented. She owed one of the maids a big hug. The bed had been turned down and there was a fire cheerfully crackling in the fireplace to combat the winter chill.

She put her shoes on the top of the table. She then peeled off her stockings and dropped them in the hamper. Just that alone felt wonderful. She went into the bathroom and gingerly removed her earrings. She put the simple studs back in so that the terrible two wouldn't yell at her for letting the holes close that soon after getting them pierced. She removed the necklace as well and put it and the earrings in the waiting velvet box. She felt . . . odd, for some reason. As if she was waiting for something.

Her answer came when movement in the mirror caught her attention as she was wiping off her makeup. Rafael stood in the bathroom doorway, leaning negligently against the door as he watched her with a soft smile on his lips. He had shed most of his tuxedo and wore only his black pants and open white shirt. "*Scusi*," he said softly. "I am looking for the most beautiful woman in the world. Have you seen her?"

She covered the sudden flutter of her heart with a wry smile. "Sorry, you've got the wrong address."

"Then you are not looking in that mirror, *cara*." He stepped up behind her and lifted her chin so she looked at their reflection. "If you could only see through my eyes," he murmured in her ear, "then you would see how beautiful you are." He nuzzled her neck and softly tasted her skin. "Do not tell me to go, Victoria. I do not have that strength."

She drew a long and trembling breath. "I don't want you to go. But . . ." She made a helpless gesture.

"But it is new for you, and you are nervous." He turned her in his arms and calmly began to remove the clips from her hair. "Do not look surprised, *cara*. Am I a fool? You believed you were ugly for many years and then lived as a male. Where in that time would you have tried to have a lover?" He combed his fingers through her hair and thoroughly demolished her styled coif. Golden locks tumbled in her eyes and others scattered in a million directions. She looked a little wild, a little untamed, and very unsure. "You break my heart when you look at me like that."

"I'm not afraid," she argued. "Just . . . understandably apprehensive."

He cocked his head. "Then you will not mind if I peel this dress off you."

Her lips curved. "I'd be grateful, actually. I can't reach the zipper. It really is beautiful, Rafe. I never thanked you properly." She rose slightly on her toes and softly pressed her lips to his. A soft sigh of pleasure was captured by his mouth when he lazily deepened the kiss, his tongue gliding over hers without hurry.

She didn't even notice that he had unzipped the dress until he tugged the straps down her shoulders. She freed her arms and he tugged lightly on the hem of the skirt. The entire dress came free and slid to the floor, leaving her in nothing but her bra and panties. She didn't even think to cover herself. He was still kissing her, still consuming her in that drugging delight, and it was the only important thing.

He lifted her off her feet and carried her into the bedroom. To feel her so soft and welcoming in his arms . . . He wanted nothing more than to take his time and savor everything about her. He did not want her to ever question again that she was loved and desired.

"I can't catch my breath," she whispered as he let her slip down his body to stand on her own feet. "I didn't expect this."

He framed her face with his hands. "It is not all about flash and frenzy." He teased her lips lightly with his and nibbled on her lower lip. "We can have that later." He slowly smiled. "I am sure we will have that many times. But not this time, *cara mia*."

She had no will to resist as he kissed her again. Every muscle went limp with pleasure until only his hands held her up. She couldn't breathe or think, but it no longer seemed important. He kissed her as if that alone was all he had ever wanted. Even when the kiss lazily deepened, he didn't overwhelm her. It was much easier to surrender when he was utterly gentle with her. She had no room for apprehension or nerves.

His lips glided along the line of her jaw. "Touch me," he murmured huskily. "I need to feel your touch."

Her hands lifted and spread across his chest slowly. Matching shivers rippled through their bodies. She felt her fingers tingling with a nearly electric charge as she softly traced the line of his muscles. The quivering in his body was a thrilling reminder that she had an entirely different strength over him as well.

She pushed at his shirt, and he shrugged out of it easily. "I'm amazed you even left it on," she said softly, a hint of amusement in her husky voice.

"I would not scare you." He slid his hands slowly up her sides and then around her back. He unhooked her bra and let it fall to the floor in a flutter of white. His breath lodged in his chest painfully as he looked at her. She was more beautiful than he remembered. "I do not want you to change more," he said, his voice thick. "You are perfection for me."

A soft moan was her only answer as his hot hands tenderly cupped her breasts. Somehow she was sure that her sensitivity had nothing to do with her growing figure and everything to do with him. It didn't seem to matter where he touched her. All that changed was the intensity of the pleasure. There was nothing that did not respond to him.

He pressed hot kisses along her strong shoulder and then down along her collar. His soul quivered with shocking emotion as he discovered the scar that sat starkly against her nearly flawless skin. His tongue traced the length of the mark before soothing it with kisses. He wanted to remove every memory of pain, every memory of fear, for the both of them. No matter how long he lived, he would never forget what she had done.

All she could manage was a whimper when his lips found one stiffened nipple. It tightened further as her breast swelled. The sensation was foreign and thrilling all at once. The ache spread like ripples in water until her body began to quiver with the need for release. How could anything that shockingly tender be so incredibly powerful?

She was barely conscious of him slowly stripping away her underwear so that she stood naked in his arms. Her eyes opened slightly and she saw the look of utter absorption on his face, the wonder in his eyes as he looked at her. He made her feel as beautiful as the diamond he had called her. "Rafe."

A shudder went through his body. He stood and lifted her into his arms to gently put her on top of the bed. With unashamed delight, she watched as he removed the last of his clothes. He was ridiculously male, unbelievably gentle. The contrast was thrilling, and even more so when she saw how aroused he was.

He eased onto the bed beside her and tangled his fingers in her hair to bring her up for another drugging kiss. When he assuaged the hunger for her lips, he began a slow exploration of her body. There was no inch that did not feel his lips or fingers, no curve or line that went unloved. Only when she was quivering wildly, her voice breathless, and her hands desperately tugging at his shoulders did he slowly make his way back up her body. His entire body was knotted and pained with violent hunger, but he leashed it desperately. He had waited too long for this moment to rush it.

"Look at me," he said thickly. Her lashes lifted to reveal darkened blue eyes swirling with need and desire and love. "Hold me. *Dio*, hold me, Victoria."

The plea shook her to her soul. She fiercely wrapped her arms around his shoulders as her legs instinctively curled around his hips. Nothing was more important than protecting this man. This incredible person who had loved her at her worst and helped her to find the best inside and out. "I love you," she whispered softly.

His control crumbled. A low sound of mingled need and elation rumbled in his chest. His kiss held both as he took her lips, and he clung to whatever will he had left as he slowly pressed into her welcoming heat. Her breath hitched but her darkening eyes told him it was not pain. Wonder slowly filled her gaze as he settled in completely. There were no words she could find to explain the sheer beauty of that moment.

There were no words for either of them. In a silence that held more promises than a single voice, he slowly took her, again and again, until she was clinging onto him with a strength that soothed him to the deepest level, bringing a sense of safety as thrilling as the feel of her body, soft and welcoming beneath him.

The shattering ecstasy that claimed them both was velvety and deep, as emotional as it was physical, and it swelled on and on until it erased every sense of self, every memory of being separate and alone. In that final moment of fusion, his lips found hers one last time as her hands framed his face. Neither was alone any longer. They never would be again.

By the time she noticed the room was getting a little chilly because the fireplace had dimmed, she was sprawled across Rafael's chest. He had rolled onto his back and tugged her on top of him, and even though he seemed to be lightly dozing, his arm still curled possessively around her waist.

She carefully disentangled herself and slid out of bed. Assorted aches made their presence known, and a tiny thrill went through her body. She looked at Rafael lying in her bed and could only marvel that someone that beautiful belonged to her. She knew that night, no matter how many others followed, would be permanently burned in her memory.

She knelt to stoke the fire and make it kick out more heat. The villa had central air and heating, but everyone kept costs down by using fireplaces for heat. She had always been warmed by the knowledge that the one family who had money to spare would be careful with it. It made them more real, more approachable.

"You left me."

The drowsy rasp of Rafael's voice teased along her nerve endings. She smiled and straightened to see him propped up in bed. "You're the insomniac," she teased as she walked over to him. "I thought you'd appreciate being left to get some rest."

"I am not capable of resting without you, *cara*." He buried his fingers in her rumpled hair and tugged her down for a lingering kiss. "Are you hungry?" he asked against her lips. "You did not eat much at the party. I believe you were quite nervous."

"I was wearing diamonds worth more than this villa in a crowd of elite sharks." She pulled a face. "I was entitled to be nervous." Her stomach rumbled lightly, and she had to grin when he arched a brow. "But I'm definitely starving. I burned a lot of energy tonight."

"*Sì*, and you will burn more as yet." He rolled out of bed as lithely as a large feline. "You start the shower and I will ring Peggy to bring us some food."

"Don't disturb her!" She crossed her arms. "It's two in the morning!"

"And the party has no doubt only just ended. She will be awake, and she will be very happy."

Red climbed her face. "You mean we snuck out way before the party ended."

He grinned. "*Sì.*" He skimmed a finger down her nose. "And I am sure that everyone there found it greatly amusing. *Nonno* will be especially happy. You made a beautiful scene, we danced as if we were already lovers, and then we snuck out together to be alone and indulge in passion." He sighed gustily. "My life is in danger, but I am a happy man."

She found herself laughing. "You are horrible, Rafe." When he tugged her into his arms, she went willingly. Her head rested on his shoulder. She liked his height as much as he liked hers. "I'm happy," she said softly. "It's a strange feeling. I'm not sure I've ever been truly happy like this before."

"That is because you are as happy with yourself as you are with your world." He tipped her chin up for another kiss. "Go start the shower and I will help you wash the 'gunk,' as you called it, from your hair."

Smiling wryly, she went into the bathroom and turned on the shower in the immense stall. She had always loved her bathroom for how ridiculously large it was, but now it had a practicality as well. Then again, maybe she wouldn't need it that long. Would she move in Rafael's room, and then they move into the master when they married? That was silly. She refused to pack up twice.

"That is a curious look," he noted as he joined her. "You look to be annoyed and yet puzzled."

"I think that sums it up." She arched a brow at him. "Our room arrangement."

The wonderful thing about how long they had known each other, and how good of friends they were, was that she did not need to say anything else. He knew exactly what she asked and why. "I would love to have you in my room, *cara*, but I would not trouble you to pack twice. We will simply alternate between rooms until we are wed. When we return from our honeymoon, we will take over the master."

"I can handle that. I hate packing." The shower was the right temperature, and she climbed in and sighed happily at the feel of the hot water. He joined her, and she could only be bemused that she felt so comfortable with him. Then again, she thought as she looked him over wistfully, he was even more gorgeous when naked *and* wet. She had many frustrated memories of him getting out of the pool like a god rising from the sea while rivulets of water streamed down his body.

"I must know what you are thinking," he murmured. "Such a curiously feminine look in your eyes, Victoria."

"Just thinking about how frustrating it was that you made me go to the pool with you. How you didn't notice me staring at you lustfully every time . . ."

His chuckle sounded low and masculine. "I was distracted by ignoring my emotions for you." Realization made his brows lift. "It suddenly comes clear to me. You are not allergic to chlorine. It was another cover."

"Yeah. I miss swimming. I liked it even when I hated how looked in a bathing suit."

"You will need a suit," he said decisively. "I will take you swimming with me here and at the *castello*. How much would I need to beg to see you in a bikini?" he asked wistfully.

"A bikini?! Me?" She sputtered as he ducked her head under the shower. "Hey!"

"Do not argue with the man who knows every inch of your body. You will be beautiful in a bikini." He skimmed his finger down the scar on her chest. As always, he felt his heart quiver at the sight of it. He didn't think he would ever get over how it felt to see it there. "This is a badge of honor."

She wouldn't argue over that one. Deciding to ignore the entire bikini conversation, she firmly scrubbed and washed away all of the gel and hairspray. It felt good to have it out of her hair, and she was oddly curious to see what her 'natural style' was once her hair had dried.

Finding out got a little delayed. Rafael insisted on helping her wash the rest of her body, and he was too sensual a man to not take advantage of her obvious weakness to his touch. "I told you," he said huskily against her neck, "you will need your strength."

"Yeah." Pinned between him and the shower wall, she couldn't help but marvel at his own strength. If things kept getting better between them as they seemed to be inclined, then she could see many happy years together in their future.

They got out of the shower and toweled off, and with tender amusement, he showed her how to use the hair dryer to dry her hair. She had always just toweled off the excess and left the rest to the air. She couldn't be displeased with the new effort, though. Her hair, once dry, fell naturally around her face in a very appealing way. "I don't think I'd ever pass as a guy again," she decided. "But I'm not unhappy about it. That time served its purpose."

"*Sì*. It led you to me." A towel knotted around his hips, he walked into the bedroom and smiled as he saw the covered tray sitting on the table. "Come eat something, Victoria, before your stomach makes another impersonation of a lioness."

"And yours is any quieter!" She swathed herself in a towel and went over to join him. A part of her wanted to be embarrassed that Peggy would have walked into the room and seen haphazardly discarded pieces of clothing and heard the shower running, but she was too bemused by the entire situation to bother.

After demolishing the food, she felt much more human again. She couldn't believe it was three in the morning and she was sitting naked in her bedroom with a lover. Her *fiancé*. And not just any lover, but potentially one who was the most amazing man in the world. Even when her 'job' ended, she knew she would always protect him.

He suddenly walked over to her and lifted her into his arms. He carried her over to the bed and dropped her down onto it. "Are you refueled, *cara*?"

"Quite." She skimmed her fingers up his arms with a smile. "But I'm not sure I could sleep right now."

Loving her all the more, his lips curved slowly. "I am sure I can help you become tired."

CHAPTER FOURTEEN

Tori didn't wake in the morning feeling as if birds were singing and the world was sunshine and roses, but she certainly woke content. She was cuddled against Rafael's side and had an arm flung across his chest possessively. While she had never been happier than knowing she was truly loved, her internal alarms now warbled very loudly. She could actually *feel* the danger hovering around Rafael.

"You are supposed to be smiling, *cara*," he murmured huskily. She looked up at him and he skimmed his fingers down her cheek. She looked rumpled, flushed, and very, very sexy. "I have you in my arms, and you are not smiling. I must not be trying hard enough to please you."

"If you tried any harder, I wouldn't be able to walk," she protested. She started laughing as she hastily rolled out of bed before he could grab her. "Don't you dare, Rafe!" She grabbed her robe and held it like a shield in front of her naked body. "As it is, we've likely missed breakfast and they'll wonder what we're up to up here."

The corner of his lips kicked up into a wicked smile. "I am sure they know, Victoria." He got out of bed and tugged her into his arms. "I will not have my wicked way with you right now." He nibbled on her chin and then her lower lip. Her ridiculously kissable mouth had tormented him for two years. It was exhilarating to finally know she was his. "I will kidnap you for lunch and have my wicked way with you then."

Her knees went weak as she held onto his arms for balance. "If you insist," she managed to say.

"I do, I assure you." He ran his thumb over her lip and cupped her cheek. "Now then," he said softly, "tell me what is wrong. There is something bothering you."

"The fact that your life is as yet in danger bothers me a lot," she shot at him. She pulled away and crossed her arms as she stalked toward the bathroom. "I woke feeling as if I could actually *see* the danger around you. Forgive me for not being all smiles."

He winced good-naturedly as she shut the door firmly. His bodyguard had a bit of a temper, which he often forgot until he provoked it on accident. Her biggest button had always been his safety, and he honestly didn't see that changing even when the danger was gone. He would have her no other way. She kept more than his physical self safe. She protected his very heart and soul.

He knocked lightly on the bathroom door and called, "Put on something pretty. We will go have breakfast in the city. I do not feel like sharing you with my family for a little bit longer."

She sighed. She wanted to tell him no, she really did, but the whole reason she had gotten that deep was because she was supposed to be his undercover bodyguard. They couldn't catch a crook without bait. That didn't mean she couldn't take extra precautions, though. "Alright."

With a grin, he grabbed his clothes from the night before so he could go back to his own room. He made a mental note to have some of his things put in her room, and vice-versa. It would be much more convenient until they married.

He caught a very quick shower and got dressed. When he went back to Tori's room, he wasn't entirely surprised to discover she was still getting ready. He could hear the muttering coming from the closet. "*Cara*," he said warmly, "anything you wear will be fine. I was merely teasing you." He stepped into the doorway and was promptly silenced as he stared at his lover in shock.

She continued to very competently assemble a small gun. "Don't look surprised," she told him. "Alex and I have both been armed more than once over the last two years. You can't handle everything with your hands. Antonio is fully aware that we're armed, and he even has copies of our licenses and permits."

He felt a little flustered. "Neither Isabelle nor I knew."

"Well, of course not." She lifted her brows at him. "Having a bodyguard was enough of a reminder of the danger you were in. Antonio decided it was best you not know all the details." She put the gun to the side and grabbed a pair of slacks. "I would have told you later if you hadn't found out now."

"*Sì*," he agreed dryly, "as I would have no doubt discovered it when I next had you naked." He felt less unnerved by the realization that his lover was armed than he might have expected to be. In a way, it made him feel better. For her safety, if not his own. He had seen firsthand just how much damage a bullet could do to someone.

The fact that she was moving and using her left arm as if she hadn't been that someone barely months before was a testament to her strength. Unable to stand it, he moved forward and tugged her into his arms. He buried his face in her hair for a moment. "Hold me, Victoria. Do not let go."

She wrapped her arms around him and held on fiercely. Too many emotions to name closed her throat. It seemed impossible to love one person that much. "I'm here, Rafe," she soothed softly. "I'm not going anywhere." She lightly framed his face with her hands when he reluctantly released her. "What brought that on?"

He lightly touched the pink scar. "I see this and I am afraid again," he admitted. "I will have nightmares forever of watching you take that bullet for me."

"At the risk of making it worse," she warned gently, "I will do it again if needed, Rafael. You know that. Tear up as many contracts as you want, but it will not change who and what I am and how I feel for you." She kissed him tenderly and then let go. "Now quit acting so emotional. Who's the girl around here?"

He found himself smiling. That was his Tori. "I believe it is you." He sighed contentedly. "And you are a very beautiful woman, Victoria."

"I'm almost starting to believe it myself," she admitted.

In less than half an hour, they headed on their way to a favored café of his. They served breakfast, and the place was quiet and intimate. Tori had been there more than once herself, though not in her 'new persona.' It felt very odd to be talking to the baristas and realize that they didn't notice she was the same person. Well, some of them didn't. A few of the people who worked there winked at her merrily; they had obviously caught on.

Coffee and breakfast in hand, Rafael and Tori caught a table near a window. She felt wired already, and she had barely touched her coffee. Her eyes moved restlessly over the entire café. It felt the same as it had the day before when she had sensed someone watching her while she was getting her hair done. There were a few other people in the café, but no one looked remarkable.

One of the baristas suddenly walked up to the table, her face pale. "How's everything?" she asked with a false cheer. She held out a note. "I was asked to give this to you."

Rafael frowned and opened the note as she hurried away. His mouth instantly went dry and he felt a chill run down his back. Tori snatched the note out of his hand and felt sick. Very clearly, it read, *Two men stand outside each door. Unless you walk out quietly, they're walking in shooting.*

Tori bore the personal evidence of their willingness to commit murder. She was not happy with this scenario. They had been planning on luring out one idiot, not an entire squadron of homicidal maniacs. She took a little breath, her mind running through every possible scenario. "Do you trust me?" she asked softly.

"With my life," he said simply.

"Let's go. And just play along with whatever I do." Hoping like hell she could act convincingly like a frightened woman when she had spent years living as a male bodyguard who was capable in most any situation, she clung onto his arm as they walked out of the café. A false sense of security. She desperately needed to build it in the enemy.

Two men stepped forward from near the door. Both wore heavy jackets with familiar bumps underneath. Tori and Alex had long before decided that holsters were far too damned obvious and had opted for other means. At that moment, her gun was in an ankle holster. As long as no one strip-searched her, they wouldn't find it.

"Come with us," one of the men said.

Rafael hesitated but went with his instincts. They had never failed him before. "Let my fiancée go," he said softly. "She is not a part of this."

The other man scoffed. "If we let her go, then our boss will have our heads. He said to grab you both, so we are." He glanced at the curb as a limo rolled up. He opened one of the doors. "Get in."

They got in, and Tori scooted all the way over into the other corner. Rafael joined her, crowding her back so that it looked as if he was protecting her. The two men got in followed by two others, the door shut, and the limo rolled off down the street. "Where's your bodyguard?" one of the men asked Rafael curtly. "I was surprised I didn't see him dogging your heels as always."

"As he was shot only months ago," Rafael retorted in a clipped voice, "you can imagine why he was not at my side. Victoria and I wished to have breakfast without *mia famiglia*. If I had realized you were such fools as to come to a public café, I would have suffered my sister and brother-in-law flirting over the breakfast table."

"Well, can't blame you for that," one of the other men admitted. "Your fiancée is hot."

Tori somehow kept her jaw from dropping. As she had thought, the men were certifiably nuts, and she wasn't entirely sure they weren't high on something with it. She kept her lips closed and burrowed closer against Rafael's back. Under the cover of hiding behind him, she had already turned on her cell phone and dialed Alex. He would be able to hear everything, and since the phone hid nicely in her bra, they wouldn't find it. Wearing a bra had *far* more practical uses than she had ever imagined, honestly.

It seemed like forever before the limo stopped. The men ushered Rafael and Tori out of the vehicle, then, to Tori's horror, separated them. Rafael was taken one way while she was escorted another. She struggled against the male holding her arm, but not yet with her full strength. "Let me go!" she snapped. "Rafe! No, let me be with him!" The one holding her was the one who had called her 'hot' so she tried to give him a pleading look. "Please!"

He paused and then cursed. "Sorry, no dice." He looked up in relief as he heard a light step. "Here she is, like you ordered."

She glanced up and felt her heart freeze. The man looking at her was handsome, but there was a coolness inside his eyes that she recognized. He would put a bullet in a man without flinching, of that she felt sure. And yet . . . something seemed slightly off about him, though she could not put her finger on it. "Don't touch me!" she snapped when he reached for her arm.

He ignored her and grabbed her much more firmly than the other man had. She knew that even her full strength would not break her free. She dug in her heels as hard as she could, but she was still dragged down a hall. The building looked like an abandoned factory of some sort, and she couldn't orient herself as to where they were located.

He swung her into a room and shut the door before releasing her. He watched her move several steps away. Calmly, he asked, "How is that bullet wound doing?"

Her eyes narrowed sharply. She didn't know how he knew, but she refused to play the bluff game. "Perfectly fine, no thanks to your buddy. If you know who I am, then why the hell did you specifically tell them to grab me?"

He reached into his jacket and emerged with a paper. He handed it to her without a word. She skimmed over it and then had to read it twice more to be sure. There was no mistake. The signature at the bottom of the document was Vincent Lucino's. The letter read, simply, that the elder Lucino was looking for a hired gun to remove the threat to his family. The utter incongruity of the years of threats of finding a hitman colliding with the fact that he had, in fact, done so, left her reeling. "Wait, you're one of the *good guys*?"

He shrugged. "I wouldn't necessarily call myself that."

"Then why haven't you shot the bastard yet?" she snapped. "If something had happened to Isabelle, or if I hadn't thrown myself over Rafael, then you can be sure *you'd* have been next on Don Lucino's list!"

"If I hadn't been here," was the retort, "then Isabelle Lucino and Gabrielle Wisteria wouldn't have found it that easy to escape. My 'men' were of the opinion that roughing them up would put pressure on Antonio Lucino. I convinced them to back off by making them think I would handle things."

Her head was still reeling, but her gut told her that he could be trusted. It was the same hunch that had told her there was more to him than met the eye. Oh, she fully believed he could still kill someone in cold blood, but why else would Vincent have hired him? You didn't get rid of crazed madmen with sunshine and lollipops. She yanked her phone out of her bra and said sharply, "Did you hear?"

"Yes," Alex responded instantly. "And Vincent has confirmed it. We have the GPS location and we're on our way, Tori! Just get Rafe out of there!"

She hung up the phone and looked at her unexpected ally. "Where is Rafe? And what's your name?"

"The top floor," he answered immediately. "And my name is Van D'Angelo."

A hired gun who was named 'the angel.' She knew she would eventually find it funny in fifty years, providing she managed to save her fiancé and actually make it to the altar with him. It was looking more and more debatable with every minute, and her nerves kept stretching more and more. "Let's end this madness. Take me to the top floor, Van."

Rafael found himself dragged upstairs and handcuffed to a steel pole that helped hold up the ceiling. The entire floor had been gutted pending a remodel, and it was an eerie collection of partially built walls and steel poles. Only a handful of windows were uncovered, and the sunlight coming in only added to the gloom. Some electric lights were on, but the bulbs were bare. He had a feeling he would never look at a horror movie the same way ever again.

He was terrified. Not only for himself, but also for Tori. Was she okay? He trusted she could defend herself, but he couldn't stop thinking of all the possible scenarios where she might end up at the mercy of those bastards. This plan was the most asinine thing he had ever agreed to do, but he couldn't be mad at Brie for thinking of it. He had thought it was a good idea at the time, too.

The crack of a whip caught his attention, and he turned as much as he could to see Martin approaching. The hair on the back of his neck stood straight up. There was something odd about the way Martin walked. The older man was weaving back and forth as if drunk, and there was a glassy sheen to his too bright eyes. The whip was in his hand, and there were assorted other alarming items tucked into the belt he wore. "You do realize," Rafael said as coolly as he could, "that murder and torture are much more severely looked upon than embezzlement, *sì*?"

Martin's response to that was to snap the whip at him. The leather strip at the end cut through cloth and skin alike as it wrapped around his arm. "I look forward to breaking you apart," Martin sneered. "A mighty Lucino, begging for his life!" He jerked on the whip and savored Rafael's flinch. A snap of his wrist made the whip let go, but he promptly attacked again, this time opening a cut along Rafael's cheek. "I'm very good with one of these," he said loftily. "Practiced by taking the heads off chickens back home."

"For a man who concocted a featherbrained scheme, the fact that you once played with chickens is not a surprise." The whip snapped across his other cheek, but he ignored the pain. "Where is Victoria?"

Martin scoffed. "Probably having some 'fun' with my bodyguard. He was insistent that he have access to the bitch." He smirked when Rafael snarled at him. "Oh, does that bother you? Too bad." He stopped abruptly and looked to the side at absolutely no one. "You lie!" he shouted at the air. "He wouldn't betray me! You said my men would, but they didn't! It was just a trick by that little 3rd District freak!" He recoiled violently and dropped to his knees with a terrified sob. "I'm sorry! I won't mention that place again!"

Rafael had known of Martin's instability, but it was many times worse to see it firsthand. Somehow, seeing this was far more frightening than the whip he carried. His skin crawled as something inside him urged him to get away. He was in the presence of evil. He just knew it inside.

Martin's head snapped up, his glazed eyes manic. He leapt to his feet and sent the whip flying for Rafael's neck.

It didn't reach him. Tori stepped in front of him and interceded the whip. The end coiled around her arm and bit into her skin. Before Martin recovered, she yanked the whip out of his hand and let it drop to the ground. "Sorry, but Rafe isn't into the kinky stuff," she said icily. Martin scrambled for the knife he wore, and she calmly lifted the gun in her other hand. "Not a chance, dipshit."

Martin stared at her in horror as he finally recognized her. He didn't doubt her aim, her skill, or willingness to shoot him. What he *did* doubt was how she had managed to get away from Vick. "You! How did you get up here?!"

"A little thing called 'stairs.' Try them sometime."

"That isn't what I meant!" he screamed. He whirled around sharply. "Vick! Vick!" He spotted movement and saw Van stepping around from behind another pillar. "There you are!" he roared. "Shoot her! Kill her! Kill them both!" He covered his head with his hands and moaned in pain. "Kill them before they kill me!" He heard the sound of a gun cocking and looked up to see Van aiming not at Tori, but at him. "No." It was a thready whisper. "You would never betray me!"

"I never worked for you," Van said quietly. "Therefore you can't say I'm betraying you."

Martin yanked what looked like a remote control out of his belt. "I have explosives!" he shouted. "I'll blow up the whole fucking building!" He began to emit a high-pitched laugh. "You won't win! It was wrong! You won't win!"

His finger started to depress a button and both Tori and Van fired. Both shots hit the center of Martin's chest. He lost his grip on the remote and toppled over. Tori leapt forward and grabbed the remote before it hit the ground. It was better safe than sorry. A putrid scent suddenly stung her nose, and she looked down to see a disgusting slime seeping out of Martin's body.

"Get back!" Van ordered sharply.

She scrambled back and put herself in front of Rafael as the slime slowly crept across the floor. It began to rise up into the air with a stench so strong and rancid that even Van's stomach churned. A malevolent face seemed to form from the slime, and it bared broken, razor edged teeth in a mockery of a smile.

The cavernous mouth opened and Van fired two more shots. They did nothing as they were absorbed by the slime. In fact, it barely spared him a glance as it began to lunge toward Tori and Rafael. Tori turned and threw her arms around Rafael to make him less of a target.

Blinding white light lit the entire area as a pure beam of it streaked through the air and slammed into the slime. It screamed with the voice of the damned and recoiled back. With a guttural roar in a language no one recognized, it changed targets and began to rush across the floor.

Tori lifted her head and instantly spotted a familiar redhead standing only feet away. "What the hell?" she said in shock. "Move!" she shouted.

Rhianna held her ground. The slime lunged forward and engulfed her entirely, and Van dropped his gun as he ran toward her to help. He was only a few steps toward her when bright white light burst through the slime and blew it away.

Remnants of it splattered against the ceiling and floor and dissolved. Rhianna looked relatively unscathed, though she had taken some nasty cuts to her arms.

On shaky legs, Tori went to Martin and grabbed the key that had fallen on the ground. She freed Rafael from the cuffs, and her stomach rebelled as she saw the bloody mess of his wrists. The cuffs had been so tight that his every movement had made them cut into his skin. "Oh god, Rafe." She dropped her head onto his shoulder.

Van picked up his fallen gun and put it away. "Eric will not be happy with you," he told Rhianna.

"Naturally not, but there was no time to be wasted." She looked at Martin's body with cool satisfaction in her eyes. "Tori, your gun repeat fires, correct?"

"Yes . . ."

"Good. Van, you were not here."

"No, ma'am." He tipped an imaginary hat and disappeared into the shadows around the room.

"I am very confused," Rafael said softly.

"You and me both!" Tori muttered.

Rhianna glanced at them. "I will handle things. Tori shot Martin twice in defense of Rafael's life. Rafael's current state is evidence enough as to why."

Tori refrained from mentioning ballistics. Rhianna's company had more power than the federal government. If she said both bullets came from Tori's gun, then sure as hell no one would question it. Just like Tori wasn't going to question the horror movie sequence she had just experienced, or Rhianna's incredible display of power.

Rhianna seemed to disappear as mysteriously as she had arrived, and only moments later, a full SWAT team of cops burst into the top floor. Alex was with them. He ran over to Tori and Rafael immediately. "Are you two okay?" he demanded sharply. He saw the state Rafael was in and began to curse softly.

"I will be fine," Rafael assured him. He cupped Tori's cheek. "Yet again, Victoria saved my life." He pressed a kiss to her forehead and pulled her into his arms, uncaring that his wounds protested the movement.

She clung onto him for a moment before forcing herself to let go. She scooped up her gun and held it out to a cop. "This is mine. My name is Tori Li. I'm Rafael's bodyguard. I can provide any documentation you need me to, including permits. Martin was threatening to blow up the building. I couldn't take any chances."

It didn't take long for the cops to find the explosives. There was enough C-4 scattered around the top floor to take out the building as well as anything else close by. Rafael was taken immediately to a hospital to be treated, but most of the wounds turned out to be minor. Doctor Singh patched both him and Tori up, and he scolded them both for being reckless.

It took even longer for statements, and neither Tori nor Rafael was very surprised to see someone from Enforcers at the station. With her presence there, it was actually not very long before they were free to go home with Alex. It was already late afternoon, and it felt like a week since that same morning.

Alex drove while Rafael rode with Tori in the backseat. Rafael couldn't bring himself to let her go just yet. She had scared him far too much lately for him to recover easily. First she had taken a bullet for him. Now she had faced a madman and some sort of manifestation of evil. He had stopped breathing when she had thrown herself over him. "No more, *cara*," he said in a quiet voice that shook slightly. "No more. You will not be in danger again. You are going to quit your job."

"And do what with my time?" she asked politely. "Sew? Knit? Please!"

"You may do whatever you like so long as you are not in danger," her fiancé retorted. "You once lamented not going to a university for a graduate degree. You may do so. It will be safe there. You will study something tame and boring like fire walking so that I do not die young of a broken heart or heart failure."

She was silent for a moment. Humor began to well, and she started laughing. "Rafe, I think you just pulled your own 'Don Lucino' act. Do you have *any* idea how you just sounded?" She lightly framed his face, careful of the bandages covering his wounds, and kissed him hard. "Fine. I'll find something safe and boring. What about trapeze acts? Can I study that?"

"Only if you wear a skimpy leotard and let me catch you." He rubbed his thumb over her cheek with a smile. "You are one-of-a-kind, Victoria. My beautiful diamond swan." His grin began to widen. "And I am sure we are embarrassing Alexander."

"Don't mind me. I'm just trying not to cry."

Tori snorted at that as they pulled into the driveway of the Lucino villa. She spotted Roberto's car, which was not a surprise, and then spotted an unfamiliar car as well. "Ugh." She sighed as she got out of Alex's car. "More visitors? I so don't want to deal with that. Can we sneak in the back?"

"Now, you know we cannot." Rafael slid an arm around her waist to keep her close as they headed for the door. "We will reassure everyone that we are fine, and then we will escape to my room and hide away for a week. Perhaps two. Then we will begin making plans for the wedding in *Italia*." He nipped at her ear teasingly. "And we will honeymoon in the *castello*."

"Can we kick everyone else out when we do? If you say yes, I might consider wearing a bikini."

"Deal," he agreed instantly with a grin. He knew a good bargain when it presented itself. Besides, he very much wanted her all to himself. Perhaps by their fiftieth anniversary, he might have recovered from the whole ordeal.

Brie and Isabelle gave glad cries when they saw them and rushed to hug both Tori and Rafael fiercely. They were mindful of Rafael's injuries but not willing to let him go for long moments. He held them just as tightly. "It is all done," he promised. "We are safe now." He glanced up at the sound of footsteps and saw Vincent and Antonio, both of whom looked older than they had the night before. "I am sorry for worrying you."

"You!" Tori aimed a finger at Vincent.

He held up his hands. "It can be discussed later, Victoria. Come into the parlor. There is someone that you need to speak with."

"Oh god," she groaned. "Now? Seriously?" She sighed as Roberto began to push her toward the parlor. "I'm going to kick your ass, Roberto."

"*Sì*, but you will need to wait until after I am wed so you may teach Gabrielle the proper etiquette for it."

Rafael glanced at his father and grandfather who both nodded. Understanding, he pulled Tori closer and began to escort her himself. "You will wish to meet this person," he told her softly. "And I hope it will finally bring you peace, *cara*."

Inside the parlor, there was a man roughly Antonio's age standing in the middle of the room. There was absolutely nothing familiar about him at all to Tori, though she felt she ought to know him. It was only when he turned and looked at her that her stomach clenched with nerves as she realized what might be happening.

He had baby blue eyes.

"Victoria," Antonio said softly, "I would like you to meet James Montgomery. He has been looking for you for many years, *cara*."

She would have run, but Rafael was still holding her. She grabbed onto his hand like a lifeline. She was barely aware of the Lucinos, Roberto, and Alex as they formed a protective shield behind her. "Is that so?" Try as she might to make her voice careless, it came out as barely a whisper.

James took a deep breath. "Your mother told me you were stillborn. I never believed her. I just . . . couldn't give up hope. Sit down, Tori," he urged. "Please at least listen to me. If after I've spoken, you want nothing to do with me, I will leave. But at least let me answer your questions."

"I am here," Rafael told Tori softly. "I will not leave you."

"Nor will we," Vincent said just as softly. "You are part of our *famiglia*."

She took a breath and slowly sat down on the settee. "Alright," she said. "Let's talk."

CHAPTER FIFTEEN

It was very uncomfortable in the parlor. Peggy brought in tea for everyone and refrained from fussing over Rafael and Tori. She would fuss over her kids when there wasn't a stranger present. She did, however, shoot James a warning look. If he hurt Tori, all bets were off.

For James, it was very painful to sit across from his daughter and realize that she not only didn't like him, but that she had every right to feel as she did. "Ask me anything," he told her. "I will not lie."

"How did you find me?"

The corner of his lips kicked up. "Your future grandfather-in-law. He called me last night and informed me that he was willing to fly me out here to meet you. As to how he found *me*, I'm not sure I want to know."

"*Sì*, you do not," Vincent said. "However, I called in a favor or two. Tori was in the system because of her childhood. You were in the system because of some petty theft when you were young. It took little work to find the connecting threads between you two."

Tori rubbed her hands over her arms. The motion reminded her of her wounded arm and she hastily dropped her hand. Rafael's arm slid around her waist and held on firmly. It was only his presence and the presence of the rest of her family that gave her strength. She could not handle this alone. "You said my . . . my mother told you I was stillborn. She threw me in the garbage. Why?"

His lashes flinched. Vincent had told him, but hearing it said again was horrifying. "We met when we were in our early twenties and stupid. We weren't serious about each other. She was seeing other men, and I was eyeing a few other women. She came to me out of the blue and raged at me for getting her pregnant. It was certainly possible I had; as I said, we were stupid." He sighed. "And I knew she was sure it was mine because she had other prospects who would have paid her a lot of money to get rid of the baby. She knew I wouldn't."

"I'm glad you didn't, obviously, but why not? You were young and stupid."

"But I love kids," he said simply. "And while she wouldn't have been my first pick for the mother of any child of mine, once you were made, I wanted to keep you. I told her she could have an abortion if she wanted, but if she was willing to deliver you, then I would take you right after birth and she'd never have to be tied down by you. She decided to deliver you under those conditions, and I agreed to help support her." He sighed. "Unfortunately, she didn't try very hard to keep you unharmed while she was pregnant. She continued to smoke and drink and do reckless things. When she entered her third trimester, I nearly took her to court over it. Then, one day, she disappeared. I went out of my mind because she was so close to delivery."

Isabelle gently rested her hands on Tori's shoulder to remind her that she was not alone. "And when she came back to you, she claimed a false birth, *sì?*"

"Said that the doctor had tried, but the baby was born dead." His hands curled into fists. "I didn't believe her. I wouldn't have imagined she had done . . . what she had done. I thought at most she would have surrendered you to the hospital or the cops, just to get back at me. Maybe I did know the truth. I just couldn't stand looking at her ever again. I moved upstate, and she moved to the Midwest. I've kept tabs on her in the time since, just in case I ever found any evidence of what she'd done. She married a while ago but doesn't have any children."

Tori let out a long breath. "The guy who picked up garbage found me right after I was dumped. Rushed me to the hospital; literally saved my life. I was in a foster home until I was eighteen and got my independence to move out here and start over. My foster parents were wonderful, but I never fit into society."

"Society," Brie disagreed fiercely, "just didn't know how to handle someone as amazing as you!"

"Vincent and Antonio told me . . . told me what has been happening. I wish saying I am sorry for not being there would make it magically better, but I know it won't." He sighed anew. "I married a while back. I have a daughter around the age of fifteen. I told my wife but did not tell my daughter what I was coming out here for. She wants a big sister, and I refused to get her hopes up. If you have no desire to know her, or me, then I will leave and not tell her. But if you'd like to have a chance to extend your family . . . then I know she and my wife will love you. *I* love you, and I'm proud of you, Tori."

"It is your decision, *cara*," Antonio told Tori. "We are your family, but if you wish to know your *papa*, then we stand by you."

Tori slowly nodded. "I guess it can't hurt. I mean, I can't hold my mother's actions against you. You didn't have any choice in the matter. And I guess it might be kind of cool to be a big sister." She snorted. "Though I think I'd be better at being a big brother, frankly. Whatever, same difference. Yeah, I'd like to know you guys. And you can come to the wedding."

Vincent nodded firmly. "I will make the arrangements for your wife and *bambina* to be flown out here soon. The wedding will be in *il castello* in Italy."

"Thank you." James got to his feet, sensing a dismissal. "I will see you soon, Tori. And thank you for giving me a chance."

"We all have our stupid moments. At least yours gave me life, so I can't be mad about it." It was also curiously reassuring to finally have answers. Someone *had* wanted her. It was something. Even still, the tension did not leave her shoulders until he had left. The door shut behind him, and she doubled over with her face in her hands. "That sucked!" She shot to her feet and rounded on Vincent. "You ever go behind my back like that again, and I'm going to find your 'hitman' and sic him on you!"

Vincent hid a grin. He was *well* pleased with Rafael's choice. He admired anyone with the nerve to yell at him. He had no doubt Tori would get along just fine with his Natalia. They were very much alike. But then, Lucinos had fabulous taste. "You were unhappy, *cara*," he said gently. "And that is not acceptable to me."

"What is this about a hitman?" Isabelle demanded. "*Nonno*, what have you not told us?"

He arched a brow. "There was danger to *mia famiglia.* It was unacceptable. I contacted a few people here in New York who put me in contact with a few others. I discovered Van D'Angelo and told him of the situation. He was aware of it because of Gabrielle's involvement as he has worked for Enforcers off and on for a few years."

"Oh god," Brie groaned as she covered her face. "Rhianna and Eric employ *hitmen*? As if they weren't scary enough!"

"He is a hired gun," he corrected, "which does involve death, *sì*. But he is an honorable man, with much integrity. He works with the police as well, though I know not his contacts there. Sometimes there are simply things that justice cannot touch, *cara*. This was one of those things."

"Does that mean things are finally done?" Rafael asked.

"I would certainly hope so," Vincent agreed. His phone began to ring, and he pulled it out. "Ah. Speaking of whom." He answered the phone and said, "*Ciao,* Van. *Grazie* for protecting *miei bambini*. I will have your payment forwarded to you."

"Don't pay me yet," Van said quietly. "I was just calling to tell you that I got my hands on Martin's files. He wasn't working alone. I don't know who his partner is, but I'm looking for him. He may be merely corrupt rather than evil, but I wish to confirm that before I call this job done. If he is a true danger, I will handle it. If he is simply corrupt, I will turn him over to the police."

"Is my family safe?"

"Best I can determine, yes, the physical danger should be past. Focus on the weddings, Don Lucino. I will handle the rest." He hung up the phone.

Vincent slowly closed his phone as well, aware that everyone watched him warily. "Van suspects there is another involved, but he does not believe there is any physical danger. Perhaps professionally you should be cautious, but the need for bodyguards has passed. I trust his instincts. Ms. Tabor told me that they are as good as fact."

"She does seem to be involved a lot, no?" Roberto murmured.

"Sorry," Brie grumbled. "Enforcers take the District and its people pretty seriously."

He lightly kissed her. "As they should, *cara mia*."

Rafael got to his feet and tugged Tori up with him. "If that is all," he said firmly, "then I am taking Victoria to my room so that we may wash away the events of the day. In fact, you may not see us again for a few days. Please ask Peggy or Marco to bring food else we waste away."

The others let them go without protest. Careful of Tori's wounded arm, he instead held her elbow to escort her up the stairs. He went directly to his room and ushered her inside. The door had barely closed behind them before he yanked her into his arms and kissed her wildly. He yanked fiercely at her clothes, desperate to have her naked so he could see she was unharmed. "*Dio*!" he said roughly. "I will never recover from these events!"

"I'm not the one who was hurt this time!" she managed to say. Something hot and wild rose inside, and she rushed open his shirt. So close. She had come so close to losing him. She didn't want to think Van's shot might have been the one to kill Martin. She wanted that satisfaction for herself. If she hadn't been there . . . a shudder ripped through her body.

She stifled a startled yelp and grabbed his shoulders for balance as he lifted her off her feet. "Your wrists!"

"I do not care!" The bed was too far away. He instead bore her down onto the floor. Only when her arms were around him, only when he was inside her once more, did the panic finally start to fade.

They did eventually make it to the bed, and she re-bandaged his wrists and arm. He insisted on tending to her injury as well, but it was already healing quickly. It didn't surprise him. Once he had made sure the tape was back in place, he lifted her left hand to his lips and kissed her engagement ring. "*Ti amo*," he said softly. "I am sorry for rushing you as I did. I should have given you more time."

"Yeah, you're just a paragon of patience," she retorted dryly. She sighed and tugged his hand to her heart. "Rafe, I'm not sorry about anything. I'm not. It was scary and it was horrible at times. But you were there. I loved you all along. I needed you to push me, to shake me up and make me see what I could be. And . . . I'm happy now. Isn't that the important part?"

He looked at her and how the evening light made her soft and sultry and so beautiful she took his breath. "You will not fly away?" he asked huskily.

She smiled. "No. I finally know where I belong." When he kissed her, she slid her arms around his neck and held on, savoring how it felt to be wanted for who she was. "I need postcards," she murmured when he lifted his head.

He arched a brow, intrigued by the very feminine smile on her lips. "What for?"

"No reason." A twinkle appeared in the corner of her eyes. "No reason at all." She laughed as he tumbled her down onto the bed once more. If this was how he intended to end all their conversations, then their future looked very bright indeed.

A cheerful Peggy brought them dinner, and they watched a movie on the television in his room. And when they were ready to sleep, Rafael, for the first time in his life, did not struggle with insomnia. With Tori in his arms, there was nothing left for him to fear. He knew she would keep him safe.

When Antonio went into his office the next morning, the contract for Rafael and Tori was sitting on his desk. Across the middle, the word 'Complete' was very clear. He left it where it was while he went to get his coffee, and it was nowhere in sight when he returned. Unsurprised, and pleased with the events, he settled into his chair. He had a wedding guest list to write for Marco, but it wasn't hard to get started. There was one name already on it.

He knew she would be pleased with the events too.

CHAPTER SIXTEEN

Eric was not a happy camper as he watched Gwyn patch up Rhianna's wounds. "You went in there by yourself," he said in a low voice. "You knew what you were up against and you didn't even tell me." Try as he might, there was a hint of pain in his voice. He and Rhianna had been best friends for two thousand years and were more like twins than mere friends.

"I've been hunting that thing my entire life," she countered softly. "It hates me more than I hate it. I know it would do anything to destroy those I love. I wasn't letting you or anyone else near it, Riku. I won't apologize for that."

Gwyn's husband, Taylor, was leaning against the wall of the office to observe. He was relatively normal, all things considered in the District, but he possessed strong gifts of his own. Among them was an ability to sense danger to those he loved. It manifested as a burning in his hands, and the fact that he was currently staring at them told Eric that he still sensed danger around Rhianna.

Rayna Mason ducked into the office and put the completed contract onto Rhianna's desk. Her hand slipped into Eric's as she leaned against his arm. She and Gwyn were a few years apart in age, but looked and acted enough alike to be twins. "There's one more, isn't there?" she asked Rhianna.

"Indeed." Freed from Gwyn, her arms now bandaged, Rhianna slipped the contract into a folder which also reflected 'Complete.' She slid the folder into a drawer labeled 'Lucino' and shut it. "Another long overdue to be done."

"Do you have more control over this scenario than you've had so far?" Taylor asked.

Her lips twisted into a half smile. "I sure hope so, Taylor."

It made none of her friends feel better to see Rayna frowning. She was Truth and had the ability to hear the truth over lies. Rhianna was telling the truth; she didn't know if she had control. It seemed more and more as evil grew in strength, her grip on events loosened. It didn't bode well.

Just what hadn't she told them yet?

⚲ ⚲ ⚲

Status: File In Progress

Analysis: What may be ugly to some can be beautiful to another if the one looking is looking with the eyes of love.

Folder Three

THERESA

CHAPTER SEVENTEEN

"Theresa!!"

The echoing bellow through the house made Theresa cringe as she tried to brush out a particularly nasty tangle from her hair. In a way, the yell did not come as a surprise; her hair always managed to knot itself just before her grandmother went on a rampage. She wrangled the snarl out and put down her brush. Somehow her fingers were steady.

She calmly left her room and headed downstairs to the den. Her grandmother waited inside. "You called?" she asked. She very nearly asked if she had bellowed, but she bit it back. She knew better.

Ruby Collins narrowed her eyes warningly. "Someone saw you having lunch with Rafael Lucino."

"And his fiancée," Theresa noted. "I work for Rafael. We were discussing a project soon to be underway that will heavily involve me."

"Fah! I care not if he is engaged! Men cannot be trusted."

She barely stifled a sigh. It wasn't the first time she had heard this tirade in the two months since she had reluctantly let Rafael take her as his date to a gala. Truthfully, she still felt surprised that Ruby had even allowed it at all. "Yes, Grandmother."

Ruby glared at her for a long moment. "You will cease wearing slacks to work!" she snapped. "Pick out long skirts and oversized sweaters. I do not want you to tempt those lascivious males in your office!"

The only 'lascivious male' in her office was one she wouldn't give the time of day. The rest were happily married or far too old. Still, she didn't argue. She had never bothered. It did no good. She had no control over her life. She could not pick her friends—she had none other than Rafael—she could not pick her clothes. She could not go to college for a higher education. She only had a GED because she hadn't been allowed to attend high school. "Very well. Is that all?"

"Don't take an attitude with me! Go to your room!"

She promptly turned on her heel and walked out. Going to her room was her only escape. She had hundreds of books crammed into her bookcases, and they allowed her to get away from her reality. A line from a favored Disney movie echoed in her mind. *When will my life begin*? At twenty-five years old, it was a good question.

The other nice thing about her room was that some strange quirk of architecture allowed her to have a perfect view of the Enforcers' building within the 3rd District some distance away. It had always been a comforting sight. She wanted to go to the District and see the magic that people whispered about. She had seen it come into the Lucinos' lives. She could use some magic of her own.

On the other side of Brooklyn, the sound of a cell phone loudly playing Celine Dion had many people staring at Van with combinations of fascination and shock. He ignored them as he moved around a corner out of sight. He sighed and answered. "Hi, Mom."

"Van!" The tone was as scolding as it was warm. "When are you coming home for a visit?"

"I told you I was in the middle of a job." He pinched the bridge of his nose. "Please don't mail me plane tickets. I can't get to my P.O. box right now. It would be a waste."

His mother sighed heavily. "Oh, come on! I don't care how busy being a private bodyguard is! You can spare a few days to come home and celebrate your father's promotion."

"I can spare a few days when I've finished this job. You want me to just abandon my client?"

"Well . . . no. I guess not. But we miss you."

He just sighed. The conversation was not a new one. His parents had no idea what he did for a living, and he took great pains to keep it that way. It meant fewer visits than they would like, and fewer than he liked as well. There were times where it was just easier to stay away. He did not regret what he did, but he sure as hell had moments where he couldn't stand to be around anyone. Not even his parents. "Look. Let me finish this, and I'll come home for a while. Okay?"

"When?"

"*Soon*." He hung up before she could do more than sputter. The phone immediately began ringing again, but this time he had been expecting the call. He hit the receive button. "D'Angelo. How is she, Officer Marks?"

Marks' sigh was audible. "Alive and recovering. A bit traumatized, of course. She thought you were going to shoot her too."

"I don't involve innocents. She didn't belong there." Van's black eyes moved sharply around the area to ensure that no one had come up while he wasn't looking. "I assume that she knows that I wasn't there?"

"Someone from Enforcers came through to make sure of it. You have very, uhm, interesting associates."

"Useful ones, anyway. Let me know when she goes home. I want to send flowers."

"Yeah, you're a real gentleman, Van."

A hint of a smile touched his lips. "Hey, just look at my record. I'm a shiny, squeaky-clean pillar of society. I even vote every time."

"You also pay your taxes, you don't litter or speed, and you freaking abide by parking laws. It'd be so much more fun keeping your record clean if you didn't make it so easy. Can't you just try to bend a normal law a bit? Make it harder for me, c'mon."

"Okay, fine." He rummaged in his pocket and found an old receipt. "Here, I just dropped a piece of trash. Find me and ticket me."

"Asshole."

Van smirked and hung up the phone. He abided by all the laws he could simply because he had to break others frequently. There were things that only he could do. Things that justice could not touch. He had a contact in every police department in the city. He had contacts in other cities as well. All knew he worked with Enforcers directly. All turned to him when there was something that needed his particular skills.

His latest job had turned into a mess of Gordian knot proportions. He didn't even know much about the man he pursued. The mysterious figure had worked with Martin Johns on the scheme, but whether he had been involved with the attempted murders of Rafael and Tori, and the kidnapping of Isabelle and Brie, Van just didn't know yet. His first step was to establish if his target was evil or merely corrupt. The latter meant going to the police. The former . . . not as much. Evil did not belong in the world. It took too many innocent lives. He just balanced the scales, as Gwyn always said.

(Two days later)

It was madness inside the Publications Office at Just In Time, Inc. Theresa had her hands full with far too many things happening at once. She stared in dismay at the shiny computer being set up on her desk and complained, "Why do I need this thing?"

The technician rummaging underneath the counter said, "Sorry, Theresa. The whole company is going digital. That means even you need to use a computer now. You've *had* email. You just weren't being forced to use it."

She heard a familiar footstep and turned to see Rafael sauntering toward her. "You know I hate these things."

"*Sì*." His voice held amusement. "But I also know that you are a quick learner and a smart woman." He tucked her hand into his elbow and firmly escorted her down an aisle of massive bookcases holding the entire history of the company. "Theresa, we are not heartless. We are asking you to do something that is quite uncomfortable, and we are asking you to go above your normal duties to begin the problematic process of scanning every file that exists here."

"Why me?" she sighed. "Rafe, really."

"Who else but you knows this place best?" he asked gently. He sighed gustily. "Perhaps I should not be appealing to your heart. Would you prefer a raise?"

"I really don't want one!" she blurted hastily.

"No? Well, too late. It was effective as of this morning." He grinned when she glared at him. If she had been anyone else, he would have expected a few curse words. He truly pitied anyone who finally managed to make her mad. The slow burners always burned the brightest. "Why would you not want a raise, Theresa?" She did not answer, but he had his suspicions. He knew who cashed her paycheck every month. "If it will ease your mind, our system is having some difficulties. It is not accepting the increase properly."

She stared at him. "You mean we're going electronic and we've already broken something."

"*Sì.* Who knew? As it stands, you will have to receive two checks." He spread his hands. "I am sorry, Theresa. But at least no one will know of your promotion should you not wish it. I know you are shy, *cara*." He flicked her in the nose lightly before tucking his hands in his pockets and walking away.

She realized her jaw was hanging open and hastily closed her mouth. A flutter of nerves in her stomach told her that he might know more about her home life than she had thought. It seemed suspect that the system would conveniently have issues with her new pay. She didn't even believe in coincidences.

She wouldn't have to give Ruby her extra pay. She could start saving money to get away. If she could just afford to get herself another place to live! Freedom. How tempting it sounded. For a chance at it, she would be willing to put up with those silly boxes of useless machinery. Well, if she didn't break one anyway.

The technician was nice enough to stay and show her how to turn on the computer, and he even left a huge book of instructions. They would be letting her learn things in pieces, thankfully. First the computer, then the scanner, then the electronic file system itself. She might even manage to get through things unscathed if they kept feeding her instructional books.

Her eyes widened as she opened her email client and saw the literally thousands of emails she had ignored by not having a computer. She groaned and dropped her head on the desk. What was *wrong* with people, anyway? Technology was making people dumber. She felt sure of it.

She did manage to get other work done, thankfully. The system threw a hissy fit when she tried to delete all the emails, and she had to make Carl come back downstairs to take care of it. While he muttered swear words at Microsoft Office, she got to work on the job she had been asked to pull for duplication. It was an old ad for a company they worked with, and they wanted some nostalgic posters for an anniversary.

She had half loaded her cart when her scalp tingled warningly. She glanced up sharply and found one of her coworkers standing in the aisle. Her shoulders tensed. "Did you need something, George?" As subtly as she could, she put the cart between them.

"When're you going to go out with me?"

"Never."

The conversation had been repeated a hundred times, but he refused to give up. She just didn't know what she was missing. Chick didn't date, and she sure as hell didn't have a man in her life. She didn't even have a woman. She was fair game. "C'mon, Theresa! I'm harmless. I'm totally healthy and I'm cute. How can you do better?"

"How about someone willing to listen when I say 'no'?" Her fingers tightened around the cart handle. "I appreciate the attention, but I'm not interested. Please leave me alone or I'll file a harassment suit."

He looked around nervously and yanked at his collar. He knew the Lucinos liked Theresa a lot. So did Tori and Alex. If they thought he was hassling her, someone would break his nose. "Okay, fine. I'll stop pestering you at work."

"At all!" she insisted as he walked away, but he didn't answer. Not that she really *wanted* to complain to Rafael or Antonio, of course. It was just a last resort. Maybe he would finally take the hint and leave her alone now. She couldn't imagine how much clearer she could make herself.

She managed to make it through the day without blowing up the computer—Carl gave her a B+ for her first day—and she gratefully left the building to head for home. She made it barely a block before her hair seemed to again warn her that trouble approached. A hand closed around her arm, and she barely bit back a yelp.

She whipped around and swung her purse at her assaulter's head, and George ducked on a shout. "Holy shit, don't kill me!"

Heart pounding, she stared at him. "You scared me!"

"I called your name but you ignored me!" He kept his hand on her arm and huffed out a breath. "Let's go get dinner."

She yanked at her arm. "I don't want to." He gave her a quick shake, and her eyes went wide. Real fear began to flutter inside her heart. Her hand tightened on her purse strap. Could she hit him hard enough to make him let go? She couldn't be sure.

"I don't know what you're such a chicken about," he shot at her, "but I'm really sick of how you think you're too good for any man. You let Rafael Lucino take you out, but you won't let me take you to even lunch? Hey, newsflash, babe, he's taken. You want a prince to rescue you or some shit?"

"Excuse me."

The chilly male voice had George slowly looking up to see a stranger standing behind Theresa. The newcomer looked handsome enough, but the hardness to his face kept him from being actually beautiful. His eyes looked as cold as his voice sounded. Inexplicably, without reason, George felt himself beginning to sweat. His skin crawled warningly. "Uh. Are we in your way?"

"Take your hand off her." The instant Theresa was freed, Van pulled her back and firmly stepped in front of her for added protection. "I believe she told you no. Would you like me to enforce the point? I would be glad to oblige."

George back-stepped so fast that he tripped over his own feet. "No! I, er, I'm good. I get it, I get it. Hands off. I won't bug her again." Hard black eyes stared at him, and he waved his hands in the air. "I'm going, I'm going!" He swung around, smacked into a store wall, and staggered back to fall on his ass. A mocking snort of derision had his color flaring red, and he scrambled up and ran away. Theresa was *crazy* if she thought she was safe with that guy!

Inexplicably, she actually did feel safe. She didn't doubt her rescuer's ability for violence, but she also didn't doubt that he would not harm her. Her hair didn't itch, and it always told her of trouble. "Thank you . . . ?" Her voice trailed off as he turned around, and she tried to keep her jaw from dropping again. Every pulse in her body began to flutter wildly as an unfamiliar yet strangely known longing rose inside. If this was the prince out to rescue her, then she was *happy* to be rescued!

"Van." A hint of a smile softened his face and warmed his eyes. "Van D'Angelo. May I escort you home?"

"Uhm. Yes. For a little ways." She fought to make her heart stop tripping over itself as she fell into step beside him. A fairly gleeful heat skipped merrily through her veins as she desperately searched for something to say that didn't involve something along the lines of 'I'm single; date me!' "Ah, thank you. For rescuing me."

"Yeah. No problem." He rubbed the back of his neck and looked for something intelligent to say. He hadn't intended to get involved, but he just hadn't been able to stand seeing her get manhandled like that. "You know that guy?"

"Work with him," she admitted.

"You should file a harassment charge."

"Yeah."

Another awkward silence fell. He finally glanced at her to see what she was thinking, and he found her smiling. "Something funny?"

She looked up at him, and her brown eyes had turned to warm whiskey from her humor. "He ran into a wall."

He felt his shoulders relax, and he had to smile in return. "I can't imagine why. I have such a comforting presence."

"You're a paragon." Her shoulders relaxed as well, and she quickly tucked her hair back when she saw strands clinging to his shirt and jeans. "My name is Theresa Adams. I really am grateful for the rescue. It was pretty scary," she admitted. She looked at her arm and saw the red marks were fading quickly. At least George hadn't bruised her.

On pure impulse, Van asked, "Can I buy you some coffee?" She looked up at him in surprise, and he felt his ears turn red. "If you say no, I'll listen. I promise."

Her gaze lowered almost shyly. "Actually . . . I wouldn't mind coffee. I'll probably be up late reading. I'll need the caffeine."

He changed direction and lightly cupped her elbow to escort her along. He realized what he had done and immediately released her to stuff his hands in his pockets. She looked at him for several moments and then lightly curled her hand around his elbow. A hint of shy pink to her cheeks made him damn tempted to lean down and kiss her. There was an honest sweetness inside her that drew him like a lodestone.

They got cups of coffee from a shop and grabbed a table in a corner. He put his back to the wall without thinking, but she didn't seem to notice anything unusual. He felt something tickle his arm and looked down to see a thick lock of her hair had wrapped around his wrist. He couldn't bring himself to free it. Somehow . . . it felt sensual. "You like to read?" he asked.

"Love it. I'll read anything and everything you give me. I probably have a million useless trivia facts inside my head. In this case, I have to learn to use a computer, and I have a book on using it. At least I'll enjoy learning. Do you read, or are you more of a movie type?"

"Books," he said fervently. "I like movies now and then, but I really love reading. I used to stuff suitcases with more books than clothes until I gave in and bought a Kindle. Instant library on the go."

She sighed wistfully. "I've thought about getting one, but technology scares me." He grinned a bit, and she stuck her tongue out at him briefly. "Don't make fun of me. I grew up in an old-fashioned household. We don't own computers. I don't even have an MP3 player. I'd break it."

"I dropped my Kindle from a ladder. If it can handle that, it can handle a technophobe. But I don't recommend any iThings. They're delicate." His heart clenched when she laughed, and he fought to ignore the needy hunger inside his body. He couldn't even tell if it was more physical or more emotional. He felt starved for her presence. He wanted to see her more. Needed to have her near. "Theresa?"

She suddenly went white and grabbed his wrist to look at his watch. "I have to get home!" She leapt to her feet. "My grandmother will be furious with me!"

He stood as well and frowned. "I'll go with you and explain."

"No!" she blurted. She shook her head hard. "Thank you, Van, but that would make it worse." She made a helpless gesture. "She hates men. *Please* don't follow me." She hesitated and then rose on her toes to briefly kiss his cheek. She tried to hurry away and was brought up short by her hair gripping his wrist. "Oh, don't do this now!" She yanked, and it finally let go.

He watched her run out and gave her a minute before he pointedly followed her. He stayed back enough that she didn't know he was there, but he wasn't sure it was necessary. She seemed blind to everything except getting home by a certain time. What the hell was going on?

The sight of the two-story house she lived in made him oddly depressed, and he didn't know why. He lingered just out of sight but could clearly hear her rattling the doorknob. "Grandmother!" she shouted. "Please, let me in!"

The retort came back, "Oh, look who finally decided to come home! Obviously you don't need a roof over your head since you don't care how much time you spend loitering at work. Go sleep in your precious lobby!"

"It won't happen again!" She struggled back tears. "Just let me in!" The door blessedly opened, and she rushed inside without looking at her grandmother. She didn't breathe again until she was safely in her bedroom.

From the outside, Van frowned darkly as he slowly walked away down the street. Something didn't feel right in the entire scenario. Maybe it was his exposure to the 3rd District, but he just could feel 'something' in the air around that melancholy house. He glanced back toward the second floor balcony, and he thought he saw a glimpse of Theresa silhouetted against the curtains. Her long hair rippled as if alive.

His job was to hunt down Martin Johns' absent partner, and the last thing he ought to be doing was getting himself tangled up in whatever problems Theresa's family had. And yet . . . maybe spending time with her might actually benefit his job as well. If *he* was going to strike at the Lucinos, he would want information. Who would be a better target than the woman who had access to all the files? He could spend a little more time with her, get to know her more, and hopefully take care of two problems at once.

What could possibly go wrong?

CHAPTER EIGHTEEN

Theresa's knees shook as she shut her bedroom door and locked it. She slowly sank down to sit on the ground and stared blindly at the opposing wall. She had no doubt that she could very well have been forced to sleep outside or at her desk. The threat had been there ever since she had become a legal adult. Just a little reminder that she was beholden to Ruby for a roof over her head.

Looking back, she knew that her grandmother's possessiveness had not changed as she grew up. It had always been over-the-top; she just hadn't thought much of it. Her parents had been murdered when she was a baby. She had always assumed that Ruby feared losing her too. But as an adult . . . strange how adults could see things differently from children. She didn't feel protected. She felt trapped.

She got to her feet and forced herself to put it aside. She would not let anything mar the one bright spot in the day: Van. She knew she didn't dare see him again, didn't dare mention him to anyone. It was enough to have met him. Perhaps meeting him was what had opened her eyes to her situation. He *did* make her feel safe. He also made her feel a laundry list of other things that were both fascinating and alarming. Maybe she could look him up when she got free, and she could ask him out.

Yeah, right. She snorted at herself as she changed into more comfortable clothes. While she could claim plenty of knowledge of the world, it came from books. Practical application had always eluded her. But . . . then again . . . maybe Van wouldn't mind being her practice buddy. He had seemed to like her well enough. She didn't know what he had intended to ask before she had noticed the time, but, maybe . . .

"Stop thinking about it!" she muttered at herself as she grabbed her brush. She started to yank it through her hair, and she felt her scalp burn briefly. She groaned as she recognized the sign. She let go of her hair, and sure enough, it now pooled on the floor. Another five inches had grown in. She snatched up the scissors she kept on her dresser and carefully trimmed it above her ankles again. She didn't dare go any higher. She chucked the hair into a basket and threw herself into her reading chair. She knew a sign when she found it.

There were times she honestly felt as if her hair was alive. It did things on its own that just couldn't be explained as an accident. It grew far too fast and far too long to keep it shorter than ankle length. She had once tried to cut it to her shoulders. It had retaliated by growing over everything like a vine. Ruby'd had to cut her free because she had ended up trussed from the ceiling. After that, they had worked to keep it at the floor. Theresa normally gave the cut hair to Ruby, but after that evening, she didn't feel right doing so. She would burn it first opportunity.

She half expected to be forbidden from going to work, but Ruby didn't say anything to her at all. She quickly hurried to the office, and she reluctantly booted up the Beast that now lived on her desk. Her eyes moved around the area quickly yet she did not see any sign of George anywhere.

"Theresa?"

She almost jumped out of her skin and swung around sharply to discover Rafael stood behind her desk. To her further astonishment, Van stood beside him. She shot to her feet. "Uhm, sorry. I'm just a bit jittery."

"*Sì*, I imagine so!" her boss scolded. "You have not been honest with me or Papa, Theresa. Why did you not tell us that you were being bothered by George?"

Her color rose as she shot a look at Van. His expression didn't change other than the slight lifting of a brow. "It wasn't a big deal until last night." She rubbed her hands over her arms. "I don't want to file a report."

Rafael wasn't surprised; Van had told him that would likely be the case. "It does not matter. George has been relieved of his duties and moved to another area. He knows he is not to speak with you again. In the meanwhile," he clapped Van lightly on the shoulder, "I would like for you to meet Van D'Angelo. He is a friend of the *famiglia*. He heard we were short on a guard for the library and Publications area and has offered his services. You may count on him, Theresa. He is an honorable man."

"We've met," she admitted softly. "I know I'm safe with him. Thank you, Rafe."

"It is my pleasure." He tapped her lightly on the nose and ambled out of the area. Only when he was in the hall did he start to whistle merrily. The moment Van had told him and Antonio that he wanted to be hired as a guard—in that particular area—both Lucinos had wondered if he had his eye on Theresa. It suited Rafael just fine. They just seemed . . . right together. It would be interesting to see how things went.

A bit awkward, Theresa linked her hands together. "You have a big mouth."

Van sighed. "You wouldn't have told either Rafael or Antonio, and we both know that something needed to be said. I think he needed more than to just be scared off or transferred, but I respect your desire to be low-profile." He leaned on the counter beside her. "If you don't want me around, I can always ask for another area."

He found himself holding his breath as she stared at him. Then, finally, a hint of a blush touched her cheeks. "No, I don't mind," she admitted softly. "And I'm sorry for rushing off last night. My grandmother is a hard woman."

He bit the tip of his tongue before he said what he really thought. "I was more worried than offended." He glanced at her desk, and his eyes warmed. "Forcing you to use a computer, huh?"

"I've only broken it once. I'm impressed with myself." She turned to sit down and unexpectedly got brought up short by her hair snagging on something. When she turned back, she realized the something happened to be Van. There were long locks wrapped around his forearms and legs alike. Bright red flooded her face as he slowly arched a brow. "I don't . . . I can't . . . oh god." She buried her face in her hands.

He studied the hair clinging onto him. As it had before, it felt sensual against his skin. He tugged gently on the confining strands, and they stubbornly held firm. They actually wound even more around him before his very eyes. Suspicions began to churn inside. He lifted his arm and looked at the hair. "Let go." His voice was soft and firm. "I am not going anywhere."

After a pause, the hair slowly unraveled and released him. It dropped back into place and pooled on the floor as if to prove it had lengthened right then and there. At least a foot of hair now sat docilely on the tile. He looked at it for a moment before reaching out and gently tugging Theresa's hands off her face. "You want to talk about this?"

"My whole life." She couldn't meet his eyes. "My hair just . . . grows. I have no control over it. We can't keep it short. I've tried. It gets mad at me." She tried to smile. "I think it's possessed."

The suspicions began to turn into alarms. He had spent far too much time in the 3rd District and worked with Enforcers for too long to dismiss something as merely a fluke. "If it does grab me again, I don't mind. I promise. I'm think I'm flattered. Hey." He lifted her chin to force her gaze up to his. "I wouldn't lie to you."

She searched his eyes and unexpectedly smiled. "I believe you." Her breath caught as his thumb rubbed over her skin softly and sent flutters of heat flickering through her nerves. Something softened in his face, and it made him unbearably beautiful as if a mask had melted away.

Both heard voices approaching, and he swiftly released her. She dropped into her seat and he walked several paces away. By the time the other employees reached them, everything looked normal. He inclined his head slightly when the two female clerks looked at him warily. "I'm the new guard."

"Uhm, okay." The blonde edged back carefully. "I'm just going to go to my desk now. Er, good morning, Theresa!" She whirled and hurried off around a large set of bookcases.

The brunette actually stood her ground though she held her purse almost like a shield. "I'm Sally. You are . . . ?"

"Van." He propped a shoulder against a bookcase. "I'm an *unarmed* security guard, if that will put your mind at ease."

Sticking a gun on a guy that mean and scary seemed entirely overkill! There didn't seem to be anything comforting about him at all. Forget protecting the library; who in their right mind would even enter the *building* with him there? "Sure, that's, ah, great." Her eyes darted around quickly. "Er, well, I'm on the clock. Later!" She dashed off hastily.

Van looked at Theresa. "I can't imagine what their problem is."

She laughed out loud and quickly slapped a hand over her mouth. Her whiskey eyes were wide over her palm and they danced with humor. She shooed him away with her other hand, and he very nearly smiled as he obligingly walked away. He had no idea why she didn't see him the way others did, and he didn't actually care. The idea of scaring her made him feel slightly ill.

He took the time to duck out of sight and sound, and he yanked out his cell phone. He hit a quick call button and waited. He watched the window as the other side rang; he had a perfectly reflected view of the open area where Theresa sat.

The other side clicked. "Enforcers."

"Theresa Adams," he said bluntly.

Rhianna hesitated audibly. "What about her?"

"Don't try that bullshit, Rhianna. I've spent too much time out there."

"Mmm. I suppose that's fair." She sighed. "Yes, I know her, Van. What's the problem?"

"Her hair. Do I need to elaborate?"

"No, of course not. But do I need to remind you that certain things leave my control once they enter the ether beyond my District?" She smiled when that was met with silence. "You really have spent too much time out here. I will be frank: yes, I know Theresa, and yes, it has to do with more than from the Lucinos and yet it also has everything to do with them. Yes, I know about the difficulties of her hair, and yes, I know exactly what's wrong. Anything beyond that, I'm simply not at liberty to tell you."

"Is she under contract?" He bit back a sigh as no answer was given. When it came to Rhianna, he couldn't assume it was an agreement. Theresa might or might not be 3rd District born. She might or might not be under an Enforcers' contract. His gut said yes to both, but he could be wrong. "Damn it, Rhianna."

"Just do what you're doing. I still don't have as much control over events as I want, Van." She gently hung up the phone.

He slowly put his phone away. He had been counting on having Enforcers at his back in case things went to hell. Being told they were effectively on their own was *not* comfortable after what he had witnessed around Martin Johns. If his partner was consumed by the same thing, and it came right for Theresa, it would get ugly. How the hell would he protect her from something that he couldn't shoot?

It did nothing to improve his mood to realize that something also felt off about the library portion of the Publications office. There were locked racks that held personnel and personal files, and he eyed them more than once as he wandered through the surprisingly cavernous area. When he found himself in front of them for the fifth time, he stopped and looked closer. What was tripping his alarms?

"Only I, Rafael, and Antonio know what's in these racks."

The sound of Theresa's voice didn't surprise him even though he hadn't heard or sensed her approach. He could normally detect anyone within a twenty-foot radius, but she slipped easily under his radar because he knew she was of no danger to him. No danger to him physically, anyway. She was Danger with a capital D to his heart and soul. He turned around and studied her. "What's in them?"

She smiled. "Things." Her gaze lowered and a hint of pink climbed her cheeks. "Uhm. I was wondering if you'd like to have lunch with me."

"Yes." As he realized how quickly he had agreed, he cleared his throat. "I would be very happy to have lunch with you."

"I'll meet you at the elevator at noon. There's a café next door that has good food." She touched his hand without any fear though she kept her touch her brief. She hurried away before anyone spotted her with him.

Not that he would knock his luck, but something had him wondering just what was going through her mind. Maybe she thought she would be safe at work where her grandmother couldn't see them. He pinched the bridge of his nose as he sighed. Yeah, she was probably under contract. This just smacked of Enforcer influence. He might have to kill someone in order to protect others, and he was falling in *love*. Incongruity. Its name was Rhianna.

Right at noon, he waited by the elevators for his 'date.' She came down the hall toward him after a moment, and he wistfully watched her hair move around her body. Will of its own or not, he liked the way it framed her full figure. He really wouldn't want to see it cut short; it just suited her. In fact, he liked everything about her exactly as it was. She had a beautifully curved shape all over, as if Nature had forgotten to use any straight lines in her figure. She looked soft and appealing and perfect. He had an inexplicable urge to cuddle, and he was assuredly *not* a cuddler.

"Van?" She tilted her head as she stopped in front of him. "You're staring."

"You seem surprised by that." He punched the elevator button.

"I suppose I am." She winced wryly. "Don't ask Rafael about his engagement party."

He made a mental note to ask at the first opportunity. "What happened?"

"It was strange. These men kept trying to ask me to dance."

"Ah." He coughed. "I assume you realize you're lovely, Theresa. Of course they would be interested." The way she eyed him assured him that he did, indeed, need to ask about the party. The idea of her not knowing what to say or do with unexpected admirers amused him more than it triggered any jealousy. Odd how that worked.

The café was not quite busy yet. They both got sandwiches and moved toward the rear of the place. He automatically put his back to the wall once more, and this time he saw her study him briefly. She smiled and shrugged it off, and his shoulders relaxed slightly. Compelled to explain, he said, "When you live putting yourself in danger, you pick up habits. I never have my back to a door."

"I can't say I blame you." She let out a quick breath. "I assume you're confused about why I asked you to lunch."

Disappointment, not a lack of surprise, made him stifle a sigh. "I will assume by your phrasing that it isn't a personal interest in getting to know me."

"Maybe a little bit," she confessed. "But mostly, really, there's something at work that I've noticed, and that I wanted to tell you. If anyone can figure it out, it's you."

His brows lifted. "You have my attention."

"Those confidential files that you kept eyeing. Something felt odd to you? It felt odd to me as well. I think someone is messing with them somehow. When I was examining them recently, I noticed that the one lock looked a bit . . . ragged."

"Like someone had tried to break it." It wasn't a question.

"Or something. I want to tell myself my imagination is overactive, but I saw you. I think you're sensitive like I am. You felt something off. You know about the problems the Lucinos have had lately. I mean, I can't imagine Rafe or Antonio hiring you without warning you about the recent trouble."

He sighed. "I did, and yes, they did." He sat back for a moment. "I'll watch the place tonight. See if we're both just overreacting. In the meantime, try not to worry about it." He felt something move and flicked a glance under the table to see that her hair had grabbed his ankle. Never one to ignore a sign, he asked, "So . . . a little bit of a personal interest?"

Her color rose. "I think we both know I'd be lying if I denied it. And you seemed to have one in me."

"Slightly more than a 'little' interest." He rubbed his thumb over the back of her hand. "I'm not exactly an expert on dating or courting or whatever the hell people call it, but I wouldn't mind playing it by ear with you. I know you're scared of your grandmother. I can be discrete."

"I've seen the way you can blend in. I believe it." She took a deep breath. "I'm kind of out of my depth." She glanced up but he didn't look surprised. "Maybe we could play it low key, and once I save enough to move, we could see what happens?"

"How about we see what happens and play it low key at the same time? Let's get to know each other. Ask me anything. I'll try to answer if I can. There are things I can't say," he warned.

"I don't mind. How about starting with the obvious?" She smiled. "Age, origins, and so on?"

"I'm twenty-nine, almost thirty, I was born in Texas where my parents still live, and as if my name wasn't a clue, yes, I have Italian blood as well. It's jumbled up with a lot of other things, though. I've been at my job for, hmm, about five years now. There was a need for my skills," he said simply. He didn't intend to keep it a secret forever, but it was assuredly not a conversation to be had in the middle of a busy café. "You?"

"I turned twenty-five a few months ago, and I'm not sure of my whole origins." She slowly stirred the lemon in her tea. "My grandmother is my mother's mother. My parents were killed when I was a baby. Grandmother has raised me since then. I don't really remember either my mom or my dad. I have some photos of them, though. I've never asked about them."

He kept his silence on his suspicions. Instead, he slowly slid his hand over hers and held on. She turned her hand over, and their fingers laced together. "I'm sorry," he told her softly. "My parents have never really understood me, but I've never doubted they loved me." He thought he had a better understanding then of why the Lucinos were drawn to Theresa; family was everything to them, and they somehow knew she needed one terribly.

They both knew it was getting to be the end of lunch, and they slowly and reluctantly pulled their hands back. They dumped their trays and stepped out into the afternoon sun. Impulsively, he grabbed her hand and held onto it as they walked. She looked up with a surprised expression that quickly turned to a smile. She rested her head against his arm on an unconsciously contented sigh.

Her scalp unexpectedly began to itch. As soon as she noticed it, she felt the tension in Van's body. She took a quick breath of fear and quickly swallowed a gasp when he swung her around the corner of the café and into an alley. He pressed her back against the side of the building. "Say nothing." His voice was nearly soundless.

She pressed her face to his shoulder and tried fight the shivers running through her body. She couldn't get warm. The itching had become a burning. She knew what it meant: her grandmother was somewhere nearby watching for her. She had completely forgotten that Ruby liked to occasionally spy on her at work. The first stirring of anger began to swell inside her heart. Why was she a prisoner?

Van's free hand gently curled around her arm, and he bent his head to say in her ear, "Breathe. Relax. Trust me. She's almost gone."

She took a long breath and was almost immediately distracted as the scent of his skin reached her. Something dangerous clung to even his scent, yet it still didn't scare her. She had been watching him all day. She could logically see why people were afraid of him. She could even see that he did nothing at all to reassure them—and she didn't blame him for it. Perhaps what drew her to him, drew them together, was more elemental than just desire. She wasn't the only one trapped in a tower; in a way, he had been just as isolated from the world.

His shoulders relaxed finally, and he eased back a bit. "It's safe." He smiled a bit wryly. "I'm sorry if I was flattening you against the wall. I didn't trust you to stay put. Frightened animals who aren't sure of their claws will always run from a threat. It was safer to stay here." His breath hitched as he saw how she looked at him. "Theresa . . . don't." Her hand came up to tenderly frame his face, and he closed his eyes. Her touch felt like heaven. "You're making it impossible to let go."

"Then don't." Her eyes searched his face. The mask had melted away again. She knew she saw the real him, and what she saw was everything she had ever wanted without knowing she wanted it. She didn't want a prince; this undercover cop was perfect. Oh, she had no proof that was his real job, but she couldn't shake her gut feeling. "Van?"

He cupped her chin and bent his head to kiss her. The whiskey colored eyes watching him widened slightly, and his body tightened greedily as he saw the color darken with a matching hunger. Her free hand settled lightly over his heart in an indelible claim. He felt something soft yet strong move against his skin and knew her hair had captured him again. It seemed superfluous to him. He had been captured the moment he saw her.

The kiss slowly deepened, and he slid his arms around her waist to bring her body close. She felt perfect. When they finally parted for air, he murmured huskily, "If I promise not to grope, can I keep holding you? I love how you feel."

"I'm a bit pudgy." It was said a bit breathlessly. "Everyone says I should lose weight."

"Don't do it on my behalf." He freed a hand to smooth her hair out of her face. At least a foot of the locks had coiled around his wrist again. "Please tell me that wasn't your first kiss. I won't be able to let you go without kissing you again."

She bit her lip and winced sheepishly. "Uhm." She sighed and rose up on her toes to kiss him again. His hands tightened, and the signal of his shaky control was wildly thrilling. It seemed oddly empowering to know she could affect this man that deeply. A gasp caught in her throat when he stole the kiss and aggressively parted her lips. If her first kiss had been a beautiful and tender thing, her second one was nothing but flash, fire, and wicked delight.

The strains of a familiar song broke the mood, and she pulled back enough to say huskily, "Your phone is playing Celine Dion."

"My mother is calling." His voice sounded rough, and his black eyes churned with emotion barely held in check. "Also, I think we might be late back to the office by now."

"I work for Italians. They understand passion. Rafael seduces Tori in his office."

He unexpectedly laughed. Though the sound came out a bit rusty from lack of use, it was still very genuine. "Does he know you know that? And does she?"

Her lips curved. "They do. They also know I'm discrete." She took a long breath and reluctantly released him. She tugged on her hair and it just as slowly let him go. Her breath wedged in her lungs as she saw his eyes flare with hunger at the feel of her hair sliding over his skin. She slowly backed up a step. His hand lifted as if to stop her, and she hurried away before she did something stupid like ask him to take her to wherever he lived. She was in way too far over her head. They needed to back up a step for a bit before they did something stupid. Why couldn't she shake the feeling that he was in danger by being involved with her?

He blew out a hard breath and grabbed his phone. "What?" he demanded.

A pause hung for a moment until his mother said drolly, "Well, that answers that. I was going to ask if you intended to bring anyone home with you on your next visit. We need to clean out the guesthouse if so. You sound . . . a bit *strained*, honey."

"Stop laughing at me." He hung up the phone with a scowl, but it shortly turned to a wry smile. His parents were going to *love* Theresa. Bringing her home wasn't exactly an option anymore. He would be damned if he let her escape from his life now. He knew he had a fight on his hands to get her to trust him to protect her, but he also had plenty of patience. He had no worries about the job taking him away, either. Everything was connected *somewhere*. He just didn't know where yet.

At the least, he finally had a good feeling of what story they were 'tangled' inside. He should have guessed. Rhianna wasn't very subtle sometimes.

CHAPTER NINETEEN

They were indeed back to work a bit late, but no one said anything about it. Most were too afraid of Van to try, and the rest liked Theresa too much to question her taste. She did encounter Roberto in the halls, though, and he winked at her saucily. The merger moved forward quickly, and she was used to seeing him as much as she saw Rafael. In fact, the merger was another thing adding to her work stress. Just In Time had more square footage for storage, and Roberto's company slowly brought over things for filing.

As she stood staring in dismay at the stacks of boxes, Sally materialized at her side. "You need to buy some jeans, girlfriend."

Theresa winced wryly. She didn't deny the charge, yet she knew her grandmother would never allow it. Maybe she could buy some and hide them at work. "I must concur. We'll need more shelving, though. That old corner where we used to stuff old supplies needs to be cleaned up and used for more storage. Antonio told me that if we need to expand into other offices on this floor or commandeer space on another floor, to just let him know. So far so good, but I'm thinking about the future. Even going electronic, we can't just destroy this stuff. It's original art."

"Agreed." Sally made notes on the iPad she held. Seeing Theresa's look, she grinned. "Technophobe."

"It's not a crime. And, hey, I haven't broken the computer more than once. Pluses for me." She scooped up a box. "One down, a million to go."

"Pebbles and road, bygones." Sally eyed her as they headed back toward the front. "You be careful, okay?"

She didn't pretend to misunderstand. "He's a good man. I feel safer with him than I do in my own house. He makes me feel happy. It's an odd feeling."

Considering they had all noticed the lingering melancholy that clung to Theresa—and the fact that she never accepted invitations to barbeques or birthday parties—it was a welcome sign that she might finally have found someone that made her happy. "You going to ask him to go with you to Italy for the wedding? You were the only one invited by the Lucinos, you know."

"I know, and I'm still not sure I can attend myself. It's complicated. But if Van wanted to go, I wouldn't mind taking him as my date." She winced wryly. "I wouldn't have minded having him as a date at the engagement party."

Sally grinned. "Hey, you looked hot, hon. You can't be that surprised. And didn't I rescue you from that tipsy guy?"

"You did, and I still owe you cookies." She put the box down on her desk and sat down with a sigh. "Back to the grindstone." A funny noise had her looking at her computer, and she groaned when she saw the infamous blue screen of death. "I didn't even touch it!"

Carl obligingly came down to fix it while she put things away. The shiny new scanner had arrived and needed to be assembled still, but the technician helpfully gave her the manual early. It seemed fascinating how fast things could change.

The rest of the day went by fairly quickly. Van very nearly offered to escort Theresa home, but he knew better. Frustration gnawed at him as he watched her walk away down the sidewalk. He very badly wanted to grab her up and steal her away to someplace he could keep her safe and secure from the rest of the world. He was driven in his life, and choice of career, by an urge to protect. This was more personal than it had ever been before.

"It is hard," Roberto murmured sympathetically from behind him. "To take that fall and know that the one you love is fragile."

Van glanced at him as he stepped forward. "Brie didn't strike me as fragile when she threw water in my face or smashed Cauly over the head before I could deal with him myself."

"She is brave, *sì*, but she is fragile. In many ways, can it not be said that the ones who are the most fragile can be the most brave? They have the most to lose." He looked the direction Theresa had gone and could just see her figure as she disappeared around a corner. "Theresa has more bravery than she knows. Yet, perhaps, she is more fragile than she knows. She has been tempered by her life. I do not know much of it, but it does not take direct knowledge to recognize the signs of mental or emotional abuse."

"Your instincts are not wrong," Van admitted. "I don't know the details yet either, but you didn't tell me anything new." Under his breath, he muttered, "Locked in a tower."

Roberto very nearly smiled. He had been wondering about that. "I have always felt there was an answer in the story that was obvious from the beginning yet never used. In every version, I have seen it." He clapped Van on the shoulder. "You are a good man, Van. And you are smart. You and Theresa can save each other. If you have need, you only have to ask and we will help. Rafe and Antonio love Theresa a great deal. She is part of their family in their hearts. Why do you think Antonio wanted Rafe to try to date her? Free her from her tower, and they will adopt her in a minute."

Van watched him walk away and smiled to himself. He could see what Rhianna had meant about things having both nothing and yet everything to do with the Lucinos. It was no coincidence that Theresa had ended up working for them. Perhaps the connection between everything was Theresa herself. It might well be that it was her story that had started it all. He would need to do some digging to be sure, but in the meantime, he had a library to babysit. Just who was tripping his internal alarms, and what were they after?

Theresa thought the entire way home about ways to play off things if Ruby noticed there was anything different. She certainly *felt* different though a look in a mirror had told her there were few lingering effects.

To her surprise, the house was blessedly empty. She hurried through to her room and took a quick shower in the attached bath. She actually enjoyed bathing despite her hair; it never retained water unless needed. By the time she got out and toweled off, her hair had already mostly dried. It was fully dry when she got dressed and went to the kitchen for food.

The door opened and closed as she stirred a pot of soup. "Welcome home, Grandma," she called. She hurried to pour a cup of hot tea and put it on the table as Ruby entered the tiny kitchen. "I made dinner."

Ruby sat down heavily at the table. "I'm not hungry." She took the tea and sipped it gingerly. "How was work?"

"Relatively normal, all things considered." Where normally she had told everything before, she found herself editing the events for once. "One of the employees got a transfer for hassling others. The scanner has been installed, and I've got the instructions to read. I had lunch with a coworker today to discuss the issues."

Ruby grunted lightly. "When do you get paid?"

"Friday, same as normal." She held onto her smile until Ruby walked out and then slowly released the breath she had been holding. She dished up a small amount of soup for herself but she didn't much feel like eating either. Lately, her grandmother had been acting . . . unusual. More tired. Sometimes in more pain as if she had been injured somehow. Something smelled rotten, and Theresa didn't know what it was or why she felt it. Maybe it would be answered by whatever Van found.

Van had been on more than one stakeout in his career. He found the ideal place to watch the restricted area from and settled in to wait. He kept one ear alert to the sounds of the quiet building, and he kept his eyes on the locked bookcases. Despite his best efforts, his mind began to wander. Was Theresa okay? Had her grandmother seen them? What was it about Ruby that he just did not trust? There were just too many loose threads in the entire scenario for him to be comfortable with anything.

A faint noise diverted his thoughts, and his eyes narrowed as he watched a small flashlight beam move across the floor. He didn't move until the figure holding the light came into view. His night vision had always been exceptional. There was nothing familiar about either male that started fiddling with the case, and they looked pitifully young. He straightened and began to move forward.

The lock wouldn't open, and the thief cursed softly as he tried to wrangle it. They had been trying for days to get in, but the stupid thing was old and rusty. The situation was not aided at all by the chills going down his back. Something dangerous lurked nearby. "Joe, you got the pliers?"

"Urk!"

It was the way he made the noise as much as the noise itself that made him whip around. Joe had been laid out flat on the ground, and another man stood with a foot on his back. Erwin almost went for the knife he wore when he saw that the newcomer held a gun very calmly and wore a guard's badge. His hands shot into the air. "Oh shit."

"Indeed." Van applied pressure to Joe's back to keep him down. "Why don't you two be the upstanding citizens I know you can be and tell me just what you're doing back here?"

Erwin tried to keep his knees from knocking. His sweaty palms felt clammy and cold. He would have tried to grab the flashlight to see the guard better, but what little he could see was *not* comforting. "We got lost."

"Very cute." Van pointedly checked the clip in the gun.

"We wanted the files on the Lucinos!" Joe blurted. "That's all! They're in these cases, and we were just going to nip them for some chick. No harm, no foul. Please don't shoot us!"

Something smelled rotten to Van. If Theresa and the Lucinos were the only ones who knew what these files were, then *she* sounded guilty. He would sooner believe in the Easter Bunny or non-partisan politics than the idea that she had any reason to steal files she could access without suspicion in the course of her normal job. She was being used. "Sit," he told Erwin.

The shorter male sat down fast enough that he almost fell on his ass. Van didn't take his eyes off the burglars or move the gun as he pulled out his cell phone and lifted it. "Officer Marks?"

"I heard. We'll be there in two minutes."

Van tucked the phone into a pocket. "Your new friends will be here shortly, kids. And I recommend a change of career. You're lucky I'm such a nice guy. My contract says I can shoot first and ask later."

Marks and two other cops arrived shortly thereafter and put both males under arrest. Van had warned Marks ahead of time that something might happen, and the veteran cop had trusted his instincts enough to be standing by. While the thugs were read their rights, Marks stepped aside with Van. "What the hell was that? They trying to frame your, ah, *friend*?"

Van ignored the subtle dig. "Sure as hell sounds like it. Do you need me, or am I free? I need to talk to her quickly and find out if my gut is right."

"Get moving. You can give a statement later." He watched Van walk out of the area and smirked as both Erwin and Joe visibly relaxed. "Aw, he was making friends again. So glad he didn't shoot them this time. It's always such a mess."

The males went glassy, and Marks' partner murmured, "You're such a dick sometimes."

"Y'take your perks where you get 'em."

Van made his way as fast as he could to where Theresa lived with Ruby. The tiny house was even more depressing in the midnight gloom than during the day. It looked completely dark and shut down for the night, but there was a very dim light coming from the room that he knew was Theresa's. She had again stayed up late to read.

She had a balcony, thankfully. He jumped up to grab the edge and hauled himself up and over the railing. He knocked very lightly on the glass doors and called softly, "Theresa? It's Van." Silence met him, but it felt deliberate. "Theresa. Please. Open the doors. I'll be quick."

The curtains parted a tiny bit, and she peeked around the edge. "You shouldn't be here," she urged just as softly. "She'll kill you!"

"I'm hard to kill. Believe me, people have *tried*." He pressed his hands to the glass. "Let me in." Let me hold you. Though the words did not come to his lips, they seemed to echo in the air around him.

She slowly reached out and unlocked the triple bolts on the doors. She tugged them open and stepped back to let him step inside. As he stared at her, she looked down quickly. She had on her normal camisole for sleeping though she had thrown on the pants as well at his knock. "What?"

"If I tell you that you're sexy, will you believe me?" he asked huskily.

She hastily grabbed her robe and pulled it on. "Unfortunately, yes, and don't you *dare* kiss me!" She struggled to free her hair from under the robe and ended up with her hands stuck. Even in the dim lamplight, her cheeks were bright as Van moved closer and helped free her. "It's worse," she admitted miserably.

He released her hair and watched almost two feet of length pool on the ground. "Without provocation?"

"It rarely needs any." She grabbed the scissors. "You want to see how bad it is?" She twisted her hair around her wrist and quickly lopped the strands off at her waist. The cut hair immediately dissolved into dust, and the shortened strands sparked at the edges before abruptly surging outward and returning to floor length. "It's not normal."

"No." He blew out a quick breath. "Theresa . . . I think you are 3rd District born." He sat down on the side of the bed and tugged her down beside him. "It would have to be your father. I couldn't get any information out of Rhianna Taber, but she admitted she knows you beyond your connection to the Lucinos. There's only one reason she would. I have other suspicions, but I can't confirm them. All I know is that we're on our own, and you've got a shitload of danger breathing down on you."

In a way, it was reassuring knowledge. "What kind of danger?"

"You were right. Someone was trying to get into the files. Two idiots trying to get the personal files on the Lucinos themselves. They said they were doing it for a 'chick', and it sure as hell makes you look guilty. On the other hand, I'm not an idiot. Have you told your grandmother about those files, or about work?"

Her mouth went dry and her heart began to beat harder. "Yes," she whispered. Her hands clenched together in her lap, and his hands covered them soothingly. "I have to tell her everything else she won't even let me keep the job at all." She leaned forward and dropped her head on his shoulder. "She's framing me. I had started to think lately that . . . that maybe she didn't love me after all, but this . . . this is not what I expected."

He pulled her onto his lap and wrapped his arms around her tightly. Little shivers rippled through her entire body and he tried to absorb them. "There may be more that we don't know. I'm going to start looking into her history. My gut tells me that she might be connected to Martin Johns somehow. I don't believe in coincidences. Brie said that it might be her fault Enforcers got involved, but I wonder if it might not be you instead."

"I started working for the Lucinos after Johns started causing trouble."

"Was it your idea or your grandmother's?"

A violent shiver ripped through her body. "Hers," she barely whispered. "It was the only job I was qualified for without going to college or having a high school degree. I never . . . I never understood why she suddenly was willing to let me work." She wrapped her arms around his neck and clung onto him with all her strength. "Why, Van?"

"I don't know, baby. I swear I'll find out." He pressed his face to her neck for a moment. He very, very badly wanted to carry her out of there and go stash her away safely at the Lucino villa or at the Viani place. He could have Tori and Alex guard her until he figured out what the hell was going on! "At least you know more of your origins," he tried to tease.

"3rd District." Longing filled her voice. "There might be somewhere I belong?"

He couldn't stand it anymore. He eased her back and smoothed her hair out of her face. "You belong with me," he urged softly. "Trust me. Let me protect you. Grab some things and leave here with me. If you can't trust me, then I'll take you to Rafael. Tori and Alex are the best I've seen at what they do."

She took a long breath and met his eyes evenly. "Who are you?"

He closed his eyes briefly and then opened them again. "It depends on how generous you want to be. The kindest term, I think, is a mercenary. Hired gun and hitman have been applied as well. I take care of things that the system can't. Vincent Lucino hired me to remove Johns; I helped kidnap Brie and Isabelle and then worked to keep them safe. I got Tori free so she could get to Rafael before it was too late. There's no knowing which of us killed Johns; I hope, for her sake, it was her. She deserved the honor." He searched her eyes and saw no condemnation. "You don't look overly surprised."

"I don't think I am. I had guessed you were an undercover cop, so I suppose I wasn't far off. Does knowing the truth change how I feel? Of course not. It just explains why others react to you the way they do." Softer, she added, "And why I feel safe with you. It's hard to not feel safe with a man who would, literally, kill to protect you." She smoothed her hand over his beloved features. "Alright. I trust you."

A heavy fist suddenly slammed on the door. "Open this door!" Ruby shouted. "I swear, you had better open this door, Theresa! I know there's someone in there with you! Unlock the damned door!" The banging grew in force.

Theresa leapt to her feet. "Get out!" she urged Van. "Hurry! She won't hurt me, but she might kill you! *Please*. Trust *me* on this."

He stood and tried to reach for her, but her hair rose up and shoved him back. He stared into her eyes for long moments before cursing under his breath. He ran out onto the balcony and swung over the side to drop down underneath where he could not be seen. He quickly made his way across the darkened landscape until he was out of sight and sound. He needed to get that research done *fast*. She could not stay there any longer.

Theresa stifled a yelp as something heavy smashed the lock and the door suddenly swung open. "Are you mad?" she demanded of her grandmother.

Ruby rushed into the room and looked around wildly. There didn't seem to be any sign of anything, and certainly Theresa was more than dressed. Overdressed, to some extent. Yet Ruby rounded on her and screamed, "Who was in here with you?"

Disdaining to lie, Theresa didn't answer the question. "I'm twenty-five, not five. Whether you like it or not, I'm a legal adult." She walked over to her closet and felt strangely calm over things. "I'm done, Grandmother. I'm leaving."

Ruby grabbed her arm and her fingers bit in painfully as she swung her around. "I will not let you waste yourself on any man! Do you think he loves you? Men don't love! They *use*! They lie and cheat and abuse the ones they profess to love! He'll tear you up and throw you aside and then you'll come crawling back to me! I won't let it happen, Theresa! I tried to teach you, but you just won't listen!"

"How do you intend to stop me?" She nearly stopped breathing as she saw the gun in her grandmother's hand. "You wouldn't shoot me."

"No, of course not." Ruby pressed the muzzle against her own head. "But you think I won't kill myself right here?"

Nausea rose and Theresa's hair seethed violently around her body. Truthfully . . . she couldn't be sure it was a bluff. It seemed like the kind of thing Ruby would do, and Theresa would never be able to live with the guilt if she was wrong. She couldn't help loving her grandmother. "You win."

"Pack." The order was curt. "I'm taking you somewhere that bastard won't find you." She whirled and stormed out.

Theresa dragged out her single suitcase and threw things inside it a bit blindly. She knew Van would find her wherever she went. She trusted him to rescue her from whatever new tower she entered, be it literal or metaphorical. She would do whatever it took to help him when he did. She was getting sick of being the meek and helpless mouse she had been for years. If she was from 3rd District, then she had the chance at a happy ending. She would damned well fight for it!

CHAPTER TWENTY

The benefit to having cultivated contacts over the years was that Van had associates in some of the strangest and yet also useful places. He had picked up people from all walks of life, and he even knew people within relatively similar fields. In this case, if he wanted to investigate Ruby's background, he needed someone experienced with digging into histories and unashamedly willing to break into a few computers as needed.

It was nearly one in the morning, but the situation was too dangerous to wait until later. He flipped through his contacts in his phone and punched one in. It took quite a few rings until the other side was finally answered, and before the other person could speak, he said, "It's Van, and I have an emergency that has put the life of an innocent young woman on the line."

Silence, then, "Shit. Let me get dressed and grab some coffee. I'll meet you at my office in fifteen." An annoyed cry from a baby had him muttering, "And you owe me for waking Jayden."

"Tell Aenya that I'll pay for the next upgrade she wants for her club."

A woman's voice groused in the background, "I'm holding you to that."

Van almost smiled as he hung up the phone and tucked it away. He had gotten to know Hiro Michaels through the Enforcers, and by far the other man was one of the best private investigators that he had known. He had been quite glad to have Hiro as an ally; it was entirely likely that Hiro might be the only one who could successfully track him even if he didn't want to be tracked.

Fifteen minutes later, he stood outside the small office that Hiro operated from. He spotted the slightly disheveled investigator approaching and asked, "Teething problems?"

"No, thankfully. Brian Matthews made a blanket that keeps that at bay." Hiro unlocked the door on a sigh and walked inside. He flicked on lights and dropped into his chair behind the desk. "Let's hear it. This ought to be good, at the least."

Van kept it as concise as he could, but he had to start at the top with the Lucinos. He finished with, "I need to act fast if I want to get Theresa out of her tower."

"No shit." Hiro was already working on the computer. "Nice to see another worthy man take the fall. The minute you mentioned you worked with Enforcers, I had a feeling you'd eventually get to this point."

"I'm not from the District."

"You didn't have to be. Did you feel at home there?" At the nod, he shrugged. "There you go. Maddie told me once that sometimes it just takes a while to find your way home. I've sure as hell seen it myself many times. I'd bet Rhianna had her eye on you from the get-go. Did she contact you the first time?"

Van winced. "Now that you mention it . . ." He blew out a breath. "It would explain a lot, that's for damned sure." He sat on the edge of the desk and watched over Hiro's head. "What are you looking for?"

"Ruby's bank deposits. Seems odd that she didn't let Theresa work until last year and doesn't work herself. Where's she getting money? I'm sure Social Security covers a bit, but it ain't going to help raise a kid and it sure as hell wouldn't have bought that house they live in. She owns it outright. No loan. Paid cash."

"Now you know why I called you at one am."

"You're still an ass." After a few more minutes, he said, "Here we go. She banks somewhere that I've accessed records before." He grinned briefly when Van lifted a brow. "You're not the only one with contacts." He ran a finger down the screen. "Check deposits of one thousand dollars every other week for the last several months. I'd bet it goes back even further. Let's see . . . Ah. Here we are."

Van leaned closer to see the scanned copy of the check. "Orson Collins. Same last name; I wonder what relation he is to her. Hang on." He grabbed his phone and began flipping through notes. "I have the info I pulled from Martin Johns' files in here."

"Gotta love modern technology. Let's see what Google says . . ." Hiro plugged the new name into the search engine and wasn't disappointed. The very first link took him to public records. "The plot thickens. Forty-five years ago, Ruby and

Orson Collins got a divorce. Records are sealed but I see some old paper clippings from a library archive that imply it wasn't precisely amicable. Looks like there was a bitter custody battle, and I see that there are reports of physical abuse."

"One of the notes I got from the file had the initials 'O.C.' in it." Van flipped pages. "OC popped up a lot. My gut said he might be the absentee partner. If we assume OC is Orson Collins, and he's obviously still in contact with his ex, then that means Ruby is using Theresa as a spy on the Lucinos for him. Johns was ruined when the scheme fell apart. Collins must have had some sort of backup."

"Something doesn't compute here for me." Hiro sat back. "Let's assume that Johns and Collins are partners and want revenge on the Lucinos for ruining them. A year in, Collins goes to his ex-wife and pays her to put their granddaughter into the company as an unwitting spy. I can't imagine any amount of money making her willing to cooperate. I would assume he's the reason she hates men, and her obsessive protection of Theresa seems to imply that she wouldn't let her out of the house willingly."

"When I went to work for Johns less than a year ago," Van said slowly, "I could only earn so much of his trust. I never knew where he got his information. I could only act quickly to keep things in line. He was a paranoid evil-possessed psychopath. Maybe he wasn't the one behind everything."

Hiro looked up sharply. "You think Collins is the root of the evil."

"There's something about what Rhianna said that's constantly bugging me." He tapped a finger on the top of the desk. "Theresa is at the heart of this. If she's under contract, it's been in place since she was a child. Who signed on her behalf? It would have to have been her grandmother; her parents were killed when she was a baby." He broke off. "Son-of-a-bitch."

Hiro closed his eyes. "Collins killed his own daughter and son-in-law, and because the son-in-law was 3rd District born, Enforcers was involved. They moved fast to protect Theresa, but it wasn't enough for Ruby, who has gone overboard in the time since. Collins showed back up, and I'd lay money on him threatening our slightly sheltered Rapunzel in order to force Ruby's compliance. You said that the evil eating Johns seemed slightly omniscient?"

"More than slightly." His voice sounded as grim as he looked. "I think it's worth noting that it couldn't stand hearing mention of the 3rd District, and it went right after Rhianna directly. If Collins was already possessed, that would be a good reason to hate his son-in-law and, by proxy, his granddaughter. Fast forward two decades and you have two possessed nutcases that Antonio and Rafael Lucino helped ruin. Rhianna set up Brie and Roberto, Alex and Bella, and Tori and Rafael—possibly to protect them from the evil itself. Say the evil knew that. It's a whole new reason to hate them."

"Throw Theresa in to unintentionally spy on them, and all of Collins and Johns' most hated people are now together. Except for the problem that they utterly failed to do anything to the Lucinos other than some surface damage to Rafael and a bullet wound to Tori that turned out to be advantageous." Hiro's stomach churned uneasily. "You didn't think the Lucinos were in any more danger physically. Of course they aren't. They have completed contracts; they're under direct protection and can't be touched. Theresa isn't. Her contract is obviously still open. And how better to strike at the Lucinos than to target her directly, when she is so close to the family that Rafael has actually referred to her as his sister to more than one person?"

Van said something explicitly rude and whirled toward the door. "No wonder Ruby is getting worse! She knows her granddaughter is right in the middle of a warzone! Theresa's been developing her courage and is at her breaking point; she can't be controlled anymore. I've got to talk to her before Collins goes after her personally!"

"Don't do anything stupid!" Hiro shouted after him. Under his breath, he added, "Things just get worse as time passes. What the hell would cause such a grudge against the District?"

Van had to cool his heels until later in the morning when he could get into the office. He knew he didn't dare return to the melancholy house so soon. He bided his time as patiently as he could, but Theresa did not show up at her normal time. He immediately left the building and called Antonio directly. "Where is Theresa?" he demanded.

Antonio blew out a breath. "I had been hoping you would know that, Van. I have not talked to her this morning, but her *nonna* called me and very politely informed me that Theresa would not be returning to work. What has been happening? You sound very strained, and it is very unlike what I have seen of you until now. You love Theresa, *sì*?"

"As if you didn't guess already." Van's eyes moved sharply over the landscape. "I think I know what's going on, and Theresa is right in the middle."

"You will handle it." Antonio's voice remained calm. "You are a good man, Van. Papa put his faith in you, and so shall I. When you have saved Theresa, you will accept your pay and use it to take her on a vacation; a cruise, I think. You will bring her home soon thereafter, however. Our library would fall apart without her, and we will need to have a party to welcome her into our family officially."

Van stared at the phone as it was hung up on the other side. Unexpected humor stirred. Vincent was the only *actual* Don Lucino, but Antonio and Rafael could both pull it off convincingly. He sure as hell wasn't going to try to disagree. If they came out of this intact, he would be more than glad to kidnap Theresa himself and hold onto her until the fear went away again. He didn't like fear very much, and like everything else, she had brought a lot of it into his life.

He knew it would be empty, but he made his way back to the maudlin house surrounded by flowers. No lights were on inside, and it just *felt* abandoned. The doors had been locked, and he broke the one on the back to get inside. The windows illuminated the structure with gloomy light, and it disturbed him to think of all the years Theresa had lived there. His eyes told him it was a perfectly lovely home, but his heart could see it for the prison had become.

He found Ruby's room on the first floor and went over it briefly. There was nothing of interest to be found; the only documents he located were ones that Hiro had already pulled from online.

Partway up the stairs, his skin crawled in a familiar way. He drew his gun and moved silently down the second floor hallway toward Theresa's room. Dead silence—unnatural silence—seemed to echo through the area. He reached for the doorknob and then quickly turned it and shoved the door open without moving into the opening. Nothing happened. He knew he wasn't alone, but his guest did not wait in the room.

He stepped inside and looked around. It definitely showed the signs of someone packing in a hurry. The balcony doors stood open and he moved over to them. A shimmer of something caught his eye and he crouched down. Long strands of brown hair glimmered in the sunlight. His breath hitched as he realized they spelled out the words '*find me*'.

His head jerked up sharply and he hit the ground fast. The bullet mostly missed him but it did graze along his arm close enough to draw blood. He looked at the doorway and found Ruby watching him with eyes too wide and too glassy. She stood on a precarious point. "Interesting introduction," he told her calmly.

Her grip on her gun was steady if white-knuckled. "You think you're any better than the people you kill?" she raged at him. "I know who you are, Van D'Angelo! Nothing but a cold-blooded murderer! I won't let my granddaughter waste herself on a man who kills for a living!"

He didn't bother to deny the charge or defend himself. It would be a waste of breath. He rolled to his feet and put his gun away. "Your ex tell you that, Mrs. Collins? Bit of a hypocrite, wouldn't you say? Where's Theresa?"

"You won't find her!" Her glassy eyes almost looked a bit mad. "She will stay there safely until Orson gets what he wants and goes away again!"

There were flaws in that logic big enough to drive a truck through, but he again didn't argue. She could not be reasoned with. He let his eyes flicker over her shoulder, and she instinctively swung around. He immediately turned and jumped over the side of the balcony. He landed relatively softly on the muddy ground and ran around the side of the building swiftly. He would have to thank Marks' teenage son for teaching him some parkour tricks; they could prove useful in the damnedest places.

He grimaced and peeled his torn shirt away from the wound. He'd had worse before, but it still hurt like hell. He kept first aid supplies in his car for just such an emergency and gingerly wrapped the graze as best he could. That done, he stared out the windshield toward the tall city buildings in the near distance. There were millions of places that Theresa could have been stashed. It would be literally like finding a needle in a haystack.

Something glimmered in the wind, and his eyes narrowed. He looked again, and he knew he couldn't be mistaken. There were very long strands of hair drifting through the air. As soon as he noticed one, he began to notice more. No one along the sidewalks had noticed them. Only his eyes could see them. It was a trail. "Better than breadcrumbs," he muttered as he started the car.

The strands in the wind eventually led him to a cluster of high-rise urban living complexes. They were the latest and greatest, and they were made of reflective glass from top to bottom. Each reached ten to twenty stories tall. The only entry points were through front doors accessible by key card or by an external glass elevator. Trying to break into one of these places would be damned impossible. Anyone and everything would see you. Hell, just using the elevator would be putting yourself on display; the elevators were not made of the same reflective glass as the buildings.

A patient man by nature, Van found it difficult to cool his heels until nighttime finally arrived. Night was never truly dark in the city, and the urban area was designed for the nightlife so it had a lot of lights and clubs nearby. He didn't even know which 'tower' Theresa was being held inside, and he carefully crept around the base of all of them. Something tickled his arm, and he looked up sharply to see strands of hair falling to the ground.

He grabbed a few from the air and saw something move in a window near the top of the ten-story building. He held his breath as he watched a thick rope of hair lower slowly toward him. It looked like an actual rope, yet he knew it was Theresa's hair. It coiled around his waist and legs tightly, and he held on as it began to swiftly bring him up the side of the building. While heights were not his favorite thing in the world, he had absolutely no fear of falling. He trusted that rope of hair more than he trusted cables or the infamous duct tape.

The window stood open, and he climbed inside it as the rope released him. He had thought that nothing more could surprise him, but he discovered very quickly that he had been wrong. He stopped short, and his eyes widened slowly as he stared at the scene in the main area of the condo.

Theresa sat in the middle of the living room floor, and her hair literally covered and climbed every surface in the area. She had been partially tied up herself, and the thick brown locks resembled vines as they engulfed the entire place. She had her face buried in her hands, but she sensed him and looked up sharply. Tears streaked her face and continued to well in her eyes. "Van?" she managed to whisper.

He knelt in front of her and reached out to cup her cheek. "I'm here," he said softly. He ignored the coils of hair that wrapped around his arms and legs. "I'm not going anywhere." He tugged her closer and kissed her deeply. A shudder ripped through his body as her arms went around his neck and clung onto him wildly. Her hair wrapped around them both, and he eased back enough to say huskily, "I think we're getting kinky now."

Her lips trembled. "I can't walk anywhere. It weighs too much. My neck is killing me. I haven't eaten since lunch."

He managed to free one hand enough to get out his pocketknife, and he flipped open the largest blade. He grabbed a handful of her hair near her waist and quickly sliced through the mass. A few more cuts freed her entirely. The cut vines immediately began to dissolve into glittering dust that disappeared from the air around them.

The ends of her cut hair sparkled but they didn't grow more than an inch. She tried to smile. "Maybe it was just going overboard for you to get up here." His arms closed around her, and her breath caught. A bit desperately, she held on in return. She couldn't tell which of them was shaking harder. "I knew you'd find me," she whispered against his neck. "I should have gone with you last night!"

"Everything happens for a reason, I think." He took a long breath. "Let's get some food into you, and I'll tell you what I've learned today." He saw her staring at his bandaged arm and glanced down to see a hint of a bloodstain through his shirt. "It's just a graze."

"Someone shot you?!" Temper started to move in her eyes. "Who would shoot at you?"

"More people than you think, actually. In this case, it was your grandmother." He got to his feet and tugged her up as well. Her hands rested passively in his, and the temper in her eyes had turned to horror. "Did she say anything when she put you in here?"

"Only that she'd be back tomorrow afternoon." She slowly reached out to touch the stain, and her lower lip quivered. "She really tried to kill you." She burrowed against his chest and curled her fingers into his shirt. Only the feel of his arms soothed her anymore. "I'm so sorry, Van! I've made things so complicated for you."

"Technically, I guess that's true." He lifted her chin and brushed a tender kiss over her lips. "Now ask me if I regret it."

She searched his eyes intently. "Do you?"

"No." His thumb rubbed over her cheekbone. "It's hard to regret finding love." He smiled when her eyes widened. "You can't be surprised." He kissed her again. "I love you very much, Theresa Adams. If you're under a contract, and I'm the one picked for you, then I'm both humbled and elated. I couldn't have asked for more."

Joy slowly turned her eyes incandescent, and her smile seemed both shy and hopeful and also utterly beautiful. "When did you realize?"

"From roughly the luncheon," he admitted. "Earlier, probably, to be honest. I knew you were going to be trouble from the moment you smiled at me the first time. I never really could keep you at a distance. I didn't even bother to try. I need you to hold me." He rubbed the back of his neck. "I sound ridiculous saying these things."

"I think you sound wonderful," she countered simply. She slid her arms around his waist. "I'm very happy to keep holding you if you'll hold me. I love you very much, Van D'Angelo, and I don't care about a contract or anything like that. I'm just happy that I have you now. *You're* my happy ending."

He lifted her off her feet for a moment and buried his face against her neck. "If we want that happy ending, we're going to have to fight for it," he warned softly. He slowly and reluctantly let her go as she eased back. "Food."

"And information," she agreed. She took a deep breath. "Just how bad is this mess?"

The explanation didn't make her feel better, and sandwich she had just eaten seemed to uneasily move in her stomach. He lifted her from where she was sitting at the counter and carried her to the loveseat. He sat down beside her and kept her curled safely in his arms. "Is there anything you can tell me?" he asked.

"Other than the 'you have good instincts' thing?" She pressed her face to his shoulder. "Even the police suspected that my grandfather murdered my parents. They called it revenge for the divorce, but there was no evidence. Why would he wait twenty years to go after my mother? I think you might have the answer: my father." A shudder ripped through her body. "And now he hates me too."

"He hated you all along, baby." His arms tightened, but he reluctantly let go as she pulled away and got to her feet. "The answer is obvious. We get out of here and stash you with the Lucinos until I can remove Collins." He studied the line of her back and tensed shoulders. "Unless it bothers you that I would."

She made a quick gesture. "If he's done everything we think he has, then I'm *glad* you have the will to do what you do." She swung around and her whiskey eyes were bright with mingled frustration and temper. "I am just getting tired of doing nothing for myself. Do I want to run and hide? Yes, I do. But I can't. I just can't, Van. I need to face this monster with you. Unknowingly, he has controlled my entire life. I have to take it back!"

He got slowly to his feet. "You do know that that goes against the grain of everything I am and do, right? I don't involve innocent parties in these situations. I could very easily call any number of people and have this tower stormed." He pulled out his cell phone. "I have Don Lucino on speed dial. He makes things happen faster than a force of nature. You'd be packed in cotton, and Alex and Tori would happily sit on you."

She lifted her chin. "Then do it. I wouldn't even be mad at you over it. I know what kind of man you are, Van. I'm asking you to let me get involved even though I'm an 'innocent party' and you love me. If you choose to take away my freedom and put me away safely, I won't fight. I respect what you are." She added softer, "I'm asking only for the same respect. I won't ever be free of the tower unless I confront the reason why I'm in it."

He held her gaze for long moments and slowly opened his hand to let the phone fall on the carpet with a thump. "I have only two conditions. One, when I think of a plan, you will follow it to the letter. You'll be looking evil in the eye, and we don't know whether it'll trigger a fight or flight in you."

"Done," she agreed immediately. She cocked her head. "What's the other condition?"

He hesitated for a moment. "I want to hold you tonight," he finally admitted softly." Just to sleep. You said I make you feel safe. You make me feel . . . loved. Peaceful." He shrugged uncomfortably. "I don't wholly have the words. I just . . . want to hold you."

"That's all you want?"

His lips twisted wryly. "I'd be lying if I said I don't want you more than I want air. But that's *your* decision to be made. I'm not going to take your free will. That sort of decision needs to be *yours* and yours alone." He reached out and skimmed the back of his fingers down her cheek. "We have a lifetime to become lovers."

When he started to pull his hand back, her fingers stopped him and held his palm against her face. Her eyes had softened and swirled with an enchanting blend of shyness and welcome. "We've been lovers from the day we met. It's just never been consummated. I'm not afraid at all. Not if it's you." She huffed out a little breath. "You can hold me tonight, but I want to hold you. And . . . I want to make love with you." She suddenly smiled. "I never realized what a beautiful phrase that is." She gave a breathless laugh when he caught her around the waist and swung up off her feet. "Oh, wow. A romantic," she teased. "Are there romances in that Kindle of yours?"

"I live with thrills and horrors. A man needs to escape somehow. Before I ruin it by not knowing where I am, point at the bedroom." He nipped teasingly at her lower lip and enjoyed hearing her breath break. "We can try out a floor when we're in my place."

She gestured down the hall. "Rug burns."

"Only on your knees."

"That sounds intriguing." She bit back a laugh as he swung her into the bedroom. "Don't drop me on the bed! It's not very bouncy."

"Remind me to invest in a better spring mattress for home." His mouth captured hers as he lowered her down to her feet once more. The playful, lighthearted desire felt perfect for that moment. His knees went weak with delight when she teasingly took control of the kiss, her hands settling feather light on his face to tug him closer. Hunger rode hard inside his body, but he ruthlessly held onto his control. He wanted a lot more than just physical release. He eased back from the kiss and smiled. "Can I undress you?"

"I'll trade you clothing for clothing."

"That's not a fair trade when you wear a bra."

"It can count with my underwear." She ignored her trembling fingers and got to work on unbuttoning his shirt. The only nerves she had were of pure need. She still did not feel embarrassed or afraid. It was hard to feel uncertain when he looked at her with desire burning in his normally cold black eyes.

He gingerly shrugged out of the shirt, mindful of his wound, and she sighed contentedly as she studied him. "Another new understanding of a phrase for me." She lightly trailed a finger down the sculpted line of his chest. "Six pack." Tempting dark hair covered his skin, and she could see silvery white lines that marked prior wounds. An oddly shaped one along his waist implied he had, indeed, been shot before. "Fast healer?"

"Depends on the injury. Bullets are easy. Paper cuts take forever." The corner of his lips curved wickedly. "Are you going to stare, or are you going to touch?" He stopped breathing as her hands slowly slid sensually up his chest and her fingertips teased over his nipples. "I think I like a well-read woman."

"I read *everything*." Her lashes lowered as he began to unbutton her blouse. "I'm afraid you won't find anything scandalous under my clothes. Not only did I not have any means of obtaining it, but it's often hard to find in my size."

Practical white silk and cotton contentedly cupped her lush breasts, and he trailed a finger down the edge where it touched her body. A flush rose along her skin temptingly. "My blood pressure couldn't handle anything scandalous," he admitted thickly. "And don't you dare lose those pounds. Wherever they're being carried is exactly where they should be. Are you healthy?"

"Ridiculously, according to my doctor."

"Then stay just like this." He curled his hands around her waist and flexed his fingers. "More for me to hold."

Solemnly, she told him, "They say that men in their thirties like softer women. It's instinct to breed."

"I'm an early bloomer." He lifted her off her feet effortlessly and buried his face between her breasts. Her hair teased along his sensitive skin, and a coil wrapped around his wrist just tight enough to keep him from escaping. He couldn't imagine why it thought he would. He could not escape if he wanted, and he sure as hell had no desire to try. "Speaking of breeding," he muttered against her skin, "I can protect you."

"Can we try for kids later?" she asked hopefully. Her heart clenched when he looked up in surprise. He looked . . . shocked, as if he hadn't thought she would want a family with him. "You have so much love inside you, Van." She unexpectedly laughed. "But we better hope for a boy. I think you'd go to pieces over a little girl!"

"We'll bribe Tori to teach her how to defend herself." He tumbled her down onto the covers of the bed and swiftly stripped her skirt away. "Kids. Later." His mouth moved voraciously over her skin until her fingers dug into his shoulders. "It's only us right now." The mental image of her rounded with child made his hands shake with longing and delight. She would be incredibly beautiful. "Maybe tomorrow."

Her laugh turned into a moan when he tugged aside her bra and his mouth hotly captured a tight nipple. "Our deal!" she managed to gasp. She tried to catch a breath as he released her and stripped away the rest of his clothes. He took care of hers as well, and when he joined her again, naked skin pressed to naked skin. It felt incredible. He burned with a heat that melted the cold inside her heart. They weren't alone anymore.

They tumbled breathlessly over the covers, and her hair tangled around them both. Hands moved everywhere, and lips found hidden secrets. Aching, desperate, he caught her underneath his body protectively. Her arms and legs alike coiled around him, and the knots in his heart eased. When he took her, he did so slowly, savoring every perfect second. Her eyes darkened erotically and her little gasp was taken by his hungry kiss as he settled in wholly. His lips moved over her face hungrily, memorizing every beloved feature. His beautiful secret princess.

Hearts had to give way to bodies at last, and they came together again and again until ecstasy finally broke free and claimed them both. They couldn't know what would happen the next day, but both knew that if this was all they would get, then it would be enough. They were together. It was all that mattered.

Sometime around midnight, Van found himself awake and thinking about everything. He went over every scenario in his mind, and he began to finally piece together a plan. Theresa stirred beside him and sleepily cuddled closer, and his arm tightened around her. She tilted her head back and looked up at him. "You should be asleep," she murmured.

"So should you." He caught a handful of her hair and watched it slip through his fingers. "Floor length again."

"I don't mind it touching the floor. Anything else is annoying. It doesn't get heavy until it pools. I think it defies gravity." She studied his face curiously. "What are you thinking?"

"I'm thinking I might just have an idea on what to do tomorrow. Does your hair always dissolve when it gets cut?"

"Actually, no." She propped herself up on an elbow. "It just does that when I cut it too fast. If I cut it carefully, it retains its form. I used to give it to Grandmother to burn, but lately I was doing it myself." Finally, belatedly, it dawned on her. "The answer was there all along," she murmured. "I was never actually trapped. I just had to see the way out."

"Roberto alluded to it yesterday, and I admit that it had been swirling in my mind." He tugged her down for a lingering kiss, and he saw her eyes darken with the same need churning inside him. "If just a kiss is going to get us going," he said huskily, "I see a happy future together looming." He kissed her again a little deeper and savored the little sound of pleasure she made. "It's tomorrow."

"Let's wait until tonight when we're in your reputedly softer bed," she countered just as huskily. "We'll celebrate breaking out of the tower." She smoothed his hair back from his eyes. She loved the way they watched her, loved the way he never wore a mask around her. "What's the plan? I can do anything."

He outlined everything, and she drew a long breath. Risky, yes, but it had a good chance of working. She knew she could handle anything if he was there with her. It was time to break out for good.

CHAPTER TWENTY-ONE

When Theresa heard a key scraping in the lock the next day, the clock read as one in the afternoon. She didn't move from where she sat on the loveseat and attempted to braid her hair. She heard the door open and said without turning, "I don't want to talk to you."

"Well, aren't you the spunky one? You're a lot like your grandmother in her youth," a man countered merrily.

She turned around quickly and discovered that Ruby stood inside the entrance with an older man beside her. He looked roughly the same age though he did not carry it nearly as well. He smiled with friendly enough attitude, but his blue eyes looked dead. A chill raced down Theresa's back. "Who are you?" she demanded.

"My name is Orson Collins, m'dear." He walked into the condo and looked around with mild curiosity. "I'm your grandfather, though Ruby would just love to pretend I don't exist." His eyes landed on her, and something unnatural and ugly moved through his gaze. "You look like your father."

"Do I? How nice since I never knew him." She got to her feet and laced her hands together tightly. It took all of her strength to stay in one place. Her entire body had tensed against her will. She looked at Ruby and found her cowering back meekly. An ugly bruise mottled her face with dark colors. She didn't bother to ask where it had come from. "What do you want, Mr. Collins?"

The smile faded from his face. "Revenge. Get me the files on the Lucinos, Theresa."

"Seeing as my grandmother had me quit, I can't imagine how I'll be allowed to get in the building."

"You can call Antonio Lucino and tell him that there was a misunderstanding and you want your job back. You will then get me all the files like a good girl and start sabotaging their precious new system."

"No."

For just a moment, his jaw actually dropped open. "Excuse me?"

"I said no. It's a word defining a denial. As in 'I will not help you ruin the Lucinos.'"

He stared at her for a moment and then calmly drew a gun from inside his jacket. He aimed it not at her, but at Ruby who went white with terror. "Do not think I will hesitate to put a bullet in her, dear." Though friendly enough, there was a bite to the tone. "I will kill her if you do not do as I tell you."

"Feel free." She shrugged lightly. "I'd be better off without her controlling my life. In fact, I'd actually *have* a life without her. I could make my own decisions, go wherever I want. Do whatever you like, *Grandfather*. I just can't care."

"You think to call my bluff?" He clicked his tongue. "I'll raise the bet, sweetheart." He cocked the gun and calmly began to depress the trigger. "I don't need her anyway."

A gun barrel suddenly pressed against his temple. Calmly, Van said, "How about I see that bet and raise it myself, Orson?"

Orson gave a bitter cackle that seared the air. "I wondered if our paths might cross! Please, D'Angelo. You think I believe you'll prove yourself a murderer right in front of Theresa? You can't kill a man in cold blood right in front of your precious little lover!"

"As a matter of fact, I can. She knows I can kill to protect her, and she is perfectly fine with that. I'm fairly sure my reflexes are faster than yours, old man. I'll shoot you before you shoot Ruby, though I can't argue that Theresa is right about being better off without either of you."

Orson abruptly threw himself backward and removed the gun from the side of his head. He swung his own weapon around toward Van, and his finger again tightened on the trigger. He spotted movement from the corner of his eye and tried to turn around again, but he was too late. The frying pan in Theresa's hands smashed into the side of his head and something crunched audibly. He dropped like a stone to the ground.

Van stared at the scene and then at Theresa. "I can't believe you did that."

"I can't believe it worked!" she retorted shakily. "I mean, it's *Disney*. When is it ever real?" A sound had her looking down sharply, and she saw an ugly ooze seeping out of Orson's pores. She stifled a yelp as Van yanked her backward, and she nearly shrieked when her hair burst out of its braid and shot forward to consume Orson. It cocooned him entirely, and the ooze could not break through the strands.

Van moved quickly though he took the care to cut her hair slowly. The ends dropped back around her waist where they sparkled, and the rest remained trussed around Orson. He had a feeling that nothing would free the old man unless the hair wanted him to be free. At a sound, his head jerked around, and he saw Ruby had picked up the fallen gun. Her hands looked steady though her body shook. The end of the barrel aimed right for his heart.

Calmly, without fear, Theresa stepped in front of him. She said nothing. Ruby's hands began to shake wildly, and she fought to keep her aim steady. Then, finally, she dropped the gun on the ground once more. Sobs wracked her body as she fell to her knees. "I just wanted you to be safe!"

The sound of sirens ripped through the building through the open window. Van glanced outside and saw several police cars and a team of SWAT members entering the building. Hiro had impeccable timing. "Cavalry."

"Get out of here." Ruby took a steadying breath. "Both of you get out of here. Let me take whatever punishment may come." She looked at Theresa and her lips trembled. "You look like your mother, too. Have the happiness we never did."

Theresa slowly nodded and ran over to the window where Van waited. He dragged out the ladder of hair they had made the night before, and he threw it out the window to create an escape. He went down first just in case she lost her balance, but she didn't have any trouble climbing down. It was quite a descent, and both winced wryly when more than one resident inside the complex stared at them in shock as they went past windows.

When they reached the ground safely, Van quickly hacked through the bottom of the ladder. The hair swiftly dissolved into shimmering dust and faded away. He turned sharply at a footstep and pulled Theresa back safely. His shoulders only relaxed when Rhianna calmly stepped forward out of the shadows. "Rhianna."

"Let's get out of here," she countered calmly. "We can talk back at Enforcers' headquarters."

"What about Orson?" Theresa whispered.

"He will be handled by other Enforcers." She gestured toward the street where a rather non-descript sedan with tinted windows sat patiently. "I know you have many questions. Come with me, and I will give you the answers."

"All of them?" Van muttered as he urged Theresa toward the car.

Rhianna smiled. "All of them."

She rode in the front seat while Van and Theresa shared the back. Van kept Theresa's hands between his in support though he didn't say anything. His gaze stayed out the window, and the mask had settled over his face again. It didn't bother her at all. She leaned her head against his shoulder and thought of a future where maybe she could convince him to do something a little less dangerous. Maybe if she was pregnant; he would hate the idea of risking their child to losing a parent the way she had.

At Enforcers HQ, they followed Rhianna up to the top floor where her office was located. She ushered them inside and shut the door. "Have a seat." She sat down behind her desk and rummaged in a drawer. She emerged with a stack of papers and offered them to Theresa.

It felt only a little surprising to see her name at the top. "I *am* under contract," she said softly. "How is it possible? Who put me under contract? My grandmother?" She skimmed through the pages and felt her heart stop as she saw the signatures at the end. "My parents? But how?"

Rhianna linked her hands on top of the desk. "Most everything you have surmised is correct but for one thing. It wasn't Ruby Collins who came to us for your protection. It was your parents. The moment your mother realized she was pregnant—pregnant with a child who would be District born—she and your father knew that you were in danger. Orson had already made noises about his hate for your parents' union. They chose to put your safety into the hands of the Enforcers."

Van lightly rested a hand on Theresa's knee. "That's how she escaped the murder."

"The exact stipulations of the contract state that she cannot be harmed by evil if it looks her directly in the eye. She also has a very powerful gift to heal should she start seeking it. That life power directly opposes evil." Rhianna sighed. "Unfortunately, healers are not exactly *resilient*. We decided to take things a step further and give her hair sentient will."

"My hair really is alive?!"

"It is both a weapon and a tool." She smiled. "Once your contract completes, it will bend to your will. You will be able to use it the way you use your hands and feet. It will grow perfectly normally unless you want it to grow more or less. Until now, it has responded purely to even your subconscious needs."

"That is daunting and yet reassuring." Theresa took a long breath and tossed the contract onto the desk. "And I think that about sums up this entire situation. I feel . . . odd. It seems so strange that I'm free now. Yet, I always could have been free if I'd just tried." She looked at Van and smiled. "I guess I just needed someone to open the window of my tower." She glanced back to Rhianna. "You said my contract isn't complete yet. What do I need to do?"

"Van knows. He is quite familiar with Enforcer contracts."

He did, and he was. "On that note, we'll take our leave." He tugged Theresa to her feet and kept her tucked safely against his side as they walked out of the office. Neither said anything as they took the elevator downstairs. His car sat outside at the curb, and it didn't surprise them at all. He opened the door and sighed. "Well."

"Yeah." She blew out a breath that turned into a smile. "Can I go home with you? Also, I need to call Antonio and Rafael and ask if I can have my job back. I suppose they will be disappointed to lose you as a guard." She tilted her head. "Will we have to travel, or can you work here?"

He lightly cupped her cheek. "I've decided to retire." His eyes softened when hers widened. "I've decided that I'm going to ask Antonio if I can stay on as a guard. Steadier pay, safer lifestyle, and a new type of job security. Of course, I'll still need to do some outside work if needed. Rhianna and Eric have repeatedly said they want to more formally keep me as a consultant, and I'd rather deal with them than the police." He winced wryly. "We'll gloss over the fact that I think that was their intent the entire time they planned to set me up with you."

"I'm not going to lie," she admitted softly, "that I had hoped you would pick a safer job. I just found you, and I don't want to lose you. If you were a normal cop, I could handle it. It's a lot harder to love a gunslinger, though."

"Gunslinger." He contemplated that. "I think that is officially the nicest thing I've been called."

"It's much more accurate," she corrected gently. She smiled. "Home?"

"First things first." He pulled a small gift out of the car and offered it. "Happy belated. I, ah, sort of picked it up for you after we met. Been holding it until now."

She tore off the paper and started laughing when she discovered herself holding a brand new Kindle. "Library on the go! Did you pre-load it with anything for me?" she teased. "You know me and technology."

"Turn it on and see it for yourself."

She pushed the button at the bottom and waited. The screen obediently lit up and went to the main menu. Her breath caught in her lungs and delight slowly spread through her heart as she saw the title of the only loaded book. *'Will you marry me?' By Van D'Angelo* She dropped the Kindle and leapt into his arms on a cry of joy. "Absolutely I will!" She held on with all her strength as he lifted her off her feet, and her hair immediately reached out to hold him as well. She kissed him with all the love in her heart, and she felt a strange heat run through her hair. It dropped free and fell into place, and she eased back in surprise. "What happened?"

He smiled and tugged her in for another kiss. "An Enforcers' contract," he murmured huskily against her lips, "is only complete when the subject's dreams come true."

"Oh." She tilted her head slightly and began to smile. Her hair lifted and tugged him closer. "Well, in that case, let's start our happy ending. Take me home, Van. We're both free of our towers now."

"How do you feel about trading a tower for a cruise ship?"

"I've always wanted to go on one," she admitted. "Why do you ask?"

He just smiled. "No reason."

EPILOGUE

Rhianna had just poured herself a cup of coffee when she saw a glow from the contract. She walked over to look at it, and smiled as she saw 'Complete' appear in red. She added her notes to the bottom and slipped it into a folder that also marked as completed. She placed it inside the Lucino drawer, closed it, and locked it tight. The word 'Finished' appeared across the front and she sat back with a sigh. Another job well done despite the difficulties.

Eric walked into her office unannounced and said without preamble, "Collins has been judged and punished. The evil inside him no longer exists. Ruby Collins has entered into a women's shelter in hopes of taking back what remaining life she will live. Seems everything is taken care of now."

"I'm glad for her. She was a pawn as well."

He studied her for long moments. More than ever, he could feel there was something she had not told him. The stirring evil that encroached more and more lately was driving her further and further away from him. "Rhi." He knelt beside her chair. "You know I love you more than anyone except Rayna. Let me help you."

She tenderly touched his cheek. "I love you, Riku, but there is nothing you can do. Just let me be alone for a while. This was harder than usual; I still feel guilty over what Tori endured."

He slowly got to his feet. "Talk to me when you can." He went into his office and shut the door quietly behind him.

She closed her eyes for long moments and then slowly opened one of the desk drawers she rarely ever accessed. Inside, sitting on a broken box, was an ancient scroll. She carefully pulled it out, treating it gingerly because of reverence and not fear for damage. It had endured for thousands of years. It would endure for thousands more.

The Ancient Greek language of the contract resembled Modern Greek in many ways but could still even confuse scholars. She read it clearly. Every word had been engraved inside her soul. Perhaps it was for that reason that the glaring red VOID across the front in English seemed harsh and cruel. She trailed a finger across the word and her lips trembled. "Eros." On a broken sound of pain, she buried her face in her arms.

When would she ever heal?

♀ ♀ ♀

Status: File Complete

Analysis: There is no tower you cannot escape from if you are willing to take a risk and cut away the invisible chains of the past. Sometimes it just takes a loving hand to open a window so you can see the answer.

Just what has been happening in Mirage while evil churns outside the District? Only one person really knows, and he has his own secrets and story to be told . . .

Bonus Folder

DAMIAN

CHAPTER ONE

Some things happened in yearly cycles on Mirage. Seasons were one. Rites of passage for princes were another. Cursed kingdoms were a third. Damian Lucksworth, prince of the Luckdom Kingdom, heard about the latest cycle while he was voluntarily mucking a stable. The stable master happened to be outside talking to a milkmaid, and the latter said, "Sounds like trouble in the northern kingdom."

The master sighed. "What else is new? And here I thought that the north would be having less trouble now that the one king returned from hiatus with a bride. What's his name? Nikolas something? Can't he help?"

"Nah, he's got his hands full already with a newborn daughter." She gestured lightly. "Anyway, the king whose kingdom just got cursed managed to get to safety. His daughter is trapped in a tower, though."

"Always with the towers."

"Why change tradition? He's calling for able-bodied princes to come try to break the curse and rescue his daughter. Whoever can do it can marry said princess and also have a chunk of the kingdom." She giggled. "I guess we don't need to worry about Prince Damian going. He's not exactly 'able-bodied' when it comes to princely duties!"

"I heard that!" Damian called. "Don't make me feed your cows herbs that'll turn them pink again!"

"Don't you dare!" she scolded. "I still haven't lived the last time down." She walked into the stables and hopped up to sit on the side of the stall. "Besides, you can't be mad at me when I'm telling the truth. We all love you, Prince Damian, but you're just not the normal princely type!"

He couldn't argue with her on that point. At twenty, he should have rescued at least *one* damsel in distress, but he just didn't really feel the need. He hated giving orders to people, even servants, and truthfully he often forgot he *had* servants—the servants, of course, loved him all the more because of it.

He couldn't ride horseback very well, but he was excellent at caring for them and raising them. He *enjoyed* working in the stables. He sucked with using a sword in combat, but he was really good with the more 'feminine' long bow. Every princess he had ever met had become one of his friends; he might make a superficial attempt at courting, but it always took less than three days to turn into friendship. To say he was vexing his parents would be to put it mildly.

As if she was following his thoughts, the milkmaid said, "Everybody's brother." She sighed gustily. "Damian, you're breaking hearts."

He grinned up at her. "I am not. You know that the princesses I know are very happy to have a male friend that they don't need to fear having designs on them or their kingdom." He hopped nimbly over the wall between stalls. "Maybe I got my prince genes crossed with a princess somewhere. I would be completely happy to have a woman sweep me off my feet and rescue me. Maybe there's a princess out there who doesn't want to be rescued."

"You're looking for love at first sight."

"Aren't we all?"

She couldn't argue with that either. "I just worry that you sitting around at home means you might miss out on something amazing." She got to her feet and winced as she heard a bellow from the direction of the castle. "The king calls for you."

"No, he *yells* for me." He sighed and put up the rake. "I guess I had best change clothes. Last time I tracked manure into the throne room, Mother almost had a heart attack. If you don't see me again, find someone to rescue me from the dungeon."

"No tower?"

"Nah, that's for women. Men get the dungeon treatment. Which is a pity since towers have a *view*." He crept around the back of the palace and quickly snuck inside and up toward his chambers. He wasted no time in stripping, bathing, and quickly putting on more acceptable clothing. Another bellow echoed, and he grimaced as he went downstairs toward the throne room. "Protect me," he muttered at a lady-in-waiting as he went past. She giggled at him, and he sighed. He opened the doors to the throne room and walked inside. "You yelled?" he asked dryly.

Predictably, his parents sat on their thrones at the other end of the room. They wore their full, heavy-duty, formal crowns. And not for the first time, he wondered why neither had neck problems from the weight. They also wore their formal robes and clothing, and he felt underdressed even in velvet. Why didn't they smother in those hundreds of layers?

"Damian." His father's brows pulled together. "What's that smell?" He groaned. "Damn it, boy, were you out doing peasant work again?"

"I, er, accidentally broke a valuable vase and that was my chosen punishment." He crossed his fingers behind his back. Really, it was always easier to make it sound like he had gotten in trouble rather than explain that he liked manual labor.

"Again with the vases. You are so clumsy," his mother scolded. She sighed. "Son, we love you dearly, but you're not living up to your potential."

"My potential, or the potential that you expect of me?"

"Don't sass me, young man!" She aimed a finger at him. "You need to get out into the world and start acting like the prince you are! You need to make a man of yourself, Damian. Go rescue a princess, slay a dragon, or *something*."

Because, of course, being a man meant being a chauvinistic jerk. He refrained from rolling his eyes. Surely princesses were getting tired of always being rescued, and he couldn't imagine the dragons were entirely sunshine and lollipops over the whole slaying thing. "Are those my only options?"

His father beetled his brows. "We are getting tired of things, Damian. You just don't take your duty seriously!" He threw a scroll at his son and it bounced off his head. "You will depart at once for the Karmic Kingdom and get rid of the curse to rescue the princess! You cannot come back unless you come back with a bride!"

Damian rubbed his head where the scroll had hit. "Seriously?"

"Very seriously!"

He stared at his parents and then picked up the scroll to look at it. It was a map of where he needed to go. The journey seemed more annoying than long. He scowled and stalked out of the throne room. "If I have kids," he muttered, "they'll get to decide for themselves how to live their lives!"

In the very center of Mirage, not far from where the River Styx attached the world to the one known as Earth, was a place of concentrated magic and beauty known as the Faerie Realm. As the name implied, it was from within this forested land that Good Faeries came forth to aid heroes on their journeys. Good Faeries had to be trained in the ways of magic and conjuration before they could be assigned, and graduating school could be a trial all by itself. Some who graduated didn't become official Good Faeries for many further years if their grades hadn't been good enough.

Unfortunately for the Realm, the latest curse and the promise of land along with the princess had brought princes and heroes out of the woodwork. Even recent graduates were being assigned to go help these able-bodied people. Faeries who returned after completing one job would be immediately sent right back out.

Elder Thom found himself in a bit of a pickle when the magic cup suddenly spit out a rune stone with a new name on it. "Damian Lucksworth." He winced. "Bad enough that we're out of faeries, but that kid doesn't know anything about what he has to do!" He drummed his fingers on his desk for a moment. With a sigh, he got to his feet. He had no choice. He had to grab Teydra. "Teydra!" he bellowed as he walked out of the consulate and crossed toward the magic streams that surrounded the Realm.

The lovely faerie lounging along the side of the stream winced and ducked down behind the spell book she held. Her shimmering cream-colored hair turned a deep pink color that matched what climbed her neck and cheeks. She peered up at Thom and tried to look innocent. "I didn't do it?"

He sighed in exasperation. It was impossible to be annoyed with Teydra. She was beautiful and charming and sweet. She was also the worst student of her graduating class, and no matter how hard she tried, she always managed to screw up even the most basic of spells.

The entire Realm loved her, but they just couldn't figure her out. She had one of the most potent gifts of all Good Faeries—they called it Mood Magic—yet she had no control over it. It manifested in the changing of her hair color to show her moods (which showed on her face anyway), and if she ever learned how to use it right, it would make her the most sought after Good Faerie on Mirage.

"Get up, girl." He offered a hand and tugged her up to her feet. Most faeries were small, but Teydra stood at an unusually taller height of five-seven that had her towering over most of her race. Save the delicacy of her frame and the glowing cerulean colored wings on her back, she could have passed for human. "What are you doing out here?"

"Studying," she admitted. "I figure if I focus on one spell hard enough, I have to eventually get it right."

"Which spell?" he asked warily.

"Summoning an enchanted sword. I figure screwing it up won't, you know, flood or burn down the Realm."

He couldn't hide his relief. "Thank you for the consideration. Now come along with me." He linked his hands behind his back as she walked beside him. "You know we're short-staffed right now."

"Yeah. It's the rescuing princesses equivalent of harvest season." She cocked her head, and one pointed ear tilted at an angle. Her long lineage was evidenced by the length and delicacy of her ears. "Do you need me to watch the Pot while you go out yourself?" It wouldn't be the first time.

"Actually, no." He handed her the stone. "You're going on a mission."

"What!" Her hair went bright red. "I can't even cast a fireball!" she yelped. "You told me I was the worst Good Faerie graduate of all time!"

"You are. But luckily for you, your charge is possibly the worst prince of all time. Perhaps your mutual ineptitude will result in some success!" He flicked a hand and a swirl of magic popped into appearance over her head. "Off with you, Teydra! You know the rules; you can't come back until he reaches the final leg of his journey."

"I'll get him killed!" she wailed, but it was too late. The magic had already sucked her up, and her lack of skill meant that she could not cast a locator to cushion the landing. She was in so much trouble!

She wasn't the only one in trouble. Damian had managed to make it a few miles away from his kingdom before he got beset by the first of what he knew would be many issues. In this case, it was a small horde of ugly demons. The natural antithesis to faeries, demons existed to *stop* heroes. Maybe it was a good sign; if they were attacking, he must have been doing something right.

He took care of the first demon relatively easily with his sword, but the other two were far bigger and far more powerful. His relatively amateurish use of the weapon could be easily countered, and one of the demons thunked him in the stomach hard enough to knock him onto his ass in the dirt.

He scrambled back up to his feet just as a strange shimmering magic appeared in the air. He and the demons looked up at the same time, and he stifled a yelp as a young woman unexpectedly flew out of the magic with a yelp of her own. She landed on his back and he once more found himself eating the dirt, though this time literally. He craned his neck enough to look back at her, and relief filled him. She had wings! "Are you a Good Faerie?"

Teydra shook her head hard to clear the spinning stars. "Uhm, yes."

"Great! Shoot the bad guys."

She blinked and focused. Her hair swiftly turned bright blue in alarm. "Uh-oh!" She grabbed her spell book out of midair and began quickly flipping pages. "It's in here somewhere! Why can't I *find* it?!"

He dropped his forehead on the ground in understanding. "Oh, god," he groaned. "They gave me the *apprentice!*" He looked up hastily when he heard movement. The demons were closing in. "Let me up!"

She scrambled off his back and fell into a flower bush. She turned pages as fast as she could in her book. "Fangs, Fauns, Figs—ah! Fireball!" She swallowed a yelp as a huge ball of fire shot from her hands. "Get down!"

He threw himself to the side and watched wide-eyed as the fireball swallowed a demon. "Okay, that could have hurt." He swung his sword at the other demon, and the blade bounced off its head. It glared at him indignantly, and he back-stepped quickly. "Anything in there for making my sword pierce armor?"

"Uhm." She flipped through the chapters. "Swords. Where are the swords?" She found a spell and aimed a hand at him. "Points right and left and up and down; make the blade sharp enough to pierce through sound!"

The sword in his hand got sharper all right. It also got bigger. It instantly multiplied in size and became so heavy that he lost his grip. The hilt hit the ground with a thud that shook the area, and the weapon wobbled precariously. He dove out of the way as the blade finally crashed over and landed on the demon. It squished flat and spewed bits of debris in all directions. He winced and swiped at the muck now on his pants. "Ugh. And I thought manure smelled!"

Teydra blew her hair out of her eyes and fell over on her back. "Darn it, Elder Thom!" A shadow moved over her face, and she opened her eyes to see Damian looking down at her. Her breath caught in her chest as she stared up at him. For just a moment, it seemed as all sound went away around her. She could see nothing except him in her sight. His shaggy green hair reminded her of her favorite meadows.

Prince, her mind reminded her pointedly. He was a *prince*. It was completely against the rules for her to be attracted to him, but, dang it, it wasn't *her* fault that he was gorgeous! Belatedly remembering her hair, she grabbed a handful and looked at it. Sure enough, it had turned purple. Not. A. Good. SIGN.

Damian had no idea why her hair kept changing color, but it fascinated him. Her cream hued eyes changed color, too. Magic rippled over her skin and lay across her cheekbones in a blend of glitter and sparkles. He had for some reason expected faeries to be fair, but she had a beautiful light chocolate color to her skin. She looked impossibly delicate, yet when he helped tug her to her feet, he discovered she stood only half a foot shorter. "I always thought faeries were smaller."

"I'm kind of tall, yes," she admitted. She rubbed the back of her neck and looked up at him shyly. "I'm Teydra. And I'm a Good Faerie but I'm kind of not officially one. I almost flunked school."

He winced. "It figures. Look, I appreciate the help, but I think I'd better handle this alone." He started to turn away and she grabbed his arm. Startled, he looked down at her. She was stronger than she looked, and she radiated a surprising heat that felt deeply alluring. He skimmed his eyes over her again, this time more wistfully. Too bad she wasn't a princess. He liked her one hell of a lot more than he had liked anyone else.

"I can't go home until I get you to your goal," she pleaded with him. "I always mess up, and Elder Thom wouldn't have sent me if he had a choice! I need to do this to prove I can be useful! I try so hard, but I always mess up! I just don't know how to be a Good Faerie, I guess. Damian, please let me help you!"

An odd sense of kinship moved through him. He knew painfully well how it felt to not fit into the expectations of other people. Maybe they weren't a bad pair; maybe they were a perfect one. And, well, it wouldn't be hardship to let her stay at his side. He totally didn't object to the very real possibility that his attraction to her might turn into love. Everything else smacked of love at first sight; it was Mirage, after all. That kind of stuff always happened. "Okay," he conceded. "You can go with me." He offered a hand. "Damian Lucksworth, prince of the Luckdom Kingdom, and heir apparent should I actually 'make a man of myself.'"

Her smile lit the area around them as she put her hand in his. "Teydra, sucky Good Faerie-in-training who can't memorize spells but can read *really* fast." Her eyes widened and she caught a breath as he brought her hand to his lips. A mottled purple and pink color swept through her hair. "I dunno, Damian. You have the princely arts down so far."

"Handshakes just don't cut it with most women; some things you learn by sheer self-defense." He walked over to his fallen sword and winced. "Dare I ask you to try to shrink it again?"

"Probably not. But canceling a spell is super easy. Even I can do that." She knelt and tapped on the sword and it glowed brightly before going back to normal. "See?" She scooped it up and offered it to him. She saw his wide-eyed look and bit back a giggle. "Magic," she told him solemnly. "I could probably lift you off the ground."

"I think I like you," he decided with a grin. He sheathed the sword again and offered her the map. "Can you read maps better than you do spell books?"

"Sure!" She opened the scroll. "Okay, I know where we're going. Follow me."

He eyed her legs and hips wistfully as he trailed behind her. He didn't object to following her anywhere. The back view was as spectacular as the front. More, actually. Her beautifully glowing wings made his fingers itch to touch.

He sighed with more exasperation than annoyance. A faerie. It just figured, didn't it, that he *still* couldn't get anything right.

CHAPTER TWO

As they walked together down the road, Damian studied his new partner curiously. Not that he knew everything about faeries in general, but he had always held a lot of beliefs that suddenly seemed wrong. "Hey, can I ask some questions?"

Teydra smiled at him. "Of course. I'll answer if I can. We don't have any secrets or stuff. I mean, even if I told you about our magic, you'd never be able to cast it. I'm not saying humans can't do it, but the elders always said it would require something dramatic for a human to cast faerie magic without having any faerie blood. I don't even know what it is."

"That's fair. How come you're this big? I don't mean your height, though. I thought faeries were much smaller."

Her hair and eyes turned a mischievous yellow color. "Like this?" Sparkles swirled around her, and she was suddenly only a foot tall. "Tada!" She flew around his head and landed light as a feather on his shoulder.

"That would be a useful skill!" he admitted wistfully. "Which is real?"

"Technically both." She sat down and braced her hands around her hips. "The big size is called our Monarch form. This size is called our Pixie form. We can use and control both from roughly about the same time that we learn to walk and fly. We're like humans in some ways, but we grow much slower."

"Let me guess. You don't walk or fly until you're five?"

"Thereabouts, yep. We grow one year for every five of yours, give or take a few." She grinned when his head swung around quickly, and she gave him a smacking kiss on his nose. "I'm technically eighty years older than you physically, but emotionally and mentally, we're the same age."

"How long do you live?" he demanded. The average for humans ranged between eighty and ninety years.

"Rarely more than five hundred, but if the magic is strong, it can be longer. We can also opt to grow older faster if we want to live among humans. Magic is awesome." She flew off his shoulder and the swirl of sparkles returned her to full size. She linked her hands behind her back as she fell once more into step beside him. Her hair shimmered and turned back to normal. "Of course, the person who sucks at magic would think so. I hope I can keep liking it even though I have trouble casting it."

"I still like women even though I'm being all but forced to marry," he offered helpfully.

She giggled. "Fair enough! Why are you, anyway?"

"Will you buy that I'm a hopeless romantic?"

"Aren't we *all* hopeless romantics at heart?"

"You haven't met my parents. I think they were in love when they got married, but their determination to foist me off on the first available princess makes me wonder." He winced wryly. "At this point, they might even be willing to settle for me marrying a servant so long as I *did* marry. I never seem to do anything right either, Teydra."

Her cream eyes darkened to gray in empathy. "The shoes they want you to wear are so small that they pinch your feet and give you no room to grow, and try as you might to walk in them, you just split the sides and end up worse than you started?"

His heart clenched in a combination of complex emotions that he couldn't wholly decipher. "Yeah," he said softly. He couldn't resist skimming his thumb across the shimmer of her cheeks. "Your shoes don't fit either, right?"

"Never have. I'm supposed to be really powerful, and I have a unique gift, but I just . . . am no good at things."

"Which gift?"

"My hair."

"The color thing? I was wondering why it did that."

A hint of pink climbed the stands. "It changes with my moods. I could be the greatest actress on Mirage—and I'm not—and my hair would give me away every time. Before you ask, yes, I know what most of the colors stand for. I even know what my gift could turn into, should I ever figure out how to control it."

He could make some guesses of his own based on their short acquaintance. The pink had to be embarrassment, and he thought the red might be shame or anger depending on the intensity. The yellow had to be playful. The purple, though, he had no idea yet. It seemed to crop up every time she looked at him for too long. It also turned gold now and then, too. "What can it become?"

"Mood influencing abilities. Like . . . I could make someone be not mad if they were really angry type stuff."

Wistfully, he asked, "Can I sneak you home in my pocket to keep my parents off my case?"

She grinned. "Only if you promise to feed me and not put me into a jar or something."

"And you'd look so cute on my dresser!" He grinned back and enjoyed watching her hair turn yellow with her lighthearted mood. A tempting thought curled through his mind before he could stop it: what color would her hair turn if he kissed her? Before he could stop himself, he reached out and tucked her hair behind her ear. Her eyes shot to his, and the silken strands turned a deep hue of purple laced with stripes of gold. His body clenched with greedy desire as he saw the look in her violet eyes and understood. Purple meant *passion*. "You're going to be trouble for me," he said softly, huskily, "aren't you?"

She took a breath that turned into a startled yelp as four bandits came lunging out of the shrubbery along the side of the road. Her eyes widened as Damian protectively yanked her closer, and her hair turned a wild combination of colors as it tried to keep up with her tumultuous emotions.

The leader of the bandits sneered at Damian. "Looks like we found ourselves another prince on his way to be a hero! It's like harvest season for us, too! Hand over your valuables, and you can be on your way."

"I'm not carrying any valuables," Damian told him in exasperation. "I only have money for food, sorry." Under his breath, he asked Teydra, "Can you turn my sword into a bow? I'm much better with one!"

"I can try," she whispered back. She took a deep breath, looked over the bandits' heads, and blurted, "Dragon!"

They whipped around instinctively, and Damian hastily shoved her to the side so he could draw his sword. He knocked one of the enemies down before the other three could turn, but things quickly turned bloody since they knew more about what they did. Teydra grabbed her spell book and flew through the pages as fast as she could. "Please work!" she blurted as she threw magic at the sword.

The blade turned into a handful of flowers. Damian couldn't pull the strike in time, and the blooms smacked a shocked bandit in the face. Angry red hives rose on his skin and he started sneezing violently. Damian blinked, realized the problem, and shoved the flowers more firmly in his face. The bandit reeled back only to trip over his own feet and face plant on the ground. "Bow!" Damian begged Teydra as he scrambled out of the way of the other two enemies.

"Oooh! Darn it!" She threw the book down and started grabbing whatever magic she could muster. "Eat a fireball, jerks!" Flames sparked along her skin and rippled down into her hands where it began to pool. The force grew hotter and hotter and bigger and bigger, and it began to drive her backwards through the dirt.

Damian quickly grabbed her around the waist to brace her, and he watched wide-eyed as the fireball grew bigger than both of them. The bandits belatedly realized they were up against something potentially painful and grabbed their fallen partners to run away. They only made it a few feet before Teydra loosed the fireball. It hit the four bandits with such force that they were sent sailing into the sky and off into the distance. Unfortunately, it had the reciprocal effect of sending her and Damian flying backwards into the bushes.

He landed first and grunted when she landed on top of him. He heard a cracking sound and opened his eyes to see broken branches about to fall. He hastily grabbed his faerie and rolled with her out of the way. The branches smashed into the ground where they had been, and dust billowed in the air. Eerie quiet finally descended.

He carefully lifted himself onto his elbows and winced as his wounds protested. He had more than a few slices from that fight. "Teydra?" He smoothed her hair out of her face, and she opened her eyes. Relief almost made him lightheaded. "Thank goodness. Are you okay?"

"Sore." She grimaced. "Very sore. And I burned my hands." She held them where he could see the ugly blisters forming across her palms. "I can heal it. One of the few spells I'm any good at is a healing one." She tried to smile. "Lucky for you." She sighed and closed her eyes again. "Goofed again. Almost killed you, too."

"You did not! Hey." He tugged a lock of her pink hair until she opened her eyes again. "You cast the fireball just fine. It was just too big. And, well, that sword had more use as a handful of posies than as itself. I can buy a bow in the next town, okay? I'm just glad we're both alive."

"People have wondered how I made it to my age," she admitted.

"Hey, I've been accused of deliberately trying to kill myself because I have no sense of self-preservation. We're even." The smile slowly faded as he stared down at her. His pulse began to pound hard and fast, an ache settling deep inside with the need to touch and caress the woman in his arms. She smelled like magic, and her lips tempted him to find out if she tasted the same. Her eyes widened suddenly and a combination of purple and pink swept through her hair. He coughed to hide a laugh. "Not that you didn't just notice, but I feel compelled to at least say out loud that, yes, I want you very badly."

"Believe me," she muttered a bit breathlessly, "I noticed!" It wouldn't have been so bad if she hadn't wanted him in return! He felt as good as he looked, and he gave off a wonderful body heat that made it darned tempting to just snuggle in and hold on. Also, if he didn't stop looking at her like that, she was going to kiss him and that would be a *really* bad idea.

His lips skimmed delicately over her forehead. "I'm beginning to read your moods," he murmured huskily. "Is the purple what I think it is?"

"Probably." She quickly pressed her fingers to his lips when his black eyes lit with greedy desire. "Okay, yes, I want you like the Styx on fire, but it's *not* an okay thing, Damian! I'm a Good Faerie-ish and you're a prince!"

"Ish."

"We're not compatible!"

"Evidence points to the contrary, Teydra." He skimmed his fingers down her arm and watched a trail of goosebumps follow behind on a delicate shiver. More purple than pink colored her hair, and the gold had come out again. "We seem very compatible. Faeries are mammals, right?"

"Well, yes, but," her breath hitched as he pressed his lips to her neck, "but that doesn't change that we're not *socially* compatible!" Her eyes went dark with distress as he lifted his head. "We need to ignore this and keep going as we are. We both have a duty to fill."

He stared at her for long moments before reluctantly releasing her and rolling to his feet. He reached down to lift her up as well and winced. "Okay. We'll pretend that nothing has changed. Let's get rid of our injuries and get back on track."

It didn't take long for her to remove the worst of the wounds on them both, and they were both very careful to keep their conversation light. Things felt a little strained initially, but eventually they fell back into easy companionship. Unfortunately for Damian, though, he got his first true test of self-control with the way her hair would turn purple and gold every time she looked at him. He still didn't know what the gold meant, and he had a feeling it might be a good thing. It was difficult enough knowing that she wanted him as badly as he wanted her!

For her part, Teydra couldn't put her finger on the color's origins either. She remembered it being important, yet she could not seem to bring up what her studies had mentioned about it. Her hair had never started turning that color until meeting Damian. What did it mean?

Perhaps miraculously, they made it the rest of the way to the city without any mishaps. It had started to become evening from afternoon, and there was still time to ask around about things. Merchants always had the latest gossip, and Damian stopped at one of the carts. "Hey, the Karmic Kingdom is cursed, right?"

"Yep. Been lots of princes and heroes through here lately." She eyed him. "You don't look like one of them."

Teydra bit her lip to hide a giggle, and he sighed. "So I've been told. What's the word on things?"

"Last I heard, it had to do with ogres or something. I think someone said the king had betrayed them in some sort of weird alliance thing."

"Ugh. Ogres. Great. They're big *and* smelly. Thanks for the information." He eyed Teydra as she turned into Pixie form and trailed along at his shoulder. "Are you trying to make me look more convincing?"

"Yup. Amazing what having a Good Faerie, even a bad one, can do for a prince's image." She landed lightly on his shoulder and poked his temple. "Ogres are better than demons, you know. They're big, but they're dumb. You'll have plenty of time to shoot them at a distance. And, really, if you beat them, then it won't matter what weapon you used, right?"

"I suppose that's true. Let's see what else people have to say."

The stories varied, of course, but the general consensus was that ogres were definitely involved. The reasons why were where people disagreed, and they ran the gamut from alliances to hunting to just random havoc. The only thing that bugged Teydra and Damian alike was that curses weren't normally an ogre's style. They tended to be more the style of wicked wizards, rogue faeries, and stuff like that. The other thing bothering them was the quantity of princes who had tried and yet apparently failed. Why hadn't they started home if they couldn't break the curse?

The Karmic Kingdom sat not far from their current destination, with only another city between where they were and where they needed to be. "Let's stay the night here," Damian offered. "We could both use the rest, and I'm not keen on camping when I seem to have an 'Accost Me' sign around my neck."

She wouldn't have minded accosting him herself, but for entirely different reasons. Even grubby and messy, he looked ridiculously gorgeous. "Fair enough. I'm hungry anyway. Casting magic can burn a lot of energy."

They got rooms at the inn and went to the dining room for dinner. He watched in bemusement as she piled her plate higher than his; apparently, she hadn't been kidding about burning energy. "So tell me about Good Faerie school," he offered as he dug into his food.

"We learn conjuration, casting, and the rules and regulations of being essentially bodyguards for people. Mostly princes and heroes, but we've been assigned to the occasional princess or bard. Depends on what they're doing and where they're doing it." She munched on a vegetable. "Once we graduate, the length of time to assignment depends on how well we did in school. A perfect student might immediately get sent out. Others like me have to wait a while."

"How old are you when you graduate?"

"Roughly eighty or so. Sixteen by your standards."

"You feel time passing the same as we do, right?"

Her gaze lowered and a hint of pink climbed her hair. "Yes."

He very badly wanted to grab her up and cuddle her tightly. She had been on standby for as long as he had been alive. No wonder she didn't have any confidence! They had never given her a chance to prove herself. "What does an unassigned faerie do?"

"Study. Tend stuff. Watch over the Magic Pot that gives assignments when there's no one else around. It's not really that bad. I've learned some different things that others don't. I'm a great cook, for example. And I play a lot of instruments. I even know how to sew really nice things. Oh! I *did* get to help out another Good Faerie," she offered. "She had to give a princess some dresses that could fit inside a walnut but become full-sized when extracted. I got to make them. I must say they were *exquisite*. When she won her prince, I made her wedding gown, too."

"Delivered in a walnut?"

"Actually, we used a normal box for that one." She grinned. "I've always thought that if I completely flunked out on being a Good Faerie that I could just set myself up as a seamstress and help out princesses in a different way entirely."

He grinned back. "Come work in my kingdom. The upper class will keep you plenty busy."

She fluttered her lashes. "I'll make a wedding dress for that bride you need to find." The reminder of why they had met immediately brought her mood back down, and she pushed her plate away. "Well."

The reminder was even less pleasant for him. He didn't think any princess would ever make him as happy as he felt when he was near his beautiful faerie. He was falling more and more in love with every passing moment, and he knew it. Some things you just couldn't mistake.

They were contemplating dessert when a traveling merchant came up to their table. "You're a prince, right?" he asked.

"I am." Damian frowned. "Is something wrong?"

"That depends on your definition of wrong. I just thought I ought to warn you if you're on your way to the kingdom. Most of the princes who have tried to get past the ogres have gotten eaten."

Teydra's eyes widened. "*Eaten*?"

"Eaten. I know, it's unusual. Just thought I should give you a heads up." He tipped his hat. "Good luck, Your Highness."

Damian looked at Teydra. "Well."

She slowly shook her head. "I don't like the sound of that, Damian. I mean, one or two princes are usually lost to every curse, but never that many! I don't think you should keep going on. You're not really good in combat, you know?"

"I know, but it's too late for me to go back. I have to keep moving forward."

Distress began to turn her hair a pale bluish-gray color. "There are other ways of proving yourself a man. You could go slay a dragon or save another kingdom where there aren't any ogres. What about going to sea?"

He sat back and lifted a brow. "Aren't Good Faeries supposed to keep their assignments on track? If I divert, you won't get to go home either, right? Why is this bothering you so much, Teydra? You can't be that worried about the ogres. Like you said, I have an advantage with a bow. Where's this fear coming from?"

"I don't know." She shook her head a little. "Logically, I completely believe you can succeed where others didn't. I can't figure out why that suddenly bothers me." His hand lightly covered hers, and she looked up quickly to find his black eyes watching her warmly. Something tender moved through his gaze. The sudden vision of him smiling at anyone else like that had her hair turning bright green with ripe jealousy. She didn't want him to go because he would win, and if he won, he would get the princess as his bride. She would have to hand him over to another woman. Sudden misery and mingled grief turned her hair black.

He didn't know what was going through her head, but he had watched the cacophony of color changes through her hair. "Teydra." He brought her hand to his cheek. "Calm down. Everything will be okay. Hey. Look at me." He lifted her chin until her eyes met his. "I know you can do anything. We'll get there together, and you'll be what makes me into a real hero. I think you're amazing."

The black melted away into gold once more as she looked at him longingly. No one had ever believed in her before. It didn't seem fair that all of this was happening. By Eros, how was any of this fair?

Her heart gave a wild lurch. Eros. The God of Love. His token color was gold. If her hair turned gold whenever she looked at Damian . . .

She shot to her feet and almost knocked over her chair. "I need to go out!" she blurted. "I'll see you later!" Without waiting for an agreement, she flew as fast as she could out of the inn. She needed to get away from him, get somewhere she could think and breathe! She didn't want to be in love with him. An attraction was okay. She could handle that. Loving him would destroy her when she couldn't keep him!

Damian very nearly went after her but forced himself to let her go. He had entirely lost what remained of his appetite, and he retired to his room for the night. He stayed up a while to read a book, and each time he heard a noise, he would listen intently to see if it was Teydra coming back. None of the noise ever came from the room beside his.

He didn't sleep at all that night. Sleeping had always been difficult enough for him without being in a foreign location. If it wasn't insomnia, it was nightmares. He hated the dark. Or rather, he hated the things that hid in the dark. He just couldn't sleep when there was absolute darkness. He kept a small lamp on his bedside at home, and even that didn't wholly help.

By the time dawn arrived, he had gotten an hour of sleep at most. Frustrated and concerned, he got dressed and went next door to scold Teydra about worrying him. The worry only compounded when he discovered her room was still empty and looked entirely untouched. Where *was* she?

He paid for both rooms and rushed out of the town. Luckily for him, she had been fleeing in her Pixie form, and she left a trail of glitter in her wake from her wings. He could just barely see it lingering in the air. His stomach churned the further he got from the city. She had gone a long way. The trail veered off the road into the thick forests, and he glanced up at the cloudy skies. They would have to move fast to get to the next town before the storm arrived. Damn it, what was wrong with her?

He unexpectedly found her sitting in the middle of a patch of flowers, and she was in her larger Monarch form. She had her face buried in her knees, and her wings drooped from her back. Painful blackness clung to her hair, and it seemed to have lost its shine. Relief at seeing her unharmed mingled with his frustration at being left behind, and he almost shouted, "Teydra!"

She stifled a yelp as she swung around. "Don't scare me!" she snapped at him.

He yanked her up off her feet and gave her a shake. "You scared *me*!" he retorted hotly. "What's wrong with you, running off like that? Were you out here all night? You could have been attacked by bandits or something!" He gave her another little shake. "Just tell me what's wrong and I'll help, okay?"

"You're what's wrong!" she shouted at him. She shoved at his shoulders but he was much bigger and stronger. Her wings fluttered madly as she fought to free herself. "Leave me alone!" She beat at his shoulder with one of her hands as tears welled in her eyes and her hair began to cycle madly through every color in existence. "I don't want to do this anymore! I can't handle it! You're going to break my heart!"

He yanked her against his aching body and kissed her with all the frustrated hunger in his soul. A shudder rippled through her body and then her fingers locked in his hair and she surged upward to deepen the kiss even further. She wrapped her arms and legs around him and held on wildly. She met and matched the aggressive thrust of his tongue, and her hair turned a vibrant shade of purple before starting to glow brightly.

It had to be the most erotic thing he had ever seen. Uncaring for time, location, or really anything else, he tumbled her down into the flowers and rushed open the laces on her dress. Delight filled him as he saw the silky corset beneath. "Who knew faeries were so wonderfully old-fashioned? You're so delicate; why do you need this thing?"

"I actually," her breath hitched on a soft whimper as his lips teased along the curves of her breasts, "actually find them comfortable. Also, it—stop, tickling me!—it also covers me well enough that if I lose my dress somehow, I'll be still dressed." A low moan vibrated in her throat as he buried his nose between her breasts. He curled his hand hotly around her waist and seared her even through the layers of cloth. She knew she should stop him, but she couldn't find the willpower. She wanted him too much. Loved him too foolishly.

Nature itself took away the problem. Lightning flashed brightly and thunder rumbled right overhead. He looked up sharply and glanced around. Even through the knots of desperate lust, he could be amused. "Never the time and place." He looked down at his faerie and found her violet eyes seething with matching emotion and bands of gold running through her purple hair. "Teydra." He started to lower his head again, and this time lightning struck close enough to shake the ground. "Whoa!" He hastily scrambled up and yanked her up as well. "We need to get moving!"

She clung onto his hand and ran quickly at his side toward the road. She felt frustrated, miserable, aching, empty, and a little bit pissed off. She tugged her laces closed with her free hand as best she could. "No more of that, Damian," she warned him fiercely. "You're supposed to be pursuing the *princess* not the *faerie*! You can't touch me again, got it? Not like you just did!"

He couldn't make a promise he wouldn't keep and therefore kept his mouth shut entirely. He didn't *want* any princess; he wanted his faerie! He would never want anyone else now that he'd had a taste of her rich magic flavor. If things went on for much longer, he would be too in love with her to ever let her go again.

Just what the hell was he supposed to do now?

CHAPTER THREE

They didn't beat the storm to the city and were forced to take shelter in an old hut along the road. They sat huddled under the roof to avoid the rain, and Teydra surprised both of them by successfully creating a small fire without blowing up anything. "I guess maybe I just needed more practice rather than more study," she murmured as she stared into the flames.

Damian couldn't help but wonder if perhaps it had more to do with whatever was between them. If he felt like he was maturing at a rapid rate by the events, he could only imagine what it was doing to her. Being an adult meant scary emotions and learning to fight for what you wanted. No matter how things ended, he would not be the same going home as he had been when he had left. "I doubt I can say the same about me and a sword. I've practiced for years. At best, I at least know the pointy end goes in the other guy."

She grinned briefly. "You're several steps ahead of some others, I'm sure." She looked at the bow and quiver of arrows he now sported. "How good are you with that anyway?"

He grabbed the bow and notched an arrow. "See for yourself." He took careful aim at a small flower in the distance. "I'll pick that flower without bruising the petals." He fired the arrow and smiled as the flower flipped into the air and landed safely on the ground. Even from a distance, it looked pristine. "See?"

"I do indeed. I can't imagine why anyone would object to you using one."

"It's a 'girl's' weapon, or so they say. Princes are supposed to be dashing and daring and swing shiny swords as they cut down dangerous villains preventing them from rescuing fair damsels in distress." He leaned back on his hands. "Weird, isn't it, that we expect that of princes, and yet kings can be completely different? I mean, presumably, a prince grows up to be a king, right?"

"Typically, yes." She smiled at him. "Speaking as a faerie who has seen a lot of princes and kings, you're not as in the minority as you think you are. Times have been changing lately, and for the better. Life happens in cycles. Every hundred years or so, things shuffle around. We're shuffling now. Did you know that a hundred years ago it was completely common for royal heirs of both genders to be banished for the silliest things? Now the boys get sent out on missions and the girls stay to be rescued. Maybe in another hundred years it'll switch."

"Can we have the towers? Dungeons are very boring."

"Well, they have no view."

He snorted softly. She really was too utterly perfect for him. And though he knew he should put it aside, he couldn't help but go over the logistics. His parents would adore her, and he knew his people would, too. The only thing he couldn't put his finger on was whether or not she would, well, be any good at being a queen. That kind of thing would really decide what outcome he worked toward. No matter how much he loved Teydra, if she would be uncomfortable or simply unsuitable as a queen, he could not put her on a throne.

That didn't mean he would walk away. Definitely not. If she couldn't rule, then he would abdicate to one of his cousins and settle into a peasant life with her. He would probably enjoy it a lot more than being a king! But if she *did* turn out to be as amazing as his gut said she might, then he would absolutely stick her on the throne beside him and they could learn together just how those heavy crowns managed to stay in place.

He sighed at his own thoughts. There were a lot of what/ifs in the scenario, and he didn't even really have the right to claim her as his own. She would fight him every inch of the way, and he couldn't blame her. They were shaking up a lot more than mere gender roles. He just didn't know what the hell to do about it.

The storm lessened within another hour and they were once more able to get on the road. It turned out to be an entirely unremarkable journey, and it put them both on the alert. Where were the bandits and the demons and the other sundry things that always plagued a prince's road?

The answer came in the form of a commotion from the small village they approached. Shouts and raucous laughter told them what they would find long before they ran into the town limits and moved toward the center. Sure enough, a pack of bandits ran amok. They tipped over some carts, uprooted gardens, grabbed purses, and generally caused a lot of low-key terror. The villagers had nothing they could say or do; it was only a farming town that served as a stopover point for the Karmic Kingdom.

Damian grabbed Teydra, and they crouched down behind the edge of a chapel. "I can pick off two of them before they get to me," he told her in a low voice. "Can you fireball at least one of the others?"

She nodded. "I think I can actually use a rooting spell to snare two of them before I use a fireball on the third." She winced. "At worst, I might accidentally make a couple trees grow under them."

"Which could be just as effective." He readied an arrow and smiled. "I know we can do this."

Strangely, she did too. She gave a little nod and moved to the side. As soon as he let the first arrow fly, she shot a blast of magic toward the two closest bandits. To her delight, roots quickly entangled them and dropped them cursing to the ground. One of the two remaining bandits rushed Damian only to be shot down, and she zipped off a fireball at the other. She winced when he evaporated into ashes. "Oops."

"I wouldn't spare him any pity," a woman said a bit shakily from behind her. "He was making some really nasty threats!"

The only two bandits who survived the ambush turned out to be the ones that had been rooted. Damian was *damned* accurate with his bow. The local guard took charge of the prisoners, and the village began to get back to its business. Everyone felt very happy with Damian and Teydra alike, and they were more than happy to share what information they had. Again, it came down to ogres and no real idea of the *actual* issue, but supposedly an escapee of the kingdom would be arriving on the morrow with more information.

Since it would be worth waiting to find out, Damian and Teydra found themselves with an entire day to waste. They hit the surprisingly busy market to see what sorts of wares were on offer, and each managed to get a new change of clothes. Teydra, showing the lovely lack of modesty that marked her race, delighted many present by stripping off her ruined dress in the market and pulling on a new tunic over her corset. Damian even had to glare at several rivals to impress the point that the faerie was *his*.

Before he said or did something really stupid, he headed for the end of the market. An old peddler selling unusual shell jewelry caught his eye, and he moved closer to look. Mixed with the shells were pearls of all colors, and he picked up a lovely necklace whose multi-hued color reminded him of Teydra's mood changing hair.

The peddler suddenly asked, "What bothers you?"

The surprisingly youthful voice coming from such an elderly face startled Damian, and he looked up to find oddly young and yet ancient blue eyes watching him. "A lot," he admitted. He put the necklace down. "I doubt you want to hear my tale of woe."

"On the contrary, son. I am quite interested. I may even be able to help you."

After a brief pause, Damian sighed. "I'm a prince who supposedly sucks at being a prince, and I'm supposed to rescue a princess from a cursed castle in order to prove myself a man. Being a prince and on a quest, I have been given a Good Faerie to aid me. Said Good Faerie is no better at her job than I am at mine, and I'm tripping over my own feet in love with her."

"Have you kissed her?"

"Unfortunately."

"That good, eh?"

"Better." He trailed a finger over a lovely statue depicting some sort of goddess rising from a scalloped shell. "She wants me in return, and I'm going crazy because her hair shows her emotions and therefore I *know* she's just as frustrated as I am. I think she's the woman of my dreams, and that really isn't so surprising since I can't seem to get anything else right. I just don't know what I'm supposed to do next."

"Hmm." The peddler contemplated things for a moment before offering, "I think I can help you. How about we make something of a deal? If you will do a few tasks for me, I can guarantee by the end of them that you will have a much better understanding of what your heart wants."

"Alright, you have a deal. Should we shake on it?"

"Actually, let us do this just a bit more formally." He offered a scroll. "This is for your sake more than mine. This scroll will be the ticket to your happy ending, Damian."

Damian took the scroll and skimmed over it quickly. It was a contract, and it clearly stated that the peddler would issue three tasks that would lead to clarification in Damian's course of action. However . . . "This part near the end. I can't read it."

"You will be able to read it when it is necessary to be read."

He looked up quickly. "You use magic?"

"I have some gifts," was the modest response. "Do we have a deal?" He offered a pen.

"Deal." Damian signed his name across the bottom of the contract and then tucked it into the quiver where he carried his arrows. "I don't object to menial or manual labor," he admitted wryly. "I rather enjoy it. What do you need me to do first?"

"Nothing very complicated, in fact. First and foremost, I need some lumber hauled in from the edges of town. You may use the cart over there for it." He smiled when Damian looked at him oddly. "Trust me when I say that the simplest of tasks can often have the most far reaching effects, young prince."

Amiable, though a bit confused, Damian grabbed the cart and lugged it toward the edge of town. Stacks of wood sat waiting to be split into lumber, and he hefted an axe to get to work. As he made the first chop, he heard an unexpected burst of giggling from a bunch of kids. He looked over curiously and felt his heart flutter in tune with his pulse.

A handful of schoolchildren clustered around Teydra, and she was telling them something that had them wide-eyed with delight. Her quick fingers fashioned wreathes of flowers for the boys and girls alike. A very little girl tugged on her leg, and she scooped her up to spin her in the air. The sunlight glowed over her wings and skin, and she seemed to sparkle with magic and beauty as she put the girl down again. She popped into Pixie form and zipped off with a giggle, and the children gave happy chase.

Breathless with wonder, he barely dragged his eyes away to get back to splitting the lumber. She loved kids. Well, of course she did. She loved a lot of things. He was willing to bet a lot of her non-Good Faerie duties had involved watching little faeries. A bit wistfully, he couldn't help but wonder what kind of mother she might be. Could humans and faeries have children together? They could always adopt if not.

He scowled and put the thoughts out of his head. He was distracting himself when he had work to do. He got down to things and shortly had the lumber split and loaded. He brought it back to the peddler and huffed out a breath. "I'm not thinking clearly. I'm getting distracted."

"Happens to the best of us, my boy. Here you go." He handed over two large buckets. "Water from the well on the other side of town, please."

"Why can't you at least challenge me? Sheesh." He hefted the buckets and carried them easily through the town toward where the well was located. He had to wait his turn since someone else was there, and he looked around curiously at the area. There seemed to be quite a bit of construction going on. "What happened over here?" he asked.

The farmer in front of him explained, "We had some damage in the last big storm before the one this morning. Lost a couple houses. We've been trying to rebuild them before winter comes in for good." He started filling his second bucket. "That your partner over there?"

"Huh?" He looked over quickly and discovered Teydra had been abandoned by the kids. Instead, she hovered over a builder's shoulder and seemed to be having a lively discussion with him over something. She adamantly shook her head and turned into Monarch form to start pointing and issuing orders. Much to Damian's bemusement, people leapt to obey. "Yeah, that's my partner. I didn't know she could take charge like that."

"She certainly knows how to make people do what is needed." He chuckled. "And I'm glad for it! Maybe I'll have a roof over my head before the next rain." He lifted his buckets. "Your turn."

"Thanks." Damian started drawing water, and he kept an eye on the scene not far away. Teydra had indeed taken charge of things. She read plans and made suggestions, and she got everyone quickly organized. He had no idea how she did it; issuing orders was on the list of princely things he had never learned. He had always assumed it was a talent he just didn't have. Teydra certainly had it. He watched her wistfully. They complemented each other perfectly. They had strengths that the other didn't, and yet they were so much alike inside.

Beginning to think about things, he carried the buckets of water back to the peddler and handed them off. The peddler merely lifted a brow with a smile. "Last but not least, would you mind terribly hitting the inn and getting the fresh baked bread the innkeeper owes me? You might have to wait for it to be packaged."

"No problem at all." He tucked his hands into his pockets and headed for the inn. The building had gotten lively later in the day, and he realized that most people went there to eat if they weren't eating at home. He ducked through the crowd and made his way toward the back where the innkeeper stood. "Bread?" he asked over the din.

She smiled. "I'll get it for you. Give me a few minutes." She ducked through the doors into the kitchen.

He turned to watch the room, and he grinned when he noticed a lovely bard sitting at the bar counter. Perched on the bard's shoulder was a Pixie-sized Good Faerie. It made him feel better to know he wasn't the only one on a quest around there. He didn't know what she was doing, but he hoped she succeeded at it.

Speaking of Good Faeries, he spotted his swinging in the front door. She had her arms full of flowers, and there was a light flush across her chocolate skin. Her creamy hair had turned a silvery hue that he thought might be happiness. She dropped off the flowers with a waitress and started laughing when she got unexpectedly hugged by her fellow faerie. The sound of her voice lifted over the room, and she drew many smiling looks. She spotted Damian then and turned toward where he stood. The silver of her hair was replaced by the unknown gold color, and her eyes shimmered purple. She smiled almost shyly at him before she got pulled into a conversation with the bard as well.

He felt an emotional fist hit him hard and powerfully. It really was too late for him. It had been too late from that first moment he had met her. He had fooled himself into thinking there might be any other outcome. What was he supposed to do next? He was supposed to fight anything and everything in order to have her for his own! He had seen plenty of evidence to prove he was right about the brilliant queen she could be. They needed to sit down and have a serious talk about things. His parents wanted him to come with a bride; they had never specified it had to be a princess, now had they?

The innkeeper suddenly offered him the basket of bread, and he quickly made his way back to the peddler. "Here you go."

The peddler smiled. "Do I sense someone might have a better idea of what he needs to do?"

"You sense right, and you were right about those tasks forcing me to think clearly. If I'd been working too hard, I would never have been able to watch Teydra as I have. I'm going to fight for her as hard as I can."

Something eternally sad moved through the gold eyes watching him. "Love is the one thing worth fighting for in life."

"Did you learn that lesson too late?" he asked softly.

"It was a bitter, painful, and perhaps a bit ironic lesson for me to learn." The peddler waved a hand. "Off with you, Damian. You have quite a fight ahead of you." To himself as Damian ran off, he murmured, "Love always waits."

Back at the inn, Damian made his way to the bar where Teydra was now sitting with the bard. The other Good Faerie was still in Pixie form and sitting on the bar top. He didn't need to ask why; the only open seat was the one they had saved for him. "Many thanks," he noted wryly as he sat down. He offered a hand to the bard. "Damian Lucksworth."

"Janaya Corgan." Her green eyes lit with humor. "I have trouble being formal with royal types. I hope you don't mind."

"I will take it as a personal favor if you aren't formal, actually, as I have trouble remembering how to be a 'royal type' to begin with." He smiled at the other faerie. "It's nice to meet you as well."

"Vriya." She slid a look at Teydra. "I've known Teydra since she was very little. I'm glad to see she's finally matured enough to actually serve in her proper role. You've been a, hmm, good influence on her."

Pink climbed Teydra's hair. Though she hadn't told Vriya everything, she knew her mentor had seen the gold from earlier. "What were you up to?" she asked Damian. "I saw you doing quite a bit of work."

"Just helping out a peddler in town." He leaned on the bar with a sigh. "It's been crazy the last few days. I need a drink."

"You and me both, friend," Janaya agreed with emphasis. She gestured lightly to the bartender. She took one of the drinks that slid her way and sighed. "Going on a quest for the one you love. Vexing, frustrating, and painful. Worse, I don't even know if I'm going to succeed. We've kind of got a station problem."

"Ah, you must love a member of the royalty." He shook his head and sniffed at his drink. "I would hope any parents just want their child to be happy."

"It's complicated," Vriya demurred. "Janaya has to fight a lot more than just station. That's why she has me to help."

He saluted with his glass. "Good luck to you."

Janaya saluted back. "Same to you." She smirked when he took a drink and then choked. "I have yet to see a member of any royal family who can keep up with a peasant in a drinking contest."

A bit challenged, he defiantly took another sip. It burned all the way down, but it wasn't that bad on the second pass. "I'm more like a peasant than a prince, thank you. I think I can hold my own."

"Uh-oh," Teydra muttered.

Vriya grinned at her. "Just let it happen. They need to unwind a bit."

Unwind they did. The challenge had been called, and the amused bartender kept track of what they consumed. It turned out that Damian *did* have the better constitution, but he didn't beat Janaya by much. They were both happily tipsy by their fourth beverages. Two more and they were wholly drunk. They sang songs together, told bad jokes, and commiserated over journeys of growth that involved bandits, demons, and sneezing flowers.

Damian squinted as he tried to focus on his new friend. "Sneezing flowers?"

"Sneezing." Janaya scowled into her nearly empty glass. "Kept hearing this little 'choo' noise. Finally figured out that it was the flowers. They were allergic to me. I shortly got covered in flower snot. I smelled like a perfume bottle for a day!"

He blinked owlishly at Teydra. "I like demons more."

She bit her lip to hide a smile. "I imagine so." She shook her head as she watched him woozily sway on his seat. "Okay, Damian. You two are done. I'm going to pour some water in you and put you to bed."

"Aww, Teydra." He grumbled as she tugged him up to his feet. The room tilted happily and he quickly grabbed her for balance. "Whee."

Now trying not to giggle, she moved him carefully toward the stairs. Such was the glamorous life of a good sidekick. She healed wounds, fireballed bandits, and kept him from drunkenly face planting on the ground or into a wall. She maneuvered him down the hall and unlocked the door to his room. She had secured it earlier while he was off doing his tasks. "In we go!" she told him cheerfully.

He sighed and leaned more heavily against her as he tried to put one foot in front of another. She dumped him on the side of the bed, and he watched her longingly as she poured him a glass of water from the pitcher. Not even being drunk made him want her less. "I love watching you move," he confessed.

A hint of pink climbed through her hair. "I walk like anyone else." She put the glass in his hand. "Drink. The last thing you need is a hangover."

He drank the water, but he kept watching her. "You sort of . . . float. And you sparkle. You taste like magic." He didn't argue when she tugged off his boots though he reached out to grab a handful of her hair. "I don't want to rescue the princess. I want to take you home. I'm so stupidly in love with you."

Gold overtook the pink in her hair and eyes alike as she looked up quickly. His eyes looked very serious despite not being sober. She could not doubt that he *believed* he meant every word. She fiercely fought to ignore the longing welling inside. She had lost track of the ways she wanted him. Emotionally and physically topped the list, but even her magic seemed to reach out hungrily for him. She struggled to ignore it to the best of her ability. "Shirt off and into bed."

He tried to take off his shirt but got tangled up partway. "Little help?"

Amused again, she helped him get free and then tossed his legs onto the bed. "Sleep, Damian." She turned to leave and his hand shot out to grab her wrist. Prepared for another test of her control, she glanced back at him. Perhaps surprisingly, there was a trace of genuine panic in his eyes. "Damian?"

"Don't go," he pleaded. "Please don't leave me. It's too dark. I can't sleep. I know you will keep away the nightmares. You protect me." He rolled onto his side and buried his face against her hip. "I don't wanna be alone."

She hadn't known he was afraid of the dark. Her lips trembled as she brushed his hair out of his eyes. How could she leave him alone? "Alright," she said softly. "I'll stay." She headed for the lamp and felt as much as heard him tense. "Trust me. You don't need the lamp if I'm here."

He bit back the protest that welled and said nothing. The light clicked off and his heart began to pound hard in rising terror. Then, suddenly, softly, he saw a soft blue glow beginning to emanate from her wings. It shrouded her in beautiful shadows and brought just enough light to the room that he could see. The soft blue hue could not disguise the gold of her hair as she returned to his side and slid onto the bed beside him. "What's the gold mean?"

"Nothing special," she lied. She tucked her legs up and had to smile as he wrapped his arms around her waist and snuggled close like a child. She couldn't quite stop herself from imagining what it would be like to have a little boy just like Damian running around. Faeries could have children with humans, and they had been crossbreeding for ages. Really, the only thing standing in front of her union with Damian was the sheer fact that she was a *Good* Faerie. It just wasn't right or fair.

He fell asleep easily in the sheltering light of her wings, and she stayed awake for a while longer. She knew it was already too late for her. He had said he was stupidly in love. A more appropriate phrase didn't exist. She was an idiot for wanting what she could not have. She would need to be Cleansed if she ever wanted to move on. Knowing it, her arms tightened around him. Could the Cleansing really even take away her memories of this most important person?

Damian woke slowly and a bit groggily as the first light of dawn began to slide in the window. He had a serious case of dry mouth but blessedly no hangover. He also felt more rested than he had in a long while. The feel of strong yet slender arms holding him had his eyes opening quickly, and he discovered himself tucked safely in Teydra's arms. His heart quivered painfully. She had held him all night. He hadn't dreamed any of that. Her wings still glowed softly, and glimmers of magic trailed through the air.

He carefully extricated himself from her grip and went to get some water to clear the taste in his mouth. He kept his back turned toward the bed, but he could see her reflection in the mirror. Her creamy hair still looked gold in color. It only turned that color for him. Striving for a distraction, he grabbed the contract from the quiver and looked at the bottom to see if he could read it yet. Surprisingly, he could.

'Mood Magic possessed by Party A shall serve as the barometer for the status of the relationship between Party A and Party B. If the color of Party A's hair turns the color of gold that heralds the presence of the God of Love, then Party B shall be given all rights and privileges to claim Party A. This contract is a binding document that can and will be Enforced to the highest degree.'

A sort of trembling began to spread from the heart outward. Her hair turned gold when she looked at him . . . because she was in love with him, too? He looked down at the contract again and finally saw the second place where her signature needed to go. If she signed, then there was nothing and no one that could stand in their way. Not even her faerie elders would be able to stop it. He didn't think she would sign it willingly, though. He would need to trick her.

He turned to put the scroll back, and his arm bumped into a statue on the dresser. The arrow held by the little cupid figurine jabbed into his skin, and he bit back a startled yelp. He looked quickly and saw only a tiny scratch. Gingerly, he moved the statue back before he did more damage. He turned around to go wake Teydra, and he came to a sharp stop as every bit of his hunger for her roared violently to life. There no longer seemed to be any way to control it. *His*. This beautiful creature belonged to him. His hands slowly curled into fists at his side, then let go. He could not fight his heart anymore.

Teydra woke to drugging pleasure radiating from the hands tenderly caressing her body. Lips teased hers lightly until she whimpered and strained upward to deepen the embrace. "Wake up and look at me," Damian's husky voice coaxed. "I need to see your eyes, my faerie."

Her lashes lifted and she caught a breath as she realized she was naked in his arms, and he wore no more clothing than she did. The wonderful heat she felt came from his bare skin against hers. "Don't," she tried to say, and the word broke in half as his mouth claimed hers hungrily. Try as she might to resist, she just could not. She would already have to be Cleansed. Why not take that one moment to be truly happy?

Magic radiated from her skin and swelled in the air. It felt thick and drugging and sensual. He lifted his head enough to ask softly, "What did you do?"

"Shielded us from prying eyes of my kind." Her hands framed his face and her lips teased his. "This is just us." Her lips trembled. "I can't let you go just yet. I will have to later, but not right now." She tugged him down for another kiss, and she let the magic inside froth until it spilled from her mouth to his. The way his pupils expanded in shocked delight made something clench low in her body. She wanted to give him everything.

Hands caressed and lingered. She watched her darker hands move across the fair skin of his chest and felt enchanted herself. Her perfect opposite. Her perfect match. She gave a breathless laugh when he pulled her up to a sitting position and buried his face against her neck. The edge of his teeth scraped teasingly in an erotic threat. "No marks," she warned huskily.

"I know someone with amazing magic. She'll make them go away again." He tugged her onto his lap. Her wings curled around them both, and he eagerly reached out to touch. To his surprised delight, they were not at all what he had expected. He had thought they would be silky like her skin, but they felt as if they were covered in tiny down feathers. He trailed fingers across the surface and watched magic ripple in his wake. Her breath broke on a moan, and her hair and eyes turned to a beautiful blend of purple and gold. "Sensitive?"

"There's," she couldn't quite bite back another whimper, "no place more sensitive." He laid her down again, and she tugged him close; she needed to feel his weight and heat. His kiss stole her breath and her soul alike, and she felt his body greedily consuming her magic like a sponge soaking up water. It would eternally make him more sensitive to all kinds of magic. Even when they parted, he would carry her gift inside for the rest of his life. It would have to be enough.

They explored every inch, caressed every line and curve, and lingered over every new secret. When neither could bear it any longer, he finally rolled onto his back and held her braced over him. He watched her eyes as he slowly took her, and the gold grew stronger than the purple. His entire body quivered violently. "I won't stop loving you!" he told her fiercely. He buried himself to the hilt and watched her head fall back helplessly. Magic glowed over her skin and wings, and she was the most incredible thing he had ever seen.

There were no more words between them as they rushed desperately toward ecstasy. A sudden memory ripped through her mind as she felt the first wild pulses of release, and she reached desperately for her magic. It locked down sharply inside her body just as the greedy tension broke and sent wicked pleasure ripping through her senses. She couldn't do anything else but hold on and ride out the storm.

He shuddered wildly as he watched magic explode like fireworks in the air around her. He dragged her down and stayed buried deep inside her throbbing body as pleasure pounded through his entire body in a magical wave. She collapsed onto his chest, and he had only enough energy left to wrap his arms around her and keep her close. Little aftershocks rippled through both of them, and he had no words. He had expected nothing of what had happened. If that was what holding out for true love got you, then he was *very* glad he had waited!

When dawn gave way to morning sun, she finally stirred in his arms and tilted her head back to look at him. "It changes nothing," she told him softly. "We both have a duty, and my elders will never approve of our union."

"And if you get pregnant?" He lifted a brow.

"I won't. I used magic to cancel my fertility." The disappointment in his eyes tore at her heart and soul. She tenderly traced his lips and cupped his cheek. "You know it would have been a bad thing."

It would have given him grounds to demand her hand, that's what it would have been! A permanent bond between them. The longing to have a child with her had been planted the day before, and now he couldn't shake it off. They could have a *family*. "I don't want duty, Teydra. I want *you*. Why should I settle for duty when love is in front of me? In front of *us*?"

"Because the expectations and rules of being a Good Faerie vastly outclass whatever you grew up with. Attraction is okay. That's kind of expected in some cases. But being lovers, let alone being mates?" She slowly shook her head. "I asked Vriya. It's just not fair to you."

"How is it not fair?"

"Because you're dependent on me!" she shouted. She jerked out of his arms and rolled to the side. She curled into herself painfully. "What you feel might not be real! It's happened before. Heroes falling for a faerie only to discover it wasn't real once they reached their goal."

He jerked her over again. "Your hair turns gold when you look at me!" he challenged.

"Yes, it does." Tears shimmered across her now black eyes. "I'll love you eternally. But you may not love me the same."

He bit back the retorts and seething anger inside. He *knew* she was wrong, damn it! And yet . . . maybe it might just be worth it to go along with things. She needed to believe in him. "Fine." He rolled out of bed and grabbed the contract. "I'll make you a deal. I'll continue this journey. I'll rescue the damned princess. But if I don't find myself in love with her, I'm coming after you. You won't be able to tell me I don't love you like I know I do!"

She hesitated. Maybe she could go without being Cleansed until she was sure. The elders wouldn't know what had happened. Only Vriya might guess, and she had vowed to keep quiet over everything. She was kinda helping Janaya on the down low, too. "Alright." Without looking or changing her mind, she flicked her fingers and her signature appeared on the bottom of the scroll. Only then realizing, she frowned at her hands. "I have control over my magic now."

He put the scroll away and knelt on the bed beside her. His fingers sank into her hair and he tugged her up for another hungry kiss. "You just needed to start using it more," he muttered against her lips. "That anti-fertility spell good for a while? I'm not letting you go yet, Teydra. Let me make memories of you. I'll never stop wanting you. You enchanted me."

She surrendered on a soft sigh and turned her face up for another kiss. She was the one who had been enchanted. They would part soon enough. One more memory would help her hold on until the end, no matter how it came.

Could he really love her?

CHAPTER FOUR

It was noon by the time they checked out of the inn. Both were miserable for different reasons though they doggedly pushed everything aside and tried to go back to being friends. Unfortunately, it had become harder than ever to ignore the attraction between them. Becoming lovers had just made the hunger deeper and more powerful. Knowing what they had together made it impossible to resist having it again. It was not aided by the fact that Damian carried Teydra's magic inside his body now. It created an odd magnetism that she had not expected.

They stopped at the market to buy some food and were halfway through their lunch when a town guard hurried up to them. "Your Highness, the escapee from the Karmic Kingdom arrived this morning."

Damian cocked his head. "Okay. What did he or she have to say?"

"She, sire. And according to what she witnessed, the ogres came to the kingdom because the king initially tried to sell his daughter to them but then changed his mind." He winced in agreement as both groaned. "The rumor is that the princess was seeing someone he did not approve of and he first thought to just hoist her off onto an easy money-making opportunity. Her protests changed his mind."

Teydra muttered, "Yeah but now he's offering her hand to whoever can rescue her from the mess he made in the first place!"

Damian sighed. "At the least, I might be able to help her out. You know. Rescue her and then get her to whomever she loves, providing he doesn't beat me there. I can completely sympathize with her." He smiled at the guard. "Thank you for the information."

"You are very welcome, sire." He bowed and took his leave.

Damian turned to Teydra. "Greed."

"It's always greed," she complained. "That explains why the ogres were so mad about things! It's still unusual for them to be chucking curses, but I almost can't blame them." She frowned. "Still, something just doesn't feel right. Just *how* did they get the power? Also, the eating princes thing isn't settling right with me, either."

"The only way we're going to know for sure is to just go there." He tugged her up to her feet. "We have only a short way to go. It'll all work out. I'll free the princess, prove that I'm yours alone, and even your elders will have to accept me."

She said nothing though she let him continue to hold her hand. It hurt too much to think about. Their time together was a lot shorter than he thought. She could not go with him into the kingdom itself. Her duty ended when he reached his destination. He would have to take everything she had taught him and do things on his own.

"Tell me about your family," he said unexpectedly, bringing her out of her thoughts. "Do you have one?"

"Uhm, kind of. My parents are both Good Faeries too, of course, and they're often on a lot of missions because they're so talented. I don't see them much though I'm sure they'll come home to celebrate me surviving my first assignment, grudging as it was for Elder Thom to send me. I've mastered my magic more, and I think I might actually be able to use my Mood Magic, too."

"You can't wait to try it out on someone."

She winced sheepishly. "I have a few classmates I wouldn't mind teaching a few lessons to, yes. They were always polite, but some of them were jerks." Apologetically, she added, "Sometimes Good Faeries forget the 'good' part of their name. They deserve a kick or two."

"Siblings?"

"Several, in fact. And, yes, same job. I kind of couldn't avoid going into things myself. I have a long lineage. I think I know why everyone enjoys their work. It's kind of thrilling to take care of someone and see them become what they are meant to be. The faeries who have lost their charges . . . I feel bad for them. I'm not sure I'd be able to handle losing you, even if—even if I didn't feel like I do."

He fought an urge to grab her into his arms. "You think you'll be sent out on more jobs now?"

"Probably." She found a smile. "It might be interesting to deal with a 'real' prince, though I think I'm fond of the 'ish' type. Maybe I can work with the non-traditional types. I'm not normal either."

"I disagree." He tugged on a lock of her hair. "Yeah, in the beginning, you definitely scared the hell out of me, but you seem to have everything down now. I think you're just a Good Faerie now. No 'ish' about it, Teydra."

"My real test is ahead, actually, so we'll see."

Silence fell between them again as they continued down the road. Even at a distance, the menacing darkness clinging to the Karmic Kingdom was very obvious. The ugly storm clouds and flickering lightning showed classic trademarks of a good old-fashioned curse. It was barely late afternoon by the time they finally reached the edges of the outlying farmlands. Damian started to go down the closest dirt road and realized that Teydra was not with him. He turned quickly. "Teydra?"

She slowly shook her head. Her hands clenched together in front of her body. "I can go no further, Damian."

"Do curses hurt faeries?"

"No." She tried to smile but couldn't manage it. "My duty has ended by successfully escorting you to your final destination. Everything from here on must be you alone. All I can do now is give you three enchanted items that may aid you in your final battles."

He grabbed her shoulders. "Why can't *you* aid me?"

"Because I can't. I've broken too many rules already. Don't make this harder than it is. You just don't know what will happen." Her eyes closed and a tear slid down her cheek. Black had slowly crept in to overtake the cream of her hair and eyes alike. "If you get to that tower and fall in love, I don't want to be there."

"It won't happen!"

"You don't know!"

"She *has* someone she loves!"

"We don't know that for sure!" she shouted. "I've seen dozens of princes or princesses be in the middle of courting or even be engaged only to have it changed overnight by the arrival of true love!" She shoved him away. "You know I'm right!"

Right about what she had seen and yet wrong about it applying to him. He already had his true love! He seethed and bit back further arguments. He knew they would get him nowhere. Her stubbornness rivaled his. "Fine. What three items are you going to give me?"

She drew a ragged breath and held up her hands. The magic came willingly when she called it, and the spell swirled through her mind without any difficulties. It seemed strange how she could remember everything now. A shimmering new long bow appeared in her hands along with a quiver of golden arrows. "An enchanted bow, to begin with." She offered it to him. "Tradition dictates a sword, but it would be useless to you. These arrows can pierce even the toughest of hides."

It weighed next to nothing in his hand, and he dropped his old one on the ground. He drew back the string and found that it was even easier than before to hold onto. Yet when he fired a test arrow at a tree, it buried itself to the end of the nock; it had gained rather than lose power. The arrows themselves glowed softly with magic. "This is amazing!"

The black in her hair began to be replaced by silver and pink. She really was getting good at it, and his praise meant everything to her. "Next will be a tool that the ogres won't like." A swirl over her hands became a golden horn. "This should render them asleep and allow you safe passage through. Break the curse and they'll have to leave. It's just the way stuff works. It might not work on all of them, though, hence the bow."

He tucked the horn into his belt. "What's the third item? I can't imagine I need anything else."

"Not need, no," she said softly, "but it is something I want you to have." She plucked a strand of her hair and offered it. "It will protect you from magical attacks. It should counter what happened when we—when we made love. My magic is inside you, Damian. You will always be sensitive from now on. My hair should keep that sensitivity from being a danger."

He twirled the hair between his fingers for a moment to admire it. He then began to wrap it firmly around his left ring finger. It felt warm and soothing, and it pulsed softly against his skin. "Teydra." He curled his other hand around the back of her neck and drew her closer. "You act like this is goodbye. I *will* come back for you." He lifted her up to her toes and kissed her tenderly, trying to give her the endless generosity of his love. She was breaking his heart with her doubt. How could she think he would ever let her go?

She clung onto him for a desperate moment but finally forced herself to let go. She took a trembling step backward as tears shimmered across her eyes. Before he could say anything, she whirled and ran away. She simply dissolved into the sunlight in mid-step. It took only a moment until it seemed as if she had never been there. All he had to show for her presence was an enchanted bow and horn, a single strand of hair, and the aching pulse of magic inside his body. He determinedly turned toward the road and got marching. The sooner this was done, the sooner he could find a way to the Faerie Realm!

The road went in only one direction, and there was nothing to block his way. Everyone who hadn't been caught by the curse had fled for their lives. The low rumble on the air told him that the ogres were still present and still hungry. He crouched down outside the partially open castle gates and peered inside carefully.

Ten or twelve pasty ogres wandered in the courtyard. They looked a strange washed out color rather than the normal green or gray that marked most others of the breed. A sort of menacing haze clung to their skin and seared the air with a disturbing scent that Damian could not place and yet felt sickened by.

He sensed movement and turned his head sharply. His jaw dropped as he saw who had joined him. "Janaya?" he whispered.

She winced. "The person I love is stuck in here. I figured the least I could do was make a go at things myself. Vriya gave me an enchanted sword, mirror, and a one-time use fireball."

He brightened. "You can use a sword?"

"Uhm, yes actually. Quite well, in fact." She looked at the bow he held out, and she began to grin. "Well, okay. This might work out perfectly. I won't tell anyone about the bow-using prince if you won't mention the sword-using bard. What else did Teydra give you?"

"A horn to put them to sleep. The other is . . . personal."

Sympathy filled her eyes. "Love is love. We can't make it comfortable. We can only be thankful to the gods that we were given the gift to begin with."

"I'm fine with it. She, on the other hand, needs to be convinced. I figure I'll break the curse and prove I'm not destined for the princess or something equally ridiculous and then help get said princess to whoever it is she *does* love so that I can then go after the one *I* want."

She blinked. "I think I followed you. Okay then. What's the plan? You put them to sleep with the horn and we rush in to kill everything else?"

"Depends on what that mirror is for."

"Vriya told me it would cancel out invisibility or morphing spells to make sure I wasn't ambushed by hidden enemies. It also reflects magic when struck."

He frowned. "If there's anything I've picked up, it's that we wouldn't have these items if they weren't needed. I'll use the horn to get everything I can and then we'll rush inside in the confusion. You have the mirror out just in case, and we'll see what is left to kill. And throw the fireball at anything that blinks funny."

"Deal." She drew her sword with one hand and held the mirror with her other. Her confidence with the weapon showed in the way she stood casually.

He lifted the horn and began to play it quickly. A haunting melody rose on the air, and the ground shook as heavy ogre bodies began to fall over. Janaya shoved the gates open and rushed inside with the mirror held like a shield. She looked around sharply and yet all of the ogres seemed to have been felled by the horn. "We're clear right now."

Damian ducked in beside her and kept an arrow notched and ready. He grimaced as he looked around the courtyard and saw the strewn bones that were all that remained of the former princes and heroes who had come through. "I don't want to be dinner."

"You'd be a bit gamey, to be sure."

Unexpectedly, the hair wrapped around his finger began to glow brightly. He felt the strange pulse of magic moving through his body, and his eyes widened as the glow expanded around him. "What's going on?"

"Uhm. Damian? Did you sleep with Teydra?" His wide-eyed look was an answer, and she winced. "There's an old legend that says that a human can learn faerie magic if it is given freely between lovers. If you got your hands on a spell book and learned the ropes, you'd be able to cast the same spells they do."

"She didn't know," he murmured mostly to himself. "The elders said it would take something dramatic for a human without faerie blood to cast faerie magic."

"I suspect I'd call what happened fairly dramatic, friend. And also useful. Hold still."

He frowned when she aimed the mirror at him. "What're you doing?"

"Nothing. I think."

He opened his mouth and then swallowed a yelp as the magic around him abruptly shot toward the mirror. It promptly ricocheted back out into the courtyard and began to bounce off every surface. An unnatural shriek filled the air and made their skin crawl. Something moved in the darkness and began to bubble across the ground like a sickening, putrid mass of festering tar. Evil. There could be no other word for it. Neither Janaya nor Damian had ever seen evil before, but they knew it for what it was. "I think we know why the ogres were acting weird," she whispered.

Several ogres lumbered up to their feet and stood swaying in place like the undead. "You take care of them!" Damian told Janaya swiftly. "I can resist magic! Let me handle the blob thing! I think I can drive it out!"

"Done!" She went running toward the ogres on a shout, and her first strike sent one of their heads flying.

He whirled and dashed off the other way. He fired off the first arrow at the blob, and it screeched again as it began to pursue him. It tried to fire a blast of ugly power at him, and the attack seemed to splash harmlessly off his skin. Strangely, rather than go after another target, the blob only seemed to become more enraged at him. He used his apparently endless supply of arrows—he liked that enchanted quiver!—to keep it at bay while he kept the corner of his eye on Janaya. She had taken a few hits, but she was winning.

The blob realized magic didn't work and rushed forward in a berserk rage. A slimy fist thumped him in the chest and knocked him backwards through a wooden coop of some kind. Rather than try to get out again, he started shooting arrows as hard and as fast as he could. "Janaya!" he shouted.

"I'm kind of busy, Damian!"

"That fireball would be appreciated!"

She glanced over, saw the tableau, and winced. "Shit!" An ogre swatted her away hard enough that she stumbled, and she had an idea. She grabbed her mirror. "Hey, ugly!" She hurled it right at the ogre's head. It grabbed it reflexively and blinked at her. Fire swirled around her now free hand. "Hold still and this'll only hurt a little!" She chucked the fireball with all her might, and it bounced off the mirror and toward the blob. The mirror shattered, and the ogre holding it was torn to bits.

Just as another grabbed her and hoisted her as if to throw her, and the blob almost closed in on Damian, the fireball landed with the force of an inferno. A horrifying scream of agony rose viciously on the air and then abruptly cut out as the blob disappeared. The ogres instantly crumbled to dust, and Janaya landed unceremoniously on the dirt. "Ouch!"

The familiar waiting silence of a normal curse filled the air in the aftermath. Damian gingerly picked his way out of the debris and plucked at the splinters in his skin. Everything seemed to hurt, and blood trickled down his face and arms. Janaya looked little better than he did as he carefully limped over. "I think we know why there were so many princes getting eaten. I guess we just needed some non-traditional fighting to take care of the problem."

"Seems so." Something unreadable moved through her eyes. "Guess you get to rescue the princess now. Can I come watch?"

"Don't see why not. It won't be dramatic." He hooked his bow over his shoulder. "Let's hope I don't get lost trying to find which tower she's in."

"The north one." She fell into step beside him.

"Oh, yeah. You mentioned you were from here." He glanced at her. "You want to go find your lover? I'm good on my own."

"It won't do me any good with the curse still in place," she noted reasonably.

"Fair enough." He gingerly stepped over and around the people who had fallen in the halls and made his way toward the entrance to the north tower. It wasn't hard to find; most castles had been built all the same. He could have navigated them in his sleep. The only fun parts of a castle were the secret passages; they were the only thing varied from place to place. His had one that went into the gardens. It would be perfect for a faerie queen.

The tower stairs were narrow enough that he and Janaya had to go single-file, and he pushed open the door at the top. He then winced in wry amusement at the highly feminine and delicate décor. "How would I ever guess a princess lived here?"

Janaya's hands clenched together. "She actually likes this stuff. It's not just because she's a princess. We all say how wonderful she will be as a queen because she loves so generously."

He paused as he reached for the bed curtain and slowly turned around. Suspicions began to churn inside. The look on Janaya's face looked one hell of a lot like the look on Teydra's face when she had let him go. "Janaya. You want to tell me what's going on? I get the feeling that you haven't told me the whole truth."

"Her name is Vanessa." Misery and longing mingled in her green eyes. "She likes to read stories to other people, and she hates sweets. Tarts are more her style. When she smiles at you, the world is perfect."

He sighed deeply. "What did her father object to more? Your station or your gender?"

"It was a bad combination of both. His bloodline would end, you see. He could have overlooked my station, but that he wouldn't get to keep his precious blue blood on the throne and maybe have to let some—gasp—adopted child into the family?" She slowly shook her head. "Ness wanted to elope with me. We thought that just getting married might make it too late for him to argue. But then he tried to sell her." Her hands clenched into fists. "She tore a strip off him, and he began to rethink."

"But it was too late."

"Yeah. I was so mad when I heard what he had offered, but then I thought maybe I could rescue her. I met Vriya on accident. She liked me. She said she has a fondness for the troublemakers of the world."

He had seen her affection for Teydra. He believed it. Delight slowly began to fill his heart. "This works out *perfectly!*"

She stared at him. "I'm beginning to think the blob hit you too hard."

He shoved the horn into her hands. "No, no! This is great! I wasn't here at all! I completely had nothing to do with this! You stormed the castle and killed the ogres and saved your love!" He grabbed her arm and shoved her toward the sleeping princess. "Kiss her awake. You're her true love, right? You can break the curse *easily*! I bet I wouldn't have even been able to wake her at all! This is *great!*"

It finally dawned on her, and she started to laugh. "You really are in love with your Good Faerie!"

"And only came here to prove that it's a real love and that I won't suddenly forget her by seeing a princess." He whirled toward the door. "Live happy and invite us to the wedding, okay? Send the invite to the Luckdom Kingdom. I have to find a way to get to my faerie!"

Helpfully, she said, "Vriya said she would wait outside the kingdom to see how I did. You might be able to find her." She smiled as she sat on the side of the bed beside Vanessa. "We'll invite you to our wedding if you invite us to yours." As he ran out, she looked down at her sleeping lover, and her eyes softened. "We all deserve a happy ending."

He had barely reached the farmlands before the storm clouds started dissipating. The gloom lifted entirely, and the people who had been lying in the fields began to stir. He spotted a familiar small figure starting to fly away and ran quickly after her. "Vriya!"

The faerie turned around in surprise. She recognized him and landed as she changed into her Monarch form. "Damian. You surprised me. You helped Janaya, I take it?"

"I did. Of course I did. I knew going in that I wouldn't miraculously fall in love with the princess just by rescuing her. I knew that even before I figured out why Janaya was there." He huffed out a breath. "The look in your eyes tells me that you suspect what I might tell you."

"Let's just say that any faerie you meet will assuredly notice." Her eyes narrowed slightly. "You want to explain?"

"I'm in love with Teydra." He shook his head quickly. "I have been from the moment I met her. We need each other, Vriya. You have to take me to her! I made her a promise that I would see if what I felt was real and if it was, I would find her. It's *real*. I'm dying without her. Let me see her, please! Here, look." He held out the scroll. "This is a legal and binding contract. She signed it herself. Her hair turned gold!"

Vriya skimmed the contract and recognized the language. She had seen more than one of these sorts of documents in her long life as a Good Faerie. They cropped up whenever a set of destined lovers needed a gentle nudge from a stronger power in the right direction. That he held the contract at all was proof of his claims. "You really love her?" she asked wistfully. "Could you make her happy?"

"I want to spend the rest of my life trying. Vriya, please. Take me to the Faerie Realm. I think it's time I did some princely things right, like rushing in to rescue my true love from the tower of her own making."

She handed the scroll back over. "The elders won't be happy with us, but I want Teydra to be happy." She offered her hand, and when he clasped it, she saw the hair around his finger. She said nothing about it. He would learn soon enough just what it entailed. She reached out for her magic and opened the portal that would take them to the Faerie Realm. Things were bound to get interesting.

CHAPTER FIVE

When Teydra walked out of her portal, the first thing she saw was a cluster of other faeries waiting. They exploded fireworks and threw streamers and confetti at her. "Congratulations, Teydra!" one of her former teachers said happily. "We always knew you could do it if you tried!" Her smile faded to a frown as she saw the black of Teydra's hair. "Honey, are you alright?"

Teydra forced the color away, and it returned to normal cream. "Just a bit sad that it's done, I guess." She linked arms with two of her friends and managed to smile. "Do we have cake to celebrate as well?"

Cake there was, along with copious other desserts and treats. Everyone felt very happy that she had so successfully done her job, and it didn't take long for them to get word that the curse had broken. Elder Thom walked into the party and announced, "Things should go back to normal. Janaya Corgan and Damian Lucksworth have gotten rid of the ogres and curse alike." He shook his head in amusement. "Lucksworth still didn't manage to act like a prince, though. Turns out Janaya is the true love of the princess."

"I'm happy to cheer on *any* type of true love!" one faerie decided merrily. He lifted his drink. "To love!"

They all happily bumped their glasses together, but Teydra was no longer smiling at all. Her heart beat wild and hard inside her chest. Damian hadn't fallen for the princess. Did that mean he would come for her? But *how*? Humans couldn't get to the Faerie Realm.

Thom looked at her for long moments. "Teydra, come walk with me, please." It wasn't quite a request.

"Yes sir." She got to her feet and kept her head down as she followed him out of the hut. "Is something wrong?"

"I was hoping you'd tell me," he said mildly. "You're not the same Teydra that left us a few days ago. This Teydra looks a bit heartbroken." He gently cuffed her chin. "She isn't smiling, and we always count on her smile. Tell me what happened, my dear."

"I would rather not." She quickly stopped walking as two small faerie children ran into her legs while shouting at each other. "Hey, easy!" She pulled them apart and knelt to look at them equally. "What's going on here?"

"He called me names!" one accused.

"He stole my homework!" the other retorted.

She gave each of them a little shake. "Stop it right now!" Her hands flickered red, and a matching color rippled down the length of her hair before dissipating. "I want you both to apologize and go play."

"I'm sorry," the first grudgingly grumbled.

"Me too," the second sighed. "Let's go get snacks from Grandma!"

They zipped off as if there had been no fight, and Thom rubbed the side of his nose thoughtfully. "Well, well," he murmured. "Someone has mastered her Mood Magic on top of everything else. You did that very well. You will be in high demand as a Good Faerie with a skill such as that. I can't imagine any hero who wouldn't find the ability to control other emotions useful."

"I'm just happy I'm not as transparent as I always used to be."

"Unfortunately," he told her gently, "you are still quite transparent to those who know you well. You may hide your hair, but you can't hide your eyes. They have yet to change from black, Teydra. Your heart is broken."

She buried her face in her hands. "I messed up so badly!"

"It can't be that bad." He took a little breath when she looked at him miserably. "I see. Well." He sighed. "I want to be surprised, but I truly can't be. It would be just like you to get yourself into this sort of a mess. You know that you will never live any sort of normal life like this. Faeries choose but one mate. You will have to be Cleansed of all memories in order to move on."

"He promised to come for me," she whispered. "If what he felt was real."

"How will he get here?" He groaned as he began to recognize what had happened. "You gave him magic."

"I couldn't control myself!" Her eyes widened. "You mean that I *actually* gave him magic? I know my magic is inside him, but you mean it's not just going to make him sensitive? He could use *actual* faerie magic?" She scowled as her hair flickered dark red with temper. "Dramatic is a word for it, I guess!"

There were some things an elder simply did not want to know. "Come with me, Teydra. You must prepare for the Cleansing."

A sudden commotion just outside the fence around the village had them turning quickly, and Teydra's eyes went wide. "Damian," she breathed. Gold and purple swept through her hair and eyes as she stared at him longingly.

Thom looked at her and then at the fence. He immediately spotted Vriya not on the side of the faeries keeping the prince out but instead on the side to let him in. Oddly, that did not much surprise him either. Teydra had an ability to touch others that had nothing to do with her Mood Magic. "What is the meaning of this?" he demanded.

Damian tried his hardest to push through the faeries determinedly blocking his way. "I want to see Teydra!" he demanded sharply. "I made her a vow that I will not break! I will have her for my queen or no one else!"

More than one jaw dropped, including Teydra's. "A prince can't marry a Good Faerie!" another elder protested. "It just doesn't happen!"

Damian held up the scroll where they could all see it. "You see this? It says that if Teydra loves me, she is mine to claim! It is overseen by a messenger of love, and it can and will be enforced!" His eyes met Teydra's, and his heart ached as he saw her obvious coloring. "I'm here," he told her softly. "I love you, Teydra."

She gave a hiccupping little sob and flew across the ground to throw herself into his arms. She wrapped her arms and wings around him as tightly as she could and clung on with all her strength. Each sob came with more force until she was wholeheartedly crying against the side of his neck. Her hair swept a bit wildly through half a dozen colors, but the gold undercoat remained the entire time. "I love you so much! Don't let me go!"

"Never!" He buried his face in her hair and held her closer.

The other faeries exchanged confused and uncertain looks. It certainly broke precedent for this to happen, yet the scroll he held was definitely familiar. Considering the fact that Good Faeries existed to help true lovers, it didn't quite seem right to break this set up just because 'it went against the rules.'

"Alright," Thom finally said. "Everyone back up a bit. Let Damian in." He almost smiled when Damian walked forward without putting Teydra down. "I think we had best treat you like we would treat anyone who sought to claim a faerie of Teydra's lineage. You must prove your worth in a magical capacity."

Teydra let go of Damian and whirled around. Distress turned her hair and eyes blue. "That's not fair, Elder Thom! He might have the ability, but he knows even less about magic than I did just a short time ago! You can't ask him to do something that he literally knows nothing about!"

"If he is the one for you, he will not need to study," the elder persisted. "Do you accept, Prince Damian?"

"In fact," came the cool retort, "I do not. You may seek to placate your people with that request, but you know as well as I do that this contract I carry is more than enough. I don't care for your acceptance, elder. As long as Teydra wants to be with me, then that is where she will be."

Teydra looked up at him in bemusement and wondered if he had any idea how utterly *royal* he sounded. He had lost something of his 'ish' as well. "I want to be with you," she told him simply. "It's all I've wanted since I met you. I just didn't know it until I realized why I hated the idea of your journey."

Thom opened his mouth but the words he wanted to say never got voiced. An icy wind swept through the area and the trees rustled in agitation. A shadow crossed over the sun and seemed to cut off its heat and light from reaching within the Realm. A familiar acrid scent stung the air, and Damian took a sharp breath. "The evil," he whispered into the eerie silence. "It came here."

Disgusting tar began to drip down through the sky. It abruptly dropped in as a whole mass and splatted into the middle of the courtyard. Several faeries screamed. Most scrambled back out of the way. Evil was not common on Mirage because of its potent magic, but all knew it when they saw it. The blob burbled over itself, and a sinister, sibilant laugh rose on the air.

When it started to creep closer, Damian reacted instinctively. He shoved Thom safely to the side and drew the enchanted bow he had been given. "I'm immune to its magic!" he shouted. "I can distract it for you to kill!"

"Our magic isn't strong enough for that!" Thom protested.

"Mine is." Teydra stepped up beside Damian and smiled tremulously at him. "I guess maybe it's a good thing that I know just how far overboard I can go." She whirled and flew around to the other side of the blob. Fire swirled around her hands, and she hurled a massive fireball at its backside. The explosion of heat had the bystanders moving back even further. Jaws dropped again as they realized that she was more powerful than they had always suspected.

Teydra and Damian worked seamlessly without words to keep the blob trapped between them. Every magical blast and every arrow chipped away a little bit more at it. When it whipped around and suddenly lunged at Teydra, Damian reacted on sheer instinct. He reached out his left hand and felt a powerful surge of knowledge through his mind. A familiar fireball formed and flew from his palm at the evil. It yelped more than shrieked and swung around to focus on him again.

It turned out that he wasn't limited to one fireball. Anything Teydra could cast, he could cast as well as long as he watched her cast it first. Neither of them had any idea why, but they didn't exactly have time to dwell on it. And when a particularly strong blast blew a hole through the center of the blob, things got even worse.

It began to ooze and spread and greedily eat up the land. Faeries quickly flew off the ground to escape, and tendrils reached up to grab them. Their very lifeforce began to be sucked away, and it would only be minutes before someone died.

A misshapen head rose from within the center of the blob and looked around wildly. Damian felt a new presence and turned sharply to discover that the old peddler had somehow come up behind him. "You!"

Teydra felt movement at the same time and also turned around quickly. An unfamiliar woman with red hair stood just behind her. She wore clothes that didn't look at all like something from Mirage, and her black eyes held what seemed like literal sparks of temper. "Who are you?" Teydra demanded. She bit back a yelp as the woman calmly walked forward. "You're going to get killed!" she wailed.

In perfect harmony, the woman and the peddler lifted their left hands and pure white magic gathered at their palms. The two attacks shot forward and merged seamlessly in the air in a nearly sensual fusion. The combined blast struck the blob and . . . obliterated it. Without any ceremony or resistance, it exploded into bits of slime that splattered onto surfaces and disappeared.

The captured faeries were released yet no one could really move or find anything to say. The woman and the peddler looked at each other for a painfully long moment and then she started to step forward. His eyes closed and he immediately dissolved into the returning sunlight. "Just a shade," she whispered achingly. She took a long breath and looked around. "Is everyone alive?"

"We seem to be." Thom studied her for a moment. "You must be Rhianna Taber from Enforcers on Earth. I've never met you, but I've sent you the completed contracts that come through our hands."

She inclined her head. "I am, and yes you have. This was something I could not ignore." She turned to where Damian and Teydra stood together. Briskly, she said, "Damian has the right of it. He and Teydra are under contract, and indeed I will Enforce the terms and conditions. Yet it would seem he has also proven himself quite the magician thanks to his ability to pull knowledge from Teydra's mind through the hair she gave him. I think perhaps you can bend the rules a bit to let him and Teydra be together."

Not a single person there dared to tell her no. The power she possessed far, *far* outclassed anything any of them had ever witnessed. "I must concur," Thom said decisively. "Damian, you may take Teydra with you if that is so her wish."

Silver color swept through Teydra's hair and eyes alike as she flew into Damian's arms. "It is!" She burst into laughter as he picked her up, turned, and started walking away. "No, no! Give Rhianna the contract! She needs it for her files!"

He chucked it over his shoulder without looking and sighed contentedly as he walked out of the village with his prize. She opened a portal that he walked through, and he told her, "We can visit of course."

"Oh of course." She swung her feet. "I can walk or fly."

"I like carrying you. It's princely."

"Do carry on then." She put her head on his shoulder and wondered why she wasn't simply glowing with joy. "What will you tell your parents?"

"They said I couldn't come back without a bride. That's what I'm doing. And I think we need to plan a big wedding. A *big* wedding. And I feel like being very royal and bossy and picky about everything."

She started giggling. "I think we're going to have a very long and fun life together. Can I sew my own wedding dress?"

"Depends. Will it fit in a walnut?"

"How about a peanut?" She gave a breathless laugh as he swooped down and kissed her with a hunger she knew would never dim. He had enchanted her heart and soul, and she wanted it no other way. "Do you know who that woman was?" she whispered against his lips.

"No, who?"

"We faeries think she's one of the two deities who watch over true lovers. I think your peddler might be the other."

It wouldn't have surprised him at all if it was true. "So we get to live happily ever after now, right? Does that mean you won't cast that anti-fertility spell anymore? If you do, I bet I can unravel it."

"You'd chance having a miniature version of either of us running around? We'll be lucky if he or she survives to a third birthday!"

He grinned wickedly. "That's okay. I know an awesome healer."

EPILOGUE

When Rhianna returned to her office in the Enforcers' Headquarters located within the 3rd District on Earth, she found her oldest friend and partner sitting behind her desk. He looked the picture of patience, but she recognized the tension in his body. She quietly shut the door behind her. "Well?"

Eric Mason got to his feet. "Are you ready to talk yet, Rhi?"

Her hesitation was obvious as she slowly sat down behind her desk. She unrolled the scroll she held and added notes to the bottom. She then slipped it into a folder that showed as 'Complete' across the front and added it to her drawer for Mirage. Aware that Eric intently watched her, she finally said, "No." She looked up at him and saw a trace of pain in his blue eyes. "You can't change anything, Riku. Talking about it right now will do nothing. I am still paying the price for the mistakes I made."

"What mistakes?" He raked his hands through his ash colored hair. "Damn it, Rhi! I just don't understand you anymore!"

Her pause was visible for a moment before she opened a small drawer in her desk. There, resting on a broken box, was a scroll written in Ancient Greek. She held it out to him calmly, though her fingers trembled lightly. "I want you to keep this for me. I don't . . . I don't know what will happen in the future. It's all grayed out around me. I only know that the end is finally coming. There will be redemption or there will be my final punishment."

He took the scroll and opened it. Though he could not read a single word of the main text, he very clearly could read the painfully bold red VOID that had been burned across the middle of the old paper. His heart began to beat harder and harder. "Does this have to do with . . . with whomever you're waiting for?"

"His spirit grows stronger." Her fingers dug into her temples to fight off an empathic and telepathic headache. The memories always overwhelmed her abilities. "I feel him all over Mirage. I saw his shade. I just don't know what I will do when—or even if—he returns to me." Her lips trembled when she tried to smile. "We didn't exactly part on good terms."

He looked down again at the VOID. "Yeah," he said very softly. "That seems to be one way of putting it."

⚲ ⚲ ⚲

Status: File Complete

Analysis: It's easy to be enchanted when love is the magic being shared.

The TABER File

Folder One

PSYCHE

CHAPTER ONE

(Ancient Greece; Roughly 2100 years ago)

Long before the world thought they were no more than myths and legends, there was a pantheon of gods and goddess that watched over the events within the land of Greece. There was Zeus, the Thunder Bearer and the king of the gods. His wife and sister was Hera, she who watched over women and marriage. Many of Zeus' brothers and sisters were in the pantheon as well, and so were many of his children. Each had a duty and role to fulfill. Most spent their days tormenting or pursuing mortals.

A part of the pantheon but not technically related to anyone within it was Aphrodite, the Goddess of Love and Beauty. She was married to Hephaestus, Hera's son, but fidelity was not precisely common among the gods. She had had many dalliances over her years, and her favored partner was Ares, the God of War. Such an unlikely union, Love and War, but it had produced a god who was arguably the busiest, most desired, and most mischievous: Eros, the God of Love and Desire.

Almost from the moment Eros was born, he used his gifts to make men and women, both mortal and god, fall in love. He would inflame their hearts with passion and he would take away desire where it was abused or not needed. Perhaps a bit ironically, the God of Desire was the only one who practiced monogamy. His mother represented polyamorous love, and he monogamous. They would inflame both equally as needed in the populous, but for their personal love lives, they had a distinct difference in preference. So, while Eros' consorts knew they may not keep him forever, but they *did* know that he was theirs for as long as he wanted them.

Even his fellow gods watched him with a bit of longing. He stood at a normal enough five-ten height for a god, and he truly epitomized perfect beauty. His golden hair curled around his sultry features, and his sky blue eyes would light with wonderful sparks whenever he felt the effects of his power. He wore a quiver of arrows on his trim hips, and a bow hooked over his shoulder where the string would cross his sculpted chest.

He was invariably putting out fires behind the other gods. Most had no concept of decorum or consent. If a mortal was assaulted by a god, he went out of his way to ensure that a future of happiness would follow. It just vexed him that he got the blame for the events happening in the first place. He didn't shoot arrows where they were unneeded; the pantheon was lusty enough without his help!

His chosen domain was hidden among the invisible clouds that supported the palace of the gods. Only his mother, father, and a few select other gods or goddesses knew how to find him. Everyone else had to call for him properly.

"Eros!"

The enraged shriek echoed through his halls as he lay perched on a cloud and watched the planet far below. He dropped his head into his hands on a groan. "By Zeus." He rolled over and sat up cross-legged to watch as his mother stormed into the area with suitable drama and flare that made her bright golden hair swirl around her shoulders and her skimpy peplos play peek-a-boo with her lush body. He merely propped his chin on his fist. "Now what has you in such a mood?"

Aphrodite scowled as she stopped in front him. She planted her hands on her hips. "My temples are being abandoned!"

He stared at her for a moment. "That is impossible. Why would they be abandoned?"

"The mortals are worshipping one of their own!" Her voice climbed on every word, and she stamped a bare foot on the ground in punctuation. "They dare compare her to me! They dare say she is more beautiful than I!" She swung away on a frustrated growl. "Go take care of her for me! Avenge your mother's pride!"

He stifled a sigh. His mother's pride demanded that he find any female who might be her rival and make sure the mortal fell in love with someone ugly. He always did as she asked—it was best to keep her happy if only for his sanity—but he always made sure the lack of appeal was only on the outside. The maidens who had dared incur Aphrodite's wrath had ended up in happy relationships anyway.

Still, this was a bit new. It was usually just people comparing a woman to Aphrodite. That this mortal was being worshipped put it into a new field. She must have been truly spectacular. Curiosity filled him and he got to his feet. "I will see to her," he offered only. A few centuries of knowing his mother told him how to divert her, and he looked at her face intently for a moment. "You may wish to stop worrying over this issue so terribly. I think I see a wrinkle."

She yelped and rushed out quickly. He grinned a bit and picked up his bow and arrows in order to descend. It would not be hard to find his target. It was obvious everyone knew who she was and where she lived. At the least, he hoped she was enjoying the worship. It could be vexing sometimes.

Down on the land, among the mortals, the young woman named Psyche was indeed being worshipped though she tried her best to protest against it. She was not a goddess, after all, and she knew the whispered tales of what Aphrodite did to rivals. Her case was not aided by the jealousy of her sisters. Though lovely, they simply did not compare.

Some sort of strange perfection imbued her features in a way that meant any man or woman who looked upon her would find her beautiful. She was a fairly normal height of five-two, but she was deceptively delicate in her frame. She had a lovely figure only just settling into its true shape, and at eighteen, it was likely she might even become more beautiful later. Rich black eyes were framed by naturally dark lashes, and her smile could light a room.

What truly elevated her though, what truly made her stand out, was her hair. The thick mane tumbled down past her shoulders in a rich red hue. No one knew where it had come from. All of her family had brown hair. Some had initially accused her mother of dallying with a god, but Psyche had the little birthmark on her foot that came down through her father's family. She was not even a half-god, though many thought she ought to be.

Of course, her adoration wouldn't have been so prominent if she had not been as beautiful inside as she was outside. She was infallibly kind and gentle, could laugh at her own mistakes, and she was the first to offer a hand if you were in trouble. Her father had been trying to keep her from breaking her heart since she was a child.

Suitors had been knocking on the door for four years. Some had offered a great deal of money and goods for her hand, but her father had refused. He would prefer to keep her unwed and at home, where she could tend to things now that her mother had passed. She didn't mind that very much; she had no desire to marry for anything less than the love her parents had shared.

She did not realize that the rejected suitors might try to force their hand until one day while she was picking grapes off the vines. She heard a footstep and turned to see one of her neighbors approaching. She liked him well enough, but her shoulders tensed a bit. Her father had warned her to not be alone with any man. "What brings you here?" she asked. She tried to subtly put the basket in front of her body.

"I have come to ask for your hand." He took off his hat earnestly. "I will treat you well, Psyche. You can sit at home all day and never work again."

Where she could be put on display like a hunting trophy. Really, how foolish did he think she was? "I am flattered, but no. My father has already declined your offer, and I am doing the same."

Something cold and ugly filled his eyes. "You will change your mind when I am done with you." He grabbed her shoulders and jerked her closer until the basket crunched between them. He tried to kiss her, but she kept jerking her head out of the way. He released her shoulder to grab her chin, and her hand suddenly shot up.

Grapes smashed into his face and briefly blinded him. She tore free of his grip and went running away into the trees as fast as she could. She felt sick and humiliated. Her panting breaths were as much from tears as they were exertion. Her day was not set to improve, however. She forgot about the dip in the landscape and went tumbling down the side of the hill. She rapped her head hard enough on the ground along the way that she was unconscious before she skidded to a stop at the bottom.

Eros knelt in the nearby trees and notched an arrow in preparation. He started to pull back the string and then lowered it again as she still did not move. Something about her seemed to powerfully draw him. He put the arrow away and hooked his bow over his shoulder as he walked forward to kneel by her side.

His breath hitched in his chest as he truly saw her for the first time. Rival his mother? Somehow she had done the impossible by being *more* beautiful. The familiar claws of desire began to rake through his body though with a potency he had never felt before. He *ached* to claim those soft lips and taste that fragrant skin. He gently reached out with his power to see her heart, and his longing only grew more powerful. She was as beautiful inside as out.

He tenderly checked her for injury and found nothing severe. He eased the bump on the back of her head and wistfully looked again at her lips. She was too good, too beautiful, even for a god. Then again, if the other gods noticed her, they might not see her as anything except a new pursuit. It made a blend of jealousy and fury churn inside his heart.

Sensing himself getting in trouble, he tried to put her down in order to walk away. He jostled his quiver in the process and jabbed his arm with the point of an arrow. A violent surge of lust ripped past his self-control, carried on a nearly cataclysmic rush of emotion. He looked down sharply, expecting to see that he had accidentally induced himself to love, but the only arrow pointed upward was an instigator. All it did was remove inhibitions on existing emotion.

It was daunting to see and feel the sheer depth of his existing emotion for this creature he held. It seemed to have been there inside him all along. Was she the one that had been foretold to walk by his side? Her breath sighed out with the scent of strawberries, and he found he did not care. He had to know her taste. He covered her eyes with his free hand so she could not see who held her, and he bent his head to claim her lips with his.

A shudder moved through his body at the perfection of her. She stirred in his grip and sighed softly into his kiss. He took it for the invitation it was and deepened the embrace with a hungry thrust of his tongue. Her hand lifted blindly and found his shoulder. It slid up to get into his hair and she held him closer as she opened her mouth and let him teach her how to kiss him in return.

He savored the feel of the desire that throbbed through her body and tingled against his nerves deliciously. It was just another reason why he ensured his consorts enjoyed their dalliances; his power would not replenish without it. Somehow this one kiss with this one woman had managed to entirely refill him. What would making love to her be like?

Realizing he was rather dangerously close to finding out right then and there, he reluctantly released her and eased back. "I suppose I ought to apologize," he murmured thickly. "Do not make me apologize. I would not mean it."

"No need, I assure you. I am fairly sure that I was a willing participant." She would have lifted her other hand but her muscles felt a bit as if they had melted. So *that* was what kissing was like. It was incredible. "Why do you cover my eyes? I do not know your voice so you must be a stranger." A hint of laughter filled her voice. "Do you think you are ugly? I think that would not matter at this point. I was happy to be kissed by you, no matter how you look."

"I do not wish you to see me." He could not resist taking another kiss from her swollen lips though he kept it light. "Count to twenty. You may open your eyes then. Your word, my lovely."

She sighed. "Very well." To prove she would keep her word, she lifted her hand to her eyes and covered his hand. It slipped away and she covered her own eyes as he tenderly placed her on the ground. She felt surprisingly cold without him holding her, and an equally strange sense of loneliness filled her. How could she miss him when she did not know him? She counted to twenty and removed her hand as she sat up and opened her eyes. There was no one around.

Heart pounding from a potent blend of love and desire and joy, Eros watched her get to her feet. Her eyes. Those beautiful eyes. Centuries before, the oracle of Delphi had found him lamenting being alone for once and not enjoying it. She had briefly entered a trace, and upon returning, told him that he would one day find his other half. His other half would be the source of his power and be the one who completed him. She would possess a power of her own that even the pantheon would have to bow down to. Most importantly, she would possess 'eyes as black as the velvet night that embraces lovers.'

He had not sensed active power inside Psyche, but perhaps she had not yet come into it. She was but a mortal age of eighteen. She had many years to mature. He would not wait for them. He would not wait to claim her as was his right. The problem of his mother remained, though; she would never approve of him having a dalliance with Psyche let alone wish to claim her as his mate.

He would have to possess Psyche in secrecy until he could convince his mother to let him keep her. He would need to keep his identity hidden even from her for fear that she might rightfully wish to brag. It would be quite a claim to say you had enraptured the God of Love himself. She deserved that right, but not yet. Somehow he would have to make her fall in love with him though she could not know his face. He *could* have used an inducer on her, but he loathed the idea of it.

She was his other half. The only creature that completed him. She was already in love with him as he had already loved her. He would simply do whatever it took to ensure she gave him her heart as willingly as he would give her his.

His eyes narrowed slightly. As soon as he punished that foul beast that had tried to assault an unwilling woman, he would put his plans into motion. Psyche would be his wife before another week passed.

CHAPTER TWO

Psyche returned home in a bemused state. She could *still* feel the lips and taste of the man who had so brazenly kissed her. Delightful pleasure still rippled through her body though it had left behind something of a powerful longing to feel more. She felt slightly achy and frustrated somehow, though she did not know what was frustrating her.

She walked into her house on a sigh and sat the basket of grapes down in the kitchen. The unexpected sound of weeping made her frown. She followed the sound into the central room and found her father on the floor. He had his face buried in his hands as sobs shook his body. She rushed swiftly to his side. "Father! What is wrong?"

He looked at her sadly. She was his most precious treasure. "My Psyche." He caught her face in his hands. "The temple oracle had a terrible vision. I went to her seeking advice for how to turn away your suitors. She told me that you are meant for no mortal man. No sooner did she see this vision than did a dark cloud pass over town. A voice spoke upon us all. You are to be given to a 'beast whose power makes Olympus shudder and that even the great Zeus himself must yield to.'"

"And if I refuse?" she whispered.

"The beast will rend our town full of despair and take away all that is loved." He pulled her into his arms and rocked her. "I would not ask it of you. We could leave the town to its own fate."

"No." She shook her head. "If this is what I am meant to do, then I will do it. My sacrifice will ensure the safety of those who live here." She thought longingly of the man who had held her. She had been hoping to seek him out and see if he would suit her. With her characteristic inner strength, she somehow reached for a smile. "I suppose I should make myself a wedding chiton."

The rush to wed her to the beast before it tore apart the town meant that many ceremonial aspects were foregone. Her sisters were very happy at the idea of ridding themselves of their so-called rival and were thus quite ready and able to help move the process along. One took upon the task of sewing the elaborate red chiton that Psyche would wear. The other fashioned the lovely veil that would hide her from her groom.

The day of the wedding, she was bathed and perfumed by her sisters and then dressed in her finery. Somehow she managed to withhold her fear and nerves as the process went on. Villagers turned out to see her leave, and many wailed and cried to the gods at the unfairness. It felt more like a funeral than a wedding day for Psyche.

Explicit instructions had been given. She was escorted beyond the town to a cliff where Zephyr, God of the Wind, would carry her to her new home. She was left alone to climb to the peak, and she had difficulty with the veil obscuring her sight. A pair of doves flew out of nowhere to aid, and they carried the veil just high enough to allow her to see. She did briefly wonder why messengers of the God of Love would help her, but finally decided it must surely be pity.

She reached the top of the cliff and found a glowing scroll hovering in the air. She gingerly reached out to take it and discovered that it was an agreement of some sort. A marriage agreement, in fact, though it did not refer to her future husband by name. They were called 'parties' instead. She could not even decipher his handwriting at the bottom; it looked more like a seal than a signature, and she had never seen the seal before. It almost resembled a heart. She skimmed over the agreement again and her eyes lingered on one line in particular. "'This agreement is a binding document that can and will be Enforced to the highest degree. This agreement is considered complete only on the basis of the signee's dreams coming true. If they do not find what they are seeking, this agreement is considered null and void."

Her dreams coming true? All she had ever dreamed of was finding someone to love and be loved by. To spend the rest of her life happy and serving the world to the best of her ability. It seemed like such an odd thing to find in an agreement that was sure to take away her dreams, but there was no going back. She lightly touched the blank space where her name was written, and her signature appeared. The scroll glowed and rolled itself up tightly, and she carefully held it tighter.

A gust of wind rippled her clothes. She looked up swiftly to discover a swirl in the air that must surely be Zephyr. Why he would aid, she did not try to guess. She stepped forward into the swirl and quickly closed her eyes as she felt her feet leave the land. Her heart pounded madly as she was carried for some distance before being gently deposited on soft grass. She opened her eyes swiftly and took in a breath of wonder.

A lush garden sat surrounded by thick trees. Lovely statues and fountains dotted the landscape, and the scent of peach trees was fragrant and wonderful. A pool for bathing had gently wafting steam curling into the air. A stone pathway led her through the glorious scenery until she discovered a beautiful palace awaiting her.

A warm power rushed over her as she stepped into the grand entry, and her veil flew back from her face. Across her mind, a strangely familiar male voice murmured, *You are my wife. I claim you as such. I have taken your veil; your innocence will be mine soon enough.*

She very nearly panicked and fled until the power curled around her tenderly and erased the fear. Somehow, she felt safe. She curled her hands together over her belly to combat lingering nerves as she moved slowly through the palace. There was much room to be had. She could do anything she wanted. There was a place for her to cook should she wish, and there was even a glorious pottery room where she could create the art she loved. It almost looked as if . . . as if she would survive whatever may come. It seemed as if she was expected to *live* there.

She stepped into the dining area and found it laid out with a suitable wedding feast, but nerves made her stomach too upset to eat anything. Again that power touched her and eased her emotions enough that she could consume even a bit. She seated herself at the lone place setting and hastily stifled a yelp as one of the statues along the wall seemed to come to life. Her wide eyes watched in disbelief as the statue picked up a tray and came to serve her. She was to have servants? *Statues*?

After she ate enough to please her watchful statue-guardian, she escaped into the garden where she had felt so secure. She remained there fashioning lovely wreaths of olive branches and flowers until the sun sank. Nerves returned with a vengeance as she got to her feet and slowly returned to the palace. A statue of a nymph came to escort her and showed her to the decadent bedroom.

She found herself left alone inside with only a single candle providing light. The moonlight could not penetrate the thick curtains at all. Her heart flipped into her throat as the door opened behind her and then shut. A soft breath extinguished the candle and plunged the room into darkness. Tears welled in her eyes and slid down her cheeks as she waited painfully for whatever terrors may come from giving herself to a beast that the gods feared.

A tender arm curled around her waist even as a familiar hand closed over her eyes. The scent of peaches seemed to imprint itself in her lungs. An equally familiar voice murmured huskily in her ear, "Fear me not, my beloved Psyche. I would *never* hurt you. You are safe with me. You will never know pain. Only pleasure awaits you within my embrace."

Her breath hitched. "You? You are . . . are my husband?" Her lips trembled. "What are you?"

"Yours." His teeth nibbled at her ear and sent flickers of delight streaming through her blood. "I am yours. Now, always, forever. You will find no greater love than what I have for you, my beloved. I am feared by the gods, yes, but you alone have nothing to fear."

Somehow she believed him. The utter tenderness in the way he held her, the emotion in his beautiful voice, soothed her nerves entirely. "Why can I not see you?" she whispered. "Can you see me?"

"I see you perfectly. You cannot see me yet. You must trust me. Trust me to know what is best. Perhaps soon there will be a day where we share the light. For now, the darkness is ours. I will come to you at every sundown. You may do whatever you wish during the day. The statues will serve your every need."

"What if I have need for you?"

Eros' heart quivered with violent emotions barely held in cheek. "Someday," he rasped. "Someday soon." When I find a way to keep you safe. "Will you trust me, my Psyche?"

She drew a long breath. "I will trust you." In a smaller voice, she asked, "There will be no pain? My sisters said that . . . that lying with a man would make a woman bleed terribly, that she would feel as if she was ripped in two."

His considerable temper nearly made his hands shake. How *dare* anyone scare a virgin in that way before her wedding night? Psyche had already been fearful because of not knowing his identity, and her sisters had dared plant that seed as well? Perhaps removing her from their clutches had been the right course even without the need to hide her away. Candidly, he admitted, "There can indeed be some pain and bleeding for a virgin if her lover does not take care with her. There will be none for you. I will ensure it."

She reached up to remove his hand from her eyes. "I will trust you, my husband." His arm loosened and she turned around in his grip. Only the trembling in her fingers gave away her lingering nerves as she reached up to touch his face. He was much taller than she had expected; she could guess him to be about four or so inches bigger than the average man. It seemed important though she could not determine why.

His hands framed her face and he drew her up to her toes as he bent his head to kiss her. His lips were hard and hungry as they fed from hers, and drugging heat flooded her body. How natural it felt to want him. How beautiful. She eagerly pressed up to return the kiss as he had taught her. The ache had returned and was starting to spread. He broke the kiss and began to nuzzle and tease the surprisingly sensitive skin behind her ear. "More?" he asked huskily.

"More." She stood meekly as he stripped away her veil and unfastened the clips at her shoulders that held her chiton in place. It fell down around her waist but a few tugs on the cord made the entire thing drop to her feet and leave her naked.

His breath wedged as he stared at her perfection. He could see every detail in the darkness, and she was too impossibly beautiful to be a mortal. She was trembling again and he quickly eased the nerves with a touch of his power. There would be *no* fear between them. She would destroy him if she feared him. Once she learned what ecstasy was like for them, he would never need to worry about her fear again.

He caught her hands and brought them to where his own chiton was fastened. "Undress me. Touch me." He curled his hands around her small waist and imagined seeing it expand with his child. She would make people fall to their knees in the streets with her radiance. He had always taken care to protect his consorts from his seed, but he would not hold back from his wife. "I want children."

Her lips quivered as she slowly unfastened the pins and let the material fall. "I might like to be a mother." A burning curiosity, need, to touch and caress with her fingers what she could not see made her reach out and press her hands to his chest. He was surprisingly hot, thrillingly powerful, and seductively soft. She could trace the line of his muscles and her mind built an image of what he must surely look like. "What are you?" she whispered.

"The man who loves you as no other ever will." He dragged her off her feet for a kiss that made the air quiver around them with the potency of its power. "Lie with me." He scooped her up and turned to lower her to the soft bed.

She gave a little gasp as whatever silky material was on it seemed to tease her sensitive skin. "It feels like a cloud!"

"Do you like it?" He shed his chiton entirely and knelt beside her on the bed. He trailed fingers slowly down her inner arm and found the tender nerves hidden there. She shivered and it was not nearly enough. He wanted to hear her crying out. He very badly wanted to hear her call his name, but he would have to wait for such a thing. He hotly caressed with his lips where his fingers had been and savored her little whimper.

She could do nothing except feel. Each erotic caress only made her body grow steadily more desperate for more of the pleasure he wrought. He seemed quite determined to map her body with his mouth, and he uncovered sensitive places she had not imagined could exist. A pulsing throb of need ran from her aching breasts to between her legs. She wanted to feel his hands there.

A soft laugh teased her ears as his teeth scraped delicately along her ribs. "Tell me," he urged huskily. "Tell me what you want. I am yours to command." He felt the little ripple of shyness inside her and vowed to remove it. There was no shame in telling a lover where you liked to be touched. "Take my hand." He put his hand into hers. "Tell me what you need."

She very nearly released him but something eased her shyness as it had eased her nerves. She brought his hand up to cover her breast, and her back arched reflexively as pleasure replaced desperation. He tenderly squeezed and caressed until she twisted beneath him. His mouth closed hotly over one taut nipple and a moan escaped her gasp. He nearly purred in response. "I love how you sound when you want me."

He moved slowly down her body and draped one of her legs over his shoulder. He was waiting when he felt her nerves surge, and he eased them again. He gave her only a breath to prepare before he found her softest flesh with his lips and fingers. Little cries answered his every caress and he savored the rising force of her hunger. His arousal pulsed and throbbed in time to her heartbeat and demanded he be inside her soon. He ignored it in favor of his hunger to please her. He loved the before as much as he loved the after of making love.

He urged her higher and higher before gently sending her over the edge. Her cry of ecstasy was the sweetest sound he had ever heard. Power ripped through his body in an unstoppable surge that stunned him. He could not resist starting to caress her again. The extra sensitivity from her release meant that it took no time at all to have her crying out for him. He wrapped his arms around her waist and rolled over to brace her on top. "Touch me," he pleaded thickly. "I must feel your hands. Taste me."

She could not resist his plea or her own desire. She felt ravenous for him somehow. There was so much more to this beautiful act than she had imagined. She sent up a mental prayer of gratitude to Eros himself, and never realized that her husband heard it and was humbled. No nerves could overcome her curiosity. She followed his example and found herself slowly savoring the flavor of his skin.

His fingers curled around her wrist and drew her hand down to his arousal. He waited, spied her expected shyness, and banished it. Her fingers curled around him to learn his shape and feel, and the surge of her surprised delight mingled with his own pleasure in a way that had him groaning.

It was his turn for surprise when soft lips suddenly teased the tip of his length. He let her pet and taste him at her will; his body was her playground the same as hers was his. The rising throb of ecstasy warned him how close he was to release, but he did not care. He tangled his fingers in her hair and urged her on when it seemed she would let go. To his delight, she teased him huskily, "More?"

"More, beloved."

The rasp of his voice made her feel strangely powerful. She had the notion she might be in danger of becoming addicted to the way he made her feel, but she was not at all bothered by the idea. She resumed her hungry caresses until his hips twisted under her and he called her name hoarsely. He was wonderfully unashamed and free, and it erased whatever lingering nerves or shyness had been inside her. She *needed* to feel him inside her where he belonged.

For just a moment, she thought she saw a gleam of bright blue eyes in the darkness as if they had glowed in response to her emotions. His hands grabbed her shoulders and he dragged her back up his body until he could consume her in a nearly bruising kiss. He rolled over to pin her, and he dragged her legs up around his waist. "Take me," he whispered fiercely, "and I will take you."

He surged forward even as she twisted upward, and he seated himself to the hilt in that first lunge. Her eyes slowly widened until the pupils disappeared into the velvet darkness, and her lips parted on a trembling breath of wonder. She could hardly believe how wonderful it felt to have him so deep. Pain? Never.

He slowly drew away and laughed richly when she tried to stop him by tightening her grip. "I am not leaving." He thrust deep again and savored her cry of delight. "See?" He took her again, and then again. Each wrought another breathless sound from her swollen lips. He fought back his release as hard as he could until she suddenly arched beneath him and he felt the searing heat of her ecstasy through his body and over his aching flesh. Only then did he let himself bury deep and stay there as matching ecstasy ripped through his body in a way he had never before experienced. It boiled out of his very soul until it consumed every drop of his existence. Finally, he knew what it meant to find the true desire born of true love.

He collapsed into her embrace and she coiled her arms around his sweaty shoulders. Loved. She felt loved all the way to her soul. Physically, certainly, but emotionally as well. Her heart and soul felt as if they were soaking up his love for her. She could feel it inside him like a beautiful glowing light.

"You have exhausted me, my beloved," he murmured thickly into her hair. "I will need to rest a bit before I can love you again." He shifted his weight so that he was lying beside her. She did not move, and he sighed as he reached out to turn her onto her side where she could snuggle against him. "I wish to hold you. Hold me in return."

She let her arm creep across his chest as she settled her head onto his shoulder. "I am happy," she murmured. "I did not expect to be. I thought . . ."

"I know what you thought." He gave a little shrug. "It was the only way to claim you as quickly as I wanted. Others would stand in the way of our union." He tucked a hand under his head and held her with his other arm. His fingers smoothed absently over her skin. "I will not apologize for what I have done."

"I do not need an apology." She closed her eyes since there was nothing to see in the dark. "What do you do during the day?"

He smiled. "I help people. I am accused of causing trouble, but it is more true that I have to clean up behind my friends." He gave a gusty sigh. "They are always demanding that I do things for them, but they never ask me for anything I want to do."

"I imagine that annoys them."

"Oh, indeed. They do not dare press the issue, though. I can make their lives quite uncomfortable."

"A man who makes the gods tremble? I imagine so." She unconsciously rubbed her cheek against his skin. She loved the scent of peaches clinging to his body. "What do you like most, my husband?"

"You." He was rewarded with a soft giggle that enchanted him. "I am fond of music and dance. I am drawn to places where people are happy, I think. I love the scent of strawberries and the taste of wine." His voice softened. "I love watching the sunrise and sunset. The sound of children laughing. Lovers embracing in the night and whispering promises to the air. If there is war, I stay away. It erases all that I hold dear."

Her lips trembled as she hid her face for a moment. How was it possible she fall in love with him so quickly? There could be no other word for the emotion inside her heart. No other word for the way she wished to be by his side and ease him if he was weary. It seemed as if there was a burden on his shoulders that she ought to be sharing though she did not know how.

His fingers stilled their stroking of her arm. A low sound of joy and wonder caught in his chest as he turned and gathered her into his arms for a powerful hug. It almost seemed as if he would never let go again. "My beloved," he whispered thickly into her hair. "Do you truly love me, my Psyche? I have given you no reason. I have asked for your blind trust."

"You have given me you." She cupped his cheek. "When you kissed me that first time, I had the thought that I might find you and see if you would suit me. I am happy enough to be here with you."

He found her lips with his and sank into the kiss as if it was the only thing in the world that he needed in order to survive. "I will touch you again," he warned huskily against her lips. His hands began to slowly stroke over her skin. "I have much to teach you. You may rest later."

She merely tugged him closer and contentedly surrendered to his embrace. She would take whatever he could give her and hope that the day came soon when they would share the light and she could have him by her side always. There was nothing else she could ever want but that simple thing.

CHAPTER THREE

A month passed in blissful serenity. Summer began to chill into autumn as Persephone returned to Hades' embrace in the Underworld, and Psyche continued to cherish every day of her new life. The days were spent with art and music and reading—she had been surprised one day by a wonderful supply of books—and her nights were filled with her husband.

He came to her after dark every evening, and he stayed by her side until the first light of dawn. She would wake alone in bed and battle back her painful loneliness by holding onto his pillow where his scent remained. Each passing day ensnared her more fully. He would never tell her details of what he did, but he would talk of himself. He was a gentle, caring, and fiercely protective man who had a bit of a temper, tendency to seek revenge for being wronged, and a strangely appealing arrogant streak.

He was also tender and loving, and he was selfless in giving himself to her. He encouraged her budding sensuality and taught her how to burn in his arms. He let her have him at her will, and he showed her how to give pleasure as thoroughly as she received it. He breathed his love with nearly every caress. When she would speak of her love, he would tremble as if he had been given a priceless reward. There was almost nothing to mar her sheer bliss and happiness with her new life.

Nothing except her growing need to have no secrets left between her and her husband. She felt as if she was only being given half of a relationship, and though the half she had was glorious, it was simply not enough anymore. The very love that allowed her to trust him implicitly was the very thing that drove her craving to remove all barriers. She very nearly prayed to the God or Goddess of Love for intervention but something made her hesitate.

Her situation was not aided by her growing loneliness. She had no one to talk to during the days. She could converse with the statues but they could not converse back. She missed people and being around others. Missed interacting and socializing. If she could simply have someone to visit with for one day, she might be happy again.

Her husband was highly sensitive to her emotions. As they lay together in bed, his fingers combed through her hair. "Tell me what you wish. I shall get it if I can. I do not like this sadness inside your heart, my beloved."

She gave a little sigh. "I am lonely. I have no one to talk to while you are away from me. I would wish you there with me during the day, but I would settle as well for a visit from someone."

He pressed his lips to the top of her head. It killed him to not yet be able to claim her entirely. His mother had been so thrilled at Psyche's supposed marriage to a 'cavernous beast' that he had not yet found a way to clarify what he had done. "Who would you visit with if you could?"

"Hmm. My father or sisters perhaps. I miss them the most."

"Your sisters are vile creatures with no love in their hearts."

She smiled at the bite in his voice. "Perhaps they are, but I cannot help loving them myself. Maybe a bit of me is a little petty as well. I would like them to see how happy I am. They were not very good at hiding their glee at my fate to be sacrificed for the village."

"Shall I dress you as a queen, my lovely wife? Deck you in fine fabrics and jewels so that they are rendered breathless with their envy?"

It was certainly tempting. "I will settle for one of those little love marks you have left before. After they tried to scare me about my wedding night, it would serve them right to see that I am treated well."

"Well?" A hint of laughter filled his husky voice as he shifted to pin her to the bed. "Treated *well*? There are far better words for how I treat you." His mouth closed hotly over her neck. "You shall have your mark, my love. And you shall have your rightful revenge. I will arrange for Zephyr to bring them to you. When you tire of them, call to Zephyr and he will take them away."

"That you can command the God of the Wind is daunting, my husband," she teased huskily as she curled a leg over his.

"He owes me a favor or two," he countered modestly. He nipped at her skin. "Now where to place that mark you wished. There are so many delightful possibilities."

She truly did not know where he had marked her until she bathed the following morning. His lips had lingered in many places and she had been so consumed with her hunger for him that she hadn't been paying attention. Much to her bemusement, she found the little red mark hovering quite blatantly over the curve of her breast where her peplos could not cover it. The peplos itself was of a fine and glorious linen in brilliant hues of gold and red that flattered her coloring. She lingered over her makeup and hair, enjoying the pampering, and then finally went to the front of her home to await her sisters.

They arrived shortly thereafter and the looks of ripe jealousy on their faces as they beheld the palace could not be mistaken. She merely smiled. "Welcome to my home, Peisma, Zelas. Please come inside."

Peisma's eyes swept over her sister's wear and envy churned in her heart. Her gaze found the little mark, and her mouth went bitter. "You look well."

"I am treated quite . . . beautifully." She led them into the dining area and gestured to two seats. "Please do sit. I have wine and cheese to enjoy."

Zelas barely withheld a yelp as a statue left his station to approach and serve the wine. "Wh-what is this? Is this magic?"

"I suppose it is." Psyche nibbled on a piece of cheese. "My husband has great power. He has ensured I do not lack for anything. I spend my days making my pottery or reading of the books he has given me. I am thinking of taking up painting. I fear I best not garden. I believe I got scolded by a statue for almost killing something."

Both sisters nearly choked on their emotions. First she had been so beautiful as to command worship. Now she had found herself treated as a queen rather than devoured by a beast. There was an obvious happiness inside her that glowed through to the outside. "So who is your husband?" Peisma asked as politely as she could.

"A good man."

"How nice for you. What does he look like?" At the silence, she made a little scoffing noise. "Surely you can share at least that much with your own sisters."

"The truth is that I do not know. There is something that keeps him from being with me during the day. He is trying, but it is not easy. I know not his face. I know only his voice and touch. The way he feels." Her voice softened. "I love him more than anything. I would ask only to see him in the light, to remove all secrets."

Zelas leaned forward. "Oh, poor Psyche." False sympathy dripped from her tone. "Such a naïve girl. You must have a demon after all. Why else would anyone wish to hide himself from someone as beautiful as you?"

Her sister leapt onto what she was thinking. "You will simply have to see him in the light, Psyche. We will worry about you until you do. What if he is a foul and vile creature?" She clicked her tongue. "What would you know of the difference, being as pure as you are?"

Psyche refrained from mentioning the fact that she had quite thoroughly examined her husband's body with her lips and fingers and had found no sign that he was anything except human. Could there be things she did not feel? Certainly so, but she did not care. "Your concern is quite touching, sisters." A hint of a bite to her tone and the snapping of sparks in her eyes were a warning that her temper stirred. "Do tell me what you would do if you were in my place."

"You must light a candle to see him." Peisma leaned over and lowered her voice. "Once you have confirmed what he is, you must take a dagger to him. Be sure to have it in your hand when you light the candle lest you must fight for your life."

It was a sickening suggestion that she might wish to kill her husband simply because he did not look a particular way. "Get out of my house." She got to her feet with regal grace. "You would make me murder the man I love." Her chin lifted. "Zephyr! My sisters are done here!"

Strangled yelps were about all that Zelas and Peisma could manage as the wind swept in and snatched them away. Psyche stormed away from the table in disgust and sought refuge in the garden bath. Her loneliness had not been assuaged. If anything, she felt even lonelier than normal. Her sisters had driven home the point that the only person who loved her was, in fact, her husband.

Desperate need welled inside her heart. She *needed* to have everything of him that she could. She wanted to love him with her eyes as thoroughly as she had with the rest of her senses. Every aspect of her self that there was, she wanted to share. The situation would have been so, so much easier if she had only been blind. She would not have had sight to share and therefore would not have craved it as terribly as she did. In fact, being blind meant he wouldn't have to hide from her at all.

Her resolve firmed as she thought about things. She could light a candle, peek at him, and be appeased until the time when they shared the light. Surely he would understand her need. It was not a lack of trust that drove her, but too much love.

The emotionally exhausting day had her actually falling asleep before he came to her that night. She woke to the feel of his hands and the taste of his kiss. He loved her with a tenderness that brought tears to her eyes and overflowed her very soul with emotion. She could only lay limply across his chest when it was done and listen to the unsteady beat of his heart even out. "I like how you wake me," she murmured in a voice still husky.

His arm coiled around her waist. "I could not resist." His other hand lifted to thread into her hair and smooth it back from her face. "They upset you."

"I should not be surprised, but I am," she admitted. "They are very jealous of me and tried to insist that you must be a demon of sorts. I threw them out. You are no demon." She rubbed her cheek against his skin. He used lotions that made his body a delightful pillow to rest upon. "I think I would have found horns and hooves by now if you were a demon."

"You may examine me again, very slowly, at any time you desire." He tugged her up for a lingering kiss. "I am merely a man that loves you." Wonder filled his voice as he murmured, "You are so beautiful to me. I could look at you forever."

It only made her wish all the more fiercely to be able to give him the same. To worship him with her eyes as she had with her hands. She let herself doze for a bit and woke around midnight. Her husband's arm was draped over her waist and she gingerly freed herself. He did not stir and his breathing did not change.

She crept over to the table where the candle sat and lit it as quietly as she could. She started to pick it up, and a hand reached past her. Her heart froze as she saw a brilliant glow enveloping the skin of her husband. Only gods glowed in such a manner. He snuffed the candle and plunged the room into darkness again.

A blend of pain and anger filled his voice as he asked, "What say you, wife? Why do you not trust me anymore?"

"I trust you!" she cried as she swung around. "I need more than what you have given me! I *need* to have everything! I want to worship you with my eyes as yours have done to me! Why do you hide from the woman who loves you as I do?"

"If you loved me," he countered harshly, "you would trust me to know what is right! Love is supposed to be blind, Psyche! It should not matter whether you see me or not!"

"You do not know how it feels!" she flung at him. A surge of power made her yelp and she threw her arms over her eyes as the palace creaked. When the power faded, she lowered her arms slowly to find herself in the middle of an empty meadow. She shivered violently for she was still naked, and a rush of power down her body clothed her in a plain peplos. It did not help much though it did ease some of the chill.

"Turn and look upon your husband," she was mocked softly. "As you so desperately wished."

She slowly turned around and found behind her a man that looked almost exactly as she had imagined him in her mind. He wore a chiton that did nothing to disguise his powerful frame. Gold hair clung to a face too beautiful to belong to a mortal. It was only when she spotted the bow and quiver he wore that understanding came. Her eyes slowly widened.

He caught her chin in his fingers. "I am Eros," he told her with a hint of bite. "You will never be loved by anyone as you are loved by me. I kept you in the dark for your own safety! My mother quite hates your very existence. She would not approve of our union. I sought for a way to keep you. Fool that I am, I will seek it still. For now, I wish not to see you for fear I may say something I regret! When you have repented what you have done, I will come for you."

"No!" She reached out desperately as he disappeared before her eyes, but though she caught a trace of pain in his eyes, it did not override the temper still there. She found herself alone, cold, and heartbroken in the middle of where her home had once stood. Wind coiled around her to return her to the cliff, and it was even colder and darker there.

A lamp appeared at her feet with a hint of a bluish glow. An unfamiliar female voice murmured across her ears, *Your lamp will not go out. It is my wedding gift to my nephew's wife. I am Artemis, young Psyche. I will watch you during the night. My twin brother Apollo shall watch you during the day.*

It was a daunting thing, and a humbling one, that the celestial twins would seek to aid her when she had been the one to ruin everything. She sank down to her knees and carefully lit the lamp. It produced light enough to see, and she wrapped her arms around herself as she stared blindly at the murky distance.

Something began to stir deep inside her mind. An odd sort of clarity moved. Images flittered past her mind as if she was watching some sort of record of events. She could even see events that had not occurred yet though they were covered in a thick gray that obscured most of them from true sight.

Understanding bloomed as she looked at what had happened. She could even see things that she did not have a legitimate reason to know about, and they all told her something that she just somehow knew was fact: she was not the only one who had not had enough trust. Eros had not trusted *her*. He had not trusted her to keep his identity a secret. She could even guess at his reasoning, but she knew he was wrong. For one thing, who would she have had to brag to while living in their secluded palace? For another thing, for a chance to know the man she loved, to simply have him, she would have gladly said not a word.

He wanted her to repent. She would carry the guilt for the rest of her life, but she could at the least prove that she truly wanted him. Truly loved him. She needed to prove she was worthy of the God of Love, and she needed also to win over his mother Aphrodite. Perhaps doing the latter might even take care of the former. She would need to find her way to Aphrodite's temple and hope she was not smited the moment she stepped inside.

With the lamp to light her way, she made her way gingerly through the night and down from the cliffs. A snowy owl arrived to aid her, and he showed the way through the thickest portions. She could somehow sense the power inside the beast and knew he must belong to Artemis. How odd that she could sense the power of the gods now. Was that from being Eros' lover, or had it come with her strange awakening?

To her surprise, she happened upon a new house as she exited the woods. A light was on inside, and she was even more surprised to see her sisters. Had they moved into their own home? Perhaps they had given up on the hope of any man wanting them. She couldn't be surprised by it. Her sisters were lovely only on the outside. A stirring inside her heart made her wish to teach them a lesson, and she approached the door.

She knocked lightly, and it was opened by Zelas. The elder female's jaw dropped briefly as she beheld who stood on her step. "Psyche?" She grabbed her sister's wrist and hurried her into the house. "Peisma!" she called. As the other joined them, she scowled at Psyche. "Why are you here and not with your precious husband? Did you do as we told you and remove such a vile beast from your life?"

"In fact," Psyche retorted coolly, "I would seem to be having a fight with my husband. It happens to all couples, I suppose. He thinks I do not trust him, and I do not think he trusts me either. But I suppose it was an inevitable moment as he feels far more deeply than any other creature alive."

"A demon?" Peisma scoffed.

A hint of a smirk touched Psyche's lips. "A god. I would seem to be the bride of Eros, the God of Love himself. I laid eyes upon him but an hour ago. He has left me in order to keep his temper, and I am seeking Aphrodite's temple to prove my worth. She does not like me. That was the whole reason for the secrecy."

Ripe jealousy rose like bile inside both Peisma and Zelas. She had married the *God of Love*?! She had been chosen by one of the most powerful of all gods, the one that even Zeus answered to. How was it fair that she be given such a thing?! "He has rejected you?" Zelas asked with as much calm as she could.

"Not rejected." Not if she could repent and prove herself worthy, at least. "We are merely apart."

As far as her sisters were concerned, that meant that she had been thrown out. Zelas grabbed Psyche's arm and forced her toward the door. "You will not stay here!" she snapped. "We do not wish to incur the wrath of the Goddess of Love! Take yourself off somewhere else and hope your husband forgives you! We have no care for you to be here!"

Psyche said nothing as she was shoved outside. The door slammed behind her and she contemplated it for a few moments. Softly, she murmured, "Such a desire to consume flesh from those you deem as beneath you. Your teeth are as sharp as your tongues." She scooped up her lamp and walked away into the nearby woods.

Zelas and Peisma did not hear her nor would they have cared. They swiftly washed and perfumed themselves and then dressed in their finest clothing. They bickered madly as they rushed from their home and toward the cliff. The swirl of wind that was Zephyr was there, and it seemed to be waiting. "We offer ourselves in place of Psyche!" Peisma announced. "We are far better than she! We deserve to be Eros' brides! We will worship the ground he walks upon and cater to his every desire!"

They tried to throw themselves into the swirl of wind but it winked out. They found themselves instead flying off the side of the cliff, and both shrieked in terror as they plummeted into the sea below. Try as they might to swim to the surface, they were dragged deeper and deeper. An odd glow appeared before them and they only briefly got a glimpse of a rather furious man holding a trident before power blasted into them.

Poseidon watched in satisfaction as the two sisters became piranhas and swam away quickly. It was the least of what they had deserved. He turned his gaze up toward the surface and sighed sadly. He could not aid Psyche directly; the best he could do was give her the vengeance she deserved for her sisters' cruelty. It would be up to the other gods to help her win over Aphrodite from her unreasonable jealousy.

Psyche was strangely aware of what he had done as she walked through the woods. It almost seemed as if the images in her mind had been crossed out in a way that meant they had happened as she had seen. It was a small comfort.

The night was growing colder. She shivered violently as she forced herself to keep walking. A few fat drops of rain landed on her skin and she looked up just as the skies opened with painful, stinging cold rain. Soaked, miserable, and more heartbroken than before as she remembered her husband's wonderfully warm arms, she tried to crouch under a tree for any semblance of protection.

A soft rumble made her look up sharply to discover that a wolf had approached. It glowed in a way not dissimilar from the owl before though it was a different sort of power. It felt rich and earthy. The wolf caught a mouthful of Psyche's peplos and tugged gently. Knowing it for a sign, she got to her feet and followed the wolf as he led her swiftly through the woods, up a rocky hillside. A cave had been opened into the backside, and the wolf urged Psyche inside. It was dry and surprisingly warm in there.

A small fire lit itself from some abandoned bits of wood. She carefully reached out to warm her hands and then scooted closer in hopes of getting dry again. Sensing the presence of a goddess still, she asked softly, "Are you . . . Demeter?"

I am, young one.

"Why do you help me?"

Because I believe that you and Eros are meant to be together. He hid himself from the eyes of his mother, but he could not hide from the rest of us. I have cursed his name for ages for his making Hades fall in love with my daughter, and she with him, but that does not mean I do not care for him.

"He is furious with me," she whispered.

He is, but he will forgive you. Love always forgives, Psyche. I have waited many centuries to see that boy take his fall, and I think he could not have chosen a better pair of arms to fall into. There is something inside you that perfectly complements him. When you come into your own, you will be equals.

It made Psyche feel a little better though she could not so easily convince herself that her husband might forgive her so quickly. She would have a great many things to do in order to repent. "Thank you," she said only.

Sleep, child. In the morning, my wolf will escort you to where Aphrodite's temple is located. Be prepared for her to treat you worse than even your sisters. She has no desire to accept you. When she learns of what has happened, she will take out her wounded vanity on you. If the tasks she gives you are too hard—and they will be hard indeed—call out to the other gods. They will offer whatever help they can.

She laid down on her side and curled up. The wolf moved closer and laid down as well to give extra warmth, and eventually she was able to fall asleep. It was not to be a restful sleep. Not any longer. Her dreams were no longer her own. Was it a gift or a curse? She honestly did not know. The one person she could ask was the one person who was too furious to see her.

How long would it take her to earn his love again?

CHAPTER FOUR

Word could travel quickly where the gods were concerned. Aphrodite may not have seen her son much over the last month, but she hadn't really cared. He was a grown man who could take care of himself. She had too many other things to deal with in the meantime.

She was busily preening in a mirror when Eris, the Goddess of Discord, strode arrogantly into the chambers. Aphrodite tolerated Eris' presence only reluctantly since she was sister to Ares. "What do you want?" she asked curtly. "I am busy."

"So has your son been," Eris countered slyly.

"Has he found himself another consort? He seemed more powerful when I saw him last. He does gain strength with each lover he takes. I do wish he had kept that lovely athlete. I would have liked sharing him."

"Oh, he has no consort. Your son is married."

Aphrodite shot to her feet so fast that her chair tipped over and clattered onto the floor. "What?!" She whipped around. "Who would he marry? He never indicated he had his eye on anyone! The other goddesses are with their same consorts or already married!"

"He took a mortal." Eris' eyes were viciously malevolent. She loved to rattle her brother's lover. She rose to the bait so nicely. Eros had been quite generous to give her this ammunition. "I think her name was . . . Psyche? Might be."

"WHAT?!" The shriek redoubled and echoed throughout the entire area, and even Eris winced. Aphrodite shoved past her informant and rushed from the place. She would have Eros' *head* if he had dared marry that outrageous, unseemly, upstart! She went to the edge of her domain and bellowed, "EROS!"

He arrived only a few minutes later. "For the love of Zeus, Mother!" He scowled at her. "I am not in the best of moods at the moment. I have no desire to deal with your temper tantrums! Whatever it is can wait!" He still felt heartbroken and miserable from Psyche's betrayal. His temper came and went, and when it went, it left him aching to see her again. How could she have not trusted him?

"Eros!" She grabbed the collar of his chiton. "Did you *dare* marry that Psyche? You swore she had been taken by a beast!"

He flicked a glance over her shoulder and saw Eris smirking at him. Fresh anger stirred anew. He would have to deal with her later. "Psyche is my other half." He met Aphrodite's eyes. "I love none as much as I love her. I *am* a beast, Mother. And she has been taken many times by me. She is my true wife."

She recoiled violently. "I forbid it!"

"It has been done." He shrugged. "I would not change it though I am quite furious with her right now. We are having our first martial spat."

"Oh?" she bit out. "Do tell what has spoiled your bliss."

"I had been keeping her in the dark to protect her from you. I came to her during the night and left her with the dawn. She did not know my name or my face. I asked her to trust me until I could make things work; I knew you would overreact as you have thus. Last night, she tried to light a candle to see me. She tried to excuse herself by saying she wished to share everything, that she wanted to worship me with her eyes, but she simply did not trust me. Love is supposed to be blind."

A part of Aphrodite almost wanted to smack him in the head. Love was to be blind, but not *that* sort of blind! *Naturally* Psyche would wish to share everything of her husband if she truly loved him. She had deserved to be given the truth. Eros was quite the one at fault for this fiasco, and Aphrodite had no doubt that he would shortly realize it himself and rush to beg forgiveness.

Over her dead body! If it had been any other female—mortal or no—she would have boxed his ears, given him a ripe lecture, and sent him to grovel. She would *never* condone his union with that comely upstart who dared compare herself with the Goddess of Beauty. She would sooner see Psyche dead than continued to be worshipped for her looks! "You are an idiot," she told him curtly. "You are the one who is blind, my son." She made a sharp gesture and a golden cage formed around him. "I will not let you go back to her when your temper cools!"

He banged on the bars but they held firm. "What are you doing?" he demanded.

"Ensuring you will not do something stupid!" She broke off and her eyes widened slightly as she heard someone praying to her. The voice was surprisingly familiar, and she looked into the distance where she could see through the eyes of her statue in the temple. A familiar redhead knelt in prayer. Nearly malicious glee filled Aphrodite. She would have a chance to get rid of her rival!

Eros cursed as she hurried off. "Mother!" he shouted. He shot a dangerous look at Eris as she ambled closer. "Your dead heart can as yet be inflamed, Discord. Do not think I will ignore your deeds."

She clicked her tongue at him mockingly. "See me shake in my sandals, Eros. By the time you get out of there, you will realize what an idiot you really are." She flew up into the air. "Maybe you should think about things, young God of Love. Who is truly to blame for your fight with your wife? I think someone else around here had a problem with trust!" She disappeared into the air.

Sobered and suddenly a bit afraid, he slowly sank down to sit on the ground. Was it his fault? His temper tried to tell him it was not, but he could not dismiss Eris' words—or his mother's. Heart pounding, he forced himself to start thinking about everything that had happened. Had he not seen something?

The wolf had taken Psyche all the way to Aphrodite's temple, and its disarray disappointed her as deeply as it upset her. It had been abandoned by the people wishing to worship her, and she was not a goddess. She did not *want* to be worshipped by any except her husband. Unable to stand the sight, she got to work cleaning everything up. She replaced the dead flowers and got the candles burning anew. She cleared debris and dusted statues. Only when everything was as it should be did she go to the altar and kneel in prayer.

She was not sure if her words were being heard until a strident feminine voice sniped behind her, "At least you are not entirely helpless! I would thank you for cleaning up, but it was your fault in the first place."

She slowly got to her feet and turned around to discover a woman too beautiful to be mortal behind her. Objectively, she was reluctantly forced to admit that, actually, she really was more beautiful than the Goddess of Beauty. She still did not feel as if she deserved worship for such a thing. "How do I address you?" she asked only. "You are my mother-in-law, and you are a goddess."

"Hmph. 'Aphrodite' will suffice." She sauntered closer. "I do not think you are that beautiful at all. You cannot hold a candle to me."

Psyche said only, "You are the Goddess of Beauty."

"I am." Her eyes narrowed as she looked down at her daughter-in-law. The mortal was a few inches shorter and overall more delicate. Even Aphrodite was reluctantly forced to admit her appeal. She could not question her son's taste; she simply did not like it. "Tell me. Do you love my son?"

Ripe agony filled Psyche's black eyes. "No one loves him more," she whispered. "Forgive me for saying so, but I believe I love him more than you do."

Aphrodite wanted to be offended, she really did, but she could feel Psyche's honesty. It would make things much simpler. She would do anything in order to get her husband back. "I shall make a deal with you. You wish to prove your worth as the bride of Eros himself? I have three tasks to set before you. Accomplish them and I will accept you as his wife, and I will personally mediate this little spat. Fail at even one, and I will see you banished for all time from his side."

Psyche took a long breath. "You have my word. What tasks do you have to place before me?"

"Come with me." She grabbed Psyche's arm and swung her around sharply.

A combination of the sharp nails digging into her arms and the disorienting transportation had Psyche's head spinning and her stomach churning. She shook off the feelings to the best of her ability and looked around quickly. She barely kept her jaw from dropping in disbelief.

They seemed to be standing inside a storehouse of some kind, and it was covered in stacks upon stacks of rice and grains that had been thoroughly mixed together. Aphrodite released her and gave her a shove forward. "Here is your task, *daughter*." She smirked. "Before you is the storeroom of the gods. We keep grains in here for our festivals. They have become quite disarrayed. There are more than a million pieces in here, and you are to sort them into individual types before sunset." She turned on her heel with a toss of her golden hair. "Have fun!" Her laughter lingered in the air long after she had disappeared.

Psyche squared her shoulders and lifted her chin. It seemed an impossible task but she would not give up. Too much was riding on her succeeding at these tasks. She knew that Aphrodite did not expect her to succeed—that she was, in fact, deliberately trying to make her fail—but it only firmed her determination.

The first thing was to make herself some room. Everything was mixed up already, so she simply started shoving and pushing it all to one side of the room. Once she had an area cleared, she lifted her skirt and filled it with the first batch of grain to begin sorting. They were all different colors, blessedly.

It still took her two hours to get the first small stacks started, and it didn't even look as if she had made a dent. She needed help. Hoping that Demeter had not led her wrong, she closed her eyes and sent up a prayer to any god who may heed her call and give her aid. That unusual knowledge she was still only just becoming accustomed to having seemed to stir, and she found herself calling out to Hestia, the Goddess of the Hearth.

There was no sound, yet she became aware that she was no longer alone. She opened her eyes quickly and discovered what looked like thousands and thousands of ants marching across the floor toward her. She did not move for fear of accidentally stepping on some. Very carefully, she knelt down. "Are . . . are you . . .?"

Across her mind, she heard a feminine voice say, *They are there to aid you, lovely Psyche. You called, and I have answered. They will tend to this impossible task. I feel it is a chance to give back to Eros for his kindness. I am grateful for the way he has honored my wish to remain untouched and has never pierced my heart with an arrow.*

"Thank you," Psyche whispered. It was humbling to hear the direct opinions of the other gods after she had indirectly been told by Eros of his difficulties with them. It seemed much as if they respected his power and did, in fact, love him a great deal, despite the problems he might cause them. Personally, she did not feel he caused any problems that were not justified.

The ants were hardworking and efficient little creatures. She moved out of their way and sat down safely to watch. With each carrying one or two grains at a time, it took only a few hours in order to get everything sorted. The individual stacks were completed and the ants had left the scene long before the sun set.

Aphrodite returned just after sunset and she was singing merrily as she entered the storage room. She broke off sharply and stopped in stunned shock as she beheld the sight of Psyche sitting calmly in front of very obviously sorted grains. She had even found the time to start storing them in barrels with labels! "How did you do this?" Aphrodite demanded harshly.

Sensing a rhetorical question, Psyche kept her mouth shut.

It was just as well. Aphrodite swung away and paced in a short circuit as she drummed her fingers on her arm. Perhaps this had been too easy. She needed to increase the danger as well as the difficulty if she was to be rid of her rival. "Well then!" She swung around and smiled though it did not reach her eyes. "Congratulations on a job well done, Psyche. I see I shall have to test you further." She made a vague gesture and a plate of scraps clattered onto the floor beside the girl. "Eat, sleep, and in the morning I shall return."

Psyche watched her sweep out with the grandeur of a queen and then gingerly poked at the scraps. They barely looked edible. It was also quite chilly in the storage room, and it was getting dark as well. She found where she had placed her lamp and lit it so that she could at least see. When she returned to the plate, she was surprised to discover it had somehow been replaced by a different one entirely. The new plate had a fresh loaf of bread and large clump of grapes on it. A glass of wine sat beside it.

Eat, a male voice said in her mind. *Eat and rest, my niece. I, Hermes, shall watch over you this night. I am the God of Good Fortune, am I not? You seem in need of a bit of fortune.*

She found herself smiling for the first time in a long while. "Thank you," she said softly. More than grateful for the food for she was very hungry, she ate both bread and grapes before gingerly sipping the wine. The warm spiciness lulled her toward sleep, and she curled up around her lamp for warmth. It would seem she had won over all of the gods except the two that counted most. Perhaps it was just the irony of her life.

She woke when the morning light came in the high windows, and she discovered a blanket had been placed over her during the night. It bore the symbol of the Queen of the Gods herself. She wrapped it further around her shoulders as she waited for Aphrodite to arrive and tell her what to do next.

Her mother-in-law arrived barely an hour later and breezed in as dramatically as she had left before. "Get up," the goddess ordered. "I am taking you to the far side of Olympus. There is a stream that flows in a place where we cannot reach easily. I wish a chalice of this water before sunset." She tossed a gold chalice to Psyche. "You will have to climb to it. I hope you are nimble."

Psyche was smart enough to close her eyes when she saw Aphrodite reaching for her arm. A quick rush of power swept over her and she opened her eyes to see that she was standing alone on an outcropping of stone. The cliffs overhead looked ragged, sharp, and near impossible to climb with two hands let alone only one. She looked around quickly and spied a sharp rock on the ground. A few minutes of work shortened her peplos to a length normally reserved for men but would better aid her efforts. She used the cloth she had removed to tie the chalice in a way where she could carry it across her body.

Her hands got gouged and torn as she climbed, and her feet fared little better. She spared some cloth to wrap all of them, but the strips were shortly bloodied. She just ignored the pain and kept moving. She had to prove she was worthy of the faith of the gods, Aphrodite's approval, and, most importantly, her husband's love.

It took a bit before she heard the waterfall that created the stream, and it gave her renewed strength. She hoisted herself up onto a ledge and discovered that she had a whole new problem. The water poured over the cliffs from just out of her reach by leaning, and the stone beside her was too flat and straight to climb. She did not have the time or energy to climb back down the way she had come in order to take a new route up to the outcropping that sat closer to the fall. It was far too wide for any mortal to jump.

She closed her eyes in order to send up a prayer but was startled out of it by the strange feeling of static along her skin. She looked up sharply and found a glorious stag standing on an outcropping over her head. He glowed softly in the light, and lightning arced between his antlers. She stopped breathing as she realized who he must surely be: Zeus, the very King of the Gods himself.

Breathe, an amused male voice said in her mind. *It would do you no good to swoon here. I admit I do not mind when a beautiful woman falls at my feet, but you belong to one of the few I would never dare challenge.*

She found a trembling smile. "I would think he was the one you would most wish to get vengeance on."

I have cursed that boy many times for the way he delights in making me want what I cannot have, so I consider it quite fair that he be enraptured by a woman himself. I would be pleased to see you keep him distracted for a long time to come, and perhaps I might find peace of my own. The stag leapt down to her level. *Onto my back, girl. I shall carry you across the divide.*

She climbed onto his back and held on tight as he ran at the divide and gracefully leapt over. She slid down to the ground again and ignored the protests her feet made when she landed. The waterfall fell close enough to spray on her face, and she filled the chalice with water. When she turned around, the stag had left her alone. She slowly sank down onto the ground to catch her breath and strength. She knew Aphrodite would locate her wherever she was with the hopes of finding her a failure.

The cawing of a crow made her look up swiftly and she found the black winged avian delicately landing near her feet. It tugged and pulled at the cloth around her damaged feet until they were revealed. Sensing yet another god's power, she said nothing. The crow brushed a wing over the wounds and yellow power flowed. The marks disappeared entirely. It looked at her expectantly and she held out her hands. They, too, were healed back to new. Duty done, the crow flew off into the sun, and she knew it had been sent by Apollo.

The sun had only just begun to sink when Aphrodite appeared on the cliff. A blend of fury and loathing turned her normally beautiful face into a displeasing mask. "So." The word was bitten off through teeth. "It would seem you are resourceful and courageous alike. I think I shall give you a task that no god let alone no mortal would ever dare accomplish."

Psyche got to her feet and braced her shoulders. She knew her mother-in-law was seeking her death rather than her worthiness, and she did not care. She would succeed, and she would win back her husband. Every event lately just felt more and more as if it was weighted in stone. It just seemed that, somehow, she could change the path the stone took if she only *knew* something. "I am ready."

"I doubt that." Aphrodite tossed her hair. "You shall find the route down into the Underworld, charm your way past Cerberus, and find Persephone herself to speak with. She and Hades have been guarding a relic of great importance that should be brought to Olympus where more gods can watch over it. I will not lie: you are very likely to die if you try this." She spread her hands wide. "You can risk your life for your love, or you can die alone and miserable. It is your choice."

Psyche drew herself up to her full height and looked Aphrodite dead in the eye. "I begin to think I know more about love than the very goddess of it. I would not try to destroy true love. I would do everything within my power to protect, cherish, and nurture it." She dropped the chalice at Aphrodite's feet where the water splashed onto the stone. Without waiting for permission, she climbed up to the next level of stone where she could safely and easily find a place to call to Zephyr and ask for journey to the River Styx that led to the Underworld.

A very shaken Aphrodite slowly knelt and picked up the chalice. She wanted to be outraged by the girl's audacity, but the words had sounded far too much like prophecy.

"Well, you just made a mess of things!"

She slowly looked up as a red light appeared and her favored lover strode out of it. He wore his normal armor as if preparing for battle but he was not armed. He never came to her armed; in fact, she was the only one he ever let down his guard for. "Ares." She closed her eyes. "I cannot shake her words."

"And rightfully so!" Temper lit his eyes warningly as he grabbed her arms and gave her a shake. "How dare you do this to our son?! You have sent Psyche to her death, and we both know it! For what? Jealousy over something she did not ask for, did not encourage, and could not change even if she wanted? You are trying to stop true love!" He gave her another shake. "You have doomed that girl, and you have doomed Eros with her! He *bound* himself to her with one of his agreements!"

She looked up in horror. Eros' agreements were powerful, profound pieces of magic that drew on the very force of love. Completing such an agreement ensured a future of happiness and joy. Failing to complete the agreement, voiding it entirely, would doom the signers to an eternity of pain, loneliness, and despair. Not even Aphrodite had the power to create such documents; they were proof that even she, the Goddess of Love, bowed to her son's gifts. "Why would he do such a thing?" she wailed.

"Is there wax in your ears?" He released her on a disgusted oath. "He *loves* her! I saw the way he looked at her when he found her. *She is his destined other half!*"

The color fled from her face as she faced what she had been confronted with: the one person who should protect love was the one who had tried to destroy it. If Dike and Aletheia, the Goddesses of Justice and Truth, had still been alive, they would have had her soundly punished for her actions. "Oh no." It was barely whispered. "We have to stop her!"

He grabbed her arm. "She is a resourceful girl, and our fellow gods and goddesses have been aiding her. We must move quickly to catch her. She may already have found Persephone!"

Aphrodite could only send up a desperate prayer of her own to the forces that lay beyond the control of the pantheon in the hopes that she had not doomed her son and his worthy lover to an early death, or worse. An eternity of suffering borne from a voided contract. She felt sick at the very idea.

CHAPTER FIVE

Aphrodite was not the only one who had been deeply cowed and forced to confront what she had done. Eros himself was in a near state of frenzy as he struggled to free himself from the cage that held him. His anger had entirely fled and left behind nothing but agony and despair. Psyche was not the one who had not held enough trust. Love was blind? The only thing blind around there was *him*. He had been blinded by his own sense of competence. He had been blinded to the very reality of love.

His wife had deserved to know all along who he was and why he could not be with her. If he put himself into her sandals, he could see himself acting the same and demanding the same. *He*, of all people, had forgotten that love demanded the giving and receiving of whole selves. True love, more than any other, was a selfish emotion that would not settle for less than everything.

The God of Love had not been willing to stand up and fight for the woman he loved. He should have claimed Psyche, told his mother off, and petitioned Zeus for approval. The Thunder God would have easily given it in exchange for a few promises to make some of his conquests easier to catch.

"Eros!" The voice barely preceded the glow that heralded Hephaestus, the blacksmith of the gods. Though he was married to Aphrodite and should have rightfully disliked her illegitimate child with Ares, he was in fact quite fond of Eros. "By Zeus, boy, what a mess you are in! Stand back from there!"

Eros backed up hastily as his stepfather hefted a mighty mallet and gave the cage a sound smack. The ceiling popped off and the bars fell onto the ground with a clatter. "Thank you," he said quickly. "Please forgive me for not staying, but I must find my wife!"

Hephaestus grabbed his arm quickly. "That is why I came to free you!" he protested urgently. "Aphrodite has sent Psyche to retrieve Pandora's Box and bring it to Olympus! She has sent your wife to her death!"

White climbed Eros' face. "What?" he barely managed to whisper. His stomach churned violently. "What has been happening?" he demanded sharply.

"Psyche offered herself to Aphrodite to prove her worth, and Aphrodite sought to either force her out of your life, or to kill her entirely! Your Psyche . . . she is *powerful*, Eros! She has a power that has reached the other gods, and even Zeus himself was willing to give her aid! But this . . ." He shook his head sharply. "This is murder! If she were a goddess, or if she were in command of whatever power she holds, she may be fine. She will charm Persephone as she has done the rest. We must hurry!"

Panic gripped Eros as he whirled and rushed from Mount Olympus. Prove her worth?! He called himself every type of fool he could as he desperately headed for the Underworld before it was too late. Another folly upon his shoulders; he had not intended to awaken her into her powers in such a way! She did not know what they were, nor did she know how to control them. He could *not* lose her!

Zephyr had dropped Psyche at the edge of the River Styx. The place was far more beautiful than she had ever imagined it might be. The river was made of a thick silver liquid that flowed between two very high cliffs. The tops of them were covered in a series of steppes and plateaus decorated in wildflowers of every type. It seemed like such an odd place to be found around the river that took the dead to the Underworld, but then again, the Styx was death, life and rebirth. She doubted even the Elysian Fields would be as beautiful as this place.

A small boat stopped beside the shore where she stood, and the creature steering it stared at her from empty eye sockets. Though a cloak covered him from head to toe, his skeletal hands and face could be seen still. Charon, the one who ferried the dead to the Underworld.

She reached for her knowledge and it came to her shortly. She reached out to touch his hands without fear, and she smiled at him. No one had ever smiled at him. The dead were in limbo until the Underworld, and living beings ran from him. The gods and goddesses barely spared him a look. "My name is Psyche. Please. I must ask for a ride to the Underworld to speak with Persephone herself."

It almost seemed as the ferryman's boney face shifted into something of a smile. It certainly softened somehow. He graciously offered a hand and helped her into the boat. When he saw her shiver as she sat down, he produced a himation from nowhere in order to wrap around her. The thick linen drape would keep her warm, and it reached her toes to maintain her modesty where her torn peplos no longer could.

He ferried her all the way to the entrance of the Underworld and just as graciously helped her from the boat again. She impulsively dropped a kiss on the top of his head in gratitude, and she unknowingly earned his eternal devotion. Nerves returned as she turned to look at the massive cavern entrance that marked the beginning of the Underworld. She did not think it was her imagination that the ceiling had stalagmites deliberately formed to resemble sharp teeth.

More sharp teeth waited further in. She had only gotten so far into the cave before a mighty snarl shook the very ground. A massive three-headed beast lunged out of the darkness and landed directly in front of her. Cerberus' heads snarled and snapped at her so close that his heated breath seared her, and yet she managed to hold her ground. She held out a trembling hand as she would to any large dog. "I am friendly. See?"

He paused before slowly lowering his heads to let each sniff at her hand in turn. Whatever he found, he liked. He laid down with a whine and let her gently scratch him behind all of his ears. She looked past him to deeper within the Underworld, and he leapt to his feet. Gently, he began to nudge her down the path. She could not help but be a bit bemused as he danced along behind her like a puppy following a favored person.

The Queen of the Underworld was sitting on her throne looking over a list of some kind when Psyche walked in. Persephone looked up, and for a moment, she could only stare. Somehow this slip of a girl had won over Charon, enchanted Cerberus, and earned the affection of nearly every god in the pantheon—and then some! "Well!" She got to her feet. "Greetings, mortal. I am Persephone."

Psyche respectfully knelt. Close. She was so close to success that she did not dare make a single mistake. "Greetings, bright one." She kept her gaze lowered. "I have been sent by Aphrodite to retrieve a relic of great power that needs to be brought to Olympus for safety."

Persephone began to frown as she realized what may be occurring. "Psyche," she kept her voice gentle, "this relic is exceptionally dangerous. We gods and goddesses can barely stand touching it. I am not certain you can handle transporting it."

"Please!" The words burst from her lips on a wave of pain. "Please let me do this! I want to prove myself worthy of being the bride of Eros! I want him to love and trust me again, the way he did before I ruined things!" She shook her head so hard that her matted red hair stung her cheeks. "Do you know how you feel to be apart from Hades for six months of every year? I have endured that every minute of the last few days!"

Persephone very badly wanted to wrap her arms around this child and promise everything would be better. The simple fact was that she could not make such a promise. Sensing there was nothing she could do, she left briefly to fetch the relic. She could not shake the feeling that something terrible was going to happen whether she did or did not hand over the relic.

She returned with the relic and brought it to Psyche. It was a small gold box of beauty and mystery sure to entice any into opening it to see what lay within. "This is it," she sighed. "You must *not* open it. Carry it swiftly from here and call to Zephyr as soon as you are beyond the entrance of the Underworld. It must arrive in Olympus quickly in order to be kept safe."

Psyche nodded fiercely. "I will not even look at it. *Nothing* would sway me." She gingerly reached out to take the box and winced hard when the metal seemed to sear into her flesh. A strange and disgusting bitter scent clung to it. Rather than risk her hands, she wrapped the box within a length of her himation. "Thank you," she told Persephone. She hesitated briefly and then rose up to kiss the goddess' cheek.

Persephone watched her hurry out and finally realized what the gods and goddesses before her had. She was truly Eros' other half. She loved just as deeply, gave just as generously, as he did. They would do truly amazing things together.

Cerberus escorted Psyche partway back toward the entrance. He left her to go the rest of the way, and she tried to hurry faster. Having gotten so used to the peplos being short, she misjudged a step and tripped over the edge of her himation. She gave a startled cry as she hit the ground with a thud, and the box tumbled away. It bounced off a rock and cracked all the way down the center.

The broken pieces clattered onto the ground and, slowly, a softly sinister laugh rolled through the air. A disgusting smell rose from the box all the stronger as an ugly black cloud began to lift into the air. A misshapen face formed within the center and bared broken, ragged teeth. On a screech of triumph, it lunged for Psyche, who could only throw her arms over her head desperately.

Eros shot in front of her at the last moment. The cloud consumed him over her terrified scream and tried desperately to devour him whole. It could not succeed. He was a god, and he was immortal. An immortal could not die. The cloud recoiled back several feet in disgust, and Eros collapsed to the ground.

Psyche scrambled to his side on a broken sound and cried out anew as she saw the condition he was in. He had been torn and ravaged by thousands of bites and cuts. He did not bleed—his immortality had halted the blood loss to save him—but he barely breathed either. His heartbeat was terrifyingly slow and halting. There seemed to be almost no life left inside his body. The cloud had devoured all but the tiny bit that could not be taken because he could not die.

She felt the cloud gathering and looked up quietly as it moved in. So be it. She would atone and she would repent in her next life for what she had caused here. She had released evil, and it had taken her husband from her. Had he forgiven her? She simply did not know. Had he saved her, or would he have protected anyone? She just . . . did not know. That sense of knowing in the back of her mind had silenced entirely.

When Ares and Aphrodite rushed into the scene, all they saw was the cloud of evil hovering over the prone forms of Eros and Psyche. A battle cry ripped from Ares' lips as his sword appeared in hand. "Athena!" he bellowed. "Artemis! To my side!"

The two goddesses appeared in their armor and with their weapons, and while Athena rushed in with Ares, Artemis stayed back to fire her arrows. She was shortly joined by Apollo, and the twins' lethal accuracy drove the evil away from the fallen lovers. The God and Goddess of War did their very best to destroy the evil, yet they knew it was futile. They had never before been able to destroy it. All they had been able to do was seal it within the box it had come from.

Zeus landed on the scene and began firing lightning bolts. The evil, perhaps sensing the fight was doomed to last forever, merely fled from the area entirely. It had been badly wounded, and it had been sealed for ages. It would take many millennia before it came into its power and sought to destroy the thing it hated most: the very power of love that brought forth life and happiness.

Weapons were lowered as eerie silence fell. A sobbing Aphrodite gathered her son in her arms and rocked him back and forth. "Does she live?" she demanded brokenly of Apollo. "Does my daughter-in-law live?"

Apollo slowly shook his head. "The evil devoured all of her life. There is nothing left. Her spirit has already fled to the Elysian Fields not far beyond here. She is gone." He waved a hand softly over Psyche's body, and it dissolved into little ribbons of silver color. It had been rendered as nothing but a shell by her death.

"We must take Eros back to Mount Olympus," Zeus ordered. "He will not be able to recover anywhere else. Ares, carry your son."

Ares knelt to take Eros from Aphrodite, and he hefted his child with little trouble despite their similar heights. Something fell out of Eros' chiton and clattered onto the floor, and all eyes lowered to see it was a scroll. Only Artemis had the courage to kneel and open it. Red color flickered in the middle of the text and abruptly formed the word VOID. The agreement had been voided. She looked up and her lips trembled. "There will be no happy ending."

They brought Eros back to Mount Olympus and moved deep within the domain to the center where the power was most concentrated. Hephaestus built a coffin of crystal for the younger god to rest within, and Apollo made a thorough examination of his wounds. When he finally gestured for the lid to be sealed, he looked old and tired. "I do not see him recovering for at least two millennia. A mortal would have died a thousand times from what he endured."

Aphrodite collapsed to her knees on a broken sob and buried her face in her hands. Athena watched her coolly for a moment before kneeling beside her. It was time for some cold, hard facts. "This is your fault, Aphrodite," she warned in a low voice. "This entire thing could have been avoided if you had merely made Psyche a goddess!"

Shocked looks were exchanged. "How could it be that simple?" Hera demanded.

Athena got to her feet on a disgusted sound. "Making Psyche a goddess means that she would be a goddess *of* something! The people would cease to worship her for her beauty and instead worship her for whatever she was in charge of doing! They would admire her no more or less than I and Artemis, and Aphrodite would be worshipped as the Goddess of Beauty once more. You shame your own power, Love Goddess, by your petty jealousy and unreasonable hate of a mortal girl!"

Ares crossed his arms. "I think it is time to point out that Psyche was *far* from mortal." He shrugged as everyone now stared at him. "Did not anyone notice how quickly we leapt to her aid? How we treated her as one of our own? It was not merely because Eros chose her. She has a gift the likes of which none of us can comprehend. We claim Eros as being more powerful than we are. Well, so is she. Given the time to mature, to grow into her power, she would be his perfect equal."

Zeus immediately turned and walked from the room. In moments, he was striding into the throne room of the Underworld where his brother and sister-in-law ruled. It did not at all surprise him to see Persephone crying in Hades' arms. She would always feel the guilt for the role she had played. "Brother, walk with me. I have a question."

Hades smoothed Persephone's hair back and tenderly kissed her before gaining his feet and crossing over to join his brother. They fell into step together as they moved toward the Elysian Fields. "This is about Psyche."

"What else?" He sighed deeply. "Has she earned a rebirth?"

"It is hard to say. She was very young, brother. Young by mortal years let alone immortal. There was a great deal of good packed inside her, but she did not do enough deeds to truly earn a rebirth." Hades stopped at the edge of the Fields and gestured within.

Zeus' heart ached as he looked and saw the spirit curled into a ball under a tree. Her misery could be felt at a distance. She would suffer eternally from her voided agreement. "What if we . . . perhaps amended the rules?"

"How so?"

"What if we were to have her reborn and *then* do the deeds needed to earn it? A debt, we shall say. I do not see it as being hard for her to do. She is the other half of the God of Love, and that means she can use the force of love energy as well. Not in the same way, perhaps, but in a way no less important or profound."

Hades thought about it critically. "I think it is very possible that we can make this happen. Should she have longevity? I do not think I am wrong in thinking you hope to buy time for Eros to recover."

"You are not wrong, and yes she should."

"Where shall we send her? Here in Greece may be too painful for her."

"I think we should let her decide the where and the when, as most spirits to be reborn do. Her gift to see the future, if that is indeed what I think it is, will dictate to her where she is needed and where she can do the most good." He lifted his hands and the voided scroll appeared on one palm even as the broken box appeared on the other. "She will remember. Hermes will see to it. It will pain her, but it would pain her more to never understand her own existence."

"She will endure, Zeus. She has a strong heart."

A wry smile tugged at his lips. "Of course she does. Things would have been so much simpler if she did not." He released the scroll and box to the ether to wait until they could be claimed by Psyche in her new life. Both he and Hades turned away from the Fields, but they knew they would not soon forget that ugly red VOID in the middle of Eros and Psyche's agreement.

One hundred years later, along the East Coast of America, before it was America, the magic boiling under the surface from the River Styx began to produce children with exceptional gifts. One of them was a girl with red hair, black eyes, and a strange ability to make things happen as she wished.

They named her Rhianna.

Status: File Voided
Analysis: Pending

Folder Two

RHIANNA

CHAPTER SIX

(Present day)

New York City was home to many things. Large buildings, big companies, millions of people, and a small den of magic. The magic was housed within the small 3rd District within the greater city, and it was overseen by one of the—arguably—biggest companies in the country. The Enforcers had been around as long as its District had, and that meant it predated the very government. Some people suspected it had been around for far, far longer than that, and that perhaps the co-owners had as well.

Rhianna Taber had never bothered to confirm or deny the rumors just as she had never bothered to confirm or deny any of the other tall tales of her District. She had watched the world change greatly over two millennia and she had seen beliefs in magic come and go. It was in a coming phase, and most people accepted 3rd District at face value as a historical landmark that might just be home to gifted humans and people who were not human at all.

Truthfully, it was more the former than the latter. Any child born in the District would be gifted. Children born to District people who lived elsewhere would be gifted. Faeries and werewolves walked alongside elves of half and whole blood. Rhianna and her partner, Eric Mason, knew every inhabitant by name. Knew every gift. Knew, in fact, where every member was even if they were beyond the limits of the District. They protected all of them.

That protection could cover everything from offering medical insurance to helping find jobs to arranging scholarships. And sometimes . . . a little bit extra was needed. Some happy endings required a bit more . . . punch. It was a punch that could only be provided when someone was placed under contract with the Enforcers. It gave liberty to Rhianna and Eric, and their associates, to do whatever was needed to ensure things ended well.

Rhianna's black eyes were warm as she studied the young woman with blue hair sitting in her guest chair. She had been expecting this visit for many years. "How goes the training, Marina?"

"It goes well. I'm almost ready to start training for the Olympics." The long-distance swimmer's hands clenched together before she blurted, "I want to try out track running!"

A delicate red brow lifted. "The water elf wants to find her land legs?" A smile tugged at her lips. "Do tell why. You were swimming before you were walking. It's often a surprise you even leave the water at all."

"I just feel like a change."

Rhianna shook her head in fond amusement. Her people knew she knew everything and yet they tried to keep secrets. "His name is Markus, correct?" She smiled when she received a wide-eyed look. "He is quite handsome. And quite the nice guy from what I hear. A track runner and trainer, right?"

"Uhm." Pink climbed Marina's pointed ears. They barely peeked out around the headband that she wore to disguise them. Her hair could be excused as being dyed, but her ears would give her away each time. "Yes." Her shoulders slumped. "He can't swim. I fished him out of the pool but he doesn't know it was me. I just can't get far from water, and he can't swim because he's *terrified* of water! It's not fair, Ms. Taber. Is there anything you can do to help me?"

"Hmm." Rhianna opened a folder on her desk as if she hadn't had the documentation sitting by for ages. "I think it's time you came under contract, Marina. This is a bit more complex than merely arranging for your training to be put on hold." She slid the document across the desk. "I will arrange for your training to be paused for two weeks, and I will also give you something to allow you to get away from the water for extended periods. At the end of the two weeks, you will have to make the choice whether to give up the water entirely or give up Markus."

"It might not be love," Marina insisted as she signed the contract. Even saying it, her stomach sank at the idea of having only one of the things she wanted so badly. "I just want to get to know him better." Her lower lip quivered. "Maybe I'll love to run as much as I love to swim." She scooped up the contract and tucked it into her backpack before she could change her mind. Her braid trailed behind her as she hurried out of the office.

Idly, from the doorway that connected Rhianna's office to his, Eric Mason asked, "Gee, I wonder whatever might happen if Markus could get over his fear and learn to swim. It's much easier for a human to adapt to the District's needs than the other way around."

Rhianna looked at him innocently. "I have no idea what you are inferring, Riku."

He snorted rudely at that and went back into his office. She just grinned. He had accused her of manipulating people since before they could walk. No one knew her better than her surrogate twin brother, but she still liked to keep him on his toes. Content, she stretched and leaned back in her chair. She loved her job. Ensuring the happiness of her people was her greatest pride and honor.

The rest of the day was a relatively normal one. She had meetings in the morning with a few associates—Enforcers had alliances with nearly every corporation in America—and she then had a lunch meeting with Eric and another Enforcer, Taylor Vincent. Taylor was a part-timer, and though not District born, he had extremely powerful gifts of his own. His wife, Gwyn, was Eric's sister-in-law, and she was the Goddess of Justice. Gwyn's almost-twin sister, Rayna, was the Goddess of Truth. Five years separated their ages but it was impossible to tell by either appearance or action.

It was for that reason that Rhianna approached the lunch table and grinned to see what Taylor was idly sketching. The depiction showed the twins racing in cloud cars as they tried to catch up to the other vehicles in front of them. Taylor's most potent gift was his art, and it was the cornerstone of the game company he owned. Rhianna dropped down into the open chair at the table and asked, "Are we branching into racing games, Taylor?"

"It's a mini-game," he answered absently. "I'm working on a sequel to *My Fair Faerie*, and I decided to bring in Rayna. She's married to the intimidating warlock that gives out quests. Can't imagine where I got that idea."

Eric smirked at him. "You're just sour that I beat you at poker."

"*You* cheated."

Rhianna sighed fondly. "Now, boys, let's play nice. Let's talk about something else. How are the other things going?"

"Just fine," Eric assured her. He dug into his peach cobbler contentedly. Both Rayna and Gwyn were exceptional cooks and kept him and Taylor happily fed. "I checked on two active works, and things are going as expected. I'd give it a few more months before it comes to fruition. On a different subject entirely, I have D.J. arranging to have the entire building baby-proofed. Glory is starting to walk."

Rhianna winced with good nature. "Uh-oh." Glory was a half-Faeriekin, half-warlock who literally charmed anyone she met. Even Rhianna had dreaded the day her niece found her feet. "We need to distract her. Teach her to garden."

"I'm working on it. She likes computers more." He grinned. "She's her mother's child."

Rayna, in addition to being Truth, was also the company hacker. She couldn't be kept out of any system, and even the government had given up trying to stop her. With a sort of 'if you can't beat them, join them' attitude, they now often hired her as a consultant. It kept Rhianna happy, too; she always made sure that Enforcers honored and respected its long-standing alliance with the feds. It had been useful more than once to call in a few favors. She kept an even closer association with the state level. Enforcers needed the authority to be able to tell police and doctors when to step back and let the District handle its own affairs.

Thinking of similar things, Taylor asked, "Is the new birthing ward at our hospital done now?"

"It is!" Rhianna bit into her *souvlaki*. She had been feeling an unusual craving for Greek food lately. There was probably something stirring somewhere from the past. It happened sometimes. Maybe the River Styx under the District was in high flow season. "Freshly painted, freshly remodeled, and they've finished hanging up all of Rayna's landscape paintings." She grinned. "Are you still trying to coax her into drawing backgrounds for your games?"

"I tried offering cookies. It didn't work. I'm hoping that, you know, I might have a trump card soon." He flipped pages and went to another drawing. He spun it around with a grin. "I'll finish it once we need it."

Half-finished on paper was a beautiful baby crib. Eric laughed and clapped Taylor on the back. "Rhi and I noticed a while ago. Congratulations, Taylor. Let us hope for the sake of everyone's sanity, your child is like you and not Gwyn."

Taylor snorted. "Heul told me the horror stories. Trust me, I agree."

Rhianna hid a smile by sipping her wine. Heul Trahern was Gwyn's eldest big brother and had raised her from the age of nine. He would certainly be the expert on her frustratingly innocent trust in the inherent good of mankind. "Speaking of Heul and birthing wards."

"Remy's recovering just nicely," Eric assured her. He smiled. "Heul is waiting on her hand and foot, despite her protests. Nicole is *very* happy with her new baby brother and is already insisting on learning to change him and clothe him."

"Naturally." Rhianna dug in her purse for money. "Her future revolves around children. She has a gift our District needs very badly; Audra can't do all of the tutoring. Having our own kindergarten will do nicely. It will prepare our young ones for the outside world." She tossed bills on the table to cover the cost of her lunch. "No food fights after I'm gone."

Eric and Taylor watched her head out of the restaurant and noted the many wistful eyes that followed her. It was neither uncommon nor unexpected. Rhianna was almost unnaturally beautiful in a way that seemed to transcend gender and perhaps beauty itself. Her thick red hair hung to just past her shoulders in a blend of curls and waves. She was fairly small at a five-two height, and she seemed deceptively slender and delicate. Her vibrant black eyes could almost literally mesmerize people.

Over the entire two thousand plus years that Eric had known her, he had only *very* occasionally seen her date anyone, and those dates had been casual to the point of almost not being dates at all. "She's waiting," he murmured.

"Yeah." Taylor sighed it as he sat back. "Do you know who she is waiting for? Neither Gwyn nor Rayna can determine it."

He hesitated visibly. "I don't know his exact identity," he said slowly, "but something terrible happened. I think this is her second life, and it happened in the first. After everything that happened to the Lucinos, I cornered her. She's been slipping away from me, and it's breaking my heart. She wouldn't tell me anything except that the 'end' is coming and she will face her final redemption or punishment. The one she's waiting for . . . his spirit is growing stronger. She doesn't know if he'll come to her again, though."

"Why not?"

His hands clenched together. "She gave me a very old contract. I can't read it because it's in Ancient Greek. But it—it is voided."

Taylor's heart stopped for a moment. No contract in Enforcers' history had ever been voided. Some had gotten painfully close though, particularly recently as Rhianna's grasp on events lessened. A voided contract meant no protection for the signee. No happy ending. Nothing but an existence of loneliness and pain or, sometimes, even death. The one person who created happy endings for others could not have her own. "I wonder what went wrong," he murmured.

"I suppose we'll find out when 'he' returns." Eric stared out the windows with eyes that could see most anything but not the futures that his sister created for everyone. Even he did not know the extent of her true power. Perhaps that, too, would finally come to light. "Just who were you?" he asked softly. "Just what story are you living?"

(Mount Olympus)

The 3rd District was not the only place of concentrated magic on the Earth. It was the only physical, reachable, place, but it was not alone. A second place was the River Styx. It ran around the world like a band, invisible beneath the surface and only accessible from the basement of the Enforcers' Headquarters. Only District members knew how to get there, and only a select few had actual access.

The third and final location was not underground but instead in the skies. Hidden beyond an invisible film of clouds that could not be seen, sensed, or touched unless you were a god was the legendary place of the Grecian Gods, Olympus itself. The closest point where it touched the Earth was the peak of Mount Olympus. Another point dipped close to the District since the Styx acted as a magnet of sorts that drew in other magical places. Most infamously, the Styx had latched onto another world entirely. The world of Mirage could only be seen on Earth as vague impressions on hot days, but it could be *clearly* seen from the land around the Styx . . . or the sky of Olympus.

It was the first thing that Eros saw when he opened his eyes for the first time in more than two thousand years. Through the cloudy glass of the casket that he rested within, he could see the obvious presence of the faerie tale world. It was not an unfamiliar world. His body had been incapacitated, but his spirit had grown enough in strength over the last few centuries that he had been able to reach out to that beautifully magical place.

He reached out and pushed aside the casket lid. It clattered onto the granite floor and sent off an eerie echoing noise. He gingerly sat up and found that there were no physical aches and pains left from his ordeal. Emotionally was another story. A living, breathing agony churned inside his heart and soul. His blue eyes were ripe with pain as he accepted how much time had passed. "Psyche." He could still smell the scent of her skin and see her mane of red hair. His beautiful wife.

He carefully got to his feet and grimaced as he realized he was still wearing the same chiton he had been wearing in the past. His bare feet made no sound as he walked slowly through the empty halls. The gods and goddesses were gone. Had *been* gone for centuries. Nothing but dust, echoes, and the lingering bitter scent of evil remained. He ignored the last for the time being. It could not touch him.

He found the old scrying pool and it still held water. A wave of his hand cleared the surface to let him look down onto the Earth. He had been somewhat prepared for it by his brief excursions outside his body, but his jaw still dropped when he saw the metropolis that his beloved Greece had become. That would take getting used to seeing!

He scoured every inch of the country with the pool, and he did not find his Psyche. He knew she lived. He had felt her more than once. He had even seen her on Mirage recently. She was out there somewhere, waiting for him. She needed him as terribly as he needed her. They could finally be together.

He sat down on the side of the pool and set about the arduous task of examining every large city. The further he moved from Greece, the stronger her power felt and the more foreign the language and land felt. He landed in a relatively new country that had veritably exploded over the last two centuries, and he found a city of sparkling lights and glass buildings. Her power permeated every mile.

The Styx itself aided him. He recognized its presence and followed it until it bubbled just under the surface of a small district that stood as a reminder of the history that had passed. The buildings looked quite old and historical though there was a single skyscraper that had been modernized. The streets *oozed* magic into the very air, and it had been saturated by his lover's beautiful power. She was far, far stronger than he remembered. She had finally settled into her gifts and almost embraced them wholly.

His breath wedged painfully in his chest as the pool suddenly revealed her to him. His eyes devoured her greedily. Her thick red mane. Her velvety black eyes. Her lithe and supple body. Had she gotten more beautiful, or had he simply forgotten how she made him feel? He knew it was not his imagination or his personal opinion that she was the most beautiful in the world. It was that very thing that had caused all of the trouble in the first place.

His impulsive nature demanded he jump out of the clouds and grab her up immediately. *That* was not a good idea at all. It, too, had caused many problems in the past. He needed to put himself into her world. He would descend, learn to live among humans, and he would put out the signals only she could read that would finally bring them together. At the least, integrating into society would not be hard. Being a god had its merits.

He strode swiftly toward the exit. Every step made a chilling darkness close behind him to cut off his return. It was no darkness that brought the restful night. It was the darkness that brought fear; it was evil itself. The acrid scent seared his sensitive nose as he continued to walk. He did not look back. Olympus was his home no longer.

The moment he broke through the invisible clouds and hovered unseen in the sky of Earth, he felt the palace seal entirely. He pressed against the entry, just out of curiosity, and it held firm. If he ever wanted to return, he would need to find another way to pierce the clouds. So be it. His future lay on the land below.

He did not go right to the district where his love waited. The way her power had saturated the land meant that she quite literally saw everything. He instead landed out of sight beyond the district and took care to mimic the average wear of the male passerby. When he became visible and stepped out of the alley, no one saw anything but a surprisingly and shockingly handsome man in blue jeans and a t-shirt. If they noticed he was barefoot, they didn't say anything. Eros only noticed it himself when he stepped on a discarded cigarette. He winced wryly and made himself some sandals while no one was watching.

The culture shock was a bit horrific. He could make himself understand the language but that did not mean he *understood* the language. These people had words that simply did not translate over for him. Everyone had interesting little devices attached to their ears that they talked into. Others were using their fingers to poke at the screen. Tiny little things were stuck in ears and attached by wires to those devices and others. Strange, giant, glowing signs seemed to be trying to sell things. Why did a partially-eaten apple need a sign that big?

It was noisy, it was smelly, and it was insane. Eros tried to duck around a corner to get out of the way of an oncoming crush, and he smacked right into a young woman. He grabbed her arm quickly to hold her on her feet. Melancholy brown eyes looked up at him. "Sorry," she sighed. "I wasn't watching."

"Neither was I."

She looked at him for a moment before cocking her head slightly. "You have an interesting accent. Sounds kind of Greek."

"Well, that is because I am." He gave her a courtly bow and quick grin. No grin greeted him in return. The God of Love was no slouch for emotions. He ducked his head and peered into her dark eyes. She stood a handful of inches shorter than his five-ten height—something he had quickly noticed was now a norm rather than a sign of being a god. "Do we have a problem, my lady?"

"I lost my sense of humor."

"Literally?"

"Seems so. Weirdly, it happened after I banged my funny bone."

He arched a pale brow. "Funny bone?"

She held out her arm and pointed to the spot in question. "Got me as to why it's called that as it isn't funny to hit. It hurts a lot. I used to laugh a lot but now nothing is funny." She offered her hand. "Priya." He studied her hand and she shook her head. "You *are* from far away. Handshake? Sign of greeting?"

"Ah." He took her hand and felt bemused by the entire thing. "Tell me, Priya. Are you gifted?"

Her eyes widened and she looked around hastily. "Uhm, maybe," she whispered. "I can sometimes feel others' emotions."

"Then I can help you." He caught her elbow and escorted her further down the sidewalk. "My name is Eros," he told her. "I am the God of Love."

New York had its crazies, to be sure, but Priya found herself unable to doubt him. He definitely looked like what she would expect from the tales of Eros: hot, sexy, and way too good for mortal women. "I need my sense of humor, not a lover."

"I did not offer to find you a lover." Though he intended to do so, given how lonely her heart felt to him. "I am a god, Priya. I can make things happen." He snapped his fingers and a scroll appeared in his hand. "If you do exactly as I tell you, then you will be happy and humorous again. Will you sign yourself into my care?"

She frowned at the scroll. "You won't own my soul, right?"

"Do not be silly. I have no need for your soul. This contract will simply allow me to do everything needed to ensure you are happy again. You may read it as slowly as you wish. It is in your language."

It was indeed. "Do you really fly and have wings and shoot people with arrows?"

The corner of his mouth kicked up into a wicked grin. "Frequently."

She huffed out a breath and signed the scroll without letting herself think about it. "You're still going to set me up, aren't you? I can feel it inside you."

He cuffed her chin. "You will have to trust my instincts to know what you need. It is my job."

"You're a matchmaker?"

"I believe I am." He looked around at the bustling streets and could see the diminished force of love. The world had become quite cynical. "In fact, I believe that is exactly what I am and should be. I suppose it is time I put my powers to good use. This world certainly needs them!" He smiled at Priya. "I could use a friend and an assistant. I cannot yet pay you, but it will not take long."

"I guess working for a god would be better than working for McDonalds." She couldn't find the ability to smile, so she hugged him instead. "I can teach you how to handle our world. I think it's probably really different for you."

She had no idea, he reflected ruefully. She proved to be a valuable ally, however, and he was as pleased personally as he was professionally to watch her 'coincidentally' meet a young doctor while having her elbow X-rayed. He obtained a small building just on the outside of Psyche's district—the 3rd District, it was called—and he opened up his new 'marriage consulting and matchmaking' business.

By the end of the first month, he was no longer feeling the culture shock as badly. He could even read a newspaper without asking Priya for a translation. They were sharing a bag of donuts before their doors opened for the day when he flipped to the business section of the paper and felt his heart stop.

The look on his face had Priya peering over to see what he was looking at. A beautiful color photo of Rhianna Taber greeted her eyes. She looked again at Eros and saw the blend of longing and suffering in his eyes. "You know Ms. Taber?"

"I did," he admitted. "A long time ago." He trailed a finger over her familiar features. He knew what she had been doing and how hard she had been working. He shoved to his feet and walked over to look out the front windows. Only a single street separated him from the one he loved. The 3rd District began right across the road. "I am so sorry I left you alone for so long, my love," he murmured achingly. "We will be together again soon."

CHAPTER SEVEN

(Two months later)

Rhianna was never not busy. There was always something to do, a meeting to attend, or simply people to watch over. At least every other day, she would see something in her dreams that meant there was someone who needed her. She would arrange the situation and get things moving; sometimes a contract was involved from the beginning, and others it came along later. It varied.

Perhaps that was why she was so puzzled one day to discover she had reached an impasse. All currently issued contracts were in a phase where she wasn't required. Others were not due to come around for another year or two. She could still feel the flow of love energy in the world and knew it was running just fine—perhaps even stronger than usual—and yet there were no new clients coming in from the outside. Even people who did not stay in the District would find their way there if they needed a happy ending. In fact, most people knew that crossing paths with the District could make dreams come true.

So what the hell was happening? She swiveled on her chair and grabbed her phone. She punched a button and waited until it picked up. "Rayna? Are you busy?"

"Define busy."

"Are you currently engaged in anything that you can't put down for five minutes to come help out your doting sister-in-law?"

"Nuh-uh. Be right up."

The delicate Faeriekin did not arrive alone. Eric was tagging along at her heels. "Rhi," he said as he walked in without looking up from a printout, "Rayna and I have almost finished reorganizing Failsafe. She has to keep getting into their system for org charts, though, as they won't provide them willingly."

Rhianna just shook her head. "Color me not surprised. They were not very happy when I called to tell them that you were on the verge of visiting. They either abide by the policies of Enforcers or they get a reboot."

Eric's presence was a bigger threat than Rhianna's for the simple fact that he only went to a company when someone royally screwed up. He typically handled the behind-the-scenes details of their various companies, and she took care of everything on the front. The contrast of their personalities—her more inviting, friendly air versus his colder, more intimidating one—made them best suited for the role they filled.

The *only* person that Eric had never been able to intimidate (other than Rhianna) was his wife, Rayna. She barely reached his shoulder in height, was even more ridiculously delicate than Rhianna, and she faced the world with the same innocent sweetness of her sister. Rhianna had known from the very beginning that Eric would need someone special, and she had been very happy to find that someone for him. "You're being followed, Rayna."

Rayna's violet eyes lit with humor as she smiled. "I can't get rid of him," she said solemnly. She giggled and dodged when he made a mock swipe for her. Her fingers skimmed down his arm tenderly for a moment before she headed over to where Rhianna's desk sat. "What do you need help with, Rhi?"

Rhianna vacated her chair. "Have a seat. I need you to hit the web and see if you can track down what the hell is going on. The flow of energy that I always sense is still moving and yet I haven't seen any signs that someone needs help."

"Huh." Eric leaned on the edge of the desk to watch as Rayna started typing. "That is a bit out of the ordinary, to be sure."

"What am I looking for?" Rayna asked.

"Anything relating to happiness, love, etcetera. The stuff that we normally take care of handling with contracts." Rhianna crossed her arms and watched over Rayna's head as she zipped through the internet like an international speed-reader. No one would ever think she hadn't learned to read until she was twenty-one. Then again, one of her gifts was her exceptional intelligence. It blended quite well with her ability to hear, see, and reveal the Truth in all living creatures.

Rhianna adored Rayna, obviously, but she always had to be *extra* careful around the tiny goddess. Rayna's ability to hear someone's heart speak the truth at the same time their voice issued a lie meant that Rhianna had to work hard to keep her associates from knowing things that she simply did not want them to know yet—if ever.

"Ah ha!" Rayna sat back happily. "I think I found our energy diverter. Look at this." She pointed at the screen. "Cupid's Grove. It's a relatively new matchmaking agency and marriage counseling services place. The marriage counselor who runs it just 'always seems to know who is right for you.' They claim a one hundred percent accuracy."

Eric whistled softly. "That's a hell of a claim. Where are they located?"

"Wow. Right outside the District. The website is just a placeholder, basically. It has the info, the reviews and references, and a downloadable questionnaire that you fill out and submit in order to book a meeting. Says he only deals with people face-to-face because he can only help people he knows."

Rhianna began to scowl. "He is messing with energies best not messed with."

Sympathetic, Rayna put a hand on her arm. "He's no different from other counselors, Rhi."

"The hell he isn't!" Little sparks filled Rhianna's eyes that Eric had always called her 'temper sparks.' "If he was like the rest, I wouldn't be feeling the flow of love energy moving stronger without at least one person knocking on my door! Mortals should *not* be interfering with this sort of thing!"

"Ah ha!" Eric shot to his feet and there was a similar temper on his face. "Damn it, Rhianna! I *knew* you were manipulating people all these years!" His hands hit the desk with a thump. "You've been setting up people like a damned matchmaker for two thousand years—including me!"

Her hands hit the desk too as she went nose-to-nose with him. "If you dare say you're mad at me for making people happy, I'm calling you a liar, and your wife will confirm it!"

Rayna was a smart cookie; she knew better than to get between Eric and Rhianna when they were going at it. The office door cautiously opened, and Taylor and Gwyn looked around the edge. Gwyn was almost perfectly identical to Rayna except for hair that was pure white and eyes that looked as much gray as violet. "Uhm." She cleared her throat. "You guys are kinda scaring the natives. Heard you downstairs."

Both heads turned. "She's finally admitted to the fact that she's the reason there are no coincidences in our district!" he snapped.

"He's just pissy because he hates when I'm right and he's not!" she snapped equally.

Rayna got to her feet and put a hand on each of their shoulders. "Okay. Fists down. Play nice."

Striving for humor to diffuse the tension—fists had indeed been known to fly in the past—Gwyn joked, "I guess that means Rhianna is the bride of Eros!"

Eric snorted. Rhianna couldn't. Something obviously shocked moved through her eyes and was noticed by all of her friends. Rayna was still touching her, and she felt the truth of the statement blasting down her nerves. Her jaw dropped. "Ohmygod she is!" she blurted.

Taylor and Eric's jaws dropped as well. "B-but!" Gwyn could barely wrap her brain around it. "But we don't remember you!" she protested. She shook her head hard. "I remember Eros! He was our favorite god 'cause he wasn't stuck-up like the others could be. Where were you, Rhi? We should remember you! It's not fair that we don't!"

"You died before I came into the picture!" Rhianna snapped. "All of you get out of my office right now!"

"Rhi, please!" Rayna tugged on her sleeve. "Let us help you!"

"*Get out!*"

Not even Eric was willing to take her on when she got that note in her voice. He and Taylor hastily escaped into his office. The twins scrambled out the front entry. Both doors slammed tight behind them. Under his breath, Taylor muttered, "I think things might finally be starting to make sense."

Eric muttered back, "We can sic the girls on her later when she hits the point of feeling guilty for yelling at them. She hates yelling at the people she loves."

"Then why do you provoke her?"

"*Someone* has to."

Rhianna scowled at both doors and tossed herself down into her chair. She was going to have to apologize to all four of them, but she just did *not* feel like it. Events of the past were still too raw and too painful for her to bear remembering. Worse still, the memories had a tendency to overwhelm her abilities and leave her psychically burnt out.

Rather than do nothing, she downloaded the questionnaire and opened it. She would fill it out, send it in, and see what happened. If the company was just a normal one with an unusually gifted owner, she would let it slide. If they were deliberately messing with the energy, she would take action. They could cause far too much trouble if they were left unchecked.

The questionnaire was surprisingly lengthy. She very nearly started just randomly answering, but something made her change her mind. What the hell. Being honest would prove whether or not they knew what they were doing.

The questions ranged from standard likes and dislikes to political and religious beliefs, and she was bemused to find that her Hellenism was listed among the Christianity, Judaism, and other sundry items. Few people believed in the Greek gods anymore; they had become nothing more than a series of myths and legends.

The next question surprised her: *Be honest. What is your ideal in a physical lover? Hair color, eyes, ethnicity, etc. Don't be ashamed if you like a type.*

She paused for a moment before marking the blond hair, blue eyes, and golden/tanned skin boxes. Her husband's image had been imprinted on her mind though she had only twice gotten to see him in the light. Her body knew his touch. Her ears knew his voice, and her lips knew his taste. She knew how he felt and how his skin always carried the scent of peaches. Only her eyes had been deprived of the chance to love him, and when she had tried to claim that chance, she had ruined it all.

A headache threatened behind her eyes and she shoved out the memories. A bit defiantly, she used the 'Other' box to write *He should look like a Greek god.* Good luck to them matching *that* one. Nothing and no one was as beautiful as a god or goddess.

She sent the questionnaire off to the email address provided and went to get herself some coffee; she badly needed caffeine. Much to her surprise, she had a response waiting for her when she returned only a few minutes later.

Greetings, Ms. Taber!

I am happy to say that I think we have the perfect *match for you! To ensure that we truly do know you as well as we think, we would love for you to come in tomorrow for a personal meeting with the counselor. We have an opening at 9:00am; the rest of his day is booked. If you cannot make it tomorrow, please let me know and I can easily find you another time.*

We look forward to meeting you at Cupid's Grove!

Priya Martinell

Administrative Assistant

Rhianna drummed her fingers on her desk for a few moments, then shrugged. She responded to say she would be there at nine and made sure to put the meeting on her calendar. They obviously did not know what they were doing, and that made her feel a bit better. She would go in, clarify her instincts, and then wash her hands of it. Maybe there was something else messing with the energy. She was going to have to apologize to Rayna and ask her to look again.

The rest of the day went normal enough for Enforcers, and her dreams that night were strangely empty. She had known she was losing her grip on events because she was too close to them, but had she passed the point where she would have even a hint of the goings-on? Perhaps the end was closer than she thought even though she had not seen evil moving for several months.

She contemplated her closet in the morning before the meeting. She really wasn't inclined to go out in her normal suits and business wear. The Grove was all but across the street from her District, and she had effectively taken the day off anyway. She grabbed the lovely yellow sundress that Brian Matthews had made her as a thank you gift and paired it with white leggings. Most yellows did not work with her coloring but not this one. Its buttery hue perfectly flattered her red hair.

She walked the blocks over to Cupid's Grove and felt the familiar tingle that meant she had left her District behind. Much to her bemusement and reluctant admiration, she rather liked the look of Cupid's Grove. It was done with a heavily Grecian architectural style, and she recognized the familiar work of Seven Wishes Design. Lexie and Joseff must have had a ball with the nearly invisible windows that made it seem as if the pillars were entirely open between them.

Her second surprise came as soon as she walked in the front door. She felt . . . strangely comfortable there. The décor likely helped, but it went deeper than that. She just felt welcome and secure in a way she normally only felt in her District.

The lovely young Indian woman behind the desk looked up curiously and began to smile. "Good morning, Ms. Taber! I'm Priya. Welcome to Cupid's Grove. Have a seat and I'll buzz Aaron that you're here."

"Thank you." Bemused because she wasn't used to people acting so blasé about her presence, she instead wandered along the lobby and admired the paintings. Most were depictions of the gods and goddesses, of course. She almost felt as if she had gone back in time. It was more nostalgic than bitter.

"Ms. Taber?" Priya called. "Aaron will see you. He's just down the hall. His office is on the left. His name is on the door."

Rhianna linked her hands behind her back as she started down the hall. It was a short one, and there were only two doors anyway. The one on the right went into what looked like a break room of sorts. The left indeed had a name placard:

Aaron Konstantinos. Of course it would be Greek. She glanced at the end of the hall and found a statue of a bow and arrow carved from olive wood.

Her ire stirred anew. She opened the door and walked in saying, "I hate to call bullshit, but I'm afraid I must. My perfect match isn't even on this plane." She broke off and stopped sharply as she reached the center of the office and realized it was empty. Were they yanking her chain?

The door shut behind her. Before she could turn, a powerful male arm slid around her waist and a hand covered her eyes. The scent of peaches crept into her lungs and dug in with velvet claws. Familiar, achingly familiar, lips tenderly skimmed over her ear. "I think that for once in your long life," an equally familiar, husky, voice murmured in Ancient Greek, "you might be wrong about something, my beloved."

Memories ambushed her on a wave of powerful emotions and dormant desires. A headache tore through her head behind her eyes, and she felt him murmur something soft and soothing. The pain evaporated, and her body lost its strength. She couldn't keep up with her own heart and mind. She barely noticed him lifting her into his arms before everything blessedly shut down and she didn't have to think or feel at all.

Her escape was only disturbed when she felt another presence invade her mind. It was not Eric despite the bond they shared. She could barely feel him at all anymore; she had thoroughly burned her telepathy out. The presence slipping past her defenses was the one person who held as much power as she did. *Come back to me, beloved,* his voice murmured soothingly. *I am here now.*

Cognizance returned in the form of feeling arms around her. A heart beat, strong and sure, under her ear, and the sound brought back memories anew. Heated summer nights where they had slept with the covers thrown off and she had used him for her pillow. The autumn chill where they had snuggled under blankets. Tender fingertips caressed her face. "Beloved. Look at me."

She forced herself to open her eyes. The face that looked down at her was the one burned into her memory. Thick blond hair that fell in loose curls around a face too handsome to belong to any mortal. Intense blue eyes that glimmered with a hint of iridescence. A mouth made for kissing. She tried to smile but it trembled. "Eros."

His fingers skimmed over her lips. "My name is Aaron now," he told her huskily. "I have placed myself within your world the way you once tried to place yourself within mine. My Rhianna." He said her name slowly, savoring it like wine. "I want to hear myself calling your name. Hear you finally calling mine." His mouth skimmed across her features and steadily lower. "Come lie with me."

Any protest died as his lips claimed hers in a kiss that seared her to her soul. Two thousand years had not gone by; he kissed her as he always had before. Hard, urgent, hungry. Her fingers fisted into his thick hair as she twisted up to meet his passion halfway. Sleeping nerves awoke with a vengeance and rushed into overdrive as pleasure flooded her body and erased loneliness. "Aaron," she whispered thickly when he lifted his head slightly.

A light shudder moved through his body. He shot to his feet with her cradled in his arms and strode swiftly down the hall. "I have need for my wife, and you have need for me." His eyes burned with bright sparks as he looked down at her. It was his desire for her that fueled his power. "Our marriage contract may be voided, but it is neither broken nor dissolved. You are still mine. I am still yours."

"I've been waiting for you." She nipped at his lower lip. It looked wonderfully bitable. "Let go of my legs." He did so, and her grip on his shoulders meant that she did not fall. She lithely boosted herself up and hooked her knees on either side of his hips. "I am stronger than I look, my husband."

He swung her with a suitably romantic flair into the bedroom, and she found a laugh welling up. She spared the room enough of a look to see that it was the same style as his office and she noticed the night sky beyond the tall windows. "It's night?"

"You had need for rest." He slowly lowered her to the bed. "I have dreamed of this. Even when I could not feel, could not reach out, I dreamed of you." He dragged her up for another of his drugging kisses. "I need to feel your body."

A moan answered him as he raked his hands down her figure and savored every supple curve even through her clothes. It was beautiful music. The act of love, of desire, always seemed more beautiful with her. "Mine."

He had never been a quiet lover. He demanded, he coaxed, and he gave. He gave so generously. There was nothing like being loved by the God of Love. Perhaps she should have known all along just who she had married. Perhaps there could have been no two thousand years of pain. No evil in the distance. She grabbed onto him with all her strength and poured herself into a kiss that made the sparks flare in his eyes.

A rough curse left his lips as he shot to his feet. He could not wait. He crossed quickly to throw the curtains closed. The room was plunged into darkness that entirely shielded him from her sight. The same was not true of him; he could see in the dark and saw her clearly.

His action rocked her to her soul. Her emotions tumbled over themselves as she tried find him in the dark. Why would he insist on darkness still? She knew his identity. The gods were gone. There was no need to hide. It couldn't be that he did not want to see her; she knew his sight was literally godlike. It had to be that he did not want her to see him. But *why*? He had absolutely no modesty or self-consciousness. What didn't he want her to see?

A memory rushed past her eyes. Her first glimpse of him when he had snuffed the candle she had lit. His bare arm had reached past her, and he had been glowing. A god only glowed when they were in their 'true' form. He was the God of Love and Desire. His true form would be his naked one. Even socks would dilute the effect. If he was wholly bared, he would reveal his true self. *He did not want her to see his true self.*

Mortals were not typically capable of beholding a god's true self because they did not have the capacity to feel deep enough emotion. If she did not feel a deep enough love or desire for her husband, she would be torn apart by her body and heart struggling to comprehend his beauty. He did not believe that her emotions went deep enough to endure. He still did not believe in her love!

His hands suddenly closed around her waist as his hot mouth caressed her neck. She began to push at his shoulders and try to twist away. "Stop!" she ordered as firmly as she could, but the rasp to her voice gave away her desire.

"Do not be afraid. I know it has been a while but—" He broke off in absolute shock as a pillow smacked him right in the nose. He released her immediately and sat up to turn on the bedside lamp. Light spilled into the room and revealed the tableau. He had stripped down to his pants, and she had gotten off the bed to back away several feet. She looked rumpled, flushed, and too damn beautiful for his sanity. He could *feel* her frustration even at range, and it was only the sparks of temper in her eyes that kept him in place. "What is wrong with you?" he demanded.

"I will not give myself to a man who won't give me all of himself in return!" she retorted hotly. "You won't give me your true self, Aaron!"

"What are you talking about?" He shot to his feet. "I have been naked with you a hundred times. You know every inch of my body. I have felt your fingers and lips everywhere. How can you say I have not given you my true self?"

A blend of humor and sadness moved through her temper as she realized that he genuinely had no idea that it was *only* her fingers and lips that knew him. She could excuse the past—he had been trying to keep his identity a secret. He had given himself away by insisting on darkness now that there was no need to hide. "You are hiding from me," she said only. "Protest all you like, I know it for fact. I will *not* accept the half-relationship that I was given before!"

He tried to grasp her shoulders and her power rose to slap him back a step. Frustration burned out of his blue eyes for long moments as he stared at her. She was not the Psyche he remembered. She was stronger, more powerful, and far more stubborn!

A flash went through his mind of the questionnaire that she had filled out. It had matched his perfectly. A one hundred percent compatibility from the part where she had admitted liking having her own way (so did he) to the part where she had confessed that she disliked yelling at loved ones but would do it anyway if they pissed her off (and so did he). Delight began to rise inside him. "You are perfect."

Red brows began to slowly lift. "Beg pardon?"

"You are perfect for me! We *matched*, Rhianna. Were you honest on your questionnaire?"

"Well . . . yes, actually." She shrugged wryly. "I figured it would reveal you as a fraud." She scowled. "I did *not* expect the God of Love to be the one messing with the energy, but I think I should have! No one else would dare."

"It is my job, my love." He grabbed her shoulders. "We matched. We matched one hundred percent. The person you are now is perfect for me. I am finally perfect for you. Give me access to your building so I may see you tomorrow."

She shook her head slightly. The way he could change gears put Taylor's cloud racing cars to shame. "Aaron, I'm sorry, but I am emotionally and mentally fried harder than an overdone *baklava*. You lost me. Again."

"Give me access to your building," he repeated patiently. "I wish to see you more."

A ladylike snort answered him. "You're a god. You can do whatever you want."

"I *want* to prove that I am hiding nothing. I want to meet you halfway. We will have an equal relationship, Rhianna. I do not want what we had before either. I will proudly claim you as mine alone. Let me see you at work. Share your world with me."

He could not possibly learn the depth of her love if he was not with her. She wasn't even sure if he ever *could* trust that she loved him as deeply as she did. What would she do if he never did? She didn't know, but she *did* know that they had a chance for the happy ending they had been deprived of before. He had forgiven her and he had come back to her. She had to take the chance that they could have it all. "Alright," she conceded. She made a slight gesture and a plastic card appeared in his hand. "You will not need to sign in nor need an escort upstairs. I'm on the top floor."

"I will be there." He dropped the card on the bed and reached out to thread his fingers into her thick red hair. "Let me kiss you one more time and then I will send you home. It will be just a kiss. You have stated your feelings and I will try to abide by them." He teasingly nibbled at her lips. "I will not promise to not kiss you."

She slowly spread her hands across his chest. Her fingertips tingled deliciously at the feel of his skin and the power that burned beneath. She rose up on her toes and took his mouth before he could take hers. It slowly deepened and unraveled with a sweetness that did not keep it from being as hungry as the rest. There was nothing quite like a man who loved to kiss, and he certainly did. She eased back a breath and said huskily, "I had forgotten how well you scattered my thoughts."

It took a great deal of willpower to resist the urge to seduce her right there. His cranky and frustrated body was only a minor problem. It was *her* hunger beating at him that drove him mad. Only he could bring her the pleasure she craved, and he knew it. Love made everything else pale in comparison. They had ruined each other for the rest of eternity from that very first night some two millennia before. "Go home," he muttered against her lips.

She blinked and was inexplicably back in her house. Her purse was even on the couch. She looked around slowly and then sank down to sit on a chair. Her lover had come back to her as she had always prayed, but he didn't even see the wall he had placed between them. She couldn't even tell him the problem! Losing her ability to see the future in no way kept her from having premonitions of the present. To tell him what was wrong would be to make worse happen.

Omniscience could be nothing but a pain in the ass sometimes. She shoved to her feet and stalked into the kitchen to find her favorite wine. She was going to have a glass, take a hot bath, and try to pretend that she would be able to get any sleep before work the following day. Thinking it, she winced as she took the first drink. She still owed Gwyn, Taylor, and Rayna an apology. (Eric deserved what he got, the fink.) She would buy some flowers and donuts on the way in. Maybe if she bribed them with sugar, they wouldn't ask any awkward questions.

Yeah. And pigs could fly.

CHAPTER EIGHT

Rhianna arrived at work the following morning to discover that the receptionist, D.J., was busily hanging new paintings that Taylor had completed. The lobby was decorated with his original art, though perhaps 'original' was not the word for them. Each fancifully depicted Rhianna and Eric's favorite jobs. They showed the Shaughnessys, the Carmichaels, and the Deases. Now being added were the paintings to represent the Lucinos.

The first showed two identical young women, one a princess and one a commoner, sitting back to back. Each looked up at a different man who was smiling at her. The second painting was split in two. The first half showed a gosling being rejected by ducks. The second half showed the now grown swan being drawn into the arms of another. The third in the series depicted a tall tower with a braid of hair spilling from the window. Shadows on the walls inside implied the owner was in a lover's arms.

The other side of the lobby had paintings of the events on Mirage. There was a new one there too; an image of a dark-skinned faerie holding an upside-down spell book while a prince holding an arrow peered over her shoulder.

Rhianna's mood lifted at the reminder of the good that had been done. She handed off one of the flowers in her hand to D.J. "Since you don't eat donuts."

"Carbs and I are not friends," he agreed with a grin. "Oh," he added as she headed for the elevator, "wolf's on grounds."

Rhianna stifled a groan. She normally loved getting a visit from her 'wolf', but she really didn't feel up to dealing with her at the moment. She was tired, frustrated, and cranky. Lucky for her, she ran into Rayna and Gwyn first on the top floor where she and Eric had their offices. "Peace offering?" She held out the flowers and box of pastry. "I'm sorry for yelling at you. I'm just touchy on the whole thing."

They both looked at her with solemn eyes and then hugged her tight. "S'okay," Gwyn told her. "We love you so we don't mind if you get mad." She pulled back and grinned impishly. "You wouldn't get mad at us if you didn't love us, so I guess we can know it's a sign that we're important to you."

"Two of my favorite people." Rhianna sighed. "Share with Taylor, please. I owe him the apology as well."

A matching impish grin lit Rayna's eyes. "But not Riku?"

"Your husband deserves what he gets, and you know it! Pleh. Anyone make coffee yet?"

"Rayna did," Taylor said from the doorway to the conference room right across the hall. "I'll grab you a cup. You look a bit peaked, Rhi. Didn't sleep well?" He grinned. "Let me guess, you spent yesterday yelling at the marriage counselor for things beyond his control."

She winced. "Yeah, I guess you could say that."

Rayna frowned thoughtfully. She was still hugging Rhianna so she could feel that what she had said was the truth, and yet . . . something felt *off* somehow. She just didn't know what. Movement in the corner of her eye had her turning her head with a smile. "Look what we found, Audra!"

Audra Shaughnessy leaned a shoulder against the door to Rhianna's office and slowly lifted a black brow. She had never seen her oldest friend in quite such a condition. Her sensitive werewolf nose scented the air, and an odd look crossed her face. "Rhi?"

Rhianna stifled a sigh. "Yes, dear?"

"What—or rather *who*—have you been doing lately that would change your scent this much? You have the scent of a male all over you! Sure as *hell* it wouldn't be there unless you'd been doing an impersonation of a clinging vine on him!"

She groaned and shoved past her friend into her office. "Damn it, Audra! Why can't you ever have any tact?" She scowled as she saw Eric watching her cautiously from the entry into his office. "Now what?" she demanded.

"Er, pardon my asking, but just what happened at Cupid's Grove yesterday? I got a headache from the backwash of your brain going into overdrive, and now I can't even reach you at all. You're completely burned out, Rhi." He frowned. "I'm worried about you."

"I'm fine, okay?"

"No, she's not." Rayna scowled. "She's cranky and frustrated!"

"Damn it, Rayna!"

Audra grinned a bit. "This gets better by the minute."

Rhianna's temper had never exactly been a tame one to begin with, and despite two millennia of learning self-control, events lately had pushed her to the edge and kept her there. The combination of physical frustration and lack of sleep on top of her burnout had her snapping, "At the risk of repeating myself, get out of my office! All of you!"

Audra straightened and leaned down until they were eye level; she stood eight inches taller than the older woman. "Quit taking out your problems on us! It's not our fault that you're getting a dose of your own medicine!"

"You have no idea what you're talking about!" she retorted hotly.

"Yeah, because someone around here never tells anyone if there's something wrong!"

"Excuse me for not wanting to concern you with things you can't help!"

"Excuse me for calling that a load of bullshit! You know damned well that you can't get a happy ending alone!"

Someone knocked very loudly on the door, and all eyes turned. Aaron struggled as hard as he could to keep from laughing out right at what he had heard and seen. He had been wondering just who would receive the sharp edge of his wife's inevitable temper. "I suppose I am interrupting, but Rhianna said that I could come by anytime." He smiled. "I am Aaron Konstantinos. I am Rhianna's husband."

Heads swung toward Rayna, but the way her jaw hung open said that he was, in fact, telling the truth. He was also a far safer target for Rhianna's temper for she knew he could give as good as he got, and she didn't risk damaging him. She snatched up the book on her desk and chucked it at his head. "You can't call yourself that!" she snapped. "I was *reborn*!"

He gracefully dodged the projectile. "I beg to differ, my love. Your heart and soul are the same as it always was, and therefore you are still my wife. It was those things that I bound myself to. I am a god." A little smirk touched his lips. "You will never escape me, Psyche."

"I am not the Psyche you knew!"

He had known that, of course, but that did not stop him from standing by his beliefs. Their contract still bound them. It would bind them until the day they ceased to exist entirely. If he ever faced a future where she left him for good, he would sacrifice every drop of his power to follow her. "No," he finally agreed softly, "but I love you no less."

Taylor and Eric exchanged a wide-eyed look as they finally realized just what story encompassed Rhianna's life. Gwyn and Rayna looked at Aaron hopefully, as if worried he did not recognize them, and he smiled. "My favorite little goddesses," he teased gently. "I am glad to see you again, Dike, Aletheia."

They gave happy cries and rushed forward to hug him tight. The moment Gwyn touched him, his brows shot up. He looked at Taylor, and Taylor just smiled. "I would assume the God of Love and Desire might sense such a thing. Yes, she's pregnant. Rayna—er, Aletheia—and Eric have a daughter already."

"I will wish to meet her and give her a blessing."

Rhianna could feel another headache brewing and pressed her fingers to her eyes. Eric studied her, studied Aaron, and then her again. "Rhi?" he asked as gently as he could. He knew she was pushing the edges of her control and he feared that she might exhaust her temper. He would not be able to handle it if temper became tears. "Did you really take the God of Love as your husband?" It was *her* truth he sought. He stood by what *she* wanted, not Aaron.

She sighed. "Kind of."

At the same time, Aaron promptly said, "She did not take me nearly often enough."

Audra barely turned a laugh into a snort. Seeing the hot look Rhianna shot at Aaron, Gwyn and Rayna grabbed their own husbands and beat a hasty retreat. None of them wanted to stick around for the fireworks. Audra feared next to nothing, and she would be damned if Rhianna suffered any longer. She strode over to Aaron and looked him dead in the eye. "I'm Audra Shaughnessy. Rhianna saved my life."

"I can see the threads in your soul from the imprint of your contract," he concurred. "I am aware of your story, she-wolf. I am pleased to see you are happy." He held out a hand with a smile. "As you like."

She sniffed at his hand intently and was not at all surprised to, at last, find the illusive tang that matched perfectly to Rhianna. She turned, looked at her friend sharply, and then left the office entirely. She had troops to rally just in case they were needed.

Rhianna had not needed the confirmation that Aaron was her perfect mate. Everything else about them fused like two halves of a whole; why shouldn't their scents do it as well? Everything she was and stood for welled inside her painfully as she fought the urge to throw herself into his arms and never let go. He could not yet give her what she needed. As long as he withheld his true self, there would never be the absolute fusion they so desperately needed in order to be happy for eternity.

She began to sway on her feet as too many years of grief and loneliness dragged her down. She would have fallen to her knees if he hadn't materialized in front of her and caught her in his arms. He was solid, safe, and secure. Her promise of a life filled with the things she had lost forever.

Tears began to well without stop. They slid down her face as she stared up at him almost blindly, and she did not know that they ran dark from the gouges on her soul. Panic briefly stopped his heart. She was far more fragile than he had believed. Those who felt the most were the ones who hurt the most. He knew it intimately. He just had not realized that she did as well.

He wrapped her fiercely in his embrace and transported them away. She needed sanctuary. She needed a place where she felt safe to break apart so that he could put her together again. "When did you last cry?" he asked her roughly as he walked through his house toward the gardens out back.

"I don't remember," she whispered. She buried her face against his shoulder. "It seemed like such a useless exercise. Tears can't change what has already been done."

"Some can. Tears hold magic, my beloved. Tears shed in grief can bring healing. Tears shed in love can create miracles." He stepped out into the lush backyard and moved toward the immense bath surrounded by peach trees. A padded bench waited, and he sat down with Rhianna still held tenderly in his arms. "Heal," he murmured into her hair. "Let go and begin to heal."

The fragrant scent of the flowers, the sweet scent of peaches, and the steamy mist of the water reminded her anew of the beautiful, happy, days before everything had fallen apart. She buried her face against his shirt and let the tears come freely. She wanted to heal. She was so tired of being unable to escape the past. The curse of her ability to love as deeply as her immortal husband.

He rocked her back and forth and sang softly in Ancient Greek. He hurt for the pain she endured, but he refused to stop the tears even though he could. They were long overdue. If she had only cried back in Greece! But, no, his leaving her had been the thing to awaken her gifts, and she had immediately set out to prove her worth. His blind stupidity had caused far, far too many problems that he now had to unravel.

The tears were eventually spent and she rested in his arms. She felt exhausted from her soul out but strangely more peaceful. She could have the strength to endure. She could find the will to continue to wait until he believed. It would come. It had to come. Whether or not it came before she faced her final judgment was the only question.

His eyes narrowed as he felt the odd sense of guilt inside her. He pulled her back and caught her face in his hands. "What are you thinking? You have nothing to be guilty over."

"Aaron." She turned her face into one of his hands. "You know what I did. I have been paying off my sin for two thousand years."

"*No.*" He shook his head hard. "Curse it to the Underworld, you are *not* paying off a sin! You have no sin! A debt, yes, you had and you have repaid." He brushed his lips over her still damp lashes as she frowned. "My beloved, you were reborn early. You had not yet earned a rebirth by dying as young as you did. Zeus and Hades bent the rules a bit to have you be reborn and *then* earn it."

"Why did they choose the time they did?" she whispered. "It was a scant hundred years later. Did they feel I needed this long to pay off my debt?"

His lips curved. "You chose the time and place. A soul that is to be reborn *chooses* its new destination. I believe that you knew that this was the place you were needed, that the 3rd District had to be made, and that only here could you truly grow into your gifts and powers."

She was not at all surprised that he knew she could see the future. She even had the feeling that he knew *why* she could, but she didn't expect him to tell her even if she asked. She had always wondered about it though she had come to accept it and use it. As always, she put it aside until it was worth thinking about. "I still have a sin, Aaron." She shook her head. "You know that the evil is growing stronger and preparing for the final siege. It's my fault it got free in the first place!"

"*It is not!*" He scowled and gave her a little shake. "If anyone is to blame, it is my mother for giving a mortal the duty of carrying that vile thing to Olympus for safety! She sent you to your death and nearly doomed the world as well for her petty jealousy!" His fingers combed back into her thick hair and held on. "I will fight by your side," he vowed fiercely. "I will fight for you as I should have from the moment I knew I was yours."

She pulled away from his grip with a decidedly rude snort. "You only became mine because you're a klutz!" As if quoting from memory, she intoned, "The god Eros looked upon the sleeping Psyche and accidentally stabbed himself with his own arrow. Upon beholding the beauty before him, lo did the arrow's power inflame his love and he sought to possess her for his own."

He just smiled. He had been expecting the accusation for a while. "I have looked upon these tales told by mortals, and many are either wrong, exaggerated, or perhaps only telling half of the truth." He tipped her chin up. "I did stab myself upon my own arrow, but it was not an arrow that induces love. It was one of my instigators, my beloved. The arrows I use to remove inhibitions on existing emotion." He tenderly caressed her lips with his. "I saw you lying there and I could see the beauty inside your heart that had caused the beauty in your face and body. I had intended to leave you be for you were too good for me—too good for even a god, my love—but I misjudged and got myself with the instigator." His lips teased hers again. "I could not let you be without claiming the kiss I craved."

She frowned. "You loved me on your own?"

"Mmm." He traced the lovely line of her cheekbone. "When I escaped you, I did not go far. I watched you." He trailed his fingers along the outside of her eyes. "Your eyes. I saw your eyes and I knew I had found my other half. It had been told to me many centuries before that my other half would have 'eyes as black as the velvet night that embraces lovers.' I knew then that I must have you no matter what else. If only I had been wise enough to understand that 'else' included my mother. Such a bitter and ironic lesson for the God of Love to learn."

She hesitated and then asked softly, "Did you ever shoot me, Aaron? The legends . . . but I don't remember it . . ."

"No." A hint of a wry and yet self-mocking smile touched his lips. "Your love was your own just as my love was my own. We are made to be together. It is our love together that gives me power. Your desire for me, my desire for you, gives me power. We belong." He rested his forehead against hers. "Tell me. Tell me what I am not giving you. I feel as if I have given you everything, Rhianna. You cannot possibly own more than you do. My very soul rests in your small hands."

She sighed and framed his beautiful face with the aforementioned hands. "Aaron. My Eros. I can't tell you what you need to give me for to tell you will make worse happen. There is a fear inside you to give me the thing you hold back. That is all I can say."

He nodded firmly. "Very well. I believe you." He smiled when her brows lifted. "I have never and will never doubt your gifts, my love. If you say I fear something, then I surely do. I will try to understand what I fear so that I may move past it. It is connected to my true self somehow?" She nodded and he kissed her nose. "I do not understand how, but perhaps the fear is inside my subconscious. I will seek it and remove it. All I ask in return is that you let me be in your life. If you cannot yet let me be your lover, then let me be your husband. Let me be your confidant and your friend. The person you turn to when you need something."

She could not deny him that when it was something she wanted just as terribly. She needed *him*. Her physical need for him, and his for her, was merely a small part of the complicated ways that they were bound. Alone. She had been so alone for so long. The curse of their voided contract. Could the void be erased and the contract made active again? She had to try. "Alright." She rested her head on his shoulder where it had always belonged. "I do love you, Aaron. Never doubt that."

"If you did not, I would seek to correct it. I would not even need arrows for it. How could you not love the God of Love?"

The arrogance was more deliberate than deeply felt, and it made her smile as he had intended. "I suppose that is true." She reluctantly straightened up. "I have work, Aaron. No doubt you do, too." She sighed. "I owe my friends *another* apology."

"I would think they rather wish an explanation."

"They can have it when I am ready. I'm too busy today."

"Are you busy tomorrow?"

"No more than normal." She tilted her head. "Why?"

"I wish to see your District." He smiled. "I have not entered it for fear you would know I was there before you were ready. I wanted you to come to me of your own will. I would like to see this beautiful place that you have given your heart to protecting."

"I could show you around," she agreed. "You will like it there, I think." She smiled as well. "We always say that those who belong in the District will eventually find their way home. People who belong nowhere else will always belong in the 3rd District. Eric and I made it to be a sanctuary."

"You will have to tell me the story tomorrow." He slowly and reluctantly released her to let her get to her feet. "Will you spend the night with me?"

"Only to sleep?"

"You know I wish more, but I trust your sight. We will be lovers when I find what it is I have not given you." He stood as well and bent to teasingly nibble at her ear. "I could shoot myself with a dulling arrow. It minimizes desire."

She shook her head. "I love the way you want me. I trust you, Aaron. Of all the gods, you never took what was not freely offered."

He shrugged. "That is not true desire, and it is certainly not love." An arrogant brow lifted. "I do not deny *influencing* someone to offer something freely, but there is nothing wrong with a dalliance purely for pleasure. My consorts were never unhappy—physically or emotionally. I did not break hearts." Under his breath, he groused, "It was my fellow gods that had that problem. People think I caused all of the mayhem, but it was all I could do to keep it to a dull roar!"

She hid a smile and patted his cheek. "There, there."

"Only you would dare placate me." He covered her hand on his cheek and leaned down to kiss her with an edge of hunger that made their hearts mutually race. She was the only one he had ever wanted enough to consider seducing against her wishes, but she was also the one that he most wanted to have willing. "I am not used to learning self-control," he muttered against her lips. He took another hard kiss. "It is a good lesson for me." His hands curved around her bottom to hold her against his aching body. "I burn for you, my beloved. Never doubt that."

Burn? She was in danger of self-combustion. She craved the feel of his hands on her body and the taste of his skin in her mouth. Her head fell to the side weakly as his knowing mouth sensitized secret nerves behind her ear. "You know that saying?" she asked huskily.

"Which?" He took a tiny nip at her earlobe. She wore clip-ons rather than piercings, and he tugged one off for better access.

"Absence makes the heart grow fonder. Beginning to think it might be abstinence."

His low laugh was as sultry as the feel of his fingers dancing down the inside of her arm. "It is an addiction with no program to cure it. We will simply have to accept that we will always crave our ecstasy. The gift for feeling true love is to feel true desire. Flames that will never extinguish." He dragged her up onto her toes and kissed her wildly for a moment before releasing her entirely and stepping back. "I will pick you up tonight to come home with me," he managed to rasp. "Off with you, temptress."

She quickly closed her eyes. Air conditioning rather than steam touched her skin a moment later and she carefully opened her eyes again to see that she was in her office. She reached up to her ear and discovered her earring was still missing. "Damn it, Aaron," she muttered.

A little 'clink' noise made her look at her desk and she saw her earring sitting on her keyboard. It was, appropriately, on the X key. The letter that in shorthand meant a kiss. The symbol had come up well after his time, but he had probably started researching modern symbolism in order to resume his duties.

"Rhianna?"

She sighed and turned to where Eric stood in the doorway to his office. "Not a single word out of you. I know I owe you an explanation, but I just can't do it yet. I'm so sorry, Riku." She broke off as he crossed the room and pulled her into his arms. All she could do was hold on in turn. Truthfully, the only person she loved more than her surrogate brother was her husband. "I think I needed that."

He let her go and skimmed a hand down her hair. "Glad to help. Now let's get your mind off things by getting some work done. You can take out your frustration on Failsafe. You get to call them and tell them that I'm coming in with new org charts and a pair of pruning shears."

She had to smile. "That sounds like a plan."

Putting her life back into its normal operations did wonders for her overall sanity and brought her temper back down to its regular level. She was able to get a great deal of work done and free up the following day to show Aaron around.

As the end of the day approached, a part of her wondered if he would just wait for her downstairs and a bit brazenly take her home. She still hadn't yet come up with an excuse for the inevitable rumor and gossip sure to fly the moment she was seen with him more than once. Only an idiot would think there was only business between them. She was hardly ashamed of her relationship, but she didn't really know what kind of relationship they *had*. They were married but not yet lovers. It made things sketchy.

He appeared out of nowhere in the middle of her office while she was shutting down her computer for the day. At her lifted brow, he told her solemnly, "I can be discrete, my beloved. I would think you ought to know that by now."

"You have a point." She went around the desk and did not protest when he tugged her into his arms. He was incapable of being near her and not touching her in some fashion. "Your place or mine?"

"Mine for now." He kissed her warmly, lingering over her flavor. "You always taste so good," he murmured thickly against her lips. "I love how you taste." He drew out another kiss until a soft purring noise emerged from her throat. "And that." His lips continued to tease hers. "I love the sounds you make." With obvious reluctance, he released her. "Welcome home."

She shook her head hard and looked around in bemusement. He had so thoroughly distracted her that she hadn't noticed the transport. Now conscious and cognizant, she was able to actually admire the décor and the way he had built his home. It held the Grecian flair, yes, but it had all of the modern amenities. She trailed fingers across the widescreen television in the living room. "A prop or do you like it?"

"I enjoy it to some extent. It is a good way to learn things. I am still learning this new world. Shall I make dinner?"

She shook her head. "Let me. I suspect I'd be eating old school if I let you be in charge. Let me offer some other cuisine as well." She shrugged out of her jacket and tossed it over the back of the couch. "I should have brought an overnight bag from home," she noted ruefully. "I am not used to spending nights elsewhere."

He paused at that. It seemed a surprising statement for a woman over two millennia old. He looked at her very seriously. "Rhianna."

She smiled as she met his eyes. "I am faithful to the man I married. Who would ever compare to my God of Love?" She heeled off her shoes and gratefully tugged off her stockings. "I'm not a virgin, though. I technically never have been. I suppose my body remembers you as thoroughly as the rest of me does. I should have clarified before that I am *emotionally* not the Psyche you remember. Everything else seems to have carried over."

"It does not bother you?" he murmured.

"Not at all. Our story never ended, Eros. We are merely in a new chapter. My rebirth was a layover of sorts. I know that now. We will take it a page at a time until you can find and eliminate what you fear." Her black eyes seemed to burn as she looked at him. "Do I want to pretend that it could be enough to have only part of you, just for a few moments of pleasure? I'd be lying to say I didn't want that. It would just never be enough for my heart and soul."

A blend of awe and pride filled him. She carried herself as regally as a queen and with the same calm confidence of any goddess. His beautiful, perfect, mate. Still, he would have to do something about her frustration soon. He could not handle knowing she suffered. "I could give you something to wear," he offered, "if you would like to not wear your suit." A bit wistfully, he added, "I miss the *peplos* you used to wear, but I think I like your suits as well. I am fond of those pants you wear."

She hid a smile. "They show off my legs?"

"They are beautiful legs. I anticipate having them wrapped around me again." He ambled down the hall and returned briefly with a t-shirt. "It will be big."

"And that works for me." Because modesty was truly ridiculous, she tugged off her blouse and pants without bothering to tell him to turn. She tugged the shirt on over her head and found the neck dipped over one of her shoulders while the ends went to her knees. He was watching her hotly, sparks in his eyes, and she could not resist yanking his chain. Without removing the shirt, she unfastened her bra, pulled down the straps, and tugged it out through a sleeve. As it dangled from her fingers, she grinned at the astonished look on his face. "Bras are a bit different from an *apodesmos*."

"So I see!" He was still not entirely sure she hadn't used some sort of magic, but he let it slide. He studied her intently in his t-shirt and finally decided, "I think I am growing fond of modern things."

"They grow on you." She wandered into the kitchen and began to poke around in the pantry and fridge. She hummed softly under her breath as she got out ground beef and the other items needed to make cheeseburgers. She would have to introduce him to sushi eventually. He had always loved fish.

The burgers were happily sizzling in a pan when she heard the sound of a familiar talk show's theme. She quirked a brow as she carried a glass of wine into the living room. She leaned over the couch to hand it to him, and she eyed the large screen. A smile started tugging at her lips. "Do I *dare* ask why you are watching Jerry Springer?"

"It reminds me of the pantheon."

She thought about that. "Hmm. I think that does sound about right. Zeus was certainly the biggest baby daddy on the block."

He choked on his wine and began laughing. "Off with you, woman!" He swatted at her halfheartedly. "You are distracting me."

She bit back a laugh as she went back into the kitchen. She would have to introduce him to a few of her favorite shows as well. The idea of snuggling on a couch to watch them together was deeply appealing. This domestic situation felt wonderful to her. What a strange feeling it was to share her life in such a way with him. They had not had this in Greece.

Arms slid around her waist. "You are sad."

"Melancholy," she corrected. She let his arms stay as she added cheese to the burgers. When he rested his chin on her shoulder, she hooked an arm around his neck. "I'm fine, Aaron. I promise. I was actually just thinking of how much I like where we are."

"I am fond of it as well," he admitted. He sniffed at the burgers as she put them onto buns. "What have you made?"

"Food." She handed him a plate with a smile. "You'll like it."

In fact, he *loved* his cheeseburger. He happily polished off his share and munched through a handful of the zucchini fries she had made as well. "I will cook tomorrow night," he told her firmly as they were cleaning up the kitchen much later. "I will ask Priya to find me some recipes tomorrow."

"She's your Eric?"

He contemplated that. "I suppose she is. I do love her a great deal. You will like her and her husband, Pablo. They are gifted as well. I believe they would have found your District if I had not found them first." He smiled as he saw her pat away a yawn. "It is getting late and it was an eventful day."

"That's one word for it. I'm using your toothbrush since I don't have one."

"I do not mind." The smile he shot at her was decidedly sensual. "Our mouths have shared space often enough."

Much to her bemusement, she had a shorter bathroom routine than he did. She only had to wash off her makeup, and he liked perfumes and lotions. Not that *she* was complaining about such a thing; she would get to sleep snuggled against that soft skinned and fragrant body. She was the first to go to bed, and she slipped under the silk covers with a contented sigh.

The lamp clicked off behind her, and she watched as he crossed to the windows to shut the heavy drapes. The room was plunged into darkness where she could not even make out his outline. Perhaps a bit ironically, he warned her, "I will not wear pajamas for your 'delicate sensibilities.' I do not own any."

She was not surprised by his actions, but she was a bit disappointed. Of course one day would not be enough. She knew that for fact though she did not know how much time it *would* take. Rather than reveal her sadness, she just snorted softly at him.

He slipped into bed beside her and snuggled up along her back. "Side, back, or stomach?" he asked her softly.

"I'm still a side sleeper."

"I still sleep on my back. Turn over."

She did so and cuddled against his side as he lifted his arm for her. He dropped it around her waist and her head found its spot on his shoulder as if no time had passed at all. She let out an unconsciously contented sigh and closed her eyes. He was a terrible distraction to her poor body, and she barely resisted an urge to start petting the peach-scented skin so deliciously close at hand.

Sensing it, he smiled. He brushed his lips over the top of her head and murmured something inaudible in Ancient Greek. He briefly encountered her instinctive resistance to his power—which in and of itself was a sign that she was his other half—and then she gave in and let him calm her nerves. She slipped asleep within the next breath.

He stared at the ceiling overhead and thought about his possible plans of action. Finally deciding he might as well do what he did best, he snuggled her closer and slept as well. Just having her in his arms where she belonged was enough for the moment.

CHAPTER NINE

Rhianna awoke alone in bed to the feel of the sunrise spilling across her face. She could still feel the warmth from where her husband had slept, and the déjà vu was briefly disorienting. Loneliness rose and threatened to close her throat. Just once . . . just once, she wanted to wake in his arms. To know he had not let go all night. But, no, that was denied to her for as long as he slept naked and the light would give away his true self.

"My beloved." His husky voice teased her ear. "Wake up, beloved. Let me see your eyes."

She opened her eyes and looked up to see him leaning over her. He was naked except for a towel knotted around his hips. She eyed it for a moment, deeply tempted to get rid of it. Why should she be denied the beauty of his body? It was not fair. "Are you taking a shower and didn't want to wake me?" she asked on a delicate yawn.

He tugged her up to a sitting position and smiled as her tousled red hair fell in her eyes. He brushed it back for her. "I was thinking we should enjoy the bath instead. You will like how it looks in the dawn."

She drummed her fingers lightly on her leg. "Hmm. Why do I not trust you . . .?"

Blue eyes lit with humor. "My only ulterior motive is to offer you something beautiful, enjoyable, and relaxing."

Pity she didn't have Rayna's ability to hear the truth. He sounded sincere enough, though. "I will settle for a shower."

"No, you will not. I have already placed soaps and towels for you." He lifted her out of bed before she could protest. "You will come enjoy the dawn with me, and I promise you will feel better after."

She could only sigh as he carried her through the house. "Why can't I tell you 'no'?"

"You cannot argue with me when you know I truly have your best interests at heart. If you did not want what I offer, your heels would dig all the way to the Styx as they did the day we met again. What I give, I give freely. I am not asking for anything in return." He teased as they entered the garden, "I will keep my towel on to prove my intentions are honorable."

Another irony, she decided, since him removing the towel would reveal his true self in the light. Keeping it on showed his as yet subconscious lack of trust in the depth of her emotions. Still . . . it *was* a step closer. Half-naked was half more than she'd had before. Her eyes ran over him wistfully. She had asked for a Greek god. She had gotten one. Her eyes at last could know what her fingers and lips did. It only stirred the craving to have more.

He smiled to himself and gently put her on her feet beside the bath. Again, she was able to see it for the first time now that she was not emotionally distraught. It was truly beautiful with lush flowers and peach trees surrounding the marble and stone pool. Statues and pillars dotted the landscape. A fountain shaped like a dolphin sat in the middle of the bath itself. "It's beautiful," she said simply.

"I thought you would approve." He waded out into the water and toward the other side where a shelf held soaps and bottles. "Come join me."

Her eyes riveted to his powerful back. Finally bared to her eyes was the fact that he bore a mark representing his power. Etched into his skin right on each of his shoulder blades was the shape of a wing. It looked black until the light flowed over it and revealed it to be the deep red hue of desire and love. Here she had thought it was just a thought of fancy that he had wings, and it turned out that he actually did. She *ached* to memorize the curves and lines with her lips. What else did she not know?

She could only sigh and strip off the borrowed shirt. She dropped it on a bench and then shed her underwear as well. She stepped down into the pool and waded in deeper. At the lowest point near the fountain, the water came up to just under her breasts. Built in benches along the sides would allow her to sink deeper and soak.

The water was covered in rose petals and they clung to her skin as she moved to where Aaron waited. Her brows lifted as he caught her around the waist and casually lifted her onto one of the lowest steps. It brought her onto eye level with him. "What are you about?" she asked warily.

"I am washing you." Suiting action to words, he began to smooth a cake of soap slowly down her arm. His fingers trailed along the sensitive nerves near her elbow and inner arm as he did, and he seemed to ignore the way her breath caught.

She told herself he was not doing it on purpose, but she knew it was a lie even before soapy hands skimmed across the inner curve of her hips and slowly upward along the base of her ribs. She wasn't breathing at all as she waited in agony for his hands to travel higher. Fingers skimmed the outer curves of her breasts and slowly trailed in toward the sensitive skin between. His lips curved as he felt the wild race of her heart. Her fingers caught his shoulders for balance and her nails bit in.

He continued his slow and thorough journey of her body. The secret nerves at the base of her spine were teased, and the heated flesh of her upper thighs were caressed. Her legs began to tremble as he worked lower. There were dozens of hotspots to be found, and he knew all of them.

By the time he had finished with the soap, it was only her grip on his arms that kept her on her feet. "Aaron." It was whispered thickly, and it sounded like a sultry siren's call. "I shouldn't let you do this."

"What I give, I give freely," he repeated huskily. He grabbed the pitcher and began to rinse her clean. The last of the soap was floating away when he tossed the pitcher aside carelessly and began the journey of her body again, but this time with his lips. He hotly caressed her breast until the taut nipple begged for his further attention. "Do I please you?" he asked thickly as he nuzzled and tasted. A moan answered him and he greedily caught the tip of her breast in his mouth. Perhaps someday milk would come from there to feed their child. How beautiful it would be.

Her knees buckled and he lifted her off her feet. He carried her to the edge of the pool and slowly lowered her to the towels waiting there. Steam curled up from her skin and a flush rode her cheeks. Her black eyes were as consuming as the night as she watched him, and the feel of her hunger for him made the sparks leap inside his eyes. He pulled himself out of the pool and leaned over her. "I will not take you." He slowly slid down her body and tormented her navel with his tongue. "I will give you what you need."

Protesting was far from her mind by that point. He was a god, but he could not turn off the sun. Either he would love her selflessly, or he would give selflessly of himself. It was the middle ground that she resisted. A hot mouth buried between her legs and the sensation made her cry out. He had revved her body so skillfully that it took him only a few moments to drive her ruthlessly to the peak and then over. The way his name broke from her lips in ecstasy raked over his aching body and made his hands shake.

She barely managed a whimper as he lied down beside her and gathered her against his chest. After the recent highs and lows, it was a blessed relief to feel nothing except that wonderful sensation of absolute pleasure. She would have tried to hold him but he had completely melted every muscle in her body.

He studied her face contentedly. The sleepy, satiated expression made her radiantly beautiful to him. It was worth every bit of his gnawing need to no longer feel her frustration beating at him. Now he could find the control to wait. "Shall I wash you again?" he asked teasingly. The little rasp to his voice gave away his need, but he did not care. Contrary to his body's annoyance, he felt incredibly full of energy and power.

She found the strength to bury her fingers in his wet hair. Drowsy black eyes opened as she smiled. "I don't think you ever had to induce anyone into wanting you, Eros. You are far too good at what you do."

"I am a firm believer in doing your best at whatever job you have. My job now is to please only one woman. I shall happily spend eternity doing so." He leaned down and kissed her slowly with a famished heat. "You are happy?"

"Depends on the context." She skimmed her fingers over his lips. "This was not fair to you, Aaron."

"I disagree. I am the one who has the problem keeping us apart. I could not handle feeling you so tangled up in your desire for me without having a way to appease it." His lips curved. "Perhaps my being so frustrated as well will drive to me to find faster what I am afraid of and remove it so I may make love to you more thoroughly. And repeatedly. And perhaps in a few ways I never taught you before. You may wish to arrange for a week of vacation."

She found herself laughing as she was reminded anew why she loved him. That wonderful, mischievous manner always lifted her spirits. Those whispers in the night two millennia before had stolen her soul. "Speaking of work, I think I am glad that I arranged to have my day free for you. I can imagine myself walking in feeling like this. I would never hear the end of it."

"I do not know why it is called 'getting laid'," he admitted wryly. "There are so many more interesting variations than merely being horizontal." He grinned when a sudden rumble from her stomach was echoed by his a moment later. "I suppose we should be less horizontal now and take care of a different sort of hunger." He rolled to his feet and winced a bit. "I would prefer a *chiton* over a towel right now," he groused as he bent and scooped her up into his arms.

She tried to hide a smile. "Chaffing?"

"Well, it certainly itches." He swung her around the corners inside the house and looked down to see her smiling. He gently placed her on her feet in the bedroom. "Have I amused you?"

Her fingers trailed up his chest and then skimmed down his jaw. "I was just thinking again that I am a lucky woman to have a man so unashamedly romantic."

A golden brow lifted arrogantly. "I invented romance."

A sudden thought of what would happen in a few months when Valentine's Day arrived made her struggle to keep back a laugh. The thought was followed by the reminder that she may not even survive to the day of lovers, and her lighthearted mood evaporated.

She was immediately drawn into his arms and rocked tenderly. "You are sad." He buried his face in her soft hair. "You were happy. What has you so unhappy, my beloved? I will be entirely yours soon enough."

Lies did not belong between them. Too many had ruined their lives already. "It's not you. It's the evil out there. It still looms, Aaron. I feel it. With every day, it grows stronger. I've had to work so quickly to ensure it cannot hurt anyone but I nearly lost someone anyway. She should never have been shot, and yet she was. I was able to use it to my advantage to help her, but it should not have happened." She dropped her head onto his shoulder. "I will carry that guilt for the rest of my life."

"Is she happy now? Healed? Healthy?"

"Of course."

"Then that is all that matters." He slowly released her and smiled because he knew she needed it. "I am going to take a shower. I will join you to make breakfast."

Entirely unsurprised, she smiled. "Alright." She watched him head into the bathroom, and she was equally unsurprised when the door shut behind him. She was becoming a bit fascinated in a strange way; his inability to be naked almost seemed to be a form of modesty. How offended would he be when he figured it out? It would be amusing, to say the least.

She had to travel around the house a bit to retrieve her clothes. Pieces had ended up all over the place. Rather than pull on her blouse and jacket again, she rummaged in his closet. He liked the same neutrals paired with jewel tones that she did. She spotted a silk shirt in warm brown and tugged it out. Once cuffed at the wrist and tied at her waist, it fit well enough to suit her. She was only going to be in her District, and her people would actually be *glad* to see her with Aaron. Just desserts, so the saying went.

She was crisping potatoes when he walked into the kitchen. His eyes lit with hungry sparks as he spotted what she wore. "And I thought you never went out without your version of body armor," he teased.

"When I'm not on the clock, I wear whatever I like. It just happens that, usually, I use my days off to stay home or visit my grandkid." She hid a smile as she heard him choke on his coffee. "Do you know the Gentle Brook Inn? It's owned and run by Madelyne and Kienan Shaughnessy. When Madelyne lost her parents, I became her legal guardian. I and Eric raised her to adulthood. She is enough like a daughter to me—and Eric and Rayna—that her son calls us his grandparents."

"Thank you for explaining," he grumbled. "I could not imagine how it be possible you have a grandchild, let alone a child, if you had not been touched by anyone except me." He nuzzled the back of her neck through her hair before getting out some eggs and frying them up. He glanced over where she had already placed strips of bacon to drain. "I have grown fond of bacon," he confessed.

She contemplated that as they were serving themselves and taking a seat at the dining table. "How are you sustaining your immortality without nectar and ambrosia?"

"It takes but one serving to make a god. We are not required to continually consume it in order to remain as gods. We chose to do so because it placed us so much higher above the normal mortals who ate the flesh of animals." The smallest hint of sarcasm had entered his tone. "I have actually discovered that I enjoy mortal living. Oh, it has its downsides, but it is nothing that I cannot overcome or avoid by my power." He arched a brow. "As you well know. I believe someone else shamelessly uses her power to have her way in things."

She just smiled. "Why have it if you do not use it? I have limitations on what I can do, though. I'm not a goddess."

Not for the first time, he could not help but think that she *should* be a goddess. She was all but one already. Truly, only a lack of full omnipotence and immortality (which was different from longevity) kept her from his station. He would have made her one right then and there, but Olympus was sealed and he had no access to nectar and ambrosia. "Would you be one if you could?" he asked softly.

She thought about it very seriously. "If it would help me better protect the people who need me, yes. What would I be a goddess *of*, though?"

He just smiled as well. "It would be interesting to find out."

After breakfast, he obligingly transported them to her home so that she could put on makeup. He watched with deep fascination at the entire process. There were many different sorts of products and items than he remembered from Ancient Greece. More colors as well. The basic ideals—emphasizing lips, eyes, and cheekbones—were familiar, though. "Why do men not wear makeup these days?" he asked as he picked up her powder and sniffed at it.

She contemplated her words and then decided that it would be something he never understood. "Cultural shift," she finally said. "It's considered feminine to wear makeup now. Men really only wear makeup if they are actors or models, and most laymen don't even realize they are." She smiled. "I have been told a dozen times that I don't need makeup, that I'm pandering to male ideology, that I am being fooled by commercialism, and that a woman should not be expected to wear makeup in order to be considered beautiful. I *like* it. I like the feel of pampering myself and knowing I'm playing up my best features. I feel naked if I'm outside without it."

It made him smile. "A part of you is still in Greece."

"Perhaps so." She offered him some lip-gloss. "I'm a bit paler than you, but we have the same hue to our skin. You can wear most anything of mine except the powder. I'll pick you up some of your own if you like. I know the modern stuff better than you do—for now."

"I would be grateful." He sniffed at the gloss. A slow and sensual smile curved his lips. "No wonder you tasted of strawberries that first day." He deliberately put on a layer. It gave his already bitable lips an effect that made them seem as if he had just kissed her. "I will kiss you again later and we will be even."

"Deal."

As he had only ever transported her in and out of her home, and he had only transported himself, he was pleasantly surprised to discover that it was actually built as a part of Enforcers HQ itself. The house was decent enough size, and it had a garden space that rivaled his. The garden was protected by glass panels over the top that let in light but were reflective on the other side so that people could not look inside. Like his home, she had decorated with their homeland in mind. "I did not realize you lived attached to where you work," he murmured.

She smiled up at him. "Nearly everyone in the District lives in a place attached to their place of work if they own the business. Eric and Rayna are on the other side of the building. Most everyone who lives here also works here. We have a large tourism trade nowadays, and we offer handmade goods as well as historical tours. We are primarily mercantile with only a small residential area. We keep it looking a bit on the rundown side so that only the people who truly belong will wish to stay. We see beyond the surface."

He certainly could see beneath the surface himself, and what he saw was a beautiful, thriving, community where everyone knew each other and shared whatever was needed with whoever was in need. He spotted several smiling glances sent toward Rhianna and impulsively caught her hand with his. Her brows lifted and he grinned. "I am enforcing the belief that you are interested in me."

She leaned her head against his arm. "As if my wearing what is obviously a man's shirt—and then being seen with a man—was not enough of a clue." She stopped walking as they reached the front gate around a beautiful bed and breakfast set behind a lush garden. "Welcome to the Gentle Brook Inn."

"Gramma!" A boy of no older than seven came rushing down the pathway and happily threw himself into Rhianna's arms. His hair was a fascinating shade of gray with only a few hints of brown to imply it had ever been anything else. Chocolate colored eyes watched his grandmother with obvious hero worship. "We have cookies."

"Well, how can I turn that down!" She snuggled him for a moment before putting him down. She knelt beside him and gestured to Aaron. "Conner, meet Aaron." She smiled up at Aaron. "This is Conner Shaughnessy. He is Madelyne and Kienan's son."

Aaron knelt as well. He could not help smiling. He had always loved children of all kinds. "I am pleased to meet you."

"I like your voice." Conner planted a kiss on his cheek. If his grandma brought him, then he must be family. "I'll tell Mommy and Daddy you're here!" He scampered back into the inn and his shoes could be heard skidding on the floors.

Aaron stood and tugged Rhianna up and then tucked her under his arm as they followed the gray-haired tornado into the building. They were promptly greeted in the lobby by a surprisingly plain woman who happily threw her arms around Rhianna. "I'm happy for you!" Madelyne exclaimed. "I was so happy when Riku called me and told me I might have a stepfather! You need to be happy, Rhianna. Tell me you're happy."

"We're getting there." Rhianna hugged her back as well. "This is Aaron Konstantinos." She winced wryly. "At least, that is who he is now. He's actually Eros, the God of Love."

Violet eyes filled with humor. "I think only a god could keep up with you, Rhianna." She turned to Aaron and studied him intently before smiling anew. She had once been wary of beautiful men, but even if Kienan had not cured her of that, she would have still been comfortable near Aaron. He radiated such a wonderful sense of compassion and acceptance into the air that she *knew* he judged only on someone's heart—if he judged at all. "My name is Madelyne, but I am Maddie to friends and family."

"Maddie it will be." He bent to kiss her cheek. "I would not mind being your stepfather. I have never been a father, but I imagine I can figure it out."

"The one god who would have a good reason for having a hundred kids has never had any?" Madelyne asked Rhianna in amusement.

Rhianna smiled. "He is also the one god who truly respected all of his consorts." She heard a footstep and looked up to see another male approaching with Conner on his shoulders. "There you are, Kienan. I was beginning to think you were lost."

Kienan Shaughnessy just grinned. As a marked contrast to his wife, he was almost as handsome as a god himself, and it was his chocolate eyes passed to his son. His hair was a thick golden brown instead. "I was in the middle of cleaning the hot spring." He eyed Aaron speculatively. "Do I like him?"

Sensing a powerfully protective nature, Aaron gave him a graceful bow. "You have my word of honor that there is nothing I could ever do to harm Rhianna. I will spend the rest of eternity filling her life with love so that she is never alone again. *She* is why I have power." He looked at Rhianna and did not bother to hide the emotion that turned his blue eyes incandescent with sparks and power. "The God of Love and Desire has need for only one woman's love and desire."

"Wow." Madelyne looked up at Kienan with a grin. "He made her blush. He's good."

Kienan was just happy to know that Rhianna would be treated the way she deserved. He considered Rhianna to be a part of his family thanks to Madelyne, and he put his family first and foremost in everything. "I'm sure that's not all he's good at."

"Behave yourself!" Rhianna scolded him, but she was smiling. "We have other places to stop. I just wanted to introduce him for now." She kissed her daughter and son-in-law's cheeks and then her grandson's puckered lips. "I will bring him over for dinner one night."

"I'll make something Greek," Madelyne offered impishly.

Aaron chuckled at that as he followed Rhianna out of the inn. "Your daughter has impeccable taste," he noted. "Her Kienan would have been chased by many of the gods if we were still in the past. I may have joined the hunt myself."

"They needed each other," she murmured. "My favorite nightingale and swan." She caught his hand and tugged him along down the sidewalk. "We have another stop to make, and a few things to see along the way. I'll tell you how it all got started."

He listened intently as she laid out the history of the 3rd District starting from the day she and Eric had realized how very different they and their families were from the rest of the tribes along the coast. His heart wept that he had not been there for her, that he had not been strong enough until recently to even reach out in another form—and only on Mirage anyway. And yet, there was pride for her accomplishments. She had done deeds worthy of her own heroic legend.

He tugged her even closer instinctively and she absently tucked a hand into the back pocket of his jeans. She smiled as she saw what they approached. Two nearly identical young men stood with a rusty haired young woman and another young woman who had pink streaks in her hair. They were arguing avidly over the clipboard that the redhead held. "Are we having trouble?" she asked dryly.

Heads swung around and smiles replaced temper. "Ms. Taber, you surprised us!" Kenneth Dease said warmly. "No trouble here; we're just not in agreement about how we want to handle the commercial we're going to be shooting for the inn. It's going to be the District's first foray into television."

His wife smirked. "You should have heard him and Kienan going at it," Sera Dease noted dryly. She studied Aaron intently for a few moments before smiling. "Welcome home."

Cameron Dease looked solemnly at Rhianna but there was a sparkle in his eyes. "Is he a keeper?"

"I like to think so." She smiled at the redhead. "I trust you to sneak me things on the side so that I can be kept up-to-date on the process, Sarah."

Sarah Dease just grinned. "It isn't much of a sneak when you announce it. And you think Cam or Ken would tell you no?" She saluted sassily. "I'll send you an email tonight with what we have so far."

Rhianna and Aaron let them be and continued on their way. They passed by a small house undergoing construction, and the front area was packed with stunning clothworks. The weaver's wife stood bickering with several exceptionally large Vikings, and there were a handful of redheads discussing colors and patterns with the weaver himself.

Rhianna murmured, "Brian and Louise Matthews. They have a little girl of about five months. The house was splitting at the seams, so to speak. You know the Traherns, of course. You hired them to do Cupid's Grove. Seven brothers matched with seven sisters because of seven wishes on a golden locket."

Aaron slid a smile at her. "You planned that one early. You must have been holding onto the golden apple for a while."

"A century or two. I would infrequently visit Greece to seek out the hidden places of my memory in order to obtain the items needed to ensure—enforce—the happiness of my people. I borrowed thread from Hestia as well."

"We will go together next time." He brought her hand to his lips and delicately teased the tender skin between her fingers with the tip of his tongue. A delicate flush climbed her face and her eyes darkened until he could barely see her expanded pupils. "I will take you to my temple and make love to you under the stars."

She refrained from mentioning the temple was a ruin and probably always surrounded by visitors. He was a god. He could make anything work. It was an encouraging sign, though, that he wanted to have her outside, even if it was in the night. "Will you disguise yourself and pretend you are seducing a poor, hapless mortal girl with your wiles?" she teased.

The sparks returned to his eyes. "I shall become a stag and chase you down, and then I will turn back and ravish you most thoroughly. Will that suit you?"

Her breath hitched as she tugged her hand free. "We have a date."

He insisted on holding her hand anyway as they continued along their way. She pointed out two couples that were window-shopping for baby furniture, and he smiled as he noticed both women were pregnant. One had hair too long to belong to a normal human, and the other was as lovely as a swan. The husband of the one with long hair looked quite hard at the edges, but Aaron could see the gentleness inside his heart. The other man had an oddly familiar shape to his face that took Aaron a moment to place. "Ah! Italian?"

"Indeed." Rhianna sighed happily at the scene. "Theresa and Van D'Angelo, and Rafael and Tori Lucino. Rafael is an associate of mine. He took over the family company a month ago. Van works as a consultant for Enforcers. He has skills of . . . particular use. Theresa is District-born. Tori is not, but she is special in her own way." Her gaze lowered. "She is the one who was wrongfully wounded."

Aaron smoothed his hand down her arm. "She is alive and she is happy. That is what is important, my beloved. And she seems to be thriving. Four months?"

"Thereabout. Theresa is at six. She is a gifted healer. I look forward to their daughter's gifts as well." She stopped outside a glittering club and lightly gestured. "Welcome to the Faerie Club. Kienan's younger sister is the owner and manager of the place. This is *the* place to be in NYC. It is so safe that parents can drop off their children without fear of harm happening to them. Aenya runs a clean ship."

He was charmed even before they went inside and found that the middle of the day made it no less lively. There were few children around since it was during school hours, but there were teens of various ages about the place along with young adults. A beautiful blonde that bore a resemblance to Kienan was on the dance floor and currently teaching a class how to do the waltz.

Rhianna looked around and was reminded again of the good that had been done. She saw Isabelle LaGuardia and Brie Viani sitting with their husbands, Alex and Roberto, and the rest of the Shaughnessy family was present as well. Taegan was teaching some of the few kids present how to do math. His wife, Kalliope, was fussing over a teenager's hair and putting it up into a fancy do. Audra was talking with her husband, Mel, and they were keeping an eye on their two children as well as the kids belonging to their siblings. Aenya's husband, Hiro, was playing at a waiter and serving tables.

The fact that all of them had day jobs, particularly Mel and Kalliope, yet they had found the time to be there when she needed them did not surprise her at all. All had completed contracts. They would instinctively respond to her call. She had wanted Aaron to see the best of her world, and it was all there in front of them.

"Rhi!" Aenya waved happily. "You saved me an email! Come look at what Heul and Remy came up with for our remodel. Van's paying," she added impishly. "He still owed me one from when he was helping Theresa."

Aaron watched Rhianna head down for a quick conversation, and he saw her stop along the way to talk to anyone who spoke up. Everyone in her District loved her as much as she loved them. They all knew who she was even if they had not met her.

Understanding began to fill him. She had said she was not his Psyche emotionally anymore, but he believed now that she was wrong. The loving, giving nature that had imbued her in the past had not gone away. She had not suddenly become more stubborn or independent. She had merely grown up. She was everything she had been before, and now also more. He would never have been able to love her in the past in the way he did right there.

"You have an interesting look on your face," Taegan noted as he stopped beside Aaron. He followed the god's gaze to where Rhianna was intently studying the plans while Aenya talked animatedly. "You didn't realize how much you love her? Odd thing for you, I think."

"I suppose even the God of Love must learn about his power firsthand. It is beginning to feel a little like destiny."

"Well, it sure wouldn't be a coincidence. Not around here anyway."

Aaron and Rhianna spent the rest of the afternoon exploring the District, and he only fell more in love with the place and its main protector as time passed. He *belonged* there. Still, he was a discrete gentleman when he chose to be. He made sure that everyone saw them part at her door and took himself away where he could not be seen before he transported himself into her living room.

He made dinner for them both and let her convince him to watch one of her favored sitcoms. Things stayed lighthearted and casual to the best of their ability, but it was not easy for either of them. He was incapable of keeping his hands off her, and the taste of strawberries on his lips had done nothing for her self-control. The interlude by the bath may as well have been a year ago. As he had said, some fires were just not meant to go out.

He borrowed her toothbrush this time and noted while she was washing her face, "We will need to place items at each other's house until we decide how to compromise on where we live. You are needed here, yet I know you were happy at my house."

"I don't mind alternating until we figure it out." She dug out one of her favorite t-shirts to sleep in and tugged it on before getting into bed. "Warm your feet before you join me. They were cold last night."

He chuckled softly. "As you wish." He padded half-naked across the room to shut the curtains and tugged off his socks as he crossed back to catch the lamp. The darkness had barely settled before he slid naked into bed beside her. She promptly turned over and scooted in where she belonged and he skimmed his fingers down her arm. A delicate shiver was his response. Her frustration gnawed at his hormones until even his teeth ached with the urge to be deep inside her. "I can ease you again," he offered huskily, a note of anticipation in his voice.

"Odd as it sounds, I don't trust you to do only that," she answered wryly. "I don't trust you in the dark, my love."

He paused for a moment as that turned over inside his mind. Why would she not trust him only in the dark? Was there a connection between whatever fear he held, his true self, and the dark? He frowned as he tried to sort it out, but it still made no sense. He would have to wait, watch, and hope she said something else that might give him a clue. Their contract would continue to remain voided until they gave all of themselves to one another. Only when it was active again could they fight for their happy ending.

Something stirred in the distance. It felt cold, slimy, and malevolent. Rhianna went very still and Aaron held her even closer. He brought her hand up to rest over his heart and laced their fingers together. "When will the war come?" he asked softly. "It is inevitable now."

"I don't know." She closed her eyes. "I only know that it will happen. If needed, I will give my life for the safety of all that lives."

He froze. "You will *not*," he vowed harshly. "You will not die on me! Enforcers needs you. The District needs you. *I* need you. I will not let you go, Rhianna. You *cannot* leave me again."

"I will try not to," she soothed. She rubbed her cheek against his skin for a moment before yawning and snuggling closer. She was asleep a few moments later.

He forced away the disturbing feeling that she was being prophetic and let himself follow her into sleep. As was his way, he woke at the first light of dawn, but he was surprised to find himself waking alone. His eyes flew wide and he discovered his lover had left him. Her side was still warm and he could still feel her skin. A sense of the house told him she was not there.

A strong and bitter sensation of loneliness filled him. He loved waking with her in his arms. The way she felt and looked so perfect. The way she had of making him feel needed, wanted, and loved. How could she have left him that way? Didn't she know how much it hurt to wake without your lover in your arms?

Actually, yes, she did. He threw an arm over his eyes as he realized that he had always left her before she woke. He had done it to protect his identity in the past, but he had no excuse for the previous morning other than 'needing to prepare the bath.' He could have done it after she woke. Why hadn't he thought to wait?

He got out of bed and got dressed. He transported himself to his home to get ready and then headed to the Grove to get some work done. Priya was not there yet, but she did not get in until eight. He walked into his office and spotted the two questionnaires on his desk. One had his name. The other had Rhianna's. They had been clipped together, and Priya had put her usual heart-shaped post-it on the top where she had written '100%!' with a smiley face.

He sank down into his chair and grabbed Rhianna's questionnaire. He slowly went down her answers to the questions about her thoughts on romance, and he grabbed a pen to circle something in particular. "Perhaps," he murmured into the quiet, "it is time I start practicing what I preach. I believe I owe my wife some long, long overdue courting."

CHAPTER TEN

Rhianna was already at work when she heard Eric enter his office. She said nothing. He walked into her space a few moments later and looked at her very intently. He slowly crossed the room and eased onto the side of her desk. "Rhi."

She looked up at him. "Yes?"

"Please tell me what's going on. Do I probably know what happened? It's likely; few don't know the tale of Psyche and Eros. What is real and what isn't, however, is what I don't know." A trace of pain lingered in his normally icy blue eyes. "You know my secrets, Rhi. You gave me my happy ending. Tell me what I need to know to help you get yours. I can't stand seeing you suffer."

She drew a long breath. "Alright." She gestured to one of the chairs. "Have a seat. This might take a few."

He tugged one closer and sat down with a wry smile. "Does it start a long, long time ago?"

Her smile was no less wry but it was also a bit sad. "Doesn't it always?"

Status: File Voided
Analysis: Pending

Folder Three
AARON

CHAPTER ELEVEN

Eric had taken the information with his characteristic ability to absorb and adapt though his face had reflected his horror for the details at times. Rhianna felt strangely peaceful now that she had gotten it off her chest. She had loathed lying to Eric and keeping him out of her life. It felt quite freeing to eliminate the last secrets between them.

Work continued on for the day with relative normalcy until roughly ten in the morning when D.J. buzzed Rhianna to tell her she had visitors that had been sent over by Cupid's Grove. She had told D.J. to consider the Grove another ally, but she had expected to see Aaron or even Priya, not referrals.

The two who showed up at her office after being escorted by a guard were a set of young women in their mid-twenties or so. Rhianna knew on one look that they were the type who would struggle to make their own happy ending. "Welcome," she said warmly as she got to her feet. "I'm Rhianna Taber. I understand you were sent over by the Grove? Have a seat and tell me what is going on."

They both sat down, and their knees bumped intimately. "Our parents are pressuring us to get married," the brunette explained. "We thought that going to the Grove might help us find true love; Mr. Konstantinos' gift to match people is almost godlike!"

Rhianna hid a smile. "So I had heard. I presume you two met that way? He matched you together?" She could certainly see where their souls would lock and fuse.

"He did but . . ." The blonde lowered her gaze. "We didn't expect to match to our own gender." She made a helpless gesture. "I'm bi, but I've been careful to date only men because I know my family would disapprove."

"I didn't even know I *was* attracted to other women," her partner admitted. "Or maybe it's just Cassie. She just . . . from the moment I met her, I've been so happy. But . . ."

"But you fear for rejection from your families," Rhianna surmised. Not for the first time, it made her blood boil. She still remembered the days when love was all that mattered, not the equipment used in the act of it. "Let me see." She tapped a finger on her chin as she let her sixth sense process. Events adjusted and she could see what needed to be done. She would have a bit of tinkering to do. "Alright then." She opened a file and began typing up a fresh contract. "I am putting you under contract with Enforcers."

The lovers exchanged a wide-eyed look. Just as people knew that dreams came true in the District, they also knew that being under contract with Enforcers, well, *enforced* that outcome. "What do we have to do?" Cassie asked.

"It will all be here within the contract. You will have to place quite a bit of trust in me." She printed out the contract and slid it across the desk. "I can see why the Grove sent you to me. Sometimes a little external force is needed." More specifically, a little external force that could change and control the future—something Aaron himself could not do. He could not change events previously set in stone, but she could. She still didn't know why.

The two young women signed without hesitation, and the blonde took possession of it. There was already a renewed spring to their step as they walked out reading over what needed to be done. As soon as the door closed behind them, Rhianna picked up her phone and made a few calls to adjust what she needed. She then emailed a copy of the contract to Rayna for her to keep an eye on.

"Got a referral, huh?" Eric leaned against the doorway. He arched a brow. "Interesting that a god can't do some things."

"If the gods could have done everything, there wouldn't have been so many of them." She tapped a finger on her lips and then picked up the phone. "I think I need to give my husband a call." She ignored Eric smirking at her. She knew he considered it his revenge that she had the same problems with Aaron that he did with Rayna. When the other side answered, she smiled. "It's Rhianna. Is Aaron busy?"

"Nope, he's between meetings. Hang on and I'll transfer you."

A click and a moment later, Aaron answered the phone smoothly, "How may I serve your desires, beloved?"

Oh, the *possibilities*. "Referrals?" she asked only.

"Ah. Naturally." The smile was in his voice. "You and I have our own strengths and gifts. Where there is some natural overlap, we still do things the other cannot. It is why we are two halves of a whole, why we are stronger together than apart. I saw that there was something I could not do and I sent them to you. I would hope you may do the same."

She could not resist teasing, "Should I be having Gwyn write up legal documents to make our alliance formal? Enforcers prides itself on having good working relationships with its allies in other fields."

He laughed softly and the sound was sultry. "You and I do many things beautifully together, and working is merely one of them. I look forward to again demonstrating my best skills for you someday soon." He gently hung up the phone.

She blew out a breath and tried to ignore the way her entire body had heated at the silky promise in his voice. She needed to re-acclimate herself to the way he turned her on with merely his words let alone if he touched her.

It stayed nicely peaceful for the rest of the morning. She had a luncheon with a few former associates that she still enjoyed speaking with, and she was bemused that they had insisted on a casual dining spot rather than the fancy places most businesspeople of her experience preferred. She liked the casual ones as well.

She got there first and was quite pleased that the staff gave her a quieter table. There was never any guilt inside her for taking advantage of her clout. It balanced for the fact that she always used her power to help others. She had taken her seat and was perusing the menu when she heard steps. She looked up and smiled. "Sullivan. Jiles. What a delight." She got to her feet to greet them properly.

Sullivan Shaughnessy was indirectly related to her thanks to Kienan and Madelyne, and there was in fact a contract in his past. Actually, his entire family for a hundred fifty years had been issued contracts. Jiles Tavoularis was Kalliope's father, and therefore he was kind of related as well. Both men were in their sixties but as fit and handsome as men two decades younger. "Rhianna." Jiles gave her cheek an affectionate kiss. "What is your secret? You simply never change."

"Good genes," she demurred modestly. Truthfully, she had never needed to worry about the fact that neither she nor Eric aged because of their longevity—and neither would Gwyn, Rayna, or Taylor. By the time people had noticed she and her partner ought to look older, the first murmurs of their power had already begun. It had never been questioned since.

They all sat down and kept the conversation light as they ordered their meals. The two men were still enjoying their retirement and being grandparents, and they had quite a few humorous tales to be told. Rhianna told them about some of Enforcers' latest business ventures and amused them both when she mentioned shamelessly intimidating competition.

They were having tea with their desserts when they were surprised by a young man in a delivery uniform walking up to the table with a bouquet of red and orange roses and forget-me-nots. He stopped beside Rhianna with a bright smile. "Hi! Rhianna Taber?"

A buzz began to rise in the entire restaurant. Sullivan and Jiles' brows seemed to lift at the same time. Very warily, Rhianna said, "Yes, I am." She eyed the flowers. "Those are not for me."

"In fact, they are." He handed them over into her arms and cleared his throat as he straightened. "I have been instructed to inform you that your loving husband sends them with his warmest regards."

As an excited clatter broke out, she closed her eyes and contemplated finding a way to kill her 'loving husband.' "Thank you," she muttered. She looked at the flowers in resignation as the boy hustled away. Red roses meant love, orange roses meant fervent passion, and forget-me-nots meant exactly what they sounded like they meant. Damn him.

Sullivan cleared his throat delicately. "Rhianna?"

She put the flowers down on the table and sought for a way to explain. "I was married a long while ago," she said carefully, "and something happened that caused us to separate. We had not seen each other in ages, and we are trying to see if we can reconcile. There are complications, unfortunately. We had trust issues."

Jiles propped his chin on his hand as he grinned. "Someone seems quite determined to overcome those issues. Will you hit me if I say that I think it's wonderful? I doubt I am the first to mention that it has always been painful to see you be alone. Some people are happy that way, but you never struck me as one of them."

"I'm not," she admitted. "I was always hoping he might forgive me and return. Unfortunately, he seems to have a few subliminal issues that he is trying to find and remove. He surprised me now, I admit, and I don't surprise easily." She winced wryly as she heard the continuing buzz in the room. "So much for him saying he would be discrete."

Sullivan grinned. "After all these years, and all of your meddling, you still thought that love could be discrete at all?"

"Touché. To be fair, he is actually quite adept at it. The fact that he came back into my life a few days ago and no one noticed is proof of it. Whatever he is up to, he is up to deliberately. He could have merely made it seem as if he was courting me, but he—" She broke off as understanding dawned. "Ah." Her smile turned wry. "He *is* courting me, but he is eliminating competition at the same time. Him courting me and my accepting would make me fair game to other interested parties."

Jiles chuckled. "As ever, you know everything. You do sound surprised though. Was there no courtship when you first met?"

"Hmm, no. Things happened quite fast. I guess he is trying to make up for lost time." She looked at the flowers with an unconscious longing. It felt kind of nice to be made to feel as if she was the only thing he wanted. She *knew* it already, yet the demonstration was wonderful. "I didn't actually intend to keep our relationship a secret forever. It's just a very complicated situation."

"You will keep us posted, yes?" Sullivan asked hopefully.

She had to laugh. "Oh, I'm sure Maddie will be quite happy to tattle on me! I'm surprised neither she nor Kienan mentioned it sooner. They met my husband just yesterday." She got to her feet and put some money on the table for her share of lunch. "I have to be heading back. It was wonderful to see you both." She scooped up her flowers and headed out past the whispers with the proud manner of a goddess.

The two friends exchanged a look before Sullivan pulled out his cell phone. They would call Kienan and Madelyne immediately and get the full scoop. If there was *anything* they could do to help, they would damned well do it!

Rhianna immediately went back to her office and ignored the giggles and grins from her employees. She put the flowers into a vase where she could admire them and turned to go to her desk. Much to her surprise, there was a gaily wrapped package sitting on the top. It was wrapped in gold paper with a white ribbon. She really didn't even need to see the signature on the card to know it was from Aaron.

She sighed and untied the ribbon. Removing the paper revealed another layer in red. Then a third in purple. She couldn't help but be impressed despite herself. A box was at last under the purple paper, and she lifted the lid to discover an assortment of custom chocolates. All of them were dark chocolate, which happened to be her favorite. She couldn't resist scooping up one and biting in, and her eyes went wide as she found herself with a mouthful of gooey cinnamon filling. A sniff of a few others revealed pomegranate and honey fillings.

The giggle that passed her lips surprised even her, and she felt glad that Eric wasn't in the office to hear her. Her impish, romantic, and sexy significant other had sent her a box of all-natural aphrodisiacs. No chocolate covered strawberries for *him*. He went right to the good stuff. As if they needed the help! Still, her non-traditional side was tickled.

The moment she realized it, she sighed and shook her head. The questionnaire she had filled out. One of the questions had been on her opinion of traditional gifts like flowers and chocolates, and she had answered that she liked them when they were adapted to the person receiving them. He had deliberately picked out things sure to stir her romantic side as well as her sense of humor. He was also deliberately playing to her senses by engaging them with aromatic scents and tastes. Odds are that she would soon be serenaded by a lyre; she had never been the saxophone type.

She couldn't resist grabbing another chocolate as she sat down and logged back onto her computer. She then promptly choked on the candy as her speakers quite merrily began to play a soft, sexy ballad rendered in a lyre and an oboe. The high notes seemed to flutter her heart, and the low notes fluttered something much lower. She grabbed her phone and punched a button. "Damn it, Rayna!"

All she got in response was an explosion of helpless giggles, and she slammed down the phone again. There was no other way the music could have gotten onto her computer. Aaron had enlisted his minions—and they had been her minions first! She sat back in her chair and drummed her fingers on her arm. Finally, with a sigh, she gave in to what he was so obviously trying to do. She rescheduled her one afternoon meeting and took the rest of the day off.

When she arrived at Cupid's Grove, Priya looked up with a smile that she hastily bit back from becoming a laugh. Rhianna merely sighed at her. "Alright. Where is he? We both know he was deliberately trying to entice me into coming to him."

Priya struggled to the best of her ability to hide her giggles. "Actually, he's not here. He had no appointments so he decided to go home. He said he was, uhm, going to get in some archery practice."

Rhianna rolled her eyes at that. She drummed her fingers on her arm for a moment as she thought about things. Perhaps it was time that Cupid got himself some competition. "Thanks, Priya." She swung around and headed out of the building. Her transportation skills were highly limited because she was not a god, but she could take herself to places that she had previously visited physically. She went home to change into casual clothes and packed herself an overnight bag. A flick of her fingers transported her to Aaron's beautiful home in the mountains and she dropped the bag inside before heading around to the gardens beyond the bath.

A large open space greeted her once she passed the line of peach trees. Several targets had been set up for practice, and her lover was calmly and expertly placing arrow after arrow into the dead center of the bulls-eye. Another bow and quiver sat nearby and she scooped it up. From ten feet behind him, she notched an arrow and let it fly. It neatly nipped over his shoulder close enough to clip a few strands of hair, flew right across the field, and smacked into the end of his last arrow with enough force to knock it out of place.

Aaron looked back over his shoulder with a slow and wicked grin. "What is that phrase mortals have? Something about 'this being war'?"

"'This means war'," she confirmed. She sauntered closer. "I think I can keep up with you, Eros. I've picked up a few skills in my life."

He tilted up her chin with his free hand and leaned down to kiss her with his familiar intensity. "And some things," he murmured huskily, "you are simply a natural at." Sparks moved across his iridescent eyes. "You taste like chocolate." He lingered over another softer kiss. "Mm. I like it. Maybe I should get some of that edible paint for us to play with."

A bit breathlessly, she asked, "Who turned you loose on the erotica sites?"

"Priya. She claimed I might as well have all of the tools of the trade, particularly since it would seem they created the word *erotic* from my name." His laugh rippled over her skin. "I think I like that."

She had always felt it was an appropriate derivation herself. "Don't think you'll distract me into losing." She pushed him back and moved up to stand beside him. "Let's see what you've got. You might be rusty after two millennia."

A little thrill rippled through him anew at the signs of her inner strength and confidence. He did not want someone he could always boss around; he wanted a partner. An equal. He lifted his bow and fired at the target, and he knocked her arrow free. The target was beginning to be a bit ragged, and he shifted to shoot the next. Her subsequent arrow knocked his out moments later.

They traded back and forth with their shots, but eventually they both just gave up and started laughing. They were simply too evenly matched. Aaron took the bows and quivers to place them aside, and then he tugged Rhianna into his arms. "I would like to declare a tie." He rubbed their noses together affectionately. "You are quite the archer, my beloved."

"It amused me to learn," she admitted. She looped her arms around his waist and smiled. "I will take it as a compliment that I can keep you on your toes. And admit that my friends are glad that I don't have arrows like you do. I'd shamelessly use them."

"You shamelessly use other things." He tucked her under his arm and escorted her back into the rest of the garden. "Come sit with me."

She took one look at the little table set with tea and cake and knew that he had indeed been deliberately luring her into coming over. She did not mind. He filled in the places in her life that her job and friends never could. "What is this?"

"I believe it is called a date." He helped her into her chair before scooting his closer so that they sat side-by-side. He brought her hand to his lips and lightly teased the skin between her fingers. "I am courting you, Rhianna. You once said you had hoped I would suit you. I realized I have been lax in that department. A married woman deserves to be courted no less than an unmarried. A married man, too," he added hopefully.

"I could be convinced to court you in return." She shook her head at him. "If, perhaps, you could ever get around to *asking* me about things. You never asked me to marry you. You never asked to court me. You didn't even ask me onto this 'date.' Sometimes a question is important even when the answer will be yes. It evens the field."

He tugged her hand to his heart and looked very seriously in her eyes. "Will you let me court you, Rhianna?" he asked softly. "Let me shower you with the love and devotion you so richly deserve. Let me ensure that there is no doubt in your mind how much I love you. I wish to tell the entire world."

She cupped his cheek with her free hand and tugged him down for a tender kiss. "Yes, you may court me," she whispered against his lips. Humor filled her eyes. "I think you already started on the 'telling the world' bit. Sending me flowers at my luncheon and declaring yourself as my husband!"

He smiled unrepentantly. "I have no desire to entertain rivals, and we both know that you starting to accept attention from any man would label you as 'single and looking' as far as the rest of the male populace was concerned. I suppose some things have not entirely changed after all this time."

"Except that I get to *choose*. It is entirely my decision. I think that I would be offended if my father was alive and you asked him for my hand."

"I would ask your entire family," he disagreed, "for I would be taking you away from them. I would not ask that they give you to me, but that they accept your decision to be taken away."

"Ooh, tactful." She reached for a slice of cake; it was chocolate, of course. "Tell me about your day, and I will tell you what I have done for your referral."

They lingered long enough in the garden that the sun was beginning to set before they realized the passage of time. It had always been that way for them, even from the beginning. They could always find something to talk about, and there was nothing sacred between them. And yet, they could be perfectly fine to be together and quiet. Both could envision wonderful times reading by a fire together, if they could get to that point where they truly lived together.

She made dinner since it was her turn, and they snuggled on the couch after to watch one of their programs. He then sat down with some questionnaires to evaluate while she read up on the business proposal that Mel had floated her direction. Once work was done for the night, they shut down everything and retired to the bedroom.

"Do you want a shower?" he asked.

"I'll catch one in the morning. I don't like showers right before bed. Makes it hard to sleep."

"I could make you tired." He teasingly nipped at her shoulder where it was bared by her nightshirt.

"You certainly could, but I will decline." She finished washing off her makeup and removed her earrings. "I once considered pierced ears, but back when I was first introduced to them, it was a bit on the barbaric side. Turned me off to the entire procedure. Rayna has tried to tell me it's very safe and relatively painless these days, but I just get the creeps."

He grinned. "So there is something that alarms the ever calm, never flustered Rhianna Taber."

She smiled at him. "I am only human."

"You are only a living being," he corrected softly. "Even gods feel fear. Perhaps we even feel all emotions more acutely."

Which was the entire reasons mortals could not behold a god or goddess in their true form. She brushed it aside; it seemed as if each day moved him closer to understanding. She could continue to be patient no matter how painful it was sometimes. "I'll wait for you in bed."

He frowned as she walked into the bedroom. "Why do you continue to sleep in that shirt? I know you do not like it, my beloved. Do you not trust me? I can abide by what you wish. I am not that much a beast."

She got under the covers. "If you can't trust me in the light, then I can't trust you in the dark." The curtains were already drawn, and she clicked off the lamp to plunge the room into darkness. "Don't forget your feet. I'd swear you had ice cubes attached to your legs."

It was just as well that it was dark for it meant she could not see his frown had deepened. He undressed for the night and slipped into bed beside her. She immediately snuggled up against his side where she belonged, and it did not take very long before her breathing evened out into the beautiful sound of sleep.

He stared at the ceiling overhead and tried to make sense of her words. She had said it before that she did not trust him in the dark. Because he had only ever made love to her in the dark? Of course he had. He had been hiding his identity from her. Yet now she inferred that he did not trust her in the light? That seemed ridiculous when he had spent the last few days with her quite vagrantly in the daylight.

But had he ever made love to her in the light?

His fingers stilled their absent stroking over her arm. No. No, he had not. Even now, past the time of deceit and lies, he had brought in the darkness that first night. He had made love to her by the pool in the light, though.

To her, not *with* her. She trusted him to not do more than ease her if they were in the light, and she did not trust him to hold back when they were in the dark. Because he had only ever made love with her in the dark, she rightfully was wary of it. No, it couldn't be that she was wary. She had said *he* was afraid of something, that he was afraid to give her something. Something that was connected to his true self.

You won't give me your true self.

Her words echoed and doubled in his head. It simply did not make sense when he had been naked with her quite frequently. He was naked right then and there. She had seen his true form plenty of—

The thoughts stumbled off and came to a halt. Horror began to slowly rise as understanding started to break through. She had *not* seen his true form. She had never *seen* him naked. Not even now that the truth was out had he ever been naked with her *in the light.* The towel by the bath. Turning off the lights and closing drapes before getting into bed. Leaving her before the dawn. Closing the door while he showered. No wonder she didn't trust him; he had painted nothing but a sign that he did not trust *her*.

But what didn't he trust? Why would he not want her to see him naked when he very much liked the way she looked at him? He had been savoring the love and desire in her eyes when she gazed at him. She was finally able to give him the same worship he had always given her . . . except while they made love. But *why?* She was all but a goddess, so—

For the second time, his thoughts stumbled off as understanding collided with hindsight. She was a mortal. He had thought of her as being almost a goddess and yet he had treated her like a mortal. *He had instinctively thought she could not handle his true self*. It was absolute bullshit, and he felt like the biggest fool in the entire universe for the second time in his life. She was his *equal*. Whether mortal or immortal, her emotions ran as deep, true, and powerfully as his did.

Agony welled anew. How he must have been hurting her! She must have been thinking all this time that he did not trust in her love. After the way they had parted in the past, he could not blame her for it at all. He had *never* questioned his decision to keep her in the dark, and he had never realized just what had really been driving it.

He had already accepted that he should have fought for her from the beginning, but now he had a much more bitter pill to swallow: he would have still screwed things up even if there had been honesty. Things had merely happened faster thanks to his deception. Even if they had seen each other during the day, even if she had known he was Eros, eventually she would have been driven to want to see him while they made love. Nothing could have stopped them from reaching the point where they were now—nothing except *her*, and she had not fully come into her power until this life.

His arm tightened around her fiercely for a moment and she mumbled something in her sleep as she cuddled even closer. One lovely leg hooked over his as if to keep him from escaping. Determination began to pound inside his heart. It was time to make them the full equals they deserved to be, and to give her the final thing that he had never given before.

He stayed up a little while longer in order to decide his course of action and finally managed to fall asleep close to midnight. The waiting would finally end tomorrow, and they could make that grab for their happy ending. It was time to change that VOID into an In Progress. They had come too far to lose now.

CHAPTER TWELVE

Rhianna awoke in the morning to the feel of fingers dancing down her arm. They skimmed up into her hair and caressed the nape of her neck. Lips teased hers. "Wake up, my beloved," Aaron's husky voice murmured. "You do not want to oversleep."

She opened her eyes to find him kneeling beside the bed. He was already dressed, and she glanced at the clock. It was indeed getting late. She freed herself from his grip and sat up with a yawn. "I don't normally oversleep. I'm still psychically burned out so some of my side gifts are muted."

He tugged her out of bed and kissed her warmly. "Go take your shower. I will make breakfast."

"Alright." She rose up on her toes to kiss him in turn before heading for the bathroom. There seemed to be something . . . different inside him. A strange sense of peace and determination that she could not put her finger on. She was really starting to dislike her burnout. She needed every advantage she could get, and she missed being able to feel Eric even at a distance.

He had baked cinnamon rolls for breakfast, and they both devoured their share happily. After they ate, he transported her back to her home where she could finish getting ready to go to work. He then transported himself to the Grove. He knew he could take the effort to learn to drive and perhaps get a vehicle, but why should he bother? If at any point he needed to go somewhere that he needed to arrive via vehicle, he could merely bribe his wife to take him. He was still tickled that she owned a motorcycle. He liked an unconventional streak in anyone.

Priya had dropped off on his desk the latest questionnaires he needed to review, and she had updated his calendar on his computer. The learning curve for the electronic beast had been interesting, to be sure. He was quite proud of himself for finally getting the hang of it. Rayna had promised him lessons later if he needed it, but so far so good.

His first meeting was at nine. He settled in with a cup of his new favorite Starbucks coffee and started going through the questionnaires for the markers he had placed. People truly did not realize just how much they gave away with a few simple questions. They left an energy fingerprint that read like neon to him. He compared those as much as he compared the answers themselves; he had matched up perfect opposites because their energies blended, and that was the important part. Likes and dislikes could be changed and expanded. It was how people grew.

He found two potential matches and clipped them together with his notes for Priya to make appointments to bring them in for more in-depth analysis. He was on his second cup of coffee by the time his client arrived, and he smiled when he saw her. She was an older woman in her mid-fifties who had been divorced for ten years. He quite looked forward to finding her love. It was beautiful at any age.

They were partway through expanding on her answers when he felt a familiar chill ripple down his skin. His head came up sharply as power moved across his eyes. Evil. It stirred. It must have surely sensed that he and Rhianna were on the cusp of becoming one. It hated nothing more than what they represented together; they alone could create the happy endings that evil sought only to destroy.

"Mr. Konstantinos?" His client frowned. "Is something wrong?" A sudden strong scent touched her nose and she pulled a face. "Ugh, that smells like rotten eggs." She gagged as the scent got stronger. "What *is* that?"

"Aaron!" Priya burst into the doorway. "Can you smell it?" He shook his head, and her heart briefly froze. Of course he wouldn't. *Humans* were sensitive to the scent added to gas, but that didn't mean gods were, too! "There's natural gas filling the building! We need to get out of here."

A chill ran down his back. "Grab the drive with our information," he ordered her as he got to his feet. Danger began to beat along his nerves as he helped his client to her feet and urged her toward the door. Natural gas. He could not smell it, but he knew it was highly flammable. Truthfully, the very fact that he could not smell it was a sign that it was directed at him. If Priya had not been there, he would have been a sitting duck.

They hustled outside and crossed the street quickly to be just inside the District. Priya was already on the phone calling 9-1-1. Their two neighboring buildings had begun to evacuate as well thanks to the smell leaking over. They went down the street rather than cross over. Oddly, that did not surprise Aaron at all.

With a roar of fire and a window-shattering explosion that also shook the ground, his building went up in a mushroom cloud of smoke and flames. Alarms started going off all over the street. People came out of other buildings to see what was going on. Sudden sirens in the distance meant that firemen had noticed and were on their way.

Aaron narrowed his eyes on the burning building as he still felt as if there was something wrong. A faint heartbeat touched his ears, and he realized that there was someone inside. It was possible. He left the back door unlocked so that the nearby homeless people had a warm spot to sleep at night.

Priya bit back a yelp as he went running for the building. "Aaron!" she wailed. "You'll get hurt!"

"Hurt?" the old woman blurted. "He'll get himself killed!"

Well, no, he wouldn't, but he would sure as hell get badly wounded. Priya barely hesitated before grabbing her cell phone. She turned and looked toward the Enforcers' tall building. She would bet that Rhianna already knew, but it was always better to be safe than sorry.

Aaron was reminded of his lack of true invulnerability when the first flaming piece of wood struck his arm. Burns and bloody wounds of other assorted shapes formed as he moved through the mess of the lobby toward the break room and the door inside that led to their storage space and back door. His slim consolation was that he might cough from the smoke but it could not do permanent damage.

He scalded his hands as he wrenched the knob to the storage area open. A plume of smoke hit him in the face and he was briefly blinded. He managed to wave it out of his face and ducked down to get inside. "Is someone here?"

A whimper responded and it did not sound human. His eyes covered the ground sharply and he found a wiggling lump under a blanket. Yanking the blanket aside revealed a bedraggled and soot-covered puppy. It was probably quite fluffy when clean, if the matted fur was any clue. He stared for a moment in sheer surprise and then scooped up the small animal into his arms. "It will be all right," he soothed. "How did you get in here?"

The acrid scent of evil touched his nose again. Understanding flashed. A trap. He had been deliberately lured back inside. He tried to kick down the back door but it seemed as if something heavy had been braced on the other side. Keeping the puppy wrapped in his jacket, he rushed back the other way as quickly as he could.

A beam crashed down from the ceiling and cut off his escape. Something moved in the corners, and even the bright glow of the fire could not banish the ugly black cloud creeping in. He held his ground without fear and wrapped the puppy tighter inside his jacket. The cloud rushed over him to consume him, and his power rose hotly. White light ripped from him and tore through the cloud. It evaporated with a scream that made chills run down even his skin.

His now torn and bloody skin. He grimaced as the pain ambushed him. A quick look down told him that he looked like a royal mess. He used another blast of raw power to break apart the beam and rushed out into the safety of the street once more. There was a large crowd of onlookers standing around, and the firemen were beginning to hook up hoses to the fire hydrants.

Priya came scrambling over to his side. Fear made her dark eyes wide. "Aaron! Oh, god. You look *horrible!* You must be in agony!" Her eyes widened more as he opened his jacket to reveal the puppy. "What the . . . how did she get in there?" She gingerly took the small creature and tried to brush at the soot. It looked like a collie of some kind and barely older than a few weeks in age.

"Aaron!" Rhianna shoved through the crowd and rushed toward him. Her black eyes had consumed her pupils in her distress, and her skin was pale. She threw herself into his arms heedless of the onlookers and clung onto him with all of her strength.

A few jaws dropped in the crowd. It was a shocking thing to see the always-collected Rhianna Taber that rattled. Rumor had already spread quickly about the fact that she was married, and now understanding began to dawn. The new marriage counselor in town, conveniently right outside her district, was her estranged husband. "Talk about a coincidence," one woman murmured.

"Rhi." Aaron held her as tightly as he could and ignored the protest of his wounds. "I am sorry, my beloved."

"Were you caught in there?" she asked against his chest.

"No." Priya scowled. "He went back inside!"

He scowled at her equally as Rhianna pulled back sharply. "You *what?!*" She narrowed her eyes as the familiar sparks of her temper appeared. "You went back into a burning building? Why?"

He shrugged. "There was a heartbeat inside. I could not let it be harmed. I am a god, my love. I cannot be killed. Perhaps I can be a bit singed, but not killed." He took the puppy and plopped it down into her arms. "You need a pet. She will suit you well." He sighed as she continued to stare at him. "I wish I could placate you by saying I would have not gone in if I had known it was merely a puppy, but I am afraid I would have done it anyway. I cherish life. I am a protector."

"Get it from your father," she muttered.

A soot-covered golden brow lifted. "I had to have something from him, did I not? It is better that it be a desire to protect than not." His lips slowly curved. "Better to make love than war, no? Still, I am amused by the way people cannot be sure of my origins. It would seem many still think I predated the gods and was adopted by Aphrodite."

"Most didn't get to see your sheer *bullheaded* stubbornness!" She plopped the dog back into Priya's arms and swung around on her heel. "Captain." She walked calmly over to where the man in charge of the firemen was standing. "Enforcers stands by to give assistance as this is close enough to our District to command our attention; the Grove is considered an ally. Was anyone injured?"

"A few passersby," he admitted. He gestured. "They are being prepared to go to the hospital."

"They will go to Enforcers' hospital and we will front the costs." She accepted his handshake and moved on to speak with the police who had arrived on the scene as well. With the same calm authority, she took charge and issued orders.

Aaron stayed back a step and watched with a smile tugging at his lips. He had been doing quite a bit of research to learn about what he had missed over two thousand years, and he had found himself fascinated by how his beautiful wife had managed to be in charge of, and stay in charge of, a multi-billion dollar company through periods of time where it had *assuredly* not been allowed for women to even contemplate working outside of a home. He thought he might finally have an answer as to how she had done it. Quite simply, who would dare tell her she couldn't?

She was natural born leader. She took charge in any situation with calm control and a sort of self-confidence that never felt arrogant. She made others feel as if they were valued equals without letting it be mistaken that her word was final. Even Eric would defer to her in the event of a tie. Her friends were perfectly fine to let her lead because she was just so damn good at it. Thinking about the events of the past, Aaron had to smile. If everything had ended happily back then, she would have taken over Olympus within the first month, and not even Zeus or Hera would have stopped her.

She strode back over to his side and ordered briskly, "You're coming home with me where I can tend to your wounds. You are not to ever visit any hospital except the one owned by Enforcers. They specifically cater to the needs of our gifted people in the District."

"Yes, beloved," he answered meekly.

She stared at him before snorting softly. "Don't try to pull that subservient attitude with me, Aaron. I know you too well." Her eyes widened as he reached for her. "Don't you *dare*." The words turned into a little gasp as he yanked her into his arms and kissed her with greedy hunger. She vaguely noted the sound of cheering in the background but found she didn't care. No level of public affection could bother her reputation. In fact, it would probably *help*.

He released her and she blew out a breath as she desperately tried to ignore her rampaging hormones. The little smirk tugging at his lips implied he could feel her frustration still, but she couldn't begrudge him his smugness. It was deserved. She shoved him back a step. "Stop that or I'll lose the ability to think." She turned to where Priya was standing with the puppy. "Priya, until Aaron can get his company up and running again, you may present yourself at Enforcers' HQ and we will find work for you to do so that you don't lack a paycheck."

"Thank you, Ms. Taber," Priya said sincerely.

"Rhianna," she corrected. She sighed and took the puppy as it was offered. She had often been intrigued by having a pet, but she had never bothered to look for one. Naturally, Aaron would have unintentionally found her a way to get her one. "Alright. I'm taking my pet and my husband home and getting them both cleaned up."

Aaron amiably walked along beside her as she strode swiftly into the District. He found himself holding the puppy again as she got out her cell phone and called Eric to tell him what had been going on. Even with good dampening on the phone, Aaron's sensitive ears could hear that Eric was not a happy warlock over events. It made him feel better. He truly wished to be friends with Eric for he knew that the other man was deeply beloved to Rhianna, and vice-versa. Naturally, he expected there to be some bickering as was with Eric and Taylor, but that was what happened when strong and dominant personalities tried to be friends. As long as it was not done in animosity, it was perfectly fine—and often entertaining to all those around.

He followed Rhianna into her house and offered the puppy. "If you will tend her, I would like a shower."

She arched a brow. "What will you do for clothes?"

"I am a god." He flicked a finger at her nose and ambled down the hall.

She just shook her head. She held the puppy up at eye level and smiled as she studied the canine face. Border collie, and what was probably a red point coat under all the soot. No more than a month old. "Alright, you. Let's see just how well you clean up."

The kitchen sink was plenty big enough for washing a small pet, and Rhianna was prepared for a fight if hers didn't like the washing. Luckily for her, the puppy seemed to enjoy the pampering as much as Rhianna enjoyed hers. Once thoroughly washed clean, the puppy was revealed to indeed have a coppery red color. She even stayed obediently in the sink while Rhianna fetched a towel to dry her.

Aaron strolled shirtless into the living room while Rhianna was using a comb to smooth out the puppy's matted fur. He dropped the shirt in his hand over the arm of the couch. "What will you name her?"

"I'm thinking Juno."

"You would name her for Hera's alternate name?"

"Do admit she was one of the nicer goddesses. Most of her bad actions were sparked by Zeus being unfaithful. Besides. She was your grandmother."

"Indeed." He grimaced as he gingerly sat down on the couch beside her. The bruises were already fading, and the wounds were showing signs of healing, but they still hurt like the fires of punishment. "I should be whole by tonight."

"Well, I am still going to bind you up." She put Juno on the floor to scamper off and explore. She briefly left to retrieve bandages and then sat down again to start wrapping up the wounds. No need for antiseptic; he couldn't catch anything. There were many benefits to being immortal. The wrapping was mostly to maintain the illusion. There had been plenty of people to see the state he was in.

As she was binding one wound, she asked softly, "Will you go home for the rest of the day since working is out? Or do you want to start taking care of calling your clients? Enforcers has a few empty office spots if you wished to use one."

"I intend to ask Priya to make the calls to tell people we are briefly closed. As for permanent space, I would like to find space in the District, yes." He smiled a bit wryly. "I love the District, Rhianna. I feel as if I *belong*. I have never felt such a sense of belonging, not even within my domain so long ago. It is true what they say. If you are drawn here, there is something you can only find here." He skimmed his free hand down her cheek. "For me, there is you. But there is more. There is . . . home."

"That's how it was for Eric and me," she admitted. "I never felt as if I belonged anywhere until we settled here and built our District. I had to accept long ago that perhaps things had happened for a reason."

He smiled. "I had also realized much the same recently. The past just would never have worked out for the simple fact that you did not know your own power, and it was this life that has allowed you to so beautifully bloom into it."

She frowned at him. "Why would my power have anything to do with it?"

"You do not understand the full scope of what you do?"

"No."

"Or see your own future?"

"No."

"Have you not ever wondered why?"

"Well, of course." She scowled. "What are you getting at, Aaron?"

His fingers tenderly caressed her cheek again. "Perhaps you should think about what complements the power of Love best, and about the things that Eric has accused you of for centuries. The gift you have . . . there is no one else with it. There will be no other. There is a very simple reason for why the gods so quickly acquiesced to you, beloved."

It made her think for a moment. Only one thing seemed to make sense, but it felt more than a bit daunting to believe *she* might have that sort of power. Very softly, she asked, "If I were to truly understand my power, would there be more I could do in order to help others?"

His heart melted. Such a typically Rhianna thing to say. While contemplating having the power to command destiny itself, she merely asked if she could do more for others. Truly, she was his other half. "Yes. There will be nothing we cannot do together."

She drew a deep breath. "It's a bit unnerving, even for me, to begin to understand. Let me process it for a while. I've learned to be patient. I will know when it is right for me to accept and take full command of my . . . gift."

"You are entitled." He kissed her softly for a moment before releasing her and testing the bandages. "They will do. After today, I will wear long sleeves until a reasonable time has passed for me to heal." He gingerly tugged on his shirt. "I will be glad for them to go. They are painful."

She smirked. "Baby." She got to her feet with a sigh. "I have to get back to work. I have a meeting this afternoon I can't put off. Juno!" she called. She knelt with a smile as the puppy bounded up to her. "Already know your name, don't you? I think you are gifted as well. Once you grow into those feet, you can be our courier. I've missed having one ever since Audra retired." She laughed as Juno happily licked her face in response. "You're welcome, I think!"

"I would like to go with you to work," Aaron offered.

"You can't sit in my meeting," she reminded him reasonably.

A brow arched arrogantly. "How little faith you have in your husband." A swirl of gold light surrounded him and he suddenly changed into a much smaller, almost cherubic, version of himself. He stood barely a foot big, and actual tiny wings had sprouted from the birthmarks on his back. He laughed richly when she gaped at him. "Where do you suppose they came up with my cherub form, beloved?" Other than a slightly stronger power, his voice sounded the same, and the masculine tones seemed quite amusing coming from someone who looked like a Disney version of a Greek statue. "Normally, only gods and goddesses can see me, but I have chosen to let you see me as well."

She felt a laugh bubbling up, and it broke out as she saw Juno watching him wide-eyed. "And puppies!"

"Ah, well, animals see clearer than most humans anyway." He landed on her shoulder. "Shall we?"

What the hell; why not? At least she wouldn't bored through her meeting, that was for certain.

CHAPTER THIRTEEN

When Rhianna walked onto the top floor with Aaron trailing along at her shoulder—leaving behind gold sparkles, the smartass—Gwyn and Rayna took one look and collapsed into a fit of the giggles. Poor Taylor and Eric could only watch them in sheer confusion; the two Faeriekin had easily tickled senses of humor, but usually it was fairly obvious what they found amusing. "Do we dare ask?" Taylor groused at Rhianna.

"Not really." She opened her office door. "By the way, the puppy is named Juno. She'll be our new courier."

"Ee!" The girlish squeal came from both sisters alike as they dropped down to scoop up Juno and smother her with cuddles and kisses. Juno's tail wagged so fast it was a blur as she happily soaked up the affection.

"I'll make a note to install a doggie door in the lobby," Eric offered dryly as he disappeared into his office.

"She needs a collar!" Rayna hopped to her feet. "C'mon, Gwyn! Let's go get one! I bet Brian'll have something." She dashed off down the hall with Gwyn and Juno close behind. "We'll bring her back later!"

Taylor just sighed and went back into Eric's office as well where they had been discussing a contract they were both overseeing. Rhianna dropped into her chair behind her desk and unlocked her computer. She was actually a bit surprised she had remembered to even lock it at all. She had been in a *bit* of a hurry the moment she had sensed Aaron in their District and gotten Priya's phone call as to why. It bothered her deeply that she had not seen it coming. Evil was truly stirring. She needed to heal from her burnout but just didn't know how.

"Beloved." Aaron ached to turn back and hold her in his arms. He very nearly decided to do so when someone knocked on the door.

"Enter," Rhianna called. She stood as a man walked into the office, and though friendly enough, there was a sort of coolness in her smile. "Assemblyman Harkin, how kind of you to join me. It's nice to meet you. I'm Rhianna Taber."

Aaron did not like Harkin on sight. He was appealing enough in the face with a pleasantly plump body, but something seemed to come through to the surface. Some sort of greasiness and lack of an ability to feel love. He didn't think he would be the only one able to see it.

Harkin gave Rhianna one of those polished political smiles that never seemed to be sincere. She had offered a hand, and he obligingly shook it. He also happened to slowly look her over in a way more than a bit derogatory, particularly as his eyes lingered on her breasts and hips. "What a delight, Ms. Taber. I am quite grateful to you for being willing to meet with me like this. I know how busy you women can be."

She freed her hand. "I do keep busy, but I make time when it is needed." She gestured to a seat and sat down herself. Under her desk, she surreptitiously rubbed her hand on her pants as if to rid herself of his touch. Aaron smirked, but she ignored him. "What can I help you with, Assemblyman?"

"I will be looking to run for re-election and I would like to receive Enforcers' support for such a thing." He gave her a placating smile. "I had explained everything in my voice mail to Eric Mason when I requested a meeting with him. I assumed he made the decisions."

She arched a brow. "Eric and I are full partners. We make mutual decisions though we will defer to each other's good judgment as needed. In the event that we are deadlocked, I am the one with the final say."

Harkin was visibly taken aback for a moment but he recovered quickly enough. "My apologies, Ms. Taber, if I offended. Women in power are still rare these days."

Bits of steam began to come out Aaron's ears. Maybe if men like this were not so quick to believe women were incapable, there might be more out there. Even in Ancient Greece, women had been respected for their skills. It was hard to not respect women as a whole when there were plenty of goddesses ready to smite anyone who dared imply they were the inferior gender. Where was Artemis when he needed her? Someone needed that smiting.

Rhianna's nails tapped lightly on the top of her desk. "I have been in power for a very long time." Her voice sounded almost gentle. "I have never had anyone question it."

Harkin loosened his collar. "Naturally not! Well, allow me to tell you where I would like to see my next term take me when it comes to the well-being of our beautiful New York."

She made notes as she listened, and she asked obligatory questions. It was purely for form. She and Eric had already compiled their list of who they would and would not support for the next round of elections—and Harkin was not on it. Rayna had been doing the research for a few months and already knew everything that might possibly be illuminated about new and old candidates.

"You certainly do have some interesting plans," she finally said when he paused. "I will pass my notes along to Eric." And enjoy watching him set them on fire. "How has your wife been lately, Assemblyman? I last saw her at Rafael and Victoria Lucino's engagement party."

A hint of pink climbed his neck. "She is well enough. She is expecting now, and rests quite a bit."

"It is probably not even his," Aaron muttered. "He has the look of a cuckold about him. And who can blame his wife? Few have Hera's patience."

Rhianna bit back a smile. "How delightful for you, Assemblyman. Congratulations to you both."

"I hear congratulations are in order for you as well, Ms. Taber. Everyone is talking about how your estranged husband has come back. Such a shame for the rest of the men of the world that such a singularly beautiful woman would not be available anymore." His eyes ran over her again. "Truly a pity. Will you retire in order to keep a home for your husband? I suppose that might be quite boring to a woman like you, though. I do hope you might consider some interesting alternatives if he can't keep you entertained."

Aaron's considerable temper blew. The sheer offensiveness of this creature in Rhianna's office could not be defined. On both the principle of it as well as a personal level, Aaron refused to condone this sort of brash attitude. There was a vast difference between genuine admiration, natural reactionary desire, and this disgusting harassment.

Before Rhianna realized what he was about to do, a familiar bow appeared in his hands. He drew out a blue tipped arrow and quite calmly fired it directly at Harkin. The other man did not feel nor sense it piercing his chest and into his heart, but he did blink rapidly a bit as if dizzy. "I feel a bit odd."

"You are a bit pale, Assemblyman." Rhianna hit a button on her intercom. "Hoang? Could you come pick up Assemblyman Harkin and escort him out to a taxi? He is not feeling well."

The guard showed up a few moments later and graciously helped a clearly disoriented Harkin out of the office. As soon as the door shut behind them, a swirl of golden light returned Aaron to normal. He leaned against Rhianna's desk and crossed his arms. "He deserved what he got."

She lifted a brow. "Do tell what it is that he got. I don't know your arrows on sight."

"Do you recall I mentioned my dulling arrows? They briefly diminish desire without erasing it. Think of a more effective variation on a cold shower." A tiny hint of menace entered his smile. "I shot that vile thing with a neutralizer instead. It permanently erases all capacity for desire so that only an inducer may return it—and it leaves behind the longing to feel desire anew." He shrugged unrepentantly. "When you are born with the capacity for lust and desire, and you abuse it, you should not be allowed to have it. It is the other side to my personal rules."

"Other side?"

"If you are born without the capacity for lust and desire, I do not induce it unless you can never be happy without it. I seek to create happiness and joy, my beloved, and that definition changes from one human to another. That creature within your office knows only greed and cruelty and personal pleasure. He deserves to live without the thing he covets most."

"You certainly won't hear me complaining about your actions. I have never actually liked him. And the women of the world will be glad to be spared his sly looks and casual grabbiness, as well. Pity you don't have something to erase his sexist attitude."

He pursed his lips. "I wonder what might happen were I to shoot him with an inducer and make him fall madly in love with his wife. Would it help?"

"Probably not. Some people can't be helped, Eros." She began to shut down her computer. "After that *delightful* meeting, I have a need to scrub myself from head to toe. Cerberus' breath smelled less than Harkin's." She smiled up at him. "Can I go home with you tonight?"

"Always." He caught her in his arms for a fierce hug before hoisting her off her feet and kissing her with a slow, famished heat guaranteed to scatter her thoughts. As they eased back, he murmured huskily, "Welcome home."

Sure enough, they were in the living room. "So glad I've gotten used to that style of travel," she sighed as she released him. Somehow her hands had ended up in his hair again. She suspected magnets existed under her skin that were drawn to his curls. "I think it's my turn to make dinner."

"Ah, but you want a bath." He flicked her nose lightly. "You can just make dinner two nights in a row later. I will get things started if you would like to go to the pool and soak. It is quite beautiful in the evening."

She asked politely, "Will you fetch me clothes from my house in order to wear?"

"You can wear my shirt tonight." He stole a kiss. "Tomorrow we shall stop at your home in the morning for you to change for work." He turned her and gave her a gentle nudge. "Go," he urged. "Relax, my beloved. I think you will find everything to be better soon enough."

She eyed him as she sensed again that he had secrets but finally sighed and grabbed some fluffy towels before heading out to the gardens. It truly did look spectacular in the evening light. Everything was illuminated in golds and reds, and she lit some lamps around the edge of the pool in order to stave off the coming night.

The water felt wonderful on her skin. Even better was scrubbing away the lingering grubby sensation of being near something icky. Much more relaxed, she sat down on one of the ledges and sank in to her neck. Jets suddenly began to pulse, and she smiled without opening her eyes. "The benefits to marrying a god."

"There are many," her husband concurred huskily.

She opened her eyes and found him wading into the pool. A towel was knotted around his hips. He watched her eyes flicker to it and briefly fill with pain before it disappeared. She said nothing, and he moved to sit on another ledge nearby. "Well, beloved." His voice was quiet and calm. "I believe it is time to talk about the past and determine our future."

She straightened up. "I see." Her fingers curled together under the water. "I guess I should start by apologizing for breaking your trust."

"No." He shook his head sharply. "The fault lies with me. I am far more at fault for what occurred than you are. I hid my identity from you and did not trust that you could keep our love a secret. I, of all people, should have understood your need for more than mere whispers in the night." His breath came out softly. "*I* am sorry. I am sorry I did not fight for you from the beginning. And I am more sorry for having made you feel rejected over and over again lately."

Her gaze lowered slightly. "Only a bit rejected."

"Now you are lying to me, love. You do not think I can see your emotions? Truly, it is a wonder that I ever had this issue at all. I am a fool, I suppose. I see you as all but a goddess and yet I instinctively treated you as a mortal. What rubbish." He got to his feet and waded closer to her. "I trust nothing more in existence than I trust the depth of your love. You feel as deeply as I do. You burn as hotly. Cry as hard. We are equals, and it is time to make us so."

Her breath hitched as he deliberately untied the towel and tossed it aside. It mattered not that the water technically covered him from the waist down—he was not *wearing* the water. No clothing barred his naked body, and it took only a moment until he began to produce that incredible glow she had only once before glimpsed. It was truly metaphysical—it hid in the darkness—but eyes would register it as nearly a halo.

She stared at him for a long moment and then inexplicably began to laugh. His brows came together with more bemusement than annoyance. "It is not very kind of you to laugh at a man who stands before you naked. What has you amused?"

The laughter only came out harder. "All this time! All this time you fretted I could not handle your true self, and *I can't want or love you any more than I do!*" She shook her head hard and tried to bite back more laughter but it felt too good to stop. "You know what it is? It's your makeup! It does nothing except emphasize what I already love and desire!"

Her laughter turned into a startled gasp as he buried his hands in her hair and jerked her up for a wild kiss. When they had to part for air, he explored the skin behind her ear until she shivered. "Mine!" he breathed huskily. "Let me love you, my Rhianna. Let me be yours again. Here, in the light."

She wound her arms around his neck and turned her head to find his lips with hers again. A blinding well of joy seemed to be rising inside her soul to erase the pain and loneliness. The gouges were beginning to heal at last. She boosted herself up and hooked her knees around his hips as he waded to the edge of the pool without releasing her from the kiss. She felt as if she was *starving* for his taste and his touch. That wonderful intimacy of being one.

He released her only to grab the towels and toss them down to protect them from the stone. He then lifted her out onto them before hauling himself out as well. His hand curled around the back of her neck and he dragged her into another consuming kiss. He could not get enough of her flavor. He felt her hands pushing at his shoulders and gave a husky laugh as he obligingly fell over on his back. His arms spread wide. "I am all yours, beloved."

For a moment, she merely stared at him and let her eyes finally learn and cherish what only her other senses had known. The blend of love, awe, and arousal in her eyes made the sparks in his iridescent eyes flare brightly. Her pleasure at seeing him was matched by his pleasure in seeing her—or rather, was *finally* matched. He groaned as her fingers began to softly explore and caress so that her senses could at last share information. "I have missed your touch," he told her roughly.

"I missed touching you." Her lips trailed along behind her fingers. "I love how it feels to want you. To be wanted by you." She laughed, and it seemed a sultry sound. "There will be no shyness inside me to banish now, Eros. I know what I want, what you want, and how to get there."

His laugh was no less tempting. "There has been no shyness since the first night." The laugh turned into a moan as her questing lips and fingers found his aching arousal. His eyes all but crossed as she slowly savored his taste. "Rhi."

The rasp to his voice made her shudder. Needing his mouth instead, she shifted back up his body and caught his face in her hands as she poured herself into a kiss that had his eyes glowing bright with power. She just did not realize that similar power briefly glowed from her eyes in turn. It, too, was meant to blend.

He caught her around the waist and rolled over to be on top. His unsteady hands raked a wild course over her body to find the most sensitive places. His heated breath murmured husky promises of love against her skin as he lingered and savored until she was crying out as she had made him cry.

As terribly as he wanted to linger, to take all of the time they had lost, her hunger was throbbing inside his body along with his own desperate need. They could linger and savor later when it had not been two thousand years since they had last loved each other. He rolled again and braced her over him. His breaths stopped entirely as he stared up at her. How was it possible she could be more beautiful to him? Perhaps it was the glow of light in her eyes that revealed her love and desire for him. "Beloved." He tried to urge her closer. "Take me as I have taken you."

She did so slowly, enjoying every moment of how he felt and how his pupils seemed to be consumed in sparks. When he was as deep as he could be, when they were finally one again, tears welled in her eyes and spilled down her cheeks. They were still a bit dark as they began to finish the healing that would erase the void on their contract and make it active once more. A happy ending. There was a chance for it.

His fingers bit into her hips and urged her to move harder and faster. Nothing seemed to matter except that glorious ecstasy luring them in. That perfect fusion of two as one. It started deep and spread wide as it consumed them, and it tore a cry from her lips that was echoed by one from him. It resonated into their very power until gold color rippled over his skin as silver rippled over hers. Where the two colors met, they merged to the radiant white light that was the power of immortal love.

He caught her when she lost the strength in her arms, and he wrapped her up fiercely in his embrace. The sound of them both struggling to catch a breath was like music, and he loved the scent of their skin lingering to mix with the flowers and peaches. *Happiness*. It glowed as deeply inside him as it did inside her. "Rhianna."

The rasp to his voice delicately teased her ears. She merely snuggled closer and tightened her arms around his chest. "Don't make me move," she murmured drowsily.

"I am afraid I must." His fingers skimmed slowly over her still sensitive skin so that her breath hitched. "I wish to take you inside and make love to you in my bed. This was an . . . appetizer." He shifted to tumble her down onto the towels and disentangled their bodies. He looked down at her and stared anew. "I cannot believe you are mine," he whispered. He scooped her up into his arms and got to his feet. "We have two millennia to make up for, beloved. I would like to take my time now."

A blend of anticipation and justifiable caution filled her. "How much time?"

"You will have to see. I will feed you after." He slowly lowered her to the bed in the nearly darkened room and deliberately turned on the lamp to spill out its golden glow. "I will love you again after I have fed you. I will spend all night loving you. Every night. For eternity." He sank into her arms for a kiss that threatened to set the sheets on fire. Against her lips, he muttered, "Perhaps in a hundred years, I will have at last recovered from two millennia without you."

She suspected it would take closer to another millennia for her, but she had no objections to the idea that things would always remain more volatile between them. Age matured everything, and the good things were like wine. And if the end truly was coming and she would not get that millennia, then at least she would this time go on knowing what it meant to be whole.

It was well after dark before their stomachs demanded another hunger be appeased. Her legs weren't the only rubbery ones as she pulled on a borrowed shirt, and she found herself giggling as she saw him struggling to put on pajama pants. "Why bother?" she asked in exasperation.

"I have learned a painful lesson about cooking while naked."

The mental image brought up fresh laughter. "That's why I always wear something, too. I may not be that built, but I have enough of a bust to be wary of leaning over a stove. Especially because I'm short!" She couldn't resist jumping onto his back and holding on tight. "Mine!"

His heart melted entirely. "Beloved." He pressed his face against the slender arms encircling his neck. "I love nothing more than I love you. I will never have enough time to make up to you what I have done."

She slid off his back and pressed her lips to one of the wing marks on his back. He had removed the bandages and barely any residue of the event of the morning remained. "Just love me," she murmured. "Just love me, and I'll call us even."

He swung around and caught her up in his arms for a fierce hug and kiss. Still holding her, he began striding toward the kitchen. "Food," he said firmly, "before you are allowed to seduce me again."

She smiled. "Was I doing that?"

"Ha!" He put her down on the couch. "I promised to make dinner. I had it prepped beforehand." Ruefully, he added, "I had a feeling we may not get to it until late."

Dinner was happily consumed by both and they went through their normal evening routine by watching their shows on his DVR. She had no makeup to wash off thanks to her bath, but she did borrow some of his lotion. She was still the first to go to bed, and when he stepped out of the bathroom, she was sitting on the side of the mattress. He cocked his head as he undressed. "Rhi?"

She stood and deliberately stripped off the nightshirt. Just as deliberately, she turned off the lamp and let the room be in darkness. Strangely, she found she could actually see his outline now. As she slowly let herself take in her true power, she seemed to be evolving somehow. "I am the light," she told him huskily. "You are the dark. There are no secrets left between us."

He pounced and tumbled her flat onto the bed. "I rather like loving you in the light where I can see the way you look when you watch me." He hotly caressed her breast. "But there is something to be said for the darkness where you have to go by touch only." He closed his eyes briefly as he let his eyesight dull a bit. He opened them again and only saw her outline. "Now we are even. I will have to stay quite close to you, beloved."

She moaned softly as his lips unerringly found a sensitive place. "If you insist."

When desire was tempered again for the time, they slept tangled together like a two-piece puzzle. Neither stirred once at all for the rest of the night, and she only began to rouse when she felt sunlight spilling on her face. She turned to escape and found herself burrowing into her husband's steady warmth. Her eyes flew wide and the first thing she saw was the wonderful rise and fall of his chest. His arms had not released her at all.

As happiness and peace welled inside her, the last lingering grasp of the past finally let go. Her empathy and telepathy returned in a rush that made her wince very lightly since it was not unlike turning on a voice mail system after a vacation. She could see and sense Eric again, and his surprised delight at feeling her in return warmed her heart.

She briefly paused before reaching out for her true power. The vision came obediently and seemed to process like a series of unconnected images inside her mind. She sorted and rejected unimportant things that could carry out their course and looked for anything she could use even when her own future was grayed out. Something, an interesting flicker, came and went as an impression of someone else's future, and she knew what needed to be done. She knew what had to be done to ensure a happy ending finally came.

Aaron stirred and his arms tightened. "I can hear your mind," he murmured sleepily. "It is buzzing in my head. You have your mental gifts back?"

"I do. I'm not burned out anymore." She rubbed her cheek against his shoulder. Her eyes stared at a future she could not yet see but somehow still sensed what it might hold. "We have a busy day, Aaron. It is time to call in my reserves and prepare them for what may be coming."

"What is coming?"

"The final confrontation."

CHAPTER FOURTEEN

They lingered over a shower together and enjoyed being able to do so. He could only watch in fascination as she shaved her legs. "Why do you do that?"

"Came up in the, hmm, early 1900s? 1920s maybe." She studied her toes and decided she needed a pedicure if they survived what lay ahead. He would enjoy one too. "Skirts got shorter and razor companies leapt on a chance to say that women were uncouth if they didn't have silky smooth skin. Turned into a societal norm like makeup usage. I rather like how it feels, actually." She shot him a slightly wicked grin. "I have a thing for smooth skin."

Very little hair covered her husband's body. It never had. Few of the gods had been hairy except for the ones who chose to grow out heavy beards. They found how they liked to look and stuck with it. She rather envied that sort of power. She had nicked herself with a razor enough times to wish a way to just be done with it.

He glided a hand down her leg and smiled. "I must admit, I grow fond of how it feels as well." If anything, it also allowed him a better view of the sleek muscles in her lovely legs. He had missed having them wrapped around him, even in sleep. "We will have to go out to dinner so you may wear a short skirt and I can admire them at my leisure."

"It's a date."

They playfully toweled each other dry, though perhaps their hands wandered a bit, and he got dressed while she pulled on another borrowed shirt. Breakfast was prepared and consumed, and he transported them to her home so she could finish getting ready. They were greeted upon their arrival by happy barks from Juno. The puppy skidded into the living room and leapt up into Rhianna's arms to enthusiastically lick her face. "Hi to you too!" she laughed. She smiled as she saw the red collar and gold tag. One side of the tag had Juno's name, and the other had the Enforcers' logo.

Aaron took charge of the puppy to take her outside while Rhianna went to change. She called D.J.'s desk while she was putting on her makeup. The receptionist was always there early because it was the only place he could get some quiet time for reading. Rhianna had made the deal with him that if he took calls from an Enforcer before the clock started, he could read as much as he liked.

"Enforcers Headquarters."

"Hello, D.J." She contemplated her eyeshadows. "I have a few calls for you to make for me. I want a meeting set up for nine am, sharp. I don't give a damn if they have previous engagements; they owe me, and they know it."

"This ought to be good. Whose arms am I twisting?"

"Mel Shaughnessy, Kenneth Dease, and Rafael Lucino. I also want Eric, Rayna, Gwyn, and Taylor to be there."

"Whoa." It was breathed softly. It was always a bit daunting when all five head Enforcers met together—it meant something big was happening—but to throw in the head members of the most famously contracted families? There was something *massive* going on this time. "I'll make the calls, Rhi," he promised. "Should I order coffee and pastries?"

"Please do. The least I can do is feed them." She disconnected the line and fastened on her earrings. They were her favorite pair; Madelyne had given them to her as a birthday gift one year. She fastened on the matching bracelet and paused to study her left hand. It was bare of rings.

Arms slid around her and strong hands slipped under hers to lace their fingers together. Aaron rested his chin on her shoulder and smiled. "I believe I owe you a ring or two, do I not? That is the custom these days. A diamond ring for engagement, and a gold ring for marriage. I do not think you are the diamond type, though." He contemplated things. "I should give you a pearl. After all, I trace origins back to the sea."

Memory made her snicker. "Technically, wasn't Zeus your grandfather *and* your cousin? Aphrodite was kind of a daughter of Uranus, so she was Zeus' aunt, right?"

"We never had much of a family tree in Olympus as much as we had a family bramble bush." He nuzzled her neck. "I shall find you a perfect pearl to be fashioned into a ring. In the meantime," he trailed his fingertips over her ring finger where power began to gather, "you shall at least have a wedding ring made from the gold that heralds my power of love."

She watched as the power solidified into a beautiful gold band with a sort of white marbling through the center. It actually glowed softly in the light. A happy thrill rippled through her soul. Such a tiny thing could make her so happy merely because of the permanence it represented. "You need one too."

He offered his other hand and opened his fingers to reveal another gold band on his palm. "Naturally, I do. I would like an engagement ring as well. Why should I not have one?"

"Why indeed!" She slipped the ring over his finger and admired it. "Would you like a pearl as well? I think it should be something associated with me instead. You claim me, I claim you."

"*Elektron*."

"*Elektron?* Oh, you mean amber?" She turned in his arms and rested her hands on his chest. "Why amber?"

"It is formed from the beauty of nature and placed under pressure to become a stone that endures for millions of years and floats upon the waves where it comes to shore." He smiled. "Pearls are born of the sea, and amber is carried upon it. It represents our similar gifts and where they overlap while letting us still be unique to one another. Perfect equals."

She could only sigh and kiss him. He had the wonderful gift to say such romantically sappy things and make them sound only beautifully sincere. "Very well. I will hunt a bit of amber if you hunt a pearl. Then we will both be suitably claimed."

"Deal." He kissed her again and then released her reluctantly. "Let us collect Juno and head into the office. I do not imagine anyone will turn down your invitation."

"Particularly since it was not an invitation. It was an order."

D.J. was an efficient secretary. By the time Aaron and Rhianna arrived, he had already gotten the conference room on the top floor set up with coffee from Starbucks and pastries from a local District bakery. Rhianna laughed at Aaron as she saw him happily consuming his beloved Starbucks. "Addict. Remind me to introduce you to a Frappuccino."

"A what?"

"Trust me."

He smiled slowly. "Always."

A justifiably confused Eric and Rayna showed up shortly thereafter. Neither commented on the emergency meeting since they knew Rhianna would explain soon enough. Instead, they focused on what they noticed immediately upon entering the room. "Welcome back," Eric told Rhianna softly. He stopped to lean down and kiss her cheek. *Do I have to like him now?* He asked it into her mind.

She shot a grin at Aaron. *I would be grateful if you did. It would be far too awkward, and far too much of déjà vu, for my brother and my husband to not get along.*

A bit mildly, Aaron spoke to them both, *Please do be aware that I can hear both of you. Do try to keep from talking about me unless it is complimentary. I do not mind that.*

Rayna was not telepathic and could not hear the conversation, but she could make a guess based on Rhianna's smirk and Eric's glare. "Oh stop it!" she scolded Eric. She hugged his arm tightly and smiled up at him. "You like him because he makes Rhi happy."

The trouble with being married to the Goddess of Truth was that telling lies, even little ones to get someone's goat, were out of the picture. She happily tattled on him frequently. "Of course I do," he sighed. "God knows—no pun intended—that she deserves some damn happiness after all this."

Deciding a diversion was in order, Rayna asked Aaron curiously, "When will you get Rhianna pregnant? She needs to be a mom again. Madelyne doesn't need her as much now, and Rhi never did get to enjoy those first early years the way I and Eric are enjoying Glory's."

Aaron shot Rhianna a decidedly sensual smile. "I am not sure if I would *get* her pregnant as much as I would *help* her with such a thing. Anything between us is always half her fault." He sighed gustily. "I do admit I would like to be a father at last. And she will be radiant when she is carrying."

Taylor and Gwyn happened to walk in the door at that point, and the former asked hopefully, "Think I'd get her to finally pose if I bribed her with handcrafted baby stuff?"

"You could always try cookies," Gwyn noted reasonably. "It works for me and Rayna when we want something."

Rhianna looked at Aaron solemnly. "Would you believe I *like* working with these smartasses?"

"Perhaps because you are one yourself?"

Hard to disagree with that one! It was also why Aaron fit in as well as he did. The subject was thankfully shelved when she spotted new arrivals in the doorway. She smiled. "Come in, gentlemen!"

Mel walked in with rightful wariness, and Kenneth and Rafael were right behind him. They were quite dissimilar men in some ways, but quite a bit alike in others. The most notable difference lay in the fact that Kenneth and Rafael were ungifted humans and Mel was a full-blooded werewolf. All were the respective leaders of their families though both Mel and Rafael's fathers were still alive. Kenneth tended to share with Cameron, but being the eldest, he typically had final say.

"I can't help but feel the same way I did many years ago when I got called into my father's office and told to get my grades up or else," Mel sighed as he sat down.

"Do admit that turned out well," Rhianna murmured.

"Am I complaining about being madly in love with a hot, though slightly cranky, wife and having two furball kids with more sass than sense? Not a lick."

Kenneth sat down beside him. "Did you know Cam's Sarah threatened at one point that she would sic your wife on our mother?"

Mel's grin looked almost menacing for a moment since it revealed his slightly, non-humanly, sharp canines. "Pity she didn't."

Rafael merely shook his head at them and bent to kiss Rhianna's cheek. "*Ciao, bella*. You are as a beautiful as ever. More, perhaps. Is this the reason why?" He lifted her now ringed left hand. "If you should have a renewal ceremony, *mia famiglia* would be honored to attend. We owe you much."

"If we do, you will." She patted his cheek affectionately. "Alright, everyone. Grab a chair. It's time we did some talking." She remained standing and was not surprised when Aaron opted to sit as well. He and Eric took the chairs at the head of the table with the others spreading out down the table from them. "I suppose I should begin by saying that I am," she glanced at Aaron and then back, "indirectly responsible for the evil that has been plaguing our world for many millennia."

"Huh." Kenneth tapped a finger lightly on the table. "How did that happen?"

"Have you heard of Eros and Psyche?"

"Sure. Oh." Mel eyed Aaron. "You know, I wondered about you. Maddie wouldn't spill the beans, but you don't smell human." He ignored the god's quick grin and turned back to Rhianna. "So the evil was released from the box you fetched from Persephone? The stories never clarified what it was, only that it killed you and would have killed Eros but not for his immortality." With a sigh, he added, "The great Greek romantic tragedy."

Rhianna held up her hands and the broken box appeared on her palms. "This and something else came to me a very long time ago. Eric and I had found the River Styx and were building our sanctuary. I was drawn to the river." Her gaze lowered. "Charon had been waiting for me faithfully. He had refused to let any but him guard the things meant for me. As soon as I had reclaimed them, I remembered it all."

"What was the other item?" Rafael asked softly.

"My marriage contract. It was voided."

Several faces paled at that revelation. "Is it still?" Gwyn whispered. Under the table, she desperately grabbed for Taylor's hand to draw on his ready strength.

"No," Eric spoke up. His eyes looked slightly shuttered. "She gave it to me to Enforce, so to speak. As of this morning, it is In Progress."

The held breaths were let out. Rhianna put the box down on the table. "This box is the infamous Pandora's Box that when opened released into our world all manner of illness and the ability to despair. As that despair got stronger, it began to . . . corrupt. Twist. And evil was born. The gods engaged it and managed to encase it once more inside the Box, and it was taken to the Underworld for guarding."

"And then your story came along." Kenneth blew out a hard breath. He felt a bit queasy. The tale of star-crossed lovers had always somehow struck a chord as if it had truly happened. Now, at least, while he knew it had, he also knew there was still a chance for a happy ending.

Aaron straightened up slightly. "I was there at the first fight against evil. I was young at the time. Young by mortal standards let alone immortal. It came right after me. It hates nothing more than the power of love. It hates nothing more than I and Rhianna for we alone can access the pure force of love energy and use it to create happy endings."

"That's why completed contracts protect people from evil," Rayna whispered.

"And why I called for Mel, Ken, and Rafe." Rhianna sat on the edge of the table. "It has been your families, as well as Rayna and Gwyn's, that have been directly involved in our fight. It has come out in stronger waves over the years. It was there subtly in the form of Richard Johnston, who abused Kay Shaughnessy. It was still as yet subtle when the hunter came after Maddie and Kienan."

"It had external forces to control," Eric picked up, "in the form of Nahga who sought to destroy Rayna and Gwyn. It was there as well inside Lorcana Dease."

Kenneth's lashes flinched slightly. "And here we always thought she was just a bitch."

"If she had not been stopped when she had, there are more terrible things she could have done." Something flickered across Gwyn's eyes as a movement of power. "She was judged and punished. I wish I could say she was a tool, Ken, but she was bad to the core to begin with. Take consolation in knowing that there is nothing to mourn."

Rafael gently clapped Kenneth on the shoulder in support and looked at Rhianna. "I will assume that the evil was then in active form when it infused the flesh of Orson Collins and Martin Johns, *sì*? That is why it hated the 3rd District and came after you directly when you came to aid me and Tori. This District represents the happy endings you and Aaron bring."

"Here is not the only place it has had trouble," Aaron offered. "There is another world attached to ours thanks to the Styx being rather sticky."

"The duct tape of magic," Rayna whispered to Gwyn, and her sister giggled.

Aaron ignored them though he briefly smiled. "Mirage has its share of bad magic—curses are vexingly common—but it did not actually manifest true evil until recently." He looked at Rhianna. "United, we are undefeatable. It could not stand up to our combined power." His left hand slid over hers on the table and their fingers laced together.

"Damn." Mel crossed his arms as he leaned back in his chair. "This is one hell of a mess we've got. Mind if I ask what happened to the rest of the pantheon?"

"Most of them chose to leave this plane when they lost the belief of the people," Rhianna offered, "but they have not left in their entirety. They linger as . . . energies in the ether. Most are near the District. They serve as guardians of sorts now that they are no longer needed. For all intents and purposes, Aaron is the only god that remains."

More than one person at the table didn't entirely agree. Rhianna should have been a goddess as well. Her power certainly rivaled one, and if gods could be made on the basis of 'heroic' deeds and 'good' actions, then she had *entirely* earned it! No one said it out loud, however. There was no knowing where the story might end.

"Alright then." Kenneth nodded firmly. "Where do we stand right now?"

"As of this immediate moment, I am placing several people under active duty. They are the ones who will aid me and Aaron in the final battle." She held up a hand and ticked off the names. "Eric, for obvious reasons. Mel, I want you and Audra alike because I have never seen any combatants as fine as werewolves. Kenneth, I am activating your wife. Her shapeshifting ability gives her a great deal of flexibility. Rafael, I am also activating Theresa."

He visibly bristled. "She is pregnant!"

Aaron inclined his head. "So she is, but she is a powerful healer. She has a completed contract that will protect her, *and* she has the additional defense that evil cannot harm her if it looks her in the eye. If she holds her ground, nothing shall get close to her at all."

Rafael still did not like it, but he knew damned well that no Enforcer would send Theresa into battle if they thought there may be a chance of her or her child being harmed. "*Scusi,* but I shall worry about her and my niece anyway," he muttered.

Mel held up a hand. "How do we intend to lure out the evil from where it is hiding? I can't imagine it would be dumb enough to come traipsing into our District when it knows there are bigger and meaner things waiting to chomp into it."

"I don't recommend actual chomping," Taylor muttered. "You'd get heartburn."

Rhianna hid a smile. "Mel is correct. It will not come down to us. And 'down' is the operative word." She gestured. "It hides in the invisible realm above our sky. The hidden domain of the gods, Mount Olympus itself. It sealed itself off as soon as Eros departed. He can't get back in without piercing through the barrier with something equally magical."

"Like . . .?"

"Good question." She spread her hands. "That is another thing I must call upon you three to do. Between the resources of your companies, you can surely locate something for us to use. It exists beyond our District at this point, and because I am so directly involved, my ability to see the future is limited. I knew only of this moment happening because I was able to see a vision of the battle to come—through someone else's eyes."

"We'll do whatever we can," Kenneth vowed. "We all owe you, Rhianna. You helped us have our dreams come true, as well as the dreams of our loved ones. The least we can do is try to help you in return."

"Thank you," she said simply. "I will let all of you go now." She smiled. "Take some pastries with you else we eat them all."

Everyone began to slowly file out. Rhianna had a conference call to complete, and Taylor had to go in to his company to work on his game. Gwyn happily commandeered Aaron to show him where Priya had been set up. There was actually an entire unoccupied suite on the first floor that would make an awesome location for a marriage counselor to operate from, but Gwyn kept that to herself. Rhianna did the recruiting stuff.

Rayna had been watching Eric quietly, and she followed him into his office. She shut the door behind herself and leaned against it. "Riku? What were you not saying? I could see the half-truth that left your lips."

He sank into his chair on a heavy sigh. "The contract is In Progress." He put the scroll on the desk and unrolled it. Sure enough, the bright red 'In Progress' was stamped across the middle. "It shouldn't be like this."

She frowned as she moved closer to look. "They have fully reconciled and are entirely one now. That was what they wanted in the past, wasn't it? Then . . . that means one of them still has a dream that has not been fulfilled." Her frown deepened. "There is a clause in this somewhere that has not been met."

"It would be so much better if I could read it," Eric muttered. "I even tried taking it to someone fluent in Ancient Greek, and she said it turned to gibberish the moment she tried to read it." He raked his hands through his hair in agitation and stirred the white streaks that were mark of his power. "How do I Enforce what I can't bloody understand?"

She slid onto his lap and curled close against his chest in an effort to comfort him. His arms went around her fiercely and he buried his face in her hair. It just seemed as if there should somehow be an easy answer. There was almost always something so simple that could guarantee everything would end well. Was the contract blurred because it *wasn't* set in stone yet?

There might still be something terrible yet to happen.

CHAPTER FIFTEEN

The rest of the day went by normally, all things considered for Enforcers. The entire building was smitten with Juno, and she was already learning the lay of the place. Until she was big enough to open doors on her own, boxes were placed beside the doors she might need to come and go from.

Rhianna was finishing up a review of a business proposal from a District member when the clock clicked over to tell her it was quitting time. She would have ignored it and kept on working, as she so often did, but the handle on the office door jiggled. She looked up and then smiled as the door popped open and Juno scampered inside. "Well, look at you!"

Aaron sauntered in behind the puppy. "Quitting time, my love." At her lifted brow, he lifted one back. "You do not think that every person in this building did not inform me that you work more than necessary because there is nothing at home to bring you there? That they have been delighted lately by the way you have taken decent time off—for the first time in centuries? That, maybe, just maybe, they are already putting things into order for Eric to run the place by himself for a month so you and I may take a long honeymoon?"

"I knew they were up to it," she admitted, "and that they were quite happy with my, hmm, *antics* these last few days. I didn't realize I had been tattled on, though." She picked up Juno when she pawed at her leg. "I suppose it makes no difference if I finish this here or at home."

"Speaking of home." He sat on the edge of her desk. "We must discuss this scenario. I do not wish to trade back and forth between our homes. I wish to live here with you in your District."

"Our," she corrected him. "You belong and it therefore belongs to you as well." She sat back in her chair. "I admit that I would rather live here permanently than anywhere else. But I would miss our garden at your home. And we could keep your home as a vacation spot. Eric and Rayna have a castle hidden in the mountains."

"I believe we should then combine our homes. It is the garden from mine that we love most from there." A gold brow lifted arrogantly. "There are many benefits to marrying a god, my beloved. I shall transport the garden down in its entirety into your garden space. There is room enough for it. We shall then merely have another built at our vacation home. Tomos and Belle of Seven Wishes would no doubt love a chance to improve upon their work."

"That plan works perfectly with me." She got to her feet and handed him Juno so that she could gather up her documents and put them in their case. "Where would we go on this honeymoon?"

He studied her for a moment, sensing that she was hiding something. Did she still think there was a chance of not having their happy ending? What had she seen? "I believe I promised someone that I would chase her through my temple. That means a trip home, at the least. We need to replace bad memories with good." His eyes softened. "It must have pained you to return there for what you needed."

"It was a guaranteed burnout for a day or two," she concurred. She smiled. "But that's not a problem now that the past is done. The memories can't overwhelm me anymore." She rose up to kiss him softly. "I love you," she breathed against his lips, and she savored seeing the way sparks flared in his eyes.

His free hand curled around the back of her neck and kept her close for another, hungrier, kiss. By the time he released her, her head was spinning in ways that had nothing to do with the fact that he had transported them home again. He put Juno down where she scampered off and then swept Rhianna up into his arms. She managed a breathless laugh as she clung to his shoulders. "Dinner?"

"Can wait." He strode down the hall. "I have a need to peel that suit off of you and love you most thoroughly. Do you mind?"

"Not at all. Please, carry on."

She later started dinner while he took care of transporting down their beautiful garden. His ability to do things like that was only a small benefit of loving, and being loved, by a god. The biggest benefit would always be the depth of his emotion, something far more profound than most other gods, by nature of who and what he was.

He returned while she was putting down food for Juno as well. "It is done now. We should enjoy it after dinner. You will love how it looks in the night. Perhaps I will love you again."

"Only perhaps?" she teased as she started dishing up their dinner. "I don't think there is much *perhaps* about it. You too thoroughly enjoy what we do to each other. Of course, you're not the only one, so don't take that as a complaint." She handed him a plate before he could grab her. "Food," she scolded lightly. "You can behave yourself at least that long."

"I am making up for lost time." He was smiling as he carried the plate over to the dining table. "No," he chided Juno when she gave him a pitiful look. "You do not get to share. You have your own food."

He and Rhianna were almost done with dinner when her cell phone began to warble. The tune seemed vaguely familiar somehow, and he looked at her in confusion. She grinned. "It's the theme from Disney's *Beauty & The Beast.* Mel's calling me." She hit the speaker button. "Good evening! Working late?"

"So to speak." Humor had warmed Mel's voice. "I might have a lead for you on how to get into Olympus. Kally brought it to my attention this afternoon. You see, we've been working with a new small business owner. He's an organic grocer. He gets in some strange and exotic items you don't always find easily in America." He coughed. "It would seem he got in some, uhm, new beans."

Aaron promptly choked on his tea. Rhianna bit her lip to hide a grin. "Do tell. What happened when he tried to plant them?"

"Weeeell, thankfully he only planted one of them as a test. It seemed to sprout overnight and he ended up with a ten-foot plant that produced no further fruit. He chopped it down for firewood and contacted us to see if we knew any way of helping him get his money back because he was swindled. It kinda tripped Kally's and my sensors." Mel snorted. "Let's face it, Rhi. When it comes to people in the District, even you, sometimes the story is obvious."

"Hard to say fairer than that," she agreed dryly. "Text me his address. Aaron and I will go tomorrow and see if we can't help him get his money back by buying the beans off him."

"With a cow?"

"Oh, very cute." She hung up on him but she was smiling. "And people wonder how these faerie tales become so prevalent. It's because there are certain ways magic can move, and it very rarely bothers to be subtle. I find the story that best works for a situation and let it grow as it naturally will—with a few twists along the way for variety." She picked up their plates and carried them into the kitchen. "Rayna made a peach pie the other day," she called. "Want some for dessert? We can eat by the pool."

"If you insist." He took the plates of pie from her so that she could fetch towels. He sighed as Juno danced at his feet. "Juno! You will trip me. Settle down." He glowered as the command fell on deaf ears. "You need training."

Rhianna arched a brow. "Sit," she ordered firmly.

Juno planted her butt and her tail wagged merrily. Aaron eyed her and then his wife. "I begin to think it is more than merely a talent that no one disobeys you. I strongly suspect you might have the ability to force compulsion."

She just smiled. "Bring the pie, dear."

The first thing they needed to do in the morning was find something valuable that they could use for trade. Why bother altering a plot that was already in their favor? They swung by the District's resident grocer to see what sorts of seeds she had that she used in her massive greenhouse (it was bigger than her actual house), and Aaron could not help but take an appreciative sniff as they walked inside. "Wonderful."

The grocer beamed at him. "I admit, I've been tempted to charge a quarter for people to come in here and just breathe. Or give in to the prodding from Enforcers to build a ventilation system that would let the smells drift over the District. I still say Frankie's bakery should be the first to do that. I wouldn't mind always smelling his cookies and cakes."

"You and me both!" Rhianna agreed. She smiled. "What can you do for us, Kasumi? We need something truly spectacular to offer in trade. Something guaranteed to spark avarice so he thinks he's swindling us."

"Let's see . . ." She flipped through seed packets. "I have some rare stuff in here. I imported this specialty herb from overseas. Gwyn had to help me wrangle it through customs, and I'm still getting calls from other farmers demanding I not monopolize it. I was thinking of letting it spread because it has such wonderful flavors. It goes with most any dish *and* I'd swear it can cure the common cold."

"I have never had a cold," Aaron told Rhianna. "I hear it is terrible."

"I had one. It wasn't that bad. Chicken pox was worse."

Kasumi looked up with wide eyes. "*You* got chicken pox?"

"I'm not a goddess," Rhianna laughed. "And do remember that Eric and I herald from a time before vaccinations and inoculations. We consider ourselves very, very lucky that we have incredibly high resistances, and *anything* we catch, we only catch once. We lucked out in getting vaccines for the truly bad things once they were offered, but we missed on chicken pox." She sighed. "It was about fifteen years ago. He caught it from a child. I babysat him until he was better, and then he had to do the same for me since he gave it to me!"

Aaron snickered softly at the mental image. Kasumi couldn't help but giggle as well. She, and everyone else, had always appreciated the way Rhianna and Eric unashamedly admitted their mistakes and guffaws. It made them real and kept them approachable to their people.

She flipped a few more packets. "Ah ha!" She tugged out the pouch and offered it to Rhianna. "Here you go, Ms. Taber. I've already got this planted, so I can harvest seeds from there to restock myself." Her smile turned impish. "We'll call it a belated wedding gift."

"I never had a wedding, actually. Just a marriage."

"Shame on you," she scolded Aaron.

"There were . . . extenuating circumstances. I do intend to remedy the situation as soon as everything is done."

Rhianna ignored that. She didn't really care one way or another about a ceremony for herself. She was considering it purely for her friends and family who wanted a chance to celebrate her happiness. Perhaps Brian would make her a wedding dress that blended modern Western style and the red *chiton* of Ancient Greece.

Seeds in hand, Aaron used his power to disguise himself and Rhianna as an elderly couple. He took the care to hide anything identifiable about them; it was critical that the grocer not realize he was dealing with Rhianna. Aaron did not have the same reputation yet, and he wasn't sure he ever would. He felt quite fine with that, actually.

It was just early enough that the grocer's shop was not busy yet. The grocer himself was an attractive young man who whistled merrily to himself as he set out the displays for the day. He seemed to sense the couple before they approached and looked up to smile. "Good morning! I'm not quite fully set up, but come in if you like."

"Actually, I wonder if you could help us." Rhianna sighed deeply. "We received this box of goodies from our daughter overseas, and as we have no aptitude for growing things, we're trying to sell or trade off the seeds. We know nothing about gardening."

"Huh. Well, I'm always open to new stuff. Let me see what you have." He took the offered packet and his eyes went wide for a moment as he realized what he held. A shrewd look quickly moved in to replace the surprise. "Hmm, well I guess I could use these. They're somewhat uncommon. Let's consider a trade, how's that?"

Rhianna lightly stepped on Aaron's foot when she sensed his rising amusement. "What did you have in mind?"

"Something that *anyone* can grow!" He disappeared inside and returned shortly with a small sack. He opened it and pulled out a handful of the beans inside. They looked like relatively normal beans in a kidney shape but they were an interesting silvery color not typically found in nature. "See these? Magic beans!"

Aaron obligingly squinted at them. "How are they magic?"

"Results will vary depending on where you plant them. I guarantee that they will produce big and beautiful plants for you to admire without worrying about killing them." He offered the bag. "Do we have a deal?"

"They are magic," Aaron told Rhianna when she pulled a skeptical look. "We cannot kill that."

"Well, since the other won't do us any good, all right." She took the bag of beans and dropped it into the satchel she wore. "Good day to you!"

"And you!" The grocer's whistling had a renewed cheer as he disappeared into his shop to put the seeds away safely.

Aaron and Rhianna left the scene and dropped the disguise once they were back inside their District. He was chuckling softly. "I am sure he is congratulating himself on a job well done at tricking us into taking these useless things off his hands."

"Some people will notice that they have a role to fill. Others will not. I suppose it depends on how many times the tale will be retold. Those told but once are the ones that are often overlooked until the end. Those that will touch many lives are the ones that often get recognized." She smiled up at him. "I love all of them, but I do admit an additional fondness for the originals. They linger in your memory."

"Or as paintings in the lobby."

"Naturally!" She sighed. "At the risk of a problem, by the way, I was not lying about having no ability to grow things. Eric is the gardener for Enforcers, and he took care of my place too. Said he'd rather put in the effort than see me always killing it. Besides. It keeps him happy and out of my hair."

"Since I have never even tried to grow something—my garden was made to be low maintenance for that very reason—I think we ought to find Eric."

They lucked out. Eric was already in the gardens in front of Enforcers HQ. The lush landscape was a defining feature of the building and lured in passersby as well as employees to sit down for a moment and relax. The warlock was covered in dirt and mulch as he turned over soil for a new section he had plotted. He changed things around once a year in order to keep it always interesting.

Rhianna stopped beside him and smiled. "Riku, got something for you."

"Huh?" He looked up and blinked as she dropped the bag in his hand. "What's this?"

"'Magic' beans."

It took him only a second before he snorted rudely. "Of course. Gee, why didn't *I* think of that? Did you trade a cow for them?"

"Herb seeds, actually. Cows are hard to parade through the middle of New York, and it's not a drought anyway. Adaptability, dear." She cocked her head. "Can you plant them?"

"Well, better me than you. They'd die within a few hours. You always overwater or smother them."

"We all have our gifts. That just isn't one of mine. I still say that it explains why you can be such a blooming idiot."

"Oh, ha ha. You're just mad that I made your potted plant take over your office as revenge for you teaching Rayna evil things."

"Yes, but they were *good* evil things, and really, every woman should know them if she has a lover stronger than she is. Every man, too, actually. It's the great equalizer for the one without the strength. You haven't heard Taylor complain."

"He's still in the racing clouds over the baby." He started digging a hole for the beans. "So we'll be woken in the middle of the night by this sucker shooting into the sky, yes? I believe that's how it's supposed to go. I'll get to cut it down after and get it out of my orchids, right?"

"You are such a whiny creature sometimes." She knelt down to lean on his shoulder as he dropped in the beans and covered them with soil. "Just replace them with morning glories when we're done."

"Dirty pool," he groused. He knew she knew morning glories were by far his favorite flower since they were the exact same color as Rayna's eyes. Their daughter had even been named for them. "Go on. Get out of my garden. There obviously won't be much time until the fight begins."

Aaron obligingly caught Rhianna's wrist and tugged her away from the scene. She glanced up to see him smiling. "Are you amused at us?" she asked curiously.

"A bit. It is more that I am happy to see the way you two snipe and bicker and love as true siblings do. Your bond is not dissimilar from that between Artemis and Apollo. It makes me feel even happier that we have come to this point in this life." He smoothed a hand down her hair tenderly. "In exchange for enduring two jealous, vain, loathsome sisters who hated you, you have now been given the unwavering love of a nearly twin brother."

"Eric was my sanity too many times to count," she murmured. "I would not have endured as long as I have without him. That's why I made sure that things would fall as needed in order for him to find Rayna. I knew from her birth that she was the right one, but I had not yet deciphered the story until she and Gwyn were given Bloody Checks. As soon as I knew that, I knew what the story would be and what I needed to do in order to ensure it happened."

"Did *he* know his role within it?"

"Nope!" Her grin looked wicked for a moment. "I got to thoroughly enjoy watching him fall in love with Sleeping Beauty and be forced to face facts that he had *always* loved her. It was there right from the beginning. Really, the way he could not stay away from her side while she slept was a *big* clue. It just needed to grow and mature as she did."

He fluttered his lashes. "And then one day she awoke, and he looked into her eyes, and he realized he had found everything he had ever wanted."

It made her laugh outright. "After everything settled and he was sulking at me over him not realizing what had been going on, I reassured him by telling him that at least he did not have to overcome a tower covered in thorny roses or a fire-breathing dragon."

"I would guess he would have rather had the tower than an encounter with the Snake God."

"Can't blame him for that, really. Still, it needed to be done. Letting Nahga escape there would have meant far worse events later."

He smiled. "You sound suspiciously like someone who controls the power of destiny."

"Who, me? I just like to have my own way in things."

The day went by with relative peace though everyone involved in the scenario was on edge. Even as the sun was setting, the first sprouts of the beanstalk had emerged from the land. Nobody was awakened in the middle of the night by any sort of earthshaking growth, but Rhianna awoke just before dawn to a vision rushing across her eyes. The symbolic shattering of a mirror.

"Aaron." She gave him a quick shake before rolling out of bed. "It's time." She dug out her rarely used jeans and a shirt she didn't mind getting grubby. There was no law that said she couldn't be comfortable when heading into what might be her final battle. Besides, she didn't *have* armor, and unlike Eric, she didn't have ritual clothing that denoted her power and bloodline.

On the other hand, she was not at all surprised to see that Aaron had chosen to shift into his familiar *chiton* and sandals. Pieces of armor had been added to the ensemble, and his bow was hooked over his shoulder. In a fight against evil, the arrows he fired would be potentially devastating. Only evil was incapable of feeling love.

They saw the beanstalk as soon as they stepped out into the murky gloom. It had grown in a spiral shape around the HQ building and it continued to spiral up until it seemed to disappear into the sky. Rhianna and Aaron made their way to the garden where it had been planted, and they found Eric standing at the base. The stalk was easily fifteen feet in diameter and would be easy to climb.

The morning wind tugged at Eric's cloak as he watched his sister approach. "I wish to go with you."

"No." Her voice booked no argument. "We need you here, Riku. Someone has to be able to kill the stalk instantly to cut off retreat once we lure the evil down. Aaron can block Olympus. We have to trap the evil here where we can finally destroy it."

He cupped her cheek. "Nothing will keep me here if you need me."

"I know." She kissed his cheek softly. She turned to start climbing the stalk and then looked back. "Riku? I just want to tell you again how much I love you. You've made my life so much better by being in it."

A little chill went down his back. That sounded suspiciously like a goodbye. "I love you too, Rhi. You know that. I don't think my life would be complete without you and Rayna in it with me."

She smiled at him for a moment and turned back to the stalk. It was not truly a climb thanks to the spiral, but it was an incline and therefore much more difficult than merely climbing stairs. They would not climb all the way to Olympus, though, as that would be silly. They only needed to get high enough in the air that it would not take much power for Aaron to fly them the rest of the way there.

That point was another few hundred feet in the air over the top of the building. The perch gave them a glorious view of the city spread out around them. It never truly slept, but it had not fully awakened for the day either. As Aaron looked out at the scenery, he murmured to Rhianna, "No one will question the beanstalk?"

"Most won't even notice it. It's a part of the magic that even I have never understood. It won't affect air traffic either. Nothing flies over the District. It messes with scanners and instrumentation. I can't imagine why."

He smiled as he lifted her into his arms. "Indeed." He flew up swiftly toward the top of the stalk and power rushed over their bodies as they passed the invisible barrier into Olympus. They emerged on the other side of the clouds, and the beanstalk ended only a few feet higher. It was covered in the bits of puffy debris that showed where it had literally smashed through the blockage.

Olympus was a ruin. It had crumbled and fallen to bits over the last few days as the evil tore it apart in its rage. The sky that always showed Mirage was now dulled and covered with a disgusting filmy substance. The bitter, putrid, stench of evil clung to the air. It smelled of blood and murder, of genocide and the slaughter of innocents.

A low rumble moved on the air as they moved deeper into the forsaken palace. The floor was gouged and cracked apart, and something acidic had burned it through in places. Columns and pillars had collapsed into rubble. The statues of the gods and goddesses had been beheaded entirely. Perhaps most tellingly, the statue of Eros had been smashed into the smallest possible pieces. The others were still partially intact, but not his.

The rumble began to become a hissing as ugly darkness moved in the corners of the place. It started to bubble and ooze out of the cracks like rancid tar, and it slowly crept across the floor. Its mere passage only seared the marble more. Rhianna slowly lifted her hands, and white and silver power began to swirl around her body. Her first strike nipped close enough to burn but not actually strike.

The blob screeched as it surged toward her like the snap of jaws. She danced back gracefully and Aaron let loose an arrow. The blob turned on him instead, and he also danced back. The tempo had been set. The lovers would flick off an attack that taunted rather than damage. They needed it to be on Earth, in the District, where they had the advantage of allies and the very sanctuary of magic.

Both lifted their hands and fired off pure white power that sensually merged halfway and sheared a hole through the blob's body. It went ballistic with rage and started lobbing blasts after blasts of necrotic power as it began to chase them blindly. Aaron grabbed up Rhianna because he could fly faster than they ran, and he plunged down past the barrier once more. The blob could not fly, but it began to creep down the beanstalk like a spreading stain of evil and decay.

"Destroy the stalk!" Aaron shouted at Eric as they approached. "Hurry!"

Eric placed his hands on the base of the stalk and his command over the element of earth rose. Withering and blackening began to rush upward as he choked the large plant of its very life. It started to dissolve upward as fast as the evil rushed down, and the two met in the middle. The blob seemed to realize what was occurring and started to climb back up the stalk, but it was too late. Power fired off from Aaron's hand and obliterated the entrance to Olympus entirely.

The blob landed on the roof of the headquarters with a splat that shook the entire building. An unnatural scream of rage welled on the air and exploded outward in a blinding rush of evil power that consumed the entire world in silence. All people dropped wherever they were. The only ones spared from the Silence were those who had completed contracts issued by either Rhianna or Aaron, and the entirety of the District itself.

Aaron landed beside Eric and gently placed Rhianna on her feet. They were joined a few moments later by Mel, Audra, Sera, and Theresa. The only outward sign of anyone's uneasiness was the way Theresa's very long hair shifted restlessly in response to her mood. "Let's do this," Sera said briskly. "I have a meeting at ten am, and my boss is a picky bastard sometimes."

The easiest way to get everyone to the roof was to take the elevator inside the building. The last flight to the actual roof was a set of stairs, and Rhianna unlocked the door at the top. The roof beyond was a mess. Broken cement and glass littered the area, and the blob's acidic presence had eaten through other places.

It spotted the small army that had arrived, and a sinister laugh rippled over the air. *You think this is enough?* The words hissed through everyone's minds in a way that made them feel a bit violated. Power flickered over the blob and it began to duplicate into shades of itself that formed into the shape of monsters and demons from lore. *There will be no more happy endings.*

Power rippled over Mel and Audra in turn, and they shifted form entirely. Fur bloomed across their bodies as their nails became claws and their faces elongated into wolf muzzles. Neither got any taller, but they certainly gained more muscle as their natural strength was bolstered. The last time Audra had taken her Battle Wolf self, she had been avenging the deaths of her clan. It seemed fitting to take it now to ensure that kind of thing never happened again. The mated pair rushed across the roof as a blur, and it was impossible to tell who let out the first snarl as they tore into several enemies.

Sera needed to have a rough understanding of whatever shape she shifted into, and she had made sure to read up on potentials the night before. Light swirled around her and replaced her tall figure with the shape of a large grizzly bear. "Cover the ones who can get hurt," she rumbled to Theresa as she lunged into the thick of things.

Theresa hurried to join Aaron and Rhianna, and her protection against evil was evident. Nothing could get close to her at all. If it approached from the front, it would meet her unwavering gaze and be repelled. Approaching from her back encountered her hair rising up as a weapon that could choke and smother.

The shades had their hands full with the lethal beasts, and that left Eric, Rhianna, and Aaron to engage the heart of the evil directly. It became a mess very quick. None of them were designed for close range battle and therefore had to focus on keeping the evil back while still trying to pick it off. They were doing damage, but the two lovers were taking it as well—and faster than Theresa could heal. More shades spilled into the fight and Eric was forced to change targets.

Aaron took the risk of shifting his bow into a sword and lunged toward the blob on the hopes that he was enough his father's son to get by. Rhianna continued to cover him with blasts of power and the bow he had conjured for her. He did well enough at first, but he misjudged a strike and received a sound thump that sent him tumbling head over heels. He cracked his head along the way and lay there for a moment, dazed.

The blob saw an opening and screeched in triumph. It would render him incapacitated again and obliterate the rest who were there. He would have no choice but to sacrifice his immortal life if he lost the ones he loved most. Like a blur of hate and dripping tar, it fired off spikes with lethal accuracy.

In an ironic twist to history repeating, they were stopped from reaching him when Rhianna leapt in front of him at the last moment. The spikes plowed through her body and blood flew. Everything and everyone froze as a tortured cry ripped from Aaron's lips. The spikes lifted Rhianna off her feet and then dropped her onto the roof with a soft thud.

Eric and Aaron scrambled to her side, and Theresa was right behind them. Tears began to well in her eyes the moment she touched Rhianna. "It's too late," she whispered. Her lips trembled as she bit back a sob. "It . . . it ripped her heart to shreds. I can't heal this! No one can!" She shook her head wildly. "How can this be?! The rest of us can't even be wounded at all, let alone killed!"

Painful understanding filled Eric. "The one person," he whispered hoarsely, "who has saved thousands of lives by issuing contracts formed from the power of love . . . is the one person who is not protected because her contract is not yet complete." He looked up sharply as he felt power rising inside Aaron. "What are you doing?"

Blue eyes faded to a dull gray color, Aaron did not look up from his wife's body resting in his arms. "I am sacrificing myself. I cannot exist without her. I have no power without her. I will follow her on. My sacrifice should be enough to destroy evil." He slowly looked up at Eric. "There will be no more contracts. The happy endings are done."

"Not just yet!" an unfamiliar male voice shouted. Red power blazed as a surge of fire and dropped a man in full ancient Grecian armor on the roof. A sword and shield appeared in his hands as he rushed toward the evil on a shout. "Wolves! Shapeshifter! Aid me! There is still time!"

Mel, Audra, and Sera hurried to join Ares as another swirl of pink and gold light deposited the beautiful figure of Aphrodite. She knelt across from her son and took his shoulders. "Do not sacrifice yourself!" she snapped at him. "It will not be enough! You must avenge your wife before you go! I will transfer my power to you; I have no need for it anymore. Do this last deed, Eros! You must!"

He closed his eyes in acceptance and opened himself to the power she poured into him. It was just barely enough to compensate for the gaping holes torn inside him by Rhianna's death. He eased her body into Eric's care and slowly got to his feet. Power blazed around him with white-hot gold color as he methodically approached the evil blob. The creature seemed to realize what a threat he was, and it tried to scramble for escape. Audra blocked its way. Another route was blocked by Mel. A third by Sera. A fourth by Ares. The only open path was directly at Aaron. The blob screamed in fury and rushed toward him to consume him.

Its scream only lifted more as he began to glow even brighter. Power ripped from his body in a blinding wave, and the blob was completely obliterated. The shockwave spread with the same suddenness as the Silence, and the darkness receded. People stirred and gained their feet as the sun and moon began to shine again upon the world.

A different sort of silence, a pained one, filled the rooftop as Aaron stopped glowing. Nobody had sustained any wounds except for him. The others had been protected by their contracts. Only one person on that roof had been at risk of death, and she had willingly paid that price for her love.

Aaron stiffly returned to her side and knelt to ease her body into his arms. A footstep had him looking up sharply and he saw the unexpected figure of Persephone approaching. Her arms held a wispy, ethereal shape that bore an uncanny resemblance to Rhianna. She knelt and gently released the spirit back into Rhianna's body. "Charon would not ferry her. She was left on the shore until I could get to her and bring her here. I had to do this. It is my atonement for so long ago."

Sunlight fell across Theresa's hands and formed into male hands that guided hers to repair the damage done internally to Rhianna's body. *Like this,* Apollo's voice told her, though in a way all could hear. *It can be done easily enough.*

Rhianna drew a sharp breath as her heart began to beat and her lungs took in air once more. Aphrodite nodded firmly. "There we are. Now. Let us be sure this cannot happen again." She held up her hands, and a crystal chalice filled with shimmering gold liquid appeared on one palm. A piece of what looked like honeycomb yet white in color appeared on her other. "A woman like this really should be a goddess as well, do you not agree?"

Aaron broke the nectar into the ambrosia so that they could be more easily consumed and then gently fed the concoction to Rhianna. Her lashes lifted enough to see what he was doing, and he smiled tremulously. "Drink," he urged her huskily. "You have far earned this right, my beloved."

She drank the entire thing, and a bright glow rippled over her body before sinking into her skin and settling. Theresa found it easier than ever to heal the last of the wounds, even without Apollo's guidance, and soon the only sign of the ordeal was the ragged and ravaged clothes that adorned Rhianna's body. Ares flicked his hand to take care of that problem, and a beautiful *peplos* of the finest linen replaced the last signs of trauma.

Rhianna's eyes opened entirely, and the familiar iridescence of immortality had come to hover in her black gaze. She blinked once before looking up at Aaron and smiling. "I'll be fine now."

"You had better be!" Audra snarled as she and Mel returned to their normal shape. "I could kick your damned ass, Rhianna! Of all the reckless, stupid things! Don't you *dare* scare me like that again!"

"I think I can promise that."

Ares, Aphrodite, and Persephone shared a smile as they got to their feet and began to walk away. "I think our job is done now," Persephone decided with a satisfied nod. "This is how it always should have been."

Ares cocked his head at his lover. "What do you suppose Rhianna is a goddess of? As Athena said, she has to be a goddess of *something.*"

A smile tugged at Aphrodite's lips as she glanced back over her shoulder to see their son and daughter-in-law embracing as if they would never let go again. "If Aaron is the God of Love, then I suppose Rhianna must surely be the Goddess of Destiny. They belong perfectly together." She rested her head on his shoulder with a contented sigh. "They are the protectors of lovers. There are plenty more happy endings to be made now. No evil will ever rise to stop them again."

EPILOGUE

Two months later, the resplendent gardens around Enforcers' Headquarters had been attacked by the gleeful designers of Seven Wishes working on provided sketches from Taylor. The entire place felt like a magical garden where dreams could come true. Under an arbor covered in grapes and wild roses, Rhianna and Aaron were finally able to renew their vows before the collected gathering of their friends and family.

Famil*ies*. The entirety of the Shaughnessy, Carmichael, Dease, and Lucino families were present. Priya and Pablo were present. Marina and Markus. Anyone who had ever been helped by either the bride or groom had been sure to put in an appearance.

Rather than exchange wedding bands, for they already wore them, Rhianna and Aaron were finally able to present one another with the custom engagement bands they had promised. Hers was a gold band set with a creamy pearl. His was a silver band set with a small bit of amber holding a very tiny forget-me-not seed inside.

The cheers reached well beyond the District as they finally shared their first kiss in their eternally joined lives. Eric walked up to the arbor where they stood and smiled as he held out a familiar scroll. "I think we need to see what this says. Don't you?"

Rhianna took it from him and slowly unrolled it. Light flickered and the word 'Complete' blazed across the center of the paper with such brilliance that everyone in the audience could see it. The cheers started anew as Rhianna whirled and threw her arms around Aaron's neck. He caught her just as close and buried his face in her hair. This was what he had wanted. His beautiful, *immortal*, lover to be by his side for all time. She would never have dared dream so big, but that was fine with him. They had finally had their dreams come true.

The reception party that followed was merry and joyful. They had foregone the whole bouquet and garter toss, though, since they had *other* ways of setting up the people who needed to be set up. Gwyn couldn't help but tease Rhianna, "I guess you'll need to enchant more file cabinets to have room for all those new contracts you two will be making. Do you have a Taber or a Konstantinos one for yourself?"

"Neither, thank you, but if that's a subtle way of asking, I'm keeping my name." She shook her head wryly. "We decided there would just be too much paperwork to get it changed. On the other hand, he's considering changing his. He says he likes the fact that it has less syllables and people won't misspell it as much."

"I only typoed it once. Sheesh."

Aaron heard the laughter and looked over with a smile. Rhianna had laughed a lot more recently than he had ever heard before. He found himself smiling and laughing more as well. The gift of their completed contract.

Cameron stepped up beside him and asked very solemnly, "So are you going to reopen your business?"

"I think I got recruited," he admitted ruefully. "She started talking about how there was an empty suite and how it would be perfect since it is on the first floor and how there really is nothing open in the District right now and that people who work there have their homes attached and since we live together . . ." He trailed off with a grin. "I did not even try to argue with her. Cupid's Grove is now a division of Enforcers."

"Huh-oh." Cameron grinned. "Taking orders from your lover. That always keeps things interesting, trust me. And since you've got, you know, *Rhianna*? Good luck, friend."

Aaron smiled toward Rhianna and was warmed when she smiled back. "I would have her no other way," he murmured softly. "She is perfect just as she is."

As the reception finally drew to a close and people began to go home, Aaron and Rhianna were hustled into a carriage that carried them to the Gentle Brook Inn where they had been reserved the largest honeymoon suite. They would spend the weekend there and then transport themselves to Greece for the first part of their month-long honeymoon.

Eric watched them ride off down the street before going into the HQ building. He quietly unfastened his tie as he rode the elevator upstairs to the top floor. Instead of going into his office, however, he went into Rhianna's. He tugged the scroll out of his jacket and unrolled it. Not so surprisingly, it had become legible now that it had been completed. Everything he had wondered about was now spelled out clearly.

He found the space at the bottom and added a few notes. An empty folder sat to the side and he tucked the scroll inside. The folder itself showed the same 'Complete', and he turned to study the as-yet empty drawers in the cabinets. He found one in line of sight to the desk and thought for a moment before writing 'Taber' across the front. He dropped the scroll inside, locked it, and the word 'Finished' appeared beneath the label.

"Riku?" Rayna stood in the doorway with Glory in her arms. She smiled. "Let's go home."

"Yeah." He crossed to her and tucked her safely under his arm as they left the office. He turned off the light and studied the darkness that filled the room. "All this time, we kept saying it. 'She should be a goddess.' 'She's all but a goddess.' 'Her power is godlike,'" he murmured. "I suppose the answer really was right there all along."

Rayna rested her head on his arm as she smiled up at him. "Isn't it always?"

"I suppose it is. What story do you suppose will be next?"

"I don't know, but I *do* know how it will end."

"Yes?"

"Happily ever after."

Status: File Complete

Analysis: The stories that take the longest to get to happy ever after are the ones with the sweetest endings.

Turn the page to come back to Mirage for one last tale that might just need some double Enforcing . . .

Bonus Folder

ELIZABELLE

CHAPTER ONE

It was that time of year again in Mirage. As surely as the seasons brought rain, flowers, falling leaves, or snow, it brought the rights of passage undertaken by all princes and heroes who sought to prove themselves in the world. Spring season was usually the 'rescue princesses' time. Summer and fall typically held the 'defeat a curse' journeys. And as the first snows began to fall and make the world into wintery wonderlands, the rite du jour was 'slay a dragon.'

The dragons were not wholly keen with the entire thing. Most were quite happy to just find a nice cave and settle in with shiny treasure to admire. The treasures typically came from their own mining and scavenging though there had been occasional raids on kingdoms; it was usually in response to someone in the kingdom doing something stupid first. And, yes, princesses had been kidnapped once in a while, but, well, even dragons got lonely. No princess nabbed by a dragon ever found her captor to be anything except polite, well mannered, and surprisingly adept at card games—and sometimes far more accurate at guessing who her true love might be.

The first snows had begun to fall. Already a few raids had happened. Thankfully, there had only been one casualty thus far, but the numbers were sure to climb. The dragons were simply at the end of their rope. The clan located off the edges of the Montgomery Kingdom had it particularly bad since the kingdom was rife with wizards and sages that drew in heroes and princes seeking advice.

"What if we made alliance?" one elder suggested to the Circle that oversaw the clan.

"You mean send in a delegate to prove we're not the ravaging beasts we're made out to be? Really, it *would* be easier if they accepted us like they do wizards. We have people who go rogue, but you can't write all of us off," another pointed out.

"I think we are in agreement, then." The first nodded his large head briefly. "I suggest we send a younger member of the clan. It's a trivial task, for one thing, and for another, he or she will be small enough to not cause an immediate alarm."

"I recommend Magnus," another offered. She sighed. "He has been driving his family crazy. He won't settle down! We keep trying to tell him that dragons don't go on adventures, but he won't listen. He's always burying his nose in books about travel. 'But why can't a dragon have an adventure? Didn't a prince marry a Good Faerie? Rules can be broken!'" She shook her head. "I remind myself he is but a whelp, but he still vexes me! At least this might make him calm down!"

"Done." The first elder inclined his head. "Coral, would you be so kind as to relay the missive to him?"

Coral rose to her full height and gracefully leapt like a large cat to the window overhead. A flap of her wings sent her soaring into the air around the massive mountain range that the clan called home. She angled down toward a remote, almost hidden, cave that had been cleverly disguised to blend into the surroundings.

She landed lightly and her talons made little clicking noises as she moved into the opening. Around two bends, the cave opened up to reveal a beautiful deposit of precious stones. Magnus was not much of a gold collector. He also did not seem to be present at first, and her eyes narrowed as she swept a quick gaze over the room.

Movement. She turned and spied the tip of a purple tail sticking out of a mound of amethysts. Clever boy. "Hmmm . . . Now wherever could he be . . .?" She moved closer and grabbed onto his tail with her jaws as if he was a pup. Dragon teeth were retractable for just such a thing, much to the gratitude of many parents. She hauled Magnus out and he gave a yelp as he found himself unceremoniously dropped on the ground. "You!" she scolded. "What are you doing, whelp?"

He scowled. "I was trying to avoid all of the antics from next door! Stupid mating season."

Mating season for dragons came about every winter, too. It was partially why it was such a good time to hunt them. Dragons in season were stronger, faster, and more territorial. Perhaps luckily for the race, dragons mated for life. An unmated dragon—like Magnus—was spared the insanity as a whole. Mated dragons really didn't think about much beyond procreation, and therefore made noisy neighbors. Once spring arrived, things would go back to normal and the mated pairs would again remember to be polite. It was the 'until spring' part that drove others nuts.

Coral sighed as she studied Magnus. It really was a shame that he was as-yet unmated himself. He was certainly one of the more handsome males around, and he had strong skills for his age of a hundred. But, since he was only the equivalent of a twenty-five-year-old human, no one was yet pressuring him to think about settling down. That would come in another fifty years. "Just you wait," she scolded him. "You'll get yours!"

"Yes, I know." He clasped a claw to his heart and took on a dramatic tone. "I will happen upon the most beautiful creature in the world—to me—and be instantly consumed with the desire to have her close to me. When mating season comes around once a year, our lives will be put on hold as we while away hours in desperate desire trying to produce a child."

A brow covered in pink scales lifted. "You won't be laughing when you get there. Also? It may be annoying to neighbors, but I've never heard a mated dragon complain about being in season. It is daunting at first until you get used to it. By the third season for a mated pair, they're quite happy for an excuse to stay in their cave together all the time—especially if they already have kids!"

He couldn't dispute that. He was actually amused by how his parents used to dump him off on a cousin or other relative to be babysat for three months. "Why are we discussing this anyway?"

"You brought it up." She sighed. "Magnus. I know you are bored. I think I might be able to help with that a bit. We need a delegate to go to the Montgomery Kingdom and petition them for alliance rather than the current status quo. We need to end this ridiculous 'prove your valor by killing a dragon' thing."

"Can I travel after I talk to them?" he asked hopefully. "I've mastered the ability to disguise myself as a human. The only thing that gives me away is scales on my neck, but a scarf covers it."

She stared at him. It normally took a dragon until at least five centuries to be able to master the ability to disguise as a different race. He was more gifted than she had believed. "Maybe," she hedged. "Why don't we see what happens at the kingdom and go from there?"

"Okay. Done." He flapped his wings and rose up into the air. The light shimmered over his rich purple hued scales and illuminated the silver stripe down his back that was mark of his noble heritage. "I'll do my best to convince them to let it be."

She watched him fly out of the cave and sighed internally again. First a prince marrying his Good Faerie, and now a dragon that didn't want to guard a cave of treasure. What next? A princess that didn't want to be rescued?

The Montgomery Kingdom was relatively normal as far as kingdoms went. It had a king and a queen, a prince that was the heir to the throne, and a princess that was amongst the most beautiful of females in her kingdom. Everything was almost perfect. Idyllic. There was really only one tiny, little problem.

"Elizabelle!!"

Elizabelle Montgomery—Liz to her friends—winced wryly as she heard her mother bellowing her name. She was busted. *Again*. Stifling a sigh, she stopped walking her favorite mare around the corral and dismounted. Those who watched her were forced to hide smiles. The status quo was apparently in shift again, what with this new generation of royalty not sticking to tradition.

Liz assuredly had the ladylike manners, gracious demeanor, and ability to make small talk with the best of her ilk. She also rode better than the masters, was better with a sword than even her brother, and she had picked up various forms of other combat by mere observation from her tower window.

Every suitor that had come by over the last six years since her sixteenth birthday had been treated to the same polite yet firm response: no way, no how. Liz was holding out for true love (which no one argued with) but the fact that true love for her meant someone willing to overlook her less than princess-ly charms implied that her search might take a while.

She ducked into the secret room near the stables to quickly change out of her leggings and tunic. She yanked on her royal dress again and hastily coiled her hair to hide all the tangles. A quick scrub of a cloth over her face removed sweat and dirt. She nearly forgot to replace her headband with her coronet and was trying to pin it into place as she hurried toward the drawing room inside the castle.

Her mother was inside and, as always, looked like she was getting ready for a ball. Liz knew some people genuinely enjoyed dressing up and being pampered, but she just wasn't one of them. In the same way some commoners were really meant to be royalty, she was one of the members of royalty meant to be common. Everyone had their own happy zone. A castle wasn't hers.

She sketched an elegant curtsey. "Yes, Mother?"

Her mother scowled at her. "Oh, don't try that sweetness thing! And don't widen your eyes so innocently, Elizabelle! I saw you from the window. I know damned well you were out in the corral again. We encouraged your wish to learn to ride because all princesses should, but you should be riding *sidesaddle*."

"It's not as easy to control a horse that way," Liz sighed. "And it's uncomfortable."

"It's more proper." That was met with a roll of the eyes, and the queen stifled a long sigh. She loved her daughter, she truly did, but she often wished she could simply understand her better. "We have tried to be lenient with you, Elizabelle, but your father and I are putting our foot down. No more riding. No more leggings. Your brother has been instructed not to teach you anything else. You will start again on the etiquette and housekeeping lessons you have shunned for so many years."

"No."

"They will—" She broke off and her eyes widened. "I'm sorry?"

"No." Liz crossed her arms. "As in 'no, I will not.' Like it or not, I'm twenty-two years old. I'm an adult. There is nothing stopping me from simply leaving home."

Her mother's eyes narrowed. "I think we disagree. We will not have our daughter off traipsing around the world without an escort!"

Hopefully, Liz asked, "If I have an escort, would you let me go?"

"Guards!" The queen turned as the door opened and two wary guards looked inside. "Escort the princess to her tower and lock her inside. She shall remain there until she comes to her senses over this ridiculous nonsense!"

With obvious reluctance, the guards moved to flank Liz. The guards and ladies-in-waiting alike adored Liz and very much wanted her to be happy—something she would never be inside the castle. Liz said nothing as the guards took her back to her tower that overlooked the barracks. They obligingly locked the door before shutting her inside, but one of them slipped her an extra master castle key *just* in case she decided she wanted to run away. They knew their princess better than her mother did.

The benefit to being 'locked' in her tower was that she could wear whatever she wanted. She bathed and changed into the tunic-dress and leggings that one of the maids had snuck in to her. She then perched in her large window to watch the courtyard on the other side of the barracks to see who was coming and going. She liked to people watch. It was fun.

Her brother, Solomon, was going through the courtyard, and he glanced up to see her. "Liz!" he scolded when he saw what she was wearing. "You'll get yourself kidnapped by a dragon if you keep being so willful!"

"I'd rather be kidnapped by a dragon than stuck here to await some idiot trying to rescue me!" she retorted. "And what are you still doing here? I thought you were leaving to go rescue some other princess."

"I got delayed by the weather and missed out." He shrugged and grinned. "No big loss. I have an adventure coming in my near future. I can feel it."

"Lucky you," she muttered.

Magnus had a healthy sense of self-preservation. He had no intentions of flying up to the castle and risking being shot down. He instead landed out of sight and changed into his human form before beginning his approach. As a human, he was just as surprisingly handsome as the dragons found him in his natural shape. His purple scales had turned into purple eyes, and his silver stripe had become silver hair. There was a slightly silver hue to his pale skin as well, and the shimmer of scales over his neck were iridescent purple.

The hue to his skin could be dismissed as a result of magical bloodlines, either faerie or mage, but the scales were a dead giveaway. He wouldn't bother with a scarf until he was trying to be incognito. For this meeting, he needed to be clear who and what he represented. There was no way this would be easy.

One thing was easy, though: getting inside. Nobody stopped him from entering the city around the castle, and he only got a few curious looks rather than outright hostility. He got even luckier when he approached the actual castle and spoke with a guard. Though obviously astonished at a dragon arriving to talk diplomacy, the guard nonetheless went to talk to the king and queen. Five minutes later, Magnus was being escorted to the throne room.

The sheer opulence of the place made his nose wrinkle slightly. He lived in a cave stuffed with treasure, and this *still* felt ostentatious. Seeing the number of robes and massive crowns that the ruling couple wore didn't make him feel any better. He could barely stand normal clothes. Weren't they smothering?

"Well!" The king's brows shot up as he beheld Magnus. "I have to admit you surprised us, er, sir. We don't often get dragons requesting audiences with us. What brings you here?"

"The ritual slaughter of my people every winter?" Magnus countered politely. "Your majesties, with all due respect, the dragons are getting quite fed up with this 'slay a dragon to prove your valor' thing. We're not all bloodthirsty, ravaging beasts. We're a civilized society. We have the occasional bad apple, but, who doesn't? We would ask for an alliance in an effort to call off this ridiculous annual hunt."

"Don't be ridiculous!" the king chided. "How else is a man supposed to prove his worth? Hunting ogres? They're not intelligent enough to be a threat."

It was almost a compliment. "Sire. Really. Look at it through our eyes. With the way your kind comes tromping through just because we're dragons, *you* come across as the bloodthirsty and brutal creatures. Tell me truly. How many times can you recall a dragon attacking a kingdom *without being slighted first*?"

"Uhm. Once or twice. Maybe three times." The king waved it aside. "The status stays where it is. We have no reason to change tradition at this time. Dragons are beasts, and beasts are for hunting and killing. An alliance is ridiculous."

A puff of smoke emerged from Magnus' nose as he snorted rudely. Before he said something in anger that he might regret, he turned and left the throne room entirely. The king had just been confronted with manners and intelligent conversation, and a request for alliance, and still had the gall to call dragons beasts?

He was partway across the courtyard when he heard someone whistle at him. He looked around quickly and then upward. A young woman was waving at him from a tower window and gesturing for him to join her. He looked around again, and a passing guard shrugged. "The princess. You can visit her. She's locked up right now. She's probably bored. We won't tell if you want to say hi."

Well, at least not *everyone* was rude. He looked up again, shrugged, and used his magic to fly himself up to the window. Dragons in human form could still fly though it did take a bit more power than normal. He landed delicately on the windowsill and stepped down into the room. "You called?" he started to ask dryly, only to break off and stare.

Delicate strands of onyx hair framed a striking face set with deep emerald eyes and ruby lips. A lithe and lovely figure matched with ivory skin made his fingers suddenly itch to touch. This gemstone princess was practically a creature of his deepest fantasy. A deep and powerful desire to mate rose hard and fast. A brief panicky thought fluttered through his mind, *She can't be my mate!*

But, really, how else was he supposed to explain his desire? It was not merely to make love to her; he very, very, *very* badly wanted to get her pregnant and see her carrying a child. That could mean only one thing. It was mating season, and he had accidentally found his mate. Trying to tell his hormones that dragons and humans probably could *not* breed kids didn't seem to do much to shut them up—and why would it, when it never worked for the same-gender pairs either? They would keep going nuts he got his mate pregnant *or* until the season ended. Of all the rotten luck!

Liz was almost not breathing as he stared at her with burning purple eyes. She didn't think it was her imagination that he was contemplating ravishing her on the floor, and the fact that she entirely didn't mind the threat told her she might be in trouble. "Hi." It came out breathless against her will. "Uhm, I'm Elizabelle Montgomery. Liz for short." She offered a hand for a handshake.

He caught her hand in his but brought it to his lips as he bowed deeply. "Magnus Silverback." A slightly deeper note to his voice was as telling as the breathless note in hers. "It's a pleasure."

Not yet it wasn't, but it probably would be! Why hadn't the princess guidebook come with a chapter on 'lusting after the wrong species'? Being a practical princess, she knew damned well the way her world worked. That much unexpected desire out of nowhere was a big damn clue that Love with a capital L was probably not far behind. She really couldn't imagine there was any other reason she had an urge to blurt, 'I'm single! I want your babies!' What the hell had brought *that* on? The desire was surprising enough without throwing in the urge to have eggs with the guy!

Rather than continue to stare into her darkened eyes, he glanced around the tower room. A smile tugged at his lips as he saw the practical décor and rather plain style of living. This was one princess who had no real care for the fancy things in life. The only gems he could spot at all were chunks of stone in the raw, like the ones he mined. "You're not normal."

She had to grin. "You have no idea." She huffed out a breath. "Magnus, you're a dragon, right?"

"Right."

"I have a big, *big* favor to ask."

"Okay . . ."

"I need you to kidnap me."

He stared at her for long moments. "I beg pardon?"

She caught his arm urgently. He stood many inches taller than her five-four frame, and he was much more powerfully built than most human men, yet she felt nothing but safe. "Please," she begged, "I can't STAND it here anymore! All they want is for me to sit around docilely and wait for some stupid hero to come save me! I want to travel, or, at the least, find some place I can live where people don't care if I use a sword and ride astride or want to wear normal clothes other than ball gowns!"

Empathy moved through him. It seemed a bit like finding a kindred spirit. "I know the feeling," he admitted softly. "All my people want me to do is settle down and guard a cave of treasure. I want adventure. To travel as well. What good are my treasures if I don't spend them on stuff?"

She took both of his hands with hers. "We could travel together. I wouldn't mind spending time with you." She grinned a bit. "I'd be lying if I tried to pretend I don't find you attractive and fascinating, and that I would absolutely not mind if you had decided to carry me away of your own will rather than me asking you to."

If she didn't stop looking at him like that, he was going to pounce on her and probably get himself shot by the guards. He felt a bit desperate to taste her. How long would he manage to keep his hands off her? She was a *princess*. Princesses did *not* become the mates of dragons, damn it! "Ground rules," he heard himself saying. "One, I think it's fair to clear the air and state that I'm badly attracted to you *but* you can trust me to protect your virtue."

She watched him from under her lashes. He should be more worried about *his* virtue. If true love came along, then she would have him. It was that simple. "Okay. And two?"

"Honesty. We have to mutually decide where we're going and what we do. We should be equals. I'd rather a friend than just a companion. I don't have many friends," he admitted.

"Me neither." She smiled. "I can agree to both, and I will be honest enough to admit I'm pretty badly attracted to you as well—as if I hadn't already implied it. Let's start with friends. Deal?"

"Deal." Though he would do his best to *keep* it as friendship until he was absolutely sure that she was his mate and he wasn't just being deviant. The only way to know for certain would be if she had the same urge to mate that he did. Considering you couldn't just *ask,* 'hey, you want to have babies?', it would be best to just see what developed. "Ready to get kidnapped?"

"Am I ever!" She rushed over to her closet and hastily threw several items into a backpack. She slipped it on and followed him over to the window. Fascinated, she watched as he jumped out and turned into his natural form before he dropped more than a foot.

He was a surprisingly handsome dragon to even her eyes. She had no way to define what his race considered beautiful, but she really liked how he looked. She kinda wanted to pet him; his scales looked really soft and shiny. He was not much bigger than ten feet overall, and he flew close enough to the window for her to climb out onto his back. The years of riding astride paid off, and she was perfectly comfortable as he flew over the courtyard wall.

A yelp rose on the air as they were spotted, and guards rushed into the throne room. "The princess was kidnapped by the dragon!" they blurted

The king shot to his feet. "So much for civilized!" he snapped. "Send out the word! Any able-bodied prince and hero in the vicinity who brings my daughter home safely may have her hand in marriage and a piece of my kingdom!" He scowled darkly as the guards ran out again. "I always knew she would get herself into trouble if she kept up being so willful! Kidnapped by a dragon!" He threw himself down into his chair with a huff. "Well, at least she'll get married and settle down after this!"

"And hopefully find true love," his wife sighed.

CHAPTER TWO

It took an hour of flight before Magnus felt it was safe to land. He touched down gently and angled a wing to help Liz slide safely to the ground. He shifted back into human form and shook his head for a moment to clear the disorienting sensation. It was always an oddity to go from ten feet to slightly less than six.

Liz grinned a bit. "Vertigo?"

"A little." He grinned back. "First time I managed this form, I tripped over my own feet because I had no idea how to get my legs to function. It was a completely new way of balancing myself. I still get kinda clumsy, just as a warning. I lose my sense of depth or forget I have longer legs relative to the placement of my knees."

She tried to bite back a snicker. "Maybe we should stop and have you watch some toddlers to see how they do it." She stretched happily and looked around. "Even just being outside the palace has made me feel better. I was getting choked in there. Apparently royals forget that being royal does not make one any less an adult once of the proper age."

"How old are you?" he asked curiously as he fell into step beside her.

"Twenty-two. You?"

"Literally one hundred, but I'm about the equivalent of a twenty-five-year-old human. We grow roughly four years for every one of yours."

"Not immortal though."

"We average about four hundred or so. We technically live as long as humans do but we just live it longer."

She blinked. "I actually understood that. Can you do that thing that faeries do where you can choose to grow old faster?"

"Sure! Any magical creature can do that." He bumped her shoulder companionably with his. "Tell me about the princess I kidnapped. Are you the heir to the throne?"

"*No,* thankfully." She shook her head. "I have an elder brother named Solomon. He's slightly younger than your mental age. He's done a few low-key type adventures, routed some ogres and the like, but nothing big yet. Keeps trying to set out and always gets waylaid. He thinks his grand adventure is coming soon. I would *happily* go on his adventures for him."

"No suitors?" It was asked casually though he felt anything but casual at the idea of competition. He might have to start eating people, and that would suck for the dragons' reputation. Also, he had heard that princes were a bit on the chewy side.

"None that have stuck!" she answered cheerfully. "First one came along when I was just sixteen." She fluttered her lashes. "How handsome he was! Fair haired and charming with blue eyes, and a nice figure of a body. He swung a dashing sword and brought me roses. He vowed to sweep me off my feet and place me in the lap of luxury."

He coughed. "And?"

"He happened to be vain as the sun will rise. I think he coiffed his hair more than a legion of princesses. He also had too high an opinion of himself. I chucked him out on his ass. Last I heard he had pissed off some witch and gotten turned into a frog. Good luck to him finding true love like *that*."

"Hmm." He was trying not to laugh. "After that?"

"Every spring, rain or shine, the line tromps through the castle. 'Be mine and I'll make you a queen!'" She clasped a hand to her heart dramatically. "'Marry me and you will never work a day!' 'Give me your hand and I will shower you in gold and silk!'" Her mocking smile softened. "There was one, though. A plain man. He was the fourth in line to inherit his kingdom. He told me he had nothing to offer except a promise to be faithful and caring. I wish I could have loved him. I couldn't, so I did the next best thing. I arranged for him to deliver a gift to a friend of mine on his way home."

"Did he find true love with her?" he asked softly.

"He did! It made me happy." She sighed. "Anyway, this coming year promises to be the worst yet. With each passing year, I've been slipping further down on the list of marriage material. Not that I'm *complaining*, but it does mean I'm scraping the bottom of the barrel. I just want to be loved. That's all." She shrugged it off. "What about you? Tell me about the dragons. Do you get the 'settle down and marry' thing, too?"

"Not until we hit the age of one-fifty. I have fifty years left before they start nagging the hell out of me. I *have* had offers, and I *have* had some lifted brows, though. Dragons mate for life," he explained, "and we have the capacity to recognize our mate on sight. I've met everyone in my clan, so everyone knows my mate isn't there yet."

She *really* wanted to ask him if he had recognized her and that was why they had both reacted as they had, but she didn't quite have the nerve for it. She didn't want to scare him off. He seemed kind of skittish. "Dragons lay eggs, right?"

"Actually, no." He smiled. "We're mammals, too. We birth live children. We only *look* like reptiles. Did you know we once had fur?" Her eyes widened and his smile deepened. "Seriously! Once we evolved to live in places other than the coldest mountains, we developed scales instead. They protect us from the changes in season. You can still see the evidence of fur in our whelps: newborn dragons have fur until they're about, hmm, one year old. The fur then falls off and scales grow in."

"I want to see a furry dragon," she sighed wistfully. "At the risk of being potentially insensitive, it sounds so cute!"

"Nope, not insensitive. It *is* cute. Seriously, if people realized how adorable baby dragons are, they wouldn't be so quick to hunt us." He scowled. "Speaking of. Your father's an ass."

"Preaching to the choir there, Magnus. Why were you here anyway?"

"We're tired of the hunting season. We thought we'd offer an alliance. But noooo. A man can only prove his valor by slaying such intelligent and powerful beasts as dragons. Never mind that we don't attack without provocation or that what few princesses were captured were usually just grabbed because the dragon was bored and wanted a friend. We make good companions."

"So far I'm happy with it," she teased him. Her breath caught anew as he looked down at her with another of those laughing smiles, and his purple eyes glowed softly. The glow shifted abruptly, and hunger tightened his face. She was definitely not mistaken about the threat of being ravished. It seemed as if he was having to exert careful control over himself for some reason. Maybe he *had* recognized her as his mate. "Magnus?"

He let out a long breath. Rather than give the whole truth, he hedged around the edges. "Winter is dragon breeding season."

"Oh." She blinked, and it dawned. "*Oh*." She winced. "And heroes *hunt* you during this time? I would not want to go near temperamental and hormonal creatures with sharp teeth unless I was bringing snacks and peace offerings!" Did that mean, then, that his desire for her would have happened for any female of any species? That was disheartening, but not entirely discouraging. "Can dragons breed with humans?" she asked skeptically. "It seems unlikely you'd be eyeing me as breeding potential if we weren't compatible. I would think nature had ways of preventing that from happening."

"I honestly don't know," he admitted, "though I concur with your assessment. You caught me off-guard. I had never wanted a human before, and I have seen a few females in my time despite being relatively cave-locked. I never saw them with more than the sort of admiration you might feel for a pretty bird." His smile turned wry. "Let's just say that my first reaction to seeing you involved things that, if I said them out loud, would get my face slapped." His sharp ears caught sound and he looked down the road to see a town not far ahead. "Ah. There we are. Resting spot!"

She would have rather found out what he had been thinking; it sounded promising. She followed his gaze down the road and sighed happily to see the town. A chance to be normal! "Do I look like a princess?"

"Hmm." He critically eyed her. "Not really. The clothes mostly hide it, and you don't have coloring that screams some specific royal bloodline. I think you'd at most be mistaken for the type of girl who could marry a prince to become a princess."

"Perfect!" She eyed his neck where the scales were visible. It was highly tempting to put her lips there. "You need a scarf." She stopped and took off her backpack to dig inside. She emerged shortly with a scarf and offered it to him. "Here you go." After he put it on, she nodded decisively. "Now you just look like a wizard who has been imbued with magic."

"As you said, perfect!" He impulsively caught her hand and held on as they continued down the road. The noise got louder as they approached, and his brows lifted as he saw the massive commotion. It looked like a bunch of people were preparing for a journey all at once. "What's going on?"

She winced as she saw the half a dozen young men in various types of armor and weaponry. "Heroes. You can't miss them. They have 'valorous type' etched into their foreheads!"

He cleared his throat and stopped an old man who was going by. "What's going on?"

The old man shook his head. "The princess of the Montgomery Kingdom was kidnapped by a dragon. The king has said that returning her safely will net her hand and a piece of the kingdom."

Liz's jaw dropped, and Magnus hastily clamped his hand over her mouth. "Don't mind her!" he blurted. "We just came from there and we didn't see anything like that at all. Are they sure she was actually kidnapped?"

"Well, the king says so, and you know how heroes are. They probably wouldn't care if she was a willing kidnappee. Throw in a beautiful princess, money, *and* dragon slaying, and you'll have every hero or prince worth his salt wanting to prove his stuff in the hopes of finding true love." The old man continued to shuffle along on his way.

Liz had a very un-princesslike urge to smack her father very hard. She could understand him misinterpreting the situation. The 'rescue my daughter and marry her' part was what bothered her. Kidnapping was completely different from curses where only true love would wake you. For all he knew, some adept guy would rescue her and not at all be her true love. Couldn't he have left it at a gold reward?

Magnus held her elbow more tightly and looked around quickly. He spotted a building with a sign that had a bed on it and hurried her that direction. He had luckily thought to bring gems with him for money, and he booked two rooms for at least the night. He urged Liz up the stairs with him and into her room. He shut the door behind himself and let out a breath. "Phew. Alright. You can let your temper loose now."

"I can't believe this!" she exploded as she threw down her backpack. "Am I the only princess in the world who thinks this is getting out of hand?"

He held up his hands soothingly. "Believe it or not, things are changing right now. You and I are proof of it. It happens in cycles. Give it another decade or two, and we'll see where the cycle is really heading. If you have a daughter someday, *she* might be the one to go on adventures and rescue silly princes who don't know better."

It made her snort with humor as he had intended. She threw herself down onto a chair with a huff. "I vote for staying here until tomorrow. They'll have all left by then. And since they'll be looking for us to be heading to ground somewhere, we're not likely to have to worry about them no matter where we go."

"Too true." He sat down across from her and grinned. "May I assume from your ire that you don't want to be rescued?"

"Meh." She made a 'maybe' gesture. "I'm not saying it wouldn't be romantic to be rescued in a time of need, but my need for rescue is a small one. Magic would be my only downfall. I'm quite skilled with a sword, and I can fight with my hands and feet as well."

"Really?" He brightened. "I'm the opposite. Magic is my thing, and if I'm in my natural form, I can claw stuff, but I lack any real physical training, *especially* with this body. Y'think you could teach me some stuff? Just some basics?"

"Sure!" She hopped to her feet. "Scarf off. I don't want to accidentally choke you." She removed the cloak she had thrown on and heeled off her shoes. "Okay. Grab me like this." She put his hands where they needed to be. "Hold on really tight." His grip tightened and she lithely twisted her body in a strange way. She promptly got free.

His eyes slowly widened. "I can't even figure out how you did that. Also, my fingers feel funny."

"Let me show you." She patiently went over the exact movements needed and how to make his human body use them. It didn't matter that he was physically stronger; if he broke free of her grip the right way, it would work on anyone of any strength. The effectiveness lay in the brief numbing of the captor's fingers.

His first attempt did nothing except make him stumble. He got free only because she lacked the strength to keep a grip. They reset and tried again, and he tried to twist himself as she had shown him. He misjudged his ratio of space, however, and threw himself off balance entirely. She tried to catch him this time and only ended up going onto the floor with him. She landed with a thump on his chest. "Ooph!" She blew locks of hair out of her eyes and smiled wryly. "Well, that's a sign of 'almost right' if ever I saw it. A little more balance and you'd have it."

There was no response and she looked down to see him staring at her with a heat that seared her to her toes. Something clenched hard and hot low inside her body with a wild rush of eager desire. She slowly reached out to touch his lips, craving the sensation of them pressed to hers. "Do dragons kiss?" she asked huskily.

His answer was to fist his hands in her hair and drag her down for a wild kiss. She shuddered in his grip and moaned softly as his tongue tangled hotly with hers. The room spun around her head as he rolled over to pin her to the cool wood floor. Her fingers found the silk of his hair and she twisted upward to fight fire with fire. Dragons not only kissed, they were also *really* good at it.

The wicked potency of the pleasure surging inside her body was stunning in its power. Nothing mattered except his taste and his touch. Nothing mattered except making love with him until she finally carried his child inside.

Child. Breeding season. Through the haze in her brain, she realized that it had gotten them both. She *had* to be his mate. She could get the whole 'he needed to mate' thing on his side. A normal desire on her side could be relatively understood, despite the crossed species thing. The fact that all *she* could think about was reproducing—where she had *never* before had the urge in more than a 'meh, someday' kind of way—was a big damn clue that they had to be mates.

She broke out of the kiss to gulp in air, and it was flavored with the oddly sweet scent of his skin. It was addicting. "Magnus." She framed his face in her hands and stared into his seething purple eyes. She did not have to look for the answer. It had been there from the beginning just as she had suspected. Love. How could she not love him? He was everything perfect for her. "If we're going to make love," she warned him thickly, "can we relocate to the bed?"

Shock pierced the intensity of his eyes as he realized how close he was to ripping off her clothes and having her right there. He released her as if burned and scooted away quickly. He averted his eyes as peach color stained his silvery cheeks. "Liz." His voice was rougher and deeper than normally possible for human voices. "I'm sorry."

"Did I look or sound like I was complaining?" She carefully sat up and looked at her hands. They were trembling as hard as her internal organs. She felt achy, frustrated, and more than a bit irked that he had stopped. "I asked for a relocation, not a ceasefire." She slid closer to him. "I've wanted you to touch me since I saw you."

His entire body quivered as she moved closer and the ripe scent of her skin gouged into his lungs. Nothing was as powerful an aphrodisiac to a dragon as the smell of his or her mate, especially at this time of year. His fingers bit into the floor hard enough to make small dents in the wood. "Move back." It came out as almost a growl.

"Magnus, am I your mate?" It was asked calmly.

His breath hissed out as her fingers trailed down his arm. Every inch of his body felt sensitized unbearably. "Yes," he bit out. "You have to be. Mating season doesn't affect a dragon unless they're mated." Fingers skimmed over the scales on his neck and he whirled to grab her arms. Wild magic poured through his eyes. "I don't think you comprehend, Elizabelle!" he snapped. "If I start to make love to you, I won't let you out of bed again until at least spring, or until you were pregnant!"

She pursed her lips as she thought about things. "Is that the only time we'd be setting the sheets on fire?"

He stared at her. "Well, no. Our relationships are always tempestuous with our mates. Breeding season just kicks it into overdrive."

"So . . . we get three months out of a year to completely indulge in desire and not worry about anyone bothering us?"

"Yes . . ."

". . . You're complaining *why*?" She eased up to nibble on his lower lip. "Not that I think we want to spend three months in this inn, beautiful as it is, but I am entirely not opposed to the concept of being your mate and, if we were so lucky, having your child." His hands fell off her arms in shock and she caught his face in her hands. A smile tugged at her lips. "Magnus. This is *Mirage*. True love comes where it chooses to come. We are part of the changing cycle, and I couldn't be happier. My true love needed to be kind of quirky, kind of different, and willing to let me be me. Also? I kind of like the whole flying thing."

He could only stare at her. A dangerous blend of love and desire tangled inside him too powerfully to be borne. "Where did you come from?" he managed to ask.

"A tower."

He couldn't help but laugh though it sounded rough. He buried his fingers in her hair and dragged her up for another hungry kiss. "I do love you," he admitted against her lips. "My true love needed to be adventurous and fun and not expect me to know everything." He rested his forehead against hers, and a hint of peach again climbed his cheeks. "I don't want to make love to you here."

"Three months would be a bit much, lovely as the place is."

"No, not that." His eyes shifted away shyly. "You'll laugh at me."

"No, I won't." She tugged him back. "What is it, Magnus?"

"I just . . ." He huffed out a breath. "I want us to be in my cave. And . . . I . . ." Much softer, he admitted, "I want to be married first. A new life. For us. Together. If we're married, then no one can take us away from each other. Even your dad would have to concede."

She took a long breath. "Okay, you're going to make me cry, and that's not fair because I'm not the crying type. Does it have to be a big ceremony?" she asked warily. "I'm not the ceremonial type."

"I'd settle for finding a judge willing to perform it," he confessed. "The problem is . . . dragons aren't governed by human laws. We would need to find someone with authority that both of our species obey. That might take a while, and the longer we go without consummating our relationship, the closer to insanity we're going to get."

She drummed her fingers on her arm as she thought quickly. "Okay. Here's what we'll do. Let's skip the kissing and cuddling thing—because even tame sparks can become infernos *fast*—and focus on finding someone that can marry us. We'll hit the road back toward the dragon lands, and once we're married, we'll hide away in your cave and hope that we get lucky enough to make our own furry baby dragon. I'll send a letter to my parents to tell them they'll be grandparents and then we can live happy ever after, right?"

He grinned. "Right."

CHAPTER THREE

It was just as well they decided to wait before becoming lovers. Both were quite famished from the trip and needed to refuel. They set out into the town once more and were relieved to notice most of the heroes had departed. Boy, were *they* in for a surprise! The tavern was open and merry, and the couple headed there for lunch.

Neither had ever been in a tavern before, and the onslaught of sounds and voices and bodies was momentarily disorienting. Both shortly adapted and grabbed seats at the only vacant table. A cheerful waitress dropped off a menu for them, and Liz contentedly studied the offerings. "What do dragons eat anyway?"

"Mostly veggies and fruit but we like bread," he answered absently.

She slowly looked up. "Dragons are *herbivores*? Then why the heck do you have those sharp teeth?"

"Fighting. They're weapons, not tools." He grinned as he perused the salad options. "Of course, we big, mighty, terrible beasts must be meat-eaters since we obviously devour whole the foolish princes who dare test our might. We even snack on princesses." He shot her a decidedly sensual look over the top of the menu. "I'm looking forward to snacking on mine."

She hastily drank her water. "You have to admit it *is* unexpected for you to be veggie eaters." She pouted. "I like red meat. Would I have to give it up?"

"Nah. We can adapt for you omnivore types. We don't eat meat because we can't digest it. It's not that we're bothered by it." He held up a hand to get their waitress' attention. When she hurried over, he smiled. "One large Veggie Lover salad for me, and a beer."

"Ale," Liz requested. She handed over the menu with a smile as well. "And the rare cut of the day."

"Sure thing. Give us 'bout half an hour for the meals." She headed behind the bar and returned shortly with their drinks. "Here you go. Enjoy."

Liz sipped her ale happily. She very rarely got to indulge in drinking anything except wine. It was such a delicate and refined drink that royalty pretty much drank nothing else. It was considered one of the reasons most royals couldn't match the endurance of peasants in a drinking contest.

She and Magnus enjoyed people-watching while they waited for their meals, and both dug in happily once they were served. They debated over dessert and then decided to split a piece of decadent chocolate cake. Dragons were herbivores, but they loved sweets in all shapes and sizes.

They were lingering over the last few bites when a conversation from the next table drifted close. "Did you hear the first set of heroes can't find the kidnapped princess?" the one woman asked her companion. "The king is getting vexed. I think I heard from someone that he might be trying to make a deal with the Wizard Rovan."

"Ugh." Her husband sat back on a scowl. "That's asking for further trouble. Isn't Rovan the one who uses all of that shady magic? The king is only going to make things worse for himself."

Liz scowled and pushed away the plate. "Well, there went my appetite."

"Mine too." Magnus got to his feet. "I'll pay for our meal and we can rest for the remainder of the day. We'll set out first thing tomorrow morning to head for the dragon settlement. We'll still be safer there than anywhere. Deals with shady wizards? That sounds like the makings of some serious trouble."

"Agreed."

They spent the rest of the afternoon relaxing at the inn. It wasn't entirely restful though. They had to keep at least a foot of space between themselves, and even that didn't help much. It seemed that the harder they fought, the worst it got. Liz had the mental impression of a piece of rubber pulled too far apart; eventually it would reach its max and yank them together without care or regard for whatever else was going on.

They set out onto the road again right after dawn the following day. Liz was armed with a sword this time thanks to a stop at a shop. "Will you protect my virtue?" Magnus teased her lightly.

She shot him a heated look. "As if you don't know that I'm the biggest danger to your virtue. Will this be easier to handle once we're lovers?"

"Not really. This is pretty much how we're going to be all season." He winced wryly. "Guess I owe an apology to some friends and neighbors for complaining about the noise they make. I have a whole new sympathy." He couldn't resist tangling his fingers into her hair for a moment. "And I think I understand what my elder was saying when she mentioned it was daunting at first but enjoyable once you got used to it."

"I do feel strangely happy," she concurred. "I mean, I'm slightly insane, half tempted to rip off your clothes, and on the point of discovering self-combustion, but I'm actually *happy*. Maybe because it feels good to want someone and be wanted that much." She shot him an impish grin. "Not to mention we both know we're *really* going to enjoy working off the frustration part. I do believe you're going to make it worth waiting for, Magnus."

"I would agree."

She lifted a brow. "Is that because you've never, hmm, *tested* this form, or because you've never mated in any sense of the word?"

He smiled. "We mate for life, remember?" He gave a gusty sigh. "Too bad you can't take a dragon form. Then we would have two ways to *test*, as you put it."

"And make enough noise to get revenge on your neighbors?"

"I'm not admitting it if it's true."

The teasing came to an abrupt halt when bushes rustled around them. Before they could move, a band of men leapt out of hiding. All were armed with enchanted weapons sure to do a lot of damage to any magical creature, even a dragon. "Ah ha!" one exclaimed. "You must be the princess we're looking for! Come with us and you'll get home safely, Your Highness."

Liz covered her face with a hand. "Uh, gentlemen, I do hate to break the bad news, but I wasn't kidnapped. I went willingly. We're on a journey." Among other things. "Do I *look* like I've been kidnapped? I mean, if *you* were going to kidnap a princess, wouldn't you lock her up somewhere?"

"That's not how it works, dear." One of the men propped his sword on his shoulder. "Rovan hired us to return you at all costs, and the dragon is to become steaks for the banquet. You're coming with us whether you like it or not." He smirked rudely when she drew her sword. "Really? What do you know about weapons?"

She calmly aimed the tip under his chin and watched him warily ease back. "A lot more than you might be comfortable admitting." She slipped the backpack off her shoulder with her free hand and held it out to Magnus. "Hold this."

"Yes, dear."

Having the element of surprise on her side allowed her to knock two of the slayers flat before the other two realized what she was doing. She competently kept the two still standing at bay before finally finding a place where she could kick one hard enough to plant him on his butt in the dirt. The last was the leader, and he was both skilled and strong. They went back and forth several times before he finally barked out something that sounded like a foreign language.

One of the downed men held up his hand and a large ball of magic formed. Magnus gave a shout as he lunged forward, but he wasn't quick enough. The blast smashed into Liz's blade and sent it reeling out of her hands. The backwash of the attack knocked her back several steps where she tripped over a stump and landed on the ground.

One of the other men had gained his feet and he grabbed Magnus. The leader reached down and hauled Liz up to her feet by her arm. Fury blazed out of his eyes. "Not bad," he grit out. "They said you were an odd one, and now I see what they mean. You should have played nice, princess. We have no reason to bring you home in one piece. They'll blame your buddy there."

She leaned back as he leaned in and nearly gagged at the stench of his breath. "I'll scream from here until next year what really happened. You can't intimidate me into anything!" Her free hand shot up and smashed into his chest with a force that made his internal organs feel strangely gooey for a moment. He staggered and she tore herself out of his grip. It tore her sleeve in the process, and the ugly bruises forming on her skin became visible.

Magnus saw red. He had been pushing the edge of his temper already with threats to his mate, but her calm handling of the ordeal had kept him tame. Seeing marks on her skin ripped aside every shred of civility. Nothing and no one *dared* harm a dragon's mate. With a quick application of the technique he had been taught, he got free of the one holding him.

A surge of bright magic changed him back into dragon shape. A snarl locked in his throat as he pounced on the first offender and broke several bones. A second barely managed a scream before claws tore him apart. Two others managed to escape. The leader grabbed up his sword and rushed in to attack, but Magnus smacked the blade away. Smoke puffed from his nose as he grabbed the man in a painful vise made from sharp claws. "Do humans fly?" he rumbled. "Let's find out!" He whirled around and hurled the man through the air with casual and almost brutal strength. He had no care for where he landed or if he would survive.

Liz had a feeling her jaw was hanging open. She had almost forgotten that her playful, sexy, would-be lover was actually a very big, very easily provoked, beast with claws and teeth. "Uhm." Her eyes widened as he moved closer, and her heart began to race. Not with fear. Strangely, she was feeling a little bit thrilled. She kind of had the feeling that only his current shape kept him from tumbling her into the bushes. "May I retract an earlier statement?" she asked breathlessly.

"Which one?" He lowered his head, and fresh rage flared as he saw the splotches of black and blue on her arm.

"I have changed my mind and I entirely don't mind being rescued, if you're doing it. It was really amazing."

A low laugh rumbled in his chest. "I didn't rescue you. I just cleaned up what you started." He delicately began to use a claw to rip her sleeve away from the shoulder entirely. That done, he softly nuzzled her arm and then began to gently lick the bruises.

Pink flushed her face. "Dare I ask?" She turned her head in surprise as she felt magic tingling through her arm. Her eyes widened slightly as she saw the bruises disappearing and felt the dull ache fading. "You can *heal*? With a *lick*?"

"Gift of a mated dragon." He watched in satisfaction as the marks faded. "I'm sure there's some rational explanation that has something to do with the chemistry that makes us mates at all, but we dragons just say that love heals and call it a gift from the God of Love." He gently closed his claws around her body. It was hard to believe that much strength was packed inside such a delicate frame. "We're getting out of here. We'll stop long enough in a town for supplies and then fly non-stop for my cave and safety."

She still wasn't wholly breathing as he flew up into the air and effectively carried her off. Marriage or no marriage, she was absolutely going to seduce him as soon as they were in his cave. It would still be a new life. Or, maybe, they might get *really* lucky and find someone to help them in the next town.

He landed just out of sight of the town and put her down. He shifted back to human, but his head hadn't stopped spinning before she leapt into his arms and kissed him wildly. He growled softly and dragged her even closer. He whirled and pinned her against the nearest tree in order to have the freedom of his hands. His fingers rushed open the laces of her tunic to find the heated flesh beneath. It never occurred to either of them that they were a hundred yards from a town and hardly somewhere private. The season had consumed them.

Perhaps luckily, a pair of doves flying by happened to coo loudly enough that it brought back a moment of cognizance. Magnus cursed ripely under his breath as he tried to lace Liz's tunic again but his shaking fingers kept interfering. Her entire body quivered violently against his, and her dazed emerald eyes looked like dark gems. "We won't survive three months," she managed to say huskily.

"Oh, we will," he muttered, "but we won't be walking after. Also? If you get pregnant early on, the season will lessen its grip because, hey, we succeeded at what it wanted."

She held up a trembling finger. "I would like to state that I wouldn't mind a month of mindless passion before we conceive and go back to the normal mindless-yet-endurable version."

"So noted." He managed to put her tunic back to rights and tucked her cloak around her shoulders again to hide her torn sleeve. "You said no kissing," he scolded her.

"It's not my fault that getting rescued by you got to me like that." She couldn't resist snuggling up against his side as they walked into the town. His skin always seemed a bit on the cool side but felt really delicious against hers. He warmed up pretty quickly, too, if she was kissing him. It would be fun to see how warm he got if she started petting him.

"Stop smiling like that," he grumbled. "You're not making my life easier, Liz." He firmly extricated his arm and poked her in the nose. "Stay here and be good. I'll buy what we need. We should reach my cave by nightfall."

"Okay." She watched him walk away and looked around curiously. The town was much like any other of its size, she supposed, since it had all the same amenities of the last one they had seen. It felt kind of boring, so maybe she wasn't cut out to travel after all. At least, not to the small places. It might be fun to visit other large cities. There was always more to do.

An elderly hand holding a red rose lowered in front of her. She turned her head quickly and discovered an old man had come up behind her silently. His was a wizened face set with surprisingly youthful blue eyes. She took the rose and smiled. "Thank you. What's this for?"

"You look a bit lost." He cocked his head slightly. "What has you troubled, my dear?

"Well . . ." She had never been the type to dump her problems on other people, yet something about this stranger just made her trust him. "I'm in a bit of a bind." She gestured to where Magnus was haggling price on bread with a baker. "We want to get married. Start a life together."

He shrewdly eyed Magnus. "Dragon, yes?"

"Yes."

"You worry that the laws of the land will not govern your union." He tugged lightly on his beard. "A fair worry, but perhaps time for a change. Now, I have a fondness for true love." Humor filled his eyes. "I imagine it is quite . . . tempestuous for you two this time of year."

"Good word for it," she muttered.

"Indeed. I think perhaps I may be able to assist you, Elizabelle." He rummaged in the pack slung across his body and emerged with a scroll. "Behold! A creation of the purest magic in the land and the force of raw love energy. A contract forged by the hands of Eros and Psyche themselves."

Her eyes slowly widened. "The God of Love?"

"And the Goddess of Destiny. They seem to be fond of you." He offered the contract.

She unrolled it and began to read. Delight slowly rose inside as she realized what she held. There, in plain language, was a marriage agreement. The seal located in the upper corner was unfamiliar somehow, yet she felt she ought to know it. "If Magnus and I sign this, we are married?" she asked eagerly. "And it says here it will be enforced. Will it?"

"You can be sure it will be Enforced to the highest degree," he promised softly.

She rolled it back up again and tucked it into a pocket inside her cloak. She rose on her toes to quickly brush a kiss over the wrinkled cheek before her. "Thank you so much!" She turned to hurry away but something made her glance back. Perhaps unsurprisingly, the old man had disappeared. She just smiled. Good spirits came in all kinds.

Magnus walked up with a large sack slung over his shoulder. "Phew! We're good to go. We'll have enough to wait out the storm likely to hit just after we get home. It's promising to be one hell of a blizzard." He winced. "We'll see if we manage to stick to our promise when we're closed in with no outside forces for a few days."

She bit back a smile. "I think we'll be fine. Let's go now. I want to see your cave!" She paused. "Uhm, not to be too *human* on you, but . . . do you have furniture? Like a bed . . . chairs . . . things other than just a cave floor and copious piles of gemstones? Blankets?"

"Blankets, yes. Furniture will have to come later. I'm sorry. I *can* promise a mattress though. I have one for my dragon form. Big and fluffy with down feathers. We might get lost in it for now, but it won't be a floor."

"That works for me."

They left town to where there was room to shift, and the storm clouds were indeed moving in overhead. This part of Mirage always got heavy snowfall when winter arrived. Magnus turned back to dragon form, and Liz climbed up onto his back. She held onto their packs as he flew low through the trees. They didn't want to fly high enough to be spotted. The storm would also buy them a few more days, thankfully.

It was hard to determine the passage of time thanks to the heavy cover, and the gloom thickened as the air got colder and colder. They circled into the mountains as the first fat flakes began to fall, and they were both lightly dusted by the time they arrived at his hidden cave. He uncovered the entrance and ushered her inside, and then closed it tightly behind himself before he shrank down to human again.

She was surprised to discover it felt warm inside the cave. "How is that possible?" she asked curiously.

"There's a vein of hot springs running under the mountains. We figured out ages ago how to divert them to warm our homes during winter times. It's especially useful since half the clan is mated and doesn't emerge during those months." He slung the packs over his shoulder and took her hand. "Come with me," he urged. "I don't know if my treasure will suit a princess, but I will share it with you gladly."

She caught her breath as he brought her around the last corner and revealed the heaps upon heaps of stone in the raw that he had mined. Torches filled the place with flickering warm light, and proudly displayed the bounty. "They're beautiful!" She reverently reached out to touch a huge deposit of emerald that was eerily like her eye color. "You mine these yourself?"

"I do." He put the packs down. Her delight at seeing his collection made him happy. "I like them, but I'd be happy to spend them. I don't have a need to hoard when I can find more. We could use them to pay for more travels. Or not." He shrugged with a wry smile. "I didn't enjoy it as much as I thought."

"I was thinking the same. Maybe I'd want to see big cities and then come home to a base. Like here." She picked up a piece of ruby and admired it. "I could make a necklace from this," she noted wistfully. Realizing what she had said, she turned with wide eyes. "I mean . . ."

"Ah ha!" He grinned. "I was wondering if you had any other talents you hadn't shared. The princess who should be adorned in jewels would rather be *making* them."

She winced wryly. "I had to do it on the sly. I always wished I could be common so I could open a trade."

He spread his hands. "Here you go," he said simply. "What I have is yours to use. If you need gold or silver, we can trade with other dragons. You can make your jewelry and then we can travel and sell it. The best of all worlds." Peach climbed his cheeks. "And, you know, if we have a baby someday. I could watch over him or her if you were working hard. Travel as a family."

She took a deep breath. It seemed like such an impossible dream that he offered her. There was no recrimination for her less than ladylike skills and graces. He loved everything about her the way she loved everything about him. If they were the new cycle, then the new cycle would be wonderful. "Magnus." She slowly drew the scroll out of her cloak. "This was given to me."

He took it and opened it. His eyes began to widen as he read. "What?" he breathed. "We're married if we sign this?"

"It is overseen and Enforced by the highest of powers. The very protectors of lovers themselves. They're real. They're not a faerie tale. All species abide by the laws of love. Neither your clan nor my family could dare argue." She held up a pen. "I don't need a ceremony. Maybe a party eventually, if anyone wants to celebrate. Will the dragons like me?" she asked hesitantly. "We've assumed they would accept us."

"It's not an assumption. They might be surprised since it's unexpected, but if we're mates, then we're mates. They'll just throw a party to celebrate and probably kidnap a human doctor so our doctors can learn what they need to take care of you as needed." He took the pen from her and signed on the line above his name. "What's the line? 'I thee wed.'"

She signed as well and smiled. "I thee wed." She thought about things for a moment. "I want to make our rings."

"Done." He dropped the scroll on the ground and pounced on her to scoop her up into his arms. Her shriek of laughter made him grin as he swung around and strode past the piles of jewels. "I have a very big bed. It has blankets. We can make a nest and not emerge for a day." The wailing of the storm overhead seemed to thicken and he slowly smiled. "Maybe three days, even."

She spotted the large and definitely fluffy bed they approached. It wasn't *too* big. He was only ten feet long, and the bed was only two feet bigger than that. She laughed again as he tossed her onto it and she sank in. "I like it!" She closed her eyes and spread her arms wide for a moment. Movement made her open her eyes once more and she looked up to see her husband kneeling beside her.

The hunger on his face stirred up every primal urge. Any hope of maintaining the lighthearted mood simply evaporated. She rose up to her knees to face him and buried her hands in his hair to drag him down for the kisses she needed more than air. His hands clenched hard around her waist as he fed from her mouth, and that wonderful low growl came from his chest.

A small gasp was all she could manage as he literally tore away her cloak and what remained of her tunic-dress. She yanked wildly at his tunic in turn and he ripped it off quickly. She tried to reach for him, but he caught her around the waist and lifted her with effortless strength to bury his face between her breasts. "I like human-type mammals," he rumbled. His teeth scraped deliciously. "So soft. Silky. Hot."

Hot? She was burning alive with the need to touch and be touched. She could feel her womb clenching and unclenching in greedy demand, and every pulse in her body throbbed with wild pleasure. "Tease later," she managed to say. "Not now. I can't stand it."

He had waited too damn long to rush that much. He ripped away her bra so that he could feast upon her damp flesh with hungry kisses. She moaned softly and another growl answered her. He yanked and tore away the rest of her clothes until she was finally naked in his arms. A bit dazed, he stared at her. He had found no treasure more beautiful than the creature in his arms. Maybe he would become a hoarder after all.

Their lips met in another desperate kiss and his breath whooshed out as she tumbled him over. She could not strip him as quickly as he had stripped her, but she was surprisingly strong and efficient. As soon as he was naked, he wrapped her within his arms and held on. The sensation of bare skin against bare skin made them both shudder.

He rolled over again and pinned her to the bed as he kissed her greedily. His freed hand slid between her legs only to find her more than ready for him. The first stroke of his fingers made her cry out. The second had her arching. It was such an erotic sight that he fought for control long enough to stroke her again.

"Hurry *up*!" she demanded breathlessly. Fingers stroked again and her breath broke on a sob. "I'm getting you back for this!"

He dragged her closer and braced himself over her. She fiercely wrapped her legs around his waist as he plunged deep into her body, and all she could manage was a strangled gasp as she felt him pulsing deep inside her body.

Nothing else mattered but the driving urge to live. To celebrate life. To create life. He drove into her again and again until her nails bit into his shoulders in desperation. When ecstasy finally arrived, it boiled up from some hidden place inside until it consumed them both in fire. Somehow, blessedly, the searing heat of his release deep inside her body seemed to help ease the demand of the season. Whether it would last or not, she didn't know, but it was enough to simply savor the lingering throb inside her entire body. She had no energy or desire to be anywhere else but there in his arms.

He had enough presence of mind to catch his weight on his arms to not smother her, but that was the extent of his ability. A little shift of her body allowed him to relax fully and they could both focus on catching their breath.

"Umph." She found the strength to wrap her arms around his shoulders. "So very worth waiting for," she sighed contentedly.

"Agreed." He turned his head to nuzzle her neck. Just the scent of her sweaty skin was enough to bring fresh desire rushing back in. She might or might not be pregnant yet. He wouldn't be sure for another few days when her body chemistry began to change and affect her scent. Only then would the season ease. In the meantime, they had a storm to enjoy. "Again?" he asked huskily as he tasted her pulse.

"If you insist," she murmured breathlessly. "But I'd recommend feeding me and letting me bathe after else I be too sore and tired for anything else."

"Feeding I can do." He slowly stroked in and out and savored the way her eyes deepened and darkened with arousal. "I can even offer a bath. Don't worry about being sore, though." He pressed deeper and caught her around the waist when she arched in reflex. "Remember what we dragons can do for our mates."

"I think I like being a dragon's mate." She was still going to have to get her revenge on him, though. Turnabout was assuredly fair play.

CHAPTER FOUR

Three blissful days passed in quiet solitude. Magnus showed Liz his portion of the hot spring that he used as a bath, and many playful moments were spent splashing each other mercilessly. They explored the stacks of gems for the best ones for their rings and finally found the ones they wanted. They could get her some tools later. They ate their meals wherever they liked, and he winced wryly when she revealed her spare clothes that she had no intention of wearing until they left the cave. It was best to not risk getting these ones ripped off too.

They made love as often as their bodies would let them. Intimacy infused the entire cave until there wasn't any place that they couldn't look at without one of them getting the giggles. Neither had ever spent that much time alone with another person let alone expected to enjoy it so deeply. It was more than just the frenzy of the season. It was the quiet moments in between where they talked, and laughed, and shared secrets.

Only one sobering moment came, and it was when she finally asked softly, "Will you age with me, Magnus?"

His fingers buried in her tangled hair. They were snuggling together under the blankets, contentedly entwined after the most recent wave of passion. "Of course," he answered simply. "I've already adjusted my aging process. All creatures with longevity are born knowing how to abandon it if needed. For as long as we are given, we will be together."

The storm had finally lessened its fury. Being as sane as they might be for the time, they reluctantly got out of bed. She got dressed in her spare clothes, and she grinned as she watched him turn to dragon and back. The process recreated clothes for him. "At least until I can get more of my own," he assured her.

"You don't need to stay in this form all the time," she noted reasonably. "I think you're quite handsome as a dragon."

"I've found I'm strangely comfortable on two legs." He grinned sheepishly. "And the longer I maintain it, the better I get at it. I might be less likely to trip you onto the floor."

"On *accident* anyway." Her brows lifted as she heard a loud scratching noise at the entrance. "Is that the equivalent of a knock?"

"It is. The one sound we can't ignore is a claw on stone." He shifted into dragon again and reached down to offer her a claw. He lifted her up to sit on his shoulder and called, "You may enter!"

A few moments later, Coral walked cautiously into the cave. "Magnus?" she asked skeptically. "We hadn't heard from you after you left, and someone said they saw you return right before the storm. Why didn't you . . ." She trailed off as she spotted Liz sitting on Magnus' shoulder. "Oh. You have a guest." It dawned and she groaned. "Tell me you didn't kidnap her from the kingdom!"

"I asked him to," Liz assured her hastily. "I'm the one who called to him. I didn't expect my father to misunderstand and overreact."

Coral eyed her knowingly and then Magnus. "I'm sure that wasn't all you two didn't expect."

Magnus eyed her back. "You sound entirely unsurprised."

"I admit I'm not." Coral shrugged with a smile. "It happens infrequently. Once or twice every few generations. It's just not talked about because the humans get so damned pissy about the silliest things. Oh, sure, half-faeries are just fine, but the gods forbid there be half-dragons running around."

Delight brightened Liz's face. "Then we *might* have a child?"

"Truth told, you two have better odds than most dragon couples. That's why we have breeding seasons, young ones. Dragons are not exceptionally fertile. Humans, however, are. We shall have to see if you have been blessed after the last few days." She smirked at Magnus. "Better sympathy now for your neighbors?"

"And then some," he grumbled. He huffed out a breath. "Liz and I are married."

Scaly brows lifted. "How is that possible?" She spotted the scroll that Liz held up, and she recognized its type immediately. She had seen one or two in her long life. "Ah. Of course. In a way, that does not surprise me either. Well then. Come along, whelps. We should go to the council and explain what has occurred."

Liz felt curiously unafraid and not nervous at all as she rode Magnus' back while he flew toward the meeting area. Coral's reaction alone had told her that she would find far more understanding here than among her own kind. As she looked around at the series of caves and cliffs scattered across the mountains that made up the clan's settlement, she decided she very much liked it there. If they could only get an alliance going! Humans and dragons would work together really well. After all, any hero worth his salt would probably be more effective with a dragon for an ally rather than an enemy.

The elders were a bit nonplussed by the willing arrival of a human princess within the settlement, but they listened intently as Magnus candidly recounted the events up to and including the realization that Liz was his mate and their marriage contract overseen by the God of Love and Goddess of Destiny. He finished the tale by saying, "We would have checked in sooner, but, well, the storm was convenient."

"There isn't a mated dragon on grounds that would begrudge you that," one elder noted dryly. He sighed gustily. "I miss those days."

Liz bit her lip to hide a smile. She had asked about what would happen when she was past her childbearing years, and Magnus had cheerfully told her that dragons had the same thing happen around the same equivalent age. Male and female alike were unable to produce children once they were more than halfway through their lifespan. It ensured that any children born to a couple would keep their parents until they were adults themselves (barring outside factors, of course).

"Well!" Another elder bent down to peer closer at Liz. "Welcome to the settlement, Liz. I think we should name you an honorary dragon and have a celebratory party to commemorate your marriage to our Magnus." She winked roguishly. "We'll then leave you two mates alone to hopefully produce our first half-dragon baby in two centuries." She patted Liz gently on the head. "You need not worry about your care during such a time. We have skilled healers, and one is old enough to have tended the last birth. You are in good claws, little dragon."

Liz looked at Magnus with a smile. "I *really* like it here. I think I finally have somewhere to fit in!"

Dragons were a resourceful lot who loved a good party. Word spread rapidly about the events and food was hastily assembled for the celebration. One of the cooks even graciously made a dish with meat in it just for Liz; breeding season was murder on energy levels, and they didn't want her to miss out on her needed nutrients just because they were herbivores. The sheer level of their consideration for her made Liz begin to realize that dragons might just be the more civilized of the two races. And she was just fine with that, really.

Those who could take a human form did so as well to help make more room for those who couldn't. They played music, laughed, danced, and had a grand time celebrating the new couple's union. Magnus introduced Liz to his parents, and she could only laugh when they both enthusiastically hugged her and thanked her for taming Magnus' adventurous spirit. Taming, nothing! They fully intended to share and enjoy it.

The party was brought to an abrupt and crashing halt by the sudden explosion of magical fireballs against the side of the mountain. "Raid!" someone shouted. "There's a raid attacking! They bear the colors of the Montgomery Kingdom and the Wizard Rovan!"

"Someone must've been watching the settlement," Coral said grimly. "To arms!" she shouted. "Drive them out but avoid bloodshed if possible! This is merely a misunderstanding!"

It was hard to call it a mere misunderstanding when Rovan was leading a small army of heroes and princes desperate to prove their valor. Liz scowled and looked around. "Alright! Who here hoards weaponry as treasure?" A few claws went up. "I need a sword and a shield. I can't promise they'll be intact when I return them. I might be bashing heads in."

Almost collectively, the entire clan fell in love. One dragon hurried off to his cave and shortly returned with a polished sword and jewel-covered shield. Liz took them gratefully and ran over to where Magnus was standing in dragon form with Coral. The fight had already started outside. More than one hero looked slightly surprised at having his life spared if he was knocked down. A rising tide of confusion began to move through some of the army.

The doors burst open and the fight poured into the celebration hall. Dragons might have been bigger targets, but they could throw magic and breathe fire. Liz darted fearlessly around legs and tails to knock back any enemy that threatened to do more permanent injury to her new family.

One prince in particular caught her eye as he dueled Coral. He was by far the most skilled of the bunch and he had already done a great deal of damage. Liz gave a little snarl and hurled her sword at him like a spear. It struck his blade with enough force to knock it out of his hand. Before he could turn, she was on him. The next thing he knew, he was flat on the stone and his head was reeling around on his shoulders.

He shook his head to clear the stars and looked up to see who had defeated him. Shock made his jaw drop. "*Elizabelle*?!"

Liz stared at him in turn. "Solomon? What are you *doing* here?" She knelt beside her brother and scowled. "Are you insane? Why didn't you or Mother and Father think to *check* before assuming I was kidnapped? This is *me*, remember? As if I would be kidnapped by anyone! *You* taught me to defend myself, and *I* invited Magnus up to my tower! Any guard would confirm it!"

He slowly sat up. "What the hell is going on?" he asked warily.

She grabbed his head and jerked it around to stare at the fight. "See that? The dragons aren't playing nice because they think you're cute. They don't want to fight! Damn it, Solomon, I'm *married* to Magnus! We're mates, and dragons mate for life. The dragons consider me one of their own now!"

His head swung back to her. "Are you serious?" he demanded.

"After three days of trying to conceive a half-dragon baby? I'm damned serious."

That was not a mental image he had needed, though he was kind of tickled at the idea of his sister as a mother. A half-dragon baby also sounded, well, really adorable. "You're happy here? Really happy?"

"Happier than I ever have been," she confirmed softly. "Solomon . . . everything we've ever thought about dragons is wrong. Magnus proved the truth of it when he tried to offer alliance. And what did our Father do? Brushed him off and called him a beast. There's so much we could learn from each other. This entire fight is pointless."

He took a long breath. "Well. I feel foolish." He let her tug him up to his feet, and he looked at Coral shamefully. "My sincerest apologies. I sought only to save my sister."

"You are forgiven," the elder assured him. "We have never held a grudge against your kind. To mark all of you as blind, bloodthirsty beasts would be to treat you no better than you have treated us." She winced. "My mate will tend to my wounds, young ones. Hurry and end this madness."

Solomon and Liz rushed into the crowd, and both began to grab as many of the humans as they could to spread the word that Liz was willing, the dragons were not evil, and this entire fight was only going to make things worse. Blessedly, heroes and princes alike were quite susceptible to the pleas of a beautiful maiden. Liz knew it, and she played it for all it was worth by sprinkling a few tears and begging for a chance to be happy with her dragon.

The fight ended swiftly thereafter and turned into an almost eerie silence. Wounds dotted both sides but there had been no casualties. Liz looked around quickly but did not spot her husband. She could see his clan mates, but not him. A cold wind touched her skin and she looked quickly toward the entrance to see it was still open. She ran swiftly toward the opening. The sound of magic made her heart skip a beat with fear. "Magnus!"

She could see the bloodstained ground where a particularly vicious fight had occurred. Snow was disturbed and shoved aside as if something large had been dragged through. She scrambled down the cliffs as fast as possible and ran to the edge where she could see the road below. Her heart stopped entirely.

A very large cage was being hauled away by oxen, and her mate was inside the cage. He looked bloody though somewhat whole overall, and he had been chained and muzzled. A man in the familiar clothes of a wizard rode at the front of the cage, and any time that Magnus tried to break free, the wizard fired off a magical blast that just did more damage.

"Rovan." Solomon had come up beside Liz. Anger darkened his face. "I didn't like it from the beginning when Father reached out to him to assist the men trying to rescue you. There were plenty of other good wizards and witches to seek aid from, and he chose the one who did nothing but bad magic."

"What would taking Magnus back to Father without me hope to accomplish?" Liz demanded sharply.

"Quite simply," an unfamiliar woman's voice said behind them, "Rovan intends to claim Magnus murdered you and should be killed. If Magnus dies, you will die as well. Mated pairs simply can't exist apart any more than lovebirds could. A failure to save you would in no way stop Rovan from claiming his reward for capturing the beast that slayed you."

The siblings turned to discover that an old woman had somehow joined them. She seemed quite beautiful especially in her advanced age, and iridescent black eyes held little bits of sparks that could only be evidence of temper. "Who are you?" Liz asked slowly.

"That is not important." She held out an interesting mask that shimmered with magic. "This is called the Mask of Illusions. It will change your appearance to suit your needs. It will serve you well in rescuing your dragon, Liz. Consider it a . . . prop on loan to you while your contract is still in progress."

Liz took the mask and studied it for a moment before turning to her brother. "I need an enchanted sword and the mantle of a dragon slayer."

"Let's see if the dragons can help." He ran back toward the hall, and she was right on his heels.

The old woman smiled to herself as she watched them go and then sighed as the old man stepped up beside her. "You didn't think to give it to her sooner."

"I assumed you would need something to do, beloved." He scowled down at her, since she stood many inches shorter. "You *should* be resting, though."

She merely snorted at him.

Upon reaching the kingdom, Magnus evaluated his options and decided to change into his human form. His wounds protested the shift, but at least they weren't spread over as large a surface. They even healed to some extent since some couldn't transfer. The muzzle also went away, but his magical chains just shrank down and continued to hold onto his wrists and ankles.

He was pissed, he was scared, and he was confused. The confusion came from much the same wonderings as Liz, but there was an additional confusion for the fact that he was pissed but not *enraged.* The breeding season had made him far more temperamental overall, yet he felt relatively normal in his anger. Maybe because Liz wasn't there? He couldn't really say. The entire thing was new to him.

Rovan eventually stopped the cage outside the castle, and guards came to escort Magnus into the throne room where the king and queen awaited. The wizard walked with a distinct swagger that made Magnus barely refrain from rolling his eyes.

The king glared intently at Magnus. "You have a lot of nerve! Coming here professing to be after alliance, and you take my daughter from me when I refuse! How can you claim to be civilized? Where is my daughter?" he demanded.

Magnus opened his mouth, and Rovan cut in with a falsely sincere tone, "I am sorry, my liege. There was nothing to be done. She has already been slain."

Magnus stared at him. He knew it was a lie. It had to be a lie. He would have felt if he had lost his mate. He would have protested the entire thing, but people in the room were already beginning to cry and wail. The queen dissolved into sobs, and the king seemed pale and sick. It was unlikely anyone would listen to the accused murderer if he tried to protest or explain reality. He needed an outsider to plead his case!

One promptly arrived in an unlikely form. The crown prince burst in the doors and demanded furiously, "Will you all cease this ridiculousness?" He stalked across the room and aligned himself beside Magnus. "Elizabelle is *alive*. Rovan is lying through his teeth in order to secure his reward! Liz was with Magnus in the settlement, certainly, but she was there *willingly*."

"Solomon, are you mad?" his father snapped.

"I am more sane than you!" He gestured at the bound dragon. "I stand by my brother-in-law! He and Liz are married, and their contract is governed by the highest of powers!"

A murmur of disgust began to run through the crowd. Several people looked ill. Vicious whispers of 'unnatural', 'immoral', and 'disgusting' began to be heard. Solomon looked around at all the people who had proclaimed to be civilized, to want their princess' happiness, and he saw finally what his sister already had. He was beginning to prefer the dragons as well.

"Enough!" the king roared as he leapt to his feet. "Fetch me a dragon slayer! This creature's head will roll!" He glared at Solomon. "And you, son, will spend a few days in the dungeon for your foolishness!"

"Why not the tower?" Solomon muttered so low only Magnus heard. "Why do we get the dungeons?"

"You don't cry," his brother-in-law muttered back.

The throne room doors opened and a figure strode inside. A cloak covered him from head to toe, and a mask under the hood kept his face hidden from view. No one who looked at him could seem to put a finger on his height or frame. Solomon and Magnus saw with eyes that loved, however, and could easily see the shorter stature and delicate frame that would not normally belong to any slayer. There was no mistaking that the person in the cloak was a woman.

The slayer stopped beside Magnus, and he barely kept the shock off his face as a familiar scent curled into his lungs. *Liz*. A second shock rippled through his heart and was followed shortly by blinding joy as he smelled something else and realized why his temper had leveled off. Their season had ended.

"You called for a slayer?" The voice that came from within the cloak was impossible for anyone to recognize, except for Solomon and Magnus. "What does he stand accused of?"

"Kidnapping and murder." The king glared malevolently at Magnus. "Your end is here, dragon! You will rue the day you met my daughter!"

"The one thing I will never do," Magnus countered softly, "is ever regret that."

The slayer drew an enchanted sword from a sheath and aimed the tip under Magnus' chin. With shocking speed and accuracy, the blade flashed through the air. It did not go for the dragon's neck, however. It shot downward and cleanly ripped through the magical binds. Shocked gasps and cries rose as Magnus was freed and turned to attack Rovan. The wizard darted away like a coward.

"What is the meaning of this?" the queen snapped.

The slayer reached up to pull down her hood and revealed ebony hair. She calmly removed the sculpted mask she wore, and everyone was immediately able to recognize her. Her armor disappeared to reveal a common tunic and leggings. She casually dropped the cloak on the floor though she retained her weapon. "Rumors of my death were highly exaggerated."

Her father and mother stared at her for long moments. "Elizabelle?" her mother asked in a trembling voice.

Liz turned a narrow look toward Rovan. "You are a lying, cheating, filthy sack of deceit and viciousness." She swung around to her parents. "Read my lips: I was not kidnapped. I was not murdered. The *closest* I have come to being in any danger was when this vile beast," she gestured at the wizard, "sent thugs after me and Magnus that threatened to assault me if I didn't return willingly."

"Then where have you been the last few days?" her father demanded.

A hint of a feminine smirk touched her lips. "Enjoying my honeymoon and dragon breeding season."

Silence fell sharply for long moments. Then, finally, the king sighed. "You are truly in love?"

"Very truly. I am happy, Father. I found where I belong."

He said nothing as he digested that. He reached a decision at last and gave a quick nod. "So be it. From this day forward, let there be al—"

"I don't think so!" Rovan snarled furiously. Magic coalesced around his hands and body. "I was promised a king's fortune, and I will have it!" He gave a bellow of rage as he hurled the blasts right at the thrones where the ruling couple sat.

It never reached them. Magnus shot across the floor and shifted to dragon form just as he reached them. The transformation created a surge of magic that repelled the attack entirely. He spread his wings wide to protect the two humans. "You won't harm my wife's parents!" he snarled. "Though they probably deserve a knock or two," he added under his breath.

A bit shakily, the queen admitted, "I begin to think you're right!"

Solomon drew the sword he wore, and he and his sister went after Rovan as one. The wizard could only fend off one of them at a time. If he tried to blast one of them, the other got in a strike with a sword. The enchanted blade did the most damage, and Rovan realized almost too late that he was outnumbered. He rushed away in a terror and scrambled out of the palace. He made it out into the city before he noticed the shadows moving in. Slowly he looked up and found several dragons hovering in the air.

His terrified shriek cut off abruptly as one of them landed directly on his back and flattened him to the ground with a bone-crunching force. His hand twitched once and then ceased to move at all. The dragon looked around at the astonished gathering of citizens and asked politely, "Oh, sorry. Was this seat taken?"

Inside the throne room, Magnus moved back to Liz's side though he did not leave his natural form. He curled a claw tenderly around her body to keep her close. Everyone watched the absolute trust with which Liz cuddled against his leg, and they at last began to see that there really was true love present.

The king slowly straightened to his full height. "As I was saying before we were interrupted . . . I am sorry." His gaze lowered. "Magnus, I ask your forgiveness. Elizabelle—Liz—my beautiful daughter, I am sorry to you as well." His chin lifted. "Let it be known that the princess has married her chosen suitor, and there is a new prince claimed by this kingdom. Let it be known also that no more will the Montgomery Kingdom condone the senseless hunting of dragons. From this day forward, there will be alliance, and we will do all within our power to bring our fellow kingdoms onboard as well!"

A resounding cheer rose, and Magnus shifted into human form. He promptly laughed as Liz leapt into his arms and kissed him quite soundly in front of the entire court. He swung her in a happy circle before tenderly lowering her to the ground. He pressed his forehead to hers. "How do you feel?" he whispered.

"I feel normal enough," she whispered back. "Should I feel odd?"

"Maybe not yet, but you will soon enough. Did you notice we didn't go nuts from that kiss?"

Delight lit her face. "Really?" A happy laugh bubbled up as she threw her arms around his neck. She turned her head and there was no mistaking the glow in her eyes as she looked at her family. "Mother, you need to learn to knit!"

Well, that called for another celebration. The kingdom threw open its doors to as many dragons as could fit, and a new party was launched. As the dragons had adapted for Liz, so did the humans adapt for the dragons, though there *was* a bit of bemused humor at the realization that dragons were vegetable eaters. The party lasted until the early hours and only broke as dawn approached and it was time for the dragons to return home.

Liz bid a tearful goodbye with her parents with the promise to visit, and for them to visit as well. She turned to hug her brother as well only to realize he had changed into durable clothes for traveling. "Are you leaving now?" she asked curiously.

"I think I am." He smiled. "I think I have a bit more to learn about our world." He kissed her cheek. "Send me word when I'm about to be an uncle, and I'll rush back. Be happy, little sister."

She kissed him in turn. "And you."

They traveled partway together before he turned go down a different road that led the opposite direction of the mountains. Magnus turned to a dragon and Liz started to climb onto his back when she spotted a familiar old man watching them with a smile. "Well, hello!" She walked over to him and held out the contract and mask. "I think I need to give these back to you, don't I? Have we fulfilled the terms?"

He opened the scroll and smiled as the word 'Complete' appeared in red across the middle. "Indeed. It was an honor to aid you." He bowed with more grace than his age implied. He tucked the scroll into his bag once more and headed down the road to where the old woman waited. Their fingers entwined with a nearly sensual sort of belonging, and they simply dissolved into the sunrise within a few steps.

"Who were they?" Magnus murmured.

Liz smiled up at him. "The protectors of lovers." She swung up onto his back gracefully. "Let's go home." She hugged him tight around the neck and sighed contentedly as his wings folded back to hug her in return. "I think we finally have our happy ending."

EPILOGUE

The 3rd District in New York City on Earth was overseen by the company known as Enforcers. The co-owners were Rhianna Taber and Eric Mason; one covered the day-to-day operations and the other worked behind-the-scenes. They had also recently added a sub-partner in order to have someone keeping a more steady watch on the world of Mirage; the two worlds were somewhat glued together, so Enforcers kept an eye on both.

Aaron Taber sauntered into his wife's office and boasted, "I knew all along that they would be perfect."

Rhianna did not look up from where she had been adding notes to their latest scroll. "You wouldn't have even noticed them if I hadn't pointed out where their paths converged."

"Hmph." He leaned on the edge of the desk and watched her put the scroll into a folder that also reflected its completion. "You would not have shared that vision if I had not said that I was intrigued by them."

"And you would not have been intrigued if I had not suggested peeking in on the current events." She opened the drawer where she kept Mirage contracts and slid the folder inside. She closed the drawer with a little snap of satisfaction. Another job well done.

When she got to her feet, she was halted from advancing around the desk by her husband's hands curling warmly around her rapidly expanding waistline. He tugged her closer and smoothed his palm tenderly over the large swell of her belly. "You should be resting. You are carrying twins, my beloved."

"I can't even break a nail without someone fretting," she complained. "The next thing I know, you're going to try to hide me away in some secret palace again!"

"He's not suicidal," came a mutter from the office beside hers, followed by a giggle from another voice.

"You two hush!" Rhianna scolded, but she was smiling. She slid her arms up around Aaron's neck and tugged him down for a lingering kiss. In the last few months, every memory of every painful moment had almost ceased to exist inside their happiness. "We do good work," she murmured.

"We do." He trailed his fingers down her cheek. "Do you suppose Solomon has a story to tell?"

"Don't we all? I suppose we'll just have to see what will happen."

"So sayeth the Goddess of Destiny?"

She just smiled. There would be hundreds of thousands of stories to be told in the future, and each would earn a special place within their files. Until the very force of love itself stopped, there would *always* be a tale to be told that would begin once upon a time, and end happily ever after.

Who could ask for more?

Status: File Complete

Analysis: Sometimes it's the dragon that wins the princess, if the dragon is the one who loves her with all his heart.

Author Notes

And that's all she wrote—almost literally. The District Series has finally come to an end. And here, at the end, I can finally say with sincerity that all along it told Rhianna's story. From the day I set out to write THE SHAUGHNESSY FILE, I knew that THE TABER FILE was where we would end. I hope you loved your journey through my magical District, and I equally hope it is one you will return to again and again.

If you loved this story, or any of my stories, please leave me a review on Amazon! Reviews are the bread and butter of an author's life, and even a simple "More, please!" will keep us going.

You can keep up with me on www.facebook.com/stacyjgarrett or www.stacyjgarrett.com or follow my blog at stacyjgarrett.wordpress.com. I sometimes lurk on Twitter (@stacyjgarrett), and Tumblr as well (stacyjgarrett.tumblr.com).

I can't wait to see you again within my magical District! Until then, keep looking for those happy ever afters!

Stacy J Garrett

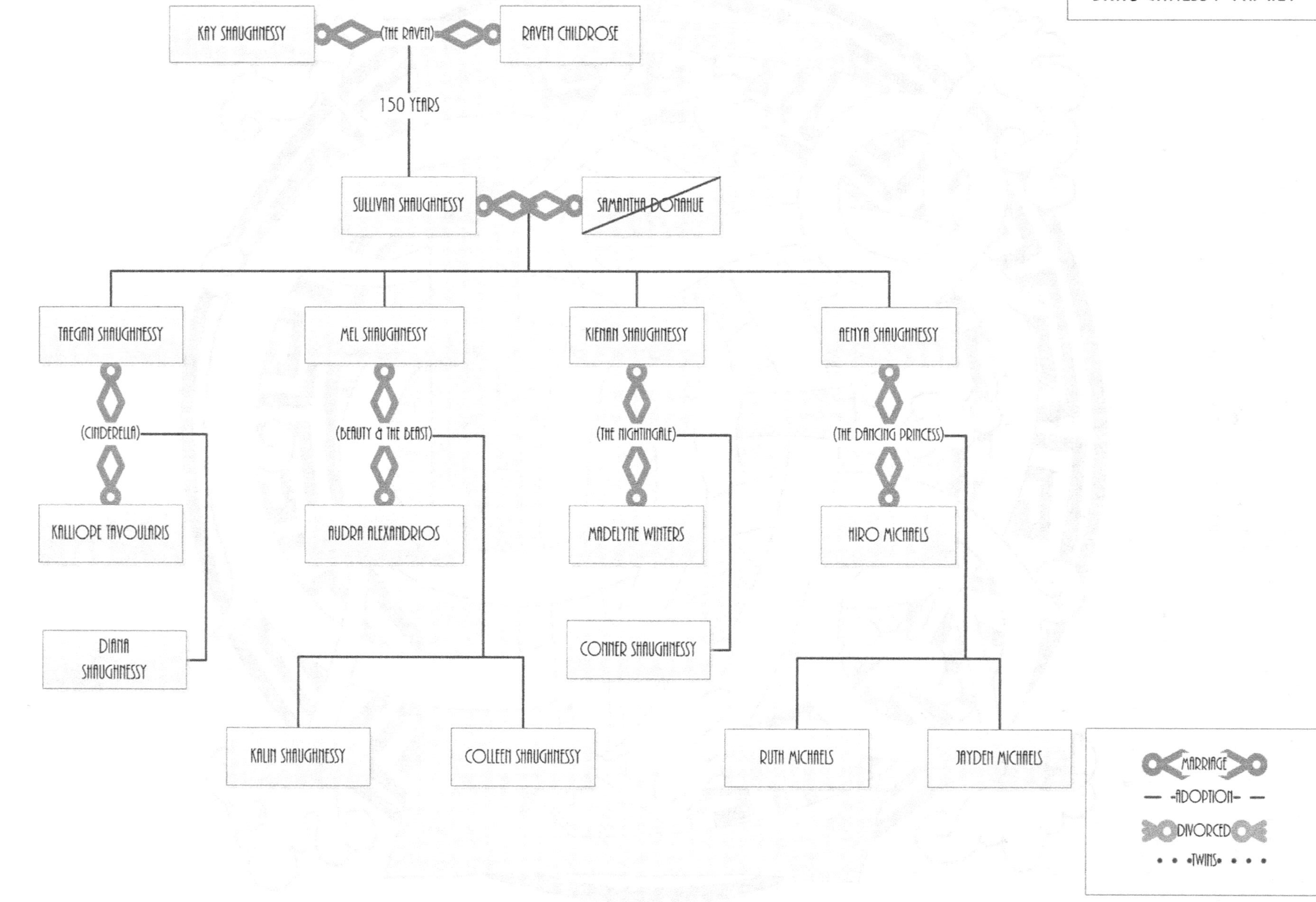

SHAUGHNESSY FAMILY
KAY SHAUGHNESSY
(THE RAVEN)
RAVEN CHILDROSE
150 YEARS
SULLIVAN SHAUGHNESSY
SAMANTHA DONAHUE
TAEGAN SHAUGHNESSY
(CINDERELLA)
KALLIOPE TAVOULARIS
DIANA SHAUGHNESSY
MEL SHAUGHNESSY
(BEAUTY & THE BEAST)
AUDRA ALEXANDRIOS
KALIN SHAUGHNESSY
COLLEEN SHAUGHNESSY
KIENAN SHAUGHNESSY
(THE NIGHTINGALE)
MADELYNE WINTERS
CONNER SHAUGHNESSY
AENYA SHAUGHNESSY
(THE DANCING PRINCESS)
HIRO MICHAELS
RUTH MICHAELS
JAYDEN MICHAELS
MARRIAGE
ADOPTION
DIVORCED
TWINS

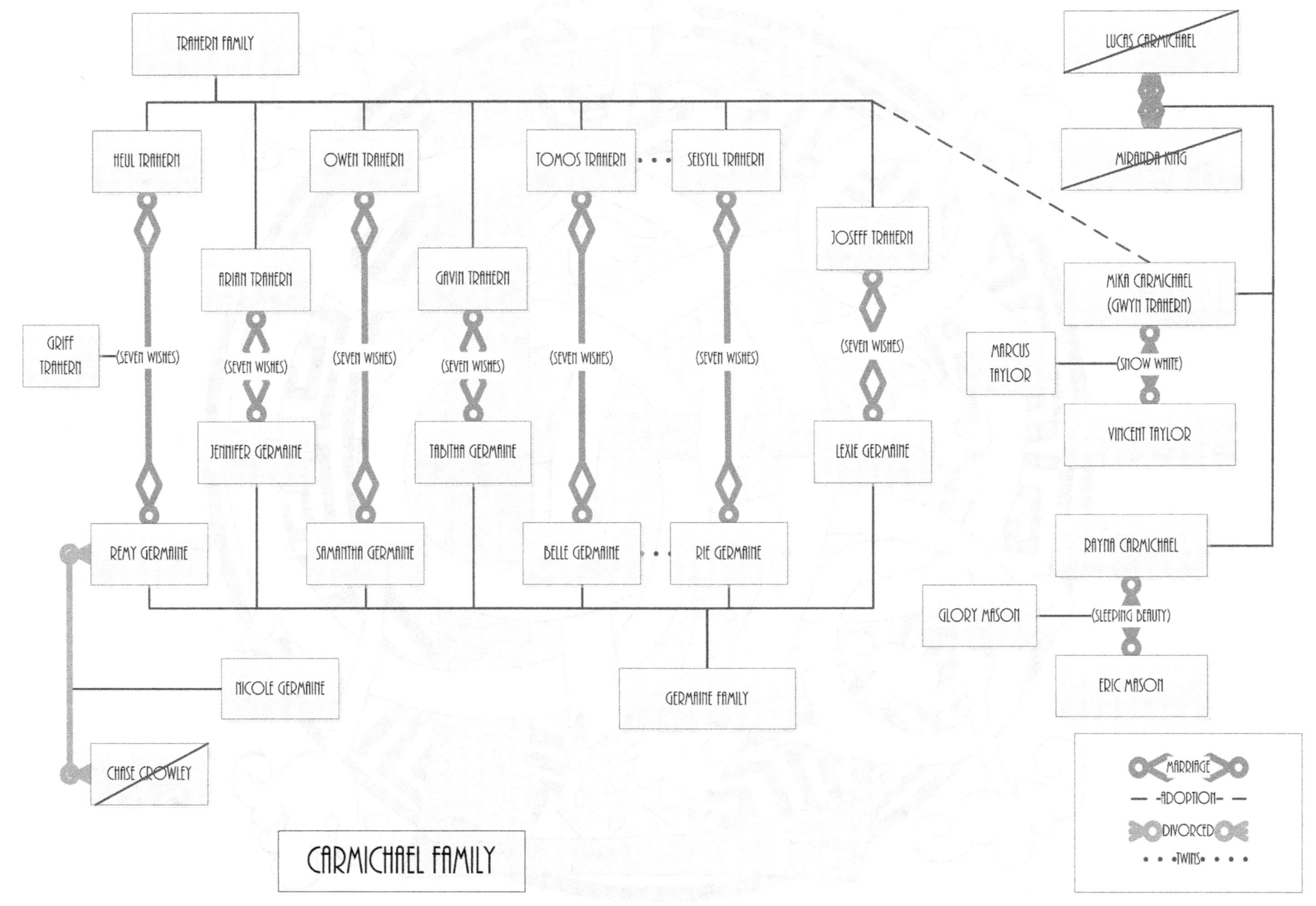

CARMICHAEL FAMILY

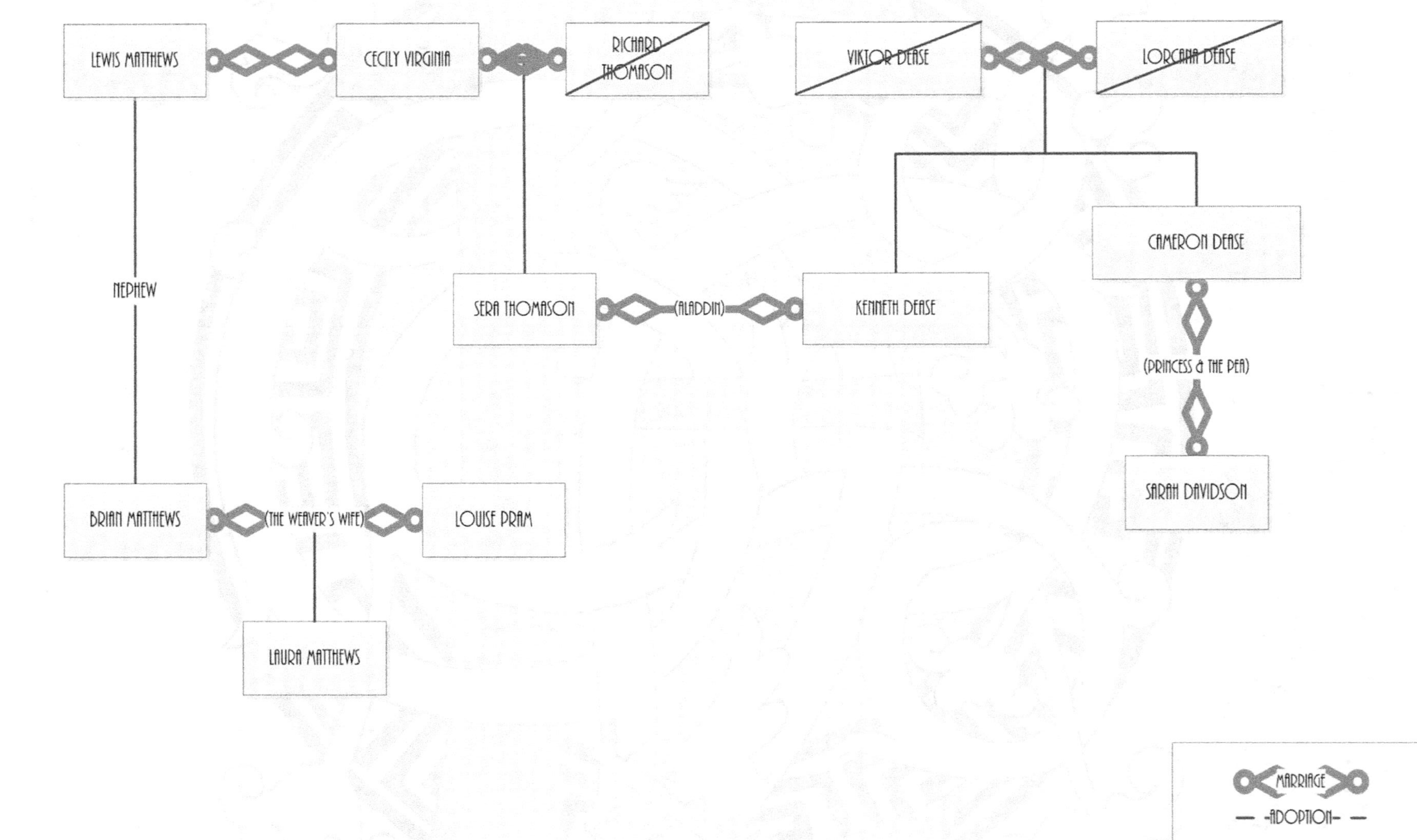

DEASE FAMILY

LUCINO FAMILY

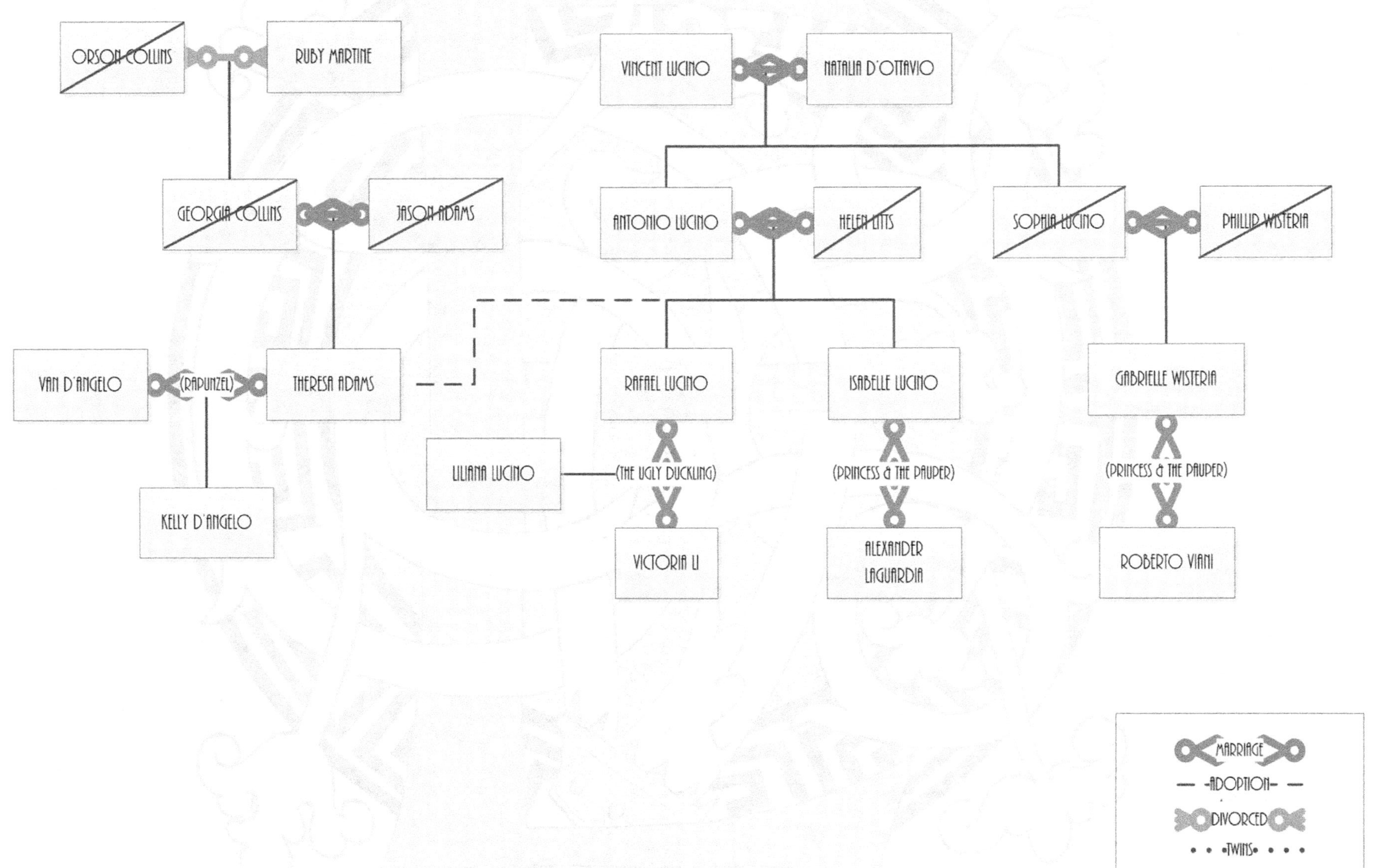

TABER FAMILY

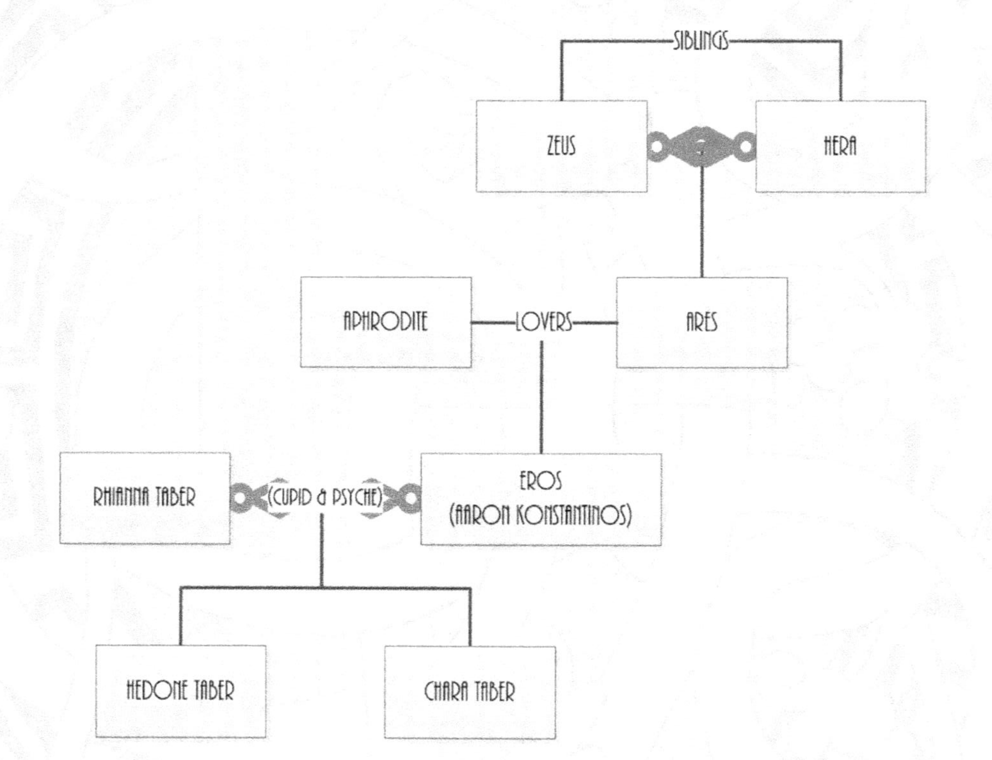

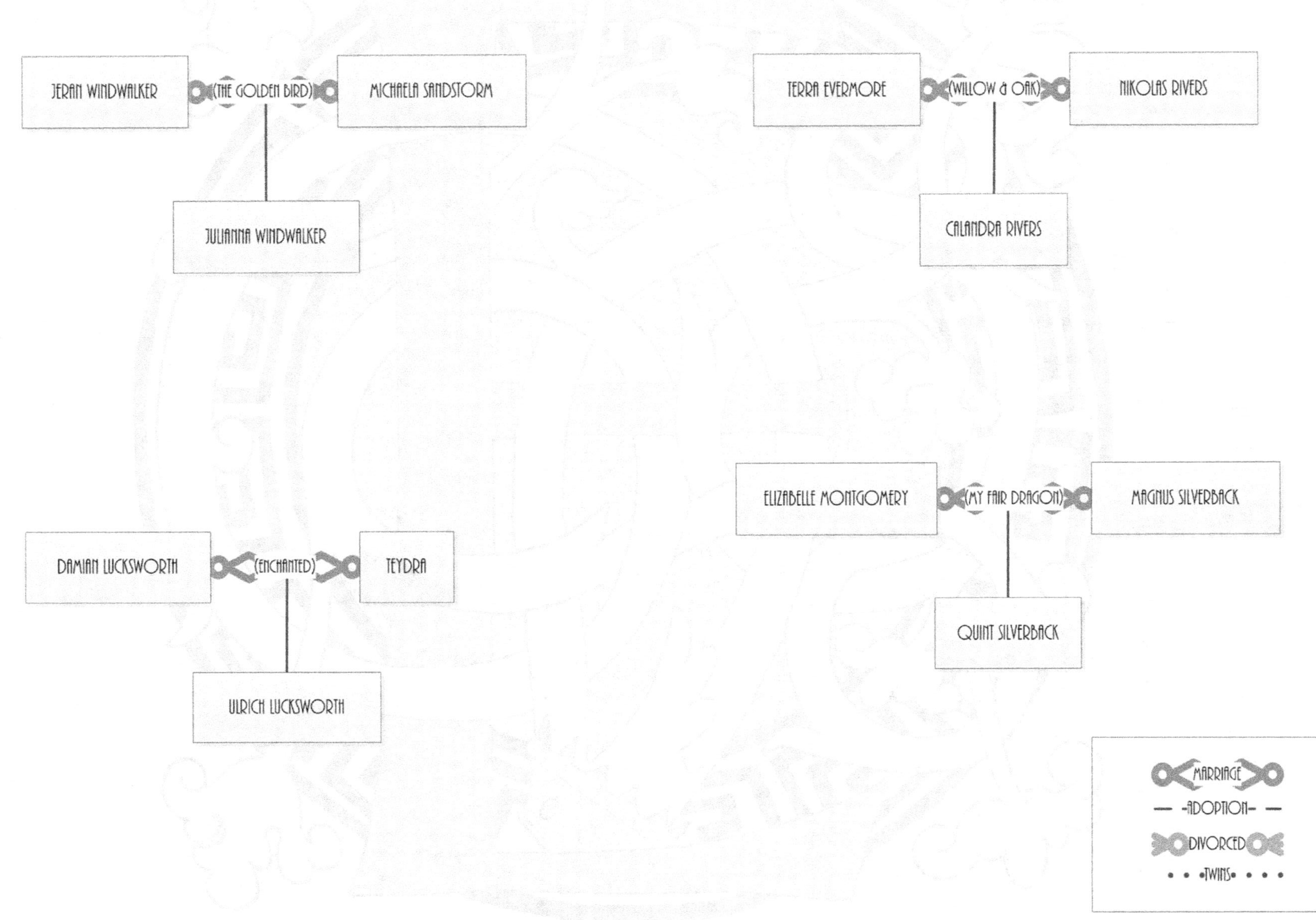
MIRAGE
JERAN WINDWALKER
(THE GOLDEN BIRD)
MICHAELA SANDSTORM
JULIANNA WINDWALKER
TERRA EVERMORE
(WILLOW & OAK)
NIKOLAS RIVERS
CALANDRA RIVERS
DAMIAN LUCKSWORTH
(ENCHANTED)
TEYDRA
ULRICH LUCKSWORTH
ELIZABELLE MONTGOMERY
(MY FAIR DRAGON)
MAGNUS SILVERBACK
QUINT SILVERBACK
MARRIAGE
-ADOPTION-
DIVORCED
•TWINS•

Stacy J. Garrett was made in England but born in Sacramento, California, and like the redwoods of the state, her roots have dug deep. Her destiny as a bard was somewhat inevitable. Little else can explain how she constantly told her mother tall tales so outlandish that she couldn't even get grounded for them. Her mother and grandmother had her reading by age three, and that love of a good story propelled her through so many books that Scholastic Books gave her a medal. A love of worlds created by others eventually brought out the desire to create her own, and she has never looked back.

Stacy has seen both good and evil in her life, and her stories, like life, have no half measures. Even in a fantasy world of dragons and faeries, even in a modern city where magic abounds, she knows that the constants of real emotion never change. Dreams come true, love can be found at first sight, princesses can rescue their princes, and maybe there really can be happily ever after. Her happy endings never come without cost, though, for she truly believes we can't appreciate the good and the joy without the bad and the pain along the way.

Her current haunt is a comfy house in her beloved Sacramento where she wrangles four feline fur-kids and consumes peppermints like mana in order to balance a calendar filled with more creative venues than a sane person should realistically undertake. If she's not chained to her desk, she's stomping through the scenery in search of equally fantastical photographs.

www.ingramcontent.com/pod-product-compliance
Lightning Source LLC
Chambersburg PA
CBHW081141300726
48982CB00006B/1022

* 9 7 8 0 9 9 9 1 0 7 0 2 7 *